PRAISE FOR CARL HIAASEN'S NOVELS

SKIN TIGHT

'The action flames, the wit's tinder dry. For snappy prose alone, not to say neat plot, it's a classic thriller' MAIL ON SUNDAY

'Taut, fast-paced action. The story jumps. The dialogue is crisp and hot ... his style has racing stripes' NEW YORK TIMES BOOK REVIEW

'Hiaasen brings classic farce to the modern thriller. There is little humour darker than his, and little funnier' EVENING STANDARD

'The story is slick, swift and gloriously, if darkly, funny. Whatever Mr Hiaasen was drinking when he wrote it – I'll have a double' SUNDAY TELEGRAPH

'A gloriously sleazy and riotously funny tale' TIME OUT

DOUBLE WHAMMY

'A careful reading of *Double Whammy* will do more to damage the Florida tourist trade than anything except an actual visit to Florida' P. J. O'ROURKE

'I went for *Double Whammy* hook, line and sinker, and I think you will too' WASHINGTON POST

'An outrageously entertaining high-protein experience' OBSERVER

'A savagely funny crime adventure ... *Double Whammy* bristles all over' MIAMI HERALD

TOURIST SEASON

'Fiendish suspense and wicked black humor ... a rollicking, exciting, exceptional book' JOHN KATZENBACH

'A remarkable example of what talented writers are doing these days with the mystery novel ... wonderful' NEW YORK TIMES BOOK REVIEW

'He may well be the funniest writer working in America today' INDEPENDENT

CARL HIAASEN OMNIBUS

TOURIST SEASON

DOUBLE WHAMMY

SKIN TIGHT

PICADOR

Tourist Season first published 1986 by G. P. Putnam's Sons Inc., New York
First published in Great Britain 1987 by Macdonald & Co Ltd
First published by Macmillan Publishers Ltd 1992 by Pan Books

Double Whammy first published in Great Britain 1988 by Mysterious Press in association
with Century Hutchinson Limited
First published by Macmillan Publishers Ltd 1990 by Pan Books

Skin Tight first published 1989 by G. P. Putnam's Sons, Inc., New York
First published by Macmillan Publishers Ltd by Macmillan London
1990 (first publication in Great Britain)

This omnibus edition published 1994 by Picador
an imprint of Macmillan Publishers Ltd
25 Eccleston Place, London SW1W 9NF
and Basingstoke

Associated companies throughout the world

ISBN 0 330 33620 7

The author gratefully acknowledges permission from ABKCO Music, Inc., to reprint
lyrics from 'Sympathy for the Devil' by Mick Jagger and Keith Richards, © 1968 by
ABKCO Music, Inc. All rights reserved.

9 8 7 6 5 4 3 2

A CIP catalogue record for this book is available from
the British Library.

Phototypeset by Intype, London
Printed and bound in Great Britain by
Mackays of Chatham PLC, Chatham, Kent

CONTENTS

FROM THE AUTHOR

This is the first time any of my novels have been collected in omnibus form, an act of sheer courage by the publisher. Looking back at these three books, it's impossible for me to trace a meaningful literary arc from one to the next. If there is a common resonance, the task of isolating it is best left to book critics, or perhaps a team of psychiatrists.

All three novels are set in South Florida, where I was born and where I still live. It's a place of extraordinary beauty, tumult, violence, and perversity—a journalist's mecca. The tone of the novels is satirical, but I promise that neither the events nor the characters are far-fetched. Pick up *The Miami Herald*, if you don't believe me.

For writers, the source of humor is often a deep personal pain. Mine comes from watching Florida destroyed by rapacious development, exploitation, and growth—all abetted by perniciously corrupt politicians. The roster of real-life scoundrels is long, so I never run short of inspiration. I also take great pleasure in concocting for my fictitious villains the most fitting and spectacular demises. Judge for yourself whether the punishments fit the crimes.

The tricky thing about satire is not selecting a target, but calibrating one's aim. I rely on my characters to do most of the work. They are neither indigenous nor unique to Florida; they simply wound up here, at the southernmost spur of America, along with four million other lemmings. In real life, I've tried (without much luck) to frighten the worst of them off. In fiction, I deal with them in other ways.

Carl Hiaasen Fort Lauderdale, Florida *January 1994*

TOURIST SEASON

For my son Scott

1

On the morning of December 1, a man named Theodore Bellamy went swimming in the Atlantic Ocean off South Florida. Bellamy was a poor swimmer, but he was a good real-estate man and a loyal Shriner.

The Shriners thought so much of Theodore Bellamy that they had paid his plane fare all the way from Evanston, Illinois, to Miami Beach, where a big Shriner convention was being staged. Bellamy and his wife, Nell, made it a second honeymoon, and got a nice double room at the Holiday Inn. The view was nothing to write home about; a big green dumpster was all they could see from the window, but the Bellamys didn't complain. They were determined to love Florida.

On the night of November 30, the Shriners had arranged a little parade down Collins Avenue. Theodore Bellamy put on his mauve fez and his silver riding jacket, and drove his chrome-spangled Harley Davidson (all the important Evanston Shriners had preshipped their bikes on a flatbed) up and down Collins in snazzy circles and figure eights, honking the horns and flashing the lights. Afterward Bellamy and his pals got bombed and sneaked out to the Place Pigalle to watch a 325-pound woman do a strip-tease. Bellamy was so snockered he didn't even blink at the ten-dollar cover.

Nell Bellamy went to bed early. When her husband lurched in at 4:07 in the morning, she said nothing. She may have even smiled just a little, to herself.

The alarm clock went off like a Redstone rocket at eight sharp. We're going swimming, Nell announced. Theodore was suffering through the please-God-I'll-never-do-it-again phase of his hangover when his wife hauled him out of bed. Next thing he knew, he was wearing his plaid swim trunks, standing on the beach, Nell nudging him toward the surf, saying you first, Teddy, tell me if it's warm enough.

The water was plenty warm, but it was also full of Portuguese men-of-war, poisonous floating jellyfish that pucker on the surface like bright blue balloons. Theodore Bellamy quickly became entangled in the burning tentacles of such a creature. He thrashed out of the ocean, his fish-white belly streaked with welts, the man-of-war clinging to his bare shoulder. He was crying. His fez was soaked.

At first Nell Bellamy was embarrassed, but then she realized that this was not Mango Daiquiri Pain, this was the real thing. She led her husband to a Disney World beach towel, and there she cradled him until two lifeguards ran up with a first-aid kit.

Later, Nell would remember that these were not your average-looking bleached-out lifeguards. One was black and the other didn't seem to speak English, but what the heck, this was Miami. She had come here resolved not to be surprised at anything, and this was the demeanor she maintained while the men knelt over her fallen husband. Besides, they were wearing authentic life-guard T-shirts, weren't they?

After ten minutes of ministrations and Vaseline, the lifeguards informed Nell Bellamy that they would have to transport her husband to a first-aid station. They said he needed medicine to counteract the man-of-war's venom. Nell wanted to go along, but they persuaded her to wait, and assured her it was nothing serious. Theodore said don't be silly, work on your tan, I'll be okay now.

And off they went. Theodore all pale-legged and stripe-bellied, a lifeguard at each side, marching down the beach.

That was 8:44 A.M.

Nell Bellamy never saw her husband again.

At ten sharp she went searching for the lifeguards, with no success, and after walking a gritty two-mile stretch of beach, she called the police. A patrolman came to the Holiday Inn and took a missing-persons report. Nell mentioned Theodore's hangover and what a lousy swimmer he was. The cop told Mrs. Bellamy that her husband had probably tried to go back in the water and had gotten into trouble in the rough surf. When Mrs. Bellamy described the two lifeguards, the policeman gave her a very odd look.

The case of Theodore Bellamy was not given top priority at the Miami Beach police department, where the officers had more catastrophic things to worry about than a drunken Shriner missing in the ocean.

The police instead were consumed with establishing the whereabouts of B. D. 'Sparky' Harper, one of the most important persons in all Florida; Harper, who had failed to show up at his office for the first time in twenty-one years. Every available detective was out shaking the palm trees, hunting for Sparky.

When it became clear that the police were too preoccupied to launch a manhunt for her husband, Nell Bellamy mobilized the Shriners. They invaded the beach in packs, some on foot, others on motorcycle, a few in tiny red motorcars that had a tendency to get stuck in the sand. The Shriners wore grim, purposeful looks; Teddy Bellamy was one of their own.

The Shriners were thorough, and they got results. Nell cried when she heard the news.

They had found Theodore's fez on the beach, at water's edge.

Nell thought: So he really drowned, the big nut.

Later the Shriners gathered at Lummus Park for an impromptu prayer service. Someone laid a wreath on the handlebars of Bellamy's customized Harley.

Nobody could have dreamed what actually happened to Theodore Bellamy. But this was just the beginning.

They found Sparky Harper later that same day, a bright and cloudless afternoon.

A cool breeze kicked up a light chop on the Pines Canal, where the suitcase floated, half-submerged, invisible to the teenager on water skis. He was skimming along at forty knots when he rammed the luggage and launched into a spectacular triple somersault.

His friends wheeled the boat to pick him up and offer congratulations. Then they doubled back for the suitcase. It took all three of them to haul it aboard; they figured it had to be stuffed with money or dope.

The water skier got a screwdriver from a toolbox and chiseled at the locks on the suitcase. 'Let's see what's inside!' he said eagerly.

And there, folded up like Charlie McCarthy, was B. D. 'Sparky' Harper.

'A dead midget!' the boat driver gasped.

'That's no midget,' the water skier said. 'That's a real person.'

'Oh God, we gotta call the cops. Come on, help me shut this damn thing.'

But with Sparky Harper swelling, the suitcase wouldn't close, and the latches were broken anyway, so all the way back to the marina the three of them sat on the luggage to keep the dead midget inside.

Two Dade County detectives drove out to Virginia Key to get the apple-red Samsonite Royal Tourister. They took a statement from the water skier, put the suitcase in the trunk of their unmarked Plymouth, and headed back downtown.

One of the cops, a blocky redhead, walked into the medical examiner's office carrying the Samsonite as if nothing were wrong. 'Is this the Pan Am terminal?' he deadpanned to the first secretary he saw.

The suitcase was taken to the morgue and placed on a shiny steel autopsy table. Dr. Joe Allen, the chief medical examiner, recognized Sparky Harper instantly.

'The first thing we've got to do,' said Dr. Allen, putting on some rubber gloves, 'is get him out of there.'

Whoever had murdered the president of the Greater Miami Chamber of Commerce had gone to considerable trouble to pack him into the red Samsonite. Sparky was only five-foot-five, but he weighed nearly one hundred ninety pounds, most of it in the midriff. To have squeezed him into a suitcase, even a deluxe-sized suitcase, was a feat that drew admiring comments from the coroner's seasoned staff. One of the clerks used up two rolls of film documenting the extrication.

Finally the corpse was removed and unfolded, more or less, onto the table. It was then that some of the amazement dissolved: Harper's legs were missing below the kneecaps. That's how the killer had fit him into the suitcase.

One of the cops whispered, 'Look at those clothes, Doc.'

It *was* odd. Sparky Harper had died wearing a brightly flowered print shirt and baggy Bermuda-style shorts. Sporty black wrap-around sunglasses concealed his dilated pupils. He looked just like any old tourist from Milwaukee.

The autopsy took two hours and twenty minutes. Inside Sparky Harper, Dr. Allen found two gallstones, forty-seven grams of partially digested stone crabs, and thirteen ounces of Pouilly Fuissé. But the coroner found no bullets, no stab wounds, no signs of trauma besides the amputations, which were crude but not necessarily fatal.

'He must have bled to death,' the redheaded cop surmised.

'Don't think so,' Dr. Allen said.

'Bet he drowned,' said the other cop.

'No, sir,' said Dr. Allen, who was probing into the lungs by now. Dr. Allen wasn't crazy about people gawking over his shoulder while he worked. It made him feel like he was performing onstage, a magician pulling little purple treasures out of a dark hole. He didn't mind having medical students as observers because they were always so solemn during an autopsy. Cops were something else; one dumb joke after another. Dr. Allen had never figured out why cops get so silly in a morgue.

'What's that greasy stuff all over his skin?' asked the red-headed detective.

'Essence of Stiff,' said the other cop.

'Smells like coconuts,' said the redhead. 'I'm serious, Doc, take a whiff.'

'No, thank you,' Dr. Allen said curtly.

'I don't smell anything,' said the assistant coroner, 'except the deceased.'

'It's coconut, definitely,' said the other cop, sniffing. 'Maybe he drowned in piña colada.'

Nobody could have guessed what actually had killed Sparky

Harper. It was supple and green and exactly five and one-quarter inches long. Dr. Allen found it lodged in the trachea. At first he thought it was a large chunk of food, but it wasn't.

It was a toy rubber alligator. It had cost seventy-nine cents at a tourist shop along the Tamiami Trail. The price tag was still glued to its corrugated tail.

B. D. 'Sparky' Harper, the president of the most powerful chamber of commerce in all Florida, had choked to death on a rubber alligator. Well, well, thought Dr. Allen as he dangled the prize for his protégés to see, here's one for my slide show at next month's convention.

2

News of B. D. Harper's death appeared on the front page of the Miami *Sun* with a retouched photograph that made Harper look like a flatulent Gene Hackman. Details of the crime were meager, but this much was known:

Harper had last been seen on the night of November 30, driving away from Joe's Stone Crab restaurant on South Miami Beach. He had told friends he was going to the Fontainebleau Hilton for drinks with some convention organizers from the International Elks.

Harper had not been wearing a Jimmy Buffett shirt and Bermuda shorts, but in fact had been dressed in a powder-blue double-knit suit purchased at J. C. Penney's.

He had not appeared drunk.

He had not worn black wraparound sunglasses.

He had not been lugging a red Samsonite.

He had not displayed a toy rubber alligator all evening.

In the newspaper story a chief detective was quoted as saying, 'This one's a real whodunit,' which is what the detective was told to say whenever a reporter called.

In this instance the reporter was Ricky Bloodworth.

Bloodworth wore that pale, obsessive look of ambition so familiar to big-city newsrooms. He was short and bony, with curly black hair and a squirrellike face frequently speckled with late-blooming acne. He was frenetic to a fault, dashing from phone to typewriter to copy desk in a blur—yet he was different from most of his colleagues. Ricky Bloodworth wanted to be much more than just a reporter; he wanted to be an authentic *character*. He tried, at various times, panama hats, silken vests, a black eye-patch, saddle shoes, a Vandyke—nobody ever noticed. He even experimented with Turkish cigarettes (thinking it debonair) and wound up on a respirator at Mercy Hospital. Even those who disliked Bloodworth, and they were many, felt sorry for him; the poor guy wanted a quirk in the worst way. But, stylistically, the best he could do was to drum pencils and suck down incredible amounts of 7-Up. It wasn't much, but it made him feel like he was contributing something to the newsroom's energy bank.

Ricky Bloodworth thought he'd done a respectable job on the first Sparky Harper story (given the deadlines), but now, on the morning of December 2, he was ready to roll. Harper's ex-wives had to be found and interviewed, his coworkers had to be quizzed, and an array of semibereaved civic leaders stood ready to offer their thoughts on the heinous crime.

But Dr. Allen came first. Ricky Bloodworth knew the phone number of the coroner's office by heart; memorizing it was one of the first things he'd done after joining the paper.

When Dr. Allen got on the line, Bloodworth asked, 'What's your theory, Doc?'

'Somebody tied up Sparky and made him swallow a rubber alligator,' the coroner said.

'Cause of death?'

'Asphyxiation.'

'How do you know he didn't swallow it on purpose?'

'Did he cut off his own legs, too?'

'You never know,' Bloodworth said. 'Maybe it started out as some kinky sex thing. Or maybe it was voodoo, all these Haitians we got now. Or *santería*.'

'Sparky was a Baptist, and the police are calling it a homicide.'

'They've been wrong before.'

Ricky Bloodworth was not one of Dr. Allen's favorite newspaper reporters. Dr. Allen regarded him as charmless and arrogant. There had been times, when the prospect of a front-page story loomed, that Dr. Allen could have sworn he saw flecks of foam on Bloodworth's lips.

Now the coroner listened to Bloodworth's typing on the end of the phone line, and wondered how badly his quotes were being mangled.

'Ricky,' he said impatiently. 'The victim's wrists showed ligature marks—'

'Any ten-year-old can tie himself up.'

'And stuff himself in a suitcase?'

The typing got faster.

'The victim was already deceased when he was placed in the suitcase,' Dr. Allen said. 'Is there anything else?'

'What about the oil? One of the cops said the body was coated with oil.'

'Not oil,' Dr. Allen said. 'A combination of benzophenone, stearic acids, and lanolin.'

'What's that?'

'Suntan lotion,' the coroner said. 'With coconut butter.'

Ricky Bloodworth was hammering away on his video terminal when he sensed a presence behind him. He turned slightly, and caught sight of Skip Wiley's bobbing face. Even with a two-day stubble it was a striking visage: long, brown, and rugged-looking; a genetic marvel, every feature plagiarized from disparate ancestors. The cheekbones were high and sculptured, the nose pencil-straight but rather long and flat, the mouth upturned with little commas on each cheek, and the eyes disarming—small and keen, the color of strong coffee; full of mirth and something else. Skip Wiley was thirty-seven years old but he had the eyes of an old Gypsy.

It made Bloodworth abnormally edgy and insecure when Skip Wiley read over his shoulder. Wiley wrote a daily column for the *Sun* and probably was the best-known journalist in Miami. Undeniably he was a gifted writer, but around the newsroom he was regarded as a strange and unpredictable character. Wiley's behavior had lately become so odd that younger reporters who once sought his counsel were now fearful of his ravings, and they avoided him.

'Coconut butter?' Wiley said gleefully. 'And no legs!'

'Skip, please.'

Wiley rolled up a chair. 'I think you should lead with the coconut butter.'

Bloodworth felt his hands go damp.

Wiley said, 'This is awful, Ricky: "Friends and colleagues of B. D. Harper expressed grief and outrage Tuesday . . ." Jesus Christ, who cares? Give them coconut oil!'

'It's a second day lead, Skip—'

'Here we go again, Mr. Journalism School.' Wiley was gnawing his lower lip, a habit manifested only when he composed a news story. 'You got some good details in here. The red Royal Tourister. The black Ray-Bans. That's good, Ricky. Why don't you toss out the rest of this shit and move the juicy stuff up top? Do your readers a favor, for once. Don't make 'em go on a scavenger hunt for the goodies.'

Bloodworth was getting queasy. He wanted to defend himself, but it was lunacy to argue with Wiley.

'Maybe later, Skip. Right now I'm jammed up for the first edition.'

Wiley jabbed a pencil at the video screen, which displayed Bloodworth's story in luminous green text. '*Brutal?* That's not the adjective you want. When I think of brutal I think of chain saws, ice picks, ax handles. Not rubber alligators. No, that's *mysterious*, wouldn't you say?'

'How about *bizarre*?'

'A bit overworked these days, but not bad. When's the last time you used *bizarre*?'

'I don't recall, Skip.'

'Try last week, in that story about the Jacuzzi killing in Hialeah. Remember? So it's too early to *bizarre* again. I think *mysterious* is the ticket.'

'Whatever you say, Skip.'

Wiley was boggling, when he wanted to be.

'What's your theory, Ricky?'

'Some sex thing, I guess. Sparky rents himself a bimbo, dresses up in this goofy outfit—'

'Perhaps a little S-and-M?'

'Yeah. Things go too far, he gags on the rubber alligator, the girl panics and calls for help. The muscle arrives, hacks up Sparky, crams the torso into the suitcase, and heaves it into Biscayne Bay.'

The goons grab the girl and take off in Sparky's car.'

Wiley eyed him. 'So you don't believe it's murder?'

'Accidental homicide. That's my prediction.' Bloodworth was starting to relax. Wiley was rocking the chair, a look of amusement on his face. Bloodworth noticed that Wiley's long choppy mane was starting to show gray among the blond.

Bloodworth said, a little more confidently, 'I think Harper's death was a freak accident. I think the girl will come forward before too long, and that'll be the end of it.'

Wiley chuckled. 'Well, it's a damn good yarn.' He stood up and pinched Ricky's shoulder affectionately. 'But I don't have to tell *you* how to hit the hype button, do I?'

For the first edition, Ricky Bloodworth moved the paragraph about the coconut oil higher in the story, and changed the word *brutal* to *mysterious* in the lead.

The rest of the afternoon Bloodworth spent on the phone, gathering mawkish quotes about Sparky Harper, who seemed venerated by everyone except his former wives. As for blood relatives, the best Bloodworth could scrounge up was a grown son, a lawyer in Marco Island, who said of his father:

'He was a dreamer, and he honestly meant well.'

Not exactly a tearjerker, but Bloodworth stuck it in the story anyway.

After finishing, he reread the piece once more. It had a nice flow, he thought, and the tone graduated smoothly: shock first, then outrage and, finally, sorrow.

It's good, a page-one contender, Bloodworth told himself as he walked down to the Coke machine.

While he was away, Skip Wiley crept up and snatched the printout of the story off his desk. He was pretending to mark it up with a blue pencil when Bloodworth came back.

'What now, Skip?'

'Your lead's no good.'

'Come on, I *told* you—'

'Hey, Ace, it's not a second-day story anymore. Something broke while you were diddling around. *News*, they call it. Check with the police desk, you'll see.'

'What are you talking about?'

Wiley grinned as he tossed the pages into Ricky Bloodworth's lap. 'The cops caught the guy,' he said. 'Ten minutes ago.'

3

Brian Keyes slouched on a worn bench in the lobby of the Dade County jail, waiting to see the creep the cops just caught. Keyes looked at his wristwatch and muttered. Twenty minutes. Twenty goddamn minutes since he'd given his name to the dull-eyed sergeant behind the bullet-proof glass.

Keyes had run into this problem before; it had something to do with the way he looked. Although he stood five-ten, a respectable height, he somehow failed to exude the authority so necessary for survival in rough bars, alleys, police stations, jails, and McDonald's drive-throughs. Keyes was adolescently slender, with blue eyes and a smooth face. He looked younger than his thirty-two years, which, in his line of work, was no particular asset. An ex-girlfriend once said, on her way out the door, that he reminded her of a guy who'd just jumped the wall of a Jesuit seminary. To disguise his boyishness, Brian Keyes had today chosen a brown suit with a finely striped Cardin tie. He was clean-shaven and his straight brown hair was neatly combed. Still, he had a feeling that his overall appearance was inadequate—not slick enough to be a lawyer, not frazzled enough to be a social worker, and not old enough to be a private investigator. Which he actually was.

So the turtle-eyed sergeant ignored him.

Keyes was surrounded by misery. On his left, a rotund Latin woman wailed into an embroidered handkerchief and nibbled on a rosary. 'Pobrecito, he's in yail again.'

On the other side, an anemic-looking teenager with yellow teeth carved an obscenity into the bench with a Phillips screwdriver. Keyes studied him neutrally until the kid looked up and snapped, 'My brother's in for agg assault!'

'You must be very proud,' Keyes said.

This place never changed. The hum and clang of the electronic doors were enough to split your skull, but the mayhem in the lobby was worse, worse even than the cell blocks. The lobby was crawling with bitter, bewildered souls, each on the sad trail of a loser. Girlfriends, ex-wives, mothers, brothers, bondsmen, lawyers, pimps, parole officers.

And me, Keyes thought. The public defender's office had tried to make the case sound interesting, but Keyes figured it had to be a lost cause. There'd be some publicity, which he didn't need, and decent money, which he did. This was a big-time case, all right. Some nut hacks up the president of the Chamber of Commerce and dumps him in the bay—just what South Florida needed, another grisly murder. Keyes wondered if the dismemberment fad would ever pass.

From the governor on down, everybody had wanted this one solved fast. And the cops had come through.

'Mr. Keyes!' The sergeant's voice echoed from a cheap speaker in the ceiling.

Keyes signed the log, clipped on a plastic visitor's badge, and walked through three sets of noisy iron gates. A trusty accompanied him into an elevator that smelled like an NFL locker room. The elevator stopped on the fifth floor.

Ernesto Cabal, alias Little Ernie, alias No-Way José, was sitting disconsolately on the crapper when the trusty opened the cell for Brian Keyes.

Ernesto held out a limp, moist hand. Keyes sat down on a wooden folding chair.

'You speak English?'

'Sure,' Ernesto said. 'I been here sixteen years. By *here* I mean here, dees country.' He pulled up his pants, flushed the john, and stretched out on a steel cot. 'They say I kill dees man Harper.'

'That's what they say.'

'I dint.'

Ernesto was a small fellow, sinewy and tough-looking, except for the eyes. A lot of cons had rabbit eyes, but not this one, Keyes thought. Ernesto's brown eyes were large and wet. Scared puppy eyes.

Keyes opened his briefcase.

'You a lawyer, Mr. Keyes?'

'Nope. I'm an investigator. I was hired by your lawyers to help you.'

'Yeah?'

'That's right.'

'You're a very young guy to be an investigator,' Ernesto said. 'How old? Dirty, dirty-one?'

'Good guess.'

Ernesto sat up. 'You any good?'

'No, I'm totally incompetent. A complete moron. Now I've got a question for you, *chico*. Did you do it?'

'I tole you. No.'

'Fine.' Keyes opened a manila file and scanned a pink tissue copy of the arrest report.

Ernesto leaned over for a peek. 'I know what that is, man.'

'Good, then explain it.'

'See, I was driving dees car and the policeman, he pull me over on a routine traffic stop . . .'

Oh boy, Keyes thought, *routine traffic stop*. This guy's been here before.

'. . . and told me I'm driving a stolen be-hickle. And the next thin I know I'm in jail and dey got me charged with first-degree murder and robbery and everythin else.'

Keyes asked, 'How did you come to be driving a 1984 Oldsmobile Delta 88?'

'I bought it.'

'I see. Ernesto, what do you do for a living?'

'I sell fruit.'

'Oh.'

'Maybe you see me at rush hour. On LeJeune Road. I sell fresh fruit in bags.'

Somewhere down the cell block another prisoner started to bang on the bars and scream that his TV was broken.

Keyes said, 'Ernesto, how much does your very best bag of fruit sell for? Top-of-the-line?'

'Mangoes or cassavas?'

'Whatever. The best.'

'Maybe one dollar . . . oh, I see what you getting at. Okay, yeah, that's right, I doan make much money. But I got some great buy on this Oldsmobile. You can't believe it.'

'Probably not.'

'I got it from a black guy.'

'For?'

'Two hundred bucks.'

Ernesto seemed to sense he was losing ground. 'Some buy. I dint believe it either.'

Keyes shrugged. 'I didn't say I didn't believe you. Now, according to the police, you were arrested on Collins Avenue on Miami Beach. You ran a series of red lights.'

'It was tree in the morning. No one was out.'

'Where did you meet the man who sold you the car?'

'Right dare on Collins. Two nights before I got busted. I met him a few blocks from the Fountain-blow. Dare's a city parking lot where I hang.'

'The one where you do all your B-and-Es?'

'Shit, you just like the policeman.'

'I need to know everything, Ernesto, otherwise I can't help. Okay, so you're hanging out, breaking into cars and ripping off Blaupunkts, whatever, and up drives this black guy in a new Olds and says, "Hey, Ernie, wanna buy this baby for two bills?" That about it?'

'Yeah, 'cept he dint know my name.'

Keyes said, 'I don't suppose you asked the gentleman where he got the car?'

Ernesto laughed—a muskrat mouth, full of small yellow teeth—and shook his head no.

'Don't suppose you asked his name, either?'

'No, man.'

'And I don't suppose you'd recognize him if you ever saw him again?'

Ernesto leaned forward and rubbed his chin intently. A great gesture, Keyes thought. Cagney in *White Heat*.

'I see dis guy somewhere before,' Ernesto said. 'I doan know where, but I know the face. Big guy. Big black guy. Gold chain, Carrera frames, nice-looking guy. Arms like this, like a foking boa constripper. Yeah, I'd know him if I saw him again. Sure.'

Keyes said, 'You had a remote suspicion that the car was hot, didn't you?'

Ernesto nodded sheepishly.

'Why didn't you unload it?'

'I was going to, man. Another day or two it'd be gone bye-bye. But it was such a great car . . . aw, you wouldn't know about thins like that, man. You prolly got a Rolls-Royce or somethin. I never had a nice car like that. I wanted to cruise around for a while, that's all. I woulda fenced it eventually.'

Keyes put the file back in the briefcase. He took out a recent photograph of B. D. Harper.

'Ever seen this man, Ernesto?'

'No.' The puppy eyes didn't even flicker.

'Ever killed anybody?'

'On purpose?'

'On purpose, by accident, any way.'

'No, sir!' Ernesto said crisply. 'Once I shot a guy in the balls. Want to know why?'

'No thanks. I read all about it on your rap sheet. A personal dispute, I believe.'

'That is right.'

Keyes rose to leave and called for a guard. Then he thought of something else. 'Ernesto,' he said, 'do you believe in black magic?'

The little Cuban grinned. '*Santería?* Sure. I doan go to those thins, but it be stupid to say I do not believe. My uncle was a *santero*, a priest. One time he brought a skull and some pennies to my mother's house. He killed a chicken in the backyard—with his teeth he killed dis chicken—and then dipped the pennies in its blood. Two days later the landlord dropped dead.' Ernesto Cabal made a chopping motion with his hand. 'Juss like that.'

'You know what I'm getting at, don't you?'

'Yes, Mr. Keyes. I never heard of no *santero* using suntan oil for anythin . . .'

Keyes started to laugh. 'Okay, Ernesto. I'll be in touch.'

'Don't you forget about me, Mr. Keyes. Dis is a bad place for an innocent man.'

Brian Keyes left the jail and walked around the corner to Metro-Dade police headquarters, another bad place for an innocent man. He shared the elevator with a tall female patrol officer who did a wonderful job of pretending not to notice him. She got off on the second floor. Keyes went all the way up to Homicide.

Al García greeted him with a grin and a soft punch on the shoulder. 'Coffee?'

'Please,' Keyes said. García was much friendlier since Keyes had left the newspaper. In the old days he was like a sphinx; now he'd start yakking and never shut up. Keyes thought it might be different this time around.

'How's business?' García asked.

'Not great, Al.'

'Takes time. You only been at it—what?—two years. And there's plenty of competition in this town.'

No fooling, Keyes thought. He had arrived in Miami in 1979 from a small newspaper in suburban Baltimore. There was nothing original about why he'd left for Florida—a better job, no snow, plenty of sunshine. On his first day at the Miami *Sun*, Keyes had been assigned the desk next to Skip Wiley—the newsroom equivalent of Parris Island. Keyes covered cops for a while, then courts, then local politics. His reporting had been solid, his writing workmanlike but undistinguished. The editors never questioned his ability, only his stomach.

There were two stories commonly told about Brian Keyes at the Miami *Sun*. The first happened a year after his arrival, when a fully loaded 727 fireballed down in Florida Bay. Keyes had rented an outboard and sped to the scene, and he'd filed a superb story, full of gripping detail. But they'd damn near had to hospital-ize him afterward: for six months Keyes kept hallucinating that burned arms and legs were reaching out from under his bed-room furniture.

The second anecdote was the most well-known. Even Al García knew about Callie Davenport. She was a four-year-old girl who'd been kidnapped from nursery school by a deranged sprinkler repairman. The lunatic had thrown her into a truck, driven out to the Glades, and murdered her. After some deer hunters found the body, Cab Mulcahy, the managing editor, had told Brian Keyes to go interview Callie Davenport's grief-stricken parents. Keyes had written a real heartbreaker, too, just like the old man wanted. But that same night he'd marched into Mulcahy's office and quit. When Keyes rushed out of the newsroom, everyone could see he'd been crying. 'That young man,' Skip Wiley had said, watching him go, 'is too easily horrified to be a great journalist.'

Besides Keyes himself, Skip Wiley was the only person in the world who knew the real reason for the tears. But he wasn't telling.

A few months later Keyes got his private investigator's license, and his newspaper friends were amused. They wondered how the hell he was going to hold together, working for a bunch of sleazoid lawyers and bail bondsmen. Brian Keyes wondered too, and wound up avoiding the rough cases. The cases that really paid.

'Still doing divorces?' Al García asked.

'Here and there.' Keyes hated to admit it, but that's what covered the rent: he'd gotten damn good at staking out nooner motels with his three-hundred-millimeter Nikon. That was another reason for Al Garciá's affability. Last year he had hired Brian Keyes to get the goods on his new son-in-law. García despised the kid, and was on the verge of outright murdering him when he called Keyes for help. Keyes had done a hell of a job, too. Tracked the little stud to a VD clinic in Homestead. Garciá's daughter wasn't thrilled by the news, but Al was. The divorce went through in four weeks, a new Dade County record.

Now Brian Keyes had a friend for life.

García poured the coffee. 'So you got a biggie, Brian.'

'Tell me about it.'

'It's a touchy one. Can't say much, especially now that you're lined up with the other side.'

'Did you work the Harper case?'

'Hell, *everybody* up here worked that case.'

Keyes tried to sip the coffee and nearly boiled his upper lip.

'Heh,' García said, 'that piece-of-shit rag newspaper you used to work for finally printed something intelligent this morning. You see it?'

'My paper was in a puddle.'

'Ha! You should have read it anyway. Wiley, the asshole that writes that column. I hate that guy normally—I really can't stand him. But today he did okay.'

Keyes didn't want to talk about Skip Wiley.

'He wrote about this case,' García went on. 'About that little scuzzball we arrested.'

'I'll be sure to get a copy,' Keyes said.

'I mean, it wasn't a hundred percent right, there was a few things he screwed up, but overall he did an okay job. I clipped it out and taped it on the refrigerator. I want my boy to read it when he gets home from school. Let him see what his old man does for a living.'

'I'm sure he'll get a charge out of it, Al. Tell me about Ernesto Cabal.'

'Dirtbag burglar.'

'Was he on your list of suspects?'

García said, 'What do you mean?'

'I mean, you've got thirty detectives working on this murder, right? You must have had a list of suspects.'

'Not on this one.'

'So what we're talking about is blind luck. Some Beach cop nails the guy for running a traffic light and, bingo, there's Mr. Sparky Harper's missing automobile.'

'Luck was only part of it,' García said sourly.

Keyes said, 'You caught Cabal in the victim's car, but what else?'

'What else do we need?'

'A witness or two might be nice.'

'Patience, Brian. We're working on it.'

'And a motive?'

García held up his hands. 'Robbery, of course.'

'Come on, Al, this wasn't a knife in the ribs. It was the ritual murder of a prominent citizen. How did Harper get into those silly clothes? Who smeared suntan oil all over him? Who stuffed a goddamn toy alligator down his throat? Who sawed his legs off? Are you telling me that some two-bit auto burglar concocted this whole thing?'

'People do crazy things for a new Oldsmobile.'

'You're hopeless,' Keyes said.

'Don't tell me you believe Cabal's story? Brian, you got to get this liberal-crusader shit out of your system. I thought two years away from that newspaper would cure you.'

'You've got to admit, it's a very weird case. You guys checked out the car, right?'

'It was clean, except for Cabal's prints.'

Keyes took out a legal pad and started jotting notes. 'What about the suitcase?'

'No prints. Its model number matches a batch sent to Jordan Marsh about a year ago, but we can't be sure. Could've just as easily come from Macy's.'

Keyes said, 'Any sign of the missing legs?'

'Nope.'

'Did you trace that terrific Hawaiian wardrobe?'

'Ugh-ugh.' García made a zipper motion across his lips.

'Oh, you got something, uh? A store, perhaps. Maybe even a salesman who remembers something odd about this particular customer—'

'Brian, back off. This is a very touchy case. If the chief even suspected I was talking to you, I'd be shaking out parking meters for the rest of my life. I think we'd better call it quits for today.'

Keyes put the legal pad back in his briefcase. 'I'm sorry, Al. I appreciate what you're doing.' Keyes was telling the truth. García didn't owe him a damn thing.

'Normally I wouldn't mind, Brian, it's just that this one is Hal's case. He's the lead detective. Went out to the scene and all. I don't want to screw it up for him.'

'I understand. What's he got you doing?'

García rolled his eyes. 'Checking out dead-enders. Take a look at this.' He slid a sheet of paper across the desk.

It was a typed letter. Keyes scanned it quickly. He started to read it again, when García snatched it away.

'Crazy, huh? It came in today's mail.'

Keyes asked for a Xerox copy.

'No way, Brian. The PD's office would cream over something like this. And it's crap, take my word for it. It's going right into the old circular file as soon as I make a couple routine calls to the feds.'

'Read it out loud,' Keyes said.

'I'll deny I ever even saw it,' García said.

'Okay, Al, you got my word. Read it, please.'

García slipped on a pair of tinted glasses and read from the letter:

> Dear Miami Chamber of Commerce:
> Welcome to the Revolution.
> Mr. B. D. Harper's death was a milestone. It may have seemed an atrocity to you; to us, it was poetry. Contrary to what you'd like to believe, this was not the act of a sick person, but the raging of a powerful new underclass.
> Mr. Harper's death was not a painful one, but it was unusual, and we trust that it got your attention. Soon we start playing for keeps. Wait for number three!
> *El Fuego,*
> Comandante, *Las Noches de Diciembre*

Al García removed his reading glasses and said, 'Not half-bad, really. For a flake.'

'Not at all,' Keyes agreed. 'What do you make of that *number-three* business? Who was victim number two?'

'There wasn't any, not that I know of.'

'So who are the Nights of December?' Keyes asked.

'A figment of some nut's imagination. "The Fire," he calls himself. *El Fuego* my ass. I'll check with the Bureau, just in case, but J. Edgar himself wouldn't have taken this one seriously. Still, I might ask around with the guys on the antiterrorism squad.'

'And then?' Keyes asked.

'A slam dunk,' García said. 'Right into the wastebasket.'

4

Cab Mulcahy poured the coffee. Skip Wiley drank.

'The beard is new, isn't it?'

'I need it,' Wiley said, 'for an assignment.'

'Oh. And what would that be?'

'That would be confidential,' Wiley said, slurping.

Cab Mulcahy was a patient man, especially for a managing editor. He had been in newspapers his entire adult life and almost nothing could provoke him. Whenever the worst kind of madness gripped the newsroom, Mulcahy would emerge to take charge, instantly imposing a rational and temperate mood. He was a thoughtful man in a profession not famous for thoughtfulness. Cab Mulcahy was also astute. He loved Skip Wiley, but distrusted him wholeheartedly.

'Cream?' Mulcahy offered.

'No thanks.' Wiley rubbed his temples briskly. He knew that the effect of this was to distort his face grotesquely, like pulling putty. He watched Mulcahy watching him.

'You missed deadline yesterday, Skip.'

'I was helping Bloodworth with his story. The kid's hopeless, Cab. Did you like my column?'

Mulcahy said, 'I think we ought to talk about it.'

'Fine,' Wiley said. 'Talk.'

'How much do you really know about the Harper case?'

'I've got my sources.'

Mulcahy smiled paternally. Wiley's column was on his desk. It lay there like a bird dropping, the first thing to await Mulcahy when he arrived at the office. He had read it three times.

'My concern,' Mulcahy began, 'is that you managed to convict Mr. Cabal in this morning's newspaper, without benefit of a trial.

You have, for lack of a better word, *reconstructed* the murder of B. D. Harper in your usual slick, readable way—'

'Thank you, Cab.'

'—without any apparent regard for the facts. This business about sexual torture, where did that come from?'

Wiley said, 'Can't tell you.'

'Skip, let me read this out loud: "Harper was tied up, spread-eagle, and subjected to vicious and unspeakable homosexual assaults for no less than five hours." Now, before you start whining, you ought to know that I took the liberty of calling the medical examiner. The autopsy showed absolutely no signs of sodomy.'

'Aw, it's the imagery that's important, Cab. The utter humiliation of this gentle man. Sodomized or not, can you deny that he was horribly humiliated by this crime?'

'Your concern for the late Mr. Harper's dignity is touching,' Mulcahy said. He turned his attention to a stack of newspaper clippings on another corner of his desk. Wordlessly he riffled through them. Wiley knew what they were: more columns.

'Here we go,' Mulcahy said, holding up one. 'On the subject of B. D. "Sparky" Harper, this is what you wrote a mere three months ago: "If there has ever been a more myopic, insensitive, and avaricious cretin to lead our Chamber of Commerce, I can't recall him. Sparky Harper takes the cake—and anything else that isn't nailed down. He is the Sultan of Shills, the perfect mouth-piece for the hungry-eyed developers, hoteliers, bankers, and lawyers who have made South Florida what it is today: Newark with palm trees." '

'I remember that column, Cab. You made me apologize to the New Jersey Tourist Bureau.'

Mulcahy leaned back and gave Skip Wiley a very hard look.

Wiley squirmed. 'I suppose you want to know why I crucified Harper a few months ago and made a hero out of him today. It's simple, Cab. Literary license. You wouldn't understand.'

'I've read a book or two. Try me.'

'I did it to dramatize the crime problem,' Wiley said. 'The Harper murder symbolizes the unspeakable mayhem in our streets. Don't you see? To make people care, I needed to bring Sparky Harper and his killer to life. Don't look at me like that, Cab. You think I'm a hypocrite? Sure, Harper was a fat little jerk. But if I put that in the paper, no one would care about the murder. I wanted to give 'em goose bumps, Cab.'

'Like the old days,' Mulcahy said with a sigh.

'What's that supposed to mean? I get more goddamned letters than I ever did. People read the hell out of my column. You should see the mail.'

'That's the trouble, Skip. I *do* see the mail. People are starting to hate you, I mean *really* hate you. Not just the usual fruit-cakes, either.'

Not true, Wiley said to himself. The people who counted were on his side.

'So you've been taking some heat, eh?'

Mulcahy looked away, out the window toward the bay.

'A few ad cancellations, perhaps? Like maybe the Richmond Department Store account—'

'Skip, that's one of about forty things on my list. It isn't funny anymore. You're fucking up on a regular basis. You miss dead-lines, you libel people, you invent ludicrous facts and put them in the paper. I've got a lawyer downstairs who does nothing but fight off litigation against your column. We've had to print seven retractions in the last four months—that's a new record, by the way. No other managing editor in the history of this newspaper can make that claim.'

Wiley was starting to feel a little sorry for Mulcahy, whom he had known for many years. Cab had been the city editor when Wiley had come to work at the *Sun.* They had been drinking buddies once, and used to go bass fishing together out in the Everglades.

It was a shame the old boy didn't understand what had to be done, Wiley thought. It was a shame the newspaper business had gotten such a frozen grip on his soul.

'The public defender's office called me this morning,' Mulcahy continued. 'Mr. Cabal's lawyer didn't appreciate your description of his client as "yellow-bellied vermin culled from the stinkpot of

Castro's jails for discharge at Mariel's harbor of shame." The Hispanic Anti-Defamation League sent a telegram voicing similar
objections. The League also notes that Señor Cabal is *not* a Mariel
refugee. He arrived in this country from Havana with his family in
1966. His older brother later received a Purple Heart in Vietnam.'

'Perhaps I got a little carried away,' Wiley said.

'Hell, Skip.' Mulcahy's voice was tired and edged with sadness.
'I think we have a big problem. And I think we're going to have
to do something. Soon.'

This was a conversation they had been having more often, so
often that Wiley had stopped taking it seriously. He got more
mail than any other writer, and the publisher counted mail as
subscribers, and subscribers as money. Wiley knew they wouldn't
lay a glove on him. He knew he was a star in the same way he
knew he was tall and brown-eyed; it was just something else
he could see in the mirror every morning, plain as day. He didn't
even notice it anymore. The only time it counted was when he
got into trouble. Like now.

'You aren't going to threaten to fire me again, are you?'

'Yes,' Mulcahy said.

'I suppose you want me to apologize to somebody.'

Mulcahy handed Wiley a list.

'I'll get right on it—'

'Sit down, Skip. I'm not finished.' Mulcahy stood up, brandishing the stack of columns. 'You know what makes me sad? You're
such a damn good writer, too good to be turning out shit like
this. Something's happened the last few months. You've been
slipping away. I think you're sick.'

Wiley winced. 'Sick?'

Mulcahy was a slim man, gray and graceful. Before becoming
an editor, he had had a distinguished career as a foreign correspondent: he had covered two wars and a half-dozen coups, and
had even been shot at three times. Wiley had always been envious
of this; in all his years as a journalist he had never once been
shot at. He had never dodged a real bullet. But Cab Mulcahy
had, and he had written poetically about the experience. Wiley
admired him, and it hurt to have the old boy talk like this.

'I took all your columns from the last four months,' Mulcahy said, 'and I gave them to Dr. Courtney, the psychiatrist.'

'Jesus! He's a wacko, Cab. The guy has a thing for animals. I've heard this from seven or eight sources. Ducks and geese, stuff like that. The paper ought to get rid of him before there's some kind of scandal—'

Mulcahy waved his hands, a signal for Wiley to shut up.

'Dr. Courtney read all these columns and he says he can chart your illness, starting since September.'

Wiley clenched his teeth so tightly his fillings nearly cracked. 'There's nothing wrong with me, Cab.'

'I want you to see a doctor.'

'Not Courtney, please.'

'The *Sun* will pay for it.'

Well, it *ought* to, Wiley thought. If I'm nuts, it's this place that's to blame.

'I also want you to go to an internist. Courtney says the mental degeneration has occurred so rapidly that it could be pathological. A tumour or something.'

'A guy who screws barnyard animals says that *I'm* pathological.'

Mulcahy said, 'He's paid for his opinions.'

'He hates the column,' Wiley said. 'Always has.' He pointed at the stack of clippings. 'I know what's in there, Cab. The one I did six weeks ago about shrinks. Courtney's still mad about that. He's trying to get back at me.'

Mulcahy said, 'He didn't mention it, although it was a particularly vile piece of writing. "Greedy, soul-sucking charlatans"— isn't that what you said about psychiatrists?'

'Something like that.'

'If I'd been here that morning, I'd have yanked that column,' Mulcahy said evenly.

'Ha!'

'Skip, this is the deal. Go see the doctors and you can keep your column, at least until we find out what the hell is wrong. In the meantime, every word you write goes through me personally. Nothing that comes out of your terminal, not even a fucking obituary, gets into this newspaper without me seeing it first.'

Wiley seemed stunned. He shrank into the chair.

'Jeez, Cab, why don't you just cut off my balls and get it over with?'

Mulcahy walked him to the door. 'Don't write about the Harper case anymore, Skip,' he said, not gently. 'Dr. Courtney is expecting you tomorrow morning. Ten sharp.'

Brian Keyes read Skip Wiley's column as soon as he got back to the office. He laughed out loud, in spite of himself. He had become amazed—there was no other word for it—at how much Wiley could get away with.

Keyes wondered if Ernesto Cabal had seen the newspaper. He hoped not. Wiley's column would absolutely ruin the young man's day.

Assuming Ernesto was innocent—and Keyes was leaning in that direction—the next step was figuring out who would have wanted B. D. Harper dead. It was a most unusual murder, and robbery seemed an unlikely motive. Dumping the body in a suitcase was like the Mob, Keyes thought, but the Mob didn't have much of a sense of humor; the Mob wouldn't have dressed Sparky up in such godawful tacky clothes, or stuffed a rubber alligator down his throat.

Finding a solid suspect besides Ernesto Cabal wasn't going to be easy. B. D. Harper had not risen to the pinnacle of his trade by making enemies. His mission, in fact, had been quite the opposite: to make as many friends as possible and offend no one. Harper had been good at this. He positively excreted congeniality.

Sparky had lived and breathed tourism. His singular goal had been to lure as many people to South Florida to spend as much money as was humanly possible in four days and three nights. He lay awake nights scheming new ways to draw people to the tropical bosom of Miami.

As a reporter, Brian Keyes had come to know B. D. Harper fairly well. There was nothing not to like; there simply was nothing much at all. He was an innocuous, rotund little man who was jolliest when Florida was crawling with snowbirds. For years Harper had run his own successful public-relations firm, staging predictable dumb stunts like putting a snow machine on the beach in January, or mailing a ripe Florida orange to every human being in Prudhoe Bay, Alaska. This was in the boom days of Miami and, in a way, Sparky Harper had been a proud pioneer of the shameless, witless boosterism that made Florida grow.

In later years, as head of the Chamber of Commerce, Harper's principal task was to compose a snazzy new bumper sticker every year:

'Miami—Too Hot to Handle!'

'Florida is . . . Paradise Found!'

'Miami Melts in Your Mouth!'

Brian Keyes's personal favorite was 'The Most Exciting City in America,' which Sparky propitiously introduced one month after Miami's worst race riot.

Harper shrewdly had peddled his lame slogans by affixing them to color posters of large-breasted women sunbathing on the beach, sprawling on the bows of sailboats, or dangling from a hang-glider—whatever Sparky could arrange. The women were always very beautiful because the Chamber of Commerce could afford to hire the top models.

The annual unveiling of the new tourism poster made Sparky Harper neither controversial nor unpopular. As far as anyone could tell, it was the only tangible thing he did all year to earn his forty-two-thousand-dollar salary.

As for the murder, Keyes thought of the usual cheap possibilities: a jealous husband, an impatient loan shark, a jilted girlfriend, a jilted boyfriend. Nothing seemed to fit. Sparky was a divorced man with a French poodle named Bambi. When he dated at all, he dated widows or hookers. He had been known to get bombed on occasion, but he never made an ass of himself in public. And he wasn't a gambler, so it was unlikely that the Mafia was into him.

Keyes guessed that whoever killed Harper might not have known him personally, but probably knew who he was. With garish methodology the killer had seemed to be making a very strong statement, which is why Keyes couldn't dismiss the 'Nights of December' letter, nutsy as it was.

Keyes decided that he needed the autopsy report. He drove to the medical examiner's office and asked for a copy. Dr. Joe Allen wasn't in, so Keyes decided to wait. As he sat in a tiled room that smelled sweetly of formalin, he started to read Allen's report line-by-line. Halfway through, his curiosity got the best of him and he unsheathed the color slides. One by one Keyes held them up to the light.

The more he studied the gruesome photographs, the more Keyes was convinced that Ernesto Cabal was telling the truth: he'd had nothing to do with B. D. Harper's murder. It was beyond Ernesto's stunted imagination to have conceived something like this.

'Don't smudge up my slides!' Dr. Joe Allen stood at the doorway, laden with files.

"Mornin', Doc.'

'Well, Brian. I hear you've hit the big time.' Joe Allen had always liked Brian Keyes. Keyes had been a solid reporter and it was a damn shame he'd given it up to become a P.I. Joe Allen wasn't crazy about private investigators.

'This was no robbery, Joe.'

'I don't know what it was,' Dr. Allen said, 'except that it was definitely death by asphyxiation.'

'Have you ever heard of a B-and-E artist to show such flair?' Keyes asked.

'It seems the police are of that opinion.'

'I'm asking for yours, Joe.'

Dr. Joe Allen had autopsied 3,712 murder victims during his long career as the Dade County coroner, so he had seen more indescribable carnage than perhaps any other human being in the whole United States. Throughout the years Joe Allen had charted South Florida's progress by what lay dead on his steel tables, and he was long past the point of ever being shocked or nauseated. He performed meticulous surgery, kept precise files, took flawless photographs, and compiled priceless morbidity data which earned him a national reputation. For example, it was Dr. Allen who had determined that Greater Miami had more mutilation-homicides per capita than any other American city, a fact he attributed to the terrific climate. In warm weather, Allen noted, there were no outdoor elements to deter a lunatic from spending six, seven, eight hours hacking away on a victim; try that in Buffalo and you'd freeze your ass off. After Dr. Allen had presented his findings to a big pathologists' convention, several other Sun Belt coroners had conducted their own studies and confirmed what became known as the Allen Mutilation Theorem.

Throughout the years a few spectacular cases stood out vividly in Dr. Allen's recollections, but the rest were just toe tags. Brian Keyes hoped Sparky Harper might be different.

The coroner put on his glasses and held up two of the more sickening slides, as if to refresh his memory. 'Brian,' he said, 'I don't think they've got the right man in jail.'

'So how do I get him out?'

'Give them a better suspect.'

'Swell, Joe. Anyone in particular?'

'In my opinion, Mr. Harper was the victim of a ritual slaying. I'd say that several persons were involved. I would also say that neither robbery nor sexual assault was the motive. I wouldn't rule out the possibility of an occult ceremony, possibly even human sacrifice. On the other hand, the body showed no common signs of torture—no cigarette burns, welts, or bruise patterns. But you can't ignore what happened to the legs.'

Keyes asked, 'What *did* happen to the legs?'

'The legs were removed after death occurred, probably so the body could be concealed in the suitcase. But it's the way the legs were removed that's so interesting.'

Keyes said, 'Joe, are you doing this just to make me sick?'

'The legs weren't just hacked off with an axe, which is the most efficient way,' said Dr. Allen, pausing to choose his words. 'It appears from the wounds that Sparky's legs might have been removed by a large animal. They might actually have been . . . twisted off.'

'God! By what, wild dogs?'

Dr. Allen shook his head somberly. 'Judging from the bite pattern, it was no dog. It was something much bigger. Don't ask me what, Brian, because I just don't know.'

'Joe, you always brighten my day.'

'Happy hunting, my friend.'

5

Brian Keyes's office was on the sixth floor of a dreary downtown bank building off SW Second Avenue, near the Miami River. The consulate of El Salvador was located down the hall, so most of the other tenants lived in perpetual fear of a terrorist attack and behaved accordingly. They all had chipped in to hire extra security guards for the lobby, but the security men had turned out to be professional burglars who one night looted the entire building of all IBM office machinery.

Brian Keyes was not affected by this crime because the only typewriter in his office was an old Olivetti portable, a leftover from his days of covering politics for the Miami *Sun*. The other items of potential value were an antique desk lamp and a telephone tape recorder, but the lamp was broken and the tape recorder was made in Korea so the burglars wanted no part of either.

The highlight of the office was a fifty-gallon salt-water aquarium, a going-away present from his friends at the newspaper. Keyes had erected it in the foyer, where a secretary ordinarily might have sat, and filled it with whiskered catfish that sucked the algae off the glass.

Except for the aquarium, the place was just as cramped, ratty, and depressing as Keyes had feared it would be. He was rarely there. Even when he had nothing to do, he'd find an excuse to leave the bank building and stroll around downtown. He had an answering service, and an electronic beeper that fit onto his belt. The beeper didn't make Keyes feel particularly important; every shyster lawyer, dope dealer, and undercover agent in Dade County wore one. It was mandatory.

On the morning of December 5, Keyes was down at Bayfront

Park, munching a sandwich and watching the tugboats, when the beeper on his belt went off loudly enough to wake a derelict two benches away.

Keyes found a pay phone and called his service. Al García was trying to reach him. It was important. Keyes phoned Homicide.

'Meet me on the beach,' García said. 'The Flamingo Isles, near Sixty-eighth and Collins. Look for the cop cars out front.'

The Flamingo Isles was not a classic Miami Beach motel. There was nothing charming about the color (silt) or the architecture (Early Texaco). At this motel there were no striped canvas awnings, no wizened retirees chirping in the lobby, no lawn chairs lined up on the front porch, no front porch whatsoever. Basically the Flamingo Isles was a dive for pimps, chicken hawks, and hookers. Rooms cost ten dollars an hour, fifteen with porno cassettes. It was rumored that some of the vestibules were equipped with hidden movie cameras to secretly record the sexual antics of Florida tourists. It was not a good place for an innocent man, but Keyes was hopeful that this was where Sparky Harper had spent his final earthly moments. If so, it meant that Harper had likely died in some bizarre sexual accident and not at the larcenous hands of Ernesto Cabal.

Keyes goosed his little MG convertible across the causeway and made it to the motel in eighteen minutes flat. Al García already was interviewing a Jamaican maid in the lobby. He kept hollering for an interpreter and the maid kept insisting in perfect English that she spoke perfect English, but García wouldn't believe her. He finally enlisted a black Miami Beach detective to take the maid's statement, and went upstairs, Keyes in tow. They entered room 223.

'Here you have it,' García said.

A pile of men's clothing lay in the middle of the floor: blue silk socks, turned inside-out; an undershirt; a pair of soiled Jockey shorts; and a powder-blue double-knit suit with a J. C. Penney label. The legs of the suit had been sheared off below the knees. Lying beneath the clothes was a pair of highly polished black Florsheims.

The room showed no signs of a mortal struggle. There was a

half-finished bottle of Seagram's and a couple cans of soda on the dresser. On the nightstand, next to the Magic Fingers machine, sat three plastic bottles of Coppertone tanning butter with coconut oil. A fingerprint man studiously dusted the containers; he was crouched on his haunches, oblivious of everything.

With a long pair of tweezers, García picked a plastic bag off the floor. The red-and-white lettering on the bag said: 'Everglades Novelties.'

'This,' García intoned, 'was used to transport the instrument of death.'

'The toy alligator?'

García nodded.

'So this is where it happened.'

'The murder? No, we don't think so.'

Suddenly a big redheaded cop barged out of the bathroom. It was Harold Keefe, the lead detective.

'Who're you?' he asked Keyes.

'A friend of Al's.' Keyes looked at García. García had an *oh shit!* look in his eyes.

'Don't touch anything,' Keefe growled on his way out the door. 'Al, don't let him touch anything, got it?'

García checked the bathroom to make sure no other detectives were sneaking around. He didn't say another word until the fingerprint man packed up his kit and left.

'Christ! I didn't know that bastard was in the john!'

'Relax, Al. He doesn't know who I am.'

García started stuffing B. D. Harper's clothing in a clear plastic evidence bag. 'Check out the stains on the floor,' he told Keyes.

Two streaks of dried blood made a wavering trail from the bedroom to the bathroom. It was not very much blood, certainly less than one would have expected.

'The lab guys are on their way,' García said, 'so I'm gonna give it to you once. Then I want you to get out of here before I get in trouble.'

'Whatever you say, Al.'

'On the night of November 30, two men rented this room for one week. They paid cash in advance, three hundred and sixty bucks.'

'What'd they look like?'

'One was described as a muscular black male in a tight yellow pullover,' García said, 'and the other was a young Latin male wearing blue jeans.'

Keyes grimaced. 'I suppose you showed Cabal's mug shot to the desk clerk.'

'Yeah, and she's seventy-five percent sure it was him.'

'Seventy-five won't cut it in court, Al.'

'Don't worry, she'll be one hundred percent positive by the time this goes to trial.'

'Anyone see them with B. D. Harper?'

'We got a couple faggots in room 225 who saw the Latin male enter this room about eleven P.M. with a chubby Anglo matching Harper's description. They heard some loud voices, and then the door slammed. The fairies peeked out just in time to see Harper being led down the stairs by the black dude and the little Cuban. Oh yeah, and the Cuban is carrying a red Samsonite.'

'So they took Harper someplace, killed him, cut his legs off, stuffed him in the suitcase, and—'

'Brought him back here,' García said. 'This is where the weird shit happens. These blood smears come from dragging the corpse into the bathroom. That's where they dress him up in that stupid flowered shirt and smear the Coppertone all over and stuff him in the suitcase.'

'Don't forget the sunglasses,' Keyes said.

'Right. Then they drive out to Key Biscayne and heave him into the bay.'

'Why all the trouble?'

García said, 'Beats the hell out of me. Anyway, the black guy and the Cuban haven't been back since early on the morning of December 1. The maid just opened the room today. She saw the blood on the floor and called the Beach police.'

'Well, this is great news, Al.'

'I'm not finished. Remember I told you I had a line on those goofy clothes? Well, I got a sales clerk at a joint down the street who says she sold them to a skinny little Cuban guy on November 29.'

'Ernesto?'

'She's eighty percent sure. The creep was wearing a floppy hat, so she's not absolutely certain.'

'Give her time,' Keyes said glumly. Things were looking bleak for Señor Cabal. Keyes wondered if he'd been wrong about the little guy. Maybe he wasn't just a crummy car burglar trying to get by.

García knotted the top of the evidence bag and scanned the room to make sure he hadn't missed anything. 'Time for you to hit the road,' he told Keyes. 'And remember, I don't know your fucking name.'

'Right Al.'

Keyes was in the parking lot, strolling toward the MG, when he heard García call from a balcony.

'Hey, Brian, you wanna *really* help your client?'

'You bet.'

'It's easy,' García shouted. 'Find the black guy.'

Keyes arrived at the county jail just as Mitch Klein was leaving. Klein was a scruffy young lawyer with the public defender's office who apparently had drawn the short straw when they farmed out Ernesto Cabal's case. As he walked out of the jail, his shirt damp and his tie loose, Klein did not look like a happy man. He looked like a man who couldn't wait to get into private practice.

Klein greeted Keyes with a lugubrious nod and said, 'What's the bad news for the day?'

'They found a motel room on the beach with Harper's clothes and some blood on the floor. Little Cuban guy rented it the night before Harper vanished.'

'Beautiful,' Klein grumbled.

'The good news is, a big black guy was working with the Cuban. He matches the description of the character Ernesto says sold him the Oldsmobile. Maybe I can find him.'

Klein rolled his eyes and made a lewd pumping motion with his right hand. 'I think Ernesto is full of shit,' he said.

Wonderful, Keyes thought, the guy's own lawyer is dumping on him.

When Keyes entered the cell, he noticed that Ernesto lay stark naked on the cot. Ernesto blinked at Keyes like a gecko lizard stunned by the sunlight.

'Dey took my close.'

'Why?'

"Fraid I'm gonna hang myself.'

'Are you?'

'Not now.'

'Glad to hear it.'

Ernesto rolled over on his stomach, exposing stringy white buttocks. Two prisoners in another cell hooted in appreciation. Ernesto ignored them.

'That man Klein wants me to cop a plea. Says he's trying to save my life. He says dey strap my ass in a lektric chair if diss case go to jury. You thin' he's right?'

Keyes said, 'I'm no lawyer.'

'Too bad. That Klein, he's got nice shoes. You could use some nice shoes, no?'

Keyes told Cabal about the Flamingo Isles motel. The Cuban sat up excitedly when he heard the part about the black man and B. D. Harper.

'Was the black guy wearing Carrera frames?'

'I don't know.'

'I'll bet it's the same dude who sold me that goddamn car.'

'I'll try to find him, Ernesto.'

'Hey, you tell Klein?'

'Yes.'

'What'd he say?'

'He said it sounded very promising.'

'I seen the black guy before.' Ernesto stood up and started pacing the cell. Keyes found his nakedness a little disconcerting. Mainly it was the tattoo: a commendable likeness of Fidel Castro's face, stenciled deftly on the tip of Ernesto's most private appendage.

'Think hard, Ernesto. Where did you see the black guy? On the beach? In a bar? At Sunday school?'

'Sone-thin like dat.' Ernesto clasped his hands behind his back and stared through the bars of the cell. 'I'm gone thin about it.'

Keyes decided it was time to break the bad news. He told Ernesto about the desk clerk at the Flamingo Isles and the saleswoman at the clothing store, about how they had looked at his mug shot and were almost positive that he was the one.

'Dumb bitches,' Ernesto said stoically.

Keyes said, 'A skinny Cuban rented that motel room, and a skinny Cuban bought those loud clothes for B. D. Harper.'

'Not *diss* skinny Cuban.'

Ernesto sat down on the cot and, mercifully, crossed his legs.

'Do you want me to get your clothes back?'

'Thas all right, man.'

'Where do I start looking for the friendly car salesman?'

'Pauly's Bar. Juss ask round. Big black guy with glasses. Not many of dose on the Beach, man.'

'Did he have an accent?'

Ernesto giggled. 'He's *black*, man. 'Course he had an accent.'

'Jamaican? Haitian? American?'

'He's no Jamaican, and he's no street nigger. Diss boy been to school.' Ernesto was very sure of himself. 'Diss man, he's slick.'

Keyes told Ernesto to think on it some more. He'd need all the help he could get. Especially at Pauly's Bar.

6

Dr. Remond Courtney didn't blink. He merely said: 'I'm not sure I heard you right, Mr. Wiley.'

'Oh, sorry.' Skip Wiley got up and ambled across the office. He leaned over and positioned his large face two inches from the doctor's nose. 'I said,' Wiley shouted, as if Courtney were deaf, 'is it really true that you have sex with mallard ducks?'

'No,' Courtney replied, lips whitening.

'Mergansers, then?'

'No.'

'Ah, so it's geese. No need to be ashamed.'

'Mr. Wiley, sit down, please. I think we're avoiding the subject, aren't we?'

'And what subject would that be, Dr. Goosefucker? May I call you that? Do you mind?'

Courtney looked down at the notebook in his lap, as if referring to something important. Actually the page was blank. 'Why,' he said to Skip Wiley, 'all this hostility?'

'Because we're wasting each other's time. There's nothing wrong with me and you know it. But you had to be an asshole and tell my boss I've got a pathological brain tumor—so here I am, about to do something truly pathological.' Wiley smiled and grabbed Dr. Courtney by the shoulders.

The psychiatrist struggled to maintain an air of superiority (as if this were just some childish prank) while trying to squirm from Wiley's grasp. But Wiley was a strong man and he easily lifted Courtney off the couch.

'I never said you had a tumor, Skip.'

Dr. Remond Courtney was remarkably calm, but he'd had plenty of practice. He was by trade a professional witness, a courthouse shrink-for-hire. He was impressive in trial—cool, self-assured, unshakable on the stand. Lawyers loved Dr. Courtney and they paid him a fortune to sit in the witness box and say their clients were crazy as loons. It was laughably easy work, and Courtney was conveniently flexible in his doctrines; one day he might be a disciple of Skinner and, the next, a follower of Freud. It all depended on the case (and who was paying his fee). Dr. Courtney had become so successful as an expert witness that he was able to drop most of his private patients and limit his psychiatric practice to three or four lucrative corporate and government contracts. Dr. Courtney had hoped this would minimize his exposure to dangerous over-the-transom South Florida fruitcakes, but he'd learned otherwise. By the time a big company got around to referring one of its employees to a psychiatrist, the screaming meemies had already set in and the patient often was receiving radio beams from Venus. The worst thing you could do in such a case, Remond Courtney believed, was lose your professional composure. Once a patient knew he could rattle you, you were finished as an analyst. Domination required composure, Dr. Courtney liked to say.

'Skip, I can assure you I never said anything about a brain tumor.'

'Oh, it's *Skip* now, is it? Did you learn that at shrink school, Dr. Goosefucker? Whenever a patient becomes unruly, call him by his first name.'

'Would you prefer "Mr. Wiley" instead?'

'I would prefer not to be here,' Wiley said, guiding Dr. Courtney toward the window of his office. Below, fifteen floors down, was Biscayne Boulevard. Courtney didn't need to be reminded of the precise distance (he'd had a patient jump once), but Skip Wiley reminded him anyway. He reminded Dr. Courtney by hanging him by his Italian-made heels.

'What do you see, doctor?'

'My life,' the upside-down psychiatrist said, 'passing before my eyes.'

'That's just a Metro bus.'

'A bus, you're right. Lots of people walking. Some taxicabs. Lots of things, Mr. Wiley.' The doctor's voice was brittle and high. He was using his arms to fend himself off the side of the building, and doing a pretty good job. After a few seconds Courtney's paisley ascot fluttered from his neck and drifted down to earth like a wounded butterfly. Skip Wiley thought he heard the doctor whimper.

'You okay down there?'

'Not really,' Courtney called up to him. 'Mr. Wiley, your time's almost up.'

Wiley dragged Courtney up through the window.

'Your ankles sweat, you know that?'

'I'm not surprised,' the doctor said.

'So you're sticking with this idea that I'm crazy? That's what you're going to tell Mulcahy?'

Courtney brushed himself off. The palms of his hands were red and abraded, and this seemed to bother him. He straightened his blazer. 'You're very lucky I didn't lose one of my contact lenses,' he told Wiley.

'You're lucky you didn't lose your goddamn life.' Plainly unsatisfied, Wiley sat down at the doctor's desk. Courtney reclaimed his spot on the couch, a brand-new spiral notebook on his lap.

'In my opinion, it started with the hurricane column,' the psychiatrist said.

'Come on, doc, that was a terrific piece.'

'It was uncommonly vicious and graphic. "What South Florida needs most is a killer hurricane . . ." All that stuff about screaming winds and crumpled condominiums. My mother saw that . . . that trash,' the doctor said with agitation, 'and the next day she put her place on the market. The poor woman's scared to death. An ocean view with a nine-point-eight-mortgage—assumable!—and still she's scared out of her mind. Wants to move to bloody Tucson. All because of you!'

'Really?' Skip Wiley seemed pleased.

'What kind of drugs,' Dr. Courtney started to ask him, 'provoke this kind of lunacy?'

But Skip Wiley already was on his way out the door, a honey-maned blur.

Cab Mulcahy strolled into the newsroom shortly after five. He was a composed, distinguished-looking presence among the young neurotics who put out the daily newspaper, and several of them traded glances that said: *Wonder what brings the old man out?*

Mulcahy was looking for Wiley. Actually, he was looking for Wiley's column. Mulcahy harbored a fear that Wiley would devise a way to sneak the damn thing into print in defiance of their agreement.

The city editor said he hadn't seen Wiley all day, and reported that no column had arrived by messenger, telephone, or teletype. The city editor also pointed out that, without a column, he was staring at a big sixteen-inch hole on the front page, with deadlines fast approaching.

'Ricky Bloodworth's offered to do the column if Wiley doesn't show up,' the city editor said.

'Has he now?'

'He worked up a couple pieces in his spare time. I saw 'em this morning, Cab, and they're not bad. A little purple, maybe, but interesting.'

'No way,' Mulcahy said. 'Tell him thanks just the same.'

The city editor looked dejected; Mulcahy knew that he had been yearning to rid himself of the Wiley Problem for a long time. The city editor did not get on well with Skip Wiley. It was a bad relationship that only got worse after Wiley let it slip that he was making five thousand dollars a year more than the city editor, not including stock options. *Stock options!* The city editor had gone home that night and kicked the shit out of his cocker spaniel.

'Did you call Wiley's house?' Mulcahy asked.

'Jenna hasn't seen him since he left for the doctor's this morning. She said he seemed fine and dandy.'

'That's what she said?'

'*Ver-batim*,' the city editor said. 'Fine and dandy.'

Mulcahy phoned Dr. Remond Courtney and told him that Skip Wiley hadn't showed up for work.

'Oh?' Dr. Courtney did not seem surprised, but it was hard to tell. Courtney was an expert at masking his reactions by saying things like *Oh* and *I see* and *Why don't you tell me about it.*

'I was wondering,' Mulcahy said impatiently, 'how things went today?'

'How things went?'

'With you and Mr. Wiley. You had an appointment, remember?'

More silence; then: 'He became abusive.'

'Became abusive? He's *always* abusive.'

'Physically abusive,' Courtney said. He was trying to remain clinical so Mulcahy wouldn't suspect how scared he'd been. 'I believe he threatened my life.'

'What did you do?'

'I talked him out of it, of course. I think we were doing much better by the end of the hour.'

'Glad to hear it,' Mulcahy said, thinking: Wiley's right, this guy is useless. 'Tell me, did Skip say where he was going after his visit?'

'No. He left in a hurry. It had been a strenuous session for both of us.'

Mulcahy said, 'So what's the verdict?'

'Verdict?'

'What the hell is wrong with him?'

'Stress, fatigue, anxiety, paranoia. It's all job-related. I suggest you give him a year off.'

'I can't do that, doctor. He's a very popular writer and the newspaper needs him.'

'Suit yourself. He's a nut case.'

A nut case who sells newspapers, Mulcahy thought ruefully. Next he tried Jenna.

'I still haven't seen him, Cab. I'm getting a little worried, too. I've got a spinach pie in the oven.'

Jenna had the most delicious voice of any woman Cab Mulcahy had ever met; pure gossamer. Even *spinach pie* came out like *Let's do it!* The day Skip Wiley moved in with Jenna was the day Cab Mulcahy decided there was no God.

'Does he usually call?' Mulcahy asked.

'He doesn't do anything in a usual way, you know that, Cab.' A silky laugh.

Mulcahy sighed. In a way it was his fault. Hadn't he introduced them to each other, Jenna and Skip, one night at the Royal Palm Club?

Jenna said, 'Skip makes contact two or three times a day, in various ways. Today—nothing, after noon.'

'What did he say,' Mulcahy ventured, 'when he ... made contact?'

'Not much. Hold on, I gotta turn down the stove. . . . Okay, let me try to remember . . . I know! He said he was on his way to get a new muffler for the car, and he also said he murdered the psychiatrist. Is that part true?'

'Of course not,' Mulcahy said.

'I'm glad. He's got such a crummy temper.'

'Jenna, did Skip mention when he might be making contact again?'

'No, he never does. He likes to surprise me, says it keeps the romance fresh. Sometimes I wonder if he's just testing me. Trust is a two-way street, y'know.'

'But he comes home for dinner?'

'Almost always,' Jenna said.

'If he comes home tonight,' Mulcahy said, by now eager to escape the conversation, 'please have him call the newsroom. It's important.'

'I'm getting worried, Cab,' Jenna said again. 'This spinach is starting to clot.'

What an actress, Mulcahy thought, she's just terrific. When Skip Wiley first seduced Jenna, he'd thought he was getting himself a gorgeous blond melon-breasted bimbo. That's how he had described her to Mulcahy, who knew better. He had warned Wiley, too, warned him to proceed with extreme caution. Mulcahy had seen Jenna in action once before; she was magnetic and purposeful far beyond Skip Wiley's ragged powers of comprehension. But Wiley hadn't listened to Mulcahy's warning, and chased Jenna shamelessly until she'd let herself get caught.

Mulcahy's speculation about Wiley's weirdness included the possibility that Jenna was the key.

Mulcahy swept the clutter from the desk into his briefcase, put on his jacket, and threaded his way through the newsroom toward the elevators.

'Cab, just a second.' It was the city editor, looking febrile.

'If Wiley doesn't show, run a feature story in his slot,' Mulcahy instructed, still walking. 'A parade story, something mild like that.

And at the bottom run a small box in italics. Say Wiley's out sick. Say the column will resume shortly.'

The city editor didn't skulk off the way Mulcahy expected him to. Mulcahy stopped short of the elevators and asked, 'What's the matter?'

'The highway patrol just called,' the city editor said uneasily. 'They found Wiley's car, the old Pontiac.'

'Where?'

'In the middle of Interstate 95. At rush hour.'

'No Wiley?'

The city editor shook his head grimly. 'Engine was running, and Clapton was blasting on the tape deck. The car was just sitting there empty in traffic. They're towing it to Miami police headquarters. I've sent Bloodworth over to see what he can find out. Want me to call you later at home?'

'Sure,' said Cab Mulcahy, more puzzled than before.

'About the column, Cab . . .'

'Yeah?'

'Sure you won't give Ricky a shot?'

Mulcahy rarely frowned or raised his voice, but he was on the verge of doing both. 'You got a parade story for tomorrow? Don't tell me you don't. There's *always* a parade in this goddamn town.'

'Yes, Cab. However, it was a very small parade today.'

'I don't care.'

'Belize Nationalism Day?'

'Perfect. Go with it. Run a nice big picture, too.'

'But, Cab . . .'

'And call Jenna. Right away.'

The screen door on Pauly's Bar was humming with flies. Inside there were six barstools, a gutted pinball machine, a boar's head, and a life-size cutout of Victoria Principal, a bourbon stain on her right breast. The bar itself was made of cheap pine and appeared to be recently repaired, bristling with fresh nails and splinters. Behind the bar was a long horizontal mirror, its fissures secured with brown hurricane tape.

At first glance Pauly's was not a raucous joint, but a careful person could sense an ominous lethargy.

Brian Keyes decided to be the perfect customer. He slipped the lumpy-faced bartender a twenty-dollar bill and discreetly assured him that no, he wasn't a cop, he was just trying to buy some information.

The bartender, who wore a mesh tank top and a shiny mail-order toupee, turned out to be somewhat helpful; after all, twenty dollars was a banner night at Pauly's. Keyes knew from looking around the place that the man he hunted would be remembered here, and he was right.

'Don't get many big niggers in here,' the bartender remarked, secreting the money in a pocket. 'Then again, they all look big at night.' The bartender laughed, and so did a greasy wino two stools down. Keyes smiled and said ha-ha, pretty funny, but this one you'd remember especially because of the fancy black sunglasses.

The bartender and the greasy wino exchanged looks, their grins getting bigger and dirtier. 'Viceroy!' the bartender said. 'Viceroy Wilson.'

'The football player?'

'Sure.'

'I don't believe it!' Keyes said.

'Well, take a look here,' and then the bartender tossed an official NFL football at Brian Keyes, knocking over his Budweiser. Viceroy Wilson, former star fullback for the Miami Dolphins, had autographed the ball with a magnificent flourish, in red ink right under the stitch.

'He's a regular,' the bartender boasted.

'No!'

'He sure is!'

'Well, I really need to talk to him.'

'He don't give autographs to just anybody.'

'I don't want an autograph.'

'Then why you asking for him? He's not a man that likes to be asked for.'

'It's personal,' Keyes said. 'Very important.'

'I'll bet,' croaked the wino. Keyes ignored him. He had a feeling these guys were full of shit anyway. Keyes was an avid football fan and, looking around, he wasn't able to picture the great Viceroy Wilson—bad hands, bankrupt and all—rubbing elbows with a bunch of pukes at Pauly's. Viceroy Wilson didn't belong in a rathole dive on South Beach; Viceroy Wilson belonged in Canton, Ohio, at the Football Hall of Fame.

'I'll get him for you,' the wino volunteered, oozing off the barstool.

'Hey, what if he don't want to be got?' the bartender said, 'Viceroy's a very private man.'

'Twenty bucks,' the wino said. Keyes handed it to him and ordered another beer. Twenty dollars apparently was now the going rate for everything at Pauly's. The wino shuffled out the door.

'Kiss your money good-bye,' the bartender said reproachfully.

'Relax,' Keyes told him, knowing it would only have the opposite effect. People in bars don't like to be told to relax.

'I'm beginning to think you're a narc!' the bartender said loudly. He calmed down when Keyes laid another twenty bucks on the bar next to the beer glass.

Forty minutes later the screen door wheezed open and stayed that way for several moments. A cool salty breeze tickled Keyes's neck. He longed to turn around but instead just sipped on the beer, pretending that the 235-pound black man (Carrera sunglasses dangling on his chest) who loomed in the tavern mirror wasn't really glaring at him as if he were the proverbial turd in the punch bowl.

'I don't think I know you,' Viceroy Wilson growled.

Brian Keyes was in the process of spinning around on the barstool, about to say something extremely witty, when a black fist the approximate size and consistency of a cinderblock slammed into the base of his neck.

At that instant Keyes's brain became a kaleidoscope, and he would later be able to recall only a few jagged pieces of consciousness.

The sound of the screen door slamming.

The taste of the sidewalk.

The cough of an automobile's ignition.

He remembered opening one eye with the dreadful thought that he was about to be run over.

And he remembered a glimpse of a vanity license tag—'GATOR 2'—as the car peeled rubber.

But Keyes didn't remember shutting his eyes and going nighty-night on the cool concrete.

'Hello?'

Brian Keyes stared up at the round, friendly-looking face of a middle-aged woman.

'Are you injured?' she asked.

'I think my spine is broken.' Keyes was lying outside Pauly's Bar. The pavement smelled like stale beer and urine. Unseen shards of an ancient wine bottle dug into his shoulder blades. It was eleven o'clock and the street was very dark.

'My name is Nell Bellamy.'

'I'm Brian Keyes.'

'Should I call an ambulance, Mr. Keyes?'

Keyes shook his head no.

'These are my friends Burt and James,' Nell Bellamy said. Two men wearing mauve fez hats bent over and peered at Brian Keyes. They were Shriners.

'What are *you* doing here?' one of them asked benignly.

'I got beat up,' Keyes replied, still flat on his back. 'I'll be fine in a month or two.' He ran a hand over his ribs, feeling through the shirt for fractures. 'What are *you* doing here?' he asked the Shriners.

'Looking for her husband.'

'Theodore Bellamy,' Nell said. 'He disappeared last Saturday.'

'Give me a hand, please,' Keyes said. The Shriners helped him to his feet. They were big, ruddy fellows; they propped him up until the vertigo went away. From inside Pauly's Bar came the sounds of breaking glass and loud shouting in Spanish.

'Let's take a walk,' Keyes said.

'But I wanted to ask around in there,' Nell said, nodding toward the bar, 'to see if anybody has seen Teddy.'

'Bad idea,' Keyes grunted.

'He's right, Nell,' one of the Shriners advised.

So they set off down Washington Avenue. They were a queer ensemble, even by South Beach standards. Keyes walked tentatively, like a well-dressed lush, while Nell handed out fliers with Teddy's picture. The Shriners ran interference through knots of shirtless refugees who milled outside the droopy boardinghouses and peeling motels. The refugees flashed predatory smiles and made wisecracks in Spanish, but the Shriners were imperturbable.

Nell Bellamy asked Keyes what had happened inside the bar, so he told her about Viceroy Wilson.

'We saw a black fellow speeding away,' Nell said.

'In a Cadillac,' Burt volunteered.

'Burt sells Cadillacs,' Nell said to Keyes. 'So he ought to know.'

The four of them had reached the southern point of Miami Beach, near Joe's Stone Crab, and they were alone on foot. This part of South Beach wasn't exactly the Boardwalk, and at night it was generally deserted except for serious drunks, ax murderers, and illegal aliens.

With Nell leading the way, the entourage strolled toward the oceanfront.

Burt remarked that he once had seen the Dolphins play the Chicago Bears in an exhibition game, and that Walter Payton had made Viceroy Wilson look like a flatfooted old man.

'That was in '75,' the Shriner added.

'By then his knees were shot,' Keyes said halfheartedly. He didn't feel much like defending any creep who'd sucker-punch him in a place like Pauly's. In all his years as a reporter he had never been slugged. Not once. He had been chased and stoned and menaced in a variety of ways, but never really punched. A punch was quite a personal thing.

'You should file charges,' Nell suggested.

Keyes felt silly. Here was this stout little woman searching godforsaken neighborhoods in the dead of night for her missing husband, while Keyes just moped along feeling sorry for himself over a lousy bump on the neck.

He asked Nell Bellamy about Theodore. She mustered herself and told, for the sixteenth time, all about the convention, the venomous jellyfish, the unorthodox lifeguards, and what the cops were saying must have happened to her husband.

'We don't believe them,' Burt said. 'Teddy didn't drown.'

'Why not?'

'Where's the body?' Burt said, swinging a beefy arm toward the ocean. 'There's been an easterly wind for days. The body should have floated up by now.'

Nell sat on a seawall and crossed her legs. She wore blue slacks and a modest red blouse, not too vivid. Biting her lip, she stared out at the soapy froth of the surf, visible even on a moonless midnight.

The loyal Shriners shifted uncomfortably, conscious of her grief. For the sake of distraction Burt said, 'Mr. Keyes, what'd you say you do for a living?'

Keyes didn't want to tell them. He knew exactly what would happen if he did: he'd have a missing-persons case he really didn't want.

'I work for some lawyers in town,' he said ambiguously.

'Research?' Nell asked.

'Sort of.'

'Do you know many people? Important people, I mean. Policemen, judges, people like that?'

Here we go, Keyes thought. 'A few,' he said. 'Not many. I'm probably not the most popular person in Dade County.'

But that didn't stop her.

'How much do you charge the lawyers?' Nell asked in a businesslike tone.

'It depends. Two-fifty, three hundred a day. Same as most private investigators.' No sense ducking it now. If the fee didn't scare her off, nothing would.

Nell got up from the seawall and daintily brushed off the seat of her pants. Excusing herself, she took the Shriners aside. Keyes watched them huddle in the penumbra of a streetlight: a chubby, pleasant-faced woman who belonged at a church bake sale, and on each side, a tall husky Midwesterner in a purple fez. Nell seemed to do most of the talking.

Keyes ached all over, but his head was the worst. He checked his pants pocket; miraculously, his wallet was still there. Just thinking about the three-mile hike back to the MG exhausted him.

After a few moments Nell approached again. She was holding a folded piece of paper.

'Do you take private cases?'

'Did I mention that my fee doesn't include expenses?'

Not even a flicker. 'Are you available to take a private case?'

'But, Mrs. Bellamy, you just met me—'

'Please, Mr. Keyes. I don't know a soul down here, but I like you and I think I can trust you. My instincts usually are very sound. Most of all, I need someone with . . .'

'Balls,' Burt said helpfully.

'You marched into that awful tavern like a trooper,' Nell said. 'That's the kind of fellow we need.'

The decent thing to do was to say no. Keyes couldn't take this nice woman's money, feeding her false hope until poor Teddy finally washed up dead on the beach. Could be weeks, depending on the tides and the wind. It would have been thievery, and Keyes couldn't do it.

'I'm sorry, but I can't help.'

'I know what you're thinking, but maybe this'll change your mind.' Nell handed him the folded paper. 'Someone left this in my mailbox at the hotel,' she explained, 'the morning my husband disappeared.'

'Read it,' said the Shriner named James, breaking his silence.

Keyes moved under the streetlight and unfolded the letter. It had been neatly typed, triple-spaced. Keyes read it twice. He still couldn't believe what it said:

> Dear Mrs. Tourist:
>   Welcome to the Revolution. Sorry to disturb your vacation, but we've had to make an example of your husband. Go back North and tell your friends what a dangerous place is Miami.
>   *El Fuego*,
>   *Comandante, Las Noches de Diciembre*

7

Brian Keyes delivered a photocopy of the new *El Fuego* letter to Homicide the next morning. Afterward he went to the office to feed the tropicals and check his messages. The Shriners had called from the county morgue to report that no one matching Theodore Bellamy's description had turned up in the night inventory of Dade County corpses. There was another call-me message from Mitch Klein, the public defender. Keyes decided not to phone back until he knew more about the letter.

At noon Keyes returned to police headquarters. 'Let's go eat,' Al García said, taking him by the arm. García didn't think it was a swell idea to be seen around the office with a private investigator. They rode to lunch in the detective's unmarked Dodge, WQBA blaring Spanish on the radio. García was nonchalantly dodging deranged motorists on Seventh Street, in the heart of Little Havana, when he stubbed out his cigarette and finally mentioned the letter.

'Same typewriter as the first one,' he said.

Keyes wasn't surprised.

'The Beach police think it's a crackpot,' García added in a noncommittal way.

'What do you think, Al?'

'I think it's too hinky for a crackpot. I think to myself, how would this *Fuego* know about Bellamy so soon? Almost before the cops! And I think, where's the connection between this Bellamy guy and B. D. Harper? They didn't even know each other, yet after each one comes these death letters. Too hinky, like I said.'

'So you're ready to spring Cabal?'

García laughed, pounding on the steering wheel. 'You're hilarious, Brian.'

'But Ernesto didn't kill Harper and he damn sure didn't snatch this drunk Shriner.'

'How do you know?'

'Because,' Keyes said, 'the guy's a burglar, not a psychopath.'

'Know what I think, brother? I think Ernesto is *El Fuego.*'

'Give me a break, Al.'

'Let me finish.' García pulled the Dodge into a shopping center and parked near a Cuban café. He rolled down the window and toyed with another cigarette. 'I think your little scuzzball client is *El Fuego*, but I also think he didn't dream up this scheme all by his lonesome. I agree with you: Cabal ain't exactly a master criminal, he's a fuckin' burglar, and not very good at that. This whole thing sounds like a bad extortion scam, and our pal Ernesto, he don't have the brains to extort a blow-job from a legless whore. So he had help. Who? you're asking me. Don't know for sure, but I'll bet it's this mysterious superhuman black dude Cabal's been crying about . . .'

Keyes related his encounter with Viceroy Wilson at Pauly's Bar.

'You deserve a good whack on the head for showing your shiny angel-food face in that snakepit,' the detective said. 'You wanna file A-and-B on the sonofabitch?'

'Just find him, Al.'

'Yes sir, Mr. Taxpayer, I'll get right on it.'

'This might help.' Keyes handed García a scribbled note that said, 'GATOR 2.' 'It's the tag on the Caddy that Wilson was driving.'

'Hey, you do good work. This'll be easy,' García said. 'Come on, let's get a sandwich and some coffee.'

Both of them ordered a hot Cuban mix and ate in the car, wax paper spread across their laps.

'Al,' Keyes said, savoring the tangy sandwich, 'what do you make of the name of this group? *Las Noches de Diciembre*—the Nights of December, right?'

García shrugged. 'Usually Cuban groups name themselves after some great date in their history, but the only thing I know happened in December is Castro came to power—nothing they'd want to celebrate. 'Course, there is another possibility.'

'What's that?'

García paused for another enormous bite. Somehow he was still able to speak. 'They got something planned for *this* December. As in, right now. And if what we've seen already is any indication'—he glanced over at Keyes—'it's gonna be a treat.'

Daniel 'Viceroy' Wilson stood six feet, two inches tall and weighed 237½ pounds. He usually wore his hair in a short Afro, or sometimes plaited, but he always kept enough of a gritty beard to make him look about half as mean as he really was.

One of the things Wilson fervently wished this afternoon, skulking in the parking lot of the world-famous Miami Seaquarium, was that he could own this fine Cadillac he was driving. It didn't seem right that it belonged to the Indian, who didn't appreciate it, didn't even use the goddamn tape deck. One time Wilson had left a Herbie Hancock cassette on the front seat, and the Indian had thrown it out the window with a bunch of Juicy Fruit wrappers and bingo tickets onto I-95. At that moment Wilson had contemplated killing the Indian, but when it came to Seminoles, one had to be careful. There was a wealth of mystical shit to be considered: eagle feathers, panther gonads, and so on. Wilson was much more fearful of Indian magic than of jail, so he let the Herbie Hancock episode slide. Besides, for the first time in years, Wilson had something to look forward to. He didn't want to spoil it by pissing off the Indian.

Still, he'd have loved to own the Caddy.

Life had not been kind to Viceroy Wilson since he was cut from the Miami Dolphins during the preseason of 1978, a month before his own Cadillac Seville had been repossessed. Since then Wilson had been through three wives, two humiliating bankruptcies, a heroin addiction, and one near-fatal shooting. Yet somehow he had managed to maintain his formidable physique in such a way that he could still bring silence to a crowded restaurant just by walking in the door. Wilson's fissured face looked every day of his thirty-six years, yet his body remained virtually unchanged from his glory days as a star fullback: taut, streamlined calves; a teenager's spare hips; and a broad, rippling wedge of a chest. Wilson's strength was in his upper body, always had been; his shoulders had been his best weapons inside the twenty-yard line.

As a rule, Viceroy Wilson didn't go around clobbering strangers in stinky taverns. He believed in the eternal low profile. He was not homesick for the Orange Bowl locker room, nor did he especially miss getting mobbed for his autograph. A free case of Colt .45 was the only reason he'd signed that football in Pauly's Bar. Generally Viceroy Wilson believed that the less he was recognized in public, the better. Part of this attitude was personal preference (autographs being a bitter reminder of the Super Bowl years), and part of it was a necessary adjustment in order to lead a successful life of crime.

Exactly why he'd sucker-punched the skinny white guy in Pauly's, Wilson wasn't sure. Something—a street instinct, maybe—told him not to let the dude get a good look at his face. Something about the back of his head said trouble. Thick brown hair, shiny, straight, razor-cut. Sculptured around the collar. Yeah, *that* was it. Cops got haircuts like that. Wilson was sure this man wasn't a cop, which made him even more of a useless jive asshole. Who else would get a haircut like that? It really annoyed Viceroy Wilson just to think about it, and he was glad he'd smacked the guy and put an end to his curiosity. Now was no time to have razor-cut strangers nosing around, asking coplike questions.

Viceroy Wilson did not think of himself as a common criminal. Since leaving the National Football League (after eight bone-battering seasons, seventy-three touchdowns, and 7,889 yards rushing), Wilson had become a dedicated anarchist. He had come to believe that all crimes were perfectly acceptable against rich people, although the term 'rich' was admittedly subjective, and varied from one night to the next.

Wilson himself was no longer rich, having been neatly cleaned out by sports agents, orthopedic surgeons, ex-wives, ex-lawyers, accountants, mortgage companies, real-estate swindlers, and an assortment of scag peddlers from Coconut Grove to Liberty City. With a shift in economic fortunes Wilson had been forced to quit shooting heroin, so he'd turned to reading in his spare time. He spent hours upon hours in the old public library at Bayfront Park, amid the snoring winos and bag ladies, and it was there Wilson decided that America sucked, especially white America. It was there that Viceroy Wilson had decided to become a radical.

He soon realized two things: first, that he was ten years too late to find a home in any sort of national radical movement and, second, there were no English-speaking radicals in all of South Florida anyway.

So for years Viceroy Wilson had quietly burgled apartments and scammed dope and boosted cars, all the while nurturing romantic hopes of one day inflicting some serious shit on the white establishment that had mangled his knees and ruined his life. Wilson remained proud of the fact that he'd never robbed a liquor store, or stolen an eight-year-old Chrysler, or snatched a purse bulging with food stamps. Politically, he was careful about picking his victims.

Then *El Fuego* came along and Viceroy Wilson felt redeemed.

He didn't know what the name *El Fuego* actually meant, but it sure sounded bad, and as long as it didn't translate into something like 'The Fart,' Wilson could live with it. They shared the name anyway, all of them. They were a team. More of a team than the goddamn Dolphins ever were.

It was four-thirty by the digital clock on the Cadillac's dash, and the last porpoise show had ended at the Seaquarium. Tourists were starting to trickle out in a splash of godawful colors.

Viceroy Wilson adjusted his Carrera sunglasses, lit up a joint, jacked up the a/c, and mellowed out behind the Caddy's blue-tinted windows. He imagined himself an invisible, lethal presence. This was fun. He liked the dirty work. 'Thirty-one Z-right,' he called it. That had been his jersey on the Dolphins: number thirty-one. And 'thirty-one Z-right' was head-down-over-right-guard, the big ball-buster. Five, six, seven nasty yards every time. Viceroy Wilson had absolutely loved it.

'Pick a pale one.' Those were his orders today. 'Pale and comely.' Now what the fuck did *that* mean? Pale was pale.

Wilson studied the tourists as they strolled by, scouting the parking lot for their precious rental cars. The boss was right: it was a bountiful crop. In no time Wilson selected a redhead, tall and creamy-skinned, with lots of cinnamon-colored freckles. Her hair was thick and permed up to bounce, and she wore a crimson halter over silky blue jogging shorts. Minneapolis, Wilson guessed, maybe Quebec. A real alien. Best of all, her husband-boyfriend-whatever was only about five-two, a hundred-ten pounds, tops. He stood there shielding his eyes from the afternoon sun, squinting pathetically as he searched for the maroon Granada or whatever it was they'd be driving.

Viceroy Wilson polished off the joint and slid out of the Cadillac. That old familiar growl was building in his throat.

Thirty-one Z-right!

Brian Keyes felt uncomfortable whenever he ventured back to the newsroom. In a way, he missed the chaos and the adrenalized camaraderie; then again, what did he expect? Him and his one-man office with a tank full of algae-sucking catfish.

Whenever Keyes revisited the *Sun*, old friends flagged him down, briefed him on the latest atrocities against truth and justice, and offered to get together at the club for a drink. Keyes was grateful for their friendliness, but it made him feel odd. He was something of a stranger now, no longer entrusted with Serious Information, the currency of big-city journalism. Nonetheless, he was glad when they waved and said hello.

This time Ricky Bloodworth was the first to corner him.

'Tell me about Ernesto Cabal,' he said breathlessly. 'I'm doing a big weekender on the Harper case.'

'Can't help you, Rick. I'm sorry, but he's a client.'

Bloodworth's voice climbed to a whine. 'You're talking like a lawyer now, not like the Brian I used to know.'

Keyes shrugged. Bloodworth was irrepressibly annoying.

'At least tell me if you think he's guilty. Surely you can do that, cantcha?'

'I think he's innocent,' Keyes said.

'Right,' Bloodworth said with an exaggerated wink. 'Sure, Brian.' He scooted back to his desk.

Keyes figured the cops hadn't told Bloodworth about the *El Fuego* letters, which was just fine. Bloodworth would have gone nuts with that stuff, and then so would the city. Nothing like a little panic to muck up an investigation.

Cab Mulcahy was waiting in his office. Slate-colored suit, crisp white shirt, navy tie. Same civilized handshake, same crinkly smile. And there was the coffeepot steaming on the corner of the desk. Same place it had been the night Brian Keyes had walked in with his resignation.

'It was good of you to come on short notice. Mind if I close the door?'

'Not at all, Cab.' Keyes had been surprised to get the message on his beeper; he'd been wondering about it all afternoon. A new job offer—that was his best guess. But why would the *Sun* want him back? The place was crawling with raw talent, kids who were plenty tough enough.

'Cab, are you going to ask me to come back to work?'

Mulcahy smiled kindly and shifted in his chair. 'To be honest, Brian, I hadn't thought about it. But if you're interested, I'm sure we can—'

'No. No, I'm not.' Keyes wondered why he didn't feel more relieved. 'I was just curious.'

'I called you,' Mulcahy said, 'because I want to hire you as a private investigator. We have a very sensitive case. You're the only one who can handle it.'

Keyes was well-versed in the rudimentary techniques of bull-shitting that the *Sun* taught all its top editors. The phrase 'You're the only one who can do it' generally translated to 'No one else will touch it.' But this time Mulcahy did not appear to be shoveling anything. He appeared to be genuinely upset.

'Brian, Skip Wiley has disappeared.'

Keyes did not move a muscle. He just looked at Mulcahy; a look of disappointment, if not betrayal. Cab Mulcahy had been afraid this might happen. He had dreaded it, but there was no other way.

'I'm sorry, Brian. I'd never ask unless we were desperate.'

'Disappeared?'

'Vanished. They found his car yesterday in the middle of I-95. He didn't show up at home last night.'

Home. Keyes chuckled: Come on, Cab, just say it, I'm not going to break down in tears. Wiley didn't show up at *Jenna's* last night. God, the old man was funny sometimes, Keyes thought. Trying to spare me a little pain. It was two years ago that Jenna had dumped him for Wiley—Wiley, of all people! Why couldn't it have been an artist, or a concert musician, or some anorexic-looking poet from the Grove? Anyone but Skip Wiley—and right in the bitter worst of the Callie Davenport business. What a couple: Jenna, who adored Godunov and Bergman; and Wiley, who once launched a write-in campaign to get Marilyn Chambers an Oscar.

'Did you call the cops?' Keyes asked.

Mulcahy shook his head and reached for the coffee. 'We decided not to. I've pretty much ruled out foul play.' He told Keyes about Wiley's eccentric behavior, and about his visit to the psychiatrist the day before.

'So you think he's hiding out?'

'I do. So does Dr. Courtney.'

Remond Courtney's opinions didn't carry much weight with Brian Keyes, who knew something of the doctor's meager talent. In the aftermath of the terrible 727 crash, when Keyes was being fingered by imaginary severed limbs, Dr. Courtney had advised him, by way of therapy, to get a job as an air-traffic controller.

'Forget that idiot shrink,' Keyes said. 'What about Jenna? What does she think?'

Mulcahy said, 'She's pretty worried. She thinks Skip might do something crazy.'

'Would that surprise you, Cab? Wiley may be talented, prolific, tough as hell—all the things you people put a premium on—but he's also a card-carrying flake. He could be anywhere. Vegas, Nassau, Juarez, who knows? Why don't you just wait a few days? He'll get so miserable not seeing his byline in the paper that he'll rush right back with a stack of fresh columns.'

'I don't think so,' Mulcahy said. 'I hope you're right but I just don't think so. I need him back now, here—where we can keep an eye on him.'

So that's it, Keyes thought. Mulcahy was worried less about Wiley's well-being than about all the trouble a man like that could create. Wiley presented an explosive public-relations problem for the Miami *Sun*; no newspaper can afford to have its star columnist turn up as the proverbial sniper in the schoolyard.

And in Skip Wiley's case, another factor loomed large: he had an enormous public following. If his column didn't appear for a few days running, lots of readers would stop buying the *Sun*. If the days turned into weeks, the attrition would show up in the next ABC audits. And if that happened, Cab Mulcahy would have to answer to the highest possible authority; good journalism is fine, but circulation is sacred. No wonder Mulcahy was nervous.

'You know him better than any of us,' Mulcahy said. 'You sat next to him in the newsroom for three years. You recognize his moods, how he thinks, *if* he thinks . . .'

'I haven't seen him since I left the paper.'

Mulcahy leaned forward. 'He hasn't changed that much, Brian. True, his behavior is a bit more extreme, and his writing is certainly more irresponsible, but he's still the same Skip Wiley.'

'Cab, you're talking to the worst possible person. You ought to know that: I can't take this case. I'm not ready to deal with him.' Keyes stood up to leave. 'Why, Cab? Why would you do this to me?'

'Because Jenna asked for you.'

Keyes sat down hard. His heart was skipping along nicely now. All he could think was: Cab better not be lying.

'I told her I didn't think it was fair,' Mulcahy said with a sigh. 'But she's very worried about him. She said it would be a great favor if I asked you to look into it, and not some stranger.'

Keyes knew it wouldn't do any good to lecture himself about Jenna, and it was pointless to act like he was going to waltz out of Mulcahy's office and forget the whole thing. The old man was right—it wasn't fair.

Mulcahy was careful not to go on too much about Jenna. 'Please, Brian, will you try to find Wiley? We'll pay you five hundred a day, plus expenses.'

'Jesus, you guys are really scared of what he might do!'

Mulcahy nodded glumly. 'He's got a considerable temper, as you know. Watching him these last few months has been unsettling, to say the least. I'm sure you read the infamous hurricane column, or maybe some of the others. "Rats as Big as Bulldogs Stalk Condo." "Snakes Infest Bathroom Plumbing at Posh Resort."

"Mystery Disease Sweeps Shuffleboard Tourney." Wiley was very shrewd about it. One day he'd write a rousing Good Samaritan column, then a funny man-on-the-street piece, then a tearjerker about some little kid with cancer . . . and then he'd quietly slip in one of those gems. He became single-minded about it. He became . . . perverse.' The editor lowered his voice. 'I think this disappearance is part of a plan. I think he intends to embarrass the newspaper in some extraordinary way.'

'You don't think he's playing games just to get a raise?'

Mulcahy shook his head firmly.

'What about the possibility that something really happened? Maybe Skip got kidnapped.'

'Maybe that's what he wants us to think,' Mulcahy said, 'but I don't buy it, Brian. No, if I know Wiley, he's out there'—Mulcahy waved a manicured hand toward the bay window—'biding his time, enjoying the hell out of this. And I want him found.'

'Suppose I do,' Keyes said.

'Call me immediately. Don't do a thing. I'm not asking you to confront him, I'd never do that. Just find him, tell me where he is. Leave the rest up to us.'

'You and Jenna?'

'He listens to her,' Mulcahy said apologetically.

'He worships her,' Keyes said. 'It's not the same thing.'

'You'll take the case?'

Keyes didn't answer right away, but he knew what he'd say. Of course he'd take the case. Part of it was the money, part of it was Jenna, and part of it was that goddamn brilliant Wiley. A long time ago it would have been pure fun, tracking down an old comrade lost on a binge. But that was before Jenna. Fun was now out of the question.

Keyes told himself: This will be a test, that's all. To see how thick is the scar.

'Let's wait twenty-four hours, Cab. In the meantime, why don't you run one of Ricky Bloodworth's columns in Skip's slot tomorrow? Run the kid's picture, too. If that doesn't make Wiley surface, then maybe you're right. Maybe it's something serious this time.'

'Brian, I don't know about Bloodworth . . .'

'I understand he's chomping at the bit. So publish one of his masterpieces. And if that doesn't bring Wiley charging back to the newsroom tomorrow, I'll take the case.'

'It's a deal. And you can start first thing.'

'We'll see,' Keyes said. 'Believe it or not, Cab, I've got other clients with worse problems than yours.'

'What could be worse than a maniac like Wiley?'

'For starters, there's a very nice lady whose husband vanished in broad daylight on Miami Beach, and there's also a not-so-nice Cuban burglar in the county jail looking at Murder One.'

'Not anymore.' It was Bloodworth himself, inserting his rodent face through a crack in the door.

'This is a private conference!' Mulcahy barked.

'Wait a second. Ricky, what is it?'

'I thought you ought to know, Brian. Just got word from the police desk.' Bloodworth waved a notebook momentously. 'Ernesto Cabal killed himself about an hour ago.'

8

Viceroy Wilson came into the room wearing tight red Jockey shorts and nothing else. This vision would have provoked cries of glee or terror from most women, but Renee LeVoux was speechless. Viceroy Wilson had stuffed a towel in her mouth before lashing her to the bed the night before.

Renee was mystified and afraid. She didn't know who this was, or where she was, or what was about to happen. She was sure of only one thing: her vacation was in shambles.

In the parking lot at the Miami Seaquarium, she had barely seen the inky specter that had swept her into the car and promised to kill her if she so much as twitched her honky lips.

The trunk of the automobile had been cramped and uncomfortable, but it had a new-car smell, which Renee thought was a good sign. She had shut her eyes and tried not to cry aloud. All she could hear was Wilson Pickett singing 'Wait Till the Midnight Hour,' which her captor had played over and over on the tape deck, full blast.

Although it had seemed like eternity, Renee LeVoux actually spent only twenty-seven minutes in the trunk of the Cadillac. Viceroy Wilson had driven straight from the Seaquarium to a cheap motor inn on the Tamiami Trail. There he'd popped the trunk and lifted Renee LeCoux over one shoulder like a sack of tangelos.

Inside the room, he'd wordlessly removed her halter and jogging shorts, gagged her, and tied her to the bed. He'd noticed that she was trembling, so he'd tossed a thin blanket across her, as if she were a horse.

Renee had slept fitfully, straining against the ropes, certain that she would awake any moment to be violated by the biggest black man she'd ever seen.

But nothing had happened. Aside from intermittently checking the knots at Renee's wrists and ankles, Viceroy Wilson had paid almost no attention to his beautiful captive. Instead he'd watched Mary Tyler Moore on television, skimmed the *New Republic,* and done one hundred push-ups, Marine-style.

The next morning, when she heard him turn on the shower, Renee began to cry again. Viceroy Wilson poked his glistening head out the bathroom door and glared. He put a finger to his lips. Renee nodded meekly and became quiet.

Viceroy Wilson had no interest in pale white girls with strawberry hair. During his time in the NFL he had known an astounding variety of women with an equally astounding range of sexual appetites. It had gotten boring toward the end, and dangerous. When Wilson had reinjured his right knee before the crucial Pittsburgh Steelers game in 1977, the Miami Dolphins had put out a press release saying it had happened in a practice scrimmage—when in fact Viceroy's knee had hyperextended on a water bed beneath two limber sisters who worked in a foundry on the Allegheny.

Later, when he became a revolutionary, Viceroy Wilson made a vow not to mix sex and sedition. He wanted to be remembered as a very professional terrorist.

He attached no symbolism to the red Jockey shorts.

'What're you lookin' at?' he asked Renee LeVoux as he toweled off.

From the bed his prisoner just stared in fright.

Moments later a key rattled in the door and another man slipped into the motel room. Viceroy Wilson greeted him with a grunt and a nod of the head. Renee was struck by the difference in the two figures and thought it odd that they could be partners. Wilson's companion was a wiry Latin-looking man who spoke sibilantly and moved catlike about the room. Craning her neck from the bed, Renee could see the two of them conferring in the kitchenette. Soon she smelled coffee and bacon, and her stomach began to make noises. Viceroy Wilson approached the bed and removed the gag from her mouth.

'If you scream, you're dead.'

'I won't, I promise.'

'Your name is Renee?'

She nodded; obviously they had her purse. 'You can have all the money in my wallet,' she offered.

'We don't want your money.' Viceroy Wilson slid one hand under her head and lifted it slightly off the pillow; with the other he held a cup of coffee to her lips. She slurped at it timorously.

'Thank you.'

'What's your boyfriend's name?'

Wilson put the coffee cup down. Renee LeVoux noticed that he had a pencil and a piece of paper.

'Why do you want to know?' she asked.

'We're going to write him a letter. Tell him you're okay.'

'Oh no!'

'Oh yes.'

Now there were two faces hovering over her, one black and indifferent, one thin and fierce. The thin man was sneering. He tore the blanket away and saw that Renee was dressed only in her panties.

'Don't hurt me!' Renee cried.

The thin man brandished a shiny knife.

'Oh please no,' Renee cried.

The black man ferociously seized the thin man by the wrist and twisted his arm. The thin man yelped and the knife fell into the bedding.

'Hay-zoose, don't ever try that shit again,' Viceroy Wilson said. He was thinking to himself: This is the problem when you work with Cuban lunatics. They can't go five minutes without pulling a pistol or a blade. They couldn't help it—it was something in their DNA molecules.

'Renee, my name is Mr. Wilson. This here is Mr. Bernal.'

Renee said, 'How do you do?'

Wilson sighed. 'We need the name of your boyfriend, and we need it now.'

'I'm not telling. I don't want you to hurt him.'

'Girl, we don't want to hurt him. We want to let him know what happened to you.'

Puzzled, Renee asked, 'What *did* happen to me?'

'You've been kidnapped by a group of dangerous radicals.'

'God! But I'm nobody.'

'That's true,' said Jesús Bernal, fishing through the bed for his blade.

'Why me? I'm just a tourist.'

'Did you enjoy the porpoise show?' Bernal asked.

Renee nodded apprehensively. 'Yes, very much. And the trained whale.'

'Shamu,' Bernal said. 'That's the whale's name.'

This guy was sickening, Wilson thought. He might even be worth killing someday.

'Did you ride the monorail?' Bernal went on mockingly. He wore a mean smile.

'No, David wanted to see the shark moat instead.'

'Now we're getting somewhere,' Wilson muttered. 'David who?'

'I won't tell you!'

Wilson slipped one hand around Renee's freckled neck. It felt soft and cool. He gave a sharp, tennis-ball squeeze; that was plenty.

'David Richaud,' Renee said, starting to sob. 'R-i-c-h-a-u-d.'

Viceroy Wilson carefully wrote down the name. 'And where are you staying?'

'At the Royal Sonesta.'

'Thank you, Renee, my sweet,' said Jesús Bernal, bobbing at the foot of the bed.

'Shut up and type,' said Wilson, shoving the paper at his companion. Bernal bounced over to the kitchen table and sat down at a portable electric typewriter.

Viceroy Wilson turned to his victim and said, 'Do you believe that fuckhead went to Dartmouth?'

Jesús Bernal may have come to the cause with impressive credentials, but he was not highly regarded by Viceroy Wilson. Jesús Bernal had once held the title of defense minister for a rabid anti-Castro terrorist group called the Seventh of July Movement. The group was named for the day in 1972 when its founders had launched a costly and ill-fated attack on a Cuban gunboat off the Isle of Pines. In later years an acrimonious dispute had arisen over the name of the group, with some members claiming that the Isle of Pines attack had actually occurred on the *sixth* of July, and demanding that the group should be renamed. A compromise was reached and eventually the terrorists became known as the First Weekend in July Movement.

Throughout the late 1970s this organization took credit for a large number of bombings, shootings, and assassination attempts in Miami and New York. According to the Indian, Bernal was named defense minister chiefly because of his Ivy League typing skills. As Viceroy Wilson knew, one of the most vital roles in any terrorist group was the composing of letters to take credit for the violence. The letters had to be ominous, oblique, and neatly typed. Jesús Bernal was very good in this assignment.

He had been recruited to *Las Noches de Diciembre* after a bitter falling-out with his comrades in the First Weekend in July Movement. Actually Bernal had been purged from the group, but he never talked about why, and Viceroy Wilson had been warned not to ask. He tolerated Bernal, but he had no instinctive fear whatsoever of the Cuban. And he was getting awful damn tired of this macho switchblade bullshit.

'We're moving out soon,' Wilson told Renee LeVoux. He balled up the towel and started to stuff it back in her mouth.

'Wait,' she whispered. 'Why did you tell me your names?'

Wilson shrugged.

'You're going to kill me, aren't you?'

'Not if you can swim,' Wilson said, inserting the gag. 'And I mean fast.'

Renee's eyes widened and she tried to scream. The more she tried, the redder she got, and all that came out was a throaty feline noise that filled the tawdry motel room. She tossed back and forth on the bed, fighting the ropes, trying to spit out the gag, until Viceroy Wilson finally said, 'Dammit!' and whacked her once in the jaw, knocking her cold.

Meanwhile, preoccupied at the Smith-Corona, the man writing for *El Fuego* began to type:

Dear Mssr. Richaud:
Welcome to the Revolution!

Four items of special interest to Brian Keyes appeared in the
Miami *Sun* of December 6.

One was a lengthy front-page story about the jailhouse suicide
of Ernesto Cabal, accused killer of B. D. 'Sparky' Harper. One
hour before the tragic incident, Cabal had complained of stomach
pains and been transported to the infirmary, where he drank a
half-pint of Pepto-Bismol and declared that he was cured. While
confined to the clinic, however, Ernesto apparently had pilfered
a long coil of intravenous tubing, which he smuggled back to his
cell. No one checked on him for hours, until they found him cold
and dead at dinnertime. Using the I.V. tube as a noose, Cabal had
managed to hang himself, naked as usual, from a water pipe. The
duty sergeant remarked to the *Sun* that it was difficult to make a
really good noose out of plastic tubing, but somehow Cabal had
done it. When asked why none of the other inmates on the cell
block had alerted the guards to Ernesto's thrashings, the sergeant
had explained that the little Cuban 'was not all that popular.'

The second item to catch Keyes's attention (he was reading on
a musty sofa next to the aquarium in his office, where he had
spent the night) was the inaugural column of Ricky Bloodworth.
The headline announced: 'Miami Rests Easier as Harper Mystery
Ends.' The column was a fulsome tribute to all the brilliant police
work that had landed Ernesto Cabal in jail and driven him to his
death. 'He knew the evidence was overwhelming and he knew
his freedom was over,' Bloodworth wrote, 'so he strangled himself
to death. He was nude, alone, and guilty as sin.' Then came a
quote from the big redheaded detective, Hal, who said that the
Harper case was closed, as far as he was concerned. 'This is one
of those rare times when justice triumphs,' Hal beamed.

Keyes noticed that there was no quote from Al García. And
there was no mention of the *El Fuego* letters.

The third article of interest was not very long, and not promi-
nently displayed. The story appeared on page 3-B, at the bottom,
beneath a small headline: 'Police Seek Missing Woman.' The

article reported that one Renee LeVoux, twenty-four years old, a
visitor from Montreal, had been abducted from the parking lot
of the world-famous Miami Seaquarium shortly before five P.M.
the previous day. Incredibly, there were no witnesses to the crime.
Miss LeVoux's male companion, whom police declined to identify,
had been knocked unconscious by a single blow to the back of
the neck, and was of no help. Anyone with information about
Miss LeVoux's whereabouts was encouraged to call a Crime Stoppers phone number.

Brian Keyes made a mental note to find out more about that
one.

Finally he spotted the one news item that he'd actually been
looking for. Mercifully it was buried on 5-B, next to the advertisements for motorized wheelchairs.

The headline said: 'County Lawyer Stabbed in Melee.' Splendid,
Keyes thought ruefully, it made the final edition after all. Keyes
wondered if the *Sun* had gotten the story right, and forced himself
to read:

> An attorney for the Dade County public defender's office
> was assaulted Wednesday night at the Royal Palm Club.
> Mitchell P. Klein, 26, was standing at the bar when he
> was suddenly attacked by another patron, police said. The
> assailant pulled Klein's hair, ripped at his clothes, and tried
> to choke him, according to witnesses. As Klein attempted to
> break away, his attacker threw him to the floor and stabbed
> him in the tongue with a salad fork, police said.
> The suspect, described as a well-dressed white male in his
> early thirties, escaped before police arrived. Witnesses said
> the man did not appear to be intoxicated. Klein was taken to
> Flagler Memorial Hospital, where he was treated for minor
> injuries and released early this morning. Due to oral surgery,
> he was unavailable for comment.

Careless reporting, Keyes grumbled, as usual.

For one thing, it hadn't been a salad fork, but one of those
dainty silver jobs designed for shrimp cocktails and lobster.

Second, he and Mitch Klein hadn't been standing at the bar; they were sitting in a booth.

Still, it *had* been a reckless gesture, something Skip Wiley himself might have tried. Keyes wondered what had gotten into him. Was he finally losing his grip? Assaulting an officer of the court in a nightclub, for God's sake, in front of a hundred witnesses. He couldn't believe he'd done it, but then he couldn't believe what Klein had said as they were talking about Ernesto's suicide.

'The only reason you're upset,' Klein had said, 'is that the case is over, and so's your payday.'

This, after Keyes had told him all about the *Fuego* letters, all about Viceroy Wilson, all about Dr. Joe Allen's opinion that Ernesto Cabal was the wrong man. After all this—and four martinis—Mitch Klein still had the loathsome audacity to say:

'Brian, don't tell me you really gave a shit about that little greaseball.'

That was the moment when Keyes had reached across the table, seized Klein by his damp curly hair, and deftly speared the lawyer's tongue with the cocktail fork. No choking. No ripping of clothes. No grappling on the floor. There was, however, a good bit of fresh blood, the sight of which surely contributed to the later embellishments of eyewitnesses.

Keyes had gotten up and left Mitch Klein blathering in the booth, the silver fork dangling from his tongue, blood puddling in the oysters Bienville.

And that had been the end of it.

Now, the next morning, Keyes was certain the cops would arrive any minute with a warrant.

Actually it turned out to be Al García, all by himself.

He knocked twice and barged in.

'What a pit!' he said, looking around.

'Why, thank you, Al.'

García sullenly peered into the murky fish tank.

'Don't smear up the glass,' Keyes said.

'Those are the ugliest guppies I ever saw,' García said.

'They're catfish,' Keyes said. 'They eat up the slime.'

'Well, they're doing a helluva job. It looks like somebody pissed in this aquarium.'

'Anything's possible,' Keyes muttered. He lay on the sofa, the newspaper spread across his chest. García picked it up and pointed to the article about Mitch Klein.

'Did you do this, Brian?'

'I got mad. Klein went to see Ernesto yesterday and told him the case was locked. Told him he didn't have a chance. Told him to plead guilty or they were going to charbroil him. Ernesto wanted to fight the charges but Klein told him to quit while he was ahead. Ernesto was going nuts in jail, all the queers chasing him. He had that incredible tattoo on his joint. The one I told you about.'

'Fidel Castro.'

'Yeah,' Keyes said. 'Well, some maniac tried to bite it off one night in the shower. Thought if he chomped off Ernesto's dick, it would kill the real Fidel in Havana. Witchcraft, he said. Somehow Ernesto got away from the guy, but he was scared out of his mind. He said he'd do anything to get out of jail. So when Klein told him he'd better plan on twenty-five to life, I guess Ernesto figured he was better off dead.'

'But Brian—'

'Why didn't that cocksucker Klein talk to me before he went over to the jail? That case wasn't locked, no way. You know I'm right, Al.'

'All I know,' the detective said, 'is that we'll never know. You gotta calm down, brother.'

Keyes closed his eyes. 'Maybe I'm just mad at myself. I should have told Klein about *El Fuego* as soon as I saw the second letter. But how was I to know the sonofabitch was in such a hurry to dump the case? Whoever heard of pleading your man five days after the goddamn crime?'

'He thought it was a loser,' García said. 'He was just trying to expedite things.'

Keyes sat up angrily, looking ragged.

'Expedite things, huh? Well, he expedited his client right into the morgue.'

García shrugged. 'You hungry?'

'I thought you were here to arrest me.'

'Naw. Klein's making noises about pressing charges. Assault with a deadly cocktail fork, something like that. Fortunately for you, nobody at the state attorney's office likes the little prick, so he's having trouble getting a warrant. He'd probably forget all about it if you'd pay his hospital bill. Can't be much—what's six little sutures on the tongue?'

Keyes smiled for the first time. 'I suppose it's the least I could do.'

'Make him an offer,' García advised. 'If you're lucky, you might not even have to say you're sorry.'

'What about the Harper case?'

'You read the paper. It's closed, man. Nothing I can do.'

'But what about Bellamy and the other *Fuego* letter?'

'Talk to Missing Persons,' García said dryly, 'and they'll call it a probable accidental drowning. And they'll say, "What letter?" '

The detective lumbered around the office, poking at books and files, flipping through notebooks, taking up time. Keyes could tell that something was bugging him.

'For what it's worth,' García said finally, 'I agree with you. There's more to the Harper murder than the late great Ernesto Cabal. I bitched and moaned about keeping the case open, but I got outvoted.'

'What're they afraid of?'

'It's the start of the season,' García said. 'Snowbirds on the wing, tourist dollars, my friend. What's everyone so afraid of? Empty hotel rooms, that's what. A gang of homicidal kidnappers is not exactly a PR man's dream, is it? The boys at the Chamber of Commerce would rather drink Drano than read *El Fuego* headlines. Not now, Brian, not during the season.'

'So that leaves me the Lone Ranger,' said Keyes.

'I'll do what I can,' García said, 'quietly.'

'Great. Can you get the state to pay my fee?'

The detective laughed. 'No, Kemosabe, but I got you a present. An honest-to-God clue. Remember the tag on the Cadillac at Pauly's Bar?'

'Sure,' Keyes said, 'GATOR 2.'

'Well, guess who it comes back to.'

'The legendary Viceroy Wilson!'

'Nope. The Seminole Nation of Florida, Incorporated.'

'Swell,' Keyes said, flopping back on the couch. 'That's some swell clue, Tonto.'

Cab Mulcahy arrived at work early, canceled two appointments, and asked his secretary to please hold all calls, except one. For the next three hours Mulcahy sat in his office and eyed the telephone. He loosened his necktie and pretended to work on some correspondence, but finally he just closed the drapes (to shield himself from the rest of the newsroom) and sat down in a corner chair. Through the window, Biscayne Bay was radiant with a sailboat regatta; Hobies skimmed and sliced fierce circles, leaping each other's wakes, orange and lemon sails snapping in the warm morning breeze. It was a gorgeous race under an infinite blue sky, but Cab Mulcahy paid no attention. It was one of the darkest days of his career. Ricky Bloodworth's column had turned out just as half-baked, unfocused, and banal as Mulcahy knew it would be. Yet he had thrown away twenty-two years of integrity and printed it anyway.

Why?

To flush Skip Wiley from his hideout.

It had seemed like a good plan. No sense blaming Keyes.

But what had Mulcahy done? He'd unleashed a monster, that's what. He glanced again at the phone. Where the hell was Wiley? How could he sit still while a jerk like Bloodworth came after his job?

Mulcahy pondered one plausible explanation: Skip Wiley was dead. That alone would account for his silence. Perhaps a robber had snatched him from his car on the expressway and killed him. It was not a pleasant scenario, but it certainly answered the big question. Mulcahy figured that death was the only thing that would slow Wiley down on a day like today. The more Cab Mulcahy thought about this possibility, the more he was ashamed of his ambivalence.

He could hear the phone ringing every few minutes outside the door, at his secretary's desk. Readers, he thought, furious readers. How could he tell them, yes, he agreed, Bloodworth's writing was disgraceful. Yes, it's a bloody travesty. Yes, he's a congenital twit and we've got no business publishing crap like that.

Much as he wanted to, Mulcahy could never say all that, because journalism was not the issue here.

There was a firm, well-rehearsed knock on the door. Before Mulcahy could get up, Ricky Bloodworth stuck his head in the room.

'I hate it when you do that,' Mulcahy said.

'Sorry.' Bloodworth handed him a stack of columns. 'Thought you might want to take a gander at these.'

'Fine. Go away now.'

'Sure, Mr. Mulcahy. Are you feeling okay?'

'A little tired, that's all. Please shut the door behind you.'

'Any one of those could run tomorrow,' Bloodworth said. 'They're sort of timeless.'

'I'll keep that in mind.'

Mulcahy sagged behind his desk and scanned the columns. With each sentence he grew queasier. Bloodworth had generously penciled his own headline ideas at the top of each piece:

'Abortion: What's the Big Deal?'

'Capital Punishment: Is the Chair Tough Enough?'

'Vietnam: Time to Try Again?'

Mulcahy was aghast. He buzzed his secretary.

'Seventy-seven calls about today's column,' she reported. 'Only three persons seemed to like it, and one of them thought it was satire.'

'Has anyone phoned,' Mulcahy asked, 'who remotely *sounded* like Mr. Wiley?'

'I'm afraid not.'

Mulcahy's stomach was on fire; the coffee was going down like brake fluid. He opened the curtains and balefully scouted the newsroom. Ricky Bloodworth was back at his desk, earnestly interviewing two husky men in red fez hats. Mulcahy felt on the verge of panic.

'Get me Brian Keyes,' he told his secretary. Enough was enough—he'd given Keyes his lousy twenty-four hours. Now it was time to find Skip Wiley, dead or alive.

9

'How's the fish?' Jenna said.

'Very good,' said Brian Keyes.

'It's a grouper. The man at the market promised it was fresh. How's the lemon sauce?'

'Very good,' Keyes said.

'It's a little runny.'

'It's fine, Jenna.'

She lowered her eyes and gave a shy smile that brought back a million memories. A smile designed to pulverize your heart. For diversion, Keyes took a fork and studiously cut the fish into identical bite-size squares.

'I liked your hair better when it was shaggy,' Jenna said. 'Now you look like an insurance man.'

'I'm in court so much these days. Gotta look straight and reliable up on the witness stand.'

Keyes wondered how much small talk would be necessary to finesse the awkward questions: Where've you been? What've you been up to? Did you get our Christmas card? He was no good at small talk, and neither was Jenna. Jenna liked to get right to the juicy stuff.

'Are you seeing anybody?'

'Not right now,' Keyes said.

'I heard you were dating a lady lawyer. Sheila something-or-other.'

'She moved,' Keyes said, 'to Jacksonville. Got on with a good firm. We're still friendly.' Surely, he thought, Jenna could see how uncomfortable this was.

'So you're living alone,' she said, not unkindly.

'Most nights, yeah.'

'You could call, just to say hi.'

'Skip doesn't like it,' Keyes said.

'He wouldn't mind,' Jenna said, 'every now and then.'

But in fact, when Jenna had first dumped him for Skip Wiley, Brian Keyes had phoned every night for three weeks, lovesick and miserable. Finally Wiley had started answering Jenna's telephone and singing 'When You Walk Through A Storm.' Immediately Keyes had quit calling.

'You look like you've lost about eight pounds,' Jenna remarked, studying him across the table.

'Nine,' Keyes said, impressed. 'You look very good.' The understatement of the century.

She had come straight from her jazz exercise class, which she taught four times a week. She was wearing a lavender Danskin, pink knit leg warmers, and white sneakers. Her blond hair was bobbed up, and she wore tiny gold earrings that caught the light each time she turned her head. Keyes noticed a fresh hint of lipstick, and the taste of an elusive perfume. As if all that weren't enough, she had a terrific new tan, which fascinated Keyes because Jenna was not a beach person.

'It's been a while since you've been here,' she said, pouring white wine.

'You've really done some work on the place.'

'Damage, you mean. It's Skip, mostly.'

Keyes pointed to a cluster of pockmarks high on the living-room wall, beneath a stuffed largemouth bass. 'Are those bullet holes?'

'Now, don't get all worried.'

Keyes got up for a closer look. 'Looks like a .38.'

'He got mad one night watching the TV news. The governor was talking about growth, how growth was so essential. The governor was saying how one thousand new people move to Florida every day. Skip's opinion about that was considerably different than the governor's. Skip didn't think the governor should have been quite so happy.'

'Why did he shoot the wall?' Keyes asked.

'Because he couldn't bring himself to shoot the TV—it's a

brand-new Trinitron,' Jenna said. 'I forgot you don't like spinach.'

'It's fine. Jenna, why is there a coffin in your living room?'

'I know, I know. I hate it, too. Skip says it makes a good cocktail table. He bought it at the flea market. He keeps his newspaper clippings inside there.'

'That's a bit odd, don't you think?' Keyes said.

'At the very least he should get it refinished.'

Keyes ate faster. This was more traumatic than he had feared. Meeting in her house—the place she shared with Wiley—had not been Keyes's idea. Jenna had insisted. She had wanted to be here, she said, in case Skip called.

If Jenna seemed genuinely worried about her lover's where-abouts, Keyes was not. His heart was with the Ernesto Cabal case—what was left of it—and tracking Skip Wiley was just a sporting way to pass some time, pay some bills ... and see Jenna again.

Keyes had a simple theory about Wiley's disappearance. He figured Skip had orchestrated the whole thing to gouge a fatter salary out of the Miami *Sun*. Wiley's usual strategy, when he wanted more money, was to arrange for friends at the Washington *Post* and the New York *Times* to call up with phony or wildly inflated job offers. Then he'd charge into Cab Mulcahy's office and threaten to defect. Mulcahy quit falling for the Fantastic Job Offer ruse about two years ago, so Keyes figured Wiley was merely trying out a new scheme.

Keyes also now realized that the idea of publishing a Ricky Bloodworth column might have backfired, and that Wiley was holed up somewhere, howling with glee over Mulcahy's torment. Keyes now believed—though he dared not tell Mulcahy—that Wiley might wait weeks before emerging. He might wait until his readers began rioting.

And Keyes also believed that Jenna might be in on it.

'Did you love me, Brian?'

'Yes.' He started to gag. He hoped it was just a fish bone going down the wrong way. Jenna came around the table and patted him on the back.

'Deep breaths,' she said soothingly. 'Don't eat so fast.'

'Why,' Keyes rasped, 'did you ask me that question?'

'Skip says you were madly in love with me.'

'I told you that myself,' Keyes said, 'about thirty thousand times.'

'I remember, Brian.'

God, there's the smile.

'How about now?' Jenna asked. 'Still feel the same way?'

Oh no, you don't. Keyes shifted into a tough-guy mode. 'This is business, Jenna. Let's talk about Skip. Where do you think he could be?'

'I don't know.'

'Oh really.'

'Brian! This isn't funny. I think he's in trouble. I think somebody's got him.'

'Why?'

'Because he's a good target,' Jenna said. She started clearing the table. 'You sit still, I'll do this. Let's see, you take your coffee black . . .'

'Cream and sugar,' Keyes said painfully. 'But I think I'll wait.'

'Okay. As I was saying, Skip's a very well-known person, a genuine celebrity. That makes him a perfect target for kidnappers. Look at Patty Hearst.'

'Or Frank Sinatra, Jr.,' Keyes said.

'Exactly.'

'You ever read *The Ransom of Red Chief*?'

'Sure,' Jenna said. 'What are you getting at?'

'Nothing.'

Every so often Keyes's attention was drawn to the coffin, which dominated Jenna's otherwise-cozy living room. The coffin was plain and vanilla-colored, made of smooth Dade County pine. A pauper's coffin. Jenna had done a valiant job of trying to disguise it as normal furniture. She had placed cocktail coasters neatly on each corner of the lid, and in the center she had stationed a blue Ming vase with fresh-cut sunflowers. For more camouflage she had added a thick stack of magazines, with *Town and Country* on top. Despite all this, there was no mistaking the coffin for anything else. Keyes wondered morbidly if he ought to peek inside, just to make sure Wiley wasn't there.

'There's been no ransom demand, has there?' he asked Jenna.

'Not yet. Let's sit on the couch.' Jenna put a James Taylor album on the stereo and went into the bedroom. When she came out, her hair was down and she was barefoot.

'If Skip wasn't kidnapped,' she said, 'then maybe Cab's right. Maybe he just went crazy and wandered off.' She curled up on the couch. 'I wish I had a fireplace.'

'It's seventy-four degrees outside,' Keyes said.

'What happened to my young romantic?'

Keyes smiled bashfully; God, she never let up. He fought to keep a proper tone to his voice. 'Is there a possibility . . . have you two been getting along?'

'Better than ever,' Jenna said. 'We made love the afternoon he left. Twice!'

'Oh.'

'Right there, where you're sitting.'

'Sorry I asked.'

Keyes kept waiting for Jenna to say: *I know how hard it was for you to take this case.* But she never did, and gave no sign of comprehending his distress.

'You've got to find him, Brian. I don't want to get the police involved, and I *don't* want a lot of publicity. It could ruin his career.'

Or cinch it, Keyes mused. He asked, 'Do you think he's gone insane?'

'I'm not sure I'd know the difference.' Jenna took off her earrings and laid them on the coffin. Elegantly she poured herself another glass of wine. Keyes sipped cautiously. The Chablis gave a dangerous urgency to his loneliness.

Jenna said, 'Lately Skip's been wilder than usual. He wakes up ranting and goes to bed ranting. You know, the usual stuff: toxic waste, oil spills, the California condor, the Biscayne Aquifer. Armageddon in general. About a week ago a man came to the door selling time-shares in Key Largo, and Skip attacked him with a marlin gaff.'

Keyes asked, 'Does he get incoherent?'

Jenna laughed softly. 'Never. He's a very cogent person, even when he's violent. He always makes perfect sense.'

'Well, if he's been kidnapped—which I doubt—all we can do is wait for a ransom demand. But if he's off somewhere in a frenzy, we've got to find him before he really hurts someone. Jenna, I need some ideas. Where the hell could he be?'

'The wilderness,' she said wistfully, gazing at her imaginary fireplace. 'That's where to start.'

'You mean the Everglades.'

'Where else? What other wilderness is there? The rest is all gone.'

Jenna was vice-secretary of the local Sierra Club, so Keyes knew it wouldn't take much to launch her off on a big speech. He had to be careful. 'Jenna, the Everglades are three times bigger than Rhode Island,' he said. 'I'll need a few more clues.'

'Oh, I don't know,' she said. The wine was almost gone. She went to the refrigerator and opened another bottle.

Remembering Jenna drunk, Keyes thought: This could be promising.

'I've got an idea,' Jenna said as she filled their glasses. 'Here, hold this.' Quickly she cleared the top of the coffin, uprooting the vase, collecting the coasters, sweeping the magazines to the carpet. Then she unfastened the clasps and opened the lid. She'd been telling the truth: the coffin was full of newspaper clippings.

Jenna dropped to her knees, the wineglass poised in her left hand. Methodically she began to explore Skip Wiley's unusual personal library. 'A few months back,' she said, 'he did a column about a place near the dike.'

Keyes knelt next to her and joined the search. Concentration was impossible, Jenna looking the way she did, smelling so warm and familiar.

'He used to go fishing at this place,' she was saying, 'when he was a boy. Not long ago he discovered that they'd built a huge development right there, next to the old dike on the edge of the Glades. A retirement community, they called it. Stocked with three thousand geezers from Jersey. Skip was livid.'

'I remember the column,' Keyes said. ' "Varicose Village." '

'Right! That'd be a good place to start. Maybe he's camping out. Planning something big.'

'Oh boy,' Keyes said.

Somehow Jenna located the column amid the random litter of Wiley's coffin. She slid over to show it to Keyes and practically nestled in his lap. He was not certain if she was doing this out of pity, or just to tease. He wanted to give her the benefit of the doubt. He also wanted to take her in his arms and make her forget all about Skip Wiley.

'The name of the place,' Jenna said, all wine-woozy, 'is Otter Creek Village. Three miles off State Road 84, it says here. Near the old bombing range.'

'I can find it.'

'He grew up not far from there,' Jenna said. 'And his family had a cabin out at Sawgrass.'

'Okay, I'll look around out there tomorrow.'

'Thank you, Brian,' Jenna said. She kissed him lightly on the lips and snuggled against his shoulder. Keyes slipped his right arm around her; it was a brotherly little hug, not a very good one. He wished he weren't so damn nervous. Still, he was thrilled to be there, alone with Jenna and no crazy Wiley, just old JT singing 'Fire and Rain' on the stereo. Keyes loved the scent of Jenna's neck, and the sweet narcotic sound of her breathing. He could have stayed that way for hours, hopelessly consumed by her presence, clutching her like a bedtime doll. With Keyes, nothing had changed; as for Jenna, it was hard to tell.

'Brian?'

'Yes, Jenna.'

'I'm getting sleepy.' She looked up from his chest. 'I think I'd better go to bed.'

She uncurled like a cat, stretching the lavender leotard in a dozen breathtaking ways. She closed the coffin, yawned, and said, 'Well.'

Keyes waited, clinging to hope.

But then she said: 'It's time for you to go home and get some rest.'

'Good idea,' Keyes said with a brave smile.

He drove off in a pinprickly sweat—euphoric, suicidal, utterly confused. All over again, he thought. God help me.

10

Overnight the weather cooled, and a fresh north wind brought an early whisper of winter.

Brian Keyes awoke at dawn, surprised by the dry chill. He slipped into blue jeans, foraged for a sweater, and went outside to crank up the car. The old MG was a marvelous summertime sportster, but on cold mornings, the engine balked. Keyes let it warm for a full ten minutes. He used the time as unwisely as possible, reliving the dinner with Jenna and devising romantic strategy.

From Miami he took the turnpike north to Road 84, a clamorous truck route that runs cross-state from Fort Lauderdale. Despite the gray gauze in the sky and the whipping wind, the highway was clogged with boxy Winnebagos, custom vans, and station wagons dragging metallic-purple bass boats—the usual weekend lemmings.

Over the years civilization doggedly had followed Road 84 toward the lip of the Everglades. Heading west, Keyes could chart the march of the chain saws and bulldozers. What once had been misty pastureland and pine barrens were now golden-age trailer parks; medieval cypress stands had been replaced by 7-Elevens and coin laundries. And spreading like a spore across the mottled landscape was every developer's wet dream, the condominium cluster.

Later as he walked along the dike, hands in his pockets, Keyes marveled at the contrast: to the western horizon, nothing but sawgrass and hammock and silent swamp; to the east, diesel cranes and cinderblock husks and high-rises. Not a hundred yards stood between the backhoes and the last of South Florida's wilderness. It had been a while since Keyes had driven this far west, and he was startled by what he saw. No wonder Skip Wiley had been so pissed off.

Keyes was nearly two miles from where he'd parked the car when he came to the Otter Creek condominium. He smiled, remembering Wiley's snide column. 'Talk about false advertising. There's no creek, and there's damn sure no otters—no live ones, anyway.'

Otter Creek Village consisted of three cheerless buildings set end-to-end at mild angles. Each warren stood five stories high and was painted white with canary-yellow trim. Every apartment featured a tiny balcony that overlooked a notably unscenic parking lot. From the dike Keyes could see a solid acre of shuffleboard courts, crisp formations of aluminum lounge chairs, and a vast ulcer-shaped swimming pool. In the center of the complex, surrounded by a twenty-foot chain-link fence, was an asphalt tennis court with faded lines and no net. The entire recreation area was outfitted with striped table umbrellas, sprouting like festive mushrooms from the concrete.

But Otter Creek was quiet today. No one floundered in the pool, and the shuffleboard courts lay deserted; the cold weather had driven the retirees inside. Keyes finally spotted one old gentleman, bundled in fluorescent rain gear, walking a hyperactive terrier along the banks of a murky manmade canal. 'Great fishing in your own backyard!' is what the Otter Creek brochure promised. Keyes didn't know much about fishing, but he had grave doubts about any creature that could procreate in such fetid water.

On the other side of the dike, in the Glades, the wind sent ripples through the dense sawgrass. Keyes broke out the binoculars and scanned the marsh. Somewhere out there, not far, stood the Wiley family cabin. Jenna had said you could find it with a good pair of field glasses, so Keyes had brought the Nikons.

Before long he spotted a row of snowy egrets, hunched along a tall fence; except it wasn't a fence, but a rooftop, an angular anomaly among the bush cattails and the scrub. Keyes trotted down the dike for a better look. The closer he got, the more the cabin showed above the swamp. The walls were made of plywood, the roof of corrugated tin. There was a crooked porch, a faded outhouse, and torn screens fluttering in the windows.

Keyes was most impressed by the fact that Wiley's cabin had been built on cypress stilts, smack in the middle of wetlands. There was no way to get there by foot.

He hiked along the dike until he drew even with the cabin; from the roof the egrets eyed him warily, flaring their nape feathers. Keyes guessed he was still a hundred yards away, with nothing but dark water and lily pads between him and the shack. He trained the Nikons and searched for signs of habitation.

The place looked empty and disused. A rusted padlock hung on the door, and the rails of the porch were plastered with petrified bird droppings. There was no boat anywhere, no smoke from the flue, no trace of a human being.

Except for the boots.

Brian Keyes knelt on the gravel of the dike and fiddled with the focus dial on the binoculars.

They were boots, all right. Brown cowboy boots, brand-new ones, judging from the shine off the toes. The boots lay on a plank beneath the warped door of the outhouse, and from their pristine condition (absent of bird speckles) it was apparent they hadn't been there very long.

Keyes knew what he had to do now: he had to find a sensible way to get out to Wiley's cabin. Swimming was out of the question. He had not quit the newspaper business to go frolic in the muck with water moccasins, not even for five hundred bucks a day.

So Brian Keyes went looking for a boat.

'Sit down, García.'

Al García settled in a chair. Harold Keefe, the big redheaded detective, cleared his throat, as if he'd been practicing for this. He picked up a copy of the Miami *Sun* and waved it in front of García's face. 'You wanna explain this!'

'Explain what, Hal?'

'This quotation here from Metro-Dade detective Alberto García. *The case is still under investigation: I can't comment.* You wanna explain that!'

García said, 'No comment is what I'm supposed to say. That's department policy. It's right there on the fucking bulletin board.'

Hal rolled up the newspaper and slammed it on the desk, as if killing a cockroach. 'Not for *this* case it's not policy. This case is closed, remember?'

García ground his teeth and tried not to say something he'd regret. 'Hal, this guy Bloodworth calls me out of the blue last night, okay? Says he's talked to these two guys, these Shriners, who tell him about their missing pal, Mr. Bellamy. You 'member Bellamy, don't you?'

Hal just scowled and waved his hand.

'Anyway,' García said, 'this hump Bloodworth says he heard there's some connection between Bellamy and Sparky Harper. Extortion letters is what he heard. Says he's writing a story on Bellamy's disappearance.'

'Oh, and that he did.' Hal fingered the newspaper. 'Ran Mr. Bellamy's picture, offered a five-thousand-dollar reward for any information, et cetera. Nothing wrong with that, García. But you didn't have to say what you said, especially the way you said it.'

'All I said was no comment.'

'And where'd you learn how to do that, the Meyer Lansky School of Public Relations? You made it sound like we're hiding something.' Hal rose to his feet. 'Why couldn't you just say the case is closed? Say we caught the killer and he tragically took his own life in jail. That's the last chapter of the Sparky Harper case. Period.'

'Then what about Bellamy?' García asked.

Hal's face was redder than García had ever seen it, and basket-ball-sized sweat marks showed under the arms of his blue poly-ester shirt. Obviously Hal had been having a crummy day.

'Bellamy was a drunk. Fell in the ocean and drowned,' Hal said. 'Forget about fucking Bellamy.'

'Then what about the *Fuego* letter?'

Hal folded his hands, a contrived gesture of civility. Harold Keefe was not a man who looked natural with folded hands. He said, 'I'm glad you mentioned the letters. We've determined that they're a hoax.'

García raised his eyebrows, but didn't say a word. He sensed that Hal was building up to something memorable.

'We showed the *Fuego* letters to Dr. Remond Courtney, the famous psychiatrist. He says the letters are phony, and the boys in the lab agree. Didn't surprise me at all, since there's been no ransom demands, no bodies . . .'

''Cept for Harper,' García mumbled.

'Forget fucking Harper! I'm talking about Bellamy and the other one.'

'What other one?'

'Here. Turned up this morning.' Hal passed a Xerox copy across the desk.

The letter was identical to the others. 'Who's Mssr. Richaud?' García asked, trying not to sound too interested.

'David Richaud is the male friend of one Renee LeVoux.' Hal pronounced it lay-vox. 'Miss LeVoux disappeared three days ago from the parking lot of the Seaquarium. Richaud filed a missing-persons report. Yesterday this letter was delivered to his hotel on Key Biscayne.'

'What's the guy's story?' asked García.

'He says the lady was kidnapped. Claims the perpetrator whacked him on the head and knocked him out.'

'You don't sound like you believe him.'

Hal laughed caustically. 'This one's got "domestic" written all over it. They had a fight, she grabs a cab and heads south with the vacation money. Richaud gets furious and figures the best way to find her is to get the cops involved. Pretty obvious, I'd say.'

'Hmmm,' said Al García.

'Which brings us to the letters.' Hal opened a drawer and pulled out a file. García knew that now was a good time to start worrying.

'Had a little talk with the chief this morning,' Hal said. Al García looked unimpressed; Hal was always having little talks with the chief.

He said, 'The chief seems to think these letters are being generated from within the police department.'

García snorted. 'He thinks *El Fuego* is a cop?'

'The chief,' Hal said sternly, 'is quite serious. He ordered me to start an internal investigation. He thinks someone around here is writing these phony letters in order to keep the Sparky Harper case alive.'

'Why?'

Hal shrugged disingenuously. 'Ambition, spite, maybe even professional jealousy. Who knows? In any case, the chief's theory makes perfect sense. Whoever's sending these crazy letters obviously is getting the names out of Missing Persons.'

Enough is enough, García thought. 'Hal,' he said, 'you're full of shit. And so's the chief.'

Hal's face turned the color of grape juice.

'Somebody's snatching tourists,' García said, 'and all you guys want to do is cover up. I got a better idea: why don't we just go out and catch the goddamn kidnappers? Come on, Hal, it'll be fun. Just like the old days, back when you were a cop and not a two-bit office politician.'

Ominously Hal opened the file. Inside was a pink memorandum, nothing else. 'Detective García,' he said, 'as of today you're on limited duty. It's indefinite, until our investigation is completed. I.A.D. wants to talk to you, so you might think about getting a lawyer.'

'Beautiful,' García muttered.

Hal slapped the file shut. 'You'll be working the late shift,' he said, 'at the motor pool.'

'Oh-oh, the combat zone.'

'It's not so bad . . . oh, by the way, there'll be some officers coming by your house later. Just to look around.'

'Hal, they'll be wasting their time. I don't own a typewriter.'

'Just the same, try to cooperate.'

'But, Hal—'

'You may go now,' said Harold Keefe, in his best high-school principal's voice, 'and try to stay out of trouble until this is over. Don't talk to any more reporters . . . or private eyes, for that matter.'

García leaned over and loudly planted his knuckles on the

desk. 'Hal,' he said, 'you're too dumb to see it, but this whole thing's gonna blow up in your fat Irish face.'

Brian Keyes drove west at a furious speed, slowing at every intersection, scouting each tacky shopping plaza. Finally he spotted a peeling sign that said 'Canoe Rentals' and screeched off the highway.

The name of the place was Mel's Bait and Tackle, and Mel himself was very busy dipping live shiners from the bait well. He told Keyes to take a seat near the soda machine and he'd get around to him in a little bit. Keyes politely mentioned that he was in a slight hurry, but he might as well have told it to the stuffed buck on the wall.

After fifteen minutes or so, Mel finally turned around, holstered his dip net, and asked Keyes what exactly he could do for him.

'I'd like to rent a canoe.'

'I'll need a deposit,' said Mel, eyeing him. 'And I'll need to know how'n hail you gonna get that canoe on toppa yore car.'

Mel had a point. The canoe was four feet longer than the MG.

'I'll need to borrow some rope.'

'No sir, you'll be need'n to *buy* some.'

'I see,' Keyes said. 'And the boat racks?'

'Those I'll rent ya.'

By the time the negotiations ended, Keyes was out thirty-seven dollars and his American Express card, which Mel confiscated as a security deposit.

Keyes made a courageous solo attempt to tie the aluminum canoe on the MG, but the boat flopped off the roof and landed with a crash on the macadam. The noise brought Mel shuffling out of the tackle shop, cursing heatedly. He was an older fellow—late fifties, paunchy, tired-looking—but he proved to be one strong son of a bitch, when it came to canoes. He told Keyes to go sit inside and read some magazines, and in five minutes the job was neatly done.

'Lemme ask you sumphin', if you don't mind,' Mel said. 'I don't see no fishing rods and I don't see no shotguns and I don't see no bow and arrow. So just where'n hail you goin' with this canoe, and what you gonna do when you get there?'

Keyes plucked the binocular case from the car and held it up for Mel to see. 'I'm a birdwatcher,' he said brightly.

Mel nodded, but he looked skeptical. 'Well,' he said after a pause, 'good luck with your snipes or woodpeckers or whatever the hail yore after. But don't put no more scratches on my damn boat!'

The canoe was lashed so tightly to the MG that the ropes sang on the highway. Back on the dike, Keyes had a hell of a time unraveling Mel's knots. Finally he was able to drag the canoe off the MG and slide it down the bank into the water. He climbed in tentatively, the oar tucked under one arm. He lowered himself to his knees and gingerly rocked the canoe, testing its stability. It seemed steady.

Keyes centered himself and began to paddle down the dike canal toward Wiley's cabin.

It was an adventurous feeling, gliding so low and alone through the Everglades. Keyes was swept away by the lushness of the scenery, a welcome distraction from his anxiety. He was no great outdoorsman but his discomfort was born of unfamiliarity, not fear. Keyes had been raised in the relentlessly civilized environs of Washington, D.C., and the only wild animals he'd ever confronted were the brazen gray squirrels of Rock Creek Park. Except for one miserable summer at a snotty boys' camp in northern Virginia, Keyes had spent almost no time out of the city. Since moving to Florida he'd heard the hoary tales of panthers, poisonous snakes, and killer alligators, and though he dismissed most of it as cracker mythology, Keyes did not savor the idea of a chance encounter. Wiley, if indeed he was out here, would be beast enough.

Keyes found a steady rhythm for the oar, and his confidence grew with each stroke. Even against the wind he made good time down the canal. By now it was an hour past noon and the gray clouds had dissipated; the sun quickly burned off the last of the morning's chill. The wetlands stirred under the heat. The cicadas and grasshoppers brassily came to life in the sawgrass, and once an old mossback terrapin clambered off the dike like a rolling helmet, plopping into the water three feet from the canoe. High overhead Keyes spotted a line of turkey vultures gliding in the thermals, scouting for carrion.

Somehow the dike sealed the Glades from the clamor of suburban Broward County; though Keyes was only a solid four-iron away from civilization, he could neither see it nor hear it. He felt himself distant, and growing tranquil.

After more than an hour he located the cabin. Keyes paddled faster, the bow of the canoe swishing through the ragged grass and pickerel weed. At fifty yards he slowed and let the canoe glide while he raised the binoculars one last time.

The western boots still lay beneath the outhouse, and the cabin still looked empty.

Brian Keyes didn't notice that the snowy egrets had flown away.

As he tied up to a rotted piling, a green chameleon scampered off the porch to munch a palmetto bug in the shadows. Keyes climbed lightly from the canoe, but the planks still shuddered under his weight. He took each step as if walking on ice, thinking: There's no way Skip Wiley could be hiding here, not the way he bangs around.

Keyes tested the padlock with a hard yank, and the rusty hasp gave way with a snap. He opened the cabin door with the toe of his sneaker and peered inside.

It looked like a dungeon for Boy Scouts.

Spiderwebs streeled from the ceiling, and a crisp snakeskin fluttered from the pine beam where it had long ago been shed. A shaky card table, once used for dining, buckled under unopened tins of Spam and sausage, the labels faded and curled. In the rear of the cabin was a bunk bed with two plastic air mattresses, each flattened and stained by mildew. In a corner two sleeping bags were rolled up tight, flecked with papery dead moths. A stack of heat-puckered magazines lay nearby; the most recent was a *Playboy* from December 1978.

In the kitchen area he found a sixty-gallon Igloo cooler; inside was a six-pack of flat Budweisers and three plastic jugs of drinking water. Keyes was about to open one of the jugs when he noticed a sediment of dubious origin suspended near the bottom. The water, he decided without tasting, had also been there a very long time.

The cabin was no larger than fifteen by thirty feet, but Keyes found plenty of crannies to explore. He was actually enjoying himself, poking through drawers and dusty cupboards, looking for signs of Wiley. He felt a little like an archaeologist over a new dig.

What finally persuaded him to retreat was the killer leaf.

Keyes had been using a whippy length of cane to clear out the spider nests, and he flicked it casually at a wrinkled gray-veined leaf beneath the card table. Suddenly the leaf sprang off the floor and, teeth bared, whistled past Keyes's ear. He stumbled out the door, shouting and brandishing the cane stick impotently. The angry bat followed him, diving in tight arcs, breaking off the attack only when hit by sunlight.

Keyes was not sure where the creature went, but he warily scanned the stratosphere from a protective crouch. He decided the bat was welcome to the solitude of the cabin; he'd wait outside for Skip Wiley or whoever owned those cowboy boots.

The afternoon passed slowly through the binoculars. Keyes didn't lay eyes on another human being, and he found himself living up to his lie, watching the birds of the Everglades: cormorants, ospreys, grackles, red-shouldered hawks, even a pair of roseate spoonbills. Finding the birds was an amusing challenge but, once spotted, they did not exactly put on a breathtaking show. The fact was, most of the birds seemed to be watching *him*.

Keyes finally was forced to avail himself of the outhouse—an act of sheer courage—and he stopped on the way out to study the mysterious cowboy boots. They were Tony Lamas, size eleven, with no name inside. Keyes was careful not to move them.

As the sun dropped and a lemon twilight settled on the shack, Keyes knew it was decision time. Once darkness came, there was no getting out of the Glades without a beacon. He'd have to spend the night with no food, no water and, most critically, no bug repellent. December wasn't a prime mosquito season, but a horsefly already had extracted a chunk of Keyes's ankle to remind him that billions of other starving insects were waiting their turns.

And then there was Mel, who had warned him to have the canoe back at dusk, or else. Keyes imagined all the random damage that a man like Mel could do with his American Express card, and decided to call it a day.

He fitted the binoculars into the case and climbed into the canoe. He slipped the half-hitch over the piling and pushed off with both hands. As the canoe skimmed away from the cabin, Keyes rose to his knees and reached for the oar.

But the oar was gone.

It *couldn't* be. But it was.

Fore and aft, the bottom of the canoe was empty. Keyes carefully turned around so he could see the cabin—it couldn't be more than twenty yards away. He needed to get back there, to get his feet on something solid. Then he'd try to figure out what the hell was going on.

He inched to the prow and found a comfortable position. With both hands Keyes began to paddle vigorously, fracturing the calm of the pond. Yet the canoe scarcely moved.

The boat was nestled firmly in a patch of hyacinth weeds. The fat green bulbs and fibrous stems clung to the hull and made it impossible to get up a head of steam. Keyes desperately needed something to hack the boat free.

The uneasiness in his gut started to feel a little like panic. He feared that he was being watched; that whoever owned the western boots had stolen the oar from the canoe, and that whoever had stolen the oar didn't want him to go.

'Skip!' Keyes shouted. 'Skip, are you there?'

But the marsh swallowed his voice, and only the shrill cicadas replied.

Keyes decided it was vital not to abandon the canoe. He regarded himself a competent swimmer, but realized that this was not Lake Louise at scenic Camp Trailblazer—this was serious swamp. With no buddy system, unless you counted eels.

Keyes couldn't be sure how deep the tea-colored water was, but he knew the weeds would make swimming treacherous. He was scared of getting tangled underwater, or sucked down by the muck. True, it was only twenty yards to the cabin, but it was a nasty goddamn twenty yards.

He leaned across the bow and began ripping up the hyacinths and tossing them aside in sodden stringy slumps. Painstakingly Keyes labored to clear a channel for the stymied canoe, but night came too quickly. He tried again to paddle by hand; this time the canoe moved six, seven, maybe eight feet before the knotted lilies seized it.

Brian Keyes was stuck. Robbed of detail, the cabin became a blocky shape in the darkness; to the east, the dike formed a perfectly linear horizon. Keyes sat back on his heels, his hands dripping water down the gunwales. His face was damp, and gnats were starting to buzz in his ears and eyes. He wasn't thinking about Mel anymore. He was thinking that this could be the worst night of his life.

Overhead, nighthawks sliced the sky, gulping bugs, and a big owl hooted twice from a faraway oak. The wind was dead now, so Keyes could hear every secret rustling in the swamp, though he could see almost nothing. After an hour he stopped trying to see at all, and just imagined—imagined that the sharp splash near the dike was only a heron spearing a minnow; imagined that the creaking plank was just a wood rat exploring the empty cabin; imagined that the piercing wail that seemed to float forever across the Glades was only a bobcat ending a hunt.

Keyes lay down in the canoe and propped his head on the leather binocular case. Even the sky was blank, held starless by the high clouds. With some effort he managed to close his eyes and tune out the traffic of the wilderness.

He thought of Jenna and felt stupid: she'd done it to him again, with one lousy dinner. He was marooned out here because he'd listened to her, and because he'd enjoyed the improbable notion that she needed him. He should have known there'd be trouble; with Jenna, you could bank on it. Keyes imagined her at that moment, puttering around the kitchen making dinner, or doing those damn Jane Fonda leg-lifts on the living-room rug. If she were worried at all, it was about Skip Wiley, not him.

Wiley. Stealing the oar from the canoe was the sort of stunt

Wiley would pull, Keyes thought. But why didn't I hear anything? Where could he be hiding? And what was he waiting for? For Christ's sake, the joke was over.

Keyes sat up slowly in the canoe, suddenly aware that the crickets and the nighthawks had fallen silent. The Everglades had become perfectly still.

Something was wrong.

Keyes knew, from watching Tarzan movies as a kid, that whenever the jungle became quiet, something terrible was about to happen. The cannibals were about to attack or the elephants were about to stampede or a leopard was about to get dinner—any of which seemed preferable to one of Skip Wiley's surprise visits. Keyes wished like hell that he'd brought the cane bough with him on board the canoe.

A shadow materialized on the porch of Wiley's cabin.

It was a man's form, erect but motionless. In the emptiness of the night Keyes could hear the man breathing. He also heard the frantic hammering of his own heart.

'Wiley?'

The figure didn't move. Featureless, it appeared to face him with folded arms.

'Skip, get me outta here, dammit.' Keyes forced a laugh, brittle with fear. With bloodless knuckles he clutched the gunwales of the canoe. 'Skip?'

The shadow on the porch stepped back until it filled the frame of the cabin door. Muscles knotting, Keyes peered at the mute figure. He felt a cool drop of sweat trickle down his spine, and he shuddered. He was ready to dive from the canoe at the first glint of a gun.

'Look, I don't know who you are, but I don't mean any harm,' Keyes said.

Nothing from the specter.

'Please, wave your hand if you can hear me,' Keyes implored.

To his astonishment, the pensive shadow raised its right hand and waved. Keyes smiled inwardly, thinking: At last, progress!— not realizing that the man's gesture was not a wave at all, but a signal.

Idiotically Keyes raised his own right hand in amiable reciprocation. He remained so transfixed by the figure at the cabin that he didn't see what he should have seen: a dark brown hand, bare and smooth, rising from the water and alighting on the starboard side of the canoe, precisely where his own hand had been.

When Keyes finally was distracted from the silent watcher, it was not by other sights or sounds, but by a paralyzing centrifugal sensation.

The canoe was spinning out from under him.

He was in the air.

He was in the water.

He was blinded, and he was choking.

He was swallowed into the throat of the swamp.

11

'Wake up, Jungle Boy!'

Brian Keyes blinked the sting from his eyes and started coughing up swamp water.

'Not even a civil hello. How do you like that?'

'Hello, Skip,' Keyes said, between hacks.

They were in a clearing, deep in a cypress hammock. Smoke hung sweetly in the night air and a fire crackled, shooting sparks into the canopy. Hands bound, Keyes sat on bare ground against the trunk of a dwarf cypress. A cool breeze announced that he'd been stripped to his underwear. A tendril of wet hydrilla weed clung to his forehead.

'Cut me loose, Skip.'

Wiley grinned, his huge elastic face full of good humor.

'What do you think of the beard, Brian?'

'Very nice. Cut me loose, you asshole.'

Chuckling, Wiley ambled back to the campfire. Keyes saw that he wasn't alone; other figures moved quietly on the fringe of the clearing, conversing in low tones. Soon Wiley returned carrying a coffee mug.

'Hot tea,' he declared. 'All natural herbs. Here, it'll put lead in your pencil.'

Keyes shook his head. 'No thanks.'

'So how're things in the private-eye business?'

'A little strange, at the moment.'

Wiley was barefoot. He wore pleated khaki trousers and a cream-colored smock with two red horizontal stripes (pseudo-African, Keyes guessed). His rebellious hair had been raked straight back, giving a blond helmet effect, and the new beard bristled thick and reddish. Keyes had to admit that Skip Wiley was still a man of considerable presence.

'I guess you want an explanation.'

'Naw,' said Keyes. 'This happens all the time.'

'You're deep in the Everglades,' Wiley said. 'This is my camp. I'm hiding out.'

'And doing the worst Kurtz I ever saw.'

'Let's wait for history to make that judgment. And stop that funny business with your hands. That's not rope, it's oiled sawgrass. You keep trying to get loose and it'll cut through the veins of your wrist. Bleed to death in nine minutes flat.'

Keyes craned a glance over his shoulder and saw that Wiley was telling the truth. He stopped struggling.

'Where are my clothes?'

'We've got 'em hung by the fire, drying out.'

'We?'

'*Las Noches de Diciembre*. The Nights of December.'

'Oh, Skip, no,' Keyes said dispiritedly. It had not occurred to him that Wiley was mixed up with the kidnappings, yet it made perfect sense. Wiley had never been predictable, except in his passion for extremes. The symbolism of Bellamy and Harper was so obvious that Keyes felt dim and stupid.

'Don't look so bummed out,' Wiley said. 'Now's a good time to meet the rest of the guys.' He clapped his enormous hands. Three figures emerged from the shadows and assembled behind him. Keyes looked up to their faces, backlighted by the fire.

'Brian, I'd like you to meet the group. The big fellow here is Viceroy Wilson—you may have heard of him.'

Keyes said, 'I think we met at Pauly's Bar.'

'Yeah,' Wilson said, 'my fist met your head.'

'And this,' Wiley said cheerfully, 'is Jesús Bernal.'

Bernal was a jittery little Latin in a stringy undershirt. Keyes immediately noticed a strong resemblance in stature and complexion to Ernesto Cabal; no wonder Al García's witnesses had been eighty percent sure.

Jesús Bernal shot Keyes a contemptuous glance before slipping into the shadows. Wilson followed in a sullen gait.

'Viceroy hates you, 'cause you look like a cop, and Jesús is just a little shy,' Wiley explained. He threw his arm around the third man. 'But here's the guy who made all this possible. Tom Tigertail. Tommy, say hi to Mr. Keyes.'

Tommy Tigertail leaned forward to study the half-naked prisoner. Tommy was a handsome young Seminole: late twenties, medium height, lean but showing plenty of muscle. He had longish black hair and a classic Creek face, with high cheekbones and Oriental eyes. He wore jeans but no shirt, just a towel slung around his neck.

'You're not hurt,' he said to Keyes.

'Naw, a little queasy is all.'

'You put up a strong fight,' Tommy said. 'Swallowed half the pond.'

'You were the one under the canoe?'

Wiley piped, 'Tommy's one helluva swimmer!'

Expressionless, Tommy walked back to the fire to join the others.

'That young man,' Wiley whispered proudly, 'is worth five million dollars. Can you believe it? He made it all on Indian bingo. Got four bingo halls in South Florida—see, gambling's legal on the reservations. Perfectly legal. You can't put a casino on Miami Beach but you could open one smack in the middle of the Big Cypress. It's goddamn brilliant irony, isn't it, Brian? Little old blue-hair paleskins from all over creation come to bet Seminole bingo and the Indians make a killing. Ha! Bury my heart at Chase Manhattan! Tommy's the business manager so the tribe cuts him in for the biggest chunk. Already he's put away five fucking million dollars!'

'So what's he doing out here instead of the Galt Ocean Mile?'

Wiley looked disappointed at the remark. 'Tommy's out here,' he said, 'because he *believes* in me. He believes in what we're doing.'

'And what is that, Skip?'

'Well, in Tommy's case, we're launching the Fourth Great Seminole War. In the case of my little Cuban friend, we are advancing the cause of international right-wing terrorism. And as far as Mr. Viceroy Wilson is concerned, we are kicking the living shit out of whitey.' Wiley bent over and dropped to a whisper again. 'See, Brian, each of these guys has his own particular constituency.

My job, as I see it, is to make them feel equally important. It's a delicate balance, believe me. These are not the most stable human beings in the world, but they've got loads of energy. It's damned inspiring.'

Keyes said, 'What about you, Skip? What's your constituency?'

'Come on!' Wiley's brow furrowed. 'You don't *know?*'

Somewhere in the brush an animal scampered, emitting a high-pitched trill. Keyes glanced toward the darkness apprehensively.

'Relax,' Wiley said. 'Just a raccoon. My constituency, Brian. Along with the eagles, the opossums, the otters, the snakes, even the buzzards. All of this belongs to them, and more. Every goddamn acre, from here west to Miami Beach and north to the big lake, belongs to them. It got stolen away, and what we're going to do . . .' Wiley made a fist and shook it. '. . . is get it back.'

Keyes thought: A cross between Dr. Dolittle and Che Guevara. Wait'll I tell Cab Mulcahy.

'Don't give me that you-poor-sick-boy look,' Wiley said. 'I'm just fine, couldn't be better. You're the one who's got a problem, Brian. A big goddamn problem, I might add. Before this is over you're gonna wish you were back at the *Sun*, covering the bozos in the mayor's race.'

Keyes said, 'I'll take some of that tea now.'

He was trying to slow Wiley down, keep him from getting too wound up. Keyes remembered what Wiley could be like on one of his fast burns, all reckless fury.

Wiley held the hot mug to Keyes's lips and let him sip.

'Brian,' he said giddily. 'We're gonna empty out this entire state. Give it back to Tom and his folks. Give it back to the bloody raccoons. Imagine: all the condos, the cheesy hotels, the trailer parks, the motor courts, the town houses, fucking Disney World— a ghost town, old pal. All the morons who thundered into Florida the past thirty years and made such a mess are gonna thunder right out again . . . the ones who don't die in the stampede.'

Skip Wiley's brown eyes were steady and intense; he was perfectly serious. Brian Keyes wondered if he was face to face with raw insanity.

'How are you going to accomplish this miracle?' he asked.

'Publicity, old pal. *Bad* publicity.' Wiley cackled. 'It's my specialty, remember? We're going to take all the postcard puffery and jam it in reverse. The swaying palms, the murmuring surf, the tropical sun—from now on, Transylvania South.'

A postcard to end all postcards, Keyes thought.

'When I say bad publicity,' Wiley went on, 'search the extreme limits of your imagination. Think back to some of the planet's great disasters—the bubonic plague, Pompeii, Hiroshima. Imagine being tourism director for the city of Hiroshima in 1946! What would you do, Brian? Or think modern times: try to sell time-shares in West Beirut! Christ, that's a tall order, but it's nothing compared to what it's going to be like down here when we're finished, me and the guys. By the time we're through, old pal, Marge and Fred and the kids will vacation in the fucking Arctic *tundra* before they'll set foot on Miami Beach.'

Wiley was pacing before the fire, his voice booming through the copse. Viceroy Wilson sat impassively on a tree stump, Kleenexing the lenses of his sunglasses. Jesús Bernal swatted at gnats and moved herky-jerky in the firelight, tossing his knife at a tree. Tommy Tigertail was out there somewhere, but Brian Keyes couldn't see him.

'Did you kill Sparky Harper?' Keyes asked Skip Wiley.

'Ho-ho-ho.'

The suntan oil, the rubber alligator, the tacky Hawaiian shirt. Keyes thought: Who else but Wiley?

'And Ted Bellamy, the Shriner?'

'I'm afraid he's dead,' Wiley said, tossing a stick in the fire.

'What about the girl at the Seaquarium?' Keyes asked.

'Brian, settle down. We're simply trying to establish credibility. Nobody took us seriously after the Harper episode. Jesús, *amigo*, get my briefcase.'

'My God, Skip, you're talking about *murder!* Three innocent people—four, if you count Ernesto Cabal. You set him up, didn't you?'

'It was Viceroy's idea, to get rid of the car,' Wiley acknowledged. 'He was your client, I know, and I'm sorry he killed himself. By the way, did you really stab his lawyer in the tongue with a shrimp fork? That was wonderful, Brian, I was so goddamn proud when I heard about it. Made me think you must've learned something, all that time sitting next to me. For what it's worth, we had planned to spring little Ernesto when the time was right.'

'*Es verdad*,' Jesús said, delivering the briefcase.

'Speak English, you schmuck,' Wiley snapped. He turned to Keyes, complaining: 'The man was born in *Trenton* and still he's doing Desi Arnaz. Drives me nuts.'

Jesús Bernal slouched away, pouting. Wiley opened the briefcase and said, 'Might as well get the preliminaries out of the way. Pay attention, Brian.' Wiley held up a pair of plaid swim trunks. 'Theodore Bellamy,' he said.

'I believe you,' said Keyes.

Next Wiley produced a crimson halter top. 'Renee What's-her-face, the Canadian girl.'

Keyes nodded blankly.

With both hands Wiley dangled a man's silver necklace with a gaudy octagonal charm. 'Sparky Harper was wearing this,' Wiley said, studying it in the firelight. 'It says "Sunshine State Booster of the Year, 1977." Got his name engraved on the back. Be sure to point that out.'

Wiley dropped the articles into the briefcase and snapped it shut. 'You'll take this back to Miami, please.'

Keyes felt relieved. He'd been contemplating the possibility of dying out here in the swamp and not liking the idea at all, dead in his underwear and covered with bug bites.

'Saw Bloodworth's column,' Wiley said. 'What a hack.'

'He's not in your league, that's for sure.'

'He's a dim-witted gerbil who can't write his name. *Strangled to death* is redundant, doesn't he know that?' Wiley fumed. 'If it'd been you, you would have put it together two days ago. You'd have connected everything—Harper, Bellamy, Renee. Hell, you would have printed our letters.'

'And you would have loved it,' Keyes said.

Wiley wasn't listening. 'Brian, I know you've still got good police sources. What do you hear?'

Viceroy Wilson edged a little closer. He was always interested in cop news.

'Metro homicide closed the Harper case when Ernesto died,' Keyes said. 'As for the other two, a big zero. Missing persons, that's all.'

'Damn!' Wiley exploded. 'Those silly shitheads have got murderous terrorists on the loose and they don't even know it! See what I mean about credibility, Brian? What do we have to do? Tell me, Viceroy, you're the historian. Did the SLA have this problem?'

'Naw, they had Patty Hearst,' Wilson replied laconically. 'Got plenty of ink. Maybe we can brainwash us some famous white bitch.'

'*Sí*,' said Jesús Bernal, digging his knife from a gumbo-limbo tree. 'Pia Zadora!'

Wiley sat cross-legged in front of Keyes. 'See what I'm up against,' he muttered.

'Skip—or is it *El Fuego* now?'

'Skip is fine.'

'Okay, what do you want from me?'

'We need a witness,' Wiley said momentously. 'Someone impeccable. Someone who can go back to Miami and attest that we are legitimate, that we're deadly serious. Brian, we want *recognition*. We want the police and the press and the politicians and the tourist board to take us seriously.'

'In other words, you want your names in the paper?'

'The Nights of December? Yes. Mine? No. Not until the time comes.' Wiley leaned closer. 'If you go back and tell the cops about me, it would complicate our plans. Jeopardize everything. Now, should you decide to play Boy Scout and spill the beans, fine. But if you do, Brian, you'll deeply regret it. All hell will break loose, and what's happened so far—the kidnappings, Sparky Harper, the rest—is gonna seem like *Mister Rogers' Neighborhood*. You understand what I'm saying? If I should pick up the *Sun* tomorrow and see my face, then me and my comrades shift into overdrive. Moderation goes out the window. And then I'm afraid some folks you and I both know, and care about, are going to wind up suddenly deceased. We're talking massacre with a capital M.'

Keyes had never seen Wiley so grim, or heard his voice so

leaden. He wondered if Wiley meant Jenna, or Cab, or friends from the newspaper.

'Brian, if we do things my way, on my schedule, the violence will be minimized—I promise. If all goes well, in a few weeks the whole truth can be told. But not now—it's too early. My name would be nothing but a distraction, a liability to the organization. So my role here—well, let it be our little secret for a while. The rest of the saga is yours to tell. In fact, that's why we invited you here. Can I offer you some softshell-turtle stew?'

Keyes said: 'Let me get this straight. I'm supposed to go back to Miami and scare the shit out of everybody.'

'Exactly,' Wiley said.

'With what, Skip? A halter top and a dime-store medallion?'

Wiley shook his head. 'Those are just freebies for the cops, old pal. No, the most significant thing you'll carry back to civilization tomorrow is *testimony*.'

Keyes was getting tired. His arms ached, his wrists hurt, and invisible insects were feasting in his crevices.

'Okay, Skip, I'll go back and tell the cops that a gang of crazed radicals dragged me out of a canoe, tied me to a tree, and gave me tea that tasted like goat piss. Is that what you want?'

'Not quite,' Wiley said. The smile was thin, the eyes cheerless. 'We want you to go back and tell everyone that you witnessed a murder.'

Keyes went cold.

Wiley stood up and smoothed his pseudo-African smock. 'Tommy! Jesús! Viceroy!' he called. 'Go get Mrs. Kimmelman.'

The morning actually had started off well for Ida Kimmelman. The arrival of the Social Security checks was always a good omen, and then her sister called from Queens to say that Joel, Ida's youngest nephew, had finally gotten into law school. It wasn't a famous law school—someplace in Ohio, with two names—but Ida went out and bought Joel a card anyway. Basically he was a good young man, a little disrespectful perhaps, but deserving of encouragement.

The truth was that Joel, as most of Ida's blood relations,

couldn't stand her. They had all been fond of Lou Kimmelman, a sweet little fellow with a teasing sense of humor, but for years the clan had puzzled over how Lou could put up with Ida's tuba voice and her incredible charmlessness. Around the apartments the same was true: Lou was popular and pitied, while Ida was barely tolerated.

When Lou finally passed on, the social invitations dried up and the fourth-floor bridge club recruited a new couple, and Ida Kimmelman was left all alone with her dog Skeeter in apartment 4-K at Otter Creek Village. Somehow the U.S. government had overlooked Lou Kimmelman's death and continued to mail a $297.75 Social Security check every month, so Ida was making out pretty well. She'd bought herself a spiffy red Ford Escort and joined a spa, and every third Tuesday she would drive Skeeter to Canine Canaan and get his little doggy toenails painted blue. Of course Ida's Otter Creek neighbors disapproved of her extravagance and thought it tacky that she boasted of her double-dipping from Social Security. Ida knew they were jealous.

She was truly ambivalent about Lou's death. On some days she felt lonely, and guessed it must be Lou she was missing. Who else had shared her life for twenty-nine years? Lou had been an accountant for a big orthopedic shoe company in Brooklyn. He had been a hard worker who had saved money in spite of Ida; Ida, who'd never wanted children of her own, who was always scheming for a new car or a tummy tuck or a new dinette. When it came time to retire, the Kimmelmans had argued about where they would go. Everyone on the block was moving to Florida, but Ida disliked everyone on the block and she didn't want to go. Instead she wanted to move to Southern California and make new friends. She wanted a condo on the beach in La Jolla.

But Lou Kimmelman had been a shrewd accountant. One painful evening, two weeks before the shoe company gave him the traditional gold Seiko sendoff, Lou had sat Ida down with the Chemical Bank passbooks and the Keogh funds and demonstrated, quite conclusively, that they couldn't afford to move to California unless they wanted to eat dried cat food the rest of their lives. Reluctantly, Ida had accepted the inevitability of Florida.

After all, it was unthinkable not to go *somewhere* after your husband retired.

So they'd bought a small two-bedroom unit at Otter Creek, three doors down from the Seligsons, and Lou Kimmelman soon became captain of the fourth-floor shuffleboard team and sergeant-at-arms of the Otter Creek Homeowners' Association.

One thing Ida Kimmelman didn't miss about Lou, now that he was gone, was how he'd sit there in his madras slacks and blinding white shoes, watching TV in their new living room (which was hardly big enough for a family of squirrels), and ask, 'Now aren't you glad we moved down here after all?'

Lou Kimmelman would say this three or four times a week, and Ida hated it. Sometimes she'd wonder bitterly if she hated Lou, too. She'd squeeze out on the balcony, which was actually more of a glorified ledge, and gaze at the parking lot and, beyond that, the emptiness of the Everglades. In these moments Ida would imagine how great it would be to have a town house on a bluff in La Jolla, where you could sip coffee and watch all those brown young men on their candy-colored surfboards. *That* was Ida Kimmelman's idea of retirement.

Instead she was stuck in Florida.

After Lou died, Ida had gathered all the bankbooks and E. F. Hutton statements and got the calculator to add up their worldly possessions—only to discover that Lou Kimmelman, damn his arithmetic, had been absolutely correct. Southern California was no more affordable than Gstaad.

So Ida laid her dream to rest with Lou, and vowed to make the best of it. Never would she admit to her Otter Creek neighbors that her unhappiness was anything but a widow's grief, or that sometimes, especially during Florida's steambath of a summer, she longed to be back up North, in the city, where one could actually walk to the grocery without an oxygen tank.

December, with its cooler nights, wasn't so unbearable. The snowbirds were trickling south and the condominium was a much livelier place than in August, when nothing moved but the mercury. Now Otter Creek Village slowly was awakening, soon to be clogged with other couples who'd discovered Florida as long-ago tourists or honeymooners and returned to claim it in their old age.

The center of social life was the swimming pool. Not much swimming took place, but there was a lot of serious floating, wading, and talking—by far the most competitive of all condominium sports.

When Ida went down to the pool, which wasn't often, she'd usually end up dominating some debate about the perilous traffic, the impossible interest rates, or the criminally high hospital bills. Each outrage was a harbinger of financial ruination, which was the favorite topic poolside at Otter Creek. Lately, since she'd discovered Lou's Social Security checks were still coming, Ida's stock speech on the economy had lost some of its fire and she'd avoided the daily discussions. Ida loved to express her opinions, but she loved her spa, too.

On the morning of December 8, Ida Kimmelman followed her morning routine: hot bagels, two cups of coffee, six ounces of prune juice, David Hartman, and the Fort Lauderdale *Sun-Sentinel*, which had terrific grocery coupons. By ten Ida was usually made-up and ready to walk Skeeter, but on this day she was running late because she had to go to Eckerd Drugs to buy a card for her nephew Joel the law student.

Ida returned to the apartment at ten-thirty to find a nasty little present from Skeeter on the shag in the bedroom. This was another reason she missed Lou, because Lou would always clean up after the dog; he never clobbered Skeeter or threatened to put him to sleep the way Ida did.

She was so mad about the mess in the bedroom that she hooked Skeeter to his leash and dragged him, yelping, down four flights of stairs. She led the dog out to the canal behind Otter Creek Village, near the Everglades dike, and unfastened the leash to let him run.

Ida noticed there was nobody out by the pool. She thought: These people! A touch of cold weather and they run indoors. The breeze felt good, too, although it puffed her new hairdo.

After fifteen minutes Ida Kimmelman got goose bumps and wished she'd brought a light sweater. She clapped her hands and shouted for Skeeter in a baritone that seemed to carry all the way to Orlando.

But Skeeter didn't come.

Ida picked up her pace along the canal, careful not to get too close. She called for Skeeter again, expecting any moment to see his beautifully barbered, AKC-registered poodle face hopping through the high grass along the banks of the canal.

But there was no sign of the little dog.

Ida trudged on, hollering, calling, cooing, thinking: He's just mad about what happened upstairs. He'll be back.

Soon she found herself standing in a field of scrub and palmetto, a full mile from Otter Creek. The sandspurs stuck to her slacks, and she cried out when a fat coppery ant chomped on her big toe.

'Skeeter darling,' Ida Kimmelman cried, the great voice fading, 'come home to Momma! Momma loves you!'

Suddenly she heard a commotion and turned to see two men waist-deep in the scrub; one black and ominous, the other small and dark. Nothing frightened Ida Kimmelman so much as the fact that the small man wore an undershirt, the mark of a true desperado.

'Have you seen my doggie?' Ida asked nervously.

The black man nodded. 'Skeeter had an accident,' he said. 'You'd better come quick.'

'What kind of accident?' Ida Kimmelman cried, forgetting her own safety and clumping after the men. 'I said, what kind of accident?'

'An eagle,' the black man said. 'A fish eagle, ma'am.'

And when Ida Kimmelman saw what was left of poor Skeeter, presented in a shoebox by the man in the undershirt, she fainted dead away. The next time she opened her eyes was in the airboat.

Standing before Brian Keyes was a plainly terrified woman in her late sixties, slightly overweight, lacquered with rouge and mascara. Her mouth was covered with two-inch hurricane tape, and her hands were tied with rope. Her shiny wine-colored hair was piled in a tangled nest on one side of her head. She was doing plenty of talking with her eyes.

Jesús Bernal cut Keyes loose and stood him up.

Skip Wiley said, 'Brian, this is Mrs. Kimmelman.'

'Skip, are you nuts?' Keyes said. 'This is kidnapping! You and your merry men are gonna wind up at Raiford.'

'Mrs. Kimmelman and her late husband discovered South Florida in 1962,' Wiley said, 'when they spent two weeks on gorgeous sun-drenched Miami Beach. Stayed at the Beau Rivage, shopped at Lincoln Road. Went to see a Jackie Gleason show live, right, Mrs. Kimmelman?'

Ida Kimmelman nodded.

'Had such a good time, they came back again and again,' Wiley said, 'and when Mr. Kimmelman, rest his soul, retired, they moved down here for good. Bought a unit out at Otter Creek Village, forty-two-five at twelve percent. A very tasteful place, Mrs. Kimmelman, I must say.'

'Mmmmmm,' Ida Kimmelman protested through the tape.

'Skip, let her go.'

'Can't do that, Brian.'

Viceroy Wilson held one of Ida Kimmelman's pale arms, and Tommy Tigertail the other. Wiley jerked his head and they led her out of the clearing into the darkness.

'Skip, I don't need to see any more. Let her go and I'll do what you want. I'll go back and tell the cops you mean business.'

'No, I think you need to be convinced,' Wiley said. 'I know *I* would. Skeptics, you and I both, Brian. Take nobody's word for anything. First law of good journalism: if your mom says she loves you, check it out first.'

Jesús Bernal handed Brian Keyes his trousers and said something sternly in Spanish.

'Put your pants on,' Wiley translated, 'and follow me.'

In great strides Wiley crashed through the brush while Keyes struggled to keep up. Sawgrass and grape-sized pine burs bit into his bare feet, but Jesús Bernal stayed close enough to prod him with his beloved knife whenever Keyes faltered.

Ahead Wiley broke from the shelter of the hammock and took a ragged trail through an open, flat expanse of swamp. A juggernaut of noise, he was just as easy to track by sight, the cream-colored smock fluttering in the gray night.

Keyes found himself trotting faster to escape the insects, but dreading what awaited him. Jesús Bernal gave no clues, grunting with each step.

After ten minutes the sprint ended abruptly at water's edge. Keyes caught his breath and studied the scene by yellow lantern light: Mrs. Kimmelman, whimpering on the ground where they had laid her; Wiley, looking haunted but anticipatory; Viceroy Wilson, cool, unexerted, and bored; Tommy Tigertail, up to his knees in the water, his back to the light; and Jesús Bernal, swatting bugs off his sweaty arms.

'Tommy,' Wiley said, panting, 'do the honors, please.'

Tommy Tigertail splashed the water with both hands and began to clap.

'Skip?' Keyes whispered.

'Shhhh!'

Tommy cupped his hands to his mouth and barked in a deep gravelly voice: 'Aaaarkk! Aaaarkk!' He slapped the water at his feet.

Skip Wiley extended the lantern and peered into the marsh. 'Here, boy!' he sang out.

'Oh God,' said Brian Keyes.

A massive shadow cut a clean V in the silky water and made no noise as it swam. Its eyes shone ruby-red, and the snaking of its prehistoric tail cast a roiling wake.

Now Brian Keyes knew what had happened to Sparky Harper.

'His name is Pavlov,' Wiley said. 'He is a North American crocodile, one of only about thirty left in the entire world. He's a shade over seventeen feet and weighs about the same as a Porsche 915. All that tonnage with a brain no bigger than a tangerine. Isn't nature wonderful, Brian? Who said God doesn't have a sense of humor?'

Keyes was awestruck. He watched Tommy Tigertail lean over to stroke the giant reptile's armored snout. From where he stood Keyes could hear its breath hissing.

'Is it . . . tame?'

Wiley laughed. 'Lord, no! He knows Tommy brings the food but there's no loyalty there, Brian. See, crocodiles are different from alligators. Tommy grew up around gators and he could tell you better than I.'

Without taking his eyes off the beast, Tommy said, 'Crocs are meaner, more aggressive. Gators get fat and lazy.'

Wiley said, 'You won't ever see a Seminole wrestle a crocodile, will you, Tommy?'

'Never,' Tommy agreed. 'Have to be crazy.'

Keyes was afraid that anything he said might hasten the ceremony, so he said nothing. If only Wiley would keep jabbering, maybe the damn crocodile would get bored and swim away. Meanwhile Ida Kimmelman was sobbing and Jesús Bernal hovered watchfully, in case she tried to get up and run. Keyes wondered if Ida had figured out the plan by now.

'This is not murder,' Wiley declared, 'it's social Darwinism. Two endangered species, Pavlov there and Mrs. Kimmelman, locked in mortal combat. To the victor goes the turf. That's how it ought to be, Brian.'

'It's not fair, Skip.'

'Fair? There are nine million Mrs. Kimmelmans between here and Tallahassee, and thirty fucking crocodiles. Is that fair? Who has the legitimate right to be here? Who does this place really belong to?'

Wiley was hitting warp speed. Keyes backed off and tried another strategy.

'Mr. Wilson,' he said, 'please don't let this happen.'

Viceroy Wilson just wanted the whole thing to be over so he could go back to the campfire and sleep off a couple joints. It wasn't his idea to do it quite this way; this was something cooked up by Wiley and the Indian. Viceroy Wilson went along to expedite the revolutionary process and also to avoid irritating the Indian, who, after all, was very generous with his Cadillac.

So Viceroy Wilson said to Keyes: 'You don't like it, close your goddamn eyes.' Which was exactly what Viceroy Wilson planned to do.

As for Pavlov, he seemed to drift leisurely in the pond not far from Tom Tigertail's ankles. The leviathan's eyes, two burning barbecue coals, gave nothing away. Keyes imagined he saw

bemusement there—as if the carnivorous dinosaur were just playing along with Skip Wiley's schemes.

At Wiley's instruction, Jesús Bernal tore the hurricane tape
from Ida Kimmelman's mouth and cut the ropes on her wrists.
Immediately she began bellowing so loudly that the crocodile was
drawn closer to shore.

'Please be quiet!' Wiley commanded.

'Who do you think you are—'

'Shut up, Mrs. Kimmelman! This is going to be a fair contest,
despite what Mr. Keyes says. You and Pavlov are going for a
swim. If you survive, you can go home.'

'But what's the meaning of this?' Ida cried.

Wiley clenched his jaw and rubbed at his temples. 'It is a
contest, pure and simple. You and Pavlov have laid claims to the
same territory'—he waved his hand at the Glades—'and always
such disputes must be settled by battle. Two primitive animals
fighting for elemental needs. It's the natural order. How's that
for *meaning?*'

'But I can't swim!' Ida Kimmelman said.

'So what? Pavlov can't play bridge. Sounds like you're even to
me.' Wiley snapped his fingers. 'Viceroy!'

Viceroy Wilson seized Mrs. Kimmelman by the shoulders and
firmly guided her toward the water. Tommy Tigertail stepped out
of the pond, drying his arms with the towel.

'Brian, this may get a little rough,' Wiley cautioned. 'You'd
better sit down.'

Keyes felt shaky and nauseated. He opened his mouth but
nothing came out. He took one queasy step toward Viceroy
Wilson, then another, and finally a scream came to his throat
and he was able to launch himself at the football player.

He grabbed on with both hands, snarling as he dug his fingernails into the jet flesh. By the look on his face, Viceroy Wilson
obviously was surprised at Keyes's strength.

Keyes felt the athlete's neck cords tighten in his grip, and saw
Mrs. Kimmelman wilt to the ground between them. The lantern
strobed, and then came shouting: 'No, Jesús! Stop!'

Skip Wiley's voice, but not in time.

Keyes felt the fiery rip beneath his right armpit and, on the inside, something metal scrape his ribs. His hands turned to cork and he fell back, gasping. A rush of heat drenched his flank. Even with Wiley and the Cuban on his back, Keyes somehow held his balance until Viceroy Wilson put him down with a vengeful right cross to the jaw.

Crumpling after the punch, Keyes dearly hoped that Wilson had knocked him out. He was hoping to awake later, when it was over, in daylight and sanity.

But Brian Keyes was not unconscious.

He lay curled on his right side, sticky with blood, looking out across the misty, lantern-lit pond. Keyes watched helplessly while Viceroy Wilson and Jesús Bernal carried Mrs. Kimmelman to the water's edge. Pavlov slowly submerged, leaving a cheerful bubble on the pond. In dread Keyes watched as the Cuban took Mrs. Kimmelman's feet and the football player grabbed her arms and they swung her twice and let go—like at a fraternity pool party. She landed in a tangle and floundered on the surface, spluttering in an enormous voice.

'Oh, stop that!' Wiley scolded, playing swim coach. 'Kick your legs and keep your head up.'

Recklessly Mrs. Kimmelman windmilled toward shore, flailing the swamp to a froth. The giant crocodile was nowhere to be seen, but ominous clouds of bottom mud stained the water. Then the silky surface of the pond seemed to bulge.

'Help!' Mrs. Kimmelman yelled.

'Keep swimming,' Wiley counseled. 'You're doing quite well.'

Brian Keyes closed his eyes when the water finally exploded.

As Ida Kimmelman went under, she thought: Damn you, Lou, are you happy now?

12

Brian Keyes shivered on the deck of a speeding airboat and watched dawn bleed across the pale Everglades sky. High on the driver's platform sat Tommy Tigertail, his black hair dancing in spikes.

Keyes lifted his head with a groan, but the Indian couldn't hear him over the din of the engine. Tommy wore a serene look as he steered deftly through the sedge.

If Skip Wiley was the ebullient nerve of *Las Noches de Diciembre*, Tommy Tigertail was the soul. He was a man of unusual temperament—taciturn, sometimes brooding, yet outwardly gracious, even warm. He was quiet not because he was shy or queer, as Jesús Bernal would whisper; Tommy was quiet because he was watchful. Never relax, never look away, never trust a white soul—the expensive lessons of history. Tommy Tigertail did not carry the pain of his ancestors for strangers to see; he carried it in his heart and dreams, which haunted him. He was tormented by the nightmare of his great-great-grandfather, Chief Tiger Tail, dying in the dank misery of a New Orleans prison barrack. Tiger Tail, who had never quit like Coacoochee, or been duped into capture like the eloquent Osceola; Tiger Tail, who had spurned the Army's demand to abandon godforsaken Florida with its fever and mosquitoes and rebuild the Seminole nation in Arkansas, of all places. Arkansas! Tiger Tail, who from the beginning had sensed the white man's mendacity and fought back brilliantly until the end, when there were virtually no warriors left. Tiger Tail, who had been captured in the battle at Palatka and shipped to a dungeon on the Mississippi, where he soon died, tubercular, homesick, and broken.

Growing up, Tommy Tigertail had memorized the broken treaties—Camp Moultrie, Payne's Landing, Fort Gibson, and the rest. These were the devices that had swept from paradise all but three hundred unconquerable Seminoles, among them Tommy's great-grandfather, then a teenager, who had hidden and fought and never touched a quill to a U.S. treaty.

Viceroy Wilson had read up on the Seminoles, who impressed him as some of the craftiest motherfuckers ever to raise a rifle. The more he read, the more Wilson was persuaded that Tommy's people had just as much fury to burn as American blacks. Viceroy Wilson was waiting for the day when the Indian's hatred percolated into raw violence or sinister magic, but so far Tommy Tigertail had kept it under rein. Moderation and manners served him well. He weaved as effortlessly through the white man's labyrinth of high finance as he did through the knotted trails of the Big Cypress. It was Tommy Tigertail who had turned the inane bingo fetish of Florida's senior citizens into a Seminole bonanza: soon after gambling was ruled to be legal on the Indian reservations, Tommy converted some old airplane hangars into the world's biggest bingo halls. Ingeniously he tailored them for the various South Florida markets: Yiddish bingo, Cuban bingo, Brooklyn bingo, and redneck bingo. The tribe got rich, and Tommy Tigertail became a tycoon without even trying. It was bingo money that bankrolled *Las Noches*, but Tommy didn't seem to care how it was spent. He said little, and carried out Skip Wiley's extravagant orders with dispassionate obedience. Around the midnight campfires it was Wiley who did the fulminating, who put the anger and the passion into words, but it was Tommy Tigertail whose spirit seemed to dominate; it was in Tommy's burnt-wood eyes that Skip Wiley found a pure purpose for his crusade.

As his airboat sliced through the morning mist, Tommy Tigertail thought for the hundredth time: It is too bad Great-great-grandfather didn't have one of these babies. They'd never have caught him.

'Slow down!' Brian Keyes croaked, teeth clicking.

Tommy Tigertail glanced down at his prisoner.

Keyes mouthed the words: 'Help me.'

The Indian cut the engine, and the airboat coasted to a stop. The silence seemed sudden and immense.

Tommy hopped off his perch and bent over Keyes.

'I'm bleeding to death,' Keyes said, fingering his sticky shirt.

'No,' Tommy Tigertail said. 'I dressed the wound myself. And gave you medicine.'

'I don't remember.'

'Button snakeroot and willow shavings.' Tommy lifted Keyes's shirt and studied the knife wound. Gently he put his hand on Keyes's belly. 'You're very cold,' he said. 'We'll wait a few minutes then.' He opened a moleskin canteen and tipped it to Keyes's mouth. The liquid was hot and smoky-tasting, stronger than any coffee known to man.

'Black tea,' explained Tommy Tigertail, 'to stop the madness.'

'Too late for that,' Keyes said with a sigh.

The Seminole wore a long-sleeved flannel shirt, denims, and western boots—the same damn boots from Wiley's cabin. Tommy Tigertail looked like no other Florida millionaire Brian Keyes had ever met.

The Indian surveyed the swamp. 'We are four miles from the road.' He climbed into the driver's seat and pointed toward the sunrise.

'When I was a boy,' he said, 'a herd of white-tailed deer lived there. Three bucks, many does. The fawns you seldom saw. In the winter, when the water disappeared, I could always find the deer grazing on the edge of this basin. When I was fifteen it was time to kill one, and I did.'

Keyes sat up, bolstered by the strange tea. Under different circumstances Tommy's version of *Bambi* would have touched him, but Keyes could scarcely listen. He was preoccupied with the selfish notion that he should be taken to a hospital as soon as possible.

Tommy Tigertail said: 'Three years ago the deer died. Five white men in a half-track ran them into the high water and killed them with shotguns. The fawns, too. I watched from this spot.' The Indian described the slaughter with no outward emotion, as if it were something he'd been expecting his whole life. It gave Keyes a fresh chill.

The Seminole said, 'You were wondering what I'm doing with Mr. Wiley. You didn't ask, but you wondered just the same. So this is my answer: your friend Mr. Wiley says there's a chance to put things right, to make those who don't belong here go away forever.'

'But it's a fantasy,' Keyes said.

Tommy Tigertail smiled handsomely, his caramel face brightening. 'Of course it's a fantasy. Of course it is!' He laughed softly, a laugh full of irony. 'Ask anybody,' Tommy said. 'Florida is the place where fantasies come true. Now, lie down, Mr. Keyes, and we will go.'

With that the Indian cranked the propeller and the two of them were drowned in noise. The airboat rocketed out of the sawgrass, and the wind shocked Brian Keyes to the spine. He huddled down, cheek to the cool aluminum deck, and counted out the miles in his pounding head.

Shortly after noon on the ninth of December, the head nurse of the emergency room at Flagler Memorial Hospital was notified by a policeman that 'a school bus with serious injuries' was on its way to the hospital.

Assuming the worst, which is the only sane way to function in Miami, the nurse immediately declared a Code Orange and scrambled every available surgeon, anesthesiologist, scrub nurse, and lab tech in the hospital. The other patients—miscellaneous gunshot victims, drug overdoses, and screeching teenagers in labor—were shuffled out of the way and told to manage as best they could. Flagler Memorial braced for full-scale carnage and catastrophe.

In no time the E. R. filled with TV crews, newspaper reporters, photographers, and personal-injury lawyers. After about an hour of waiting, everyone got cranky and wanted to know what was the damn story with this busload of mangled orphans. Where were the choppers? And the ambulances? Where the hell were the grieving parents?

The head nurse was getting baleful glares from the orthopedic surgeons ('It's Sunday, for Chrissakes!') when the bus finally clattered up to the emergency-room door.

It was not a school bus, though once it might have been. And in fairness to the cop who radioed it in, the bus had the right

colors, yellow and black; the yellow being paint and the black
being rust.

The driver, a phlegmatic fellow with a Budweiser in one hand,
seemed extremely surprised to be met by bright lights and Minicams and an army of tense-looking people dressed in white.
Drunk as he was, the driver could sense their collective disappointment.

For the bus was not packed with seriously injured children,
but perfectly healthy migrant workers—Jamaicans, Haitians,
Dominicans, and Mexicans, all sweaty and dusty and peeved that
their day in the tomato fields had been cut short.

'I don't understand,' the nurse said, scanning the dark faces.
'Where's the emergency?'

'There's your fuckin' emergency,' the bus driver said, waving a
stubby arm. 'Up top.'

The nurse stood on the tips of her white shoes and saw what
the driver was talking about: a young man strapped to the rack
on top of the bus. He looked damp and half-conscious, his clothes
soaked with blood. For some reason a briefcase had been placed
under his lolling head.

'Humph!' said the nurse, turning to face the throng. 'Relax,
everybody.'

A pair of orderlies clambered atop the bus and untied Brian
Keyes. As they placed him on a stretcher and carried him into
the hospital, the emergency room emptied with a groan. Only
one reporter hung around to ask questions, and that was Ricky
Bloodworth.

Nobody bothered to retrieve the briefcase from the top of the
migrant bus. Miraculously it remained there, unsecured, almost
halfway back to Immokalee, until the bus accidentally struck an
opossum crossing Route 41. The jolt launched the briefcase—
containing all Skip Wiley's vital evidence—off the roof of the
bus into the Tamiami Canal, where it sank unopened into a
gator hole.

Al García was in a bellicose mood. He hated the night shift if he
couldn't be out on the streets, and he couldn't be on the streets

if he was running the motor pool. The motor pool was a terrible place for a detective; there was nothing to investigate. The highlight of the evening was when one of the K–9 guys drove in with chunks of dead cat all over the backseat of the squad car. The cop said the cat had gone crazy and attacked his K–9 German shepherd and the dog didn't have a choice but to fight back—it was just a terrible thing to see. García said sure, pal, and wrote it up anyway, musing over the sick possibilities.

Al García did not want his career to end this way, in a stale little office on a parking lot full of police cars.

He was still furious about the two goons from I.A.D. who had foraged through his house, hunting for a typewriter that wasn't there. They'd each carried Xerox copies of the *El Fuego* letters to compare with anything they found. But all they'd discovered was a bunch of hand-scrawled hate letters García had once written to Lee Iacocca, the president of Chrysler Motors. For some reason almost every cop car in America is made by Chrysler, and Al García calculated that he'd spent at least forty thousand hours of his life riding in Chrysler-made automobiles: Furies, LeBarons, Diplomats, Monacos, Darts, you-name-it. Al García was an expert on Chryslers, and he hated the damn things. Hated the steering, hated the shocks, hated the brakes, hated the radios. García especially hated the seats. He had hemorrhoids the size of bell peppers and it was all Lee Iacocca's fault. So García had dashed off a few appropriate missives, which he wisely never sent. Typically the letters would begin: 'Dear Shit-for-Brains.' For some reason the guys from I.A.D. found this fascinating. They sealed the letters in a plastic bag and exchanged congratulatory whispers. García gave them the finger on their way out the door.

He didn't really expect to see the I.A.D. boys again anytime soon, so he was mildly surprised when one of the assholes appeared that night at the motor pool. García remembered that his name was Lieutenant Bozeman. He was very young to be a lieutenant, and much too sharply dressed to be a good cop.

'I hope you need a car,' García said. 'You like cats?'

Bozeman helped himself to a seat. He took a notebook from his coat.

'Just a few questions, sergeant, if you don't mind.'

'I *do* mind, dipshit. I'm very busy right now, in case you didn't notice. I got six marked units waiting to have the tires rotated, I got a rear bumper missing off a paddy wagon, and the transmission just dropped out of an undercover car in the middle of the Rickenbacker Causeway. Much as I'd love to help you, I got no time.'

Bozeman said, 'Harold Keefe thinks you wrote the *Fuego* letters.'

'Why would I do a stupid thing like that?'

'To make him look bad.'

'Hal doesn't need my help.'

Bozeman scribbled something in the notebook.

'Weren't you passed over for a promotion last year?'

'Yeah,' García said. 'Failed the swimsuit competition. So what?'

Scribble, scribble. The scratch of the pen jangled García's nerves.

'You don't like Detective Keefe very much, do you, García?'

'I love Detective Keefe,' García said. He leaned over and beckoned Bozeman with a fat brown finger. 'I love Hal very much,' García whispered. 'In fact, I *want* him.'

'That's not funny,' Bozeman said stiffly.

'You're right, it's very sad. See, Hal doesn't want me . . . what did you say your first name was?'

'I didn't.'

Bozeman started jotting again. García firmly took him by the wrist. 'I like you, too, lieutenant.'

'Stop it!'

'Please don't be shy. Are you married?'

'Sergeant, that's enough.'

García frowned. 'You don't want me either?'

'No!'

'Then why are you getting a lump in your pants, you little fruit!'

Bozeman pulled away, as if burned on a stove. García wheezed with laughter and pounded on the desk.

'You!' Bozeman tried very hard to look icy, Bronson-style, but was betrayed by his crimson blush. 'You're nothing but a psychopath, Sergeant García.'

'And you're nothing but a well-dressed sack of shit.' García stood up and exhaled straight into the lieutenant's face. 'Now get out of here before I launch that Bic pen up your Brooks Brothers ass. And put this in your notebook: whoever wrote those *Fuego* letters is crazier than me, and he's for real.'

After the I.A.D. guy left, García didn't have much to do so he scrounged up a police manual and looked up 'moral turpitude.' The definition wasn't so bad but, Christ, those two words really jumped off the page. Especially *turpitude*, which inspired images of Great Danes and Reddi Wip and double-jointed cheerleaders. Certainly wouldn't go over very big back at the homestead. If I.A.D. dumps on me, García thought, maybe they'll have the decency to go with simple 'insubordination.' With a creep like Bozeman, who could tell.

Ricky Bloodworth's story began like this:

> A local private investigator was stabbed and left for dead along an Everglades highway Sunday.
>
> Police said Brian Keyes, 32, was attacked and dumped on the Tamiami Trail about fifteen miles east of Naples. Keyes was spotted by a passing bus driver and transported to Flagler Memorial Hospital, where he was listed in stable condition following surgery.
>
> Keyes, a former Miami newspaper reporter, told the *Sun* that he was on a canoe trip when he was abducted, robbed, and stabbed by two Slavic men wearing wigs and Halloween masks.

Bloodworth finished typing and took the story to Cab Mulcahy's office. Mulcahy sat behind the desk, dictating letters, trying to conceal his wretchedness. He wore an expensive knit sports shirt—a classy lemon pastel, not a crease anywhere.

The old boy never came in on weekends; Bloodworth wondered what was up.

'You said you wanted to see this?'

'Yes, Ricky, have a seat.' Mulcahy took the story and read it.

It took him a long time; he seemed to read each sentence twice.

'Is it the byline?' Bloodworth asked worriedly.

Mulcahy glanced up. 'What?'

'My byline. I changed it.' Bloodworth walked around the desk and pointed over the editor's shoulder. 'See? Richard L. Bloodworth. Instead of Ricky.'

'Oh yes.'

'I think it looks better,' Bloodworth said. 'More professional.'

What had really happened was this: Ricky Bloodworth had eaten breakfast with a correspondent from the New York *Times*, who explained that the *Times* simply didn't hire people named *Ricky*. How about just plain Rick? Bloodworth had asked. Well, *Rick* was a swell name for a Little League coach, the reporter had said, as kindly as he could, but it was hardly appropriate for a world-class journalist. Bloodworth was devastated by this revelation because he'd spent half his adult life sending résumés to Abe Rosenthal without even a postcard in reply. Now he knew why. He pressed the *Times* man for more tips and the fellow told him that everybody on the *Times* used middle initials in their bylines because surveys showed that middle initials enhanced credibility twenty-three percent among newspaper readers.

Ricky Bloodworth thought this was a great idea, and he'd quickly fallen in love with the way *Richard L. Bloodworth* looked on the screen of his word processor.

'So, you like it?' he asked Mulcahy.

'It's fine,' Mulcahy said, paying no attention whatsoever. Personally he didn't care if Bloodworth called himself *Richard L. Douchebag*. Mulcahy was more concerned about Brian Keyes.

'What else did he say?'

'Not much. They gave him a shot at the hospital and he got real spacey,' Bloodworth said. 'Kept asking for Jenna.'

Mulcahy groaned inwardly. 'Did he mention anyone else?'

'No. It sure is a strange tale. What do you suppose he was doing way out there in a canoe?'

'I've got no idea.' Mulcahy handed Bloodworth the story. 'Good job, Richard L. The new byline looks splendid.'

'Thanks,' Bloodworth said, beaming. 'I'm gonna use it on the column, too.'

Cab Mulcahy's ulcer quivered. 'Ricky, I meant to tell you: the column's been put on hold for now. We need you on general assignment.'

'Sure, Cab,' Bloodworth said in a wounded voice. Then, rebounding: 'Tell you what. I'm gonna go see Brian again tomorrow. Try to get a blow-by-blow.'

Mulcahy shook his head. 'Let him rest.'

'But it'd be a terrific second-day feature—'

'The man just got his thorax stitched back together. Give him a break, okay? Besides, somebody gets stabbed every thirty seconds in Miami. It's not news anymore. Maybe in Spudville, Iowa, but not here.'

Not news. That was all Ricky Bloodworth needed to hear.

He retreated to his desk and practiced typing his new byline. He even experimented with different middle initials, just to gauge the effect: Richard A. Bloodworth, Richard B. Bloodworth, Richard C. Bloodworth and so on. There was something about having a vowel for a middle initial that struck Bloodworth as impressive, and he wondered if his mother would get upset if he changed his middle name from Leon to Attenborough.

Bloodworth was still mulling the notion an hour later when an editor handed him a police bulletin about some old lady who'd turned up missing from her Broward condominium. As he skimmed the police report about Mrs. Kimmelman's disappearance, Ricky Bloodworth suddenly remembered something else Brian Keyes had whispered from his Demerol fog on the stretcher, something even odder than the business about the Slavic kidnappers.

'Ida is dead,' Keyes had told him.

Richard L. Bloodworth emptied his typewriter and started working the phones like a dervish.

13

Skip Wiley had a plan.

That's what he told them—the Indian, the football player, and the Cuban—whenever they got restless.

Trust me, boys, I have a plan!

And he was such a convincing eccentric that they usually calmed down. Wiley overpowered them—even Viceroy Wilson, who thought Wiley would've made a righteous TV preacher. Of all *Las Noches de Diciembre*, only Wilson was absolutely certain of Wiley's sanity. As much as he hated honkies, Wilson found Skip Wiley vastly amusing.

Jesús Bernal, on the other hand, was not amused. He thought Wiley was a reckless lunatic, and wasted no opportunity to say so. Bernal believed discipline was essential for revolution; Wiley, of course, believed just the opposite.

Usually it was Viceroy Wilson who was left to suffer the Cuban's ravings because the Indian just ignored both of them. Without Wiley around, Tommy Tigertail invariably climbed into his airboat and roared into the Everglades without a word. Viceroy Wilson didn't mind, as long as Tommy left the keys to the Cadillac.

On the morning of December 10, Skip Wiley was gone and the Indian had vanished, leaving Viceroy Wilson alone with Jesús Bernal. At Wiley's instruction, the two of them were driving to Miami on an important mission.

'He's *loco*,' Bernal was saying. 'Did you see his eyes?'

'He just drank a six-pack,' Wilson reminded him.

'Crazy fucker. All this work and what do we have to show for it? *Nada*. Remember all the publicity he promised? NBC! Geraldo Rivera! *Mother Jones!* Ha!'

Jesús Bernal no longer spoke Spanish in the presence of Viceroy

Wilson because Wilson had promised to kill him if he did. The mere sound of people speaking Spanish gave Viceroy Wilson a terrible headache. Opera had the same effect.

'The man's got a plan,' Wilson said, 'so chill out.'

'What plan? He's a fucking nut!' Bernal nervously knotted the tail of his undershirt. 'We're all going to wind up in prison, except him. He'll be at the Betty Ford Clinic while you and me do twenty-five at Raiford, getting butt-fucked in the showers.'

'Be a good experience for you.'

'Don't tell me about *plans*,' the Cuban groused.

Viceroy Wilson slid Lionel Richie into the tape deck.

'Oh, man, turn the jungle drums down—' Jesús Bernal reached for the volume knob but Wilson forcefully intercepted his arm. 'Okay, okay! Christ, take it easy.' Bernal couldn't see Viceroy Wilson's eyes behind the Carrera sunglasses; it was just as well.

'So tell me about Dartmouth,' Wilson said in a phony Ivy League tone. 'Did you excel?'

'That wasn't me, that was another Jesús Bernal. I'm a different person now.'

'Too bad,' Wilson said. 'Tell me about the First Weekend in July Movement.'

'Never!'

Wilson chuckled dryly. He'd done a little checking at the Miami Public Library.

'Why'd they kick you out?'

'They didn't kick me out, *coño*, I quit!'

Viceroy Wilson didn't like the sound of *coño*, but he let it slide. He was having too much fun. He'd been waiting for this since the first time Jesús Bernal had flashed his switchblade. Jesús was a bully, his mean streak carefully rehearsed; Viceroy Wilson would have loved to play football against Jesús Bernal. Just one play. Thirty-one Z-right.

'So tell me about the bombs.'

Bernal sneered.

'Come on, Jesús. I read where you were in charge of munitions.'

'I held the title of defense minister!'

'Yeah, that was later. I'm talking about 1978, June 1978.'

Bernal's upper lip twitched. He stared out the car window and started humming 'All Night Long,' drumming on his knee.

Viceroy Wilson said, 'June 15, 1978.'

'Turn up the music.'

This is what had happened on the afternoon of June 15, 1978: Jesús Bernal manufactured a letter bomb which was meant to kill a well-known Miami talk-show host. This TV celebrity had been foolhardy enough to suggest that the United States should send emergency medical supplies to a rural province in Cuba, where a deadly strain of influenza had afflicted hundreds of children.

The talk-show host had actually made this appeal for Cuba on the air. In Dade County, Florida.

Jesús Bernal, munitions man for the First Weekend in July Movement, saw the talk show and flew into action. It had taken only two hours to fashion an inconspicuous letter bomb with gunpowder, C-4, glass, wire, gum, and blasting caps. He'd addressed the package to the talk-show star at the television studio, and put it in a mailbox at Southwest Eighth Street and LeJeune Road (the same intersection where, years later, poor Ernesto Cabal would peddle his mangoes and cassavas).

At 4:10 P.M. on June 15, 1978—ten minutes after Jesús Bernal had deposited the lethal package—the mailbox blew up. No one was killed. No one was injured. It wasn't even a particularly loud explosion, by Miami standards.

Jesús Bernal knew he was in trouble. Frantically he'd telephoned seven Cuban radio stations and announced that the First Weekend in July Movement was responsible for the bombing. They all wanted to know: what bombing?

Two days later, on orders from above, Jesús Bernal had tried again. Another letter bomb, another mailbox. Another premature detonation. This time it had made the newspapers: *Feds Seek Postal Prankster*.

When Jesús Bernal had translated this headline for the *comandante* of the First Weekend movement, the old man had erupted in fury, waving the newspaper with a scarred and trembling fist.

We are terrorists, not pranksters! And you, Jesús, are a *maricón!* Make another bomb, a big one, and kill the *coño* on TV . . . or else. The *comandante* was a revered veteran of the Bay of Pigs, and was to be obeyed at all costs. Jesús worked swiftly.

It was the third bomb that made the pages of *Time* and *U.S. News & World Report*, where Viceroy Wilson read about it years later in the stacks of the public library. The third bomb was a delicate yet extremely powerful device that was meant to blow up a car. Jesús Bernal spent four days building the bomb in the kitchen of a Little Havana rooming house. He had personally transported the device to the television station, where he'd meticulously affixed it to a forest-green El Dorado which, in the darkness of the night, appeared identical to the one driven by the seditious TV talk-show host.

Unfortunately, the El Dorado was not identical; in fact, it was not the right automobile. The El Dorado that blew up on the Dolphin Expressway on June 22, 1978, actually belonged to a man named Salvatore 'The Cleaver' Buscante, a notorious loan shark and pornographer who had often played gin with Meyer Lansky.

The headline the next day said: *Anti-Castro Terrorists Claim Credit for Mob Hit; Feds Puzzle Over Cuban Connection.*

Jesús Bernal immediately was expelled from the First Weekend in July Movement, and ordered at gunpoint to leave Florida. He spent ten miserable months in Union City before being recalled by the *comandante*, who had come to miss Bernal's public-relations acumen. So what if he'd bombed the wrong guy? He got press, didn't he?

Over the protests of almost all the First Weekend in July's hardcore soldiers, the *comandante* had promoted Jesús Bernal to defense minister and bought him an IBM Selectric. From then on, the First Weekend was known for having the most impeccable press releases in the hemisphere. In his new role Jesús Bernal was an innovator: he even sent communiqués on embossed letter-heads—italic for bombings, boldface for political assassinations. Even the most skeptical commandos had to admit that the kid from Dartmouth had style. Soon the First Weekend in July became the preeminent anti-Castro group in the United States.

In the summer of 1981, under Bernal's inspired guidance, the terrorists launched an ambitious PR campaign to discredit Fidel Castro. Although this effort again won national publicity, it also led to Jesús Bernal's second and final banishment from the First Weekend in July.

The linchpin of the campaign had been a 'letter' from a renowned Swiss doctor reporting that President Castro was dying of a rare venereal disease transmitted by poultry. The malady supposedly was manifested by a number of grotesque symptoms, the mildest of which was drooling insanity. Of course the Swiss letter had been invented by none other than Jesús Bernal, but the document was accepted in Miami so unquestionably, and with such patriotic fervor, that Bernal decided to unleash it in Cuba as well. He hatched a daring scheme and persuaded the *comandante* to donate $19,022—a sum which, sadly, represented the entire treasury of the First Weekend in July Movement.

Not surprisingly, Jesús Bernal picked the first weekend of July in 1981 as the time of attack: the weekend Fidel would finally fall. In Little Havana, the air filled with intrigue and jubilation.

But not for long. On July 4, 1981, a low-flying DC-3 cargo plane dumped six metric tons of anti-Castro leaflets on the resort city of Kingston, Jamaica. The townspeople were baffled because the literature was printed in Spanish; only the words *Castro* and *syphilis* seemed to ring a bell among some Jamaicans. One of the leaflets was shown to the island's prime minister, who immediately cabled Fidel Castro to express sorrow over the president's unfortunate illness.

Later, under scornful grilling by the *comandante*, Jesús Bernal admitted that no, he'd never studied aerial navigation at Dartmouth. Bernal argued that it had been an honest mistake—from thirteen thousand feet, Kingston didn't look *that* different from Havana. Then Jesús had flashed his trump card: a copy of the New York *Times*. Three paragraphs, page 15a, in the International News roundup: *Tourist Bus Damaged by Falling Air Cargo*.

But the *comandante* and his men were not mollified: Jesús Bernal was purged forever from the First Weekend in July Movement.

'I know all about the bombs,' Viceroy Wilson said as they drove to Miami, several years later. 'You're just doing this to redeem yourself.'

'Ha! I am a hero to all freedom fighters.'

'You're a pitiful fuck-up,' Wilson said.

'Look who's talking, goddamn junkie spook.'

'What you say?'

Thank God the music was up so loud.

'Nothing,' Jesús Bernal said. 'You missed the damn exit.' He was getting mad at Viceroy Wilson. 'You never even said thanks.'

'Thanks for what?' Wilson asked from behind his sunglasses.

'For slicing that guy back in the swamp when he tried to strangle you.'

Wilson laughed. 'A mosquito, man, that's all he was.'

'You looked pretty uptight when that mosquito grabbed your neck. Your eyeballs almost popped out of your chocolate face, that little mosquito was squeezing so hard.'

'Sheee-iiit.'

'Yeah, you owe me one, *compadre.*'

'You're the one should be thanking *me*. You been waitin' your whole Cuban life to stab somebody in the back and now you did it. Guess that makes you a man, don't it? Say, why don't you call up your old dudes and see if they'll take you back.' Viceroy Wilson grinned nastily. 'Maybe they'll make you minister of switchblades.'

Jesús Bernal scowled and mumbled something crude in Spanish. 'I spit on their mothers,' he declared. 'If they got on their knees I wouldn't go back. Never!'

This was a total lie: Jesús Bernal yearned to abandon Skip Wiley's circus and rejoin his old gang of dedicated extortionists, bombers, and firebugs. In his heart Jesús Bernal believed his special talents were being wasted. Whenever he thought about Wiley's crazy plan he got a sour stomach that wouldn't go away. Somehow he couldn't visualize the masses ever mobilizing behind *El Fuego*; besides, if Wiley had his way, there'd be no masses left to mobilize—they'd all be heading North. These doubts had begun the day Ernesto Cabal hanged himself; guilt was a deadly emotion for a stouthearted terrorist, but guilt is what Jesús Bernal felt. He didn't feel particularly good about feeding strangers to crocodiles, either. It wasn't that the Cuban sympathized with *gringo* tourists, but Wiley's peculiar method of murder did not seem like the kind of political statement *Las Noches de Diciembre* ought to be making. And if nothing else, Jesús Bernal considered himself an expert on political statements.

'This is the place,' Viceroy Wilson announced.

Great, thought Jesús Bernal. He wished Wiley would just let him alone with the typewriter and plastique.

Wilson parked the car in front of a two-story office building on Biscayne Boulevard at Seventy-ninth. A sign out front said: 'Greater Miami Orange Bowl Committee.'

'Comb your hair,' Wilson grumbled.

'Shut up.'

'You look like a damn *Marielito*.'

'And you look like my father's yard man.'

The lady at the reception desk didn't like the looks of either of them. 'Yes?' she said with a polite Southern lilt unmistakable in its derision.

'We're here about the advertisement,' Viceroy Wilson explained, shedding his Carreras.

'Yes?'

'The ad for security guards,' Jesús Bernal said.

'Security guards,' Wilson said, 'for the Orange Bowl Parade.'

'I see,' said the Southern lady, warily handing each of them a job application. 'And you both have some experience?'

'Do we ever,' said Viceroy Wilson, smiling his touch-down smile.

When Brian Keyes awoke, the first thing he noticed was a woman on top of him in the hospital bed. Her blond head lay on his shoulder, and she seemed to be sleeping. Keyes strained to get a glimpse of her face, but every little movement brought a fresh volt of pain.

The woman weighed heavily on his chest; his ribs still ached from the surgery. Keyes stared down at the soft hair and sniffed for fragrant clues; it wasn't easy, especially with the tube up his nose.

'Jenna?' he rasped.

The woman on his chest stirred and gave a little hum of a reply.

'Jenna, that you?'

She looked up with a sleepy-eyed hello.

'You sound just like George Burns. Want some water?'

Keyes nodded. He let out a sigh when Jenna climbed out of bed.

'Where'd you get the nurse's uniform?'

'You like it?' She hitched up the hem. 'Check out the white stockings.'

Keyes sipped at the cold water; his throat was a furnace.

'What time is it? What day?'

'December 10, my love. Ten-thirty P.M. Way past visiting hours. That's why I had to wear this silly outfit.'

'You'd make a spectacular nurse. I'm getting better by the second.'

Jenna blushed. She sat at the foot of the bed. 'You looked so precious when you were asleep.'

Keyes shut his eyes and faked a snore.

'Now stop!' Jenna laughed. 'You look precious anyway. Aw, Brian, I'm so sorry. What happened out there?'

'Skip didn't tell you?'

She looked away. 'I haven't talked to him.'

Keyes thought: She must think I've had brain surgery.

'What happened out there?' she asked again.

'I got knifed by one of Skip's *caballeros*.'

'I don't believe it,' Jenna said.

Pausing only for gulps of water, Keyes related the sad tale of Mrs. Kimmelman. For once Jenna seemed to focus on every word. She was curious, but unalarmed.

'That poor woman. Do you think she died?'

Keyes nodded patiently. 'I'm pretty sure.'

Jenna stood up and walked to the window. 'The weather got muggy again,' she remarked. 'Three gorgeous days with a little winter, and then poof, Sauna City. My folks already had three feet of snow.'

'Jenna?'

When she turned to face him, her eyes were moist. She was trying to keep it inside, trying to recoup like the magnificent actress she was.

'I'm s-s-so sorry,' she cried. 'I didn't know you'd get hurt.'

Keyes held out his hand. 'I'm all right. C'mere.'

She climbed back into bed, sobbing on his shoulder. At first the pain was murderous, but Jenna's perfume was better than morphine. Keyes wondered what he'd say if a real nurse walked in.

Jenna sniffed. 'How's Skip?'

'Skip's a little crazy, Jenna.'

'Of course he is.'

'Slightly crazier than usual,' Keyes said. 'He's killing off tourists.'

'I figured it'd be something like that. But it's not really murder, is it? I mean *murder* in the criminal way.'

'Jenna, he fed an old lady to a crocodile!'

'He sent me a Mailgram,' she said.

'A Mailgram?'

'It said: "Dear Jenna, burn all my Rolodex cards at once. Love, Skip." '

Keyes asked, 'Did you do it? Did you burn the Rolodex?'

'Of course not,' Jenna said, as if the suggestion were preposterous. 'The message obviously is in code, which I haven't yet figured out. Besides, he keeps the Rolodex inside that darned coffin, which gives me the creeps.'

Keyes grimaced, not from pain.

'Look at all these tubes,' Jenna said. 'There's one in your chest and one up your nose and another stuck in your arm. What's in that bottle?'

'Glucose. Tomorrow I'm back on solids and in three days I'll be out of here. Jenna, where's Skip now?'

'I've no idea.'

'You've got to find him. He's killed four people.'

'Not personally he hasn't.' Jenna pulled back the sheet. 'Let me see your stitches.'

Keyes turned to one side and lifted his right arm.

'Oh, boy,' said Jenna, whistling.

'Nasty, huh?'

'Looks like a railroad track.' She traced the wound with a finger, light as a feather. Keyes shivered pleasurably.

'Did the knife hit your lung? Or was it a knife?' Jenna asked.

'Nicked it,' Keyes said.

'Ouch,' Jenna whispered. She stroked his forehead and smiled. 'How do you feel? I mean *really*.'

Keyes flushed. He knew what she meant. Really.

'Woozy,' he said, thinking: Something extraordinary is happening here; maybe Wiley's under the bed.

'Too woozy? What if I took this one away . . . would you be all right? Could you breathe?'

'Well, let's find out,' Keyes said. Of course she couldn't be serious. Not *here*. He removed the oxygen tube and took three breaths.

'Okay?' Jenna asked.

Keyes nodded; it was pain he could live with.

Jenna slid out of bed and unbuttoned her starched nurse's uniform. Suddenly she was standing there in bra and panties and white hospital hose. She had a deliciously naughty look on her face. Keyes didn't think he'd seen that particular look before.

'I think we should make love,' Jenna announced.

Keyes was stupefied. Considering what had happened the last few days, maybe he was due for a miracle. Maybe this was God's way of balancing fate. Or maybe it was something else altogether. Keyes didn't care; it was bound to be his last spell of infinite pleasure until Skip Wiley was caught or killed.

'It's possible I still love you, Brian,' said Jenna, slipping out of her bra. 'Mind if I lock the door?'

'What about the nurses?'

'We'll be oh-so-quiet.' Jenna stepped out of her panties. She looked radiant, her new tan lines providing a phenomenal lesson in contrasts. Keyes had never seen her velvet tummy so brown, or her breasts so white.

He said: 'I'm a wreck. I need to shave.'

Then he said: 'I don't know if I can do this.'

And then he decided to just shut up and let things happen, because he really couldn't be sure that this wasn't some splendid Dilaudid dream, and that Jenna wasn't just your usual breathtaking nude mirage in white hospital stockings.

She studied him from an artist's pose, arms folded, a finger on her lips. 'This is going to be tricky. I guess I'd better get on top.' And she did.

Smothered in delight, Keyes kissed Jenna's neck and throat and collarbone and whatever else he could get his mouth on. He half-hugged her, using the arm that wasn't attached to the intravenous tube, and played his fingers down her spine. Jenna seemed to enjoy it. She arched, then pressed down hard with her hips. Her aim was perfect.

'Have you missed me, Brian?'

'Yup.' Which was all the breath he had left.

Jenna sat up, straddling him. Her eyes were liquid and, for once, not so far away. She swayed gently with a hand on each bed rail, as if riding a sled.

'Am I hurting you?' she asked with one of those killer smiles. 'I didn't think so.'

Partly out of passion and partly to get the weight off his tortured diaphragm, Keyes pulled her down. He kissed her lightly on the mouth and right away she closed her eyes. At first she was tentative, maybe even nervous, but soon she started doing all the amazing things she used to do when they were lovers; things he'd never forgotten but never thought he'd experience again.

Lovemaking with Jenna had always been an emotional workout for Brian Keyes—shock therapy for the heart. True to form, his brain shut down the moment she pressed against him. He totally forgot where he was and why he was there. He forgot his stitches, he forgot his collapsed lung, and he forgot the tube gurgling out of his side. He forgot the nurse, who was pounding on the door. He even forgot Ida Kimmelman and the goddamn crocodile.

He forgot everything but Jenna and Wiley.

'What about Skip?' he whispered between nibbles. 'I thought you were madly in love with Skip.'

'Hush now,' Jenna said, guiding his free hand. 'And try not to kick the I.V.'

14

Jesús Bernal finally got a chance to build another bomb, thanks to Ricky Bloodworth.

On the morning of December 12, the Miami *Sun* published its first front-page story about *Las Noches de Diciembre*. It was not a flawless piece of journalism but it stirred excitement at Skip Wiley's Everglades bivouac.

The lead of the story focused on the ominous *El Fuego* letter discovered in Ida Kimmelman's condominium mailbox. A trusting Broward County detective had read the contents to Ricky Bloodworth (*Dear Otter Creek Shuffleboard Club: Welcome to the Revolution!*) and Bloodworth realized he had a hot one. He worked the phones like a boiler-room pro, pestering every cop he knew until he unearthed the fact that this *Fuego* letter was the fourth of its kind. Thus the murder of B. D. 'Sparky' Harper finally was linked to the disappearance of the Shriner, the abduction of the Canadian woman at the Seaquarium, and now the unsolved kidnapping of Ida Kimmelman. Of course, neither the police nor Ricky Bloodworth knew precisely what had happened to the last three victims—who could have guessed?—but it was still quite a list. Especially if you tacked on the savage stabbing of private investigator Brian Keyes.

This front-page attention thrilled Skip Wiley, and in a brief campfire ceremony he thanked his fellow radicals for their patience. 'Remember ye this day!' he told them. 'On this day we are born to the eyes of America. Today the Miami *Sun*, tomorrow *USA Today!*'

None of the conspirators were identified in Bloodworth's story, and Brian Keyes's description of his 'Slavic' abductors was repeated as if it were an established fact. Wiley admired the yarn as a stroke of originality.

There was one significant error in Ricky Bloodworth's story

which, when read aloud by Jesús Bernal, made Skip Wiley roll his eyes, Viceroy Wilson laugh out loud, and Tommy Tigertail shrug. It was a shrug Tommy saved for extremely stupid behavior by white people. Somehow Ricky Bloodworth had managed to screw up the name of Wiley's group and referred to it throughout the story as *Las* Nachos *de Diciembre*, which translates exactly as one might suppose. Skip Wiley had been in the newspaper business too long not to be tickled by this mistake, but Jesús Bernal was apoplectic. 'Nachos!' he shrieked. 'This is your brilliant publicity coup? We are now world-famous nachos!' With that Jesús Bernal shredded the newspaper and declared that he'd never experienced such humiliation in all his days in the underground. Skip Wiley suspected that, more than anything, Bernal resented the Mexican insinuation.

'Relax,' he told Jesús. 'We'll straighten this out soon enough, won't we?'

Several persons were deeply displeased to see Ricky Bloodworth's story. One was Cab Mulcahy, who sensed Skip Wiley's demented hand behind the *El Fuego* caper. Mulcahy could see disaster looming. For the newspaper. For himself. For all Miami. He shriveled at the vision of a handcuffed Wiley being led up the steps of the Dade County Courthouse—wild-eyed and foamy-mouthed, bellowing one of his dark axioms. Every major paper in America would cover the extravaganza: *Columnist Goes on Trial as Mass Murderer*. It would be better than Manson because Skip Wiley was more coherent. Skip Wiley was a hell of a quote.

Despite his premonitions, Cab Mulcahy knew there was little he could do until he was absolutely sure.

Another person who cringed at the sight of Richard L. Bloodworth's byline was Detective Harold Keefe, who'd nearly succeeded in convincing the police hierarchy that a renegade cop had dreamed up those crazy letters. Harold Keefe had refused to speak with Bloodworth the night before and now was sorry he hadn't. Keefe could have used the opportunity to drop the dime on Al García and derail all this freaky *Las Noches* crap. Now it was too late, a veritable disaster. The chief was furious, I.A.D. was on red alert, and the Chamber of Commerce was handing out cyanide capsules.

As Harold Keefe studied the front page of the Miami *Sun*, he decided to retaliate swiftly, utilizing the police department's vast apparatus for equivocation. He would compose a public statement to put the whole Nacho case in a sober perspective. The wording would be dicey, considering the publicity, but Keefe would stick to the original platform: The murder of B. D. Harper is unrelated to the subsequent disappearance of tourists . . . No evidence of foul play . . . The *Fuego* letters are a sick hoax perpetrated by a disgruntled policeman (for support, quote from Dr. Remond Courtney's report to the chief) . . . Close by saying the whole matter remains under investigation . . . an *internal* investigation. Pretty tidy, Keefe thought.

He recorded two versions of the statement, a thirty-second loop for radio and two fifteen-second sound bites for TV. The tapes were copied and the cassettes distributed to broadcast reporters in the lobby of police headquarters. Full texts of the press release (in English, Spanish, and Creole) were hand-delivered to all Miami newspapers; a studio eight-by-ten of Harold Keefe was conveniently included in the package.

Keefe's statement was released just in time for the noon news on radio and television.

Tommy Tigertail was driving east on Alligator Alley when he heard the broadcast. He turned around and cruised back to tell Skip Wiley.

'I'll be damned, a cover-up!' Wiley exclaimed. The Indian had found him fishing near the secret campsite. Wiley was dressed in a buckskin jacket and Fila tennis shorts; he wore an Australian bush hat with a red emblem on the crown. He listened closely to Tommy Tigertail's account of the police press release, and winced at the mention of Dr. Remond Courtney

'I wonder what happened to Brian,' Wiley said irritably. 'He was our ace in the hole, our smoking gun. I even gave him the briefcase—it was all the proof those moron cops would ever need.'

'So what do we do?' the Indian asked.

'Strike again,' advised Jesús Bernal, who had wandered out of the hammock to eavesdrop. 'Strike again, and strike dramatically.'

Wiley's bestubbled face cracked into a grin. 'Jesús, *mi hermano*, do you still have some C-4?'

'*Sí.*'

'*Bueno,*' said Wiley, humoring him with Spanish. 'Make me a bomb.'

'Yes, sir!' Bernal said, scarcely concealing his rapture. 'What kind of bomb?'

'A bomb that goes off when it's supposed to.'

'*Claro!* Do not worry.'

'Please don't blow up my car,' Tommy Tigertail said.

Among those who had no intention of waiting for a bomb were the residents of Otter Creek Village, where the abduction of Ida Kimmelman had set off a minor panic. Newly hired security guards now patrolled the shuffleboard courts until midnight—security guards with guns! Furthermore, the Otter Creek Safety Committee declared that all condominium owners should henceforth walk their dogs *en masse*, for protection. This was a drastic measure that only promoted more hysteria at Otter Creek—a herd of yipping, squatting miniature poodles dragging scores of Sansa-belted retirees across the landscaping. Fearful of kidnappings, some of the oldsters armed themselves with sharp umbrellas or canisters of Mace, which they often used on one another in the heat of competition for shrubs and hydrants. Indelible terror seized the residents when the actual text of the *El Fuego* letter appeared in the newspaper; within hours forty-seven units at Otter Creek were put up for sale. Contracts on fourteen other apartments, including a penthouse with a whirlpool, were canceled. Overnight the parking lot seemed to fill with mustard-colored moving vans and station wagons with New York tags.

This was the first wave out of Florida.

It was exactly the way Skip Wiley had dreamed it.

One morning Brian Keyes looked up and saw the round, friendly face of Nell Bellamy. For a second he thought he was back on the sidewalk outside Pauly's Bar.

'Hello again.'

'Hi,' Keyes said.

'I read about your accident.'

'It wasn't exactly an accident,' Keyes said. 'Why are you whispering?'

'It's a hospital. I always whisper in hospitals.' Nell Bellamy looked embarrassed.

Keyes said, 'It was nice of you to come.'

'How are you feeling? The nurses said you had a little setback.'

'Tore a few stitches the other night. One of those things.' The cost of Jenna's heavenly visit; the next morning he'd felt like a gutted carp.

Nell tucked another pillow under his head. 'Did you see the paper? They think it's a gang of . . . maniacs.'

Brian Keyes knew why Nell Bellamy had come, and it was time to tell the truth. As a reporter, he'd always tried to do these melancholy chores over the phone, never in person. On the phone you could just close your eyes and take a deep gulp and say, 'Ma'am, I'm sorry to have to tell you this, but—' and then the rotten news. Your little boy got hit by a truck. Your sister was a passenger on that 727. They found your daughter's body, Mrs. Davenport. Sometimes Keyes couldn't bring himself to do it, and he'd play the line-is-busy game with his editor. *Sorry, can't get a comment from the family. The line's been busy all afternoon.* And then if the editor persisted, Keyes would dial his own phone number and hold the receiver away from his ear, so the busy signal would be audible.

Unfortunately, Nell Bellamy wasn't on the other end of a telephone. She was standing intently at the rail of the hospital bed, bracing for what her ace private investigator was about to say.

'Mr. Keyes, I've a feeling you found out something important.'

Keyes couldn't bear to look in her eyes, so he concentrated on the buttons of her crisp blouse. 'Mrs. Bellamy, I'm sorry to have to tell you this, but your husband is dead. I think he was murdered.'

Nell Bellamy sat down, neat and plump, in a chair by the window. 'Oh, Teddy,' she said softly.

At that moment Brian Keyes could have murdered Skip Wiley, could have grabbed his wild blond mane and snapped his neck.

In his derangement Wiley had come to see his own life as a headline, getting bigger and more sensational each day. Everything *El Fuego* said and did, or ordered done, was devised with one test: how it would look in print. Sparky Harper gagging on a rubber alligator, for instance—masterful, in a way. For days Keyes had been thinking about Wiley's macabre front-page reality. Now he thought: Skip ought to be here to watch this woman cry.

'I think it was the same people who stabbed me,' Keyes said. 'They're very dangerous, Mrs. Bellamy. They're fanatical.'

'The Nachos?' Nell Bellamy asked. 'But why would they kill my husband? He's just a realtor.'

'They're killing off tourists,' Keyes said.

Nell nodded as if she understood, as if Florida was finally making sense. 'Well, the police warned me not to believe the newspaper.'

'The police are wrong, Mrs. Bellamy.'

'A detective told me Teddy must've drowned. He said there's no such thing as The Nachos.'

'They had Teddy's swimming trunks,' Keyes said.

'Oh no,' Nell said, stricken. 'What did they do to him? I mean, how . . .?'

Keyes felt terrible. He held out his hand and Nell Bellamy took it. 'They told me it was quick and painless,' he said. 'I'm very sorry.'

From nowhere Nell produced a handful of pink Kleenexes and dabbed at her eyes. 'You're a brave man, Mr. Keyes. Risking your life the way you did.' She composed herself and took a paisley checkbook from her purse. 'How much do I owe you?'

'Put that away,' Keyes said. 'Please, Mrs. Bellamy.'

'You're very kind.'

No, I'm not, Keyes said to himself.

'Is there any chance,' Mrs. Bellamy said, 'of finding Teddy's body?'

'None,' said Keyes, thinking of Pavlov the crocodile.

The door opened and the two beefy Shriners came into the room. They wore business suits and mauve fez hats.

'You're a popular fellow,' Burt the Shriner said. 'Lots of visitors. Mr. Mulcahy from the newspaper was here. So was Detective Keefe. Later there was a Sergeant García, kind of a rude fellow. Also some television types asking for an interview. One of those Live-Eye jobs.'

'We told them to come back another day,' said the Shriner named James, 'when you were up to snuff.'

'I asked Burt and James to keep an eye on the door,' Nell Bellamy explained. 'Hope you don't mind.'

'Not at all. Thank you.' Keyes knew what García and the other visitors had wanted: a firsthand account of his *noche* with *Las Noches*. Cab Mulcahy doubtlessly had figured out the Wiley connection. Keyes wondered what the old boy would do now.

'We knew it'd be like Grand Central Station up here after that newspaper article,' Burt said. 'We thought you'd appreciate a little peace and quiet.' He looked at Mrs. Bellamy and said, 'So what's the verdict, Nellie?'

'Mr. Keyes says the newspaper was right.'

'Slavic murderers! Wearing wigs!'

'No,' Brian Keyes said. 'That part was wrong.'

'But the part about Ted being killed, that was true,' Nell told the Shriners. 'They stole his bathing trunks.'

'Lord God,' Burt said, 'those bastards.'

James put a meaty arm around Nell Bellamy's shoulders and she went for the Kleenex again.

Burt waited a decent interval, then asked: 'What are the chances that the police will catch these people?'

'Fifty-fifty,' Keyes replied, without conviction.

'Not good enough,' James said.

'Piss poor,' Burt concurred. 'Mr. Keyes, what's your timetable? Are you going to stick with this case?'

'Absolutely.'

'Good. We'd like to tag along.'

'Nellie's going back to Evanston,' James said protectively. 'Tonight.'

'But not us, no sir, we've got a score to settle,' Burt declared. 'What about it, Mr. Keyes? We're not professionals, not like you, but we can take care of ourselves. I'm pretty good with a handgun—'

'*Pretty* good!' James interjected. 'Jeez.'

'And James himself has some martial-arts experience. Black belt, yellow belt, you name it. Plus a pilot's license. What about it, Mr. Keyes, think you could use some help?'

Well, hell, thought Brian Keyes, why not?

'I'd be grateful,' Keyes told them.

'Good, then it's settled.'

'Just one thing.'

'Yes, Mr. Keyes?'

'About those hats. You have to wear them all the time?'

There was an awkward moment of silence, as if Keyes had breached some sacred Shriner wont. Burt and James glanced at one another, and even Nell Bellamy looked up, her face mostly hidden by a mask of pink tissue.

'It's a fez,' Burt said, touching the purple crown. 'What about it?'

'Would you like one?' James offered. 'Maybe without a tassel.'

'Never mind,' Keyes said. He pressed the button to ring for a nurse. It was time to check out.

The annual competition for Miami's Orange Bowl queen had attracted the usual chorus line of debutantes, fashion models, ex-cheerleaders, and slick sorority tarts.

Jesús Bernal, who'd spent the whole day building a bomb, was overwhelmed. As far as he was concerned, this was a dandy way to take your mind off plastique.

'You ever seen this much pussy?' he asked Viceroy Wilson.

'Sure,' Wilson said. 'Dallas. Super Bowl Eight.'

Two touchdowns, three blow-jobs, and a cowgirl sandwich. God, he was such a lowlife in those days. All hard-on, no purpose. Wilson shook his head at the memory and lighted a joint.

'Not here!' Bernal snapped. 'Remember, we're supposed to be security guards.'

'Well, I feel so secure I'm gonna smoke some weed.'

They stood in darkness at the rear of the Civic Center. The

stage was bathed in kliegs. It was dress rehearsal and the audi-torium was empty, except for a skeleton orchestra, some TV technicians, and the contestants themselves. The women milled onstage, tugging at their gumdrop-colored swimsuits and poofing their hair. The air conditioning was running full blast, and Jesús Bernal had never seen so many erect nipples in one congregation.

'The fourth one from the left,' Bernal said. 'Her name is Maria.'

'No way,' said Viceroy Wilson. He really couldn't see a damn thing with the sunglasses on.

'How about the redhead? Rory McWhat's-her-face.'

'Forget it, Hay-zoos. She don't have a prayer. Freckles look rotten on TV.'

'She made it to the semifinals,' Bernal said.

'Sympathy vote. Mark my words.'

Viceroy Wilson was having as good a time as his abstemious revolutionary ethic would allow. Whenever Wilson found himself distracted by lust, he sublimated rigorously. And whenever he sublimated, he was struck by a vestigial urge to run with a foot-ball. Right now he wanted to run down the center aisle, hurdle onstage, and steamroller the emcee. The emcee had a voice that could take the paint off your car.

'They're going to fire your ass for smoking,' Bernal scolded. 'You'll wreck everything.'

'Know what you need? You need about eight Quaaludes. Calm your Cuban ass right down.'

Jesús Bernal was appalled at the lack of regimentation within *Las Noches de Diciembre.* Viceroy Wilson, who personified the insubordination, wouldn't have lasted ten minutes with the First Weekend in July. Using drugs during a mission! The Cubans would have wasted him immediately.

'Any sisters make the semis?' Wilson asked.

'*Nadie,*' Jesús Bernal reported. 'Seven Anglos, three Cubans.'

'God damn, that figures.'

Jesús Bernal could no longer see Viceroy Wilson's face, only a sphere of bluish smoke behind the sunglasses. Bernal knew that Wilson was worried about the Indian's Cadillac, which they'd double-parked in front of the Hyatt Regency. Bernal himself was anxious about the car, and for the same reason. The double-parking had nothing to do with it.

Skip Wiley had ordered them to interrupt their mission and stop at the Civic Center. A scouting assignment, Wiley had explained, extremely important.

Drive carefully, Wiley had added. Very carefully.

Which only reinforced Jesús Bernal's belief that Wiley was especially crazy when it came to risking other people's asses. A reputable terrorist simply would not dally in downtown Miami with a freshly assembled bomb in the trunk of his Cadillac. Bombs, like pizzas, are made for speedy delivery.

'Straighten up,' Wilson said, stubbing out the joint. 'Some-body's coming.'

A man with a walkie-talkie charged up the aisle. He was the chief of security for all Orange Bowl festivities.

'What's that smell?' he demanded, looking straight at Jesús Bernal.

'*No sé*,' Bernal replied.

'Caught some kids smoking dope in the back row and threw 'em out,' Wilson said. 'Broke their fingers first.'

'Good work, Mr. Wilson.'

The security chief was a big Dolphins fan, so he was overjoyed to have the legendary Viceroy Wilson on his staff.

'So, you enjoying the pageant?' he chirped.

'Loving it,' Wilson said. 'Who's your pick?'

'Rory McAllister. Little redhead with the nice ass. Second from the right.'

'*Sí, es muy bonita*,' Jesús Bernal said.

'Tell me, my man, why don't I see any black women up on that stage?'

The security chief lost his locker-room grin and wilted back a few steps. 'Gosh, I don't know. That's a stumper. Want me to ask the judges?'

'Yeah,' Viceroy Wilson said. 'Do that.'

'Right away, Mr. Wilson. And, hey, good work rousting those dopers!' The security chief hurried away.

Jesús Bernal and Viceroy Wilson strolled to the foot of the stage and stared up at the beauty contestants, who were practicing the winner's walk. Back straight, boobs out, buttocks tight, big smile. To Jesús Bernal each of the women seemed six feet tall, perfect and impenetrable.

'Number five,' Wilson said in a disinterested tone. 'That's your winner.'

Jesús Bernal found a program and read aloud: 'Kara Lynn Shivers. Sophomore, University of Miami. Majoring in public relations. Hobbies: Swimming, mime, and French horn. Hair: blond. Eyes: hazel.'

'Height?' Wilson said.

'Five-eight.'

'She weighs one-twenty.'

'One hundred ten,' Bernal said 'That's what it says here.'

'Vanity.' Wilson coughed. 'The bitch is lying.'

Bernal shrugged. 'Whatever you say. Is one-twenty too heavy?'

Wilson smiled, thinking of all those NFL linebackers. Somebody yelled 'Cut!' and the emcee swaggered across the stage, trailing a microphone cord. He leaned over and spoke to Wilson and Bernal. 'You guys are too close to the action. We got the top of your heads in that last shot.'

The emcee sounded quite annoyed. Viceroy Wilson had never seen such large bright teeth on a white person. You could tile a swimming pool with teeth like that.

Jesús Bernal stuck out his chest and tapped the badge that was pinned to the pocket of his gray security-guard uniform.

The emcee said, 'Hey, I'm superimpressed, okay? Now, get away from the stage. You're making the girls nervous and you're fucking up the take. *Comprende?*'

From somewhere inside Viceroy Wilson came a wet growling noise. Jesús Bernal seized him by the arm and tried to pull him away from the stage, but it was too late. Wilson reached up and grabbed one of the emcee's black nylon ankles.

'Let go, you!' the emcee cried.

'Let go, Viceroy,' Jesús Bernal pleaded.

'Aarrrummmm, rrmmmmmm,' Viceroy Wilson said.

Then the emcee was a blur, the microphone flying one way, a

black shoe flying the other. The emcee's blow-dried head hit the stage with a crack that carried to every corner of the acoustically perfect auditorium. A few of the beauty contestants shrieked 'Oh Jerry!' and ran to the young man's aid; others just stared with pained expressions at the prone tuxedo.

The security chief sprinted down the aisle and bounded on-stage. 'My God, what happened here? Back off, girls, give him air. Give him air.'

Jesús Bernal glanced at Viceroy Wilson and thought: The dumb spade just ruined everything.

'The man slipped on a puddle,' Bernal told the security chief.

'Naw, it was an epileptic attack,' said Viceroy Wilson.

'Get a doctor!' the security chief hollered into his K-Mart walkie-talkie. 'Somebody get a doctor.'

'An epilepsy doctor,' advised Viceroy Wilson.

Kara Lynn Shivers gracefully dropped to her knees and cradled the emcee's head. Discreetly she removed some tissue from the left cup of her bathing suit and began dabbing the emcee's fore-head. The injured man gazed up at Kara Lynn's perfect sopho-more breasts with a stunned but tranquil look.

'I told you she's gonna win,' Viceroy Wilson whispered. 'This'll be so damn easy.'

'Let's move,' Jesús Bernal said, commando style. 'We've got to find the golf course before it gets dark.'

'Hay-zoos, lemme tell you something,' Wilson said, taking his time. 'If your little box of Tinker Toys goes off before we get there, just 'member the last thing you're gonna see on this earth is my black face—and I'll be chewing on your fuckin' guts all the way to hell.'

15

Like all terrible golfers, Dr. Remond Courtney believed that nothing was too extravagant for his game. He wore Arnold Palmer sweaters and Tom Watson spikes, and carried a full set of Jack Nicklaus MacGregors, including a six-wood that the Golden Bear himself couldn't hit if his life depended on it.

And like all terrible golfers, Dr. Courtney preferred to play very early in the morning, embracing the myth that golf balls fly farther in cool weather. Since he had no true friends at the Palmetto Country Club, Dr. Courtney often recruited his patients to play golf with him. This worked out fine if the patients were fairly stable, but occasionally one would go completely berserk. This usually happened on the back nine, which was lousy with water hazards, and Dr. Courtney would wave the other golfers to play through while he took an hour to tranquilize his partner. Some Thursdays a round of golf for Dr. Courtney was almost as grueling as a day at work, which is why he had no qualms about writing off all his MacGregors as a hefty tax deduction.

On December 13, Dr. Remond Courtney hitched up his pretentious tweed knickers and teed off at 7:08 A.M. The foursome included one of his patients—a vastly improved schizophrenic named Mario Groppo—and two total strangers from Seattle. The strangers were engineers for Boeing, the aerospace company, and they tended to shank the ball off the tee. Predictably, Mario Groppo would hook the ball on one hole and slice the ball on the next. Nobody in the foursome could putt worth a damn.

As for Dr. Remond Courtney, his golf swing was so unusual that from a distance he appeared to be beating a snake to death. It was a very violent golf swing for a psychiatrist. He managed an eight on the first hole and still won it by two strokes. It looked like it was going to be a long morning.

By the fifth tee, Dr. Courtney had become confident enough in his partners' ineptitude that he'd started betting on every hole. Poor Mario Groppo promptly dropped thirty dollars and appeared headed for a major anxiety attack; the Seattle tourists went to the bourbon flask early and lost their amiable out-of-towner dispositions. Every time Dr. Courtney would bend over a putt, one of them would fart or sneeze in flagrant violation of golf etiquette. The psychiatrist haughtily ignored this rudeness, no matter how many strokes it cost.

The foursome made the turn with Dr. Courtney leading the Seattle engineers by four and seven strokes respectively, while Mario Groppo sweated bullets somewhere around twenty over par.

Weatherwise it was a fine Florida day. The sky was china blue and a light breeze fought off the lethal humidity. As they strolled down the twelfth fairway, the psychiatrist sidled up to Mario and said, 'So how are we feeling today, Mr. Groppo?'

'Just fine,' replied Mario, fishing in his golf bag for a five-iron.

'Come now,' Dr. Courtney said. 'Something's troubling you, isn't it?'

'I'm lying three in the rough. That's all that's troubling me.'

'Are you sure? I've got some Thorazine in my golf bag.'

'I'm fine,' Mario said impatiently. 'Thanks anyway.'

Dr. Courtney patted him on the back and gave a doctorly wink. 'When you want to talk, just let me know. I'll set aside some time.'

Dr. Courtney and the Boeing engineers put their shots smack on the green, while Mario Groppo dumped his five-iron in the back bunker.

'Too much club,' the psychiatrist remarked.

'Too much mouth,' sniped one of the guys from Boeing.

Dr. Courtney snorted contemptuously and marched toward the green, his putter propped like a musket on his shoulder.

While the other golfers lined up their putts, poor Mario Groppo waded into the sand trap, a canyon from which he could barely see daylight.

'I'll hold the stick,' Dr. Courtney called.

Over the lip of the bunker Mario could make out the tip of the flagstick, Dr. Courtney's pink face and, beyond that, the visors of the two Seattle tourists, waiting their turns.

The psychiatrist kept shouting advice. 'Bend the left knee! Keep the club face open! Hit behind the ball!'

'Oh shut up,' Mario Groppo said. He grimaced at the idea of surrendering another ten bucks to Remond Courtney.

Mario glared down at the half-buried Titleist and grimly dug his spikes into the sand. He took one last look at the flag, then swung the wedge with a mighty grunt.

To everyone's surprise, Mario's golf ball leapt merrily from the sand trap, kissed the green, and rolled sweetly, inexorably toward the hole.

'All right!' exclaimed one of the Seattle tourists.

'I don't believe it,' sniffed Dr. Courtney as Mario's ball dropped with a plunk.

At that instant the twelfth green of the Palmetto Country Club exploded in a hellish thunderclap. The bomb, hidden deep in the cup, launched the flagstick like a flaming javelin. The air crackled as a brilliant orange plume unfurled over the gentle fairways.

There was no time to run, no time to scream.

His face scorched and hair smoldering, poor Mario Groppo found himself lost in a crater. Haplessly he weaved in circles, using his sand wedge as a cane. 'Holy God!' he mumbled, squinting through the smoke and silicate dust for some sign of the doomed threesome. 'Holy Jesus God!' he said, as the sky rained wet clumps of sod and flesh, twisted stems of golf clubs, and bright swatches of Izod shirts.

Mario sat down in the dirt. In a daze he thought he heard a man's voice, and wondered if one of the other golfers had been spared.

'Hello! I'm right here!' Mario cried. 'Over here!'

But the voice that replied was much too far away, and much too sonorous. The voice rose in proclamation from a stand of tall Australian pines bordering the thirteenth fairway.

'*Bon voyage*, Dr. Goosefucker!' the voice sang out. 'Welcome to the Revolution!'

Jenna stood at the door, hands on her hips. 'Boy, everybody in Miami's looking for you!' She wore an indigo Danskin and a white terrycloth headband. Her forehead was damp; the Jane Fonda workout video was on the television.

'May I come in?' Brian Keyes asked.

'Of course. I'm making granola bars. Come sit in the kitchen and talk.'

Jenna was in her element, and Keyes knew he'd have to take it slowly. One wrong move and it was lights out.

'Cab called. He's hunting all over for you.'

'I'll bet.'

'What about these cops?' Jenna emptied a box of raisins into a mixing bowl. 'Cab says the cops want to talk to you about what happened. Hey, are you feeling okay? How come you left the hospital so soon?'

'I got better,' Keyes said, 'thanks to this incredible nurse.'

No reaction. Jenna stood at the kitchen counter with her back to him. She was stirring the granola mix.

'You're really something,' Keyes said playfully. 'I got in all kinds of trouble, you know.'

'What kind of trouble?'

'The doctors chewed me out, moved me to a private room. They said we violated about five hundred hospital rules. The whole wing was talking about it.'

'Yeah? You like carobs? I'm gonna add some carobs.'

'I hate granola bars.'

'These are homemade.' Jenna's stirring became rhythmic.

'I talked to Skip today.' She glanced over her shoulder at Keyes. 'He wanted me to tell you how sorry he was about the Cuban. He said the little fellow means well; he just gets carried away with the knife. I told Skip you were doing better and he was quite relieved. He wanted me to tell you it won't happen again.'

'How thoughtful,' Keyes said acidly. 'Where is the Madman of Miami, anyhow?'

'We didn't talk about that,' Jenna said. She was padding around the kitchen in jazz exercise tights and no shoes. 'Skip made a bunch of new rules,' she said. 'Rule number one: Don't ask where he is. Rule number two: Don't use his name over the telephone. Rule number three: No more horny love letters.'

'Jenna, you've got to help me find him.'

'Why? He's done nothing wrong. He told me he's got a clear conscience. Here, want a taste of this?' She thrust a wooden spoon in his mouth. 'See, that's good stuff.'

'Not bad,' Keyes said, thinking: She's at it again.

Jenna poured the granola butter into a pan, and put the pan in the oven. She took a bottle of white wine from the refrigerator and poured herself a glass.

'Fewer calories than you think,' she said, her green eyes sparkling through the wine crystal.

'You sure look great.'

'As soon as the granola bars are done, I'm leaving town,' Jenna announced.

Keyes said nothing.

'I'd ask you to stay for dinner, but I've got to catch a plane.'

'I understand,' Keyes said. 'Where you going?'

'Wisconsin. T'see my folks.'

No hesitation; she had it all worked out. Keyes admired her preparation. If he didn't know her so well he might've believed her. He tried to stall.

'May I have some wine?'

'Unh-unh,' Jenna said. 'Better not. You know how you get.'

'Sleepy is how I get.'

'No, sexy and romantic is how you get.'

'What's wrong with that?'

'Tonight it's wrong.'

'It wasn't wrong in the hospital, was it?'

'Not at all,' Jenna said. 'It was perfect in the hospital.' She kissed him on the forehead; a polite little kiss that told Keyes his time was running out. She might as well have tapped her foot and pointed at the clock.

He stood up and took her hands. 'Please help me.'

'I can't,' Jenna said firmly. She looked him straight in the eyes, and Keyes realized that, for her, this was no dilemma. She wasn't torn over loyalties. Skip Wiley came first, second, and third.

Keyes guessed how it must have started: a spark of an idea —maybe Jenna's, maybe Skip's—something mentioned over

dinner, maybe even in the sack. A fantastic notion to turn back
time, to drive out the carpetbaggers, to reclaim the land by painting it as treacherous and uninhabitable. And to do it all with sly
tricks and egregious pranks—Armageddon, with mirrors. Wiley
would have embraced the idea, embellished it, talked it to life,
and made it all seem possible. And Jenna, having started the
spark or at least fanned it, would have slipped back to watch her
passionate genius turn the whimsy into reality—watching with
love and amazement, but not paying quite enough attention. So
that when the killing started, and she finally understood how far
he had carried the scheme, there was nothing to do but let him
finish. The alternative was betrayal: to destroy Skip and orphan
this dream, the thing they had created together.

'Is he going to stop this craziness?' Keyes asked.

'I don't think so,' Jenna said, looking away.

'Then he'll be caught,' Keyes said, 'or killed.'

'Oh, I doubt that.' She removed her headband and plucked off
her tiny gold earrings. 'I know Skip, and he's way ahead of
everybody. Even you, my love. Now, scoot out of here and let
me pack. I've got a ten-o'clock plane.'

Brian Keyes retreated to the living room and sat dejectedly on
the coffin-turned-coffee-table.

'What are you doing?' Jenna asked from the kitchen doorway.
'Brian, it's time to go.'

'Did you hear what happened today? Today it was a goddamn
bomb. Three people blown to bits. You think that's cute? The old
Wiley sense of humor—you find bombs amusing?'

'Not particularly.' Jenna paused, frowning briefly, and something crossed her face that Keyes seldom had seen. Guilt,
remorse . . . something. 'Don't jump to conclusions about Skip,'
she said finally. 'That shrink had lots of enemies.'

'This isn't a game of Clue,' Keyes said. 'Your boyfriend has
become a murderer.'

'It's not like you to get so melodramatic,' Jenna said
impatiently. 'Why can't you just leave it alone? Get busy on your
other cases and forget about it. You did your job: you found Skip.
When he's ready to come back, he will. That's what I told Cab

this morning, but he's just like you. He thinks Skip has some kind of crazy death wish. Nothing could be sillier, Brian. I'm really disappointed in you guys.' She was twirling the headband on her index finger, and looking very self-assured.

'Brian, you've got two problems Skip doesn't have.'

'What's that?' Keyes asked, sensing defeat.

'Your ego and your heart.'

'Well, pardon me.' Now it was time to go. He didn't have to take this Joyce Brothers shit from a woman who bakes her own granola bars.

Halfway out the door he turned and said, 'Jenna, what about the other night in the hospital? What *was* all that?'

'That was a moment, Brian, yours and mine.' She smiled; the first soft smile of the whole evening. 'It was one lovely moment, and that's all. Why does there have to be more? Why do you guys think there's always a Big Picture? Honest to God, Brian, sometimes I think the newspaper business fucked you up forever.'

Jenna hardly ever used the word 'fuck.' Keyes figured she really must be agitated.

'Have a good trip,' he said. 'Give your parents my best.'

'Aw, you're sweet,' Jenna said. 'You get some rest while I'm gone. Forget about Skip, forget about me, forget about the Big Picture. Everything's going to work out fine.'

Ninety minutes later she left the house carrying a canvas travel bag and a tin of hot granola bars. She wore tight jeans, a loose long-sleeved blouse, and white heels. Her hair was pinned in a prim bun.

The drive to the airport was vintage Jenna—no recognition or regard for curbs, stop signs, traffic lights, or pedestrians. Brian Keyes kept a distance of two or three blocks, wincing at Jenna's close calls. He had borrowed a rental car from one of the Shriners because Jenna surely would've recognized the MG, by sound if not by sight.

She parked in the long-term garage at Miami International. Slouching low in the driver's seat, Keyes whizzed right past her and found a spot on the next level. He bolted from the car, raced down the stairwell, and caught sight of Jenna disappearing into the elevator. He ran all the way to the terminal building and waited.

Even in a crowd she was impossible to miss. She had a classic airport walk, sensual but aloof; men always moved out of the way to watch Jenna's jeans go by, back and forth, a divine natural metronome.

Keyes followed her until she stopped at the Bahamasair ticket counter. He hid behind a pillar, scouting for Skip Wiley.

'Want us to take over?'

Keyes wheeled around. 'Jesus Christ!'

'Didn't mean to frighten you.'

It was Burt the Shriner.

'Where'd you come from?' Keyes asked.

'Right behind you. Ever since you came in.'

'And your pal?'

'He's around the corner. Keeping an eye on your lady friend.'

Keyes was impressed; these guys weren't half-bad.

'She's on her way to Nassau,' Burt reported. 'Her ticket was prepaid.'

'By whom?'

'The Seminole Nation of Florida, Incorporated. Does that make any sense, Mr. Keyes?'

'I'll explain later.'

Keyes peered around the pillar at the Bahamasair counter, but Jenna was gone.

'Shit!'

'Don't worry,' Burt said. 'James is close behind.'

'We're too damn late.' Keyes broke into a run.

Because of the phenomenal number of airplane hijackings from Miami, the FAA had installed sophisticated new security measures designed to prevent anyone with bombs, guns, or invalid coach-class tickets from entering the flight concourse. The most effective of all these security steps was the hiring of squads of fat, foul-tempered, non-English-speaking women to obstruct all runways and harass all passengers.

In tracking Jenna, James the Shriner made it no farther than

Concourse G, where a corpulent security guard named Lupee pinned him to the wall and questioned him relentlessly in Portuguese. The focus of her concern was the fez that James was wearing, which she tore off his head and ran through the X-ray machine several times, mashing it in the process. In the meantime Bahamasair Flight 123 to Nassau departed.

'I blew it,' James apologized afterward in the coffee shop. 'I'm sorry.'

'Don't worry,' Keyes said. 'You didn't have a chance.'

'Not one-on-one,' Burt agreed. 'Mr. Keyes, our information says that your lady friend is traveling alone.'

Somehow Burt had secured a printout of the passenger manifest (he wouldn't say how, and Keyes could only assume a fraternal Masonic connection with one of the ticket agents). With the Shriners staring over his shoulder, Keyes ran his finger down the passenger list. Wiley wouldn't be using his own name, nor would he settle for a simple Smith or Jones as an alias.

'Who are we hunting?' Burt asked.

'A very cunning fruitcake.'

'What did you say his name was?'

'I didn't,' Keyes said.

He found whom he was looking for, assigned to seats 15-A and 15-B:

'Karamazov, Viceroy.'

'Karamazov, Skip.'

Keyes crumpled the passenger manifest into a ball and disgustedly tossed it over his shoulder. The Shriners smoothed it out and studied the names.

'A real wiseass,' Burt said. 'This friend of yours, he seems to be enjoying all this, doesn't he?'

'Sure looks that way,' Keyes grumbled, trying to remember where the hell he'd left his passport.

16

They found Skip Wiley snoring beneath a baby-blue umbrella on Cable Beach. He wore ragged denim cutoffs and no shirt. A pornographic novel titled *Crack of Dawn* was open across his lap. A half-empty bottle of Myers's rum perspired in a plastic bucket of ice, protected by the shade of Wiley's torso.

Brian Keyes removed the rum and dumped the ice cubes over Wiley's naked chest.

'Christ on a bike!' Wiley sat up like a bolt.

'Hello, Skip.'

'You're one cruel fucker.' Wiley reached for a towel. 'Introduce me to your friends.'

'This is Burt and this is James.'

'Love the hats, guys. Sorry I missed the sale.' Wiley shook hands with the Shriners. 'Pull up some beach and have a seat. Terrific view, just like on *Love Boat*, huh?'

Burt and James silently agreed; they had never seen the ocean so glassy, so crystalline blue. It truly was a tropical paradise. The cabdriver had said that one of the James Bond movies had been filmed in this cove, and from then on the Shriners had felt they were on a great adventure. They didn't know what to make of this fellow under the beach umbrella, but they'd already agreed to let Brian Keyes do the talking.

'Where's Jenna?' Keyes asked. He liked to start with the easy questions.

'House hunting,' Wiley said. 'I can't stand this goddamn hotel. Full of American rubes and geeks pissing away Junior's college fund at the blackjack tables. It's pathetic.' Wiley poured himself an iceless rum and cranberry juice. 'How're the ribs, Brian?'

'Getting better.' Keyes was scouting the shoreline.

'Relax, he's not here.'

'Who?'

'Viceroy, that's who! So you can unpucker your asshole. I sent him on some errands because I wanted privacy. Now you show up with these burly bookends.'

'They're friends of Theodore Bellamy.'

'I see,' Wiley said, scratching his head. 'So we're here for vengeance, are we? Brian, I hope you explained to your companions that they are now on foreign soil and treading in a country that takes a dim view of kidnapping and murder. A country that respects the rights of all foreign nationals and adheres to the strictest legal tests for extradition.'

'Meaning what?' Burt demanded.

'Meaning you and your bucket-headed partner are on your way to Fox Hill Prison if you fuck with me,' Skip Wiley said, waving his rum glass. 'I'm a guest here, an honored guest.'

This problem had occurred to Brian Keyes as soon as he set foot in Nassau. He had no idea how one would go about kidnapping Skip Wiley and hauling him back to Florida. By boat? Barge? Private helicopter? And if one succeeded, then what? No charges had been filed against Wiley in the States because no one, besides Keyes and possibly Cab Mulcahy, knew the true identity of *El Fuego*.

'Did you kill Dr. Courtney?' Keyes asked.

'Ho-ho-ho.'

'Why'd you do it?'

'Please,' Wiley said, raising a hand, 'we've been through all this.'

'You need help, Skip.'

'I've got all the help I need, Ace. Look, you're lucky I'm still talking to you. I gave you everything you'd need to turn the cops loose like a bunch of bloodhounds.'

'I lost the briefcase.'

'Swell, just swell.' Wiley laughed sourly. 'Some fucking private eye you turned out to be. I will admit one thing: that was a great line you fed Bloodworth about Slavic crazoids in fright wigs. Just the right nuance of xenophobia.'

'I was hoping nobody'd believe it.'

Wiley's cavernous grin disappeared and his lively brown eyes hardened. 'Tell your friends to take a stroll,' he said under his breath. 'I want to talk to you.'

Keyes motioned to the Shriners and they trudged down the beach, glancing over their shoulders every few steps.

'So talk,' Keyes said to Wiley.

'You think I'm just a deranged egomaniac?'

'Oh no, Skip, you're completely normal. Every newspaper has at least one or two reporters who moonlight as mass murderers. It's a well-known occupational hazard.'

Wiley sniffed scornfully. 'Let me assure you, my young friend, that I'm not crazy. I know what I'm doing, and I know what I've done. You're fond of the word *murderer*—fine. Call me whatever you want. Zealotry can be grueling, that's for sure; don't think it doesn't take a toll on the psyche—or the conscience. But just for the record, it's not my name that's important, it's the group's. Recognition is damned essential to morale, Brian, and morale is vital to the cause. These fellas deserve some ink.'

'But a revolution? Skip, really.'

'Revolution?—perhaps you're right; perhaps that's hyperbole. But Jesús and Viceroy are fond of the imagery, so I indulge them.' Wiley tossed his rum glass into the sand. 'So there'll be no revolution, in the classic sense, but chaos? You bet. Shame. Panic. Flight. Economic disaster.'

'Pretty ambitious,' Keyes said.

'It's the least I can do,' Wiley said. 'Brian, what is Florida anyway? An immense sunny toilet where millions of tourists flush their money and save the moment on Kodak film. The recipe for redemption is simple: scare away the tourists and pretty soon you scare off the developers. No more developers, no more bankers. No more bankers, no more lawyers. No more lawyers, no more dope smugglers. The whole motherfucking economy implodes! Now, tell me I'm crazy.'

Brian Keyes knew better than to do that.

Wiley's long hair glinted gold in the Bahamian sun. He wore a look of lionly confidence. 'So the question,' he went on, 'is how to scare away the tourists.'

'Murder a few,' Keyes said.

'For starters.'

'Skip, there's got to be another way.'

'No!' Wiley shot to his feet, uprooting the beach umbrella with his head. 'There . . . is . . . no . . . other . . . way! Think about it, you mullusk-brained moron! What gets headlines? Murder, mayhem, and madness—the cardinal Ms of the newsroom. That's what terrifies the travel agents of the world. That's what rates congressional hearings and crime commissions. And that's what frightens off bozo Shriner conventions. It's a damn shame, I grant you that. It's a shame I simply couldn't stand up at the next county commission meeting and ask our noble public servants to please stop destroying the planet. It's a shame that the people who poisoned this paradise won't just apologize and pack their U-Hauls and head back North to the smog and the blizzards. But it's a proven fact they won't leave until somebody lights a fire under 'em. That's what *Las Noches de Diciembre* is all about. *"Cops Seek Grisly Suitcase Killer"* . . . *"Elderly Woman Abducted, Fed to Vicious Reptile"* . . . *"Golf Course Bomb Claims Three on Tricky Twelfth Hole"* . . . *"Crazed Terrorists Stalk Florida Tourists."* ' Wiley was practically chanting the headlines, as if he were watching them roll off the presses at the New York *Post*.

'Sure, it's cold-blooded,' he said, 'but that's the game of journalism for you. It's the only game I know, but I know how to win.'

'The old hype button,' Keyes said.

'You got it, Ace!' Wiley slapped him on the shoulder. 'Let's go find your funny friends.'

They walked up Cable Beach. Keyes sidestepped the wavelets but Wiley crashed ahead, kicking water with his enormous slabs of feet. He cocked his head high, chin thrust toward the sun.

'If you hate tourists so much,' Keyes said, 'why'd you come here, of all places?'

'Sovereignty,' Wiley replied, 'and convenience. Besides, the Bahamas is different from Florida. The A.Q. here is only forty-two.'

A.Q., Keyes remembered, stood for Asshole Quotient. Skip Wiley had a well-known theory that the quality of life declined in direct proportion to the Asshole Quotient. According to Wiley's reckoning, Miami had 134 total assholes per square mile, giving it the worst A.Q. in North America. In second place was Aspen, Colorado (101), with Malibu Beach, California, finishing third at 97.

Every year Skip Wiley wrote a column rating the ten most unbearable places on the continent according to A.Q., and every year the city editor diligently changed 'Asshole Quotient' to 'Idiot Quotient' before the column could be published. The next day Wiley would turn in a new column apologizing to his readers because he'd neglected to count one more total asshole, that being his own editor. And of course Wiley's editor would immediately delete *that*, too. After a few years it was obvious that even Skip Wiley couldn't get the word *asshole* into the Miami *Sun*, but the whole newsroom looked forward to the annual struggle.

'The great thing about the Bahamas,' Wiley was saying, 'is that they don't let the tourists stay. Trying to buy property here is like trying to get a personal audience with the pope. Damn near impossible without the right connections. So, Mr. and Mrs. Mickey Mouse Ears from Akron can come and tinkle away all their money, but then it's bye-bye, leavin' on a jet plane. Punch out at immigrations. Too bad they didn't think of this system in Florida.'

'Florida's not an island, Skip.'

Wiley hopped over two Bahamian children who were wrestling in the water. His gravelly, melodic laughter mixed with their giggles and carried into the surf.

'Don't you think this has gone far enough?' Keyes asked.

'I was waiting for you to say that,' Wiley said, marching ahead. 'Mr. I'm-Only-Trying-to-Help, that's you. A real killjoy.'

Keyes stopped walking. The blue water curled over his tennis shoes. 'I hate to see people die, that's all,' he said to Wiley.

'I know you do,' Wiley said, looking back. 'So do I. Believe it or not.' He didn't need to say any more. They were both remembering little Callie Davenport.

Up ahead a crowd of bathers gathered noisily in a circle under some slash pines. Keyes and Wiley heard the sound of men shouting and, in the distance, a siren.

Keyes thought of Burt and James and started running, his sneakers squishing in the sand. Wiley put on a sudden burst of speed and caught him by the arm.

'Wait a minute, Ace, better let me check this out.'

On the fringe of the melee Keyes counted four Bahamian policemen, each wearing a pith helmet and crisp white uniform. They carried hard plastic batons but no sidearms. Wiley strolled up and started chatting with one of the cops; he came back with the bad news.

'I'm afraid your friends had to learn the hard way.'

From a distance Keyes watched the Bahamian officers lead Burt and James away from the beach. The purple fez hats were easy to follow, bobbing above the jolly crowd.

'What the hell happened?' Keyes asked, contemplating a rescue attempt.

'Stay here,' Wiley cautioned, 'unless you're into bondage.'

What had happened was this: on their reluctant trek down Cable Beach, the keen-eyed Shriners had spotted none other than Viceroy Wilson, the fugitive football star, coming toward them. As usual Wilson was wrapped safely behind his Carrera sunglasses and, as usual, he was stoked to the gills, having scored some primo Jamaican herb off a busboy at the hotel. Viceroy Wilson had never been to the islands, and the striking display of Bahamian womanhood along the beach had seriously diverted his attention from the revolution. Wilson was so preoccupied that he hadn't noticed the two husky purple-hatted honkies in gray suits stalking him among the bathers.

The Shriners had struck swiftly, with a sinister rustle of polyester. Burt had seized Viceroy Wilson's left arm and James had grabbed the right, pivoting and twisting in a very sophisticated karate maneuver. Unfortunately, the people who invented karate never got to practice on 235-pound former NFL fullbacks with sequoia-sized arms. Viceroy Wilson had disrespectfully flattened the Shriners and broken hard for the hotel. Robbed of agility by the marijuana, he'd tripped on an Igloo cooler and gone down. The Shriners had been upon him quickly, puffing and grunting and attaching themselves to his powerful torso. Somehow Viceroy

Wilson had risen to his feet and galvanized his famous legs. The old reflexes had taken command; with Shriners clinging to his thighs, Wilson churned along the beach. It was a memorable sight, and several quick-witted tourists had turned their home-movie cameras toward the combat. Viceroy Wilson was all elbows and knees and speed, and the Shriners had fallen away, tassels spinning. Eventually the police had arrived and arrested Burt and James for assault. The officers apologized profusely to Skip Wiley, for they specifically had been recruited to keep watch over Wiley's entourage, a commitment guaranteed by a generous cash gratuity.

'I told your bookends to behave,' Wiley said reproachfully as they watched the police van drive off.

Keyes asked wearily, 'Are they going to jail?'

'Naw, to the airport. They'll be deported as undesirables. Certainly can't argue with that.'

They returned to the shade of the blue umbrella. Keyes sat down in the cool sand. Wiley stretched out on the patio chair.

'They're going to figure out it's you,' Keyes said. 'The cops, the press. Somebody'll put it together.'

'Not for a while.' Wiley squinted into the sun. 'You weren't thinking about squealing, were you?'

Keyes shook his head and looked away, out at the gentle waves. *Of course I'm thinking about it, you jerk.*

'Because I meant what I said before,' Wiley said. 'If the cops catch on to me too soon, we're in trouble. And if they do catch on, I'll know it was you. Nobody else.'

'But, Skip, there's all kinds of clues. Wilson and the Cuban, they're leaving a trail—'

'Fine, no problem. That we can survive. Besides, they're secretly dying to be famous again. Me—I've got to work in the background right now. Too much planning to be done, juking here and there. I can't have Metro Homicide sniffing after me; it plays hell with the creative process. See, if I'm exposed as *El Fuego*, I'll lose my leverage with the troops. It'll mean I'm not so shrewd, not so clever, not so irreplaceable. They'll stop listening to me, Brian, and that's big goddamn trouble. Some of the things these fellas want to do, some of the people they want to snuff!

Lose me and you lose the voice of reason. Then it's Bloodbath City, old pal, and that ain't standard Wiley hyperbole. That's a goddamn fact.'

Keyes studied his unraveled friend and thought of the Ida Kimmelman ceremony. Skip's threat of a massacre seemed deadly serious.

Keyes said, 'If you've got them so mesmerized, convince them to call it off.'

Wiley answered with a snort. 'Never! The cause is just. The dream is pure.' He pointed a finger at Keyes. 'It's up to you and Cab and the others to end the violence. How? Accept the Nights of December as a legitimate terrorist cell. Give us a forum. Pass the message that we're serious, that we'll continue the campaign until the exodus is fully under way. Ha! Imagine: bumper-to-bumper from Key West to Jacksonville: U-Hauls, Winnebagos, Airstreams, station wagons, moving vans, buses, eighteen-wheelers. All northbound!' Wiley sat up animatedly. 'Brian, in the last hour we've been talking, 41.6 morons moved into the state of Florida. They are arriving at the rate of a thousand a day. One thousand each and every day! There is *no place to put them*! The land is shriveling beneath us, the water is poison, the air is rancid.' Wiley threw back his head. 'Lord, such a simple equation. Nature's trying to tell us it's time to move on.'

'The last of the Malthusians,' Keyes said.

'Hell, Malthus only *dreamed* a nightmare like Interstate 95. He never had to drive the fucking thing.'

Keyes thought: He seems to have his mind made up. Maybe I'll have to kill him after all. Certainly not now, not on a crowded beach in the afternoon. But maybe soon.

Wiley propped his fuzzy chin on his knuckles and grew silent. He watched the arrival of a gleaming cruise ship across the harbor. Its alabaster decks were lined with bright specks of tourists snapping pictures and flailing idiotic hellos toward the peddlers on the dock. Wiley looked quite amused. Brian Keyes wished he could penetrate his old friend's twisted swamp of a brain; he felt more helpless than ever.

Wiley said: 'I suppose you want to hear what's next.'

'You bet.'

'It's a real beaut.'

'Let's have it.'

'Okay,' Wiley said. 'We're going to violate the most sacred virgin in all Miami.'

'Can you be a little more specific?'

''Fraid not, Brian. You're a bright young man, you figure it out.'

'When you say violate, you mean rape.'

'Hell no!' Wiley was indignant. 'I can't believe you'd think such a thing. All the years we've known each other—Christ, do I look like a rapist?'

Keyes didn't answer because sometimes Skip Wiley *did* look like a rapist.

'The word "violate"—'

'Dust off your dictionary, Ace. We're going to desecrate an immaculate princess. That's all the clues for you.'

Wiley dug into his jeans and came up with a silver traffic whistle, which he blew three times, loudly.

'What the hell is that?' Keyes asked, realizing that it was too late.

'Time for you to say good-bye to Goombayland.'

Keyes caught sight of four starch-shirted Bahamian cops running down the beach, kicking up sand with their black boots, and waving batons.

'Oh shit,' Keyes muttered.

'Look at them move,' Wiley marveled. 'Isn't bribery wonderful?'

Keyes quickly reviewed his options. Physical resistance was out of the question; the policemen looked like four scowling black locomotives. Running also seemed futile—there was nowhere to go where he wouldn't shine like a two-hundred-watt bulb. He considered plunging into the surf and swimming for freedom, but was dissuaded by the probability of being mortally gnawed by a bull shark, or mowed down by a ski boat. In the end, Keyes meekly presented himself to the Bahamian officers. The tropical sunshine seemed to evaporate as they encircled him.

'Take it easy, men,' Skip Wiley said, unfurling from the beach chair. 'He's obviously harmless.'

Eight rock-hard hands clamped onto Brian Keyes.

'I guess this means you and Jenna aren't inviting me up for conch chowder.'

''Fraid not, Brian.' Wiley yawned, stretching his ropy brown arms. 'Have a safe trip home.'

'When am I gonna see you again, Skip?'

'Soon,' Wiley said. 'On national TV. Now, if you'll excuse me, I'm late for my windsurfing lesson.'

17

'Kara Lynn.'

'Yes, Mr. Mayor.'

'What do you think about famine?'

Kara Lynn Shivers considered the question carefully. 'Which famine, Mr. Mayor?'

'World famine,' the mayor said, 'in general.'

'Well, in general,' Kara Lynn said, 'I think famine is a truly terrible thing.'

'If you were selected our Orange Bowl queen,' the mayor went on, 'would you work to end world famine?'

'Tirelessly, Mr. Mayor.'

The other judges nodded approvingly. They liked Kara Lynn Shivers better than the other semifinalists, and they'd already made up their minds. If only the mayor would hurry up with the last interview.

'How would you do it?' the mayor asked.

'Do what?' Kara Lynn said.

'Stop famine.'

'I didn't say I could stop it,' Kara Lynn said with a trace of sarcasm. In the third row she spotted her father, grimly making a slashing motion across his throat.

'But I'd certainly try,' she said, softening. 'As you know, I'm majoring in public relations, Mr. Mayor, and I could use those special skills to bring the world's attention to the plight of its starving children. I would consider that my first priority as Orange Bowl queen.'

The mayor beamed. Kara Lynn's father let out a sigh of relief.

'Thank you, Kara Lynn,' the mayor said. 'We'll adjourn until tonight.'

'Thank you, Mr. Mayor,' Kara Lynn said. Then, nodding sweetly toward the other judges, 'Thank *all* of you.'

And now, she thought, you can all go back to the Hyatt and whack off.

Kara Lynn Shivers, nineteen years old, blond, hazel-eyed, five-foot-eight, one hundred twenty pounds (Viceroy Wilson was on the money), had become a cynical young woman. She despised beauty pageants and all the fraudulent insouciance they required. Though she had won many titles—Little Miss Mass Transit, Miss Anglo Miami and, of course, Stone Crab Queen—each new tiara only added to Kara Lynn's deepening misery. Offstage she had no smiles, no charms, no patience. She was all used up.

It was her father's fault. He was the one who'd made her learn 'Eleanor Rigby' on the French horn. 'The judges'll love it,' he'd said, and they always did.

It was her father who made her, at age six, change her name from Karen Noreen because 'Noreen belongs in the 4-H, not Atlantic City.'

It was her father who dragged her to Geneva, at age nine, to be ministered by 'the greatest ambidextrous orthodontist in all Europe.'

Kara Lynn Shivers suspected there was something seriously hinky with her father—not for wanting his little princess to be a star (a harmless fantasy), but for suggesting that no price was too high.

It was her father who'd mailed off a stack of bikini Polaroids to *Playboy* magazine, then to *Penthouse*, then *Oui*, and after countless rejections announced that Kara Lynn needed bigger breasts. Kara Lynn didn't want bigger breasts. Her little breasts were just fine; round, perky, very cute. No one ever complained about her breasts except her father, who hadn't seen them naked since she was a kid anyway.

One afternoon, a few months before the Orange Bowl pageant, Kara Lynn's father secretly invited a renowned plastic surgeon to the house. Kara Lynn had just returned from exercise class in a pink body stocking. She was in the kitchen, fixing a pitcher of iced tea, when the two men slipped up behind her.

'Well, what do you think?' her father had asked.

'No sweat,' the surgeon had said. 'B-cup, or C?'

'Stay away from my tits!' Kara Lynn had cried, reaching for a steak knife.

'But, buttercup, I'm only trying to help.'

'They're my tits, Dad. You stay away!'

'Forty million people watch that parade on New Year's Eve. Don't you want to make a good impression?'

Kara Lynn's mother was no help.

'Your father just wants the best for you,' she'd said. 'What's so wrong with that?'

'Mother!'

'It'll be a lovely Christmas present.'

'But I don't want new boobs for Christmas,' Kara Lynn said, 'I want a Volkswagen.'

On the night of December 16, Kara Lynn Shivers and her original breasts charmed a small but enthusiastic crowd at the Civic Center, and the judges unanimously crowned her Miami's Orange Bowl queen. A surprise guest, Julio Iglesias, presented Kara Lynn with a bouquet of roses. She smiled expertly and accepted Julio's kiss, but her heart was not aflutter. After the television lights went dark, Jerry, the oily emcee, thanked Kara Lynn for reviving him after his altercation with the black security guard. Jerry told Kara Lynn he was 'wiped out emotionally' by her rendition of 'Eleanor Rigby,' and asked if she'd join him for a drink.

'You just want a blow-job,' Kara Lynn said. 'What's that got to do with world famine?'

Kara Lynn Shivers decided that the Orange Bowl would be her last beauty pageant. She was right.

The week of December 16 was the busiest yet for *Las Noches de Diciembre*. Three more tourists vanished, a drunken college kid was eaten alive by a wild crocodile, and the bucolic Hibiscus Kennel Club was the grisly scene for what became known as the Trifecta Massacre. The national wire services were slowly awakening to Florida's newest crime wave, and no less an authority than the New York *Times* published its own priceless account: *Abductions of Florida Tourists Trouble Some Authorities.*

It was the worst week in the entire life of Detective Harold Keefe.

With Skip Wiley out of the country, Jesús Bernal went hog-wild with bombs. He built three of them, and typed up a preliminary list of targets:

1. Detective Harold Keefe.
2. Anyplace with lots of tourists.
3. Anyplace with lots of Communists.

The first bombing was not a total success.

On the morning of December 17, Harold Keefe left his house at the usual time and took his usual route to the Metro-Dade Police Department. From keen surveillance Jesús Bernal knew that between 7:38 and 7:46 A.M., Detective Keefe would pass through the toll plaza on the Dolphin Expressway. He also knew that Keefe would use the lane marked Trucks-Change-Receipts. Jesús Bernal was ready. He got to the toll booth at 7:25 A.M., tied up the cashier, and watched for Harold Keefe's unmarked black Plymouth Volare.

Harold Keefe was not at his most observant early in the morning. He scarcely glanced at the lean Cuban cashier who dropped his change—'Sorry, meester!'—and crawled under his car, groping (Keefe assumed) for the quarter. And he paid no attention to the faint plink of metal on metal.

Which was the sound of Jesús Bernal attaching the remote-control bomb.

'Have a nice day!' Bernal waved as Harold Keefe drove away.

Sixty seconds later the bomb exploded, lifting the black Volare out of rush-hour traffic and dropping it into a drainage culvert.

Harold Keefe was not killed. The Miami *Sun* described his wounds as 'massive foot injuries,' which is another way of saying that the detective's toes were blown off, every single one; other than that, Harold Keefe hopped away without a scratch. It was one of the strangest bombings anyone could remember, and it was not what Jesús Bernal had in mind.

The second bomb was more powerful, and its results more spectacular. It blew up on the night of December 18, during the first race at the Hibiscus Kennel Club before a record crowd of 14,501 spectators (including two-thirds of the county commission). The Kennel Club bomb actually was a small land mine, a rudimentary imitation claymore, which Jesús Bernal had buried on the second turn of the track. The greyhound that triggered the mine was a speedy dam named Blistered Sister who went off at 20-to-1. Literally. One second there were eight lank dogs churning along the rail, and the next they were airborne, inside-out. It was a mess. The blast took out a sixty-foot stretch of racetrack and disrupted betting for hours. Blistered Sister, whose brindle carcass landed closest to the finish wire, was ruled the winner and paid out $40.60 on a $2 ticket. As the kennel crews repaired the mangled track with a backhoe and shovels, a taut, unfamiliar voice rang out of the public-address system:

'*Hola*, Pari-Mutuel Wagerers,' the voice said. 'Welcome to the Revolution!'

Only the county commissioners seemed alarmed.

The third bomb was the one Jesús Bernal saved. He'd looked all over Miami for a gathering of Communists to blow up, but found none. He knew they were there—they *had* to be. Bernal didn't want to waste this bomb because it was a real masterpiece; his ticket back to the First Weekend in July. He decided to save the bomb until some Communists popped up. If worse came to worst, he could always plant it at ACLU.

While Jesús Bernal scurried around town with his C-4 and blasting caps, Tommy Tigertail and Viceroy Wilson (back from Nassau, still celibate) picked off three more tourists.

'We need the stats,' Skip Wiley had urged by telegram.

'Stats?' mumbled the Indian.

Viceroy Wilson understood perfectly.

The kidnappings were nothing fancy: a young surfer at the Pompano Pier, lured to a waiting Cadillac with a lid of fresh Colombian red; and a middle-aged couple from White Plains who mysteriously vanished from their front-row table during Jackie Mason's second show at the Diplomat.

At midweek, Tommy Tigertail delivered some grim news.

'Pavlov is sick,' he told Viceroy Wilson at the Everglades campsite.

'I'll bet it was that goddamned surfer,' Wilson said.

'No,' the Indian said, 'it's the water. He needs salt water.'

Viceroy Wilson scanned the pond for the ominous brown log that was Pavlov's snout. From a distance—a safe distance—the monster looked just fine.

'This is a North American crocodile. His habitat is salt water,' Tommy explained. 'He's been out here two weeks and now he needs to go home.'

'Fine with me,' Viceroy Wilson said.

The second they got the ropes on Pavlov, Viceroy saw what the Indian was talking about. The big croc was listless and cloudy-eyed. Even its hiss sounded anemic.

Hauling Pavlov from the bowels of the Glades to the shores of Biscayne Bay turned out to be a day-long endeavor. Even in a state of lethargy the crocodile was formidable cargo, and its disposition did not improve as the trip wore on. The Indian had rented a tractor-trailer for the journey, but there wasn't enough room in the cab for all three commandos. Viceroy Wilson decided that Jesús Bernal, by virtue of his switchblade prowess, was best equipped to ride in back with the giant reptile. Every time Tommy Tigertail took a sharp corner the trailer came alive with muffled hissing and Spanish invective.

At dusk they pulled off the Seventy-ninth Street Causeway, dragged Pavlov out of the rig, and prodded him into the salty shallows of Biscayne Bay. The croc swam east, never looking back, propelled by that massive rhythmic tail. Pavlov did not stop swimming for thirty hours. He crossed the bay, entered the Atlantic through Haulover Cut, and churned north along the Gold Coast. It was as if, Skip Wiley mused later, the great beast somehow had been imbued with the spirit of *Las Noches;* as if it had drawn inspiration from its captors.

To Viceroy Wilson, the explanation was more elementary; Seminole magic. The damn Indian had worked a spell.

Pavlov stopped swimming when he reached the famous Ft. Lauderdale beachfront. There, in darkness, he dragged his thousand pounds ashore and made for the party lights of the Barbary Coast Hotel. Later, in daylight, beachgoers would trace the crocodile's lethal path by the trench in the sand.

Wiley's mystical notions aside, what probably happened was that the croc merely grew tired of fighting the ocean currents and came ashore to rest. Once on land, its nostrils got wind of the Barbary's luxuriant saltwater swimming pool, and Pavlov had decided to enjoy himself.

Besides being young, drunk, and stupid, Kyle Griffith (University of Georgia, Class of '87) had no good reason to be in that swimming pool at four in the morning. A bad reason for being there—nude, save for a foam-rubber hat that said 'Go Bulldawgs!'—was that Griffith's dithering Sigma Nu brothers had dared him to jump thirty feet from the balcony of the hotel room to the warm pool, which lay in darkness so complete that even a seventeen-foot crocodile could be invisible.

Having eaten prodigiously in recent days, Pavlov was not very hungry. A snack would have been fine, perhaps a coot or a small garfish. But once Kyle Griffith hit the water, Pavlov's dinosaural instincts took over. The crocodile seized the bewildered Sigma Nu by the legs and submerged to the bottom of the swimming pool, where the beast lay motionless for several minutes, as if contemplating the wisdom of its own gluttony. In the end, of course, the college kid was consumed, though Pavlov regurgitated the silly rubber hat.

This onslaught of violent and weird events destroyed Detective Harold Keefe's hoax theory (not to mention his career) and convinced the civic leaders of Dade County that a ruthless band of psychopaths was indeed roaming the streets.

Toeless and sullen, Keefe was spared the shame of a demotion and allowed to take a generous disability leave from the police department.

On the morning of December 20, while Brian Keyes was on the phone to the U.S. State Department, three uniformed police officers arrived at his office and politely requested his company downtown. Keyes had been expecting the visit, and was in no mood to argue. He had spent the week dodging Ricky Bloodworth and trying to negotiate the release of the two Shriners from a Bahamian prison, where they were being held on vague charges of espionage and lobster poaching. Keyes sent word to Skip Wiley that enough was enough, the joke was over, but all he got back was a cable that said: 'Don't you have work to do?' Eventually Burt and James were fined five thousand dollars each and placed on a nonstop Nassau-to-Chicago flight. Keyes had been playing dumb with the State Department when the cops showed up.

At police headquarters Keyes was led to a soundproof conference room and told to wait. The windowless suite was newly carpeted and smelled like paint. On the wall hung a blackboard on which someone had chalked the words '*Las Noches de Diciembre?* Nights of December?' After a few minutes Al García strolled in, grinning like a whale.

'No more motor pool!' he chortled. 'Welcome to the big time.'

'Big time, Al?'

'My very own task force. Can you believe it, Brian, they put *me* in charge.'

'In charge of what?'

'In charge of solving the *Las Noches* murders.'

'No offense, Al,' Keyes said, 'but why you?'

'Well, the gang has a Spanish name. I'm a Spanish cop.' García laughed until he turned red. He sat down at the head of a long table and lit a cigarette. 'It's all top secret, this task force, and let's keep it thataway. We don't want to cause a panic, close the hotels, God forbid. It's the season, y'know.'

García was still chuckling. Keyes knew he didn't give a shit about the hotels.

'How big is your task force?'

'Four detectives, including me, plus a guy at the FBI if we need him. We got a real code name and everything: Fuego One.'

'I like it,' Keyes said. Almost time for the big decision. García was finished circling.

'So, my friend, you've had quite a time of it, eh?'

'Quite a time,' Keyes agreed.

'Let's talk about it.' García fished a spiral notebook from his rumpled jacket. 'What do you know about this outfit?'

'I know they set up Ernesto Cabal for a fall. The poor putz had nothing to do with Sparky Harper's death, just like I tried to tell you weeks ago.'

García frowned. 'I'm sorry, man. Really. He looked hot, and he was all we had at the time.'

'And that's it? *Adiós*, Ernesto.'

'What do you want, five Hail Marys? I said I was fucking sorry, and I am. Don't forget I didn't kill Cabal, Brian, he killed himself. A little more patience and the *hijo de puta* mighta walked out of jail a free man.'

Keyes said, 'He was scared, that's all.'

'Yeah, man, well, I'm kinda scared too. I'm scared these nuts are gonna murder more innocent people. And I'm scared that I'm going to have to look at more legless dead bloated bodies. But most of all I'm scared of what my wife's going to do when I tell her I have to work through Christmas! So, rest in peace and forgive me, Ernesto'—García made a perfunctory sign of the cross—'but I got to get busy.'

'I'll try to help, Al.'

'Excellent. You can start by telling me who you saw out there in the Glades. Anybody interesting?'

'Guy named Jesús Bernal.'

'Hey, our bomber! Sloppy fucker, too. Left his fingerprints all over the piping. Buys the wire in Hialeah.' García jotted in his notepad. 'He the one who jammed the shiv in your ribs?'

'I think so,' Keyes said.

'What about your pal from Pauly's joint, the football hero?'

'Viceroy Wilson. Yeah, him too.'

'He must be *El Fuego*.'

Keyes thought: There it is. Time to shut up or throw in Wiley. Once it was done, there'd be no going back.

'Al, I'm not sure.'

'About what?'

'*El Fuego*. See, there were four of them, and they never mentioned it.'

García's cigarette toggled excitedly. 'Four of them! Who were the other two?'

'There was an Indian.'

'A raghead Indian or a Tonto Indian?'

'A Seminole. Tommy Tigertail, they call him.'

'The man with the Cadillac,' García said. He jotted down Tommy's name and asked, 'How about number four?'

'White male, late thirties.' Keyes shrugged. 'It was dark, like I said.' So that was the decision: to get Skip Wiley himself. Keyes knew he stood a better chance of finding him quietly, with no police sirens. Most of all he was worried about Wiley's threat of a bloodbath; what had seemed unthinkable three weeks ago seemed imminent now.

García sat back and folded his puffy hands. 'Something's bothering me, *amigo*. I think to myself, why the hell would these maniacs snatch mild-mannered Brian Keyes, of all people? I mean, if they weren't gonna kill you, then why take the risk? They just want to chat or what?'

'They wanted me to witness a murder,' Keyes said.

'And did you?'

'Yes, I think so. Ida Kimmelman was the woman's name.'

'The Broward condo queen,' García muttered, writing intently.

'They fed her to a crocodile,' Keyes said.

'Who?'

'Wilson and Bernal. They threw her in a pond—why are you looking at me like that?'

Al García capped his pen. 'Go on, Brian.'

'I'm not making this up. They threw her in the water and a crocodile ate her.'

Lost in thought, García gnawed on a thumbnail. He'd heard about the college kid who got gobbled up in Lauderdale and pondered the connection—after all, how many crocodiles could there be?

Keyes said: 'They did it for effect. For headlines, that's all.'

'Why didn't you report this a week ago?'

'And read about it on the front page? No way, that's exactly what they wanted. I wasn't about to let them use me.'

'Very noble,' García said caustically. 'Really showed 'em who's boss. By the way, hotshot, you been reading the fucking newspaper this week? Your pals out there in the swamp make Richard Speck look like Soupy Sales.'

'For God's sake, Al, it's not like I've been on vacation. What do you think I've been working on?'

'Tell me more.'

'I'd like to.'

'Excellent.' García tapped his pen on the table.

'Al, they're planning something big.' Without naming Skip Wiley, Keyes recounted the enigmatic threat to 'violate the most sacred virgin in all Miami.'

'Sounds like Rape City.'

'I think it's worse than that.'

'Maybe you could find that camp again.'

'Not in a million years,' Keyes said. He was telling the truth.

'I'll get a chopper and we'll take a SWAT team.'

'How about the National Guard?'

'Don't laugh,' García said. 'They've promised whatever I need.'

'Find the Cuban and the football player,' Keyes advised, 'and that'll be the end of it. No more kidnappings.'

'Brian, I get the feeling you're holding back.' García peered over the top of his reading glasses. 'Tell me you're not holding back.'

'Al, I don't remember much. I was busy losing three units of blood.'

'Yeah, well, maybe something'll come back to you.' García waved good-bye with the cigarette. 'We'll talk again. Sanchez will give you a lift downtown.'

Keyes started to get up from the table.

'By the way,' García said, 'that was a helluva funny piece in the *Sun* today. D'you see it?'

'My paper was in a puddle.'

'Well, I got it in my coat somewhere. Clipped it out. Here it is . . . I hate to admit it, but I actually started to miss this asshole's column while he was out sick.'

'May I?' Keyes asked. Apprehensively he lifted the folded newspaper clipping from García's brown paw. He opened it at arm's length, as if it were radioactive.

'Go ahead, read it,' Al García said. 'It's funny as hell. All about his vacation in the Bahamas. The guy's got a regular way with words.'

'So he does,' said Brian Keyes, trying not to appear dumb-founded by what he saw.

In print.

With a studio photo.

Under a headline that said:

Wiley Returns.

18

Nassau—The worst thing about visiting the Bahamas is Americans like me. The hotels are lousy with us.

Americans with terrible manners.

Americans who talk like the rest of the world is deaf.

And dress like the rest of the world is blind.

I come here seeking solitude, an oasis for recuperation, and all I get is a jackhammer sinus headache that won't go away. From Bay Street to the baccarat salons, there's no escaping this foul plague of tourists.

In Florida we've grown accustomed to their noisome behavior (and tolerate it, as avarice dictates we must), but there is something obscene about witnessing its infliction upon the people of a foreign country.

Frankly, we ought to be ashamed of ourselves.

Perhaps it's basic pioneer spirit that compels Americans each vacation season to evacuate their hometowns and explore new lands. Fine. But how do you justify fluorescent Bermuda shorts? Or *E.T.* beach sandals? What gives us the right to so offend the rest of civilization?

Ah, but look who's talking.

The other day I tried windsurfing, an absurd sport that requires one to balance perilously on a banana-shaped piece of fiberglass while steering the seas with a flimsy canvas sheet.

Windsurfing lessons in the Bahamas cost $45, a bargain for vacationing yahoos who firmly believe that the more dangerous an enterprise, the more you should pay for it. And for a thirty-seven-year-old degenerate in my addled condition, windsurfing is fraught with exciting little dangers:

lacerations, compound fractures, groin pulls, spinal paralysis—not to mention toxic jellyfish, killer sharks, sea urchins, and sting rays.

Windsurfing probably is not as dangerous as, say, flying a slow U-2 over Cuba, but there isn't a jock pilot in the whole damn Air Force who's ever had to worry about losing his swimtrunks (and self-esteem) before a beachload of gawking, tittering, shrimp-skinned tourists.

Which is what happened to me at high noon yesterday when I was blindsided by a thunderous breaker.

My Bahamian windsurfing instructor, Rudy, had every right to laugh; it was a stupendous moon job.

After my spill (and near-drowning), I loudly accused him of supplying faulty equipment. Replied Rudy: 'De only 'quipment dat fawlty, mon, is you drunken old body.'

He was right. You can't surf with a bottle of Myers's under your arm. Stupid bloody tourist.

Wiley Returns.

'How could you print that crap?' Brian Keyes demanded.

'Calm down,' said Cab Mulcahy, 'and close the door.'

But Keyes could not be calm, not with Wiley's elongated face leering from the pages of the Miami *Sun*. That the newspaper would revive his column was beyond belief, a monstrous gag. Wiley had the gun, and Mulcahy had just handed him the bullets, gift-wrapped.

'Cab, you don't know what you're getting into.'

'I'm afraid I do.' Mulcahy looked chagrined. 'Skip's involved with these terrorists, isn't he?'

'He's not just *involved*, Cab, he's running the whole damn show. He's the Number One Nacho.'

'You're certain, Brian?'

'Absolutely.'

The editor closed his eyes. 'How bad?'

'Imagine General Patton on acid.'

'I see.'

They sat in morose silence, pretending to gaze out Mulcahy's office window. On Biscayne Bay the waves had turned to slate under pickets of bruised thunderclouds, advancing from the east. It was probably raining like hell in the Bahamas.

'He called yesterday from Nassau,' Mulcahy began. 'Said he was feeling better. No more visceral rage, he said; back to big-league journalism. He sent the column by telex—totally harmless, no preaching, no politics. You've got to admit, it's good for a chuckle. I told Skip we'd run it after he came back to Florida and we had a long talk, to which he replied: "In due time." '

'So you published the damn thing anyway.'

'I was outvoted,' Mulcahy said.

'By whom?'

'By the only one who matters.'

'Cardoza?' Keyes asked.

Cardoza was the publisher.

'The prince himself,' Mulcahy said. 'Two weeks is a long time without your clean-up hitter, Brian. I told him Skip was still under the weather, suffering from exhaustion, the whole nine yards. But Cardoza read the column and said Skip sure didn't *write* like he was exhausted so we might as well print the column. And that was it, end of argument. Listen, we were getting a lot of mail, a *lot*, including some cancellations. You would've thought we yanked *Doonesbury* or *Peanuts*.'

Keyes said, 'Did you tell Cardoza everything?'

'About as much as you told the cops.'

Keyes shrugged. *Touché.*

'This is grand,' Mulcahy said sardonically. 'Here we are, two truth-seekers who for once actually get hold of the truth. So what do we do? We hide it. Swallow it. Smother it. You should be telling the police, and I should be telling my readers, but look at us—the original chickenshit twins. We're both worried about that crazy sonofabitch—as if he deserves our concern—and we're both telling ourselves that there's got to be another way. Except there isn't, is there? It's gone too damn far. People are dead, the cops are rabid, and the city's in an uproar. Meanwhile our old pal Wiley is hiding somewhere out there, dreaming up a punch line for this hideous joke.'

'What do you want to do?' Keyes asked.

'Go to the cops,' Mulcahy said. 'Right now.'

Keyes shook his head. 'Skip said there'd be a bloodbath if his name got out.'

'Bloodbath—he used that word?' Mulcahy asked incredulously.

'Yep. "Massacre," too, if I'm not mistaken. We've got to think about this carefully, Cab. Think about what they've already done—the kidnappings, the bombings. Look what they did to Dr. Courtney and that detective, Keefe. I don't think Wiley's bullshitting when he talks bloodbath. They've got the credentials now.' Keyes didn't mention his fear for Jenna or for Mulcahy himself.

'All right, suppose we tell the police but embargo all the press.'

'Be serious,' Keyes said. 'Once the cops heard Wiley's name they'd leak like the Haitian navy. And when the radio and TV folks get wind of it, the *Sun* will have no choice. You'll have to go with the story. Out front, too.'

'We have to get him back from the Bahamas,' Mulcahy asserted. 'I'm going to try the embassy.'

'It won't work, Cab. Skip's untouchable over there. I found out he entered the island on a fake passport, but nobody in Nassau seems to care. Apparently he's bribed everyone but the prime minister.'

'So what the hell do we do?'

Keyes said, 'I think we've got to play rough. You've got the one thing he cares about, that column.'

'Yeah,' Mulcahy said, 'and every damn word goes through me.'

Keyes thought about that.

'I know a little something about the Bahamas government,' he said. 'They're hypersensitive about their national image.'

'What are you suggesting?'

'Suppose you rewrote Skip's next column.'

'Suppose I let Bloodworth try it,' Mulcahy said.

'Oh boy.' In Wiley's words, rewriting was a mortal sin, punishable by castration. Spray-painting the Sistine Chapel, he used to call it.

Keyes thought he noticed the old boy's eyes twinkle.

'Suppose I gave it to Bloodworth and told him to punch up the lead. Make it more hard-hitting. Asked him to tinker with some of Skip's more energetic passages.'

'Might turn into something the Bahamians wouldn't like,' Keyes mused. 'Might wear out Skip's welcome real quick.'

'I can't believe we're talking about this.'

'Suppose it works,' Keyes said. 'Let's say he comes back to Miami. Then what?'

'Intercept him at the airport,' Mulcahy said. 'Turn him in, take him out of circulation. Get him some professional help.'

'He could always plead insanity.'

'I'm considering it myself,' Mulcahy muttered. 'After twenty-two years you'd think I could spot a psychopath in my own newsroom.'

'On the contrary,' said Keyes. 'The longer you're in the business, the harder it gets.'

Mulcahy was one of those rare editors who'd gone into news-papers for all the right reasons, with all the right instincts and all the right sensibilities. He was a wonderful fluke—fair but not weak, tough but not heartless, aggressive but circumspect. The Wiley situation was tearing him up.

Mulcahy toyed with a memo, shredding the edges. 'I pulled his personnel file today, just for kicks. Jesus Christ, Brian, it's full of wild stuff. Stuff I'd forgotten all about.'

The episodes had escalated in gravity:

December 13, 1978. Skip Wiley reprimanded for impersonating National Security Adviser Zbigniew Brzezinski in an effort to obtain box seats to an NFL playoff game.

April 17, 1980. Wiley reprimanded after filing an IRS return listing his occupation as 'prophet, redeemer, and sage.'

July 23, 1982. Wiley suspended two days with pay after using obscene cuneiform symbols to describe Senator Jesse Helms of North Carolina.

March 7, 1984. Wiley suspended five days with pay after telling a radio-talkshow audience that Florida's entire supply of drinking water had been poisoned by Bolivian drug dealers.

October 3, 1984. Wiley suspended three days without pay for

allegedly assaulting a Jehovah's Witness with a long-handled marlin gaff.

'I guess I wasn't paying attention,' Mulcahy said, 'on purpose.' He leaned forward and dropped his voice to a whisper. 'Brian, do you really think he's crazy? I mean, *crazy* crazy?'

'I'm not sure. Skip is no drooling yo-yo. If he were, we'd have nothing to worry about. You could let him write all he wants—who'd give a shit? Whatever he wrote wouldn't make sense anyway—if he were *crazy* crazy.'

'Are you saying—'

'He makes some sense, yes,' Keyes said. 'Wiley's goddamn plan makes sense because it seems to be working. He's got the entire Gold Coast terrified, your venerable newspaper included. I saw where the big Teamsters' convention was moved to Atlantic City—'

Mulcahy nodded lugubriously.

'And *The Battle of the Network Bimbos* or whatever—switched from Key Biscayne to Phoenix, of all places.'

'Tucson,' Mulcahy corrected.

'You see my point.'

'It'll wear off,' Mulcahy said. 'Panic always does.'

'Not if the tourists keep disappearing.'

'He's wiring us a new column tomorrow afternoon. I'll give it to Ricky for a good butchering and we'll publish it Sunday. See if *that* doesn't bring the bastard back from his tropical vacation.'

Keyes said, 'If it doesn't, we'll have to think of something else.' He made the *something else* sound ominous.

Mulcahy sighed. 'I'd still hate to see him die.'

Keyes had saved the worst for last. 'Skip's planning something horrendous,' he told Mulcahy. 'I don't know the details, but it's going to happen soon. He said they're going to violate a sacred virgin, whatever that means.'

Mulcahy mulled the possibilities.

'The mayor's wife?'

'Naw, not Skip's type,' Keyes said.

'A nun, then—you think they'd snatch an actual nun?'

'I doubt it, Cab. Skip's very big on symbolism. I think a nun is off the mark.'

'How about a celebrity? Hey, Liza Minnelli is playing the Eden Roc this month.'

'Skip can't stand Liza Minnelli,' Keyes noted.

'There you go!'

'The most sacred virgin in all Miami—Liza Minnelli?'

'Well, shit,' Mulcahy said. 'You got a better idea?'

Brian Keyes did have an idea, but it wasn't one that Mulcahy especially wanted to hear. Keyes hoped that Cab might think of it on his own.

'If you were Skip and you wanted to get the world's attention,' Keyes said, 'you'd try something drastic, something beyond the realm of merely heinous.'

'Don't try to cheer me up.'

'And if you were Wiley,' Keyes went on, 'you'd want—no, you'd *demand*—maximum exposure.'

Mulcahy's chin came off his chest. 'Maximum exposure?'

'We're talking television,' Keyes said. 'Network television.' That's what Skip had promised at Cable Beach.

'Oh no.' Mulcahy sounded like a man whose worst nightmare was coming true.

'Cab, what's the most fantastic spectacle in Miami, the event watched every year by the entire country?'

'The Orange Bowl Parade, of course.'

'And who's the star of the parade?'

'Holy shit,' Mulcahy groaned. He thought: If Brian's right, this is even worse than a nun.

'The Orange Bowl queen.'

'Right,' Keyes said, 'and when is the Orange Bowl Parade?'

'The last night of December!' Mulcahy exclaimed.

'The very last night of December,' said Brian Keyes. '*La Ultima Noche de Diciembre.*'

19

The conference table had been carved into the likeness of a Florida navel orange. A big one. The table filled the Chamber of Commerce with its roundness and orangeness. And at the crown of the orange, where the stem had been hewn, sat the chairman of the Orange Bowl Committee.

'Have a seat, Mr. Keyes,' he said.

Brian Keyes slipped into a leather chair. He couldn't take his eyes off the damn table. Once upon a time it must have been a beautiful slab of white walnut, before they'd varnished it into such a florid atrocity.

'You know most everyone here,' the chairman said.

Keyes scanned familiar faces: the Miami chief of police, the Dade County chief of police, two vice-mayors, a few ruddy Chamber of Commerce types (including the late Sparky Harper's successor), Cab Mulcahy, looking dyspeptic, and, of course, Al García from the newly mobilized Fuego One Task Force. García was sitting at the giant orange's navel.

The air was blue with cigarette smoke and sharp with the aroma of fresh coffee. Everyone had their own ashtray, their own glass of ice water, and their own packet of press clippings about the tourist murders. The mood of the group was funereal.

'Let's start with Sergeant García,' the Orange Bowl chairman said, consulting a legal pad. 'Did I pronounce that correctly?'

'Yes, sir.' The words hissed through clenched teeth. García had promised the chief he'd be polite. The Orange Bowl chairman was a doughy white-haired Florida cracker who was still getting used to the whole idea of Cubans.

'The name of the gang is *Las Noches de Diciembre*, or the Nights of December,' García began. 'It's an extremist organization but

we're not sure about its politics or its motives. We do know
they use murder, kidnapping, torture, and bombing. So far they
haven't asked for ransom or anything else. All they seem to want
is publicity. Their targets are mainly tourists, although we think
they also whacked Mr. B. D. Harper.'

'Whacked?' said the chairman.

'Murdered,' Keyes explained.

'Yes, murdered,' Al García said, 'with a capital M. These bozos
mean business.'

'Bozos?' the chairman said tentatively, glancing around the
table.

'The bad guys,' Keyes explained.

'*Las Noches*,' García said.

That was the extent of García's formal presentation. He hated
meetings like this; they reminded him of *Sesame Street*. García
took off his tinted reading glasses and fished in his pockets for
a cigarette.

The Orange Bowl man cleared his throat and said: 'Sergeant,
do we know exactly who these people are?'

'Some of them.'

García took his time with the Bic lighter.

'The gang has at least four members. A white male, mid-thirties,
identity unknown.' García gave a sideways glance toward Keyes.
'There is a young Seminole Indian named Tigertail. The bomber,
the one who did the Palmetto Country Club job—he's an old
acquaintance. A Cuban right-winger named Jesús Bernal.'

'How do you spell that?' the chairman asked, pen poised over
the legal pad.

'J-e-s-ú-s,' García said impatiently.

'Oh. Just like *our* Jesus, only pronounced different.'

'Yeah,' García said. 'And the last name is B-e-r-n-a-l.'

'What does that mean?' the chairman asked. 'In English.'

'It means "Jesús Bernal," ' García grumbled. 'It's his fucking
name, that's all.'

The Dade County police chief looked sick to his stomach.

García said, 'The fourth suspect you all know. His name is
Daniel Wilson, AKA Viceroy.'

'Oh no,' said the chairman. 'One of the Dolphins.'

'Old number thirty-one,' one of the vice-mayors lamented.

Everyone at the orange table was a big football fan, and the mention of Viceroy Wilson's name ignited a paroxysm of nostalgia.

'It's hard to understand,' the chairman said sadly. 'Our town was very good to that boy.'

Brian Keyes didn't need the NAACP to tell him there were no black faces sitting at the orange table.

'Well,' García said. 'Mr. Wilson apparently has a beef against society. A serious beef. They all do.'

'Which one is *El Fuego?*' somebody asked.

'Don't know,' García replied.

'What does that mean, *El Fuego?*' the chairman asked.

'The Fire. The Flame. Take your pick.' García was annoyed. He hadn't come to teach Spanish 101.

'When can you arrest these men?' the chairman demanded.

'When I find 'em.' García motioned toward Cab Mulcahy. 'There'll be a story in tomorrow's newspaper that ID's the three known suspects and asks for the public's help in locating them. We sent over some mug shots this morning with Mr. Bloodworth.'

'We're running the pictures,' Mulcahy said, 'on the front page.'

'That'll help,' García said. 'But somehow I don't think these guys are going to sit still and let us find them. I think we're going to have to wait till they appear. And they *will* appear. Mr. Keyes here is a private investigator, a pretty good one. As you know, he was abducted by *Las Noches* a couple of weeks ago and roughed up pretty good. Brian, tell 'em the good news.'

Keyes said, 'We have reason to believe that they plan to kidnap the Orange Bowl queen.'

Everyone at the table sat back in their chairs like they'd been punched in the chest. There was plenty of nervous whispering.

'That's the craziest stunt I ever heard,' said somebody in a bright blazer. Actually, several of the men wore identical bright blazers. The blazers were orange.

'We're taking this threat very seriously,' interjected the Dade County police chief, always jittery among civic-leader types.

'We think it's going to happen during the parade,' Brian Keyes said, touching off another round of white-establishment gasping.

'Good Lord!'

'They're going to kidnap the Orange Bowl queen in the middle of the parade?'

'On national goddamn TV? In front of Jane fucking Pauley?'

'And Michael Landon?'

''Fraid so,' Al García said.

Jane Pauley and Michael Landon were scheduled to host the King Orange Jamboree Parade from an elevated booth on Biscayne Boulevard. Jane Pauley and Michael Landon were big celebrities, but García tapped his cigarette ashes all over the orange walnut to let everyone know he didn't give a shit about that. Brian Keyes admired the way García had taken over the meeting from the guys in the blazers.

One of the vice-mayors turned to Keyes and said: 'You've met these people. What do you think—would they listen to reason?'

'Doubtful,' said Keyes. 'Very doubtful.' If necessary he was prepared to tell them what happened to Ida Kimmelman, just so they'd give up the idea of trying to bargain with *El Fuego*.

'Mr. Keyes,' a vice-mayor said, 'what is it they want?'

'They want us to leave,' Keyes said.

'All of us,' García added, 'from Palm Beach to Key West.'

'I don't understand,' the vice-mayor said.

'They want Florida back,' Keyes said, 'the way it was.'

'The way it was *when?*'

'When it wasn't fucked up with so many people,' García said.

The table erupted in snorts and sniggering, and the men in the blazers seemed to shake their heads gravely in syncopation. 'Why doesn't this kind of shit ever happen to Disney World?' one of them said mournfully.

The Orange Bowl chairman decided he'd heard enough dire news from the private eye and the rude detective, so he turned to the police chiefs for encouragement.

'Gentlemen, surely you're not just going to sit and wait for these outlaws to show up and disrupt the parade. They must be arrested as soon as possible, before New Year's Eve. It's bad enough that the press already knows about them.'

'It's pretty tough to keep the lid on mass murder,' remarked the Miami police chief. 'God knows we've tried.'

'We're doing all we can to find these people,' added the Dade County police chief. 'We've got every available detective working the case, but it's tough. Especially around Christmas. Half the department's on leave.'

The Orange Bowl chairman said grumpily, 'I don't want your excuses. I want to hear exactly what you're doing to catch these killers!'

The police chiefs turned to Al García, who'd been waiting patiently for the ball to bounce back his way.

'Right now we've got six undercover guys in Little Havana looking for Jesús Bernal,' García said. 'We've got eight more over in Liberty City searching for Viceroy Wilson. The Indian—well, he's a problem. Looks like he just disappeared off the planet. Anyhow, we got plenty of reward money out on the street—just how much, I can't say, but it's more than my whole damn pension. We've doubled the patrols at every big South Florida tourist attraction—the Seaquarium, Ocean World, Six Flags, the racetracks, the beaches. There was a rumor that the Monkey Jungle might be next so we've got a sniper team waiting upwind. What's more, we got choppers and airboats searching the Glades for *El Fuego*'s camp. We even hired our own Indian guide.'

A nearsighted Miccosukee, García noted silently, but he was better than nothing.

One of the vice-mayors suggested that warnings be posted in all the major tourist hotels.

'Are you out of your mind?' screeched Sparky Harper's Chamber of Commerce successor. 'Are you *trying* to cause panic?'

'No one would panic,' the vice-mayor said defensively, 'if the warnings were worded properly.'

'Perhaps in small type,' the chairman suggested.

'And perhaps in Chinese,' said Al García.

The chairman glowered. 'Sergeant, you don't seem to understand what's at stake here.'

'Human lives,' the detective said, raising his hands. 'That's all,
far as I'm concerned.'

'It's much more than that,' the Orange Bowl chairman snapped.
'NBC is here! Let's not forget that. And let's not forget the theme
of this year's parade: "Tropical Tranquility." '

Brian Keyes desperately looked across the table at Cab Mulcahy.
The managing editor's eyelids closed slowly, like a dying iguana's.

'Look,' García said, 'you guys have to put on a parade and I
have to solve murders. Maybe even prevent 'em, if possible. So
listen real good 'cause here's the plan: we're gonna have cops
crawling all over Biscayne Boulevard on New Year's Eve. We're
gonna have the Orange Bowl queen so completely surrounded
by police that you might as well paint a badge on her goddamn
float. I don't care what it looks like on television. Fuck NBC.
Fuck Jane Pauley. Fuck Alf Landon.'

'*Michael* Landon,' Keyes whispered.

'Him, too.'

The Orange Bowl chairman looked like he'd have killed for a
Maalox. He said, 'Sergeant, that's the worst plan I ever heard. It
would be catastrophe, image-wise.'

'I agree,' said Sparky Harper's successor.

'This is not a military parade,' scoffed another Chamber of
Commerce man.

'Now, wait a minute,' said one of the orange-blazer guys.
'Maybe we can compromise. Suppose we have the police wave
batons and march in lockstep behind the queen's float! I'd say
that would look mighty darn impressive. And no one would
suspect a thing.'

'How about screw the batons,' said Al García.

'Then plainclothes,' suggested the Dade County police chief.

'Maybe,' García said.

'And have them hiding in the crowd,' the Orange Bowl chairman said. 'Not in the blessed parade.'

'Won't work,' Keyes said. 'I've been stuck in that crowd before,
when I covered the parade for the *Sun*. You can't move—it's like
acres of human taffy. Something happens and it'd take you five
minutes to reach the float, and that's too long.'

The Orange Bowl chairman was not persuaded. He scrunched his blackberry eyes and said, 'There will be no police marching in this parade! We're selling Tropical Tranquility, not *Dragnet.*'

'Okay, if that's the way you want it,' García said. 'How about we just stash a midget with a MAC-10 underneath the queen's gown?'

'Al, please,' groaned the Dade County police chief.

'No one would notice a thing,' García said mischievously, 'except maybe the midget.'

'Don't you have another plan?' pleaded one of the blazers.

'Yeah, matter of fact, I do.' García winked at Brian Keyes. 'I sure do.'

Skip Wiley's Christmas column arrived from Nassau by telex on Saturday, December 22.

Cab Mulcahy read it carefully before he summoned Ricky Bloodworth to his office.

'You've been doing a fine job on the terrorist story,' Mulcahy said. This was a shameless lie, but Mulcahy had no choice. Bloodworth was a sucker for phony compliments.

'Thanks, Cab,' he said. 'Did you hear? *Time* magazine called.'

'Really.'

'Yup. Wanted all my clips on *Las Nachos.*'

'*Las* Noches,' Mulcahy corrected.

'Right. But isn't that great? About *Time* magazine?'

'Terrific,' Cab Mulcahy said, thinking: Does this chowderhead really believe *Time* magazine wants to hire him?

'Ricky, I need your help.'

Bloodworth's squirrelly features furrowed. 'Sure, Cab, anything at all.'

'I got this column from Skip Wiley'—Mulcahy waved the telex—'and, frankly, it's not up to par.'

Ricky Bloodworth didn't say anything immediately, but his eyes brightened with an it's-too-good-to-be-true look.

'You want to substitute one of mine!'

'Not exactly,' Mulcahy said.

'I've already got a Christmas column worked up,' Bloodworth

persisted. 'Christmas in Palm Beach. I interviewed Rose Kennedy's butler. It's a nice little story, Cab. Rose Kennedy bought the butler a Chevrolet last Christmas, and you know what he got for her? You'll never guess.'

'Probably not.'

'Two tickets to *Torch Song Trilogy*.'

'Ricky . . .'

'Don't you think that's a good Christmas story?'

'Very moving, but not precisely what I had in mind.'

God forgive me, thought Cab Mulcahy as he handed Wiley's column to Ricky Bloodworth.

'I want you to punch up Skip's piece,' Mulcahy said. 'Really make it sing.'

Bloodworth skimmed the column warily. 'Geez, Cab, I don't know about this.'

'Do it as a favor,' Mulcahy said, 'for me.'

'But what's Skip going to say?'

'Let me worry about that.'

'He can get pretty nasty, Cab. He punched me once,' Bloodworth said, 'in the groin area.'

'Skip punched you?'

Bloodworth nodded. 'He said I burned one of his sources.'

'Did you?'

'It was a misunderstanding. I didn't know the guy was off-the-record. Anyway, he gave me a helluva quote.'

'So,' Mulcahy said, 'you printed his name in the story.'

'Right.'

'What happened?'

'I think the guy got fired.'

'I see.'

'And possibly indicted,' Bloodworth said.

'Hmmm.' Mulcahy thought: When it's all over, I'm getting rid of this asshole. Send him up to the Okeechobee bureau to cover Cucumber Jubilees for the rest of his life.

'The whole thing was just a misunderstanding, but Skip was totally irrational about it. He blamed me for everything.'

'Did he now?' Mulcahy's ulcer was shooting electric messages.

Bloodworth said, 'The point is, I don't want Skip to go on the warpath again. He's a violent man.'

'Ricky, let me worry about it. Just take a crack at the column, all right?'

It had arrived as a lovely little piece, one of Wiley's traditional holiday tearjerkers. It began like this:

> Rollie Artis rowed out to sea last Thursday dawn.
>
> You could watch him from Cable Beach, paddling out Nassau harbor, his thick black arms flashing at the oars.
>
> Rollie went to hunt for conchs, which was his livelihood, as it was his father's. And, as his father, Rollie Artis was a splendid diver with strong lungs and sharp eyes and an instinct for finding the shellfish beds.
>
> But on Thursday the winds were high and the water was ferocious, and the other conch divers had warned Rollie not to try it.
>
> 'But I got to,' he had said. 'If I don't go fishin', there be no Christmas for my babies this year.'
>
> At dusk Rollie's wife Clarisse waited on the dock behind the Straw Market; waited, as she always did, for the sight of the bright wooden skiff.
>
> But Rollie Artis never returned. The next morning the seas calmed and the other fishermen searched for their friend. Not a trace was found. A few of the men were old enough to remember that the same thing had happened to Rollie's father, on another winter's day. An act of God, the old divers said; what else could explain such a tragic irony?
>
> Yesterday, at Rollie's house in Queen's Park, Clarisse put up a yule tree and sang to her two small children. Christmas carols. And the song of a fisherman.

Ricky Bloodworth took Wiley's column to his desk and slaughtered it. It took less than an hour. Cab Mulcahy was surprised at Bloodworth's aptitude for turgidity; it came naturally to the kid.

This, unedited, is what he brought back:

The Bahamas Coast Guard has some real explaining to do.

Nassau fisherman Rollie Artis disappeared from sight last Thursday and nobody except his fishing pals seem to give a hoot.

In our country, Artis would have been the object of a massive air-and-sea rescue effort. But in the Bahamas, nobody lifts the first helicopter. Is it money? Manpower? Equipment? Makes you wonder where all those tourist tax dollars are going—especially when you consider what they're gouging for a decent hotel room these days on Paradise Island.

It also makes you wonder about a supposedly modern government that fails to enforce basic safety regulations for boaters. If a law had forced Rollie Artis to carry life jackets, he might be alive today. And if his boat had been properly equipped with an outboard motor, he might have made it back to port.

He might have been home for Christmas.

Ever since its independence the Bahamas has been telling the world community what a prosperous advanced nation it has become. Well, it's time to start acting like one. It's time this little country, which so loves rich foreigners, took an equal interest in the fate of its own people—especially the poor and feckless.

Cab Mulcahy nearly gnawed through his upper lip as he read Ricky's rewrite.

'I thought Skip was being a little too sentimental,' Bloodworth explained. 'I think he really missed the big picture.'

'Yes,' Mulcahy said pensively. 'You've turned a sentimental anecdote about a missing fisherman into a blistering indictment of a friendly foreign government.'

'Exactly,' Bloodworth said proudly. 'The column's got some guts to it now.'

'Guts.'

'Cab, isn't that what you wanted?'

'Oh yes. This is perfect.'

'You know,' Bloodworth said, 'normally I'd ask for a byline on the column, since I rewrote it and all. But under the circumstances, I think I'd like to leave my name off. Just keep it our secret.'

'Smart move,' Mulcahy said.

'Otherwise Skip might get the wrong idea.'

'I understand.'

'Because if he gets upset—'

'I told you, I'll handle it. Don't worry.'

'Thanks, Cab.'

Forty minutes after Richard L. Bloodworth left, Mulcahy had not moved from his desk. He looked rumpled and dispirited.

The city editor strolled in and said, 'I hear Ricky's polished up Wiley's column.'

Listlessly Mulcahy handed it to him.

The city editor didn't know what to say. He was the one who'd always said Bloodworth showed promise. Consequently, he felt duty-bound to offer something positive.

'Well,' the city editor said, not taking his eyes off the page, 'Ricky certainly doesn't pull any punches, does he?'

'He's an insensitive cretin. A menace.'

'He's a pretty good police reporter, Cab.'

'I never said he wasn't.'

'So what do you want me to do?'

'Smooth the wrinkles and run it Monday.'

'But that's Christmas Eve,' the city editor said. 'I thought we were using it Christmas Day.'

'I refuse to do that to our readers,' Mulcahy said. 'Not on Christmas.'

'But what'll I run in Wiley's slot Christmas Day?'

'I don't know,' Mulcahy said. 'A prayer would be nice.'

20

The Shivers family lived in a beautiful old home next to a golf course in Coral Gables. It was a two-story house, white Florida stucco with red barrel-tile roof. An ancient ficus tree cloaked the front lawn. In the driveway were a BMW, a Lincoln, and a new Volkswagen. Brian Keyes parked behind the VW.

A short man with a fresh tan and a pointy chin answered the door. He was trim, almost youthful, and dressed stem-to-stern in L. L. Bean. He definitely belonged to the BMW.

'Reed Shivers,' he said with a collegiate handshake. 'Come in, Mr. Keyes.'

They sat in an elegant living room with plenty of soft camel furniture. In one corner stood a tall, woodsy-smelling Christmas tree; some of its ornaments were made of blown glass.

'Pumpkin!' Reed Shivers called. 'Come here!'

At first Brian Keyes thought Shivers might be shouting to a pet beagle.

'My daughter,' Shivers said. 'She'll be down in a minute, I'm sure. Would you like coffee?'

'Thanks,' Keyes said. 'No sugar.'

'Not in this house,' Shivers said. 'We watch our diets. You'll see for yourself.'

Shivers poured the coffee from a silver pot.

'So you're a private detective.'

'Yes,' Keyes said restlessly.

'I'm a tax lawyer, myself.'

'So I heard.'

Shivers waited, thinking the private eye would ask about what it's like to be an important tax attorney in Miami. Keyes sipped at his coffee and said nothing.

'I'm just curious,' Shivers said. 'How much money do private investigators make?'

'At least a million a year,' Keyes said. 'Sometimes two million. I lose track.'

Reed Shivers whistled. 'Wow! You've got good shelters, I presume.'

'The best.'

'Oil, right?'

'Concrete.'

'Hmmm-mmm,' said Reed Shivers.

Keyes wondered how this clown ever made it through Yale Law.

'Pumpkin pie!' Shivers hollered again. 'I don't know what's keeping her, Mr. Keyes.'

'Before your daughter gets here, I'd like to offer some advice.'

'Certainly.'

'Don't let her ride that float in the Orange Bowl Parade.'

'You're joking.'

'Not at all,' Keyes said. 'The people who've made this threat are very violent. And ingenious. No one knows what they might do.'

'Sergeant García said it was a kidnapping plot.'

'It's a bit more complicated than that.'

'You think they might try to harm Kara Lynn?'

'It's very possible,' Keyes said.

'But there'll be cops all over the place!'

Keyes put down his coffee cup, aiming for a linen doily. 'Mr. Shivers, I just want you to be aware of the risks. The risks are substantial.'

Reed Shivers looked annoyed. 'Some risk. An Injun, a Cuban, and a washed-up spade ballplayer. Don't tell me a hundred well-armed policemen can't stop a bunch of losers like that!'

'Mr. Shivers, losers get lucky. If one nut can shoot the damn President in Dealey Plaza, a whole gang of nuts can sure as hell snatch your precious little Pumpkin off Biscayne Boulevard.'

'Shhhh.'

Kara Lynn Shivers stood at the French doors.

'Sugar doll! Come here and meet Mr. Keyes.'

Reed Shivers whispered: 'Isn't she spectacular?'

She was. She wore tight jeans, white sneakers, and a gray Miami Hurricanes sweatshirt. Kara Lynn Shivers greeted Brian Keyes with an expert smile. It was one of the best smiles he'd seen in a long time.

'So you're my bodyguard,' she said.

'It wasn't my idea,' Keyes said.

'I can think of worse assignments,' Reed Shivers said with a locker-room wink.

Keyes said, 'Kara Lynn, I'm going to tell you what I told your dad: I think you ought to drop out of the parade next week. I think you're in serious danger.'

Kara Lynn looked at her father.

'I already told him,' Shivers said. 'It's out of the question.'

'Do I get a choice?'

'Of course, buttercup.'

'Then I want to hear what Mr. Keyes has to say.'

Kara Lynn Shivers was quite beautiful, which wasn't surprising; one did not get to be Orange Bowl queen by looking like a woodchuck. What did surprise Brian Keyes was the wit in Kara Lynn's gray-green eyes and the steel in her voice. He had expected a chronic case of airheadedness but found just the opposite. Kara Lynn seemed very self-assured for nineteen, and canny—light-years ahead of her old man. Still, Keyes was wary. He had stopped falling in love with beauty queens when he was twenty-six.

'One reason Sergeant García asked me to keep an eye on you,' Keyes said, 'is because I'm the only person who's seen the terrorists face-to-face. At least, I'm the only one still alive. They're treacherous and unpredictable. And clever—I can't over-emphasize that. These guys are damn clever. Now, your father's right: there will be scores of plainclothes police all up and down the parade route. You won't see them, and neither will the folks watching on TV, but they'll be there, with guns. Let's hope *Las Noches* know it; then maybe they'll think twice before trying anything.'

'Dad, suppose something happens,' Kara Lynn said.

'We pay the ransom, of course. I've already called Lloyd's about a kidnap policy and arranged the very best—the same one all the top multinationals have on their executives.'

'That's not what I meant,' Kara Lynn said sharply. 'Suppose there's a shoot-out during the parade, with all those little kids in the crowd. Somebody might get killed.'

'Now, darling, these police are expert marksmen.'

'Mr. Shivers,' Keyes said, 'you've been watching way too much TV.'

Kara Lynn started to smile, then caught herself.

'In the first place, this gang doesn't ask for ransoms. They don't need your money,' Keyes said. 'And your daughter's absolutely right about the shooting. Once it starts, somebody's going to die. As for all those cops being crack shooters, I guarantee you that half of them couldn't hit the SS *Norway* with a bazooka at ten paces.'

'Thank you, Mr. Keyes,' Reed Shivers said acidly, 'for your reassurance.'

'I'm not paid to give pep talks.'

'Dad—' Kara Lynn said.

'Sweetie, it's the *Orange Bowl Parade*. Forty million people will be watching, including all the top talent agents in Hollywood and New York. Jane Pauley's going to be there. In person.'

Kara Lynn knew the forty-million figure was a crock.

'Dad, it's a parade, not a moon shoot.'

Reed Shivers' voice quavered. 'It's the most important moment of your whole life!'

'And maybe the last,' Keyes said. 'But what the hell. It'd be worth it just to see little Pumpkin's face in *People* magazine, right?'

'Shut up, you creep!' Pink in the face, Shivers bounced to his feet and assumed a silly combative stance. With one hand Brian Keyes shoved him back into the folds of the camel sofa.

'Don't be an asshole,' Keyes said. 'This is your daughter's life we're talking about.'

Reed Shivers was so angry his body seemed to twitch. It was not an image the L. L. Bean people would have chosen for the spring catalog.

'If it's so damn dangerous,' Shivers rasped, 'why won't they just cancel the parade?'

Keyes chuckled. 'You know Miami better than that. Christ himself could carry the cross down Biscayne Boulevard and they'd still run the Orange Bowl Parade, right over his body.'

'Mr. Keyes,' Kara Lynn said, 'can I talk to my father for a minute, alone?'

Keyes walked out to the game room, which was walled in chocolate-brown cork. It was Sunday so there was nothing but football on the wide-screen television: Keyes turned it off. He counted sixteen golfing trophies in one maple bookcase. On the bar was a framed color photograph of Reed Shivers with his arm around Bob Hope. In the picture Shivers looked drunk and Bob Hope looked taxidermied.

Keyes went to the billiard table and glumly racked up the balls. Guarding the girl had been García's idea; Keyes wasn't thrilled about it but he'd taken the job anyway. With Skip Wiley out of reach in the Bahamas there wasn't much else to do. No fresh tourist corpses had popped up and even the Trifecta Massacre had turned into a dead end, the bomber having made a clean getaway. Now it was a waiting game, and Kara Lynn was the bait.

Keyes scratched the cue ball just as she walked in. She closed the door behind her.

'Look, don't get mad, but I've decided to go ahead and be in the parade.'

'Swell,' Keyes said. 'I hope your father knows probate.'

'You're really trying to scare me. Well, I'm scared, okay? I honestly am.' She really was.

'Then don't be stubborn.' Keyes propped the cue stick in a corner.

'Look,' Kara Lynn said, 'if I drop out, they'll just get somebody else, one of the runners-up. Let me tell you, Mr. Keyes, some of those girls would ride in that parade no matter what. They'd *pay* to do it. So if I quit, it won't change a thing. The Nights of December will still have somebody to kidnap, or try to. It might as well be me.'

'Besides,' Keyes said, 'it'll make great television.'

Kara Lynn glared at him. 'You think I like this whole setup?'

'Don't you want to be a star?'

'I'd much rather be alive.' Kara Lynn shrugged. 'My dad wants to see his little girl on NBC. Let him have his moment, Mr. Keyes. He says it's safe.'

'Your dad's a real piece of work.'

'I told you not to get mad.'

Keyes smiled in spite of himself. It wasn't easy, being a tough guy. 'Okay, I'm not mad.'

'Good.' Kara Lynn went to the bar and fixed herself a club soda. She tossed a cold can of Coors at Keyes. He caught it one-handed.

'I've never had a bodyguard before,' she said. 'How does this work?'

'Well, for the next week or so, it's just you and me, with some discreet assistance from Dade County's finest. The most important thing is that you're never alone when you're out of this house. We want the bad guys to see that you're not a sitting duck, that you've got protection—though I use the term loosely. You want to go shopping, I'll carry the groceries. You want to play tennis, I'll carry the rackets. You want to go to the beach, I'll carry the Coppertone.'

'What if I want to go on a date?'

'No dates.'

'Says who?'

'The eminent Orange Bowl Committee. They would prefer that you not go anywhere at night. I think that's a good idea.'

'Oh, just a great idea.'

'Your boyfriend can come by the house to visit. Watch TV. Play Trivial Pursuit. Smoke dope. Doesn't matter to me.'

'Can we make love?'

Keyes reddened. 'If you're quiet about it,' he said. 'I need my sleep.'

Kara Lynn laughed. 'I'm just kidding. I don't have a boyfriend; we broke up after I won this stupid contest. Mr. Keyes—'

'It's Brian, please. I get a new gray hair every time a pretty girl calls me mister.'

'All right . . . Brian, will you carry a gun?'

'Sometimes. And a nifty Dick Tracy police radio.'

'What kind of gun?' asked Kara Lynn.

'Never mind.' It was a Browning nine-millimeter. Keyes hated the damn thing. The holster bled all over his shirts.

'Can I ask you something?' she said. 'I don't want to hurt your feelings, but when they told me about a bodyguard I expected somebody . . .'

'A little larger?'

'Yeah. More imposing.'

'Imposing is my specialty,' Keyes said. 'But you want to know why they didn't send a big gorilla cop instead of a skinny private eye.'

Kara Lynn nodded. Her eyes were just dynamite.

Keyes said, 'The eminent Orange Bowl Committee felt that it would be a catastrophe, image-wise, if it became known that the Orange Bowl queen was under police protection. The eminent Orange Bowl Committee felt that the scoundrels of the press would seize upon such a nugget and blow it way out of proportion. They feared that surrounding a beauty queen with heavily armed police would create the wrong kind of publicity. Detract from their splendid program. Make people too scared to come to the parade. So the civic fathers decided to hide the cops and hire a freelance undercover baby-sitter. Me.'

'Unbelievable,' Kara Lynn said. 'Those jerks.'

'I know you'd feel safer with Clint Eastwood,' Keyes said. 'So would I.'

'You'll do fine.'

'Your dad doesn't like me.'

'But I do,' Kara Lynn said, 'and I'm the queen, remember? When do you start?'

'My stuff's in the car.'

'The gun, too?'

'Would you forget about the gun!'

'As long as *you* don't forget whose adorable little ass is on the line here.' Kara Lynn patted her blue-jeaned rump. 'Mine! I know you're no Dirty Harry, but promise me that you actually know how to use the gun, Brian. Promise me that much, please?'

*

The next day was Christmas Eve, and Skip Wiley assembled three-fourths of the Nights of December in his rented villa near Lyford Cay, on the outskirts of Nassau.

Tommy Tigertail had elected to stay deep in the Everglades, tending to bingo business, but Jesús Bernal and Viceroy Wilson had jumped at the chance to get out of South Florida, particularly since their photographs had been published on the front page of the Miami *Sun*. To be sure, neither picture bore much resemblance to the two men sitting on Skip Wiley's sundeck. The photograph of Jesús Bernal with a Snidely Whiplash mustache had been taken in 1977 after his arrest for illegal possession of a surface-to-air missile. He looked about fourteen years old. The picture of Viceroy Wilson was no better; it actually had been clipped from an old Miami Dolphins yearbook. Wilson was decked out in his aqua jersey and shoulder pads, pretending to stiff-arm an invisible tackler. He was wearing the same phony scowl that all the bubblegum companies want football players to wear in their pictures; Viceroy Wilson's real scowl was much more effective.

No photograph of the Indian had appeared in the Miami media because no photograph was known to exist.

Skip Wiley didn't seem too concerned about the mug shots as he cracked jokes and handed out cold Heinekens to his visitors.

Viceroy Wilson peered over the rims of his sunglasses. 'How come the papers don't mention your name?' he asked Wiley.

'Because Mr. Brian Keyes apparently is covering up for me. Don't ask me why, boys. A misguided act of friendship, I suppose.'

'The cops searched my mother's house this morning,' Jesús Bernal blurted angrily. 'My sister's house, last night. They're all over Little Havana, like rats, those cops.'

'An occupational hazard,' Wiley said. 'You should be used to it by now.'

'But they broke down her door!' Bernal cried. 'Fucking animals. This guy García, he's going to pay. "Scum of the earth," he called us. It was in the papers. *Scum of the earth!* Cubans know how to deal with traitors like that.'

'Here we go again,' Viceroy Wilson said. 'The Masked Avenger.'

'You shut up!'

Wilson laughed and attacked a plate of johnnycake.

'Go easy on the bread,' Wiley said. 'Remember, you've got to drop ten pounds this week.'

Viceroy Wilson shoveled a thick slice into his cheeks. 'And who the fuck are you,' he said, spitting crumbs, 'Don Shula?'

'Aren't we testy this morning? You boys must have had a bumpy flight.' Wiley festively stacked the empty green beer bottles. 'I know just the thing to cheer you up. Jenna's doing a plum pudding!'

'Count me in,' said Viceroy Wilson.

'And I think there might be a little something for both of you under the Christmas tree.'

'No shit?' Jesús Bernal said brightly. 'Well, God bless *Las Noches de Diciembre*, each and every one.'

But the Nights of December never got to open their gifts. Hitting the newsstands of Nassau that afternoon was the Miami *Sun*, featuring Skip Wiley's doctored Christmas column. Within thirty minutes the prime minister himself called an emergency cabinet meeting and declared that the story about the fisherman Rollie Artis was 'an insult to the sovereignty and self-respect of the Bahamas.' The minister of home affairs immediately drafted a deportation order, to which each cabinet member affixed his signature. At approximately six P.M., just as Jenna's plum pudding ignited, six uniformed Bahamian immigration officers burst into Wiley's palatial manor house and ordered him out of the commonwealth forever. No amount of proffered cash or traveler's checks would change their minds.

It wasn't until much later, on the midnight flight to Haiti, that Jenna got up the courage to show Skip Wiley what had been done to his column.

'Bloodworth!' he gasped. 'That wretched nematode!'

'It sure was a mean trick,' Jenna allowed.

'Sacrilege!' Wiley said, his brown eyes smoldering.

'But clever,' Jenna remarked. 'Wouldn't you say?'

'Well, now it's our turn to be clever,' Wiley said, slipping the column into his jacket. 'Jenna, as soon as we get to Port-au-

Prince, send a message to Tommy back at camp. Have him Federal Express me the Nielsens from last New Year's Eve. And the Arbitrons, too, if he can get his hands on 'em.'

'What now, Skip?'

'Don't worry, darling, the strategy stays the same.' Wiley patted her knee. 'Full speed ahead.'

21

From a bare-bulb warehouse off Miami Avenue, Jesús Bernal placed a phone call to the secret headquarters of the First Weekend in July Movement.

'*El Comandante, por favor*,' he said.

From the other end came thick Cuban voices, the sound of chairs scraping, a door opening. The telephone clanged as if someone had dropped it into a steel drum.

'Hey!' Jesús Bernal said angrily. '*Oye!*'

'*Qué pasa, chico?*' It was the Mixmaster rasp of the *comandante* himself. In his mind's eye Jesús could picture the old bastard sucking on a wet cigar, his strained twisted fingers like a vulture talon clutching the receiver. Jesús Bernal could picture those mean brown eyes, narrowing at the sound of his voice.

'It's me,' Jesús said in Spanish. 'Have you seen the newspapers, *Comandante?*'

'*Sí.*'

Proudly Jesús said, 'I am famous.'

'So is Ronald McDonald.'

'I was expelled from the Bahamas,' Jesús declared.

'For what? Stealing coconuts?'

Jesús began to fume. 'It is important work.'

'It is girl's play.'

'I bombed a Miami policeman!'

'You bombed his fucking feet,' the *comandante* said. 'I read the papers, *chico*. All these years and you are still the worst bomber I ever saw. You couldn't blow up a balloon.'

After a pause, the old man said. 'Tell me, who is this *El Fuego?*'

'I am *El Fuego*,' Jesús answered.

The *comandante* cackled. 'You are a shit-eating liar,' he said, again in Spanish.

Jesús grimaced. 'All right. *El Fuego* is a powerful Anglo. He is also a crazy man, he wants to give Florida back to the Indians and the raccoons. He recruited me for the dirty work.'

'And to write the communiqués.'

'*Claro.*'

'It is the one talent you seem to have.'

Jesús Bernal smiled hopefully. There was a long silence on the other end. He heard the sound of a match striking wood; the old man's damn cigar had just gone out.

'The FBI has been asking about you,' the *comandante* growled. 'It's a bad idea, you calling me.'

Jesús Bernal swallowed hard. 'I want to come back to the movement. My work here is finished. This organization, it is not disciplined, *Comandante*. There is drug use . . . and liquor. And the crazy man, *El Fuego*, he's always making jokes.'

'I'm not surprised. It is all very funny.'

'Please, *Comandante*, read the papers! Haven't I proven myself?'

'You bombed a fucking golf course,' the old man said.

'A vital strategic target,' Jesús countered.

'*Coño!* A Russian freighter is a strategic target, but a golf course is . . . a goddamn golf course. And these were not Communist soldiers you killed, they were rich Americans. I'm surprised Fidel himself didn't send you a medal.'

By now Jesús was trembling. His voice skipped like a teenager's. He cupped his hand over the mouthpiece so Viceroy Wilson couldn't hear him begging.

'Please, *Comandante*, I've committed many bombings, kidnappings, even murders—all in the name of The Cause. What must I do to convince you to take me back?'

'Do something serious,' the old man said, his chest rattling. 'And do it right.'

Jesús Bernal slammed down the phone and cursed. He returned to the sawhorse where Viceroy Wilson was working, snatched a hammer, and started whaling on a two-by-four. The warehouse was hazy with sawdust and marijuana smoke.

'So you didn't get the job,' Wilson said through a mouthful of nails.

'I thought you didn't understand Spanish,' Bernal snapped.

'In 1977 we had a placekicker named Rivera,' Wilson said. 'From Mexico, I think. Used to give Spanish lessons on the team plane. One Sunday in Kansas City the motherfucker missed four straight field goals inside the thirty and we lost the game. That night a bunch of us got together and called Immigration.'

'You had him arrested?'

'The next day at practice.' Viceroy Wilson shrugged. 'Football's a tough sport, man.'

'So now you're going to tell Wiley I want out.'

'Naw,' Wilson said. 'Not if you stay through New Year's. After that, I don't give a fuck what you do.'

'I'm thinking of starting my own group,' Jesús Bernal confided.

'What you gonna call it?'

'I haven't decided.'

'How about: The Ernesto Cabal Cabal.'

'Go to hell,' said the Cuban, still sensitive on the Ernesto issue.

'This new group,' Viceroy Wilson said, 'what's the mission this time?'

'Invade Havana.'

'Naturally.' With switchblades, no doubt. Viceroy Wilson started hammering again. Every once in a while he'd step back to see how the thing was taking shape.

Tommy Tigertail sat on a blanket in the corner, beneath a somber daguerreotype of Thlocko-Tustenugee, Chief Tiger Tail. Tommy's eyes were open but unfocused; fresh from an Everglades passage, he had only just learned that Pavlov had been shot the week before in a beachfront swimming pool by the Fort Lauderdale SWAT team. Grief had robbed the Indian of all energy, and he had dropped his hammer and sat down in a trance. He feared it would be a night of dreams, when his fingers again would claw the wet bars of the dungeon where his great-great-grandfather had perished. On such nights Tommy's soul wandered, keeping company with his warrior ancestor. Tommy knew what would happen if his soul should not return from its journey by dawn: He would forever become part of his own nightmare, and never awake from it. This was the fate of many anguished Seminoles, whose souls suddenly fled in the night; for Tommy Tigertail, such a death would be infinitely worse than anything the white policemen might do to him.

'Look at that crybaby,' Jesús Bernal said, scowling at the heart-sick Indian. 'Somebody shot his pet lizard.'

'You shut up,' Viceroy Wilson hissed at the Cuban, 'or I'll nail your nuts to your nose.'

Tommy Tigertail was the closest thing to a brother that Viceroy had found in the Nights of December. Between them was an unspoken bond that had nothing to do with the use of the Cadillac; it was a bond of history. In his post-heroin library days Viceroy Wilson had studied the Seminole Wars, and knew that Tommy's people had fought not just to keep their land, but to protect the runaway slaves who had joined them on the Florida savannas. The magnificence of that struggle was not lost on Viceroy Wilson; he knew Tommy would never give him up. Viceroy had never trusted anyone so completely.

Jesús Bernal sensed that it was unwise and perhaps dangerous to make fun of the Indian, so he changed the subject.

'I'm going to show the *comandante* a thing or two,' he said determinedly.

'That's cool,' said Viceroy Wilson, turning back to his work, 'long as you wait till after New Year's.'

'We'll see about that, *negrito*,' Jesús said bravely, after Viceroy Wilson had cranked up the circular saw and could not possibly hear him.

22

Brian Keyes never thought of himself as lonely, but there were times when he wondered where all his friends had gone. As a rule private detectives are not swamped with party invitations and that part Keyes didn't mind; he wasn't a lampshade-and-kazoo type of guy. But there were nights when a phone call from any sociable nonfelon would have been a welcome surprise on the old beeper. It wasn't loneliness, really; aloneness was more like it. Keyes had felt it as soon as he'd quit the *Sun*; it was as if the quintessential noise of life had suddenly shrunk by fifty decibels. On some days the quiet tortured him; the office, the apartment, the stake-outs. Sometimes he wound up talking to the car radio; sometimes the damn thing talked back. Two years away from the *Sun* and Keyes still longed for the peculiar fraternity of the city room. It ruled your whole damn life, the newspaper, and even if it made vulgar cynical bastards out of everybody, at least the bastards were there in the empty times. Day or night you could walk into the *Sun* and find somebody ready to sneak out for a beer or sandwich. These days Keyes ate alone, or with clients so scuzzy he wanted to gag on the corned beef and rye.

Which is why he came to enjoy guarding Kara Lynn Shivers. The first couple days she'd treated him with the same frostiness and suspicion she held for most men, but gradually she had warmed up. The less they talked about the beauty-queen racket, the happier Kara Lynn seemed. She was good company, nothing like Keyes had expected. It seemed a miracle that she had emerged from the cloying parentage of Reed Shivers so independent, unspoiled, and classy. It also was amazing that her sense of humor had survived, as had some soft and thoughtful edges. Talking to Kara Lynn was so easy that Keyes had to remind himself that this was not prom week, it was a serious assignment, and the package did not include true confessions. He was getting paid a small truckload of money to do one job: deliver Kara Lynn Shivers safe, pristine, and magnificent aboard the queen's float.

Two days after Christmas, five days before the big parade, Kara Lynn came downstairs wearing a sassy lemon-yellow tennis skirt and a matching knit vest. She handed Brian Keyes one of her father's expensive boron tennis rackets and said, 'Come on, Marlowe, we're going to the club.'

Keyes wasn't in a clubby mood. He'd spent a second straight morning at the airport, watching Customs in case Wiley tried to slip through. As usual, Miami International was a zoo—and there'd been no sign of Skip.

'I'm beat,' Keyes told Kara Lynn. 'Besides, I'm lousy at tennis.'

'Not with those legs,' Kara Lynn said. 'Now, come on.'

They took her VW. It was only a ten-block ride, a winding circle around the Coral Gables golf course. Keyes drove. In the rearview, two cars back, was a Cadillac Seville with tinted windows. It was the worst tail job Keyes had ever seen—if that's what it was. On an open stretch Keyes coasted the VW and the Caddy backed off by half a mile. Then it turned off and disappeared.

Kara Lynn was very cool; she hadn't turned around once.

'Do you have your own gun?' she asked casually.

'It's in the trunk.'

'There is no trunk.'

'There is too,' Keyes said, 'in the MG.'

'Brilliant,' she said. 'How much did you say they were paying you?'

Keyes gave her a that's-very-funny look.

'Who do you think was following us?'

'Maybe nobody. Maybe the bad guys.'

'They wouldn't try anything now, not before the parade.'

'Who knows,' Keyes said. 'We're dealing with a special brand of fruitcake.' He pulled into the clubhouse parking lot.

Kara Lynn asked, 'How are you going to play tennis in those ratty sneakers?'

'Badly, I'm sure.' The shoes weren't the worst of it. Keyes was wearing raggedy cutoff jeans and a Rolling Stones concert T-shirt.

'Take my arm,' Kara Lynn said, 'otherwise they'll think you're a caddy.'

Keyes dragged himself around the tennis court for a solid hour, volleying like a madman, all speed and no finesse. His stitches throbbed constantly and his right lung was on fire. The only thing that kept him going was the long-legged sight of Kara Lynn rushing the net, her lips set intently, cheeks flushing pink, blond hair shimmering with each step. When it came to tennis, she was a very serious young lady. Nothing fancy, no power to speak of, but clean precise strokes. Tricky, too.

She beat him 6–4, 3–6, 7–6. A drop shot got him. He made a valiant stab, but wound up straddling the net. He was too exhausted to feel embarrassed.

Afterward Kara Lynn led him into the clubhouse lounge. Keyes took a quick survey and concluded that he was the only person in the whole joint without an alligator on his shirt. Even the bartender had one. Keyes thought he'd died and gone to Preppie Heaven.

Several fragrant young men stopped Kara Lynn for a peck on the cheek. Kiss, kiss. Howya doing. Looking great. Bye now. Keyes himself got a few curious stares.

'You ever see *Goodbye, Columbus*?' he said to Kara Lynn when they sat down. 'I feel just like the schmuck in that movie, and you're the Ali MacGraw part.'

'Oh please.'

'It was before your time. Forget about it.'

'I like the Rolling Stones,' Kara Lynn volunteered.

'Yeah?'

'Your T-shirt's pretty pitiful, but the Stones are all right.'

She ordered a club soda. Keyes asked for a draft.

'I was kidding about the shirt,' Kara Lynn said.

'And my sneakers.'

'No, I was serious about the sneakers.' She gave his arm a little pinch. Keyes grinned. He was starting to feel warm and comfortable and incredibly witty. Time to watch out. Book of Jenna, Chapter One.

'Why'd you leave the newspaper?' Kara Lynn asked. Some

weight-lifter-type with an enormous head of curly blond hair waved at her from across the lounge and pointed to his drink. She shook her head no, and turned away.

'You want to join him, it's okay,' Keyes said. 'I'll sit up at the bar.'

'Oh no you won't. Tell me why you quit the newspaper.'

Keyes gulped the beer. 'Because I made a mistake.'

'Everybody makes mistakes.'

'Not big ones. Not in that business.'

'Oh, come on. How bad could it be?'

'The worst.' Keyes set down the mug and leaned forward. 'Let me explain something. Your dad's a bigshot lawyer. If he goofs up, he waltzes into court, files a new motion, and fixes it. The client never knows. If a surgeon screws up, he digs a little deeper, adds a few extra stitches, and makes it all right. In most jobs it's like that—there's always a way out. But what I did, I can't fix. It's done forever. Once the paper rolls off the press, that's it. Sure, you can publish a correction or a bloody apology, but there's no guarantee that the right people will see it. Some folks will only remember what you wrote the first time, and if what you wrote was wrong, that's how they'll remember it.'

'Did you get fired?'

'I resigned. My boss never knew why.'

'You were scared to tell him.'

'No, I was scared to hurt him.'

Kara Lynn twirled the ice cubes in her club soda.

'Do you miss it?'

'Sometimes,' he said, 'I miss the people. Some of the smartest people I know work in that business. And some of the screwiest. That's what happens when you chase the truth for too long; you finally catch up with it and you're never the same. Screwed up for life.' He was thinking of Skip Wiley.

Kara Lynn was a terrific listener. She was *too* good. Keyes wondered if she was petrified with boredom.

But then she said: 'Tell me about being a private eye.'

'One thrill after another: *Mr Keyes, here's two grand. Find out if my wife's sleeping with her psychiatrist. Take some pictures, too.*'

'Still chasing the truth,' said Kara Lynn.

'Yeah. But it's a cheap grimy truth. Gets in your hair, your clothes. Under your goddamn fingernails. I never felt like this when I was a reporter, honest to God.'

'You're pretty unhappy, Brian.'

'That makes two of us, Cinderella.'

'Why, whatever do you mean? I'm the Orange Bowl queen, remember? I've got a thousand-dollar savings bond, a new wardrobe, a singing coach, and a four-year scholarship.' Kara Lynn shook loose her ponytail and struck a haughty profile. 'What more could a girl want?' Then she cracked up laughing.

Keyes laughed too.

The gorilla with the curly blond hair was waving again.

'I think Hercules wants to buy you a drink,' Keyes said.

'Yeah, time to go.' Kara Lynn signed the tab. Keyes didn't feel the least bit odd about it; Reed Shivers would find a way to write it off.

'Do me a favor, Brian.'

'Sure.'

'When we walk out of here, would you hold my hand?'

'Why?'

'Because it's more polite than saying, "fuck off." Which is what I'd like really to tell these jerks, but I can't. Not here at Dad's club.'

As they rose from the table, Keyes tucked the tennis racket under his left arm and put his right arm around Kara Lynn's shoulders. They walked out that way, right past the Old Spice preppies. It felt just fine.

'You're a good sport,' Kara Lynn said when they got to the car, 'and I was right about your legs. You ran me ragged out there.'

Brian Keyes wasn't listening.

The Seville was parked across the street, in the shade of a banyan tree. A thin dark man in an undershirt sat on the fender, drumming his hands on the side of the car. The man wasn't paying attention; he wasn't doing what he'd been told.

'Get in the car,' Keyes said to Kara Lynn. 'The police radio's under the front seat. Try to call García.'

Kara Lynn got in the driver's side of the VW and rolled down the window. 'Where are you going?'

'That's the asshole who stabbed me.'

'Brian—'

But he was already gone, strolling across the parking lot. He looked perfectly calm, a tennis bum on his way home. Kara Lynn could hear him whistling a song. 'Yesterday,' it sounded like. She saw Keyes slip the leather sheath off her father's tennis racket.

'Oh no,' Kara Lynn said.

Jesús Bernal did not recognize Brian Keyes immediately. He wouldn't have been looking for him, anyway. Jesús Bernal's mission was to scout for cops; Skip Wiley had wanted to know if there were policemen assigned to the girl. So far, Bernal hadn't seen the first patrol car; the lunatic Wiley was wrong again, as usual. Bernal was just about ready to call it quits and cruise back to the warehouse when the tennis player ambled up to him.

'Hey, *muchacho*, remember me?'

Bernal looked hard at the boyish face and, after a moment or two, remembered.

But not fast enough.

Keyes swing the tennis racket and hit Jesús Bernal flush in the face. A nicely timed forehand smash. Broke three strings on the racket.

The Cuban's head bounced off the Cadillac's bumper. He landed faceup on the pavement, snorkeling his own blood. The undershirt hung in shreds from the hood ornament.

Keyes bent over Jesús Bernal and whacked him again, this time a solid backhand to the throat. The Cuban kicked his legs and made a sound like a garbage disposal.

'Gggrrrnnnn,' he burbled.

'You should see my serve,' said Brian Keyes.

Kara Lynn Shivers pulled the VW alongside the Cadillac. Keyes got in and she stomped the accelerator.

'God Almighty, you killed him!'

'No such luck. You get hold of the cops?'

'No, the radio—' She was too excited to talk.

'Find a phone booth,' Keyes said.

'Brian, he looked . . . really . . . dead!'

'He wasn't. Not by a long shot. I gotta call García. Find a goddamn phone booth.'

She nodded, and kept nodding, like a dashboard puppy. She was scared as hell.

'Was he one . . . of . . . them?' Kara Lynn spoke in breathless gulps, as if she'd been crying, but she hadn't. Her knuckles were red on the steering wheel.

Keyes touched her arm, felt her flinch.

'Kara Lynn, it'll be all right.' But he was thinking: Maybe this means Wiley's back.

'It's scary,' Kara Lynn said shakily, staring hard at the road ahead. 'It's insane.'

'Honest to God, it'll be all right.'

23

When Sergeant Al García's squad finally got to the country club, all they found beneath the banyan tree were radial tire tracks, a syrupy puddle of blood, and several kernels of corn, which turned out to be human teeth. The police searched all night for the Seville. They roared in convoys through Coral Gables and Little Havana, stopping every Cadillac in sight, rousting every poor sap in an undershirt.

Yet the Fuego One Task Force did not find the injured Jesús Bernal, and by eight o'clock the next morning Al García's phone was ringing off the hook. Reed Shivers. The chief. The Orange Bowl chairman. Ricky Bloodworth. The Chamber of Commerce. Even NBC, for Christ's sake.

García carried three Styrofoam cups of black coffee to his office and locked the door behind him. He dialed the Shivers house and Brian Keyes picked up on the first ring.

'He got away,' the detective said.

'You don't say.'

'Hey, it's not our fault Shirley Temple couldn't figure out the police radio.'

'She was scared stiff,' Keyes said. 'I was on the phone five minutes later. Five lousy minutes.'

'That's all it takes,' García said. 'If it makes you feel any better, the sonofabitch leaked pretty good. He's got to be hurting.'

Hurt or not, it was unimaginable that Jesús Bernal would turn up at a hospital; he was probably out in the Glades drinking Tommy Tigertail's home-brewed medicines. Which meant he was probably going to recover.

Brian Keyes figured Jesús Bernal probably could make a career out of getting revenge.

'Al, they've got to call off the parade.'

'Not in a billion years,' García said.

'But this clinches it—it proves these idiots are serious about taking Kara Lynn. After yesterday they're going to try twice as hard.'

'We'll be ready.' García slugged down the coffee; he figured he'd need a gallon of caffeine to brave the waiting shitstorm.

'How's the queen holding up?' he asked.

'Mildly terrified. All of a sudden she's not sure who's more dangerous, *Las Noches* or me. She wants to call the whole thing off but Daddy's leaning hard. It's been a very lively morning.'

García asked, 'Did you call your Shriner pals up North?'

'Yeah. They're on board.'

'Excellent! Remember, *chico*, not a word to a soul.'

'You got it.'

'The dudes in the orange blazers, they'd have a stroke.'

'Not to mention your badge,' Keyes said.

Jesús Bernal lay shirtless on a blue shag carpet remnant. His eyes were shut and his breath whistled through raw gums. His throat shone purple and swollen. Every once in a while his hands tremored and drew into bony fists. Macho dreaming, Viceroy Wilson thought. Intermittently he checked on Bernal, then went ahead hammering and sawing and drilling as if he were alone in the warehouse, which was no bigger than a garage.

Time was running out. The Indian had sent lumber and palmetto trimmings, but no manpower. Wilson had been working like hell, living on wheat germ milkshakes; he'd dropped five pounds in two days.

The sound of an automobile outside startled him. It wasn't the Seville, either; Wilson knew the hum of the Caddy like he knew his own mother's voice. Stealthily he set down the tools and picked up a sawed-off shotgun. He heard footsteps at the warehouse door. The lock rattled. Wilson brought the gun to his shoulder.

The door opened and Skip Wiley stalked in.

'A little jumpy, aren't we?' he said.

Tommy Tigertail stood behind him.

They stared at Viceroy Wilson until he lowered the sawed-off. Wiley came up and gave him a hug. 'You're doing damn fine,' he said. 'Damn fine.'

Viceroy Wilson was not wild about hugs; a handshake would have sufficed. 'So you're back from the tropics,' he said to Wiley, 'looking tan and tough.'

'Horseshit. I look like hell.' But he didn't. Wiley's face was bronze and his beard was golden-red from the sun. He was wearing a brightly striped soccer jersey with the words 'Cap Haitien' printed across the front pocket.

'D'you join a fucking spa?' Wilson said.

'Hardly.' Wiley stooped over the snoring, sawdust-sprinkled form of Jesús Bernal. 'Looks meaner with no teeth, doesn't he?'

'Sorry sack of shit,' Wilson said.

'I know, I know. That's Item One on the agenda.'

Skip Wiley removed his panama hat and prowled the small warehouse, examining Viceroy Wilson's creation in the bleak light of the bare sixty-watt bulb. Tommy Tigertail stood in a corner, his features unreadable in the shadow. Viceroy Wilson popped a can of Heineken and waited for the fun to begin; he needed a breather, anyway.

Wiley sat down on a sawhorse and folded his arms. 'Wake him up,' he told the Indian.

Tommy prodded Jesús Bernal with the hard toe of his boot. The Cuban moaned and rolled over, burying his face in the crook of an elbow. Tommy poked him again, decisively. Jesús sat up snuffling and rubbing his eyes. His fractured nose was the shape of a question mark and the rest of his face was a grid: the perfect imprint of a Spalding tennis racket.

'How you feeling?' Skip Wiley asked.

'Thiddy,' the Cuban said. 'Damn thiddy.'

'I'll get you some new teeth,' Wiley promised.

'Manks a mot.' Jesús sounded like he was talking through a mouthful of marbles.

Wiley clasped his hands evangelically. 'Well,' he said, 'I'm delighted we're all here. The rainbow coalition, together again. And only four days left!'

'Mank God,' muttered Jesús Bernal. 'Idth aah turding duh thid.' *It's all turning to shit*, is what Jesús was trying to say.

Skip Wiley took a loud breath and stared down at the dusty floor. All at once the cheeriness seemed to drain from his expression; his mouth, always on the verge of smiling, suddenly turned thin and severe; the merry brown eyes shrank and turned dull. The transformation was so palpable and so volcanic that even Jesús Bernal was moved to silence.

'The reason I came back,' Wiley said somberly, 'is to prevent disaster. To save us from international ridicule.'

As he looked up, the pale light snared his chin, the ridge of his long nose, the blond crest of his forehead. The others were struck by Wiley's flickering visage. He reminded Jesús Bernal of a priest in the confessional, and Viceroy Wilson of a Basin Street scat singer. And when Tommy Tigertail looked at Wiley, he was reminded of an animal spirit he had once encountered at the sacred Green Corn dance.

'Our moment is at hand,' Wiley told them. 'And this is no time to be losing ground or getting careless. We've had a rotten week. First we're booted out the Bahamas—humiliating, but not calamitous—and then yesterday we nearly blow it for good. Yesterday'— he glanced down at the Cuban—'we had extreme major fuckage.'

'Unngh,' Bernal remarked defensively.

'The whole idea,' Wiley said, his voice building, 'of surveilling Kara Lynn Shivers was to determine if she was under police protection. I assumed we all understood that it was vitally important to remain invisible.'

The word *invisible* seemed to snake through the warehouse and wrap around the Cuban's neck.

'Now, Jesús,' Wiley went on, 'since your teeth got knocked out and your larynx looks like an avocado, I'm not going to make you tell me precisely what happened. Not now, anyway. Today I want you to rest, and I want you to stay here until I tell you to leave. Because, as we speak, every police officer in Dade County is out looking for you. If you were captured—and I realize that might appeal to your grandiose appetite for martyrdom—but *if* you were captured, there's no telling what they'd do to make you talk.'

'No mucking way,' Bernal said.

'Let's not take the chance. You stay put,' Wiley said. 'Gentlemen, we've had a major setback: we've lost the element of stealth.'

'But Keyes already knew the plan,' Tommy Tigertail said.

'Of course, of course—but look . . .' Wiley was trying to come up with a good Seminole-type metaphor. 'Tommy, it's the difference between knowing there's a panther hiding in the swamp, and seeing that panther with your own eyes. What's more frightening: wondering where it is, or finding it?'

The Indian didn't need it spelled out for him. Neither did Viceroy Wilson. They knew the magnitude of Bernal's transgression.

'Judging by the paper this morning, yesterday's clumsy episode has taken some of the luster from our mission,' Wiley said sardonically. 'In all my life I've never heard of a professional terrorist being subdued by a putz with a tennis racket.'

'Eaaamy,' replied Jesús Bernal, probably in Spanish.

'Lucky he didn't kill you,' Viceroy Wilson said.

'Lucky's the right word,' Wiley added. 'Lucky all we lost is a car.'

'What?' Wilson cried.

'I'm sorry, old man, but the cops put a BOLO out on the Caddy so I had Tommy get rid of the darn thing.'

'No!'

'I dumped it in a rockpit,' the Indian said.

With the roar of a wounded grizzly, Viceroy Wilson hurled himself upon Jesús Bernal and began pummeling him ferociously in the ribs and kidneys.

'Ged ob me, you addhoe!' the toothless Cuban howled. 'Hep!'

With great effort Tommy Tigertail was able to pull Viceroy Wilson away from Jesús Bernal. Once separated, the two revolutionaries glowered at each other, panting like leopards.

Skip Wiley rose to his feet. 'Look what's happening here! Ten days ago *Las Noches* was unstoppable, fearless, indivisible. Now we're trying to maim and mutilate each other. Last week we were front-page news and today the paper's making fun of us. Did you see the *Sun*? Did you see the bloody cartoon? Bearded guy supposed to look like Che Guevara, with a beret and machine gun, except he's got a tennis racket smashed over his head! Funny, huh? Vaudeville terrorists, that's us. That's the Nights of December. And instead of going out to redeem ourselves with some serious extremism, what do we do? We sit in this rathole and hold our own tag-team wrestling match. Don't you see, this is exactly what they want! They're trying to destroy us from within!'

Tommy Tigertail thought Wiley was giving García and the other white men entirely too much credit. Brian Keyes was the only one who worried Tommy.

'The sad truth is, we've lost our psychological advantage,' Skip Wiley said, 'and we've got to get it back. That's why I've divined a new plan.'

'What new plan?' asked Viceroy Wilson. He couldn't bear the thought of learning a whole new plan; he thought the old plan was all right.

'Nupid! Mus plain nupid!' Jesús Bernal whined. Not only was it stupid, it was downright suicidal to change the plan so late in the game; it went against all basic terrorist training. It was unthinkable.

'Lighten up, comrades,' Skip Wiley said. 'We're not tossing out the old plan, just embellishing it.'

'Tell them,' the Indian said. 'Tell them your idea.'

So Wiley told them all about it. 'Not just one princess, but two!' he concluded merrily. 'Double your pleasure, double your fun!'

Viceroy Wilson liked what he heard; the new plan was Wiley's cleverest yet. Phase One would wreak bedlam, knock everybody off-balance; the perfect setup. Phase One also required a helicopter, and Viceroy Wilson had always wanted to ride in a helicopter. Tommy Tigertail approved of the plan too, mainly because it afforded him a couple days of working deep in the Everglades, alone with his people.

Only Jesús Bernal opposed Skip Wiley's new plan. He lay on the warehouse floor, carping unintelligibly, growing more and more miserable as Wiley issued orders. The beating he'd gotten from that *maricón* Keyes and the cruel scolding he'd gotten from *El Fuego* had plunged Jesús Bernal into a familiar well of self-pity. Unable to be understood in any language, he found himself ignored. And worse, patronized. That Wiley had decided upon such a reckless change of strategy without consulting him—him, the most seasoned of all the terrorists!—infuriated Jesús Bernal. It was infamy repeating itself; it was the First Weekend in July Movement all over again.

When it came time for the Cuban's assignment, Skip Wiley announced that *Las Noches* once again would be needing Bernal's unique skills at the Smith-Corona; there were historic communiqués to be written! Jesús assented halfheartedly, hoping that in the dim light the other conspirators could not see the disloyalty in his eyes, or his sneer of contempt. Jesús Bernal made a private and fateful decision: he would proceed with a plan of his own. He would humble them all: the arrogant Indian, the stoned-freak nigger and the *culebra* cop García. Keyes, too; Keyes would suffer in failure. And when it was over, on New Year's Day, *El Comandante* would beg Jesús Bernal to return and lead the holy struggle against the Bearded One. It would be most satisfying to watch the old man grovel. Ha!

And Wiley, damn him—who said he was such a genius? If Wiley was so smart, Jesús thought, how could he have forgotten about the third bomb, the most powerful of all? How could he forget to inquire what had become of it? What kind of leader was so careless to let such a thing pass?

So tonight when it becomes an issue, thought Jesús Bernal, I can look him square in the eye, on the way out the door, and say: *But, El Fuego, you never asked. You never asked.*

Richard L. Bloodworth had spent the day at the Metro-Dade police station, lying in wait for Sergeant Al García. Bloodworth could be excruciatingly patient. He passed the time introducing himself to secretaries and patrolmen, upon whom he proudly foisted newly printed business cards on which the 'Ricky' had been replaced with the staid 'Richard L.' Most of those who received Bloodworth's business card tore it up the minute he was out of sight, but a few tucked it away in a drawer or a wallet. Someday, Bloodworth hoped, one of these drones would call with a hot tip, maybe even a ticket to the front page.

At first Al García had no intention of letting Ricky Bloodworth slither within striking distance. Their last exchange had been brief and unfortunate:

Bloodworth: Sergeant, these terrorists act like real scum of the earth, don't they?

García: Yeah. Get out of my office.

The next morning the detective had picked up the paper and seen this impolitic headline: *Cop Labels Terrorists Scum of Earth*.

Al García believed that no good could ever come from a newspaper interview, and that only idiots spoke to newspaper reporters. He explained this to the chief when the chief phoned to ask why the Miami *Sun* was getting jerked around. As often happened, the chief did not agree with Al García's philosophy and remarked on the detective's poor attitude. The chief argued that it was vital for the head of the Fuego One Task Force to keep a high law-and-order profile until the Orange Bowl Parade. That meant cooperating with the press.

So Ricky Bloodworth finally got an audience with the sergeant. The reporter came in wearing a lawyerly three-piece suit. He said hello to García and shook hands amiably, as if being forced to wait seven and a half hours was the most natural thing in the world.

Bloodworth took out a notebook, uncapped a red pen, and jotted García's name at the top of a page. The detective watched the ritual with a sour face.

'Before I forget, I'd like you to have one of these.' Bloodworth handed García a business card.

'I'll treasure it always,' García said. 'What's the L stand for?'

'Lancelot,' Bloodworth said. That was one of the drawbacks about the new byline; people were always asking about the middle initial. Leon was such a nerdy name that Bloodworth had scrapped it. Lancelot was more fitting.

Bloodworth asked his first question.

'Sergeant, exactly what happened last night?'

'The suspect escaped.'

'Jesús Bernal, the famous terrorist?'

'Yeah.'

'What about the vigilante with the tennis racket?'

'We're waiting,' García said, 'for him to come forward.'

Bloodworth scrawled in the notebook.

'Do you intend to press charges?'

'What for?'

'Assault, of course. According to witnesses, he simply walked up to Mr. Bernal and beat him senseless with the tennis racket, without any provocation.'

García said, 'That's still under investigation.'

Bloodworth scribbled some more. He was starting to remind García of that young shithead Bozeman from Internal Affairs.

'Any idea what Mr. Bernal was doing in Coral Gables?'

'Nope,' Garcia said.

Bloodworth dutifully wrote 'NO IDEA' in his notebook.

'Sergeant, I'm still puzzled about how this went down.'

García hated it when jerks like Bloodworth tried to talk like cops.

'What do you mean *went down?* Down where?' García said.

'I mean, how could it happen? Here's one of the most wanted men in Florida lying unconscious in a pool of blood on a busy public street—and the police still manage to lose him. How in the world did he get away?'

García shrugged. He thought: Let's see you *quote* a shrug, asshole.

'It seems simply . . . inconceivable,' Bloodworth remarked.

Al García realized that, in effect, he'd just been called a Jell-O-brained moron. That was the beauty of a snotty word like *inconceivable*.

'The one thing everybody wants to know,' Bloodworth continued, 'is where the Nights of December are going to attack next.'

'I'd like to know, myself.'

'You have no idea?'

'Nope,' García lied.

Again Bloodworth wrote, 'NO IDEA.'

'Let me bum a cigarette,' the detective said.

'Sorry, but I don't smoke.'

'Then what's that in your vest? It looks like a pack of cigarettes.'

Bloodworth smiled sheepishly and took out a small Sony Pearlcorder. 'A tape recorder,' he explained unnecessarily.

'Oh,' García said. 'Is it on?'

'Well, yes.'

'Can I see it?'

Ricky Bloodworth handed the miniature recorder to García.

'Quite a little gadget,' the detective said. 'You keep the First Amendment in here, do you?'

'Very funny.' Bloodworth's bluish mouth opened in a round ratlike smile, all incisors.

García set the Pearlcorder flat on the desktop, its tiny reels still spinning. He reached into his holster and took out his Smith and Wesson service revolver.

'What are you going to do?' Bloodworth asked.

'Watch.'

With the butt of the pistol, García pounded the Sony to tiny pieces. He gave the pieces back to Bloodworth, along with a tangle of brown ribbon.

'Don't ever tape me again,' García said, 'not without asking.'

Bloodworth stared in disbelief at the expensive Japanese debris.

'What's the matter with you?' he cried. 'Everybody uses tape recorders. It's just a tool, for God's sake . . . for accuracy . . . to make me a better reporter.'

'Brain surgery wouldn't make you a better reporter,' García said. 'Now get out of here before I have you strip-searched.' So much for cooperating with the press.

'This is . . . an outrage,' Bloodworth stammered.

'Simply inconceivable,' García agreed.

For half an hour Bloodworth sat on the steps of the police station and morosely flipped through his notebook. García had given him practically nothing, not one damn usable quote. It had been a dry week, too, newswise. Until last night, *Las Noches* had been quiet: no more kidnappings or murders to goose the story back to page one. Bloodworth was getting itchy. He wondered if Cab Mulcahy would let him do a column about Al

García and the bumbling Fuego One Task Force. He wondered what García's boss would say if he found out about the tape-recorder incident.

A local TV crew marched up the steps, around Bloodworth, into police headquarters. He thought: What if García had given them an interview, too? What if the detective actually said something important on television? Identified *El Fuego*, for instance? Bloodworth's flesh turned clammy. Christ! He'd completely forgotten to ask Sergeant García about *El Fuego*.

In a panic, Bloodworth dashed back up the steps. He couldn't go back to the newsroom empty-handed, too much was riding on this story—a raise, his very own column, maybe even a job with the New York *Times*. The stakes were too fantastic to let an oafish Cuban cop ruin everything.

Bloodworth hopped off the elevator at Homicide, but the TV crew was nowhere in sight. He scurried from office to office, unimpeded. At the end of a long hall, he finally spotted the bright TV lights.

It was too late. Through the window of a soundproof interview room, Bloodworth saw Al García talking expansively to a pretty brunette television reporter. She was holding a microphone and he was smiling like it was cocktails at the Four Seasons. The camera rolled.

Bloodworth watched in wretched helplessness, struggling to read the detective's lips. García glanced at Bloodworth's face in the window and mouthed three words: 'Up your ass.'

In a fury, Bloodworth retreated to García's empty office, where he fumed and cursed and looked at his wristwatch every thirty seconds. How long could it last? What could he be telling her? Bloodworth felt a damp stripe settle down the back of his shirt. He was getting beaten, beaten badly. By a TV bimbo.

A man with a plastic badge that said 'Mail Room' came in and piled papers and packages on García's desk.

As soon as the messenger left, Bloodworth slid over and sifted through the goodies. A two-page memo on weapons training. A ten-page memo on pensions. An invoice for softball uniforms.

Crap!

Next he sampled the unopened mail, scanning the return

addresses. He found something from the FBI fingerprint section in Washington and held it to the light, without success; the clever Feebs used opaque envelopes.

Underneath the stack of letters was a brown box the size of a toaster.

A bright red courier sticker was glued to the box: Same-day service, fourteen bucks. Oddly, whoever had sent the parcel had tied a luxurious bow in the twine, the kind of bow you'd see on a Fifth Avenue Christmas package.

The address label had been typed neatly:

> To Sgt. Alberto García, Maggot and Traitor
> Metro-Dade Police Pig Department
> Miami, City of Pigs, Florida

Ricky Bloodworth excitedly opened his notebook and copied everything.

In the upper-left-hand corner, on the top of the box, the sender had written:

'*De un guerrero y patriota.*'

From a warrior and patriot.

Ricky Bloodworth went to the door and peered down the hallway. Amazingly, the TV lights were still blazing away. God Almighty, he thought, not even Joe Wambaugh yaps this much.

Bloodworth returned to the desk and picked up the brown box. It was much lighter than he expected. Bloodworth shook it cautiously at first, then briskly. Nothing. It was packed solid.

Bloodworth trembled at the thought of what he was about to do.

We're talking felony, he told himself. This is police evidence, no doubt about it.

But screw García—he busted my tape recorder.

Ricky Bloodworth put the box under one arm and hurried out of the Homicide office. He went down three flights of stairs and came out in the Traffic Division, which was deserted. He found an empty rest room and locked himself in a stall that reeked of ammonia and bad cologne.

The reporter sat on a toilet and set the box on his lap. He

propped his notebook on the tissue rack. He stuck the red pen behind his left ear.

Bloodworth's heart was drumming. He actually felt himself getting hard—that's how much he loved this job. Ricky savored his coup: a treasure chest of clues from the Nights of December. An exclusive, too . . . that was the part that gave him a hard-on.

He had already decided what he would do. As soon as he was done peeking, he'd send the package right back to García. He'd wrap it exactly the same and steam the labels—who would ever know?

Lovingly Ricky Bloodworth rubbed the smooth brown paper, fingered the frayed twine.

Then he pinched one end of the magnificent bow and pulled, pulled on it until the knot popped.

And a savage furnace swallowed him.

Tore the air from his lungs.

And the flesh from his cheeks.

Until the universe turned molten white.

24

It had always puzzled Cab Mulcahy that Mr. Cardoza took such an ardent personal interest in the Miami *Sun*. Traditionally publishers love to meddle with the news operation (because that's the most exciting part of a newspaper, the only part worth dicking around with), but Cardoza was not a typical publisher. He had little understanding of the tenets of journalism with no paternal affection for the newspaper, for his fortunes did not singularly rise or plummet with the *Sun*. Rather, Cardoza was a boundless entrepreneur, a man who loved the variety of making money; a man with dozens of incongruous irons in the fire. He owned a soccer team in St. Kitts, a stock car in Darlington, a chain of family cinemas, four butcher shops, a Liberian oil tanker, three thousand coin-operated condom machines, and a phosphate mine. Any single one of those enterprises, Cab Mulcahy thought, was infinitely more amusing as a money toy than the frequently struggling Miami *Sun*, of which Cardoza owned fifty-one percent. Which automatically made him publisher and meddler-for-life.

On the evening of December 28, a Friday, Cab Mulcahy was summoned from an opulent pre-Orange Bowl cocktail party to explain to Mr. Cardoza why Skip Wiley's column had not appeared in the paper since Christmas Eve.

The publisher did not particularly wish to see Mulcahy in person; and he certainly had no intention of visiting the newsroom. Cardoza preferred to do business office-to-office, by telephone—distance yields perspective, he liked to say. Also, he got a kick out of hanging up on people.

At the appointed hour, Cardoza dialed Mulcahy's desk.

'I didn't think much of that Christmas Eve column,' he began.

'Me neither,' Mulcahy said.

'Who gives a shit about some native fisherman who can't swim? It seems to me Mr. Wiley can do better.'

'He's still not himself,' Mulcahy said.

'He gets paid to be himself,' Cardoza said. 'A small fortune, he gets paid. And here it's Christmas week, tourist season, when our circulation's supposed to shoot sky-high, and where's our star clean-up hitter? Every day I pick up the newspaper, and nothing. No Skip Wiley. The *Sun*'s dead without him. Lies there like a dog turd on my front lawn.'

Mulcahy said, 'Really, Mr. Cardoza, I wouldn't go that far.'

'Oh you wouldn't? You'd like to hear the cancellation figures, maybe. Or take a few hours to read some of the mail we've been getting.'

'That's not necessary.'

For years Cab Mulcahy had tried to tell Cardoza that he overestimated Wiley's popularity, that no single writer could pull enough support to significantly boost or bust the circulation numbers. Whether that was true or not, it was what Mulcahy chose to believe. However, as a pure businessman Cardoza felt that he appreciated the concept of a Good Product far better than some ivory-tower editor. And in Cardoza's predominant and immutable view, what made the Miami *Sun* a Good Product were Skip Wiley, Ann Landers, and Dagwood Bumstead. On some days Wiley alone was worth the twenty-five cents.

'Where the hell is he?' Cardoza demanded.

'I don't know,' Mulcahy said. 'I expect him back in town on Christmas Day.'

'Send someone to Nassau,' Cardoza barked through the speaker box. 'Do whatever you have to do.'

Mulcahy rubbed the back of his neck and closed his eyes. It was fortunate that Cardoza couldn't see him. 'Skip's not in the Bahamas anymore,' he said. 'Apparently he was deported from the islands on the twenty-fourth.'

'Deported!' Cardoza huffed. 'For what?'

'It's quite a long list, sir.'

'Give me the high points.'

'Attempted bribery, possession of a controlled substance, and behaving as an undesirable, whatever that means. For what it's worth, the embassy says Wiley was set up. Apparently that column about the fisherman didn't go over too well with the Bahamian government.'

'Now everybody's a goddamn critic,' Cardoza said.

'All I know is that they put him on a plane,' Mulcahy said. 'At gunpoint.'

'Why didn't we think of that?'

Though miserly with compliments, Cardoza privately held great admiration for Cab Mulcahy; he couldn't imagine anyone trying to manage so many deeply disturbed individuals as there were in the newsroom. It was a disorderly place where eccentricity, torpor, petulance, even insubordination were tolerated, so Cardoza stayed far away, where it was safe. He stayed near the money.

'God knows I'd never tell you how to run that operation, Cab, but I do want to see Skip Wiley in my newspaper again. That means you'd better find him. I want a New Year's column from that crazy sonofabitch, you understand? Don't tell me he's sick and don't tell me he's exhausted, and don't fucking tell me that he's not himself. Just tell me that he's writing again, understand?'

'Yes, sir, but apparently—'

And Cardoza hung up.

All week long Cab Mulcahy had been waiting for the phone call or telegram, waiting for that familiar profane foghorn greeting. Waiting in vain. He couldn't believe that Skip Wiley had docilely accepted the butchery of the Christmas column; he couldn't believe that Wiley had suppressed what must have been a colossal homicidal rage.

Was Skip that far gone?

In the meantime, the Nights of December had fallen quiet and dropped off the front page, much to the relief of the men in the orange blazers. Scores of suspects had been rounded up, including a few men who might have vaguely resembled Jesús Bernal or Daniel 'Viceroy' Wilson; all were released or charged with unrelated crimes. There was also talk of a summit with Seminole tribal elders to seek assistance in locating Tommy Tigertail, but the

Seminoles refused to go near the police station and the cops refused to enter the reservation, so the meeting never materialized.

The morning edition of the *Sun* had carried four stories about the upcoming Orange Bowl festivities (including a color photograph of twenty newly arrived Shriners, jovially polishing their Harleys), but in the whole newspaper there was only one item about *Las Noches de Diciembre*. It was a short feature story and a cartoon, beneath a headline that said: *Tennis Buff Boffs Bomb Suspect.*

It was only now, rereading it in print, that Cab Mulcahy realized how trenchantly the presentation of Ricky Bloodworth's article— the tone, the headline, the slapstick cartoon—struck at the very manhood of the Nights of December. It worried Mulcahy. Coupled with Wiley's ominous silence, it worried him profoundly.

He looked out at the newsroom just in time to see a lean figure running toward the office, weaving through the desks and video-display terminals. It was Brian Keyes.

'He called!' Keyes said breathlessly. 'Twenty minutes ago. The bastard left a message on my beeper.'

'What did he say?'

'He said he's gonna phone here, your office. Wants to talk to both of us.'

'It's about damn time,' Mulcahy said, feeling a little better about the prospects. He took off his black dinner jacket and hung it over a chair.

As they waited for the phone to ring, Mulcahy busied himself by brewing a fresh pot of coffee. His hands shook slightly as he poured it. Keyes scooped a handful of peppermint candies from a jar on the secretary's desk and ate them mechanically, one by one.

'What are we going to say?' Mulcahy asked. 'When he calls, what the hell are we supposed to say?'

'We've got to convince him it's all over,' Keyes said. 'Tell him we know the whole plan. Tell him if he tries anything at the parade, *Las Noches* are as good as dead. Tell him it'll make Bonnie and Clyde look like Sunday at the beach.'

Mulcahy nodded neutrally. Might work, might not. With Skip, who the hell could ever tell?

'I think we ought to concede some minor points,' Mulcahy suggested. 'He'll never give up if he thinks it's been a total loss.'

'You're right,' Keyes said. 'Congratulate him on all the ink they got. The newsmagazines, the *Post*, *USA Today*. Tell him the Nights of December made their point. They got everybody's attention.'

'Which is true.'

'Of course it's true.'

'But is it enough for Skip?'

Keyes and Mulcahy looked at each other with the same answer.

'What are we going to do,' Keyes asked, 'when he tells us to go beat our meat?'

Mulcahy stroked his chin. 'We could talk to Jenna.'

'Forget it,' Keyes said sharply. 'Lost cause.'

'Then it's over. Bloodbath or not, we go to the cops.'

'Yup.' Keyes glanced at the telephone.

'Imagine the headlines, Cab.'

'God help us.'

The phone rang. Once. Twice. Mulcahy swallowed hard and answered on the third ring.

'I see,' he said after a few seconds.

Keyes excitedly pointed to the speaker box. Mulcahy shook his head unhappily. Then he hung up. His face was like gray crepe.

'That wasn't him,' Mulcahy said. 'It wasn't Wiley.'

'Then who was it?'

'Sergeant García,' he said gravely. 'Apparently the Nights of December just blew up the one and only Richard L. Bloodworth.'

The bomb that exploded in Ricky Bloodworth's lap was powerful by Little Havana standards, but not utterly devastating. To build it, Jesús Bernal had hollowed a round Styrofoam lobster float and packed the core with generous but unmeasured amounts of Semtex-H, C-4, and old gunpowder. Then he ran a fuse through the middle and plugged the ends with gasoline-soaked Jockey shorts and two Army blasting caps. Next Bernal had meticulously embedded into the Styrofoam ball hundreds of two-penny nails (the sharp ends facing out), as well as assorted slivers of rusty cola cans and soup tins. It was not a bomb designed to wipe out embassies or armored limousines; this was, in the terrorist vernacular, an antipersonnel device. Bernal had packed the bristling lobster buoy into an empty one-gallon paint drum and threaded the fuse through a hole in the lid. The fuse became part of the magnificent bow that adorned the deadly brown box—an inspired touch of which the Cuban was especially proud.

Yet, as always, Jesús Bernal had a problem with quality control. He had envisioned a weapon that would fire shrapnel in all directions at an equal force, leaving no square centimeter of human flesh unpunctured. The paint can, Bernal had determined, would itself disintegrate into jagged fragments and become part of the lethal payload.

Fortunately for Ricky Bloodworth, that is not what happened. Fortunately, Jesús Bernal had failed to seal properly the bottom of the paint can, which blew off at the instant of explosion and gave the bomb something it was never supposed to have: rocket thrust.

In what the Metro-Dade Bomb Squad calculated was no more than two-thousandths of a second, Jesús Bernal's prize package blasted off from Ricky Bloodworth's lap on a nineteen-degree trajectory, passed cleanly through three ply-wood toilet stalls, and detonated in the men's urinal. The rest room was gutted.

An hour later, when Cab Mulcahy and Brian Keyes arrived, men in white lab coats were balanced on stepladders, scraping what appeared to be chunks of pink bubble gum off the charred rest-room ceiling.

'Mr. Bloodworth's fingertips,' Al García explained. 'We've found seven out of ten, so far.'

'How is he?' Mulcahy asked.

'He's got a nosebleed like Victoria Falls,' the detective said, 'but he'll make it.'

Luckily, the police station was only five minutes from Flagler Memorial Hospital. Ricky Bloodworth had arrived in the emergency room semiconscious and suffering from hand injuries, lacerations and second-degree burns over his face and groin.

'The tip of his cock got fried—don't ask me how,' García said. 'He's also deaf, but the doctor says that might be temporary.'

Mulcahy stepped gingerly through the smoky chamber, his shoes crunching on a carpet of broken mirror, splintered wood, and powdered tile. Pretzeled by the blast, naked water pipes sprouted from the walls and floor, dripping milky fluid.

Brian Keyes knelt next to the bomb-squad guys as they picked through the ceramic ruins of the urinal. 'Look at all these damn nails,' Keyes said.

'Two hundred seven,' said one of the bomb experts, 'and still counting.'

Keyes looked up and saw Mulcahy with his black tie loosened and French sleeves rolled up. He had a notebook out, and was descending on Al García. Keyes had to grin: the old boy looked right at home.

Mulcahy asked García: 'How do you know this was the Nights of December?'

'Your Mr. Bloodworth's been working on the story, right? That makes him a prime target.' García eyed the notebook uneasily. 'Besides, the boys here tell me this looks like another Jesús Bernal special.'

'What was Ricky doing down here?' Keyes said.

'Probably taking a dump,' García said.

'Come on, Al, this is Traffic. Why wouldn't he be upstairs in Homicide?'

''Cause I kicked his sleazy ass out when I caught him trying to tape-record me. Had one of those little James Bond jobs tucked in his vest.'

Mulcahy frowned. 'I'm sorry abut that, Sergeant. That's strictly against newsroom policy.'

'Fucking A.'

'When you saw him last,' Keyes said, 'did he have a package?'

'Nope,' García said. 'But here's my theory, Brian. After I chase him out of here, he goes home, finds this hinky package in the mailbox, freaks out, and comes racing back to show me. On the way upstairs he stops in the john and bang!'

'How'd he get the box past the security desk in the lobby?' asked Mulcahy. A damn good question, Keyes thought.

But García just chuckled. 'You could waltz a Pershing missile by those bozos downstairs and they'd never look twice.'

At first Keyes didn't want to believe that Bloodworth himself had been the target, or that Skip Wiley might have ordered his execution. It was something Wiley had threatened for years around the newsroom, but then so had almost every other reporter. Bloodworth was always on somebody's shit list.

Yet Keyes couldn't deny that the bombing made perfect sense, considering what Bloodworth had written about *Las Noches*, and considering what had happened to Wiley's Christmas column. Keyes felt guilty about his role in the Bahamas scheme; Cab Mulcahy felt much worse. Across the rubble the two men exchanged anguished glances and shared the same chilling thought: Skip wasn't kidding about a bloodbath. Imagine a bomb like this, in a crowd . . .

If this was Wiley's way of warning Keyes and Mulcahy to keep their silence, it worked.

With a gloved hand, one of the bomb-squad guys displayed a twisted scrap of tin which still bore a red-and-white soup label. 'Minestrone,' he announced. 'This baby was sharpened with a diamond file.'

'Cute,' Mulcahy said, pocketing the notebook. 'Come on, Brian, let's go see Ricky.'

Within minutes of the explosion, the emergency room of Flagler Memorial had been occupied by a clamorous army of journalists, each resolved to make Richard L. Bloodworth a hero of the Fourth Estate. News-wise, it would have been a better story (and certainly less work) if Ricky had been killed outright, but near-martyrdom was better than nothing. The mere fact that the Nights of December had bombed a news reporter guaranteed international headlines, and the event was sure to draw the Big Boys from New York—the networks, the *Times* and *Sixty Minutes*, all of whom would do anything to get out of Manhattan in the winter. The locals realized that now was the time to score the big interview, before Diane Sawyer strolled into town and scooped them all.

Two policemen escorted Brian Keyes and Cab Mulcahy through the mob and hustled them into a laundry elevator. Five minutes later they stood at the door of Bloodworth's private tenth-floor room.

The hospital's official press release had listed Ricky in satisfactory condition, but in no sense of the word did he seem satisfactory. He looked like he'd stuck his head into a bonfire—burnt ears curled up like fortune cookies, hairless eyelids swollen tight, the seared nose and cheeks stained burgundy with surgical antiseptic. He looked like a barbecued mole.

Cab Mulcahy quaked at the sight of his wounded reporter. Like a stricken father, he stood at the side of the bed, lightly touching Bloodworth's arm through the sheets.

Bloodworth made a singsong noise and Keyes edged closer. It was hard to tell through the bruised slits, but Ricky's eyes seemed to be open.

'Grunt if you can hear me,' Keyes said.

Bloodworth made no sound.

'Brian, he's deaf, remember?'

'Oh yeah.' Keyes made an 'okay' signal with his thumb and forefinger. Bloodworth smiled feebly.

'Good boy,' Mulcahy said. 'You're going to be just fine. We'll take care of everything.'

Bloodworth raised his right hand to return the gesture, a poignant if somewhat palsied effort. Keyes noticed that each of Ricky's fingers was bandaged to the second joint; in fact, the fingers seemed oddly stubbed. Keyes lifted the sheet and checked Bloodworth's left hand—same thing. Al García wasn't kidding: Jesús Bernal's bomb had sheared all Ricky's fingertips. Not even the thumbs had been spared. Evidently he had been holding the box at the moment of explosion.

'Oh brother,' Keyes said, replacing the sheet.

'Everything's going to be just fine,' Mulcahy said to Bloodworth.

'He's never gonna type again,' Keyes whispered.

'Ssshhhh!'

'Or bite his nails, for that matter.'

'We'll get the best plastic surgeon in Miami,' Mulcahy vowed. He was wondering what in the world to do with a deaf reporter with no fingertips. For his suffering Ricky certainly deserved something, Mulcahy thought, something generous but safe. Perhaps a lifetime column on the food page—even Bloodworth couldn't screw up a casserole recipe.

'Too bad he can't tell us what happened,' Keyes said.

Ricky Bloodworth had no intention of telling anyone what had happened; even an elephant-sized dose of painkillers had not dulled his sense of survival. Maimed or not, he knew he'd be fired, perhaps even indicted, if it ever became known that he'd snatched the brown package from Sergeant García's desk. It was better to let the world think the bomb had been meant for him—better for his career, better for the story. And why should that lout García get any attention, anyway?

Through a haze, Bloodworth saw Cab Mulcahy holding up a notebook. On it the editor had written: 'You are going to make it okay.'

Bloodworth smiled and, with one of his nubs, gave a tremulous thumbs-up.

Keyes took the notebook and wrote: 'Where did you get the package?'

Bloodworth shrugged lamely.

'I guess he doesn't remember much,' Mulcahy said.

'Guess not.'

Next Keyes printed: 'Are you strong enough to write a note for the cops?'

Bloodworth squinted at the pad, then shook his head no.

'We'd better let him rest,' Mulcahy said.

'Sure.'

'I don't know what to tell the wolf pack downstairs,' Mulcahy fretted.

'Hell, Cab, they're the competition. Don't say a damn thing.'

'I can't do that.'

'Why not? You're the *Sun*'s reporter on this one, aren't you?

So just keep your mouth shut and write the story. Write the hell out of it, too.'

Amused, Mulcahy said, 'Well, why not?'

He winked at Bloodworth and turned for the door. Bloodworth grunted urgently.

'He wants to say something,' Keyes said. He laid the notebook on Ricky's chest and fitted the pen into his gauzed claw.

Bloodworth wrote laboriously and in tall woozy letters:

'PAGE ONE?'

Keyes showed the notebook to Mulcahy and said, 'Can you believe this?'

A nurse came in and gave Ricky Bloodworth an enormous shot. Before drifting off, he saw Keyes and Mulcahy waving good night.

Outside the hospital, Keyes said, 'It's getting late, Cab, I'd better head back to the house.' Dismally he wondered what a nail bomb could do to Reed Shivers' cork billiard room.

'Go on ahead,' Mulcahy said. 'If our pal calls, you'll be the first to know.'

Back in the newsroom, the other reporters and editors were surprised to see Cab Mulcahy sit down at a video-display terminal and begin to write. Before long his presence seemed to galvanize the whole staff, and the Friday-night pace of the newsroom quickened into something approaching gusto.

The spell was interrupted by the city editor, who, after circling reluctantly, finally stepped forward to give Cab Mulcahy the message.

'From Wiley,' the city editor said uneasily. 'He phoned while you were out.'

Mulcahy's ulcer twinged when he saw the message.

'I say yes, you say no,' it read. 'You say stop, and I say go, go, go.'

25

From the hospital Brian Keyes drove straight to Coral Gables to check on Kara Lynn. He rang the bell three times before Reed Shivers opened the door.

'Nice of you to show up,' Shivers said archly. He wore a monogrammed wine-colored robe and calfskin slippers. A walnut pipe bobbed superciliously in the corner of his mouth.

'Nice to see you, too, Mr. Hefner.'

'Don't be a wise guy—where've you been? You're getting big bucks to be a baby-sitter.'

'There's been another bombing,' Keyes said, brushing past him. 'A newspaper reporter.'

'The Nachos again?' All the Anglos in Miami had started calling Wiley's gang the Nachos because it was so much easier to pronounce than *Las Noches de Diciembre*.

'Where's Kara Lynn?' Keyes asked.

'Out in the game room working her fanny off. Try not to interrupt.'

Keyes examined Reed Shivers as he would a termite. 'After all this, you still want your daughter to ride in that parade?'

'They have dogs, Mr. Keyes, dogs trained to sniff out the bombs.'

'You're incredible.'

'We're talking about a career decision here.'

'We're talking murder, Mr. Shivers.'

'Not so loud!'

Keyes heard music coming from the game room. It sounded like the Bee Gees, *Stayin' alive, stayin' alive, oooh-oooh-oooh-oooh*. The bass guitar thumped through the wall.

'Jazz aerobics,' Shivers explained. 'Since Kara Lynn can't go out to class, the teacher came here. I thought that was damned considerate.'

Keyes went into the game room. The stereo was extremely loud. The pool table had been rolled to one wall. In the middle of the carpet, Kara Lynn was stretched out, grabbing her heels.

Keyes smiled.

Then he looked up and saw Jenna.

'Oh God, no,' he said, but the words were lost in the music. Jenna and Kara Lynn were so absorbed that neither noticed him standing there gaping.

Their choreography was enthralling; each woman gracefully mirrored the other, stretching, dipping, arching, skipping, kicking. Keyes was transfixed by the vision—the two of them in sleek leotards and practically nothing else, both with their blond hair up in ponytails. Of course there was no mistaking one for the other: Jenna was bustier, fuller in the hips, and she had those gold earrings. Kara Lynn was taller, with long thoroughbred legs. Tennis legs.

Brian Keyes could not have dreamed up a more stunning, or baffling, apparition. He turned off the stereo, leaving the dancers stranded in mid-jumping jack.

'Whoa!' Jenna said, dropping her arms to her sides.

'Hey! What's the idea?' Kara Lynn was a little annoyed.

'I'll explain,' Keyes said.

Jenna turned around and stared. 'Brian!' She seemed shocked to see him.

'Hey there,' Keyes said. 'Since when do you make house calls?'

'Oh boy.'

Kara Lynn looked quizzically at Jenna, then back at Keyes. The prickly silence gave it all away.

'So you two know each other,' said Kara Lynn.

'Long time ago,' Keyes said.

'Not so long,' said Jenna, talking with her eyes.

Kara Lynn looked embarrassed. 'I'm going to get some lemonade.'

When she was gone, Jenna said, 'How'd you find me here?'

'Don't flatter yourself. I wasn't even looking.' Keyes felt rotten. And angry. 'Tell me what's going on,' he said.

Jenna dabbed her forehead with a towel that matched her pink lipstick. 'Kara Lynn's been a student of mine for two years. She's a good dancer and quite athletic, in case you didn't already know.'

Keyes let that one slide.

'She said she couldn't come to class this week—something about a parade curfew—so I offered to stop by here for a short workout. I don't know what you're being so snotty about.'

'Where's Skip?' The eternal question; Keyes wondered why he even bothered.

'I'm not sure. This is some room, huh?'

'Jenna!'

'Time for sit-ups.'

'Stop.'

But in an instant she was supine, arms locked behind her neck. 'Hold my legs. Please, Brian, don't be a pill.'

He got down on all fours and braced her ankles with his hands. He thought: She really is on another planet.

'One . . . two . . . three . . .' She was as limber as a whip.

'Where's Wiley?' Keyes asked.

'Seven . . . eight . . . I got one for you . . . what are *you* doing here?' With each sit-up Jenna emitted a soft round cry, half-moan and half-grunt. Keyes was intimately familiar with the sound.

'I've been hired to keep an eye on Kara Lynn,' he said.

'You? Come on, Bri . . .'

'Your deranged boyfriend plans to kidnap her during the Orange Bowl Parade, or didn't you know?'

'Fourteen . . . fifteen . . . Jeez, I said *hold* my legs, don't fracture them . . . you're wrong about Skip . . .'

'Did he send you here?' Keyes asked.

'Don't be silly . . . he doesn't even know I'm back in the country . . . supposed to be house-hunting in Port-au-Prince . . .'

'Holy Christ.' Keyes couldn't imagine Skip Wiley loose on the streets of Port-au-Prince. The government of Haiti was not known for its sense of humor.

'Twenty-four . . . twenty-five . . . Tell me the truth, Brian, are you sleeping with this kid?'

'No.' Why did he answer?—it was none of her damn business. 'Jenna, I just don't want her to get hurt.'

'Skip wouldn't do that . . .'

'No? He blew up Ricky Bloodworth tonight.'

'Mmmm . . . all the way?'

'He's still breathing, if that's what you mean.'

Jenna was tiring, but not much.

'Thirty-nine . . . forty . . . Skip promised he wouldn't hurt the girl . . . ease up a little on the left leg . . . hey, you still miss me?' She caught his eye, beamed. Full of confidence, like she could jerk the leash anytime she wanted.

'Do you want Skip to die?' Keyes said tonelessly. He'd had about all he could take.

'Forty-six, forty-seven . . . course not . . . do you?'

'No.' But don't ask me why not, Keyes thought, because the bastard richly deserves it.

'Brian . . . don't let anything happen to him.'

That was it. One the count of forty-nine he stopped her, slipped a hand behind her head and held her there, in a sitting position. Probably with more firmness than was necessary.

'Just one more!' Jenna protested.

'Know what he said, Jenna? He said there'd be a bloodbath if I told the cops about him. Said lots of people would die.'

'Baloney.' She strained against his grip. 'He's just bluffing.'

Keyes said, 'Look here at my clothes—what do you suppose that is?'

'A-1 Sauce?'

'It's blood, you bubblehead! Human blood. I knelt in a big warm puddle of it tonight over at police headquarters. You should have been there, the place looked like Beirut.'

'Let me go,' Jenna said.

'So what do you make of all these darned murders?' he said. 'Pretty hilarious, huh?'

'Brian, just stop it.'

'No, goddammit, look at me!' But she wouldn't.

'Look at these bloodstains and tell me Wiley's a big hero,' he said angrily. 'Tell me how proud you are, go ahead, Jenna. The man's a genius, all right. Takes a real visionary to bomb a moron in a toilet.'

She squirmed loose and shot to her feet. Her face was pink and she was breathing hard.

Keyes said, 'Jenna, you can end all this—it's not too late. Do everyone a favor and turn him in.'

She shook her head once and spun away, out the door.

'I'm going for pizza,' Kara Lynn announced.

'Not alone you're not,' Keyes said.

'It'll make you chubby,' Reed Shivers added. 'The only Orange Bowl queen with a mozzarella tummy.'

'That's enough, Daddy. I'm hungry.'

'Then we'll get it delivered,' Keyes said. He picked up the telephone in the game room and stared at it. The phone was made out of an actual bottle of Seagram's; Reed Shivers had ordered it specially from a golf catalog.

'What do you like on your pizza?' Keyes asked.

Kara Lynn shrugged. 'Mushrooms, anchovies.'

'No pizza!' her father said. 'Pumpkin, we've got publicity stills tomorrow, remember?'

'Screw it,' said Kara Lynn.

'That's the spirit,' Keyes cheered.

'But it's *swimsuit*,' Shivers pleaded.

'And I'll look sensational, Daddy. Tiny tits and all.'

Keyes changed his mind about having the pizza delivered. Kara Lynn obviously needed to get out of the house.

'You ever been to Tony's?' he said. 'Great pizza.'

'Let's go.'

'At least go easy on the cheese,' Reed Shivers said, pouting into his pipestem.

They took the MG. It was a chilly night, full of stars. The brisk air whistled through a rusty hole in the floorboard, and the car got cold quickly.

'The heater's busted,' Keyes said. 'I got an extra sweater in the back.'

'I'm okay.' Kara Lynn cupped her hands and blew into them softly. Keyes could see the gooseflesh on her bare arms.

'How far to Tony's?' she asked.

'I've got no idea,' Keyes said. 'I made it up.'

'Oh.'

'To get us away from Professor Higgins.'

'Daddy's not a bad guy,' Kara Lynn said, 'but he can be such a pain in the ass.'

Keyes drove north down LeJeune Road. Just for the hell of it, he squared the block at Miracle Mile to make sure they weren't being followed again.

'Is the Pizza Hut okay?'

'Sure,' Kara Lynn said.

They got a booth in the corner, away from the jukebox and video games. Keyes ordered a pizza with mushrooms, pepperoni, and anchovies. Kara Lynn looked like she was freezing in her dance tights, so Keyes went out to the car and got his spare sweater, a gray cotton pullover.

With a nod of thanks, she slipped it on over the leotard. Keyes wondered why she was so quiet; it wasn't a hostile silence, or even a sulk. It reminded him of the first few days at the house, when she was sizing him up. Kara Lynn was a pro when it came to withdrawal, a real blank page when she wanted to be.

'What's on your mind?' he finally asked.

'I was just wondering about you and Jenna.'

'Ancient history.'

'Go on.'

'Very boring.'

'I'll bet.'

'And painful.'

'Oh.' She took a sip of diet cola, a concession to her father. 'Didn't mean to pry.'

'Forget it,' Keyes said. 'But do me a favor: no more aerobics classes until after the parade.'

'How come?'

'Call it a security precaution.'

'For heaven's sake, you're not saying Jenna's dangerous!'

You don't know the half of it, Keyes thought. 'Did Jenna ever say anything about the Orange Bowl?'

'Sure. She wished me luck before the pageant—even sent a bouquet of wild sea oats to the dressing room.'

'She would have made a great florist.'

'Actually she's the one who convinced me to enter the contest. To be honest, I was burned out on the darned things. Besides, I didn't think I had a chance—you should've seen some of the other girls. But Jenna said to give it a try. Strike a blow for small-breasted women, she said.'

'A great florist and a great psychologist,' Keyes said. So Jenna was in on it from the beginning. What the hell did he expect? He decided to leave it at that, though. Jenna wouldn't be back, and there was no use scaring Kara Lynn.

'She says I look like her, ten years ago.'

'Maybe a little,' Keyes said. It wasn't the beauty they had in common, so much as the aura—an aura of absolute control. The ability to conquer with a shy glance or the slightest of smiles.

'I hope I look that good when I'm twenty-nine,' Kara Lynn remarked.

'You will.'

A waitress brought the pizza, hot and pungent. They attacked it hungrily. Keyes got tomato sauce on both his sleeves. Kara Lynn rolled her eyes, pretending to be mortified.

'Have you had many girlfriends?' she asked.

'Thousands. I was once engaged to half the Rockettes.'

'You don't like this subject, do you?'

'Look, I never asked you what it's like to be the Stone Crab queen, with a dozen greaseball contest judges staring up your crotch. I never asked because it seemed personal and none of my business, and I knew you wouldn't want to talk about it.'

'You're right. It's awful, that's why.'

'It *looks* awful,' Keyes said. 'I don't know how you do it.'

Kara Lynn plucked an anchovy from the pizza and dropped it neatly on a napkin; a little anchovy graveyard. 'It's easy to become Stone Crab queen,' she said. 'All you have to do is get some black heels and a bikini and learn to play "Eleanor Rigby" on the French horn.'

'You got my vote.'

'I hate it. All of it.'

'I know.'

'Half the girls get boob jobs and butt tucks,' Kara Lynn said. 'Nobody does anything about it.'

'What happens to them when there's no more beauty pageants?'

'Two, three years of modeling. A few local TV commercials if you're lucky. Guy once offered me three grand to lie on the hood of a Dodge truck and say: *I got my Ram Charger at Cooley Motors.* Real Shakespearean television. Daddy had a seizure when I turned it down.'

'What do you really want to do, Kara Lynn?'

'Stop world famine, of course.'

Keyes laughed. 'And after that?'

'See Europe.'

Keyes cut another slice of pizza but it surrendered grudgingly. A web of cheese hung elastically from his mouth to the platter.

'What about you, Brian? Your life all mapped out?'

Keyes chewed pensively.

'Someday I'm going to buy a sailboat,' he said. 'Move down to Islamorada, live off seaweed and lobsters. Let the sun fry me so brown that my hide gets tough as a turtle shell. I think I'd make a helluva good sea turtle—hey, don't look at me like that.'

'But you're serious!'

'A turtle's got no natural enemies,' Keyes said.

Kara Lynn felt warm. She liked the cozy smell of the sweater. 'Can I come visit you down there?'

'You bet. Fix up a nice big plate of sargassum. We'll pig out.'

Kara Lynn watched him so closely that Keyes began to feel a little uncomfortable. She was zeroing in on something. The old Jenna antennae started to twitch.

'What do you think about me, Brian?'

'I like you,' he said. 'I like you very much.'

'She really hurt you, didn't she?'

Out of the blue. Just when he'd started to relax.

'Who?' he said inanely.

'Jenna. One look at the two of you together—'

'Forget the two of us together.'

'I'm sorry. No more soap opera, I promise.' She folded her arms and sat back. Her gray-green eyes captured him, froze him in one place. Nineteen years old, no one should have a look that good, Keyes thought.

'I can't figure out what I like so much about you,' Kara Lynn said. 'But I think it's your attitude.'

'I've got a miserable attitude.'

'Yeah, you come on that way but it's bullshit, isn't it, Marlowe? Some of it's an act.'

'Until I grow my turtle shell.'

'What I like,' said Kara Lynn, 'is your attitude toward me. You're the first man who hasn't treated me like a porcelain doll. You don't pamper, you don't drool, and you don't try to impress me.'

Keyes smiled wanly. 'Somehow I knew there was no danger of that.'

'And I like the way you tell the truth,' she said. 'For instance, I think you told the truth just now when you said you liked me. I think you really do.'

'Sure.'

'I think you wouldn't mind if I kissed you.'

Keyes opened his mouth but nothing came out. He felt a little shaky. Like prom night, for God's sake.

Kara Lynn reached over and took his arm. She pulled him gently. 'Meet you halfway,' she said.

They kissed across the table. It was a long kiss, and Keyes nearly got lost in it. He also managed to plant his left elbow in the pizza.

'You're nervous,' she said.

'You're a client. That makes me nervous.'

'Naw. Pretty girls make you nervous.'

'Some of them, yeah.'

In the MG on the way home, she sat much closer.

'You're worried about me,' Kara Lynn said.

'I don't want you in this stupid parade.'

She held onto his right arm with both hands. 'I've got to do it. It's either me or some other girl.'

'Then let it be some other girl.'

'No, Brian.'

Things were changing—all of a sudden the stakes couldn't be higher. The harrowing parameters of his nightmare had become perceptible; and locked inside them, Kara Lynn Shivers and Skip Wiley.

Keyes wondered if the maniac had phoned Cab Mulcahy, like he promised.

'You're frightened, aren't you?' Kara Lynn asked.

'Yup.'

'We'll be all right,' she said. Like Jenna used to say.

The house was dark when Keyes pulled into the driveway. The shaggy-headed palms hung still in the crisp night. Grackles bickered high in the old ficus tree. From the flowerbed a disinterested calico cat watched them come up the walk.

Keyes waited on the second step while Kara Lynn unlocked the front door. He went in first, switched on a small lamp in the hall, checked around.

'Everything's fine,' he said. And out of habit took a step toward the guest room where he slept.

'No,' Kara Lynn whispered, taking his hand. 'Come upstairs.'

26

Skip Wiley stormed into the warehouse shortly after noon on the twenty-ninth of December, the day after the bombing at police headquarters.

'Where is Jesús?' Wiley demanded.

'Don't know,' Viceroy Wilson said.

'He was gone when we got here,' said Tommy Tigertail.

Both men were shirtless, with leather carpentry belts strung from their waists. The Indian had a red bandanna around his neck, and his caramel chest was beaded with perspiration. Viceroy Wilson wore gray sweatpants and faded aqua wristbands, which kept his hands dry.

They had worked unceasingly since dawn, and the skeletal contraption had grown to fill the warehouse from floor to ceiling.

'It's coming along,' Wiley said halfheartedly. 'You're doing fine.'

He paced with agitation, gnawing his lower lip, hands crammed in the pockets of his jeans. With each step his track shoes squeaked on the dusty concrete—a noise that only added to the tension. *El Fuego* was on the threshold of eruption; Viceroy Wilson and Tommy Tigertail could sense it.

In slow motion Skip Wiley picked up an iron mallet. He studied it methodically, weighed it in each hand, then began to pound the aluminum door like a gong. With every swing came a new expletive. 'That crazy-cretinous-brainless-shitheaded putz of a Cuban!' he grunted. 'Worthless-misguided-suicidal-goddamn miscreant!'

Viceroy Wilson flinched each time the mallet landed, the noise amplified in his skull by forty freshly ingested milligrams of methamphetamine.

'Why didn't he tell me about this?' Wiley cried. 'Who ordered him to go bomb that reptile Bloodworth?'

'Maybe he thought it would make up for the tennis thing,' Tommy Tigertail said.

'Rubbish! Even after my lecture on solidarity, he pulls a silly stunt like this! No wonder the other crazy Cubans kicked him out. I should have known better—I should have listened to you guys.'

Viceroy Wilson resisted the temptation to rub it in. Actually he was somewhat puzzled by Skip Wiley's anger. He figured that after all that had happened, Wiley ought to be elated to see Ricky Bloodworth go up in smoke. And if a new wave of counter-publicity was what Wiley sought, the bombing had been a bon-anza: *Las Noches* were all over the morning papers and TV. But Viceroy Wilson listened unquestioningly to the harangue because he simply couldn't bring himself to defend Jesús Bernal. He'd warned the little bastard to chill out until after New Year's.

'Insubordination!' Wiley bellowed. 'A group like ours can't survive with insubordination. You know what this is? A test, that's what. That slippery hot-blooded weasel is trying to push me as far as he can. He thinks I'm not tough enough. He wants *mucho macho*. He wants machetes and machine pistols and night-scopes. He wants us to dress in fatigues and crawl through mine-fields and bite the necks off live chickens. That's his idea of revolution. No subtlety, no wit, no goddamn style.'

Wiley was getting hoarse. He dropped the iron mallet. Viceroy Wilson handed him a jar of cold Gatorade.

'We need to find him,' the Indian said.

'Damn soon,' added Wilson.

Wilson wiped his mouth. 'Any clues?'

Viceroy Wilson shook his head. In one corner of the warehouse, on Bernal's pitiful carpet remnant, sat the Smith-Corona type-writer. It was empty.

'He won't be back,' Tommy Tigertail said.

'A loose cannon,' growled Wiley, subsiding a bit.

Viceroy Wilson decided there was no point in keeping Jesús Bernal's secret. 'The other night he was on the phone to his old dudes. Trying to get back on the A-team.'

'The First Weekend in July?'

'They told him no way,' Wilson said.

'So he decided to put on a one-man show,' Wiley said.

'Looks that way.'

'Well, that's gratitude for you.'

'Let's try to find him,' Tommy Tigertail repeated, with consternation.

'Hopeless,' Skip Wiley said. 'Anyway, he'll crawl back when he gets lonely—or when he can't stand the heat from García.'

'Oh fine,' Viceroy Wilson grumbled. 'Just what we need.'

Wiley said, 'Besides, I hate to completely give up on the guy.' What he really hated was the thought that anyone could resist his charisma or so blithely spurn his leadership. Recruiting a hard-core case like Jesús Bernal had been a personal triumph; losing him stung Skip Wiley's ego.

'Look, I've got to know,' he said. 'Are you boys still with the program?'

'Tighter than ever,' Viceroy Wilson said. The Indian nodded in agreement.

'What about the chopper?'

'Watson Island. Nine tonight,' Wilson said. 'The pilot's cool. Free-lance man. Does some jobs for the Marine Patrol, the DEA and the blockade-runners, too. Long as the price is nice.'

'And the goodies?' Wiley asked.

'Safe and sound,' Tommy Tigertail reported.

'Nobody got hurt?'

The Indian smiled—these white men! 'No, of course not,' he said. 'Everybody had a ball.'

Wiley sighed. 'Good, then we're on—with or without our Cuban friend.' He reached into a pocket and came out with something in the palm of his hand. To Viceroy Wilson the object looked like a pink castanet.

'What the hell,' Wiley said. He carefully placed the object on the keyboard of Jesús Bernal's abandoned typewriter. 'Just in case he comes back.'

It was a brand-new set of dentures.

*

Cab Mulcahy had waited all night for Skip Wiley to call again. He'd attached a small tape recorder to the telephone next to the bed and slept restlessly, if at all. There was no question of Wiley reaching him if he'd wanted—Skip knew the number, and had never been shy about calling. Back when he was writing in full stride, Wiley would phone Mulcahy at least once a week to demand the firing or public humiliation of some mid-level editor who had dared to alter the column. These tirades normally lasted about thirty minutes until Wiley's voice gave out and he hung up. Once in a while Mulcahy discovered that Skip was right—somebody indeed had mangled a phrase or even edited a fact error into the column; in these instances the managing editor would issue a firm yet discreet rebuke, but Wiley seldom was satisfied. He was constantly threatening to murder or sexually mutilate somebody in the newsroom and, on one occasion, actually fired a speargun at an unsuspecting editor at the city desk. For weeks there was talk of a lawsuit, but eventually the poor shaken fellow simply quit and took a job with a public-relations firm in Tampa. Wiley had been remorseless; as far as he was concerned, anyone who couldn't weather a little criticism had no business in journalism anyway. Cab Mulcahy had been dismayed: firing a spear at an editor was a sure way to bring in the unions. To punish Wiley, Mulcahy had forced him to drive out to the Deauville Hotel one morning and interview Wayne Newton. To no one's surprise, the resulting column was unprintable. The speargun episode eventually was forgiven.

As a habit Skip Wiley called Mulcahy's home only in moments of rage and only in the merciless wee hours of the morning, when Wiley could be sure of holding the boss's undivided attention. Which is why Cab Mulcahy scarcely slept Friday night, and why he was so fretful by Saturday morning when Skip still hadn't phoned. Keyes called twice to see if Wiley had made contact, but there was nothing to report; both of them worried that Skip might have changed his mind. By midafternoon Mulcahy—still unshaven, and rambling the house in a rumpled bathrobe—was battling a serious depression. He feared that he had missed the only chance to reason with Wiley or bring him in for help.

He was fixing a tuna sandwich on toast when the phone finally rang at half-past five. He hurried into the bedroom, closed the door, punched the tape recorder.

'Hello?'

'You viper!'

'Skip?'

'What kind of snake would let Bloodworth sodomize a Christmas column!'

'Where are you, buddy?'

'At the Gates of Hell, waiting. I told 'em to save you a ringside seat at the inferno.'

Mulcahy was impressed by Wiley's vitriol; not bad for a five-day-old rage. 'I'm sorry, Skip. I should never have done it. It was wrong.'

'Immoral is what it was.'

'Yes, you're right. I apologize. But I don't think morality is your strong suit, at the moment.'

'Whoa,' Wiley said. 'Blowing up Ricky Bloodworth was *not* my idea, Cab. It was one of those things that happens in the fever of revolution. Corrective measures are under way.'

'He's going to recuperate. You're damn lucky, Skip.'

'Yeah, I paid a visit to the hospital.'

'You did? But there's supposed to be a police guard!'

Wiley said, 'Don't get all upset. The kid was thrilled to see me. I brought him a stuffed skunk.'

Mulcahy decided to make his move. A conversation with Wiley was like a freight train: you either got aboard fast or you missed the whole damn thing.

'If you're in town, why don't you stop by the house?'

'Thanks, but I'm extremely busy, Cab.'

'I could meet you somewhere. At the club, maybe.'

'Let's cut the crap, okay?'

'Sure, Skip.'

'Keyes isn't as smart as he thinks.'

'Oh.'

'Neither are you.'

'What do you mean?'

'In due time, old friend.'

'Why are you doing this?' The wrong thing to say—Mulcahy knew it immediately.

'Why am I doing this? Cab, don't you read your own newspaper? Are you blind? What do you see when you stare out that big bay window, anyway? Maybe you can't understand because you weren't here thirty years ago, when it was paradise. Before they put parking meters on the beach. Before the beach disappeared. God, Cab, don't tell me you're like the rest of these migratory loons. They think it's heaven down here as long as the sun's out, long as they don't have to put chains on the tires, it's marvelous. They *think* it's really paradise, because, compared to Buffalo, it is. But, Cab, compared to paradise . . .'

'Skip, I know how you feel, believe me. But it'll never work.'

'Why not?'

'You can't evacuate South Florida, for God's sake. These people are here to stay.'

'That's what the cavemen said about tyrannosaurus.'

'Skip, listen to me. They won't leave for a bloody hurricane— what makes you think they'll move out after a few lousy bombs?'

'When the condos fail, the banks fail. When the banks fail, it's bye-bye lemmings.' Wiley sounded impatient. 'I explained all this to Keyes.'

'Okay, I understand it,' Mulcahy said. 'I understand perfectly. Just tell me, what's this business about "violating a sacred virgin"? How does that fit into your theory?'

'I thought you smartasses had it all figured out.'

'Well, if it's the Orange Bowl queen, forget it. The police are everywhere.'

'Maybe, maybe not.'

Mulcahy said, 'Skip, you're going to get yourself shot.'

'I'm not planning on it.'

'What *are* you planning?'

'To be on the front page of your newspaper again tomorrow.'

'Tomorrow?' Mulcahy found it difficult to sound nonchalant. 'But the parade's not for two days.'

'This is a little preview, Cab.'

Mulcahy was flustered. 'What kind of preview?'

Wiley said, 'You'll have to wait and see. As a courtesy, I'm advising you to budget some space for tomorrow's front page.'

Mulcahy took a deep breath. 'No, Skip.'

There was a pause; then Wiley laughed disbelievingly. 'What do you mean *no?*'

'I won't put the Nights of December on page one. I'll bury the story, so help me God.'

'You can't,' Wiley said, sounding vastly amused. 'Don't you see, you're powerless. You can't ignore the news unless you're ready to forsake the public trust—and you're not, Cab. I'll bet on it. You're too honorable, too ethical, too everything. The integrity of that newspaper is sacred to you, probably the only thing sacred in your life. Diddling around with my column is one thing, but censorship's another. You wouldn't do it, not in a million years. You're at the mercy of the news, old friend, and right now the news is me.'

'Skip, I still run this paper,' said Mulcahy, his voice taut. He was choking the phone with both hands.

'And you do a swell job running the paper,' Wiley said. 'But if you don't think I know how to make the front page after all these years, then it's *your* brain that's turned to Rice-a-Roni. Now I've really got to sign off. My schedule is extremely tight.'

'No, Skip, hold on just a second. I want you to please, please stop killing these innocent people—'

'Dammit, I haven't. Not one. Not innocent.'

'Just stop the murders, please. As a friend I'm begging you. The cops are going to figure it out and they'll track you down. Why don't you end this thing and turn yourself in. You need—'

'What do I need? Help? I need help? Come on, Cab, lighten up. Melodrama doesn't suit you. I've got to run.'

'Skip, if you hang up, I'm calling García. I'm going to give him your name, tell him everything.'

'Brian didn't explain the rules.'

'I can't go along anymore, threats or not. Bloodbath, my ass—I mean, what more can you do, Skip? You even blew up one of my reporters.'

'So you're going to put all this in the newspaper?'

'Absolutely.'

'Then do me a favor,' Wiley said seriously.

'What?'

'Make sure you run a good picture. I'm partial to the right-side profile, the one where I'm wearing the corduroy jacket. The dark brown one.'

'Yeah, I remember,' Mulcahy said dejectedly.

'What about Cardoza?'

'He's next on my list, after the cops.'

'S'pose he wants his New Year's column.'

'Don't even think about it,' Mulcahy said.

'Fine. Be that way. The paper's dull as dishwater.'

'I'll handle Cardoza,' Mulcahy said.

'I'm sure. But in the meantime, Cab, watch the heavens.'

'What do you mean?'

'Watch the heavens! Got that?'

'Yes,' Mulcahy said. He didn't like the sound of things. He would have preferred that Wiley not bother giving any more clues. 'Look, Skip, why don't you call Brian?'

'He's busy nymphet-sitting.'

'Talk to him!'

'Nah.'

'Okay, then he wanted me to tell you something. He wanted me to tell you that it's hopeless, that what you're doing is sheer suicide. He wanted me to tell you that whether you know it or not, it's all over.'

'Ho-ho-ho,' Skip Wiley said, and hung up.

Right away Cab Mulcahy put in a call to Al García, but the entire Fuego One Task Force was out in the Everglades on a tip. A deer hunter had stumbled into a fresh campsite that looked promising; García wasn't expected back in the office until morning. Mulcahy left an urgent message.

Next he tried Keyes, but Brian was gone too. There was a photo session out on the beach. Reed Shivers explained—the Orange Bowl queen at sunset. The languid look, very artsy. Keyes had tagged along to keep an eye on things; took the gun but not his beeper.

'Shit,' Mulcahy said.

Cardoza was strike three. The publisher was attending the Palm Beach premiere of a new Burt Reynolds movie. Afterward was a cookout at Generoso Pope's.

Cab Mulcahy fixed himself a pitcher of martinis, sat down with Mozart on the stereo, and waited for the telephone to ring. It was the lousiest Saturday night of his life, and it was about to get worse.

One of Sparky Harper's only legacies was the annual pre-Orange Bowl Friendship Cruise. Each year, on the Saturday evening before the Monday parade, a large contingent of visiting dignitaries, politicians, VIPs and wealthy tourists set sail from the Port of Miami for a two-day junket to Freeport and Key West. Sparky Harper had inaugurated the Friendship Cruise as a goodwill gimmick, and also as a secret favor to one of his ex-wives' brothers, who ran a lucrative catering firm for the cruise lines. For the first few years, the Orange Bowl queen contestants had been invited along on the cruise, as had all the Orange Bowl football players. However, the Chamber of Commerce quietly discontinued this policy in the late 1970s following an unseemly episode involving a lifeboat, a young beauty queen, and three University of Oklahoma sophomore linebackers. Once the beauty contestants and the football players had been banned from the ship, Sparky Harper had found himself with loads of empty chairs and four hundred pounds of surplus Gulf shrimp. It was then he had gotten the idea to invite journalists—but not just any journalists: travel writers. Sparky Harper and the Greater Miami Chamber of Commerce adored travel writers because travel writers never wrote stories about street crime, water pollution, fish kills, beach erosion, refugees, AIDS epidemics, nuclear accidents, cocaine smuggler, gunrunners, or race riots. Once in a while, a daring travel writer would mention one of these subjects in passing, but strictly in the context of a minor setback from which South Florida was pluckily rebounding. For instance, when huge tracts of Miami Beach began to disappear into the ocean, leaving nothing but garish hotels at water's edge, a decision was made to hastily build a new beach out of dredged-up rock, shells, and coral grit. Once this was done, Sparky Harper mailed out hundreds of impressive aerial photographs to newspapers everywhere. Sure enough, many travel writers soon journeyed to Miami and wrote about the wondrous new beach without ever mentioning the fact that you needed logger's boots to cross it without lacerating the veins of your feet. As a rule, travel writers wrote only about the good stuff; they were A-okay in Sparky's book. So, with the endorsement of the Chamber of Commerce, in 1980 Sparky Harper invited fifty travel writers from newspapers all across North America to come to Miami during Orange Bowl Week and sail the Friendship Cruise. Of course, 1980 was the year of the Liberty City riots and the Mariel boatlift, so only nine travel writers showed up, several of them carrying guns for protection. The following year the turnout was much better, and the year after that, better still. By the time of Sparky Harper's death, the Friendship Cruise was widely regarded by American travel writers as one of the premier junkets in the business.

This year the Chamber of Commerce unanimously had voted to dedicate the event to Sparky Harper's memory. On the night of December 29, four weeks after Sparky's murder, a crowd of 750 gathered at the Port of Miami and listened as the mayor of Miami read a brief tribute to the slain public-relations wizard. Afterward the crowd streamed up the gangplank and boarded the SS *Nordic Princess*, where an orgy of eating and drinking and banal joke-telling commenced.

The SS *Nordic Princess* was a sleek cruise liner, and nearly brand-new. Built on a fiord in Norway, she was 527 feet long and carried a gross tonnage of 16,500. She had seven decks, four hundred cabins, two heated swimming pools, five restaurants, eight bars, a spa, a library, a bowling alley, fifty slot machines, and a video arcade. There was also a branch of Chase Manhattan on the gambling mezzanine. The *Nordic Princess* was served by a crew of three hundred, mostly Dominicans and Haitians, with a few obligatory white Englishmen to serve as bell captains and maître d's.

Many of the passengers on the Friendship Cruise had never before sailed on an ocean liner. One of them was Mack Dane, the new travel writer from the Tulsa *Express*. Dane was a spry and earnest fellow in his mid-sixties who had spent most of his newspaper career trying to cover the oil industry. As a reward for his thirty-two years of service (and also to get him out of the way to make room for a young reporter), the *Express* had 'promoted' him to the travel beat. The Orange Bowl was his first assignment, the Friendship Cruise his maiden voyage.

Like most of the guests aboard the *Nordic Princess*, Mack Dane was tickled to be in Miami in December. He had just spoken to his daughter back in Oklahoma and learned that there was three feet of fresh snow and a wind chill of forty-two below, and that the dog had frozen to the doorstep.

As the ship glided out of Government Cut, Mack Dane found his way to the top deck and strategically positioned himself near a tray of fresh stone crabs and jumbo shrimp. Christmas lights were strung festively from the ship's smokestacks, and a live *salsa* band was performing a medley of Jimmy Buffett tunes in a fashion that no one had ever dreamed possible. A strong breeze blew in from the ocean, pushing clouds and a promise of light rain. Mack Dane grabbed another banana daiquiri. He was having a grand time. He wondered if any of his fellow travel writers were young and pretty.

Two tourists stood at the rail and waved at the tiny figures of snook fishermen out on the jetty. Mack Dane watched the tourists for a few minutes and decided to interview them for his story. They looked like a reasonable couple.

'The Gilberts,' they said warmly. 'Montreal.'

Sam Gilbert was about forty years old. He wore pale yellow slacks and an expensive toupee that was having a rough go of it with the wind. Other than that, he was a handsome-looking gentleman with a pleasant smile. His wife appeared to be in her late thirties. She was dressed in a tasteful beige pantsuit, a sheer silk scarf tucked around her neck. His hair was so unnaturally blond that it was attracting fireflies, but other than that Mrs. Gilbert looked like a friendly and decent person.

'This your first cruise?' Mack Dane asked.

'Yes,' Mrs. Gilbert said. 'We had to book four months in advance. This is a very popular trip.'

Mack Dane told them he was a travel writer, and a guest of the Chamber of Commerce.

'You didn't have to pay?' Mrs. Gilbert said.

'Well, no.'

'What a great job,' said Sam Gilbert.

'First trip to Miami?' Mack Dane asked.

'Right,' Gilbert said. 'We're here to see the Irish stomp the Huskers.' Notre Dame was playing the University of Nebraska in the Orange Bowl football game on New Year's Day. According to many sportswriters, the game would determine the national collegiate football championship.

'I don't like football,' Mrs. Gilbert confided. 'I'm here for the sunshine and shopping.'

'We just bought a winter home in Boca Raton,' Sam Gilbert said. 'Not a home, actually, a condominium.'

'Sam's a doctor,' Mrs. Gilbert explained.

Mack Dane felt like another drink. The *Nordic Princess* was out to sea, rocking ever so lightly in the northeast chop. Behind her, the skies of Miami glowed a burnished orange from the sodium anticrime lights.

'So it's safe to say you're really enjoying this trip,' Mack Dane said.

'Oh yes.' Mrs. Gilbert noisily attacked a stone-crab claw. Mack Dane wondered if she'd considered removing the shell first.

'Put in your article,' she said, 'that Dr. and Mrs. Samuel Gilbert of Montreal, Canada, are having the time of their lives.'

Sam Gilbert said, 'I wouldn't go that far.'

'Mr. Dane, could you do us a favor? Could you take our picture?'

'Sure.' Mack Dane put away his notebook and wiped his hands on a cocktail napkin that was decorated with the seal of the State of Florida. Mrs. Gilbert handed him a small thirty-five-millimeter camera with a built-in flash and built-in focus and built-in light meter.

The Gilberts posed arm-in-arm against the rail of the ship. Sam Gilbert wore his doctor face while Mrs. Gilbert kept reaching up and fiddling with his toupee, which, in the strong wind, had begun to resemble a dead starling.

Mack Dane squinted through the viewfinder and tried to frame the Gilberts romantically, with the lights of Miami shining over their shoulders. At first it was a perfect picture—if only there'd been a full moon! Then something went wrong. Suddenly Mack Dane couldn't see the Gilberts anymore; he couldn't see anything through the camera except a white light. He figured something broke on the focus.

But when he took the camera away from his face, Mack Dane realized that the white light was real: a beam piercing down from the heavens. Or from something *in* the heavens. Something that hovered like a dragonfly high above the SS *Nordic Princess*.

'A helicopter,' Mack Dane said. 'A big one.' He knew the sound of a chopper. He'd flown them lots of times out to the oil rigs.

The Gilberts craned their necks and stared into the sky, shielding their eyes from the powerful search beam. The other partiers crowded together, pointing. The *salsa* band took a break.

Mack Dane said, 'It's coming down.'

The helicopter did seem to be descending slowly, but it was no longer in a hover, it was flying in a slow arc. Trailing behind the chopper was a long advertising banner.

'This is really tacky,' Sam Gilbert said.

Mack Dane put on eyeglasses and turned in circles, trying to read the streamer. In four-foot letters it said: 'AVAST AND AHOY: WELCOME TO THE REVOLUTI—'

'Revoluti?' puzzled Sam Gilbert.

'Maybe it's a new perfume,' said his wife.

Mack Dane wondered if some letters had fallen off the advertisement.

The helicopter dropped lower and lower, and soon the partiers aboard the Friendship Cruise found themselves drowned to silence by the rotor noise. When the chopper was no more than one hundred feet above the deck, the banner was cut loose. It fluttered into the sea like an enormous confetti. The crowd ooooohhhed, and a few even applauded.

Mack Dane noticed that the top deck—the Royal Sun Deck, according to the ship's guide—was filling with tourists and VIPs and travel writers who had come up from below to investigate the commotion. Before long, people were packed elbow to elbow. In the meantime, the captain of the SS *Nordic Princess* had grown concerned about the reckless helicopter and cut his speed to eight knots.

'Hello, folks!' said a brassy male voice. Somebody on the helicopter had an electric bullhorn.

'Having a good time in Florida?' the voice called.

'Yeaaaah!' shouted the partiers, their faces upturned brightly. Some of the stuffy civic-leader types—the mayor, the Orange Bowl committeemen, the Chamber of Commerce life members— were miffed at the interruption of the cruise but, not wanting to spoil anyone's fun, said nothing.

The loud voice in the helicopter said: 'How would all of you like some genuine Florida souvenirs?'

'Yeaaaaah!' shouted the partiers.

'Well, here you go!' the voice said.

A door on the side of the helicopter opened and a white parcel plummeted toward the deck of the *Nordic Princess*. It was followed by another and another. At first Mack Dane thought the objects might be miniature parachutes or beach towels, but when one landed near his feet he saw that it was only a shopping bag from Neiman-Marcus. Soon the deck was being rained with shopping bags from all the finest department stores—Lord and Taylor, Bloomingdale's, Macy's, Burdine's, Jordan Marsh, Saks. Once the travelers realized what was happening, the Friendship Cruise quickly dissolved into a frenzied scrabble for the goodies.

Mack Dane thought: This is some advertising gimmick.

To her credit, Mrs. Gilbert held her own against stiff competition. She outmuscled a jewelry dealer from Brooklyn and the vicious wife of a Miami city commissioner to capture three of the prized shopping bags.

'Look, Sam!'

'Really,' Sam Gilbert muttered.

'What did you win?' Mack Dane asked.

'I'm not sure,' Mrs. Gilbert said. The shopping bags were stapled shut. She ripped one open and fished inside.

Her hand came out with a bracelet. The bracelet had a pattern of pale yellow chain, and looked like rubber. The odd thing was, it appeared to be moving.

It was a live snake.

Mrs. Gilbert was speechless. Her eyelids fluttered as the snake coiled around her creamy wrist. Its strawberry tongue flicked in and out, tasting her heat.

'Jesus Christ,' said her husband.

It was not a big snake, maybe three feet long, but it was dark brown and fat as a kitchen pipe. The snake was every bit as bewildered as the Gilberts.

Behind Mack Dane a woman shrieked. And across the deck, another. A man yelled out, 'Oh my God!' and fainted with his eyes open. As if jarred from a trance, Mrs. Gilbert dropped the brown snake and back-pedaled; her jaw was going up and down, but nothing was coming out.

By now each of the shopping bags (exactly two hundred in all) had been opened with the same startling results.

The sundeck of the *Nordic Princess* was crawling with snakes. King snakes, black snakes, blue runners, garter snakes, green snakes, banded water snakes, ring-necked snakes, yellow rat snakes, corn snakes, indigo snakes, scarlet king snakes. Most of the snakes were harmless, except for a handful of Eastern diamondback rattlers and cottonmouth water moccasins, like the one in Mrs. Gilbert's prize bag. Skip Wiley had not planned on dropping any poisonous snakes—he didn't think it necessary— but he'd neglected to tell Tommy Tigertail and his crew of Indian snake-catchers. The Seminoles made no distinction, spiritual or taxonomical, between venomous and nonvenomous snakes; all were holy.

As the reptiles squirmed across the teakwood, the crowd panicked. Several men tried to stomp on the snakes; others rushed forward brandishing deck chairs and fire extinguishers. Many of the snakes became agitated and began snapping in all directions.

Mrs. Gilbert, among others, was bitten on the ankle.

Her husband the doctor stood there helplessly.

'I'm just a radiologist,' he said to Mack Dane.

The captain of the *Nordic Princess* looked down from the wheel-room and saw bedlam on his ship. To restore order, he blew the ship's tremendous horn three times.

'What does that mean?' cried Sam Gilbert, who was carrying his wife around on his back.

Mack Dane did not care to admit that although he was a travel writer, he knew nothing about ocean liners. So he said: 'I think it means we abandon ship.'

'Abandon ship!' screamed Mrs. Gilbert.

And they did. They formed a flying wedge, hundreds of them, and crashed through the rails and ropes of the upper deck. The Gilberts were among the first to go, plunging seventy feet into the Atlantic Ocean, leaving the ship to the damnable snakes.

As soon as he hit the water, Mack Dane was sorry he'd said anything about jumping overboard. The water was chilly and rough, and he wondered how long he could stay afloat. It also occurred to him, in hindsight, that sharks might be infinitely worse than a bunch of frightened snakes.

The *Nordic Princess* came dead in the water, towering like a gray wall above the frantic swimmers. Fire bells rang at both ends of the ship. Mack Dane could see crew members on every deck throwing life preservers and lowering the dinghies. The ocean seemed full of shrieking people, their heads bobbing like so many coconuts.

Mack Dane noticed that the mystery helicopter was circling again, firing its hot-white spotlight into the water. Occasionally the beam would fix on the befuddled face of a dog-paddling tourist.

From the helicopter drifted a melody, muted by the engines and warped by the wind. It was not a soothing song, either. It was Pat Boone sounding like Brenda Lee. It was the theme from the motion picture *Exodus*.

A good-looking man in a business suit who was treading water near Mack Dane raised up a fist and hollered at the helicopter: 'You sick bastards!'

Mack Dane recognized the man as the mayor of Miami.

'Who are those guys up there?' Mack Dane asked. He was thinking about the story he'd have to write, if he survived.

'Fucking Nachos,' the mayor said. He kicked hard and swam off toward the SS *Nordic Princess*.

Mack Dane watched the chopper climb sharply and bank east, against the wind. The white spotlight vanished and the cabin door closed. In a few moments all that was visible were three pinpoints of light—red, green, and white—on the fuselage, although the racket of the propellers remained audible, dicing the night air.

An empty lifeboat drifted toward Mack Dane and he pulled himself aboard. He peeled off his blazer and laid it on his lap. As he was helping a young couple from Lansing, Michigan, climb in, Mack Dane saw a diamondback rattlesnake swim by. It looked miserable and helpless.

'What a night,' said the man from Lansing.

Something about the sound of the helicopter changed. Mack Dane looked for the lights and spotted them about a mile east of the ship, and low to the purple horizon. The rotor engines sounded rough, the pitch rising.

'Something's not right,' Mack Dane said.

The next sound was a wet roar, dying among the waves. Then the sky turned quiet and gray. The helicopter was gone. A plume of smoke rose off the water, marking the grave as surely as a cross. A few minutes later, the rain came.

27

Miraculously, none of the voyagers from the *Nordic Princess* perished in the Atlantic Ocean. Many had snatched life jackets before leaping overboard; others proved competent if not graceful swimmers. Some of the tourists were too drunk to panic and simply lolled in the waves, like polyester manatees, until help arrived. Others, including the Gilberts, were saved by strong tidal currents that dragged them to a shallow sandbar where they waited in waist-deep water, their hair matted to pink skulls, each of them still wearing a plastic nametag that said, 'Hi! I'm—'. Luckily a Coast Guard cutter had arrived swiftly and deployed inflatable Zodiac speedboats to round up the passengers. By midnight, all 312 missing persons had been retrieved. The rescue had unfolded so quickly that all thirteen victims of poisonous snakebites made it to the hospital with time to spare and only transient hallucinations. A survey of other casualties included one possible heart attack, seven broken bones, four man-of-war stings, and a dozen litigable whiplashes.

Although the thrust of the rescue efforts concentrated around the cruise ship, a small contingent of Coast Guardsmen launched a separate search for the mystery helicopter one mile away. A slashing rain and forty-mile-per-hour gusts made the task dangerous and nearly impossible. As the night wore on, the waves grew to nine feet and the searchers reluctantly gave up.

The next morning, in a misty sprinkle, a sturdy shrimp trawler out of Virginia Key came upon a fresh oil slick a few miles off Miami Beach. Floating in the blue-black ooze was a tangle of debris: two seat cushions and a nest of electronic wiring from the helicopter, an album sleeve from an old Pat Boone record, a bloodied white-and-aqua football jersey, an Australian bush hat with a red emblem on the crown, and two dozen empty plastic shopping bags from Saks Fifth Avenue. Judging by the location of the slick, the helicopter had gone down in 450 feet of water. When the skies cleared, the Coast Guard sent two choppers of its own, but no more wreckage was found. A forensics expert from the Navy later reported to the Fuego One Task Force that no one could have survived the crash, and that there was virtually no chance of recovering any bodies. The water, he said, was full of lemon sharks.

Terrorist Believed Dead After Aerial Assault on Cruise Ship.

Skip Wiley had been right. The wild saga of the *Nordic Princess* appeared in sixty-point type across the front page of the Miami *Sun* the next morning. Cab Mulcahy had been left with no choice, for Wiley had shrewdly selected the day of the week with the most anemic competition for news space—the President was giving a speech on abortion, a bus filled with pilgrims crashed in India, and a trained chimpanzee named Jake upchucked in the space shuttle. The sensational story of *Las Noches* got big play all over the country, and wound up on the front pages of the Washington *Post*, the Atlanta *Journal* and *Constitution*, the Los Angeles *Times*, the Chicago *Tribune* and the Philadelphia *Inquirer*. The version that appeared in the Miami *Sun* was the most detailed by far, though it made no mention of Wiley's role; Mulcahy was still trying to reach Al García to tell him.

Only one other newspaper devoted as much space to the *Nordic Princess* story as did the *Sun*, and that was the Tulsa *Express*. (Old Mack Dane had outdone himself, dictating thirty-eight breath-taking inches of copy to the national desk over a Coast Guards-man's marine-band radio.) As for the broadcast media, NBC had capitalized on its extra Orange Bowl manpower and diverted camera crews to the Port of Miami, Coast Guard headquarters, and Flagler Memorial Hospital. Heroes, victims, witnesses, and distant relatives flocked to the bright television lights, hoping to be interviewed by Jane Pauley or someone equally glamorous. By Sunday noon, much of the United States had heard or seen the story about killer snakes from the sky and the gang of South Florida crazies known as the Nights of December.

The chairman of the Orange Bowl Committee didn't know whether to laugh or blow his brains out. In the space of forty-eight hours at the apogee of the tourist season, homicidal lunatics had detonated a newspaper reporter and launched an aerial attack against a domestic ocean liner. That was the bad news. The good news was: the bastards were dead. The parade was saved.

At 8:30 A.M. on Sunday, December 30, a press conference was staged at the office of the Greater Miami Chamber of Commerce, in the hallowed room with the table shaped like a giant navel orange. Sitting around the table's upper hemisphere were the chairman of the Orange Bowl Committee (at the stem), then Sergeant Al García, Sparky Harper's successor at the Chamber of Commerce, the mayors of Miami and Dade County, the police chiefs of Miami and Dade County, and an officer from the Coast Guard, who wished he were someplace else. The lower half of the table was occupied by reporters and cameramen, including a crew from the CBS *Morning News*.

The Orange Bowl chairman stood up and spoke nervously into a microphone at a portable podium. He read from a prepared statement:

'Ladies and gentlemen, thank you for coming on such short notice. At approximately 9:16 last night, the cruise ship SS *Nordic Princess* was accosted by an unmarked, unidentified helicopter off the coast of Miami Beach, Florida. At the time of the attack, the cruise ship was under lease to the Greater Miami Chamber of Commerce as part of the Orange Bowl Jamboree festivities. As a result of hostile actions undertaken by occupants of the helicopter, more than three hundred persons were forced to abandon the ocean liner in an emergency Mayday. I am happy to report that all those passengers, including myself and several others in this room, were safely rescued. All of us wish to extend our heartfelt thanks to Commander Bob Smythe and the United States Coast Guard for their quick and decisive action.'

Commander Bob Smythe smiled wanly as a half-dozen motor-drive Nikons went off in his face. He couldn't wait for his transfer to Charleston to come through.

'Shortly after the incident involving the *Nordic Princess*,' the Orange Bowl man continued reading, 'the suspect helicopter flew away from the cruise ship in an easterly direction. At approximately 9:21 P.M., the aircraft experienced engine trouble and apparently went down at sea. No radio contact was ever made with the helicopter, so the nature of its distress may never be known.'

The Orange Bowl chairman paused for a drink of water. He was unhappy with the tone of the press release, which had been composed hastily by a high-priced public-relations man. The PR man was a former Washington magazine editor who was reputed to be the model of glibness in crisis situations, but the Orange Bowl chairman was unimpressed. The press release sounded stiff and tedious, like it had come out of the Pentagon. The Orange Bowl chairman didn't know much about good writing, but he knew 'Tropical Tranquillity' when he saw it—and this wasn't it. He wondered why it was so hard to find a good cheap hack.

'At approximately 6:07 this morning, a commercial fishing vessel discovered fuel residue and evidence of helicopter wreckage approximately six miles off Miami Beach. Navy and Coast Guard personnel searched the area thoroughly and found no signs of survivors. Because of the preponderance of carnivorous deep-water marine species, it is highly unlikely that any human remains will be recovered.

'However, one item found in the debris has been conclusively identified as the property of Daniel Wilson, age thirty-six, a former professional football player who had been sought as a suspect in several recent kidnappings.'

The Orange Bowl chairman reached into a brown grocery bag and pulled out the dark-stained Miami Dolphins jersey belonging to Viceroy Wilson. At the sight of the number 31, the photographers became frenzied.

'According to Sergeant Al García of the Metro-Dade police, Mr. Wilson was an active member of a small terrorist group known as *Las Noches de Diciembre*. This organization, also known as the Nights of December, has claimed credit for several recent kidnappings, homicides, and bombings in the Miami area, including the so-called Trifecta Massacre at the Hibiscus Kennel Club. The Nights of December also are prime suspects in a bombing incident two days ago in which a local journalist was seriously injured. We have strong reason to believe it was Mr. Wilson and three other members of this radical cell who carried out last night's attack on the *Nordic Princess*, and who died in the subsequent helicopter crash. While every effort is being made to verify this information, we feel confident that a sinister and senseless threat to our community has been removed, and that the people of South Florida can celebrate the new year—and the Orange Bowl festival—without fear or worry. Thank you all very much.'

The Orange Bowl chairman sat down and wiped the back of his neck with a crisp white handkerchief. He had no intention of uttering another word, or doing anything to ruin his slick job of delivering the press release. He'd even improvised a bit, changing the distasteful and tourist-repellent phrase 'oil slick' to 'fuel residue' in the third paragraph.

As soon as the reporters began firing questions, the Orange Bowl chairman motioned Al García to the podium.

The detective approached the long-necked microphone with extreme caution, as if it were a flamethrower.

'What about Jesús Bernal?' a TV reporter shouted.

'No comment,' García said. He felt like having a cigarette, but the chief had ordered him not to smoke in front of the cameras.

'Where did all the snakes come from?' someone asked.

'I've got no idea,' said Al García. The sound of two dozen scribbling felt-tip pens clawed at his nerves.

'What about the banner?' a radio reporter said. 'Did you find the banner?'

'No comment.'

'Where did the chopper come from?'

'No comment.'

Several reporters began to complain about all the *no comments* and threatened to walk out of the press conference. The Dade County mayor excitedly whispered something to the chief of police, who leaned across and excitedly whispered something to Al García. The detective glared at all of them.

'Seems I've been authorized to answer your questions,' García told the reporters, 'as long as it won't interfere with the investigation. About the helicopter—we haven't traced it yet. It was a rebuilt Huey 34, probably stolen up in Lauderdale or Palm Beach.'

'What about Jesús Bernal?' asked a man from a Cuban radio station.

Al García decided to give the guys in the orange blazers something to think about. 'We have no evidence that Mr. Bernal was aboard the helicopter last night,' he said.

The Orange Bowl chairman shot to his feet. 'But he probably was!'

'We have no such evidence,' García repeated.

'What about the banner?' the radio reporter asked.

'We recovered it this morning, tangled up in a swordfish line. The streamer was rented yesterday afternoon from Cairo Advertising at the Opa-locka Airport. Three individuals were seen attaching the letters. A white male, bearded, late thirties, wearing an Australian bush hat; a black male, approximately the same age but heavyset, wearing a football jersey; a younger, dark-skinned male, clean-shaven, described as either a Mexican or a native American Indian. The banner on the chopper basically said the same thing as all the previous communiqués—"Welcome to the Revolution" et cetera.'

'Those men seen at the airport,' a TV reporter said, 'those were The Nachos?'

'*Las Noches*,' García snapped.

'Who paid for the banner?' somebody shouted.

'Apparently the white male.'

'How much?'

The Orange Bowl chairman sensed that it had been a tactical mistake to let Al García stand at the microphone. The idiot was actually answering the journalists' questions. The more García talked, the more frenetically the reporters wrote in their notebooks. And the more they wrote in their notebooks, the more stories would appear in the newspapers and the more airtime the dead Nachos would get. More was not what the Orange Bowl Committee wanted to see.

The chairman stood up and said with a smile, 'I think that's all for now.' But he was completely ignored by everyone, including Al García.

'The white male suspect paid three hundred dollars cash for use of the advertising streamer,' García said.

'Could that man have been *El Fuego*?' a reporter asked.

'It's possible, yeah.'

'Did he give a name at the airport?'

'Yes, he did,' García said.

Then all at once, like a flock of crows: 'What?'

García glanced over at the police chief. The chief shrugged. The Orange Bowl chairman waved a chubby hand, trying to get somebody's attention.

'The suspect did use a name at the airport,' García said, 'but we believe it was an alias.'

'What was it?'

'In fact, we're ninety-nine percent sure it was an alias,' the detective said, fading from the microphone.

'What was it, Al? What?'

'Well,' García said, 'the name the suspect gave was Hugo. Victor Hugo.'

There was a lull in the questioning while the reporters explained to each other who Victor Hugo was.

'What about motive?' somebody shouted finally.

'That's easy,' García replied. 'They attacked the ocean liner for the same reason they marinated Sparky Harper in Coppertone. Publicity.' He smiled with amusement at all the busy notebooks. 'Looks to me like they got exactly what they wanted.'

The press conference had taken a perilous turn, and the Orange Bowl chairman could no longer contain his rising panic. Squeezing to the podium, he discreetly placed a stubby hand between García's shoulder blades and guided the detective to the nearest available chair. Then the Orange Bowl man boldly seized the neck of the microphone himself. 'Ladies and gentlemen,' he said cordially, 'wouldn't you rather hear the mayor's firsthand account of his escape from the *Nordic Princess*?'

Brian Keyes watched the press conference on a television in Kara

Lynn Shivers' bedroom. Her father was out playing golf and her mother was eating quiche with the Junior League.

Kara Lynn was curled up on the bed in bikini panties and a lemon T-shirt. Keyes wore cutoffs. He squeezed her hand as they listened to Al García talking to the reporters. When the mayor got up and started to tell about the helicopter attack, Keyes punched the remote control and switched to a basketball game.

For a long time he didn't say anything, just stared at the TV screen. Kara Lynn put her arms around him and kissed him on the neck.

'It's really over,' she whispered.

'I don't know,' Keyes said distantly. He kept visualizing that crackpot Wiley, strolling into the Opa-locka Airport with his bush hat and two hundred bags of wild snakes. Keyes tried to imagine the scene later, aboard the Huey, Wiley and his portable record player; Wiley trying to explain *Exodus* to Viceroy Wilson.

'The only one left is that Cuban,' Kara Lynn said.

'Maybe.' Keyes tried to think of Skip Wiley as dead and could not. The obstacle was not grief; it was plain disbelief. It was not beyond Wiley to have rented an aged and dangerously unreliable helicopter, or to have hired an inept pilot. What was uncharacteristic was for Wiley to have placed himself so squarely in jeopardy. All through December he had kept a safe distance from the actual terrorism, sending Wilson or Bernal or the Seminole to take the big risks. Why the sudden bravery? Keyes wondered. And what a convenient way to die. He had felt a little guilty that he could summon so little sadness for his old friend—but then again, maybe it was too soon for mourning.

'The late Victor Hugo,' Keyes mused. Wiley must have known how his friends would smile at that one; he was forever edifying his own legend.

'*Les Misérables*,' Kara Lynn said. 'Sounds like Mr. Fuego had a sense of humor.'

'Sick,' Keyes said. 'Sick, sick, sick.' Wiley would be better off dead, he thought, before the incredible dismal truth were known. With Wiley dead, Kara Lynn would be safe. So would the newspaper; Cab Mulcahy could return to the world of honest journalism. It would be better for almost everybody if Wiley were lost at sea, everybody except Jenna—Jenna was another issue. She hadn't been aboard that helicopter. Keyes knew it instinctively. Jenna's talent was creating catastrophes, then avoiding them.

'I want this to be the end,' Kara Lynn said quietly.

'Well, maybe it is.'

'But you don't believe they're really dead,' she said.

'The way it happened, it's too perfect.'

'The Prince of Cynics. You don't believe life can ever be perfect?'

'Nope,' Keyes said. 'Death, either.'

Later, when Kara Lynn was in the shower, Al García phoned.

'It's about damn time,' Keyes groused.

'Been kinda hectic around here,' the detective said. 'I saw this stack of messages from you and Mulcahy. Figured your conscience finally woke up.'

'We had our reasons, Al. Now it's time to talk.'

'Oh, I can't wait. But it just so happens I already got a line on *El Fuego*.'

So García knew.

Keyes felt lousy about not telling him in the first place, but Wiley's threats had seemed serious and, in retrospect, believable. García would have to understand.

'When we were doing routine checks on Wilson and Bernal, I had a pal search the morgue at the newspaper,' the detective said. 'Easy, really. I guess it's all on computer now. Funny thing, Brian. About four months ago your asshole buddy Wiley does this story on whatever happened to Daniel Viceroy Wilson, the famous football star. Very sympathetic. Hard-times-for-the-troubled-black-athlete number. Typical liberal shit. Anyway, three weeks later, guess what? Guy does a column about Jesús Bernal. *Our* precious Jesús. *Fire burns in the breast of a young Cuban freedom fighter*—that's how the story starts off. Makes me sick, too, I gotta tell you. Nearly tossed my black beans. So I'm thinking, what a weird coincidence this is: two of the four Nights of December getting a big ride in the newspaper just before the ca-ca hits the fan. So, for the hell of it, what d'you suppose I do?'

'Pull all Wiley's columns.'

'Right. Big stack of 'em, and they're full of geeks and cons and losers . . . shit, if you threw them all together you'd have the scariest nest of bizarros in the history of the planet Earth. Took me a week to wade through that crap, too—hey, the guy can write, I told you that. He can put the words together okay, but it's his attitude that hacks me off. Such an arrogant hump. Anyway, out of all these columns, guess who pops up next? Your Indian, Brian, the guy with the airboat, Tommy Tigerpaws or whatever the hell it is. A fucking full-blooded gator-wrestling white-hating Seminole Indian. I got more stuff out of Wiley's column than I've been able to squeeze out of the whole Seminole tribe. Turns out ole Tommy's richer than your average Colombian snow-bird. And he's also very bitter about all the bad shit to come down on his ancestors—for that I can't blame him, Brian. That was *your* people too. The Cubans had nothing to do with screwing the Indians out of Florida.'

'Al, let's—'

'I'm almost done, *amigo*. So after all this I look on my desk and what have I got? I got an angry black racist football player, a crazy bomb-happy Cuban revolutionary, and a filthy-rich Indian with a bingo chip on his shoulder. Three of the four. So the rest was easy, even for a dumb cop like me—the trick was to read everything Wiley wrote for the last two years. *Cristo!* What a strange guy.'

'Funny you didn't mention all this at the press conference,' Keyes said.

'Gee, guess I forgot.'

Which meant García wasn't ready to buy the chopper crash.

'It bugs me,' he said. 'I think to myself, why would *El Fuego* pick a stunt like this to show his face?'

'If only they'd found some bodies,' Keyes said. The words sounded stark and bloodless, but he meant them. He said to García: 'What do we do now?'

'The smart guys in the suits say it's all over.'

'What do you say, Al?'

'I say we wait till after the parade before we open the fucking champagne.'

'Good idea. In the meantime, I'll stick with the queen.'

'One more thing, Brian. Since I'm nice enough not to immediately throw your ass in jail for obstruction, the least you could do is stop by later and tell me about your crazy batshit friend.'

'Yeah,' Keyes said, 'I guess I'd better.'

28

As Al García hung up, he chided himself for not hollering more at Brian Keyes. He didn't know why Keyes had held back about Skip Wiley all these weeks, but he certainly would find out. The gamesmanship of trading information always irritated García, but he accepted it as essential to the job. Reporters, cops, politicians, private detectives—all gifted in the coy art of you-tell-me, I-tell-you. Afterward you felt like either an oracle or a whore.

García assumed there was a compelling reason for what Keyes had done. There better have been. A trade-off of some sort, maybe even extortion. Wiley seemed capable of anything.

Besides, the question had diminished in urgency since the helicopter crash. No sooner had the Sunday press conference ended than the chief had slipped García a terse note: 'Consider disbanding Fuego One Task Force. We could have a press release ready by tomorrow A.M.'

García had acknowledged the suggestion without committing to it. As all good detectives, he had learned to subsist on the bittersweet. Good guys, bad guys, you had to watch your step. He'd met crooks to whom he'd entrusted his life, and cops who'd steal crackers from the blind. García was seldom moved by the wisdom of his superiors, and more often dazzled by the cleverness of the criminal mind. The *Fuego* case had been a peculiar challenge; all along he had felt as if he were battling two sides, *Las Noches* and the Miami establishment.

The detective was ambivalent about the mysterious helicopter crash. Part of him wanted to believe that the Nights of December was dead. It had nothing to do with the Orange Bowl or civic boosterism or preserving the tourist trade. Rather, it seemed a marvelous example of bad guys getting their due; justice in the biblical sense. And as a practical matter, there was no tidier way to solve a homicide than to have all your suspects suddenly croak. God knows the small fortune it would save the taxpayers.

On the other hand was the tug of professional pride: García didn't like the Chamber of Commerce opening and closing his murder cases. The self-congratulatory tone of the TV press conference had been farcical; the truth was, García's crack squad never had come close to finding, much less capturing, *Las Noches de Diciembre*. It had been a frustrating assignment for a cop unaccustomed to being outwitted, and García didn't like the taste of it. To see Skip Wiley and his weird crew vanquished by a sputtering old Army helicopter seemed mundane and anticlimactic. From García's view, it would have been immensely more satisfying to have tracked the bastards to their Everglades hideout and smoked them in a blazing firefight.

Which is why he wasn't ready to call it quits.

Intuition told García that the ending didn't fit. A bunch of crazy Cubans or Nicaraguans?—sure, that's the sort of fuck-up you'd expect, running a chopper clean out of fuel. But from the very first victim, the Nights of December had been different. They had approached each act of violence with a certain selectivity and élan. Choking Sparky Harper with a toy alligator was more than murder; it was terrorism with imagination. It was the stamp of a blade like Wiley.

Wiley—who, in Al García's opinion, was too damn smart to flame out over the deep blue sea. It'd be just like that cagey sonofabitch to fake his own death, lull everyone to sleep, then swoop down on the Orange Bowl parade and snatch the queen— just like he'd planned all along.

The detective crumpled the chief's directive and dropped it into a trashcan. He flipped through a stack of clippings until he came to the infamous hurricane column:

> What South Florida needs most is a killer hurricane, sudden and furious, an implacable tempest that would raze the concrete shorelines and rake away the scum and corruption . . .

As he read it for the second time, García felt the hairs prickle on the back of his neck.

> The tidal surge, a swollen gargoyle of a wave, is born beyond the Gulf Stream. Gaining size and thunder by the minute, it races under a deafening wind toward Florida's sleeping coastline. In purple darkness it pulverizes Miami Beach with a twenty-foot wall of water, flooding Carl Fisher's billion-dollar island of muck. Picture it: corpses upon corpses, clogging the flooded lobbies of once-majestic condominiums; dead dreamers, swollen, blue-veined, carplike.
>
> They will die in bewilderment, in the fierce arms of the beloved ocean that brought them here in the first place. Fools! the wind will scream, fools all.

García thought: These are the words of a pathologically bitter man, if not a certified fruitcake. He was dying to hear what Keyes could tell him about the guy.

Somebody rapped lightly on the door.

'Come on in, Brian,' García said.

The door flew open with a crash.

García's left hand found the butt of his revolver but he changed his mind. Nothing like a sawed-off shotgun to argue for prudence.

'*Buenas noches*,' the detective said to the man in the soiled undershirt.

'Hello, maggot,' said Jesús Bernal. 'Let's go for a ride, just you and me.'

Since spurning the Nights of December, Jesús Bernal had slipped into a desperate and harried state. He had pinned his grandiose hope of redemption on his last homemade bomb, only to see it claim the wrong victim, some goofball news reporter. Once again serendipity had taunted Bernal, reducing his most passionate and calculated crimes to slapstick. His long career as a terrorist had been marred by such misfortune, and he had come to fear that he might be forever cheated of his place in radical history, that he had blown his last big chance. That morning's press conference had pitched the little Cuban into an orgy of self-pity—he had screeched at the television screen, pummeled the walls, kicked holes in the doors of his motel room. He *knew* that the helicopter stunt was a frivolous idea, that the first plan had been the best. He had *tried* to teach the others about discipline and efficiency, about the fatal dangers of impetuosity. But that fuckhead Wiley was beyond reason, and the dope-wasted nigger and the creepy Seminole Indian had trailed along like zombies. They were babies playing a man's game. Now they were dead, and so for all practical purposes was *Las Noches de Diciembre*, leaving Jesús Bernal an orphan of the cause. Wretchedly he wondered what his ex-comrades in the First Weekend in July Movement were saying about him; he could hear the *comandante*'s sneering laughter. Who could blame the old fart? For all the fanfare about *Las Noches*, nothing historic had been proven, nothing of permanence achieved. So there was no point calling the old man to beg again for readmission.

Bernal knew his options were limited. Strategically, it would be futile to revive the name of the organization—as far as the world was concerned, the Nights of December no longer existed. Even the fucking stationery was useless.

One possibility was to start his own underground terrorist movement. To hell with the crazy Wileys and the feeble old Bay of Piggers; it was time for daring new blood. Yet there was still the problem of credibility, and shedding the stigma of recent failures.

Which was why Jesús Bernal sneaked into Metro-Dade police headquarters on Sunday evening, December 30.

If all went as planned, Jesús figured he'd never again have to worry about his future; he would be the Reggie Jackson of South Florida terrorism, a free-agent superstar-assassin. The First Weekend in July, Omega Seven, Alpha 66—they'd all be knocking down his door. Then maybe he *would* form his own gang, recruiting only the best from the others and leaving the faggots and doddering old men to their Eighth Street parades.

Even before the helicopter accident, Jesús Bernal had unilaterally decided to select a new victim. To impress the *comandante*, the target would have to be a person of prominence and formi-

dable authority. And most important, the chosen prey must represent an abhorrence to The Cause—either compromise, complicity,
or total apathy.

Bernal's brightest hope was Sergeant Al García.

The chubby turncoat had invited trouble during the press conference by noting there was no evidence of Jesús being aboard
the ill-fated Huey. In his emotionally bruised and paranoid state,
Bernal perceived this remark as a slur, something meant to por-
tray him as a sniveling coward who cringed in the background
while his brethren risked their lives. In fact, García had mentioned
Jesús Bernal only to annoy the guys in the orange blazers; he
never thought it would precipitate this kind of visit.

'Take the back stairs,' Bernal commanded.

The police station was all but empty on a Sunday night and
they saw no one on the stairwell. The two men emerged from a
doorway on the northwest side and crossed the jail parking lot,
concealed by a tall hedge. Bernal walked stiffly, the shotgun
pointed down and held close to his right leg; from a distance he
looked like a man with a slight limp.

García's unmarked police car was parked on Fourteenth Street.
'You drive,' Bernal said. 'And stay off the freeways.'

They headed south, crossed the Miami River drawbridge, and
stopped at the busy traffic light at Northwest Seventh Street.

'Which way?' García asked.

Jesús Bernal hesitated. 'Just a second.' Across his lap lay the
shotgun, its barrel gaping from the crook of his arm. The gun
was an over-and-under model, cut back to fourteen inches. Al
García didn't need the training manual to figure out what a
sawed-off could do. It was pointed at his kidneys.

'Turn right,' Bernal said hoarsely. García could make out the
faint cross-hatch imprint of the tennis racket on his abductor's
face. He also noticed that Bernal's nose was badly broken, though
his teeth were straight and gleaming.

They spoke Spanish to each other.

'Where are we going?' García asked.

'Why, you worried?' Bernal said tautly. 'You think a badge and
a gun makes you a hero! Makes you a genuine American! I beg

your pardon, Mr. *Policía*. You are no hero, you're a coward. You turned your back on your true country.'

'What do you mean?' García asked, biting back anger.

'Do you not have family in Cuba?'

'An uncle,' the detective replied. 'And a sister.'

Bernal poked the shotgun into García's neck. The barrel was cold and sharp. 'You abandoned your own sister! You are a shit-eating worm and I should kill you right now.'

'She chose to stay behind, my sister did.'

'*No creo—*'

'It's true,' García said. 'She married a man in the army.'

'Such shit! And your uncle—what lie have you invented for him?'

'He is a doctor in Camaguey, with a family. Four children. This is not a lie.'

'Such shit!'

'Put the gun down before somebody sees it,' García warned.

Reluctantly Jesús Bernal lowered the sawed-off. He held it across his knees, below the dashboard.

'You think it was easy for me?' García said. 'You think it was easy to leave, to start over? I came here with nothing.'

Jesús Bernal was unmoved. 'Why are you not fighting for your family's liberation?' he demanded.

Rather than say something he might eternally regret, García said nothing. Psychology was not his strong suit; he was a firm believer of the fist-in-the-face school of criminal therapy.

Jesús Bernal was a mangy bundle of nerves. He smelled like he hadn't bathed for a month and his black hair was a dull curly mat. His high-topped sneakers tapped the floorboard, while his free hand knotted and reknotted the tail of his threadbare under-shirt. He fidgeted like a little kid whose bladder was about to burst.

'What do you think about this, Mr. *Policía?* Me catching you, instead of the other way around!' Jesús flashed his new dentures. 'Cut over to the Trail and we'll head for the Turnpike.'

'But you said no freeways.'

'Shut up and do as I say.' Bernal reached over and ripped

the microphone from García's police radio. He threw it out the window. 'You get lonely, you talk to me.'

García shrugged. 'Nice night for a drive.'

'Hope you got plenty of gas,' Bernal said. 'García, I want to ask you something, okay? How does a scum like you sleep at night? What kind of lullabies does a *buitre* sing? When you close your eyes, do you see your sister and your uncle in Cuba, eh? Do you feel their torture and suffering, while you get fat on American ice cream and go to jai-alai with your Anglo pals? I have often wondered about traitors like you, García.

'When I was very young, my job was to visit the businessmen and collect contributions for *La Causa*. I had four blocks on *Calle Ocho*, three more on Flagler Street downtown. A man named Miguel—he owned a small laundry—once gave three thousand dollars. And old Roberto, he ran *bolita* from a café. *Zorro rojo*, the red fox, we called him; Roberto could well afford to be a generous patriot. Not all these businessmen were happy to see me at their door, but they understood the importance of my request. They hated Fidel, with their hearts they hated him, and so they managed to find the money. This is how we survived, while traitors like you ignored us.'

'Chickenshit shakedowns,' García muttered.

'Shut up!'

García picked up the turnpike at the Tamiami Trail and drove south. Traffic thinned out and, on both sides of the highway, chintzy eggshell apartments and tacky tract-house developments gave way to pastures, farmland, and patches of dense glades. García now had no doubt that Bernal planned to kill him. He guessed, cynically, that it would probably be a simple execution; kneeling on the gravel of some dirt road, mosquitoes buzzing in his ears, the shotgun blast devoured by the empty night. The fucking turkey buzzards would find him first. The *buitres*.

Maybe it wasn't such a bad idea to piss the little runt off. Maybe he'd get excited, maybe a little careless.

'So what about your pals?'

'Idiots!' Bernal said.

'Oh, I'm not so sure,' García said. 'Some of that stuff was ingenious.'

'That was mine,' Bernal said. 'The best stuff was mine. The kennel club bombing—I thought it up myself.'

'A pile of dead dogs. What the hell did *that* prove?'

'Quiet, *coño*. It proved that no place was safe, that's what it proved. No place was safe for tourists and traitors and carpetbaggers. Any idiot could see the point.'

García shook his head. Carpetbaggers—definitely a Skip Wiley word.

'Dead greyhounds,' García said mockingly. 'I'm sure Castro couldn't sleep for days.'

'Just drive, goddammit.'

'I never understood your stake in the group,' García went on. 'I think, what the hell does a hardcore like Jesús care about tourists and condos? I think, maybe he just wants his name in the papers. Maybe he's got nowhere else to go.'

Bernal made a fist and pounded the dash. 'See, this is why you're such a dumb cop! Figure it out, García. What really happened to the movement? Everyone in Miami got fat and happy, like you. Half a million Cubans—they could stampede Havana anytime they wanted, but they won't because most of them are just like you. Greedy and prosperous. Prosperity is killing anticommunism, García. If our people here were starving or freezing or dying, don't you think they'd want to go back to Cuba? Don't you think they'd sign up for the next invasion? Of course they would, by the thousands. But not now. Oh, they are careful to wave flags and pledge money and say *Death to the bearded one!* But they don't mean it. You see, they've got their IRAs and their Chevrolets and their season tickets to the Dolphins, and they don't give a shit about Cuba anymore. They'll never leave Florida as long as life is better here, so the only thing for us to do is make life worse. That's exactly what the Nights of December had in mind. It was a good plan, before the great Señor Fuego cracked up, a good plan based on sound dialectic. If it came to pass that all the snowbirds fled north—chasing their precious money— then Florida's economy would disintegrate and finally our people would be forced into action. And Cuba is the only place for us to go.'

García's patience was frayed. He knew all about Jesús Benal

Rivera, born in Trenton, New Jersey, son of a certified public accountant and product of the Ivy League; a man who had never set foot on the island of Cuba.

'You're a phony,' García told him, 'a pitiful phony.'

Bernal raised the stubby shotgun and placed the barrel against the detective's right temple.

García pretended not to notice. He drove at a steady sixty-five, hands damp on the wheel. Bernal would never shoot him while the car was going so fast. Even with the gun at his head García was feeling slightly more optimistic about his chances. For ten miles he had been watching a set of headlights in the rearview mirror. Once he had tapped his brakes, and whoever was following had flashed his brights in reply. García thought: Please be a cop.

After a few tense moments Bernal put the shotgun down. 'Not now,' he said, seemingly to himself. 'Not just yet.' García glanced over and saw that a crooked smile had settled across the bomber's griddled features.

The Turnpike ended at Florida City, and the MG was running on fumes. Brian Keyes coasted into an all-night service station but the pumps were off and he had to wait in line to pay the attendant. He watched helplessly as the taillights of Al García's car disappeared, heading toward Card Sound.

Catching up would take a miracle.

Keyes had arrived at police headquarters just as Jesús Bernal and García were getting in the car. He had spotted the shotgun, but there had been no time to get help; all he could do was try to stay close and hope Bernal didn't see him.

Everything was going smoothly until he'd checked the gas gauge.

Keyes hurriedly pumped five dollars' worth. He ran back to the bullet-proof window and pounded on the glass.

'Call the police!' he shouted at the attendant. The man gave no sign of comprehending any language, least of all English.

'A policeman is in trouble,' Keyes said. He pointed down the highway. 'Get help!'

The gas station attendant nodded vaguely.

'No credit çards,' he said. 'Much sorry.'

Keyes jumped into the MG and raced down U.S. Highway One. He turned off at Card Sound Road, a narrow and seemingly endless two-lane lined with towering pines. The road ahead was black and desolate, not another car in sight. Keyes stood on the accelerator and watched the speedometer climb to ninety. Mosquitoes, dragonflies, and junebugs thwacked the car, their jellied blood smearing the windshield. Every few miles the headlights would freeze a rabbit or opossum near the treeline, but there was no sign anywhere of human life.

As the road swung east, Keyes slowed to check some cars at a crab shanty, then at Alabama Jack's, a popular tavern, which had closed for the night. At the toll booth to the Card Sound Bridge, he asked a sleepy redneck cashier if a black Dodge had come through.

'Two Cubans,' she reported. ''Bout five minutes ago. I 'member cause they didn't wait for change.'

Keyes crossed the tall bridge at a crawl, studying the nocturnal faces of the crabbers and mullet fishermen lined along the rail. Soon he was on North Key Largo, and more alone than ever. This end of the island remained a wilderness of tangled scrub, mahogany, buttonwood, gumbo-limbo, and red mangrove. The last of the North American crocodiles lived in its brackish bogs; this was where Tommy Tigertail had recruited Pavlov. There were alligators, too, and rattlers, gray foxes, hordes of brazen coons, and the occasional shy otter. But mostly the island was alive with birds: nighthawks, ospreys, snowy egrets, spoonbills, limpkins, parrots, blue herons, cormorants, the rare owl. Some slept, some stalked, and some, like the scaly-headed vultures, waited ominously for dawn.

Keyes turned off on County Road 905, drove about half a mile, and parked on the shoulder. He rolled down the window of the MG and the tiny sports car immediately filled with insidious bootblack mosquitoes. Keyes swatted automatically, and tried to listen above the humming insects and the buzz of the nighthawks for something out of place. Perhaps the sound of a car door slamming, or human voices.

But the night surrendered no clues.

He went another mile down the road and parked again; still nothing but marsh noises and the salty smell of the ocean. After a few minutes a paunchy raccoon waddled out of the scrub and stood on its hind legs to investigate; it blinked at Keyes and ambled away, chirping irritably.

He started the MG and headed down 905 at high speed to blow the mosquitoes out of the car. He was driving so fast he nearly missed it, concealed on the east side of the highway, headfirst in a dense hammock. A glint of chrome among the dark green woods is what caught Keyes's eye.

He pumped the brakes and steered off the blacktop. He slipped out of the sports car and popped the trunk. Groping in the dark, he found what he was looking for and crept back to the spot.

The black Dodge was empty and its engine nearly cold to the touch.

The two men stood alone at the end of a rutted limestone jetty, poking like a stone finger into the sea. A warm tangy wind blew from the northeast, mussing García's thin black hair. His mustache was damp from sweat, and his bare arms itched and bled from the trek through the hammock. The detective had given up all hope about the car in the rearview mirror; it had turned off in Florida City.

Jesús Bernal seemed not to notice the cloud of mosquitoes swarming around his head. García thought: perhaps they don't sting him—his blood is poisoned and the insects know it.

Fevered with excitement, Bernal's face glistened in the water's reflection. His eyes darted ratlike and his head jerked at each muffled animal noise from the woods behind them. In one hand Bernal clutched the sawed-off shotgun, and with the other waved a heavy police flashlight, lacing amber ribbons in the blackness.

Jesús was already contemplating the journey back to the car, alone. The shotgun probably would be empty by then, useless. He grew terrified just thinking about the ordeal—what good was a flashlight against panthers! He imagined himself imprisoned all night by the impenetrable hammock; at first disoriented, then panicked. Then lost! The sounds alone might drive him insane.

For Jesús Bernal was scared of the dark.

'What's the matter?' García asked.

'Nothing.' Bernal ground his dentures and made the fear go away. 'This is where we say *adiós*.'

'Yeah?' García thought it seemed an odd place for an execution. The jetty provided no concealment and the echo of gunfire would carry for miles across the water. He hoped a boat might pass soon.

Jesús Bernal fumbled in his khaki trousers and came out with a brown letter-sized envelope, folded in half.

'Open it,' he wheezed. 'Read it aloud.' He aimed the flashlight so García could make out the document, which had been typed neatly. It appeared much longer than any of the communiqués from the Nights of December.

'What is this, you writing a book?' the detective grumbled.

'Read!' Bernal said.

García took his eyeglasses from a shirt pocket.

There were two identical sections, one in English and one in Spanish:

'I, Alberto García Delgado, hereby confess myself as a traitor to my native country of Cuba. I admit to the gravest of crimes: persecuting and harassing those brave revolutionaries who would destroy the dictator Castro, and who would liberate our suffering nation so that all Cuban peoples may return. With my despicable crimes I have dishonored these patriots and shamed my own heritage, and that of my father. I deeply regret my seditious behavior. I realize that I can never be forgiven for using my police authority to obstruct what was good and just. For this reason, I have agreed to accept whatever punishment is deemed fitting by my judge, the honorable Jesús Bernal Rivera—a man who has courageously dedicated his life to the most noble of revolutionary callings.'

García thrust the document back at Jesús and said, 'I'm not signing it, *chico*.' He knew time was short.

'Oh, I think you'll reconsider.'

'No way.'

García lunged forward, his arms reaching out for the shotgun.

Jesús pulled the trigger and an orange fireball tore the detective off his feet and slammed him to the ground.

He lay on his back, staring numbly at the tropical stars. His head throbbed, and his left side felt steamy and drenched.

Jesús Bernal was a little wobbly himself. He had never before fired a shotgun, and discovered that he had not been holding the weapon properly. The recoil had hammered him squarely in the gut, knocking the wind out. A full minute passed before he could speak.

'Get up!' he told García. 'Get up and sign your confession. It will be read on all the important radio stations tomorrow.'

'I can't.' García had no feeling on his left side. He probed gingerly with his right hand and found his shirt shredded and soaked with fresh blood. Jagged yellow bone protruded from the pulp of his shoulder. He felt dizzy and breathless, and knew he would soon be in shock.

'Get up, *traidor!*' Jesús Bernal stood over the detective and waved the gun like a sword.

García thought that if he could only get to his feet he might be able to run to the woods. But when he tried to raise himself from the gravel, his legs convulsed impotently. 'I can't move,' he said weakly.

Jesús Bernal angrily stuffed the document into his pocket. 'We'll see,' he said. 'We'll see about this. Are you prepared to receive your sentence?'

'Yeah,' García groaned. 'What the hell.'

Bernal stalked to the tip of the jetty. 'I chose this spot for a reason,' he said, pointing the gun across the Atlantic. 'Out there is Cuba. Two hundred miles. It is nearer than Disney World, Mr. *Policía*. I think it's time you should go home.'

'I don't believe this,' said Al García.

'Are you much of a swimmer?' Jesús Bernal asked.

'Not when I'm fucking paralyzed.'

'Such a baby. But, you see, this is your sentence. The sentence which—you have agreed—befits your treasonous crimes. Alberto García, maggot and traitor, I hereby command you to return at once to Cuba. There you will join the underground and fight the devil in his own backyard. This is how you will redeem yourself. Perhaps you may someday be a hero. Or at least a man.'

'How about shark food?' García said. Even with two good arms he was a rotten swimmer. He knew he'd never make it as far as Molasses Reef, much less Havana harbor. It was a funny idea, really. García heard himself laugh out loud.

'What's so goddamn hilarious?'

'Nothing, commander.'

The detective began to think of his family. Dreamily he pictured his wife and his children as he had last seen them. At dinner, two nights ago. They all seemed to be smiling. He thought: I must have done *something* right.

He opened his eyes and turned his head to see the tops of Jesús Bernal's moldy sneakers.

'Up!' Bernal cried. He kicked at García, once, twice, three times, until the detective lost count. They were not hard kicks, but diabolically aimed.

Bernal bent down until their faces were inches apart. 'Get your stinking ass off the ground,' Bernal said, his breath sour and sickening.

Once more García tried to sit up, but rolled sideways instead. He nearly passed out as his full weight landed on his mangled arm.

Bernal resumed kicking and García rolled again, the limestone and coral digging into his flesh.

'Go!' Bernal shouted, prodding with his feet. 'Go, go, go!'

García landed in the water with a muted splash. The salt scoured his wounds and a sudden coldness seized his chest, robbing him of all breath. García did not know how deep the water was, but it didn't matter. He could have drowned in a saucepan. Somehow he clawed to the surface and slurped air.

He looked up toward the jetty and saw Bernal's stringy silhouette, the shotgun raised over his head in triumph. Jesús played the flashlight across the waves.

'You'd better get started!' he called exuberantly. 'Head for Carysfort Light. It's a good place to rest. By daybreak you'll be ready to go again. Hurry, *mi guerrero*, onward to Cuba! She is not as far as you think.'

García was too weak to float, much less swim. Hungrily he gulped breath after breath, but it was not enough. A marrow-deep pain began to smother his conscious thought, and he sensed himself slipping away. He paddled mindlessly with his good arm; he didn't care that he was going in circles, as long as his head stayed above water.

'You look like a fool!' Jesús Bernal yelled giddily. 'A fat little clown!'

Another gunshot split the night and Jesús Bernal commenced a curious dance, hopping like a marionette. In his deepening fog Al García thought: The idiot is shooting into the sky, like frigging New Year's Eve.

Still another shot went off, and then more, until the crackles blended to a dull resonance, like a church bell. García wondered why he saw no firebursts from the mouth of the sawed-off.

Jesús Bernal's queer dance became palsied. Suddenly he stopped hopping, bent over double and emitted a horrific wail. The shotgun and the flashlight clattered to the rocks.

But García himself was out of strength. His arm felt like cement, and his will to save himself evaporated under a warm wave of irrepressible fatigue. He was sliding downward into euphoria, away from all pain. The ocean took him gently and closed his tired eyes, but not before he saw a final shot shear the crown of Jesús Bernal's head and leave him twitching in a heap on the jetty.

29

'Nice shooting, Ace,' Al García said feebly.

'I hate that damn gun.' Brian Keyes had needed six rounds from the Browning to put a bullet where he'd wanted. His hands still tingled from the shots.

'Which hospital is nearest?'

'Homestead,' García said, shivering. 'Call my wife, would you?'

'When we get there.'

'I'm pissed you didn't tell me about your pal Wiley.'

'He said he'd kill lots more people if I did.'

García coughed. 'It couldn't have been much worse than it was.'

'Oh no? You saw what that bomb did to the john—now imagine the same thing at the parade, with all those kids. A holocaust, Al. He seemed capable of anything.'

'You shoulda told me anyway,' García said. 'Shit, this hurts. I'm gonna sleep for a while.' He shut his eyes and sagged down in the passenger seat. Soon Keyes could hear his breathing, a weak irregular rasp.

Keyes drove like a maniac. Droplets of salt water trickled from his hair into his mouth and eyes; he was soaked to the skin. García's blood dappled his shirt and pants. As he wheeled the MG back onto Highway One, a sharp pain pinched under his right arm. Keyes wondered if he had torn open the old stab wound while carrying García piggyback through the hammock.

The trip to Farmer's Hospital from Key Largo took twenty minutes. García was unconscious when they arrived at the emergency room, and was immediately stripped and taken to surgery.

Keyes telephoned García's wife and told her to come down right away, Al had been hurt. Then he tried Jenna. He let it ring fifteen or twenty times but no one picked up. Was she gone? Hiding? Dead? He considered driving up to the house and breaking in, but it was too late and he was too exhausted.

He made one more phone call, to Metro-Dade Homicide. He told them where to find Jesús Bernal's body. Soon the island would be crawling with reporters.

Keyes looked up at the clock and smiled at the irony; two-thirty in the morning. Too late to make the morning papers.

The phone jarred Cab Mulcahy from his sleep at seven-thirty.

'I got a message you called. What's up?' It was Cardoza.

Mulcahy sat round-shouldered on the edge of the bed, rubbing sleep from his eyes. 'It concerns Skip Wiley,' he said fuzzily.

He told Cardoza about Wiley's criminal involvement with the Nights of December, omitting nothing except his own knowledge.

'Goddamn!' Cardoza exclaimed. 'Maybe that explains it.'

'What?'

'Wiley sent me a New Year's column yesterday but I damn near tossed it out. I thought it was a fake, some asshole playing a joke.'

'What does it say?' Mulcahy asked. He was not surprised that Wiley had ignored the chain of command and appealed directly to the publisher. Skip knew how much Cardoza loved his stuff.

Cardoza read part of the column aloud over the phone.

'It sounds like a confession,' Mulcahy said. It was actually quite remarkable. 'Mr Cardoza, we have to write about all this.'

'Are you kidding?'

'It's our job,' Mulcahy said.

'Making a blue-chip newspaper look like a nuthouse—that's our job?'

'Our job is printing the truth. Even if it's painful and even if it makes us look foolish.'

'Speak for yourself,' Cardoza said. 'So what exactly do we do with this column? It's not the least bit funny, you know.'

'I think we run it as is—right next to a lengthy story explaining everything that's happened the last month.'

Cardoza was appalled. In no other business would you wave your stinky laundry in the customers' faces; this wasn't ethics, it was idiocy.

'Don't go off half-cocked,' Cardoza told Mulcahy. 'I heard on the radio that the whole gang is dead. I assume that means Mr. Wiley, too.'

'Well, tonight's the big parade,' Mulcahy said. 'Let's wait and see.'

Cardoza was stunned by the revelation about Skip Wiley. Of all the writers at the paper, Wiley had been his favorite, the spice in the recipe. And though he had never actually met the man, Cardoza felt he knew him intimately from his writing. Undoubtedly Wiley was impulsive, irreverent, even tasteless at times— but homicidal? It occurred to Cardoza that a newspaper this size must be riddled with closet psychopaths like Wiley; the potential for future disasters seemed awesome. Expensive disasters, too. Lawyerly-type disasters.

'You sure we have to print this?' Cardoza said.

'Absolutely,' Cab Mulcahy replied.

'Then go ahead,' the publisher growled, 'but when the calls start pouring in, remember—I'm out of town.'

The crusty businessman in Cardoza—which was to say, *all* of Cardoza—immediately thought of selling the newspaper, getting out before they straitjacketed the whole building. Just last week he'd had an excellent offer from the Krolman Corporation, makers of world-famous French bidets. A bit overcapitalized, but they'd cleared thirty million last year after taxes. Cardoza had been impressed by the bottom line—thirty mil was a lot of douching. Now the Krolman boys were looking to diversify.

The publisher's fingers were flying through the Rolodex even as he hung up on Cab Mulcahy.

Reed Shivers pounded loudly on the door to the guest room. 'Young man, I want to speak with you!'

'Later,' Keyes mumbled.

'No, not later. Right now! Open this door!'

Keyes let Shivers in and met him with a scowl. '*Open this door right now! What do I look like, the Beaver? Gee, Dad, I was only trying to get some sleep.*'

'That's enough, Mr. Keyes. You said you were going to be gone for one hour last night—one hour! The housekeeper says you got in at six.'

'A situation came up. I couldn't help it.'

'So you just run off and forget all about my daughter,' Reed Shivers said.

'There was a squad car at each end of the block.'

'All alone, the night before the big parade!'

'I said I couldn't help it,' Keyes said.

Kara Lynn walked in wearing a shapeless pink robe and fuzzy bedroom slippers. Her hair was pinned up and her eyes were sleepy. Without makeup she looked about fourteen years old.

'Hi, guys,' she said. 'What's all the racket?'

Right away she saw that Brian had slept in his street clothes. She stared at the sticky brown stain on his clothes, somehow knowing what it was. She also noticed that he still wore his shoulder holster. The Browning semiautomatic lay on a night-stand next to the bed. It was the first time she had ever seen it. It seemed unwieldy, and out of place in a bedroom.

'The Cuban's dead,' Keyes said flatly.

Reed Shivers rubbed his chin sheepishly. It occurred to him that he had underestimated Keyes or, worse, misread him entirely.

'Bernal kidnapped García last night and I had to shoot him,' Keyes said.

Kara Lynn gave him a long hug, with her eyes closed. Keyes stood there stiffly, not knowing how to respond in front of her father. Reed Shivers looked away and made a disapproving cluck.

Keyes said, 'I expect there'll be some police coming by a little later to ask me some questions.'

Reed Shivers folded his arms and said, 'Actually this is extremely good news. It means all those damn Nachos are dead. According to the papers, this Cuban fellow was the last one.' He tugged his daughter safely back to arm's reach. 'Pumpkin, don't you see? The parade's going to be wonderful—there's no more threat. We won't be needing Mr. Keyes anymore.'

Kara Lynn looked up at Brian questioningly.

'Let's play it safe, Mr. Shivers. I've got my doubts about that helicopter crash. Sergeant García and I agree that everything should stay the same for tonight. Nothing changes.'

'But it was on TV. All those maniacs are dead.'

'And what if they're not?' Kara Lynn said. 'Daddy, I'd feel better if we stuck to the plan. Just for tonight.'

'All right, cupcake, if you'll sleep easier. But as of tomorrow morning, no more bodyguard.' Reed Shivers marched down the hall, still wondering about that hug.

Brian Keyes closed the door quietly and locked it. He took Kara Lynn's hand and led her to the bed. They lay down and held one another; he, hugging a little tighter. Keyes realized that he had crossed a cold threshold and could never return to what he was, what he had trained to be—a professional bystander, an expertly detached voyeur who was skilled at reconstructing violence after the fact, but never present and never participatory. For reporters, the safety net was the ability to walk away, polish it off, forget about it. It was as easy as turning off the television, because whatever was happening always happened to somebody else; reality was past tense and once removed, something to be observed but not experienced. Two years ago, at such a newsworthy moment, Keyes himself would have been racing south with the wolf pack, jogging through the hammock to reach the jetty first, his notebook flipped open, his eyes sponging up each detail, counting up the bullet holes in the corpse, by now gray and bloodless. And two years ago he might have gotten sick at the sight and gone off to vomit in the woods, where the other reporters couldn't see him. Later he would have stood back and studied the death scene, but could only have guessed at what might have happened, or why.

'We don't have to talk about it,' Kara Lynn said. She stirred against him. 'Let's just lie here for a little while.'

'I had no choice. He shot García.'

'This was the same man we saw outside the country club. You're certain?'

Keyes nodded.

He said, 'Maybe I ought to say a prayer or something. Isn't that what you're supposed to do when you kill somebody?'

'Only in spaghetti westerns.' She slid her arms around his waist. 'Try to get some rest. You did the right thing.'

'I know,' he said dully. 'The only thing I feel guilty about is not feeling guilty. The sonofabitch deserved to die.'

The words came out soulless. Kara Lynn shuddered. Sometimes he frightened her, just a little.

'Hey, Sundance, you want to see my gown?'

'Sure.'

She bounced up from the bed. 'Stay right here, don't move,' she said. 'I'll model it for you.'

'I'd like that,' Keyes said. 'I really would.'

At noon Al García awoke. He gazed around the hospital room and felt warmed by its pale yellow walls and the slivered shadows from the venetian blinds. He was too drugged to pay much attention to the burning in his arm or the huge knot on the base of his neck or the burbling sound from inside his chest. Instead the detective was washed by a mood of elemental triumph: he was alive and Jesús Bernal was dead. Deader than a goddamn cockroach. Al García relished the role of survivor, even if he owed his life not to his own faltering reflexes, but to Brian Keyes. The kid had turned out to be rock steady, and strong as a bear to haul him out of the ocean the way he had.

Groggily García greeted his wife, who offered spousely sympathy but peppered him with questions that he pretended not to hear. Afterward, an orthopedic surgeon stopped in to report that although García's left arm had been saved, it was too early to know if the muscles and bones would mend properly; the shoulder basically was being held together by steel pins and catgut. García worriedly asked if any shotgun pellets had nicked the spine, and the doctor said no, though the initial fall on his neck had caused some temporary numbness. García wiggled the toes on both feet and seemed satisfied that he would walk again.

He was drifting off to sleep when the chief of police showed up. García winked at him.

'The doctors say you're going to make it,' the chief whispered.

'Piece-a-cake,' García murmured.

'Look, I know this is a bad time, but the media's gone absolutely batshit over this shooting. We're trying to put together a short release. Is there anything you can tell me about what happened out there?'

'Found the body?'

'Yes,' the chief replied. 'Shot four times with a nine-millimeter. The last one really did the trick, blew his brains halfway to Bimini.'

'Fucker blasted me with a sawed-off.'

'I know,' the chief said. 'The question is, who blasted him?'

'Tomorrow,' García said, closing his eyes.

'Al, please.'

'Tomorrow, the whole story.' Or as much of it as was absolutely necessary.

'Okay, but I've got to say *something* to the press this afternoon. They're tearing around like a pack of frigging hyenas.'

'Tell 'em you don't know nuthin'. Tell 'em I haven't regained consciousness.'

'That might work,' the chief mused.

'Sure it'll work. One more thing . . .' García paused to adjust the plastic tube in his nose. 'Tell the nurses I want a TV.'

'Sounds reasonable.'

'A color TV for tonight.'

'Sure, Al.'

'Don't want to miss the parade.'

30

In the mid-1800s Miami was known as Fort Dallas. It was a mucky, rutted, steaming, snake-infested settlement of two hundred souls, perennially under attack from crafty Seminoles or decimated by epidemics of malaria. This was a time long before Fisher, Flagler, and other land grabbers arrived to suck their fortunes out of North America's most famous swamp. It was a time when the local obsession was survival, not square footage, when the sun was not a commodity but a blistering curse.

No one knew what Fort Dallas might eventually become, not that knowing would have altered its future. The dream was always there, sustenance against the cruel hardships. Then, as now, the smell of opportunity was too strong to ignore, attracting a procession of grafters, con artists, Confederate deserters, geeks, bushwackers, rustlers, Gypsies, and slave traders. Their inventiveness and tenacity and utter contempt for the wilderness around them would set the tone for the development of South Florida. They preserved only what was free and immutable—the sunshine and the sea—and marked the rest for destruction, because how else could you sell it? In its natural state, the soggy frontier south of Lake Okeechobee simply was not marketable. Still, the transformation of the face of the land began slowly, not so much because of the Indians or the terrain as because of the lagging technology of plunder. Finally came the railroads and the dredge and the bulldozer, and the end of Fort Dallas.

For thirty years, beginning around the turn of the century, South Florida grew at an astonishing pace. Rabid opportunists seized as much land as they could, swapped it, platted it, sold it. Where there was no land they dredged it from the bottom of Biscayne Bay, manufactured an island, named it after a flower or a daughter or themselves, and peddled it as a natural oasis. All this was done with great efficiency and enthusiasm, but with no vision whatsoever.

Those wheeler-dealers who didn't blow their brains out after the Hurricane of '26 or hang themselves after the real-estate bust were eventually rewarded with untold wealth. Today they were venerated for their perseverance and toughness of spirit, and some even had public parks named after them. These characters are regarded as the true pioneers of South Florida.

It is their descendants, the heirs to paradise (and to the banks and the land), who put on the annual Orange Bowl Parade.

The pageant began a half-century ago as an honest parade, Main Street entertainment for little children and tourists. But with the ascension of television the event grew and changed character. Gradually it became an elaborate instrument of self-promotion, deliberately staged to show the rest of the United States (suffering through winter) a sunny, scenic, and sexy sanctuary. The idea was to make everybody drop their snow shovels and hop the next jumbo jet for Florida. To this end, the Orange Bowl Parade was as meticulously orchestrated as a nuclear strike. Those who would appear on camera were carefully selected: high-school bands from Bumfuck, Iowa, awe shining from their sunburned faces as they bugled down Biscayne Boulevard; a sprinkling of Caribbean blacks and South American Hispanics, evidence of Miami's exotic but closely supervised cultural mix; the most innocuous of TV celebrities, delighted to shill for the tourist board in exchange for comped rooms at the Fontainebleau.

From the Chamber of Commerce point of view, the most essential ingredient was subliminal sex. You cannot sell sun-drenched beaches without showing tanned female cleavage; Middle America hungered for it. Thus the pageant always featured droves of women in brief but not-quite-nasty bathing suits. The favored choice of models was the pneumatic blond teenager, suggestively hugging a neoprene palm tree or riding a stuffed alligator and smiling so fixedly that any idiot could see her makeup had been put on with a trowel.

Every year the Orange Bowl Committee chose a sunny new

theme, but seldom did it touch on Florida's rapacious history. Swamp wars and slave raids and massacres of Indian children did not strike the Orange Bowl fathers as suitable topics for a parade; a parade intended purely as a primetime postcard.

As noted, this year's slogan was 'Tropical Tranquillity.'

At six P.M. the floats and clowns and high-school bands collected in the parking lots across from the Dupont Plaza Hotel. Dusky clouds rolled in from the north, smothering the vermilion sunset and dropping temperatures. The wind came in chilly gusts; some of the girls in bathing suits sneaked back to the dressing rooms to tape Band-Aids over their nipples, so they wouldn't be embarrassed if it got cold.

Before the parade could begin, a huge balloon replica of some comic-strip character with teeth like Erik Estrada's broke from its tether and drifted toward the high-voltage power lines. A policeman with a rifle shot it down, the first casualty of the evening.

Traditionally, the order of march began with a police honor guard and ended, a mile or so later, with the queen's float. This year the regimen would be different. Al García had insisted that a troop of cops be positioned within shouting distance of Kara Lynn Shivers, but the Orange Bowl Committee absolutely refused, fearing Major Image Problems if TV cameras were to show uniformed police in the same frame as the queen. Brian Keyes had suggested a compromise, which was accepted: a colorful contingent of Shriners on motorcycles was inserted between the queen's float and the City of Miami (Marching) SWAT Team.

The Shriners would be led, of course, by Burt and James, packing handguns in their baggy trousers. Of the forty men behind them, only twenty would actually belong to the Evanston Shrine; the rest would be motorcycle cops secretly conscripted by Al García. This part of the plan had never been revealed to the Orange Bowl Committee or to the Chamber of Commerce. However, to anyone paying close attention, it was obvious from the pained expressions on these unusually young and muscular-looking Shriners that something was screwy. The way they wore the fez hats, for one thing: straight up, instead of cocked ten degrees, jocular-Shriner style.

There was even more firepower: thirty undercover officers armed with machine pistols (and a mug shot of Viceroy Wilson burned into their memories) would move through the crowd, flanking Kara Lynn's float. From above, eight police sharp-shooters with nightscopes would watch from various downtown buildings along Biscayne Boulevard and Flagler Street, the parade routes.

The queen's float shimmered gold and royal blue, by virtue of seventy-thousand polyethylene flower petals stapled to a bed of plywood, plaster, and chickenwire. The motif was 'Mermaid Magic,' featuring Kara Lynn in a clinging burnt-orange gown, her hair in tendrils under the Orange Bowl tiara, her cheeks glistening as if kissed by the sea. There had been a brief debate about whether or not she should wear a rubber fish tail, and though her father endorsed the idea ('More camera time, sweetcakes'), she declined firmly.

Kara Lynn's throne was a simulated coral reef built on the front end of the float. From this perch she would smile and wave to the throngs while a hidden stereo broadcasted actual underwater recordings of migrating sperm whales. Meanwhile the four runner-up contestants, dressed in matching tuna-blue mermaid gowns, would pretend to cavort in an imaginary lagoon behind Kara Lynn's reef. In rehearsal, with all the blond beauty queens making swimming motions with their arms, someone remarked that it looked like a Swedish version of the Supremes.

The queen's float had been constructed around a Datsun pickup truck, which would power it along Biscayne Boulevard. The truck's cab had been camouflaged as a friendly octopus in the mermaid lagoon; the driver of the float and Brian Keyes would be sitting inside. The windshield of the pickup had been removed to permit a sudden exit, just in case.

Despite these extraordinary precautions and the preponderance of high-powered guns, the pre-parade atmosphere was anything but tense. Even the Orange Bowl committeemen seemed loose and confident.

The sight of so many policemen, or the knowledge of their

presence, was reassurance enough for those to whom the parade meant everything. These, of course, were the same buoyant optimists who believed that the violent events of the weekend had conclusively ended Miami's drama.

The parade was due to begin at seven-thirty P.M. sharp, but it was delayed several minutes because of a problem with one of the floats. Acting on a confidential tip, U.S. customs agents had impounded the colorful entry sponsored by the city of Bogotá, Colombia, and were busily hammering sharp steel tubes through the sides of the float in search of a particular white flaky powder. Failing in that, they brought in four excitable police dogs to sniff every crevice for drugs. Though no contraband was found, one of the German shepherds peed all over the Colombian coffee princess and the float was immediately withdrawn. It was the only one in the whole pageant made with real carnations.

At 7:47 P.M., the West Stowe, Ohio, High School Marching Band and Honor Guard stepped onto Biscayne Boulevard, struck up a unique rendition of Jim Morrison's 'Light My Fire,' and the King Orange Jamboree Parade was under way. The skies were cloudy but the wind had steadied and there was no trace of rain. Standing five-deep along both sides of the boulevard was an enormous crowd of 200,000, most of whom had paid at least twelve bucks to park their expensive late-model cars in one of the most dangerous urban neighborhoods in the western hemisphere.

At precisely 8:01, the kliegs lighted up in the blue NBC booth, washing co-hosts Jane Pauley and Michael Landon in an unremitting white glare.

A teleprompter mounted on brackets above the cameras began to scroll. His cheeks burnished and his New Testament curls showing spangles of sun-induced blondness, Michael Landon spoke first to America, sticking faithfully to the script:

> Hello everybody and welcome to Miami, Florida. What a night for a parade! [Cut to three-second shot of majorette with baton.] It's a mild sixty-seven degrees here in South Florida, with a tangy sea breeze reminding us that beautiful

Biscayne Bay and the Atlantic Ocean are just over my shoulder. Down below, on Biscayne Boulevard, the King Orange Jamboree is in full swing. [Cut for four-second shot of swaying palm trees and Cooley Motors float.] The theme of this year's pageant is Tropical Tranquillity, and for the past week I've been enjoying just that, as you can see from my sunburn [sheepish smile]. Now I'd like to introduce my co-host for tonight's Orange Bowl pageant, the lovely and talented Jane Pauley. [Cut to close-up Pauley, then two-shot.]

Pauley: Thanks, Michael. We have had a great stay down here, though it looks like you spent a bit more time at the beach than I did. [Landon medium smile.] There's a lot of excitement in this town, and not just over the parade. As you know, tomorrow night the University of Nebraska Cornhuskers and the Fighting Irish of Notre Dame square off for the national college football championship in the Orange Bowl. NBC will carry that game live, and it looks like the weather's going to be perfect. Michael, who're you rooting for? [Cut to Landon close-up.]

Landon: I like Nebraska, Jane.

Pauley: Well, I think I'm going with Notre Dame.

Landon: Ah, still an Indiana girl.

Pauley [laughing]: You betcha. [Cut from two-camera to close-up.] On a serious note [turning to camera], if you've been following the news recently you probably know that this South Florida community has been struggling with a tragic and frightening crisis for the past month. A terrorist group calling itself the Nights of December has taken credit for a series of bombings, kidnappings, and other crimes in the Miami area. At least ten persons, many of them tourists, are known to have been killed. Now, as you may have heard, several alleged members of this terrorist group are believed to have died in a helicopter accident over the weekend. And last night, the last known member of this extremist cell was shot to death after abducting a Dade County police officer. It has been a trying time for the citizens down here, and in spite of all this difficulty they still managed to make us feel warm and welcome. [Cut to Landon, nodding appreciatively.] And, Michael, I know you'll agree as we watch some of these amazing floats go by: It's shaping up as another spectacular Orange Bowl extravaganza! [Cut to shot over Landon shoulder as he enjoys parade.]

Landon [big smile]: Is it ever! And look at some of these bathing beauties! I may never go back to Malibu.

The parade slowly headed north up the boulevard, past the massive gray public library and Bayfront Park, wino mecca of the eastern seaboard.

The cab of the pickup truck was oppressively stuffy under heavy layers of plaster and plastic. To keep from suffocating, Keyes held his face close to the open windshield, which also functioned as the smiling mouth of the friendly octopus. The driver of the float noticed the gun beneath Keyes's jacket, but said nothing and appeared unconcerned.

From inside the float, Keyes found it difficult to see much of anything past the prancing rear-ends of the four blue mermaids. Occasionally, when they parted, he caught a glimpse of Kara Lynn's bare shoulders on the front of the float. As for peripheral vision, he had none; the faces of the spectators were invisible to him.

To offset the racket from the Shriners' Harley Davidsons, the sperm-whale music had been cranked up to maximum volume. Keyes ranked the whales in the same melodic category as Yoko Ono and high-speed dental drills. It took every ounce of concentration to follow the chatter on the portable police radio that linked him to the command center. Each new block brought the same report: everything calm, so far.

When Kara Lynn's float reached the main grandstands, it came to a stop so that she and the other Orange Bowl finalists could wave at the VIPs and pose for the still photographers. Brian Keyes tensed as soon as he felt the Datsun brake; it was during this pause, scheduled for precisely three minutes and twenty seconds, that Keyes expected Skip Wiley to make his move, while the TV cameras settled on Kara Lynn. Forewarned, the police snipers focused their infrared scopes while the plainclothesmen slid through the cheering crowd to take preassigned positions along the curb. On cue, Burt and James led the Shriner cavalcade into an intricate figure-eight that effectively encircled the queen's float with skull-buzzing motorcycles.

But nothing happened.

Kara Lynn dutifully waved at everyone who vaguely looked important, flash bulbs popped, and the parade crawled on. The floats crossed the median at NE Fifth Street and headed south back down the boulevard, past the heart of the city's infant skyline. At Flagler Street the procession turned west, and away from the bright television lights. Instantly everyone relaxed and the floats picked up speed for the final leg. Kara Lynn quit waving; her arms were killing her. It was all she could do to smile.

At North Miami Avenue, one of the undercover cops calmly called over the radio for assistance. Some ex-Nicaraguan National Guardsmen who were picketing the U.S. immigration office now threatened to crash the parade if they did not immediately receive their green cards. A consignment of six officers responded and easily quelled the disturbance.

A block later, one of the motorcycle cops disguised as a Shriner reported sighting a heavyset black male resembling Daniel 'Viceroy' Wilson, watching the parade from the steps of the county courthouse.

As the queen's float passed the building, Keyes leaned out of the octopus's mouth to see a squad of officers swarm up the marble steps like indigo ants. The search proved fruitless, however; three large black men were briefly detained, questioned, and released. They were, in order of size, a Boca Raton stockbroker, a city councilman from Cleveland, and a seven-foot Rastafarian marijuana wholesaler. None bore the slightest resemblance to Viceroy Wilson, and the motorcycle cop's radio alert was dismissed as a false alarm.

Al García refused to take any painkillers while he watched the parade from his hospital room in Homestead. He wanted to be fully cognizant, and he wanted his vision clear. Two young nurses asked if they could sit and watch with him, and García was delighted to have company. One of the nurses remarked that Michael Landon was the second-handsomest man on television, next to Rick Springfield, the singer.

As the floats rolled by, García impatiently drummed the plaster cast that was glued to his left side. He worried that if trouble broke out, the TV cameras wouldn't show it; that's the way it worked at baseball games, when fans ran onto the field. Prime time was too precious to waste on misfits.

Finally the queen's float came into view, emitting a tremulous screech that García took for brake trouble, when actually it was just the whale music. One of the nurses remarked on how gorgeous Kara Lynn looked, but García wasn't paying attention. He put on his glasses and squinted at the dopey octopus's smile until he spotted Keyes, his schoolboy face bobbing in and out of the shadow. Pain and all, García had to chuckle. Poor Brian looked wretched.

At 8:55, the last marching band clanged into view playing something by Neil Diamond. The NBC cameras cut back to Jane Pauley and Michael Landon in the blue booth:

> Pauley: Another thrilling Orange Bowl spectacle! I don't know how they do it, year after year. [Cut to Landon.]
>
> Landon: It's amazing, isn't it, Jane? I'd just like to thank NBC and the Orange Bowl organizers for inviting us to spend New Year's Eve in beautiful South Florida. One of the local weathermen just handed me a list of temperatures around the country and, before we sign off, I'd like to share some of these [holds up temp list]. New York, twenty-one . . .
>
> Pauley [VO]: Brrrrr.
>
> Landon: Wichita, nine below; Knoxville, thirty-nine; Chicago, three degrees and snow! Indianapolis—Jane, are you ready? [Cut to Pauley.]
>
> Pauley: Oh boy, let's have it.
>
> Landon: Six degrees!
>
> Pauley [pinning on a Go Irish! button]: Home sweet home.

Well, I promised everyone I'd bring back some fresh oranges, but I'm just sorry there's no way to package this magnificent Miami sunshine. Thanks for joining us . . . good night, everybody.

Landon [two-shot, both waving, major smiles]: 'Night, everybody. Happy New Year!

García reached for the remote control and turned the channel. A show about humorous TV bloopers came on and García asked the nurse for a shot of Demerol. He lay thinking about the killing of Jesús Bernal and the peaceful parade, and contemplated the possibility that the madness was really over. He felt immense relief.

Ten minutes later the phone rang, sounding five miles away. It was the chief of police.

'Hey, Al, how you feeling?'

'Pretty damn good, boss.'

'We did it, huh?'

García didn't want to quibble. 'Yeah,' he said.

'Did you see the pageant?'

'Yeah, it was just great.'

'Looks like the Nachos are history, buddy.'

'Looks that way,' García said, thinking: This is the same bozo who thought *I* wrote the *Fuego* letters. But this time he just might be right. It looks like Wiley took the deep-six after all.

'What do you say we shitcan the task force?' the chief said.

'Sure.' There was no good argument against it. The parade was over, the girl was safe.

'First thing tomorrow I'll do up a release.'

'Fine, boss.'

'And, Al, on my honor: you're getting all the credit on this one. All the credit you deserve.'

For what? García wondered as he hung up. It wasn't like I shot down the goddamn chopper myself.

After the parade, Brian Keyes drove back to the Shivers house and started packing. Reed Shivers and his wife got home thirty minutes later.

'See, all that panic for nothing,' Shivers said smugly.

'I get paid to panic,' Keyes said, stuffing his clothes into a canvas athletic bag. He felt drained and empty. The end wasn't supposed to have been this easy, but Wiley's moment had come and gone—if the bastard really had been alive, Keyes thought, he would have shown up. With bells on.

'Where's Kara Lynn?' Keyes asked.

'She went to a wrap party with the other girls,' Mrs. Shivers said.

'A wrap party.'

'A little tradition in beauty pageants,' Mrs. Shivers explained. 'Girls only.'

'You'd best be off,' Reed Shivers said. He was trying to light his pipe, sucking on the stem like a starving carp. 'There was a lady from the Eileen Ford agency in the stands—she picked up on Kara Lynn right away. I'm expecting a call anytime.'

'Wonderful,' Keyes said. 'Book a room at the Plaza.'

The Shiverses walked him to the door.

'Is your friend going to be all right?' Mrs. Shivers asked. 'The Cuban policeman.'

'I think so. He's a tough guy.'

'You're a brave young man yourself,' she said. Her tone of voice made it plain that she was addressing the hired help. 'Thank you for all you've done for Kara Lynn.'

'Yes,' Reed Shivers said grudgingly. He extended his golden-brown hand; a Yale man's polite but superior handshake. 'Drive carefully now,' he said.

'Good night, Mr. and Mrs. Cleaver.'

They nodded blankly and shut the front door.

Keyes was standing at the trunk of the MG, squirming out of the shoulder holster, when a brown Buick pulled into the driveway and Kara Lynn got out. She had changed into blue jeans and a papery white sleeveless blouse; she carried her Orange Bowl gown on a plastic hanger.

'Where you going, Marlowe?'

'Back to the other side of town.'

A female voice from the Buick shouted: 'Kara, is that him?'

Kara Lynn smiled bashfully and waved her friends to leave. The Buick honked twice as it sped off.

'We had a little wine,' she said. 'I told 'em about you.'

Keyes laughed. 'The private eye in the octopus.'

Kara Lynn laid the gown across the hood of the sports car and glanced up at the house, checking for her parents at the window. Then she put her arms around Keyes and said, 'Let's go somewhere and make love.'

Keyes kissed her softly. 'Your folks are waiting inside. Somebody from a model agency is supposed to call.'

'Who cares?'

'Your old man. Besides, I'm worn out.'

'Hey, don't look so blue. We made it.' Playfully she took his hands and placed them on her buttocks. 'The mother lode is safe,' she said, kissing him hard. 'Good work, kiddo.'

'I'll call you tomorrow.'

A yellow porch light came on over the front door.

'Daddy waits,' said Kara Lynn, frowning.

Keyes climbed into the MG and started the engine. Kara Lynn scooped up her gown and pecked him on the cheek. 'Did I mention,' she said in a breathy Marilyn voice, 'that I wasn't wearing any panties tonight?'

'I know,' Keyes said. 'It wasn't all bad, the view from the octopus.'

On the way back to his apartment, he stopped at the office to check for burglaries and collect his mail, which consisted of a dozen bills, two large checks from the Miami *Sun*, and a *National Geographic* with an albino something on the cover. Lost somewhere in the debris on Keyes's desk was a checkbook, and he decided to locate it, just in case he ever needed to buy groceries again. Afterward he tried to clean the aquarium, which had been consumed by an advancing greenish slime that threatened to overtake its borders.

These chores were undertaken mainly to stuff his mind with distractions and delay the inevitable. It was nearly one A.M. when Keyes finished, and he lay down on the battered sofa and fell asleep. Before long he felt the coarse grip of the Browning semiautomatic in his right hand. He looked down and saw that his hand was covered with lustrous black mosquitoes, which were swelling up and bursting one by one, little blood balloons. A bony-looking puppet appeared and began to dance, and the Browning went off. The bullets traveled slowly, leaving orange contrails. One after another they puffed into the limestone around the puppet's feet. Just as the puppet's likeness changed from Jesús Bernal to Ernesto Cabal, one of the bullets smashed its head into a thousand wooden splinters. The slivers flew in all directions, twanging the puppet strings which led to the sky. In the dream Brian Keyes saw himself racing toward the broken puppet and snatching the strings with blood-splashed hands. Then he was airborne over the ocean, clinging for life. In a wispy cloud high above, a familiar man with long blond hair and Gypsy eyes twitched the puppet strings and muttered about the usurious price of coffins.

31

Port-au Prince, Haiti. December 28th—By the time this is published, I might be dead or in jail, or hiding in some bleak rathole of a country where I'd never get to read it anyway. Which would be a shame.

But I suppose I've got it coming.

For many years I've written a daily column for this newspaper, a column that achieved an unforeseen but gratifying popularity. I admit that the reportage was not always faultless, but I never strayed too far from the truth. Besides, you folks knew what you were getting.

I probably could have continued to grind out fifteen inches of daily outrage, insult, poignancy, and sarcasm until I got old and my brain turned to porridge. See, I had a nifty deal going here at the paper. The brass liked me, and to keep me contented paid a salary nearly commensurate with my talents. This is what happens when you sell the merchandise: they make it worth your while.

About six weeks ago something changed. Whether it was my job attitude, spiritual diet, or moral equilibrium, I can't say. Things got out of hand, I suppose. The simple and convenient view is that I went berserk, which is possible though unlikely. In my business you learn that sanity, not insanity, is the greater riddle—and that there's nothing so menacing as a sane person suddenly alerted to his own fate.

One thing is true. Over time I came to see the destiny of Florida in a singularly horrid vision, and I took steps to change that destiny. Extreme steps. I assembled a few choice acquaintances and we made some moves, as they say.

In my ardor I might have committed a few unforgivable felonies, but my mission was to save the place and to inspire those who *cared, and to that noble end I suppose I'd break almost any law. Which they say I did.*

For once it was a fair fight, both sides battling with tantamount weapons: publicity versus counterpublicity. Their ammunition was fantasy and whitewash, and ours was the meanest of truths, random crime, and terror. What better way to destroy bogus mail-order illusions!

The odious reality is that we live on a peninsula stolen from the Indians, plundered by carpetbaggers, and immorally occupied by Yankee immigrants who arrive at the rate of one thousand per day, Okies in BMWs.

Most of us born here were always taught to worship growth, or tolerate it unquestioningly. Growth meant prosperity, which was defined in terms of swimming pools and waterfront lots and putting one's kids through college. So when the first frostbitten lemmings arrived with their checkbooks, all the locals raced out and got real-estate licenses; everybody wanted in on the ground floor. Greed was so thick you had to scrape it off your shoes.

The only thing that ever stood between the developers and autocracy was the cursed wilderness. Where there was water, we drained it. Where there were trees, we sawed them down. The scrub we simply burned. The bulldozer was God's machine, so we fed it. Malignantly, progress gnawed its way inland from both coasts, stampeding nature.

Today the Florida most of you know—and created, in fact—is a suburban tundra purged of all primeval wonder save for the sacred solar orb. For all you care, this could be Scottsdale, Arizona, with beaches.

Let me fill you in on what's been going on the last few years: the Glades have begun to dry up and die; the fresh water supply is being poisoned with unpotable toxic scum; up near Orlando they actually tried to straighten a bloody river; in Miami the beachfront hotels are pumping raw sewage into the Gulf Stream; statewide there is a murder every seven hours; the panther is nearly extinct; grotesque three-headed nuclear trout are being caught in Biscayne Bay; and Dade County's gone totally Republican.

This is terrible, you say, but what can we do?

Well, for starters, you can get out.

And since you won't, I will.

It's been pure agony to watch the violent taking of my homeland, and impossible not to act in resistance. Perhaps, in resisting, certain events happened that should not have, and for these I'm sorry. Unfortunately, extremism seldom lends itself to discipline.

At any rate, my pals and I certainly got your attention, didn't we?

By the time this is published—if it's published—I certainly won't be where I am now, so I don't mind revealing the location: a palm-shaded porch of an old hotel on a mountainside overlooking the sad city of Port-au-Prince. Above my head is a wooden paddle fan that hasn't turned since the days of Papa Doc. It's humid here, but no worse than SW Eighth Street in July, and I'm just fine. I'm sitting on a wicker chaise, sipping a polyester-colored rum drink and listening to last year's NBA All-Star game on French radio. Upstairs in my hotel room are three counterfeit passports and $4,000 U.S. cash. I've got a good idea of where I've got to go and what I've got to do.

Evidently this will be my last column, but whatever you do, please don't phone up and cancel your subscription to the paper. The Sun is run by mostly decent and semi-talented journalists who deserve your attention. Besides, if you quit reading it now, you'll miss the best part.

Historically, the function of deranged radicals is to put in motion what only others can finish; to illuminate by excess; to stir the conscience and fade away in exile. To this end, the Nights of December leaves a worthy legacy.

Welcome to the Revolution.

For the first time in nearly half a century, the front page of the Miami *Sun* on New Year's Day did not lead with a story or photograph of the Orange Bowl Parade. Instead, the paper was dominated by three uncommon pieces of journalism.

The farewell column of Skip Wiley appeared in a vertical slot along the left-hand gutter, beneath Wiley's signature photo. Stripped across the top of the newspaper, under the masthead, was a surprisingly self-critical article about why the *Sun* had failed to connect Wiley to *Las Noches de Diciembre* even after his involvement became known to a certain high-ranking editor. This piece was written, and written well, by Cab Mulcahy himself. Therein shocked Miami readers learned that Wiley's cryptic 'where I've got to go, and what I've got to do' referred to the planned, but unconsummated, kidnapping of the Orange Bowl queen during the previous night's parade.

The other key element of the front page was a dramatic but incomplete account of the killing of fugitive terrorist Jesús Bernal on a limestone spit in North Key Largo. This story carried no byline because it was produced by several reporters, one of whom had confirmed the fact that private investigator Brian Keyes had fired the fatal shots from a nine-millimeter Browning handgun, which he was duly licensed to carry. Keyes's presence at the remote jetty was unexplained, although the newspaper noted that he recently had been hired as part of a covert Orange Bowl security force. The only other witness to the Bernal shooting, Metro-Dade Police Sergeant Alberto García, was recovering from surgery and unavailable for comment.

When Brian Keyes woke up in the dinginess of his office, Jenna sat at the desk, reading the morning paper.

'When are you gonna learn to lock the door?' she asked. She handed him the front page. 'Take a look. The puddy tat's out of the bag.'

Keyes sat up and spread the newspaper across his knees. He tried to read, but his eyes refused to focus.

'I figured you'd be decked out in black,' he said groggily.

'I don't believe he's dead,' Jenna said. 'I will not believe it, not till I see the body.' Case closed. She forced a smile. 'Hey, Bri, seems you're a big hero for killing that Cuban kidnapper.'

'Yeah, I look like a big hero, don't I?'

He glanced at Wiley's column. 'December 28—the day before the helicopter crash. When's the last time you heard from him?'

'Same day. I got a telegram from Haiti.'

'What did he say?' Keyes asked.

'He said to spray the lawn for chinch bugs.'

'That all?'

She pursed her lips. 'He also said if anything happens, he wants to be buried in that pine coffin he got from the swap meet. Buried with all his old newspaper clippings, of course.'

'Very touching.'

'I think he stole the idea from the Indian,' Jenna said. 'Seminole warriors are always buried with their weapons.'

Keyes stumbled downstairs to a vending machine and bought three cups of coffee. Jenna took one look and said she didn't want any, so Keyes drank them all.

It put him in a perfect mood for Skip Wiley's farewell column, which Keyes found mawkish and disorganized and only slightly revelatory. He was more interested in Cab Mulcahy's companion story. In it, the managing editor explained that Wiley's key role in the Nights of December had not been exposed because of a threat that many more tourists and innocent persons would be murdered. For several days the information about Wiley was withheld while an investigator hired by the *Sun* searched for him; in retrospect, Mulcahy had written, this decision was ill-advised and probably unethical.

'Poor Cab,' Keyes said, not to Jenna but himself. He felt hurt and embarrassed for his friend.

Jenna came around from behind the desk and sat on the tattered sofa next to Keyes. 'Skip really got carried away,' she said, stopping just short of remorse.

'He carried all of us away,' Keyes said, 'everyone who cared about him. You, me, Mulcahy, the whole damn newspaper. He carried all of us right into the toilet.'

'Brian, don't be this way.'

Jenna wasn't wearing any makeup; she looked like she hadn't slept in two days. 'It was a good cause,' she said defensively. 'Just poor administration.'

'What makes you think he's not dead?'

'Intuition.'

'Oh really.' Keyes eyed her with annoyance, as he would a stray cat.

He said, 'I can't imagine Skip passing up that parade. National television, half the country tuned in. It was too good to resist— if he's not dead, he's in a coma somewhere.'

'He's not dead,' Jenna said.

'We'll see.'

Jenna had never heard him so snide.

'What's with you?' she asked.

'Aw, nothing. Blew a guy's head off last night and I'm still a little bushed. Wanna go for a Danish?'

Jenna looked shaky. 'Oh Brian,' she said.

A plaintively rendered *oh Brian* usually would do the trick; a guaranteed melt-down. This time Keyes felt nothing but a penetrating dullness; not lust or jealousy, rage or bitterness.

'He was supposed to meet me at Wolfie's this morning, but he never came,' she admitted. 'I'm kind of worried.' Her eyes were red. Keyes knew she was about to turn on the waterworks.

'He can't be dead,' she said, choking out the words.

Keyes said, 'I'm sorry, Jenna, but you did the worst possible thing; you encouraged the bastard.'

'I suppose,' she said, starting to sob. 'But some of it sounded so harmless.'

'Skip was about as harmless as a 190-pound scorpion.'

'For instance, dropping those snakes on the ocean liner,' she said. 'Somehow it didn't seem so terrible when he was arranging it. The way he told it, it was supposed to be kind of funny.'

'With goddamn rattlesnakes, Jenna?'

'He didn't tell me *that* part. Honest.' She reached out and put her arms around him. 'Hold me,' she whispered. Normally another foolproof heartbreaker. Keyes took her hand and patted it avuncularly. He didn't know where it had gone—all his feeling for her—just that it wasn't there now.

'It wasn't all Skip's fault,' Jenna cried. 'This was building up for years, poisoning him from the inside. He felt a *duty*, Brian, a duty to be the sentinel of outrage. Who else would speak for the land? For the wild creatures?'

'Save your Sierra Club lecture for the first-graders, okay?'

'Skip was not a bad man, he has a vision of right and wrong.

He's a principled person who took things too far, and maybe he paid for his mistakes. But he deserves credit for his courage, and for all his misery he deserves compassion, too.'

'What he deserved,' Keyes said, 'was twenty-five-to-life at Raiford.' Ten innocent people were dead and here was Jenna doing Portia from the *Merchant of Venice*. He let go of her hand and stood up, not wishing to test his fortitude by sitting too close for too long. He said, 'You'd better go.'

'I took the bus,' Jenna sniffled. 'Can you give me a lift?'

'No, I can't.'

'But I really don't want to be alone, Brian. I just want to lie in a hot bath and think sunny thoughts, a hot bath with kelp crystals. Maybe you could come by tonight and keep me company?'

In the tub Jenna would be unstoppable. 'Thanks anyway,' Keyes said, 'but I'm going to the football game.'

He gave her ten bucks for a cab.

She looked at the money, then at Brian. Her little-girl-lost look, a pale version at that.

'If he's dead,' she said softly, 'what'll we do?'

'I'll varnish the coffin,' Keyes said, 'you spray the chinch bugs.'

32

The annual Orange Bowl Football Classic began at exactly eight P.M. on January 1, when the Fighting Irish of Notre Dame kicked off to the University of Nebraska Cornhuskers before a stadium crowd of 73,411 and an estimated worldwide television audience of forty-one million people. The A. C. Nielsen Company, which rates TV shows based on sample American homes, later calculated that the Notre Dame–Nebraska football game attained a block-buster rating of 23.5, giving it a 38 share of all households watching television that Tuesday night. These ratings were all the more remarkable considering that, for obvious reasons, the second half of the Orange Bowl game was never played.

Midway through the first quarter the rains came; stinging needles that sent a groan through the crowd and brought out a sea of umbrellas.

Brian Keyes huddled sullenly in the rain and wished he'd stayed home. He had decided to attend the game only because he couldn't reach Kara Lynn, and because he'd gotten a free ticket (the Chamber of Commerce, showing its gratitude). Unfortunately, his seat was in the midst of the University of Nebraska card section, where raucous fans held up squares of bright poster-board to spell out witty messages like 'Mash the Irish!' in giant letters. No sooner had Keyes settled in when some of the rooters had handed him two red cards and asked if he wouldn't mind being their semicolon. Keyes was worse than miserable.

On the field Nebraska was humiliating Notre Dame; no real surprise, since the no-neck Cornhuskers outweighed their opponents by an average of thirty-two pounds apiece. Many of the fans, already sopped and now bored, wondered whose brilliant idea the four-point spread was. By half-time the score was 21–3.

The second-string running back for Notre Dame was a young man named David Lee, who stood six-feet-four and weighed a shade under two hundred pounds and was about as Irish as Sonny Liston. Though nominally listed on the team roster as a senior, David Lee was actually several dozen credits short of sophomore status—this, despite majoring in physical education and minoring in physical therapy. David Lee's grade-point average had recently skied to 1.9, slightly enhancing his chances of graduating from college before the age of fifty—provided, of course, he was not first drafted by a professional football team.

Which now seemed unlikely. During the first half of the Orange Bowl game, David Lee attempted to run with the football three times. The first effort resulted in a five-yard loss, the second a fumble. The third time he actually gained twelve yards and a first down. Unfortunately the only two pro football scouts in the stadium missed David Lee's big run because they spent the entire second quarter stuck in line at the men's room, fighting over the urinals with some Klansmen from Perrine.

David Lee's fortunes changed at halftime. As the two teams filed off the field and entered the tunnels leading to the lockers, a muscular Orange Bowl security guard pulled the young halfback aside and asked to speak with him privately. The guard informed David Lee that there was an emergency phone call from his parents in Bedford-Stuy, and escorted him to a stale-smelling broom closet below the stands in the southwest corner of the stadium. Once inside the room, which had no telephone, the security guard locked the door and said:

'Do you know who I am?'

'No, sir,' David Lee replied politely, as even mediocre Notre Dame athletes were taught to do.

'I'm Viceroy Wilson.' And Wilson it was, not at all dead.

'Naw!' Lee grinned. 'C'm on, man!' He studied the security guard's furrowed face and saw in it something familiar, even famous. 'Shit, it's really you!' Lee said. 'I can't believe it—*the* Viceroy Wilson. Man, how come you wound up with a shitty job like this?'

The young man had obviously not been reading anything but the sports pages in Miami.

'Having a rough time tonight?' Wilson asked.

'You got that right,' David Lee said. 'Those honky farmboys are built like garbage trucks.'

'Field looks pretty slippery, too. Hard to make your cuts.'

'Damn right. Hey, what about my momma and daddy?'

'Oh, I lied about that. Lemme see your helmet, bro.'

Lee handed it to him. 'Fits you pretty good.'

'Yeah,' Viceroy Wilson said, squeezing it down over his ears. 'Lemme buy it from you.'

'Sheeiiit!' David Lee laughed. 'You really sumthin.'

'I'm serious, man.' Viceroy Wilson pulled out a wad of cash. 'A thousand bucks,' he said, 'for the whole uniform, 'cept for the cleats. I got my own fuckin' cleats.'

The money was Skip Wiley's idea; Viceroy was just as amenable to punching the young man's lights out and stripping him clean.

David Lee fondled the crisp new bills and peered at the visage inside the gold Notre Dame helmet. He wondered if the Carrera sunglasses were some kind of gag.

'Is it a deal or not?' Wilson asked.

'Look, the coach is gonna freak. How about after the game?'

'This *is* after the game. Believe me, son, the game is over.' Viceroy Wilson nonchalantly handed the college halfback another one thousand dollars.

'Two grand for a football uniform!'

'That's right, bro.'

'You want the jock strap, too?'

'Fuck no!'

When he finally made it back to the Notre Dame locker room, David Lee stood naked except for his spikes and athletic supporter. After apologizing for interrupting the team prayer, he soberly told the coach he had been robbed and molested by a gang of crazed Mariel refugees, and asked if he could sit out the rest of the game.

The Orange Bowl Football Classic is as famous for its prodigal halftime production as for its superior brand of collegiate football. The halftime show is unfailingly more extravagant and fanciful than the Orange Bowl parade of the previous evening because the Halftime Celebration Committee adopts its own theme, hires its own professional director, recruits its own fresh-faced talent, and performs for its own television crew. The effect is that of a wearisome Vegas floor show played out across ten acres of Prescription Athletic Turf by four hundred professional 'young people' who all look like they just got scholarships at Brigham Young. In recent years the TV people realized that lipsynching by the New Christy Minstrels and clog-dancing by giant stuffed mice in tuxedos were not enough to prevent millions of football viewers from going to the toilet and missing all the important car commercials, so the halftime producers introduced fireworks and even lasers into the Orange Bowl show. This proved to be a big hit and new-car sales went up accordingly. Each year more and more spectacular effects were worked into the script, and themes were modernized with the 18-to-34-year-old consumer in mind (though a few minor Disney characters were tossed in for the children). In the minds of the Orange Bowl organizers, the ideal halftime production was conceptually 'hip,' visually thrilling, morally inoffensive, and unremittingly middle-class.

The emcee of the Orange Bowl halftime show was a television personality named John Davidson, selected chiefly because of his dimples, which could be seen from as far away as the stadium's upper deck. Standing in an ice-blue spotlight on the fifty-yard line, John Davidson opened the festivities with a tepid medley of famous show tunes. Soon he was enveloped by a throng of prancing, dancing, capering, miming, rain-soaked Broadway characters in full costume: bewhiskered cats, Yiddish fiddlers, gorgeous chorus girls, two Little Orphan Annies, three Elephant Men, a Hamlet, a King of Siam, and even a tap-dancing Willy Loman. The theme of the twenty-two-minute extravaganza was 'The World's a Stage,' an ambitious sequel to previous Orange Bowl halftime galas such as 'The World's a Song,' 'The World's a Parade,' and more recently, 'The World's a Great Big Planet.'

The heart of the production was the reenactment of six legendary stage scenes, each compressed to eighty-five seconds and supplemented when necessary with tasteful bilingual narration. The final vignette was a soliloquy from *Hamlet*, which did not play well in the downpour; fans in the upper levels of the Orange Bowl could not clearly see Poor Yorick's skull and assumed they were applauding Señor Wences.

Afterward all the performers gathered arm-in-arm under a vast neon marquee and, to no one's surprise, sang 'Give My Regards to Broadway.' Then the floodlights in the stadium dimmed and the slate rainclouds overhead formed an Elysian backdrop for the emotional climax, a holographic tribute to the late Ethel Merman.

The audience had scarcely recovered from this boggling spectacle of electronic magic—scenes from *Gypsy* projected in three dimensions at a height of thirty stories—when the lights winked on and John Davidson strode to midfield.

'Ladies and gentlemen,' he said, with a smile bright enough to bleach rock, 'if I may direct your attention to the east zone, it's my great pleasure to introduce this year's Orange Bowl queen, the beautiful Kara Lynn Shivers!'

In the stands, Brian Keyes went cold. In his obsession with the parade he had forgotten about the game, and the traditional halftime introduction of the queen and her court. It was a brief ceremony—a few of the prize-winning floats circling once in front of the stands before exiting the east end zone. As Kara Lynn's father had griped, it was hardly worth getting your hair done for, eleven crummy minutes of airtime.

But eleven minutes was plenty long enough. An eternity, Keyes thought. A horrible certainty possessed him and he jumped to his feet. Where were the cops—where were the goddamn cops?

The mermaid float entered first, still trumpeting sperm-whale music; then came floats from Cooley Motors, the Nordic Steamship Lines, and the Palm Beach Lawn Polo Society. The procession was supposed to end with a modest contingent of motorcycle Shriners from Illinois, who had been awarded a halftime slot following the untimely cancellation of the entry from Bogotá.

However, something foreign trailed the betasseled Shriners into the stadium: a strange unnamed float. Curious fans who thumbed through their Official Orange Bowl Souvenir Programs found no mention of this peculiar diorama. In their reserved box seats along the forty-yard line, members of the Orange Bowl Committee trained binoculars on the interloper and exchanged fretful whispers. Since the NBC cameras already had discovered the mystery float, intervention was out of the question, image-wise; besides, there was no reason to suspect anything but a harmless fraternity prank.

Though its craftsmanship was amateurish (forgivable, considering its humble warehouse origins), the float actually made a quaint impression. It was an Everglades tableau, almost childlike in simplicity. At one end stood an authentic thatched chickee, the traditional Seminole shelter; nearby lay a dugout canoe, half-carved from a bald cypress; steam rose from a black kettle hung over a mock fire. Grazing in a thicket, presumably unseen, was a stuffed white-tailed deer; a similarly preserved raccoon peered down from the lineated trunk of a synthetic palm. The centerpiece was a genuine Indian, very much alive and dressed in the nineteenth-century garb of trading-post Seminoles: a round, brimless straw hat, baggy pants, gingham shirt, a knotted red kerchief, and a tan cowskin vest. Somewhat anachronistically, the nineteenth-century Indian was perched at the helm of a modern airboat, gliding through the River of Grass. A long unpolished dagger was looped in the Seminole's snakeskin belt and a toy Winchester rifle lay across his lap. His smooth youthful face seemed the portrait of civility.

Brian Keyes sprang for the aisle the moment he saw the Indian. Frantically he tried to make his way down from the stands, but the Nebraska card-flashers (*Irish Suck!*) were embroiled in a heated cross-stadium skirmish with the Notre Dame card section (*Huskers Die!*). Keyes pushed and shoved and elbowed his way along the row but it was slow going, too slow, and some of the well-fed Cornhusker faithful decided to teach this rude young fellow some manners. They simply refused to move. Not for a semicolon, they said; set your butt down.

As the floats trundled past the stands, wind-whipped rains lashed the riders and sent the ersatz Broadway actors scurrying off the field for cover. Kara Lynn was drenched and miserable, but she continued to wave valiantly and smile. Through a pair of field glasses (and from the dry safety of a VIP box) Reed Shivers assayed his daughter's bedraggled visage and noted that her makeup was running badly, inky rivulets marring impeccable cheeks—she looked like something from a Warhol movie. Reed Shivers anxiously wondered if it was time to buy the lady from the Eileen Ford Agency another drink.

Reed Shivers and almost everyone else in the Orange Bowl did not yet realize that the Nights of December were alive and well. Nor did they know with what ease Skip Wiley's troops had carried out the assault on the *Nordic Princess*, the ditching of the stolen Huey, and the staging of their own deaths: the gang had simply performed flawlessly (minus Jesús Bernal, who'd vanished before Wiley had revealed the scheme's final refinement, and who'd gone to his death haplessly believing that the helicopter crash was an accident).

Tommy Tigertail had played a heroic role as captain of the clandestine rescue boat, a twenty-one-foot Mako powered by a two-hundred-horsepower Evinrude. Posing as a mackerel fisherman, he had plowed rough seas for an hour, staying close to the ocean liner but attracting no notice. His night vision had proved crucial when they had all bailed out—the pilot, Skip Wiley, and Viceroy Wilson. The ocean had been a turbid and treacherous soup, littered with sinking or half-sunk chopper wreckage, but within minutes the Indian had found all his comrades and pulled them safely into the speedboat.

The daring helicopter pilot had been rewarded with twenty thousand dollars of bingo skim, a phony passport, and a first-class plane ticket to Barbados. The Nights of December had dried off, checked into a Coconut Grove hotel, and gone back to work.

The news of Jesús Bernal's violent fate had darkened Skip Wiley's mood, but he'd refused to let it drag him down. Bernal's passing had not similarly moved Viceroy Wilson, who merely remarked how inconsiderate it was for Hay-Zoos to have ripped off his private shotgun, and how supremely stupid to have used it on a cop. Tommy Tigertail had had absolutely nothing to say about the neurotic Cuban's death; he had understood Jesús even less than Jesús had understood him.

In truth, Bernal's death had changed nothing. *Las Noches* had gone ahead with the mission, working with a vigor and *esprit* that had warmed Wiley's heart. At the vortex of the plan was a rejuvenated, rock-hard, and recently drug-free Viceroy Wilson, much more than a shadow of his former self.

Viceroy had had no trouble choosing Notre Dame's uniform over the apple-red jersey of the University of Nebraska.

The reasons were simple. First, Nebraska's agri-business hegemony represented a vile anathema to Wilson, whose radical sympathies were more logically drawn to the Irish Republican Army, and thus Notre Dame.

Second, and most important, Notre Dame was the only one of the teams with a number thirty-one on its roster.

In reconstructing Viceroy Wilson's movements about the stadium that night, it was determined that several fans saw him emerge from the broom closet at 9:40 P.M. Ten minutes later he was observed, in uniform, ordering a jumbo orange juice at the concession stand in Section W.

Four minutes after that, he was seen eating a raisin bagel in a box seat at the Notre Dame twenty-yard line. When the rightful occupant returned from the souvenir shop and requested that Viceroy move elsewhere, Wilson inconsiderately mutilated the man's shamrock umbrella and popped him in the face. No one in the stands called the police; it seemed more properly a matter for the NCAA.

An eight-minute period elapsed during which no one reported seeing number thirty-one—then half the households of America did, courtesy of NBC.

While the other football players clustered in the southwest tunnel, Viceroy Wilson broke onto the field in a casual but self-assured trot. Many Notre Dame fans applauded, thinking the halftime show was finally over but wondering why the rest of the green-and-gold did not follow. They wondered, too, why a second-rate fumbler like David Lee would be given the honor of leading the Fighting Irish into battle.

They were stunned by what happened next.

Number thirty-one ran a perfect beeline down the center of

the football field, each great stride splashing in the soggy turf.
For Miami Dolphin fanatics, it was an unmistakable if ghostly
reprise—the familiar numeral on the jersey; the right shoulder,
drooping ever so slightly, as if bracing for a high tackle; the thick
arms pumping like watchgears, the black hands locked in fists;
and of course that triangular wedge of muscle from the shoulders
to the hips. All that was missing was a football.

By the time Viceroy Wilson crossed the fifty-yard line, he was
in full gait and no $3.50-an-hour security guard on the face of
the earth could have caught him. Viceroy's mad dash seemed to
freeze the authorities, who did not wish to shoot, maim, or
otherwise embarrass any Notre Dame player. Maybe the kid was
psyching himself for the game, or maybe just showing off for
South Bend. After all, there were TV cameras everywhere.

In the midst of Viceroy Wilson's virtuoso run, two other disturb-
ances erupted in the stadium.

First, the Seminole float rumbled and began to shudder at the
tail of the procession—it appeared as if it was about to blow apart.
The Shriners slowed their motorcycles and wheeled around,
believing that the dim-witted Indian had accidentally started up
the airboat.

At the same instant John Davidson was accosted at midfield by
a bald, barefoot, russet-bearded man who was dressed as the King
of Siam. It was, of course, Skip Wiley.

Unintelligible bits of their argument went out over the stadium
sound system and then a struggle began. The two men tumbled
out of the spotlight.

Seconds later the King of Siam appeared alone, holding Davidson's cordless microphone.

The crowd seemed greatly confused about whether this was part
of the official program; half of them clapped and half murmured.

Skip Wiley beamed up at the stands and said, 'Please allow me
to introduce myself, I'm a man of wealth and taste.'

Brian Keyes had extricated himself from the card-flashers and
was bounding down the stadium, four steps at a time, when he
heard it.

Skip Wiley shouted to the heavens: 'Been around for long, long
years. Stolen many a man's soul and faith.'

Swell, Keyes said to himself, he's doing the Stones.

From the crest of the queen's float, Kara Lynn Shivers stopped waving at the crippled Cub Scouts in Section Q and turned to see what was going on. She did not recall 'Sympathy for the Devil' being listed in the Orange Bowl music program. Nor did she recognize the bald performer in the gold Oriental waistcoat.

'Pleased to meet you,' Wiley sang, 'hope you guess my name. . . .'

In the NBC trailer the assistant producer barked into his mike: 'Keep two cameras on that asshole!' Which was the prevailing sentiment among his forty-one million viewers.

Skip Wiley's performance was queer enough to draw almost everyone's attention away from Viceroy Wilson—everyone except the Shriners. Reacting swiftly, Burt and James led the motorcycle squadron across the east zone to intercept the hulking ex-fullback. It was the ultimate test of Viceroy's reborn skill, zigging and juking through the stolid heart of the Evanston Shrine; stiff-arming fenders where necessary; using his All-Pro shoulder to knock the cyclists off balance; an elbow to the fez, a fist to the throat (in the old days, fifteen yards and loss of down). With each collision Viceroy Wilson gave a contented growl. *Thirty-one Z-right.* This was the only part he'd ever missed, the purity of contact. Galvanized by adrenaline, he rejoiced in the shining justice of his run—the abused black hero outwitting, outflanking, outmuscling the whitest of the white establishment, impotent against his inevitable assault on precious honky womanhood. In Wilson's wake the bruised Shriners squirmed in the slop, pinned beneath their spangled Harleys; defeated, Viceroy mused, by their own gaudy materialism. And all this played out with splendid irony in the theater of his past heroics.

With the pursuers in chaos, all that stood between Viceroy Wilson and the Orange Bowl queen was the United States Marine Corps Honor Guard, whose members had no intention of breaking formation or soiling their dress blues. Wilson threaded them effortlessly and bounded onto the mermaid float.

'Oh shit,' said Kara Lynn Shivers.

'Come on, girl,' Viceroy Wilson said, catching his wind.

'Where we going?' Kara Lynn asked.

'Into history.'

The tuna-blue mermaids shrieked as Wilson slung the queen over his shoulder and sprinted back upfield.

At that second the Seminole airboat shot off the Everglades float, splintering plywood, disemboweling the stuffed deer, leveling the chickee; the aviation engine expelling a suffocating contrail of rain and kerosene fumes over the stands. The airboat's aluminum hull pancaked on the slick football turf and hydroplaned; it was perfect, the Indian thought, gaining speed—you couldn't ask for a better surface.

Brian Keyes had finally reached the ground level and was vaulting the fence when he found the cops he'd been looking for. Five of Miami's finest. Dogs, nightsticks, the works. Keyes protested at the top of his lungs but they pinned him to the fence anyway, and there, stuck like a moth, he watched the whole terrible scene unfold—the airboat wheeling circles; Viceroy running with Kara Lynn slung over his shoulder; Skip crooning at the microphone.

On the field Burt and James had righted their bikes and resumed the chase. The key element now was speed, not agility: dodging a Harley Davidson was one thing, outrunning it was impossible. Viceroy Wilson had no illusion about this: he was counting heavily on the Indian.

Tommy Tigertail was a wizard with the airboat. He cut the field in half and slid the howling craft between Wilson and the frowning white riders in purple hats. The Indian spun the boat on a dime, throwing a sheet of rain and loose sod into the teeth of the Shriners. James lost control and went down in a deep skid, chewing a trench from the Notre Dame forty-yard line to the Nebraska thirty-five. He did not get up. Burt alertly veered from the airboat's backwash and, to avoid the flying muck, crouched behind his customized Plexiglas windshield.

The airboat bounded up alongside Viceroy Wilson and coasted to a stop. Wilson heaved Kara Lynn Shivers onto the deck as if she were a sandbag. By now the stadium crowd had figured out that this was not part of the show and started to scream witlessly. The Orange Bowl chairman was on his feet, yelling for the cops, while Sparky Harper's Chamber of Commerce successor frantically tried to sabotage the cables on one of NBC's portable Mini-cams. Meanwhile some of the real Notre Dame football players ambled onto the field to watch the commotion; Tommy Tigertail feared that they might soon get chivalrous notions.

'Hurry,' he said to Viceroy Wilson.

Wilson had one foot in the airboat when Burt's Harley buzzed him like a fat chrome bee. Viceroy looked down to discover that his right leg—his bad leg—was stuck fast in a Shriner death hug. With his other leg Wilson kicked and bucked like a buted-up racehorse. The motorcycle fell from under Viceroy's attacker but somehow Burt kept his balance and his grip, and wound up on his feet. Wilson thought: This guy would have made a helluva nose tackle.

'Let the girl go!' Burt commanded.

'Get in,' Tommy Tigertail said to Wilson.

'I can't shake loose!'

The pain in Viceroy's knee—famously mangled, prematurely arthritic, now barely held together with pins and screws—was insufferable, worse than anything he remembered from the old days.

'Hurry!' said the Indian. He jiggled the stick and the airboat jerked into gear. They were on a drier patch of the field so the boat moved forward in balky fits. Tommy was aching to throttle up to top speed; through the cutting rain he had spotted a phalanx of helmeted police advancing from the north sidelines. In the bow Kara Lynn sat up, shivering in the deluge.

'Let her go!' Burt bellowed, tugging and twisting Wilson's leg until number thirty-one clung to the hull by only the tips of his fingers. A deep-bone pain began to rake Viceroy's mind and seep his resolve. He suddenly felt old and tired, and realized he'd spent all his stamina on that glorious run.

The Indian decided it was time to go—the police were trotting now, yellow-fanged K-9 dogs at their heels. Tommy hopped off the driver's platform, grabbed Viceroy Wilson by the wrists, and yanked with all his strength. Burt lost his grip and fell backward, the purple fez tumbling off. Wilson landed in the boat with a grunt.

Kara Lynn tried to scrabble out, but the airboat was already moving too fast. She huddled with her legs to her chest, hands pressed to her ears; the thundering yowl of the engine was a new source of pain.

She saw the sturdy Shriner running alongside the airboat, his sequined vest flapping. He kept shouting for Tommy to stop.

He had a small brown pistol in one hand.

Viceroy Wilson rose to the prow, breadloaf arms swaying at his sides, keeping steady but favoring his right leg. He tore off the Notre Dame helmet and hurled it vainly at the dogged Shriner.

Viceroy's bare mahogany head glistened in the rain; the stadium lights twinkled in the ebony panes of his sunglasses. He scowled imperiously at Burt and raised his right fist in a salute that was at least traditional, if not trite.

'Down!' the Indian shouted. The airboat was hurtling straight for one of the goalposts—Tommy would have to make an amazing turn. 'Viceroy, get down!'

Kara Lynn saw a rosy flash at the muzzle of Burt's pistol, but heard no shot.

When she turned, Viceroy Wilson was gone.

With a grimace Tommy Tigertail spun the airboat in a perilous fishtailing arc. It slid sideways against the padded goalpost and bounced off. The Marching Cornhusker majorettes dropped their batons and broke rank, leaving Tommy a clear path to escape. With Kara Lynn crouched fearfully in the bow, the airboat skimmed out of the stadium through the east gate. A getaway tractor-trailer rig had been parked on Seventh Street but the Indian knew he wouldn't need it; the swales were ankle-deep in rainwater and the airboat glided on mirrors all the way to the Miami River.

Viceroy Wilson lay dead in the east end zone. From the Goodyear blimp it appeared that he was splayed directly over the F in 'Fighting Irish,' which had been painted in tall gold letters across the turf.

A babbling congress of cops, orange blazers, drunken fans, and battered Shriners had surrounded the Super Bowl hero. Brian Keyes was there, too, kneeling down and speaking urgently into

Viceroy Wilson's ear, but Viceroy Wilson was answering no questions. He lay face up, his lips curled in a poster-perfect radical snarl. His right hand was so obdurately clenched into a fist that two veteran morticians would later be unable to pry it open. Centered between the three and the one of the kelly-green football jersey was a single bullet hole, which was the object of much squeamish finger pointing.

'I'm telling ya,' the Notre Dame coach was saying, 'he's *not* one of ours.'

Outside the Orange Bowl, on Fourteenth Avenue, the King of Siam flagged a taxi.

33

Keyes made it from the stadium to Jenna's house in twenty minutes.

'Hey, there,' she said, opening the screen door. She was wearing a baggy sweatshirt with nothing underneath.

Keyes went into the living room. The coffin was padlocked.

'Open it,' he said.

'But I don't have a key,' Jenna said. 'What's the matter—he's alive, isn't he?'

'Surprise, surprise.'

'I told you!' she exclaimed.

'Put on some goddamn clothes.'

She nodded and went to the bedroom.

'Do you have a hammer?' Keyes called.

'In the garage.'

He found a sledge and carried it back to the living room. Jenna cleared the vase and magazines off the macabre coffee table. She was wearing tan hiking shorts and a navy long-sleeved pullover. She had also put on a bra and some running shoes.

'Look out,' Keyes said. He pounded the padlock three times before the hasp snapped.

Inside the cheap coffin, Skip Wiley's detritus looked as muddled and random as before—yellowed newspaper clippings, old notebooks, mildewed paperbacks, library files purloined from the *Sun*'s morgue. Keyes sifted through everything in search of a single fresh clue. The best he could do was a sales receipt from a Fort Lauderdale marine dealer.

'Skip bought a boat last week,' Keyes said. 'Twenty-one-foot Mako. Eighteen-five, cash. Any idea why?'

'Nuh-uh.'

'When's the last time he was here?'

'I'm not sure,' Jenna replied.

Keyes grabbed her by the arms and shook hard. He frightened her, which was what he wanted. He wanted her off balance.

Jenna didn't know how to react, she'd never seen Brian this way. His eyes were dry and contemptuous, and his voice was that of an intruder.

'When was Skip here?' he repeated.

'A week ago, I think. No, last Friday.'

'What did he do?'

'He spent half the day reading the paper,' Jenna said. 'That much I remember.'

'Really?'

'Okay, let me think.' She took a deep theatrical breath and put her hands in her pockets. 'Okay, he was clipping some stuff from the newspaper—that, I remember. And he was playing his music. Steppenwolf, real loud . . . I made him turn it down. Then we grilled some burgers with mushrooms, and the Indian man came over and they left. That's what I remember.'

'He didn't say a word about the Nights of December?'

'No.'

'And you didn't ask?'

'No,' Jenna said. 'I knew better. He was really wired, Brian. He was in no mood for questions.'

'You're useless, you know that?'

'Brian!'

'Where's the garbage?'

'Out on the curb.' Jenna started sniffling; it sounded possibly authentic.

Keyes walked to the street and hauled the ten-gallon bag back into the house. He used a car key to gash it open.

'What're you doing now?' Jenna asked.

'Looking for Wheaties boxtops. Didn't you hear?—there's a big sweepstakes.'

He kicked through guava rinds, putrid cottage cheese, eggshells, tea bags, melon husks, coffee grounds, yogurt cartons, chicken bones, and root-beer cans. The newspapers were at the very bottom, soggy and rancid-smelling. Keyes used the toe of his shoe to search for the front page from Friday, December 28. When he found it, he motioned Jenna over. She made a face as she tiptoed through the rank mush.

'This is the one he was clipping?' Keyes asked.

'Right.'

Keyes got on his knees and went through the newspaper, page by sodden page. Jenna backed away and sat on the floor. Pouting would be a waste of energy; Brian scarcely even noticed she was in the room.

He found Skip Wiley's scissor holes in the real-estate section. A long article had been clipped from the bottom of the first page, and a large display advertisement had been cut out of Page F-17.

Keyes held up the shredded newsprint for Jenna to see; she shrugged and shook her head. 'Stay here,' he said. 'I need to use your phone.'

Three minutes later he was back. He took her by the hand and said, 'Let's go, we're running out of time.' Keyes had called a librarian at the *Sun*. Now he knew what Wiley had clipped out. He knew everything.

'What about this mess?' Jenna complained.

'This is nothing,' Keyes said, yanking her out the front door. 'This is a picnic.'

They arrived at the Virginia Key marina within minutes of one another, Skip Wiley by car, the Indian by airboat. The Indian's round straw hat had blown off during the ride and his wet black hair was windswept behind his ears. Wiley had changed to a flannel shirt, painter's trousers, and a blue Atlanta Braves baseball cap.

The Mako outboard had been gassed up and tied to a piling. The marina was dark and, once Tommy stopped the airboat, silent. He carefully lifted Kara Lynn into the outboard; she was limp as a rag and her eyes were closed. Her blond hair hung in a stringy mop across half of her face.

'I gave her something to drink,' the Indian said, hopping out. 'She'll sleep for a time.'

'Perfect,' Wiley said. 'Look, Tom, I'm damn sorry about Viceroy.'

'It was my fault.'

'Like hell. All he had to do was duck down, but the big black jackass decides to pull a Huey Newton. He really disappointed me, him and his Black Power bullshit—it wasn't the time or place for it, but the sonofabitch couldn't resist. A regular moonchild of the sixties.'

Tommy Tigertail's eyes dulled with grief. 'I'll miss him,' he said.

'Me too, pal.'

'I found these in the airboat.' Tommy held up Viceroy Wilson's cherished sunglasses.

'Here,' Wiley said. He fitted the glitzy Carreras onto the Indian's downcast face. 'Hey, right out of *GQ*!'

'Where's that?' Tommy asked. With the glasses he looked like a Tijuana hit-man.

A pair of pelicans waddled up the dock to see if the two men were generous anglers. The Indian smiled at the goofy-looking birds and said, 'Sorry, guys, no fish.'

A red pickup truck with oversized tires pulled into the lot. The driver turned the headlights off and sat with the engine running.

Wiley worriedly glanced over his shoulder.

'It's all right,' Tommy said. 'That's my ride.'

'Where you off to?'

'I've got a skiff waiting at Flamingo, down in the back country. There's an old chickee up the Shark River, nobody knows about it. The last few weeks I've had it stocked with supplies—plenty to last me forever.' Tommy Tigertail had stored enough for two men. Now there would be only one.

'You've been so damn generous,' Wiley said. 'I wish you could stay and watch the fun.'

'If I remained here,' Tommy said, 'I'd bring nothing but pain to my people. The police would never leave them alone. It's better to go far away, where I can't be found.'

'I'm really sorry,' Wiley said.

'Why?' The Indian wore a look of utter serenity. In a voice that carried a note of private triumph he said, 'Don't you see? This way I will not die in prison.' That much he owed his ancestors.

'If you ever get down to Haiti,' Wiley said, 'look me up in the phone book. Under E for Exile.'

'Stay out of trouble,' Tommy Tigertail advised. 'Stay free.'

Wiley scratched his neck and grinned. 'We pulled some outstanding shit, didn't we?'

'Yes,' Tommy said. 'Outstanding.' He shook Wiley's hand and gave him the red kerchief from around his neck. 'Good-bye, Skip.'

''Bye, Tom.'

The Indian walked briskly to the pickup truck. An ancient Seminole with thin gray hair and a walnut face sat behind the wheel.

'Let's go, Uncle Billie,' Tommy said.

They could see Skip Wiley toiling at the console of the sleek boat, warming the big engine. He was singing in a stentorian cannon that crashed out over the carping gulls and the slap of the waves.

Rode a tank, held a general's rank, when the blitzkrieg raged and the bodies stank . . .

'Who is the strange one with the beard?' the old Seminole wanted to know.

'With any luck,' Tommy Tigertail said affectionately, 'the last white man I'll ever see.'

When they reached the toll booth to the Rickenbacker Causeway, Jenna sat up and asked, 'Where we going?'

'For a boat ride,' Brian Keyes replied.

'I thought we were going to the police. Don't you think that's a better idea?'

'The goddamn marines would be a better idea, if I had that kind of time.'

Keyes knew exactly what the cops were doing—setting up a vast and worthless perimeter around the Orange Bowl. The city was howling with sirens; every squad car in Dade County was in motion. There were no helicopters up because of the bad weather—and without choppers, Keyes knew, the cops could forget about catching the Indian.

Jenna shifted apprehensively. She said, 'I think you ought to drop me off here. This whole thing is between you and Skip.'

Keyes drove faster down the causeway. Years ago—a lifetime ago—he and Jenna used to park there at night and make love under the trees, and afterward marvel at how the skyscrapers glittered off the bay. Since then, the causeway had become extremely popular with ski-mask rapists and icepick murderers, and not many unarmed couples went there to neck anymore.

Jenna said, 'Why don't you let me out?'

'Not here, it's way too dangerous,' he said. 'I'm curious—why'd you stop by the office today?'

'Just lonely,' Jenna said. 'And I was worried sick about Skip . . . I thought you might know something.'

Keyes glanced at her and said, 'Your little chore was to keep me company, right?'

'That's the dumbest thing I ever heard.'

'You were in on the whole thing.'

'I hate you like this,' Jenna said angrily. 'So damn smug, you think you've got it all figured out. Well, you don't . . . there's one thing you never figured out: why I left you for Skip.'

'That's true,' Keyes said, remembering how nasty she could get. She sat ramrod straight in the seat, chin out, a portrait of defiance.

'The choice was easy, Brian. You're a totally passive person, an incurable knothole peeper, a spy.'

Keyes thought: This is going to be a beaut.

Jenna said, 'You're a follower and a chaser and chronicler of other human lives, but you will not fucking *participate*. I wanted somebody who would. Skip isn't afraid to dance on the big stage. He's the sort of person you love to watch but would hate to be, because he takes chances. He's a leader, and leaders don't just get followed—they get chased. That's not your style, Brian, getting chased. The thing about Skip, he makes things happen.'

'So did Juan Corona. You two would make a swell couple.'

Keyes found himself strangely unperturbed by Jenna's emasculatory harangue; maybe there was hope for him yet. He hit the brakes and the MG skidded off the road into some gravel. He backed up to the gate of the Virginia Key marina.

'I believe that's your car,' he said to Jenna.

'Where?'

He pointed. 'Next to the boat ramp. The white Mercury.'

'My car's in the shop,' Jenna snapped.

'Really? Shall we go check the license tag?'

Jenna turned away.

'Skip borrowed it,' she said almost inaudibly.

Keyes saw her hand move to the door handle. He reached across the seat and slapped the lock down.

'Not yet,' he warned her. 'You're not going anywhere.'

'Hey, what is this?'

'It's called deep trouble, and you're in the middle, Miss Granola Bar.'

'All I ever knew were bits and pieces, that's all,' she insisted. 'Skip didn't tell me everything. He was always dropping little hints but I was scared to ask for more. I didn't know about the new boat and I sure don't know where he is right now. Honest, Brian, I thought the stunt with the ocean liner was it; his big plan. I didn't know anything about tonight, I swear. I wasn't even sure he was still alive.'

Her eyes couldn't get more liquid, her voice more beseeching. A metamorphosis in thirty seconds.

Keyes said, 'You promised he wasn't going to hurt Kara Lynn.'

'Maybe he's not,' Jenna said ingenuously. 'Maybe he's already let her go.'

'Yeah, and maybe I'm the Prince of Wales.'

Keyes drove past the Miami Marine Stadium and turned down a winding two-lane macadam. The shrimper's dock was at the dead end of the road, on a teardrop-shaped lagoon.

The shrimper's name was Joey and he owned three small trawlers that harvested Biscayne Bay by night. He worked out of a plywood shack lighted by bare bulbs and guarded by a pair of friendly mutts.

Joey was dipping shrimp when Keyes drove up.

'I don't know if you remember me,' Keyes said. 'I interviewed you a few years back for a newspaper story.'

'Sure,' said Joey, peering past the end of his cigar. 'You were askin' about pollution, some damn thing.'

'Right. Look, I need a boat. It's sort of an emergency.'

Joey glanced over at Jenna sitting in the car.

'Damn fine emergency,' he said. 'But you don't need a boat, you need a water bed.'

'Please,' Keyes said. 'We need a ride to Osprey Island.'

'You and the girl?'

'That's right. It's worth a hundred bucks.'

Joey hung the net on a nail over the shrimp tank. 'That island's private property, son.'

'I know.'

'It's black as a bear's asshole and fulla bugs. Why the hell you wanna go over there on a night like this?'

'Like I said, it's an emergency,' Keyes said. 'Life and death.'

'Naturally,' Joey muttered. He took the hundred dollars and struggled into his oilskin raingear. 'There's more weather on the way,' he said. 'Go fetch your ladyfriend. We'll take the *Tina Marie*.'

Osprey Island was a paddle-shaped outcrop in east Biscayne Bay, about five miles south of the Cape Florida lighthouse. There were no sandy beaches, for the island was mostly hard coral and oolite rock—a long-dead reef, thrust barely above sea level. The shores were collared with thick red mangrove; farther inland, young buttonwoods, gumbo-limbo, sea grape, and mahogany. An old man who had lived there for thirty years had planted a row of royal palms and a stand of pines, and these rose majestically from the elevated plot that had been his homestead, before he fell ill and moved back to the mainland. All that remained of the house was a concrete slab and four cypress pilings and a carpet of broken pink stucco; a bare fifty-foot flagpole stood as a salt-eaten legacy to the old man's patriotism and also to his indelible fear that someday the Russians would invade Florida, starting with Osprey Island.

Like almost everything else in South Florida, the islet was dishonestly named. There were no white-hooded ospreys, or fish eagles, living on Osprey Island because the nesting trees were not of sufficient height or maturity. A few of the regal birds lived on Sand Key or Elliott, farther south, and occasionally they could be seen diving the channel and marl flats around the island bearing their name. But if it had been left up to the Calusa Indians, who had first settled the place, the island probably would have been called Mosquito or Crab, because these were the predominant life forms infesting its fifty-three acres.

There was no dock—Hurricane Betsy had washed it away in 1965—but a shallow mooring big enough for one boat had been blasted out of the dead coral on the lee side. With some difficulty of navigation, and considerable paint loss to the outboard's hull, Skip Wiley managed to locate the anchorage in pitch dark. He waded ashore with Kara Lynn deadweight in his arms. The trail to the campsite was fresh and Wiley had no trouble following it, although the sharp branches snagged his clothes and scratched his scalp. Every few steps came a new lashing insult and he bellowed appropriate curses to the firmament.

At the campsite, not far from the old cabin rubble, Wiley placed Kara Lynn on a bed of pine needles and covered her with a thin woolen blanket. Both of them were soaked from the crossing.

Wiley swatted no-see-'ems in the darkness for three hours until he heard the hum of a passing motorboat. Finally! he groused. The Marine Patrol on its nightly route. Wiley had been waiting for the bastard to go by; now it was safe.

When the police boat was gone he built a small fire from dry tinder he had stored under a sheet of industrial plastic. The wind was due east and unbelievably strong, scattering sparks from the campfire like swarms of tipsy fireflies. Wiley was grateful that the woods were wet.

He was fixing a mug of instant bouillon when Kara Lynn woke up, surprising him.

'Hello, there,' Skip Wiley said, thinking it was a good thing he'd tied her wrists and ankles—she looked like a strong girl.

'I know this is a dumb question—' Kara Lynn began.

'Osprey Island,' Wiley said.

'Where's that?'

'Out in the bay. Care for some soup?'

Wiley helped her sit up and pulled the blanket around to cover her back and shoulders, which were bare in the parade gown. He held the cup while she drank.

'I know who you are,' Kara Lynn said. 'I read the big story in the paper today—was it today?'

Wiley looked at his wristwatch. It was half-past three in the morning. 'Yesterday,' he said. 'So what did you think?'

'About the story?'

'No, the column.'

'You've done better,' Kara Lynn said.

'What do you mean?'

'Can I have another sip? Thanks.' She drank a little more and said: 'You're sharper when you don't write in the first person.'

Wiley plucked at his beard.

'Now, don't get mad,' Kara Lynn said. 'It's just that some of the transitions seemed contrived, like you were reaching.'

'It was a damn tough piece to write,' Wiley said thoughtfully.

'I'm sure it was.'

'I mean, I couldn't see another way to do it. The first-person approach seemed inescapable.'

'Maybe you're right,' Kara Lynn said. 'I just don't think it was as effective as the hurricane column.'

Wiley brightened. 'You liked that one?'

'A real scorcher,' Kara Lynn said. 'We talked about it in class.'

'No kidding!' Skip Wiley was delighted. Then his smile ebbed and he sat in silence for several minutes. The girl was not what he expected, and he felt a troubling ambivalence about what was to come. He wished the Seminole sleeping drink had lasted longer; now that Kara Lynn was awake, he sensed a formidable undercurrent. She was a composed and resourceful person—he'd have to watch himself.

'What's the matter?' Kara Lynn asked.

'Why aren't you crying or something?' Wiley grumbled.

Kara Lynn looked around the campsite. 'What would be the point?'

Wiley spread more tinder on the fire and held his hands over the flame. The warmth was comforting. He thought: Actually, there's nothing to stop me from leaving now. The job is done.

'Do you know Brian Keyes?'

'Sure,' Wiley said, 'we worked together.'

'Was he a good reporter?'

'Brian's a good man,' Wiley said, 'but I'm not so sure if he was a good reporter. He wasn't really suited for the business.'

'Apparently neither were you.'

'No comparison,' he scoffed. 'Absolutely no comparison.'

'Oh, I'm not sure,' Kara Lynn said. 'I think you're two sides to the same coin, you and Brian.'

'And I think you read too much *Cosmo*.' Wiley wondered why she was so damned interested in Keyes.

'What about Jenna?' Kara Lynn asked. 'You serious about her?'

'What is this, the Merv show?' Wiley ground his teeth. 'Look,' he said, 'I'd love to sit and chat but it's time to be on my way.'

'You're going to leave me out here in the rain? With no food or water?'

'You won't need any,' he said. ''Fraid I'm going to have to douse the fire, too.'

'A real gentleman,' Kara Lynn said acerbically. She was already testing the rope on her wrist.

Wiley was about to pour some tea on the flames when he straightened up and cocked his head. 'Did you hear something?' he asked.

'No,' Kara Lynn lied.

'It's a goddamn boat.'

'It's the wind, that's all.'

Wiley set down the kettle, took off his baseball cap, and went crashing off, his bare bright egg of a head vanishing into the hardwoods. Thinking he had fled, Kara Lynn squirmed to the campfire and turned herself around. She held her wrists over the bluest flame, until she smelled flesh. With a cry she pulled away; the rope held fast.

When she looked up, he was standing there. He folded his arms and said, 'See what you did, you hurt yourself.' He carried her back to the bed of pine needles and examined the burns. 'Christ, I didn't even bring a Band-Aid,' he said.

'I'm all right,' said Kara Lynn. Her eyes teared from the pain. 'What about that noise?'

'It was nothing,' Wiley said, 'just a shrimper trolling offshore.' He tore a strip of orange silk from the hem of her gown. He soaked it in salt water and wound it around the burn. Then he cut another length of rope and retied her wrists, tighter than before.

The rain started again. It came in slashing horizontal sheets. Wiley covered his eyes and said, 'Shit, I can't run the boat in this mess.'

'Why don't you wait till it lets up?' Kara Lynn suggested.

Her composure was aggravating. Wiley glared down at her and said, 'Hey, Pollyanna, you're awfully calm for a kidnap victim. You overdosed on Midol or what?'

Kara Lynn's ocelot eyes stared back in a way that made him shiver slightly. She wasn't afraid. *She was not afraid*. What a great kid, Wiley thought. What a damn shame.

They huddled under a sheet of opaque plastic, the raindrops popping at their heads. Wiley tied Tommy's red kerchief around the dome of his head to blot the rain from his eyes.

'Tell me about Osprey Island,' Kara Lynn said, as if they were rocking on a front porch waiting for the ice-cream truck.

'A special place,' he said, melancholic. 'A gem of nature. There's a freshwater spring down the trail, can you believe it? Miles off the mainland and the aquifer still bubbles up. You can see coons, opossums, wood rats drinking there, but mostly birds. Wood storks, blue herons. There's a bald eagle on the island, a young male. Wingspan is ten feet if it's an inch, just a glorious bird. He stays up in the tallest pines, fishes only at dawn and dusk. He's up there now, in the trees.' Wiley's ancient-looking eyes went to the pine stand. 'It's too windy to fly, so I'm sure he's up there now.'

'I've never seen a wild eagle,' Kara Lynn remarked. 'I was born down here and I've never seen one.'

'That's too bad,' Skip Wiley said sincerely. His head was bowed. Tiny bubbles of water hung in his rusty beard. It didn't make it any easier that she was born here, he thought.

'It'll be gone soon, this place,' he said. 'A year from now a sixteen-story monster will stand right where we're sitting.' He got to his knees and fumbled in the pocket of his trousers. He pulled out some damp gray newspaper clippings, folded into a square. 'Let me give you the full picture,' he said, unfolding them, starting to read. Kara Lynn looked over his shoulder.

'*Welcome to the Osprey Club . . . Fine living, for the discriminating Floridian.* Makes you want to puke.'

'Pretty tacky,' Kara Lynn agreed.

'A hundred and two units from two-fifty all the way up to a million-six. Friendly financing available. Vaulted ceilings, marble archways, sunken living rooms, Roman tubs, atrium patios with real cedar trellises, boy oh boy.' Wiley looked up from the newspaper advertisement and gazed out at the woodsy shadows.

'Can't someone try to block it?' Kara Lynn suggested. 'The Audubon people. Or maybe the National Park Service.'

'Too late,' Wiley said. 'See, it's a private island. After old man Bradshaw died, his scumball kids put it up for sale. Puerco Development picks it up for three mil and wham, next thing you know it's rezoned for multifamily high-rise.'

'Didn't you do a column on this?' she asked.

'I sure did.' One of Wiley's many pending lawsuits: a gratuitous and unprovable reference to Mafia connections.

'Back to the blandishments,' he said, 'there'll be four air-conditioned racketball courts, a spa, a bike trail, a tennis complex, a piazza, two fountains, and even a waterfall. Think about that: they're going to bury the natural spring and build a fiberglass waterfall! Progress, my darling. It says here they're also planting something called a *lush greenbelt*, which is basically a place for rich people to let their poodles take a shit.'

Kara Lynn said: 'How will people get out here?'

'Ferry,' Wiley answered. 'See here: *Take a quaint ferry to your very own island where the Mediterranean meets Miami!* See, Kara Lynn, the bastards can't sell Florida anymore, they've got to sell the bloody Riviera.'

'It sounds a bit overdone,' she said.

'Twenty-four hundred square feet of overdone,' Wiley said, 'with a view.'

'But no ospreys,' said Kara Lynn, sensing the downward spiral of his emotions.

'And no eagle,' Wiley said glumly.

He acted as if he were ready to leave, and Kara Lynn knew that if he did, it would be over.

'Why did you pick me?' she asked.

Wiley turned to look at her. 'Because you're perfect,' he said. 'Or at least you represent perfection. Beauty. Chastity. Innocence. All tanned and blond, the golden American dream. That's all they really promise with their damn parade and their unctuous tourist advertising. Come see Miami, come see the girls! But it's a cheap tease, darling. Florida's nothing but an adman's wet dream.'

'That's enough,' Kara Lynn said, reddening.

'I take it you don't think of yourself as a precious piece of ass.'

'Not really, no.'

'Me, neither,' Wiley said, 'but we are definitely in the minority. And that's why we're out here now—an object lesson for all those bootlicking shills and hustlers.'

Wiley crawled out from under the plastic tent and rose to his full height, declaring, 'The only way to reach the greedy blind pagans is to strike at their meager principles.' He pointed toward the treetops. 'To the creators of the Osprey Club, that precious eagle up there is not life, it has no real value. Same goes for the wood rats and the herons. Weighed against the depreciated net worth of a sixteen-story condominium after sellout, the natural inhabitants of this island do not represent life—they have no fucking value. You with me?'

Kara Lynn nodded. She still couldn't see the big bird.

'Now,' Wiley said, 'if you're the CEO of Puerco Development, what has worth to you, besides money? What is a life? Among all creatures, what is the one that cannot legally be extinguished for the sake of progress?' Wiley arched his eyebrows and pointed a dripping finger at Kara Lynn's nose. 'You,' he said. 'You are, presumably, inviolate.'

For the first time in the conversation, it occurred to Kara Lynn that this fellow might truly be insane.

Wiley blinked at her. 'I'll be right back,' he said.

This time she didn't move. Wet and cold, she had come to cherish the meager protection of the plastic shelter. Wiley returned carrying a short wooden stake. An orange plastic streamer was attached to the blunt end.

'Survey markers,' Kara Lynn said.

'Very good. So you know what it means—construction is imminent.'

'How imminent?' she asked.

'Like tomorrow.'

'Tomorrow's the groundbreaking?'

'Naw, that was Christmas Eve. Purely ceremonial,' Wiley said. 'Tomorrow is much more significant. Tomorrow's the day they start terrain modification.'

'What's that?'

'Just what it says.'

Kara Lynn was puzzled. 'I don't see any bulldozers.'

'No, those would be used later, for contour clearing.'

'Then what do they use for this "terrain modification"?' she asked.

'Dynamite,' Skip Wiley replied. 'At dawn.'

OSPREY ISLAND

Kara Lynn thought she might have heard him wrong, thought it might have been a trick of the wind.

'Did you say dynamite?' she asked.

'Eight hundred pounds,' Skip Wiley said, 'split into three payloads. One at the northwest tip, another at the southeast cove. The third cache, the big one, is right over there, no more than twenty yards. Can you see it? That galvanized box beneath those trees.'

From where she sat Kara Lynn saw nothing but shadows.

'I . . . I don't . . .' She was choking on fear, unable to speak. Hold on, she told herself.

'They do it by remote control,' Wiley explained, 'from a barge. We passed it on the way out, anchored three miles off the island. You were asleep.'

'Oh . . .' The plan was more terrible than she had imagined; all the stalling had been futile, a wasted strategy.

'They have to do it at dawn,' Wiley went on, 'some kind of Army Corps rule. Can't bring boats any closer to the island because the blast'll blow the windows out.'

He ambled to the campfire and stood with his back to her for several moments. His naked cantaloupe head twitched back and forth, as if he were talking to himself. Abruptly he turned around and said, 'The reason for the dynamite is the coral. See—' He kicked at the ground with his shoe. 'Harder than cement. They need to go down twenty-four inches before pouring the foundation for the condo. Can't make a dent with shovels, not in this stuff . . . so that's why the dynamite. Flip of a switch and—poof— turn this place into the Bonneville flats. Eight hundred pounds is a lot of firecracker.'

Kara Lynn steadied herself just enough to utter the most inane question of her entire life: 'What about me?'

Wiley spread his arms. 'No life forms will survive,' he said in a clinical tone. 'Not even the gnats.'

'Please don't do this,' Kara Lynn said.

'It's not me, Barbie Doll, it's progress. Your beef is with Puerco Development.'

'Don't leave me here,' she said, just shy of a beg.

'Darling, how could I save you and not save that magnificent eagle? Or the helpless rabbits and the homely opossums, or even the lowly fiddler crabs? It's impossible to rescue them, so I can't very well rescue you. It wouldn't be fair. It would be like . . . playing God. This way is best, Kara Lynn. This way—for the first time in nineteen pampered years—you are truly part of the natural order. You now inhabit this beautiful little island, and the value of your life is the same as all creatures here. If they should survive past dawn, so shall you. If not . . . well, maybe the good people of Florida will finally appreciate the magnitude of their sins. If Osprey Island is leveled in the name of progress, I predict a cataclysmic backlash, once the truth is known. The truth being that they blew up the one species they really care about—a future customer.'

Kara Lynn was running low on poise. 'The symbolism is intriguing,' she said, 'but your logic is ridiculous.'

'Just listen,' Wiley said. From a breast pocket he took another clipping and read: ' "Officials in South Florida estimate that adverse publicity surrounding December's tourist murders has cost the resort area as much as ten million dollars in family and convention trade." ' Wiley waved the clip and gloated. 'Not too shabby, eh?'

'I'm impressed,' Kara Lynn said archly. 'A month's worth of killing and all you've got to show for it is one dinky paragraph in *Newsweek*.'

'It's the lead Periscope item!' Wiley said, defensively.

'Terrific,' Kara Lynn said. 'Look, why don't you let me go? You can do better than this.'

'I think not.'

'I can swim away,' she declared.

'Not all tied up, you can't,' Wiley said. 'Besides, the water's lousy with blacktip sharks. Did you know they spawn at night in the shallows? Aggressive little bastards, too. A bite here, a bite there, a little blood and pretty soon the big boys pick up the scent. Bull sharks and hammerheads big enough to eat a goddamn Datsun.'

'That'll do,' said Kara Lynn.

Something rustled at the edge of the clearing. A branch cracking in the storm, she thought. Skip Wiley cocked his head and peered toward the sound, but the hard rain painted everything gray and hunched and formless. The only identifiable noises were raindrops slapping leaves, and the hiss of embers as the campfire died in the downpour.

Wiley was not satisfied. Like an ungainly baseball pitcher, he wound up and hurled the survey stake end-over-end into the trees.

The missile was answered by an odd strangled peep.

Wiley chuckled. 'Just as I thought,' he said, 'a wood stork.'

Just then the thicket ruptured with an explosion so enormous that Kara Lynn was certain that Wiley had accidentally detonated the dynamite.

When she opened her eyes, he was sitting down, slack-jawed and pale. The red kerchief was askew, drooped over one eye. Both legs stuck straight out, doll-like, in front of him. He seemed transfixed by something close at hand—a radiant splotch of crimson and a yellow knob of bone, where his right knee used to be. Absently he fingered the frayed hole in his trousers.

Kara Lynn felt a surge of nausea. She gulped a breath.

Brian Keyes moved quickly out of the trees.

His brown hair was plastered to his forehead; rain streamed down his cheeks. His face was blank. He was walking deliberately, a little hurried, as if his flight were boarding.

He strode up to Skip Wiley, placed a foot on his chest, and kicked him flat on his back. A regular one-man cavalry! Kara Lynn was elated, washed with relief. She didn't notice the Browning in Brian's right hand until he shoved the barrel into Wiley's mouth.

'Hello, Skip,' Keyes said. 'How about telling me where you anchored the boat?'

Wiley's wolfish eyes crinkled with amusement. He grunted an indecipherable greeting. Keyes slowly withdrew the gun, but kept it inches from Wiley's nose.

'Holy Christ!' Wiley boomed, sitting up. 'And I thought you were dangerous with a typewriter.'

'You're losing blood,' Keyes said.

'No thanks to you.'

'Where's the boat?'

'Not so fast.'

Keyes fired again, the gun so close to Wiley's face that the charge knocked him back down. Wiley clutched at his ears and rolled away, over the sharp corrugated coral. The bullet had thwacked harmlessly into the stucco rubble of the old cabin.

Kara Lynn cried out involuntarily—she was afraid she'd have to watch a killing. Keyes came over, untied her, and gave a gentle hug. 'You okay?'

She nodded. 'I want to get out of here. They're going to dynamite this place—'

'I know.' He had to find Wiley's boat.

Joey the shrimper had been generous enough to provide a tin of smoked amberjack and a jug of water before letting them off, but he had not been generous enough to wait around. Muttering about the obscene cost of fuel, he had aimed the *Tina Marie* away from the island, leaving his passengers to find their own way back to the mainland.

Keyes stood over Wiley and ordered him to sit up.

'You're in an ugly mood,' Wiley said nervously. His ears rang. He felt like he was talking down a tunnel.

Keyes took off his shirt and tied it around Wiley's mutilated leg. 'We haven't got much time,' he said.

Wiley studied Brian intently; the gun made him a stranger. The violent eruption was unnerving enough, but what sobered Wiley even more was the look of chilling and absolute indifference. This was not the same polite young man who'd sat next to him in the newsroom; Wiley feared a loss of leverage. Against this

Brian Keyes, in this place, Wiley's weapons were greatly limited. Right away he ruled out charm, wit, and oratory.

'How'd you find me?'

'Never mind,' Keyes said.

'Jenna told you, right?'

'No.' So she had known. Of course she knew. 'Give me the keys to the Mako,' Keyes said.

Grudgingly Wiley handed them over.

He pointed at Kara Lynn. 'It's the girl, isn't it? You fell for her! That's why you're in Charlie Bronson mode—defending the fair maiden. Just your luck, Brian. Seems like I'm always screwing up your love life.'

Keyes didn't know how much longer he could hold up. He wanted to go now, while he still had the strength, while he was still propelled by whatever it was that let him pull the trigger one more time.

'Kara Lynn, would you like to know a secret about Mr. Keyes?'

She said nothing, knowing that it wasn't finished yet. Not as long as Wiley could speak.

'Don't you want to hear a war story?' Wiley asked.

'Shut up,' Keyes said.

'You want the boat? Then you've got to listen. *Politely.*'

Keyes grabbed Wiley's wrist and looked at the watch. It was half-past five; they'd be cutting it close.

'A few years back, a little girl was kidnapped and murdered,' Wiley said, turning to Kara Lynn, his audience. 'After the body was found, Brian was supposed to go interview the parents.'

'The Davenports,' Keyes said.

'Hey, let me tell it!' Wiley said indignantly.

The rain had slackened to a sibilant drizzle. Keyes tore a piece of plastic from Kara Lynn's makeshift poncho and sat down on it. He felt oppressively lethargic, bone-tired.

'Brian came back with a great piece,' Wiley said. 'Mother, weeping hysterically; father, blind with rage. *Tomorrow would be Callie Davenport's fourth birthday. Her room is full of bright presents, each tenderly wrapped. There's a Snoopy doll from Uncle Dennis, a Dr. Seuss from Grandpa. Callie won't be there on her birthday, so the packages may sit there for a long time. Maybe forever. Her parents simply can't bear to go in her bedroom.'*

Keyes sagged. He couldn't believe that Wiley remembered the story, word for word. It was amazing.

'A real tearjerker,' Wiley pronounced. 'That morning half of Miami was weeping into their Rice Krispies.' He seemed oblivious of pain, of the thickening puddle of blood under his leg.

'Kara Lynn,' he said, 'in my business, the coin of the realm is a good quote—it's the only thing that brings a newspaper story to life. One decent quote is the difference between dog food and caviar, and Brian's story about Callie Davenport was choked with lyrical quotes. *"All I want," sobbed the little girl's father, "is ten minutes with the guy who did this. Ten minutes and a clawhammer." A neighbor drove Callie's mother to the morgue to identify her daughter. "I wanted to lie down beside her," Mrs. Davenport said. "I wanted to put my arms around my baby and wake her up . . ."* '

Keyes said, 'That's enough.'

'Don't be so modest,' Wiley chided. 'It's the only thing you ever wrote that made me jealous.'

'I made it all up,' Keyes said, taking Kara Lynn's hand. He was hoping she'd squeeze back, and she did.

Wiley looked perturbed, as if Brian had spoiled the big punch line.

'I drove out to the house,' Keyes said in a monotone. 'I was expecting a crowd. Neighbors, relatives, you know. But there was only one car in the driveway, they were all alone . . . I knocked on the door. Mrs. Davenport answered and I could see in her eyes she'd been through hell. Behind her, I saw how they'd put all of Callie's pictures out in the living room—on the piano, the sofas, the TV console, everywhere . . . you never saw so many baby pictures. Mr. Davenport sat on the floor with an old photo album across his lap . . . he was crying his heart out . . .

'In a nice voice Mrs. Davenport asked me what I wanted. At first I couldn't say a damn thing and then I told her I was an insurance adjustor and I was looking for the Smiths' house and I must have got the wrong address. Then I drove back to my apartment and made up the whole story, all those swell quotes. That's what the *Sun* printed.'

'The ultimate impiety,' Wiley intoned, 'the rape of truth.'

'He's right,' Keyes said. 'But I just couldn't bring myself to do it, to go in that house and intrude on those people's grief. So I invented the whole damn story.'

'I think it took guts to walk away,' Kara Lynn said.

'Oh please.' Wiley grimaced. 'It was an act of profound coward-ice. No self-respecting journalist turns his back on pain and suffer-ing. It was an egregious and shameful thing, Pollyanna, your boyfriend's no hero.'

Kara Lynn stared at Wiley and said, 'You're pathetic.' She said it in such a mordant and disdainful way that Wiley flinched. Obviously he'd misjudged her, and Keyes too. He had saved the Callie Davenport story all these years, anticipating the moment he might need it. Yet it had not produced the desired effect, not at all. He felt a little confused.

Keyes said to Kara Lynn, 'I had to quit the paper. I'd stepped over the line and there was no going back.'

'At least I hawk the truth,' Wiley cut in. 'That's what this campaign is all about—dramatizing the true consequence of folly.' He struggled wobbly to his feet. He gained balance by clutching a sea-grape limb and shifting all weight to his left side. The other leg hung like a dead and blackening trunk.

'Brian, I don't know if you'll ever understand, but try. All that wretched grief the Davenports spent on their little girl is exactly what I feel when I think what's happened to this place. It's the same sense of loss, the same fury and primal lust for vengeance. The difference is, I can't turn my back the way you did. My particular villain is not some tattooed sex pervert, but an entire generation of blow-dried rapists with phones in their Volvos and five-million-dollar lines of credit and secretaries who give head. These are the kind of deviants who dreamed up the Osprey Club, idiots who couldn't tell an osprey from a fucking parakeet.'

Kara Lynn was amazed at Wiley's indefatigable fervor. Brian Keyes was not stirred; he'd heard it all before. Overhead the skies were clearing as the last of the rain clouds scudded west. On the horizon shone a tinge of magenta, the first promise of dawn. Time was running out and there was one last chore.

'Skip—'

'Brian, Kara Lynn, can you imagine the Asshole Quotient on this island one year from now? You'll need the goddamn Census Bureau just to count up all the gold chains—'

Keyes slipped the Browning into his belt. 'Where's the boat, Skip?'

'I changed my mind,' he said peevishly. 'You'll have to find it yourself. If you don't, we all go boom together. That's a much better story, don't you think? *Condo Island Blast Claims Three.*'

'Try four,' Keyes said.

Wiley fingered his beard. His needle-sharp eyes went from Keyes to Kara Lynn and back. 'What are you talking about?'

'She's here, Skip.'

'Jenna?'

Keyes pointed to the hardwoods.

'Jenna's on the island?'

'I thought we'd play some bridge,' said Keyes.

'Why'd you bring her!' Wiley demanded angrily.

'So we'd be even.'

Wiley said, 'Brian, I had no idea you were such a mean-spirited sonofabitch.' He looked profoundly disappointed.

'Wait here,' Keyes said. Quickly he went into the woods.

'Did you know about this?' Wiley asked Kara Lynn.

'What're you so upset about?' she said. 'It'll make a better story, right?'

Mulling options, Wiley nibbled his lower lip.

Keyes returned, leading Jenna by the hand. At the sight of her, Wiley's face drained.

'Oh boy,' he said in a shrunken voice.

'I'm sorry, Skip,' Jenna said. She acted embarrassed, mortified, like a teenager who'd just wrecked her father's brand-new car.

'She's a little shy,' Keyes explained. 'She didn't want you to know she was here.'

'I ruined everything,' Jenna said. She gasped when she saw

Wiley's mangled knee but made no move to dress the wound. Florence Nightingale Jenna was not.

Wiley looked at his watch. It said 6:07. Dawn came at 6:27 sharp.

'Skip's through talking,' Keyes said to Jenna. 'He's said everything he could possibly say. Now all four of us are going to get aboard the boat and get the hell off this island before it blows up.'

Wiley kneaded the calf of his right leg. 'I can't believe you actually shot me,' he said.

'I thought it might shut you up.'

'Just what the hell were you aiming for?'

'What's the difference?' Keyes said.

Kara Lynn had climbed the old homestead plot. The elevation was scarcely ten feet, but it was high enough to afford a view of the surrounding waters, now calm. A distant wisp of brown diesel smoke attracted her attention.

'I think I see the barge,' she said.

Keyes said, 'What's it going to be, Skip?'

Wiley gazed at Jenna; Keyes figured it was about time for a big sloppy hug. They both looked ten years older than before, yet still not quite like a couple.

'There's a mooring at the north end, on the lee side, opposite the way you came,' Wiley said tiredly. 'That's where the Mako's anchored up. You'd best get going.'

'We're *all* going,' Keyes said.

'Not me,' Wiley said. 'You can't make me, podner.' He was right. The gun didn't count for anything now.

'Hey, there's an eagle,' Jenna said.

The bird was airborne, elegantly soaring toward the pines. It carried a silvery fish in its talons.

'Just look at that,' Wiley marveled, his eyes brightening beneath the Seminole bandanna. He took off his baseball cap in salute.

'It's a gorgeous bird,' Kara Lynn agreed, tugging on Brian's arm. Time to go, she was saying, step on it.

'Skip, come with us,' Keyes urged.

'Or what? You gonna shoot me again?'

'Of course not.'

Wiley said, 'Forget about me, pal. I'm beginning to like it here.' He held out his arms and Jenna went to him. Wiley kissed her on the forehead. He touched her hair and said, 'I don't suppose you want to keep a one-legged lunatic company?'

Jenna's eyes, as usual, gave the answer. Keyes saw it and looked away. He'd seen it before.

'Aw, I don't blame you,' Wiley said to her, 'the bugs out here are just awful.' He patted her on the butt and let go.

To Keyes he whispered, 'Help her pick out a new coffee table, okay?'

'Skip, please—'

'No! Go now, and hurry. These radio-controlled devices are extremely precise.'

Keyes led the two women across the clearing. Jenna trudged ahead woodenly, but Keyes and Kara Lynn paused at the crest of the homesteader's hill. They looked back and saw Wiley in the clearing, leaning against the rusty flagpole. His arms were folded, and on his face was a broad and euphoric and incomprehensible grin.

'Hey, Brian,' he shouted, 'I didn't finish my story.'

Keyes almost laughed. 'Not now, you asshole!' The guy was unbelievable.

'But I never told you—they called.'

'Who?'

'The Davenports. They phoned the day your piece ran, but you were already gone.'

Keyes groaned—the bastard always wanted the last word.

Anxiously he shouted back, 'What did they want?'

'They wanted to say thanks,' Wiley hollered. 'I couldn't believe it! They actually wanted to say thanks for butting out.'

Keyes waved one last time at his old friend.

Lost forever, his odyssey now measured in minutes, Skip Wiley swung a ropy brown arm in reply. He was still waving his cap when Brian Keyes, Jenna, and Kara Lynn Shivers disappeared into the buttonwood.

*

They found the trail and, ten minutes later, the mooring where he outboard was anchored. The tide was up so they had to wade, skating their feet across the mud and turtle grass. Jenna lost her footing and slipped down, without a word, into the shallows. Keyes grabbed her under one arm, Kara Lynn got the other. Together they hoisted her into the boat.

The engine was stone cold.

With trembling fingers Keyes turned the key again and again. The motor whined and coughed but wouldn't start.

'You flooded it,' Kara Lynn said. 'Let it sit for thirty seconds.'

Keyes looked at her curiously but did what he was told. The next time he turned the key, the Evinrude roared into life.

'Dad's got a ski boat,' Kara Lynn explained. 'Happens all the time.'

Keyes jammed down the throttle and the Mako chewed its way off the flat, churning marl and grass, planing slowly. Finally it found deeper water, flattened out and gained speed. Already the rim of purple winter sky was turning yellow gold.

'How much time?' Jenna asked numbly.

'Three, four minutes,' Keyes guessed.

They had to circle Osprey Island to reach the marked channel that would take them to safety.

'Brian!' Jenna blurted, pointing.

Keyes jerked back on the stick until the engine quit. The boat coasted in glassy silence, a quarter-mile off the islet. They all stared toward the stand of high pines.

'Oh no,' Kara Lynn said.

Keyes was incredulous.

Jenna said, 'Boy, he never gives up.'

Skip Wiley was in the trees.

He was dragging himself up the tallest pine, branch by branch, the painstaking, web-crawling gait of a spider. How with a smashed leg Wiley had climbed so high was astonishing. It was not a feat of gymnastics so much as a show of reckless nerve. He hung in the tree like a broken scarecrow; ragged, elongated, his limbs bent at odd angles. From a distance his skull shone three-toned—the russet beard; the jutting tanned face; the alabaster pate. In one hand was Tommy Tigertail's red bandanna—Wiley was waving it back and forth and shrieking at the top of his considerable lungs; plangent gibberish.

'Brian, he wants us to come get him!'

'No,' Keyes said, 'that's not it.'

It was sadder than that.

The object of Wiley's expedition was perched at the top of the forty-foot pine. With its keen and faultless eyes it peered down at this demented, blood-crusted creature and wondered what in the world to do. As Skip Wiley advanced, he brayed, flailed his bright kerchief, shattered branches—but the great predator merely blinked and clung to its precious fish.

'He's trying to save the eagle,' Brian Keyes said. 'He's trying to make the eagle fly.'

'God, he is,' said Kara Lynn.

'Fly,' Jenna murmured excitedly. 'Fly away, bird!'

'Oh please,' Kara Lynn said.

That is how they left him—Skip Wiley ascending, insectine, possessed of an unknowable will and strength; the eagle studying him warily, shuddering its brown-gold wings, weighing a decision.

Brian Keyes turned the ignition and the boat shot forward in a widening arc. The Mako was very fast, and Osprey Island receded quickly in the slick curling seam of the speedboat's wake. Within minutes they were far away, safe, but none of them dared to look back.

Off the bow, at the horizon, the sun seeped into a violet sky.

Somewhere out on Biscayne Bay, a flat red barge emitted three long whoops of warning, the most dolorous sound that Brian Keyes had ever heard. He clung to the wheel and waited.

'Fly!' he whispered. 'Please fly away.'

DOUBLE WHAMMY

In memory of Clyde Ingalls

1

On the morning of January 6, two hours before dawn, a man named Robert Clinch rolled out of bed and rubbed the sleep from his eyes. He put on three pairs of socks, a blue flannel shirt, olive dungarees, a Timex waterproof watch, and a burgundy cap with a patch stitched to the crown. The patch said: 'Mann's Jelly Worms.'

Clinch padded to the kitchen and fixed himself a pot of coffee, four eggs scrambled (with ketchup), a quarter-pound of Jimmy Dean sausage, and two slices of whole-wheat toast with grape jam. As he ate, he listened to the radio for a weather report. The temperature outside was forty-one degrees, humidity thirty-five percent, wind blowing from the northeast at seven miles per hour. According to the weatherman, thick fog lay on the highway between Harney and Lake Jesup. Robert Clinch loved to drive in the fog because it gave him a chance to use the amber fog lights on his new Blazer truck. The fog lights had been a $455 option, and his wife, Clarisse, now asleep in the bedroom, was always bitching about what a waste of money they were. Clinch decided that later, when he got home from the lake, he would tell Clarisse how the fog lights had saved his life on Route 222; how a wall-eyed truck driver with a rig full of Valencia oranges had crossed the center line and swerved back just in time because he'd seen the Blazer's fancy fog lights. Robert Clinch was not sure if Clarisse would bite on the story; in fact, he wasn't sure if she'd be all too thrilled that the truck hadn't plowed into him, vanquishing in one fiery millisecond the expensive Blazer, the sleek bass boat, and Robert Clinch himself. Clarisse did not think much of her husband's hobby.

Robert Clinch put on a pair of soft-soled Gore-Tex boots and slipped into a vivid red ski vest that was covered with emblems from various fishing tournaments. He went out to the garage where the boat was kept and gazed at it proudly, running his hand along the shiny gunwale. It was a Ranger 390V, nineteen and one-half feet long. Dual livewells, custom upholstery and carpeting (royal blue), and twin tanks that held enough fuel to run all the way to Okeechobee and back. The engine on the boat was a two-hundred-horsepower Mercury, one of the most powerful outboards ever manufactured. A friend had once clocked Bobby Clinch's boat at sixty-two miles per hour. There was no earthly reason to go so fast, except that it was fun as hell to show off.

Robert Clinch loved his boat more than anything else in the world. Loved it more than his wife. More than his kids. More than his girlfriend. More than his double-mortgaged home. Even more than the very largemouth bass he was pursuing. Riding on the lake at dawn, Robert Clinch often felt that he loved his boat more than he loved life itself.

On this special morning he decided, for appearance's sake, to bring along a fishing rod. From a rack on the wall he picked a cheap spinning outfit—why risk the good stuff? As he tried to thread the eight-pound monofilament through the guides of the rod, Clinch noticed that his hands were quivering. He wondered if it was the coffee, his nerves, or both. Finally he got the rod rigged and tied a plastic minnow lure to the end of the line. He found his portable Q-Beam spotlight, tested it, and stored it under a bow hatch inside the boat. Then he hitched the trailer to the back of the Blazer.

Clinch started the truck and let it warm. The air in the cab was frosty and he could see his breath. He turned up the heater full blast. He thought about one more cup of coffee but decided against it; he didn't want to spend all morning with a bursting bladder, and it was too damn cold to unzip and hang his pecker over the side of the boat.

He also thought about bringing a gun, but that seemed silly. Nobody took a gun to the lake.

Robert Clinch was about to pull out of the driveway when he got an idea, something that might make his homecoming more bearable. He slipped back into the house and wrote a note to Clarisse. He put it on the dinette, next to the toaster: 'Honey, I'll be home by noon. Maybe we can go to Sears and look for that shower curtain you wanted. Love, Bobby.'

Robert Clinch never returned.

By midafternoon his wife was so angry that she drove to Sears and purchased not only a shower curtain but some electric hair curlers and a pink throw rug too. By suppertime she was livid, and tossed her husband's portion of Kentucky fried chicken over the fence to the Labrador retriever next door. At midnight she phoned her mother in Valdosta to announce that she was packing up the kids and leaving the bum for good.

The next morning, as Clarisse rifled her husband's bureau for clues and loose cash, the county sheriff phoned. He had some lousy news.

From the air a cropduster had spotted a purplish slick on a remote corner of Lake Jesup known as Coon Bog. On a second pass the cropduster had spotted the sparkled hull of a bass boat, upside down and half-submerged about fifty yards from shore. Something big and red was floating nearby.

Clarisse Clinch asked the sheriff if the big red thing in the water happened to have blond hair, and the sheriff said not anymore, since a flock of mallard ducks had been pecking at it all night. Clarisse asked if any identification had been found on the body, and the sheriff said no, Bobby's wallet must have shaken out in the accident and fallen into the water. Mrs. Clinch told the sheriff thank you, hung up, and immediately dialed the Visa Card headquarters in Miami to report the loss.

'What do you know about fishing?'

'A little,' said R. J. Decker. The interview was still at the stage where Decker was supposed to look steady and taciturn, the stage where the prospective client was sizing him up. Decker knew he was pretty good in the sizing-up department. He had the physique of a linebacker: five-eleven, one hundred ninety pounds, chest like a drum, arms like cable. He had curly dark hair and sharp brown eyes that gave nothing away. He often looked amused but seldom smiled around strangers. At times he could be a very good listener, or pretend to be. Decker was neither diffident nor particularly patient; he was merely on constant alert for jerks. Time was too short to waste on them. Unless it was absolutely necessary, like now.

'Are you an outdoorsman?' Dennis Gault asked.

Decker shrugged. 'You mean can I start a campfire? Sure. Can I kill a Cape buffalo barehanded? Probably not.'

Gault poured himself a gin and tonic. 'But you can handle yourself, I presume.'

'You presume right.'

'Size doesn't mean a damn thing,' Gault said. 'You could still be a wimp.'

Decker sighed. Another macho jerk.

Gault asked, 'So what kind of fishing do you know about?'

'Offshore stuff, nothing exotic. Grouper, snapper, dolphin.'

'Pussy fish,' Gault snorted. 'For tourists.'

'Oh,' Decker said, 'so you must be the new Zane Grey.'

Gault looked up sharply from his gin. 'I don't care for your attitude, mister.'

Decker had heard this before. The *mister* was a nice touch, though.

Dennis Gault said, 'You look like you want to punch me.'

'That's pretty funny.'

'I don't know about you,' Gault said, stirring his drink. 'You look like you're itching to take a swing.'

'What for?' Decker said. 'Anytime I want to punch an asshole I can stroll down to Biscayne Boulevard and take my pick.'

He guessed that it would take Gault five or six seconds to come up with some witty reply. Actually it took a little longer.

'I guarantee you never met an asshole like me,' he said.

Decker glanced at his wristwatch and looked very bored—a mannerism he'd been practicing.

Gault made a face. He wore a tight powder-blue pullover and baggy linen trousers. He looked forty, maybe older. He studied Decker through amber aviator glasses. 'You don't like me, do you?' he said.

'I don't know you, Mr. Gault.'

'You know I'm rich, and you know I've got a problem. That's enough.'

'I know you kept me suffocating in your neo-modern earth-tone lobby for two hours,' Decker said. 'I know your secretary's name is Ruth and I know she doesn't keep any Maalox tablets in her desk because I asked. I know your daddy owns this skyscraper and your granddad owns a sugar mill, and I know your T-shirt looks like hell with those trousers. And that's all I know about you.'

Which was sort of a lie. Decker also knew about the two family banks in Boca Raton, the shopping mall in Daytona Beach, and the seventy-five thousand acres of raw cane west of Lake Okeechobee.

Dennis Gault sat down behind a low Plexiglas desk. The desk looked like it belonged in a museum, maybe as a display case for Mayan pottery. Gault said, 'So I'm a sugar daddy, you're right. Want to know what I know about you, Mr. Private Eye, Mr. Felony Past?'

Oh boy, thought R. J. Decker, this is your life. 'Tell me your problem or I'm leaving.'

'Tournament fishing,' Gault said. 'What do you know about tournament fishing?'

'Not a damn thing.'

Gault stood up and pointed reverently to a fat blackish fish mounted on the wall. 'Do you know what that is?'

'An oil drum,' Decker replied, 'with eyes.' He knew what it was. You couldn't live in the South and not know what it was.

'A largemouth bass!' Gault exclaimed.

He gazed at the stuffed fish as if it were a sacred icon. It was easy to see how the bass got its name; its maw could have engulfed a soccer ball.

'Fourteen pounds, four ounces,' Gault announced. 'Got her on a crankbait at Lake Toho. Do you have any idea what this fish was worth?'

Decker felt helpless. He felt like he was stuck in an elevator with a Jehovah's Witness.

'Seventy-five thousand dollars,' Gault said.

'Christ.'

'Now I got your attention, don't I?' Gault grinned. He patted the flank of the plastic bass as if it were the family dog.

'This fish,' he went on, 'won the Southeast Regional Bass Anglers Classic two years ago. First place was seventy-five large and a Ford Thunderbird. I gave the car to some migrants.'

'All that for one fish?' Decker was amazed. Civilization was in serious trouble.

'In 1985,' Gault went on, 'I fished seventeen tournaments and made one hundred and seven thousand dollars, Mr. Decker. Don't look so astounded. The prize money comes from sponsors—boat makers, tackle manufacturers, bait companies, the outboard marine industry. Bass fishing is an immensely profitable business, the fastest-growing outdoor sport in America. Of course, the tournament circuit is in no way a sport, it's a cutthroat enterprise.'

'But you don't need the money,' Decker said.

'I need the competition.'

The Ted Turner Syndrome, Decker thought.

'So what's the problem?'

'The problem is criminals,' Gault said.

'Could you be more specific?'

'Cheats.'

'People who lie about the size of the fish they catch—'

Gault laughed acidly. 'You can't lie about the size. Dead or alive, the fish are brought back to the dock to be weighed.'

'Then how can anybody cheat?'

'Ha!' Gault said, and told his story.

There had been an incident at a big-money tournament in north Texas. The contest had been sponsored by a famous plastic-worm company that had put up a quarter-million-dollar purse. At the end of the final day Dennis Gault stood on the dock with twenty-seven pounds of largemouth bass, including a nine-pounder. Normally a catch like this would have won a tournament hands down, and Gault was posing proudly with his string of fish when the last boat roared up to the dock. A man named Dickie Lockhart hopped out holding a monster bass—eleven pounds, seven ounces—which of course won first place.

'That fish,' Dennis Gault recalled angrily, 'had been dead for two days.'

'How do you know?'

'Because I know a stiff when I see one. That fish was cold, Mr. Decker, icebox-type cold. You follow?'

'A ringer?' It was all Decker could do not to laugh.

'I know what you're thinking: Who cares if some dumb shit-kicker redneck cheats with a fish? But think about this: Of the last seven big-money tournaments held in the United States, Dickie Lockhart has won five and finished second twice. That's two hundred sixty thousand bucks, which makes him not such a dumb shitkicker after all. It makes him downright respectable. He's got his own frigging TV show, if you can believe that.'

Decker said, 'Did you confront him about the ringer?'

'Hell, no. That's a damn serious thing, and I had no solid proof.'

'Nobody else was suspicious?'

'Shit, *everybody* else was suspicious, but no one had the balls to say boo. Over beers, sure, they said they knew it was a stiff. But not to Dickie's face.'

'This Lockhart, he must be a real tough guy,' Decker said, needling.

'Not tough, just powerful. Most bass pros don't want to piss him off. If you want to get asked to the invitationals, you'd better be pals with Dickie. If you want product endorsements, you better kiss Dickie's ass. Same goes if you want your new outboard wholesale. It adds up. Some guys don't like Dickie Lockhart worth a shit, but they sure like to be on TV.'

Decker said, 'He's the only one who cheats?'

Gault hooted.

'Then what's the big deal?' Decker asked.

'The big deal'—Gault sneered—'is that Lockhart cheats in the big ones. The big deal is that he cheats against *me*. It's the difference between a Kiwanis softball game and the fucking World Series, you understand?'

'Absolutely,' Decker said. He had heard enough. 'Mr. Gault, I really don't think I can help you.'

'Sit down.'

'Look, this is not my strong suit. . . .'

'What is your strong suit? Divorces? Car repos? Workmen's comp? If you're doing so hot, maybe you wouldn't mind telling me why you're moonlighting at that shyster insurance agency where I tracked you down.'

Decker headed for the door.

'The fee is fifty thousand dollars.'

Decker wheeled and stared. Finally he said, 'You don't need a P.I., you need a doctor.'

'The money is yours if you can catch this cocksucker cheating, and prove it.'

'Prove it?'

Gault said, 'You were an ace photographer once. Couple big awards—I know about you, Decker. I know about your crummy temper and your run-in with the law. I also know you'd rather sleep in a tent than a Hilton, and that's fine. They say you're a little crazy, but crazy is exactly what I need.'

'You want pictures?' Decker said. 'Of fish?'

'What better proof?' Gault glowed at the idea. 'You get me a photograph of Dickie Lockhart cheating, and I'll get you published in every blessed outdoors magazine in the free world. That's a bonus, too, on top of the fee.'

The cover of *Field and Stream*, Decker thought, a dream come true. 'I told you,' he said, 'I don't know anything about tournament fishing.'

'If it makes you feel any better, you weren't my first choice.'

It didn't make Decker feel any better.

'The first guy I picked knew plenty about fishing,' Dennis Gault said, 'a real pro.'

'And?'

'It didn't work out. Now I need a new guy.'

Dennis Gault looked uncomfortable. 'Distracted' was the word for it. He set down his drink and reached inside the desk. Out came a fake-lizardskin checkbook. Or maybe it was real.

'Twenty-five up front,' Gault said, reaching for a pen.

R. J. Decker thought of the alternative and shrugged. 'Make it thirty,' he said.

2

To Dr. Michael Pembroke fell the task of dissecting the body of Robert Clinch.

The weight of this doleful assignment was almost unbearable because Dr. Pembroke by training was not a coroner, but a clinical pathologist. He addressed warts, cysts, tumors, and polyps with ease and certitude, but corpses terrified him, as did forensics in general.

Most Florida counties employ a full-time medical examiner, or coroner, to handle the flow of human dead. Rural Harney County could not justify such a luxury to its taxpayers, so each year the county commission voted to retain the part-time services of a pathologist to serve as coroner when needed. For the grand sum of five thousand dollars Dr. Michael Pembroke was taking his turn. The job was not unduly time-consuming, as there were only four thousand citizens in the county and they did not die often. Most who did die had the courtesy to do so at the hospital, or under routine circumstances that required neither an autopsy nor an investigation. The few Harney Countians who expired unnaturally could usually be classified as victims of (a) domestic turmoil, (b) automobile accidents, (c) hunting accidents, (d) boating accidents, or (e) lightning. Harney County had more fatal lightning strikes than any other place in Florida, though no one knew why. The local fundamentalist church had a field day with this statistic.

When news of Robert Clinch's death arrived at the laboratory, Dr. Pembroke was staring at a common wart (*verruca vulgaris*) that had come from the thumb of a watermelon farmer. The scaly brown lump was not a pleasant sight, but it was infinitely preferable to the swollen visage of a dead bass fisherman. The doctor tried to stall and pretend he was deeply occupied at the microscope, but the sheriff's deputy waited patiently, leafing through some dermatology pamphlets. Dr. Pembroke finally gave up and got in the back of the squad car for the short ride to the morgue.

'Can you tell me what happened?' Dr. Pembroke asked, leaning forward.

'It's Bobby Clinch,' the deputy said over his shoulder. 'Musta flipped his boat in the lake.'

Dr. Pembroke was relieved. Now he had a theory; soon he'd have a cause-of-death. In no time he could return to the wart. Maybe this wouldn't be so bad.

The police car pulled up to a low red-brick building that served as the county morgue. The building had once been leased out as a Burger King restaurant, and had not been refurbished since the county bought it. While the Burger King sign had been removed (and sold to a college fraternity house), the counters, booths, and drive-up window remained exactly as they had been in the days of the Whopper. Dr. Pembroke once wrote a letter to the county commission suggesting that a fast-food joint was hardly the proper site for a morgue, but the commissioners tersely pointed out that it was the only place in Harney with a walk-in freezer.

Peering through the plate-glass window, Dr. Pembroke saw a pudgy man with a ruddy, squashed-looking face. It was Culver Rundell, whose shoulders (the doctor remembered) had been covered with brown junctional moles. These had been expertly biopsied and found to be nonmalignant.

'Hey, doc!' Culver Rundell said as Dr. Pembroke came through the door.

'Hello,' the pathologist said. 'How are those moles?' Pathologists seldom have to deal with whole patients so they are notoriously weak at making small talk.

'The moles are coming back,' Culver Rundell reported, 'by the hundreds. My wife takes a Flair pen and plays connect-the-dots from my neck to my butthole.'

'Why don't you come by the office and I'll take a look.'

'Naw, doc, you done your best. I'm used to the damn things,

and so's Jeannie. We make the best of the situation, if you know what I mean.'

Culver Rundell ran a fish camp on Lake Jesup. He was not much of a fisherman but he loved the live-bait business, worms and wild shiners mainly. He also served as official weighmaster for some of America's most prestigious bass tournaments, and this honor Culver Rundell owed to his lifelong friendship with Dickie Lockhart, champion basser.

'Are you the one who found the deceased?' Dr. Pembroke asked.

'Nope, that was the Davidson boys.'

'Which ones?' Dr. Pembroke asked. There were three sets of Davidson boys in Harney County.

'Daniel and Desi. They found Bobby floating at the bog and hauled him back to the fish camp. The boys wanted to go back out so I told 'em I'd take care of the body. We didn't have no hearse so I used my four-by-four.'

Dr. Pembroke climbed over the counter into what once had been the kitchen area of the Burger King. With some effort, Culver Rundell followed.

The body of Robert Clinch lay on a long stainless-steel table. The stench was dreadful, a mixture of wet death and petrified french fries.

'Holy Jesus,' said Dr. Pembroke.

'I know it,' said Rundell.

'How long was he in the water?' the doctor asked.

'We were kind of hoping you'd tell us.' It was the deputy, standing at the counter as if waiting for a vanilla shake.

Dr. Pembroke hated floaters and this was a beaut. Bobby Clinch's eyes were popping out of his face, milkballs on springs. An engorged tongue poked from the dead man's mouth like a fat coppery eel.

'What happened to his head?' Dr. Pembroke asked. It appeared that numerous patches of Robert Clinch's hair had been yanked raw from his scalp, leaving the checker-skulled impression of an under-dressed punk rocker.

'Ducks,' said Culver Rundell. 'A whole flock.'

'They thought it was food,' the deputy explained.

'It looks like pickerel weeds, hair does. Especially hair like Bobby's,' Rundell went on. 'In the water it looks like weeds.'

'This time of year ducks'll eat anything,' the deputy added.

Dr. Pembroke felt queasy. Sometimes he wished he'd gone into radiology like his dumb cousin. With heavy stainless surgical shears he began to cut Robert Clinch's clothes off, a task made more arduous by the swollen condition of the limbs and torso. As soon as Clinch's waterlogged dungarees were cut away and more purple flesh was revealed, both Culver Rundell and the sheriff's deputy decided to wait on the other side of the counter, where they took a booth and chatted about the latest scandal with the University of Florida football team.

Fifteen minutes later, Dr. Pembroke came out with a chart on a clipboard. He was scribbling as he talked.

'The body was in the water at least twenty-four hours,' he said. 'Cause of death was drowning.'

'Was he drunk?' Rundell asked.

'I doubt it, but I won't get the blood tests back for about a week.'

'Should I tell the sheriff it was an accident?' the deputy said.

'It looks that way, yes,' Dr. Pembroke said. 'There was a head wound consistent with impact in a high-speed crash.'

A bad bruise is what it was, consistent with any number of things, but Dr. Pembroke preferred to be definitive. Much of what he knew about forensic medicine came from watching reruns of the television show *Quincy, M.E.* Quincy the TV coroner could always glance at an injury and announce what exactly it was consistent with, so Dr. Pembroke tried to do the same. The truth was that after the other two men had left the autopsy table, Dr. Pembroke had worked as hastily as possible. He had drawn blood, made note of a golf-ball-size bruise on Bobby Clinch's skull and, with something less than surgical acuity, hacked a Y-shaped incision from the neck to the belly. He reached in, grabbed a handful of lung, and quickly ascertained that it was full of brackish lake water, which is exactly what Dr. Pembroke wanted to see. It meant that Bobby Clinch had drowned, as suspected. Further proof was the presence of a shiny dead minnow in the right bronchus, indicating that on the way down Bobby Clinch had inhaled violently, but to no avail. Having determined this, Dr. Pembroke had wasted not another moment with the rancid body; had not even turned it over for a quick look-see before dragging it into the hamburger cooler.

The pathologist signed the death certificate and handed it to the deputy. Culver Rundell read it over the lawman's shoulder and nodded. 'I'll call Clarisse,' he said, 'then I gotta hose out the truck.'

The largemouth bass is the most popular gamefish in North America, as it can be found in the warmest waters of almost every state. Its appeal has grown so astronomically in the last ten years that thousands of bass-fishing clubs have sprung up, and are swamped with new members. According to the sporting-goods industry, more millions of dollars are spent to catch large-mouth bass than are spent on any other outdoor activity in the United States. Bass magazines promote the species as the workingman's fish, available to anyone within strolling distance of a lake, river, culvert, reservoir, rockpit, or drainage ditch. The bass is not picky; it is hardy, prolific, and on a given day will eat just about any God-awful lure dragged in front of its maw. As a fighter it is bullish, but tires easily; as a jumper its skills are admirable, though no match for a graceful rainbow trout or tarpon; as table fare it is blandly acceptable, even tasty when properly seasoned. Its astonishing popularity comes from a modest combination of these traits, plus the simple fact that there are so many largemouth bass swimming around that just about any damn fool can catch one.

Its democratic nature makes the bass an ideal tournament fish, and a marketing dream-come-true for the tackle industry. Because a largemouth in Seattle is no different from its Everglades cousin, expensive bass-fishing products need no regionalization, no tailored advertising. This is why hard-core bass fishermen everywhere are outfitted exactly the same, from their trucks to their togs to their tackle. On any body of water, in any county rural or urban, the uniform and arsenal of the bassing fraternity are unmistakable. The universal mission is to catch one of those freakishly big bass known as lunkers or hawgs. In many parts of the country, any fish over five pounds is considered a trophy, and it is not uncommon for the ardent basser to have three or four such specimens mounted on the walls of his home; one for the living room, one for the den, and so on. The geographic range of truly gargantuan fish, ten to fifteen pounds, is limited to the humid Deep South, particularly Georgia and Florida. In these areas the quest for the world's biggest bass is rabid and ruthless; for tournament fishermen this is the big leagues, where top prize money for a two-day event might equal seventy-five thousand dollars. If the weather on these days happens to be rotten or the water too cold, a dinky four-pound bass might win the whole shooting match. More than likely, though, it takes a lunker fish to win the major tournaments, and few anglers are capable of catching lunkers day in and day out.

Weekend anglers are fond of noting that the largest bass ever caught was not landed by a tournament fisherman. It was taken by a nineteen-year-old Georgia farm kid named George W. Perry at an oxbow slough called Montgomery Lake. Fittingly, young Perry had never heard of Lowrance fish-finders or Thruster trolling motors or Fenwick graphite flipping sticks. Perry went out fishing in a simple rowboat and took the only bass lure he owned, a beat-up Creek Chub. He went fishing mainly because his family was hungry, and he returned with a largemouth bass that weighted twenty-two pounds four ounces. The year was 1932. Since then, despite all the space-age advancements in fish-catching technology, nobody has boated a bass that comes close to the size of George Perry's trophy, which he and his loved ones promptly ate for dinner. Today an historical plaque commemorating this leviathan largemouth stands on Highway 117, near Lumber City, Georgia. It serves as a defiant and nagging challenge to modern bass fishermen and all their infernal electronics. Some ichthyologists have been so bold as to suggest that the Monster of Montgomery Lake was a supremely mutant fish, an all-tackle record that will never be bested by any angler. To which Dickie Lockhart, in closing each segment of *Fish Fever*, would scrunch up his eyes, wave a finger at the camera, and decree: 'George Perry, next week your cracker butt is history!'

There was no tournament that weekend, so Dickie Lockhart was taping a show. He was shooting on Lake Kissimmee, nor far from Disney World. The title of this particular episode was 'Hawg Hunting.' Dickie needed a bass over ten pounds; anything less wasn't a hawg.

As always, he used two boats; one to fish from, one for the film crew. Like most TV fishing-show hosts, Dickie Lockhart used videotapes because they were cheaper than sixteen-millimeter, and reusable. Film was unthinkable for a bass show because you might go two or three days shooting nothing but men casting their lures and spitting tobacco, but no fish. With the video, a bad day didn't blow the whole budget because you just backed it up and shot again.

Dickie Lockhart had been catching bass all morning, little two- and three-pounders. He could guess the weight as soon as he hooked up, then furiously skitter the poor fish across the surface into the boat. 'Goddammit,' he would shout, 'rewind that sucker and let's try again.'

During lulls in the action, Dickie would grow tense and foul-mouthed. 'Come on, you bucket-mouthed bastards,' he'd growl as he cast at the shoreline, 'hit this thing or I'm bringing dynamite tomorrow, y'hear?'

Midmorning the wind kicked up, mussing Dickie Lockhart's shiny black hair. 'Goddammit,' he shouted, 'stop the tape.' After he got a comb from his tacklebox and slicked himself down, he ordered the cameraman to crank it up again.

'How do I look?' Dickie asked.

'Like a champ,' the cameraman said thinly. The cameraman dreamed of the day when Dickie Lockhart would get shitfaced drunk and drop his drawers to moon his little ole fishing pals all across America. Then Dickie would fall out of the boat, as he often did after drinking. Afterward the cameraman would pretend to rewind the videotape and erase this sloppy moment, but of course he wouldn't. He'd save it and, when the time was right, threaten to send it to the sports-and-religion network that syndicated Dickie Lockhart's fishing show. Dickie would suddenly become a generous fellow, and the cameraman would finally be able to afford to take his wife to the Virgin Islands.

Now, with the tape rolling, Dickie Lockhart was talking man-to-man with the serious bass angler back home. Dickie's TV accent was much thicker and gooier than his real-life accent, an exaggeration that was necessary to meet the demographic of the show, which was basically male Deep Southern grit-suckers. As he cast his lure and reeled it in, Dickie Lockhart would confide exactly what brand of crankbait he was using, what pound line was on the reel, what kind of sunglasses (amber or green) worked better on a bright day. The patter carried an air of informality and friendliness, when in fact the point was to shill as many of Dickie Lockhart's sponsors' products as possible in twenty-four minutes of live tape. The crankbait was made by Bagley, the line by Du Pont, the reel by Shimano, the sunglasses by Polaroid, and so on. Somehow, when Dickie stared into the camera and dropped these bald-faced plugs, it didn't seem so cheap.

At about noon a third bass boat raced up to the fishing spot, and Dickie started hollering like a madman. 'Goddammit, stop the tape! Stop the tape!' He hopped up and down on the bow and shook his fist at the man in the other boat. 'Hey, can't you see we're filming a goddamn TV show here? You got the whole frigging lake but you gotta stop here and wreck the tape!' Then he saw that the other angler was Ozzie Rundell, Culver's brother, so Dickie stopped shouting. He didn't apologize, but he did pipe down.

'Didn't mean to interrupt,' Ozzie said. He was a mumbler. Dickie Lockhart told him to speak up.

'Didn't mean to interrupt!' Ozzie said, a bit louder. In his entire life he had never boated a bass over four pounds, and was in awe of Dickie Lockhart.

'Well?' Dickie said.

'I thought you'd want to know.'

Dickie shook his head. He kicked a button on the bow and used the trolling motor to steer his boat closer to Ozzie's. When the two were side by side, Dickie said impatiently, 'Now start over.'

'I thought you'd want to know. They found Bobby Clinch.'

'Where?'

'Dead.'

Ozzie would get around to answering the questions, but not in the order he was asked. His mind worked that way.

'How?' Dickie said.

'In Lake Harney.'

'When?'

'Flipped his boat and drowned,' Ozzie said.

'Goddamn,' said Dickie Lockhart. 'I'm sorry.'

'Yesterday,' Ozzie said in conclusion.

Dickie turned to the cameraman and said, 'Well, that's it for the day.'

Ozzie seemed thrilled just to be able to touch the deck of the champion's boat. He gazed at Dickie Lockhart's fishing gear the way a Little Leaguer might stare at Ted Williams' bat. 'Well, sorry to interrupt,' he mumbled.

'Don't worry about it,' Dickie Lockhart said. 'They stopped biting two hours ago.'

'What plug you usin'?' Ozzie inquired.

'My special baby,' Dickie said, 'the Double Whammy.'

The Double Whammy was the hottest lure on the pro bass circuit, thanks in large measure to Dickie Lockhart. For the last eight tournaments he'd won, Dickie had declared it was the amazing Double Whammy that had tricked the trophy fish. His phenomenal success with the lure—a skirted spinnerbait with twin silver spoons—had not been duplicated by any other professional angler, though all had tried, filling their tackleboxes with elaborate variations and imitations. Most of the bassers caught big fish on the Double Whammy, but none caught as many, or at such opportune times, as Dickie Lockhart.

'It's a real killer, huh?' Ozzie said.

'You betcha,' Dickie said. He took the fishing line in his front teeth and bit through, freeing the jangling lure. 'You want it?' he asked.

Ozzie Rundell beamed like a kid on Christmas morning. 'Shoot yeah!'

Dickie Lockhart tossed the lure toward Ozzie's boat. In his giddiness Ozzie actually tried to catch the thing in his bare hands. He missed, of course, and the Double Whammy embedded its needle-sharp hook firmly in the poor man's cheek. Ozzie didn't seem to feel a thing; didn't seem to notice the blood dripping down his jawline.

'Thanks!' he shouted as Dickie Lockhart started up his boat. 'Thanks a million!'

'Don't mention it,' the champion replied, leaning on the throttle.

3

R. J. Decker had been born in Texas. His father had been an FBI man, and the family had lived in Dallas until December of 1963. Two weeks after Kennedy was shot, Decker's father was transferred to Miami and assigned to a crack squad whose task was to ensure that no pals of Fidel Castro took a shot at LBJ. It was a tense and exciting time, but it passed. Decker's father eventually wound up in a typically stupefying FBI desk job, got fat, and died of clogged arteries at age forty-nine. One of Decker's older brothers grew up to be a cop in Minneapolis. The other sold Porsches to cocaine dealers in San Francisco.

A good athlete and a fair student in college, R. J. Decker surprised all his classmates by becoming a professional photographer. Cameras were his private passion; he was fascinated with the art of freezing time in the eye. He never told anyone but it was the Zapruder film that had done it. When *Life* magazine had come out with those grainy movie pictures of the assassination, R. J. Decker was only eight years old. Still he was transfixed by the frames of the wounded president and his wife. The pink of her suit, the black blur of the Lincoln—horrific images, yet magnetic. The boy never imagined such a moment could be captured and kept for history. Soon afterward he got his first camera.

For Decker, photography was more than just a hobby, it was a way of looking at the world. He had been cursed with a short temper and a cynical outlook, so the darkroom became a soothing place, and the ceremony of making pictures a gentle therapy.

Much to his frustration, the studio-photography business proved unbearably dull and profitable. Decker did weddings, bar mitzvahs, portraits, and commercial jobs, mostly magazine advertisements. He was once paid nine thousand dollars to take the perfect picture of a bottle of Midol. The ad showed up in all the big women's magazines, and Decker clipped several copies to send to his friends, as a joke on himself.

And, of course, there were the fashion layouts with professional models. The first year Decker fell in love seventeen times. The second year he let the Hasselblad do the falling in love. His pictures were very good, he was making large sums of money, and he was bored out of his skull.

One afternoon on Miami Beach, while Decker was on a commercial shoot for a new tequila-scented suntan oil, a young tourist suddenly tore off her clothes and jumped into the Atlantic and tried to drown herself. The lifeguards reached her just in time, and Decker snapped a couple of frames as they carried her from the surf. The woman's blond hair was tangled across her cheeks, her eyes were puffy and half-closed, and her lips were gray. What really made the photograph was the face of one of the lifeguards who had rescued the young woman. He'd carefully wrapped his arms around her bare chest to shield her from the gawkers, and in his eyes Decker's lens had captured both panic and pity.

For the hell of it Decker gave the roll of film to a newspaper reporter who had followed the paramedics to the scene. The next day the Miami *Sun* published Decker's photograph on the front page, and paid him the grand sum of thirty dollars. The day after that, the managing editor offered him a full-time job and Decker said yes.

In some ways it was the best move he ever made. In some ways it was the worst. Decker only wished he would have lasted longer.

He thought of this as he drove into Harney County, starting a new case, working for a man he didn't like at all.

Harney was Dickie Lockhart's hometown, and the personal headquarters of his bass-fishing empire.

Upon arrival the first thing Decker did was to find Ott Pickney, which was easy. Ott was not a man on the move.

He wrote obituaries for the Harney *Sentinel*, which published two times a week, three during boar season. The leisurely pace of the small newspaper suited Ott Pickney perfectly because it left plenty of time for golf and gardening. Before moving to Central Florida, Pickney had worked for seventeen years at the Miami *Sun*, which is where Decker had met him. At first Decker had assumed from Ott's sluggish behavior that here was a once-solid reporter languishing in the twilight of his career; it soon became clear that Ott Pickney's career had begun in twilight and grown only dimmer. That he had lasted so long in Miami was the result of a dense newsroom bureaucracy that always seemed to find a place for him, no matter how useless he was. Ott was one of those newspaper characters who got passed from one department to another until, after so many years, he had become such a sad fixture that no editor wished to be remembered as the one who fired him. Consequently, Ott didn't get fired. He retired from the *Sun* at full pension and moved to Harney to write obits and grow prizewinning orchids.

R. J. Decker found Pickney in the *Sentinel's* newsroom, such as it was. There were three typewriters, five desks, and four telephones. Ott was lounging at the coffee machine; nothing had changed.

He grinned when Decker walked in. 'R.J.! God Almighty, what brings you here? Your car break down or what?'

Decker smiled and shook Ott's hand. He noticed that Ott was wearing baggy brown trousers and a blue Banlon shirt. Probably the last Banlon shirt in America. How could you not like a guy who wasn't ashamed to dress like this?

'You look great,' Decker said.

'And I feel great, R.J., I really do. Hey, I know it's not exactly the big city, but I had my fill of that, didn't I?' Ott was talking a little too loudly. 'We got out just in time, R.J., you and me. That paper would have killed both of us one way or another.'

'It tried.'

'Yeah, boy,' Ott said. 'Sandy, get over here! I want you to meet somebody.' A wrenlike man with thick eyeglasses walked over and nodded cautiously at Decker. 'R.J., this is Sandy Kilpatrick, my editor. Sandy, this is R. J. Decker. R.J. and I worked together down in the Magic City. I wrote the prose, he took the snapshots. We covered that big voodoo murder together, remember, R.J.?'

Decker remembered. He remembered it wasn't exactly a big voodoo murder. Some redneck mechanic in Hialeah had killed his wife by sticking her with pins; safety pins, hundreds of them. The mechanic had read something about voodoo in *Argosy* magazine and had totally confused the rituals. He loaded his wife up on Barbancourt rum and started pricking away until she bled to death. Then he pretended to come home from work and find her dead. He blamed the crime on a Haitian couple down the street, claiming they had put a hex on his house and Oldsmobile. The cops didn't go for this and the redneck mechanic wound up on Death Row.

As Ott was reinventing this story, Sandy Kilpatrick stared at R. J. Decker the way visitors from Miami got stared at in this part of Florida. Like they were trouble. Kilpatrick obviously had heard Ott's voodoo-murder story about four hundred times and soon started to shrink away.

'Nice meeting you,' Decker said.

Kilpatrick nodded again as he slipped out of the office.

'Good kid,' Ott Pickney said avuncularly. 'He's learning.'

Decker helped himself to a cup of coffee. His legs were stiff from the long drive.

'What the hell brings you here?' Ott asked amiably.

'Fish,' Decker said.

'Didn't know you were a basser.'

'I thought I'd give it a try,' Decker said. 'They say Harney's a real hotspot for the big ones.'

'Lunkers,' Ott said.

Decker looked at him quizzically.

'In these parts, they're not *big ones*, they're lunkers,' Ott explained. 'The most mammoth bass in the hemisphere.'

'Hawgs,' Decker said, remembering one of Dennis Gault's phrases.

'Sure, you got it!'

'Where's the best place to try, this time of year?'

Ott Pickney sat down at his desk. 'Boy, R.J., I really can't help you much. The man to see is Jamie Belliroso, our sports guy.'

'Where can I find him?'

'Maui,' Ott Pickney said.

Jamie Belliroso, it turned out, was one of a vanishing breed of sportswriters who would accept any junket tossed their way, as long as gourmet food and extensive travel were involved. This month it was a marlin-fishing extravaganza in Hawaii, sponsored by a company that manufactured polyethylene fish baits. Jamie Belliroso's air fare, room, and board would all be paid for with the quiet understanding that the name of the bait company would be mentioned a mere eight or ten times in his feature article, and that the name of the company would be spelled correctly—which, in Belliroso's case, was never a sure thing. In the meantime, the blue marlin were striking and Jamie was enjoying the hell out of Maui.

'When will he be back?' Decker asked.

'Who knows,' Ott said. 'From Hawaii he's off to Christmas Island for bonefish.'

Decker said, 'Anyone else who could help me? Someone mentioned a guide named Dickie Lockhart.'

Ott laughed. 'A *guide*? My friend, Dickie's not a guide, he's a god. A big-time bass pro. The biggest.'

'What does that mean?'

'It means he wouldn't be seen in the same boat with a greenhorn putz like you. Besides, Dickie doesn't hire out.'

Decker decided not to mention Dennis Gault's grave allegations. Ott was obviously a huge fan of Dickie Lockhart's. Decker wondered if the whole town was as starstruck.

'There's a couple good guides work out on the lake,' Ott suggested. 'Think they're up to two hundred dollars a day.'

The world has gone mad, Decker thought. 'That's too rich for my blood,' he said to Ott.

'Yeah, it's steep all right, but they don't give the tourist much choice. See, they got a union.'

'A union?' It was all too much.

'The Lake Jesup Bass Captains Union. They keep the charter rates fixed, I'm afraid.'

'Christ, Ott, I came here to catch a fish and you're telling me the lake's locked up by the fucking Izaak Walton division of the

Teamsters. What a swell little town you've got here.'

'It's not like that,' Ott Pickney said in a you-don't-understand tone. 'Besides, there's other options. One, rent yourself a skiff and give it a shot alone—'

'I wouldn't know where to start,' Decker said.

'Or two, you can try this guy who lives out at the lake.'

'Don't tell me he's not in the union?'

'He's the only one,' Ott said. 'When you meet him you'll know why.' Ott rolled his eyeballs theatrically.

Decker said, 'I sense you're trying to tell me the man is loony.'

'They say he knows the bass,' Ott said. 'They also say he's dangerous.'

Decker was in the market for a renegade. The mystery man sounded like a good possibility.

'What does he charge?' Decker asked, still playing the rube.

'I have no idea,' Ott said. 'After you see him, you may want to reconsider. In that case you can hook up with one of the regulars out of Rundell's marina.'

Decker shook his head. 'They sound like hot dogs, Ott. I just want to relax.'

Ott's brow wrinkled. 'I know these folks, R.J. I like 'em, too. Now I won't sit here and tell you bassers are completely normal, 'cause that's not true either. They're slightly manic. They got boats that'll outrace a Corvette, and they're fairly crazy out on the water. Just the other day I wrote up a young man who flipped his rig doing about sixty on the lake. Hit a cypress knee and punched out.'

'He died?'

'It was dawn. Foggy . Guess he was racing his pals to the fishing hole.' Pickney chuckled harshly. 'No brakes on a boat, partner.'

'Didn't the same thing happen a few years ago in one of those big tournaments?' Decker said. 'I read about it in the Orlando papers. Two boats crashed on the way out.'

Ott said, 'Yeah, over on Apopka. Officially it's a grand-prix start, but the boys call it a blast-off. Fifty boats taking off from a dead stop.' Ott shaped his hands into two speedboats and gave a demonstration. 'Kaboom! Hell, those tournaments are something else, R.J. You ought to do a color layout sometime.'

'I've heard all kinds of stuff goes on. Cheating and everything.'

'Aw, I heard that too, and I just can't believe it. How in the world can you cheat? Either you've got fish on a stringer, or you don't.' Ott sniffed at the idea. 'I know these folks and I don't buy it, not for a second. Texas, maybe, sure. But not here.'

Ott Pickney acted like it was all city talk. He acted like the desk made him an authority—his desk, his newsroom, his town. Ott's ego was adapting quite well to the rural life, Decker thought. The wise old pro from Miami.

Pickney perked up. 'You on expense account?'

'A good one,' Decker said.

'Buy me lunch?'

'Sure, Ott.'

'The guy at the lake, his name is Skink. As I said, they talk like he's only got one oar in the water, so watch your step. One time we sent a kid to write a little feature story about him and this Skink took an ax and busted the windows out of the kid's car. He lives in a cabin off the old Mormon Trail. You can't miss it, R.J., it's right on the lake. Looks like a glorified outhouse.'

'Skink what?' Decker asked.

'That's his whole name,' Ott Pickney said. 'That's all he needs up here.' He rolled his chair back and clomped his shoes up on the bare desk. 'See, sport, you're not in Miami anymore.'

The man named Skink said, 'Go.'

'I need to talk to you.'

'You got thirty seconds.' The man named Skink had a gun. A Remington, Decker noted. The rifle lay across his lap.

It was a large lap. Skink appeared to be in his late forties, early fifties. He sat in a canvas folding chair on the porch of his cabin. He wore Marine-style boots and an orange rainsuit, luminous even in the twilight. The shape and features of his face were hard to see, but Skink's silver-flecked hair hung in a braided rope down his back. Decker figured long hair was risky in this part of the woods, but Skink was substantial enough to set his own style.

'My name is Decker.'

'You from the IRS?' The man's voice was deep and wet, like mud slipping down a drain.

'No,' Decker said.

'I pay no taxes,' Skink said. He was wearing a rainhat, though it wasn't raining. He was also wearing sunglasses and the sun was down. 'I pay no attention to taxes,' Skink asserted. 'Not since Nixon, the goddamn thief.'

'I'm not from the government,' Decker said carefully. 'I'm a private investigator.'

Skink grunted.

'Like Barnaby Jones,' Decker ventured.

Skink raised the rifle and aimed at Decker's heart. 'I pay no attention to television,' he said.

'Forget I mentioned it. Please.'

Skink held the gun steady. Decker felt moisture bead on the back of his neck. 'Put the gun away,' he said.

'I don't know,' Skink said. 'I feel like shooting tonight.'

Decker thought: Just my luck. 'I heard you do some guiding,' he said.

Skink's gun lowered a fraction of an inch. 'I do.'

'For bass,' Decker said. 'Bass fishing.'

'Hundred bucks a day, no matter.'

'Fine,' Decker said.

'You'll call me captain?'

'If you want.'

Skink lowered the rifle all the way. Decker reached into his pocket and pulled out a one-hundred-dollar bill. He unfolded it, smoothed it out, and offered it to Skink.

'Put it away. Pay when we get your fish in the boat.' Skink looked annoyed. 'You act like you still want to talk.'

For some reason the banjo music from *Deliverance* kept tinkling in Decker's head. It got louder every time he took a good look at Skink's face.

'Talk,' Skink said. 'Quick.' He reached over and set the rifle in a corner, its barrel pointing up. Then he removed the sunglasses. His eyes were green; not hazel or olive, but deep green, like Rocky Mountain evergreens. His eyebrows, tangled and ratty, grew at an angle that gave his tanned face the cast of perpetual anger. Decker wondered how many repeat customers a guide like Skink could have.

'Do you fish the tournaments?'

'Not anymore,' Skink said. 'If it's tournament fish you're after, keep your damn money.'

'It's cheaters I'm after,' Decker said.

Skink sat up so suddenly that his plastic rainsuit squeaked. The forest-green eyes impaled R. J. Decker while the mouth chewed hard on the corners of its mustache. Skink took a deep breath and when his chest filled, he looked twice as big. It was only when he got to his feet that Decker saw what a diesel he truly was.

'I'm hungry,' Skink said. He took ten steps toward his truck, stopped, and said, 'Well, Miami, come on.'

As the pickup bounced down the old Mormon Trail, Decker said, 'Captain, how'd you know where I was from?'

'Haircut.'

'That bad?'

'Distinctive.'

'Distinctive' was not a word Decker expected to hear from the captain's lips. Obviously this was not the type of fellow you could sort out in a day, or even two.

Skink steered the truck onto Route 222 and headed south. He drove slow, much slower than he had driven on the trail. Decker noticed that he hunched himself over the wheel, and peered hawklike through the windshield.

'What's the matter?' Decker asked.

'Hush.'

Cars and trucks were flying by at sixty miles an hour. Skink was barely doing twenty. Decker was sure they were about to get rear-ended by a tractor-trailer.

'You all right?'

'I pay no attention to the traffic,' Skink said. He turned the wheel hard to the right and took the truck off the road, skidding in the gravel. Before Decker could react, the big man leapt from the cab and dashed back into the road. Decker saw him snatch something off the center line and toss it onto the shoulder.

'What the hell are you doing?' Decker shouted, but his voice died in the roar of a passing gasoline tanker. He looked both ways before jogging across the highway to join Skink on the other side.

Skink was kneeling next to a plump, misshapen lump of gray fur.

Decker saw it was a dead opossum. Skink ran a hand across its furry belly. 'Still warm,' he reported.

Decker said nothing.

'Road kill,' Skink said, by way of explanation. He took a knife out of his belt. 'You hungry, Miami?'

Decker said uneasily, 'How about if we just stop someplace and I buy you supper?'

'No need,' Skink said, and he sawed off the opossum's head. He lifted the carcass by its pink tail and stalked back to the truck. Decker now understood the reason for the fluorescent rainsuit; a speeding motorist could see Skink a mile away. He looked like a neon yeti.

'You'll like the flavor,' Skink remarked as Decker got in the truck beside him.'

'I think I'll pass.'

'Nope.'

'What?'

'We both eat, that's the deal. Then you get the hell out. Another day we'll talk fish.'

Skink pulled the rainhat down tight on his skull.

'And after that,' he said, turning the ignition, 'we might even talk about cheaters.'

'So you know about this?' Decker said.

Skink laughed bitterly. 'I do, sir, but I wisht I didn't.'

Clouds of insects swirled in and out of the high-beams as the truck jounced down the dirt road. Suddenly Skink killed the lights and cut the ignition. The pickup coasted to a stop.

'Listen!' Skink said.

Decker heard an engine. It sounded like a lawn mower.

Skink jumped from the truck and ran into the trees. This time Decker was right behind him.

'I told the bastards,' Skink said, panting.

'Who?' Decker asked. It seemed as if they were running toward the noise, not away from it.

'I told them,' Skink repeated. They broke out of the pines, onto a bluff, and Skink immediately shrank into a crouch. Below them was a small stream, with a dirt rut following the higher ground next to the water. A single headlight bobbed on the trail.

Decker could see it clearly—a lone rider on a dirt bike. Up close the motorcycle sounded like a chainsaw, the growl rising and falling with the hills. Soon the rider would pass directly beneath them.

Decker saw that Skink had a pistol in his right hand.

'What the hell are you doing?'

'Quiet, Miami.'

Skink extended his right arm, aiming. Decker lunged, too late. The noise of the gun knocked him on his back.

The dirt bike went down like a lame horse. The rider screamed as he flew over the handlebars.

Dirt spitting from its rear tire, the bike tumbled down the embankment and splashed into the stream, where the engine choked and died in bubbles.

Up the trail, the rider moaned and began to extricate himself from a cabbage palm.

'Christ!' Decker said, his breath heavy.

Skink tucked the pistol in his pants. 'Front tire,' he reported, almost smiling. 'Told you I was in the mood to shoot.'

Back at the shack, Skink barbecued the opossum on an open spit and served it with fresh corn, collards, and strawberries. Decker focused on the vegetables because the opossum tasted gamy and terrible; he could only take Skink's word that the animal was fresh and had not lain dead on the highway for days.

As they sat by the fire, Decker wondered why the ferocious mosquitoes were concentrating on his flesh, while Skink seemed immune. Perhaps the captain's blood was lethal.

'Who hired you?' Skink asked through a mouthful of meat.

Decker told him who, and why.

Skink stopped chewing and stared.

'You know Mr. Gault?' Decker asked.

'I know lots of folks.'

'Dickie Lockhart?'

Skink bit clean through a possum bone. 'Sure.'

'Lockhart's the cheater,' Decker said.

'You're getting close.'

'There's more?' Decker asked.

'Hell, yes!' Skink tossed the bone into the lake, where its splash startled a mallard.

'More,' Skink muttered. 'More, more, more.'

'Let's hear it, captain,' Decker said.

'Another night.' Skink spit something brown into the fire and scowled at nothing in particular. 'How much you getting paid?'

Decker was almost embarrassed to tell him. 'Fifty grand,' he said.

Skink didn't even blink. 'Not enough,' he said. 'Come on, Miami, finish your damn supper.'

4

Ott Pickney stopped by the motel before eight the next morning. He knocked loudly on R. J. Decker's door.

Groggily, Decker let him in. 'So how'd it go?' Ott asked.

'A lively night.'

'Is he as kooky as they say?'

'Hard to tell,' Decker said. Living in Miami tended to recalibrate one's view of sanity.

Ott said he was on his way to a funeral. 'That poor fella I told you about.'

'The fisherman?'

'Bobby Clinch,' Ott said. 'Sandy wants a tearjerker for the weekend paper—it's the least we can do for a local boy. You and Skink going out for bass?'

'Not this morning.' Skink had left the proposition in the air. Decker planned to meet him later.

Ott Pickney said, 'Why don't you ride along with me?'

'To a funeral?'

'The whole town's closing down for it,' Ott said. 'Besides, I thought you might want to see some big-time bassers up close. Bobby had loads of friends.'

'Give me a second to shower.'

Decker hated funerals. Working for the newspaper, he'd had to cover too many grim graveside services, from a cop shot by some coked-up creep to a toddler raped and murdered by her babysitter. Child murders got plenty of play in the papers, and a shot of the grieving parents was guaranteed to run four columns, minimum. A funeral like that was the most dreaded assignment in journalism. Decker didn't know quite what to expect in Harney. For him it was strictly business, a casual surveillance.

Maybe even Dickie Lockhart would show up, Decker thought as he toweled off. He was eager to get a glimpse of the town celebrity.

They rode to the graveyard in Ott Pickney's truck. Almost everyone else in Harney owned a Ford or a Chevy, but Ott drove a new Toyota flatbed. 'Orchids,' he explained, a bit defensively, 'don't take up much space.'

'It's a fine truck,' Decker offered.

Ott lit a Camel so Decker rolled down the window. It was a breezy morning and the air was cold, blowing dead from the north.

'Can I ask something?' Ott said. 'It's personal.'

'Fire away.'

'I heard you got divorced.'

'Right,' Decker said.

'That's a shame, R.J. She seemed like a terrific kid.'

'The problem was money,' Decker said. 'He had some, I didn't.' His wife had run off with a timeshare-salesman-turned-chiropractor. Life didn't get any meaner.

'Jesus, I'm sorry.' The divorce wasn't really what Ott wanted to talk about. 'I heard something else,' he said.

'Probably true,' Decker said. 'I did ten months at Apalachee, if that's what you heard.'

Pickney was sucking so hard on the cigarette that the ash was three inches long. Decker was afraid it would drop into Ott's lap and set his pants on fire, which is what had happened one day in the newsroom of the Miami *Sun*. None of the fire extinguishers had been working, so Ott had been forced to straddle a drinking fountain to douse the flames.

'Do you mind talking about it?' Ott said. 'I understand if you'd rather not.'

Decker said, 'It was after one of the Dolphin games. I was parked about four blocks from the stadium. Coming back to the car, I spotted some jerkoff breaking into the trunk, trying to rip off the cameras. I told him to stop, he ran. He was carrying two Nikons and a brand new Leica. No way was I going to let him get away.'

'You caught up with him?'

'Yeah, he fell and I caught up to him. I guess I got carried away.'

Pickney shook his head and spit the dead Camel butt out the window. 'Ten months! I can't believe they'd give you that much time for slugging a burglar.'

'Not just any burglar—a football star at Palmetto High,' Decker said. 'Three of his sisters testified that they'd witnessed the whole thing. Said Big Brother never stole the cameras. Said he was minding his own business, juking on the corner when I drove up and asked where I could score some weed. Said Big Brother told me to get lost, and I jumped out of my car and pounded him into dog meat. All of which was a goddamn lie.'

'So then?'

'So the state attorney's office dropped the burglary charge on Mr. Football Hero, and nailed me for agg assault. He gets a scholarship to USC, I get felony arts-and-crafts. That's the whole yarn.'

Pickney sighed. 'And you lost your job.'

'The newspaper had no choice, Ott.' Not with the boy's father raising so much hell. The boy's father was Levon Bennett, big wheel on the Orange Bowl Committee, board chairman of about a hundred banks. Decker had always thought the newspaper might have rehired him after Apalachee if only Levon Bennett wasn't in the same Sunday golf foursome as the executive publisher.

'You always had a terrible temper.'

'Luck, too. Of all the thieves worth stomping in Miami, I've got to pick a future Heisman Trophy winner.' Decker laughed sourly.

'So now you're a . . .'

'Private investigator,' Decker said. Obviously Ott was having a little trouble getting to the point.

The point being what in the hell Decker was doing as a P.I. 'I burned out on newspapers,' he said to Ott.

'With your portfolio you could have done anything, R.J. Magazines, free-lance, the New York agencies. You could write your own ticket.'

'Not with a rap sheet,' Decker said.

It was a comfortable lie. A lawyer friend had arranged for

Decker's criminal record to be legally expunged, wiped off the computer, so the rap sheet wasn't really the problem.

The truth was, Decker had to get away from the news business. He needed a divorce from photography because he had started to see life and death as a sequence of frames; Decker's mind had started to work like his goddamn cameras, and it scared him. The night he made up his mind was the night the city desk had sent him out on what everybody figured was a routine drug homicide. Something stinky dripping from the trunk of a new Seville parked on the sky level of the Number Five Garage at Miami International. Decker got there just as the cops were drilling the locks. Checked the motor drive on the Leica. Got down on one knee. Felt the cold dampness seep through his trousers. *Raining like a bitch*. Trunk pops open. *A young woman, used to be, anyway*. Heels, nylons, pretty silk dress, except for the brown stains. *Stench bad enough to choke a maggot*. He'd been expecting the usual Juan Doe—Latin male, mid-twenties, dripping gold, no ID, multiple gunshot wounds. *Not a girl with a coat hanger wrapped around her neck*. Not Leslie. Decker refocused. *Leslie*. Jesus Christ, he knew this girl, worked with her at the paper. Decker fed the Leica more film. She was a fashion writer—who the fuck'd want to murder a fashion writer? *Her husband, said a homicide guy*. Decker bracketed the shots, changed angles to get some of the hair, but no face. Paper won't print faces of the dead, that's policy. He fired away, thinking: I know this girl, so why can't I stop? *Leica whispering in the rain, click-click-click*. Oh God, she's a friend of mine so why the fuck can't I stop. *Husband told her they were flying to Disney World, big romantic weekend, said the homicide man*. Decker reloaded, couldn't help himself. *Strangled her right here, stuffed her in the trunk, grabbed his suitcase, and hopped a plane for Key West with a barmaid from North Miami Beach*. She'd only been married what, three months? *Four, said the homicide guy, welcome to the Magic Kingdom. Haven't you got enough pictures for Chrissakes?* Sure, Decker said, but he couldn't look at Leslie's body unless it was through the lens, so he ran back to his car and threw up his guts in a puddle.

Three days later, Levon Bennett's son tried to steal R. J. Decker's cameras outside the stadium, and Decker chased him down and beat him unconscious. Those are my eyes, he'd said as he slugged the punk. Without them I'm fucking blind, don't you understand?

At Apalachee he'd met a very nice doctor doing four years for Medicare fraud, who gave him the name of an insurance company that needed an investigator. Sometimes the investigator had to take his own pictures—'sometimes' was about all Decker figured he could handle. Besides, he was broke and never wanted to see the inside of a newsroom again. So he tried one free-lance job for the insurance company—took a picture of a forty-two-foot Bertram that was supposed to be sunk off Cat Island but wasn't—and got paid two thousand dollars. Decker found the task to be totally painless and profitable. Once his rap sheet was purged, he applied for his P.I. license and purchased two cameras, a Nikon and a Canon, both used. The work was small potatoes, no Pulitzers but no pain. Most important, he had discovered with more and more cases that he still loved the cameras but could see just fine without them—no blood and gore in the darkroom, just mug shots and auto tags and grainy telescopic stills of married guys sneaking out of motels.

None of this he told Ott Pickney. Being a private detective isn't so bad, is what he said, and the pay's good. 'It's just temporary,' Decker lied, 'until I figure out what I want to do.'

Ott managed a sympathetic smile. He was trying to be a pal. 'You were a fine photographer, R.J.'

'Still am,' Decker said with a wink. 'I waltzed out of that newspaper with a trunkload of free Ektachrome.'

The funeral was like nothing R. J. Decker had ever seen, and he'd been to some beauties. Jonestown. Beirut. Benghazi.

But this was one for the books. The L. L. Bean catalog, to be exact.

They were burying Bobby Clinch in his bass boat.

Actually, part of the boat. The blue metal-flake hull had been sawed up and hewn into a coffin. It wasn't a bad job, either, especially on short notice.

Clarisse Clinch thought it a ghastly idea until the Harney

County Bass Blasters Club had offered to pay the bill. The funeral director was a dedicated fisherman, which made it easier to overlook certain state burial regulations concerning casket material.

R. J. Decker resisted the urge to grab an F-1 and shoot some pictures. The last thing he needed in the viewfinder was a shrieking widow.

The thirty-acre cemetery was known locally as Our Lady of Tropicana, since it had been carved out of a moribund citrus grove. The mourners stood in the sunshine on a gentle green slope. The preacher had finished the prayer and was preparing to lay Bobby Clinch's soul to rest.

'I know some of you were out on Lake Jesup this morning and missed the church service,' the preacher said. 'Clarisse has been kind enough to let us open the casket one more time so you boys—Bobby's fishing buddies—can pay your eternal respects.'

Decker leaned over to Ott Pickney. 'Which one is Lockhart?'

'Don't see him,' Ott said.

A line of men, many dressed in khaki jumpsuits or bright flotation vests, a few still sloshing in their waders, filed by the sparkly blue casket. The undertaker had done a miraculous job, all things considered. The bloatedness of the body's features had been minimized by heavy pink makeup and artful eye shadows. Although the man in the casket did not much resemble the Bobby Clinch that his pals had known, it could easily have been an older and chubbier brother. While some of the fishermen reached in and tugged affectionately at the bill of Bobby's cap (which concealed what the ducks had done to his hair), others placed sentimental tokens in the coffin with their dead companion; fishing lures, mostly: Rapalas, Bombers, Jitterbugs, Snagless Sallies, Gollywompers, Hula Poppers, River Runts. Some of the lures were cracked or faded, the hooks bent and rusted, but each represented a special memory of a day on the water with Bobby Clinch. Clarisse made an effort to appear moved by this fraternal ceremony, but her thoughts were drifting. She had already had a line on a buyer for her husband's Blazer.

Ott Pickney and R. J. Decker were among the last to walk by the casket. By now the inside looked like a display rack at a tackle shop. A fishing rod lay like a sword at the dead man's side.

Ott remarked, 'Pearl Brothers did a fantastic job, don't you think?'

Decker made a face.

'Well, you didn't know him when he was alive.'

'Nobody looks good dead,' Decker said. Especially a floater.

Finally the lid was closed. The bier was cleared of flowers, including the impressive spray sent by the Lake Jesup Bass Captains Union—a leaping lunker, done all in petunias. With the ceremony concluded, the mourners broke into small groups and began to trudge back to their trucks.

'I gotta get some quotes from the missus,' Ott whispered to Decker.

'Sure. I'm in no particular hurry.'

Ott walked over and tentatively sat down on a folding chair next to Clarisse Clinch. When he took out his notebook, the widow recoiled as if it were a tarantula. R. J. Decker chuckled.

'So you like funerals?'

It was a woman's voice. Decker turned around.

'I heard you laugh,' she said.

'We all deal with grief in our own way.' Decker kept a straight face when he said it.

'You're full of shit.' The woman's tone stopped just short of friendly.

Mid-thirties, dark blue eyes, light brown hair curly to the shoulders. Decker was sure he had seen her somewhere before. She had an expensive tan, fresh from Curaçao or maybe the Caymans. She wore a black dress cut much too low for your standard funeral. This dress was a night at the symphony.

'My name is Decker.'

'Mine's Lanie.'

'Elaine?'

'Once upon a time. Now it's Lanie.' She shot a look toward Ott Pickney. Or was it Clarisse? 'You didn't know Bobby, did you?' she said.

'Nope.'

'Then why are you here?'

'I'm a friend of Ott's.'

'You sure don't look like a friend of Ott's. And I wish you'd please quit staring at my tits.'

Decker reddened. Nothing clever came to mind so he kept quiet and stared at the top of his shoes.

Lanie said, 'So what did you think of the sendoff?'

'Impressive.'

' "Sick" is the word for it,' she said.

An ear-splitting noise came from the gravesite. Bobby Clinch's customized bass-boat casket had slipped off the belts and torn free of the winch as it was being lowered into the ground. Now it stood on end, perpendicular in the hole; it looked like a giant grape Popsicle.

'Oh Jesus,' Lanie said, turning away.

Cemetery workers in overalls scrambled to restore decorum. Decker saw Clarisse Clinch shaking her head in disgust. Ott was busy scribbling, his neck bent like a heron's.

'How well did you know him?' Decker asked.

'Better than anybody,' Lanie said. She pointed back toward the driveway, where the mourners' cars were parked. 'See that tangerine Corvette? That was a present from Bobby, right after he finished second in Atlanta. I've only given two blowjobs in my entire life, Mr. Decker, and that Corvette is one of them.'

Decker resisted asking about the other. He tried to remember the polite thing to say when a beautiful stranger struck up a conversation about oral sex. None of the obvious replies seemed appropriate for a funeral.

The woman named Lanie said,. 'Did you get a look inside the coffin?'

'Yeah, amazing,' Decker said.

'That fishing rod was Bobby's favorite. A Bantam Maglite bait-caster on a five-foot Fenwick graphite.'

Decker thought: Oh no, not her too.

'I gave him that outfit for Christmas,' Lanie said, adding quickly: 'It wasn't my idea to bury him with it.'

'I wouldn't have thought so,' Decker said.

They watched the cemetery workers tip Bobby Clinch's coffin back into the grave, where it landed with an embarrassing thud.

Hastily the diggers picked up their shovels and went to work. Lanie slipped on a pair of dark sunglasses and smoothed her hair. Her motions were elegant, well-practiced in the kind of mirrors you'd never find in Harney. The lady was definitely out-of-town.

'It wasn't what you think. Bobby and me, I mean.'

'I don't think anything,' Decker said. Why did they always have this compulsion to confess? Did he look like Pat O'Brien? Did he look like he cared?

'He really loved me,' Lanie volunteered.

'Of course he did,' Decker said. The Corvette was proof. A greater love hath no man than an orange sports car with a T-top and mag wheels.

'I hope you find out what really happened,' she said. 'That's why you're here, isn't it? Well, you're going to earn your fee on this one.'

Then she walked away. R. J. Decker found himself concentrating on the way she moved. It was a dazzlingly lascivious walk, with a sway of the hips that suggested maybe a little booze for breakfast. Decker had done worse things than admire a woman's legs at a funeral, but he knew he should have been thinking about something else. Why, for example, the grieving mistress knew more about him than he knew about her. He got up and strolled after her. When he called her name, Lanie turned, smiled, didn't stop walking. By the time Decker caught up she was already in the Corvette, door locked. She waved once through the tinted windows, then sped off, nearly peeling rubber over his feet.

When Decker got back to the grave, Ott Pickney was finishing his interview.

He nodded good-bye to Clarisse. 'A cold woman,' he said to Decker. 'Something tells me Bobby spent too much time on the lake.'

As they walked to the truck, Decker asked about the fishing rod in the coffin.

'Looked a beauty,' Ott agreed.

'Yes, but I was wondering,' Decker said. 'Guy goes fishing early one morning, flips his boat, falls in the lake . . .'

'Yeah?'

'How'd they ever find the rod?'

Ott shrugged. 'Hell, R.J., how do I know? Maybe they snagged it off the bottom.'

'Thirty feet of brown water? I don't think so.'

'Okay, maybe he didn't bring it with him. Maybe he left it at home.'

'But it was his favorite rig.'

'What are you getting at?'

'I just think it's odd.'

'Bass fanatics like Bobby Clinch got a hundred fishing poles, R.J., a new favorite every day. Whatever catches a lunker.'

'Maybe you're right.'

'You need to relax,' Ott said, 'you really do.'

They climbed in the Toyota and like clockwork Pickney lit up a Camel. He couldn't do it outdoors, in the fresh air, Decker thought; it had to be in a stuffy cab. He felt like getting out and hiking back to the motel. Give himself some time to think about this Lanie business.

'Clarisse didn't give me diddly for this story,' Ott complained. 'A bitter, bitter woman. I'd much rather have been interviewing your saucy new friend.'

Decker said, 'Who was she, anyway?'

'A very hot number,' Ott said. 'Don't tell me she's already got your dick in a knot.'

'She seemed to know who I am. Or at least what I do.'

'I'm not surprised.'

'She said her name was Lanie.'

'Lovely, lovely Lanie,' Ott sang.

'Then you know her.'

'R.J., everybody knows Lanie Gault. Her brother's one of the biggest bass fishermen in the country.'

Dickie Lockhart missed the big funeral because he had to fly to New Orleans and meet with his boss.

The boss was the Reverend Charles Weeb, president, general manager, and spiritual commander of the Outdoor Christian

Network, which syndicated Dickie Lockhart's television show.

Lockhart was not a remotely religious person—each Sunday being occupied by fishing—so he'd never bothered to ascertain precisely which denomination was espoused by the Reverend Charles Weeb. Whenever the two men met, Weeb never mentioned sin, God, Jesus Christ, the Virgin Mary, or any of the A-list apostles. Instead Weeb mainly talked about ratings and revenues and why some of Lockhart's big sponsors were going soft on him. During these discussions the Reverend Charles Weeb often became exercised and tossed around terms like 'shithead' and 'cocksucker' more freely than any preacher Dickie Lockhart had ever met.

Two or three times a year, Lockhart would be summoned to New Orleans for a detailed review of *Fish Fever*, Lockhart's immensely popular television show. The Reverend Charles Weeb, who naturally had his own evangelical show on the Outdoor Christian Network, seemed to possess an uncommon interest in Lockhart's low-budget fishing travelogue.

On the day of Bobby Clinch's funeral the two men met in a pink suite in a big hotel on Chartres Street. The room was full of fruit baskets and complimentary bottles of booze. On a credenza by the door stood an odd collection of tiny statuary—plastic dashboard saints that various hotel workers had dropped off so that the Reverend Weeb might bestow a small blessing, if he had time.

'Nutty Catholics,' Weeb grumbled. 'Only know how to do two things—screw and beg forgiveness.'

'Can I have an apple?' Dickie Lockhart asked.

'No,' said Charles Weeb. He wore an expensive maroon jogging suit that he'd bought for cash on Rodeo Drive in Beverly Hills. As always, his straw-blond hair looked perfect. Weeb also had straw-blond eyebrows which, Dickie Lockhart guessed, were combed with as much care as the hair.

Weeb propped his Reeboks on the coffee table, slipped on a pair of reading glasses, and scanned the latest Nielsens.

'Not too terrible,' he said.

'Thank you,' Lockhart said. Meetings were not his strong suit;

he was already daydreaming about Bourbon Street, and what might happen later.

'You want to explain Macon?' Charlie Weeb said, peering over the rims.

Lockhart shrank into the sofa. He had no idea what the boss was talking about. Had he missed a fishing tournament? Maybe a promotional gig for one of the top sponsors? Wasn't Macon where Happy Gland Fish Scent was manufactured?

'Macon,' Weeb sighed. His tone was that of a disappointed parent. 'We lost Macon to that shiteating cocksucker.'

'Spurling?'

'Who else!' Weeb crumpled the Nielsens.

Ed Spurling hosted a show called *Fishin' with Fast Eddie*, which was broadcast by satellite to one hundred and seventeen television stations. One more, counting Macon.

In the fierce battle for TV bass-fishing supremacy, Ed Spurling was Dickie Lockhart's blood rival.

'Macon,' Dickie said morosely. Georgia was damn good bass country, too.

'So it's one hundred twenty-five stations to one-eighteen,' the Reverend Charles Weeb remarked. 'Too damn close for comfort.'

'But we've got some overlap,' Lockhart noted. 'Mobile, Gulfport, and Fort Worth.'

Weeb nodded. 'Little Rock too,' he said.

These were cable systems that carried both bass programs; a few markets could easily support more than one.

'Guess I forgot to tell you,' Weeb said. 'You lost the dinnertime slot in Little Rock. They bumped you to Sunday morning, after *Ozark Bowling*.'

Lockhart groaned. Spurling's lead-in was Kansas City Royals baseball, a blockbuster. It didn't seem fair.

'You see what's happening,' the reverend said darkly.

'But the show's doing good. Did you see the one from Lake Jackson?'

'Shaky lens work.' Weeb sneered. 'Looked like your video ace had the DTs.'

'We do our best,' the fisherman muttered, 'on a thousand lousy bucks per episode.' That was the *Fish Fever* budget, excluding Dickie Lockhart's salary. Travel money was so tight that Lockhart drove a Winnebago between locations to save on motels.

Weeb said, 'Your show needs a damn good jolt.'

'I caught three ten-pounders at Lake Jackson!'

'Spurling's got a new theme song,' Weeb went on. 'Banjos. Mac Davis on the vocals. Have you heard it?'

Lockhart shook his head. He wasn't much for arguing with the boss, but sometimes pride got the best of him. He asked Charles Weeb, 'Did you see the latest BBRs?'

Published by *Bass Blasters* magazine, the Bass Blasters Ratings (BBR) ranked the country's top anglers. The BBR was to bass fishing what the Nielsens were to the TV networks.

'Did you notice who's number one?' Dickie Lockhart asked. '*Again.*'

'Yeah,' Weeb took his sneakers off the coffee table and sat up. 'It's a good fucking thing, too, because right now all we got going for us is your name, Dickie. You're a winner and viewers like winners. 'Course, I see where Mr. Spurling won himself a tournament in mid-Tennessee—'

'The minor leagues, Reverend Weeb. I smoked him at the Atlanta Classic. He finished eighth, and no keepers.'

Weeb stood up and smoothed the wrinkles from his expensive jogging suit. Then he sat down again. 'As I said, we're very pleased you're on top. I just hate to see you slipping, that's all. It happens, if you're not careful. Happens in business, happens in fishing too. One and the same.'

Weeb tore open a fruit basket and tossed Lockhart an apple. Lockhart felt like telling Weeb how much his jogging suit looked like K-Mart pajamas.

The Reverend Charles Weeb said, 'This is the majors, Dickie. If you don't win, you get benched.' He took off his glasses. 'I truly hope you keep winning. In fact, I strongly recommend it.'

On this matter, of course, Dickie Lockhart was way ahead of him.

5

Decker honked twice as he drove up to Skink's shack. Short, polite honks. The last thing he wanted to do was surprise a man in a shooting mood.

The shack had a permanent lean, and looked as if a decent breeze could flatten it. Except for the buzz of horseflies, the place stood silent. Decker stuck his hands in his pockets and walked down to the lake. Across the water, several hundred yards away, a sleek boat drifted with two fishermen, plugging the shoreline. Every time one of them cast his lure, the shiny monofilament made a gossamer arc over the water before settling to the surface. The pointed raspberry hull of the fishermen's boat glistened under the noon sun. Decker didn't even bother to try a shout. If Skink were fishing, he'd be alone. And never in a boat like that.

Decker trudged back to the shack and sat on the porch. Seconds later he heard a cracking noise overhead, and Skink dropped out of an old pine tree.

He got up off the ground and said, 'I'm beginning not to despise you.'

'Nice to hear,' Decker said.

'You didn't go inside.'

'It's not my house,' Decker said.

'Precisely,' Skink grumped, clomping onto the porch. 'Some people would've gone in anyway.'

Daylight added no nuances or definition to Skink's appearance. Today he wore camouflage fatigues, sunglasses, and a flowered shower cap from which sprouted the long braid of silver-gray hair.

He poured coffee for Decker, but none for himself.

'I got fresh rabbit for lunch,' Skink said.

'No thanks.'

'I said *fresh*.'

'I just ate,' Decker said unconvincingly.

'How was the funeral?'

Decker shrugged. 'Did you know Robert Clinch?'

'I know them all,' Skink said.

'Lanie Gault?'

'Her brother's the big tycoon who hired you.'

'Right.' Decker had been relieved when Ott had told him that Dennis Gault was Lanie's brother. A husband would have been disconcerting news indeed.

Decker said, 'Miss Gault thinks there's something strange about the way Bobby Clinch died.'

Skink was on his haunches, working on the fire. He didn't answer right away. Once the tinder was lit, he said, 'Good rabbit is tough to come by. They tend to get all the way smushed and there's no damn meat left. The best ones are the ones that just barely get clipped and knocked back to the shoulder of the road. This one here, you'd hardly know it got hit. Meat's perfect. Might as well dropped dead of a bunny heart attack.' Skink was arranging the pieces on a frypan.

'I'll try a bite or two,' Decker said, surrendering.

Only then did Skink smile. It was one of the unlikeliest smiles Decker had ever seen, because Skink had perfect teeth. Straight, flawless, blindingly white ivories, the kind nobody is born with. TV-anchorman-type teeth—Skink's were that good.

Decker wasn't sure if he should be comforted or concerned. He was still thinking about those teeth when Skink said: 'I was at the Coon Bog Saturday morning.'

'When it happened?'

'Right before.'

'They said he must've been doing sixty knots when the boat flipped.'

Skink basted the sizzling rabbit with butter. He looked up and said, 'When I saw the boat, it wasn't moving.'

'Was Clinch alive?'

'Hell, yes.'

Decker said, 'Then the accident must have happened after you left.'

Skink snorted.

'Did he see you?' Decker asked.

'Nope. I was kneeling in the trees, skinning out a rattler. Nobody saw me.' He handed Decker a hunk of fried meat.

Decker blew on it until it cooled, then took a small bite. It was really very good. He asked, 'What made you notice Clinch?'

'Because he wasn't fishing.'

Decker swallowed the meat, and out came a quizzical noise.

'He wasn't fishing,' Skink repeated, 'and I thought that was damn strange. Get up at dawn, race like mad to a fishing hole, then just poke around the lily pads with a paddle. I was watching because I wanted to see if he'd find what he was looking for.'

'Did he?'

'Don't know. I left, had to get the snake on ice.'

'Christ,' Decker said. He reached into the frypan and gingerly picked out another piece of rabbit. Skink nodded approvingly.

Decker asked, 'What do you make of it?'

Skink said: 'I'm working for you, is that right?'

'If you'll do it, I sure need the help.'

'No shit.' The pan was empty. Skink poured the gloppy grease into an old milk carton.

'Bass were slapping over that morning,' he said, 'and not once did that fucker pick up a rod and cast. Do you find that strange?'

'I suppose,' Decker said.

'God, you need a lesson or two,' Skink muttered. 'Guys like Clinch love to catch bass more than they love to screw. That's the truth, Miami. You put 'em on a good bass lake at dawn and they get *hard*. So the question is, why wasn't Bobby Clinch fishing on the Coon Bog last Saturday?'

Decker had nothing to offer.

'You want to hear something even stranger?' Skink said. 'There was another boat out there too, and not far away. Two guys.'

Decker said, 'And they weren't fishing either, were they, captain?'

'Ha-ha!' Skink cawed. 'See there – those rabbit glands went straight to your brain!'

Decker's coffee had cooled, but it didn't matter. He gulped the rest of it.

Skink had become more animated and intense; the cords in his neck were tight. Decker couldn't tell if he was angry or ecstatic. Using a pocket knife to pick strings of rabbit meat from his perfect teeth, Skink said: 'Well, Miami, aren't you going to ask me what this means?'

'It was on my list of questions, yeah.'

'You'll hear my theory tonight, on the lake.'

'On the lake?'

'Your first communion,' Skink said, and scrambled noisily back up into the big pine.

Ott Pickney had left Miami in gentle retreat from big-city journalism. He knew he could have stayed at the *Sun* for the rest of his life, but felt he had more or less made his point. Having written virtually nothing substantial in at least a decade, he had nonetheless departed the newspaper in a triumphant state of mind. He had survived the conversion to cold type, the advent of unions, the onslaught of the preppy cubs, the rise of the hotshot managers. Ott had watched the stars and starfuckers arrive and, with a minimum of ambition, outlasted most of them. He felt he was living proof that a successful journalist need not be innately cunning or aggressive, even in South Florida.

In Ott's own mind, Harney was the same game, just a slower track.

Which is why he half-resented R. J. Decker's infernal skepticism about the death of Bobby Clinch. A foolhardy fisherman wrecks his boat and drowns—so what? In Miami it's one crummy paragraph on page 12-D; no one would look twice. Ott Pickney was peeved at Decker's coy insinuation that something sinister was brewing right under Ott's nose. This wasn't Dade County, he thought, and these weren't Dade County people. The idea of an organized cheating ring at the fish tournaments struck Ott as merely farfetched, but the suggestion of foul play in Robert Clinch's death was a gross insult to the community. Ott resolved to show R. J. Decker how wrong he was.

After the funeral, Ott went back to the newsroom and stewed

awhile. The *Sentinel*'s deadlines being what they were, he had two days to play with the Clinch piece. As he flipped through his notebook, Ott figured he had enough to bang out fifteen or twenty inches. Barely.

In an uncharacteristic burst of tenacity, he decided to give Clarisse Clinch another shot.

He found the house in chaos. A yellow moving van was parked out front; a crew of burly men was emptying the place. Clarisse had set up a command post in the kitchen, and under her scathing direction the movers were working very swiftly.

'Sorry to intrude,' Ott said to her, 'but I remembered a couple more questions.'

'I got no answers,' Clarisse snapped. 'We're on our way to Valdosta.'

Ott tried to picture Clarisse in a slinky, wet-looking dress, sliding long-legged into a tangerine sports car. He couldn't visualize it. This woman was a different species from Lanie Gault.

'I just need a little more about Bobby's hobby,' Ott said. 'A few anecdotes.'

'Anecdotes!' Clarisse said sharply. 'You writing a book?'

'Just a feature story,' Ott said. 'Bobby's friends say he was quite a fisherman.'

'You saw the coffin,' Clarisse said. 'And you saw his friends.' She clapped her hands twice loudly. 'Hey! Watch the ottoman, Pablo, unless you want to buy me a new one!'

The man named Pablo mumbled something obscene.

Clarisse turned back to Ott. 'Do you fish?'

He shook his head.

'Thank God there's at least one of you,' she said.

Her eyes flickered to a bookcase in the living room. Ott noticed that there were no books on the shelves, only trophies. Each of the trophies was crowned with a cheap gold-painted replica of a jumping fish. Bass, Ott assumed. He counted up the trophies and wrote the number '18' in his notebook. One of the movers unfolded a big cardboard box and began wrapping and packing the trophies.

'No!' Clarisse said. 'Those go in the dumpster.'

The mover shrugged.

Ott followed the widow to the garage. 'This junk in here,' she was saying, 'I've got to sell.'

Bobby Clinch's fishing gear. Cane poles, spinning rods, flipping rods, bait-casting rods, popping rods, fly rods. Ott Pickney counted them up and wrote '22' in his notebook. Each of the outfits seemed to be in immaculate condition.

'These are worth a lot of money,' Ott said to Clarisse.

'Maybe I should take out an ad in your newspaper.'

'Yes, good idea.' All Harney *Sentinel* reporters were trained in the paperwork of classified advertising, just in case the moment arose. Ott got a pad of order forms out of the glove box in the truck.

'Twenty-two fishing rods,' he began.

'Three pairs of hip waders,' Clarisse said, rummaging through her husband's bass trove.

'Two landing nets,' Ott noted.

'Four vests,' she said, 'one with Velcro pockets.'

'Is that an electric hook sharpener?'

'Brand new,' Clarisse said. 'Make sure you put down that it's brand new.'

'Got it.'

'And I don't know what to do about *this*.' From under a workbench she dragged what appeared to be a plastic suitcase with the word 'PLANO' stamped on the top. 'I can't even lift the darn thing,' she said. 'I'm afraid to look inside.'

'What is it?' Ott asked.

'The mother lode,' Clarisse said. 'Bobby's tacklebox.'

Ott hoisted it by the handle, then set it down on the kitchen counter. It must have weighed fifty pounds.

'He has junk in there from when he was ten years old. Lures and stuff.' Clarisse's voice sounded small; she was blinking her eyes as if she were about to cry, or at least fighting the urge.

Ott unfastened the clasps on the tacklebox and opened the lid. He had never seen such an eclectic collection of gadgets: rainbow-colored worms and frogs and plastic minnows and even tiny rubber snakes, all bristling with diamond-sharpened hooks. The lures were neatly organized on eight folding trays. Knives, pliers, stainless-steel hook removers, sinkers, swivels, and spools of leader material filled the bottom of the box.

In a violet velvet pouch was a small bronze scale used for weighing bass. The numerals on the scale optimistically went up to twenty-five pounds, although no largemouth bass that size had ever been caught.

Of the scale, Clarisse remarked: 'That stupid thing cost forty bucks. Bobby said it was tournament-certified, whatever that means. All the guys had the same model, he said, so nobody could cheat on the weight.'

Ott Pickney carefully fitted the bronze scale back in its pouch. He returned the pouch to Bobby Clinch's tacklebox and closed the latches.

Clarisse sat down on the concrete steps in the garage and stared sadly at the bushel of orphaned fishing poles. She said, 'This is what Bobby's life was all about, Mr. Pickney. Not me or the kids or the job at the phone company . . . just this. He wasn't happy unless he was out on the lake.'

Finally a decent quote, Ott thought, and scribbled feverishly in his notebook. *He wasn't happy unless he was fishing on the lake.* Close enough.

It wasn't until later, as Ott Pickney was driving back to the newspaper office, that it hit him like a fist in the gut: R. J. Decker was right. Something odd was going on.

If Bobby Clinch had taken the tacklebox on his fateful trip, it surely would have been lost in the boat accident.

So why had he gone to Lake Jesup without it?

Skink's boat was a bare twelve-foot skiff with peeling oars and splinters on the seat planks.

'Get in,' he told R. J. Decker.

Decker sat in the prow and Skink shoved off. It was a chilly night under a muffled sky; an unbroken mat of high gray clouds, pushed south by a cold breeze. Skink set a Coleman lantern in the center of the skiff, next to Decker's waterproof camera bag.

'No bugs,' Skink remarked. 'Not with this wind.'

He had brought two fishing rods that looked like flea-market specials. The fibreglass was brown and faded, the reels tarnished and dull. The outfits bore no resemblance to the sparkling master-piece that Decker had seen displayed so reverently in Bobby Clinch's casket.

Skink rowed effortlessly; wavelets kissed at the bow as the little boat crossed Lake Jesup. Decker enjoyed the quiet ride in the cool night. He was still slightly uneasy around Skink, but he was beginning to like the guy, even if he was a head case. Decker had met a few like Skink, eccentric hoary loners. Some were hiding, some were running, some just waiting for something, or some-one, to catch up. That was Skink, waiting. Decker would give him plenty of room.

'Looks like no one else is out tonight,' he said to Skink.

'Ha, they're everywhere,' Skink said. He rowed with his back to Decker. Decker wished he'd take off the damn shower cap, but couldn't figure a way to broach the subject.

'How do you know which way to go?' he asked.

'There's a trailer park due northwest. Lights shine through the trees,' Skink said. 'They leave 'em on all night, too. Old folks who live there, they're scared if the lights go off. Wild noises tend to get loud in the darkness—you ever noticed that, Miami? Pay attention now: the boat is the face of a clock, and you're sittin' at midnight. The trailer park lights are ten o'clock—'

'I see.'

'Good. Now look around about two-thirty, see there? More lights. That's a Zippy Mart on Route 222.' Skink described all this without once turning around. 'Which way we headed from camp, Miami?'

'Looks like due north.'

'Good,' Skink said. 'Got myself a fuckin' Eagle Scout in the boat.'

Decker didn't know what this giant fruitcake was up to, but a boat ride sure beat hell out of an all-night divorce surveillance.

Skink stopped rowing after twenty minutes. He set the lantern on the seat plank and picked up one of the fishing rods. From the prow Decker watched him fiddling with the line, and heard him curse under his breath.

Finally Skink pivoted on the seat and handed Decker the spin-ning rod. Tied to the end of the line was a long purple rubber lure. Decker figured it was supposed to be an eel, a snake, or a worm with thyroid. Skink's knot was hardly the tightest that Decker had ever seen.

'Let's see you cast,' Skink said.

Decker held the rod in his right hand. He took it back over his shoulder and made a motion like he was throwing a baseball. The rubber lure landed with a slap four feet from the boat.

'That sucks,' Skink said. 'Try opening the bail.'

He showed Decker how to open the face of the reel, and how to control the line with the tip of his forefinger. He demonstrated how the wrist, not the arm, supplied the power for the cast. After a half-dozen tries, Decker was winging the purple eel sixty-five feet.

'All right,' Skink said. He turned off the Coleman lantern.

The boat drifted at the mouth of a small cove, where the water lay as flat as a smoky mirror. Even on a starless night the lake gave off its own gray light. Decker could make out an apron of pines along the shore; around the boat were thick-stemmed lily pads, cypress nubs, patches of tall reeds.

'Go to it,' said Skink.

'Where?' Decker said. 'Won't I get snagged on all these lilies?'

'That's a weedless hook on the end of your line. Cast just like you were doing before, then think like a nightcrawler. Make it dance like a goddamn worm that knows it's about to get eaten.'

Decker made a good cast. The lure plopped into the pads. As he retrieved it, he waggled the rod in a lame attempt to make the plastic bait slither.

'Jesus Christ, it's not a fucking *breadstick*, it's a snake.' Skink snatched the outfit from Decker's hands and made a tremendous cast. The lure made a distant plop as it landed close to the shoreline. 'Now watch the tip of the rod,' Skink instructed. 'Watch my wrists.'

The snake-eel-worm skipped across the lily pads and wriggled across the plane of the water. Decker had to admit it looked alive.

When the lure was five feet from the boat, it seemed to explode. Or something exploded beneath it. Skink yanked it back, hard, but the eel flew out of the water and thwacked into his shower cap.

Decker's chest pounded in a spot right under his throat. Only bubbles and foam floated in the water where the thing had been.

'What the hell was that?' he stammered.

'Hawg,' Skink said. 'Good one, too.' He unhooked the fake eel from his cap and handed the fishing rod back to Decker. 'You try. Quick now, while he's still hot in the belly.'

Decker made a cast in the same direction. His fingers trembled as he jigged the rubber creature across the surface of the cove.

'Water's nervous,' Skink said, drying his beard. 'Slow it down a tad.'

'Like this?' Decker whispered.

'Yeah.'

Decker heard it before he felt it. A jarring concussion, as if somebody had thrown a cinderblock in the water near the boat. Instantly something nearly pulled the rod from his hands. On instinct Decker yanked back. The line screeched off the old reel in short bursts, bending the rod into an inverse U. The fish circled and broke the surface on the starboard side, toward the stern. Its back was banded in greenish black, its shoulders bronze, and its fat belly as pale as ice. The gills rattled like dice when the bass shook its huge mouth.

'Damn!' Decker grunted.

'She's a big girl,' Skink said, just watching.

The fish went deep, tugged some, sat some, then dug for the roots of the lilies. Awestruck, Decker more or less hung on. Skink knew what would happen, and it did. The fish cleverly wrapped the line in the weeds and broke off with a loud crack. The battle had lasted but three minutes.

'Shit,' Decker said. He turned on the lantern and studied the broken end of the monofilament.

'Ten-pounder,' Skink said. 'Easy.' He swung his legs over the plank, braced his boots on the transom, and started to row.

Decker asked, 'You got another one of those eels?'

'We're going in,' Skink said.

'One more shot, captain—I'll do better next time.'

'You did fine, Miami. You got what you needed, a jolt of the ballbuster fever. Save me from listening to a lot of stupid questions down the road.' Skink picked up the pace with the oars.

Decker said, 'I've got to admit, it was fun.'

'That's what they say.'

During the trip back to shore, Decker couldn't stop thinking about the big bass, the tensile shock of its strength against his own muscles. Maybe there was something mystical to Bobby Clinch's obsession. The experience, Decker admitted to himself, had been exhilarating and pure; the solitude and darkness of the lake shattered by a brute from the deep. It was nothing like fishing on the drift boats, or dropping shrimp off the bridges in the Keys. This was different. Decker felt like a little kid, all wired up.

'I want to try this again,' he told Skink.

'Maybe someday, after the dirty work is over. You want to hear my theory?'

'Sure.' Decker had been waiting all damn night.

Skink said: 'Robert Clinch found out about the cheating. He knew who and he knew how. I think he was after the proof when they caught him on the bog.'

'Who caught him? Dickie Lockhart?'

Skink said, 'Dickie wasn't in the other boat I saw. He's not that stupid.'

'But he sent somebody to kill Bobby Clinch.'

'I'm not sure of that, Miami. Maybe it was a trap, or maybe Clinch just turned up in the worst place at the worst time.'

'What was Bobby looking for?' Decker asked.

Skink made three swipes of the oars before answering. 'A fish,' he said. 'A particular fish.'

That was Skink's theory, or what he intended to share of it. Twice Decker asked Skink what he meant, what particular fish, but Skink never replied. He rowed mechanically. The only sounds on the lake were his husky breaths and the rhythmic squeak of the rusty oarlocks. Slowly the details of the southern shoreline, including the crooked silhouette of the cabin, came into Decker's view. The trip was almost over.

Decker asked, 'You come out here every night?'

'Only when I'm in the mood for fish for dinner,' Skink replied.

'And you always use that big purple worm?'

'Nope,' Skink said, beaching the boat with a final stroke, 'what I usually use is a twelve-gauge.'

When R. J. Decker got back to the motel, he found a note from the night manager on the door. The note said Ott Pickney had called, but it didn't say why.

Decker already had the key in the lock when he heard a car pull in and park. He glanced over his shoulder, half-expecting to see Ott's perky Toyota flatbed.

What he saw instead was a tangerine Corvette.

6

Decker had a poor memory for names. Terrific eye for faces, but no name recollection whatsoever.

'It was a spring-fashion shoot,' Lanie Gault prodded. 'You acted like you'd rather be in Salvador.'

'I think I remember now,' Decker said. 'On Sanibel Beach, right?'

Lanie nodded. She sat on the edge of the bed, looking relaxed. Strange motel room, strange man, but still relaxed. Decker was not nearly so comfortable.

'Must have been five, six years ago,' he said. Trying to be professional, trying not to look at her legs.

'You've put on some weight,' Lanie said. 'It's good weight, though, don't worry.'

Decker turned on the television, looking for Letterman. He stopped flipping channels when he found one of those dreadful syndicated game shows. He sat down heavily and pretended to watch the tube.

'Do I look any different?' Lanie asked. She didn't say it as if she were begging a compliment.

'You look great,' Decker said, turning from the TV.

'Believe it or not, I think I've still got the swimsuit I wore for the pictures.'

On this detail Decker's memory was clear. Yellow one-piece thong, the kind that required some touch-up shaving.

Lanie said, 'You screwed one of the other models, didn't you?'

Decker sighed.

'She was talking about it on the drive back to Boca.'

'I hope she was kind,' Decker said. Diane was her name. A very nice lady. Hadn't seemed like the magpie type, but here you had it. He'd kept a phone number, except now she was married to a large Puerto Rican police captain. Her number was filed under S, for suicide.

Lanie Gault kicked her sandals off and sat cross-legged on the bedspread. She wore a fruity-colored sleeveless top and white shorts. Her arms and legs, even the tops of her feet, were a golden tan. So were her neck and chest, the part Decker could see. He wondered about the rest, wondered if it was worth a try. Bad timing, he decided.

'Can we turn that shit down, please?' Lanie said. On the television a young couple from Napa had just won an Oldsmobile Cutlass, and the audience was going nuts.

Decker twisted down the volume.

She said, 'Look, I'm sorry about this morning. I'd had a couple martinis to get me going.'

'Don't blame you,' Decker said.

'I must have sounded like a coldhearted whore, which I'm not.'

Decker went along with it. 'It was a tough funeral,' he said, 'especially with the wife there.'

'You said it.'

'Before you tell me about Bobby,' Decker said, 'I'd like to know how you knew about me. And why I was here.' He guessed it was her brother but he wanted to make sure.

'Dennis called me,' Lanie said.

'Why?'

'Because he knows I've got a personal interest. Or maybe he's just feeling guilty about Bobby and wants me to know he's not giving up on it.'

Or maybe he wants you to try me out, Decker thought.

Lanie said, 'I met Bobby Clinch at a bass tournament in Dallas two summers ago. I was doing outdoor layouts for the Neiman-Marcus catalog—beach togs, picnic wear, stuff like that. Dennis happened to be in town for this big tournament, so I drove out to the reservoir one afternoon, just to say hi. Must have been sixty boats, a hundred guys, and they all looked exactly the same. They dressed alike, walked alike, talked alike, chewed tobacco alike. All dragging fish to be weighed. Afterward they gathered around this tall chalk-board to see who was ahead in the points. Christ, I thought I'd died and gone to redneck hell.'

'Then Bobby came along.'

'Right,' Lanie said. 'He said hello, introduced himself. It sounds corny, but I could tell he was different from the others.'

'Corny' was not the word for how it sounded. Decker listened politely anyway. He figured there was a love scene coming.

Lanie said, 'That night, while the rest of the guys were playing poker and getting bombed, he took me out on the reservoir in his boat, just the two of us. I'll never forget it, it was a crescent moon, not a cloud anywhere.' She laughed gently and her eyes dropped. 'We wound up making it out on the water. In the bow of Bobby's boat was this fancy pedestal seat that spun around . . . and that's what we did. Lucky we didn't capsize.'

This girl, Decker thought, has a wondrous imagination.

'Bobby wasn't one of these full-time tournament freaks,' Lanie said. 'He had a good job laying cable for the phone company. He fished four, maybe five pro events a year, so he wasn't a serious threat to anybody. He had no enemies, Decker. All the guys liked Bobby.'

'So what made him different?' Decker asked.

'He enjoyed himself more,' Lanie said. 'He seemed so happy just to be out there . . . and those were the best nights for us, after he'd spent a day on the lake. Even if he hadn't caught a thing, he'd be happy. Laughing, oh brother, he'd laugh at the whole damn ritual. Bobby loved fishing, that's for sure, but at least he saw how crazy it looked from the outside. And that's more than I can say for my brother.'

R. J. Decker got up and switched off the TV. This was the part he'd been waiting for.

'Did Dennis tell you exactly why he hired me?'

'No,' Lanie said, 'but it can only be one thing. The cheating.'

As if it were no secret.

'Dennis knows Dickie Lockhart's been rigging the tournaments,' she said. 'It's all he talks about. At first he actually tried to hire some killers. He said that's what Hemingway would have done.'

'No, Hemingway would have done it himself.'

'About six months ago Dennis flew down two mob guys from Queens. Offered them eighty-five grand to bump off Dickie and grind the body into puppy chow. My brother didn't know one of the creeps was working for the feds—Sal something-or-other. He blabbed the whole crazy story. Luckily no one at the FBI believed it, but for a while Dennis was scared out of his pants. At least it cured him of the urge to kill Dickie Lockhart. Now he says he'll settle for an indictment.'

'So your brother's next move,' R. J. Decker said, 'was to hire me.'

Lanie shook her head. 'Bobby.'

Decker had been hoping she wouldn't say that.

'Dennis met Bobby on the pro circuit and they hit it off right away. They even fished together in a few of the buddy tournaments, and always finished in the loot. Dennis told Bobby his suspicions about Lockhart and offered him a ton of money to get the proof.'

'What could Bobby do that your brother couldn't do himself?'

'Snoop,' Lanie said, 'inconspicuously. Everybody knows Dennis has a hard-on for Dickie Lockhart. Dickie knows it too, and he's damn careful with Dennis around. So my brother's plan was to pull out of the next few tournaments—claim the family business as an excuse—and hope that Dickie got careless.'

'With Bobby Clinch watching every move.'

'Exactly.'

Decker asked, 'How much money did Dennis offer him?'

'Plenty. Bobby wasn't greedy, but he wanted enough to be able to get out of his marriage. See, he wanted Clarisse to have the house, free and clear. He'd never just walk out on her and the kids.'

R. J. Decker wasn't exactly moved to tears. Lanie's story was mucky, and Decker was ready to say goodnight.

'Did your brother know about you and Bobby?' he asked.

'Sure he did. Dennis never said a word, but I'm sure he knew.' Lanie Gault put her hands under her chin. 'I thought he might bring it up, after Bobby was killed. Just a note or a phone call—

something to let on that he knew I was hurting. Not Dennis. The sonofabitch has Freon in his veins, I'm warning you. My brother wants to nail Dickie Lockhart and if you happen to die in the chase he won't be sending a wreath to the funeral. Just another replacement. Like you.'

The possibility of being murdered over a dead fish did not appeal to R. J. Decker's sense of adventure. He had photographed men who had died for less, and many who had died for more. Over the years he had adopted a carrion fly's unglamorous view of death: it didn't really matter how you got that way, it stunk just the same.

'You think Lockhart killed your boyfriend?' Decker asked Lanie.

'Who else would do it?'

'You're sure it was no accident?'

'Positive,' Lanie said. 'Bobby knew every log in that lake. He could've run it blindfolded.'

Decker was inclined to believe her. 'Who owns Dickie's TV show?' he asked.

'The Outdoor Christian Network. You heard of it?'

'TV Bible geysers,' Decker said.

Lanie straightened, as if working out a crick in her spine. 'More than old-time religion,' she said. 'OCN is quite the modern conglomerate. They're into health insurance, unit trusts, oil futures, real-estate development . . .'

'I'll check into it,' Decker promised. 'I'm tired, Lanie. I've got a rotten drive tomorrow.'

She nodded, got up, and slipped into her sandals. She stood in front of the mirror and brushed through her hair in brisk, sure strokes.

'One more thing,' Decker said. 'Out at the cemetery, how did you know which one was me? Sanibel was a long time ago.'

Lanie laughed. 'You kidding?'

'Don't tell me I stood out.'

'Yeah, you did,' she said, 'but Dennis wired me a picture, in case I wasn't sure.'

'A picture.'

Lanie reached in her purse. 'Courtesy of the booking desk at the Dade County Jail.'

Decker recognized the old mug shots. Cute move, Dennis. Just a touch of the hot needle.

'I've seen friendlier smiles,' Lanie said, studying the police photos. 'You still taking pictures, Decker?'

'Once in a while.'

'Maybe you could do me sometime. I'm thinking of going back into modeling.' Lanie put the purse under her arm and opened the door. 'It's been so long I've probably forgotten how to pose.'

You're doing just fine, Decker thought. 'Good night,' he said.

Decker had to go back to Miami to soup some film for an insurance-fraud trial, set for the coming week. He figured he'd use the long drive to decide what to do about Dennis Gault and the fishing scam. His instincts about the cast of characters told him to drop the case—but what about the death of Bobby Clinch?

As he packed his suitcase Decker heard himself say: So what? He hated the way he sounded because he sounded like every lazy asshole cop or P.I. he'd ever met. Big cases, big problems. Go for the easy bucks, that would be the advice.

Yet Decker knew he couldn't drop it now. Bobby Clinch got killed because he went snooping for a secret fish; such a remarkable crime couldn't easily be ignored. The idea that somebody had become homicidal over a largemouth bass was perversely appealing to Decker, and it made him want very much to get a picture of the guys who did it.

First he needed to meet with Gault again, a distasteful prospect. He could do it this evening, back in Miami; it wouldn't take long. From the motel room Decker called and made reservations for the following night on a seven-P.M. United flight to New Orleans. The Cajun Invitational Bass Classic was this week's stop on the professional fishing tour, and a good place for Decker to get his first glimpse of Dickie Lockhart in action. He had seen the famous TV angler's face on a billboard across from a bait shop on Route 222: 'Dickie Lockhart Loves Happy Gland Fish Scent! So Do Lunker Bass!' Decker had been so intrigued by the billboard that he'd asked a man at the bait shop if the Happy Gland company made a formula for humans. The man at the bait shop dutifully checked behind the counter and said no.

Before leaving Harney, Decker tried to call Ott Pickney at the newspaper. Sandy Kilpatrick, the birdlike editor, said Ott had gone out early to do some interviews. The note of concern in Kilpatrick's voice suggested that pre-lunchtime enterprise was uncharacteristic behavior for Ott. Decker left a message to have Ott call him that night in Miami.

At that moment Ott Pickney was slurping down black coffee at Culver Rundell's bait shop on the southern shore of Lake Jesup. Culver Rundell was behind the counter and his brother Ozzie was out back dipping shiners. Ott was trying to strike up a conversation about Bobby Clinch. Ott had set his reporter's notebook on the counter twenty minutes earlier, and the pages were still blank.

'Sorry I'm not much help,' Culver Rundell said. 'Bobby was a nice guy, a pretty good basser. That's about all I can tell you. Also, he favored spinnerbaits.'

'Spinnerbaits.'

'Over plastic worms,' Culver Rundell explained.

Ott Pickney could not bring himself to transcribe this detail.

'I understand you were here when they brought in the body,' Ott said.

'I was. The Davidson boys found him. Daniel and Desi.'

'How awful,' Ott said.

'It was my truck that took him to the morgue.'

Ott said nothing about the autopsy. Dr. Pembroke was third on his list of interview subjects.

'I hated to miss the funeral,' Culver Rundell said, 'but we had one hellacious busy morning.'

'The casket was made out of Bobby's boat.'

'So I heard!' Culver said. 'What a neat idea. I wisht I coulda seen it.'

Ott tapped his Bic pen on the counter and said amiably, 'I was amazed how handsomely they did it.'

'What I heard,' said Culver Rundell, 'is they got a regular oak coffin from Pearl Brothers, sanded off the finish, and paneled it with long strips from the hull of the boat. Cost another two grand, I know for a fact. The bass club is paying.'

Ott Pickney said, 'And who would have done the work, the funeral home?'

'Naw, it was Larkin's shop.'

Larkin was a carpenter. He had done all the benches at the Harney County Courthouse, and also the front doors on the new U.S. Post Office.

'He's the best in town,' Culver Rundell remarked. He thought he was doing Larkin a favor, a little free publicity for the business.

'Well, he did a damn fine job with the coffin,' Ott said. He left two one-dollar bills on the countertop, said good-bye, and drove immediately to Larkin's shop. Ott hoped there would be something left to see, though he had no idea exactly what to look for.

The shop was more of an old A-frame barn with a fancy new electric garage door, the kind used on those big import-export warehouses in western Dade County. The door to the wood shop was up. Ott saw plenty of raw furniture but no carpenters. It turned out Larkin wasn't there; it was a slow morning, so he'd gone fishing. Naturally.

A young black apprentice carpenter named Miller asked the reporter what he wanted.

'I'm doing a story about Bobby Clinch, the young man who died in that terrible boating accident at the Bog.'

'Yeah,' Miller said. His workshirt was soaked. Sawdust and curlicued pine shavings stuck to his coal-black arms. He looked as if he were in the middle of a project, and wanted to get back to it.

Pushing things, Ott Pickney said, 'This shop did the custom work on the coffin, right?'

'Yeah,' Miller said, 'the boat job.'

'It was really something,' Ott said. 'How did you guys do that? You won't mind if I take some notes—'

'Mr. Larkin did it all by himself,' Miller said. 'I guess he knew the deceased.'

That last word rattled Ott. He glanced up from the notebook to catch the cutting look in Miller's eye. The look said: Don't patronize me, pal, I got better things to do.

'Blue metal-flake casket, man. Looked like a giant fucking cough drop.'

Ott cleared his throat. 'I'm sure they meant well . . . I mean, it was supposed to be symbolic. Sort of a farewell gesture.'

'I'll give you a farewell gesture—' Miller said, but then the phone rang in the far corner of the workshed. The apprentice hurried off, and Ott quietly poked through the shop. He wondered why he'd never gotten the hang of talking to black people, why they always looked at him as if he were a cockroach.

Miller was talking in a loud voice into the phone. Something about a walnut dining table and an unpaid bill.

Ott Pickney slipped out the front way, then walked around to the back of the shop where Miller couldn't see him. Against one wall stood two long green dumpsters filled with fresh-cut lumber remnants. They were the sweetest-smelling dumpsters Ott had ever come across. He stood on his tiptoes and looked inside. In the first he saw a pile of wooden chips, blocks, odd triangles and rectangles, a broken sawhorse, a hogshead, empty cans of resin and varnish; Mr. Larkin's predictable junk.

At the second dumpster Ott found a similar jumble of pulp, plywood, and two-by-fours, but also something else: molded chunks of blue-sparkled fiberglass. It was the remains of Bobby Clinch's Ranger bass boat, sawed to pieces in the customizing of the fisherman's coffin.

Ott boosted himself, using an empty gallon can of Formsby's turned upside down. He stuffed the notebook into the back pocket of his trousers and stretched over the rim of the dumpster so his arms could reach the wreckage. As he sifted through the fiberglass scraps, Ott realized it was impossible to tell how these jigsawed pieces had ever comprised a nineteen-foot boat.

The one fragment he recognized was the console. Ott found it in the bottom of the dumpster.

Every expensive bass boat has a console, a recessed cockpit designed to give anglers the same sensation as if they were racing the Daytona 500 instead of merely demolishing the quietude of a lake.

To Ott Pickney, the cockpit of Bobby Clinch's fishing boat more closely resembled the pilot's deck of a 747. Among the concave dials were a compass, a sonic depth recorder, a digital tachometer, an LED gauge showing water temperature at five different depths, power-tilt adjusters, trim tabs, a marine radio and an AM-FM stereo, with a tape deck. All these electronics obviously were ruined from being submerged in the lake, but Ott was fascinated anyway. He hoisted the console out of the dumpster to take a closer look.

He set the heavy piece on his lap and imagined himself at the controls of a two-hundred-horsepower speedboat. He pretended to hunker behind the Plexiglass windshield and aim the boat along a winding creek. The only trouble was, the steering wheel wouldn't budge in his hands.

Ott turned the console over, thinking the shaft had gotten snarled in all the loose wiring. But that wasn't the problem; the problem was a short length of black nylon rope. The rope had been wrapped tightly around the base of the steering column beneath the console, where it wouldn't be seen. Ott plucked fruitlessly at the coils; the rope had been tied on with authority. The steering was completely jammed.

Which meant, of course, that the direction of Bobby Clinch's boat had been fixed. It meant that Clinch himself needn't have been at the wheel at the instant of the crash. It meant that the fisherman probably was already dying or injured when the ghost-driven bass boat flipped over and tunneled bow-first into the chilly water.

Ott Pickney did not grasp this scenario as swiftly as he might have. It was dawning on him slowly, but he became so engrossed in the contemplation that he lost track of his surroundings. He heard footsteps and looked up, expecting to see Miller, the carpenter's black apprentice. Instead there were three other men, dressed in the standard local garb—caps, jeans, flannel shirts. One of the visitors carried a short piece of lumber, a second carried a loop of heavy wire; the other just stood dull-eyed, fists at his side. Ott started to say something but his greeting died beneath the grinding whine of a carpenter's table saw; Miller back at work inside the shed. The three men stepped closer. Only one was a local, but he recognized Ott Pickney and knew that the reporter could identify him. Unfortunately for Ott, none of the men wished to see their names in the paper.

7

Dennis Gault was holding a stack of VCR cassettes when he answered the door. He was wearing salmon shorts and a loose mesh top that looked like it would have made an excellent mullet seine. Gault led R. J. Decker to the living room, which was filled with low flat-looking furniture. The predominant hue was cranberry.

Gault put a cassette in the video recorder and told Decker to sit down. 'Want a drink?' Gault asked. He smelled like he was on his tenth Smirnoff.

Decker took a cold beer.

A fishing show came on the television screen. Gault used the remote control to fast-forward the tape. Two guys in a bass boat, Decker could tell; casting and reeling, casting and reeling, occasionally hauling in a small fish. Fast-forward was the only way to endure this, Decker decided.

A commercial came on and Gault abruptly hit the freeze button. 'Theeeeere's Dickie!' he sang derisively.

On the screen Dickie Lockhart stood by the side of a lake, squinting into the sun. He was wearing a crisply pressed basser's jumpsuit, desert tan; his cap was off and his hair was blow-dried to perfection. He was holding up a sixteen-ounce bottle of Happy Gland Fish Scent, and grinning.

'Does that stuff really work?' Decker asked. A bit off the point, but he was curious.

'Hard to say,' Gault replied. 'Stinks like a sack of dead cats, that's for sure.'

He speeded the tape forward until he found the segment he'd been searching for. He froze the picture as the angler in the bow of the boat hoisted a fat black bass to show the camera.

'There! Look now, pay attention!' Gault said. Excitedly he shuffled on bare knees across the floor to the television screen, one of those custom five-foot monsters that eats up the whole wall. 'There, Decker, look. This fish is a ringer!'

'How can you tell?'

'See here, the eyes are flat. Not cloudy yet, but flat as tile. And the color's washed out of the flanks. No vertical stripes, not a one. Muck is the color of this fish.'

'It doesn't look too healthy,' Decker agreed.

'Healthy? Man, this fish is DOA. Check the dorsal. The guy is fanning the fins for the camera. Why? 'Cause they'd fold up otherwise. This fish is de-fucking-ceased.'

'But they just showed the fisherman reeling it in,' Decker said.

'Wrong. Now watch.' Gault backed up the tape and replayed the fight. The rod was bent, the water around the boat boiled and splashed—but the angles and the editing of the video made it impossible to see the actual size of the bass. Until the fisherman lifted it for the camera.

'That rookie caught a fish,' Gault said, 'but not *this* fish.' He hit a button and rewound the tape. 'Want to watch another one?'

'That won't be necessary,' Decker said.

'You see how easy it is to cheat.'

'For a TV show, sure.'

'It's even easier in a tournament,' Gault said, 'especially when your partner's in on it. And the weighmaster too. Not to mention the goddamn sponsors.' He went to the kitchen and came back with a beer for Decker and a fresh vodka-tonic for himself.

'Tell me about what happened in Harney,' he said.

'Met a guy named Skink,' Decker said.

Gault whistled and arched his eyebrows. 'A real fruitbar. I fished with him once on the St. John's.'

'He's going to help me catch Lockhart.'

'Not on my nickel!' Gault protested.

'I need him.'

'He's a maniac.'

'I don't think so.'

'He eats dead animals off the road!'

'Waste not, want not,' Decker said. 'He's the only one up there I'd trust. Without him I quit the case.'

Gault folded his hands. Decker drank his beer.

'All right,' Gault said, 'but be careful. That guy's got Texas Tower written all over him, and neither of us wants to be there if he ever reaches the top.'

What Gault meant was: If there's trouble, don't drag my name into it.

'What else did you do?' he asked Decker.

'Went to a funeral.'

Gault licked his lower lip nervously.

'Robert Clinch,' Decker said, 'late of your hire. Nice of you to tell me.'

Gault toyed with the stack of fishing videotapes, pretending to organize them. Without looking up, he asked, 'Do they know what exactly happened?'

'The coroner says it was accidental.'

Gault smiled thinly. 'We know that's horseshit, don't we? The only question in my mind is: How'd they do it?'

Decker said, 'My question is: Who?'

'Who? Dickie Lockhart, that's who!' Gault said. 'Don't be stupid, man. Dickie knew I was closing in and he knew Bobby was working for me. What do you mean—*who*?'

'You're probably right,' Decker said, 'but I'd like to be sure.'

'Haven't you been listening? Christ, don't tell me I've hired a complete moron.'

'I met your sister,' Decker said. He liked to save the best for last.

'Elaine?' Gault said. He looked most uncomfortable, just as Decker had expected. It was worth the wait.

'We had a nice chat,' Decker said. He wanted Gault to be the one who finished the conversation. He didn't want to be the one to take it any further, but he had to. He needed to find out if Gault knew everything.

'You didn't tell me a couple important things. You didn't tell me about Clinch and you didn't tell me you had a sister up in Harney.' Decker's voice had the slightest sting of irritation.

'She gets around, my sister.' Gault drained his glass. His face was getting red.

Stubborn bastard, Decker thought, have it your way.

'You knew she was having an affair with Bobby Clinch,' he said evenly.

'Says who?' Gault snapped. The red became deeper.

'Lanie.'

'*Lanie?*'

'That's what they call her.'

'Oh, is it now?'

'Personally, I don't care if she's screwing the entire American Legion post,' Decker said, 'but I need to know what you know.'

'You better shut your mouth, ace!' Gault's face was actually purple now.

Decker thought: We really hit a nerve here. But from the murderous looks he was getting, he figured now wasn't the time to pursue it. He got up and headed for the door but Gault grabbed his arm and snarled, 'Wait just a minute.' Decker shook free and—rather gently, he thought—guided Gault backward until his butt hit the sofa.

'Good-bye now,' Decker said.

But Gault had lost it. He lunged and got Decker by the throat. Gagging, Decker felt manicured fingernails digging into the meat of his neck. he stared up the length of Gault's brown arms and saw every vein and tendon swollen. The man's cheeks were flushed, but his lips twitched like bloodless worms.

The two men toppled across the low sofa with Gault on top, amber eyeglasses askew. He was spitting and hollering about what a shiteating punk Decker was, while Decker was trying to squirm free from the neckhold before he passed out. His vision bloomed kaleidoscopic and his skull roared. The blood in his head was trying to go south but Dennis Gault wouldn't let it.

A cardinal rule of being a successful private investigator is: Don't slug your own clients. But sometimes exceptions had to be made. Decker made one. He released his fruitless grip on Gault's wrists and, in a clumsy but effective pincer motion, hammered him in the ribs with both fists. As the wind exploded from Gault's lungs, Decker bucked him over and jumped on top.

Dennis Gault had figured R. J. Decker to be strong, but he was unprepared for the force now planted on his sternum. As his own foolish rage subsided, he fearfully began to wonder if Decker was just getting warmed up.

Gault felt but never saw the two sharp punches that flattened his nose, shattered his designer frames, and closed one eye. Later, when he awoke and dragged himself to the bathroom, he would marvel in the mirror that only two punches could have done so much damage. He found a pail of ice cubes waiting on the night-stand, next to a bottle of aspirin.

And a handwritten note from R. J. Decker: 'The fee is now one hundred, asshole.'

Harney was such a small county that it was difficult to mount a serious high-school athletic program. There was, after all, only one high school. The enrollment fluctuated from about one hundred and seventy-five to two hundred and ten, so the pool of sports talent was relatively limited. In those rare and precious years when Harney High fielded a winning team, the star athletes were encouraged to flunk a year or two in order to delay gradu-ation and prolong the school's victory streak. A few idealistic teachers spoke out against this unorthodox display of school spirit, but the truth was that many of the top jocks were D students anyway and had finally intended to spend six or seven years in high school.

Football was the sport that Harney loved most; unfortunately, the football team of Harney High had never compiled a winning record. One season, in desperation they even scheduled three games against the wimpiest parochial schools in Duval County. Harney lost every game. The coach was fired, and moved out of town.

Consequently the Harney High athletic department decided to concentrate on another sport, basketball. The first order of busi-ness was to build a gymnasium with a basketball court and some portable bleachers. The second move was to send a cautious delegation of coaches and teachers into the black neighborhood to recruit some good basketball players. A few old crackers in Harney huffed and swore about having to watch a bunch of skinny spooks tear up and down the court, and about how it wasn't fair to the good Christian white kids, but then it was pointed out that the good Christian white kids were mostly slow and fat and couldn't make a lay-up from a trampoline.

Once the basketball program was established, the team performed better than anyone had expected. The first year it made it to the regionals, the next to the state playoffs in the Class Four-A division. True, the star center of the Harney team was twenty-seven years old, but he looked much younger. No one raised a peep. As the team kept winning, basketball eventually captured Harney County's heart.

The Harney High basketball team was called the Armadillos. It was not the first choice of names. Originally the school had wanted its team to be the Rattlers, but a Class AA team in Orlando already claimed that nickname. Second choice was the Bobcats, except that a Bible college in Leesburg had dibs on that one. It went on like this for several months—the Tigers, the Hawks, the Panthers; all taken, the good names—until finally it came down to either the Owls or the Armadillos. The school board voted to name the team the Owls since it had six fewer letters and the uniforms would be much less expensive, but the student body rebelled and gathered hundreds of signatures on a typed petition declaring that the Harney Owls was 'a pussy name and nobody'll ever go to any of the damn games.' Without comment the school board reversed its vote.

Once the Harney Armadillos started kicking ass on the basketball court, the local alumnae decided that the school needed an actual mascot, something on the order of the famous San Diego Chicken, only cheaper. Ideas were submitted in a local contest sponsored by the *Sentinel*, and a winner was chosen from sixteen entries. Working on commission, one of the matrons from the Sewing Club stitched together an incredible costume out of old automobile seat covers and floormats.

It was a six-foot armadillo, complete with glossy armored haunches, a long anteater nose (salvaged from a Hoover canister vacuum), and a scaly tail.

The mascot was to be known as Davey Dillo, and he would perform at each of the home games. By custom he would appear before the opening tipoff, breakdancing to a tape of Michael Jackson's 'Billie Jean.' Then at halftime Davey Dillo would stage a series of clumsy stunts on a skateboard, to whatever music the band had learned that week.

Davey Dillo's was not a polished act, but the youngsters (at least those under four) thought it was the funniest thing ever to hit the Harney gymnasium. The grown-ups thought the man inside the armadillo costume had a lot of guts.

On the evening of January 12 the Harney Armadillos were all set to play the Valencia Cropdusters in a battle for first place in the mid-state Four-A division. Inside the gymnasium sat two hundred fans, more than the coaches and cheerleaders had ever seen; so many fans that, when the national anthem was sung, it actually sounded on key.

The last words—'home of the brave!'—were Davey Dillo's regular cue to prance onto the basketball court and wave a single sequined glove on one of his armadillo paws. Then he would start the dance.

But on this night the popular mascot did not appear.

After a few awkward moments somebody cut off the Michael Jackson tape and put on Ricky Scaggs, while the coaches ordered the players to search the gym. In all two years of his existence, Davey Dillo had never missed a sporting event at Harney High (even the track and field), so nobody knew what to think. Soon the crowd, even the Valencia High fans, began to chant, 'We want the Dillo! We want the Dillo!'

But Davey Dillo was not in the locker room suiting up. He wasn't oiling the wheels on his skateboard. He wasn't mending the pink-washcloth tongue of his armadillo costume.

Davey Dillo—rather, the man who created and portrayed Davey Dillo—was missing.

His identity was the worst-kept secret in Harney County. It was Ott Pickney, of course.

8

R. J. Decker lived in a trailer court about a mile off the Palmetto Expressway. The trailer was forty feet long and ten feet wide, and made of the finest sheet aluminum. Inside the walls were covered with cheap paneling that had warped in the tropical humidity; the threadbare carpet was the color of liver. For amenities the trailer featured a badly wired kitchenette, a drip of a shower, and a decrepit air conditioner that leaked gray fluid all over the place. Decker had converted the master closet to a darkroom, and it was all the space he needed; it was a busy week if he used it more than once or twice.

He didn't want to live in a trailer park, hated the very idea, but it was all he could afford after the divorce. Not that his wife had cleaned him out, she hadn't; she had merely taken what was hers, which amounted to practically everything of value in the marriage. Except for the cameras. In aggregate, R. J. Decker's camera equipment was worth twice as much as the trailer where he lived. He took no special steps to protect or conceal the cameras because virtually all his trailer-park neighbors owned free-running pit bulldogs, canine psychopaths that no burglar dared to challenge.

For some reason the neighbors' dogs never bothered Catherine. Decker was printing film when she dropped by. As soon as he let her in the door, she wrinkled her nose. 'Yuk! Hypo.' She knew the smell of the fixer.

'I'll be done in a second,' he said, and slipped back into the darkroom. He wondered what was up. He wondered where James was. James was the chiropractor she had married less than two weeks after the divorce.

The day Catherine had married Dr. James was also the day

Decker had clobbered the burglar. Catherine had always felt guilty, as if she'd lighted the fuse. She'd written him two or three times a month when he was at Apalachee; once she'd even mailed a Polaroid of herself in a black bra and panties. Somehow it got by the prison censor. 'For old times,' she'd printed on the back of the snapshot, as a joke. Decker was sure Dr. James had no idea. Years after the marriage Catherine still called or stopped by, but only at night and never on weekends. Decker always felt good for a little while afterward.

He washed a couple of eight-by-tens and hung the prints from a clothesline strung across the darkroom. He could have turned on the overheads without harm to the photographs, but he preferred to work in the red glow of the safelight. Catherine tapped twice and came in, shutting the door quickly. She knew the routine.

'Where's the mister?' Decker asked.

'Tampa,' Catherine said. 'Big convention. Every other weekend is a big convention. What've we got here?' She stood on her toes and studied the prints. 'Who's the weight-lifter?'

'Fireman out on ninety-percent disability.'

'So what's he doing hulking out at Vic Tanny?'

'That's what the insurance company wants to know,' Decker said.

'Pretty dull stuff, Rage.' Sometimes she called him Rage instead of R.J. It was a pet name that had something to do with his temper. Decker didn't mind it, coming from Catherine.

'I've got a good one cooking,' he said.

'Yeah? Like what?'

She looked great in the warm red light. Catherine was a knock-out. Was, is, always will be. An expensive knockout.

'I'm investigating a professional fisherman,' Decker said, 'for cheating in tournaments. Allegedly.'

'Come on, Rage.'

'I'm serious.'

Catherine folded her arms and gave him a motherly look. 'Why don't you ask the paper for your old job back?'

'Because the paper won't pay me a hundred large to go fishing.'

Catherine said, 'Wow.'

She smelled wonderful. She knew Decker liked a certain perfume so she always wore it for him—what was the name? He couldn't remember. Something fashionably neurotic. Compulsion, that was it. A scent that probably wouldn't appeal to Dr. James, at least Decker hoped not. He wondered if Catherine was still on the same four-ounce bottle he'd bought for her birthday three years ago.

Decker tweezered another black-and-white of the goldbrick fireman out of the fixer and rinsed it down.

'No pictures of fish?' Catherine asked.

'Not yet.'

'Somebody is really gonna pay you a hundred thousand?'

'Well, at least fifty. That's if I get what he wants.'

She said, 'What are you going to do with all that money?'

'Try to buy you back.'

Catherine's laugh died in her throat. She looked hurt. 'That's not really funny, R.J.'

'I guess not.'

'You didn't mean it, did you?'

'No, I didn't mean it.'

'You've got a nasty streak.'

'I was beaten as a child,' Decker said.

'Can we get out of here? I'm getting high on your darn chemicals.'

Decker took her to a barbecue joint on South Dixie Highway. Catherine ordered half a chicken and iced tea, he had beer and ribs. They talked about a thousand little things, and Decker thought about how much fun it was to be with her, still. It wasn't a sad feeling, just wistful; he knew it would go away. The best feelings always did.

'Have you thought about New York?' Catherine asked.

The free-lance speech. Decker knew it by heart.

'Look at Foley. He had a cover shot on *Sports Illustrated* last summer,' she said.

Foley was another photographer who'd quit the newspaper and gone free-lance.

'Hale Irwin,' Decker said derisively.

'What?'

'That was Foley's big picture. A golfer. A fucking golfer, Catherine. That's not what I want to do, follow a bunch of Izod shirts around a hot golf course all day for one stupid picture.'

Catherine said, 'It was just an example, Rage. Foley's had plenty of business since he moved to New York. And not just golfers, so don't give me that pissed-off look.'

'He's a good shooter.'

'But you're better, by a mile.' She reached across the table and pinched his arm gently. 'Hey, it doesn't have to be heavy-duty. No Salvadors, no murders, no dead girls in Cadillacs. Just stick to the soft stuff, Rage, you've earned it.'

Decker guessed it was about time for the all-that-wasted-talent routine.

Catherine came through. 'I just hate to see you wasting all your talent,' she said. 'Snooping around like a thief, taking pictures of . . .'

'Guys who cheat insurance companies.'

'Yeah.'

Decker said, 'Maybe you're right.'

'Will you think about New York?'

'Take some of these ribs, I can't eat 'em all.'

'No, thanks, I'm full.'

'So tell me about the quack.'

'Stop it,' Catherine said. 'James's patients are wild about him. He's very generous with his time.'

'And the spine-cracking business is good.'

'Good, but it could be better,' Catherine said. 'James is talking about moving.'

Decker grinned. 'Let me guess where.'

Catherine reddened. 'His brother's got a practice on Long Island. It's going gangbusters, James says.'

'No shit?'

'Don't look so cocky, R.J. This has nothing to do with you.'

'So you wouldn't come see me,' Decker said. 'I mean, if I were to move to New York and you somehow wound up on Long Island, you wouldn't drop by and chat?'

Catherine wiped her hands on a napkin. 'Jesus, I don't know.'

Her voice was different now, the airy confidence gone. 'I don't know what I've done, R.J. Sometimes I wonder. James is special and I realize how lucky I am, but still . . . The man irons his socks, did I tell you that?'

Decker nodded. 'You called me from your honeymoon to tell me that.' From Honolulu she'd called.

'Yeah, well.'

'That's okay,' Decker said. 'I didn't mind.' It was better than losing her completely. He would miss her if the sock-ironing chiropractor whisked her away to New York.

'You know the hell of it?' Catherine said. 'My back's still killing me.'

Decker's telephone was ringing when he returned to the trailer. The man on the other end didn't need to identify himself.

'Hello, Miami.'

'Hey, captain.' Decker was surprised. Skink would do anything to avoid the phone.

'The Armadillo is dead,' said Skink.

Decker figured Skink was talking about his supper.

'You listening?' Skink said.

'The armadillo.'

'Yeah, your little pal from the newspaper.'

'Ott?'

'Officially he's only missing. Unofficially he's dead. You better get up here. It's time to go to work.'

Decker sat down at the kitchen counter. 'Start at the beginning,' he said. Gruffly Skink summarized the facts of the disappearance, closing with a neutral explanation of Ott Pickney's alter ego, Davey Dillo.

'They say he was very convincing,' Skink said, by way of condolence.

Decker had a hell of a hard time imagining Ott in an armadillo costume on a skateboard. He had a harder time imagining Ott dead.

'Maybe they just took him somewhere to put a scare in him,' he speculated.

'No way,' Skink said. 'I'll see you soon. Oh yeah—when you

get to Harney, don't check in at the motel. It's not safe. You'd better stay out here with me.'

'I'd rather not,' Decker said.

'Aw, it'll be loads of fun,' Skink said with a grunt. 'We can roast weenies and marshmallows.'

Decker drove all night. He shot straight up Interstate 95 and got off at Route 222, just west of Wabasso. Another ninety minutes and he was in Harney County. By the time he got to Skink's place on the lake, it was four-thirty in the morning. Already one or two bass boats were out on the water; Decker could hear the big engines chewing up the darkness.

At the sound of Decker's car Skink clumped onto the porch. He was fully dressed—boots, sunglasses, the orange weathersuit. Decker wondered if he slept in uniform.

'That's some driving,' Skink said. 'Get your gear and come on inside.'

Decker carried his duffel into the shack. It was the first time he had ventured beyond the porch, and he wasn't sure what to expect. Pelts, maybe. Wallpaper made from rabbit pelts.

As he pushed past the screen door, Decker was amazed by what he saw: books. Every wall had raw pine shelves to the ceiling, and every shelf was lined with books. The east wall was for classic fiction: Poe, Hemingway, Dostoyevsky, Mark Twain, Jack London, Faulkner, Fitzgerald, even Boris Pasternak. The west wall was for political biographies: Churchill, Sandburg's Lincoln, Hitler, Huey Long, Eisenhower, Joseph McCarthy, John F. Kennedy, even Robert Caro's Lyndon Johnson, though it looked like a book-club edition. The south wall was exclusively for reference books: the *Britannica, Current Biography*, the *Florida Statutes*, even the *Reader's Guide to Periodic Literature*. This was the wall of the shack that leaned so precipitously, and now Decker knew why; it held the heaviest books.

The shelves of the north wall were divided into two sections. The top was philosophy and the humanities. The bottom half was for children's books. The Hardy Boys, Tom Swift, Dr. Seuss. *Charlotte's Web* and the Brothers Grimm.

'What're you staring at?' Skink demanded.

'These are great books,' Decker said.

'No shit.'

In the middle of the floor there was a bare mattress and army blanket, but no pillow. The Remington was propped in a corner. The Coleman lantern hung from a slat in the ceiling; it offered only a fuzzy white light that would flare or dim as the mantle burned down. Decker thought Skink must do his reading in the daytime, or else he'd go blind.

Another car pulled up outside the shack. Decker glanced at Skink. He looked as if he were expecting somebody. He pushed open the screen door and a cop walked in; a state trooper. Stiff cowboy-style hat, pressed gray uniform (long sleeves of course). On one shoulder was a patch shaped like a Florida orange. The cop was almost as big as Skink. He was younger, though—a wedge of muscle from the waist up.

Decker noticed that this state trooper was different from most. Most were big, young, lean, and white. This trooper was black. Decker could not imagine a more miserable place than Harney County to be a black cop.

'This is Jim Tile,' Skink said. 'Jim, this is the guy I told you about.'

'Miami,' Tile said, and shook Decker's hand. Skink dragged a rocker and a folding chair in from the porch. Tile took off his hat and sat down in the rocker, Decker took the chair and Skink sat on the bare pine floor.

Decker said, 'What happened to Ott?'

'He's dead,' Skink said.

'But what the hell happened?'

Skink sighed and motioned to Jim Tile. 'Yesterday morning,' the trooper said, in a voice so deep it seemed to shake the lantern, 'I was on road patrol about dawn. Out on the Gilchrist Highway where it crosses Morgan Slough.'

'Some of the guys fish the slough when the water's up,' Skink cut in. 'You need a johnboat, and no outboard. Ten minutes from the highway and you're into heavy bass cover.'

Jim Tile said, 'So I see a pair of headlights back in the scrub. I can tell it's a truck. I pull off and park. Ten minutes go by and the truck hasn't moved, though the lights are still on. If it's two kids screwing they wouldn't be leaving the headlights on, so I go to check it out.'

'You're alone?' Decker asked.

Tile laughed. 'Nearest backup is in frigging Orlando. Yeah, I'm alone, you could say that. So I take my pumpgun and my Kevlar light and start slipping toward the truck through the scrub, moving close as I can to the big cypresses so whoever's back there won't see me. All of a sudden I hear a door slam and the truck comes tearing out of the bush. I go down in a crouch and jack a round into the shotgun, but they never slow down, just hit the highway and take off.'

'Three guys,' Skink said.

'In a dark green pickup,' Tile said. 'I'm pretty sure it was a Ford, but it wasn't local. I didn't catch the tag.'

'Did the men see you?' Decker asked.

'The one on the passenger side, no doubt about it.'

'Did you recognize him?'

'Let him finish, Miami,' Skink said.

'So I go down to where the truck was parked,' Tile said, 'right on the edge of the slough. I mean, from the tire tracks you could see they'd backed right up to the water. I figure they're poaching gators or maybe jacklighting a deer that came down to drink. Makes sense, except the ground is completely dry and clean. No blood, no skin, no shells, no nothing.'

'Except this,' Skink said. He reached into his rainsuit and took out a notebook. He handed it to R. J. Decker. It was a news reporter's notebook, the standard pocket-size spiral. On the front, written in blue ink, were the words: 'PICKNEY/CLINCH OBIT.' Decker could tell from the thinness of the notebook that some of the pages had been torn out. Those that remained were blank.

'It was under some palmetto,' Jim Tile said, 'maybe thirty feet from where the truck was parked.'

'You didn't find anything else?' Decker asked.

'No, sir.'

'Did you report this?'

'Report what?' Tile said. 'A truck parked in the bushes? Show me the law against that.'

'But you found this notebook and it belongs to a missing person.'

Skink shook his head. 'The basketball team says he's missing but nobody's filed a report yet. The sheriff may or may not get around to it.'

'What are you saying?' Decker asked.

'The sheriff's name is Earley Lockhart,' Skink said, 'as in Dickie. As in uncle. And, for what it's worth, he has a twelve-pound bass hanging behind his desk. Jim, tell Mr. Decker about your outstanding relationship with the Harney County sheriff's department.'

'No relationship,' Jim Tile said. 'Far as they're concerned, I don't exist. Wrong color. Wrong uniform.'

Skink said, 'Jim and I go way back. We depend on each other, especially when there's trouble. That's why Jim brought me the Armadillo's notebook.'

'But how do you know he's dead?' Decker said.

Skink stood up and turned off the Coleman. Out on the porch he picked up one of his spinning rods. 'You wanna drive?' he said to Jim Tile.

'Sure,' said the trooper, 'give Mr. Decker a ride in a real po-leece car.'

'I've had the privilege,' Decker said.

'Who was the guy in the truck, the one who recognized you?' Decker asked.

He was sitting in the back of the patrol car, behind the steel grate. Jim Tile was at the wheel; he glanced over at Skink, a crinkled orange mass on the passenger's side, and Skink nodded that it was all right.

'Man named Ozzie Rundell,' Jim Tile said.

'Halfwit,' Skink grumbled.

'Has he got a brother?' R. J. Decker had heard of Culver Rundell. Ott had mentioned him at Bobby Clinch's funeral. He'd said he was surprised not to see Culver at the service.

'Yeah, Culver,' Jim Tile said. 'He runs a bait shop on Lake Jesup.'

Decker thought it was probably the same one he'd stopped at a few days earlier. Culver couldn't have been the man behind the counter.

'He's smarter than Ozzie,' Skink remarked, 'but mildew is smarter than Ozzie.'

They were on a two-lane blacktop, no center line, no road signs. Decker didn't recognize the highway. Jim Tile was driving fast, one hand on the wheel. Through the grate Decker could see the speedometer prick ninety. He was glad there was no fog.

'How'd you meet the captain?' he asked Jim Tile.

'Used to work for him,' the trooper said.

'In Tallahassee,' Skink added. 'Long time ago.'

'What kind of work?' Decker asked.

'Scut work,' Skink said.

Decker was too tired to pursue it. He stretched out in the back seat and started to doze. He kept thinking about Ott Pickney and wondering what he was about to see. Skink and Jim Tile were silent up front. After about fifteen minutes Decker felt the patrol car brake and pull off the pavement. Now it bounced along with the sound of sticks and leaves scratching at the undercarriage.

Decker opened his eyes and sat up. They were at Morgan Slough.

Jim Tile got out first and checked around. The cool darkness was ebbing from the swamp; another half-hour and it would be dawn. Skink took his fishing rod from the car and went to the edge of the water, which was the burned color of black tea. The slough was a tangle of lilies and hydrilla, dead branches and live cypress knees. In the tall boughs hung tangled tresses of Spanish moss. The place looked prehistoric.

Jim Tile stood with his hands on his hips. Skink started to cast, reel in, cast again.

'What's going on?' Decker said, shaking off his drowsiness. The crisp winter air had a faint smoky smell.

'The plug I'm using is called a Bayou Boogie,' Skink said. 'Medium-fast sinker, two sets of treble hooks. I sharpened 'em earlier, before you got here. You probably noticed I put new line on the reel since you and I went out.'

'I didn't notice,' Decker muttered. All this way for a goddamn fishing lesson. Didn't these people ever just come out and say something?

'Fifteen-pound test Trilene,' Skink went on. 'You know how much weight this stuff'll lift?'

'No idea,' Decker said.

'Well—there we go!' Skink's fishing rod bent double. Instead of setting the hook, he pumped slowly, putting his considerable muscle into it. Whatever it was on the end of the line barely moved.

'You're snagged on a stump,' Decker said to Skink.

'Don't think so.'

Slowly it was coming up; somehow Skink was pulling the thing in. He pumped so hard that Decker was sure the rod would snap, then Skink would slack up, reel fast, and pump again. The line was stretched so tautly that it hummed.

'You're almost there,' Jim Tile said.

'Get ready!' Skink's voice strained under the effort.

He gave a mighty pull and something broke water. It was an iron chain. Skink's fishing lure had snagged in one of the links. Jim Tile knelt down and grabbed it before it could sink back into the slough. He unhooked the fishing lure, and Skink reeled in.

By now Decker knew what was coming.

Hand over hand, Jim Tile hauled on the chain. The wrong end came up first; it was an anchor. A new anchor, too, made of cast iron. A clump of hydrilla weed hung like a soggy green wig from the anchor's fork.

Jim Tile heaved it on shore. Wordlessly he started working toward the other end, the submerged end of the chain.

Instinctively, R. J. Decker thought of his cameras. They were locked in his car, back at Skink's shack. He felt naked without them, like the old days. Certain things were easier to take if you were looking through a camera; sometimes it was the only protection you had, the lens putting an essential distance between the eye and the horror. The horror of seeing a dead friend in the trunk of a Seville, for example. The distance existed only in the mind, of course, but sometimes the inside of a lens was a good place to hide. Decker hadn't felt like hiding there for a long time, but now he did. He wanted his cameras, longed for the familiar weight around his neck. Without the cameras he wasn't sure if he could look, but he knew he must. After all, that was the point of getting out of the business. To be able to look again, and to feel something.

Jim Tile struggled with the chain. Skink knelt beside him and loaned his weight to the tug.

'There now,' Skink said, breathing hard. The other end of the chain came out of the water in his right hand.

'Get it done,' said Jim Tile.

Tied to the end of the chain was a thin nylon rope. Skink's massive hands followed the rope down until the water was up to his elbows. His fingers foraged blindly below the surface; he looked like a giant raccoon hunting a crawfish.

'Ah!' he exclaimed.

Jim Tile stood up, wiped his hands on his uniform, and backed away. With a primordial grunt Skink lifted his morbid catch from the bottom of Morgan Slough.

'Oh God,' groaned R. J. Decker.

Ott Pickney floated up dead on the end of a fish stringer. Like a lunker bass, he had been securely fastened through both lips.

9

They were driving back toward Harney on the Gilchrist Highway.

'We can't just leave him there,' R. J. Decker said.

'No choice,' Skink said from the back seat of the patrol car.

'What do you mean? We've got a murder here. Last time I checked, that's still against the law, even in a shitbucket town like this.'

Jim Tile said, 'You don't understand.'

Skink leaned forward and mushed his face against the grating. 'How do we explain being out in the slough? A spade cop and a certifiable lunatic like me.' And an ex-con, Decker thought. From under the flowered shower cap Skink winked at him. 'It's Jim I'm really worried about, Miami. They'd love a shot at State Trooper Jim Tile, am I right?'

Decker said, 'Screw the locals, then. Go to the state attorney general and get a grand jury. We've got two dead men, first Clinch and now Ott Pickney. We can't let it lie.'

'We won't,' said Jim Tile.

Terrific, Decker thought, the three musketeers.

'What are you so afraid of?' he asked the trooper. 'You think they'd really try to frame us?'

'Worse,' said Jim Tile. 'They'll ignore us. Clinch was already ruled an accident.'

'But Ott's floating out there on a fish stringer,' Decker said. 'I think somebody might legitimately raise the question of foul play.'

Jim Tile pulled the car off the pavement and stopped. They were a mile and a half outside the town limits. A pair of headlights approached from the other direction.

'Duck down,' Jim Tile said.

Skink and Decker stayed low until the other car had passed. Then Skink climbed out with his fishing rod. 'Come on,' he said to Decker, 'we'll hoof it from here. It's best that nobody sees Jim with the two of us.'

Decker got out of the car. The sky in the east was turning a metallic pink.

'Explain it to him,' Jim Tile said to Skink, and drove away.

Decker started trudging down the highway. He felt a hundred years old. He wished he were back in Miami, that's how rotten he felt. He was trying to remember if Ott Pickney had any kids, or an ex-wife somewhere. It was entirely possible there was nobody, just the orchids.

'I'm sorry about your friend,' Skink said, 'but you've got to understand.'

'I'm listening.'

'The body will be gone by noon, if it's not already. They'll be back for it. They saw Jim Tile out by the slough, and that was that.'

Decker said, 'We should've stayed there. Jim could have called for help on the radio.'

Skink marched ahead of Decker and turned around, walking backward so he could face him directly. 'The sheriff's office scans all police frequencies. They would've picked up the call and sent a couple of marked cars. Next thing you know, the locals grab jurisdiction and they're questioning you and me, and they're calling Tallahassee about poor Jim Tile—how there's all these irregularities in his report, how uppity and uncooperative he is. Whatever bullshit they can make up, they will. You know how many black troopers there are in this whole state? Not enough for a goddamn basketball team. Jim's a good man and I'm not gonna let him get hung by a bunch of hicks. Not over a fish, for Christ's sake.'

Decker had never heard Skink say so much in one breath. He asked, 'So what's the plan?'

Skink stopped backward-walking. 'Right now the plan is to get off the road.'

Decker spun around and saw a pickup truck coming slowly down the highway. Rays from the new sun reflected off the windshield, making it impossible to see who was driving, or how many there were up front.

Skink tugged Decker's arm and said, 'Let's stroll through the woods, shall we?'

They left the pavement and walked briskly into a stand of tall pine. They heard the truck speed up. When it was even with them, it stopped. A door slammed, then another.

Skink and Decker were twenty-five yards from the highway when the first shots rang out. Decker hit the ground and pulled Skink with him. A bullet peeled the bark off a tree near their feet.

Decker said, 'I'm sure glad you're wearing that orange raincoat, captain. Bet they can only see us a mile or two away.'

'Semiautomatic?' Skink asked through clenched teeth.

Decker nodded. 'Sounds like a Ruger Mini-14.' Very popular with the Porsche-and-power set in Miami, but not the sort of bang-bang you expected upstate.

The rifle went off again, so rapidly that it was impossible to tell the fresh rounds from the echoes. The slugs slapped at the leaves in a lethal hailstorm. From where they huddled Decker and Skink couldn't see the truck on the highway, but they could hear men's voices between the volleys.

'Will they come for us?' Decker whispered.

'I expect.' Skink's cheek was pressed against a carpet of pine needles. A fire ant struggled in the tangle of his mustache; Skink made no move to brush it away. He was listening to the ground.

'There's only two of them,' he announced.

'Only?' One with a Ruger was plenty.

Skink's right hand fished under his rainsuit and came out with the pistol.

Decker heard twigs crackle at the edge of the pine.

'Let's run for it,' he said. They wouldn't have a prayer in a shoot-out.

'You run,' Skink said.

And draw fire, Decker thought. What a grand idea. At least in Beirut you had a chance because of the doorways; doorways made excellent cover. You simply ran a zigzag from one to another. Right now there wasn't a doorway in sight. Even the trees were too skinny to offer protection.

Decker heard footsteps breaking the scrub a few yards behind him. Skink motioned for him to go.

He bunched up on his knees, dug his toes into the moist dirt, and pushed off like a sprinter. He ran erratically, weaving through the pine trunks and hurdling small palmetto bushes. A man shouted and then the gunfire started again. Decker flinched as bullets whined off the tree trunks—low, high, always a few feet behind him. Whoever was shooting was running too, and his aim was lousy.

Decker didn't know the terrain so he picked his openings as they appeared. He spotted promising cover across a bald clearing and he pumped for it, holding his head low. He almost made it, too, when something struck him in the eyes and he crumpled in pain.

A rifle slug had caught a pine branch and whipped it flush across Decker's face. He lay panting on the ground, his fists pressed to his eyes. Maybe they would think he'd been hit. Maybe they would go looking for Skink.

Abruptly the shooting was over.

Decker heard honking. Somebody was leaning on the horn of the truck; long urgent blasts. From the highway a man shouted somebody's name. Decker couldn't make out the words. He took his hands from his face and was relieved to discover that he wasn't blind. His cheeks were wet from his eyes, and his eyes certainly stung, but they seemed to be working.

It was not until he heard the pickup roar away that Decker dared to move, and then he wasn't sure which way to go. The direction that made the most sense was away from the road, but he didn't want to abandon Skink, if Skink were still alive.

Decker crawled to a tree and stood up, cautiously aligning his profile with the trunk. Nothing moved in the clearing; the morning lay dead silent, the songbirds still mute with fear.

What the hell, Decker thought. At the top of his lungs he shouted, 'Skink!'

Something big and pale moved at the edge of the woods across the clearing. It made a tremendous noise. 'I told you to call me captain!' it bellowed.

Skink was fine. He stood stark naked except for his military boots. 'Look what that asshole did to my suit!' He held up the plastic rain jacket. There were three small holes between the shoulder blades. 'I got out of it just in time,' Skink said. 'Hung it on a limb. When I rustled the branch the guy squared around perfectly and cut loose. He was looking the wrong place, slightly.'

Hairy and bare-assed, Skink led Decker to the body. The dead man had a black crusty circle between his sandy eyebrows. His mouth was set in an O.

'You were right about the Ruger,' Skink said. The rifle lay at the man's side. The clip had been removed.

'To answer your question, no, I've never seen him before,' Skink said. 'He's hired help, somebody's out-of-town cousin. His pal stayed at the treeline as a lookout.'

'I'm sure they figured one gun was enough,' Decker said.

'Guy's all of thirty years old,' Skink mused, looking down at the dead man. 'Stupid jerkoff.'

Decker said, 'May I assume we won't be notifying the authorities?'

'You learn fast,' Skink said.

In the mid-1970s a man named Clinton Tyree became governor of Florida. He was everything voters craved: tall, ruggedly handsome, an ex-college football star (second-team All-American lineman), a decorated Vietnam veteran (a sniper once lost for sixteen days behind enemy lines with no food or ammunition), an eligible bachelor, an avid outdoorsman—and best of all, he was native-born, a rarity at that time in Florida. At first Clinton Tyree's political ideology was conservative when it was practical to be, liberal when it made no difference. At six-foot-six, he looked impressive on the campaign trail and the media loved him. He won the governorship running as a Democrat, but proved to be unlike any Democrat or Republican that the state of Florida had ever seen. To the utter confusion of everyone in Tallahassee, Clint Tyree turned out to be a completely honest man. The first time he turned down a kickback, the bribers naturally assumed that the problem was the amount. The bribers, wealthy land developers with an eye on a particular coastal wildlife preserve, followed with a second offer to the new governor. It was so much money that it would have guaranteed him a comfortable retirement anywhere in the world. The developers were clever, too. The bribe money was to emanate from an overseas corporation with a bank account in Nassau. The funds would be wired from Bay Street to a holding company in Grand Cayman, and from there to a blind trust set up especially for Clinton Tyree at a bank in Panama. In this way the newly acquired wealth of the newly elected governor of Florida would have been shielded by the secrecy laws of three foreign governments.

The crooked developers thought this was an ingenious and foolproof plan, and they were dumbfounded when Clinton Tyree told them to go fuck themselves. The developers had naively contributed large sums to Tyree's gubernatorial campaign, and they could not believe that this was the same man who was now—on a state letterhead!—dismissing them as 'submaggots, unfit to suck the sludge off a septic tank.'

The rich developers were further astounded to discover that all their conversations with the governor had been secretly tape-recorded by the chief executive himself. They learned about this when carloads of taciturn FBI agents pulled up to their fancy Brickell Avenue office tower, stormed in with warrants, and arrested the whole gold-chained gang of them. Soon the Internal Revenue Service merrily leapt into the investigation and, within six short months, one of the largest land-development firms in the Southeastern United States went belly-up like a dead mudfish.

It was an exciting and historic moment in Florida history. Newspaper editorials lionized Governor Clint Tyree for his courage and honesty, while network pundits promoted him as the dashing harbinger of a New South.

Of course, the people who really counted—that is, the people with the money and the power—did not view the new governor as a hero. They viewed him as a dangerous pain in the ass. True, every slick Florida politician got up and preached for honest government, but few vaguely understood the concept and even fewer practiced it. Clint Tyree was different; he was trouble. He was sending the wrong message.

With Florida no longer virgin territory, competition was brutal among greedy speculators. The edge went to those with the proper grease and the best connections. In the Sunshine State growth had always depended on graft; anyone who was against corruption was obviously against progress. Something had to be done.

The development interests had two choices: they could wait for Tyree's term to expire and get him voted out of office, or they could deal around him.

Which is what they did. They devoted their full resources and attention to corrupting whoever needed it most, a task accomplished with little resistance. The governor was but one vote on the state cabinet, and it was a simple matter for his political enemies to secure the loyalty of an opposing majority. Money was all it took. Similarly, it was simple (though slightly more expensive) to solidify support in the state houses so that Clinton Tyree's oft-used veto was automatically overridden.

Before long the new governor found himself on the losing side of virtually every important political battle. He discovered that being interviewed by David Brinkley, or getting his picture on the cover of *Time*, meant nothing as long as his colleagues kept voting to surrender every inch of Florida's beachfront to pinky-ringed condominium moguls. With each defeat Clint Tyree grew more saturnine, downcast, and withdrawn. The letters he dictated became so dark and profane that his aides were terrified to send them out under the state seal, and rewrote them surreptitiously. They whispered that the governor was losing too much weight, that his suits weren't always pressed to perfection, that his hair was getting shaggy. Some Republicans even started a rumor that Tyree was suffering from a dreaded sexual disease.

Meanwhile the rich developers who had tried to bribe him finally went to trial, with the governor sitting as the chief witness against them. It was, as they say, a media circus. Clinton Tyree's friends thought he held up about as well as could be expected; his enemies thought he looked glazed and unkempt, like a dope addict on the witness stand.

The trial proved to be a tepid victory. The developers were convicted of bribery and conspiracy, but as punishment all they got was probation. They were family men, the judge explained; churchgoers, too.

By wretched coincidence, the day after the sentencing, the

Florida Cabinet voted 6–1 to close down the Sparrow Beach Wildlife Preserve and sell it to the Sparrow Beach Development Corporation for twelve million dollars. The purported reason for the sale was the unfortunate death (from either sexual frustration or old age) of the only remaining Karp's Seagrape sparrow, the species for whom the verdant preserve had first been established. With the last rare bird dead, the cabinet reasoned, why continue to tie up perfectly good waterfront? The lone vote against the land deal belonged to the governor, of course, and only afterward did he discover that the principal shareholder in the Sparrow Beach Development Corporation was none other than his trusted running mate, the lieutenant governor.

The morning after the vote, Governor Clinton Tyree did what no other Florida governor had ever done. He quit.

He didn't tell a soul in Tallahassee what he was doing. He simply walked out of the governor's mansion, got in the back of his limousine, and told his chauffeur to drive.

Six hours later he told the driver to stop. The limo pulled into a bus depot in downtown Orlando, where the governor said goodbye to his driver and told him to get the hell going.

For two days Governor Clinton Tyree was the subject of the most massive manhunt in the history of the state. The FBI, the highway patrol, the marine patrol, the Florida Department of Law Enforcement, and the National Guard sent out agents, troops, psychics, bloodhounds and helicopters. The governor's chauffeur was polygraphed seven times and, although he always passed, was still regarded as a prime suspect in the disappearance.

The search ended when Clinton Tyree's notarized resignation was delivered to the Capitol. In a short letter released to the press, the ex-governor said he quit the office because of 'disturbing moral and philosophical conflicts.' He graciously thanked his friends and supporters, and closed the message by quoting a poignant but seemingly irrelevant passage from a Moody Blues song.

After Clint Tyree's resignation, the slimy business of selling off Florida resumed in the state capital. Those who had been loyal to the young governor began to give interviews suggesting that for two whole years they'd known that he was basically a nut. A few intrepid reporters depleted precious expense accounts trying to track down Clinton Tyree and get the real story, but with no success. The last confirmed sighting was that afternoon when the fugitive governor had vanished from the downtown Orlando bus depot. Using the name Black Leclere, he had purchased a one-way ticket to Fort Lauderdale, but never arrived. Along the way the Greyhound Scenic Cruiser had stopped to refuel at an Exxon station; the driver hadn't noticed that the tall passenger in a blue pinstriped suit who had gotten off to use the men's room had never come back. The Exxon station was located across from a fruit stand on Route 222, four miles outside the town limits of Harney.

Clinton Tyree had selected Harney not only because of its natural beauty—the lake and the ranchlands, the cypresses and the pines—but also because of its profound political retardation. Harney County had the lowest voter registration per capita of any county in Florida. It was one of the few places to be blacklisted by both the Gallup and Lou Harris pollsters, due to the fact that sixty-three percent of those interviewed could not correctly name a vice-president, any vice-president, of the United States. Four out of five Harney citizens had not bothered to cast ballots during the previous gubernatorial election, mainly because the annual bull-semen auction was scheduled the same day.

This was a town where Clinton Tyree was sure he'd never be recognized, where he could build himself a place and mind his own business and call himself Rajneesh or Buz, or even Skink, and nobody would bother him.

Skink waited all day to get rid of the body. Once darkness fell, he took the truck and left R. J. Decker in the shack. Decker didn't ask because he didn't want to know.

Skink was gone for an hour. When he got back, he was regarbed in full fluorescence. He stalked through the screen door and kicked off his Marine boots. His feet were bare. He had two limp squirrels under one arm, fresh roadkills.

'The Armadillo is still there,' he reported.

Immediately Decker guessed what had happened: Skink had

hauled the other body out to Morgan Slough. And he probably had hooked it on the same fish stringer.

'I can't stay here,' Decker said.

'Suit yourself. Sheriff cars all over the place. There's a pair of 'em parked out on the Mormon Trail, and they hate it out there, believe me. Could be something's in the wind.'

Decker sat on the bare wooden floor, his back rubbing against the unvarnished planks of a bookcase. He needed sleep, but every time he closed his eyes he saw Ott Pickney's corpse. The images were indelible. Three frames, if he'd had a camera.

First: the crest of the skull breaking the surface, Ott's hair dripping to one side like brown turtle grass.

Then a shot of the bloodless forehead and the wide-open eyes focused somewhere on eternity.

Finally: a full pallid death mask, fastened grotesquely on the stringer with a loop of heavy wire, and suspended from the water by Skink's tremendous arms, visible in the lower-left-hand corner of the frame.

That was how R. J. Decker was doomed to remember Ott Pickney. It was a curse of the photographic eye never to forget.

'You look like you're ready to quit,' Skink said.

'Give me another option.'

'Keep going as if nothing happened. Stay on Dickie Lockhart's ass. There's a bass tournament this weekend—'

'New Orleans.'

'Yeah, well, let's go.'

'You and me?'

'And Mr. Nikon. You got a decent tripod, I hope.'

'Sure,' Decker said. 'In the car.'

'And a six-hundred-millimeter, at least.'

'Right.' His trusty NFL lens; it could peer up a quarterback's nostrils.

'So?' Skink said.

'So it's not worth it,' Decker said.

Skink tore off his shower cap and threw it into a corner. He pulled the rubber band out of his ponytail and shook his long hair free.

'I got some supper,' he said. 'I'll eat all of it if you're not hungry.'

Decker rubbed his temples. He didn't feel like food. 'I can't believe they'd kill somebody over a goddamn fish.'

Skink stood up, holding the dead squirrels by their hind legs. 'This thing isn't about fishing.'

'Well, money then,' Decker said.

'That's only part of it. If we quit, we miss the rest. If we quit, we lose Dickie Lockhart, probably forever. They can't touch him on the killings, not yet anyway.'

'I know,' Decker said. There wouldn't be a shred of evidence. Ozzie Rundell would go to the chair before he'd rat on his idol.

Decker asked, 'Do you think they know it's us?'

'Depends,' Skink said. 'Depends if the other guy in the pickup saw our faces this morning. Also depends if the Armadillo told 'em about you before he died. If he told 'em who you are, then you've got problems.'

'Me? What about you? It was your gun that waxed the guy.'

'What gun?' Skink said, raising his hands. 'What gun you talking about, officer?' He flashed his anchorman smile. 'Don't worry about me, Miami. If you've got the urge to worry, worry about setting up some good fish pictures.'

Skink cooked the squirrels on sticks over the outdoor fire. Decker drank a cold beer and felt the night close down over Lake Jesup. They ate in silence; Decker was hungrier than he'd thought. Afterward they each popped open another beer and watched the embers burn down.

'Jim Tile is with us the whole way,' Skink said.

'Is it safe?' Decker asked. 'For him, I mean.'

'Not for him, not for us. But Jim Tile is a careful man. So am I. And you—you're catching on.' Skink balanced the beer can on one knee. 'There's an Eastern nonstop to New Orleans,' he said, 'leaves about noon from Orlando.'

Decker glanced over at him. 'What do you think?'

Skink said, 'Probably smart if we drive separate.'

Decker nodded. They'll never let him on the plane, he thought, not dressed like that. 'Then I guess I'll see you at the airport.'

Skink dumped a tin of water on the last of the coals. 'Where you headed tonight?' he asked.

'There's somebody I need to see,' Decker said, 'though I'm not sure where she's staying. Actually, I'm not even sure she's still in town. It's Dennis Gault's sister.'

Skink snorted. 'She's still in town.' He peeled off his rainsuit. 'She's at the Days Inn, least that's where the little gumdrop Vette is parked.'

'Thanks, I can find it. What about the deputies up on the Trail?'

'Long gone,' Skink said. 'Shift ended a half-hour ago.'

He walked Decker to the car.

'Be careful with that lady,' Skink said. 'If you get the urge to tell her your life story, I understand. Just leave out the part about today.'

'I'm too damn tired,' Decker sighed.

'That's what they all say.'

10

She was still at the Days Inn. Room 135. When she answered
the door she wore a nightshirt. One of those expensive silky tops;
it barely came down far enough to cover her pale yellow panties.
R. J. Decker noticed the color of her panties when she reached
up to get a robe from a hook on the back of the closet door.
Decker did a pitiful job of trying not to stare.

Lanie said, 'What's in the bag?'

'A change of clothes.'

'You going somewhere?'

'Tomorrow.'

'Where?'

'Up north a ways.'

Lanie sat in the middle of the bed and Decker took a chair. An
old James Bond movie was on television.

'Sean Connery was the best,' Lanie remarked. 'I've seen this
darn thing about twenty times.'

'Why are you still in town?' Decker asked.

'I'm going tomorrow, too.'

'You didn't answer the question. Why are you still here? Why
didn't you go home after Bobby's funeral?'

Lanie said, 'I went out to the cemetery today. And yesterday. I
haven't felt like leaving yet, that's all. We each deal with grief in
our own way—isn't that what you said?'

Very sharp, Decker thought. He just loved it when they filed
stuff away. 'Know what I think?' he said. 'I think the Gault family
needs to be tested. Scientifically, I mean. I think maybe there's a
genetic deficiency that prevents you people from telling the truth.
I think the Mayo Clinic might be very interested.'

She rolled her eyes, a little ditty right out of high school. It
was supposed to be cool but it came off as nervous.

'I won't stay long,' Decker said, 'but we need to talk.'

'I don't feel like talking,' Lanie said, 'but you're welcome to stay as long as you like. I'm not tired.'

She crossed her legs up under the robe and glanced over at him. Something in the stale motel room smelled fresh and wonderful, and it definitely wasn't Parfum de Days Inn. It was Lanie; she was one of those women who just naturally smelled like a spring day. Or maybe it just seemed that way because she looked so good. Whatever the phenomenon, Decker had the sense to realize he was in trouble, that by walking into her room and letting her hop into bed he had lost all leverage, all hope of getting any answers. He knew he was wasting his time, but he didn't feel like leaving.

'You look like hell,' Lanie said.

'Been a long day.'

'Hot on the trail?'

'Oh, right.'

'Anything new about Bobby's death?'

'I thought you didn't feel like talking,' Decker said.

'I'm curious, that's all. More than curious. I loved him, remember?'

'You keep saying that,' Decker said, 'like you've got to keep reminding yourself.'

'Why don't you believe me?'

Lee Strasberg material. Lanie the wounded lover. Her tone of voice was exquisite—hurt but not defensive. And not a flicker of doubt in those beautiful eyes; in fact, she looked about ready to cry. It was such a splendid performance that Decker reconsidered the question: Why didn't he believe her?

'Because Bobby Clinch wasn't your type,' he said.

'How do you know?'

'That Corvette parked outside. That's you, Lanie. Bobby was pure pickup truck. You might've liked him, laid him, maybe even given him that blowjob you're so proud of, but you didn't love him.'

'You can tell all this from looking at a damn car!'

'I'm an expert,' Decker said, 'it's what I do.' It was true about cars; there was no better clue to the total personality. Any good cop would tell you so. Decker hadn't thought much about the psychology of automobiles until he became a private investigator and had to spend half his time tracing, following, and photographing all kinds. On long surveillances in busy parking lots he made a game of matching shoppers to their cars, and had gotten good at it. The make, model, color, everything down to the shine on the hubcaps was a clue to the puzzle. Decker's own car was a plain gray 1979 Plymouth Volaré, stylistically the most forgettable automobile Detroit ever produced. Decker knew it fit him perfectly. It fit his need to be invisible.

'So you think I belong back in Miami,' Lanie was saying sarcastically. 'Who can you picture me with, Decker? I know—a young Colombian stud! Rolex, gold necklace, and black Ferrari. Or maybe you figure I'm too old for a coke whore. Maybe you see me on the arm of some silver-haired geezer playing the ponies out at Hialeah.'

'Anybody but Bobby Clinch,' Decker said. 'Steve and Eydie you weren't.'

Of course then the tears came, and the next thing Decker knew he had moved to the bed and put his arms around Lanie and told her to knock off the crying. Please. In his mind's eye he could see himself in this cheesy scene out of a cheap detective movie; acting like the gruff cad, awkwardly consoling the weepy long-legged knockout, knowing deep down he ought to play it as the tough guy but feeling compelled to show this warm sensitive side. Decker knew he was a fool but he certainly didn't feel like letting go of Lanie Gault. There was something magnetic and comforting and entirely natural about holding a sweet-smelling woman in a silken nightie on a strange bed in a strange motel room in a strange town where neither one of you belonged.

A Bell Jet-Ranger helicopter awaited the Reverend Charles Weeb at the Fort Lauderdale Executive Airport. Weeb wore a navy pin-striped suit, designer sunglasses, and lizard boots. He was traveling with a vice-president of the Outdoor Christian Network and a young brunette woman who claimed to be a secretary, and who managed to slip her phone number to the chopper pilot during the brief flight.

The helicopter carried the Reverend Charles Weeb to a narrow dike on the edge of the Florida Everglades. Looking east from the levee, Weeb and his associates had a clear view of a massive highway construction site. The land had been bulldozed, the roadbed had been poured, the pilings had been driven for the overpasses. Dump trucks hauled loose fill back and forth, while graders crawled in dusty clouds along the medians.

'Show me again,' Weeb said to the vice-president.

'Our property starts right about there,' the vice-president said, pointing, 'and abuts the expressway for five miles to the south. The state highway board has generously given us three interchanges.'

Generously my ass, thought Weeb. Twenty thousand in bonds to each of the greedy fuckers.

'Give me the binoculars,' Weeb said.

'I'm sorry, sir, but I left them at the airport.'

'I'm going to go sit in the helicopter,' the brunette woman whined.

'Stay right here,' Weeb growled. 'How'm I supposed to see the lake system without the binoculars?'

'We can fly over it on the way back,' the vice-president said. 'The canals are almost done.'

Vigorously Weeb shook his head. 'Dammit, Billy, you did it again. People don't buy townhouses on *canals*. "Canal" is a dirty word. A canal is where raw sewage goes. A canal is where ducks fuck and cattle piss. Who wants to live on a damn canal! Would you pay a hundred-fifty grand to do that? No, you'd want to live on a *lake*, a cool scenic lake, and lakes is what we're selling here.'

'I understand,' said the vice-president. Lakes it is. Straight, narrow lakes. Lakes you could toss a stone across. Lakes of identical fingerlike dimensions.

The company that OCN had hired was a marine dredging firm whose foremen were, basically, linear-minded. They had once dredged the mouths of Port Everglades and Government Cut, and a long stretch of the freighter route in Tampa Bay. They had worked with impressive speed and efficiency, and they had worked in a perfectly straight line—which is desirable if you're digging a ship channel but rather a handicap when you're digging a lake. This problem had been mentioned several times to Reverend Charles Weeb, who had merely pointed out the fiscal foolishness of having big round lakes. The bigger the lake, the more water. The more water, the less land to sell. The less land to sell, the fewer townhouses to build.

'Lakes don't have to be round,' the Reverend Weeb said. 'I'm not going to tell you again.'

'Yes, sir.'

Weeb turned to the west and stared out at the Glades. 'Reminds me of the fucking Sahara,' he said, 'except with muck.'

'The water rises in late spring and early summer,' the vice-president reported.

'Dickie promises bass.'

'Yes, sir, some of the best fishing in the South.'

'He'd better be right.' Weeb walked along the dike, admiring the spine of the new highway. The vice-president walked a few steps behind him while the secretary stayed where she was, casting glances toward the blue-tinted cockpit of the Jet-Ranger.

'Twenty-nine thousand units,' Weeb was saying, 'twenty-nine thousand families. Our very own Christian city!'

'Yes,' the vice-president said. It was the name of the development that gnawed at him. Lunker Lakes. The vice-president felt that the name Lunker Lakes presented a substantial marketing problem; too colloquial, too red behind the neck. The Reverend Charles Weeb disagreed. It was his audience, he said, and he damn well knew what they would and would not buy. Lunker Lakes was perfect, he insisted. It couldn't miss.

Charlie Weeb was heading back to the chopper. 'Billy, we ought to start thinking about shooting some commercials,' he said. 'Future Bass Capital of America, something like that. Fly Dickie down and get some tape in the can. He can use his own crew, but I'd like you or Deacon Johnson to supervise.'

The vice-president said, 'There's no fish in the lakes yet.'

Weeb climbed into the chopper and the vice-president squeezed in beside him. The secretary was up front next to the pilot. Weeb didn't seem to care.

'I know there's no fucking fish in the lakes. Tell Dickie to go across the dike and shoot some tape on the other side. He'll know what to do.'

The Jet-Ranger lifted off and swung low to the east.

'Head over this way,' the vice-president told the pilot, 'where they're digging those lakes.'

'What lakes?' the pilot asked.

Skink was late to the airport. R. J. Decker was not the least bit surprised. He slipped into a phone booth and called the Harney *Sentinel* to see if anything had broken loose about the shootings. He had a story all made up about going to meet Ott at the pancake house but Ott never showing up.

Sandy Kilpatrick got on the phone. He said, 'I've got some very bad news, Mr. Decker.'

Decker took a breath.

'It's about Ott,' Kilpatrick said. His voice was a forced whisper, like a priest in the confessional.

'What happened?' Decker said.

'A terrible car accident early this morning,' Kilpatrick said. 'Out on the Gilchrist Highway. Ott must have gone to sleep at the wheel. His truck ran off the road and hit a big cypress.'

'Oh Jesus,' Decker said. They'd set up the wreck to cover the murder.

'It burned for two hours, started a mean brushfire,' Kilpatrick said. 'By the time it was over there wasn't much left. The remains are over at the morgue now, but . . . well, they're hoping to get enough blood to find out if he'd been drinking. They're big on DUI stats around here.'

Ott's body would be scorched to a cinder. No one would ever suspect it had been in the water, just as no one would guess what had really killed him. The cheapest trick in the book, but it would work in Harney. Decker could imagine them already repainting the death's-head billboard on Route 222: 'DRIVE SAFELY. DON'T BE FATALITY NO. 5.'

He didn't know what to say now. Conversations about the

newly dead made him uncomfortable, but he didn't want to seem uncaring. 'I didn't think Ott was a big drinker,' he said lamely.

'Me neither,' Kilpatrick said, 'but I figured something was wrong when he didn't show up for the basketball game night before last. He was the team mascot, you know.'

'Davey Dillo.'

'Right.' There was a pause on the end of the line; Kilpatrick pondering how to explain Ott's armadillo suit. 'It's sort of an unwritten rule here at the newspaper,' the editor said, 'that everybody gives to the United Way. Just a few bucks out of each paycheck—you know, the company's big in civic charity.'

'I understand,' Decker said.

'Well, Ott refused to donate anything, said he didn't trust 'em. I'd never seen him so adamant.'

'He always watched his pennies,' Decker said. Ott Pickney was one of the cheapest men he'd ever met. While covering the Dade County courthouse he'd once missed the verdict in a sensational murder trial because he couldn't find a parking spot with a broken meter.

Sandy Kilpatrick went on: 'Our publisher has a rigid policy about the United Way. When he heard Ott was holding back, he ordered me to fire him. To save Ott's job I came up with this compromise.'

'Davey Dillo?'

'The school team needed a mascot.'

'It sure doesn't sound like Ott,' Decker said.

'He resisted at first, but he got to where he really enjoyed it. I heard him say so. He was dynamite on that skateboard, too, even in that bulky costume. Someone his age—the kids said he should have been a surfer.'

'Sounds like quite a show,' Decker said, trying to imagine it.

'He never missed a game, that's why I was worried the other night when he didn't show. Only thing I could figure is that he'd gone out Saturday night and tied one on. Maybe went up to Cocoa Beach, met a girl, and just decided to stay the weekend.'

Ott sacked out with a beach bunny—the story probably was all over Harney by now. 'Maybe that's it,' Decker said. 'He was probably on his way home when the accident happened.' This was Ott's old pal from Miami, lying through his teeth. If Kilpatrick only knew the truth, Decker thought. He said, 'Sandy, I'm so sorry. I can't believe he's dead.' That part was almost true, and the regret was genuine.

'The service is tomorrow,' Kilpatrick said. 'Cremation seemed the best way to go, considering.'

Decker said good-bye and hung up. Then he called a florist shop in Miami and asked them to wire an orchid to Ott Pickney's funeral. The best orchid they had.

11

Jim Tile was born in the town of Wilamette, Florida, a corrupt and
barren flyspeck untouched by the alien notions of integration, fair
housing and equal rights. Jim Tile was one of the few blacks ever
to have escaped his miserable neighborhood without benefit of a
bus ride to Raiford or a football scholarship. He attributed his
success to good steady parents who made him stay in school, and
also to his awesome physical abilities. Most street kids thought
punching was the cool way to fight, but Jim Tile preferred to
wrestle because it was more personal. For this he took some grief
from his pals until the first time the white kids jumped him and
tried to push his face in some cowshit. There were three of them,
and naturally they waited until Jim Tile was alone. They actually
got him down for a moment, but the one who was supposed to
lock Jim Tile's arms didn't get a good grip and that was that. One
of the white kids ended up with a broken collarbone, another
with both elbows hyperextended grotesquely, and the third had
four broken ribs where Jim Tile had squeezed him in a leg scissors.
And they all went to the hospital with cowshit on their noses.

After high school Jim Tile enrolled at Florida State University
in Tallahassee, majored in criminal justice, was graduated, and
joined the highway patrol. His friends and classmates told him
that he was nuts, that a young black man with a 4.0 grade average
and a college degree could write his own ticket with the DEA or
Customs, maybe even the FBI. Jim Tile could have taken his pick.
Besides, everybody knew about the highway patrol: it had the
worst pay and the highest risks of any law-enforcement job in
the state—not to mention its reputation as an enclave for hard-
core rednecks who, while not excluding minority recruits, hardly
welcomed them with champagne and tickertape parades.

In the 1970s the usual fate of black troopers was to get assigned to the lousiest roads in the reddest counties. This way they could spend most of their days writing tickets to foul-mouthed Klansmen farmers who insisted on driving their tractors down the middle of the highway in violation of about seventeen traffic statutes. Two or three years of this challenging work was enough to inspire most black troopers to look elsewhere for employment, but Jim Tile hung on. When other troopers asked him why, he replied that he intended someday to become commander of the entire highway patrol. His friends thought he was joking, but when word of Jim Tile's boldly stated ambition reached certain colonels and lieutenants in Tallahassee he was immediately reassigned to patrol the remote roadways of Harney County and faithfully protect its enlightened citizenry, most of whom insisted on addressing him as Boy or Son or Officer Zulu.

One day Trooper Jim Tile was told to accompany a little-known gubernatorial candidate on a campaign swing through Harney. The day began with breakfast at the pancake house and finished with a roast-hog barbecue on the shore of Lake Jesup. The candidate, Clinton Tyree, gave the identical slick speech no less than nine times, and out of utter boredom Jim Tile memorized it. By the end of the day he was unconsciously muttering the big applause lines just before they came out of the candidate's mouth. From the reactions—and penurious donations—of several fat-cat political contributors, it was obvious that they had gotten the idea that Clinton Tyree was letting a big black man tell him what to say.

At dusk, after all the reporters and politicos had polished off the barbecue and gone home, Clinton Tyree took Jim Tile aside and said:

'I know you don't think much of my speech, but in November I'm going to be elected governor.'

'I don't doubt it,' Jim Tile said, 'but it's because of your teeth, not your ideals.'

After Clinton Tyree won the election, one of the first things he did was order Trooper Jim Tile transferred from Harney County to the governor's special detail in Tallahassee. This unit was the equivalent of the state's Secret Service, one of the most prestigious assignments in the highway patrol. Never before had a black man been chosen as a bodyguard for a governor, and many of Tyree's cronies told him that he was setting a dangerous precedent. The governor only laughed. He told them that Jim Tile was the most prescient man he'd met during the whole campaign. An exit survey taken on election day by the pollster Pat Caddell revealed that what Florida voters had liked most about candidate Clinton Tyree was not his plainly spoken views on the death penalty or toxic dumps or corporate income taxes, but rather his handsome smile. In particular, his teeth.

During his brief and turbulent tenure in the governor's mansion, Clinton Tyree confided often in Jim Tile. The trooper grew to admire him; he thought the new governor was courageous, visionary, earnest, and doomed. Jim Tile was probably the only person in Florida who was not surprised when Clinton Tyree resigned from office and vanished from the public eye.

As soon as Tyree was gone, Trooper Jim Tile was removed from the governor's detail and sent back to Harney in the hopes that he'd come to his senses and quit the force.

For some reason he did not.

Jim Tile remained loyal to Clinton Tyree, who was now calling himself Skink and subsisting on fried bass and dead animals off the highway. Jim Tile's loyalty extended so far as to driving the former governor to the Orlando airport for one of his rare trips out of state.

'I could take some comp time and come with you,' Jim Tile volunteered.

Skink was riding in the back of the patrol car in order to draw less attention. He looked like a prisoner anyway.

'Thanks for the offer,' he said, 'but we're going to a tournament in Louisiana.'

Jim Tile nodded in understanding. 'Gotcha.' Bopping down Bourbon Street he'd be fine. Fishing the bayous was another matter.

'Keep your ears open while I'm gone,' Skink said. 'I'd steer clear of the Morgan Slouth, too.'

'Don't worry.'

Skink could tell Jim Tile was worried. He could see distraction in the way the trooper sat at the wheel; driving was the last thing on his mind. He was barely doing sixty.

'Is it me or yourself you're thinking about?' Skink asked.

'I was thinking about something that happened yesterday morning,' Jim Tile said. 'About twenty minutes after I dropped you guys off on the highway, I pulled over a pickup truck that nearly broke my radar.'

'Mmmm,' Skink said, acting like he couldn't have cared less.

'I wrote him up a speeding ticket for doing ninety-two. The man said he was late for work. I said where do you work, and he said Miller Lumber. I said you must be new, and he said yeah, that's right. I said it must be your first day because you're driving the wrong damn direction, and then he didn't say anything.'

'You ever seen this boy before?'

'No,' Jim Tile said.

'Or the truck?'

'No. Had Louisiana plates. Jefferson Parish.'

'Mmmm,' Skink said.

'But you know what was funny,' Jim Tile said. 'There was a rifle clip on the front seat. No rifle, just a fresh clip. Thirty rounds. Would have fit a Ruger, I expect. The man said the gun was stolen out of his truck down in West Palm. Said some nigger kids stole it.'

Skink frowned. 'He said that to your face? *Nigger* kids? What the hell did you do when he said that, Jim? Split open his cracker skull, I hope.'

'Naw,' Jim Tile said. 'Know what else was strange? I saw two jugs of coffee on the front seat. Not one, but two.'

'Maybe he was extra thirsty,' Skink said.

'Or maybe the second jug didn't belong to him. Maybe it belonged to a buddy.' The trooper straightened in the driver's seat, yawned, and stretched his arms. 'Maybe the man's buddy was the one with the rifle. Maybe there was some trouble back on the road and something happened to him.'

'You got one hell of an imagination,' Skink said. 'You ought to write for the movies.' There was no point in telling his friend about the killing. Someday it might be necessary, but not now; the trooper had enough to worry about.

'So you got the fellow's name, the driver,' Skink said.

Jim Tile nodded. 'Thomas Curl.'

'I don't believe he works at Miller's,' Skink remarked.

'Me neither.'

'Suppose I ask around New Orleans.'

'Would you mind?' Jim Tile said. 'I'm just curious.'

'Don't blame you. Man's got to have a reason for lying to a cop. I'll see what I can dig up.'

They rode the last ten miles in silence; Jim Tile, wishing that Skink would just come out and tell him about it, but knowing there were good reasons not to. The second man was dead, the trooper was sure. Maybe the details weren't all that important.

As he pulled up to the terminal, Jim Tile said, 'This Decker, you must think he's all right.'

'Seems solid enough.'

'Just remember he's got other priorities. He's not working for you.'

'Maybe he is,' Skink said, 'and he just doesn't know it.'

'Yet,' said Jim Tile.

R. J. Decker was pacing in front of the Eastern Airlines counter when Skink lumbered in, looking like a biker who'd misplaced all his amphetamines. Still, Decker had to admit, the overall appearance was a slight improvement.

'I took a bath,' Skink said, 'aren't you proud?'

'Thank you.'

'I hate airplanes.'

'Come on, they're boarding our flight.'

At the gate Skink got into an argument with a flight attendant who wouldn't let him carry on his scuba gear.

'It won't fit under the seat,' she explained.

'I'll show you where it fits,' Skink growled.

'Just check the tanks into baggage,' Decker said.

'They'll bust 'em,' Skink protested.

'Then I'll buy you new ones.'

'Our handlers are very careful,' the flight attendant said brightly.

'Troglodytes!' said Skink, and stalked onto the airplane.

'Your friend's a little grumpy this morning,' the flight attendant said as she took Decker's ticket coupon.

'He's just a nervous flier. He'll settle down.'

'I hope so. You might mention to him that we have an armed sky marshal on board.'

Oh, absolutely, Decker thought, what a fine idea.

He found Skink hunkered down in the last row of the tail section.

'I traded seats with a couple Catholic missionaries,' Skink explained. 'This is the safest place to be if the plane goes down, the last row. Where's your camera gear?'

'In a trunk, don't worry.'

'You remembered the tripod?'

'Yes, captain.'

Skink was a jangled mess. He fumed and squirmed and fidgeted. He scratched nervously at the hair on his cheeks. Decker had never seen him this way.

'You don't like to fly?'

'Spent half my life on planes. Planes don't scare me. I hate the goddamn things but they don't scare me, if that's what you're getting at.' He dug into a pocket of his black denim jacket and brought out the black sunglasses and the flowered shower cap.

'Please don't put those on,' Decker said. 'Not right now.'

'You with the fucking FAA or what?' Skink pulled the rainhat tight over his hair. 'Who cares,' he said.

The man looks miserable, Decker thought, a true sociopath. It wasn't the airplane, either, it was the people; Skink plainly couldn't stand to be out in public. Under the rainhat he seemed to calm. Behind the charcoal lenses of the sunglasses, Decker sensed, Skink's green eyes had closed.

'Pay no attention to me,' he said quietly.

'Take a nap,' Decker said. The jet engines, which seemed anchored directly over their heads, drowned Decker's words; the plane started rolling down the runway. Skink said nothing until they were airborne.

Then he shifted in his seat and said: 'Bad news, Miami. The Rundell brothers are on this bird. Picking their noses up in first class, if you can believe it. Makes me sick.'

Decker hadn't noticed them when he boarded; he'd been pre-occupied with Skink. 'Did they see you?'

'What do you think?' Skink replied mordantly.

'So much for stealth.'

Skink chuckled. 'Culver damn near wet his pants.'

'He'll be on the phone to Lockhart the minute we're on the ground.'

'Can't have that,' Skink said. He stared out the window until the flight attendants started moving down the aisle with the lunch trays. Skink lowered the tabletop at his seat and braced his logger's arms on it.

'Ozzie and Culver, they don't know your face.'

'I don't think so,' Decker said, 'but I can't be sure. I believe I stopped in their bait shop once.'

'Damn.' Skink smoothed the plastic cap against his skull and fingered his long braid of hair. Decker could tell he was cooking up a scheme. 'Where does this plane go from New Orleans?' Skink asked.

'Tulsa.'

'Good,' Skink said. 'That's where you're going. As soon as you get there, hop another flight and come back. You got plenty of cash?'

'Yeah, and plastic.'

'It's cash you'll need,' Skink said. 'Most bail bondsmen don't take MasterCard.'

Whatever the plan, Decker didn't like it already. 'Is it you or me who's going to need bail?'

'Aw, relax,' Skink said.

But now it was impossible.

When the stewardess brought the food, Skink glowered from under his cap and snapped: 'What in the name of Christ is this slop?'

'Beef Wellington, muffins, a fresh garden salad, and carrot cake.'

'How about some goddamn opossum?' Skink said.

The flight attendant's blue buttonlike eyes flickered slightly. 'I don't think so, sir, but we may have a chicken Kiev left over from the Atlanta flight.'

'How about squirrel?' Skink said. 'Squirrel Kiev would be lovely.'

'I'm sorry, but that's not on the menu,' the stewardess said, the lilt and patience draining from her voice. 'Would you care for a beverage this morning?'

'Just opossum hormones,' Skink said, 'and if I don't get some, I'm going to tear this goddamn airplane apart.' Then he casually ripped the tray table off its hinges and handed it to the flight attendant, who backpedaled in terror up the aisle.

She was calling for her supervisor when Skink rose from his seat and shouted, 'You promised opossum! I called ahead and you promised to reserve a possum lunch. Kosher, too!'

R. J. Decker felt paralyzed. Skink's plan was now evident, and irreversible.

'Fresh opossum—or we all die together!' he proclaimed. By now pandemonium was sweeping the tail section; women and children scurried toward the front of the aircraft while the male passengers conferred about the best course of action. Skink's size, apparel, and maniacal demeanor did not invite heroic confrontation at thirty thousand feet.

To Decker it seemed like every passenger in the airplane had turned around to stare at the lunatic in the flowered shower cap.

The aisle cleared as a man with a badge on his shirt came out of first class and hurried toward the trouble.

'Remember, you don't know me!' Skink whispered to Decker.

'No kidding.'

The sky marshal, a short stocky man with a bushy mustache, asked R.J. Decker if he would mind moving up a few rows for the remainder of the flight.

'Gladly,' Decker said.

The sky marshal carried no gun, just a short billy club and a pair of handcuffs. He sat down in Decker's seat.

'Are you the man with the opossum?' Skink asked.

'Behave yourself,' the sky marshal said sternly, 'and I won't have to use these.' He jangled the handcuffs ominously.

'Please,' Skink said, 'I'm a heavily medicated man.'

The sky marshal nodded. 'Everything is fine now. We're only a half-hour from New Orleans.'

Soon the plane was calm again and lunch service was resumed. When Decker turned around he saw Skink and the sky marshal chatting amiably.

After landing in New Orleans, the pilot asked all passengers to remain seated for a few minutes. As soon as the cabin door opened, three city policemen and two federal agents in dark suits boarded the plane and led Skink away in handcuffs and leg irons. On the way out he made a point of kissing one of the flight attendants on the earlobe and warning the pilot to watch out for windshear over Little Rock.

The Rundell brothers watched in fascination.

'Where they taking him?' Ozzie wondered.

'The nuthouse, I hope,' said Culver. 'Let's get going.'

R. J. Decker stayed on the plane to Tulsa. Except for one drunken tourist wearing a Disney World tank top and Pluto ears, it was a peaceful flight.

12

On the night of January 15, Dickie Lockhart got dog-sucking drunk on Bourbon Street and was booted out of a topless joint for tossing rubber nightcrawlers on the dancers. The worms were a freebie from a national tackle company whose sales reps had come to town for the big bass tournament. The sales reps had given Dickie Lockhart four bags of assorted lures and hooks, plus a thousand dollars cash as incentive to win the tournament using the company's equipment. Dickie blew the entire grand in the French Quarter, buying rock cocaine and rainbow-colored cocktails for exquisitely painted women, most of whom turned out to be flaming he-she's out trolling for cock. In disgust Dickie Lockhart had retreated to the strip joints, where at least the boobs were genuine. The trouble happened when he ran out of five-dollar bills for tips; finding only the slippery rubber nightcrawlers in his pockets, he began flicking them up at the nude performers. In his drunken state he was vastly entertained by the way the gooey worms clung to the dancers' thighs and nipples, and would occasionally tangle in their pubic hair. The nightcrawlers looked (and felt) so authentic that the strippers began shrieking and clawing at their own flesh; one frail acrobat even collapsed and rolled about the stage as if she were on fire. Dickie thought the whole scene was hysterical; obviously these girls had never been fishing. He was mildly baffled when the bouncers heaved him out of the joint (hadn't they seen him on TV?), but took some satisfaction when other patrons booed the rough manner in which he was expelled.

Afterward he had a few more drinks and went looking for his boss, the Reverend Charles Weeb. Drunk was the only condition in which Dickie Lockhart could have made this decision; as a rule one did not pop in on Reverend Weeb unless one was invited.

Dickie lurched up to the top-floor suite of the swank hotel on Chartres Street and pounded on the door. It was almost midnight.

'Who is it?' a female voice asked.

'DEA!' said Dickie Lockhart. 'Open the fuck up!'

The door opened and a beautiful long-haired woman stood there; at least she seemed beautiful to Dickie Lockhart. An apparition, really. She was wearing canvas hip waders and nothing else. Her lovely breasts poked out in a friendly way from under the suspenders. For a moment Dickie almost forgot he was supposed to be with the DEA.

'I got a warrant for Charles Weeb,' he snarled.

'What's with the fishing rod?' the naked wader asked.

Dickie Lockhart had been carrying a nine-foot boron fly rod all night long. He couldn't remember why. Somebody in a bar had given it to him; another damn salesman, probably.

'It's not a fishing rod, so shut up!'

'Yes, it is,' said the woman.

'It's a heroin probe,' Dickie Lockhart said. 'Now stand back.' He brushed past her and marched into the living room of the suite, but the reverend was not there. Dickie headed for the master bedroom, the woman clomping after him in the heavy waders.

'Have you got a warrant?' she asked.

Dickie found the Reverend Charles Weeb lying on his back in bed. Another young woman was on top of him, bouncing happily. This one was wearing a Saints jersey, number 12.

From behind Dickie Lockhart the bare-breasted wader announced: 'Charlie, there's a man here to arrest you.'

Weeb looked up irritably, fastened his angry eyes on Dickie Lockhart, and said: 'Be gone, sinner!'

It occurred to Dickie that maybe it wasn't such a hot idea to stop by unannounced. He went back to the living room, turned on the television, and slumped on the couch. The woman in the waders fixed him a bourbon. She said her name was Ellen O'Something and that she had recently been promoted to executive secretary of the First Pentecostal Church of Exemptive Redemption, of which the Reverend Charles Weeb was founder and spiritual masthead. She apologized for answering the door half-naked, said the waders weren't really her idea. Dickie Lockhart said he understood, thought she looked darn good in them. He told her to watch out for chafing, though, said he spoke from experience.

'Nice fly rod,' she remarked.

'Not for bass,' Dickie Lockhart said. 'The action's too fast for poppers.'

The woman nodded. 'I was thinking more about streamers,' she said. 'A Muddler Minnow, for instance. Say a four or a six.'

'Sure,' Dickie Lockhart said, dumbstruck, dizzy, madly in love. 'Sure, with the boron you could throw a size four, you bet. Do you fish?'

At that moment the Reverend Charles Weeb thundered into the room with a mauve towel wrapped around his midsection. The apparition excused herself and clomped off to a bedroom. Dickie Lockhart's heart ached. He was sure he'd never see her again, Charles Weeb would make sure of that.

'Son, what in the name of holy fuck is the matter with you?' the clergyman began. 'What demon has possessed you, what poison serpent, what diseased fucking germ has invaded your brain and robbed you of all common sense? What in the name of Our Savior Jesus were you thinking when you knocked on my door tonight?'

'I'm fairly plastered,' Dickie Lockhart said.

'Well, so you are. But see what you've done. That young lady in there—'

'The quarterback?'

'Hush! That young lady was on the brink of a profound revelation when you burst in and interrupted our collective concentration. I don't appreciate that, Dickie, and neither does she.'

'The night's young,' Dickie Lockhart said. 'You can try again.'

The Reverend Weeb glowered. 'Why did you come here?'

Dickie shrugged. 'I wanted to talk.'

'About what?' Weeb hiked up the towel to cover the pale fatty roll of shrimp-colored belly. 'What was so all-fired important that you would invade my personal privacy at this hour?'

'The show,' Dickie said, emboldened by Ellen's bourbon. 'I just don't think you fully appreciate the show. I think you take me for granted, Reverend Weeb.'

'Is that right?'

Dickie Lockhart stood up. It wasn't easy. He pointed the nine-foot boron fly rod directly at Reverend Weeb's midsection, so that the tip tickled the gray curly hair.

'Catching bass is not easy,' Dickie Lockhart said, his own anger welling, fueled by a mental image of his beloved Ellen O'Something bouncing on top of this flabby rich pig. 'Catching bass is not a sure thing.'

Weeb said, 'I understand, Dickie.' He had dealt with angry drunks before and knew that caution was the best strategy. He didn't like the fishing rod poking into his tummy, but realized that only his pride was in danger. 'Overall, I think you do a hell of a job with *Fish Fever*, I really do.'

'Then why do you treat me like shit?'

'Now, I pay you very well,' Weeb said.

With his wrist Dickie Lockhart started whipping the rod back and forth, filling the room with sibilant noise. Weeb had a hunch it would hurt like hell if the tip thwacked across his bare flesh, and he edged back a step.

'I heard,' said Dickie Lockhart, 'that you been talking to Ed Spurling.'

'Where did you hear that?' A new look came into the minister's eyes, a look of nervousness.

'Some boys that fish with Ed. Said Ed told 'em that the Outdoor Christian Network wanted to buy his TV show.'

Weeb said, 'Dickie, that's ridiculous. We've got the best bass show in all America. Yours. We don't need another.'

'That's what I said, but those boys that fish with Ed told me something else. They said Ed was bragging that you promised to make him number one within two years. Within two years, they said, *Fish Fever* would be out of production.'

These redneck assholes, Weeb was thinking, what a grapevine they had. It was too bad Ed Spurling couldn't keep his damn mouth shut.

'Dickie,' Weeb said, 'somebody's pulling your leg. I never met

Spurling in my life. I don't blame you for being upset, buddy, but I swear you've got nothing to worry about. Look, of all the pro bass anglers in the world, who did I ask to do the promotion footage for Lunker Lakes? Who? You, Dickie, 'cause you're the best. All of us at OCN feel the same way; you're our number-one man.'

Lockhart lowered the fishing rod. His eyes were muddy, his arms like lead. If he didn't pass out soon he'd need another bourbon.

Soothingly the Reverend Charles Weeb said, 'Don't worry, son, none of what you heard is true.'

'Sure glad to hear it,' Dickie said, 'because there's no telling what would happen if I found out otherwise. No telling. Remember the guy from the zoning board down in Lauderdale, the one you told me to take fishing that time? Man, he had some wild stories about that Lunker Lagoon.'

'Lunker Lakes,' Weeb said tersely.

'He says he got himself a brand-new swimming pool, thanks to you. With a sauna in the shallow end!'

'I wouldn't know.'

Dickie broke into a daffy grin. 'And I'm trying to imagine what your faithful flock might do if they found out their shepherd was double-boffing a couple of sweet young girls from the church. I'm wondering about that, Reverend Weeb.'

'I get the point.'

'Do you really?' Dickie Lockhart wielded the fly rod swordlike and, with an artful flick, popped the knot on Charlie Weeb's bath towel, which dropped to his ankles.

'Aw, what a cute little thing,' Dickie said with a wink. 'Cute as a junebug.'

Weeb flushed. He couldn't believe that the tables had turned so fast, that he had so carelessly misjudged this nasty little cracker bastard. 'What do you want?' he asked Dickie Lockhart.

'A new contract. Five years, no cancellation. Plus ten percent of first-run syndication rights. Don't look so sad, Reverend Weeb. I'll make it easy for you: you don't have to announce it until after I win the tournament this week. I'll show up at the press conference with the trophy, put on a good show.'

'All right,' Weeb said, cupping his hands over his privates, 'what else?'

'I want the budget doubled to two thousand per show.'

'Fifteen hundred tops.'

'Fine,' Dickie said. 'I'm not a greedy man.'

'Anything more?' asked Reverend Weeb.

'Yeah, go get Ellen and tell her I'm giving her a ride home.'

Lake Maurepas, where the Cajun Invitational Bass Classic was to be held, was a bladder-shaped miniature of the immense Lake Pontchartrain. Located off Interstate 55 northwest of New Orleans, the marshy and bass-rich Maurepas was connected to its muddy mother at Pass Manchac, a few miles south of the town of Hammond. It was there that that R. J. Decker and Skink took a room at a Quality Court motel. At the Sportsman's Hideout Marina they rented a small aluminum johnboat with a fifteen-horsepower outboard, and told the lady at the cash register they'd be going out at dusk. The lady looked suspicious until Skink introduced himself as the famous explorer Philippe Cousteau, and explained he was working on a documentary about the famous Louisiana eel spawn, which only took place in the dead of night. Yes, the lady at the cash register nodded, I've heard of it. Then she asked for Philippe's autograph and Skink earnestly replied (in a marvelous French accent) that for such a beautiful woman, a mere autograph would never do. Instead he promised to name a new species of mollusk in her honor.

It had taken the better part of the morning to get Skink arraigned and bailed out of jail, and by now it was the middle of the day; not hot, but piercingly bright, the way it gets in January in the Deep South. Skink said there was no point in going out on the water now because the bass would be in thick cover. He curled up on the floor of the motel room and went to sleep while Decker read the New Orleans *Times-Picayune*. On the back page of the local section was a small item about a local man who had disappeared on a fishing trip to Florida and was presumed drowned somewhere in the murky vastness of Lake Okeechobee. The young man's name was Lemus Curl, and except for the absence of a blackened bullet hole in his forehead, the picture in the paper matched the face of the man whom Skink had shot dead near Morgan Slough; the man who had tried to murder them with the rifle. Obviously it was Lemus Curl's brother whom Jim Tile had stopped for speeding shortly afterward. Interestingly, the same Thomas Curl was quoted in the newspaper as saying that his brother had slipped off the dike and tumbled into the water on the west side of the big lake. The article reported that Lemus Curl had been tussling with a hawg bass at the time of the tragic accident. Decker thought this last detail, though untrue, lent a fine ironic touch to the story.

Skink snored away and Decker felt alone. He felt like calling Catherine. He found a pay phone outside the lobby of the Quality Court. She answered on the fifth ring, and sounded like she'd been sleeping.

'Did I wake you?'

'Hey, Rage, where you at?'

'In a motel outside New Orleans.'

'Hmmm, sounds romantic.'

'Very,' Decker said. 'My roommate is a 240-pound homicidal hermit. For dinner he's fixing me a dead fox he scraped off the highway near Ponchatoula, and after that we're taking a leaky tin boat out on a windy lake to spy on some semi-retarded fishermen. Don't you wish you were here?'

'I could fly in tomorrow, get a hotel in the Quarter.'

'Don't be a tease, Catherine.'

'Oh, Decker.' She was stretching, waking up, probably kicking off the covers. He could tell all that over the phone. 'I had to get up early and take James to the airport,' she said.

'Where to now?'

'San Francisco.'

'And of course he didn't want you to come along.'

'That's not true,' Catherine said. 'Those conventions are a bore, and besides, I've got plans of my own. What are you doing out in the bayous?'

'Rethinking Darwin,' Decker said. 'Some of these folks didn't evolve from apes; it was the other way around.'

'You should have gotten a nice room downtown.'

'That's not what I meant,' Decker said. 'The fish people, I'm talking about.'

'Take notes,' Catherine said, 'it sounds like it'll make a terrific movie. *Attack of the Fish People*. Now, be honest, Rage, wouldn't you rather be shooting pictures of golfers?'

Decker said, 'I'd better go.'

'That's it?'

'I've got a lot to tell you, but not over the phone.'

'It's all right,' Catherine said. 'Anytime you want to talk.' He wished she'd been serious about flying up to New Orleans, though it was a nutty scheme. She would have been safer in San Francisco with her chiropractor.

'I'll call you when I get back,' Decker said.

'Take care,' Catherine said. 'Slurp an oyster for me.'

At dusk Skink was ready to roll. Shower cap, weathersuit, mosquito netting, lamps, flippers, regulator, scuba tank, dive knife, spear-gun and, purely for show, a couple of cheap spinning rods. R. J. Decker was afraid the johnboat would sink under the weight. He decided there was no point in bringing the cameras at night; a strobe would be useless at long distance. If his theory was correct, Dickie Lockhart wouldn't be anywhere near the lake anyway.

They made sure they were alone at the dock before loading the boat and shoving off. It was a chilly night, and a northern breeze stung Decker's cheeks and nose. At the throttle, Skink seemed perfectly warm and serene behind his sunglasses. He seemed to know where he was going. He followed the concrete ribbon of I-55, which was sunk into the marshlands on enormous concrete pilings. The highway pilings were round and smooth, as big as sequoias but out of place; the cars that raced overhead intruded harshly on the foggy peace of the bayous. After twenty minutes Skink cut off the motor.

'I prefer oars,' Skink said, but there were none in the boat. 'You can hear more with oars,' he remarked.

R. J. Decker noticed what he was talking about. Across the

water, bouncing off the pilings, came the sound of men's voices; pieces of conversation, deep bursts of laughter, carried by the wind.

'Let's drift for a while,' Skink suggested. He picked up one of the fishing poles and made a few idle casts. Darkness had settled in and the lake was gray. Skink cocked his head, listening for clues from the other boat.

'I think I see them,' Decker said. A fuzzy pinprick of white light, rocking.

'They've got a Coleman lit,' Skink said. 'Two hundred yards away, at least.'

'They sound a helluva lot closer,' Decker said.

'Just a trick of the night.'

After a few minutes the light went out. Skink and Decker heard the ignition sounds of a big engine. It was probably a bass boat. Swiftly Skink hand-cranked the outboard and aimed the johnboat toward the other craft. Legs wide, he stood up as he steered, though Decker couldn't imagine how he could safely navigate around the highway pilings, not to mention the submerged stumps and brushpiles that mined the lakeshore. Every so often Skink would cut the outboard and listen to make sure the other boat was still moving; as long as their engine was running, they'd never know they were being followed. Sitting on two hundred horses, you can't hear yourself think.

After a few minutes the other boat stopped and the Coleman lantern flickered on again. The men's voices were faint and more distant than before.

'We'll never get close,' Skink muttered, 'unless we walk it.'

Fortuitously the wind pushed the johnboat into a stand of lily pads. Hand over hand, Skink used the roots to pull them to shore, where Decker tied the boat to a sturdy limb. He grabbed a flashlight and hopped out after Skink. They followed a ragged course along the shoreline for probably four hundred yards, taking tentative spongy steps and using the flashlight sparingly. They passed through a trailer park with particular stealth, not wishing to be mistaken for bears and blasted to oblivion. Far removed from his native territory, Skink's nocturnal instincts remained sound; his path brought them out of the bogs within thirty yards of where the bass boat floated.

The lantern illuminated two men, not the Rundell brothers. 'Local boys,' Skink whispered. 'Makes sense. Need someone who knows the water.' The anglers were not casting their fishing lines; rather, they seemed to be studying the water. The deck of the boat bristled with rods, each with a line out. In the penumbra a half-dozen red floats were visible bobbing around the sides of the boat. 'Livebaiters,' Skink explained. 'My guess is worms.'

R. J. Decker said, 'It could be anybody out for a night on the lake.'

'No,' Skink said, 'these boys are out to load the boat.'

And they were. Every so often one of the poles would bend and flutter, and a bass would splash out in the pads. Quickly one of the men would snatch the rig and reel in the fish as fast as he could. The bass were quickly unhooked and put in a livewell under a hatch in the stern.

This methodical fish-collecting went on for two hours, during which Skink said little and scarcely moved a muscle. Decker's legs were cramping from sitting on his haunches, but it was impossible to stand up and stretch without being seen. Mercifully, as the wind stiffened and the temperature dropped, the two poachers finally called it quits. They reeled in the worms, stored the rods, cranked the big engine, and motored slowly—confoundingly so—up the southeastern shore of the lake. The boat stayed unusually close to the elevated highway, maneuvering in and out of the pilings; occasionally the lantern light flickered across the faces of the two men as they leaned over the gunwales, peering at something which neither Decker nor Skink could see.

Of course it was Skink who led the way back to the johnboat. By the time they got there, the marsh was empty and silent; the other men had finished their business and roared away.

Skink stripped down to his underwear and began fitting his considerable bulk into a wetsuit.

'I was afraid of this,' Decker said. Pitch black, fifty degrees, and this madman was going in. Decker couldn't wait to see the look on the game warden's face.

'Can you drive the boat?' Skink asked.

'I think I can handle it.'

'Take me along the pilings, the same way our buddies went.'

Decker said, 'I wouldn't dive in this soup.'

'Who's asking you to? Come on, let's move.'

They motored down the lake to the poacher's bass hole. Skink strapped on a yellow scuba tank, adjusted his headlamp, and slipped over the side. He fitted a nylon rope around his waist and tied it to the transom of the boat. One sharp tug was a signal to stop, two meant reverse, and three tugs meant trouble. 'In that case do your best to haul me in,' Skink advised. 'If you can't manage, then get the hell out of here, I'm gator chow.'

Decker steered the boat anxiously, monitoring Skink's progress by the bubbles surfacing in the foamy wake. He wondered what the fish and turtles must think, confronted in their inky element by such a hoary gurgling beast. The engine's throttle was set as low as it would go, so the johnboat moved at a crawl; Skink was a heavy load to tow.

When he found what he was searching for, Skink tugged so hard that the rope nearly pulled the stern under. Immediately Decker shifted to neutral so the propellor wouldn't be spinning perilously when Skink came up.

He burst to the surface like a happy porpoise. He held a wire cage, three feet by three. Inside the trap were four healthy largemouth bass, which flapped helplessly against the mesh as Skink hoisted their manmade cell into the bow. He turned off the regulator, spit out the mouthpiece, and tore off his mask.

'Jackpot!' he said breathlessly. 'Lookit here.'

Hanging from the fish cage was an eight-foot length of heavy monofilament line, transparent from more than a few feet away. Skink had cut one end with his dive knife. 'They tied it to a willow branch—you'd never see it unless you knew where to look,' he said. 'Get the wirecutters, Miami.'

Decker clipped the hinges off the fish cage. Skink reached in and took out the bass one by one, gently releasing each fish back into the lake. It was an oddly tender moment; Skink's grin was as warm as the glow from the lantern. After the bass were freed, he returned the empty cage to the water and tied it to the same dry bough.

Decker had to admit that it was an ingenious cheat. Salt the lake with pre-caught fish and scoop them out on tournament day. Dennis Gault was right; these boys would do anything to win. The more he thought about it, the more disgusted Decker got. The poachers had corrupted this beautiful place, polluted its smoky mystery. He couldn't wait to see their faces when they discovered what had happened, couldn't wait to take their pictures.

Probing the waters around the highway pilings, Decker and Skink located three more submerged cages, each stocked with the freshly caught bass. They counted eleven fish in all, four in the final trap; lifting the largest by its lower lip, Skink estimated its weight at nine and a half pounds. 'This bruiser would have bought dirty Dickie first place,' he gloated. '*Adiós*, old girl.' And he let the fish go.

That left two smaller bass flopping in the mesh, their underslung jaws snapping in mute protest while starved burgundy gills flared in agitation.

'Sorry fellas,' Skink said. 'You're the bait.' With a pair of blunt-nosed pliers he carefully clipped the first two spines of the dorsal fin on each bass.

'What're you doing?' R. J. Decker asked.

'Marking them,' Skink replied, 'that's all.'

With the fish still trapped, he securely rewired the door of the cage and eased it below the surface. He made sure it was tied securely to the concrete beam where Dickie Lockhart would be looking for it. By that time, of course, the bass champion would be in a state of desperate panic, wondering not only who was sabotaging his secret fish cages but also how in the world he would ever win the tournament now.

13

The day the Cajun Invitational Bass Classic was to begin, Dennis Gault was hundreds of miles away in Miami. Though it nettled him to miss the competition, strategy dictated that he sit out the tournament. He wanted Dickie Lockhart to feel safe and secure, knowing his archenemy wasn't around to spy on him. He wanted Dickie and his gang to let their guard down.

Gault spent most of the morning in a surly mood, barking at secretaries and hanging up on commodity brokers who wanted the scoop on the new cane crop. In the morning paper he checked the weather in New Orleans and was elated to see that it was windy and cold; this meant rugged fishing. R. J. Decker called briefly to say things were going well, but offered no details. The other thing he didn't offer was an apology for smashing Dennis Gault's nose. Gault was miffed at Decker's icy attitude but thrilled by the idea that the drama finally had begun. Gault's hatred for Dickie Lockhart consumed him, and he would not rest until the man was not just broken but scandalized.

The cheating was only part of it; Gault would have rigged some bass tournaments himself, had he found trustworthy conspirators. The more virulent seed of Dennis Gault's resentment was knowing that a dumb hick like Dickie was part of the bass brotherhood—the Good Old Boy that Gault himself could never be. Dickie was the champ, the TV personality, the world-famous outdoorsman; he could scarcely balance a checkbook or tie a Windsor, but he knew Curt Gowdy personally. In a man's world, that counted for plenty.

Losing to Lockhart in a bass tournament was bad enough, but watching impotently while the asshole outsmarted everybody else was intolerable. Dennis Gault's venom toward Dickie and his crowd spilled from a deep well. It was the way they looked at him when he showed up for the tournaments; he was the outsider, the dilettante with the money. Their eyes said: You don't belong on this lake, mister, you belong on a golf course. He was constantly referred to as The Rich Guy from Miami. Coral Gables would have been fine, but *Miami*. He might as well have dropped in from Bolivia as far as the other bassers were concerned. To a man they were rural Deep Southerners, with names like Jerry and Larry, Chet and Greg, Jeb and Jimmy. When they talked it was bubba-this and brother-that, between spits of chaw. When Dennis Gault opened his mouth and all that get-me-my-broker stuff came out, the bassers looked at him as if he were a peeling leper.

Naively Gault had thought this antagonism might abate as his angling skills improved and he began to win a few tournaments. Things only got worse, of course, due in large measure to his own abysmal judgment. For instance, Dennis Gault insisted on driving his burgundy Rolls Corniche to all the fishing tournaments. The purple vision of such a car towing a bass boat down the Florida Turnpike was enough to stop traffic, and it positively ruined the bucolic ambience of any dockside gathering. Many times Gault would return from a hard day of fishing to find his tires flattened, or see that some mischiefmaker had parked his burgundy pride beneath a tree filled with diarrhetic crows. But Gault was a peculiar man when it came to personal tastes; his father had driven a Rolls and by God that's what Dennis would drive. He did not like pickup trucks, but a pickup would have helped him crack the bass clique. With the Corniche he stood no chance.

The incident with the helicopters is what sealed his excommunication.

Long before he had collected any evidence against Dickie Lockhart, Dennis Gault had proposed a monitoring program to deter cheating in the big-money tournaments. Rumors of flagrant bass-planting had surfaced even in the usually booster-minded outdoor magazines, and a few unseemly scandals had come to light. Consequently, professional tournament organizers were in a mood to mend their tarnished image. More as a public-relations gambit than anything, they had agreed to try Dennis Gault's unusual experiment.

This was his plan: to have independent spotters in helicopters follow the fishermen and keep an eye on them during the competition. Gault even offered to pay for the chopper rentals himself, an offer which was snapped up immediately.

The problem with the plan was that largemouth bass don't much care for noise, and helicopters make plenty. The fish didn't like the penetrating thrum of the big machines, nor the waves the aircraft kicked up on the water. This was quickly evident in the Tuscaloosa bass tournament, where Gault's airborne scheme was tried for the first and last time. Whenever the helicopters would appear and hover over the bass boats, the fish would go deep and quit eating. The wind from the rotors made it impossible to cast a lure, and blew the caps and forty-dollar Polaroid sunglasses off several irritated contestants. The whole thing was a truly terrible idea, and on the second day of the experiment two of the helicopters were actually shot out of the sky by angry bass fishermen. Because no one was seriously injured, the offenders were assessed only ten penalty pounds apiece off their final stringers. Dennis Gault finished in fourteenth place and was banished from the national Competition Committee forever.

Which was probably just as well. Soon afterward Gault had come to suspect Dickie Lockhart of cheating, and his obsession took root like a wild and irrational vine. It twisted itself so ferociously around Gault's soul that even knowing of R. J. Decker's progress in Louisiana only agitated him; Gault itched to be there to share in the stalk, though he knew it would have been a grave mistake. On the telephone Decker had addressed him in the same cold tones as the fishermen always did, as if he were a spoiled wimp, and this began to bother Gault too. Sometimes Decker seemed to forget he was hired help.

The way this is going, Gault thought, I'll be the last to know if something shakes loose.

So he made a call and asked Lanie for another favor.

Decker got up before dawn, struggled into his blue jeans, and threw on a musty blue pea jacket. The DJ on the clock radio announced that it was forty-eight degrees in downtown Hammond. Decker shivered, and put on two pairs of socks; living in the South Florida heat turned your blood to broth.

Skink sat on the floor of the motel room and flossed his teeth. He wore only Jockey shorts, sunglasses, and the flowered bathcap. Decker asked if he wanted to go along but Skink shook his head no. The twang of the floss against gleaming bicuspids sounded like a toy ukulele.

'Want me to bring back some coffee?' Decker asked.

'A rabbit would be good,' Skink said.

Decker sighed and said he would be back before ten. He got in the rental car and headed for the dock at Pass Manchac. On old Route 51 he encountered a steady stream of well-buffed Jeeps, Broncos, and Blazers, all towing bass boats to Lake Maurepas. Many of the trucks had oversize tires, tinted windows, and powerful fog lights that shot amber spears through the soupy-blue bayous. These vehicles served as the royal carriages of the top bass pros, who had won them in various fishing tournaments; a tournament wasn't even worth entering unless a four-wheel-drive was one of the prizes. Many of the bassers won three or four a year.

At the fish camp the mood was solemn and businesslike as the sleek boats were backed off galvanized trailers into the milky-green water. The anglers all wore caps, vests, and jumpsuits plastered with colorful patches advertising their sponsors' products; everything from bug spray to chewing tobacco to worms was shilled in this manner. Most of the fishermen wore Lucite goggles to protect their faces during the breakneck race to the bass hole. This innovation had recently been introduced to the bassing world after one unlucky angler died hitting a swarm of junebugs at fifty knots; one of the brittle beetles had gone through his left eyeball like a bullet and tunneled straight into his brain.

R. J. Decker sipped coffee from a Styrofoam cup and stood among a throng of wives, girlfriends, and mechanics waiting for the tournament to begin. A tall chalk scoreboard posted outside the Sportsman's Hideout displayed the roster of forty entrants, which included some of the most famous bass fishermen of all time; Jimmy Houston of Oklahoma, Larry Nixon of Texas, Orlando Wilson of Georgia, and of course the legendary Roland Martin of Florida. Revered in the world of fishing, these names meant absolutely nothing to R. J. Decker, who recognized only one entry on the Cajun Invitational chalkboard: Dickie Lockhart.

But where was the sonofabitch? As the headlights of the trucks sporadically played across the water, Decker scrutinized the faces of the anglers, now hunkered behind the consoles of their boats. They looked virtually identical with their goggles and their caps and their puffed ruddy cheeks. Dickie's boat was out there somewhere, Decker knew, but he'd have to wait until the weigh-in to see him.

At precisely five-thirty a bearded man in khaki trousers, a flannel shirt, and a string tie strode to the end of the dock and announced through a megaphone: 'Bass anglers, prepare for the blast-off!' In unison the fishermen turned their ignitions, and Lake Maurepas boiled and rumbled and swelled. Blue smoke from the big outboards curled skyward and collected in an acrid foreign cloud over the marsh. The boats inched away from the crowded ramp and crept out toward where the pass opened its mouth to the lake. The procession came to a stop at a lighted buoy.

'Now the fun starts,' said a young woman standing next to R. J. Decker. She was holding two sleeping babies.

The starter raised a pistol and fired into the air. Instantly a wall of noise rose off Maurepas; the race was on. The bass boats hiccuped and growled and then whined, pushing for more speed. With the throttles hammered down, the stems dug ferociously and the bows popped up at such alarming angles that Decker was certain some of the boats would flip over in midair. Yet somehow they planed off perfectly, gliding flat and barely creasing the crystal texture of the lake. The song of the big engines was that of a million furious bees; it tore the dawn all to hell.

It was one of the most remarkable moments Decker had ever seen, almost military in its high-tech absurdity: forty boats rocketing the same direction at sixty miles per hour. In darkness.

Most of the spectators applauded heartily.

'Doesn't anyone ever get hurt?' Decker asked the woman with the two babies, who were now yowling.

'Hurt?' she said. 'No, sir. At that speed you just flat-out die.'

Skink was waiting outside the motel when Decker returned. 'You got the cameras?' he asked.

'All ready,' Decker said.

They drove back to the Sportsman's Hideout and rented the same johnboat from the night before. This time Decker asked for a paddle. The cashier said brightly to Skink: 'Are you finding enough of those eels, Mr. Cousteau?'

'*Sí*,' Skink replied.

'*Oui!*' Decker whispered.

'*Oui!*' Skink said. 'Many many eels.'

'I'm so glad,' the cashier said.

Hastily they loaded the boat. Decker's camera gear was packed in waterproof aluminum carriers. Skink took special care to distribute the weight evenly, so the johnboat wouldn't list. After the morning's parade of lightning-fast bass rigs, the puny fifteen-horse outboard seemed slow and anemic to Decker. By the time they got to the secret spot, the sun had been up an hour.

Skink guided the johnboat deep into the bullrushes. The engine stalled when the prop snarled in thick grass. Skink used his bare hands to pull them out of sight, away from the pass. Soon they seemed walled in by cattails, sawgrass and hyacinth. Directly overhead was the elevated ramp of Interstate 55; Decker and Skink were hidden in its cool shadow. Wordlessly Skink shed the orange rainsuit and put on a full camouflage hunting outfit, the type deer hunters use. He threw one to R. J. Decker and told him to do the same. The mottled hunting suit was brand-new, still crinkled from the bag.

'Where'd you get this?' Decker asked.

'Borrowed it,' Skink said. 'Put the tripod up front.' By swinging the plastic paddle he cleared a field of view through the bullrushes. He pointed and said, 'That's where we pulled the last trap.'

Decker set the tripod in the bow, carefully tightening the legs. He attached a Nikon camera body with a six-hundred-millimeter lens; it looked like a snub-nosed bazooka. He had decided on black-and-white film; as evidence it was much more dramatic than a tiny Kodachrome slide. Color was for vacation snapshots, black-and-white was for the grit of reality. With a long lens the print would have that grainy texture that seemed to convey guilt, seemed proof that somebody was getting caught in the act of something.

Decker closed one eye and expertly focused on the strand of monofilament tied to the concrete piling.

'How long do we wait?' he asked.

Skink grunted. 'Long as it takes. They'll be here soon.'

'How can you be sure?'

'The fish,' Skink said. He meant the two bass he had left in the fish trap, the ones he had marked with the pliers. 'The longer you leave 'em, the worse they look. Bang their heads against the wire, get all fucked up. They'd stand out bad at the weigh-in. The trick is to get 'em fresh.'

'Makes sense,' Decker said.

'Well, these boys aren't stupid.'

On this point Decker and Skink disagreed.

After fifteen minutes they heard the sound of another boat. Skink slid to his knees and Decker took his position at the tripod camera. A boat with a glittering green metal-flake hull drifted into the Nikon's frame; the man up front held a fishing rod and used a foot pedal to control a small electric motor. The motor made a purring sound; it was designed to maneuver the boat silently, so as not to frighten the bass. The angler seated in the stern was casting a purple rubber worm and working the lure as a snake, the way Skink had showed Decker that night on Lake Jesup.

Unfortunately, neither of the men in the green boat happened to be Dickie Lockhart searching for his traps; they were just ordinary fishermen. After a while they glided away, still working the shoreline intently, seldom speaking to one another. Decker didn't know if the men were contestants in the big tournament, but thought they probably must be, judging by the grim set to their jawlines.

An hour passed and no other boats went by. Skink leaned back, propping his shoulders against the plastic cowling of the outboard motor. He looked thoroughly relaxed, much happier than he had seemed in the motel room. A blue heron joined them in the shade of the highway. Head cocked, it waded the shallows in slow motion, finally spearing a small bluegill. Skink laughed out loud and clapped his hands appreciatively. 'Now, that's fishing!' he exclaimed, but the noise startled the gangly bird, which squawked and flapped away, dropping the bluegill. No bigger than a silver dollar, the wounded fish swam in addled circles, flashing in the brown water. Skink leaned over and snatched it with one sure swipe.

'Please,' Decker protested.

Skink shrugged. 'Gonna die anyway.'

'I promise, we'll get a big lunch at Middendorf's—'

But it was too late. Skink gulped the fish raw.

'Christ.' Decker looked away. He hoped like hell they wouldn't see any snakes.

'Protein,' Skink said, muffling a burp.

'I'll stick to Raisin Bran.'

Stiffly Decker stood up to stretch his legs. He was beginning to think Dickie Lockhart wouldn't show up. What if he'd gotten spooked by finding the other traps empty? What if he'd decided to play it safe and fish honestly? Skink had assured him that no such change of plans was possible, too much was at stake. Not just first-place prize money but crucial points in the national bass standings—and don't forget the prestige. Damn egos, Skink had said, these boys make Reggie Jackson seem humble by comparison.

'Any sign of the Rundell brothers this morning?' Skink asked.

'Not that I saw,' Decker said.

'You can bet your ass they'll show up at the weigh-in. We'll have to be careful. You look worried, Miami.'

'Just restless.'

Skink sat forward. 'You been thinking about the dead guy back in Harney, am I right?'

'Dead guys, plural.'

'See why Bobby Clinch got killed in the Coon Bog,' Skink said.

'He was looking for fish cages, same as we were last night. Only Bobby wasn't too careful. The Bog is probably where Dickie hides some big mother hawgs.'

Decker said, 'It's not just Clinch that bothers me, it's the other two.'

Skink propped his chin in his hands. He was doing his best to appear sympathetic. 'Look at it like this: the creep I killed probably killed your pal the Armadillo.'

'Is that how you look at it?'

'I *don't* look at it,' Skink said, 'period.'

'He shot at us first,' Decker said, almost talking to himself.

'Right.'

'But we should have gone to the cops.'

'Don't be a jackass. You want your fucking name in the papers? Not me,' Skink said, 'I got no appetite for fame.'

Decker had been dying to ask. 'What exactly did you do,' he said to Skink, 'before this?'

'Before this?' Skink plucked off his shades. 'I made mistakes.'

'Something about you does look familiar,' Decker said. 'Something about the mouth.'

'Used to leave it open a lot,' Skink said.

'I think it's the teeth,' Decker was saying.

Skink's forest-green eyes sparkled. 'Ah, the teeth.' He grinned, quite naturally.

But R. J. Decker couldn't make the connection. The brief governorship of Clinton Tyree had occurred before Decker's newspaper days and before he paid much attention to statewide politics. Besides, the face now smiling at him from beneath the flowered bathcap was so snarled and seamed that the governor's closest friends might have had trouble recognizing him.

'What's the story?' Decker asked earnestly. 'Are you wanted somewhere?'

'Not wanted,' Skink said. 'Lost.'

But before Decker could press for more, Skink raised a fishy brown finger to his lips. Another boat was coming.

Coming fast, and from the opposite direction. Skink motioned to Decker and they shrank to the deck of the narrow johnboat. The sound of the other outboard stopped abruptly, and Decker heard men's voices behind them. The voices seemed very close, but he was afraid to get up and look.

'You have a talk with that fuckin' guy tonight!' said one man.

'I said I would, didn't I?' Another voice.

'Find out if he was followed or what.'

'He woulda said somethin'.'

'Mebbe. Mebbe he's just bean a smardass. Ever thoughta that?'

'I'll talk to him. Christ, was it the third piling or the fourth?'

'The fourth,' said the first voice. 'See, there's the line.'

The fishermen had spotted the submerged trap. Decker carefully lifted himself from the bottom of the johnboat and inched toward the camera in the bow. Skink nodded and motioned that it was safe to move. The poachers' voices bounced back and forth off the concrete under I-55.

"Least the fuckers didn't find this one.'

'Pull it up quick.'

Decker studied the two men through the camera. They had their backs toward him. Under the caps one looked blondish and one had thick black hair, like Dickie Lockhart's. Both seemed like large men, though it was difficult to tell how much of the bulk was winter clothing. The bass boat itself was silver and blue, with an unreadable name in fancy script along the side. Decker kept the camera trained on the fishermen. His forefinger squeezed the shutter button while his thumb levered the rewind. He had snapped six frames and still the men had not turned around.

It was maddening. Decker could see that they had the fish cage out of the water. 'They won't turn around,' he whispered to Skink. 'I haven't got the picture yet.'

From the back of the boat Skink acknowledged with a grunt. He flipped his sunglasses down. 'Get ready,' he said.

Then he screamed, a piercing feral cry that made Decker shiver. The unhuman quavering echo jolted both fishermen and caused them to drop the wire cage with a commotion. Clutching their precious captive bass, they wheeled to face a screeching bobcat, or maybe even a panther, but instead saw only the empty mocking glades. Swiftly, Decker fired away. His camera captured every detail of bewilderment in the two men's faces, including the bolt of fear in their eyes.

Two men who definitely were not Dickie Lockhart.

14

'So what now?'

'Eat,' Skink said through a mouthful of fried catfish. They sat at a corner table in Middendorf's. No one seemed to notice their camouflage suits.

Decker said, 'Wait till Gault hears we tailed the wrong guys.'

Skink had momentarily turned his attention to a bowl of drippy coleslaw. 'Maybe not,' he said. 'Maybe they work for Lockhart.'

Decker had considered that possibility. Perhaps Dickie was too cautious to pull the fish traps himself. All he'd have to do was recruit some pals for the deed, and rendezvous later on the lake to pick up the purloined bass. Some of those boys would do anything Dickie Lockhart told them, as long as he promised to put them on TV.

The other possible explanation of what had happened that morning made just as much sense: R. J. Decker had simply photographed the wrong gang of cheaters.

Either way, the faces on film were not the ones Dennis Gault wanted to see.

'You know damn well Dickie's got the tournament rigged.'

'Of course,' Skink said. 'But there's a billion places to hide the bass around here. Bayous far as the eye can see. Shit, he could sink the traps out on Pontchartrain and we'd grow old lookin' in that soup.'

'So we staked out the obvious place,' Decker said gloomily.

'And got ourselves some obvious assholes.' Skink signaled a waitress for more catfish. 'It'll all work out, Miami. Go to the weigh-in, see what happens. And eat your goddamn hush puppies, all right? Worse comes to worst, I'll just shoot the motherfucker.'

'Pardon?'

'Lockhart,' Skink said.

'Come on.' Decker vainly searched Skink's face for some sign that he was joking.

'Gault would love it,' Skink said. 'Damn, I got a mouthful of bones here. How hard is it to properly fillet a fish? Doesn't take a fucking surgeon, does it?' A waitress warily approached the table but Decker motioned her away.

'We're not killing Dickie,' he whispered to Skink.

'I've been thinking about it,' Skink said, not lowering his voice even a little. 'Who gives a shit if Lockhart croaks? His sponsors? The network? Big deal.' Skink paused to chew.

'I'll get the damn photograph,' Decker said.

'Be lots easier just to shoot his ass. Fella I know in Thibodaux, he'd lend me a deer rifle.'

'No!' Decker snapped, but he saw that the idea had already lodged itself like a tick, somewhere behind those infernal sunglasses. 'It's crazy,' Decker said. 'You mention it again and I'm gone, captain.'

'Oh, relax,' Skink said.

'I mean it!'

Skink reached over and speared a hush puppy from Decker's plate. 'I warned you,' he said playfully. 'You had your chance.'

The bass boats were as haphazard in their return as they had been regimented in departure. The weigh-in was set for four-thirty, and the fishermen cut wild vectors across Lake Maurepas to beat the deadline. They came from all directions; wide open seemed to be the only speed they knew. The ramp at Pass Manchac was bustling with spectators, sponsors, and even a local television crew. A monumental glass aquarium—a grudging concession to conservationists—had been erected near the scoreboard, ostensibly to keep the caught bass alive so they could be freed later. As the catches were brought in, the fish were weighed, measured, and photographed by a Louisiana state biologist. Then they were dropped into the greenish tank, where most of them promptly turned belly-up and expired in deep shock.

The all-important weight totals went up on the big scoreboard. The angler with the biggest fish would receive ten thousand dollars; heaviest stringer was twenty grand, plus a new bass boat, a vacation trailer, and a Dodge Ram four-by-four, which would most likely be traded back for cash.

Decker waited alone because Skink had gone back to the motel. He had mumbled something about not wanting to bump into the Rundell brothers—and there they were, slurping beer by the gas pumps. Ozzie was such a pitiable dolt, yet it was he who'd driven the getaway truck from the scene of Ott Pickney's murder. Decker played with the idea of sneaking up to Ozzie and whispering something terrifying into his ear, just to get a reaction. A fatal angina attack, maybe.

But Decker decided to keep a safe distance, on the off-chance Culver might remember him from the bait shop.

The ritual of the weigh-in—the handshakes, the hushed gathering around the scales, the posting of the results—held Decker's attention at first, but after a while his thoughts drifted back to Skink. It occurred to him that Skink was starting to unravel, or maybe just finishing the process, and that for all his backwoods savvy the man might become a serious liability. Decker wished Jim Tile were around to settle Skink down, or at least advise Decker how to handle him.

A burst of applause sprang from around the stage and the rest of the crowd rose on tiptoes, straining to see. A lean, tan, and apparently well-known fisherman was parading a stringer of three immense bass the way a triumphant boxer brandishes the championship belt. The scorer climbed a stepladder and wrote '21–7' in chalk next to the name of Ed Spurling. By four pounds he had become the new leader of the Cajun Invitational Bass Classic.

Grinning handsomely, Fast Eddie Spurling slipped the fat fish into the gigantic aquarium and clasped his hands over his head. Reflexively, and without purpose, Decker snapped a few pictures.

The cheaters in the green boat arrived ten minutes before the deadline. They wore no smiles for the fans. Only four bass hung on their stringer, including the two wan specimens that Skink had marked the previous night in the fish trap. Decker got off four frames before the cheaters slung their catch onto the scale and trudged off in a sulk. 'Eight-fourteen,' the weighmaster droned through a megaphone. Tenth place, Decker noted; it wasn't Lockhart, but it still felt good.

Dickie's boat was the last one to reach the dock. The crowd rustled and shifted; some of the other anglers craned their necks and muttered nervously, but a few pretended not to notice the champ's arrival. Ed Spurling popped a Budweiser and turned his back on the scene. He was talking to a bigshot from the Stren line company.

Dickie Lockhart pulled off his goggles, smoothed his jumpsuit, and ran a comb through his unnaturally shiny hair. All this, before bounding out of the boat. 'Hey,' he said when a fan called out his name. 'How you? Hey there! Nice to see ya,' as he threaded through the spectators. A crew from *Fish Fever* filmed the victory march.

Dickie's driver, a local boy, remained on his knees in the back of the bass boat, trying to grab the fish out of the livewell. He seemed to be taking a long time. Eventually even Ed Spurling turned to watch.

There were five bass in all, very nice ones. Decker figured the smallest to be four pounds; the biggest was simply grotesque. It had the color of burnt moss and the shape of an old stump. The eyes bulged. The mouth was as wide as a milkpail.

Dickie Lockhart's helper carried the stringer of fish through the murmuring throng to the weighmaster, who dumped them in a plastic laundry basket. The hawg went on the scale first: twelve pounds, seven ounces. When the weight flashed on the official Rolex digital readout, a few in the crowd whistled and clapped.

Ten grand, Decker thought, just like that. He snapped a picture of Dickie cleaning his sunglasses with a bandanna.

The entire stringer went next. 'Thirty-oh-nine,' the weighmaster bellowed. 'We've got us a winner!'

Decker noticed that the applause was neither unanimous nor ebullient, save for the beer-drooling Rundells, Dickie's most loyal worshipers.

'Polygraph!' a basser from Reserve shouted angrily.

'Put him on the box,' yelled another, one of Ed Spurling's people.

Dickie Lockhart ignored them. He grabbed each end of the stringer and lifted the bass for the benefit of the photographers. True-life pictures, he knew, were the essence of product-endorsement advertisements in outdoor magazines. Each of Dickie's many sponsors desired a special shot of their star and the prize-winning catch, and Lockhart effusively obliged. By the time he had finished posing and deposited the big fish into the tank, the bass were so dead that they sank like stones. The scorer chalked '30–9' next to Dickie's name on the big board.

R. J. Decker's camera ran out of film, but he didn't bother to reload. It was all a waste of time.

The weighmaster handed Lockhart two checks and three sets of keys.

'Just what I need,' the TV star joked, 'another damn boat.'

R. J. Decker couldn't wait to get out, and he pushed the rental car, an anemic four-cylinder compact, as fast as it would go. On Route 51 a gleaming Jeep Wagoneer passed him doing ninety, minimum. The driver looked like Ed Spurling. The passenger had startling straw-blond hair and wore a salmon jogging suit. They both seemed preoccupied.

At the motel the skinny young desk clerk flagged Decker into the lobby.

'I gave the key to your lady-friend,' he said with a wink. 'Didn't think you'd mind.'

'Of course not,' Decker said. Catherine—she'd come after all. He almost ran to the room.

The moment he opened the door Decker realized that Skink could no longer be counted among the sane; he had vaulted the gap from eccentric to sociopath.

Lanie Gault was tied up on the floor.

Not just tied up but tightly wrapped—wound like a mummy from shoulders to ankles in eighty-pound monofilament fishing line.

She was alive, at least. Her eyes were wide open, but upside-down it was hard to read the emotions. Decker noticed that she was naked except for bikini panties and gray Reebok sneakers. Her mouth was sealed; Skink had run a strip of hurricane tape several times around Lanie's head, gumming her curly brown hair. Decker decided to save the tape for last.

'Don't move,' he said. As if she'd be going out for cigarettes.

Decker dug a pocket knife from his camera bag. He knelt next to Lanie and began sawing through the heavy strands. Skink had wrapped her about four hundred times, spun her like a top, evidently; cutting her free took nearly thirty minutes. He took extra care with the tape over her mouth.

'Christ,' she gasped, examining the purple grooves in her flesh. Decker helped her to the bed and handed her a blouse from her overnight bag.

'You know,' Lanie said, cool as ever, 'that your friend is totally unglued.'

'What did he do to you?'

'You just saw it.'

'Nothing else?'

'This isn't enough?' Lanie said. 'He strung me up like a Christmas turkey. The weird thing was, he never said a word.'

Decker was almost afraid to ask: 'Why'd he take your clothes off?'

Lanie shook her head. 'He didn't, that was me. Thought I'd surprise you when you got back. I was down almost to the bare essentials when Bigfoot barged in.'

'We're sharing the room,' Decker said lamely.

'Cute.'

'He sleeps on the floor.'

'Lucky for you.'

Decker said, 'He didn't act angry?'

'Not really. Annoyed, I guess. He tied me up, grabbed his gear, and took off. Look at me, Decker, look what he did! I got stripes on my tits, stripes all over.'

'They'll go away,' Decker said, 'once the circulation comes back.'

'That line cut into the back of my legs,' Lanie said, examining herself in the mirror.

'I'm sorry,' Decker said. He was impressed that Lanie was taking it so well. 'He didn't say where he was going?'

'I told you, he didn't say a damn thing, just sang this song over and over.'

Decker was past the point of being surprised. 'A song,' he repeated. 'Skink was singing?'

'Yeah. "Nights in White Satin." '

'Ah.' Moody Blues. The man was a child of the Sixties.

'He's not much of a crooner,' Lanie grumbled.

'As long as he didn't hurt you.'

She shot him a look.

'I mean, besides tying you up,' Decker said.

'He didn't try to pork me, no,' Lanie said, 'and he didn't stick electrodes into my eyeballs, if that's what you mean. But he's still totally nuts.'

'I'm aware of that.'

'I could call the cops, you know.'

'What for? He's long gone.'

Not so long, Lanie thought, maybe fifteen minutes. 'Mind if I take a shower?'

'Go ahead.' Decker slumped back on the bed and closed his eyes. Soon he heard water running in the bathroom. He wished it were rain.

Lanie came out, still dripping. Already the purple ligature bars were fading.

'Well, here we are,' she said, a bit too brightly. 'Another night, another motel. Decker, we're in a rut.'

'So to speak.'

'Remember the last time?'

'Sure.'

'Well, don't get too damn excited,' she said, scowling. She wrapped herself in the towel.

Decker had always been a sucker for fresh-out-of-the-shower women. With considerable effort he pushed ahead with purposeful conversation. 'Dennis told you I was here.'

'He mentioned it, yeah.'

'What else did he mention?'

'Just about Dickie and the tournament, that's all,' Lanie said. She sat on the bed and crossed her legs. 'What's with you? I came all this way and you act like I've got a disease.'

'Rough day,' Decker said.

She reached over and took his hand. 'Don't worry about your weird friend, he'll find his way back to Harney.'

Decker said, 'He forgot his plane ticket.' Not to mention the insistent New Orleans bail bondsman; the airline disturbance was a federal rap.

'He'll be fine,' Lanie said. 'Put him on a highway and he'll eat his way home.'

Decker perked up. 'So you know about Skink?'

'He's a legend,' Lanie said. She started unbuttoning Decker's shirt. 'One rumor is he's a mass murderer from Oregon. Another says he's ex-CIA, helped kill Trujillo. One story goes he's hiding from the Warren Commission.'

'Those are first-rate,' Decker said, but he had nothing more plausible to offer in the way of Skink theories. A bomber for the Weather Underground. Owsley's secret chemist. Lead singer for the Grass Roots. Take your pick.

'Come under the covers,' Lanie said, and before Decker knew it the towel was on the floor and she was sliding between the muslin sheets. 'Come on, you tell me about your rough day.'

This, thought Decker, from a woman who'd just been strung up nude by a madman. Good old irrepressible Lanie Gault.

Later she got hungry. Decker said there was a good burger joint down the street, but Lanie nagged him into driving all the way to New Orleans. She tossed her overnight bag in the back seat and announced that she'd get her own room in the Quarter because she didn't want to stay at the Quality Court, in case Skink returned. Decker didn't blame her one bit.

They went to the Acme for raw oysters and beer. Lanie kept making suggestive oyster remarks while Decker smiled politely, wishing like hell he were back in Miami, alone in his trailer. He had enjoyed rolling around in bed with her—at least he'd thought so at the time—but was having difficulty recalling any of the prurient details.

Shortly after midnight he excused himself, went to a pay phone on Iberville, and called Jim Tile in Florida. Decker told him what had happened with Skink, Lanie, and the bass tournament.

'Man,' the trooper said. 'He tied her up?'

'And took off.'

'Come on home,' Tile said.

'What about Skink?'

'He'll be all right. He gets these moods.'

Decker told Tile about Skink's histrionics on the airplane. 'He has arraignment tomorrow,' Decker said. 'In the federal building on Poydras. If he calls, Jim, please remind him.'

Tile said, 'Don't hold your breath.'

Lanie had ordered another dozen on the half-shell while Decker was on the phone.

'I'm stuffed,' he said, but ate one anyway.

'Dennis says you're getting close to Lockhart.'

She'd been trying all night to find out what happened with the tournament. Decker hadn't said much.

Lanie said, 'I heard on the radio that Dickie won.'

'That's right.' Radio? What kind of radio station covers a fish tournament? Decker wondered.

'Did he cheat again?' Lanie asked.

'I don't know. Probably.' Decker paused. 'I'll send your brother a full report.'

'He'll be pissed.'

Tough shit, Decker wanted to say. But instead: 'We're not giving up.'

'You and Bigfoot?'

'He's got a particular talent.'

'Not with women,' Lanie said.

Decker dropped her off at the Bienville House. His feelings were not the least bit wounded when she didn't invite him to stay the night.

*

He took his time driving back to Hammond. It was past two in the morning, but I-10 was loaded with big trucks and semis, citybound. Their headlights made Decker's eyes water.

At the junction near Laplace he decided to take Route 51 instead of the new interstate. The bumpy unlit two-lane was Skink's kind of highway. Decker flicked on his brights and drove slowly, hoping against all reason to spot the big orange rainsuit skulking roadside. By the time Decker reached Pass Manchac all he'd seen was a gray fox, two baby raccoons, and a fresh-dead water moccasin.

Decker pumped the brakes as he drove by the Sportsman's Hideout. Someone had left the spotlights on at the dock. It made no sense; the tournament was over, the bassers long gone. Decker negotiated a sleepy U-turn and went back.

When he got out of the car, he noticed that the lake air was not nearly as chilly as the night before. Too late for the fishermen, the wind had finally shifted from north to south; it was a balmy Gulf breeze that made the spotlights tremble on the poles.

One of the beams aimed at the tournament scoreboard, another more or less at the giant aquarium.

Decker wondered if anyone had remembered to free the bass. He strolled down to the docks to see.

The aquarium pump labored, grinding noisy bubbles. The water had turned a silty shade of brown. With the back of his hand Decker wiped a window in the condensation and peered into the glass tank. Right away he spotted three dead fish, gaping and jelly-eyed, rolling slow-motion with the current along the bottom. Decker felt like a tourist at some Charles Addams rendition of Marineland.

The shadow of something larger drifted over the dead bass. Decker glanced toward the top of the ten-foot tank, but looked away when the spotlight caught him flush in the eyes.

To escape the glare he climbed the wooden stairs to the weighmaster's platform, which overlooked both the scoreboard and the release tank. From this vantage Decker spotted more dead bass floating on the surface, and something else, whorling slowly in the backwash of the pump. The form was big-shouldered and brown—at first Decker thought it might be a sea cow, somebody's sick idea of a joke.

When the thing drifted by, he got a better look.

It was a man, floating facedown; a chunky man dressed in a brown jumpsuit.

Decker watched the corpse go around the tank again. This time, when it floated by, he grabbed the stiff cold shoulders and flipped it over with a splash.

Dickie Lockhart's eyes stared wide but were long past seeing. He wore a plum-sized bruise on his right temple. If the blow hadn't killed him outright, it had definitely rendered him unfit for a midnight swim.

The killer's final touch was diabolical, and not without wit: a fishing lure, the redoubtable Double Whammy, had been hooked through Dickie Lockhart's lower lip. It hung off Dickie's face like a queer Christmas ornament. Unfortunately, being just as dead as Dickie, none of the bass in the aquarium could appreciate the piquancy of the killer's gesture.

R. J. Decker lowered the corpse back into the water and walked quickly to the car. The scene screamed for a photograph, but it screamed something else too. Decker heard it all the way back to the motel and even afterward, deep into fitful dreams.

15

According to his official church biography, Charles Weeb had turned to God after an anguished boyhood of poverty, abuse, and neglect. His father had died a drunk and his mother had died a dope fiend, though not before selling Charlie's two sisters to a Chinese slavery ring in exchange for sixty-five dollars and three grams of uncut opium.

The imagined fate of the missing Weeb sisters was a recurring theme in Charlie's TV sermons on the Outdoor Christian Network; nothing sucked in money faster than a lingering close-up of those snapshots of the two little girls, June-Lee and Melissa, under the plaintive caption: 'WHAT HAS SATAN DONE WITH THESE ANGELS?'

The Reverend Charles Weeb knew, of course. The angels in question were both alive and well, and presumably still working for Mr. Hugh Hefner in the same capacity that had first attracted Reverend Weeb's attention. He had personally clipped their child-hood photographs from the pages of *Playboy* magazine—that hokey section featuring family pictures of the centerfold as a little girl. Charlie Weeb had long since forgotten the real names of these models, or even what month and year they had starred in the publication. However, he wasn't the least bit worried that the pictures would be recognized and his scheme revealed, since no devout OCN viewer could ever admit to looking at such a magazine. The Reverend Charles Weeb made sure to regularly warn his flock that *Playboy* was a passport to hell.

In fact Charlie Weeb had no sisters, just an older brother named Bernie, who had been busted selling phony oil leases from a North Miami boiler room and was now doing seven years for wire fraud. Weeb's father had been a shoe salesman with an ulcer intolerant of alcohol; his mother was not a dope fiend but a successful real-estate agent, and from her Charlie Weeb had drawn the inspiration for his dream project in Florida, Lunker Lakes.

The Weeb family had never been particularly religious, so neighbors were surprised, even somewhat skeptical, to learn that little Charlie had grown up to become a fundamentalist preacher. The Weebs, after all, were Jewish. Acquaintances were even more puzzled to turn on the television and see Charlie going on about his wretched parents and kidnapped sisters. Bernie the Bum was the only one whom the neighbors remembered.

Charles Weeb's path to religious prominence had been a curious and halting one. After being expelled from the Citadel for moral turpitude, he had spent ten years chasing fads, hoping to hit it big. 'Eighteen-to-twenty-five alive!' was Charlie's slogan, because that was always his target market. His schemes were always about two years too late and fifty percent undercapitalized. For a while he ran a health-food store in Tallahassee, then a disco in Gulf Shores, then a hot-tub factory in Orlando. Though his track record made him look like a loser, Charlie Weeb was basically a clever man; no matter how catastrophically his enterprises failed, Weeb's bank account always prospered. In the late 1970s the IRS expressed an avid interest in Charlie Weeb's fortunes; this he took as a signal to find God, and quickly. Thus was born the First Pentecostal Church of Exemptive Redemption.

Charlie Weeb didn't own an actual church, but he had something even better: a TV station.

For two million dollars he had purchased a small UHF operation whose programming consisted entirely of game shows, Atlanta Braves baseball, and *The Best of Hee-Haw*. Nothing changed for four months, until one Sunday morning a man with straw-blond hair and messianic eyebrows stood behind a cardboard pulpit and introduced himself as the Most Holy Reverend Charles Weeb. From now on, he said, WEEB-TV would be the voice of Jesus Christ.

Then, live on the air, Charlie Weeb healed a crippled cat.

Hundreds of viewers saw it. The calico kitten limped to the

stage and—after a tremulous Reverend Weeb prayed for its soul and passed a hand over its furry head—the animal scampered away, cured.

The following Sunday Charlie Weeb performed the same miracle on a gimpy beagle. The Sunday after that, a shoat. Two weeks later, a baby llama, on loan from a traveling circus.

Weeb saved the master coup for Christmas Sunday, the start of a ratings-sweep week. Before the biggest TV audience ever, he healed a lamb.

It was a magnificent performance, full of biblical symbolism. Few viewers who saw the nappy dull-eyed critter rise off the floor were not deeply moved. No one in Charlie Weeb's flock seemed to mind that the miracle took about an hour longer than expected; they figured that, it being a busy Christmas, God was running a little late. In fact, the reason for the delay in the much-promoted lamb healing was that Charlie Weeb's assistant had injected way too much lidocaine into the animal's hind legs before the show, so it took an extra long time for the effect of the drug to wear off.

The Reverend Weeb nearly preached himself hoarse over that lamb, and after the Christmas miracle he swore off healings forever. By then it didn't matter; his reputation had been made. Soon stations all over the South were airing Weeb's show, *Jesus in Your Living Room*, and weekly mail donations were topping in the six figures. In TV evangelism Charlie Weeb finally had hooked into a popular trend before it tapped out.

This time he decided to take a chance. This time he funneled the profits into expansion instead of Bahamian bank accounts. With Weeb's preacher hour as its blockbuster leadoff, the Outdoor Christian Network was inaugurated with sixty-four stations as prepaid subscribers. The OCN format was simple: religion, hunting, fishing, farm-stock reports, and country-music-awards shows. Even as Charlie Weeb branched the OCN empire into real estate, investment banking, and other endeavors, he could scarcely believe the rousing success of his TV formula; it confirmed everything he had always said about the state of the human race.

Initially Weeb had refused to believe that grown men would sit for hours watching fishing programs on cable TV. In person the act of fishing was boring enough; watching someone else do it seemed like a form of self-torture. Yet Weeb's market researchers convinced him otherwise—Real Men tuned in to TV fishing, and the demographics were rock-solid for beer, tobacco, and automotive advertising, not to mention the marine industry.

Weeb scanned the projections and immediately ordered up a one-hour bass-fishing program. He personally auditioned three well-known anglers. The first, Ben Geer, was rejected because of his weight (three hundred and ninety pounds) and his uncontrollable habit of coughing gobs of sputum into the microphone. The second angler, Art Pinkler, was witty, knowledgeable, and ruggedly handsome, but burdened with a squeaky New England accent that spelled death on the Q meter. The budget was too lean for speech lessons or overdubbing, so Pinkler was out; Charlie Weeb needed a genuine redneck.

Which left Dickie Lockhart.

Weeb thought the first episode of *Fish Fever* was the worst piece of television he had ever seen. Dickie was incoherent, the camera work palsied, and the tape editors obviously stoned. Still Dickie had hauled in three huge largemouth bass, and the advertisers had loved every dirt-cheap minute. Baffled, Weeb stuck with the show. In three years, *Fish Fever* became a top earner for the Outdoor Christian Network, though in recent months it had lost ground in several important markets to Ed Spurling's rival bass show. Spurling's program was briskly edited and slickly packaged, which appealed to Charlie Weeb, as did anything that made wads of money and was not an outright embarrassment. Sensing that Dickie Lockhart's days as the Baron of Bass might be numbered, the Reverend Weeb had quietly approached Fast Eddie Spurling to see if he could be bought. The two men were still haggling over salaries by the time the Cajun Invitational fishing tournament came along, when Dickie found the preacher with two nearly naked women.

Lockhart's demand for a lucrative new contract was an extortion that Reverend Weeb could not afford to ignore; competition had grown cutthroat among TV evangelicals—the slightest moral stain and you'd be off the air.

As he had vowed, Dickie Lockhart won the New Orleans tournament easily. Charlie Weeb didn't bother to show up at the victory party. He scheduled a press conference for the next morning to announce Dickie Lockhart's new cable deal, and phoned the TV writer of the *Times-Picayune* to let him know. Then he called a couple of hookers.

At five-thirty in the morning, a city policeman knocked on the double door to Charlie Weeb's hotel suite. The cop recognized one of the hookers but didn't mention it. 'I've got bad news, Reverend,' the policeman said. 'Dickie Lockhart's been murdered.'

'Jesus help us,' Charlie Weeb said.

The cop nodded. 'Somebody beat him over the head real good. Stole his truck, his boat, all his fishing gear. The cash he won in the tournament, too.'

'This is terrible,' said Reverend Weeb. 'A robbery.'

'We'll know more tomorrow, when the lab techs are done,' the cop said on his way out. 'Try to get some rest.'

'Thank you,' said Charlie Weeb.

He was wide-awake now. He paid off the hookers and sat down to write his Sunday sermon.

R. J. Decker was not exactly flabbergasted to wake up in the motel room and find that Skink had not returned. Decker had every reason to suspect that it was he who had murdered Dickie Lockhart—first of all, because Skink had talked so nonchalantly about doing it; second, the perverse details of the crime seemed to carry his stamp.

Decker showered in a daze and shaved brutally, as if pain would drive the fog from his brain. The case had turned not only more murderous but also more insane. The newspapers would go nuts with this stuff; it was probably even a national story. It was a story from which Decker fervently wished to escape.

After checking out of the motel, he packed his gear into the rental car and drove toward Pass Manchac. It was nine in the morning—surely somebody had discovered the gruesome scene by now.

As he drove across the water Decker's heart pounded; he could see blue lights flashing near the boat ramp. He pulled in at the Sportsman's Hideout, got out of the car, and wedged into the crowd that encircled the huge bass aquarium. There were five police cruisers, two ambulances, and a fire truck, all for one dead body. It had been three whole hours since Dickie's remains had been fished from the tank, strapped to a stretcher, and covered with a green woolen blanket; no one seemed in a hurry to make the trip to the morgue.

The crowd was mostly men, some of whom Decker recognized even without their caps as contestants from the bass tournament. Two local detectives with pads and pencils were working the spectators, hoping to luck into a witness. A pretty young woman leaned against one of the squad cars. She was sobbing as she talked to a uniformed cop, who was filling out a pink report. Decker heard the girl say her name was Ellen. Ellen O'Leary. She had a New Orleans accent.

Decker wondered what she knew, what she might have seen.

In the back of his mind Decker harbored a fear that Skink might show up at the dock to admire his own handiwork, but there was no sign of him. Decker slipped into a phone booth and called Dennis Gault at home in Miami. He sounded half-asleep.

'What do you want?'

What do you want? All charm, this guy.

'Your pal Dickie's landed his last lunker,' Decker said.

'What do you mean?'

'He's dead.'

'Shit,' Gault said. 'What happened?'

'I'll tell you about it later.'

'Don't leave New Orleans,' Gault said. 'Stay put.'

'No way.' Just what I need is that asshole jetting up for brunch at Brennan's, Decker thought. He's probably icing a Dom Perignon already.

In an oddly stiff tone Gault asked, 'Do you have those pictures?' As if it made a difference now.

Decker didn't answer. Through the pane in the phone booth he was watching Thomas Curl and the Rundell brothers in the parking lot of the marina. One of the local detectives was interviewing the three men together; when Ozzie talked, his head bobbed up and down like a dashboard puppy. The cop was scribbling energetically in his notebook.

'What number you at?' Dennis Gault asked over the phone.

'Seventy,' Decker replied. 'As in miles per hour.'

The tire blew on Interstate 10, outside of Kenner. The spare was one of those tiny toy tires now standard equipment on new cars. To get to the spare Decker had to empty the trunk of his duffel and camera gear, which he stacked neatly by the side of the highway. He had gotten the rental halfway jacked when he heard another car pull up behind him in the emergency lane; by the emphysemic sounds of the engine, Decker knew it wasn't a cop.

Not even close. It was a brown 1974 Cordoba, its vinyl roof puckered like a sun blister. Two-for-four on the hubcaps. Three men got out of the rusty old tank; judging by their undershirts and tattoos, Decker assumed they were not from the Triple-A. He pried the crowbar out of the jack handle and held it behind him.

'Gentlemen,' he said.

'Whatsamatter here?' said the largest of the trio.

'Flat tire,' Decker said. 'I'm fine.'

'Yeah?'

'Yeah. Thanks anyway.'

The men didn't exactly take the hint. Two of them ambled over to where Decker had laid the camera bag, tripod, and galvanized lens cases. One of the jerks poked at the camera with the toe of his boot.

'Whatsis?' he said.

'Beer money,' said the other.

Decker couldn't believe it. Broad daylight, cars and trucks and Winnebagos cruising by on the interstate—and these pussbuckets were going to roll him anyway. Damned Nikons, he thought; sometimes they seemed to be the root of all his troubles.

'I'm a professional photographer,' Decker said. 'Want me to take your picture?'

The two thinnest men looked expectantly toward the bigger one. Decker knew the idea appealed to them, although their leader needed a little convincing. 'A nice eight-by-ten,' Decker said affably, 'just for fun.' He knew what the big guy was thinking: Well, why not—we're going to steal the damn things anyway.

'Stand in front of the car and I'll get a shot of all three of you together. Go ahead, now.'

Decker walked over to the camera bag and inconspicuously set the crowbar inside. He picked up a bare F-3 camera body, didn't even bother to screw on a lens. These morons wouldn't know the difference. Shrugging, murmuring, slicking their hair with brown bony hands, the highwaymen struck a pricelessly idiotic pose in front of the dented Cordoba. As he pressed the shutter, Decker almost wished there were film in the camera.

'That's just great, guys,' he said. 'Now let's try one from the side.'

The big man scowled.

'Just a joke,' Decker said. The two thin guys didn't get it anyway.

'Enougha this shit,' the leader of the trio said. 'We want your goddamn car.'

'What for?'

'To go to Florida.'

Of course, Decker thought, Florida. He should have known. Every pillhead fugitive felon in America winds up in Florida eventually. The Human Sludge Factor—it all drips to the South.

'One more picture,' Decker suggested. He had to hurry; he didn't want to get mugged, but he didn't want to miss his plane, either.

'No!' the big man said.

'One more picture and you can have the car, the cameras, everything.'

Decker kept one eye on the interstate, thinking: Don't they have a highway patrol in Louisiana?

'You guys got some cigarettes? That would be a good shot, have a cigarette hanging from your mouth.'

One of the thin guys lighted a Camel and wedged it into his

lips at a very cool angle. 'Oh yeah,' Decker said. 'That's what I mean. Let me get the wide-angle lens.'

He went back to the camera bag and fished out a regular fifty-millimeter, which he attached to the Nikon. He picked up the crowbar and slipped it down the front of his jeans. The black iron felt cold against his left leg.

When he turned around, Decker saw that all three men now sported cigarettes. 'The girls down in Florida are gonna love this picture,' he said.

One of the thin guys grinned. 'Good pussy in Florida, right?'

'The best,' Decker said. He moved up close, clicking away. The men stunk like stale beer and tobacco. Through the lens Decker saw rawboned ageless faces; they could have been twenty years old, or forty-five. Classic cons. They seemed mesmerized by the camera, or at least by Decker's hyperactive choreography. The leader of the trio plainly was getting antsy; he couldn't wait to kick Decker's ass, maybe even kill him, and get moving.

'Almost done,' Decker said finally. 'Move a little closer together . . . that's good . . . now look to my right and blow some smoke . . . great! . . . keep looking out at the water . . . that-is-perfect!'

Staring obediently at Lake Pontchartrain, the three men never saw Decker pull out the crowbar. With both hands he swung as hard as he could, a batter's arc. The iron blade pinged off the top of their skulls one by one, as if Decker were playing a human xylophone. The robbers fell in a wailing cross-eyed heap.

Decker had expected less noise and more blood. As the adrenaline ebbed, he looked down and wondered if he had hit them more than once. He didn't think so.

Now it was definitely time to go; the flat tire was Hertz's problem. Decker quickly loaded his stuff into the Cordoba. The key was in the ignition. A blue oily pistol lay on the front seat. He tossed it out the window on his way to the airport.

16

The first person R. J. Decker called when he got back to Miami was Lou Zicutto. Lou was branch claims manager of the mammoth insurance company where Decker worked part-time as an investigator. Lou was a spindly little twit, maybe a hundred twenty pounds, but he had a huge florid head, which he shaved every day. As a result he looked very much like a Tootsie Pop with lips. Despite his appearance, Lou Zicutto was treated respectfully by all employees and coworkers, who steadfastly believed that he was a member of the Mafia who could have them snuffed with a single phone call. Lou himself did nothing to discourage this idea, even though it wasn't true. Except for the fancy stationery, Decker himself didn't see much difference between the mob and an insurance company, anyway.

'Where ya been?' Lou Zicutto asked. 'I left a jillion messages.' Lou had a raspy cabdriver voice, and he was always sucking on menthol cough drops.

'I've been out of town on a case,' Decker said. He could hear Lou slurping away, working the lozenges around his teeth.

'We got Núñez this week, remember?'

Núñez was a big fraud trial the company was prosecuting. Núñez was a stockbroker who stole his own yacht and tried to scuttle it off Bimini for the insurance. Decker had shot some pictures and done surveillance; he was scheduled to testify for the company.

'You're my star witness,' Lou said.

'I can't make it, Lou, not this week.'

'What the hell you mean?'

Decker said, 'I've got a conflict.'

'No shit you got a conflict. You got a big fucking conflict with me, you don't show up.' The cough drops were clacking furiously. 'Two million bucks this creep is trying to rip us for.'

'You got my pictures, the tapes, the reports—' Decker said.

'Your smiling face is what the lawyers want,' Lou Zicutto said. 'You be there, Mr. Cameraman.' Then he hung up.

The second person Decker tried to call was Catherine. The first time, the line was busy. He tried again two minutes later and a man answered. It sounded like James, the chiropractor; he answered the phone the way doctors do, not with a civil hello but with a 'Yes?' Like it was a pain in the ass to have to speak to another human being.

Decker hung up the phone, opened a beer, and put a Bob Seger album on the stereo. He wondered what Catherine's new house looked like, whether she had one of these sunken marble tubs she'd always wanted. A vision of Catherine in a bubble bath suddenly swept over Decker, and his chest started to throb.

He was half-asleep on the sofa when the phone rang. The machine answered on the third ring. Decker sat up when he heard Al García's voice.

'Call me as soon as you get in.'

García was a Metro police detective and an old friend. Except he didn't sound so friendly on the machine; he sounded awfully damn professional. Decker was a little worried. He drank two cups of black instant coffee before calling back.

'Hey, Sarge, what's up?'

García said, 'You at the trailer?'

'No, I'm in the penthouse of the Coconut Grove Hotel. They're having a Morgan Fairchild lookalike contest and I'm the judge for the swimsuit competition.'

Normally García would have donated some appropriately lewd counterpunchline, but today all he offered was a polite chuckle.

'We need to talk,' the detective said mildly. 'See you in about thirty.'

García was sitting on something, that much was certain. Decker shaved and put on a fresh shirt. He could easily guess what must have happened. A Louisiana cop probably had found those three dirtbags that Decker had clobbered along the interstate. They would have sworn that this scoundrel from Miami had flagged them down and robbed them, of course. A tracer on the Hertz car would have yielded Decker's name and address, and from then on it was only a matter of professional courtesy. Al García was probably bringing a bench warrant from St. Charles Parish.

Decker was not especially eager to return, or be returned, to Louisiana. He figured he could beat the phony assault rap from the highway robbers, but what if the Lockhart case broke open in the meantime? Decker didn't want to be around if Skink got arrested.

Skink was the big problem. If Decker hadn't enlisted the mad hermit into the case, Dickie Lockhart would still be alive. On the other hand, it was probably Lockhart who had arranged the murders of Robert Clinch and then Ott Pickney. Decker didn't know exactly what to do next; it was a goddamn mess. He had come to like Skink and he hated the thought of him going to the gas chamber over a greedy sleazoid such as Lockhart, but murder was murder. As he straightened up the trailer—a week's worth of moldy laundry, mainly—Decker toyed with the idea of telling García the whole story; it was so profoundly weird that even a Miami cop might be sympathetic. But Decker decided to hold off, for the moment. There appeared to be a good chance that Skink might never be found, or even identified as a suspect. Decker also understood that Skink might see absolutely nothing wrong in what he did, and would merely appear one day to take full credit for the deed. This was always a possibility when dealing with the chronically unraveled.

The news from Louisiana was relatively sparse. In the two days Decker had been back in Florida, the local newspapers had run only a couple of four-paragraph wire stories about Dickie Lockhart's murder at the bass tournament—robbery believed to be the motive; no prints, no suspects; services to be held in Harney County. The stories probably would have gotten better play had it not been for the biannual mass murder in Oklahoma; this time it was twelve motorists shot by a disgruntled toll-booth operator who was fed up with people not having exact change.

After trying Catherine, Decker had made three attempts to reach Dennis Gault. Various disinterested secretaries had reported that the sugarcane baron was on long distance, in a conference, or out of town. Decker had not left his name or a message. What he had wanted to tell Gault was that the case was over (obviously) and that he was pocketing twenty grand of the advance for time and expenses. Gault would bitch and argue, but not too much. Not if he had any brains.

Al García showed up right on time. Decker heard the car door slam and waited for a knock. Then he heard another car pull up the gravel drive, and another. He looked out the window and couldn't believe it: Al's unmarked Chrysler, plus two green-and-whites—a whole damn posse for a lousy agg assault. Then a terrible thought occurred to him: What if it were something more serious? What if one of those Louisiana dirtbags had actually died? That would explain the committee.

The cops were out of their squad cars, having a huddle in front of Decker's trailer. García's cigarette bobbed up and down as he talked to the uniformed officers.

'Shit,' Decker said. The neighbors would be absolutely thrilled; this was good for a year's worth of gossip. Where were the pit bulls when you needed them?

Decker figured the best way to handle the scene was to stroll outside and say hello, as if nothing were out of the ordinary. He was two steps from opening the door when something the approximate consistency of granite crashed down on the base of his neck, and he fell headlong through a dizzy galaxy of white noise and blinding pinwheels.

When he awoke, Decker felt like somebody had screwed his skull on crookedly. He opened his eyes and the world was red.

'Don't fucking move.'

A man had him from behind, around the neck. It was a military hold, unbreakable. One good squeeze and Decker would pass out again. A large gritty hand was clapped over his mouth. The man's chin dug into Decker's right shoulder, and his breath whistled warmly in Decker's ear.

Even when Decker's head cleared, the red didn't go away. The intruder had dragged him into the darkroom, turned on the photo light, and locked the door. From somewhere, remotely, Decker heard Al García calling his name. It sounded like the detective was outside the trailer, shouting in through a window. Probably didn't have a search warrant, Decker thought; that was just like García, everything by the bloody book. Decker hoped that Al would take a chance and pop the lock on the front door. If that happened, Decker was ready to make some serious noise.

Decker's abductor must have sensed something, because he brutally tightened his hold. Instantly Decker felt bug-eyed and queasy. His arms began to tingle and he let out an involuntary groan.

'Ssshhh,' the man said.

Forced to suck air through his nose, Decker couldn't help but notice that the man smelled. Not a stink, exactly, but a powerful musk, not altogether unpleasant. Decker tuned out García's muffled shouts, closed his eyes, and concentrated. The smell was deep swamp and animal, sweet pine tinged with carrion. Mixed in were fainter traces of black bog mud and dried sweat and old smoke. Not tobacco smoke, either, but the woodsy fume of campfires. Suddenly Decker felt foolish. He abandoned all thought of a struggle and relaxed in the intruder's bearlike grip.

The voice in his ear whispered, 'Nice going, Miami.'

R. J. Decker was right. Al García didn't have a search warrant. What he had, stuffed in an inside pocket of his J. C. Penney suit jacket, was a bench warrant for Decker's arrest, which had been Federal Expressed that morning all the way from New Orleans. The warrant was as literate and comprehensible as could be expected, but it did not give Al García the right to bust down the door to Decker's trailer.

'Why the hell not?' asked one of the uniformed cops.

'No PC,' García snapped. PC was probable cause.

'He's hiding in the can, I bet.'

'Not Decker,' García said.

'I don't want to wait around,' the other cop said.

'Oh, you got big plans, Billy?' García said. 'Late to the fucking opera maybe?'

The cop turned away.

García grumbled. 'I don't want to wait either,' he said. He was tired of hollering through Decker's window and he was also pissed off. He had driven all the way out here as a favor, and regretted it. He hated trailer parks; trailer parks were the reason God invented tornadoes. García could have sent only the green-and-whites, but Decker was a friend and this was serious business. García wanted to hear his side of it, because what the Louisiana people had told him so far was simply not believable.

'You want me to disable his vehicle?' asked the uniformed cop named Billy.

'What are you talking about?'

'Flatten the tires, so he can't get away.'

García shook his head. 'No, that won't be necessary.' The standards at the police academy had gone to hell, that much was obvious. Anybody with an eighteen-inch neck could get a badge these days.

'He said he'd be here, right?' the other cop asked.

'Yeah,' García mumbled, 'that's what he said.'

So where was he? Why hadn't he taken his own car? García was more miffed than curious.

The cop named Billy said, 'Suppose the jalousies on the back door suddenly fell out? Suppose we could crawl right in?'

'Suppose you go sit under that palm tree and play with yourself,' García said.

Christ, what a day. It began when the Hialeah grave robbers struck again, swiping seven human skulls in a predawn raid on a city cemetery. At first García had refused to answer the call on the grounds that it wasn't really a murder, since the victims of the crime were already dead. One of them in particular had been dead since before Al García was born, so he didn't think it was practical, or fair, that he should have to reinvestigate. Everybody in the office had agreed that technically it wasn't a homicide; more likely petty larceny. What could a crumbly old skull be worth on the street? they had asked. Fifteen, twenty bucks, tops.

Unfortunately, it developed that one of the rudely mutilated cadavers belonged to the uncle of a Miami city commissioner, so the case had hastily been elevated to a priority status and all detectives were admonished to keep their sick senses of humor to themselves.

About noon García had to drop the head case when a real murder happened. A Bahamian crack freak had carved up his male roommate, skinned him out like a mackerel, and tried to sell the fillets to a wholesale seafood market on Bird Road. It was one of those cases so bent as to be threatened by the sheer weight of law-enforcement bureaucracy—the crime scene had been crawling not just with policemen, but with deputy coroners, assistant prosecutors, immigration officers, even an inspector from the USDA. By the time the mess was cleaned up, García's bum shoulder was throbbing angrily. Pure, hundred-percent stress.

He had spotted the express packet from New Orleans when he got back to the office. A perfectly shitty ending to a shitty day. Now R. J. Decker had made like a rabbit and García was stuck in a crackerbox trailer park trying to decide if he should leave these moron patrolmen to wait with the warrant. He was reasonably sure that, left unsupervised, they would gladly shoot Decker or at least beat the hell out of him, just to make up for all the aggravation.

'Screw it,' García said finally, 'let's go get some coffee and try again later.'

'He'll be back,' Decker said when he heard the police cars pull away.

Skink had let go of his neck. They were still in the darkroom, where Skink's fluorescent rainsuit shone almost white in the wash of the red bulb. Skink appeared more haggard and rumpled than Decker remembered; twigs and small pieces of leaf hung like confetti in his long gray braid. His hair stuck out in clumps from under the shower cap.

'Where have you been?' Decker asked. His neck was torturing him, like someone had pounded a railroad spike into the crown of his spine.

'The girl,' Skink said. 'I should have known.'

'Lanie?'

'I got back to the room and there she is, half-undressed. She said you'd invited her to fly up—'

'No way.'

'I figured,' Skink said. 'That's why I tied her up, so you could decide for yourself what to do. You cut her loose, I presume.'

'Yeah.'

'And screwed her too?'

Decker frowned.

'Just what I thought,' Skink said. 'We've got to get the hell out of here.'

'Listen, captain, that cop is a friend of mine.'

'Which one?' With one blackened finger Skink scratched absently at a brambly eyebrow.

'The Cuban detective. García's his name.'

'So?'

'So he's a good man,' Decker said. 'He'll try to get us a break.'

'*Us?*'

'Yeah, with the New Orleans people. Al could make it as painless as possible.'

Skink studied Decker's face and said, 'Hell, I guess I squeezed too tight.'

They went to a Denny's on Biscayne Boulevard, where Skink fit right in with the clientele. He ordered six raw eggs and a string of pork sausages. Decker's neck had stiffened up, and he had the worst headache of his life.

'You could have just tapped me on the shoulder,' he complained.

'No time to be polite,' Skink said, without a trace of apology. 'I did it for your own good.'

'How'd you get in, anyway?'

'Slim-jimmed the back door. Two minutes later and your bosom buddy García would have had you in bracelets. Eat something, all right? We got a long damn ride.'

Decker had no intention of taking a long damn ride with Skink, and no intention of getting picked up as an accessory to murder.

He had decided not to turn Skink in to the police, but the man would have to make his own escape; the partnership was over.

Skink said, 'Your neighbors'll raise hell about the dead dogs.'

'Oh?'

'Couldn't be helped,' Skink said, slurping a drip of yolk from his mustache. 'Self-defense.'

'You killed the pit bulldogs?'

'Not *all* of them. Just the ones that were chasing me.'

Before Decker could ask, Skink said, 'With a knife. No one saw a thing.'

'God.' Decker's brainpan felt like the bells of Notre Dame. He noticed that his fingers twitched when he tried to butter a biscuit. It dawned on him that he was not a well person, that he needed to go to a doctor.

But before he abandoned Skink he wanted to ask about Dickie Lockhart. He wanted to hear Skink's version, in case it never came out.

'When you left the motel in Hammond,' Decker began, 'where'd you go?'

'Back to the lake. Bor rowed a boat and found Dickie's fish traps.'

'You're kidding.'

Skink beamed. A brown clot of sausage was stuck between his two front teeth. 'The boat I took was Ozzie Rundell's,' he said. 'Dumb fucker left the keys in the switch and a map in the console.'

'A depth chart of Lake Maurepas,' Decker guessed, 'with the trap sites marked.'

'Marked real clear, too,' Skink said, 'in crayon, just for Ozzie.'

It made sense. While Dickie Lockhart was celebrating his victory, the Rundells would sneak out on the lake to clean up the evidence. Dickie was so cheap he probably used the same traps over and over.

'Those fish he won with were Florida bass,' Skink was saying. 'Probably trucked in from Lake Jackson or maybe the Rodman. That mudhole Maurepas never saw bass that pretty, you can bet your ass—'

'What'd you do after you found the traps?' Decker cut in.

Skink set down his fork. 'I pulled the plug on Ozzie's boat and swam to shore.'

'Then?'

'Then I stuck out my thumb, and here I am.'

Two cops came in, walking the cowboy walk, and took a booth. Cops ate at Denny's all the time, but still they made Decker nervous. They kept glancing over at Skink—hard glances—and Decker could tell they were dreaming up an excuse for a hassle and ID check. He laid a ten on the table and headed for the car; Skink shuffled behind, shoving a couple of biscuits into the pockets of his rainsuit. No sooner were they back on the boulevard than Decker spotted another patrol car in the rearview. The patrol car was following closely, and Decker could only assume that Al García had put out the word. When the blue lights came on, Decker dutifully pulled over.

'Hell,' Skink said.

Decker waited until both cops were out of the car, then he punched the accelerator and took off.

Skink said, 'Sometimes I like your style.'

Decker guessed he had a three-minute lead. 'I'm going to turn on Thirty-sixth Street,' he said, 'and when I hit the brakes, you bail out.'

'Why?' Skink asked calmly.

Decker was pushing the old Plymouth beyond its natural limits of speed and maneuverability. It was one of those nights on the boulevard—every other car was either a Cadillac or a junker, and nobody was going over thirty. Decker was leaving most of his tread on the asphalt, and running every stoplight. The rearview was clear, but he knew it wouldn't take long for the cops to radio for backup.

'You might want to try another road,' Skink suggested.

'You're a big help,' Decker said, watching a bus loom ahead. He took a right on Thirty-fifth Street and braked the car so hard he could smell burnt metal. 'Get going,' he said to Skink.

'Are you crazy?'

'Get out!'

'*You* get out,' Skink said. 'You're the dumb shit they're after.'

Impatiently Decker jammed the gearshift into park. 'Look, all they got me for is agg assault and, after this, a misdemeanor resisting. Meanwhile, you're looking at murder-one if they put it all together.'

With a plastic crunch Skink turned in his seat. 'What the hell are you talking about?'

'I'm talking about Dickie Lockhart.'

Skink cackled. 'You think *I* killed him?'

'It crossed my mind, yeah.'

Skink laughed some more, and punched the dashboard. He thought the whole thing was hilarious. He was hooting and howling and kicking his feet, and all Decker wanted to do was push him out of the car and get going.

'You really don't know what happened, do you?' Skink asked, after settling down.

Decker killed the headlights and shrank down in the driver's seat. He was a nervous wreck, couldn't take his eyes off the mirrors. 'What don't I know?' he said to Skink.

'What the goddamn warrant says, you don't even know. Jim Tile got a copy, airmail. He read it to me first thing this morning and you should hear what it says, Miami. Says you murdered Dickie Lockhart.'

'Me?'

'That's what it says.'

Decker heard the first siren and went cold.

Skink said, 'You got set up, buddy, set up so good it's almost a thing of beauty. The girl was bait.'

'Go on,' Decker said thickly. He was trying to remember Lanie's story, trying to remember some of the holes.

'Don't even think about turning yourself in,' Skink said. 'García may be your pal but he's no magician. Now please let's get the hell out of here while we still can. I'll tell you the rest as we go.'

17

They ditched the Plymouth back at the trailer park and took a bus to the airport, where Decker rented a white Thunderbird from Avis. Skink did not approve; he said they needed a four-by-four truck, something on the order of a Bronco, but the Avis people only had cars.

Sticking in the heavy traffic, they drove around Little Havana for two hours while Decker quizzed Skink about what had happened at Lake Maurepas.

'Who whacked Lockhart?' he asked.

'I don't know that,' Skink said. 'This is what I do know, mostly from Jim Tile and a few phone calls. While you were banging Gault's sister, somebody clubbed Dickie to death. First thing the next morning, Gault himself flies to New Orleans to offer the cops a sworn statement. He tells them an ex-con photographer named Decker was trying to blackmail Dickie over the bass cheating. Says you approached him with some photographs and wanted a hundred K—he even had a note in your handwriting to that effect.'

'Jesus,' Decker groaned. It was the note he had written the night Gault had fought with him—the note raising his fee to one hundred thousand dollars.

Skink went on: 'Gault tells the cops that he told you to fuck off, so then you went to Lockhart. At first Dickie paid you—thirty grand in all, Gault says—'

'Cute,' Decker muttered. Thirty had been his advance on the case.

'—but then Dickie gets tired of paying and says no more. You go to New Orleans to confront him, threaten to expose him at the big tournament. There's an argument, a fight ... you can script the rest. The cops already have.'

'And my alibi witness is the real killer's sister.'

'Lanie wasted no time giving an affidavit,' Skink said. 'A very helpful lady. She says you poked her, drove her back to New Orleans, and dropped her at a hotel. Says you told her you had to go see Dickie on some business.'

'I can pick 'em,' Decker said mordantly.

Skink fidgeted in the car; his expression had grown strained. The press of the traffic, the din of the streets, bothered him. 'Almost forgot,' he said. 'They got the blackmail photographs too.'

'What photographs?'

'Of Dickie pulling the fish cages,' Skink replied. 'Beats me, too. You're the expert, figure it out.'

Decker was astounded. 'They got actual pictures?'

'That's what the DA says. Very sharp black-and-whites of Dickie doing the deed.'

'But who took 'em?'

'The DA says you did. They traced an empty box of film to a wholesale shipment of Kodak that went to the photo lab at the newspaper. The newspaper says it was part of the batch you swiped on your way out the door.'

'I see.' Skink was right: it was almost a thing of beauty.

Skink said, 'Are you missing any film?'

'I don't know.'

'The junk we shot in Louisiana, where's that?'

'Still in my camera bag,' Decker said, 'I guess.'

'You guess.' Skink laughed harshly. 'You better damn well find out, Miami. You're not the only wizard with a darkroom.'

Decker felt tired; he wanted to close his eyes, cap the lens. Skink told him they should take U.S. 27 up to Alligator Alley and go west.

'We'd be safer in the city,' Decker said. He didn't feel like driving the entire width of the state; the drumbeat pain on his brainstem was unbearable. The Alley would be crawling with state troopers, too; they had an eye for sporty rental cars. 'Where exactly did you want to go?' he asked Skink.

'The Big Cypress is a good place to hide.' Skink gave him a sideways glance.

'Not the swamp-rat routine,' Decker said, 'not tonight. Let's stay in town.'

'You got somewhere that's safe?'

'Maybe.'

'No hotels,' Skink hissed.

'No hotels.'

Decker parked at the curb and studied the house silently for several moments. It seemed impressively large, even for Miami Shores. There were two cars, a Firebird and a Jaguar sedan, parked in a half-circle gravel driveway. The sabal palms and seagrape trees were bathed by soft orange spotlights mounted discreetly around the Bermuda lawn. A Spanish archway framed the front door, which was made of a coffee-colored wood. There were no iron bars across the front window, but Decker could see a bold red sticker advertising the burglar alarm.

'You gonna sit here and moon all night?' Skink said.

They got out and walked up the driveway, the gravel crunching noisily under their feet. Skink had nothing to say about the big house; he'd seen plenty, and most were owned by wealthy and respectable thieves.

Indelicately Decker asked him to stand back a few steps from the door.

'So they don't die of fright, is that it?' Skink said.

Catherine answered the bell. 'Rage,' she said, looking more than a little surprised.

She wore tight cutoff jeans and a sleeveless lavender top, with no brassiere. Decker was ticked off that James the doctor had let her answer the door in the middle of the night—they could have been any variety of nocturnal Dade County creep: killers, kidnappers, witch doctors looking for a sacrificial goat. What kind of a lazy jerk would send his wife to the door alone, with no bra on, at eleven-thirty?

'I would've called,' R. J. Decker said, 'but it's kind of an emergency.'

Catherine glanced at Skink and seemed to grasp the seriousness of the situation.

'Come on in, guys,' she said in a friendly den-mother tone. Then she leaned close and whispered to Decker: 'James is here.'

'I know.' The Jag was the giveaway.

A snow-white miniature poodle raced full speed into the foyer, its toenails clacking on the tile. The moment it saw Skink, the dog began to snarl and drool deliriously. It chomped the cuff of his orange rainsuit and began tearing at the plastic. Wordlessly Skink kicked the animal once, sharply, skidding it back down the hall.

'Sorry,' Decker said wanly.

'It's okay,' Catherine said, leading them into the kitchen. 'I hate the little bastard—he pees in my shoes, did I tell you that?'

Out of nowhere Skink said: 'We need a place for the night.'

Catherine nodded. 'There's plenty of room.' An emergency is right, she thought; that would be the only thing to get Decker to stay under the same roof.

Skink said: 'Decker's hurt, too.'

'I'm all right.'

'What is it?' Catherine asked.

'I almost broke his neck,' Skink said, 'accidentally.'

'It's just a sprain,' Decker said.

Then James the doctor—Catherine's husband—walked into the kitchen. He wore a navy Ralph Lauren bathrobe that stopped at his pale hairless knees; he also wore matching blue slippers. Decker was seized by an urge to repeatedly slap the man in the face; instead he just froze.

James studied the two visitors and said, 'Catherine?' He wanted an explanation.

Both Catherine and Decker looked fairly helpless, so Skink stepped forward and said, 'This is your wife's ex-husband, and I'm his friend.'

'Oh?' In his lifetime James had never seen anything like Skink up close, but he was doing his best to maintain a man-of-the-house authority. To Decker he extended his hand and said, 'R.J., isn't it? Funny we haven't met before.'

'Uproarious,' Decker said, giving the doctor's hand an exceedingly firm shake.

'They're spending the night,' Catherine told her husband. 'R.J.'s trailer flooded.'

'There's been no rain,' James remarked.

'A pipe broke,' Catherine said impatiently.

Good girl, Decker thought; still quick on her feet.

'I'm going to fix these fellows some tea,' she said. 'Everybody into the living room, now, scat.'

The living room had been designed around one of those giant seven-foot televisions of the type Decker had seen at Dennis Gault's condominium. Every chair, every sofa, every bar stool had a view of the screen. James the chiropractor had been watching a videocassette of one of the 'Star Wars' movies. 'I've got all three on tape,' he volunteered.

Decker was calming down. He had no reason to hate the guy, except maybe for the robe; anyway, it was Catherine who had made the choice.

James was slender and somewhat tall—taller than Decker had expected. He had a fine chin, high cheekbones, and quick aggressive-looking eyes. His hair was reddish-brown, his skin fair. His long delicate hands were probably a competitive advantage in the world of chiropractic. On the whole he was slightly better-looking than Decker had hoped he would be.

'I've seen some of your photographs, and they're quite good,' James said, adding: 'Catherine has an old album.'

A double beat on the word *old*. In a way Decker felt a little sorry for him, having two surly strangers in the house, and a wife expecting him to be civil. The man was nervous, and who wouldn't be?

Bravely James smiled over at Skink, a dominating presence in his fluorescent rainsuit. James said, 'And you must be a crossing guard!'

Catherine brought cinnamon tea on a plain tray. Skink took a cup and drank it down hot. Afterward his dark green eyes seemed to glow.

As Catherine poured him another cup, Skink said: 'You're quite a beautiful girl.'

Decker was dumbstruck. James the doctor was plainly mortified. Skink smiled luminously and said, 'My friend was an idiot
to let you go.'

'Thank you,' Catherine said. She didn't act put out at all, and
she certainly didn't act threatened. The look on her face was
charmed and knowing. It was, Decker thought irritably, as if she
and Skink were sharing a secret, and the secret was about him.

'Catherine,' James said sternly, changing the subject, 'have you
seen Bambi?'

'He was playing in the hall a few minutes ago.'

'He looked a little tired,' Decker offered.

'Bambi?' Skink made a face. 'You mean that goddamn yappy
dog?'

James stiffened. 'He's a pedigree.'

'He's a fucking rodent,' Skink said, 'with a perm.'

Catherine started to laugh, caught herself. Even in his jealous
snit, Decker had to admit they made a comical foursome. He was
glad to see that Skink's momentary charm had evaporated; he
was much more likable as a heathen.

James glared at him and said, 'I didn't get your name.'

'Ichabod,' Skink said. 'Icky for short.'

Decker suspected, and fervently hoped, that Ichabod was not
Skink's real name. He hoped that Skink had not chosen this
particular moment, in front of these particular people, to bare
the murky secrets of his soul. Catherine was known to have that
effect on a man.

Inanely Decker said to James, 'This is quite a place. Your practice must be going great guns.'

'Actually,' James said, 'I picked up this house before I became
a doctor.' He seemed relieved not to be talking about the poodle
or his wife's good looks. 'Back when I was in real estate,' he said,
'that's when I lucked into the place.'

'What kinda real estate?' Skink asked.

'Interval-ownership units,' James replied, without looking at
him.

'Timeshares,' Catherine added helpfully.

On the sofa Skink shifted with an audible crinkle. 'Timeshares,'
he said. 'Whereabouts?'

Catherine pointed to several small plaques hanging on one of the walls. 'James was the top salesman three years in a row,' she said. It didn't sound like she was bragging; it sounded like she said it to get it out of the way, knowing James would have mentioned it anyway.

'And where was this?' Skink pressed.

'Up the coast north of Smyrna,' James said. 'We did very well for a stretch in the late seventies. Then Tallahassee cracked down, the media went sour on us, and the interval market dried up. Same old tune. I figured it was time to move along to something else.'

'Boom and bust,' Decker played along. 'That's the story of Florida.' Was it purely the money, he wondered, that had attracted Catherine to this lanky twit? In a way he hoped it was that simple, that it was nothing more.

Skink got up and crunched over to examine the plaques. Catherine and James couldn't take their eyes off him; they had never had such a wild-looking person roaming their house.

'What was the name of your project?' Skink asked, toying with his silvery braid.

'Sparrow Beach,' James said. 'The Sparrow Beach Club. Seems like ancient history now.'

Skink gave no reply, but let out a soft and surprising noise. It sounded to R. J. Decker like a sigh.

'Is your friend all right?' Catherine asked later.

'Sure,' Decker said. 'He prefers to sleep outdoors, really.'

In the middle of James's monologue about his sales triumphs at Sparrow Beach, Skink had turned to Catherine and asked if he could spend the night in the backyard. Decker could tell he was brooding, but had no private moment to ask what was wrong. Catherine had loaned Skink an old blanket and in a flat voice Skink had thanked her for the hospitality and lumbered out the back door. He had ignored James completely.

Skink settled in under a tall avocado tree, and from the window Decker could see him sitting upright against the trunk, facing the narrow waterway that ran behind Catherine's house. Decker had an urge to join him there, under the stars.

'Let James have a look at your neck,' Catherine said.

'No, I'll be fine.'

'Lie down here,' James instructed, making room on the sofa. 'Lie down on your stomach.'

The next thing Decker knew, James was hunched over him with one knee propped on the sofa for leverage. Intently he kneaded and probed the back of Decker's neck, while Catherine watched cross-legged on an ottoman.

'That hurt?' James asked.

Decker grunted. It did hurt, but the rubbing helped; James seemed to know what he was doing.

'Brother, you're really out of alignment,' he said.

'That's a medical term?'

'Full traction is what you need. Slings and weights. Thermal therapy. Ultrasound. You're too young for Medicare, otherwise I'd fix you right up with a twelve-week program.' James worked his fingers along Decker's spine. He seemed at ease now, enjoying the role of expert. 'Have you got any insurance?' he asked.

'Nope,' Decker said.

'Workmen's comp? Maybe you're in an HMO.'

'Nope.' The guy was unbelievable; the pitchman's spark was probably left over from his days of peddling condos.

'I must caution you,' James went on, 'that injuries such as this should never go untreated. Your neck has been wrenched badly.'

'I'm aware of that,' Decker said, wincing under the chiropractor's explorations. 'Tell me, what's the difference between this and a massage?'

'I'm a doctor, that's the difference. Don't move now. I think I've got an extra brace in the trunk of the car.'

After James had left the room, Catherine came over and knelt down on the floor next to Decker. 'Tell me what's happened, Rage.'

'Somebody's trying to frame me for a murder.'

'Who? Not the Fish People!'

'Afraid so,' Decker said. He was ready for a trenchant scolding—this was Catherine's specialty—but for some reason (probably pity) she refrained.

'The guy out back, Grizzly Adams—'

'He's all right,' Decker said.

'James is scared of him.'

'So am I, but he's all I've got.'

Catherine kissed him lightly on the ear. 'Is there anything I can do?'

For one flushed moment Decker felt his heart stop. Bump, bump—then dead air. All from a whiff of perfume and a silly peck on the earlobe. It was so wonderful that Decker almost forgot she'd dumped him for a guy who wore ninety-dollar bathrobes.

Catherine said, 'I want to help.'

'Does James have a broker?' Decker asked.

'Yes. Hutton, Shearson, somebody big like that. It's a VIP account, that much I know. They sent us a magnum of champagne last Christmas.'

Decker said, 'This is what I need. Tell James you got a tip at the beauty parlor—'

'Oh, please.'

'Or wherever, Catherine, just tell him you got a tip on a stock. It's traded as OCN, I think. The Outdoor Christian Network. See if your husband's broker can send over a prospectus. I need a copy as soon as possible.'

She said, 'He'll think it's odd. We never talk about his investments.'

'Try it,' Decker said. 'Play dumb and sweet and just-trying-to-help. You can do it.'

'You're still an asshole, Rage.'

'And you're still a vision, Catherine. Would your husband get too terribly upset if you and I took off our clothes and hopped in the shower? We can tell him it's part of my medical treatment. Hot-water traction, they call it.'

At that moment James walked in, too preoccupied to notice his wife scooting back to the ottoman. James was carrying a foam-padded brace, the kind that fastens around the neck like a collar.

'That man,' he said indignantly, 'has built a bonfire in our backyard!'

Catherine went to the window. 'For heaven's sake it's not a *bonfire*,' she said. 'It's just a barbecue, honey, no worse than you and your hibachi.'

'But the hibachi is gas,' James protested.

R. J. Decker pushed himself off the sofa and went to see for himself. Skink huddled in a familiar pose beneath the avocado tree; crouched on his haunches, tending a small campfire.

'He looks like a damn hobo,' James said.

'That's enough,' Catherine snapped. 'He's not hurting anybody.'

Decker observed that Skink had fashioned a rotisserie spit out of dead branches. He was cooking a chunk of gray meat over the fire, rotating it slowly by hand.

'What do you suppose he's got there?' Catherine said.

'Probably something gross he scrounged from the garbage,' James said. 'Or maybe a duck out of that filthy canal.'

In the flickering shadows Decker couldn't be sure, but he had a pretty good idea what his friend was fixing for dinner. It was Bambi, of course. Skink was serenely roasting the doctor's pet poodle.

18

R. J. Decker took a bed in one of the guestrooms, but he couldn't sleep. Dancing on the walls were cartoon sheep in red tuxedos—wallpaper for a baby's room, obviously, but Catherine had never been too wild about kids. On this matter the chiropractor had failed to change her mind. Still, Decker admired his optimism for leaving the nursery wallpaper up.

When Decker closed his eyes, the tuxedoed sheep were replaced by the face of Dennis Gault: the seething visage of a man trying to strangle him. Decker wondered if the fistfight at Gault's condominium had been an act like everything else; he wondered if Gault were really that clever or ballsy, or if things had just fallen right. Decker couldn't wait to meet up with Gault and ask him. Afterward it would be nice to choke the sonofabitch so decisively that his eyeballs would pop out of his skull and roll across his fancy glass desk like a couple of aggies.

At about three o'clock Decker gave up on sleep and got out of bed. From the window there was no sign of Skink's campfire, or of Skink himself. Decker assumed—hoped, at least—that he was curled up in the bushes somewhere.

For Decker, being in the same house with Catherine was unnerving. Though it was also the house of James, Catherine's tastes predominated—smart and elegant, and so expensive that Decker marveled how such a destitute mongrel as himself had managed to keep her as long as he had. If only he could steal a few moments alone with her now, but how? Skink wanted to be on the road before dawn—there was little time.

Barefoot, and wearing only his underwear, Decker made his way through the long hallways, which smelled of Catherine's hair and perfume. A couple of times, near doorways, Decker had to step carefully over the white beams of photosensitive alarm units, which were mounted at knee-level throughout the house.

Photoelectronic burglar alarms were the latest rage among the rich in Miami, thanks to a widely publicized case in which a whole gang of notorious cat burglars was captured inside a Star Island mansion after tripping the silent alarm. The gang had comprised bold Mariel refugees relatively new to the country and unschooled in the basic skills and technology of modern burglary. While looting the den of the mansion, one of the Cuban intruders had spotted a wall-mounted photoelectronic unit and naturally assumed it was a laser beam that would incinerate them all if they dared cross it. Consequently, they did not. They sat there all night and, the next morning, surrendered sheepishly to police. The incident made all the TV news. Photoelectronic burglar alarms became so popular that burglars soon began to specialize in stealing the alarms themselves. In many of the houses where such devices were installed, the alarm itself was more valuable than anything else on the premises. For a while, all the fences in Hialeah were paying twice as much for stolen burglar alarms as they were for Sony VCRs, but even at five hundred a pop it was virtually impossible for thieves to keep up with the demand.

Tiptoeing around the alarm beams, Decker found the master bedroom at the far west end of Catherine's house. He listened at the door to make sure nothing was going on, and was greatly relieved to hear the sound of snoring.

Decker slipped into the room. He stood at the door until his eyes adjusted; the window shades were drawn and it was very dark. Gradually he inched toward the source of the snoring until his right foot stubbed a wooden bed poster. Decker bit back a groan, and one of the two forms in the big bed stirred and turned slightly under the covers. Decker knelt by the side of the bed, and the form snored directly into his face.

'Catherine,' he whispered.

She snored again, and Decker remembered how difficult it was to wake her up. He shook her gently by the shoulder and said her name again. This time she swallowed, sighed, and groggily opened her eyes. When she saw who it was, she sat up immediately.

She put her hand on the back of Decker's head and pulled him close. 'What are you doing here?'

'Hey, careful with the neck,' Decker whispered back.

Catherine glanced at her husband to make sure he was still dozing. Decker had counted on James being a sound sleeper; unlike surgeons or obstetricians, chiropractors rarely had to go tearing off to the hospital in the middle of the night. Back spasms could wait. James was probably accustomed to getting a full nine hours.

'What is it, Rage?' Catherine said into his ear. Her hair was tangled from sleep, and her eyes were a little puffy, but Decker didn't care at all. He kissed her on the mouth and boldly slipped a hand under her nightshirt.

During the kiss Catherine sort of gulped, but still she closed her eyes. Decker knew this because he peeked; he had to. Some women closed their eyes during kissing just to be polite, but Catherine never did unless she was honestly enjoying herself. Decker was pleased to see her eyes shut. The activity beneath the nightshirt was another matter. With an elbow Catherine deftly had pinned his hand to her left breast; obviously that was as far as Mr. Hand would be allowed to go. It was all right with Decker; the left one had always been his favorite, anyway.

Catherine pulled away and said, 'You're nuts. Get outta here.'

'Come to my room,' Decker said.

Catherine shook her head and gestured toward her husband.

'Leave him here,' Decker said playfully.

'He'll notice if I get out of bed.'

'Just for a few minutes.'

'No—'

So he kissed her again. This time she gave a shy purr, which Decker correctly read more as tolerance than total surrender. The second kiss lasted longer than the first, and Decker was getting fairly heated up when James suddenly rolled over, snorted, and said, 'Cath?'

Carefully she lay down on the pillow, Decker's hand still resting on her breast. 'Yes, hon?' she said.

Cath.

Hon.

Very sweet, Decker thought, a regular goddamn testimonial to marital bliss. He started to remove his hand but Catherine wouldn't let him. Decker smiled in the dark.

'Cath,' James said torpidly, 'did Bambi ever come in?'

'No, honey,' she said. 'He's probably out on the porch. Go back to sleep now.'

Catherine held motionless until James's breathing grew thick and regular. Then she turned her back to him so that she and Decker were face-to-face at the edge of the bed.

'Go back to your room,' she whispered. 'Give me about ten minutes.'

'Thatta girl,' Decker said, rising off his knees. 'One more kiss.'

Catherine said, 'Ssshhh,' but she kissed him back. This time she let her tongue sneak into his mouth.

'We'll need your boat.'

Catherine and Decker opened their eyes mid-kiss and stared at each other. The whisper did not belong to James.

'The boat,' Skink said.

Catherine saw his tangled face looming impassively over Decker's shoulder.

'I don't mean to interrupt,' Skink said, 'but there's some cops out front.'

Decker stood up and fought back a panic. It had to be Al García. He knew about the divorce, and Catherine would have been high on his list of interviews. The surprising thing was that he'd come in the dead of night—unless, of course, he knew Decker was inside the house.

Which any nitwit could have figured out from the rental car out front. Decker wondered if maybe deep down he wanted to go back to jail—what else could explain such carelessness? Skink took care of survival in the boonies, but the city was Decker's responsibility and he kept making dumb mistakes.

'Your boat,' Skink said again to Catherine, 'it's tied up out back.'

She whispered, 'I don't know where the keys are.'

'I don't need the keys,' Skink said, no longer making an effort to talk quietly. 'We'll leave 'er up at Haulover, but don't go looking right away.'

The doorbell rang, followed by three sharp knocks.

James sat up in bed and reached for a lamp on the nightstand. Blearily he eyed Decker and Skink. 'What's going on?'

Catherine was out from the covers, brushing her hair in the mirror. 'You better get moving,' she said to Decker's reflection. 'I'll keep them at the door.'

'We'll need a head start.'

'Don't worry, Rage.'

The doorbell rang again. The knocks turned to pounding.

Skink handed Decker his jeans and shoes.

'What's going on?' James the doctor wondered. 'Where's the damn dog?'

Since the truck they'd been driving was registered to Dickie Lockhart, and since the New Orleans police had temporarily impounded it along with everything else belonging to Dickie, the Rundell brothers had been forced to take a Trailways all the way back to Florida. On the trip they talked primarily about two things—how their hero had died, and what had happened to their precious bass boat.

Dim as they were, even the Rundells realized that not much could be done for Dickie, but the boat was another issue. It had been stolen and then scuttled in the middle of Lake Maurepas, where it had turned up as bottom clutter on Captain Coot Hough's Vexilar LCD Video sonic fish-finder. Once the lost boat had been pinpointed, the Rundells had recruited an amateur salvage team made up of fellow bass anglers, who raised the vessel with a hand-cranked winch mounted on a borrowed construction barge. The sight of their sludge-covered beauty breaking the surface was the second saddest thing Ozzie Rundell had ever seen—the first being Dickie Lockhart's blue-lipped corpse in the big fish tank.

On the long bus ride back to Harney, Ozzie and Culver puzzled over who might have stolen their boat and why. The prime suspect seemed to be the violent hermit known to the Rundells only as Skink. A peculiar and vividly garbed man matching his description had been spotted on the lake by several other anglers, though no one had reported witnessing the actual sinking of the boat. What Skink was doing in Louisiana was a mystery that the Rundells did not contemplate for long—he was there, that's all that mattered. They clearly remembered the sky marshals leading him off the airplane in New Orleans, and they remembered the look of latent derangement in his eyes. Certainly the man was capable of stealing a boat; the riddle was finding a plausible motive. With a fellow like Skink, unadulterated malice might have been enough, but the Rundells remained doubtful. Culver in particular suspected revenge, or a plot hatched by one of Dickie Lockhart's jealous competitors. In the world of professional bassing it was well known that the Rundell brothers were the most loyal of Dickie's retinue, and in Culver's mind it made them likely targets.

If Culver were outwardly angry about the destruction of their prized fishing boat, Ozzie seemed more wounded and perplexed. He was particularly incredulous that Skink would commit such an atrocity against them for no apparent reason. In the ten-odd years since the shaggy woodsman had come to live on Lake Jesup, Ozzie had probably not exchanged a half-dozen words with him. On the rare occasions when Skink came to town, he purchased lumber and dry goods and used books from the Faith Farm—or so Mrs. Coot Hough had gossiped—but never once had he come into the bait shop for tackle or lures (though he was reputed to be an expert angler). Ozzie's only close encounters with the man were the many times he'd had to swerve to avoid the crouched figure plucking animal carcasses off the Gilchrist Highway or Route 222. Nearly all the citizenry of Harney had occasionally come across Skink and his fresh roadkills, and the general assumption was that he ate the dead critters, though no one could say for a fact. The only person known to have a friendly relationship with Skink was Trooper Jim Tile of the state highway patrol. Occasionally fishermen out on Lake Jesup would see Jim Tile sitting at Skink's campfire, but none of them knew the trooper well enough to ask about it. Actually no one in Harney, not even the blacks, knew Jim Tile much better than they knew Skink.

Which was why Ozzie was so stunned to hear his brother

announce that they would visit the trooper as soon as they got home.

'We'll get some answers out of that nigger,' Culver said.

'I don't know,' Ozzie mumbled. He wasn't keen on confrontations. Neither was Culver, usually, but Dickie's murder had set him on edge. He was talking big and mean, the way he sometimes did after drinking.

Ozzie Rundell had a perfectly good reason for not wanting to see Jim Tile face-to-face: Jim Tile had been out at Morgan Slough the night Ott Pickney was killed, the night Ozzie was driving Tom Curl's truck. As they were speeding out from the trail, Ozzie had spotted the trooper on foot. What he didn't know was whether or not Jim Tile had spotted him too. Ozzie had assumed not, since nothing terrible had happened in the days that followed, but he didn't want to press his meager luck. He felt he should explain to his brother the risks of visiting Jim Tile, but as usual the words wouldn't come out. The day after the newsman's death, Ozzie had assured Culver that everything had gone smoothly at the slough, and hadn't mentioned the black trooper. If Ozzie revealed the truth now, Culver would be furious, and Ozzie was in no mood to get yelled at. The closest thing to a protest he could muster was: 'A trooper is the law. Even a nigger trooper.'

Culver scowled and said, 'We'll see about that.'

Jim Tile lived alone in a two-bedroom apartment on Washington Drive, in the black neighborhood of Harney. He had been married for three years until his wife had gone off to Atlanta to become a big-time fashion model. Jim Tile could have gone with her, since he had been offered an excellent job with the Georgia Bureau of Investigation, but he had chosen to stay with the highway patrol in Florida. His loyalty had been rewarded with a protracted tour of duty in the most backward-thinking and racist county in the state. To stop a car for speeding in Harney was to automatically invite a disgusting torrent of verbal abuse—the whites hated Jim Tile because he was black, and the blacks hated him for doing a honky's job. Rough words were expected, and occasionally somebody would sneak up and cut the tires on his patrol car late at night, but it seldom went any further. In all the years only one person had been foolhardy enough to try to fight Trooper Jim Tile. The boy's name was Dekle, and he was eighteen, as big and white as a Frigidaire, and just about as intelligent. Dekle had been doing seventy in a school zone and had run down a kitten before Jim Tile caught up and forced him off the road. At the time Jim Tile was new to Harney, and the Dekle boy remarked how he had never seen a chocolate state trooper before. Now you have, said Jim Tile, so turn around and put your hands on the roof of the car. At which point Dekle punched Jim Tile with all his strength and was astounded to see the trooper merely rock back slightly on his heels, when any other human being would have fallen flat on his back, out cold. The fight did not last long, perhaps thirty seconds, and years afterwards Dekle's right arm still hung like a corkscrew and he still got around with the aid of a special Lucite cane, which his mother had purchased from a mail-order house in Tampa. Even in a place where there was no shortage of booze or stupidity, no one in Harney had since gotten drunk enough or dumb enough to take a poke at the black trooper. Most folks, including Ozzie Rundell, wouldn't consider giving the man any lip.

They found the apartment on Washington Drive easily; Jim Tile's black-and-tan Ford police cruiser was out front.

Culver parked his mother's truck. He got a pistol from under the front seat and tucked it into the back of his dungarees.

'What's that for?' Ozzie asked worriedly.

'It's a bad neighborhood, Oz.'

'I ain't going in there with a gun,' Ozzie said in a brittle voice. 'I ain't!'

'Fine,' Culver said. 'You sit out here in the parking lot with all these jigaboos. I'm sure they'll love the prospect of a fat little cracker boy like you.'

Ozzie looked around and knew that his brother was right. The streets were full of black faces, including some frightfully muscular teenagers slam-dunking basketballs through a rusty hoop nailed to a telephone pole. Ozzie decided he didn't want to stay in the truck after all. He followed Culver up to Jim Tile's apartment.

The trooper was finishing dinner, and getting ready to go out on the night shift. He came to the door wearing the gray, sharply pressed trousers of his uniform, but no shirt. The Rundell brothers were awestruck by the dimensions of his chest and arms.

After stammering for a second, Culver finally said, 'We need to talk about the guy lives up on the lake.'

'Our boat got sunk,' Ozzie warbled, without explanation.

Jim Tile let them in, motioned toward two chairs at the dinette. The Rundell brothers sat down.

'Skink is his name, right?' Culver said.

'What's the connection,' Jim Tile asked mildly, 'between the man on the lake and your boat?'

Ozzie started to say something, got lost, and looked to his brother for help. Culver said, 'We heard Mr. Skink is the one who sunked it.'

Jim Tile said, 'Well, Mr. Skink is out of town.'

'It happened out of town,' Culver said. 'At a tournament up in Louisiana.'

'Did you go to the police?' Jim Tile asked.

'Not yet,' Culver said. He had wanted to, but Thomas Curl had said it was a bad idea. He said the police would be busy with Dickie's murder, and it wouldn't be right to bother them over a bass boat. Besides, the boat *had* been recovered out of the water, and it was Thomas Curl's opinion that it could be repaired. Ozzie said great, but Culver didn't like the idea. Culver wanted a brand-new boat, and he wanted the man named Skink to buy it for him.

'Well, if you haven't talked to the police in Louisiana, then I suggest you do,' Jim Tile said. 'Once there's a warrant, one of Sheriff Lockhart's deputies can go out to Lake Jesup and arrest him.'

Culver Rundell doubted if Sheriff Earley Lockhart was much interested in a boat theft, not with his famous nephew turning up murdered in Louisiana. Earley had caught a flight to New Orleans two days after the killing, and had not yet returned. Before leaving, the sheriff dramatically informed the Harney *Sentinel* that his presence had been requested to assist in the homicide investigation, but in reality the Louisiana authorities merely wanted somebody to accompany Dickie's autopsied body back to Florida.

'It's a jurisdictional problem,' Trooper Jim Tile said to the Rundell brothers. 'I really can't help.'

'You can take us to see Mr. Skink,' Culver said.

'Why? You know where he lives—drive out there yourself.'

To Ozzie's ear, Jim Tile's response sounded as close to a definite no as you could get. But Culver wasn't giving up.

'No way,' Culver said. 'I heard he's got a big gun, shoots at people just for the fun of it. He doesn't know me or my brother, and he might just open fire if we was to drive up unannounced. You, he knows. Even if he's crazy as they say, he won't shoot a damn police car.'

The low, even tone of Jim Tile's voice did not change. 'I told you, he's out of town.'

'Well, let's go see.'

'No,' said Jim Tile, rising. 'I have to go to work.'

'Momma's truck,' Ozzie blurted. 'Maybe we oughta go, Culver.'

Annoyed, Culver glanced at his brother. 'What are you talking about?'

'I'm worried about Momma's truck out there. Maybe we should go.'

'The truck'll be fine,' Culver said.

'I don't know,' Jim Tile said, parting the venetian blinds. 'It's a pretty rough neighborhood.'

Ozzie looked stricken.

'Oh, settle down,' Culver said angrily. Then, to Jim Tile: 'You, why won't you help us? I lost a twenty-thousand-dollar rig because of that bastard!'

Jim Tile was still looking out the window. 'So that's your mother's pickup?'

'Ours is in the impound, up New Orleans,' Ozzie said.

'The red one,' Jim Tile said.

'Yeah,' Culver grunted, secretly impressed that the trooper would remember the color.

Then Jim Tile said to Ozzie: 'What about the green one?'

The color washed out of Ozzie's cheeks. His eyelids fluttered, as if he were about to faint.

'What green one?' Culver said, slow to put it together.

'The one your brother was driving week before last,' Jim Tile said, 'out on the Gilchrist. About dawn, one morning.'

'When?' Ozzie hiccuped. 'Wasn't me. Our truck is red.'

'You and two other guys,' Jim Tile said, 'and the truck was green. Out-of-state tags.'

Finally Culver was picking up on the train of conversation. He tried to help Ozzie as best he could, even though he felt like strangling him.

'I remember that day,' Culver improvised, watching his brother's eyes grow big. 'You and some boys went fishing up at the slough. I remember 'cause you took a couple Shakespeare plug rods out of the shop, along with some Johnson spoons and purple skirts.'

Ozzie's lips were like chalk. His bottom jaw went up and down until finally he said, 'Oh, yeah.'

Culver said, 'I remember 'cause you didn't want to try live shiners, even though I told you to. You said there was too much heavy cover, so you'd prefer dragging those damn weedless spoons.'

Jim Tile was buttoning his shirt. 'So, Ozzie,' he said, 'you guys catch anything?'

'Sure,' Ozzie said, glancing at the door, as if he were about to run.

'What'd you catch?'

'Our truck is red,' Ozzie Rundell said, licking his lips. His shoulders twitched and his eyes rolled up and fixed on the ceiling. His cheeks puffed out, like he was trying to fart.

'Pardon me?' Jim Tile said, bending over to tie his shoes.

'That's Momma's pickup outside,' Ozzie said in a very high voice. He was gone, unglued, lost in a pathetic blubbering panic. Culver shook his head disgustedly.

'I asked what you caught,' Jim Tile said, 'out at Morgan Slough.'

Ozzie smiled and smacked his lips. 'One time Dickie gave me a tacklebox,' he said.

'All right, that's enough,' Culver broke in.

'Ozzie?' said Jim Tile.

'The day in the truck?'

'The green truck, yes.'

'I was driving, that's all. I didn't drown nobody.'

'Of course not,' Jim Tile said.

'That's it,' said Culver Rundell. 'Shut the fuck up, Oz.'

Culver had the gun out. He was holding it with two hands, pointing it at Jim Tile's heart. Jim Tile glanced down once, but seemed to pay no more attention to the gun than if it were just Culver's fly unzipped.

'Let's go,' Culver said in a husky whisper.

But Jim Tile merely walked into the bedroom, stood at the dresser, and adjusted his trooper's Stetson.

'Now!' Culver shouted. Ozzie stared at the handgun and covered his ears.

Jim Tile reached for a bottle of cologne.

Culver exploded. 'Nigger, I'm talking to you!'

Only then did Jim Tile turn to give Ozzie Rundell's brother his complete and undivided attention.

19

The boat was an eighteen-foot Aquasport with a two-hundred-horse Evinrude outboard; smooth trim, dry ride, very fast. Skink liked it quite a bit. He liked it so much he decided not to ditch it at Haulover docks after all, but to drive it up the Intracoastal Waterway all the way to Pier 66, in Fort Lauderdale. The morning was biting cold, and R. J. Decker would have preferred to travel by car, but there was no point to raising the issue. Skink was having a ball, his silvery ponytail strung out behind him like a rope in the breeze. At the Dania Beach bridge he cut the throttle down to idle speed and the Aquasport coasted into a slow crawl.

'What's up?' Decker asked.

Skink said, 'Manatee zone.'

In the wintertime giant manatees migrate with their young to congregate sluggishly in the warm sheltered waters of the Intracoastal. During manatee season boaters are required by law to go slow, but each year dozens of the gentle mammals are run down and sliced to ribbons by reckless tourists and teenagers. The fine for such a crime costs the offending boater no more than a new pair of Top-Siders, and is not much of a deterrent. During the last days of his governorship, Clinton Tyree had lobbied for a somewhat tougher law. His version would have required anyone who killed a manatee to immediately forfeit his boat (no matter how luxurious) and pay a ten-thousand-dollar fine or go to jail for forty-five days. The Tyree amendment would have also required the manatee killer to personally bury the dead animal himself, at a public ceremony.

Not surprisingly, the governor's proposal was quietly rejected.

R. J. Decker knew none of this, so he was somewhat perplexed when Skink took a hawklike interest in another boat, speeding south down the waterway in the predawn twilight. It was a gaily colored ski boat full of young men and women returning from a night of serious dockside partying. Skink waved furiously and shouted for them to slow down, watch out for the sea cows, but the kids just stared back with radish-colored eyes—except for the driver, who made the awful mistake of flipping Skink the magic digit. Later the girls from the ski boat would tell the marine patrol that their boyfriends had gravely underestimated the size and temperament of the old hippie, just as they had underestimated the speed of the Aquasport. Were it not for the other stranger dragging the old hippie off them, the girls said, their boyfriends might have been seriously killed. (At this point the girls were doing all the talking because the young men were still being X-rayed at Broward General Hospital for broken bones. The doctors marveled that they had been able to swim so far in such a traumatized condition.)

To convince Skink to quit pummeling the speeders, Decker had had to agree to let him sink their ski boat, which he did by shooting three holes in the hull. Then he scrupulously idled the Aquasport all the way to the Port Everglades inlet, and from there it was full throttle again to Pier 66. By now Decker was cold and wet and eternally grateful to be off the water. They caught a cab to the Harbor Beach Marriott, got a room, and fell asleep—Decker splayed on the kingsize bed, Skink in a ball on the floor. At noon they woke up and started working the phones.

Jim Tile got off the road at nine in the morning. When he got back to the apartment, he fixed himself four poached eggs, three hunks of Canadian bacon, and a tumbler of fresh-squeezed orange juice. Then he took off his trousers, went to the bathroom, and changed the dressing on the bullet wound in his right thigh. Afterward he put on a gray sweatsuit, fixed himself some hot tea, and sat down with the newspaper. He did all this without saying a word to the Rundell brothers, who were still bound and gagged on the floor. In truth Culver didn't feel slighted (he had passed out from pain many hours before), but Ozzie was dying to talk. Ozzie was scared out of his mind.

'Thur?' he said.

Jim Tile lowered the newspaper, reached down, and yanked the towel from Ozzie's mouth.

'Sir, is my brother dead? Thank you. For taking the towel, I mean, thanks.'

Jim Tile said, 'Your brother is not dead.'

'What's wrong with him? His face don't look right.'

'His jaw's broken,' Jim Tile said. 'And all his fingers too.' It had happened when Jim Tile had wrenched the pistol away, after Culver had shot him and ruined a perfectly good uniform.

'He needs a doctor, bad,' Ozzie said plaintively.

'Yes, he does.' Jim Tile hadn't meant to break Culver's jaw in so many places, and he was annoyed at himself for punching the man too hard. Culver wouldn't be doing any chatting for a long time, so now the information would have to come from Ozzie, one of the most witless and jumble-headed crackers that Jim Tile had ever met.

Culver moaned and strained against the ropes. Ozzie said, 'Oh Jesus, he's hurt bad.'

'Yes, he is,' Jim Tile said. 'You can take him to the doctor after we have our talk.'

'Promise?'

'You've got my word.'

'Is Culver going to jail?'

'Well, I don't know. Attempted murder of a police officer, that's a life term here in Florida. Agg assault, use of a firearm in the commission of a felony, and so on. I just don't know.'

Ozzie said, 'What about me?'

'Oh, same goes for you. You're his partner, right?'

Ozzie's eyes got wet. 'Momma 'spects the truck back long time ago.'

'She'll be worried,' Jim Tile said.

'Can we go soon?'

Jim Tile folded up the newspaper and leaned forward. 'First you answer some questions.'

'Okay, but go slow.'

'Did Dickie Lockhart get you boys to kill Bobby Clinch?'

'No, Jesus! Honest we didn't.' Ozzie's nose was running. 'I liked Bobby, so'd Culver—'

'Then who killed him?' Jim Tile asked.

'I don't know.' Ozzie sniffed loudly, trying to get the snot off his upper lip. 'I got no idea,' he said.

Jim Tile believed him. He said, 'Tell me about Mr. Pickney.'

'Who? Help me out.'

'The guy who played Davey Dillo at the high school.'

'Oh, the reporter,' Ozzie said. 'Sir, I didn't drown nobody.'

'Who did?'

Culver made a gurgling sound, opened his eyes—showing the whites—and shut them slowly again. Ozzie cried and said, 'We gotta get the truck back to Momma.'

'Then tell me about Morgan Slough.' Jim Tile held a teacup to Ozzie Rundell's lips. He took a loud sip, swallowed twice, and began to talk. Jim Tile sat back and listened, saving his questions for the end. He figured the least interruption would confuse Ozzie beyond redemption.

'Okay, a few days after Bobby Clinch died, Tom and Lemus came by the bait shop for coffee. They were saying how somebody was trying to make it look like Dickie done it, except it was an accident—Doc Pembroke even said so. But Tom and Lemus, they said how somebody went to the newspaper with a made-up story that Dickie kilt Bobby, and now this detective from Miami was goin' around asking about Bobby and what happened at the Coon Bog. Culver ast who would try to set Dickie Lockhart up like that, but Tom said there were about a million guys jealous of Dickie would do it in a flash. He said they'd try to make it look like Bobby caught Dickie cheating in some tournament.

'So Culver hears all this and gets worried because, right before the Curl boys come by, this reporter fella had been in asting about Bobby's boat and the funeral and such—see, they sawed up his Ranger into a coffin. Mr. Pinky, he seemed real interested so Culver told him Larkin's place had done the carpenter work. The man said thanks and went off.

'Jeez, when Tom and Lemus hear all this they say we've got to get over to Larkin's right away. Culver was busy with some customers so he told me to ride along in the truck, which I did. On the way over Tom and Lemus said if we don't do something fast, the newspaper's gonna do a big write-up about how Dickie murdered Bobby Clinch, which we all knew was a lie, but still it would ruin Dickie and make him lose the TV show. They said we better stop this guy and I said yeah, but that was before I knew what they meant. What they meant by stopping him. Sir, can I have some more tea?'

Jim Tile held the cup for Ozzie.

'The green truck, that was Tom and Lemus's,' Ozzie said.

'Oh,' said Jim Tile.

'Anyway, we get to Larkin's and there's the guy out back by the dumpster. Ott Pinky. I recognized him right off, and Lemus says: Is that the guy? And I say yeah, it is.' Ozzie paused. 'I got in the back of the truck, the green truck.'

Jim Tile said, 'And Mr. Pickney rode up front? Between the Curl boys.'

'Yes, sir. There's a deer camp on the Sumter property. Maybe sixteen miles out. We took him there for the rest of the day. See, I thought mainly they was just gonna ast him questions.'

Jim Tile said, 'What did you see, Ozzie?'

'Mainly I stayed in the truck.'

'Then what did you hear?'

Ozzie looked down. 'Jesus, I don't know. Mainly some yelling. . . .' The words tumbled slowly, trailed off. Jim Tile imagined Ozzie's fevered brain cells exploding like popcorn.

The trooper said, 'What did Ott tell them?'

'We made a fire, drank some beer, fell asleep. About three hours before dawn we headed for the slough.'

'Was Mr. Pickney still alive?'

'He didn't tell them hardly nothing, according to Tom and Lemus.' Ozzie was untracked again, answering Jim Tile's questions in no particular sequence.

Jim Tile said, 'You were the driver, that's all?'

'He was still alive when we got there. Banged up but still alive. See, I thought they was gonna let him go. I thought they was through with him. Tom and Lemus, they said to stay in the truck and I did. But it got cold and I couldn't figure what was takin' so long. Finally I got out to whizz and that's when I heard the splash.'

Jim Tile said, 'You didn't see anything?'

'It was a damn big splash.' Ozzie sneezed, and more gunk came out of his nose. He said, 'Truth is, I didn't really want to look.'

Jim Tile untied Ozzie's wrists and ankles and helped him to his feet. Together they carried Culver out to the pickup and laid him on the flatbed. Ozzie put the tailgates back up. Jim Tile got an extra pillow and a blanket from his apartment.

'Think you'd best get him over to the hospital in Melbourne,' Jim Tile said. 'Nobody here in town can fix that jawbone.'

Ozzie nodded glumly. 'I gotta go by the house and fetch Momma.' He got in the truck and started the ignition.

Jim Tile leaned in the driver's window and said, 'Ozzie, you understand what happens if I have to arrest you.'

'Culver goes to jail,' Ozzie said wanly.

'For the rest of his natural life. When he gets to feeling better, please remind him, would you?'

'I will,' said Ozzie. 'Sir, I swear I don't think he meant to shoot you.'

'Of course he did,' said Jim Tile, 'but I'm inclined to let the whole thing slide, long as you boys stay out of my way for a while.'

Ozzie was so relieved that he nearly peed his pants. He didn't even mind that the black man had called *them* boys. Basically Ozzie was happy to still be alive. The trooper could have killed them both and gotten away with it, yet here he was, being a true Christian and letting them go.

'Just one favor,' Jim Tile said, resting a coal-black arm on the door of the truck.

'Sure,' Ozzie said.

'Where can I find Thomas Curl?'

Richard Clarence Lockhart was buried on January 25 at the Our Lady of Tropicana cemetery outside Harney. It was a relatively small turnout, considering Dickie's fame and stature in the county, but the low attendance could be explained easily enough.

By unfortunate coincidence, the day of the funeral was also opening day of the Okeechobee Bass Blasters Classic, so almost all Dickie's friends and colleagues were out fishing. Dickie would certainly forgive them, the preacher had chuckled, especially since the tournament required a nonrefundable entry fee of two thousand dollars per boat.

Dickie Lockhart was buried in a handsome walnut coffin, not a bass boat. The hearse bearing the coffin was escorted to Our Lady of Tropicana by three police cars, including a trooper's cruiser driven, none too happily, by Jim Tile. Dickie Lockhart's casket was closed during the eulogy, since the mortician ultimately had been frustrated in his cosmetic efforts to remove the Double Whammy spinnerbait from Dickie's lip; in the clammy New Orleans morgue the lure's hook had dulled, while Dickie's skin had only toughened. Rather than further mutilate the facial features of the deceased, the mortician had simply advised Dickie's sister to keep the coffin closed and remember him as he was.

Ozzie Rundell was extremely grateful. He couldn't have borne another glimpse of his murdered idol.

Culver Rundell did not attend the funeral, since he was hospitalized with thirty-nine linear feet of stainless-steel wire in his jaws. On Culver's behalf, the bait shop had ordered a special floral arrangement topped by a ceramic jumping fish. Unfortunately the ceramic fish was a striped marlin, not a largemouth bass, but no one at the funeral was rude enough to mention it.

The Reverend Charles Weeb also did not attend the funeral, but on behalf of the Outdoor Christian Network he sent a six-foot gladiola wreath with a white ribbon that said: 'Tight Lines, Old Friend.' This was the hit of the graveside service, but the best was yet to come. The next morning, at the closing of the regular Sunday broadcast of *Jesus in Your Living Room*, Charlie Weeb offered a special benediction for the soul of his dear, dear friend Dickie Lockhart, the greatest bass fisherman in the history of America. Then Dickie's face appeared on the big screen behind the pulpit, and the assembled flock lip-synched to a Johnny Cash recording of 'Nearer, My God, to Thee.' At the end of the song everybody was weeping, even Charlie Weeb, the man who had so often privately referred to Dickie Lockhart as a shiftless pellet-brained cocksucker.

Twenty-five minutes after the church show was over and the audience was paid, the Reverend Charles Weeb strolled into a skybox in the Superdome, which had been rented for the big press conference. If Charlie Weeb was disappointed in the sparse turnout of media, he didn't show it. He wore his wide-bodied smile and a cream-colored suit with a plum kerchief in the breast pocket. At his side stood a rangy tanned man with curly brown hair and a friendly, toothy smile. Right away the man reminded some of the photographers of Bruce Dern, the actor, but it wasn't. It was Eddie Spurling, the fisherman.

'Gentlemen,' said Charlie Weeb, still in character, 'am I a happy man today! Yes indeed, I am. It is my pleasure to announce that, beginning this week, Eddie Spurling will be the new host of *Fish Fever.*'

There were only two print reporters in the room, but Weeb politely waited for them to jot the big news in their spiral notebooks.

Weeb continued: 'As you know, for some time Eddie's been the host of his own popular bass show on a competing network. We are most pleased to have stolen him away, since it means—as of yesterday—an additional seventy-four independent cable stations switching to the Outdoor Christian Network for the upcoming fishing season.' Charlie Weeb allowed himself a brief dramatic pause. 'And let me say that although all of us will miss Dickie Lockhart and his special brand of outdoor entertainment, I'm certain that his fans will find Eddie Spurling just as exciting, just as informative, and just as much fun to fish with every week. All of us here in the OCN family couldn't be more pleased!'

Eddie stepped forward and tipped an invisible cap. He was looking pretty pleased himself, and for good reason. January had been a fabulous month. Without winning a single bass tournament he had doubled both his salary and his national TV exposure, and had also landed the lucrative six-figure endorsement contract for Happy Gland Fish Scent products. The Happy

Gland package (entailing print, TV, billboard, and radio commercials) was the envy of the professional bass-fishing circuit, a prize held exclusively for the past five years by Dickie Lockhart. With Lockhart's sudden death, the Happy Gland people needed a new star. The choice was an obvious one; the ad agency didn't even bother to hold auditions. Henceforth every bottle of Bass Bolero, Mackerel Musk, and Catfish Cum would bear the grinning likeness of Fast Eddie Spurling.

'Any questions?' asked Charlie Weeb.

The reporters just looked at one another. Each of them was thinking he would go back to the newsroom and kill the editor who sent him on this assignment.

Weeb said, 'I've saved the best for last. Girls, bring out the visuals.'

Two young women in opalescent bathing suits entered the skybox carrying an immense gold-plated trophy. The trophy easily stood five feet off the ground. On the corners of the base of the trophy were toy-size figures of anglers holding fishing rods, bent in varying degrees of mythic struggle. At the crown of the trophy was an authentic largemouth bass in a full body mount. As bass went, it was no hawg, but poised on the trophy it did look impressive.

'Well, there!' said the Reverend Weeb.

'What did you win it for?' one of the reporters asked Eddie Spurling.

'I didn't win it,' Fast Eddie said, 'not yet.'

'Gentlemen, read what it says on the trophy, look closely,' said Charlie Weeb. 'This is probably the biggest trophy most of you ever saw, including Eddie here, who's won some pretty big ones.'

'None this big,' Eddie Spurling said admiringly.

'Damn right,' Weeb said. 'That's because it's the biggest trophy ever. And it's the biggest trophy ever because it goes to the winner of the biggest fishing tournament ever. Three weeks from today, gentlemen, on the edge of the legendary Florida Everglades, fifty of the best bass anglers in the world will compete for a first prize of two hundred and fifty thousand dollars.'

'Christ,' said one of the reporters. Finally something to scribble.

'The richest tournament ever,' Charlie Weeb said, glowing. 'The Dickie Lockhart Memorial Bass Blasters Classic.'

Ed Spurling said, 'At Lunker Lakes.'

'Oh yes,' said the Reverend Weeb, 'how could I forget?'

20

Al García was dog-tired. He'd been up since six, and even after four cups of coffee his tongue felt like mossy Styrofoam. His bum left shoulder was screaming for Percodans but García stuck with plain aspirin, four at a pop. It was one of those days when he wondered why he hadn't just retired on full disability and moved quietly to Ocala; one of those days when everything and everybody in Miami annoyed the shit out of him. The lady at the toll booth, for instance, when she'd snatched the dollar bill out of his hand—a frigging buck, just for the matchless pleasure of driving the Rickenbacker out to Key Biscayne. And the doorman at the Mayan high-rise condo. *Let's see some identification, please.* How about a sergeant's badge, asshole? The thing was, the doorman—dressed in a charcoal monkey suit that must have cost four bills—the doorman used to work for fucking Somoza. Used to pulverize peasant skulls on behalf of the Nicaraguan National Guard. García knew this, and still he had to stand there, dig around for his shield *and* a driver's license, before the goon would let him inside.

To top it off, the rich guy he's supposed to interview comes to the door wearing one of those faggy thong bathing suits (candy-apple red) that make it look like you've got a python between your legs.

'Come on in, Sergeant,' said Dennis Gault. 'Tell me the news.'

'What news?' García looked the place over before he sat down. Nice apartment. Thick, fluffy carpet—no rug-burn romances for this stud. Swell view of the Atlantic, too. Got to cost a million-three easy, García thought. You can't buy a toilet on the island for under two-fifty.

Gault said, 'About Decker—didn't you catch him?'

'Not yet.'

'Grapefruit juice? O.J.?'

'Coffee if you got it,' García said. 'You must be headed down to the beach.'

'No,' Gault said, 'the sauna.' After he poured García's coffee, he said, 'I thought that's why you called—Decker, I mean. I figured you boys would've found him by now.'

You boys. Fine, be that way, García thought. 'We almost had him last night, but he got away.'

'Got away?' Dennis Gault asked.

'As in, eluded us,' García said. 'Stole a boat and took off across the bay. By the time we got a chopper up, it was too late.'

'Sounds like you boys fucked up.'

'We prefer to think of it as a missed opportunity.' García smiled. 'Very good coffee. Colombian?'

'Yeah,' Dennis Gault said. He dumped a squirt of vodka into his grapefruit juice.

'The reason I'm here,' García said, 'is I need you to tell me everything about what happened with Decker.'

Gault sat down, tugged irritably at his cherry swimtrunks. García figured they must be riding clear up the crack of his buttocks.

'Hell, I flew to New Orleans and gave a full statement,' Gault said. 'How many times do I have to go over it?'

García said, 'I've read your statement, Mr. Gault. It's fine as far as it goes. But, see, working the Miami angle, I need a few more details.'

'Such as?'

'Such as how did Decker choose you?' García was admiring the empty coffee cup. It looked like real china.

Gault said, 'My feelings about Dickie Lockhart were no secret, Sergeant. I'm sure Decker talked to some fishermen, heard the stories. Once he took those photographs, I was the logical choice for a buyer—he knew I hated Dickie, knew I wanted to see him discredited. Plus he knew I was a man of means. He knew I could afford his price, no matter how ludicrous.'

Man of means. García was in hog heaven. 'He told you all this, Decker did?'

'No, I don't recall that he did. You asked how he picked me and I'm telling you it wasn't too damn difficult.'

García said, 'How did he first contact you?'

'He called.'

'Your secretary just patched him right through?'

'Of course not,' Gault said. 'He left a message. Left about seventeen messages before finally I got fed up and picked up the phone.'

'That's good,' García said. From the inside of his tan suit coat he produced a small notebook and wrote something down. 'Seventeen messages—your secretary's bound to remember the name, don't you think? She probably wrote his number in a desk calendar somewhere. Even a scrap of paper would be a help.'

'I don't know,' Gault said. 'That was weeks ago. She probably tossed it by now.'

Al García left his notebook open on his lap while Gault repeated his story that R. J. Decker had demanded one hundred thousand dollars for the photographs of Dickie Lockhart cheating.

'I told him he was nuts,' Gault said. 'I told him to take a flying fuck.'

'But you saw the pictures.'

'Yeah, and it was Dickie, all right, pulling fish cages in a lake somewhere. Illegal as hell.'

García said, 'So why didn't you buy them?'

'For the obvious reasons, that's why.' Gault pretended to be insulted.

'Too much money,' García said. 'That's the most obvious one.'

'Forget the money. It would have been wrong.'

'Wrong?'

'Don't look at me like that,' Gault said. 'You're looking at me like I was a common criminal.'

Maybe worse, García thought. He had already decided that Dennis Gault was a liar. The question was, how far did it go?

'The note,' the detective said. 'Asking for a hundred grand—'

'I gave it to the cops in New Orleans.'

'Yes, I know. But I was wondering what Decker meant— remember he used the word "fee". Like it was a real case. He said, "The fee is now a hundred grand," something like that.'

Gault said, 'Hell, I knew exactly what he meant.'

'Sure, but I was thinking—why he didn't use the word "price"? I mean, he was talking about the price of the photographs, wasn't he? It just seemed like a funny choice of words.'

'Not to me,' Gault said.

'When did he give you the note?'

'Same day he showed me the pictures, January 7, I guess it was.' Gault got up and went to the bathroom. When he came back he was wearing a monogrammed terrycloth robe over the skimpy red thong. It had gotten chillier in the apartment.

'After I told Decker to get lost, he went right to Lockhart for all the marbles. It was pure blackmail: Pay me or I give the pictures to my pals at the newspaper. Naturally Dickie paid— the poor schmuck had no choice.'

García said, 'How do you know all this?'

Gault laughed caustically and slapped his hands on his knees. 'From R. J. Decker!' he said. 'Decker told my sister Elaine. Turns out he was banging her—I'm sure New Orleans must've filled you in. Anyway, Decker told Elaine he squeezed thirty grand out of Dickie before Dickie cut him off. At the tournament Decker went to see him about it, and you know the rest.'

'Decker doesn't sound too bright.'

'Then why haven't you caught him?'

'What I meant,' García said evenly, 'is that it wasn't too bright for him to blab all this shit to your sister.'

Dennis Gault shrugged and stood up. 'You know how it is—in the sack you'll say anything. Besides, you never met Elaine. Talking is her second-favorite thing.' Gault flashed García a sly, frat-house sort of look. García thought this showed real class, a millionaire pimping his own sister. With each passing minute the homicide detective was growing to doubt Mr. Gault's character.

He said, 'Maybe Decker was just bragging.'

'Bragging, passing the time, waiting for his dick to get hard again, I don't know. Whatever the reason, he told Elaine.' Gault took García's coffee cup. 'What about Decker's partner, this Skink maniac?'

'We don't even know his real name,' García said.

'He's a nut case, I've met him. Tell your boys to be damn careful.'

'You bet,' García said, rising. 'Thanks for the coffee. You've been most helpful.'

Gault twirled the sash of his robe as he walked the detective to the door. 'As you can tell, I had no love for Dickie Lockhart. If anything else had happened to him—a plane crash, prostate cancer, AIDS—you wouldn't have heard a peep out of me. Hell, I would've thrown a party. But murder—not even a cheating motherfucker like Dickie deserved to be murdered in cold blood. That's why I went to the police.'

'Sort of a civic duty,' García said.

'Exactly.' Before Gault said good-bye, something occurred to him: It would be best to end the interview on a light and friendly note. He said to García, 'You're from Cuba, right?'

'A long time ago.'

'There's some hellacious fishing down there, south of Havana. Castro himself is a nut for largemouth bass, did you know that?'

'I read something about it.'

Gault said, 'For years I've been trying to pull some strings and wrangle an invitation, but it's damn tough in my position. I'm in the sugar business, as you know. The Bearded One doesn't send us many valentines.'

'Well, you're the competition,' García said.

'Still, I'm dying to try for a Cuban bass. I've heard stories of sixteen-, eighteen-pound hawgs. What's the name of that famous lake?'

García said, 'I forget.'

'Did you do much fishing,' Gault asked, 'when you lived there?'

'I was just a small boy,' García said. 'My great-uncle did some fishing, though.'

'Is that right?'

'He was a mullet man.'

'Oh.'

'He sold marlin baits to Hemingway.'

'No shit!' Dennis Gault said. Now he was impressed. 'I saw a movie about Hemingway once,' he said. 'Starred that Patton guy.'

Back at police headquarters, Al García sat down at his desk and slipped a cassette into a portable tape recorder. The date of January 7 had been written in pencil on the label of the cassette. It was one of three used in R. J. Decker's answering machine. García had picked them up at the trailer after he got the search warrant.

He closed the door to his office, and turned the volume on the tape machine up to number ten on the dial. Then he lit a cigarette and pressed the Play button.

There were a few seconds of scratchy blank tape, followed by the sound of a phone ringing. The fourth ring was interrupted by a metallic click and the sound of R. J. Decker's voice: 'I'm not home now. Please leave a message at the tone.'

The first caller was a woman: 'Rage, it's me. James is on another trip and I'm in the mood for pasta. How about Rita's at nine?'

In his notebook García wrote: *Ex-wife*.

The second caller was also a woman: 'R.J., it's Barbara. I'm sorry about canceling the other night. How about a drink later to make up for it?'

García wrote: *Some girl*.

The third caller was a man: 'Mr. Decker, you probably don't know me but I know of you. I need a private investigator, and you come highly recommended. Call me as soon as possible—I guarantee it'll be worth your time. The number is 555–3400. The name is Dennis Gault.'

In his notebook Al García wrote: *Bad guy*.

For several days Decker and Skink stayed inside the hotel room, waiting for things to cool off. Decker had done what he could over the phone, and was eager to get on the road. For his part, Skink had shrunk into a silent and lethargic melancholy, and exhibited no desire to do anything or go anywhere.

Finally, the afternoon Catherine arrived, Skink briefly came to life. He went outside and stood on the beach and started shooting at jetliners on final approach to the Fort Lauderdale-Hollywood airport.

Catherine had shown up with a recent stock prospectus from the

Outdoor Christian Network, which was listed on the New York exchange as Outdoor ChristNet. Decker was no whiz when it came to stocks, so he had telephoned a reporter friend on the business desk of the Miami *Sun*. The reporter had done a search on OCN in the newsroom computer and come up with some interesting clips, which Catherine had picked up before she left Miami. From the file it was obvious that OCN's rapid growth in the Sun Belt cable market had flooded the company with fluid capital, capital which the Reverend Charles Weeb and his advisers were plowing pell-mell into Florida real estate. The prospectus made several tantalizing references to an 'exciting new waterfront development targeted for middle-income family home buyers' but neglected to mention the protracted and somewhat shady process by which Lunker Lakes had escaped all zoning regulations known to man. The word 'kickback,' for example, appeared nowhere in the stock brochure. The newspaper articles dwelt on this aspect of the controversial project, and indeed it was the only angle that seemed to interest Skink in the slightest. He asked where exactly Lunker Lakes would be located, then took the prospectus and newspaper clippings from Decker's hands and read them closely.

Then he pulled the flowered shower cap down tight on his hair, excused himself with a mumble, walked outside, and waited on the beach. The first incoming jet was an Eastern 727 from La Guardia; the second was a United DC-10 from Chicago via St. Louis; the third was a Bahamas Air shuttle carrying day gamblers back from Freeport. None of the airliners went down or even smoked, though Skink was sure he dinged the bellies a couple of times. The noise of the gunfire was virtually smothered by the roar of the jets and the heavy-metal wail of Bon Jovi from some teenybopper's boom box. In all Skink got off eleven rounds from the nine-millimeter Browning before he spied the lifeguard's Jeep speeding toward him down the beach. The Jeep was at least three-quarters of a mile away, giving Skink plenty of time to jog back to the hotel, duck into a john in the lobby, and work on his appearance.

When he got back to the room, the shower cap and sunglasses were in his pocket, the orange rainsuit was folded under one arm, and his long braid of hair was tucked down the back of his shirt. R. J. Decker asked what happened and Skink told him.

'Excellent,' Decker said. 'Let's see, by my estimate that means we're now wanted by the Metro-Dade police, the highway patrol, the marine patrol, and now the FAA and FBI. Am I leaving anybody out?'

Skink settled listlessly on the floor.

Catherine said, 'R.J., you've got to get him out of the city.'

Decker said, 'My father, rest his soul, would be so proud to know that he raised a fugitive. Not every FBI man can make that claim.'

'I'm sorry,' Skink sighed.

It was the most pathetic thing Decker had ever heard him say— and in one way the scariest. Skink acted like he was on the brink of losing it. Decker leaned over and said, 'Captain, why were you shooting at airplanes?'

'Look who they're bringing,' Skink said. 'They're bringing the suckers to Lunker Lakes. The Reverend Weeb's lucky lemmings.' He seemed out of breath. He motioned for Catherine to hand him the OCN prospectus. With a brown crusty finger he went down the names of directors.

'These guys,' he said hoarsely. 'I know a few.'

'From where?' Catherine asked.

'It's not important. Twenty-nine thousand units in the Everglades is what's important. Christian city, my ass. It's the crime of the damn century. These guys are like cockroaches, you can't fucking get rid of 'em.'

Decker said, 'It's too late, captain. Dredging started a year ago.'

'Jesus,' Skink said, biting his lip. He put on his sunglasses and bowed his head. He didn't look up for some time. Decker glanced over at Catherine. She was right: they had to get Skink back to the woods.

From the hallway came sounds of men talking but trying not to be heard. Then a knock on the door to the next room; another knock across the hall.

'Hotel security,' a male voice said.

R. J. Decker motioned Skink toward the bathroom. He nodded

and crab-walked across the floor, shutting the door behind him. Quickly Decker peeled off his shirt and drew the shades. 'Take off your shoes,' he whispered to Catherine, 'and lie down here on the bed.' She figured out the plan immediately. She was down to bra and panties and under the covers before Decker even got a good peek.

A man knocked three times on the door.

'Whoze it?' Decker hollered. 'Go 'way.'

'Hotel security, please open up.'

'We're sleeping!'

Another voice: 'Police!'

Decker stomped to the door as noisily as possible. He cracked it just enough to give the men a narrow view of Catherine in the bed.

'What's the problem?' Decker demanded.

A blue-suited young man with a walkie-talkie stood next to a disinterested uniformed cop. The security man said, 'Sir, there was an incident out on the beach. A man with a gun—nobody was hurt.'

'That's damn good to hear,' Decker said impatiently.

The cop said, 'You haven't seen anyone unusual up on this floor?'

'For the last couple hours I haven't seen nuthin',' Decker said, 'except stars.' He nodded over his shoulder, toward Catherine. The security man looked a little embarrassed.

The policeman said, 'Big scruffy guy with a bright hat and ponytail. Witnesses saw him run into this hotel, so we're suggesting that all guests stay in their rooms for a while.'

'Don't you worry,' Decker said.

'Just for a while,' the security man added, 'until they catch him.'

When Decker shut the door, Catherine sat up in bed and said, 'Stars? You saw stars?'

'Don't you dare move,' Decker said, diving headfirst into the sheets.

Thomas Curl was not a happy man. In the past few weeks he had made more money than he or three previous generations of

Curls had ever seen, yet Thomas was not at peace. First of all, his brother Lemus was dead, and for a while Thomas had been stuck with the body. Since he had told everyone, including his daddy, that Lemus had accidentally drowned on a fishing trip to Florida, there was no way he could bring back a body with a bullet hole in the head. People would ask many questions, and answering questions was not Thomas Curl's strong suit. So, after discovering Lemus' turtle-eaten corpse on the fish stringer in Morgan Slough, and mulling it over for two days, Thomas decided what the hell and just buried his brother in a dry sandy grave on some pastureland east of the Gilchrist. The whole time he worked with the shovel he had a feeling that every turkey buzzard in Florida was wheeling in the sky overhead, waiting to make a smorgasbord of Lemus' remains. Afterward Thomas took off his bass cap and stood by the grave and tried to remember a prayer. The only one he could think of began: 'Now I lay me down to sleep . . .' Close enough.

Almost every night Thomas Curl reflected sadly on how Lemus had died, how he had let him dash off into the scrub by himself, and how all of a sudden he didn't hear Lemus' Ruger anymore. And how Thomas had panicked and leapt into the green pickup and taken off, pretty sure that his brother was already dead—and how he'd returned with a borrowed coon dog and found some heavy tracks and blood, but no body. At that moment he had expected never to see his brother again, and later at the slough was horrified to the point of nausea. On orders Thomas had gone there to check on things, just to make sure the nigger cop hadn't found Ott Pickney's body. But there was poor Lemus, strung up in the black water with the other one, and it was then Thomas Curl realized the dangerous magnitude of the opposition. Thomas was not the brightest human being in the world, but he knew a message when he saw one.

So he had buried Lemus, torched Ott Pickney's body in a phony truck accident, and driven straight back to New Orleans, where, again, things didn't go as smoothly as he'd hoped. Thomas expressed the view that he shouldn't be blamed for every little loose end, and was curtly instructed to return to Florida immediately. Not Harney, either, but Miami.

Thomas Curl was not wild about Miami. Back when he was still boxing he had trained one summer at the Fifth Street Gym, out on the beach. He remembered staying in a ratty pink hotel with two other middleweights, and he remembered getting drunk on Saturday nights and, out of sheer boredom, beating the shit out of skinny Cuban refugees who lived in the city parks. Thomas remembered Miami as a hot and unfriendly place, but then again, he was young and homesick and broke. Now he was grown-up, thirty-five pounds heavier, and rolling in new money.

To boost his spirits, Thomas Curl splurged and got a room at the Grand Bay Hotel. The room came with a fruit basket and a sunken bathtub. He was sucking on a nectarine and soaking in the tub when Dennis Gault called back.

Thomas Curl said, 'Hey, they got a phone in the goddamn john.'

'Welcome to the city, Jethro.' Gault was in a brusque mood. Dealing with this moron was at least two notches below dealing with Decker. Gault said, 'A cop came to see me.'

Thomas Curl spit the nectarine pit into his soapy hand. 'Yeah? They caught 'em yet?'

'No,' Gault said, 'but the way things are shaping up, maybe it's best if they don't.'

'Hell you mean?'

Gault said, 'This cop, fucking Cuban, he doesn't believe a word I say.'

'Who cares, long as New Orleans believes you.'

'Ever heard of extradition?' Gault snapped. 'This guy can cause us major problems, son. He can keep Decker away from the Louisiana people a long time. Sit on him for weeks, listen to his story, maybe even buy it.'

'No way,' Curl said.

'We can't take the chance, Thomas.'

'I done enough for you.'

Gault said, 'This one's not for me, it's for your brother.'

In the tub Thomas reached over and turned on the hot water. He was careful not to get the telephone wet, in case it might electrocute him.

Gault said, 'I need you to find Decker. Before the cops.'

'What about that crazy gorilla?'

'They probably split up by now.'

'I don't want to fuck with him. Culver said he's mean as a moccasin.'

Gault said, 'Culver's afraid of a tit in the dark. Besides, from what Elaine says, Skink isn't the type to stick with Decker. They probably split up, like I said.'

Thomas Curl was not convinced. He remembered the neatly centered bullet hole in his brother's forehead.

'What's the pay?'

'Same as before,' Gault said.

'Double if I got to deal with the gorilla.'

'Hell, you ought to do it for free,' Gault said. Greed was truly a despicable vice, he thought. 'For Christ's sake, Thomas, these are the guys who killed Lemus. One or both, it's up to you. Decker's the one that worries me most. He's the one that could hurt us in court. We're talking hard time, too.'

Thomas Curl did not like the idea of being sent to the state penitentiary even for a day. There was also something powerfully attractive, even romantic, about avenging his brother's death.

'Where do I start?' he asked.

'Way behind, unfortunately,' Gault said. 'Decker's already running. The trick is to find out where, because he sure as hell won't be coming your way.'

'Not unless I got somethin' he wants,' said Thomas Curl.

21

Catherine said: 'This won't work, not with him in the bathroom.'
She got out of bed and began to dress.

From behind the bathroom door, a voice grumped: 'Pay no attention to me.'

Decker dolefully watched Catherine button her blouse. This is what I get, he thought; exactly what I deserve. He said to her, 'This man's a distraction, you're right.'

'I don't know what I was thinking,' Catherine said, stepping into a pink slip. 'James is furious as it is, and now I'm an hour late.'

'Sorry,' Decker said.

'Here, give me a hand with this zipper.'

'Nice skirt,' Decker said. 'It's silk, isn't it?'

'I can't stand these damn zippers on the side.'

Decker peeked at the label. 'Jesus, Catherine, a Gucci.'

She frowned. 'Stop it, R.J. I know what you're up to.'

As always.

Decker rolled out of bed and groped around the floor for his jeans. It was dark outside, time to go. Muffled scraping noises emanated from the bathroom. Decker couldn't imagine what Skink was doing in there.

Catherine brushed out her hair, put on some pale pink lipstick.

'You look positively beatific,' Decker said. 'Pure as the driven snow.'

'No thanks to you.' She turned from the mirror and took his hands. 'I'd give anything to forget about you, you bastard.'

Decker said, 'Could try hypnosis. Or hallucinogens.'

Catherine put her arms around him. 'Cut the bullshit, pal, it's all right to be scared. This is the most trouble you've ever been in.'

'I believe so,' Decker said.

Catherine kissed him on the neck. 'Watch out for yourself, Rage. And him too.'

'We'll be fine.' He handed Catherine her Louis Vuitton purse and her one-hundred-percent-cashmere sweater.

Before she walked out the door she said, 'I just want you to know, it wouldn't have been a mercy fuck. It would have been the real thing.'

Decker said, 'I got that impression, yeah.'

He couldn't believe how much he still loved her.

Somehow Skink had wedged himself between the bathroom sink and the toilet, compressed his bulk into a massive, musty cube on the tile floor. At first Decker couldn't even pinpoint the location of his head; the wheezing seemed to come from under the toilet tank. Decker knelt down and saw Skink's scaly face staring out from behind the water pipes. He looked like a bearded iguana.

'Why'd you turn on the light?' he asked.

'So I wouldn't step on your vital organs.'

'Worse things could happen,' Skink said.

Freud would have a picnic, Decker thought. 'Look, captain, we've got to get going.'

'I'm safe right here,' Skink observed.

'Not really,' Decker said. 'You're hiding under a toilet in a hundred-dollar beachfront hotel room. Someone's bound to complain.'

'You think?'

Decker nodded patiently. 'It's much safer back in Harney,' he said. 'If we leave now, we'll be back at the lake by midnight.'

'You mean it?'

'Yes.'

'I'll kill you, Miami, if this is a trap. I'll fucking cut out your bladder and wring it in your hair.'

'It's no trap,' Decker said. 'Let's go.'

It took forty-five minutes to disengage Skink from the plumbing. In the process the sink snapped clear off its legs; Decker left it lying on the bed.

In the lobby of the hotel he rented a Ford Escort. He got it out of the underground parking and pulled around back to the hotel's service entrance, where Skink was waiting by the dumpsters. As Skink got in the car, Decker noticed something white tucked under one arm.

'Whatcha got there?' he said.

'Seagull.' Skink held up the limp bird by its curled orange feet. 'Hasn't been dead more than ten minutes. I scarfed it off the grille of that seafood truck.'

'Lucky us,' Decker said thinly.

'You hungry? We can stop and make a fire once we get out of this traffic.'

'Let's wait, okay?'

'Sure,' Skink said. 'It'll keep for a couple hours.'

Decker headed west from the beach on the Seventeenth Street Causeway, past Port Everglades and the Ocean World aquarium. It was typical January beach traffic, bumper-to-bumper nitwits as far as the eye could see. Every other car had New York plates.

Skink fit the dead bird into the glove compartment and covered it with a copy of the rental agreement. He seemed in a much better mood already. He put on his sunglasses and flowered shower cap, and turned around to get his fluorescent rainsuit from the back seat. Through the rear window he noticed a dark blue Chrysler sedan following two car-lengths behind. He spotted a plastic bubble on the dashboard; not flashing, but a bubble just the same. The driver's face was obscured by the tinted windshield, but a red dot bobbed at mouth-level.

'Your buddy García smoke?'

Decker checked the rearview. 'Oh, shit,' he said.

Skink struggled into the rainsuit, adjusted his sunglasses, and said, 'Well, Miami, what's it going to be?'

The blue light on the Chrysler's dashboard was flashing now. Hopelessly Decker scanned the traffic on the causeway; it was jammed all the way to the next traffic signal, and beyond. There was nowhere to go. Al García was up on his bumper and flashing his brights. Decker figured he had a better chance one-on-one, with no Fort Lauderdale cops. He decided to stop before it turned into a convoy.

He pulled into the parking lot of a liquor store. With the big

Chrysler García easily blocked off the little Escort, parked, kept the blue light turning. A bad sign, Decker thought.

He turned to Skink: 'I don't want to see your gun.'

'Relax,' Skink said. 'Mr. Browning sleeps with the fishes.'

Al García approached the car in a bemused and almost casual manner. At the driver's window he bent down and said, 'R.J., you are the king of all fuckups.'

'Sorry I stood you up the other day,' Decker said.

'Everyone but the National Guard is looking for you.'

'Now that you mention it, Al, aren't you slightly out of your jurisdiction? I believe this is Broward County.'

'And you're a fleeing felon, asshole, so I can chase you wherever I want. That's the law.' He spit out his cigarette and ground it into the asphalt with his shoe.

Decker said, 'So what'd you do, follow Catherine up from Miami?'

'She's a slick little driver, she gave it her best.'

Decker said, 'I didn't kill anybody, Al.'

'How about Little Stevie Wonder there?'

Skink blinked lizardlike behind his sunglasses.

'Come on, R.J., let's all of us go for a ride.' García was so smooth he didn't even unholster his gun. Decker was impressed; you had to be. Now if only Skink behaved.

Skink retrieved his dead seagull from the glove box and Decker locked up the rental car. García was waiting in the Chrysler. 'Who wants to ride shotgun?' he asked affably.

Decker said, 'I thought you'd want both us ruthless murderers to sit back in the cage.'

'Nah,' Al García said, unplugging the blue light. He got back into traffic, turned off Seventeenth Street on Federal Highway, then cut back west on Road 84, an impossible truck route. Decker was surprised when he didn't turn south at the Interstate 95 exchange.

'Where are you going?'

'The Turnpike's a cleaner shot, isn't it?' the detective said.

'Not really,' Decker said.

'He means north,' Skink said from the back seat. 'To Harney.'

'Right,' Al García said. 'On the way, I want you guys to tell me all about bass fishing.'

The news from Lunker Lakes was not good.

'They died,' reported Charlie Weeb's hydrologist, some pinhead hired fresh out of the University of Florida.

'Died?' said the Reverend Weeb. 'What the fuck are you talking about?'

He was talking about the bass—two thousand yearling large-mouths imported at enormous cost from a private hatchery in Alabama.

'They croaked,' said the hydrologist. 'What can I say? The water's very bad, Reverend Weeb. Tannic acid they can tolerate, but the current phosphate levels are lethal. There's no fresh oxygen, no natural water flow. Whoever dredged your canals—'

'*Lakes*, goddammit!'

'—they dredged too deep. The fish don't last more than two days.'

'Jesus Christ Almighty. So what're we talking about here—stinking dead bass floating all over the place?'

The hydrologist said, 'I took the liberty of hiring some local boats to scoop up the kill. With this cool weather it's not so bad, but if a warm front pushes through, they'd smell it all the way to Key West.'

Weeb slammed down the phone and groaned. The woman lying next to him said, 'What is it, Father?'

'I'm not a priest,' Weeb snapped. He didn't have the energy for a theology lesson; it would have been a waste of time anyway. The girl worked at Louie's Lap-Dancing Palace in Gretna. She said her whole family watched him every Sunday morning on television.

'I never been with a TV star before,' she said, burrowing into his chest. 'You're a big boy, too.'

Charlie Weeb was only half-listening. He missed Ellen O'Leary; no one else looked quite as fine, topless in the rubber trout waders. No one soothed him the way Ellen did, either, but now she was gone. Took off after Dickie Lockhart's murder. One more disappointment in a week of bleak disappointments for the Reverend Charles Weeb.

'How much do I owe you?' he asked the lap dancer.

'Nothing, Father.' She sounded confused. 'I brought my own money.'

'What for?' Weeb looked down; he couldn't see her face, just the top of her head and the smooth slope of her naked back.

'I got a favor to ask,' the lap dancer said, whispering into his chest hair. 'And I wanna pay for it.'

'What on earth are you talking about?'

'I want you to heal my poppa.' She looked up shyly. 'He's got the gout, my poppa does.'

'No, child—'

'Some days he can't barely get himself out of bed.'

Weeb shifted restlessly, glanced at his wristwatch.

'I'll give you two hundred dollars,' the girl declared.

'You're serious?'

'Just one little prayer, please.'

'Two hundred bucks?'

'And a hum job, if you want it, Father.'

Charlie Weeb stared at her, thinking: It's true what they say about the power of television.

'Come, child,' he said softly, 'let's pray.'

Later, when he was alone, the Reverend Charles Weeb thought about the girl and what she'd wanted. Maybe it was the answer he'd been looking for. It had worked before, in the early years; perhaps it would work again.

Charlie Weeb drank a Scotch and tried to sleep, but he couldn't. In recent nights he had been kept awake by the chilling realization that Lunker Lakes, his dream city, was in deep trouble. The first blow had come from the Federal Deposit Insurance Corporation, whose auditors had swept into the offices of First Standard Eurobank of Ohio and discovered that the whole damn thing was on the verge of insolvency. The problem was bad loans, huge ones, which First Standard Eurobank apparently handed out as freely as desk calendars. The Outdoor Christian Network, doing business as Lunker Lakes Ltd., had been the beneficiary of just such unbridled generosity—twenty-four million dollars for site planning and construction. On paper there was nothing unusual about the loan or the terms of repayment (eleven percent over ten years), but in reality not much money ever got repaid. About six thousand dollars, to be exact. Wanton disorganization ruled First Standard Eurobank's collections department—as patient and amiable a bunch of Christian soldiers as Charlie Weeb had ever met. He kept missing the bimonthly payments and they kept saying don't worry and Charlie Weeb *didn't* worry, because this was a fucking bank, for God's sake, and banks don't go under anymore. Then the FDIC swooped in and discovered that First Standard Eurobank had been just as patient and flexible with all its commercial customers, to the extent that virtually nobody except farmers were being made to repay their loans on time. Suddenly the president of the bank and three top assistants all moved to Barbados, leaving Uncle Sam to sort out the mess. Pretty soon the bad news trickled out: First Standard Eurobank was calling in its bad loans. All over the country big-time land developers headed for the tall grass. Charlie Weeb himself had been dodging some twit from *The Wall Street Journal* for five days.

What aggravated Weeb was that he had intended all along to pay back the money, but at a pace commensurate with advance sales at Lunker Lakes. Unfortunately, sales were going very slowly. Charlie Weeb couldn't figure it out. He fired his marketing people, fired his advertising people, fired his sales people—yet nothing improved. It was maddening. The lakefront models were simply beautiful. Three bedrooms, sunken bath and sauna, cathedral ceilings, solar heating, microwave kitchens—'Christian town-home living at its finest!' Charlie Weeb was fanatical about using the term 'town home,' which was a fancy way of saying two-story condo. The problem with using the word 'condo' was, as every idiot in Florida knew, you couldn't charge a hundred and fifty thousand for a 'condo' fourteen miles away from the ocean. For this reason any Lunker Lakes salesman who spoke the word was immediately terminated. Condos carried a hideous connotation, Charlie Weeb had lectured—this wasn't a cheesy high-rise full of nasty old farts, this was a *wholesome family community*. With fucking bike paths!

And still the dumb shits couldn't sell it. A hundred-sixty units in the first four months. A hundred-sixty! Weeb was beside himself. Phase One of the project called for eight thousand units. Without Phase One there would be no Phase Two, and without Phase Two you could scrap the build-out projections of twenty-nine thousand. While you're at it, scrap the loans, the equity, even the zoning permits. The longer the project lagged, the greater the chances that all the county commissioners who had so graciously accepted Charlie Weeb's bribes would die or be voted out of office, and a whole new set would have to be paid off. One white knight could gum up the works.

The Reverend Charles Weeb had even deeper concerns. He had been so confident of Lunker Lakes that he had broken a cardinal rule and sunk three million dollars of his own personal, Bahamian-sheltered money into the project. The thought of losing it made him sick as a dog. Lying in bed, juggling the ghastly numbers in his head, Weeb also realized that the Outdoor Christian Network itself was probably not strong enough to survive if Lunker Lakes were to go under.

So he had to do something to raise money, lots of it. And fast. This was the urgency behind scheduling the new Dickie Lockhart Memorial Bass Blasters Classic on such short notice. Lunker Lakes was starving for publicity, and the TV coverage of the tournament was bound to boost sales—provided they could paint some of the buildings and get a few palm trees planted in time.

Trucking in two thousand young bass had been, Weeb thought, dastardly clever. For authenticity he had also planned to salt the lakes with a dozen big Florida hawgs a few days before the tournament. And, of course, he fully intended for Eddie Spurling to win the whole shebang with the fattest stringer of monster bass conceivable. Charlie Weeb had yet to discuss the importance of this matter with Eddie, but he was sure Eddie would understand. Certain details had to be arranged. Nothing could be left to chance—not on live cable television.

Charlie Weeb was feeling downright optimistic until he learned about the fish kill. He never imagined that all the bass would die, but he really didn't care to hear some elaborate scientific explanation. He knew this: Under no circumstances would the fishing tournament be canceled. If necessary he would simply purchase another truckload of bass, and somehow slip them into the lake the day of the tournament. Maybe the pinhead hydrologist could work a few miracles, buy him a few extra hours. It could be done, Charlie Weeb was sure.

As a long-term sales gimmick, the big bass tournament held much promise. However, the short-term fiscal crisis demanded immediate attention.

To this end the lap dancer from Louie's had given Charlie Weeb new spiritual inspiration.

He sat up in bed and reached for the phone.

'Deacon Johnson, please.'

A sleepy voice came on the line.

Weeb said, 'Izzy, wake up. It's me.'

'It's three in the morning, man.'

'Tough shit. Are you listening?'

'Yeah,' said Deacon Johnson.

'Izzy, I want to do a healing on Sunday's show.'

Deacon Johnson coughed up something in his throat.

'You sure?' he said.

'Positive. Unless you got any other brilliant ideas to solve the cash-flow problem.'

Deacon Johnson said, 'Healings are tricky, Charles.'

'Hell, you don't have to tell me! That's why I quit doing 'em. But these are desperate times, Izzy. I figure we tape a couple fifteen-second promos tomorrow, start pushing the thing hard. Goose the ratings by the weekend—I bet we'll do a million-two.'

'A million-two?' Deacon Johnson said. 'For a sheep?'

'Screw the sheep. I'm talking about a real person.'

Deacon Johnson didn't respond right away. The Reverend Weeb said, 'Well?'

'We've never done a human being before, Charles.'

'We've never dropped twenty-four mill before, Izzy. Look, I

want you to set it up the same as we did with the animals. Find me a good one.'

Deacon Johnson was not enthusiastic, but he knew better than to balk.

'Get me a little kid if you can,' Charlie Weeb was saying, 'or a teenager. No geezers and no housewives.'

'I'll try,' said Deacon Johnson. The logistics of the feat would be formidable.

'Blond, if possible,' Weeb went on. Every heartbreaking detail spelled more money—he knew this from his experience promoting the tragic tale of June-Lee and Melissa, the two mythical Weeb sisters sold into Chinese slavery. 'No redheads,' Weeb instructed Deacon Johnson. 'You get me a little blond kid to heal, Izzy, and I swear we'll do a million-two.'

Deacon Johnson said, 'I guess you wouldn't consider a practice run. Say, with a goat.'

22

An hour out of Fort Lauderdale, Skink started to pluck the dead seagull in the back seat. Every so often he threw a handful of gray-white feathers out the window. García adjusted the rearview and watched, disbelieving. After R. J. Decker explained the custom, García decided to pull off the Turnpike for a dinner break. They dropped Skink near the Delray Beach overpass to let him roast the bird in private. García offered some matches, but as he got out of the car Skink mumbled, 'Don't need any.'

Decker said, 'We're driving into town for some burgers. Meet you back here in about an hour.'

'Fine,' Skink said.

'You'll be waiting, right?'

'Most likely.'

A hunching ursine shape in the darkness, Skink gathered kindling as they drove away.

Waiting in a line of cars at the Burger King drive-through, García said to Decker, 'So the bottom line is, these Gomers are murdering each other over fish.'

'It's money too, Al. Prizes, endorsements, TV contracts, Fishing's just the sizzle. And not all these guys are dumb peckerwoods.'

The detective chuckled. 'Guess not. They tricked your ass, didn't they?'

'Nicely,' Decker said. On the trip he had told García about Dennis Gault, the photographs, Dickie Lockhart, and Lanie. The part about Lanie was not Decker's favorite. 'All I can figure,' he said, 'is she remembered my name from that fashion shoot in Sanibel. Probably read about the Bennett case too—it made all the papers.' The *Sun*'s unsparing headline had read:

'STAFF PHOTOG CONVICTED IN BEATING OF PREP FOOTBALL STAR.'

García said, 'Gault must've creamed when his sister suggested you for the mark. Big ex-con photographer with a bad temper, down on his luck.'

'Made to order,' Decker agreed glumly.

'What about the pictures of Lockhart cheating? New Orleans sent Xerox copies, but still they look pretty good.'

Decker said, 'They've got to be tricked up.'

'Just so you know, I served a warrant on your trailer. Took every single roll from your camera bag—had our lab soup the film.'

'And?'

'Garbage. Surveillance stuff for that insurance case, that's all. No fish pictures, R.J.'

There you had it. Lanie had probably swiped the good stuff out of his bag at the motel in Hammond. Her brother would've had no trouble finding a good lab man to doctor the prints. Decker said, 'Jesus, Al, what the hell do I do now?'

'Well, in my official capacity as a sworn law-enforcement officer of the state of Florida, I'd advise you to turn yourself in, agree to the extradition, and trust your fate to the justice system. As a friend, I'd advise you to stay the fuck out of Louisiana until we get you some alibi witnesses.'

'*We?*' Decker was surprised. 'Al, you'll get in all kinds of trouble if they find out you're helping me. You're probably already in the jackpot for taking a duty car out of Dade County.'

García smiled. 'Didn't I tell you? I went on sick leave two days ago. Indefinite—doctor says my damn shoulder's out of whack again. The lieutenant wasn't thrilled, but what's he gonna do? Half the guys retire they get a lousy hangnail. Me, I get popped point-blank with a sawed-off and I only miss twenty-three days. They can't bitch about a week here and there for therapy.'

'Sick leave,' Decker mused. 'That explains your unusually charming disposition.'

'Don't be a smartass. Right now I'm the only friend you got.'

'Not quite,' Decker said.

According to Ozzie Rundell, Thomas Curl's Uncle Shawn lived just outside of Orlando. He ran a moldy roadside tourist trap called Sheeba's African Jungle Safari, located about four miles west of the Disney World entrance on U.S. 92. Ozzie had offered to draw a map, but Jim Tile said no thanks, he didn't need directions.

The broken-down zoo wasn't hard to find. In the six years since Shawn Curl had purchased the place from Leroy and Sheeba Barnwell, the once-exotic menagerie had shrunk to its current cheerless census of one emaciated lion, two balding llamas, three goats, a blind boa constrictor, and seventeen uncontrollably nasty raccoons. A big red billboard on U.S. 92 promised a 'DELIGHTFUL CHILDREN'S PETTING ZOO,' but in actuality there was nothing at Sheeba's to pet; not safely, anyway. Shawn Curl's insurance company had summarily canceled his policy after the ninth infectious raccoon bite, so Shawn Curl had put up a twelve-foot hurricane fence to keep the tourists away from the animals. The only consistent money-making enterprise at the African Jungle Safari was the booth with plastic palm trees where, for $3.75, tourists could be photographed draping the blind boa constrictor around their necks. Since snakes have no eyelids, the tourists didn't know that the boa constrictor was blind. They were also unaware that, except for a tiny space where the feeding tube fit, the big snake's mouth had been expertly stitched shut with a Singer sewing machine. In these litigious times, Shawn Curl wasn't taking any more chances.

He didn't know what to think when the musclebound black state trooper walked into the gift shop; Shawn Curl had never seen a black trooper in Orlando before. He noticed that the man walked with a slight limp, and thought probably he had been hired for just that reason—to fill some stupid minority handicap quota. Shawn Curl decided he'd better be civil, or else the big spade might snitch on him to the Fish and Game Department for the way the wild animals were being treated.

'What ken we do you for, officer?'

Jim Tile stood at the counter eyeing a display of bootleg Mickey Mouse dolls. Each stuffed Mickey had a Confederate flag poking out of its paw. Jim Tile picked up one of the Mickeys and turned it over.

' "Made in Thailand," ' he read aloud.

Shawn Curl coughed nervously.

'Nine-fifty for one of these?' the trooper asked.

Shawn Curl said, 'Not for you. For you, half-price.'

'A discount,' Jim Tile said.

'For all peace officers, yessir. That's our standard discount.'

Jim Tile put the mouse doll back on the counter and said, 'Does Disney know you're selling this crap?'

Shawn Curl worked his jaw sideways. 'Far as I know it's all legal, officer.'

Jim Tile looked around the gift shop. 'They could sue you for everything,' he said, 'such as it is.'

'Hey, I ain't dune nuthin' nobody else ain't dune.'

After scanning the shelves—cluttered with painted coconut heads, rubber alligators, chipped conch shells, bathtub sharks, and other made-for-Florida rubbish—Jim Tile's disapproving brown eyes settled again on the bogus Mickey Mouse doll. 'The Disney people,' he said, 'they won't go for this. That rebel flag is enough to get their lawyers all excited.'

Exasperated, Shawn Curl puffed out his cheeks. 'Who sent you here, anyway?'

'I'm looking for young Thomas.'

'He ain't here.'

The trooper said, 'Tell me where I can find him.'

'S'pose you got a warrant.'

'What I got,' said Jim Tile, 'is his uncle. By the balls.'

A family of tourists walked in, the kids darting underfoot while the mother eyed the merchandise uneasily. The father peered tentatively at the zoo grounds through a window behind the cash register. Jim Tile guessed they wouldn't stay long. They didn't. 'Raccoons, that's all,' the father had reported back to his wife. 'We've got zillions of raccoons back in Michigan.'

When they were alone again, Jim Tile said, 'Shawn, give me your nephew's address in New Orleans. Right now.'

'I'll give it to you,' Shawn Curl said, scribbling on the back of a postcard, 'but he ain't there.'

'Where can I find him?'

'Last time he come through he was on his way to Miami.'

'When was that?'

'Few days ago,' said Shawn Curl.

'Where's he staying?'

'Some big hotel.'

'You're a big help, Shawn. I guess I'll have to call Disney headquarters after all.'

Shawn Curl didn't like that word, *Headquarters.* In a sulky voice he said, 'The hotel is the Grand Biscayne Something. I don't remember the whole name.'

'Why was Thomas going down to Miami?'

'Business, he said.'

'What business is he in?'

Shawn Curl shrugged. 'Promotions is what he calls it.'

Jim Tile said, 'I couldn't help but notice that big Oldsmobile out front, the blue Nine-eight. It looks brand-new.'

Warily Shawn Curl looked at the trooper. 'No, I had it awhile.'

'Still got the sticker in the window,' Jim Tile remarked, 'and the paper license tag from the dealer.'

'So?'

'Did Thomas give you that new car?'

Shawn Curl drew a deep breath. What was the world coming to, that a nigger could talk to him like this? 'Maybe he did give it to me,' Shawn Curl said. 'There's no law 'ginst it.'

'No, there isn't,' Jim Tile said. He thanked Shawn Curl for his time, and walked toward the door. 'By the way,' the trooper said, 'that lion's humping one of your llamas.'

'Shit,' said Shawn Curl, scrambling to find his pitchfork.

The three boys went to the high-school basketball game but they didn't stay long. Kyle, the one with the phony driver's license, had three six-packs in the trunk, along with his stepfather's .22-caliber rifle. Jeff and Cole, both of whom were on the verge of flunking out anyway, cared even less about high-school basketball than Kyle. The game was just their excuse to get out of the house, something to tell the parents. The teenagers left before the first half was over. Kyle drove to the usual spot, a country dumpsite miles west of the city, and there they gulped down the six-packs while plinking bottles, soda cans, and the occasional hapless rat. Once the beer and ammunition were used up, there was only one thing left to do. Jeff and Cole called it 'bum-bashing,' though it was Kyle, the biggest one, who claimed to have invented both the phrase and the sport. That's what everyone at the high school said, anyway: It must have been Kyle's idea.

Every winter transients flock to Florida as sure as the tourists and turkey buzzards. Their numbers are not so great, but often they are more visible; sleeping in the parks and public libraries, panhandling the street corners. The weather is so mild that there is almost no outdoor place that a bum would find uninhabitable in southern Florida. Paradise is how many of them would describe it. Some towns address the problem with less tolerance than others (Palm Beach, for example, where loitering is treated the same as ax-murder), but usually the bums get by with little fear of incarceration. The reason is simple, and in it lies another prime attraction for the nation's wandering winos: there is no room for them in South Florida's jails because the jails already are too crowded with dangerous criminals.

Beginning in late December, then, the transients start appearing on the streets. Rootless, solitary, and unwelcome, they are ideal victims for the randomly violent. Kyle and his high-school friends discovered this the very first time. On a five-dollar bet from Cole, Kyle slugged a wino under a bridge. The boys ran away, but nothing happened. Of course the transient never reported the attack—the local cops would have laughed at him. A week later the teenagers tried it again when they discovered an old longhair sleeping on a golf course in Boca Raton. This time Jeff and Cole pitched in, while Kyle added a few whacks with his stepfather's four-iron. This time when they ran away, the kids were laughing.

Soon bum-bashing became part of the weekly recreation; a thrill, something to do. The boys were easily bored and not all that popular at school, shunned by the jocks, dopers, and surfers alike. So whenever Kyle could get the car and swipe some beer money, Jeff and Cole were raring to go. Shooting the rifle always seemed to put them in the right mood.

As soon as they left the dump they started scouting for bums to bash. It was Jeff who spotted the guy curled up beneath the Turnpike overpass. Kyle drove by once, turned the car around, and drove past again. This time he parked fifty yards down the road. The three teenagers got out and walked back. Kyle liked the way it was shaping up—a dark stretch of highway with practically no traffic.

Skink was nearly asleep, stretched out halfway up the concrete embankment and faced away from the road. He heard someone coming, but assumed it was only Decker and the Cuban detective. As the men got closer, their footsteps did not alarm Skink nearly so much as their whispering. He was turning over to take a look just as Kyle ran up and kicked him brutally in the head.

Skink rolled down the embankment and lay still, facedown on the flat ground.

'Hey, Mr. Hobo,' said Kyle, 'sorry I busted your shades.' He held up the broken sunglasses for the others to see.

Jeff and Cole each took a turn kicking Skink in the ribs. 'I like his outfit,' Jeff said. He was a bony kid with volcanic pustular acne. 'This'd be great for hunting,' he said, fingering the rainsuit.

'Then take it,' Kyle said.

'Yeah, go ahead,' Cole said, 'even though it's about ten sizes too big.'

'You'll look like an orange tepee,' Kyle teased.

Jeff knelt and tried to roll Skink on his back. 'He's a big sum-bitch,' he said. 'Gimme a hand.'

They turned Skink over and stripped him.

'He looks dead,' Cole remarked.

'Check out the ponytail,' Jeff said. He had climbed into Skink's enormous rainsuit. The hood flopped down over his eyes, and the legs and arms were way too long. The other boys laughed as Jeff did a little jig under the highway bridge. 'I'm Mr. Hobo!' he sang. 'Dead Mr. Hobo! Have a drink, make a stink—'

Jeff stopped singing when he saw the stranger. The man was sprinting toward them from across the road. Jeff tried to warn Kyle but it was too late.

The man took down both Kyle and Cole with a diving knee-high tackle. On the ground it was madness. The man hit Cole three times, crushing his nose and shattering his right cheekbone with an eggshell sound that made Jeff want to gag. While this was going on, Kyle, who was taller than the stranger, managed to get on his feet and grab the man around the neck, from behind. But the stranger, still on his knees, merely brought both elbows up sharply into Kyle's groin. Sickened, Jeff watched his other friend crumple. Then the man was on top of Kyle, aiming tremendous jackhammer punches at the meat of his throat.

Jeff turned from the scene to run but he stumbled inside the baggy rainsuit, got up, faltered again. A hand gripped the back of his neck and something cold pressed against the base of his skull. A gun.

'Don't move, you little fuckwad.' A tough-looking dark man with a mustache.

He dragged Jeff back to the overpass, where the bigger stranger was still straddling Kyle and wordlessly redesigning the young man's face.

'Stop it!' yelled the dark man with the gun. 'Decker, stop!'

But R. J. Decker couldn't stop; he couldn't even hear. Al García's voice echoed under the bridge but not a word reached Decker's ears. All that registered in his consciousness was the sight of a face and the need to punish it. Decker was working mechanically, his knuckles raw and bloody and numb. He stopped punching only when heavy damp arms encircled his chest and lifted him in the air, as if he were weightless, and suspended him there for what seemed like a very long time. Coming down, unwinding finally, the first thing Decker could hear was the furious sound of his own breathing. The second thing, from the beast with the big arms, was a tired voice that said, 'Okay, Miami, I'm impressed.'

23

Skink slipped unconscious in the back seat. His head sagged against R. J. Decker's shoulder and the breath rattled deep in his ribs. Decker felt warm drops seeping through his shirt.

'He's lost that eye,' Al García said grimly, chewing on a cigarette as he drove.

Decker had seen it too. Skink's left eye was a jellied mess—Kyle, the big kid, had been wearing Texas roach-stomper boots. A whitish fluid oozed down Skink's cheek.

'He needs a doctor,' Decker said.

So did the teenage thugs, García thought, but they would live—no thanks to Decker. Barehanded he would have killed them all if Skink hadn't stopped him. García felt certain that the kids wouldn't tell the police about the beating—Jeff, the acne twerp, was the type to spill the beans and the others knew it. Together they'd invent some melodramatic story of what happened under the bridge, something that would play well at school. García was pretty sure two of them would spend the rest of the semester in the hospital, anyway.

Decker felt exhausted and depressed. His arms ached and his knuckles stung. He touched Skink's face and felt a crust of blood on the big man's beard.

'Maybe I ought to give up,' Decker said.

'Don't be a moron.'

'Once we get him to a doctor, you drop me off on the highway and haul ass back to Dade County. Nobody'll know a thing.'

'Fuck you,' García said.

'Al, it's not worth it.'

'Speak for yourself.' It was Skink. He raised his head and wiped his face with the sleeve of his rainsuit. With a forefinger he probed his broken eye socket and said, 'Great.'

'There's a hospital near the St. Lucie exit,' García said.

Skink said, 'Naw, just keep driving.'

'I'm sorry, captain,' Decker said. 'We shouldn't have left you alone.'

'Alone is how I like it.' He slid over to the corner of the back seat. His face sank into the shadow.

García pulled off the Turnpike at Fort Pierce and stopped at a Pic 'n' Pay convenience store. Decker got out to make a phone call. While he was gone Skink stirred again and straightened up. In the washhouse light his face looked pulpy and lopsided; García could tell he was in agony.

He said, 'Hang in there, Governor.'

Skink stared at him. 'What, you lifted some fingerprints?'

García nodded. 'From a brass doorknob. That night at the chiropractor's house. Got a solid match from the FBI on an ancient missing-persons case.'

'A closed case,' Skink said.

'A famous case.'

Skink gazed out the window of the car.

'Who else knows?' he said.

'Nobody but me and some G-7 clerk at the Hoover Building.'

'I see.'

García said, 'For what it's worth, I don't like quitters, Mr. Tyree, but I suspect you had your reasons.'

'I'll make no goddamn apologies,' Skink said. After a pause he added: 'Don't tell Decker.'

'No reason to,' said Al García.

Decker came back with hot coffee and Danish. Skink said he wasn't hungry. 'Keep your eyes out, though,' he added when they were back on the road.

'I got you something,' Decker handed him a brown bag.

Skink opened it and grinned what was left of his TV smile.

Inside the bag was a new pair of black sunglasses.

Just before midnight he suddenly groaned and passed out again. Decker tore up his own shirt for a compress bandage and wrapped the bad eye. He held Skink's head in his lap and told García to drive faster.

Minutes after they crossed the county line into Harney, a highway-patrol car appeared in the rearview mirror and practically glued itself to the Chrysler's bumper.

'Oh hell,' Al García said.

But R. J. Decker was feeling much better.

Deacon Johnson was proud of himself. He had gone down to the welfare office near the Superdome and found a nine-year-old blond girl who was double-jointed at the elbows. When she popped her bony arms out they looked magnificently grotesque, an effect that would be amplified dramatically by Charlie Weeb's television cameras. Deacon Johnson asked the girl's mother if he could rent her daughter for a couple of days and the mother said sure, for a hundred bucks—but no funny business. Deacon Johnson said don't worry, ma'am, this is a wholesome Christian enterprise, and led the little girl to his limousine.

At the downtown production studios of the Outdoor Christian Network, Deacon Johnson took the little girl, whose name was Darla, to meet the famous Reverend Charles Weeb.

Twirling his eyeglasses in one hand, Weeb looked relaxed behind his desk. He wore a powder-blue pullover, white parachute pants, and a pair of black Nike running shoes. A young woman with astounding breasts was trimming his famous cinnamon-blond eyebrows.

Deacon Johnson said, 'Darla, show the preacher your little trick.'

Darla took one step forward and extended both arms, as if awaiting handcuffs.

'Well?' said Charlie Weeb.

Darla closed her eyes, strained—and chucked her elbows out of joint at preposterous angles. The sockets emitted two little pops as they disengaged.

The statuesque eyebrow barber nearly wilted.

'Bravo!' said Charlie Weeb.

'Thank you,' said Darla. Her pale arms hung crookedly at her sides.

'Izzy, whadya think?' Weeb said. 'I think we're talking the big P.'

'Polio?' Deacon Johnson frowned.

'Why the hell not?'

Deacon Johnson said, 'Well, it's very uncommon these days.'
'Perfect.'

'Except everybody knows there's a vaccine.'

'Not in the bowels of Appalachian coal country,' Charlie Weeb said. 'Not for a poor little orphan girl raised on grubworms and drainwater.'

Darla spoke up. 'I live in a 'partment on St. Charles,' she said firmly. 'With my momma.'

'Talk to this child,' Charlie Weeb said to Deacon Johnson. 'Explain how TV works.'

It was a good thing for Charlie Weeb that there was no audience for the dress rehearsals. At first Darla insisted on popping her elbows in and out, in and out—just to show off—and it took Deacon Johnson quite some time to make her understand the theatrical importance of timing. At a given cue Darla was supposed to roll her eyes, loll her tongue, and fall writhing onto the stage; when she rose again to face the cameras and audience, her polio would be cured. To demonstrate the success of his ministrations, the Reverend Charles Weeb would then toss her a beach ball.

The cue for Darla's fit was to be when Weeb raised his arms and implored: 'Lord Jesus, mend this poor Christian creature!' The first few times, Darla jumped the gun badly, collapsing on the word 'Jesus' so that the sound of her limp form hitting the stage stepped all over Charlie Weeb's big climax. Once Deacon Johnson had coached Darla past this problem, the next challenge was teaching her to catch the beach ball. The first few times she simply let the ball bounce off her chest, and the noise of it smacking the lanyard mike nearly blew out the engineer's eardrums. Darla dropped the ball so many times in rehearsal that the Reverend Weeb lost his Christian temper and called her a 'palsied little twat'—a term which, fortunately, the child did not understand. When Weeb demanded that they go back to the lidocaine-injection method, Deacon Johnson quickly intervened and suggested now was a good time for lunch.

Miraculously, the live Sunday broadcast went off without a hitch. The crew did an extraordinary job making Darla appear sallow and gray and mortally ill. When the cue came, she collapsed perfectly and—after much thrashing—arose beaming and cherubic and healed. Reviewing the videotapes later, the Reverend Weeb marveled aloud at how deftly and invisibly little Darla had reengaged her elbow joints. Only on slo-mo could you see her do it. And, at the end, she even caught the beach ball. Charlie Weeb had been so genuinely overjoyed that he hadn't even needed the glycerine tears.

They ran the 800 number for five full minutes on the TV screen following Darla's performance. That evening, when Charlie Weeb got the final figures from the phone bank, he called Deacon Johnson at home.

'Guess the totals, Izzy.'

'I really don't know. A million?'

Weeb cackled and said, 'Guess again, sucker.'

Deacon Johnson was too tired to guess. 'I don't know, Charles,' he said.

'How does a million-four sound?' the Reverend Weeb exulted.

The deacon was amazed. 'Holy shit,' he said.

'Exactly,' said Charlie Weeb. 'Are you thinking what I'm thinking?'

Thomas Curl had been thoroughly enjoying himself at the Grand Bay Hotel and he was annoyed that he had to depart so suddenly. One morning, while eating eggs Benedict in the sunken bathtub, he had received a strange and unsettling phone call. Thomas Curl could tell by the scratchy conversation that it was long distance, and he could tell by the voice that it wasn't either Dennis Gault or his Uncle Shawn, the only two men who knew where to find him. The voice sounded to Thomas Curl like it might belong to a nigger, but Curl couldn't be sure. Whoever it was had called him by name, so Curl had hung up the phone immediately and decided to check out of the hotel. He was worried that the black-sounding voice might turn out to be Decker's crazy gorilla friend Skink, who would think nothing of breaking into a fancy suite and drowning someone in a sunken tub.

Thomas Curl took a more modest room at the Airport Marriott and shrewdly registered under the name 'Juan Gómez,' which he figured was the Miami equivalent of John Smith. The fact that Thomas Curl looked about as Hispanic as Cale Yarborough didn't stop him, and his Juan Gómez signature drew scarcely a raised eyebrow from a desk clerk named Rosario.

That evening, after a room-service steak, Thomas Curl went to work. R. J. Decker's address was in the phone book, and now it was only a matter of finding a decent map of Dade County.

The Palmetto Expressway, Thomas Curl decided, was worse than anything in New Orleans, worse even than Interstate 4 in Orlando. Thomas Curl had always considered himself a fast and sharp-witted driver, but the Palmetto shattered his confidence. It was as if he'd stalled out in the center lane, with bleating semis and muffler-dragging low-riders and cherry Porsches speeding past on both sides. Thomas Curl had heard the wild tales about Miami drivers, and now he could go back home and say it was all true. They were moving so damn fast you couldn't even flip them the finger.

He was delighted when he found his exit and got on a street with actual traffic lights. The trailer park was at the dark end of a dead-end street. Thomas Curl poked the car around slowly until he found the mailbox to R. J. Decker's mobile home. The lights were off and the trailer looked empty, as Thomas Curl knew it would be. An older gray sedan, a Dodge or Plymouth, sat in the gravel drive; the rear tires looked low on air, as if the car hadn't been driven recently. Curl parked behind it and cut off his headlights. He took a sixteen-inch flathead screwdriver from under the front seat. He was not the world's greatest burglar but he knew the fundamentals, including the fact that trailers usually were a cinch.

Another cardinal rule of burglary was: Leave your gun in the car unless you want another nickel tacked onto your prison sentence. Thomas Curl began to have second thoughts about this rule after he had gotten the screwdriver stuck in Decker's back door, and after a neighbor's sixty-five-pound pit bulldog came trotting over to investigate the racket. As the dog bared its teeth and emitted a tremulous rumble, Thomas Curl could not help thinking how nice it would have been to be holding either the shotgun or the pistol, both locked in the trunk of his car.

The pit bull got a running start before it leapt, so it landed on Thomas Curl with maximum impact. He crashed against the aluminum wall and lost his wind, but somehow kept his balance. The dog crouched at his feet and snarled hotly. The animal seemed genuinely surprised that it had failed to knock its victim down, but Thomas Curl was a muscular and stocky fellow with a low center of gravity.

The next time the dog jumped, Thomas Curl recoiled and tried to shield his face with his right arm, which is where the animal sank its yellow fangs. At first Thomas Curl felt no pain, only an unbelievable pressure. He stared at the dog and couldn't believe it. Eyes wide, its pale muzzle splotched with Curl's blood, the frenzied animal twisted and turned as it dangled from the arm; it was trying to tear the flesh from Thomas Curl's bone.

Curl swallowed his scream. With his left hand he feverishly groped for the long screwdriver, still wedged in the doorjamb. He found it, grunted as he yanked it free, and poised it firmly in his good fist.

With all his strength Thomas Curl lifted his right arm as high as his head, so that the pit bull hung before him at eye level, squirming and frothing. With one jagged downward thrust Thomas Curl disemboweled the animal. Its wild eyes went instantly dull and the legs stopped kicking, but still the powerful jaws held fast to Curl's thick arm. Moments passed and Curl stood rigid, waiting for the animal's muscles to slacken in death. Yet even as its guts dripped on the cold doorstep, steaming the night air, the dog's jaws would not let go.

Thomas Curl braced against waves of nausea. The screwdriver slipped from his good hand and pinged off the concrete stoop.

At a nearby trailer the porch light came on, and an elderly man in a long undershirt poked his head out. Thomas Curl quickly turned his back so that the neighbor would not see the dead dog on his arm. By the fresh light Curl noticed that in his panic he had succeeded in breaking the doorjamb. With his good hand he turned the knob, and lurched inside R. J. Decker's trailer.

Curl lay faceup on a sofa, the big dog across his chest. He stayed there for what seemed like an hour, until he could no longer tolerate the weight of the animal and the raw odor of its blood. In the darkness he could only imagine what his right arm looked like; he felt the first stinging tickle of a vile infection, and the burning throb of torn muscles. He realized that before long the dog's body would stiffen, and it would become virtually impossible to pry its jaws. Angrily Thomas Curl balled his left fist and tested his strength. Still supine, he aimed a fierce upper cut at the pit bull's head. The punch made little noise and had no effect, but Thomas Curl did not stop. He shut his eyes and imagined himself on the bag at the Fifth Street Gym, and punched left-breathe-left in a steady tempo. For the heavy bag drill his ex-manager used to play 'Midnight Rambler' on the PA, so Curl ran the tune through his skull while he pounded on the pit bull. With each impact a ferocious bolt shot from his mangled arm into the vortex of his neck. The pain was miserable, but his alone; like any punching bag, the dog felt nothing. Its grip was immovable and, Thomas Curl began to fear, supernatural.

He dragged himself off the sofa, flipped on the kitchen lights, and began to tear Decker's trailer apart, looking for a tool. A wooden broom handle proved impotent against the demonic mandibles; a hammer satisfying to the grip, but messy and ineffectual. Finally, hanging from a pegboard in a utility closet, Thomas Curl found what he was looking for: a small hacksaw. He struggled into the narrow bathroom and knelt down. With his deadening right arm he slung the dog carcass into the shower stall, and gazed numbly at the livid mess. Thomas Curl didn't know whether he was just exhausted or going crazy, but he found it difficult to distinguish which flesh was his and which belonged to the animal. From the knotted muscle of his shoulder to the pinkish tail of the dog corpse seemed a single evil mass. Thomas Curl's left hand searched the tile until his fingers found the steel teeth of the hacksaw. He took a breath, and did what he had to.

Catherine was alone in bed when the doorbell rang.

James the doctor was gone again, this time to Montreal for a big trade show. He and several other chiropractors had agreed to endorse a new back-pain product called the Miracle VibraCouch, and the Canadian trade show was to be the scene of its unveiling. Saying good-bye at the car, James had promised to bring back videotapes of all the excitement, and Catherine had said that'll be wonderful and pecked him on the cheek. James had asked her which model VibraCouch would go best in the Florida room, the tartan or the dusty rose, and Catherine had said neither, I don't want an electric couch in my house, thank-you. James was pouting as he drove away.

When the bell rang, Catherine slipped into a short chiffon robe and padded barefoot to the door. The house was bright, and the clock in the alcove said nine-thirty. She'd overslept again.

Through a window she saw the gray Plymouth Volaré parked in the driveway. Catherine smiled—here we go again. She checked herself in the mirror and said what the hell, it's hopeless this early in the morning. When she opened the door she said, 'Great timing as usual, Rage.'

But the man turned around and it wasn't R.J. It was a heavyset stranger wearing R.J.'s brown leather coat. Catherine had bought the coat for him at a western shop near Denver. The stranger wore it on his shoulders like a cape. Maybe it wasn't R.J.'s coat after all, Catherine thought anxiously; maybe it was one just like it.

''Scuze me,' said the man, 'you Mrs. Decker?'

'Stuckameyer,' Catherine said. 'I used to be Mrs. Decker.'

The man had thin sandy hair, a flat crooked nose, and tiny dull eyes. He handed Catherine a crisp brown office envelope containing a sheaf of legal papers. Catherine scanned them and looked up quizzically.

'So?' she said. 'These are my old divorce papers.'

'But that *is* you? Catherine Decker.'

'Where'd you get this stuff?' she said irritably.

'I found it,' the man said, 'at Mr. Decker's.'

Catherine studied him closely. She saw that he was also wearing one of R.J.'s knit shirts. She tried to slam the door but the man blocked it with a black round-toed boot.

'Don't be a dumb cunt,' he said.

Catherine was turning to run when she saw the pistol. The

man pointed it with his right hand extended from under the leather coat. Something round and mottled and awful was attached to the stranger's arm. It looked like a football with ears.

'Oh Jesus,' Catherine cried.

'Don't mind him,' the man said, 'he don't bite.'

He pushed his way into the house and shut the door. He shifted the pistol to his other hand, and tucked the dog-headed arm back under the coat.

'Decker's in some deep shit,' said the stranger.

'Well, I don't know where he is.' Catherine pulled her robe tight in the front.

Thomas Curl said, 'You know why I'm here?'

'No, but I know who you are,' Catherine said. 'You're one of the Fish People, aren't you?'

24

Jim Tile's patrol car passed García on Route 222 and led them into town, which was as dark as a mortuary. The trooper took them directly to the house of an old black doctor, who packed and dressed Skink's seeping eye wound. Silently Decker and García watched the old man dance a penlight in front of Skink's haggard face and peer into the other eye for quite a long time. 'He needs a neurologist right away,' the doctor said finally. 'Gainesville's your best bet.'

Skink himself said nothing. When they got back to the cabin, he curled up on a mattress and went to sleep. Jim Tile got the campfire going. Al García selected an oak stump of suitable width and sat down close to the flames. 'Now what?' he said. 'We tell ghost stories?'

R. J. Decker said, 'This is where he lives.'

'Unbelievable,' the detective muttered.

Jim Tile went to the car and came back with two black-and-white photographs, eight-by-tens. 'From our friends in the bayou,' he said, handing the pictures to R. J. Decker.

'Christ,' Decker mumbled. They were the caught-in-the-act shots of the bass cheaters in the reeds at Lake Maurepas—except that Dickie Lockhart's head had been supered onto one of the other men's body. Decker recognized the mug of Dickie from the bunch he'd shot at the Cajun Classic weigh-in. Looking at the doctored photographs made him feel angry and, in a way, violated.

'Somebody swiped my film and had some fun in the darkroom,' he said to Jim Tile. 'I've seen better phonies.'

'Sure fooled New Orleans homicide.'

'It's still bush,' Decker snapped. 'I can find a half-dozen expert witnesses to say these are tricked.'

Al García took the prints from Decker and studied them. 'Nifty,' he said. 'That's how they do it, huh?'

'In cages, yeah.'

'And how long will those fish stay alive?'

Decker shrugged. 'Couple days, I guess.'

Jim Tile said, 'There's some other things you ought to know.' He told them about his conversation with Ozzie Rundell, and Ozzie's version of Ott Pickney's murder.

'He also says Lockhart didn't kill Robert Clinch.'

'You believe that?' Decker asked.

Jim Tile nodded.

García said, 'Had to be Gault.'

'That's my guess too,' the trooper agreed, 'but I'm not sure why he'd do it.'

R. J. Decker thought about it. Why would Dennis Gault order the murder of a man he had recruited to work for him? Lanie might know; she might even be part of the reason.

Jim Tile said, 'There's a guy named Thomas Curl, a real shit-kicker. He and his brother killed your friend Ott. My bet is they did Bobby Clinch too.'

'The Louisiana boys,' Decker said.

Jim Tile said, 'It just so happens that Lemus Curl is missing. Family says he fell into Lake Okeechobee.'

García looked curiously at Decker, who tried not to react.

'But the other Curl,' Jim Tile went on, 'Thomas Curl, is in Miami.'

'Fuck me,' said Al García.

Decker said, 'Let me guess: Curl is looking for me.'

'Most likely,' Jim Tile said. 'By phone I tracked him to some ritzy hotel in the Grove, but then he took off.'

'What's the connection to Gault?'

'He paid for Curl's room,' Jim Tile said.

He took a piece of paper from his left breast pocket, unfolded it carefully and handed it to Decker. 'Meanwhile,' Jim Tile said, 'Mr. Gault is going fishing.'

It was a promotional flier for the Dickie Lockhart Memorial Bass Blasters Classic. In the firelight García read it aloud over

Decker's shoulder: 'The richest tournament in history. Entry fee is only three thousand dollars, but hurry—the field will be limited to fifty boats.'

Decker couldn't believe it, the ballsiness of these guys. 'Three thousand bucks,' he said.

'It is amazing,' Jim Tile remarked. Long ago he had given up trying to understand the cracker mentality. He wondered if the Cuban cop would have the same difficulty.

García said, 'Dennis Gault I can figure out. He's a greedy little egomaniac who wants trophies for his penthouse. But what's the rest of the shit with this tournament?'

Decker explained the Outdoor Christian Network and its vast stake in the Lunker Lakes development. 'They're going to use the TV fish hype to sell townhouses. Everybody does it these days. Mazda has golf, Lipton has tennis, OCN has bass. The demographics match up nicely.'

Al García looked extremely amused. 'You're telling me,' he said, 'that grown men will sit down for hours in front of a television set and watch other men go fishing.'

'Millions,' Decker said, 'every weekend.'

'I don't ever want to hear you talk about crazy Cubans,' García said, 'never again.'

A flicker of a smile crossed Jim Tile's face, and then he grew serious. 'Gault is the big problem,' he said. 'He's the one who can put Decker in prison.'

'He'd rather have him dead,' García noted.

Decker knew the detective was right. By now Dennis Gault surely understood that a trial could be disastrous; the evidence against Decker was entirely circumstantial, and Gault couldn't risk taking the witness stand himself. There were neater ways to close a murder case, and one was to make the prime suspect vanish. That, Decker thought, would be Thomas Curl's department.

García said to Decker, 'We need to get to Gault before Curl gets to you.'

'That's brilliant, Al.'

'Any ideas, smartass?'

'Yes, as a matter of fact. My idea is that you plant your lazy Cuban butt right here for a day or so, and keep an eye on our sick friend.' Decker turned to Jim Tile. 'I need a favor from you.'

'Starting tonight,' the trooper said, 'I'm on vacation.'

'Good,' Decker said. 'You feel like taking a drive to the beach?'

Jim Tile chuckled. 'My Coppertone's already packed.'

Crescent Beach is a few miles south of St. Augustine. The broad expanse of sand is sugary white, but packed so hard you could drive a truck to the water's edge without fear of getting stuck. For a long time Crescent Beach and adjacent communities existed in a rare and splendid quiet. To the south, Daytona got all the publicity and the crowds to go with it; to the north, the beach at Jacksonville was still clean enough to keep the city folks home on weekends. As the condo market boomed in the seventies, though, developers scouted and scoured all of the state's ocean-front possibilities, and spied lovely Crescent Beach as a promoter's wet dream—the perfect escape. See Florida as it used to be! Enjoy the solitude of long romantic walks, the Atlantic nipping at your toes! Lie down among the dunes! The dunes became a crucial selling point for North Florida's long-ignored beaches, because the people in South Florida didn't know what a dune was—the developers had flattened them all back in the fifties. True, by Northern standards Florida dunes weren't much to write home about—stubbled little hillocks, really—but the condo salesmen made the most of them and customers thought they were quaint. Once the building boom took hold south of Jacksonville and the beachfront became clogged with exclusive resorts and high-rises and golf communities, the state was forced to start buying up the remaining dunes, making parks, and nailing boardwalks every whichway to keep the dunes from getting leveled. Mysteriously, tourists would drive for miles and pay admission just to see a three-foot crest of sand with a few strands of sea oats—a genuine touch of wilderness among the cabanas.

Lanie Gault had not chosen Crescent Beach for its dunes. She hadn't chosen it at all; a lover had bought the condo and given it to her for Valentine's Day in 1982. He was a wonderful and basically harmless man, had his own insurance company, and Lanie didn't mind that he was married. He wasn't the sort of guy you wanted to have around *all* the time anyway. Every other weekend was just fine. It lasted for about two years until his wife found out—somebody called her up with the juicy details. The insurance man couldn't figure out who would do such a thing, but Lanie knew. It was her brother. Dennis never admitted to making the phone call, but Lanie had no doubt he was the one. Dennis couldn't stand the insurance man (nothing new) and for months had been telling her to clear the deed and dump the guy, he's bad news. He *isn't* bad news, Lanie had argued, thinking: He's just slightly boring. When the wife found out, Lanie was angry with her brother but also a little relieved. A few days later the insurance man came to the condo and told her he was moving back to St. Louis and kissed her good-bye. Lanie cried and said she understood and asked if he wanted her to give the condo back. The insurance man said heavens no, it's all yours, just don't tell anyone where you got it. A week later Lanie put in brand-new wine carpeting and decided maybe her heart wasn't truly broken after all.

Lanie's condominium was on the east wing of the ninth floor, and featured a scallop-shaped balcony with an ocean view. One of the things she liked about the building was the security—not only a gatehouse at the entrance, but an armed guard in the lobby and a closed-circuit TV bank. Nobody got upstairs without clearance, and the security people had strict instructions to phone ahead, no matter what. Given such procedures, Lanie was understandably alarmed to be awakened by someone knocking on the door. She squirmed across the king-size bed and snatched the phone off the nightstand and called the desk. The guard said, 'It's the police, Miss Gault, we had to let them up.'

When she opened the door, she saw the problem. Jim Tile was wearing his state trooper's uniform.

'Can I help you?' Lanie asked.

'Not me,' Jim Tile said, 'my friend.'

R. J. Decker peeked around the corner of the doorway. 'Remember me? We exchanged bodily fluids not long ago.'

Lanie looked stunned to see him. 'Hi,' she said tentatively.

The two men walked in; Jim Tile courteously removing his Stetson, Decker closing the door behind them. 'I can see you're wondering how to play this scene,' he said to Lanie, 'because you don't know how much I know.'

'What do you mean?'

Decker opened the living-room curtains without remarking on the view. 'Lovey-dovey is one way to go. You know the bit: *Where you been? I missed you. Why haven't you called?* But that's only good if I don't know that you went to the New Orleans cops. And if I don't know you helped your brother set me up.'

Lanie sat down and fiddled with her hair. Jim Tile went to the kitchen and fixed three glasses of orange juice.

'Another way to go,' Decker continued, 'is the Terrified Witness routine. Murder suspect barges into your apartment, scares the shit out of you. *Please don't hurt me. I'll do anything you want, just don't hurt me.* That's if you're trying to sell me the idea that you really believe I killed Dickie Lockhart. Which is horseshit.'

Lanie smiled weakly. 'Any other choices?'

'Try the truth,' said Decker, 'just as an experiment.'

'You got a tape player?' Jim Tile asked.

Lanie said, 'On the balcony, with the beach stuff.' She shook her head no when Jim Tile offered a glass of juice.

The trooper went outside and got the portable stereo. He came back and set it up on the coffee table in the living room. There was already a cassette in the tape player.

Jim Tile punched the Record button. He said, 'You don't mind?'

'Hey, that's my Neil Diamond you're erasing,' Lanie complained.

'What a loss,' Decker said.

Jim Tile fiddled with the volume dial. 'Nice box,' he said. 'Graphic equalizers and everything.'

'Let's start with Dennis,' Decker said.

'Forget it, R.J.'

Jim Tile said, 'She's right. Let's don't start with her brother. Let's start with Robert Clinch.'

Lanie stared coldly at the big black man. 'I could get you in a lot of trouble.'

'Don't flatter yourself,' said Jim Tile.

Decker was impressed at how unimpressed Jim Tile was. He said, 'Okay, princess, guess who killed Bobby.'

'Dickie Lockhart did.'

'Wrong.'

'Then who?'

Jim Tile got up and opened the glass doors to the balcony. A cool breeze stirred the curtains. Lanie shivered.

Decker said, 'Dennis didn't think much of your affair with Bobby Clinch, did he? I mean, a sexy high-class girl like you can't be sneaking off with a grotey redneck bass fisherman.'

'What?' Lanie looked aggravated, not cool at all.

Jim Tile said, 'Your brother had Robert Clinch killed. He hired two men to do it. They waited for him at the Coon Bog that morning, jumped him, then rigged his boat for a bad wreck. Dennis wanted everyone to think Dickie was behind it.'

'No,' said Lanie, glassy-eyed.

She really doesn't know, Decker thought. If she's acting, it's the performance of her life.

'Bobby wasn't getting anywhere on the cheating,' she said numbly. 'Dickie's people were too slick. Dennis was impatient, he was riding Bobby pretty hard. Then . . . well.'

'He found out you and Bobby were involved.'

Lanie gave a shallow laugh. 'The sportfucking, he didn't mind. A different fella each night and he'd never say a word to me. Whenever things got serious is when he acted weird. Like when Bobby said he was going to leave his wife and go away with me, Dennis got furious. But still he would never do what you say. Never!'

Decker said, 'Lanie, he needed you more than he needed Bobby.'

'For what, Decker? Needed me for what?'

Decker tapped his chest. 'For me.'

By now Lanie was crying. Not the best job of crying Decker had ever seen, but still pretty convincing. 'What are you saying?' she hacked between sobs. 'You think I was whoring for my own brother! I cared for Bobby, you don't believe me but it's true.'

Jim Tile was not moved. In years of writing traffic tickets, he'd heard every imaginable tale of woe. With his usual remoteness he said, 'When's the last time you spoke to him?'

'Bobby? I saw him the night before he died. We had a drink at a shrimp place over in Wabasso.'

'Did he tell you he was going to the lake?'

'Of course he did—he was so excited. He'd gotten a tip that Dickie was hiding his fish cages in the Coon Bog. Bobby was thrilled as anything. He couldn't wait to find the bass and call Dennis.'

Decker said, 'Where did the tip come from?'

'Some guy who called up Bobby, wouldn't give his name.'

'It was a setup,' Jim Tile said, 'the phone call.'

'Now, wait,' Lanie said. She kept looking down at the tape player.

Time's up, Decker thought. He sat next to Lanie and said, 'Call me nosy, but I'd like to know why you framed me.'

Lanie didn't answer. Decker took one of her hands and held it very gently, as if it were a baby animal he was afraid of squeezing. Lanie looked frightened.

'It was your brother's idea, wasn't it?'

'At first he talked about blackmail,' she said. 'He asked if I knew any good photographers who could follow Dickie and get the pictures without him knowing. I thought of you, and Dennis said fine. He said to keep you interested and I said okay, anything to get back at Dickie for what he did.'

'What you *thought* he did,' Decker interjected.

'Dennis said it was Dickie who killed Bobby. I believed him, why shouldn't I? It made sense.'

Jim Tile said, 'So Dickie's murdered, then what?'

'Dennis calls me in New Orleans.'

Decker said, 'Just what the hell were you doing there anyway?'

'He sent me,' Lanie said. 'To make sure you weren't goofing off, he said. He was pissed off because you weren't telling him much on the phone.'

'So you drag me into bed, then steal my film?'

'Who dragged who?' Lanie said sharply. 'About the film, I'm sorry. It was a shitty thing to do. Dennis said he was dying to see what you'd got. Said the stuff belonged to him anyway.'

Decker held her hand just a little tighter. 'And you actually believed all this?' he asked agitatedly. 'These errands didn't strike you as a little odd? No light bulb flashed on in your beautiful size-four brain?'

'No,' Lanie snapped, 'no light bulbs.'

Jim Tile said, 'Getting back to Dickie's murder . . .'

'Yeah,' Lanie said, shifting her eyes to the trooper. 'That morning Dennis called me in New Orleans, all upset. He said Decker had gone and killed Lockhart. Dennis was afraid.'

Jim Tile said, 'He told you he might be a suspect.'

'Right. He said Decker was trying to frame him, and he asked me to go to the police.'

'And lie?'

'He's my brother, for God's sake. I didn't want him to go to jail over a crazy goddamn fish murder. Bobby's death was bad enough, I didn't want to lose Dennis too. So I went down and gave a very brief statement.' She looked at Decker again. 'I said you dropped me off on your way to see Dickie Lockhart. That's all.'

'It was plenty,' Decker said. 'Thanks a heap.'

'Dennis sounded desperate.'

'And with good reason.'

'I still don't believe you,' Lanie said.

'Yes, you do,' said Jim Tile.

It was all Decker could do to hold his temper. 'Any other little Dennis favors we should know about?'

Lanie said, 'Can you turn that thing off?'

Jim Tile stopped the tape machine.

Lanie got up and led them through the apartment to the second bedroom. She opened the door as quietly as she could. The room was totally dark; the shades were not only drawn, but the cracks were sealed with hurricane tape. Lanie turned on the ceiling light.

A young long-haired woman lay in bed, a pink cotton blanket pulled up to her chin. Her bluish eyelids were half-closed and she breathed heavily, with her mouth open. Some pills and a half-empty bottle of Dewar's sat on the nightstand.

Jim Tile looked at R. J. Decker, who said, 'I've seen her before. At the tournament in New Orleans.'

'Name's Ellen O'Leary,' Lanie said in a dull voice. 'She's not feeling well.'

In a fury Decker pushed Lanie Gault to the wall, pinned her arms.

'No more games,' he said. 'Who's this girl?'

'I *don't* know,' Lanie cried.

'You just came home one night and there she was, passed out in bed?'

'No, a man brought her. Dennis asked me to look after her.'

Decker said, 'You're a very sick lady, Elaine.'

'Easy, man,' said Jim Tile. He sat down on the bed next to Ellen O'Leary and studied the labels on the pill bottles. 'Nembutals,' he said to Decker.

'Swell, a Norma Jean cocktail.'

'Just to make her sleepy,' Lanie insisted. 'She'll be all right, R.J. Every night I give her soup. Would you get off me, please?'

Decker grabbed Lanie's arm and led her out of the bedroom. Jim Tile flushed the pills down the toilet and went to the kitchen to fix coffee for the woman named Ellen. He was wondering how much stranger things would get.

Decker himself was frazzled. Lanie was impossible.

'What did your brother say about this woman?' he asked her.

'He said to keep an eye on her, that's all. Keep her sleepy and out of trouble. He said she was a danger to herself and others.'

'I'll bet.'

Lanie asked if she could get dressed. Decker said yes, but he wouldn't let her out of his sight. Lanie didn't object. Casually she stripped off her nightshirt and stood naked in front of the mirror, brushing out her hair while Decker watched impassively. Finally she put on jeans and a University of Miami sweatshirt.

Decker said, 'You know a man named Thomas Curl?'

'Sure, that's the guy who brought Ellen,' Lanie answered. 'He works for Dennis.'

By the way she said it, Decker could tell she really didn't know. Even Lanie wasn't that good.

'Thomas Curl killed Bobby,' he said.

'Stop it,' Lanie said, 'right now.' But it was obvious by her expression that she was putting it all together.

In the other room Jim Tile carried Ellen to the shower. He propped her under a cold drizzle for ten minutes until she spluttered and bent over to vomit. Then he toweled her off and put her back in bed. Once her stomach settled, she sat up and sipped some coffee.

Jim Tile closed the door and said, 'You want to talk?'

'Where am I?' Ellen asked thickly.

'Florida.'

'I must've got sick—did I miss it?'

'Miss what?' Jim Tile asked.

'Dickie's funeral.'

'Yes, it's over.'

'Oh.' Ellen's eyes filled up.

Jim Tile said, 'Dickie was a friend of yours?'

'Yes, officer, he was.'

'How long did you know him?'

'Not long,' answered Ellen O'Leary, 'just a few days. But he cared for me.'

'When's the last time you saw him?'

Ellen said, 'Right before it happened.'

'The murder?'

'Yes, officer. I was up in the hotel with him, celebrating after the bass tournament, when Thomas Curl came to the door and said he needed to see Dickie right away.'

'Then what happened, Ellen?'

'They went off together and Dickie didn't come back. I fell asleep—we'd had an awful lot of champagne. The next morning I heard on the radio what happened.'

Jim Tile refilled her coffee cup. 'What did you do then?' he asked.

'I was so upset, I called Reverend Weeb,' she said, 'and I asked him to say a prayer for Dickie's soul. And Reverend Weeb said only if I came over and knelt down with him.'

'I bet you weren't in the mood for *that*.'

'Right,' Ellen said. She didn't understand how the black trooper could know about Reverend Weeb's strange ways, but she was grateful for the compassion.

Jim Tile opened the bedroom door and asked Decker and Lanie to come in.

'Ellen,' he said, 'tell Miss Gault who came and got Dickie Lockhart the night he was killed.'

'Thomas Curl,' said Ellen O'Leary.

Lanie looked stricken. 'Are you sure?'

'I've known him since high school.'

'God,' Lanie said dejectedly.

Ellen tucked an extra pillow under her head. 'I'm feeling lots better,' she said.

'Well, I feel like hell,' said Lanie.

The phone rang. Jim Tile told her to answer it, and motioned Decker to pick up the kitchen extension.

The caller was Dennis Gault.

'Hi,' Lanie said, with the trooper standing very close behind her.

'How's it going, sis?' Gault asked.

'Fine,' Lanie said. 'Ellen's still sleeping.'

'Excellent.'

'Dennis, I'd like to go out, catch some sun, do some shopping. How much longer with the babysitting?'

'Look, Elaine, I don't know. The cops still haven't caught Decker.'

'Oh, great.' Perfect sarcasm. Decker listened admiringly—she really could have been a star of stage and screen.

'What if they don't catch him?' she said.

'Don't be ridiculous.'

'Dennis, I want Tom to come get this girl.'

'Soon,' Gault promised. 'I sent him down to Miami on some business. He'll pick up Ellen when he gets back. Relax, wouldya, sweet thing?'

'Miami,' Lanie repeated.

'Yeah,' her brother said, 'we're getting ready for the big tournament.'

'Oh boy,' said Lanie, thinking: I hope you drown, you murdering bastard.

25

The fire died slowly, and as it did Al García poked and speared the embers in a feeble attempt to revive the flames. Soon a gray curling mist cloaked the lake and settled over the detective's shoulders like a damp shroud. Small creatures scuttled unseen through the woods, each crackling twig reminded García that he was desperately removed from his element, the city. Even from the lake there were noises—what, he couldn't imagine—splashes and gurgles of all dimensions. García wondered about bears; what kind, how big. The weight of the Colt Python under his arm was a small comfort, but he knew the gun was not designed to kill bears. García was no outdoorsman, his main exposure to the wilderness being old reruns of *The American Sportsman*. Two things he remembered most vividly about the TV show were ferocious bears the size of Pontiacs, and convivial campfire scenes where all the men slugged down beers and feasted on fresh venison. García seemed to recall that there were always at least ten heavily armed guys around Curt Gowdy at the camp, plus a camera crew. And here he was, practically all alone with a dead fire.

Halfheartedly García collected some kindling and tossed it into the embers. He put his cigarette lighter to the pile, but the wood sparked and in a moment went cold. The detective unscrewed the top of his disposable lighter and dumped the fluid on the sticks. Then he leaned over and touched a match to the fire, which promptly blew up in his face.

After García picked himself off the ground, he sat down lugubriously by the smouldering campfire. Gingerly he explored his face and found only minimal damage—his eyebrows were scorched and curlicued, and his mustache gave off an acrid smell. García jumped at the low rumble of laughter—it was Skink, hulking in the doorway of the shack.

'Honest to God,' the big man said. In three minutes the fire was ablaze again. Skink made coffee, which García accepted gratefully. There was something odd about the governor's appearance, and it took the detective several moments to figure it out.

'Your eye,' he said to Skink.

'What of it?'

A new eye stared from the socket where the heavy gauze had been packed. The new eye was strikingly big, with a startling yellow iris and a pupil as large as a half-dollar. García couldn't help but notice that the new eye was not a perfect fit for the hole in Skink's face.

'Where did you get it?' García asked.

'Does it look okay?'

'Fine,' the detective said. 'Very nice.'

Skink clomped into the shack and came back with a stuffed barn owl, an erect, imperious-looking bird. 'I tie this on the roof to keep the crows and grackles away,' he said. Admiring the taxidermied owl at arm's length, Skink said, 'If looks could kill.'

García asked, 'Will it still scare the birds? With one eye, I mean.'

'Hell, yes,' Skink said. 'Even more so. Just look at that vicious fucker.'

The owl's frozen gaze was still fierce, García had to admit. And Skink himself looked exceptional; while his new eye did not move in concert with its mate, it still commanded attention.

'I'll give it a try,' Skink said, putting on his sunglasses.

After they finished the coffee, Skink got the Coleman lantern and led García down to the water. He told him to get in the rowboat. García shared the bow with an old tin bucket, a nylon castnet folded inside. Skink rowed briskly across the lake, singing an old rock song that García vaguely recognized: *No one knows what it's like to be the bad man, to be the sad man* . . . More like the madman, García said to himself.

He was impressed by Skink's energy, after the savage beating he'd taken. The wooden boat cut the water in strong bolts, Skink pulling at the oars with a fervor that bordered on jubilation. Truly he was a different man than the bloodied heap wheezing in the back seat of García's car. If the pain still bothered him, Skink didn't show it. He was plainly overjoyed to be home, and on the water.

After twenty minutes Skink guided the rowboat into a cove on the northern shore, but he didn't break his pace. With his good eye he checked over his shoulder and kept a course for the mouth of a small creek that emptied into the lake between two prehistoric live oaks. To García the creek seemed too narrow even for the little skiff, yet it swallowed them easily. For fifty yards it snaked through mossy bottomland, beneath lightning-splintered cypress and eerie tangled beards of Spanish moss. García was awestruck by the primordial beauty of the swamp but said nothing, afraid to disturb the silence. Skink had long stopped singing.

Eventually the creek opened to a blackwater pond rimmed by lily pads and mined with rotting stumps.

Skink removed his sunglasses and tucked them into the pocket of his weathersuit. He turned from the oars and motioned for the castnet. Awkwardly García handed it to him; the lead weights were heavy and unwieldy. Standing wide-legged, Skink clenched the string in his teeth and hurled the net in a smooth low arc; it opened perfectly and settled to the water like a gossamer umbrella. When he dragged the net back into the boat, it was spangled with fish, flashing in the mesh like pieces of a shattered mirror. Skink filled the tin bucket with water and emptied the fish into it. Then he refolded the net and sat down, facing Al García.

'Golden shiners,' he announced. Skink plucked one out of the bucket and swallowed it alive.

García stared at him. 'What do they taste like?' he asked.

'Like shiners.' Skink took another fish from the bucket and thwacked it lightly against the gunwale, killing it instantly. 'Watch here,' he said to García.

Leaning over the side of the skiff, Skink slapped the palm of his hand on the water, causing a loud concussion. He repeated this action several times until suddenly he pulled his hand from the pond and said, 'Whooo, baby!' He dropped the dead shiner and beneath it the black water erupted—a massive fish, as bronze and broad as a cannon, engulfed the little fish where it floated.

'*Cristo!*' gasped Al García.

Skink stared at the now-silken surface and grinned proudly. 'Yeah, she's a big old momma.' He tossed another shiner, with the same volcanic result.

'That's a bass?' García asked.

'Hawg,' Skink said. 'The fucking monster-beastie of all time. Guess her weight, Sergeant.'

'I've got no idea.' In the fickle light of the lantern García looked hard for the fish but saw nothing; the water was impenetrable, the color of crude oil.

'Name's Queenie,' Skink said, 'and she weighs twenty-nine pounds, easy.'

Skink tossed three more shiners, and the bass devoured them, soaking the men in her frenzy.

'So this is your pet,' García said.

'Hell, no,' Skink said, 'she's my partner.' He handed the bucket to Al García. 'You try,' he said, 'but watch your pinkies.'

García crippled a shiner and tossed it into the pond. Nothing happened, not a ripple.

'Spank the water,' Skink instructed.

García tried, timidly, making more bubbles than noise.

'Louder, dammit!' Skink said. 'That's it. Quick, now, drop a shiner.'

No sooner had the tiny fish landed—still wriggling, this one— than the monster-beastie slurped it down. The noise was obscene.

'She likes you,' Skink said. 'Do it again.'

García tossed another baitfish and watched it disappear. 'You learn this shit from Marlin Perkins?' he said.

Skink ignored him. 'Give me the bucket,' he said. He fed the big fish the rest of the dying shiners, save one. Skink held it between his thumb and forefinger, tickling the water. He used the fish as a silvery wand, tracing figure-eights by the side of the rowboat. From its unseen lair deep in the pond, the big fish rose slowly until its black dorsal punctured the velvet surface. As the fish hung motionless, García for the first time could see its true size, and appreciate the awesome capacity of its underslung jaw. The bass glided slowly toward Skink's teasing shiner; frenzy had been replaced by a delicate deliberation. Skink's fingers released the baitfish, which disappeared instantly into the white maw— yet the fish did not swim away, nor did Skink withdraw his hand. Amazingly, he took the bass by its lower lip, hoisted it from the pond, and laid it carefully across his lap. 'There now, momma,' Skink said. Dripping in the boat, the fish flared its gills and snapped at air, but did not struggle. It was, García thought, a magnificent gaping brute—nearly thirty pounds of iridescent muscle.

'Sergeant,' Skink said, 'say hi to Queenie.'

García did not wish to seem rude, but he didn't feel like talking to a fish.

'Come on,' Skink prodded.

'Hey, Queenie,' said the detective, without conviction. He was very glad his lieutenant couldn't see him.

Skink kept a thumb curled in the bass's lower lip, and slipped the other hand under its bloated pale belly. He lifted the bass and propped it long-wise on his shoulder, like a barrel. Skink's face was side-by-side with that of the monster bass, and Al García found himself staring at (from left to right) the eyes of a fish, a man, and a stuffed owl.

As if cuddling a puppy, Skink pressed his cheek against Queenie's scaly gillplates. 'Meet the new boss,' he whispered to the fish, 'same as the old boss.'

Al García didn't know what the hell he was talking about.

The Reverend Charles Weeb arrived at Lunker Lakes just in time to see the second batch of fish die. The hydrologist was crestfallen but said there was nothing to be done. Under a gray sky Weeb stood on the bank next to the young scientist and counted the fish as they bobbed to the surface of the bad water. At number seventy-five, Weeb turned and stalked back to the model townhome that was serving as tournament headquarters.

'Cancel tomorrow's press tour,' he snapped at Deacon Johnson, who obediently lunged for his Rolodex.

To the hydrologist Weeb said: 'So how long did this bunch live?'

'Eighteen hours, sir.'

'Shit. And the trip down from Alabama was . . .?'

'About two days,' the hydrologist said.

'Shit.' Lunker Lakes had now claimed four thousand young bass, and Charlie Weeb was deeply worried. For now he was thinking in the short-term.

'I can get another two thousand,' he said to the hydrologist.

'I wouldn't recommend it,' the man said. 'The water's still sub-standard.'

'*Substandard?* What you're really saying is these fish stand a better chance in a sewer, is that right?'

'I wouldn't go quite that far,' the hydrologist said.

'Okay, pencil-neck, let's hear the bad news.' Weeb shut the door to his private office and motioned the young man to a Chippendale chair. 'You like this unit? We've got your atrium doors, your breakfast bay, your cathedral ceiling—did I mention solar heat? See, I've got to sell twenty-nine thousand of these babies and right now they're moving real fucking slow. It's gonna get slower if I got a dead-fish problem, you understand?' Charlie Weeb inhaled two Chiclets. 'I'm selling a *new* Florida here, son. The last of the frontier. My buyers are simple folks who'd rather go fishing than get fried to raisins on the beach. Lunker Lakes is their kind of place, an outdoor community, see? Walk out the back door with your fishing pole and reel in a whopper. That's the way I dreamed it, but right now . . . well.'

'We're talking cesspool,' the hydrologist said bluntly. 'I did some more tests, very sophisticated chemical scans. You've got toxins in this water that make the East River seem like Walden Pond. The worst concentration is in the bottom muck—we're talking in Guinness-record PCBs.'

'How?' Charlie Weeb yowled. 'How can it be poisoned if it's pre-dredged?'

The hydrologist said, 'I was puzzled too, until I checked down at the courthouse. This used to be a landfill, Reverend Weeb, right where the lakes are.'

'A dump?'

'One of the biggest—and worst,' the hydrologist reported

grimly. 'Four hundred acres of sludge, rubbers, dioxins, you name it. EPA never did find out.'

Charlie Weeb said, 'Lord God!'—an exclamation he almost never used off the air.

'In layman's terms,' the hydrologist concluded, 'when you dredged Lunker Lakes, you tapped into twenty-four years' worth of fermented battery acid.'

Charlie Weeb coughed his gum into the trashcan. His mind was racing. He visualized the disastrous headlines and rubbed his eyes, as if to make the nightmare go away. Silently he cursed himself for succumbing to the South Florida real-estate disease when he could have played it safe and gone for tax-free muni bonds—the OCN board *had* left it up to him. Through his befogged paroxysm of self-pity Weeb remotely heard the hydrologist explaining how the lakes could be cleansed and made safe, but the project would take years and cost millions . . .

First things first, thought Charlie Weeb. The poster on the wall reminded him that the big tournament was only four days away. The immediate priority was getting some new fish.

'If I could get the tanker truck here before dawn,' Charlie Weeb said, 'get the bass in the water early, would they live until sunset?'

'Probably.'

'Thank God it's a one-day tournament,' Weeb said, thinking aloud.

'Can't say how healthy they'd be,' the hydrologist cautioned. 'They may not feed at all.'

'They don't need to,' Weeb said, leaving the man thoroughly confused. 'Get those fucking dead fish out of my sight, every one,' the preacher ordered, and the hydrologist fled to round up some boats.

Fast Eddie Spurling was next on Charlie Weeb's agenda. Eddie came in wearing a Happy Gland fishing cap and a shiny silver Evinrude jacket. Tucked into his cheek was a plug of Red Man tobacco so big it would have gagged a hyena. It was all Weeb could do to conceal his disgust; Eddie Spurling was about the biggest Gomer he'd ever met.

'The fish are dying,' Eddie said, his voice pained.

'You noticed.'

'Why?'

'Don't worry about it,' Weeb said. 'Sit down, please.'

'I hate to see 'em dying like that.'

Not half as much as I do, Weeb thought morosely. 'Eddie,' he began, 'have you given much thought to the big tournament? Have you got a plan for winning?'

Eddie Spurling shifted the tobacco to his other cheek. Chewing hard, he said, 'Truthfully, I figured buzzbaits would do it, but now I don't know. There's not much cover in this water. 'Fact, there's not much *anything* in this water. I didn't even see any garfish down there, and those suckers could live in a toilet bowl.'

Weeb frowned.

'Jelly worms,' Eddie declared through his chaw. 'Rig 'em Texas-style, I think that'll be the ticket, sir.'

Charlie Weeb sat forward and put on his eyeglasses. 'Eddie, it's very important that you win this tournament.'

'Well, I'll damn sure try.' He flashed a mouthful of wet brown teeth. 'Prize money like that—you kidding?'

'Trying is fine,' Weeb said, 'very admirable. But this time we may need to do more. A little insurance.'

Weeb was not surprised that Eddie looked confused.

'You're the new star at OCN, we got a lot riding on you,' Charlie Weeb said. 'If you win, we all win. And Lunker Lakes too. This is a tremendous opportunity, Eddie.'

'Well, sure.'

'Opportunities like this don't come along every day.' Weeb rocked back and folded his hands behind his head. 'I've been having this dream, Eddie, and you're in it.'

'Yeah?'

'That's right. In my dream, the sun is shining, the lakes are clear and beautiful. Thousands of happy home-buyers are gathered around, and the TV is there too, waiting for the end of the big tournament. All the other fishermen are back at the dock except you, Eddie.'

'Ugh.'

'Then, only seconds before the deadline, I see your boat cutting across the water. You pull up with a big smile on your face, get out, wave at the cameras. Then you reach down and pull up the biggest stringer of largemouth bass anyone's ever seen. The whole joint goes wild, Eddie. There you are, standing under the Lunker Lakes sign, holding up these giant mother fish. God, it's a vision, don't you agree?'

'Sure, Reverend Weeb, it'd be a dream come true.'

Charlie Weeb said, 'Eddie, it *will* come true. I'm trucking in some big fucking bass from Alabama. They're yours, partner.'

'Wait a minute.'

'With the water this bad, I can't chance keeping the biggest ones in Lunker Lakes,' Weeb said. He unrolled a map across the kitchen counter. 'Here we are,' he said, pointing, 'and here's the Everglades dike. All you got to do is tie the boat at the culvert, hop the levee, and pull the cages.'

'Cages—fish cages?'

'No, *tiger* cages, Eddie—Christ, what do you think?'

Eddie Spurling said, 'I ain't gone cheat.'

'Pardon me?'

'Lookit, I'll scout the lakes and dump some brush piles a few days ahead. Stock 'em with bass before the tournament day and mark the spots. Hell, everybody does that—how about it?'

Charlie Weeb shook his head. 'The fish will croak, Eddie, that's the problem. I got two thousand yearlings coming in the night before and I'll be lucky if they hang on until dusk. Worse comes to worst, you might be the only guy in the tournament to bring in a live bass.'

'But I ain't gone cheat.'

Reverend Weeb smiled patiently. 'Eddie, you just bought that big place outside Tuscaloosa—what, sixty acres, something like that. And I notice your wife's driving a new Eldorado ... well, Eddie, I look at you and see a man who's enjoying himself, am I right? I see a man who likes being number one, for a change. Some men get a chance like this and they blow it—think of Dickie Lockhart.'

Eddie Spurling didn't want to think about that fool Dickie

Lockhart. What happened to Dickie Lockhart was a damn fluke. Eddie ground his Red Man to a soggy pulp. 'You got a place I could spit this?' he asked.

'The sink is fine,' Weeb said. Angrily Eddie Spurling drilled the wad straight into the disposal.

'So what's it gonna be,' Charlie Weeb said. 'You want to be a star, or not?'

Later that afternoon, Deacon Johnson knocked on the door to Reverend Weeb's private office. Inside, Reverend Weeb was getting a vigorous back rub and dictating a Sunday sermon for transcription.

'Who you got lined up for the healing?' Weeb grunted, the masseuse kneading his freckled shoulder blades.

'No kids,' Deacon Johnson reported glumly. 'Florida's different from Louisiana, Charles. The state welfare office threatened to shut us down if we use any kids on the show.'

'Pagan assholes!'

Charlie Weeb had planned a grand healing for the morning of the big bass tournament. A lavish pulpit was being constructed as part of the weigh station.

'Now what?' he said.

'I'm going down to the VA tomorrow to look for some cripples,' Deacon Johnson said.

'Not real cripples?'

'No,' said the deacon. 'With some of the vets, it comes and goes. They stub their toe, they get a wheelchair—it's all in their head. I think we can find one to play along.'

'Be careful,' Reverend Weeb said. 'All we need is some fruitcake Rambo flashing back to Nam on live TV.'

'Don't worry,' Deacon Johnson said. 'Charles, I thought you'd like to hear some good news.'

'Absolutely.'

Deacon Johnson said, 'The tournament's full. Today we got our fiftieth boat.'

'Thank God.' The hundred-fifty grand in entry fees would almost cover costs. 'Anybody famous?' Weeb asked.

'No, couple of brothers,' Deacon Johnson said. 'In fact, Eddie said he never even heard of them. Tile is the name. James and Chico.'

The preacher chuckled and rolled over on his back. 'Long as the check cleared,' he said.

26

Catherine was astonished when they went through the Golden Glades interchange and the toll-booth lady hardly looked twice at Lucas.

'I can't believe it,' Catherine said as they drove away.

Behind the wheel, Thomas Curl scowled. 'What the hell *would* she say?'

When they had pulled up to the booth, Curl had reached out with his dog-headed arm to get the ticket. The toll-booth lady glanced benignly at the pit bull, which was decomposing rather noticeably.

'Have a nice day,' the toll-booth lady said. 'I'm all out of Milkbones.'

'Thanks just the same,' said Thomas Curl, driving on.

He had named the dead dog head Lucas.

'Why not Luke?' Catherine asked.

'What a dumb name for a dog.'

Thomas Curl held the pistol tightly with his left hand; that's why he'd had to reach for the toll ticket with his right arm, the dog arm. That's the one he steered with. Catherine could see that it was grossly swollen with infection. The puss-lathered flesh had turned gray, with lightning streaks of crimson.

'You should see a doctor.'

'After I see Dennis,' Thomas Curl said. 'And after I see your goddamn husband.' Curl was sweating like a pig.

Catherine said, 'He's not my husband anymore.'

'I still plan to kill him, on account of Lemus.'

'See if I care,' said Catherine, staring out the window, seemingly enjoying the ride.

Thomas Curl didn't know what to make of her. The girl should have been frightened to death.

'Wait'll he finds out where you are.'

'Decker? What makes you think he still cares?' she bluffed.

Thomas Curl laughed coarsely. 'He's only got about a million fucking pitchers.'

'Of me?'

'Fucking A. Under the bed, in the closet, probably in his underpants drawer too. Didn't you know that?'

Catherine didn't know about the pictures. She wondered which ones R.J. had kept, which ones he liked best.

'My husband's a doctor. He could take a look at that arm when he gets back tonight.' Another bluff. James would have passed out at the sight.

'No way,' Thomas said. 'We're headed for Lauderdale.' He looked down at the dog head and smiled. 'Ain't that right, Lucas boy?'

Catherine was not surprised when Lucas made no reply, but Thomas Curl frowned unhappily. 'Lucas, you hear me? Goddammit, puppy, speak!'

The festering dog head clung mutely to his arm.

Thomas Curl shoved the barrel of the pistol into one of the animal's piebald ears.

'Please don't,' Catherine cried, raising her arms.

No longer paying even cursory attention to the highway, Thomas glared down at Lucas and bared his own teeth. 'My daddy said you got to show 'em who's boss. Dogs is like wives, he said, you can't let 'em have their way once else they run wild. Ain't that right, Lucas boy?'

Again nothing.

Thomas Curl cocked the pistol. 'Bad dog, Lucas!'

Catherine covered her mouth and let out a muffled little bark.

Curl grinned and leaned closer. 'Hear that?'

Catherine barked again. It was better than having him fire a gun inside the car, doing seventy.

'That's my puppy,' Curl said, oblivious. He laid the pistol in his lap and patted the crown of the dead dog's head. 'You good boy, Lucas, I knew all along.'

'Ruff!' said Catherine.

*

Skink netted more shiners and made Al García practice with the fish until nearly dawn. Finally they let the monster-beastie rest, and Skink rowed back across Lake Jesup. As they dragged the skiff ashore, García noticed two cars parked behind Skink's truck at the shack. One belonged to Trooper Jim Tile. The other was a tangerine Corvette.

'Company,' Skink said, removing his raincap.

The four of them were sitting around the campfire: Decker, Tile, Lanie Gault, and a woman whom Skink did not recognize. Decker introduced her as Ellen O'Leary.

'How's the eye?' Jim Tile asked.

Skink grinned and took off his sunglasses. 'Good as new,' he said. Everyone felt obliged to say something nice about the owl eye.

'You hungry?' Skink said. 'I'll take the truck and find some breakfast.'

'We hit the Mister Donut on the way in,' Decker said.

'Thank you anyway,' Lanie added.

Skink nodded. 'I am, sort of,' he said. 'Hungry, I mean. You please move the cars?'

'Take mine,' Lanie said, fishing the keys out of her jeans. 'Better yet, I'll go with you.'

'Like hell,' Decker said.

'I don't mind,' said Skink, 'if you don't.'

'No more rope tricks,' Lanie said. It was her cockteasing voice; Decker recognized it. She got in the passenger side of the Corvette. Skink squeezed himself behind the wheel.

'Hope she likes possum omelets,' Decker said.

Skink and Lanie were gone a long time.

Al García told Decker the plan, beginning with: 'The man's totally crazy.'

'Thanks for the bulletin.'

Jim Tile said, 'He knows about things. You can trust him.'

Skink's plan was to crash the big bass tournament and ruin it. His plan was to sabotage the Lunker Lakes resort on national television.

García said to Jim Tile: 'You and me are fishing together.'

'In the tournament?'

'He's already paid our entry fee,' García said. 'The best part is, we're supposed to be *hermanos*. Brothers.'

Jim Tile shook his head. He was smiling. 'I like it. I don't know why, but I do.'

In a faint voice Ellen O'Leary said, 'You don't look that much alike.'

'In the eyes we do,' García said, straight-faced. 'This is going to be fun.'

'Fun' is not the word R. J. Decker would have chosen. Things had gotten dangerously out of hand; suddenly a one-eyed road-side carnivore with possible brain damage was running the whole program. Even more astounding, García was going along with it. Decker couldn't imagine what could have happened while he and Jim Tile were up at Crescent Beach.

'This is all fascinating,' Decker said, 'and I wish both of you the best of luck in the tournament, but my immediate problem is Dennis Gault. Murder-one, remember?'

By way of interagency updating, Jim Tile said to García: 'The sister is taken care of. As a state's witness, forget it.' He held up the tape cassette.

'Good work,' García said. He turned to Ellen O'Leary. 'What about you, miss?'

Ellen looked worriedly at Jim Tile. The trooper said, 'She can put Tom Curl with Dickie Lockhart right before the murder.'

'Not bad,' García said. 'R.J., I can't figure what you're so worked up about. Sounds to me like an easy *nolle prosse*.'

'If you don't mind,' Decker said. 'Gault set me up on a murder charge. He also arranged to kill my friend Ott. At this very moment he's got some halfwit redneck hitman out looking for me. I would prefer not to wait three or four months for the New Orleans district attorney to settle the issue.'

García raised a fleshy brown hand. 'Yeah, I hear you, *chico*. Why don't I just pop big Mr. Gault at the fish tournament? Irritate the hell out of him, wouldn't it?'

'Good TV, too,' Jim Tile remarked.

'Pop him for what?' Decker asked.

García paused to light a cigarette. 'Filing false information, for starters. He lied to me—I don't like that. Obstruction, that's another good one. I haven't used it in years, so why not.'

Decker said, 'It's chickenshit, Al.'

'Better than nothing,' Jim Tile said.

García watched a blue smoke ring float into the oaks. 'Best I can do,' he said, 'until we find Tom Curl and have a serious chat with the boy.'

'You think he'll flip?' Decker said.

'Sure.' Al García smiled. 'If I ask real nice.'

Skink jacked the Corvette up to ninety on the Gilchrist. He felt obliged to do it, seeing as how he'd probably never get another chance. It truly was quite a car. He loved the way its snout sucked up the road.

In the passenger seat Lanie tucked her long legs beneath her bottom and turned sideways to watch him drive. Skink didn't like being watched, but he said nothing. It had been a long time since he had shared a moment with a beautiful woman; that was one price of hermitage. He remembered how good judgment went out the window in such times, so he warned himself to be careful, there was work to do. His head was killing him too; the pain had returned as soon as he'd gotten off the lake. A specialist was out of the question. There was no time.

Lanie popped a Whitney Houston tape in the cassette player and started keeping time with her bare feet. Without looking away from the road, Skink reached over and jerked the tape out of the dash. Then he threw it out the window.

'Got any Creedence?' he said.

In the seat Lanie whirled and, through the rear window, watched Whitney Houston bounce and shatter and unspool on the highway. 'You're crazy,' she snapped at Skink. 'You're buying me a new tape, buster.'

Skink wasn't paying attention. He had spotted something far ahead in the road; a motionless brown lump. He started braking the sports car, pumping slowly so it wouldn't leave rubber or spin out. When it finally came to a stop on the shoulder, he flicked on the emergency flashers and got out. He made sure to take the keys.

The thing in the road was a dead armadillo. After a brief examination Skink carried it by its scaly tail back to the Corvette.

Lanie was aghast. Skink tossed the carcass in the back and started the car.

'Ever had one?'

Lanie shook her head violently.

'Makes one hell of a gumbo,' he said. 'Use the shell as a tureen, if you do it right. Holds about two gallons.'

Lanie leaned back to see where the armadillo had landed, how much of a mess had been made on the upholstery.

'It's fresh, don't worry,' Skink said. He wheeled the Corvette around and headed back.

'Okay, who are you? Really.'

Skink said, 'You've seen who I am.'

'Before this,' Lanie said. 'You must have been . . . *somebody*. I mean, you didn't grow up on roadkills.'

'Unfortunately, no.'

Lanie said, 'I like you. Your hands especially. The day we first met I noticed them, when you were tying me with that plastic rope.'

'Fishing line,' Skink said, 'not rope. I'm glad there's no hard feelings.'

'You can't blame me for being curious.'

'Sure I can. It's none of your damn business who I am.'

'Shit,' Lanie said, 'you're impossible.'

Skink hit the brakes hard and downshifted. The sports car fishtailed severely and spun off the Gilchrist and came to rest in a field of crackling dry pastureland.

'My Vette is now parked in cowshit,' Lanie observed, more perturbed than frightened.

Skink took his hands off the steering wheel.

'Want to know who I am? I'm the guy who had a chance to save this place, only I blew it.'

'Save what?'

Skink made a circular gesture. 'Everything. Everything that

counts for anything. I'm the guy that could have saved it, but instead I ran. So there's your answer.'

'Clue me in, please.'

'Don't worry, it's ancient history.'

Lanie said, 'Were you famous or something?'

Skink just laughed. He couldn't help it.

'What's so funny?' she asked. He had a terrific smile, no doubt about it.

'No more damn questions.'

'Just one,' Lanie said, moving in. 'How about a kiss?'

It didn't stop at just one, and it didn't stop with just kissing. Skink was impressed by both her energy and agility—unless you had circus experience, it wasn't easy getting naked in the bucket seat of a Corvette. Skink himself tore the inseam of his orange weathersuit in the struggle. Lanie had better luck with her jeans and panties; somehow she even got her long bare legs wrapped around him. Skink admired her tan, and said so. She hit a button and the seat slid down to a full recline.

Once she was on top Lanie allowed her breasts to brush back and forth against Skink's cheeks. She looked down and saw that he seemed to be enjoying himself. His huge boots were braced against the dashboard.

'What do you like?' she asked.

'Worldly things.'

'You got it,' Lanie said. 'We're going to do it and then we're going to lie here together and talk, all right?'

'Sure.'

She pressed down hard and began to rock her hips. 'Get to know each other a little better.'

'Fine idea,' Skink said.

Then she leaned down, snuck her tongue in his ear, and said, 'Leave the sunglasses on, okay?'

Even for Lanie Gault, the owl eye would have been a glaring distraction.

Later that afternoon, after Lanie was gone and Jim Tile had stashed Ellen O'Leary at his apartment, Skink took the truck to town. He came back towing a dented old boat trailer with a sagging rusty axle. In the flatbed of the pickup truck was a six-horsepower Mercury outboard that had seen brighter days. There was also a plastic forty-gallon garbage bucket, eight feet of aquarium tubing, and four dozen D-size batteries, which Skink had purchased at Harney Hardware.

He was fiddling with his trash-bucket contraption when Decker came up and said, 'Why'd you let her go?'

'No reason to keep her.'

To Decker the reason seemed obvious. 'She'll run straight to her brother.'

'And tell him what?'

'Where I am, for starters.'

'You won't be here that long,' Skink said. 'We're all heading south. Jim Tile and the Cuban—they been practicing?'

'All day,' Decker said. 'García's hopeless.'

'He can play captain, then.'

Decker needed to ask something else but he didn't want to set Skink off.

'She doesn't know the plan, does she?'

It was another way of asking what had happened in the Corvette. Skink clearly didn't want to talk about it.

'Some of us know how to get laid with our mouths shut,' he said sourly. 'No, she doesn't know the damn plan.'

Decker was getting ominous vibrations; maybe the beating in Delray had loosened a few more bolts in the big man's brainpan. Skink was forever pulling guns, and he looked like he wanted to pull one now. Decker asked Jim Tile for a ride to town, to make some phone calls. Al García went along; he was out of cigarettes.

'Town's a bad idea,' Jim Tile said, heading away from Harney on Route 222. 'The three of us shouldn't be seen together. There's a Zippy Mart about eight miles along here.'

Decker said, 'This idea of his . . . I don't know, Jim.'

'It's his last chance,' the trooper said. 'You saw how bad he looks.'

'Then let's get him to a hospital.'

'It's not the eye, Decker. Or what those kids did to him. He's all beat up inside. He's done it to himself, you understand? Been doing it for years.'

Al García leaned forward in the back seat and said, 'What's the harm, R.J.? The man wants to make a point.'

Decker said, 'Skink I almost understand. But why are you guys going along?'

'Maybe we got a point to make, too,' Jim Tile said.

After that, Decker left it alone.

'Relax,' García told him. 'Couple old road cops like us need a break in the monotony, that's all.'

At the Zippy Mart, Jim Tile waited in the car while García went to buy his cigarettes and Decker used the pay phone. It had been several days since he had left Miami and, assuming he'd still have to make a living when this case was over, he thought it a wise idea to check his messages. He dialed his number, then punched the playback code for the tape machine.

The first voice made him wince. Lou Zicutto from the insurance company: 'Hey, douche-bag, you're lucky Núñez came down with mono. We got a two-week postponement from the judge, so this time no excuses—be there with your negatives. Otherwise just go ahead and buy yourself some fucking crutches, got it?'

What a prince to work for.

Decker didn't recognize the second voice, didn't need to: 'I got your wife, Mr. Decker, and she's just as pretty as the pitchers. So we're gonna trade: her tight little ass for yours. Call me . . . make it Friday at the Holiday Inn, Coral Springs. We'll be registered Mr. and Mrs. Juan Gómez.'

Decker hung up and sagged against the wall.

Al García, who'd come out of the store whistling, grabbed Decker by the arm. 'What is it, man?'

Jim Tile came up and took the other side.

'He's got Catherine,' Decker said tonelessly.

'Fuck.' García spit on the pavement.

'It's Tom Curl,' said the trooper.

R. J. Decker sat on the fender of Jim Tile's car and said nothing for five minutes, just stared at the ground. Finally he looked up at the other two men.

'Is there a place around here to buy a camera?' he asked.

27

When they got back to Lake Jesup, Jim Tile told Skink what Thomas Curl had done.

The big man sat down heavily on the tailgate of the truck and wrapped his arms around his head. R. J. Decker took a step forward but Jim Tile motioned him back.

After a few moments Skink looked up and said, 'It's my fault, Miami.'

'It's nobody's fault.'

'I'm the one who shot—'

'It's nobody's fault,' Decker said again, 'so shut up.' The less said about Lemus Curl, the better. Especially in the presence of cops.

Skink pulled painfully at his beard. 'This could screw up everything,' he said hoarsely.

'I would say so,' Al García grunted.

Skink took off the sunglasses. His good eye was red and moist. He gazed at Decker, and in a small brittle voice, said: 'The plan can't be changed, it's too late.'

'Do what you have to,' Decker said.

'I'll kill him afterward,' Skink said, 'I promise.'

'Thanks anyway, but it won't come to that.'

'This thing—' Skink paused, raked feverishly at his beard. He was boiling inside. He pounded his fists against the fender of the truck. 'This thing I have to do—it's so important.'

Decker said, 'I know, captain.'

'You'd understand better if you knew everything.' Skink spoke solemnly. 'If you knew it all, then you'd see the point.'

'It's all right,' Decker said. 'Go ahead with your plan. I've got one of my own.'

Skink grinned and clapped his hands. 'That's the spirit!' he said. 'That's what I like to hear.'

Al García and Jim Tile exchanged doubtful glances. In its own way, R. J. Decker's scheme was every bit as loony as Skink's.

Like a surgeon inspecting his instruments, Dennis Gault laid out his tournament bass tackle on the pile carpet and took inventory: six Bantam Magnumlite 2000 GT plugging reels, eight Shimano rods, four graphite Ugly Stiks, three bottles of Happy Gland bass scent, a Randall knife, two cutting stones, Sargent stainless pliers, a diamond-flake hook sharpener, Coppertone sunblock, a telescopic landing net, two pairs of Polaroid sunglasses (amber and green), a certified Chatillion scale and, of course, his tacklebox. The tacklebox was the suitcase-size Plano Model 7777, with ninety separate compartments. As was everything in Dennis Gault's tournament artillery, his bass lures were brand-new. For top-water action he had stocked up on Bang-O-Lures, Shad Raps, Slo Dancers, Hula Poppers, and Zara Spooks; for deep dredging he had armed himself with Wee Warts and Whopper Stoppers and the redoubtable Lazy Ike. For brushpiles he had unsheathed the Jig-N-Pig and Double Whammy, the Bayou Boogie and Eerie Dearie, plus a rainbow trove of Mister Twisters. As for that most reliable of bass rigs, the artificial worm, Dennis Gault had amassed three gooey pounds. He had caught fish on every color, so he packed them all: the black-grape crawdad, the smoke-sparkle lizard, the flip-tail purple daddy, the motor-oil moccasin, the blueberry gollywhomper, everything.

Gault arranged them lovingly; there was plenty of room.

The most critical decision, the one over which he pondered longest, was what strength fishing line to put on the reels. Good line is paramount; the slenderest of plastic threads, it is all that ties the angler to his wild and precious trophy. The longer a bass stays on the line, the greater its chances of escape. Since every fish that breaks off or throws the hook is money down the drain, the goal of the professional bass angler is to lose no fish whatsoever. Consequently, in tournaments there is not even the pretense of an actual battle between fisherman and fish. The

brutish deep dives and graceful acrobatics of a hooked largemouth
bass are not tolerated in the heat of serious angling competition.
In fact, the standard strategy is to strike the fish with all your
might and then drag the stunned creature into the boat as rapidly
as possible. In tournaments it is not uncommon to see five-pound
bass being skipped helplessly across the water in this manner.

Obviously, heavy line was essential. For the Dickie Lockhart
Memorial Classic, Dennis Gault selected a twenty-pound pink
Andes monofilament—limp enough to cast the lure a modest
distance in a light wind, yet sturdy enough to straighten the spine
of any mortal largemouth.

Gault was ironing a Bass Blasters patch onto the crown of his
cap when the phone rang. It was Lanie, calling from a truck stop
halfway between Harney and Fort Lauderdale.

'Ellen O'Leary is gone,' she said. 'Decker came to the condo
and got her.'

'Nice work,' her brother said snidely.

'What'd you expect me to do? He had that big black guy with
him, the trooper.'

Gault was determined not to let anything spoil the tournament
for him.

'Don't worry about it,' he said.

'What about New Orleans?' Lanie asked.

'Forget about it,' Gault said, 'and forget about Decker. Tom
Curl is taking care of it.'

Lanie knew what that meant, but she swept the thought from
her mind. She pretended it meant nothing. 'Dennis, I told them
about the affidavit, about how I lied.'

She thought he would be furious, but instead he said: 'It doesn't
really matter.'

Lanie wanted Dennis to say something more, but he didn't.
She wanted to hear all about the tournament, what tackle he
planned to use, where he'd be staying. She wanted him at least
to sound pleased that she'd called, but he sounded only bored.
With Dennis, everything was business.

'I've got to pack,' he said.

'For the tournament?'

'Right.'

'Could I come along?'

'Not a good idea, Elaine. Lots of tension, you know.'

'But I have a surprise.'

'And what might that be?'

'Not much, big brother. Just a tip that'll guarantee you win the Lockhart Memorial.'

'Really, Elaine.' But she had him hooked.

Lanie said, 'You know a man they call Skink?'

'Yes. He's crazy as a bedbug.'

'I don't think so.'

There was an edgy pause on the other end of the line. Dennis Gault was thinking sordid and unpleasant thoughts about his sister and the hermit. He wondered where his mother had gone wrong raising Elaine.

'Dennis, he's got a huge fish.'

'Is that what he calls it? His fish?'

Lanie said, 'Be that way. Be an asshole.'

'Finish your fairy tale.'

'He's raised this giant mutant bass, he's very proud of it. He makes it sound like a world record or something.'

'I seriously doubt that.'

Lanie said, 'Then later he mentions he's got friends fishing in this tournament.'

'*Later?* You mean after tea and crumpets?'

'Drop it, Dennis. It wasn't exactly easy getting this guy to open up. He'd make Charles Bronson seem like the life of the party.'

'What else did he say?'

'That he and the fish were going on a trip this weekend.'

Gault snorted. 'He and the fish. You mean like a date?'

Lanie let him think about it. Dennis Gault didn't take a long time.

'He's going to plant the bass at Lunker Lakes,' he said, 'so his friends can win the tournament.'

'That's what I figured.'

'Not a bad day's work, even if you've got to split the prize money three ways.'

'Instead of just two,' Lanie said.

'What?'

'You and me, half and half,' she said, 'if you win with Skink's fish.'

Dennis Gault had to laugh. She was something, his sister. If she were a man, she'd have steel ones.

'Deal?' Lanie said.

'Sure, fifty-fifty.' Gault really didn't give a damn about the money anyway.

'I'm not riding in it,' Al García said.

'It's all I could find, with a trailer hitch,' Jim Tile explained.

García said, 'It's a fucking garbage truck, Jim. An eleven-ton diesel garbage truck!'

'It's perfect,' Skink said. 'It's you.'

He had strapped the wooden skiff to the secondhand trailer; even with the outboard engine it was a light load. He one-handed the tongue of the trailer and snapped it down on the ball of the hitch.

García stared in dismay. The peeling old boat was bad enough by itself, but hitched to the rump of a garbage truck it looked like a flea-market special. 'Gypsies wouldn't ride in this fucking caravan,' the detective said. 'What happened to your cousin's lawn truck?'

'Axle broke,' said Jim Tile.

'Then let's rent a regular pickup.'

'No time,' Skink said.

'Then let's all ride with you,' García said.

'No way,' Skink said. 'We can't be seen together down there. From this moment on, you don't know me, I don't know you. Bass is the name of the game, no socializing. It's just you and Jim Tile, brothers. That's all.'

García said, 'What if something happens—how do we reach you?'

'I'll be aware. You got the map?'

'Yep.' To demonstrate, García patted a trouser pocket.

'Good. Now, remember, get one of those big Igloos.'

'I know, the sixty-gallon job.'

'Right. And an aquarium pump.'

Jim Tile said, 'We've got it all written down.'

Skink smiled tiredly. 'So you do.' He tucked his ropy gray braid down the back of his weather jacket. The trooper had advised him to do this to reduce his chances of getting pulled over for no reason on the Turnpike; long hair was a magnet for cops.

As Skink climbed into the truck, he said, 'Decker make his phone call?'

'Yeah,' Jim Tile said, 'he's already gone.'

'God, that's the one thing I'm worried about,' Skink said. 'I really like that boy.' He pulled the raincap tight on his skull. He lifted the sunglasses just enough to fit a finger underneath, working the owl eye back into its socket.

'How you feeling?' Jim Tile asked.

'Better and better. Thanks for asking. And you, Señor Smartass Cuban, remember—'

'I'll be gentle with her, governor, don't worry.'

'—because if she dies, I'll have to kill somebody.'

With that Skink started the ignition, and the truck jostled down the dirt cattle path toward the Mormon Trail.

Tied upright in the flatbed was the big plastic garbage pail, criss-crossed with ropes and elastic bungy cords. Fastened crudely to the top of the pail was a battery-powered pump, obviously rebuilt, from which sprouted clear life-giving tubes. Inside the plastic container was precisely thirty gallons of Lake Jesup's purest, and in that agitated but freshly oxygenated water was the fish called Queenie, flaring her fins, jawing silent fulminations. The hugest largemouth bass in all the world.

After they checked in at the motel, Thomas Curl told Catherine to take off her clothes. She got as far as her bra and panties and said that was it.

'I want you nekked,' Curl said, brandishing the pistol. 'That way you won't run off.'

Catherine said, 'It's too cold.'

Curl got a thin woolen blanket from the closet and threw it at her. 'Now,' he said.

Catherine fingered the blanket. 'Awfully scratchy,' she complained.

Thomas Curl cocked the pistol. He didn't aim it directly at her, but pointed it up, drawn back over his left shoulder, gunslinger-style. 'Strip,' he said.

Reluctantly she did as she was told. The fact that Thomas Curl's minimal brain was racked by infection weighed heavily in Catherine's decision. Anyone else she would have tried to talk out of it, but this was not a well person; he had become febrile, rambling, alternately manic and torpid. He had given up all attempts to prize the dead dog head from his arm. It was his friend now.

Thomas Curl watched intently as Catherine wrapped herself twice around in the blanket and sat down at the head of the bed.

'You got the nicest tits,' he said.

'Bet you say that to all your kidnap victims.'

'I think I might like to poke you.'

'Some other night,' said Catherine.

Slowly, like a sleepy chameleon, Thomas Curl closed his puffy eyes by degrees. His head drooped to one side, and would have drooped even more except that his temple came to rest on the muzzle of the pistol. For a moment Catherine was sure she'd be rinsing brains out of her hair, but abruptly Thomas Curl woke up. He uncocked the gun and slid it into his belt. With his dog arm he motioned to the telephone on the nightstand. 'Call your doctor husband,' he said. 'Tell him everything's peachy.'

Catherine dialed the number of the hotel in Montreal, but James was not in his room. She hung up.

'I'll try later,' she said.

Unsteadily Thomas Curl made his way to the bed. The stench from the dead dog head was overpowering.

'Can we open a window?' Catherine asked.

'Lie down.'

'What for?'

With his good arm he flattened her on the bed. Using torn

strips of bed linen, he tied her to the mattress. Catherine was impressed by the strength of the knots, considering his limited dexterity.

Thomas Curl unplugged the phone and tucked it under his right arm. 'Don't try nuthin' funny,' he said to Catherine.

'Are you leaving?'

'Lucas has to go for a walk.'

Catherine nodded.

'I'm taking the phone,' said Curl.

'Could you pick up some food?' she asked. 'I'm starving.'

Thomas Curl threw R. J. Decker's coat over his shoulders. 'Burger King'll have to do,' he said.

'Wendy's has a salad bar,' Catherine suggested.

'All right,' Curl said, 'Wendy's.'

He wasn't very hungry. He picked at some french fries while Catherine ate her salad and sipped a Diet Coke. Curl had had so much trouble untying her that he'd just cut the linen with a pocket-knife.

'Did Lucas enjoy his walk?' she said.

'He was a good boy,' Curl said, patting the dog head. 'A good boy for daddy.'

He put the phone back in the wall and told Catherine to try Montreal again. This time James answered.

'How's the convention?' Catherine said. 'Lots of laughs?'

Thomas Curl moved close to her on the bed and took out the gun, as a reminder.

Catherine said to James: 'Just so you won't worry, I'm going up to my sister's in Boca for a few days. In case you called home and I wasn't there.' They talked for a few minutes about the weather and the encouraging advance orders for the electric vibrating chiropractic couch, and then Catherine said goodbye.

'That was good,' Thomas Curl said, munching a cold french fry. 'You like him as much as Decker?'

'James is a sweetheart,' Catherine said. 'If it's money you're after, he'd pay anything to get me back.'

'It's not money I'm after.'

'I know,' she said.

'So now he won't be worried, your doctor won't? When you're not home?'

'No, he's having a ball,' Catherine said. 'He got interviewed for *Vertebrae Today.*'

Curl burped.

'A chiropractic magazine,' Catherine explained. She herself was not overwhelmed with excitement.

The phone rang. Catherine started to reach for it, but Curl thwacked her arm with the butt of the gun. When he answered, a man's voice said: 'It's me. Decker.'

'You here yet?'

'On the way,' Decker said. He was at a service plaza in Fort Pierce, gassing up Al García's car.

'You ready to trade?'

'Absolutely,' Decker said. 'How's Mrs. Gómez?'

Curl put the receiver to Catherine's cheek. 'Tell him you're fine,' he said.

'R.J., I'm fine.'

'Catherine, I'm sorry about this.'

'It's okay—'

Curl snatched the phone back and said: 'This is the way we're going to do it: a straight-up trade.'

'Fair enough, but I choose the place.'

'Fuck you, bubba.'

'It's the only way, Tom. It's the only way I can make sure the lady walks free.'

Curl rubbed his brow. He wanted to stand firm, but his mind could not assemble an argument. Every thought that entered his head seemed to sizzle and burn up in the fever. As Decker instructed him when and where to go, Thomas Curl repeated everything aloud in a thick, disconnected voice. Luckily Catherine jotted the directions on a Holiday Inn notepad, because Curl forgot everything the instant he hung up.

'Hungry, Lucas?' He opened the brown grocery bag. He had stopped at the store and bought the dog a little treat.

Catherine eyed the package. 'Gaines Burgers?'

'His favorite,' Curl said. He unwrapped one of the patties and mashed it between the dog's jaws, still fixed obdurately to his own arm. The red meat stuck to the animal's dried yellow fangs. 'You like that, dontcha, boy?'

Catherine said, 'He's not hungry, Tom. I can tell.'

'Guess you're right,' Curl said. 'Must be all the traveling.'

28

Deacon Johnson tapped lightly on the door. For once, Reverend Weeb was alone.

'Charles, you'd better come see.'

'What now?' the preacher said irritably.

He followed Deacon Johnson out of the townhouse office, through the courtyard, down a sloping walk to a boat ramp on the newly sodded shore of Lunker Lake Number One. Many of the anglers had begun to arrive, so the ramp was crowded with needle-shaped bass boats, each attached to a big candy-colored Blazer, Jeep, or Bronco. In the midst of the gleaming congregation was an immense army-green garbage truck with a warped old skiff hitched to its bumper.

Two men leaned impassively against the truck; one was tall and muscular and black, the other roundish and Latin-looking. The rest of the bass fishermen studied the unusual newcomers from a distance, and chuckled in low voices.

Charlie Weeb approached the men and said, 'If you're looking for the dump, it's out Road 84.' He pointed west, toward the dike. 'That way.'

Jim Tile said, 'We're here for the bass tournament.'

'Is that right?' Weeb eyed the rowboat disdainfully. 'Sorry, son, but this event's not open to the general public.'

Al García said, 'We're not the general public, son. We're the Tile Brothers.' Coolly he handed Charlie Weeb the receipt for the registration fee. Without a glance, Weeb passed it to Deacon Johnson.

'It's them, all right,' Deacon Johnson reported. 'Boat number fifty, all paid up.'

'You don't look like brothers,' Reverend Weeb said accusingly.

'*Se, es veridad,*' Jim Tile said.

'Fo sho,' added Al García.'We true be bros.'

They had practiced the routine on the long ride down. Jim Tile had done much better learning Spanish than Al García had done learning jive. Still, it achieved the desired effect.

Charlie Weeb puckered his cheeks and anxiously ran a manicured hand through his perfect blond hair. 'Gentlemen, excuse me for a sec,' he said, and took Deacon Johnson aside.

'This is some fucking joke.'

'It's no joke, Charles.'

'Spic and spade brothers? I'd call that a joke.' Weeb was spitting, he was so exasperated. 'Izzy, tonight we're flying in one thousand loyal Christian prospective homesite buyers. I promised them to do a healing, I promised them to have some world-class bass fishing, and I promised to get their shining faces on national cable TV. All this, Izzy, in order to *sell some fucking lots.*'

'Keep your voice down, Charles.' Even at a whisper, Reverend Weeb could rattle the china.

Deacon Johnson took him by the arm and edged away from the newcomers. Standing in the rank shadow of the garbage truck, Deacon Johnson said, 'We've taken their money, Charles, we've got to let them fish.'

'Screw the entry fee. Give it back.'

'Oh fine,' Deacon Johnson said, 'and when the newspapers call, you explain why you did it.'

The thought of bad publicity sent a cold razor down Charlie Weeb's spine.

Almost plaintively he said: 'These folks I'm bringing down, Izzy, they don't want to see a spic and a spade in this family-oriented development. The folks at home who watch my show, they don't want to see 'em either. I'm not here to pass judgment, Izzy, I'm here for the demographics. Fact is, my people are the whitest of the white. Soon as they spot those two guys, that's the ball game. They'll think everything they heard about South Florida is true, niggers and Cubans everywhere. Even on the bass lakes.'

Deacon Johnson said, 'There's forty-nine other boats in this tournament, Charles. Just tell your cameramen to stay off the little wooden one. As for the garbage truck, we'll park it out back in the construction lot. Loan these guys a decent rental car to get around the property. Anyone asks, tell 'em they work here.'

'Good idea,' Weeb said. 'Say they pour asphalt or something. Excellent.' Sometimes he didn't know what he'd do without Izzy.

Deacon Johnson said, 'Don't worry, Charles, just look at them—they don't have a chance. It'll be a holy miracle if that termite bucket doesn't sink at the dock.'

All Charlie Weeb could say was: 'Whoever heard of a spic and a spade in a pro bass tournament?'

But the mysterious Tile Brothers were already putting their boat in the water.

The next day was practice day, and in keeping with tradition the anglers gathered early at the boat ramp to exchange theories and cultivate possible excuses. Because no one had fished Lunker Lakes before, the talk was basically bullshit and idle speculation. The bass would be schooled by the culverts. No, they'd be holding deep. No, they'd be bedded in the shallows.

Only Charlie Weeb and his men knew the truth: there were no bass except dead ones. The new ones were on the way.

Eddie Spurling realized that something was terribly wrong, but he didn't say a word. Instead of mingling with his pals over coffee and biscuits, he strolled the shore alone in the predawn pitch. A couple of the other pros sidled up to make conversation, but Eddie was unresponsive and gloomy. He didn't show the least interest in Duke Puffin's deep-sonic crankbait or Tom Jericho's new weedless trolling motor.

While the mockingbirds announced sunrise, Eddie Spurling just stared out at the still brown canals and thought: This water's no damn good.

Al García and Jim Tile were the last to get started. They'd been briefly delayed when Billie Radcliffe, a very white young man from Waycross, Georgia, said to Jim Tile: 'Where's your cane pole, Uncle Remus?' Jim Tile had felt compelled to explain the importance of good manners to Billie Radcliffe, by way of breaking every single fishing rod in Billie Radcliffe's custom-made bass boat. This had been done in a calm and methodical way, and with no interference, since Al García and his Colt Python had supervised the brief ceremony. From then on, the other fishermen steered clear of the Tile Brothers.

It was just as well. All the practice at Lake Jesup had been in vain: Al García proved to be the world's most dangerous bass angler. On four occasions he snagged Jim Tile's scalp with errant casts. Three other times he hooked himself, once so severely that Jim Tile had to cut the barbs off the hooks just to remove them from García's thigh.

Casting a heavy plug rod required a sensitive thumb, but invariably García would release the spool too early or too late. Either he would fire the lure straight into the bottom of the boat, where it shattered like a bullet, or he would launch it straight up in the air, so it could plummet dangerously down on their heads. In the few instances when the detective actually managed to hit the water, Jim Tile put down his fishing rod and applauded. They both agreed that Al García should concentrate on steering the boat.

With the puny six-horse outboard, it took them longer to get around the canals, but by midday they reached the spot Skink had told them about, at the far western terminus of Lunker Lake Number Seven. Charlie Weeb's landscapers had not yet reached this boundary of the development, so the shores remained as barren white piles of dredged-up fill. The canal ended at the old earthen dike that separated the lush watery Florida Everglades from concrete civilization. Charlie Weeb had pushed it to the brink. This was the final barrier.

Jim Tile and Al García had the Number Seven hole to themselves, as Skink had predicted they would. It was too sparse, too bright, and too remote for the other bassers.

García nudged the skiff to shore, where Jim Tile got out and collected several armfuls of dead holly branches from a heap left by the bulldozers. Hidden under a tarp in the boat were three wooden orange crates, which they had brought from Harney in the bin of the garbage truck. García tied the crates together while Jim Tile stuffed the dead branches between the slats. Together they lowered the crates into the water. With a fishing line, Al García measured the depth at thirteen feet. He marked the secret spot by placing two empty Budweiser cans on the bank.

This was to be Queenie's home away from home.

'Oldest trick in the book,' Skink had told the detective two nights before. 'These big hawgs love obstructions. Lay back invisible in the bush, sucking down dumb minnows. Find the brushpile, you find the fish. Make the brushpile, you win the damn tournament.'

That was the plan.

Jim Tile and Al García felt pretty good about pulling it off; there wasn't another boat in sight.

There was, however, a private helicopter.

The Tile Brothers hadn't bothered to look up, since it flew over only once.

But once was all that Dennis Gault's pilot needed to mark his map. Then he flew back to the heliport to radio his boss.

That evening, after the practice day, the mood at the boat ramp ranged from doubtful to downhearted. No one had caught a single bass, though none of the fishermen would admit it. It was more than a matter of pride—it was the mandatory furtiveness of competition. With two hundred and fifty thousand dollars at stake, lifelong friendships and fraternal confidences counted for spit. No intelligence was shared; no strategies compared; no secrets swapped. As a result, nobody comprehended the full scope of the fishless disaster that was named Lunker Lakes. While scouting the shoreline, a few anglers had come across dead yearling bass, and privately mulled the usual theories—nitrogen runoff, phosphate dumping, algae blooms, pesticides. Still, it wasn't the few dead fish as much as the absence of live ones that disturbed the contestants; as the day wore on, optimism evaporated. These were the best fishermen in the country, and they knew bad water when they saw it. All morning the men tried to mark fish on their Hummingbird sonars, but all that showed was a deep gray void. The banks were uniformly steep, the bottom uniformly flat, and the lakes uniformly lifeless. Even Dennis Gault was worried, though he had an ace up his L. L. Bean sleeve.

At dusk the anglers returned to the boat ramp to find banners streaming, canned country music blaring, and an elaborate rectangular stage rising—a pink pulpit at one end, the bass scoreboard at the other. The whole stage was bathed by hot kliegs while the OCN cameramen conducted their lighting checks. Over the pulpit hung a red-lettered banner that said: 'JESUS IN YOUR LIVING ROOM— LIVE AT FIVE!' And over the scoreboard hung a blue-lettered banner that said: 'Lunker Lakes Presents the Dickie Lockhart Memorial Bass Blasters Classic.' Every possible camera angle was cluttered with the signs and logos of the various sponsors who had put up the big prize money.

Once all the bass boats had returned to the dock, the Reverend Charles Weeb ambled centerstage with a cordless microphone.

'Greeting, sportsmen!'

The tired anglers grumbled halfheartedly.

'Understand it was tough fishing out there today, but don't you worry!' shouted Charlie Weeb. 'The Lord tells me tomorrow's gonna be one hell of a day!'

The PA system amplified the preacher's enthusiasm, and the fishermen smiled and applauded, though not energetically.

'Yes, sir,' Charlie Weeb said, 'I talked to the Lord this afternoon, and the Lord said: "Tomorrow will be good. Tomorrow the hawgs will be hungry!" '

Duke Puffin shouted, 'Did he say to use buzzbaits or rubber worms?'

The bass fishermen roared, and Reverend Weeb grinned appreciatively. Anything to loosen the jerks up.

'As you know,' he said, 'tonight is barbecue night at Lunker Lakes. Ribs, chicken, Okeechobee catfish, and all the beer you can drink!'

The free-food announcement drew the first sincere applause of the evening.

'So,' Reverend Weeb continued, 'I got two air-conditioned buses ready to take y'all to the clubhouse. Have a good time tonight, get plenty of rest, and tomorrow you put some big numbers on that bass board, because the whole country'll be watching!'

Eagerly the anglers filed onto the buses. Jim Tile and Al García made a point of sitting in the very front. No one spoke a word to them.

As soon as the buses pulled away, Weeb tossed the microphone to an OCN technician, grabbed the young hydrologist backstage, and said: 'It's here, I hope.'

'Yes, sir, just give the word.'

To the grips Weeb yelled: 'Turn those kliegs around! Light the ramp—hurry up, asshole, while we're still young!'

Out of the settling darkness a gleaming steel tanker truck appeared. Although it looked like an ordinary oil-company truck, it was not. The driver backed cautiously down the slick boat ramp, and three feet from the water's edge he braked the tanker with a gaseous hiss.

'Nice park job,' the hydrologist said.

The driver hopped out waving a clipboard.

'Two thousand fresh basserinos,' he said. 'Who signs for these?'

After the barbecue Jim Tile and Al García drove the loaner car back to the lodge, where they got the bad news.

The raid had failed.

The Broward SWAT team had swept with lethal certainty into Room 1412 of the Coral Springs Holiday Inn and brusquely arrested one Mr. Juan Gómez, suspected kidnapper. Unfortunately he turned out to be a genuine Juan Gómez, computer software salesman. Furthermore, the young lady he had been diddling in his motel room turned out not to be the missing Catherine Stuckameyer, but rather the nineteen-year-old daughter of the founder of Floppy World, one of Juan Gómez's biggest retail clients.

By the time the confusion was sorted out and the SWAT team returned to the Holiday Inn, the other Juan Gómez, the one whose real name was Thomas Curl, had fled his room for parts unknown. Evidence technicians spent hours analyzing the Gaines Burger particles.

Al García had arranged the raid without telling R. J. Decker, who had fiercely rejected the idea of a police rescue attempt. He had insisted on handling Thomas Curl himself because

Catherine's life was at stake, so Jim Tile and Al García had backed off and pretended to go along with it. As soon as Decker left Harney, García got on the phone to his lieutenant in Miami, who got on the phone to the Broward sheriff's office. There was a delay of several hours in the police bureaucracy, mainly because no Catherine Stuckameyer had officially been reported missing and the authorities suspected it was just another lonely rich wife skipping out. By the time the SWAT team moved in, and found the right motel room, it was too late.

'They fucked it up,' García said, slamming down the phone. 'Can you believe it, now they're pissed off at me! Some pinhead *gringo* captain's saying I made 'em look bad, says there's still no evidence of a kidnap. Fucking GI Joes with their greasepaint and their M-16s hit the wrong damn room, it's not my fault.'

'Meanwhile,' Jim Tile said, 'we've lost Curl, Decker's ex, and even Decker himself.'

'So the hotshot gets his way after all. It's his ball game now.' García threw down his bass cap and cursed. 'What the hell else can we do?'

'Go fishing,' the trooper said. 'That's all.'

It was half-past midnight when someone knocked on the door of Dennis Gault's room. He couldn't imagine who it might be. He had elected not to stay at Lunker Lakes Lodge with the others because all the parties would be raucous and distracting, and because the other anglers would ignore him as always. Besides, there was sawdust all over the carpets, and the walls reeked of fresh paint; obviously the place had been slapped together in about two weeks, just for the tournament.

So Gault had taken a suite at the Everglades Hilton, where he always stayed in Fort Lauderdale. Only Lanie, his secretaries, and a few lady friends knew where to find him. Which was why he was puzzled by the midnight visitor.

He listened at the door. From the other side the sound of a man's labored breathing and a faint buzzing noise. 'Who is it?'

'Me, Mr. Gault.'

He recognized the voice. Angrily Gault opened the door, but

what he saw stole his breath away. 'Mother of Jesus!'

'Hey, chief,' said Thomas Curl, 'nice pajamas.' He swayed in and crashed down into an armchair.

'Uh, Tom—'

'What's the matter, chief?'

Gault stared numbly. What could he say? Curl looked like death on a bad day. His eyes were swollen slits, his face streaked with purple. Sweat glistened on his gray forehead and a chowder-white ooze flecked the corners of his lips.

'What happened to you, Tom?'

'Mrs. Decker's safe in the trunk, don't worry.' Curl wiped his mouth on the sleeve of his jacket. 'Say, chief, those the shiniest damn pajamas I ever saw.'

Dennis Gault's gaze fixed on Curl's right arm. 'What . . . what the fuck is that?' he stammered.

'Lucas is his name,' Curl said. 'He good boy.'

'Oh, Christ.' Now Gault realized where the buzzing sound had come from. From the flies swarming around the dog head.

'I's raised around puppies,' Curl said, 'mostly mutts.'

Gault said, 'It's not good for you to be here.'

'But I got a few hours to kill.'

'Before you meet Decker?'

'Yep.' Curl spotted a decanter of brandy on a sideboard. Mechanically Gault handed it to him. Curl drew three hard swallows from the bottle. His eyes glowed after he put it down. 'I'll need a bass boat,' he said, smacking his lips.

Gault scribbled a phone number on a napkin. 'Here, this guy's got a Starcraft.'

'Anything'll do.'

'You all right?' Gault asked.

'I'll be fine. Clear this shit up once and for all.' Curl noticed Gault's fishing gear laid out meticulously on the carpet. 'Nice tackle, chief. Looks straight out of the catalog.'

'Tom, you'd better go. I've got to be up early tomorrow.'

'I ain't been sleepin much, myself. Lucas, he always wants to play.'

Dennis Gault could scarcely breathe, the stink was so vile. 'Call me day after tomorrow. I'll have a little something for you.'

'Real good.'

'One more thing, Tom, it's very important: everything's set for tonight, right? With Decker, I mean?'

'Don't you worry.'

Gault said, 'You can handle it alone?'

'It's my rightful obligation.'

At the door, Thomas Curl drunkenly thrust out his right hand. 'Put her there, chief.' Gault shook the rotted thing without daring to look.

'Well, tight lines!' said Curl, with a sloppy but spirited sailor's salute.

'Thank you, Tom,' said Dennis Gault. He closed the door, dumped the brandy, then bolted into a scalding shower.

29

The phone calls started as soon as they turned in.

When Al García answered, the voice on the other end said: 'Why don't you go back to Miami, spic-face?'

When Jim Tile answered, the message was: 'Don't show your lips on the lake, nigger.'

After the fourth call, García turned on the light and sat up in bed. 'It's bad enough they give us the worst damn room in the place, and now this.'

'Nice view of the dumpster, though,' Jim Tile said. When he swung his bare brown legs out from under the covers, García noticed the bandage over Culver Rundell's bullet hole.

'It's nothing, just a through-and-through,' the trooper said.

'One of these bass nuts?'

Jim Tile nodded.

'Well, shit,' García said, 'maybe we oughta take the phone calls more seriously.'

'They're just trying to scare us.'

The phone started ringing again. Jim Tile watched it for a full minute before picking up.

'You're gator bait, spook,' the caller drawled.

The trooper hung up. His jaw was set and his eyes were hard. 'I'm beginning to take this personally.'

'You and me both.' García grabbed his pants off the chair and dug around for the cigarette lighter. When the phone rang again, the detective said, 'My turn.'

Another Southern voice: 'Lucky for you, grease floats.'

García slammed down the receiver and said, 'You'd think one of us would have the brains to pull the plug out of the wall.'

'No,' said Jim Tile. He was worried about Skink, and Decker. One of them might need to get through.

'I can't imagine these jerks are actually worried about us winning, not after seeing the boat,' García said. 'Wonder what they're so damn scared of.'

'The sight of us,' Jim Tile said. He lay back on his pillow and stared at the ceiling. García lit a cigarette and thumbed through a Lunker Lakes sales brochure that some lady had given him at the barbecue.

It was half-past two when somebody outside fired a rifle through their window and ran.

Angrily Jim Tile picked up the phone and started dialing.

As he shook the glass out of his blanket, Al García asked, 'So who you calling, *chico*, the Fish and Game?'

'I think it's important to make an impression,' the trooper said. 'Don't you?'

To get on the dike, Eddie Spurling had to drive to the west end of Road 84, then zig north up U.S. 27 to the Sawgrass Fish Camp. Here the dike was accessible, but wide enough for only one vehicle; at three in the morning Eddie didn't anticipate oncoming traffic. He drove the Wagoneer at a crawl through a crystal darkness, insects whorling out of the swamp to cloud the headlights. Every so often he had to brake as the high-beams froze some animal, ruby-eyed, on the rutted track—rabbits, raccoons, foxes, bobcats, even a fat old female otter. Eddie marveled at so much wildlife, so close to the big city.

It took an hour to make the full circuit back to where the flood levee abutted Lunker Lake Number Seven. When he reached the designated spot, Eddie Spurling turned off the engine, killed the lights, rolled down his window, and gazed off to the west. The Everglades night was glorious and immense, the sweep of the sky unlike anything he'd seen anywhere in the South; here the galaxy seemed to spill straight into the shimmering swamp.

When Eddie looked east he saw blocked and broken landscape, the harsh aura of downtown lights, the pale linear scar of the nascent superhighway and its three interchanges, built especially for Charlie Weeb's development. There was nothing beautiful about it, and Eddie turned away. He put on his cap, snapped his down vest, and stepped out of the truck into the gentle hum of the marsh.

Water glistened on both sides of the dike. Under a thin fog, Lunker Lake Number Seven lay as flat and dead as a cistern; by contrast, the small pool on the Everglades side was dimpled with darting minnows and waterbugs. The pocket was lushly fringed with cattails and sawgrass and crisp round lily pads as big as pizzas. Something else floated in the pool—a plastic Clorox bottle, tied to a rope.

Eddie Spurling noticed how out of place it looked; obscene, really, like litter. The whole idea of it made him mad—Weeb and his damn Alabama importers. Eddie carefully made his way down the slope of the dike, his boots sliding in the loose dirt. At the edge of the pool he found a long stick, which he used to snag the floating bleach bottle.

He got hold of the rope and pulled it hand over hand. The fish trap was unexpectedly heavy; leaden almost. Must've got tangled in the hydrilla weed, Eddie thought.

When the cage finally broke the surface, he dropped the stick and grabbed the mesh with his fingers. Then he pulled it to shore.

Eddie shone his flashlight in the cage and said, 'My God!' He couldn't believe the size of it—a coppery-black bass of grotesque proportions, so huge it could've been a deep-sea groper. It looked thirty pounds. The hawg glared at Eddie and thrashed furiously in its wire prison. Eddie could only stare, awestruck. He thought: This is impossible.

On the other side of the pond something made a noise, and Eddie Spurling went cold. He recognized the naked click of a rifle hammer.

A deep voice said: 'Put her back.'

Eddie swallowed dryly. He was almost too terrified to move.

The gun went off and the Clorox bottle exploded at his feet. After the echo faded, the voice said: 'Now.'

Rubber-kneed, Eddie lowered the fish cage back into the pool, letting the wet rope pay through his fingers.

Across the pond, the rifleman rose from the cattails. By the size of the silhouette Eddie Spurling saw that the man was quite large. His appearance was made more ominous by military fatigues and some sort of black mask. The man sloshed through the marsh and hiked up the side of the dike. Eddie thought about running but there was no place to go; he thought about swimming but there was a problem with snakes and alligators. So he just stood there, trying not to soil himself.

Soon the rifleman loomed directly above him, on the dike.

'Kill the flashlight,' the man said.

He was close enough for Eddie to make out his features. He had long dark hair and a ratty beard and a flowered plastic cap on his head. The mask turned out to be sunglasses. The rifle was a Remington.

'I'm Fast Eddie Spurling.'

'Who asked?'

'From television?'

'I watch no television,' said the rifleman.

Eddie tried a different approach. 'Is it money you want? The Jeep? Go ahead and take it.'

Without blinking, the rifleman turned and blasted the tinted windshield out of Eddie Spurling's Wagoneer. 'I got my own truck, thanks,' he said. Then he shot out the fog lights, too.

Eddie was sweating ice water.

The man said, 'That's some fish, huh?'

Eddie nodded energetically. 'Biggest I ever saw.'

'Name's Queenie.'

'Real nice,' Eddie said desperately. He was quite certain the hairy rifleman was going to kill him.

'You're probably curious what happened to yours.'

'They weren't really mine,' Eddie said.

The man laughed thinly. 'You just came all the way out here to say hello.'

Eddie said, 'No, sir, I came to let 'em go.'

'How about I just shoot off your pecker and get it over with?'

'Please,' Eddie cried. 'I mean it, I was about to set them fish free. Check the truck if you don't believe it. If I was gonna take 'em, I'd have brung a livewell, right? I'd have brung the damn boat, wouldn't I?'

The rifleman seemed to be thinking it over.

Eddie went on: 'And why would I be here three hours before the tournament and risk having 'em croak on me?'

The man said, 'You're not one of the cheaters?'

'No, and I don't aim to start. I couldn't go through with it, so screw Charlie Weeb.'

The rifleman lowered his gun. 'I let those ringer bass go.'

Eddie Spurling said, 'Well, I'm glad you did.'

'Three hawgsters. One must've gone at least eleven-eight.'

'Well,' said Eddie, 'maybe I'll catch him someday, when he's bigger.'

The man said: 'What about Queenie? What would you have done about her?'

Without hesitating Eddie said, 'I'da let her go, too.'

'I bet.'

'What would be the point of killing her, mister? Suppose I took that monster and stuffed her. Every time I'd walk in the den she'd be staring down from the wall, the awful truth in those damn purple eyes. I couldn't live with it, mister. That's why I say, you didn't need the gun. I'da let her go anyway.'

The rifleman stood there, showing nothing. The sunglasses scared the hell out of Eddie.

'I've got a boy, mister, age nine,' Eddie said. 'You think I could lie to my boy about a fish like that? Say I caught it when I didn't?'

'Some men could.'

'Not me.'

The rifleman said: 'I believe you, Mr. Spurling. Now, get the fuck out of here, please.'

Eddie obediently scrambled up the bank of the dike. He hopped in the Jeep without even brushing the broken glass off the seat.

''Can you turn this thing around okay?'

'Yeah,' Eddie said, 'I got four-wheel drive.' In the dark he groped nervously for the keys.

'The seam of the universe,' the rifleman mused. 'This dike is like the moral seam of the universe.'

'It's narrow, that's for sure,' Eddie said.

'Evil on the one side, good on the other.' The man illustrated by pointing with the Remington.

Eddie stuck his head out the window and said very politely: 'Can I ask what you plan to do with that big beautiful bass?'

'I plan to let her go,' the man said, 'in about five minutes.' He didn't say where, on which side of the seam.

Eddie knew he shouldn't press his luck, knew he should just get the hell away from this lunatic, but he couldn't help it. The fisherman in him just had to ask: 'What's she weigh, anyhow?'

'Twenty-nine even.'

'Holy moly,' Fast Eddie Spurling gasped.

'Now get lost,' said the rifleman, 'and good luck in the tournament.'

After Eddie had gone, Skink hauled the big fish out of the pool. He propped the cage yoke-style across his shoulders and carried it across the dike to Lunker Lakes. He put it back in the water while he searched the banks until he found the two beer cans marking the spot where Jim Tile and Al García had sunk the brushpile.

Skink hoisted the cage once more and moved it to the secret spot. This time he removed the big bass, pointed her toward the submerged obstruction, and gently let her go. The fish kicked once, roiled, and was gone. 'See you tonight,' Skink said. 'Then we go home.'

Rifle in hand, he stood on the dike for two hours and watched the night start to fade. On the Everglades side, a heron croaked and redwings bickered in the bullrushes; the other side of the dike lay mute and lifeless. Skink waited for something to show in Lunker Lake Number Seven—a turtle, a garfish, anything. He waited a long time.

Then, deep in worry, he trudged down the dike to where he'd left his truck. To the east, at the dirty rim of the city, the sun was coming up.

At that moment R. J. Decker parked his car behind a row of construction trailers at Lunker Lakes. Dawn was the best time to move, because by then most rent-a-cops were either asleep or shooting the shit around the timeclock, waiting to punch out. Decker spotted only one uniformed guard, a rotund and florid fellow who emerged from one of the trailers just long enough to take a leak, then shut the door.

Decker checked the camera again. It was a Minolta Maxxum, a sturdy thirty-five millimeter he'd picked up at West Palm Beach discount house that took credit cards. He was thinking that a Kodak or a Sure-Shot might have worked just as well, but he'd been in such a hurry. He opened the back of the frame and inspected the loading mechanism; he did the same with the motor-drive unit.

Satisfied, Decker capped the lens, closed up the camera, and locked it in the glove compartment of Al García's car. Then he got the bolt-cutters out of the trunk and snuck up to the supply shed, where he went to work on the padlock.

The blast-off for the Dickie Lockhart Memorial Bass Blasters Classic was set for six-thirty, but the anglers arrived very early to put their boats in the water and test their gear and collect free goodies from tackle reps up and down the dock. The fishermen knew that whoever won this tournament might never have to wet a line again, not just because of the tremendous purse but because of the product endorsements to follow. The bass lure that took first prize in the Lockhart undoubtedly would be the hottest item in freshwater bait shops for a year. There was no logic to this fad, since bass will eat just about anything (including their own young), but the tackle companies did everything in their power to encourage manic buying. Before the opening gun they loaded down the contestants with free plugs, jigs, spinners, and of course rubber worms, displayed in giant plastic vats like so much hellish purple pasta.

The morning was cool and clear; there was talk it might hit eighty by midafternoon. Matronly volunteers from The First Pentecostal Church of Exemptive Redemption handed out Bible tracts and served hot biscuits and coffee, though many contestants were too tense to eat or pray.

At six sharp a burgundy Rolls-Royce Corniche pulled up to the ramp at Lunker Lake Number One. Dennis and Lanie Gault got out. Lanie was dressed in a red timber jacket, skintight Gore-Tex dungarees, and black riding boots. She basked in the stares from the other contestants and dug heartily into a bag of hot croissants.

With an air of supreme confidence, Dennis Gault uncranked his sparkling seventeen-foot Ranger bass boat off the trailer into the water. One by one, he meticulously stowed his fishing rods, then his toolbox, then his immense tacklebox. Hunkering into the cockpit of the boat, he checked the gauges—water temperature, trim tilt, tabs, tachometer, fuel, batteries, oil pressure. He punched a button on his sonic fish-finder and the screen blinked a bright green digital good-morning. The big Johnson outboard turned over on the first try, purring like a tiger cub. While the engine warmed up, Dennis Gault stood at the wheel and casually smoothed the creases of his sky-blue jumpsuit. He squirted Windex on the lenses of his amber Polaroids and wiped them with a dark blue bandanna. Next he slipped on his monogrammed weather vest, and tucked a five-ounce squirt bottle of Happy Gland into the pocket. In accordance with prevailing bass fashion, he spun his cap so that the bill was at his back; that way the wind wouldn't tear it off his head at fifty miles an hour.

Dennis Gault had expected to hear the usual cracks about the Rolls and what a pompous ass he was, but for once the other bass anglers left him alone. In fact, Gault was so absorbed in his own pretournament ritual that he almost missed the highlight of the morning.

It started as a pinprick on the eastern horizon, but it came faster than the sunrise; a strange pulsing light. The bass fishermen clustered on the dock to watch. They figured one of the big bait companies was pulling a stunt for a new commercial. Some stunt it was, too.

Soon the sky over Lunker Lakes throbbed in piercing aquamarine. On a forty-foot screen mounted behind the stage, the face of Reverend Charles Weeb appeared for the morning benediction; it was a taped message (for Charlie Weeb seldom rose before ten), but none of the contestants was in the mood to hear what the Old Testament said about fishing. They were riveted on what was slowly rolling toward them down the road.

It was a convoy of police cars.

Highway-patrol cruisers, to be exact; sixteen of them, their flashing blue lights slicing up the darkness. Dead last in the procession was a garbage truck with a rowboat hooked to the bumper.

Dennis Gault did not like the looks of things. He wondered if the cops had come to arrest somebody, possibly even him. He shot a worried glance at Lanie, who shrugged and shook her head.

The first eight troopers peeled off to one side of the boat ramp and parked bumper-to-bumper; the last eight parked in similar formation on the other side, forming a broad V-shaped alley for Al García and Jim Tile in the garbage truck.

Each of the state troopers got out and stood by his car. They wore seriously neutral expressions, and showed no reaction to the OCN Minicams filming their arrival. To a man, the troopers were young, ramrod-straight, clean-cut, muscular, and heavily armed. They were some of Jim Tile's best friends on the force, and they were white, which definitely made an impression.

The old wooden skiff was lowered into the lake without incident.

Deacon Johnson was up early. The importance of the day weighed heavily, and he had reason to be anxious. He put on his favorite desert-tan leisure suit, buffed his cream-colored shoes, and trimmed his nose hairs. At the breakfast table he chewed halfheartedly on raisin bagels, scanned the sports page to make sure they hadn't screwed up the big display ad for the tournament, then called for the limousine.

He decided to give the VA hospital one more try.

This time, two doctors were waiting at the admissions desk.

Deacon Johnson smiled and stuck out his hand, but the doctors regarded it as if it were a rattlesnake.

'I'm sorry,' one said, 'but you'll have to leave.'

'You've been upsetting the patients,' said the other.

'Isn't there one,' Deacon Johnson said, 'who wants to be on TV?'

'They said you offered them money.'

'I had to,' Deacon Johnson lied. 'FCC rules.'

'Money,' the doctor went on, 'in exchange for lying about their illnesses.'

'Not lying—*dramatizing*. There's a big difference.' Deacon Johnson folded his arms indignantly. 'We run a thoroughly Christian enterprise at OCN.'

'Several of the patients became quite upset when you were here before.'

'I certainly meant no harm.'

'They've discussed violence,' said the other doctor, apparently a psychiatrist.

'Violence?' said Deacon Johnson.

'That's why we can't let you back inside.'

'But there was one, Corporal Clement. He expressed an interest in appearing with Reverend Weeb today.'

The two doctors traded glances.

'Clement,' Deacon Johnson repeated, spelling out the name. 'The fellow with the trick knees.'

The psychiatrist said, 'I'm afraid Corporal Clement has been moved inpatient to the sixth floor.'

'It appears he got into the pharmacy last night,' the other doctor explained.

'He won't be available for television appearances,' the psychiatrist added. 'Please go now, Mr. Johnson, before we call for Security.'

Deacon Johnson got back in the limo and sulked.

'Where to?' the driver asked.

'You know this town?'

'Born and raised,' the driver said.

'Good. Find me some bums.'

Charlie Weeb would be royally ticked off; he'd specifically said no street people, it was too risky. Lofty standards were fine and dandy, but Deacon Johnson was running out of time. The healing was only hours away.

The limousine driver took him to the dissolute stretch of Fort Lauderdale beach known as the Strip, but there all the bums had bleached hair and great tans. 'Too healthy-looking,' Deacon Johnson decided.

'There's a soup kitchen down Sunrise Boulevard,' the driver said.

'Let's give it a try.'

Deacon Johnson saw that the driver was right about the soup kitchen: wall-to-wall winos; sallow, toothless, oily-haired vaga-bonds, the hardest of the hard-core. Some were so haggard that no makeup artist could possibly have rendered them presentable in time for the show. Worse, most of the men were too hung-over to comprehend Deacon Johnson's offer; the money they understood just fine, it was the part about dressing up and rehearsing that seemed to sail over their heads.

'It's television, for Christ's sake,' Deacon Johnson implored.

The men just grinned and scratched themselves.

In desperation, Deacon Johnson selected a skinny bum named Clu, who was in a wheelchair. The driver lifted Clu into the backseat of the limo and folded the wheelchair into the trunk.

As they rode back to Lunker Lakes, Deacon Johnson said: 'Are you sure you can rise up?'

'You bet.'

'On command?'

'You bet.'

Clu wore a mischievous smile that made Deacon Johnson wonder. 'So what's wrong with your legs?' he asked.

'Not a thing,' Clue replied.

'Then why the wheelchair?'

'I got it on a trade,' Clu said. 'Three cans of Sterno and a wool sock. Pretty good deal, I'd say.'

'Indeed,' Deacon Johnson said. 'And how long ago was this?'

'Nineteen and eighty-one,' said Clu, still smirking.

'And you've been in the chair ever since?'

'Every minute,' Clu said. 'No need to get up.'

Deacon Johnson leaned forward and told the limo driver to pull over.

'Get out,' he said to Clu.

'What for?'

'It's just a test,' Deacon Johnson said. 'Get out and walk around the car.'

When the driver opened the door, Clu tumbled facedown onto the pavement. The driver reached down to help him, but Deacon Johnson shook his finger.

He said, 'Can you rise up, son?'

Clu tried with all his might until he was pink in the face, but his skinny legs would not work. 'I don't believe this,' he whined.

'Just as I thought,' said Deacon Johnson stiffly.

On the ground Clu continued to grunt and squirm. 'Let me work on this a minute,' he pleaded.

'Give him back the damn wheelchair,' Deacon Johnson snapped at the driver, 'and let's go.'

Just when he was certain that the grand TV mega-healing would have to be called off, or at least scaled back to a sheep or a cat, Deacon Johnson spotted the blind man.

The man was alone on a bus bench outside the entrance to Lunker Lakes; beneath the big cedar billboard, in fact, directly under the second L. That he would be sitting right there at such a crucial moment seemed like a heavenly miracle, except that Deacon Johnson didn't believe in miracles. Plain old dumb luck was more like it. He told the limo driver to stop.

The blind man did not have a guide dog or a white cane, so Deacon Johnson was hopeful that they could do business.

He walked up to him and said hello. The man didn't move one bit, just stared straight ahead. Deacon Johnson could see nothing but his own natty reflection in the dark glasses.

'May I ask,' Deacon Johnson said, 'are you blind?'

'I suppose,' the man said.

'May I ask how blind?'

'Depends what you mean.'

'Can you see what that billboard says?' Deacon Johnson pointed to a big Toyota sign a quarter-mile down the road.

The man said, 'Not hardly.'

Deacon Johnson held a hand in front of the man's face. 'Can you see that?'

The man nodded yes.

'Very good.' Thank God, Deacon Johnson thought. For

coaching purposes, partly blind was perfect. As a telegenic bonus, the man appeared sickly but not morbidly sunken, like some of the bums at the soup kitchen.

Deacon Johnson introduced himself and said, 'Have you heard of the Outdoor Christian Network?'

'Yes,' the blind man said.

'Then you've heard of the Reverend Charles Weeb, how he heals people on national television?'

'I watch no television.'

'Yes, I understand, but at least have you *heard* of Reverend Weeb's healings? The reason I ask, he's having one today. Right here, inside this gate.'

'A healing.'

'On live satellite television,' Deacon Johnson said. 'Would you be interested?'

The man toyed with his beard.

'For five hundred dollars,' Deacon Johnson said.

'And would I be healed?'

'Let me say, Reverend Weeb gets excellent results. With the Lord's help, of course.' Deacon Johnson circled the blind man and assessed his camera presence. 'I think the Lord would probably like us to shave you,' he said. 'And possibly cut your hair— the braid could be a distraction.'

The blind man raised a middle digit in front of Deacon Johnson's face. 'Can you see that?' he said.

Deacon Johnson chuckled weakly. 'I underestimated you, sir. Let's make it a thousand dollars.'

'For a thousand bucks I take a shower,' the blind man said, 'that's all.'

When the man stood up he towered over Deacon Johnson. He pulled on a flowered plastic cap and smoothed it flat over his skull. Then, with thick callused fingers, he pinched Deacon Johnson's elbow and held on.

'Lead the way,' the blind man said.

The instant the other bass boats roared away, Al García felt sure that he and Jim Tile would be drowned, that the roiling wakes would swamp the wooden skiff and it would sink upside-down, trapping them both in a cold underwater pocket.

This did not happen. The skiff proved not only stable but also dry. It was, however, maddeningly slow—made even slower by the sloshing heft of the Igloo cooler, which was filled with fresh Lake Jesup water especially for Queenie. That, added to the considerable weight of the two men, the tackle, the gas tank, the lunchboxes, the anchor, and the bait (several pounds of frozen Harney County shiners, Queenie's favorite) was almost too much for the tired little six-horse Mercury to push.

García puttered down the canal on a straight course for Lunker Lake Number Seven. With one hand he steered the engine. With the other he idly trolled a fishing line baited with a misshapen jangling monstrosity of a lure. 'Looks like an elephant IUD,' García had told the perky but unappreciative sales rep who'd given it to him on the dock. 'Maybe one of Cher's earrings.'

It was a long slow ride, and the rhythmic drone of the outboard eventually brought on drowsiness. García was half-dozing when something jolted his hands; he opened his eyes to see the tip of the fishing rod quiver and dip. Remembering what Skink had taught him, he jerked twice, solidly, and a stubborn tug answered at the end of the line. Without much effort the detective reeled in his catch, a feisty black fish no more than twelve inches long.

Jim Tile said, 'I believe that's a baby bass.'

'I'll be damned,' said Al García. 'Throw him in the cooler.'

'What for?'

'So we can show the governor we got one fair and square.'

'It's awfully small,' Jim Tile remarked, releasing the bass into the Igloo.

'A fish is a fish,' the detective said. 'Come on, Jimbo, get in the goddamn tournament spirit.'

Then the engine quit; coughed twice, spit blue smoke, and died. Al García removed the cowling and tinkered fruitlessly for ten minutes, then traded places so the trooper could give it a try.

Jim Tile repeatedly pulled the starter cord, but the Mercury showed no sign of life. After the tenth try, he sat down and said, 'Damn.'

The wooden skiff hung motionless in the canal, not another bass boat in sight.

'We got a long ways to go,' García said.

On a hunch, Jim Tile disengaged the fuel line and sniffed the plug.

'Something's wrong,' he said.

García winced. 'Don't tell me we're out of gas.'

Jim Tile hoisted the heavy aluminum fuel tank and unscrewed the lid. He peered inside, then put his nose to the hole.

'Plenty of gas,' he said dismally, 'only somebody's pissed in it.'

30

The night had taken a toll on both of them.

Catherine felt gritty and cramped from being curled in the trunk of the car. Her knees were scuffed and her hair smelled like tire rubber from using the spare as a pillow. She had cried herself to sleep, and now, in the white glare of morning, the sight of Thomas Curl's pistol made her want to cry again. Thinking of Decker helped to hold back the tears.

Curl himself had deteriorated more than Catherine had thought possible, short of coma or death. He could no longer move his right arm at all; the muscle was as black and dead as the dog head that hung from it. Gunk seeped from Curl's eyes and nose, and overnight his tongue had bloomed swollen from his mouth, like some exotic scarlet fruit. On the boat he practically ignored Catherine, but murmured constantly to the rictal dog while stroking its petrified muzzle. By now Catherine was used to everything, even the smell.

Thomas Curl had been drinking ferociously since before dawn, and she surmised that this alone had kept the pain of infection from consuming him. He drove the boat slowly, steering with his knees and squinting against the sun. They passed several fishermen on the canal, but apparently none could see the pistol poking Catherine's left breast. If they noticed the pit bull's head, they didn't let on.

'I'm a rich man, Lucas,' Thomas Curl said to the dog. 'I got enough money for ten of these speedboats.'

Catherine said, 'Tom, we're almost there.' She felt the muzzle of the gun dig harder.

'Lucas, boy, we're almost there,' Thomas Curl said.

With this announcement he threw himself against the throttle and the Starcraft shot forward, plowing aimlessly through a stand of thick sawgrass. Catherine let out a cry as the serrated stalks raked her cheeks, drawing blood. The boat broke out of the matted grass, leapt the water, and climbed a mudbank. The prop stuck hard, and there they sat.

'This is the place,' Thomas Curl declared.

'Not quite,' Catherine said.

'He'll find us, don't you worry,' Curl said. 'He's got a nose for your little pussy, I bet.'

'Cute,' Catherine said. 'You ought to work for Hallmark, writing valentines.'

She used the hem of her skirt to dab the cuts on her face. Half-staggering, Curl got himself out of the boat. The pistol was still in his good hand.

'Don't bother with the leash,' he said to Catherine.

'Right,' she said. There was no leash, of course. She climbed out of the beached Starcraft and instantly cursed Thomas Curl for not letting her wear any shoes.

While she stooped to pick the nettles from her feet, Curl cocked his head and cupped an ear with his gun hand. 'What is it?' he said excitedly.

'What is what?' Catherine asked, but he wasn't speaking to her.

'What is it, boy?'

Somewhere in the deep rotting bog of Thomas Curl's brain, his dog was barking. Curl dropped to a crouch and lowered his voice.

'Lucas hears something comin',' he said.

Catherine heard it too. Her heart raced when she spotted R. J. Decker, hands in his pockets, walking along the bank of the canal.

She waved and tried to shout, but nothing came out. Decker waved back and grinned, the way he always did when he hadn't seen her for a while. Grinned like nothing was wrong, like no gangrenous madman was jabbing a loaded pistol into Catherine's nipple while shouting at a severed dog head on his arm: 'Heel, boy, heel!'

'Easy, Tom,' said R. J. Decker.

'Shut up, fuckhead.'

'Did we get up on the wrong side of the bed?'

'I said shut up, and don't come no closer.'

Decker stood ten feet away. Jeans, flannel shirt, tennis shoes. A camera hung from a thin strap around his neck.

'You remember the deal,' he said to Curl. 'A straight-up trade: Me for her.'

'What kind of deal you offer Lemus?'

Decker said, 'I didn't shoot your brother, but I will say he had it coming.'

'So do you, fuckhead.'

'I know, Tom.'

R. J. Decker could see that something was monstrously wrong with Thomas Curl, that he was a sick man. He could also see that something ghastly had happened to Curl's right arm, and that this might be a cause of his distress.

Decker said, 'That a dog, Tom?'

'The hell does it look like?'

'It's definitely a dog,' Catherine said. 'A pit bull, I believe.'

'I used to know a dog like that,' Decker said affably. 'Lived in my trailer park. Poindexter was its name.'

Thomas Curl said, 'This one is Lucas.'

'Does he do any tricks?'

'Yeah, he chews the balls off fuckheads like you.'

'I see.'

Catherine said, 'You're hurting me, Tom.'

'Take the gun out of there.' Decker spoke calmly. 'Let her go now, that was the deal.'

'I'll show you the deal,' said Thomas Curl. With his tumid red tongue he licked the tip of the gun barrel and placed it squarely between Catherine's light brown eyebrows. He twisted the muzzle back and forth, leaving a wet round imprint on her forehead.

'That's the deal Lemus got,' said Thomas Curl. 'Dead-center bull's-eye.' He poked the gun back in her breast.

The touch of blue steel on her face had made Catherine shiver. She thought she might even faint; in a way, she wished she would. Falling facedown in the sawgrass would be better than this. And Decker—she could have clobbered him, standing there like it was the checkout line of the supermarket. The one time she wanted to see the hot streak, the dangerous temper. Normally she detested violence, but this would have been an exception; Catherine would have been delighted to watch her ex-husband strangle Thomas Curl with his bare hands.

'I got to kill you both,' Curl said. He was fighting off deep tremors. Sweat gathered in big drops on his cheeks, and his breath came in raspy bursts.

Decker knew he could take him, probably with one good punch. If only the pistol weren't aimed point-blank at Catherine's heart. Oh, Catherine. Decker had to be careful, he was so close to the edge.

'A deal is a deal,' Decker said.

'Hell, I can't let her go now.'

'She won't tell,' Decker said. 'She's got a husband to think about.'

'Too bad,' Thomas Curl growled. Suddenly one eye looked bigger than the other. He started rocking slightly, as if on the deck of a ship.

Curl said, 'Let's get it over with, I don't feel so good.'

He pushed Catherine toward Decker, who pulled her close with both hands. 'Rage, please,' she whispered.

Curl said, 'So who wants it first?' When neither of them answered, he consulted his faithful pal. 'Lucas, who gets it first?'

'Tom, one final favor before you do this.'

'Shut up.'

'Take our picture together, okay? Me and Catherine.'

Curl sneered. 'What the hell for?'

'Because I love her,' Decker said, 'and it's our last moment together. Forever.'

'You got *that* right.'

'Then please,' Decker said.

Catherine squeezed his hand. 'I love you too, Rage.' The words sounded wonderful, but under the circumstances Decker wasn't sure how to take it; guns make people say the darnedest things.

He lifted the Minolta from around his neck. Thomas Curl tucked the pistol under his right arm and took the camera in his good hand. He examined it hopelessly, as if it were an atom-splitter.

'My daddy's just got a Polaroid.'

'This is almost the same,' Decker said reassuringly. 'You look through that little window.'

'Yeah?' Thomas Curl raised the camera to his big eye.

'Can you see us?'

'Nope,' Curl said.

Decker took two steps backward, pulling Catherine by the elbows.

'How about now, Tom?'

Curl cackled. 'Hey, yeah, I see you.'

'Good. Now . . . just press that black button on top.'

'Wait, you're all fuzzy-looking.'

'That's all right.'

Curl said, 'Shit, might as well have a good final pitcher, considering. Now, how do I fix the focus?'

Catherine squeezed Decker's arm. 'Fuck the focus,' she said under her breath. 'Go for his gun.'

But in a helpful tone Decker said, 'Tom, the focus is in the black button.'

'The same one?'

'Yeah. It's all automatic, you just press it.'

'I'll be damned.'

Decker said, 'Isn't that something?'

'Yeah,' Thomas Curl said, 'but then where does the pitcher come out?'

'Jesus,' Catherine sighed.

'Underneath,' Decker lied. For the first time he sounded slightly impatient.

Curl turned the camera upside-down in his hand. 'I don't see where.'

'Trust me, Tom.'

'You say so.' Curl raised the Minolta one more time. It took several drunken moments to align the viewfinder with his eye.

'Lucas, don't the two of them look sweet?' Curl hacked out a cruel watery laugh. 'First I shoot your pitcher, then I shoot your goddamn brains out.'

He located the black button with a twitching forefinger. 'Okay, fuckheads, say cheese.'

'Good-bye, Tom,' said R. J. Decker.

There was no film loaded in the camera, only fourteen ounces of water gel, a malleable plastic explosive commonly used at construction sites. For Decker it was a simple chore to run bare copper wires from the camera's batteries directly into the hard-packed gelatin, a substance so volatile that the charge from the shutter contact provided more than enough heat.

As chemical reactions go, it was simple and brief.

At the touch of the button the Minolta blew up; not much in the way of flash, but a powerful air-puckering concussion that tore off Thomas Curl's poisoned skull and launched it in an arc worthy of a forty-foot jump shot. It landed with a noisy sploosh in the middle of the canal.

Catherine was transfixed by how long it took for Curl's headless body to fold up and collapse on the reddening mud; minutes, it seemed. But then, in the pungent gray haze of the killing, every scene seemed to happen in slow motion: R.J. tossing the gun into the water; R.J. dragging the corpse to the boat; R.J. sliding the boat down the bank; R.J. lifting her easily in his arms, carrying her away to someplace safe.

They took turns rowing. Every time they squeaked past another bass boat, they got the same mocking look.

'I don't give a shit,' Al García said to Jim Tile. 'You notice, they don't seem to be catching fish.'

This was true; García and Jim Tile did not know why, nor did they give it much thought as they rowed. Their concern was for one fish only, and they still had a long way to go. As for the other contestants, they might have been interested to know that Charlie Weeb's hydrologist had warned this would happen, that the imported bass might not feed in the bad water. Even had the pros known the full truth, it was unlikely they would have given up and packed their rods—not with so much at stake. Deep in every angler's soul is a secret confidence in his own special prowess that impels him to keep fishing in the face of common sense, basic science, financial ruin, and even natural disasters. In the maddening campaign at Lunker Lakes, whole tackleboxes were emptied and no secret weapon was left unsheathed. The putrid waters were plumbed by lures of every imaginable size and color, retrieved through every navigable depth at every possible speed. By midday it became obvious that even the most sophisticated angling technology in the world would not induce these fish to eat.

As they tediously rowed the skiff through the network of long canals, Jim Tile and Al García detected angst on the faces of other competitors.

'They don't look like they're having much fun,' García said.

'They don't know what fun is,' said Jim Tile, taking his turn at the oars. 'This here's fun.'

With each pull the truth was sinking in: even if they reached the brushpile and did what Skink told them, they'd probably never get back to the dock by sunset. Not rowing.

But they had to try.

'Step on it, *chico*,' Al García said. 'Oxford's gaining on us.'

At that moment, on the westernmost end of Lunker Lake Number Seven, Dennis Gault was refolding the waterproof map that his helicopter pilot had marked for him. Lanie was up in the pedestal seat, reading from a stack of *Cosmos* she'd brought along to kill time. Her nose shone with Hawaiian tanning butter.

Dennis Gault breathed on his sunglasses and wiped each lens with a tissue. He tested them against the sun before putting them on. Scanning his arsenal, he selected a plug-casting outfit with a brand new Double Whammy tied to the end of the line. He tested the sharpness of the hook against his thumbnail, and grinned in self-satisfaction when the barb stuck fast. Then he squirted the lure three times with Happy Gland Bass Bolero.

Finally Gault was ready. He reared back and fired the spinner bait to the exact spot where the sunken brushpile should have been.

'Come on, mother,' he said. 'Suck on this.'

31

'Explain to me,' the Reverend Charles Weeb said from the barber chair, 'exactly how that shit got on the air.'

'The promo spot?' Deacon Johnson asked.

'Yes, Izzy. With all the police cars.'

'It was a live remote, Charles, just like you wanted. "We interrupt our regular programming to take you to the Dickie Lockhart Memorial Bass Blasters blah, blah, blah. Tune in later for the exciting finish." '

'Sixteen frigging cop cars, Izzy—it looked like a dope raid, not a fishing tournament.'

'It wasn't like we invited them.'

'Oh no,' Charlie Weeb said, 'you went one better. You beamed them into eleven million households.'

Deacon Johnson said, 'We'd already paid for the satellite time, Charles. I think you're overreacting.'

Weeb squirmed impatiently while the barber worked on his bushy blond eyebrows. He thought: Maybe Izzy's right, maybe the cop cars weren't so bad. Might even get viewers curious, jack up the ratings.

'May I bring him in now?' Deacon Johnson asked.

'Sure, Izzy.' Weeb was done with his haircut. He gave the barber a hundred dollars and told him to go home. Weeb checked himself in the mirror and splashed on some Old Spice. Then he went to the closet and selected a pale raspberry suit, one of his favorites. He was stepping into the shiny flared trousers when Deacon Johnson returned with the designated sinner.

'Well, you're certainly a big fella,' Weeb said.

'I must be,' said the man.

'Deacon Johnson tells me you're blind.'

'Not completely.'

'Well, no, of course not,' Reverend Weeb said. 'No child of God is completely blind, not in the spiritual sense. His eyes are your eyes.'

'That's damn good to know.'

'What's your name, sinner?'

'They call me Skink.'

'What's that, Scandinavian or something? *Skink.*' Weeb frowned. 'Would you mind, Mr. Skink, if today you took a biblical name? Say, Jeremiah?'

'Sure.'

'That's excellent.' Reverend Weeb was worried about the man's braided hair, and he pantomimed his concern to Deacon Johnson.

'The hair stays,' Skink said.

'It's not that bad,' Deacon Johnson interjected. 'Actually, he looks a little like one of the Oak Ridge Boys.'

Charlie Weeb conceded the point. He said, 'Mr. Skink, I guess they told you how this works. We've got a dress rehearsal in about twenty minutes, but I want to warn you: the real thing is much different, much more . . . emotional. You ever been to a televised tent healing before?'

'Nope.'

'People cry, scream, drool, tremble, fall down on the floor. It's a joyous, joyous moment. And the better *you* are, the more joyous it is.'

'What I want to know,' Skink said, 'is do I really get healed?'

Reverend Weeb smiled avuncularly and flicked the lint off his raspberry lapels. 'Mr. Skink, there are two kinds of healings. One is a physical revelation, the other is spiritual. No one but the Lord himself can foretell what will happen this afternoon—probably a genuine miracle—but at the very least, I promise your eyes will be healed in the spiritual sense.'

'That won't help me pass the driver's test, will it?'

Charlie Weeb coughed lightly. 'Did Deacon Johnson mention that we pay in cash?'

At five sharp, the special live edition of *Jesus in Your Living Room* flashed via satellite across the far reaches of the Outdoor Christian

Network. Radiant and cool, the Reverend Charles Weeb appeared behind his pink plaster pulpit and welcomed America to the scenic and friendly new community of Lunker Lakes, Florida.

'We are particularly delighted to be joined by hundreds of Christian brothers and sisters who flew all the way down here to share this exciting day with us. Thank you all for your love, your prayers, and your down payments . . . as you've seen for yourself, Florida is still a paradise, a place of peacefulness, of inner reflection, of celebrating God's glorious work by celebrating nature . . .'

Camera number one swung skyward.

'And see there, as I speak,' said Reverend Weeb, 'eagles soar over this beautiful new Elysium!'

The high-soaring birds were not eagles, but common brown turkey vultures. The camera man was under strict instructions to avoid close-ups.

Camera number two panned to the audience—starchy, contented, attentive faces, except for one man in the front row, who was not applauding. He wore an ill-fitting sharkskin suit, a frayed straw hat, and black sunglasses. He did not look like a happy Christian soldier; more like Charles Manson on steroids. Camera two did not linger on his face for long.

Charlie Weeb didn't call on him for twenty minutes. By that time the audience throbbed in a damp and weepy frenzy. As Weeb had predicted, fat women were fainting left and right. Grown men were bawling like babies.

At a nod from Reverend Weeb, two young deacons in dovewhite suits led the blind man to the stage.

'You poor wretched sinner,' Weeb said. 'What is your name?'

'Jeremiah Skink.'

'Ah, Jeremiah!'

The audience roared.

'Jeremiah, do you believe in miracles?'

'Yes, Brother Weeb,' Skink said. 'Yes, I do.'

'Do you believe the Lord is here at Lunker Lakes today?'

'I believe he's here with you,' Skink said, reciting the lines, which had been cut drastically due to problems at rehearsal.

'And, Jeremiah, do you believe he watches over his children?'

'He loves us all,' Skink said.

'You have been blind, lo, for how long?'

'Lo, for quite a while,' Skink said.

'And the doctors have given up on you?'

'Totally, Reverend Weeb.'

'And you've even given up on yourself, haven't you, brother?'

'Amen,' Skink said, as a Minicam zoomed in on the sunglasses. He was mad at himself for caving in about the straw hat and sharkskin suit.

Reverend Weeb dabbed his forehead with a kerchief and rested a pudgy pink hand on Skink's shoulder.

'Jeremiah,' he said momentously, 'on this glorious tropical day that God has given us, on a day when Christian sportsmen are reaping fortunes from these pristine waters behind us, on such a day it is God's wish that you should see again. You should see the glory of his sunshine and his sky and the breathtaking natural beauty of his modestly priced family town-home community. Would you like to see that, Jeremiah? Would you like to see again?'

'You bet your ass,' Skink said, deviating slightly from the script.

Reverend Weeb's eyebrows jumped, but he didn't lose tempo. 'Jeremiah,' he went on, 'I'm going to ask these good Christian people who are witnessing with us today at Lunker Lakes to join hands with one another. And all of you at home, put down your Bibles and join hands in your living room. And I myself will take your hands, Jeremiah, and together we will beseech Almighty Jesus to bless you with the gift of sight.'

'Amen,' Skink said.

'Amen!' echoed the crowd.

'Make this sinner see!' Reverend Weeb cried to the heavens.

'See!' the crowd shouted. 'See! See!'

Skink was getting into the act, in spite of himself. 'See me, feel me!' he hollered.

'See him, feel him!' the audience responded. A strange new verse, but it had a pleasing cadence.

Hastily Reverend Weeb steered the prayer chant back to more

conventional exhortations. 'God, save this wretched sinner!'

'Save him!' echoed the crowd.

Like a turtle suddenly caught on the highway, Reverend Weeb retracted his neck, drew in his extremities, and blinked his eyes. The trance lasted a full minute before he snapped out. Raising his arms above his head, he declared: 'The time is nigh. Jesus is coming to our living room!'

The audience waited rapturously. The Minicam was so close you could have counted the pores on Charlie Weeb's nose.

'Jeremiah?' he said. 'Repeat after me: "Jesus, let me see your face." '

Skink repeated it.

'And, "Jesus, let me see the sunshine.' "

'Jesus, let me see the sunshine.'

'And, "Jesus, let me see the pure Christian glory of your newest creation, Lunker Lakes." '

'Ditto,' Skink said. Now came the fun part.

'The Lord has spoken,' Weeb declared. 'Jeremiah, my dear Christian brother, remove thy Wayfarers!'

Skink took off the sunglasses and tucked them in the top pocket of the suit. A ripple of shock passed through the audience. Skink had not allowed the makeup girls near his face. The Minicams backed off fast.

Averting his eyes, Reverend Weeb bellowed: 'Jeremiah, are you truly healed?'

'Oh yes, Brother Weeb.'

'And what is it you see?'

'A great man in a raspberry suit.'

The audience applauded. Many shouted febrile praises to the heavens.

Beaming modestly, Reverend Weeb pressed on: 'And, Jeremiah, above my head there is a joyous sign—a sign invisible to your eyes only a few short moments ago. Tell us what it says.'

This was Skink's big cue, the lead-in to the live tournament coverage. Since it was assumed he would still be mostly blind after the healing, Skink had been asked to memorize the banner and pretend to be reading it on the air. The banner said: 'Lunker

Lakes Presents the Dickie Lockhart Memorial Bass Blasters Classic.'

But those were not the words that Skink intended to say into the microphone.

Charlie Weeb waited three long beats. 'Jeremiah?'

Skink raised his eyes to the banner.

'Jeremiah, please,' Weeb said, 'what does the sign say?'

'It says: "Squeeze My Lemon, Baby." '

A hot prickly silence fell over the stage. Terror filled the face of the Reverend Charles Weeb. His mouth hung open and his gleaming bonded caps clacked vigorously, but no spiritual words issued forth.

The big blind man with the pulpy face began to weep.

'Thank you, Lord. Thank you, Brother Weeb. Thanks for everything.'

With that, Skink turned to face camera one.

And winked.

And when he winked, the amber glass owl eye popped from the hole in his head and bounced on the stage with the sharp crack of a marble. They heard it all the way in the back row.

'Oh, I can see again, Brother Weeb,' the formerly blind man cried. 'Come, let me embrace you as the Lord embraced me.'

With simian arms Skink reached out and seized the Minicam and pulled it to his face.

'Squeeze my lemon, baby!' he moaned, mashing his lips to the lens.

In the crowd, thirteen women fainted heavily out of their folding chairs.

This time it was for real.

'Want a beer?' Lanie asked.

'No,' said Dennis Gault.

'A Perrier?' Lanie dug into the ice chest.

'Quiet,' her brother said.

He had been casting at the brushpile for a long time without a nibble. He had tried every gizmo in the tacklebox, plus a few experimental hybrids, but returned to the Double Whammy out of stubbornness. It had been Dickie Lockhart's secret lure, every-body knew that, so Dennis Gault was dying to win the tourna-ment with it. Flaunt it. Rub it in. Show the cracker bastards that their king was really dead.

Gault knew he was in the right spot, for the sonic depth-finder provided a detailed topography of the canal bottom. The brushpile came across as a ragged black spike on an otherwise featureless chart; an elliptical red blip shone beneath it.

That was the fish.

From the size of the blip, Dennis Gault could tell the bass was very large.

It did not stay in one place, but moved slowly around the fringes of the submerged crates. Gault aimed his casts accordingly.

'Why won't the damn thing eat?' Lanie asked.

'I don't know,' Gault said, 'but I wish you'd be quiet.'

Lanie made a face and went back to her magazines. She wanted her brother to win the tournament as much as he did, but she didn't fully understand why he took it so seriously—especially since he didn't need the money. At least Bobby Clinch had had good reasons to get tense over fishing tournaments; he was trying to keep groceries on Clarisse's table and gas in Lanie's Corvette.

She spun in the pedestal seat so the sun was at her back, and flipped to an article on bulimia.

Thirteen feet beneath the bass boat, in a tea-colored void, the great fish sulked restively. A primitive alarm had gone off somewhere in its central nervous system; a survival warning, powerful but unselective. The great fish could not know what triggered the inner response—acute oxygen depletion, brought about by toxins in the water—but she reacted as all largemouth bass do when sensing a change in the atmosphere.

She decided to gorge herself.

Loglike, she rose off the bottom and hung invisible beneath the floating shadow. She waited under the boat for the familiar rhythmic slapping noise, and peered through liquid glass for the friendly face of the creature who always brought the shiners. The hunger had begun to burn in her belly.

Glancing at the screen of the depth-finder, Dennis Gault said: 'My God, the damn thing's right under us.'

'I sure don't see it,' Lanie said.

'Under the boat,' her brother said. 'Right there on the sonar.'

The fish was so close that he didn't need to cast. He merely dropped the spinnerbait straight down, counted to twelve, and began the slow retrieve. The lure swam unmolested past the brushpile and rattled up, up, up toward the surface. Its rubber skirt shimmied, and its twin spoons twirled. Its mechanical agitation exuded the fear of the pursued, yet it did not behave like a frog or a minnow or even a crawdad. In fact, it resembled absolutely nothing in nature—yet the great fish engulfed it savagely.

Dennis Gault had never felt such a force. When the fish struck, he answered three times, jerking with all his might. The rod bowed and the line twanged, but the thing did not budge. It felt like a cinderblock.

'Sweet Jesus,' Gault said. 'Elaine, I've got it!'

She dropped her magazine and went fumbling for the landing net.

'No, not yet!' Her brother was panting so heavily that Lanie wondered if she should get a brown bag ready.

The great fish had begun to do something that no bass had ever been able to do to Dennis Gault—it was taking line. Not just in a few heady spurts, either, but in a sizzling streak. Gault pressed his thumb to the spool and yelped as the flesh burned raw before his eyes. The bass never slowed.

With his free hand Gault turned on the ignition and put the boat in reverse: he would back down on the beast, as if it were a marlin or a tuna.

'What should I do?' Lanie asked, moving to the back of the boat.

'Take the wheel when I say so.'

Forty yards away, the fish broke the surface. Too heavy to clear the water, it thrashed its maw in seismic rage, the lure jingling in its lower lip. To Dennis Gault the freakish bass seemed as murky and ominous as a bull alligator. He couldn't even guess at the weight; its mouth looked as broad as a basketball hoop.

'Holy shit,' Lanie said, dazzled.

'Here, take it.' Gault motioned her to the steering wheel. 'Take it straight back on top of this bitch.' He stood up and stuck the butt of the rod in his belly, levering his back and thigh muscles into the fight. The fish seemed oblivious. For every foot of line Dennis Gault gained, the giant bass would reclaim two.

'Faster,' Gault told his sister, who nudged the throttle. She had never driven a Ranger before, but figured it couldn't be much different from the Vette.

Motoring in reverse, the boat gradually ate up the distance between Dennis Gault and the thing on the end of his line. After several brief surges, the bass bore deep and hunkered on the bottom to regain its wind.

Gault held such faith in his expensive tackle and in his knowledge of fish behavior that he felt confident tightening the drag on his reel. The purpose was to prevent the bass from running out any more line, and for any other hawg the strategy might have worked: the twenty-pound monofilament was extremely strong, the graphite rod pliant but stout. Finally, and most important to Gault's reasoning, the fish should have rightfully been exhausted after such an extraordinary battle.

Gault twisted the drag down so that nothing smaller than a Mack truck could have stolen more line. Then he began to reel.

'I think it's coming,' he announced. 'By God, the fucker's giving up.'

The great fish bucked its head and resisted surrender, but Gault was able to lift her off the bottom. Unlike the wily old lunkers of well-traveled farm ponds and tourist lakes, this bass had never before felt the sting of the hook, had never struggled against invisible talons. She had acquired no tricks to use on Dennis Gault and his powerful noise machine; all she had was her strength, and in the bad water there was little of it left.

Gault savored the feel of the fish weakening, and a faint smile came over his face. If Dickie weren't already dead, he thought, the sight of this monster hanging at the dock would kill him. Gault checked to make sure the landing net was within reach.

Then the line went slack.

For a sickening moment Gault thought the bass had broken off, but then he figured it out. The bass was coming in fast. He reeled frenetically, trying to bring the line tight.

'Elaine, it's running at us—go the other way!'

She jammed the engine in gear and the boat churned forward, roiling the water to a foam.

The great fish came to the top; a big bronze drainpipe, hovering behind the stern. It was dark enough and deep enough to be the shadow of something, not the thing itself. For the first time Dennis Gault realized its true dimensions and felt a hot rush. This fish was undoubtedly a world record; already he could see his name on the plaque. Already he could picture the bass mounted on the wall behind his desk; the taxidermist would brighten its flanks, touch up the gills, put some fury back in the dull purple eyes.

The fury was there now, only Dennis Gault couldn't see it.

When he pulled on the line, the bass obligingly swam toward the boat. 'Get the net,' he shouted at his sister. 'Give me the goddamn net.'

Then, with a kick of its tail, the fish sounded.

'Reverse!' Dennis Gault cried.

Lanie jerked on the throttle as hard as she could, and the big outboard cavitated loudly as it backed up. It was then, with the boat directly overhead, that the fish exhibited what little guile nature had invested in her pebble-sized brain. She changed direction.

'No-no-no-no!' Dennis Gault was shrieking.

The boat was heading one way, the bass was going the other. Gault braced his knees against the gunwale. He clutched the butt of the rod with both hands.

The line came tight.

The rod doubled until the tip pricked the water. 'Stop!' Dennis Gault grunted. 'Stop, you sorry-dumb-dirty-fat-mother—'

The great fish did not stop.

With the drag cranked down, Dennis Gault could give her no line. All he could do was hang on.

'Let go!' Lanie pleaded.

'No fucking way,' said Dennis. 'This fish is mine.'

Lanie watched helplessly as her brother pitched over the transom. The last she saw of him were the soles of his Top-Siders.

The splash was followed by a dreadful low whine, but it was not Dennis' scream. His scream had died when he hit the propeller, which was turning (according to the dash-mounted tachometer) at precisely four thousand revolutions per minute. The propeller happened to be a brand-new turbo model SST, so the three cupped stainless blades were as sharp as sabers. Dennis Gault might as well have fallen facefirst into a two-hundred-horsepower garbage disposal. Grinding was the sound that his sister had heard.

Lanie cut off the engine and stood up to see what had happened.

'Dennis?' Timorously she peered into the cloudy water, darkening from tea to rust.

A rag-sized swatch of sky-blue fabric floated up; a piece of Dennis Gault's official Bass Blasters jumpsuit. When Lanie saw it, she knew there was no point in diving in after her brother. She held on to the side of the boat with both hands, leaned over, and daintily tossed her croissants.

A hundred yards away, at the point where Charlie Weeb's canal met the dike, the great fish crashed to the surface, shook its head, and threw the hook.

32

They sat on the hood of the car, parked among the bass trucks. They had a good view of the stage, the weigh-in station, the ramp, and the dock. The sun was starting to slip behind a low bank of copper clouds, and some of the boats were heading in.

'You all right?' Catherine asked. She had showered and brushed out her hair and changed clothes. Decker had stopped at a shopping mall and bought her some slacks and a kelly-green blouse; she'd been touched that he still remembered her size.

'I'm fine,' Decker said. His mental lens had preserved Thomas Curl in three frames, none of them pretty.

Catherine said, 'James'll never believe all this.'

Decker looked at her in an odd way. Immediately she felt rotten about mentioning her husband.

Decker said, 'See the excitement you're missing, not being married to me?'

'I don't remember it quite like this.'

'I do,' Decker said, 'just like this.' He smiled and gave her hand a little squeeze. Catherine felt relieved; he'd be all right. She slid off the car and went to scout the food at the buffet, which was set up near the stage.

From out of somewhere Skink materialized and stole Catherine's place on the hood.

'Nice threads,' Decker said.

'First suit I've worn in years.'

'The hat's a treat too.'

Skink shrugged. 'You missed the show.'

'What happened?'

'Preacher tried to heal me.'

Decker laughed a little as Skink told the story.

'That explains where the crowd went,' he said.

'Scattered like hamsters,' Skink said. 'Worst part is, I lost the damn eye. Just kept rolling.'

'We'll get you a new one.'

'Not an owl this time, either. I'd prefer a boar—one of those big nasty bastards.'

Up to this moment, Decker had been watching the boats race in. Now he turned to Skink and in a quiet voice said, 'I'm in some trouble, captain.'

Skink clicked his tongue against his teeth.

'I killed that man,' Decker said.

'Figured as much.'

'There was no other way.'

Skink asked what happened to the body, and Decker told him. 'Don't worry about it,' he said. 'You did good.'

'Don't worry about it?'

'You heard me.'

Decker sighed. He felt detached and fuzzy, as if he were having an out-of-body experience. He felt as if he were in a tall tree looking down on himself and this hoary character in a straw hat, a bad suit, and sunglasses. From this vantage Skink would have made a fine photographic portrait; like one of those debauched-looking acid dealers at Woodstock. Or maybe Altamont. One of those guys who looked too old and too hard for the crowd.

Decker decided to tell Skink why he'd come back to Lunker Lakes. He was bound to ask, anyway.

'When I found Catherine,' Decker said, 'I got to thinking about Dennis Gault.'

'He's *the* case in New Orleans, the whole thing,' Skink repeated. 'It's a joke, so forget about it. You're clear.'

Decker said, 'I wasn't thinking about New Orleans, captain. I was thinking about Bobby Clinch and Ott Pickney and Dickie Lockhart. In relation to Gault, I mean.'

'And Catherine.'

'Yes. Catherine too.'

'True,' Skink said, 'Mr. Gault is not a very nice man.'

Decker took a short breath and said, 'I was seriously thinking about killing him.'

'Now that you got the hang of it, right?'

Decker was stung by Skink's sarcasm. And a sterling example you are, he thought. 'I don't know what I'll do when I see him. Could be I won't be able to stop myself.'

'Don't give me that cuckoo's-nest routine,' Skink said. 'Do you really want to do it? Or do you want yourself to want to? Think about it. Tom Curl was a different story—your girl was involved. That was rescue; this is revenge. Even a one-eyed basket case like me can see you don't have the stomach for it, and I'm glad.'

Decker turned away.

'But the best reason not to kill the bastard,' Skink added, 'is that it's simply not necessary.'

'Maybe you're right.'

'I don't think you understand.'

'Doesn't matter.' Decker hopped off the hood. He spotted Catherine on her way back with a couple of chili dogs. 'I think it's best if we take off before the festivities,' he said wearily.

Skink shook his head. 'It's best if you stay,' he said. 'Besides, I need a favor.'

'Naturally.'

'You know how to work one of these damn TV cameras?'

Later, when *The Wall Street Journal* and others would reconstruct the collapse of the Outdoor Christian Network, some of Charlie Weeb's colleagues and competitors would say he was a fool not to pull the plug on the Lunker Lakes show the instant Skink French-kissed the Minicam. However, such a judgment failed to take into account the pressure from Weeb's corporate sponsors, who had paid extraordinary sums to finance the bass tournament and definitely expected to see it (and their fishing products) on national television. To these businessmen, the attempted faith-healing was merely a gross and irritating preamble to the main event. The weigh-in itself was attended by no less than the entire board of directors of the Happy Gland fish-scent company, who had flown down from Elijay, Georgia, with the expectation that Eddie Spurling, their new spokesman, would win the Lockhart

Memorial hands down. Charlie Weeb had assured them of this in the most positive terms.

So, even after Skink's performance, little thought was given to aborting the program. In fact, there was no time between the church show and the tournament for Weeb to contemplate the scope of the catastrophe, broadcast-wise. He knew it was bad; very bad. Before his eyes the sea of faithful Christian faces had dissipated; the first ten rows in front of the stage now were empty, with some of the chairs overturned by hasty departures. A few people milled around the boat docks, while others hovered at the free buffet. Most apparently had retreated to the charter buses, where they huddled in their seats and recited appropriate Bible tracts. They couldn't wait to get out of Lunker Lakes.

As soon as Skink had leapt off the stage in pursuit of his eyeball, Charlie Weeb had cut to a commercial and gone searching for Deacon Johnson, who had presciently commandeered the limousine and struck out for parts unknown. Weeb's principal inquiry—as enunciated in a gaseous torrent of obscenities—concerned the selection of Mr. Jeremiah Skink as a subject worthy of healing. It was Reverend Weeb's opinion that Skink was more demented than disabled, and that his schizoid tendency toward self-mutilation should have been evident to Deacon Johnson (who, after all, was being paid two hundred thou a year to prevent such embarrassments).

Failing to locate Deacon Johnson, Charlie Weeb returned to the stage and tried to make the best of things. His image as a faith-healer was damaged, perhaps irreparably, but that concerned him less than the mounting specter of financial ruin. Word had filtered back to Weeb that many of the pilgrims who had signed new contracts for Lunker Lakes homesites were having second thoughts—a half-dozen had even demanded their deposits back. Weeb's stomach had churned sourly at the news.

What he now needed—in fact, the only thing that would save the project—was a big warm Southern finish. Specifically: a beaming, tanned, lovable, good ole boy in the person of Eddie Spurling, with a string of lunker bass. That would put the mood right.

So Charlie Weeb seized the microphone and talked a blue streak as the boats roared in. He talked about sunshine, balmy climate, calm waters, central air, adjustable mortgages, bike paths, rec rooms, low maintenance fees, the Olympic-size swimming pool, everything but fish.

Because there weren't any.

Every boat was coming back empty. The OCN sports reporter would stick a mike in front of the angler and the angler would straighten his cap and spit some chaw and grumble about it being one of those days, and then the sports reporter would smile lamely and say better luck next time.

Those gathered dockside—primarily the sponsors and tackle reps and devoted relatives of the contestants—could not recall such a dismal day of bass fishing, even in the weeks after Hurricane Camille had torn up the South.

Skink himself was worried by what he saw, but there was nothing to do but wait. Surely somebody had caught some fish.

As the pattern became clear to Charlie Weeb, he found it increasingly difficult to put a positive spin on the day's events. A weigh-in with nothing to weigh was extremely dull television, even by cable standards. To fill the air time until Eddie Spurling arrived, Weeb ordered the director to run some how-to fishing videos supplied by the big tackle companies.

With only ten minutes until deadline, and the winter sun nearly gone, forty-seven bass boats had checked in at the ramp. The empty scoreboard mocked Charlie Weeb. He could no longer summon the courage to look at the Happy Gland entourage.

Where were Eddie Spurling and his ringers?

Backstage the young hydrologist approached Reverend Weeb and said, 'Bad news—the water's worse today than ever.'

'Get out of my sight,' Weeb said. He didn't give a damn anymore about the water—Eddie's fish would be fine, since they were coming out of the Everglades.

With a grave look, the hydrologist said, 'You're about to have a major problem.'

'And you're about to get a size-ten Florsheim up your ass, so get lost.'

Weeb's earpiece crackled and the TV director said: 'How much longer?'

'We got three boats out,' the preacher said. 'Sit tight, it'll be worth it.'

It was.

Naturally Skink was first to hear them. He hopped off Decker's car and ambled down to the dock. The other onlookers gave way, recognizing him instantly as the deranged Cyclops whom Reverend Weeb had tried to cure. Skink stood alone until Decker and Catherine came down, holding hands.

'Listen,' Skink said.

Decker heard the boat. Whoever it was, he was approaching very slowly—a behavior virtually unknown in professional bass-fishing circles.

'Engine trouble?' Decker said.

Skink shook his head. A mischievous grin split his face.

Catherine said, 'This ought to be good.'

Suddenly the dock was washed in hot light as the kliegs came on. An OCN cameraman, a wiry young man with curly red hair, hustled across the boat ramp with the Minicam balanced on one shoulder. Without explanation he handed the camera and battery pack to R. J. Decker, and bounded away.

'Prior engagement,' Skink explained. Catherine couldn't be sure, but she thought he winked his good eye behind the sunglasses.

Decker got the Minicam focused while Catherine fitted the headset over his ears. In the earphone he could hear the director hollering for Camera Two to get steady.

'This is a breeze,' Decker said. A four-year-old could work the zoom.

Skink rubbed his leathery hands together. 'Lights! Camera!'

Decker aimed down the lake and waited. Before long a bass boat chugged into view. It was Fast Eddie Spurling, going slow. The reason was obvious.

He was towing two other boats.

'Is it Spurling?' the TV director barked at Camera Two.

'Yep,' Decker said.

The word was relayed to Reverend Weeb, who got on the PA system and beckoned all within earshot at once to the dock area. Even those who had fled to the buses emerged to see what was going on.

'Go right, Rudy,' the director instructed Decker, and Decker obliged, as Rudy would have.

As the procession of boats tediously made its way up Lunker Lake Number One, a few people in the crowd (specifically, those with binoculars) began to react alarmingly. Curious, Charlie Weeb stepped down from the stage to join his congregation at water's edge.

R. J. Decker was doing quite well with the TV camera. Through the viewfinder everything was in perfect focus.

There was Eddie Spurling half-turned in the driver's seat as he checked the crippled boats on his towline.

The first was the wooden skiff—there were Jim Tile and Al García, sitting aft and stern. They toasted the TV lights with cans of Budweiser.

Charlie Weeb let out a whimper. 'Mother of God, it's the Tile Brothers.' He had completely forgotten about the spic and the spade. 'Get the camera offa them!' the preacher screamed.

Slowly R.J. Decker panned to the second boat, and when he did his knees nearly crimped.

It was the Starcraft, and it wasn't the way Decker had left it.

Catherine said, 'Oh no,' and moved behind Skink. She leaned her head against his back, and closed her eyes.

The boat was full of buzzards.

There was a ragged cluster of at least a dozen—burly fearless birds; oily brown, stooped-shouldered, with raw pink heads and sharp ruthless eyes. They belched and shifted and blinked in the bright light, but they didn't fly. They were too full.

'Tough customers,' Skink whispered to Decker.

Numbly Decker let the TV camera peer into the boat. He ignored the disembodied voice shrieking from his earpiece.

The buzzards stood in a litter of human bones. The bones were clean, but occasionally one of the rancid birds would bend down and pick savagely, as a possessive gesture to the others. The biggest buzzard, a dishevelled male with a stained crooked beak, palmed a bare yellow skull in its talons.

'Looks like a dog,' Skink said, puzzled.

'It's Lucas,' Catherine sighed. 'Rage, I want to go home.'

As soon as Eddie Spurling tied off the boats, Charlie Weeb barged forward and said, 'Why'd you tow those fuckers in?'

'Because they ast me to.'

'So where's the fish?'

'No fish,' Eddie Spurling reported. 'I got skunked.'

Weeb sucked on his upper lip. He had to be careful what he said. There was a decent-sized crowd now; the other contestants had hung around just to see how the famous TV fisherman had fared.

'What do you mean, no fish—how is that possible?' Weeb spoke in a low strained voice. He used his eyes to grill Eddie about the ringers—where the fuck were they!

'Damn rascals just weren't bitin'.'

'You're in big trouble, Eddie.'

'Naw, I don't think so.'

The sports reporter from OCN poked his microphone into Spurling's face and asked the star of *Fish Fever* what had happened.

'Just one of those days,' Fast Eddie mused, 'when you feel like a spit-valve on the trombone of life.'

Al García and Jim Tile climbed out of the skiff with the Igloo cooler. Skink was waiting for them.

'We didn't get Queenie,' García said.

'I know.'

García looked at Jim Tile, then at Skink.

Skink said, 'Bet you boys had some engine trouble.'

'I don't believe this,' García said. He realized what had happened, but he didn't know why.

'What's going on, jungle man?'

'Change of plans,' Skink said. 'Late-breaking brainstorm.'

Jim Tile was thinking about it. 'The Starcraft isn't one of the tournament boats.'

'No,' Skink said, 'it's not. Ask Decker about that one.'

García said, 'That means there's another guy still out on the water.'

'Right,' said Jim Tile. 'Dennis Gault.'

Skink looked pleased. 'You boys are pretty sharp, even for cops.'

Al García remembered what Skink had taught him about the huge fish. 'Just what the hell have you done?' he asked.

'It's not me, *señor*. I just arranged things.' Skink flipped open the lid of the Igloo and saw García's little bass, darting in the clean water. 'I'll be damned, Sergeant, I'm proud of you.'

Jim Tile said, 'Sir, there's something you ought to know.'

'In a minute, Trooper Jim. First let's get this little scupper to the weigh station.' By himself Skink hoisted the heavy cooler and elbowed his way through the crowd. 'You won't believe this,' he was saying over his shoulder to Tile and García, 'but I believe you're the only boat that caught fish.'

'That's what we're trying to tell you,' García said, huffing behind.

Skink climbed the stage and carried the cooler to the scale. He took out the little bass and carefully set him in the basket. Behind them onstage the digital scale lighted up with glowing six-foot numerals: '14 oz.'

'Ha-ha!' Skink cawed. He found the stage mike and boomed into the PA system: 'Attention, K-Mart shoppers! We've got a winner.'

'Shitfire,' Charlie Weeb muttered. The voice on the PA sounded just like the blind man. First a boatload of buzzards, and now what?

As the queasy preacher followed the OCN cameraman to the weigh station, it occurred to him it wasn't red-haired Rudy, but someone else with the Minicam, someone Weeb didn't recognize. It made little sense, but in the unremitting chaos of the day it seemed a negligible mystery.

The blind man was not onstage when Charlie Weeb got there, but another nightmare awaited him.

The Tile Brothers.

'Hola,' Jim Tile said to Charlie Weeb. *'Es muy grande* fish, no?'

'Check it out, bro,' Al García said.

Charlie Weeb got a bilious taste in his throat. 'It appears that you are indeed the winner,' he said. The Minicam was right in his face—all America was watching. Somehow Weeb composed himself and raised the puny bass for the camera. Two girls in orange bikinis rolled out the immense trophy, and two more carried out a giant cardboard facsimile of the check for two hundred and fifty thousand dollars.

'That's righteous,' Al García said, causing Jim Tile to wince, 'but where be the real thing?'

'Ah,' Weeb said. How could he go on TV and say that, after all this, the check was missing? That he and Deacon Johnson were the only two human beings with the combination to the safe, and now Deacon Johnson was gone?

Sensing trouble, Jim Tile asked, '*¿Donde está el cheque?*'

'I'm sorry,' Reverend Weeb said, 'but I don't speak Cubish.'

By way of translation, Al García said: 'Where's the fucking bread, *por favor*?'

Weeb attempted several explanations, none persuasive and none contradicting the fact that he had promised to present the check to the winners on national television on the day of the tournament. The crowd, especially the other bass anglers, became unruly and insistent; much as they resented the Tile Brothers, they resented even more the idea of any fisherman getting stiffed. Even the sulking Happy Gland contingent joined the fracas.

'I'm sorry,' Weeb said finally, raising his palms, 'there's been a slight problem.'

Al García and Jim Tile looked at one another irritably.

'You do the honors,' García said.

Jim Tile dug a badge and some handcuffs out of his jacket.

Charlie Weeb's lushly forested eyebrows seemed to wilt. A buzz went through the audience.

'Cut, Rudy, cut!' the director was hollering into R. J. Decker's ear, but Decker let it roll.

In perfect English, Jim Tile said, 'Mr. Weeb, you're under arrest for fraud—'

'And grand larceny,' García interjected. 'And any other damn thing I can think of.'

'And grand larceny,' Jim Tile continued. 'You have the right to remain silent—'

Just then a sorrowful cry sheared the dusk. It rose up from the water in a guttural animal pitch that made García flinch and shiver.

Jim Tile bowed his head. He'd tried to tell him.

Decker dropped the Minicam and ran toward the boat ramp.

Skink was on his knees in the shallow water. All around him fish were rising in convulsions, finning belly-up, cutting the glassy surface in jerky zigzag vectors.

Skink scooped up one of the addled bass as it swam by and held it up, dripping, for Decker and the others to see.

'They're all dying,' he cried.

'Take my boat,' Eddie Spurling offered. 'I got six of the damn things.'

'Thank you,' Skink said hoarsely. Decker and Catherine climbed in after him.

'I hope you find her,' Fast Eddie called as the boat pulled away. He would never forget the sight of that magnificent beast in the fish cage; he couldn't bear the thought of her dying in bad water, but it seemed inevitable.

In the bass boat Skink stood up and opened the throttle. First the straw hat blew off, then the sunglasses. Skink didn't seem to care. Nor did he seem to notice the gnats and bugs splattering against his cheeks and forehead, and sticking in his beard by the glue of their own blood. In the depthless gray of early night, Skink drove wide open as if he knew the canals by heart, or instinct. The boat accelerated like a rocket; Decker watched the speedometer tickle sixty and he clenched his teeth, praying they wouldn't hit an alligator or a log. Catherine turned her head and clung to his chest with both arms. Except for the bone-chilling speed, it might have been a lovely moment.

Over the howl of the engine, Skink began to shout.

'Confrontation,' he declared, 'is the essence of nature!'

He shook his silvery braid loose and let his hair stream out behind him.

'Confrontation is the rhythm of life,' he went on. 'In nature violence is pure and purposeful, one species against another in an act of survival!'

Terrific, Decker thought, Marlin Perkins on PCP. 'Watch where you're going, captain!' he shouted.

'All I did with Dennis Gault,' Skink hollered back, 'was to arrange a natural confrontation. No different from a thousand other confrontations that take place every night and every day out here, unseen and uncelebrated. Yet I knew Gault's instincts as well as I knew the fish. It was only a matter of timing, of matching the natural rhythms. Putting the two species within striking distance. That's all it was, Miami.'

Skink pounded the steering wheel ferociously with both fists, causing the speeding boat to skitter precipitously off its plane.

'But goddamn,' he groaned. 'Goddamn, I didn't know about the water.'

Decker rose beside him at the console and casually edged his knee against the wheel, just in case. 'Of course you didn't know!' Decker shouted. He ducked, unnecessarily, as they roared beneath an overpass for the new superhighway.

'We're running through poison,' Skink said, incredulously. 'They built a whole fucking resort on poison water.'

'I know, captain.'

'It's my fault.'

'Don't be ridiculous.'

'You don't understand!' Skink turned around and said to Catherine: 'He doesn't understand. Do you love this man? Then make him understand. It's my fault.'

Shielding her face from the cold, Catherine said, 'You're being too hard on yourself. That's what I think.'

Skink smiled. His classic anchorman teeth were now speckled with dead gnats. 'You're quite a lady,' he said. 'I wish you'd dump your doctor and go back—'

Suddenly, in front of them, another boat appeared. Just a flat shadow hanging in the darkness, dead across the middle of the canal. Someone in a yellow rain slicker was sitting in the bow of the boat, hunched in the seat.

Skink wasn't even looking, he was talking to Catherine, who

had opened her mouth to scream. Desperately Decker leaned hard left on the steering wheel and drew back on the throttle. Fast Eddie's boat nearly went airborne as it struck the other craft a glancing mushy blow on the stern. They spun twice before Decker found the kill switch that cut the engine.

Skink, who had been thrown hard against the engine, got to his feet and took a visual survey. 'This is the place,' he said.

The other boat had been bumped up against the bank. Decker waited for his heart to stop hammering before he called to the person in the yellow slicker: 'You all right?'

'Screw you!'

'Lanie?'

'Always the vixen,' Skink said. He was stripping off the cheap sharkskin suit that Deacon Johnson had given him for the healing.

'Who is that woman?' Catherine asked.

'Gault's sister,' Decker replied.

'Screw both of you!' Lanie shouted. She was standing in the bow, pointing angrily at them.

'So, where's Dennis?' Decker asked.

'Change the subject,' Skink advised. He was naked now. He was on his knees, leaning over the side of the boat, unwittingly mooning Decker and Catherine. He slapped the flat of his palm on the water.

'I hope your fish croaks,' Lanie shouted at Skink, 'like all the rest.' Her voice broke. 'Like Dennis.'

Catherine said, 'Have I missed something?'

Skink furiously pulled a dead yearling from the canal and heaved it to shore. He slapped and slapped, but no fish rose off the bottom, no fish came to his hand.

Decker rummaged through Eddie's boat until he found a spotlight, which plugged into the boat's cigarette lighter. With Skink still hanging over the side calling and slapping for Queenie, Decker worked the beam along the shoreline. Once he inadvertently flashed it in Lanie's direction; she cursed and spun around in the pedestal seat to face the other way.

Decker spotted the body floating at the end of the canal, near the flood dike. He lowered the twin trolling motors and steered Eddie's boat along the yellow path of the spotlight.

Catherine craned to see what it was, but Decker put his hand on her shoulder.

Dapper Dennis Gault was in shreds. He floated facedown, snarled in twenty-pound fishing line.

'The rhythm of confrontation,' Skink said. 'In a way, I almost admire the sonofabitch.'

Decker knew there was nothing to be done.

'This is some sport,' Catherine remarked.

Skink and Decker saw the great fish simultaneously. She surfaced on her side, feebly, near Gault's bloated legs. Her gills had bled from red to pink, and her flanks had blackened. She was dying.

'No, you don't,' Skink said, and dove in. For a big man he made a small splash, entering the water like a needle.

Catherine stood up to watch with Decker. Their breath came out in soft frosty puffs.

'I got her!' Skink shouted. 'But damnation!'

Somehow he had become entangled in Dennis Gault's body. For several moments the water churned in a macabre one-sided duel, stiff dead limbs thrashing against the living. Catherine was terrified; it looked as if Gault had come back to life. Skink was in great pain, the foul brackish water searing his raw eye socket. All at once he seemed to be slipping under.

R. J. Decker picked up Fast Eddie's fish gaff and stuck it hard in the meat of Gault's shoulders. He pulled brutishly at the corpse with all his weight, and Skink kicked away, free. He cradled the sluggish fish with his bare arms. He swam with his head out, on his back, otter-style. He was fighting to catch his breath.

'Thanks, Miami,' he wheezed. 'Take care.'

With four kicks he made it to shore, and carried the great fish up the slope. Decker didn't need the spotlight to track him—a naked white Amazon running splayfooted along the embankment. He was singing, too, though the melody was indistinct.

Decker gunned the engine and beached the bass boat with a jolt. He jumped ashore and reached out his hand for Catherine.

Together they jogged toward the flood dike, but Skink was far ahead. Even toting the fish, he seemed to be running twice as fast.

From the canal behind them, Lanie Gault called Skink's name. Decker heard two shots and reflexively he dragged Catherine to the ground. They looked up to see two small flares explode overhead, drenching the night in vermilion. In a strange way it reminded Decker of the warm safe light of the darkroom. He had no idea why Lanie had fired the flare gun; maybe it was all she had.

They got up and started running again, but by this time Skink had already crested the dike. When they reached the other side, he was gone, vanished into the seam of the universe. As the flares burned out, the red glow drained from the sky and the crystal darkness returned to the marsh.

A washboard ripple lingered on the quiet pool. Frogs peeped, crickets trilled, waterbugs skated through the bullrushes. There was no sign of the great fish, no sign of the man.

'Hear it?' Decker asked.

Catherine brushed the insects away and strained to listen. 'I don't think so, Rage.'

'Something swimming.' The gentlest of motions, receding somewhere out in the Glades. Decker was sure of it.

'Wait,' Catherine said, taking his arm, 'now I do.'

SKIN TIGHT

Acknowledgment

For his advice, expertise, and good humor,
I am grateful to Dr. Gerard Grau, and also to his
former surgical nurse Connie, who is my wife.

1

On the third of January, a leaden, blustery day, two tourists from Covington, Tennessee, removed their sensible shoes to go strolling on the beach at Key Biscayne.

When they got to the old Cape Florida lighthouse, the young man and his fiancée sat down on the damp sand to watch the ocean crash hard across the brown boulders at the point of the island. There was a salt haze in the air, and it stung the young man's eyes so that when he spotted the thing floating, it took several moments to focus on what it was.

'It's a big dead fish,' his fiancée said. 'Maybe a porpoise.'

'I don't believe so,' said the young man. He stood up, dusted off the seat of his trousers, and walked to the edge of the surf. As the thing floated closer, the young man began to wonder about his legal responsibilities, providing it turned out to be what he thought it was. Oh yes, he had heard about Miami; this sort of stuff happened every day.

'Let's go back now,' he said abruptly to his fiancée.

'No, I want to see what it is. It doesn't look like a fish anymore.'

The young man scanned the beach and saw they were all alone, thanks to the lousy weather. He also knew from a brochure back at the hotel that the lighthouse was long ago abandoned, so there would be no one watching from above.

'It's a dead body,' he said grimly to his fiancée.

'Come off it.'

At that instant a big, lisping breaker took the thing on its crest and carried it all the way to the beach, where it stuck—the nose of the dead man grounding as a keel in the sand.

The young man's fiancée stared down at the corpse and said, 'Geez, you're right.'

The young man sucked in his breath and took a step back.

'Should we turn it over?' his fiancée asked. 'Maybe he's still alive.'

'Don't touch it. He's dead.'

'How do you know?'

The young man pointed with a bare toe. 'See that hole?'

'That's a hole?'

She bent over and studied a stain on the shirt. The stain was the color of rust and the size of a sand dollar.

'Well, he didn't just drown,' the young man announced.

His fiancée shivered a little and buttoned her sweater. 'So what do we do now?'

'Now we get out of here.'

'Shouldn't we call the police?'

'It's our vacation, Cheryl. Besides, we're a half-hour's walk to the nearest phone.'

The young man was getting nervous; he thought he heard a boat's engine somewhere around the point of the island, on the bay side.

The woman tourist said, 'Just a second.' She unsnapped the black leather case that held her trusty Canon Sure-Shot.

'What are you doing?'

'I want a picture, Thomas.' She already had the camera up to her eye.

'Are you crazy?'

'Otherwise no one back home will believe us. I mean, we come all the way down to Miami and what happens? Remember how your brother was making murder jokes before we left? It's unreal. Stand to the right a little, Thomas, and pretend to look down at it.'

'Pretend, hell.'

'Come on, one picture.'

'No,' the man said, eyeing the corpse.

'Please? You used up a whole roll on Flipper.'

The woman snapped the picture and said, 'That's good. Now you take one of me.'

'Well, hurry it up,' the young man grumped. The wind was blowing harder from the northeast, moaning through the whippy

Australian pines behind them. The sound of the boat engine, wherever it was, had faded away.

The young man's fiancée struck a pose next to the dead body: She pointed at it and made a sour face, crinkling her zinc-coated nose.

'I can't believe this,' the young man said, lining up the photograph.

'Me neither, Thomas. A real live dead body—just like on the TV show. Yuk!'

'Yeah, yuk,' said the young man. 'Fucking yuk is right.'

The day had begun with only a light, cool breeze and a rim of broken raspberry clouds out toward the Bahamas. Stranahan was up early, frying eggs and chasing the gulls off the roof. He lived in an old stilt house on the shallow tidal flats of Biscayne Bay, a mile from the tip of Cape Florida. The house had a small generator powered by a four-bladed windmill, but no air-conditioning. Except for a few days in August and September, there was always a decent breeze. That was one nice thing about living on the water.

There were maybe a dozen other houses in the stretch of Biscayne Bay known as Stiltsville, but none were inhabited; rich owners used them for weekend parties, and their kids got drunk on them in the summer. The rest of the time they served as fancy, split-level toilets for seagulls and cormorants.

Stranahan had purchased his house dirt-cheap at a government auction. The previous owner was a Venezuelan cocaine courier who had been shot thirteen times in a serious business dispute, then indicted posthumously. No sooner had the corpse been air-freighted back to Caracas than Customs agents seized the stilt house, along with three condos, two Porsches, a one-eyed scarlet macaw, and a yacht with a hot tub. The hot tub was where the Venezuelan had met his spectacular death, so bidding was feverish. Likewise the macaw—a material witness to its owner's murder—fetched top dollar; before the auction, mischievous Customs agents had taught the bird to say, 'Duck, you shithead!'

By the time the stilt house had come up on the block, nobody was interested. Stranahan had picked it up for forty thousand and change.

He coveted the solitude of the flats and was delighted to be the only human soul living in Stiltsville. His house, barn-red with brown shutters, sat three hundred yards off the main channel, so most of the weekend boat traffic traveled clear of him. Occasionally a drunk or a total moron would try to clear the banks with a big cabin cruiser, but they did not get far, and they got no sympathy or assistance from the big man in the barn-red house.

January third was a weekday and, with the weather blackening out east, there wouldn't be many boaters out. Stranahan savored this fact as he sat on the sun deck, eating his eggs and Canadian bacon right out of the frying pan. When a pair of fat, dirty gulls swooped in to nag him for the leftovers, he picked up a BB pistol and opened fire. The birds screeched off in the direction of the Miami skyline, and Stranahan hoped they would not stop until they got there.

After breakfast he pulled on a pair of stringy denim cutoffs and started doing push-ups. He stopped at one hundred five, and went inside to get some orange juice. From the kitchen he heard a boat coming and checked out the window. It was a yellow bonefish skiff, racing heedlessly across the shallows. Stranahan smiled; he knew all the local guides. Sometimes he'd let them use his house for a bathroom stop, if they had a particularly shy female customer who didn't want to hang it over the side of the boat.

Stranahan poured two cups of hot coffee and went back out on the deck. The yellow skiff was idling up to the dock, which was below the house itself and served as a boat garage. The guide waved up at Stranahan and tied off from the bow. The man's client, an inordinately pale fellow, was preoccupied trying to decide which of four different grades of sunscreen to slather on his milky arms. The guide hopped out of the skiff and climbed up to the sun deck.

'Morning, Captain.' Stranahan handed a mug of coffee to the guide, who accepted it with a friendly grunt. The two men had known each other many years, but this was only the second or third occasion that the captain had gotten out of his boat and come up to the stilt house. Stranahan waited to hear the reason.

When he put down the empty cup, the guide said: 'Mick, you expecting company?'

'No.'

'There was a man this morning.'

'At the marina?'

'No, out here. Asking which house was yours.' The guide glanced over the railing at his client, who now was practicing with a fly rod, snapping the line like a horsewhip.

Stranahan laughed and said, 'Looks like a winner.'

'Looks like a long goddamn day,' the captain muttered.

'Tell me about this guy.'

'He flagged me down over by the radio towers. He was in a white Seacraft, a twenty-footer. I thought he was having engine trouble but all he wanted was to know which house was yours. I sent him down toward Elliott Key, so I hope he wasn't a friend. Said he was.'

'Did he give you a name?'

'Tim is what he said.'

Stranahan said the only Tim he knew was an ex-homicide cop named Gavigan.

'That's it,' the fishing guide said. 'Tim Gavigan is what he said.'

'Skinny redhead?'

'Nope.'

'Shit,' said Stranahan. Of course it wasn't Timmy Gavigan. Gavigan was busy dying of lung cancer in the VA.

The captain said, 'You want me to hang close today?'

'Hell, no, you got your sport down there, he's raring to go.'

'Fuck it. Mick, he wouldn't know a bonefish from a sperm whale. Anyway. I've got a few choice spots around here—maybe we'll luck out.'

'Not with this breeze, buddy; the flats are already pea soup. You go on down south, I'll be all right. He's probably just some process-server.'

'Somebody's sure to tell him which house.'

'Yeah, I figure so,' Stranahan said. 'A white Seacraft, you said?'

'Twenty-footer,' the guide repeated. Before he started down the stairs, he said, 'The guy's got some size to him, too.'

'Thanks for the info.'

Stranahan watched the yellow skiff shoot south, across the flats, until all he could see was the long zipper of foam in its wake. The guide would be heading to Sand Key, Stranahan thought, or maybe all the way to Caesar Creek—well out of radio range. As if the damn radio still worked.

By three o'clock in the afternoon, the wind had stiffened, and the sky and the water had acquired the same purple shade of gray. Stranahan slipped into long jeans and a light jacket. He put on his sneakers, too; at the time he didn't think about why he did this, but much later it came to him: Splinters. From running on the wooden deck. The raw two-by-fours were hell on bare feet, so Stranahan had put on his sneakers. In case he had to run.

The Seacraft was noisy. Stranahan heard it coming two miles away. He found the white speck through his field glasses and watched it plow through the hard chop. The boat was heading straight for Stranahan's stilt house and staying clean in the channels, too.

Figures, Stranahan thought sourly. Probably one of the park rangers down at Elliott Key told the guy which house; just trying to be helpful.

He got up and closed the brown shutters from the outside. Through the field glasses he took one more long look at the man in the Seacraft, who was still a half-mile away. Stranahan did not recognize the man, but could tell he was from up North—the guy made a point of shirt-sleeves, on this kind of a day, and the dumbest-looking sunglasses ever made.

Stranahan slipped inside the house and closed the door behind him. There was no way to lock it from the inside; there was no reason, usually.

With the shutters down the inside of the house was pitch-black, but Stranahan knew every corner of each room. In this house he had ridden out two hurricanes—baby ones, but nasty just the same. He had spent both storms in total darkness, because the wind knifed through the walls and played hell with the lanterns, and the last thing you wanted was an indoor fire.

So Stranahan knew the house in the dark.

He selected his place and waited.

After a few minutes the pitch of the Seacraft's engines dropped an octave, and Stranahan figured the boat was slowing down. The guy would be eyeing the place closely, trying to figure out the best way up on the flat. There was a narrow cut in the marl, maybe four feet deep at high tide and wide enough for one boat. If the guy saw it and made this his entry, he would certainly spot Stranahan's aluminium skiff tied up under the water tanks. And then he would know.

Stranahan heard the Seacraft's engines chewing up the marly bottom. The guy had missed the deep cut.

Stranahan heard the big boat thud into the pilings at the west end of the house. He could hear the guy clunking around in the bow, grunting as he tried to tie it off against the tide, which was falling fast.

Stranahan heard—and felt—the man hoist himself out of the boat and climb to the main deck of the house. He heard the man say: 'Anybody home?'

The man did not have a light step; the captain was right—he was a big one. By the vibrations of the plankboards, Stranahan charted the intruder's movements.

Finally the guy knocked on the door and said: 'Hey! Hello there!'

When no one answered, the guy just opened the door.

He stood framed in the afternoon light, such as it was, and Stranahan got a pretty good look. The man had removed his sunglasses. As he peered into the dark house, his right hand went to the waist of his trousers.

'State your business,' Stranahan said from the shadows.

'Oh, hey!' The man stepped backward onto the deck, forfeiting his silhouette for detail. Stranahan did not recognize the face— an odd and lumpy one, skin stretched tightly over squared cheek-bones. Also, the nose didn't match the eyes and chin. Stranahan wondered if the guy had ever been in a bad car wreck.

The man said: 'I ran out of gas, and I was wondering if you had a couple of gallons to get me back to the marina. I'll be happy to pay.'

'Sorry,' Stranahan said.

The guy looked for the source of the voice, but he couldn't see a damn thing in the shuttered-up house.

'Hey, pal, you okay?'

'Just fine,' Stranahan said.

'Well, then, would you mind stepping out where I can see you?'

With his left hand Stranahan grabbed the leg of a barstool and sent it skidding along the bare floor to no place in particular. He just wanted to see what the asshole would do, and he was not disappointed. The guy took a short-barreled pistol out of his pants and held it behind his back. Then he took two steps forward until he was completely inside the house. He took another slow step toward the spot where the broken barstool lay, only now he was holding the pistol in front of him.

Stranahan, who had squeezed himself into a spot between the freezer and the pantry, had seen enough of the damn gun.

'Over here,' he said to the stranger.

And when the guy spun around to get a bead on where the voice was coming from, Mick Stranahan lunged out of the shadows and stabbed him straight through with a stuffed marlin head he had gotten off the wall.

It was a fine blue marlin, maybe four hundred pounds, and whoever caught it had decided to mount only the head and shoulders, down to the spike of the dorsal. The trophy fish had come with the Venezuelan's house and hung in the living room, where Stranahan had grown accustomed to its indigo stripes, its raging glass eye and its fearsome black sword. In a way it was a shame to mess it up, but Stranahan knew the BB gun would be useless against a real revolver.

The taxidermied fish was not as heavy as Stranahan anticipated, but it was cumbersome; Stranahan concentrated on his aim as he charged the intruder. It paid off.

The marlin's bill split the man's breastbone, tore his aorta, and severed his spine. He died before Stranahan got a chance to ask him any questions. The final puzzled look on the man's face suggested that he was not expecting to be gored by a giant stuffed fish head.

The intruder carried no identification, no wallet, no wedding ring; just the keys to a rented Thunderbird. Aboard the Seacraft, which was also rented, Stranahan found an Igloo cooler with two six-packs of Corona and a couple of cheap spinning rods that the killer had brought along just for looks.

Stranahan heaved the body into the Seacraft and took the boat out into the Biscayne Channel. There he pushed the dead guy overboard, tossed the pistol into deep water, rinsed down the decks, dove off the stern, and swam back toward the stilt house. In fifteen minutes his knees hit the mud bank, and he waded the last seventy-five yards to the dock.

That night there was no sunset to speak of, because of the dreary skies, but Stranahan sat on the deck anyway. As he stared out to the west, he tried to figure out who wanted him dead, and why. He considered this a priority.

2

On the fourth day of January, the sun came out, and Dr. Rudy Graveline smiled. The sun was very good for business. It baked and fried and pitted the facial flesh, and seeded the pores with vile microscopic cancers that would eventually sprout and require excision. Dr. Rudy Graveline was a plastic surgeon, and he dearly loved to see the sun.

He was in a fine mood, anyway, because it was January. In Florida, January is the heart of the winter tourist season and a bonanza time for cosmetic surgeons. Thousands of older men and women who flock down for the warm weather also use the occasion to improve their features. Tummy tucks, nose jobs, boob jobs, butt jobs, fat suctions, face lifts, you name it. And they always beg for an appointment in January, so that the scars will be healed by the time they go back North in the spring.

Dr. Rudy Graveline could not accommodate all the snowbirds, but he did his damnedest. All four surgical theaters at the Whispering Palms Spa were booked from dawn to dusk in January, February, and halfway into March. Most of the patients asked especially for Dr. Graveline, whose reputation greatly exceeded his talents. While Rudy usually farmed the cases out to the eight other plastic surgeons on staff, many patients got the impression that Dr. Graveline himself had performed their surgery. This is because Rudy would often come in and pat their wrinkled hands until they nodded off, blissfully, under the nitrous or I.V. Valium. At that point Rudy would turn them over to one of his younger and more competent protégés.

Dr. Graveline saved himself for the richer patients. The regulars got cut on every winter, and Rudy counted on their business. He reassured his surgical hypochondriacs that there was nothing abnormal about having a fifth, sixth, or seventh blepharoplasty in as many years. *Does it make you feel better about yourself?* Rudy would ask them. *Then it's worth it, isn't it? Of course it is.*

Such a patient was Madeleine Margaret Wilhoit, age sixty-nine, of North Palm Beach. In the course of their acquaintance, there was scarcely a square inch of Madeleine's substantial physique that Dr. Rudy Graveline had not altered. Whatever he did and whatever he charged, Madeleine was always delighted. And she always came back the next year for more. Though Madeleine's face reminded Dr. Graveline in many ways of a camel, he was fond of her. She was the kind of steady patient that offshore trust funds are made of.

On January fourth, buoyed by the warm sunny drive to Whispering Palms, Rudy Graveline set about the task of repairing for the fifth, sixth, or seventh time (he couldn't remember exactly) the upper eyelids of Madeleine Margaret Wilhoit. Given the dromedarian texture of the woman's skin, the mission was doomed and Rudy knew it. Any cosmetic improvement would have to take place exclusively in Madeleine's imagination, but Rudy (knowing she would be ecstatic) pressed on.

Midway through the operation, the telephone on the wall let out two beeps. With a gowned elbow the operating-room nurse deftly punched the intercom box and told the caller that Dr. Graveline was in the middle of surgery and not available.

'It's fucking important, tell him,' said a sullen male voice, which Rudy instantly recognized.

He asked the nurse and the anesthetist to leave the operating room for a few minutes. When they were gone, he said to the phone box: 'Go ahead. This is me.'

The phone call was made from a pay booth in Atlantic City, New Jersey, not that it would have mattered to Rudy. Jersey was all he knew, all he needed to know.

'You want the report?' the man asked.

'Of course.'

'It went lousy.'

Rudy sighed and stared down at the violet vectors he had inked around Madeleine's eyes. 'How lousy?' the surgeon said to the phone box.

'The ultimate fucking lousy.'

Rudy tried to imagine the face on the other end of the line, in New Jersey. In the old days he could guess a face by the voice on the phone. This particular voice sounded fat and lardy, with black curly eyebrows and mean dark eyes.

'So what now?' the doctor asked.

'Keep the other half of your money.'

What a prince, Rudy thought.

'What if I want you to try again?'

'Fine by me.'

'So what'll *that* cost?'

'Same,' said Curly Eyebrows. 'Deal's a deal.'

'Can I think on it?'

'Sure. I'll call back tomorrow.'

Rudy said, 'It's just that I didn't count on any problems.'

'The problem's not yours. Anyway, this shit happens.'

'I understand,' Dr. Graveline said.

The man in New Jersey hung up, and Madeleine Margaret Wilhoit started to squirm. It occurred to Rudy that maybe the old bag wasn't asleep after all, and that maybe she'd heard the whole conversation.

'Madeleine?' he whispered in her ear.

'Unngggh.'

'Are you okay?'

'Fine, Papa,' Madeleine drooled. 'When do I get to ride in the sailboat?'

Rudy Graveline smiled, then buzzed for the nurse and anesthetist to come back and help him finish the job.

During his time at the State Attorney's Office, Mick Stranahan had helped put many people in jail. Most of them were out now, even the murderers, due to a federal court order requiring the state of Florida to seasonally purge its overcrowded prisons. Stranahan accepted the fact that some of these ex-cons harbored bitterness against him, and that more than a few would be delighted to see him dead. For this reason, Stranahan was exceedingly cautious about visitors. He was not a paranoid person, but took a practical view of risk: When someone pulls a gun at your front door, there's really no point to asking him what he wants. The answer is obvious, and so is the solution.

The gunman who came to the stilt house was the fifth person that Mick Stranahan had killed in his lifetime.

The first two were North Vietnamese Army regulars who were laying trip wire for land mines near the town of Dak Mat Lop in the Central Highlands. Stranahan surprised the young soldiers by using his sidearm instead of his M-16, and by not missing. It happened during the second week of May 1969, when Stranahan was barely twenty years old.

The third person he killed was a Miami holdup man named Thomas Henry Thomas, who made the mistake of sticking up a fried-chicken joint while Stranahan was standing in line for a nine-piece box of Extra Double Crispy. To supplement the paltry seventy-eight dollars he had grabbed from the cash register, Thomas Henry Thomas decided to confiscate the wallets and purses of each customer. It went rather smoothly until he came down the line to Mick Stranahan, who calmly took away Thomas Henry Thomas's .38-caliber Charter Arms revolver and shot him twice in the right temporal lobe. In appreciation, the fried-chicken franchise presented Stranahan with three months' worth of discount coupons and offered to put his likeness on every carton of Chicken Chunkettes sold during the month of December 1977. Being broke and savagely divorced, Stranahan took the coupons but declined the celebrity photo.

The shooting of Thomas Henry Thomas (his obvious character flaws aside) was deemed serious enough to dissuade both the Miami and metropolitan Dade County police from hiring Mick Stranahan as an officer. His virulent refusal to take any routine psychological tests also militated against him. However, the State Attorney's office was in dire need of a streetwise investigator, and was delighted to hire a highly decorated war veteran, even at the relatively tender age of twenty-nine.

The fourth and most important person that Mick Stranahan

killed was a crooked Dade County judge named Raleigh Goomer. Judge Goomer's specialty was shaking down defense lawyers in exchange for ridiculous bond reductions, which allowed dangerous felons to get out of jail and skip town. It was Stranahan who caught Judge Goomer at this game and arrested him taking a payoff at a strip joint near the Miami airport. On the trip to the jail, Judge Goomer apparently panicked, pulled a .22 somewhere out of his black nylon socks, and fired three shots at Mick Stranahan. Hit twice in the right thigh, Stranahan still managed to seize the gun, twist the barrel up the judge's right nostril, and fire.

A special prosecutor sent down from Tampa presented the case to the grand jury, and the grand jury agreed that the killing of Judge Goomer was probably self-defense, though a point-blank nostril shot did seem extreme. Even though Stranahan was cleared, he obviously could no longer be employed by the State Attorney's Office. Pressure for his dismissal came most intensely from other crooked judges, several of whom stated that they were afraid to have Mr. Stranahan testifying in their courtrooms.

On June 7, 1988, Mick Stranahan resigned from the prosecutor's staff. The press release called it early retirement, and disclosed that Stranahan would be receiving full disability compensation as a result of injuries suffered in the Goomer shooting. Stranahan wasn't disabled at all, but his family connection with a notorious personal-injury lawyer was sufficient to terrify the county into paying him off. When Stranahan said he didn't want the money, the county promptly doubled its offer and threw in a motorized wheelchair. Stranahan gave up.

Not long afterwards, he moved out to Stiltsville and made friends with the fish.

A marine patrol boat pulled up to Mick Stranahan's place at half-past noon. Stranahan was on the top deck, dropping a line for mangrove snappers down below.

'Got a second?' asked the marine patrol officer, a sharp young Cuban named Luis Córdova. Stranahan liked him all right.

'Come on up,' he said.

Stranahan reeled in his bait and put the fishing rod down. He dumped four dead snappers out of the bucket and gutted them one at a time, tossing their creamy innards in the water.

Córdova was talking about the body that had washed up on Cape Florida.

'Rangers found it yesterday evening,' he said. 'Lemon shark got the left foot.'

'That happens,' Stranahan said, skinning one of the fish filets.

'The M.E. says it was one hell of a stab wound.'

'I'm gonna fry these up for sandwiches,' Stranahan said. 'You interested in lunch?'

Córdova shook his head. 'No, Mick, there's some jerks poaching lobster down at Boca Chita so I gotta be on my way. Metro asked me to poke around out here, see if somebody saw anything. And since you're the only one out here . . .'

Stranahan glanced up from the fish-cleaning. 'I don't remember much going on yesterday,' he said. 'Weather was piss-poor, that I know.'

He tossed the fish skeletons, heads still attached, over the rail.

'Well, Metro's not all that excited,' Córdova said.

'How come? Who's the stiff?'

'Name of Tony Traviola, wise guy. Jersey state police got a fat jacket on him. Tony the Eel, loan-collector type. Not a very nice man, from what I understand.'

Stranahan said, 'They think it's a mob hit?'

'I don't know what they think.'

Stranahan carried the filets into the house and ran them under the tap. He was careful with the water, since the tanks were low. Córdova accepted a glass of iced tea and stood next to Stranahan in the kitchen, watching him roll the filets in egg yolk and bread crumbs. Normally Stranahan preferred to be left alone when he cooked, but he didn't want Luis Córdova to go just yet.

'They found the guy's boat, too,' the marine patrolman went on. 'It was a rental out of Haulover. White Seacraft.'

Stranahan said he hadn't seen one of those lately.

'Few specks of blood was all they found,' Córdova said. 'Somebody cleaned it pretty good.'

Stranahan laid the snapper filets in a half inch of oil in a frying pan. The stove didn't seem to be working, so he got on his knees and checked the pilot light—dead, as usual. He put a match to it and, before long, the fish started to sizzle.

Córdova sat down on one of the wicker barstools.

'So why don't they think it was the mob?' Stranahan asked.

'I didn't say they didn't, Mick.'

Stranahan smiled and opened a bottle of beer.

Córdova shrugged. 'They don't tell me every little thing.'

'First of all, they wouldn't bring him all the way down to Florida to do it, would they, Luis? They got the exact same ocean up in Jersey. So Tony the Eel was already here on business.'

'Makes sense,' Córdova nodded.

'Second, why didn't they just shoot him? Knives are for kids, not pros.'

Córdova took the bait. 'Wasn't a knife,' he said. 'It was too big, the M.E. said. More like a javelin.'

'That's not like the guineas.'

'No,' Córdova agreed.

Stranahan made three fish sandwiches and gave one to the marine patrolman, who had forgotten about going after the lobster poachers, if there ever were any.

'The other weird thing,' he said through a mouthful of bread, 'is the guy's face.'

'What about it?'

'It didn't match the mug shots, not even close. They made him through fingerprints and dentals, but when they got the mugs back from the FBI it looked like a different guy altogether. So Metro calls the Bureau and says you made a mistake, and they say the hell we did, that's Tony Traviola. They go back and forth for about two hours until somebody has the brains to call the M.E.' Córdova stopped to gulp some iced tea; the fish was steaming in his cheeks.

Stranahan said, 'And?'

'Plastic surgery.'

'No shit?'

'At least five different operations, from his eyes to his chin. Tony the Eel, he was a regular Michael Jackson. His own mother wouldn't have known him.'

Stranahan opened another beer and sat down. 'Why would a bum like Traviola get his face remade?'

Córdova said, 'Traviola did a nickel for extortion, got out of Rahway about two years ago. Not long afterwards a Purolator truck gets him, but the robbers turn up dead three days later—without the loot. Classic mob rip. The feds put a warrant out for Traviola, hung his snapshot in every post office along the Eastern seaboard.'

'Good reason to get the old schnoz bobbed,' Stranahan said.

'That's what they figure.' Córdova got up and rinsed his plate in the sink.

Stranahan was impressed. 'You didn't get all this out of Metro, did you?'

Córdova laughed. 'Hey, even the grouper troopers got a computer.'

This was a good kid, Stranahan thought, a good cop. Maybe there was hope for the world after all.

'I see you went out and got the newspaper,' the marine patrolman remarked. 'What's the occasion, you got a pony running at Gulfstream?'

Hell, Stranahan thought, that was a stupid move. On the counter was the *Herald*, open to the page with the story about the dead floater. Miami being what it is, the floater paragraph was only two paragraphs long, wedged under a tiny headline between a one-ton coke bust and a double homicide on the river. Maybe Luis Córdova wouldn't notice.

'You must've got up early to get to the marina and back,' he said.

'Grocery run,' Stranahan lied. 'Besides, it was a nice morning for a boat ride. How was the fish?'

'Delicious, Mick.' Córdova slapped him on the shoulder and said so long.

Stranahan walked out on the deck and watched Córdova untie his patrol boat, a gray Mako outboard with a blue police light mounted on the center console.

'If anything comes up, I'll give you a call, Luis.'

'No sweat, it's Metro's party,' the marine patrolman said. 'Guy sounds like a dirtbag, anyway.'

'Yeah,' Stranahan said, 'I feel sorry for that shark, the one that ate his foot.'

Córdova chuckled. 'Yeah, he'll be puking for a week.'

Stranahan waved as the police boat pulled away. He was pleased to see Luis Córdova heading south toward Boca Chita, as Luis had said he would. He was also pleased that the young officer had not asked him about the blue marlin head on the living-room wall, about why the sword was mended together with fresh hurricane tape.

Timmy Gavigan had looked like death for most of his adult life. Now he had an excuse.

His coppery hair had fallen out in thickets, revealing patches of pale freckled scalp. His face, once round and florid, looked like somebody had let the air out.

From his hospital bed Timmy Gavigan said, 'Mick, can you believe this fucking food?' He picked up a chunk of gray meat off the tray and held it up with two fingers, like an important piece of evidence. 'This is your government in action, Mick. Same fuckers that want to put lasers in outer space can't fry a Salisbury steak.'

Stranahan said, 'I'll go get us some take-out.'

'Forget it.'

'You're not hungry?'

'I got about five gallons of poison in my bloodstream, Mick. Some new formula, experimental super juice. I told 'em to go ahead, why the hell not? If it kills just one of those goddamn cells, then I'm for it.'

Stranahan smiled and sat down.

'A man came out to see me the other day. He was using your name, Tim.'

Gavigan's laugh rattled. 'Not too bright. Didn't he know we was friends?'

'Yeah, that's what I mean. He was telling people he was you, trying to find out where my house was.'

'But he didn't tell *you* he was me?'

'No,' Stranahan said.

Gavigan's blue eyes seemed to light up. 'Did he find your place?'

'Unfortunately.'

'And?'

Stranahan thought about how to handle it.

'Hey, Mick, I haven't got loads of time, okay? I mean, I could check out of this life any second now, so don't make me choke the goddamn story out of you.'

Stranahan said, 'It turns out he was a bad guy from back East. Killer for the mob.'

'*Was?*' Gavigan grinned. 'So that's it. And here I thought you'd come by just to see how your old pal was hanging in.'

'That, too,' Stranahan said.

'But first you want me to figure it out, how this pasta-breath tied us together.'

'I don't like the fact that he was using your name.'

'How d'you think I feel?' Gavigan handed Stranahan the dinner tray and told him to set it on the floor. He folded his papery hands on his lap, over the thin woolen blanket. 'How would he know we was friends, Mick? You never call, never send candy. Missed my birthday three years in a row.'

'That's not true, Timmy. Two years ago I sent a strip-o-gram.'

'You sent that broad? I thought she just showed up lonely at the station and picked out the handsomest cop. Hell, Mick, I took her to Grand Bahama for a week, damn near married her.'

Stranahan was feeling better; Timmy knew something. Stranahan could tell from the eyes. It had come back to him.

Gavigan said, 'Mick, that girl had the finest nipples I ever saw. I meant to thank you.'

'Anytime.'

'Like Susan B. Anthony dollars, that's how big they were. Same shape, too. Octagonal.' Gavigan winked. 'You remember the Barletta thing?'

'Sure.' A missing-person's case that had turned into a possible kidnap. The victim was a twenty-two-year-old University of Miami student. Victoria Barletta: brown eyes, black hair, five eight, one hundred and thirty pounds. Disappeared on a rainy March afternoon.

Still unsolved.

'We had our names in the paper,' Gavigan said. 'I still got the clipping.'

Stranahan remembered. There was a press conference. Victoria's parents offered a $10,000 reward. Timmy was there from Homicide, Stranahan from the State Attorney's Office. Both of them were quoted in the story, which ran on the front pages of the *Herald* and the *Miami News*.

Gavigan coughed in a way that startled Mick Stranahan. It sounded like Timmy's lungs had turned to custard.

'Hand me that cup,' Gavigan said. 'Know what? That was the only time we made the papers together.'

'Timmy, we got in the papers all the time.'

'Yeah, but not together.' He slurped down some ginger ale and pointed a pale bony finger at Stranahan. 'Not together, bucko, trust me. I save all the clippings for my scrapbook. Don't you?'

Stranahan said no.

'You *wouldn't*.' Gavigan hacked out a laugh.

'So you think this Mafia guy got it out of the papers?'

'Not the Mafia guy,' Gavigan said, 'but the guy who hired him. It's a good possibility.'

'The Barletta thing was four years ago, Timmy.'

'Hey, I ain't the only one who keeps scrapbooks.'

He yawned. 'Think hard on this, Mick, it's probably important.'

Stranahan stood up and said, 'You get some rest, buddy.'

'I'm glad you took care of that prick who was using my name.'

'Hey, I don't know what you're talking about.'

'Yeah, you do.' Gavigan smiled. 'Anyway, I'm glad you took care of him. He had no business lying like that, using my name.'

Stranahan pulled the blanket up to his friend's neck.

'Good night, Timmy.'

'Be careful, Mick,' the old cop said. 'Hey, and when I croak, you save the newspaper clipping, okay? Glue it on the last page of my scrapbook.'

'It's a promise.'

'Unless it don't make the papers.'

'It'll make the damn papers,' Stranahan said. 'Buried back in the truss ads, where you belong.'

Timmy Gavigan laughed so hard, he had to ring the nurse for oxygen.

3

Four days after the Mafia man came to murder him, Mick
Stranahan got up early and took the skiff to the marina. There
he jump-started his old Chrysler Imperial and drove down to
Gables-by-the-Sea, a ritzy but misnomered neighborhood where
his sister Kate lived with her degenerate lawyer husband and
three teenaged daughters from two previous marriages (his, not
hers). The subdivision was nowhere near the ocean but fronted
a series of man-made canals that emptied into Biscayne Bay.
No one complained about this marketing deception, as it was
understood by buyers and sellers alike that Gables-by-the-Sea
sounded much more toney than Gables-on-the-Canal. The price
of the real estate duly reflected this exaggeration.

Stranahan's sister lived in a big split-level house with five bedrooms, a swimming pool, a sauna, and a putting green in the
yard. Her lawyer husband even bought a thirty-foot sailboat to
go with the dock out back, although he couldn't tell his fore from
his aft. The sight of the sparkling white mast poking over the top
of the big house made Stranahan shake his head as he pulled
into the driveway—Kate's husband was positively born for
South Florida.

When Stranahan's sister came to the door, she said, 'Well, look
who's here.'

Stranahan kissed her and said, 'Is Jocko home?'

'His name's not Jocko.'

'He's a circus ape, Katie, that's a fact.'

'His name's not Jocko, so lay off.'

'Where's the blue Beemer?'

'We traded it.'

Stranahan followed his sister into the living room, where one of the girls was watching MTV and never looked up.

'Traded for what?'

'A Maserati,' Kate said, adding: 'The sedan, not the sporty one.'

'Perfect,' Stranahan said.

Kate made a sad face, and Stranahan gave her a little hug; it killed him to think his little sister had married a sleazeball ambulance chaser. Kipper Garth's face was on highway billboards up and down the Gold Coast—'If you've had an accident, somebody somewhere owes you money!!! Dial 555-TORT.' Kipper Garth's firm was called The Friendly Solicitors, and it proved to be a marvelously lucrative racket. Kipper Garth culled through thousands of greedy complainants, dumping the losers and farming out the good cases to legitimate personal-injury lawyers, with whom he would split the fees fifty-fifty. In this way Kipper Garth made hundreds of thousands of dollars without ever setting his Bally loafers on a courtroom floor, which (given his general ignorance of the law) was a blessing for his clients.

'He's playing tennis,' Kate said.

'I'm sorry for what I said,' Stranahan told her. 'You know how I feel.'

'I wish you'd give him a chance, Mick. He's got some fine qualities.'

If you like tapeworms, Stranahan thought. He could scarcely hear Kate over the Def Leppard video on the television, so he motioned her to the kitchen.

'I came by to pick up my shotgun,' he said.

His sister's eyes went from green to gray, like when they were kids and she was onto him.

'I got a seagull problem out at the house,' Stranahan said.

Kate said, 'Oh? What happened to those plastic owls?'

'Didn't work,' Stranahan said. 'Gulls just crapped all over 'em.'

They went into Kipper Garth's study, the square footage of which exceeded that of Stranahan's entire house. His shotgun, a Remington pump, was locked up with some fancy filigreed bird guns in a maplewood rack. Kate got the key from a drawer in her husband's desk. Stranahan took the Remington down and looked it over.

Kate noticed his expression and said, 'Kip used it once or twice up North. For pheasant.'

'He could've cleaned off the mud, at least.'

'Sorry, Mick.'

'The man is hopeless.'

Kate touched his arm and said, 'He'll be home in an hour. Would you stay?'

'I can't.'

'As a favor, please. I'd like you to straighten out this lawsuit nonsense once and for all.'

'Nothing to straighten out, Katie. The little monkey wants to sue me, fine. I understand.'

The dispute stemmed from a pending disbarment proceeding against Kipper Garth, who stood accused of defrauding an insurance company. One of Kipper Garth's clients had claimed eighty percent disability after tripping over a rake on the seventeenth hole of a golf course. Three days after the suit had been filed, the man was dumb enough to enter the 26-kilometer Orange Bowl Marathon, dumb enough to finish third, and dumb enough to give interviews to several TV sportscasters.

It was such an egregious scam that even the Florida Bar couldn't ignore it, and with no encouragement Mick Stranahan had stepped forward to testify against his own brother-in-law. Some of what Stranahan had said was fact, and some was opinion; Kipper Garth liked none of it and had threatened to sue for defamation.

'It's getting ridiculous,' Kate said. 'It really is.'

'Don't worry, he won't file,' Stranahan said. 'He couldn't find the goddamn courthouse with a map.'

'Will you ever let up? This is my husband you're talking about.'

Stranahan shrugged. 'He's treating you well?'

'Like a princess. Now will you let up?'

'Sure, Katie.'

At the door, she gave him a worried look and said, 'Be careful with the gun, Mick.'

'No problem,' he said. 'Tell Jocko I was here.'

'Not hello? Or maybe Happy New Year?'
'No, just tell him I was here. That's all.'

Stranahan got back to the marina and wrapped the shotgun in an oilcloth and slipped it lengthwise under the seats of the skiff. He headed south in a biting wind, taking spray over the port side and bouncing hard in the troughs. It took twenty-five minutes to reach the stilt house; Stranahan idled in on a low tide. As soon as he tied off, he heard voices up above and bare feet on the planks.

He unwrapped the shotgun and crept up the stairs.

Three naked women were stretched out sunning on the deck. One of them, a slender brunette, looked up and screamed. The others reflexively scrambled for their towels.

Stranahan said, 'What are you doing on my house?'

'Are you going to shoot us?' the brunette asked.

'I doubt it.'

'We didn't know this place was yours,' said another woman, a bleached blonde with substantial breasts.

Stranahan muttered and opened the door, which was padlocked from the outside. This happened occasionally—sunbathers or drunken kids climbing up on the place when he wasn't home. He put the gun away, got a cold beer, and came back out. The women had wrapped themselves up and were gathering their lotions and Sony Walk-Mans.

'Where's your boat?' Stranahan asked.

'Way out there,' the brunette said, pointing.

Stranahan squinted into the glare. It looked like a big red Formula, towing two skiers. 'Boyfriends?' he said.

The bleached blonde nodded. 'They said this place was deserted. Honest, we didn't know. They'll be back at four.'

'It's all right, you can stay,' he said. 'It's a nice day for the water.' Then he went back inside to clean the shotgun. Before long, the third woman, a true blonde, came in and asked for a glass of water.

'Take a beer,' Stranahan said. 'I'm saving the water.'

She was back to her naked state. Stranahan tried to concentrate on the Remington.

'I'm a model,' she announced, and started talking. Name's Tina, nineteen years old, born in Detroit but moved down here when she was still a baby, likes to model but hates some of the creeps who take the pictures.

'My career is really taking off,' she declared. She sat down on a bar stool, crossed her legs, folded her arms under her breasts.

'So what do you do?' she asked.

'I'm retired.'

'You look awful young to be retired. You must be rich.'

'A billionaire,' Stranahan said, peering through the shiny blue barrel of the shotgun. 'Maybe even a trillionaire. I'm not sure.'

Tina smiled. 'Right,' she said. 'You ever watch *Miami Vice*? I've been on there twice. Both times I played prostitutes, but at least I had some good lines.'

'I don't have a television,' Stranahan said. 'Sorry I missed it.'

'Know what else? I dated Don Johnson.'

'I bet that looks good on the résumé.'

'He's a really nice guy,' Tina remarked, 'not like they say.'

Stranahan glanced up and said, 'I think your tan's fading.'

Tina the model looked down at herself, seemed to get tangled up in a thought. 'Can I ask you a favor?'

A headache was taking seed in Mick Stranahan's brain. He actually felt it sprouting, like ragweed, out of the base of his skull.

Tina stood up and said: 'I want you to look at my boobs.'

'I have. They're lovely.'

'Please, look again. Closer.'

Stranahan screwed the Remington shut and laid it across his lap. He sat up straight and looked directly at Tina's breasts. They seemed exquisite in all respects.

She said, 'Are they lined up okay?'

'Appear to be.'

'Reason I ask, I had one of those operations. You know, a boob job. For the kind of modeling I do, it was necessary. I mean, I was about a thirty-two A, if you can imagine.'

Stranahan just shook his head. He felt unable to contribute to the conversation.

'Anyway, I paid three grand for this boob job and it's really helped, workwise. Except the other day I did a *Penthouse* tryout and the photog makes some remark about my tits. Says I got a gravity problem on the left side.'

Stranahan studied the two breasts and said, 'Would that be your left or my left?'

'Mine.'

'Well, he's nuts,' Stranahan said. 'They're both perfect.'

'You're not just saying that?'

'I'll prove it,' he said, thinking: I can't believe I'm doing this. He went to the pantry and rummaged noisily until he found what he was searching for, a carpenter's level.

Tina eyed it and said, 'I've seen one of those.'

'Hold still,' Stranahan said.

'What are you going to do?'

'Just watch the bubble.'

The level was a galvanized steel ruler with a clear cylinder of amber liquid fixed in the middle. Inside the cylinder was a bubble of air, which moved in the liquid according to the angle being measured. If the surface was dead level, the bubble sat at the midway point of the cylinder.

Stranahan placed the tool across Tina's chest, so that each end rested lightly on a nipple.

'Now look down slowly, Tina.'

' 'Kay.'

'Where's the bubble?' he said.

'Smack dab in the center.'

'Right,' Stranahan said. 'See—they're lined up perfectly.'

He lifted the ruler off her chest and set it on the bar. Tina beamed and gave herself a little squeeze, which caused her to bounce in a truly wonderful way. Stranahan decided to clean the shotgun one more time.

'Well, back to the sunshine,' Tina laughed, sprinting bare-assed out the door.

'Back to the sunshine,' Mick Stranahan said, thinking that there was no sight in the world like a young lady completely at ease with herself, even if it cost three grand to get that way.

At four-thirty, the red Formula full of husky boyfriends roared up. Stranahan was reading on the sun deck, paying little attention to the naked women. The water was way too shallow for the ski boat, so the boyfriends idled it about fifty yards from the stilt house. After a manly huddle, one of them hopped to the bow and shouted at Mick Stranahan.

'Hey, what the hell are you doing?'

Stranahan glanced up from the newspaper and said nothing. Tina called out to the boat, 'It's okay. He lives here.'

'Put your clothes on!' hollered one of the guys in the boat, probably Tina's boyfriend.

Tina wiggled into a T-shirt. All the boyfriends appeared to be fairly agitated by Stranahan's presence among the nude women. Stranahan stood up and told the girls the water was too low for the ski boat.

'I'll run you out there in the skiff,' he said.

'You better not, Richie's real upset,' Tina said.

'Richie should have more faith in his fellow man.'

The three young women gathered their towels and suntan oils and clambered awkwardly into Stranahan's skiff. He jacked the outboard up a couple notches, so the prop wouldn't hit bottom, and steered out toward the red Formula in the channel. Once alongside the ski boat, he helped the girls climb up one at a time. Tina even gave him a peck on the cheek as she left.

The boyfriends were every bit as dumb and full of themselves as Stranahan figured. Each one wore a gold chain on his chest, which said it all.

'What was that about?' snarled the boyfriend called Richie, after witnessing Tina's good-bye peck.

'Nothing,' Tina said. 'He's an all-right guy.'

Stranahan had already let go, and the skiff had drifted a few yards beyond the ski boat, when Richie slapped Tina for being such a slut. Then he pointed out at Stranahan and yelled something extremely rude.

The boyfriends were quite surprised to see the aluminum skiff coming back at them, fast. They were equally amazed at the nimbleness with which the big stranger hopped onto the bow of their boat.

Richie took an impressive roundhouse swing at the guy, but

the next thing the other boyfriends knew, Richie was flat on his back with the ski rope tied around both feet. Suddenly he was in the water, and the boat was moving, and Richie was dragging in the salt spray and yowling at the top of his lungs. The other boyfriends tried to seize the throttle, but the stranger knocked them down quickly and with a minimum of effort.

After about three-quarters of a mile, Tina and the other women asked Stranahan to please stop the speedboat, and he did. He grabbed the ski rope and hauled Richie back in, and they all watched him vomit up sea water for ten minutes straight.

'You're a stupid young man,' Stranahan counseled. 'Don't ever come out here again.'

Then Stranahan got in the skiff and went back to the stilt house, and the Formula sped away. Stranahan fixed himself a drink and stretched out on the sun deck. He was troubled by what was happening to the bay, when boatloads of idiots could spoil the whole afternoon. It was becoming a regular annoyance, and Stranahan could foresee a time when he might have to move away.

By late afternoon most of the other boats had cleared out of Stiltsville, except for a cabin cruiser that anchored on the south side of the radio towers in about four feet of water. A very odd location, Stranahan thought. On this boat he counted three people; one seemed to be pointing something big and black in the direction of Stranahan's house.

Stranahan went inside and came back with the shotgun, utterly useless at five hundred yards, and the binoculars, which were not. Quickly he got the cabin cruiser into focus and determined that what was being aimed at him was not a big gun, but a portable television camera.

The people in the cabin cruiser were taking his picture.

This was the capper. First the Mafia hit man, then the nude sunbathers and their troglodyte boyfriends, now a bloody TV crew. Stranahan turned his back to the cabin cruiser and kicked off his trousers. This would give them something to think about: moon over Miami. He was in such sour spirits that he didn't even peek over his shoulder to see their reaction when he bent over.

Watching the sun slide low, Mick Stranahan perceived the syncopation of these events as providential; things had changed on the water, all was no longer calm. The emotion that accompanied this realization was not fear, or even anxiety, but disappointment. All these days the tranquility of the bay, its bright and relentless beauty, had lulled him into thinking the world was not so rotten after all.

The minicam on the cabin cruiser reminded him otherwise. Mick Stranahan had no idea what the bastards wanted, but he was sorely tempted to hop in the skiff and go find out. In the end, he simply finished his gin and tonic and went back inside the stilt house. At dusk, when the light was gone, the boat pulled anchor and motored away.

4

After quitting the State Attorney's Office, Stranahan had kept his gold investigator's badge to remind people that he used to work there, in case he needed to get back inside. Like now.

A young assistant state attorney, whose name was Dreeson, took Stranahan to an interview room and handed him the Barletta file, which must have weighed four pounds. In an officious voice, the young prosecutor said:

'You can sit here and make notes, Mr. Stranahan. But it's still an open case, so don't take anything out.'

'You mean I can't blow my nose on the affidavits?'

Dreeson made a face and shut the door, hard.

Stranahan opened the jacket, and the first thing to fall out was a photograph of Victoria Barletta. Class picture, clipped from the 1985 University of Miami student yearbook. Long dark hair, brushed to a shine; big dark eyes; a long sharp nose, probably her old man's; gorgeous Italian smile, warm and laughing and honest.

Stranahan set the picture aside. He had never met the girl, never would.

He skimmed the statements taken so long ago by himself and Timmy Gavigan: the parents, the boyfriend, the sorority sisters. The details of the case came back to him quickly in a cold flood.

On March 12, 1986, Victoria Barletta had gotten up early, jogged three miles around the campus, showered, attended a 9 A.M. class in advanced public relations, met her boyfriend at a breakfast shop near Mark Light Field, then bicycled to an 11 A.M. seminar on the history of television news. Afterwards, Vicky went back to the Alpha Chi Omega house, changed into jeans, sneakers, and a sweatshirt, and asked a sorority sister to give her a lift to a doctor's appointment in South Miami, only three miles from the university.

The appointment was scheduled for 1:30 P.M. at a medical build-ing called the Durkos Center. As Vicky got out of the car, she instructed her friend to come back at about 5 P.M. and pick her up. Then she went inside and got a nose job and was never seen again.

According to a doctor and a nurse at the clinic, Vicky Barletta left the office at about 4:50 P.M. to wait on the bus bench out front for her ride back to campus. Her face was splotched, her eyes swollen to slits, and her nose heavily bandaged—not exactly a tempting sight for your average trolling rapist, Timmy Gavigan had pointed out.

Still, they both knew better than to rule it out. One minute the girl was on the bench, the next she was gone.

Three county buses had stopped there between 4:50 and 5:14 P.M., when Vicky's friend finally arrived at the clinic. None of the bus drivers remembered seeing a woman with a busted-up face get on board.

So the cops were left to assume that somebody snatched Vic-toria Barletta off the bus bench moments after she emerged from The Durkos Center.

The case was treated like a kidnapping, though Gavigan and Stranahan suspected otherwise. The Barlettas had no money and no access to any; Vicky's father was half-owner of a car wash in Evanston, Illinois. Aside from a couple of cranks, there were no ransom calls made to the family, or to the police. The girl was just plain gone, and undoubtedly dead.

Rereading the file four years later, Mick Stranahan began to feel frustrated all over again. It was the damnedest thing: Vicky had told no one—not her parents, her boyfriend, nobody—about the cosmetic surgery; apparently it was meant to be a surprise.

Stranahan and Timmy Gavigan had spent a total of fifteen hours interviewing Vicky's boyfriend and wound up believing him. The kid had cried pathetically; he used to tease Vicky about her shnoz. 'My little anteater,' he used to call her. The boyfriend had been shattered by what happened, and blamed himself: His birthday was March twentieth. Obviously, he sobbed, the new nose was Vicky's present to him.

From a homicide investigator's point of view, the secrecy with which Victoria Barletta planned her doctor's visit meant something else: It limited the suspects to somebody who just happened to be passing by, a random psychopath.

A killer who was never caught.

A victim who was never found.

That was how Mick Stranahan remembered it. He scribbled a few names and numbers on a pad, stuffed everything into the file, then carried it back to a pock-faced clerk.

'Tell me something,' Stranahan said, 'how'd you happen to have this one downtown?'

The clerk said, 'What do you mean?'

'I mean, this place didn't used to be so efficient. Used to take two weeks to dig out an old case like this.'

'You just got lucky,' the clerk said. 'We pulled the file from the warehouse a week ago.'

'This file here?' Stranahan tapped the green folder. 'Same one?'

'Mr. Eckert wanted to see it.'

Gerry Eckert was the State Attorney. He hadn't personally gone to court in at least sixteen years, so Stranahan doubted if he even remembered how to read a file.

'So how's old Gerry doing?'

'Just dandy,' said the clerk, as if Eckert were his closest, dearest pal in the world. 'He's doing real good.'

'Don't tell me he's finally gonna pop somebody in this case.'

'I don't think so, Mr. Stranahan. He just wanted to refresh his memory before he went on TV. The Reynaldo Flemm show.'

Stranahan whistled. Reynaldo Flemm was a television journalist who specialized in sensational crime cases. He was nationally famous for getting beaten up on camera, usually by the very hoodlums he was trying to interview. No matter what kind of elaborate disguise Reynaldo Flemm would devise, he was always too vain to cover his face. Naturally the crooks would recognize him instantly and bash the living shit out of him. For pure action footage, it was hard to beat; Reynaldo Flemm's specials were among the highest-rated programs on television.

'So Gerry's hit the big time,' Stranahan said.

'Yep,' the clerk said.

'What did he say about this case?'

'Mr. Eckert?'

'Yeah, what did he tell this TV guy?'

The clerk said, 'Well, I wasn't there for the taping. But from what I heard, Mr. Eckert said the whole thing is still a mystery.'

'Well, that's true enough.'

'And Mr. Eckert told Mr. Flemm that he wouldn't be one bit surprised if someday it turns out that Victoria Barletta ran away. Just took one look at her face and ran away. Otherwise, why haven't they found a body?'

Stranahan thought: Eckert hasn't changed a bit, still dumb as a bull gator.

'I can't wait to see the show,' Stranahan remarked.

'It's scheduled to be on March twelfth at nine P.M.' The clerk held up a piece of paper. 'We got a memo from Mr. Eckert today.'

The man from New Jersey did not call Dr. Rudy Graveline again for four days. Then, on the afternoon of January eighth, Rudy got a message on his beeper. The beeper went off at a bad moment, when Rudy happened to be screwing the young wife of a Miami Dolphins wide receiver. The woman had come to Whispering Palms for a simple consult—a tiny pink scar along her jawline, could it be fixed?—and the next thing she knew, the doctor had her talking about all kinds of personal things, including how lonely it got at home during the football season when Jake's mind was on the game and nothing else. Well, the next thing she knew, the doctor was taking her to lunch in his black Jaguar sedan with the great Dolby sound system, and the football player's wife found herself thinking how the rich smell of leather upholstery made her hot, really hot, and then—as if he could read her mind—the doctor suddenly pulled off the Julia Tuttle Causeway, parked the Jag in some pepper trees, and started to gnaw her panties off. He even made cute little squirrel noises as he nuzzled between her legs.

Before long the doctor was merrily pounding away while the football player's wife gazed up at him through the spokes of the walnut steering wheel, under which her head had become uncomfortably wedged.

When the beeper went off on Dr. Graveline's belt, he scarcely missed a beat. He glanced down at the phone number (glowing in bright green numerals) and snatched the car phone from its cradle in the glove box. With one hand he managed to dial the long-distance number even as he finished with the football player's wife, who by this time was silently counting down, hoping he'd hurry it up. She'd had about all she could take of the smell of new leather.

Dr. Graveline pulled away just as the phone started ringing somewhere in New Jersey.

The man answered on the fourth ring. 'Yeah, what?'

'It's me. Rudy.'

'You been jogging or what?'

'Something like that.'

'Sounds like you're gonna have a fuckin' heart attack.'

Dr. Graveline said: 'Give me a second to catch my breath.'

The football player's wife was squirming back into her slacks. The look on her face suggested disappointment at her partner's performance, but Rudy Graveline did not notice.

'About the deal,' he said. 'I don't think so.'

Curly Eyebrows in New Jersey said: 'Your problem musta gone away.'

'Not really.'

'Then what?'

'I'm going to get somebody local.'

The man in New Jersey started to laugh. He laughed and laughed until he began to wheeze.

'Doc, this is a big mistake. Local is no good.'

'I've got a guy in mind,' Dr. Graveline said.

'A Cuban, right? Crazy fuckin' Cuban, I knew it.'

'No, he's not a Cuban.'

'One of my people?'

'No,' Rudy said. 'He's by himself.'

Again Curly Eyebrows laughed. 'Nobody is by himself, Doc. Nobody in this business.'

'This one is different,' Rudy said. Different wasn't the word for it. 'Anyway, I just wanted to let you know, so you wouldn't send anybody else.'

'Suit yourself.'

'And I'm sorry about the other fellow.'

'Don't bring up that shit, hear? You're on one of those cellular phones, I can tell. I hate them things, Doc, they ain't safe. They give off all kinds of fucked-up microwaves, anybody can listen in.'

Dr. Graveline said, 'I don't think so.'

'Yeah, well, I read where people can listen to their blenders and hair dryers and shit. Pick up everything you say.'

The football player's wife was brushing on fresh makeup, using the vanity mirror on the back of the sun visor.

The man in Jersey said: 'Your luck, some broad's pickin' us up on her electric dildo. Every word.'

'Talk to you later,' Rudy said.

'One piece of advice,' said Curly Eyebrows. 'This guy you lined up for the job, don't tell him your life story. I mean it, Doc. Give him the name, the address, the dough, and that's it.'

'Oh, I can trust him,' Dr. Graveline said.

'Like hell,' laughed the man in New Jersey, and hung up.

The football player's wife flipped the sun visor up, closed her compact, and said, 'Business?'

'Yes, I dabble in real estate.' Rudy zipped up his pants. 'I've decided to go with a Miami broker.'

The woman shrugged. She noticed her pink bikini panties on the floor-mat, and quickly put them in her purse. They were ruined; the doctor had chewed a hole in them.

'Can I drive your car back to the office?' she asked.

'No,' said Rudy Graveline. He got out and walked around to the driver's side. The football player's wife slid across the seat, and Rudy got in.

'I almost forgot,' the woman said, fingering the place on her jaw, 'about my scar.'

'A cinch,' the doctor said. 'We can do it under local anesthetic, make it smooth as silk.'

The football player's wife smiled. 'Really?'

'Oh sure, it's easy,' Rudy said, steering the Jaguar back on the highway. 'But I was wondering about something else . . .'

'Yes?'

'You won't mind some friendly professional advice?'

'Of course not.' The woman's voice held an edge of concern.

'Well, I couldn't help but notice,' Dr. Graveline said, 'when we were making love . . .'

'Yes?'

Without taking his eyes off the road, he reached down and patted her hip. 'You could use a little suction around the saddlebags.'

The football player's wife turned away and blinked.

'Please don't be embarrassed,' the doctor said. 'This is my specialty, after all. Believe me, darling, I've got an eye for perfection, and you're only an inch or two away.'

She took a little breath and said, 'Around the thighs?'

'That's all.'

'How much would it cost?' she asked with a trace of a sniffle.

Rudy Graveline smiled warmly and passed her a monogrammed handkerchief. 'Less than you think,' he said.

The cabin cruiser with the camera crew came back again, anchored in the same place. Stranahan sighed and spit hard into the tide. He was in no mood for this.

He was standing on the dock with a spinning rod in his hands, catching pinfish from around the pilings of the stilt house. Suspended motionless in the gin-clear water below was a dark blue log, or so it would have appeared to the average tourist. The log measured about five feet long and, when properly motivated, could streak through the water at about sixty knots to make a kill. Teeth were the trademark of the Great Barracuda, and the monster specimen that Mick Stranahan called Liza had once left thirteen needle-sharp incisors in a large plastic mullet that some moron had trolled through the Biscayne Channel. Since that episode the barracuda had more or less camped beneath Stranahan's place. Every afternoon he went out and caught for its supper a few dollar-sized pinfish, which he tossed off the dock, and which the barracuda devoured in lightning flashes that churned the water and sent the mangrove snappers diving for cover. Liza's teeth had long since grown back.

Because of his preoccupation with the camera boat, Mick Stranahan allowed the last pinfish to stay on the line longer than he should have. It tugged back and forth, sparkling just below the surface until the barracuda ran out of patience. Before Stranahan could react, the big fish rocketed from under the stilt house and severed the majority of the pinfish as cleanly as a scalpel; a quivering pair of fish lips was all that remained on Stranahan's hook.

'Nice shot,' he mumbled and stored the rod away.

He climbed into the skiff and motored off the flat, toward the cabin cruiser. The photographer immediately put down the video camera; Stranahan could see him conferring with the rest of the crew. There was a brief and clumsy attempt to raise the anchor, followed by the sound of the boat's engine whining impotently in the way that cold outboards do. Finally the crew gave up and just waited for the big man in the skiff, who by now was within hailing distance.

A stocky man with a lacquered helmet of black hair and a stiff bottle-brush mustache stood on the transom of the boat and shouted, 'Ahoy there!'

Stranahan cut the motor and let the skiff coast up to the cabin cruiser. He tied off on a deck cleat, stood up, and said, 'Did I hear you right? Did you actually say *ahoy*?'

The man with the mustache nodded uneasily.

'Where did you learn that, watching pirate movies? Jesus Christ, I can't believe you said that. *Ahoy there!* Give me a break.' Stranahan was really aggravated. He jumped into the bigger boat and said, 'Which one of you assholes is Reynaldo Flemm? Let me guess; it's Captain Blood here.'

The stocky man with the mustache puffed out his chest and said, 'Watch it, pal!' —which took a certain amount of courage, since Mick Stranahan was holding a stainless-steel tarpon gaff in his right hand. Flemm's crew—an overweight cameraman and an athletic young woman in blue jeans—kept one eye on their precious equipment and the other on the stranger with the steel hook.

Stranahan said, 'Why have you been taking my picture?'

'For a story,' Flemm said. 'For television.'

'What's the story?'

'I'm not at liberty to say.'

Stranahan frowned. 'What's it got to do with Vicky Barletta?'

Reynaldo Flemm shook his head. 'In due time, Mr. Stranahan. When we're ready to do the interview.'

Stranahan said, 'I'm ready to do the interview now.'

Flemm smiled in a superior way. 'Sorry.'

Stranahan slipped the tarpon gaff between Reynaldo Flemm's legs and gave a little jerk. The tip of the blade not only poked through Reynaldo Flemm's Banana Republic trousers, but also through his thirty-dollar bikini underpants (flamenco red), which he had purchased at a boutique in Coconut Grove. The cold point of the gaff came to rest on Reynaldo Flemm's scrotum, and at this frightful instant the air rushed from his intestinal tract with a sharp noise that seemed to punctuate Mick Stranahan's request.

'The interview,' he said again to Flemm, who nodded energetically.

But words escaped the television celebrity. Try as he might, Flemm could only burble in clipped phrases. Fear, and the absence of cue cards, had robbed him of cogent conversation.

The young woman in blue jeans stepped forward from the cabin of the boat and said, 'Please, Mr. Stranahan, we didn't mean to intrude.'

'Of course you did.'

'My name is Christina Marks. I'm the producer of this segment.'

'Segment of what?' Stranahan asked.

'Of the Reynaldo Flemm show. *In Your Face*. You must have seen it.'

'Never.'

For Reynaldo, Stranahan knew, this was worse than a gaff in the balls.

'Come on,' Christina Marks said.

'Honest,' Stranahan said. 'You see a TV dish over on my house?'

'Well, no.'

'There you go. Now, what's this all about? And hurry it up, your man here looks like his legs are cramping.'

Indeed, Reynaldo Flemm was shaking on his tiptoes. Stranahan eased the gaff down just a notch or two.

Christina Marks said: 'Do you know a nurse named Maggie Gonzalez?'

'Nope,' Stranahan said.

'Are you sure?'

'Give me a hint.'

'She worked at the Durkos Medical Center.'

'Okay, now I remember.' He had taken her statement the day after Victoria Barletta had vanished. Timmy Gavigan had done the doctor, while Stranahan had taken the nurse. He had scanned the affidavits in the State Attorney's file that morning.

'You sure about the last name?' Stranahan asked.

'Sorry—Gonzalez is her married name. Back then it was Orestes.'

'So let's have the rest.'

'About a month ago, in New York, she came to us.'

'To me,' croaked Reynaldo Flemm.

'Shut up,' said Stranahan.

Christina Marks went on: 'She said she had some important information about the Barletta case. She indicated she was willing to talk on camera.'

'To me,' Flemm said, before Stranahan tweaked him once more with the tarpon gaff.

'But first,' Christina Marks said, 'she said she had to speak to you, Mr. Stranahan.'

'About what?'

'All she said was that she needed to talk to you first, because you could do something about it. And don't ask me about what, because I don't know. We gave her six hundred bucks, put her on a plane to Florida, and never saw her again. She was supposed to be back two weeks ago last Monday.' Christina Marks put her hands in her pockets. 'That's all there is. We came down here to look for Maggie Gonzalez, and you're the best lead we had.'

Stranahan removed the gaff from Reynaldo Flemm's crotch

and tossed it into the bow of his skiff. Almost instantly, Flemm leapt from the stern and bolted for the cabin. 'Get tape of that fucker,' he cried at the cameraman, 'so we can prosecute his fat ass!'

'Ray, knock it off,' said Christina Marks.

Stranahan liked the way she talked down to the big star. 'Tell him,' he said, 'that if he points that goddamn camera at me again, he'll be auditioning for the Elephant Man on Broadway. That's how seriously I'll mess up his face.'

'Ray,' she said, 'did you hear that?'

'Roll tape! Roll tape!' Flemm was all over the cameraman.

Wearily, Stranahan got back into his skiff and said, 'Miss Marks, the interview is over.'

Now it was her turn to be angry. She hopped up on the transom, tennis shoes squeaking on the teak. 'Wait a minute, that's it?'

Stranahan looked up from his little boat. 'I haven't seen Maggie Gonzalez since the day after the Barletta girl disappeared. That's the truth. I don't know whether she took your money and went south or what, but I haven't heard from her.'

'He's lying,' sneered Reynaldo Flemm, and he stormed into the cabin to sulk. A gust of wind had made a comical nest of his hair.

Stranahan hand-cranked the outboard and slipped it into gear.

'I'm at the Sonesta,' Christina Marks said to him, 'if Maggie Gonzalez should call.'

Not likely, Stranahan thought. Not very likely at all.

'How the hell did you find me, anyway?' he called out to the young TV producer.

'Your ex-wife,' Christina Marks called back from the cabin cruiser.

'Which one?'

'Number four.'

That would be Chloe, Stranahan thought. Naturally.

'How much did it cost you?' he shouted.

Sheepishly, Christina Marks held up five fingers.

'You got off light,' Mick Stranahan said, and turned the skiff homeward.

5

Christina Marks was in bed, reading an old *New Yorker*, when somebody rapped on the door of the hotel room. She was hoping it might be Mick Stranahan, but it wasn't.

'Hello, Ray.'

As Reynaldo Flemm breezed in, he patted her on the rump.

'Cute,' Christina said, closing the door. 'I was getting ready to turn in.'

'I brought some wine.'

'No, thanks.'

Reynaldo Flemm turned on the television and made himself at home. He was wearing another pair of khaki Banana Republic trousers and a baggy denim shirt. He smelled like a bucket of Brut. In a single motion he scissored his legs and propped his white high-top Air Jordans on the coffee table.

Christina Marks tightened the sash on her bathrobe and sat down at the other end of the sofa. 'I'm tired, Ray,' she said.

He acted like he didn't hear it. 'This Stranahan guy, he's the key to it,' Flemm said. 'I think we should follow him tomorrow.'

'Oh, please.'

'Rent a van. A van with smoked window panels. We set the camera on a tripod in back. I'll be driving, so Willie gets the angle over my ... let's see, it'd be my right shoulder. Great shot, through the windshield as we follow this big prick—'

'Willie gets carsick,' Christina Marks said.

Reynaldo Flemm cackled scornfully.

'It's a lousy idea,' Christina said. She wanted him to go away, now.

'What, you trust that Stranahan?'

'No,' she said, but in a way she did trust him. At least more than she trusted Maggie Gonzalez; there was something squirrely about the woman's sudden need to fly to Miami. Why had she said she wanted to see Stranahan? Where had she really gone?

Reynaldo Flemm wasn't remotely concerned about Maggie's motives—good video was good video—but Christina Marks wanted to know more about the woman. She had better things to do than sit in a steaming van, tailing a guy who, if he caught them, would probably destroy every piece of electronics in their possession.

'So, what other leads we got?' Reynaldo Flemm demanded. 'Tell me that.'

'Maggie's probably got family here,' Christina said, 'and friends.'

'Dull, dull, dull.'

'Hard work is dull sometimes,' Christina said sharply, 'but how would you know?'

Flemm sat up straight and flared his upper lip like a chihuahua. 'You can't talk to me like that! You just remember who's the star.'

'And you just remember who writes all your lines. And who does all your dull, dull research. Remember who tells you what questions to ask. And who edits these pieces so you don't come off looking like a pompous airhead.' Except that's exactly how Reynaldo came off, most of the time. There was no way around it, no postproduction wizardry that could disguise the man's true personality on tape.

Reynaldo Flemm shrugged. His attention had been stolen by something on the television: Mike Wallace of CBS was a guest on the Letterman show. Flemm punched up the volume and inched to the edge of the sofa.

'You know how old that geezer is?' he said, pointing at Wallace. 'I'm half his age.'

Christina Marks held her tongue.

Reynaldo said, 'I bet *his* producer sleeps with him anytime he wants.' He glanced sideways at Christina.

She got up, went to the door, and held it open. 'Go back to your room, Ray.'

'Aw, come on, I was kidding.'

'No, you weren't.'

'All right, I wasn't. Come on, Chris, close the door. Let's open the wine.'

'Good night, Ray.'

He got up and turned off the TV. He was sulking.

'I'm sorry,' he said.

'You sure are.'

Christina Marks held all the cards. Reynaldo Flemm needed her far worse than she needed him. Not only was she very talented, but she knew things about Reynaldo Flemm that he did not wish the whole world of television to know. About the time she caught him beating himself up, for example. It happened at a Hyatt House in Atlanta. Flemm was supposed to be out interviewing street-gang members, but Christina found him in the bathroom of his hotel room, thwacking himself in the cheek with a sock full of parking tokens. Reynaldo's idea was to give himself a nasty shiner, then go on camera and breathlessly report that an infamous gang leader named Rapper Otis had assaulted him.

Reynaldo Flemm had begged Christina Marks not to tell the executive producers about the sock incident, and she hadn't; the weeping is what got to her. She couldn't bear it.

For keeping this and other weird secrets, Christina felt secure in her job, certainly secure enough to tell Reynaldo Flemm to go pound salt every time he put the make on her.

On the way out the door, he said, 'I still say we get up early and follow this Stranahan guy.'

'And I still say no.'

'But, Chris, he *knows* something.'

'Yeah, Ray, he knows how to hurt people.'

Christina couldn't be sure, but she thought she saw a hungry spark in the eyes of Reynaldo Flemm.

The next morning Stranahan left the skiff at the marina, got the Chrysler and drove back across the Rickenbacker Causeway to the mainland. Next to him on the front seat was his yellow notepad, open to the page where he had jotted the names and numbers from the Barletta file. The first place he went was the

Durkos Medical Center, except it wasn't there anymore. The building was now occupied entirely by dentists: nine of them, according to Stranahan's count from the office directory. He went looking for the building manager.

Every door and hallway reverberated with the nerve-stabbing whine of high-speed dental drills; soon Stranahan's molars started to throb, and he began to feel claustrophobic. He enlisted a friendly janitor to lead him to the superintendent, a mammoth olive-colored woman who introduced herself as Marlee Jones.

Stranahan handed Marlee Jones a card and told her what he wanted. She glanced at the card and shrugged. 'I don't have to tell you nothing,' she said, displaying the kind of public-spirited cooperation that Stranahan had come to appreciate among the Miami citizenry.

'No, you don't have to tell me nothing,' he said to Marlee, 'but I can make it possible for a county code inspector to brighten your morning tomorrow, and the day after that, and every single day until you die of old age.' Stranahan picked up a broom and stabbed the wooden handle into the foam-tile ceiling. 'Looks like pure asbestos to me,' he said. 'Sure hate for the feds to find out.'

Marlee Jones scowled, exhibiting an impressive array of gold teeth: bribes, no doubt, from her tenants. She shuffled to a metal desk and opened a bottom drawer and got out a black ledger. 'All right, smartass, what was that name?'

'Durkos.' Stranahan spelled it. 'A medical group. They were here as of March twelfth, four years ago.'

'Well, as of April first, four years ago, they was gone.' Marlee started to close the ledger, but Stranahan put his hand on the page.

'May I look?'

'It's just numbers, mister.'

'Aw, let me give it a whirl.' Stranahan took the ledger from Marlee Jones and ran down the columns with his forefinger. The Durkos Medical Trust, Inc., had been sole tenant of the building for two years, but had vacated within weeks after Victoria Barletta's disappearance. The ledger showed that the company had paid its lease and security deposits through May. Stranahan thought it was peculiar that, after moving out, the medical group never got a refund.

'Maybe they didn't ask,' Marlee Jones said.

'Doctors are the cheapest human beings alive,' Stranahan said. 'For fifteen grand they don't just ask, they hire lawyers.'

Again Marlee Jones shrugged. 'Some people be in a big damn hurry.'

'What do you remember about it?'

'Who says I was here?'

'This handwriting in the ledger book—it's the same as on these receipts.' Stranahan tapped a finger on a pile of rental coupons. Marlee Jones appeared to be having a spell of high blood pressure.

Stranahan asked again: 'So what do you remember?'

With a groan Marlee Jones heaved her bottom into the chair behind the desk. She said, 'One night they cleared out. Must've backed up a trailer truck, who knows. I came in, the place was empty, except for a bunch of cheapo paintings on the walls. Cats with big eyes, that sorta shit.'

'Were they all surgeons?'

'Seemed like it. But they wasn't partners.'

'Durkos the main man?'

'Was no Durkos that I heard of. Big man was a Doctor Grave-yard, something like that. The other four guys worked for him. How come I know this is, the day after all the stuff is gone, a couple of the other doctors showed up dressed for work. They couldn't believe their office was emptied.'

Graveline was the name of the surgeon who had operated on Vicky Barletta. There was no point to correcting Marlee Jones on the name. Stranahan said, 'This Dr. Graveyard, he didn't tell the other doctors about the move?'

'This is Miami, lots of people in a big-time hurry.'

'Yeah, but not many pay in advance.'

Marlee Jones finally laughed. 'You right about that.'

'Did anybody leave a forwarding address?'

'Nope.'

Stranahan handed Marlee Jones the ledger book.

'You be through with me?' she asked.

'Yes, ma'am.'

'For good?'

'Most likely.'

'Then can I ask who is it you're workin' for?'

'Myself,' said Mick Stranahan.

Since the day that the Durkos Medical Center had ceased to exist, the life of Nurse Maggie Orestes had gotten complicated. She had gone to work in the emergency room at Jackson Hospital, where one night she had met a man named Ricky Gonzalez. The reason for Ricky Gonzalez's visit to the emergency room was that he had accidentally been run over by a turbocharged Ferrari during the annual running of the Miami Grand Prix. Ricky was a race-car promoter, and he had been posing for pictures with Lorenzo Lamas in pit row, not paying close attention when the Ferrari had roared in and run over both his feet. Ricky broke a total of fourteen bones, while Lorenzo Lamas escaped without a scratch.

Nurse Maggie Orestes attended to Ricky Gonzalez in the emergency room before they put him under for surgery. He was young, dashing, full of promises—and so cheerful, considering what had happened.

A month later they were married at a Catholic church in Hialeah. Ricky persuaded Maggie to quit nursing and be a full-time hostess for the many important social functions that race-car promoters must necessarily conduct. Maggie had hoped she would come to enjoy car racing and the people involved in it, but she didn't. It was noisy and stupid and boring, and the people were worse. Maggie and Ricky had some fierce arguments, and she was on the verge of walking out of the marriage when the second pit-row accident happened.

This time it was a Porsche, and Ricky wasn't so lucky. After the service they cremated him in his complimentary silver Purolator racing jacket, which turned out to be fireproof, so they had to cremate that portion twice. Lorenzo Lamas sent a wreath all the way from Malibu, California. At the wake Ricky's lawyer came up to Maggie Gonzalez and told her the bad news: First, her husband had no life insurance; second, he had emptied their joint bank accounts to pay for his cocaine habit. Maggie had known nothing about the drug problem, but in retrospect it explained her late husband's irrepressible high spirits and also his lack of caution around the race track.

A widowhood of destitution did not appeal to Maggie Gonzalez. She went back to being a nurse with a plan to nail herself a rich doctor or at least his money. In eighteen months she had been through three of them, all disasters—a married pediatrician, a divorced radiologist, and a urologist who wore women's underwear and who wound up giving Maggie a stubborn venereal disease. When she dumped the urologist, he got her fired from the hospital and filed a phony complaint with the state nursing board.

All this left Maggie Gonzalez with a molten hatred of men and a mind for vengeance.

Money is what pushed her to the brink. With the mortgage payment on her duplex coming due, and only eighty-eight bucks in the checking account, Maggie decided to go ahead and do it. Part of the motive was financial desperation, true, but there was also a delicious hint of excitement—payback, to the sonofabitch who'd started it all.

First Maggie used her Visa card to buy a plane ticket to New York, where she caught a cab to the midtown offices of Reynaldo Flemm, the famous television journalist. There she told producer Christina Marks the story of Victoria Barletta, and cut a deal.

Five thousand dollars to repeat it on camera—that's as high as Reynaldo's people would go. Maggie Gonzalez was disappointed; it was, after all, one hell of a story.

That night Christina Marks got Maggie a room at the Goreham Hotel, and she lay there watching Robin Leach on TV and worrying about the risks she was taking. She remembered the State Attorney's investigator who had questioned her nearly four years ago, and how she had lied to him. God, what was she thinking of now? Flemm's people would fly straight to Miami and interview the investigator—Stranahan was his name—and he'd tell them she'd never said a word about all this when it happened. Her credibility would be shot, and so would the five grand. Out the window.

Maggie realized she had to do something about Stranahan.
And also about Dr. Rudy Graveline.

Graveline was a dangerous creep. To rat on Rudy—well, he had warned her. And rewarded her, in a sense. A decent severance, glowing references for a new job. That was after he closed down the Durkos Center.

Lying there, Maggie got another idea. It was wild, but it just might work. The next morning she went back to Christina Marks and made up a vague story about how she had to go see Investigator Stranahan right away, otherwise no TV show. Reluctantly the producer gave her a plane ticket and six hundred in expenses.

Of course, Maggie had no intention of visiting Mick Stranahan. When she got back to Florida, she drove directly to the Whispering Palms Spa and Surgery Center in beautiful Bal Harbour. Dr. Rudy Graveline was very surprised to see her. He led her into a private office and closed the door.

'You look frightened,' the surgeon said.

'I am.'

'And a little bouncy in the bottom.'

'I eat when I'm frightened,' Maggie said, keeping her cool.

'So what is it?' Rudy asked.

'Vicky Barletta,' she said. 'Somebody's making a fuss.'

'Oh.' Rudy Graveline appeared calm. 'Who?'

'One of the investigators. A man named Stranahan.'

'I don't remember him,' Rudy said.

'I do. He's scary.'

'Did he speak to you?'

Maggie shook her head. 'Worse than that,' she said. 'Some TV people came to my place. They're doing a special on missing persons.'

'Christ, don't tell me.'

'Stranahan's going to talk.'

Rudy said, 'But what does he know?'

Maggie blinked. 'I'm worried, Dr. Graveline. It's going to break open all over again.'

'No way.'

Maggie's notion was to get Stranahan out of the way. Whether

Dr. Graveline bribed him, terrorized him, or worse was immaterial; Rudy could get to anybody. Those who stood in his way either got with the program or got run over. One time another surgeon had done a corrective rhinoplasty on one of Rudy's botched-up patients, then badmouthed Rudy at a medical society cocktail party. Rudy got so furious that he paid two goons to trash the other doctor's office, but not before stealing his medical files. Soon, the other doctor's surgical patients received personal letters thanking them for being so understanding while he battled that terrible heroin addiction, which now seemed to be under control. Well, almost . . . By the end of the month, the other doctor had closed what was left of his practice and moved to British Columbia.

Maggie Gonzalez was counting on Rudy Graveline to overreact again; she wanted him worried about Stranahan to the exclusion of all others. By the time the doctor turned on the tube and discovered who was the real threat, Maggie would be long gone. And out of reach.

She went on: 'They won't leave me alone, these TV people. They said the case is going to a grand jury. They said Stranahan's going to testify.' She fished in her purse for a tissue. 'I thought you ought to know.'

Rudy Graveline thanked her for coming. He told her not to worry, everything was going to be fine. He suggested she get out of town for a few weeks, and she said that was probably a good idea. He asked if there was anywhere in particular she wanted to go, and she said New York. The doctor said New York is a swell place to visit around Christmas time, and he wrote out a personal check for twenty-five hundred dollars. He recommended that Maggie stay gone for at least a month, and said to call if she needed more money. *When*, Maggie said. Not *if* she needed more money, but when.

Later that same afternoon, Dr. Rudy Graveline had locked his office door and made a telephone call to a seafood restaurant in New Jersey. He talked to a man who probably had curly eyebrows, a man who promised to send somebody down around the first of the year.

On the day that Tony Traviola, the first hitman, arrived to kill Mick Stranahan, Maggie Gonzalez was in a tenth-floor room at the Essex House hotel. The room had a view of Central Park, where Maggie was taking skating lessons at Donald Trump's ice rink. She planned to lay low for a few more weeks, maybe stop in for a chat at *20/20*. A little competition never hurt. Maybe Reynaldo Flemm would get worried enough to jack up his offer. Five grand sucked, it really did.

Dr. Rudy Graveline made an appointment with the second killer for January tenth at three in the afternoon. The man arrived at Whispering Palms a half-hour early and sat quietly in the waiting room, scaring the hell out of the other patients.

Rudy knew him only as Chemo, a cruel but descriptive nickname, for he truly did appear to be in the final grim stages of chemotherapy. Black hair sprouted in random wisps from a blue-veined scalp. His lips were thin and papery, the color of wet cement. Red-rimmed eyes peered back at gawkers with a dull and chilling indifference; the hooded lids blinked slowly, pellucid as a salamander's. And the skin—the skin is what made people gasp, what emptied the waiting room at Whispering Palms. Chemo's skin looked like breakfast cereal, like somebody had glued Rice Krispies to every square centimeter of his face.

This, and the fact that he stood six foot nine, made Chemo a memorable sight.

Dr. Graveline was not alarmed, because he knew how Chemo had come to look this way: It was not melanoma, but a freak electrolysis accident in Scranton, many years before. While burning two ingrown hair follicles off the tip of Chemo's nose, an elderly dermatologist had suffered a crippling stroke and lost all hand-eye coordination. Valiantly the old doctor had tried to complete the procedure, but in so doing managed to incinerate every normal pore within range of the electrified needle. Since Chemo had eaten five Valiums for breakfast, he was fast asleep on the table when the tragedy occurred. When he awoke to find his whole face blistered up like a lobster, he immediately garrotted the dermatologist and fled the State of Pennsylvania forever.

Chemo had spent the better part of five years on the lam, seeking medical relief; ointments proved futile, and in fact a faulty prescription had caused the startling Rice Krispie effect. Eventually Chemo came to believe that the only hope was cosmetic surgery, and his quest for a miracle brought him naturally to Florida and naturally into the care of Dr. Rudy Graveline.

At three sharp, Rudy motioned Chemo into the consultation room. Chemo ducked as he entered and shut the door behind him. He sat in an overstuffed chair and blinked moistly at Dr. Graveline.

Rudy said: 'And how are we doing today?'

Chemo grunted. 'How do you think?'

'When you were here a few weeks ago, we discussed a treatment plan. You remember?'

'Yep,' Chem said.

'And a payment plan, too.'

'How could I forget?' Chemo said.

Dr. Graveline ignored the sarcasm; the man had every right to be bitter.

'Dermabrasion is expensive,' Rudy said.

'I don't know why,' Chemo said. 'You just stick my face in a belt sander, right?'

The doctor smiled patiently. 'It's a bit more sophisticated than that—'

'But the principle's the same.'

Rudy nodded. 'Roughly speaking.'

'So how can it be two hundred bucks a pop?'

'Two hundred and ten,' Rudy corrected. 'Because it requires uncommonly steady hands. You can appreciate that, I'm sure.'

Chemo smiled at the remark. Rudy wished he hadn't; the smile was harrowing, a deadly weapon all by itself. Chemo looked like he'd been teething on cinderblocks.

'I *did* get a job,' he said.

Dr. Graveline agreed that was a start.

'At the Gay Bidet,' Chemo said. 'It's a punk club down on South Beach. I'm a greeter.' Again with the smile.

'A greeter,' said Rudy. 'Well, well.'

'I keep out the scum,' Chemo explained.

Rudy asked about the pay. Chemo said he got six bucks an hour, not including tips.

'Not bad,' Rudy said, 'but still . . .' He scribbled some figures on a pad, then took a calculator out of his desk and punched on it for a while. All very dramatic.

Chemo stretched his neck to look. 'What's the damage?'

'I figure twenty-four visits, that's a minimum,' Rudy said. 'Say we do one square inch every session.'

'Shit, just do it all at once.'

'Can't,' Rudy lied, 'not with dermabrasion. Say twenty-four visits at two ten each, that's—'

'Five thousand and forty dollars,' Chemo muttered. 'Jesus H. Christ.'

Dr. Graveline said: 'I don't need it all at once. Give me half to start.'

'Jesus H. Christ.'

Rudy put the calculator away.

'I just started at the club a week ago,' Chemo said. 'I gotta buy groceries.'

Rudy came around the desk and sat down on the edge. In a fatherly tone he asked: 'You have Blue Cross?'

'The fuck, I'm a fugitive, remember?'

'Of course.'

Rudy shook his head and mused. It was all so sad, that a great country like ours couldn't provide minimal health care to all its citizens.

'So I'm screwed,' Chemo said.

'Not necessarily.' Dr. Graveline rubbed his chin. 'I've got an idea.'

'Yeah?'

'It's a job I need done.'

If Chemo had had eyebrows, they would have arched.

'If you could do this job,' Rudy went on, 'I think we could work a deal.'

'A discount?'

'I don't see why not.'

Idly, Chemo fingered the scales on his cheeks. 'What's the job?'

'I need you to kill somebody,' Rudy said.

'Who?'

'A man that could cause me some trouble.'

'What kind of trouble?'

'Could shut down Whispering Palms. Take away my medical license. And that's for starters.'

Chemo ran a bloodless tongue across his lips. 'Who is this man?'

'His name is Mick Stranahan.'

'Where do I find him?'

'I'm not sure,' Rudy said. 'He's here in Miami somewhere.'

Chemo said that wasn't much of a lead. 'I figure a murder is worth at least five grand,' he said.

'Come on, he's not a cop or anything. He's just a regular guy. Three thousand, tops.' Rudy was a bear when it got down to money.

Chemo folded his huge bony hands. 'Twenty treatments, that's my final offer.'

Rudy worked it out in his head. 'That's forty-two hundred dollars!'

'Right.'

'You sure drive a hard bargain,' Rudy said.

Chemo grinned triumphantly. 'So when can you start on my face?'

'Soon as this chore is done.'

Chemo stood up. 'I suppose you'll want proof.'

Rudy Graveline hadn't really thought about it. He said, 'A newspaper clipping would do.'

'Sure you don't want me to bring you something?'

'Like what?'

'A finger,' Chemo said, 'maybe one of his nuts.'

'That won't be necessary,' said Dr. Graveline, 'really it won't.'

6

Stranahan got Maggie Orestes Gonzalez's home address from a friend of his who worked for the state nursing board in Jacksonville. Although Maggie's license was paid up to date, no current place of employment was listed on the file.

The address was a duplex apartment in a quiet old neighborhood off Coral Way, in the Little Havana section of Miami. There was a chain-link fence around a sparse brown yard, a ceramic statue of Santa Barbara in the flower bed, and the customary burglar bars on every window. Stranahan propped open the screen door and knocked three times on the heavy pine frame. He wasn't surprised that no one was home.

To break into Maggie Gonzalez's apartment, Stranahan used a three-inch stainless-steel lockpick that he had confiscated from the mouth of an infamous condominium burglar named Wet Willie Jeeter. Wet Willie got his nickname because he only worked on rainy days; on sunny days he was a golf caddy at the Doral Country Club. When they went through Wet Willie's place after the arrest, the cops found seventeen personally autographed photos of Jack Nicklaus, going back to the 1967 Masters. What the cops did not find was any of Wet Willie's burglar tools, due to the fact that Wet Willie kept them well hidden beneath his tongue.

Stranahan found them when he visited Wet Willie in the Dade County Jail, two weeks before the trial. The purpose of the visit was to make Wet Willie realize the wisdom of pleading guilty and saving the taxpayers the expense of trial. Unspoken was the fact that the State Attorney's Office had a miserably weak case and was desperate for a deal. Wet Willie told Stranahan thanks anyway, but he'd just as soon take his chances with a jury.

Stranahan said fine and offered Wet Willie a stick of Dentyne, which the burglar popped into his mouth without thinking. The chewing dislodged the steel lockpicks, which immediately stuck fast in the Dentyne; the whole mess eventually lodged itself in Wet Willie's throat. For a few hectic minutes Stranahan thought he might have to perform an amateur tracheotomy, but miraculously the burglar coughed up the tiny tools and also a complete confession. Stranahan kept one of Wet Willie's lockpicks as a souvenir.

The lock on Maggie's door was a breeze.

Stranahan slipped inside and noticed how neat the place looked. Someone, probably a neighbor or a relative, had carefully stacked the unopened mail on a table near the front door. On the kitchen counter was a Princess-model telephone attached to an answering machine. Stranahan pressed the Rewind button, then Play, and listened to Maggie's voice say: 'Hi, I'm not home right now so you're listening to another one of those dumb answering machines. Please leave a brief message and I'll get back to you as soon as possible. Bye now!'

Stranahan played the rest of the tape, which was blank. Either Maggie Gonzalez wasn't getting any calls, or someone was taking them for her, or she was phoning in for her own messages with one of those remote pocket beepers. Whatever the circumstances, it was a sign that she probably wasn't all that dead.

Other clues in the apartment pointed to travel. There was no luggage in the closets, no bras or underwear in the bedroom drawers, no makeup on the bathroom sink. The most interesting thing Stranahan found was crumpled in a waste basket in a corner of the living room: a bank deposit slip for twenty-five hundred dollars, dated the twenty-seventh of December.

Have a nice trip, Stranahan thought.

He let himself out, carefully locking the door behind him. Then he drove three blocks to a pay phone at a 7-Eleven, where he dialed Maggie's phone number and left a very important message on her machine.

At the end of the day, Christina Marks dropped her rented Ford Escort with the hotel valet, bought a copy of the *New York Times* at the shop in the lobby, and took the elevator up to her room. Before she could get the key out of the door, Mick Stranahan opened it from the other side.

'Come on in,' he said.

'Nice of you,' Christina said, 'considering it's my room.'

Stranahan noticed she had one of those trendy leather briefcase satchels that you wear over your shoulder. A couple of legal pads stuck out the top.

'You've been busy.'

'You want a drink?'

'Gin and tonic, thanks,' Stranahan said. After a pause: 'I was afraid the great Reynaldo might see me if I waited in the lobby.'

'So you got a key to my room?'

'Not exactly.'

Christina Marks handed him the drink. Then she poured herself a beer, and sat down in a rattan chair with garish floral pillows that were supposed to look tropical.

'I went to see Maggie's family today,' she said.

'Any luck?'

'No. Unfortunately, they don't speak English.'

Stranahan smiled and shook his head.

'What's so funny?' Christina said. 'Just because I don't speak Spanish?'

Stranahan said, 'Except for probably her grandmother, all Maggie's family speaks perfect English. Perfect.'

'What?'

'Her father teaches physics at Palmetto High School. Her mother is an operator for Southern Bell. Her sister Consuelo is a legal secretary, and her brother, whats-his-name . . .'

'Tomás.'

'Tommy, yeah,' Stranahan said. 'He's a senior account executive at Merrill Lynch.'

Christina Marks put down her beer so decisively that it nearly broke the glass coffee table. 'I sat in the living room, talking to these people, and they just stared at me and said—'

'*No habla* English, *señora*.'

'Exactly.'

'Oldest trick in Miami,' Stranahan said. 'They just didn't want to talk. Don't feel bad, they tried the same thing with me.'

'And I suppose you know Spanish.'

'Enough to make them think I knew more. They're worried about Maggie, actually. Been worried for some time. She's had some personal problems, Maggie has. Money problems, too— that much I found out before her old lady started having chest pains.'

'You're kidding.'

'Second oldest trick,' Stranahan said, smiling, 'but I was done anyway. I honestly don't think they know where she is.'

Christina Marks finished her beer and got another from the small hotel refrigerator. When she sat down again, she kicked off her shoes.

'So,' she said, 'you're ahead of us.'

'You and Reynaldo?'

'The crew,' Christina said, looking stung.

'No, I'm not ahead of you,' Stranahan said. 'Tell me what Maggie Gonzalez knows about Vicky Barletta.'

Christina said, 'I can't do that.'

'How much did you promise to pay?'

Again Christina shook her head.

'Know what I think?' Stranahan said. 'I think you and Ray are getting the hum job of your lives.'

'Pardon?'

'I think Maggie is sucking you off, big-time.'

Christina heard herself saying, 'You might be right.'

Stranahan softened his tone. 'Let me give you a hypothetical,' he said. 'This Maggie Gonzalez, whom you've never seen before, shows up in New York one day and offers to tell you a sensational story about a missing college coed. The way she tells it, the girl came to a terrible and ghastly end. And, conveniently, the way she tells it can't ever be proven or disproved. Why? Because it happened a long time ago. And the odds are, Christina, that Victoria Barletta is dead. And the odds are, whoever did it isn't about to come forward to say that Reynaldo Flemm got it all wrong when he told the story on national TV.'

Christina Marks leaned forward. 'Fine. All fine, except for one thing. She names names.'

'Maggie does?'

'Yes. She describes exactly how it happened and who did it.'

'And these people—'

'Person, singular.'

'He? She?'

'He,' Christina said.

'He's still alive?'

'Sure is.'

'Here in town?'

'That's right.'

'Jesus,' Stranahan said. He got up and fixed himself another gin. He dropped a couple of ice cubes, his hands were shaking so much. This was not good, he told himself, getting so excited was definitely not good.

He carried his drink back to the living room and said, 'Is it the doctor?'

'I can't say.' It would violate a confidence, Christina Marks explained. Journalists have to protect their sources.

Stranahan finished half his drink before he spoke again. 'Are you any good?'

Christina looked at him curiously.

'At what you do,' he said irritably, 'are you any damn good?'

'Yes, I think so.'

'Can you keep the great Reynaldo out of my hair?'

'I'll try. Why?'

'Because,' Stranahan said, 'it would be to our mutual benefit to meet once in a while, just you and me.'

'Compare notes?'

'Something like that. I don't know why, but I think I can trust you.'

'Thanks.'

'I'm not saying I do, just that it's possible.'

He put down the glass and stood up.

'What's your stake in this?' Christina Marks asked.

'Truth, justice, whatever.'

'No, it's bigger than that.'

She was pretty sharp, he had to admit. But he wasn't ready to tell her about Tony the Eel and the marlin head.

As she walked Stranahan to the door, Christina said, 'I spent some time at the newspaper today.'

'Reading up, I suppose.'

'You've got quite a clip file,' she said. 'I suppose I ought to be scared of you.'

'You don't believe everything you read?'

'Of course not.' Christina Marks opened the door. 'Just tell me, how much of it was true?'

'All of it,' Mick Stranahan said, 'unfortunately.'

Of Stranahan's five ex-wives, only one had chosen to keep his last name: ex-wife number four, Chloe Simpkins Stranahan. Even after she remarried, Chloe hung on to his name as an act of unalloyed spite. Naturally she was listed in the Miami phone book; Stranahan had begged her to please get a nonpublished number, but Chloe had said that would defeat the whole purpose. 'This way, any girl who wants to call up and check on you, I can tell them the truth. That you're a dangerous lunatic. That's what I'll tell them when they call up, Mick—*honey, he was one dangerous lunatic.*'

Christina Marks had gotten all the Stranahan numbers from directory assistance. When she had called Chloe from New York, Chloe assumed it was just one of Mick's girlfriends, and had given a vitriolic and highly embellished account of their eight-month marriage and nine-month divorce. Finally Christina Marks had cut in and explained who she was and what she wanted, and Chloe Simpkins Stranahan had said: 'That'll cost you a grand.'

'Five hundred,' Christina countered.

'Bitch,' Chloe hissed. But when the cashier's check arrived the next afternoon by Federal Express, Chloe faithfully picked up the phone and called Christina Marks (collect) in New York and told her where to locate her dangerous lunatic of an ex-husband.

'Give him a disease for me, will you?' Chloe had said and then had hung up.

The hit man known as Chemo was not nearly as resourceful

as Christina Marks, but he did know enough to check the telephone book for Stranahans. There were five, and Chemo wrote them all down.

The day after his meeting with Dr. Rudy Graveline, Chemo went for a drive. His car was a royal blue 1980 Bonneville, with tinted windows. The tinted windows were essential to conceal Chemo's face, the mere glimpse of which could cause a high-speed pileup at any intersection.

Louis K. Stranahan was the first on Chemo's list. A Miamian would have recognized the address as being in the middle of Liberty City, but Chemo did not. It occurred to him upon entering the neighborhood that he should have asked Dr. Graveline whether the man he was supposed to kill was black or white, because it might have saved some time.

The address was in the James Scott housing project, a bleak and tragic warren where few outsiders of any color dared to go. Even on a bright winter day, the project gave off a dark and ominous heat. Chemo was oblivious; he saw no danger here, just work. He parked the Bonneville next to a fenced-in basketball court and got out. Almost instantly the kids on the court stopped playing. The basketball hit the rim and bounced lazily out of bounds, but no one ran to pick it up. They were all staring at Chemo. The only sound was the dental-drill rap of Run-D.M.C. from a distant quadrophonic blaster.

'Hello, there,' Chemo said.

The kids from the project glanced at one another, trying to guess how they should play it; this was one of the tallest white motherfuckers they'd ever seen this side of the Interstate. Also, one of the ugliest.

'Game's full,' the biggest kid declared with a forced authority.

'Oh, I don't want to play,' Chemo said.

A look of relief spread among the players, and one of them jogged after the basketball.

'I'm looking for a man named Louis Stranahan.'

'He ain't here.'

'Where is he?'

'Gone.'

Chemo said, 'Does he have a brother named Mick?'

'He's got six brothers,' one of the basketball players volunteered. 'But no Mick.'

'There's a Dick,' said another teenager.

'And a Lawrence.'

Chemo took the list out of his pocket and frowned. Sure enough, Lawrence Stranahan was the second name from the phone book. The address was close by, too.

As Chemo stood there, cranelike, squinting at the piece of paper, the black kids loosened up a little. They started shooting a few hoops, horsing around. The white guy wasn't so scary after all; shit, there were eight of them and one of him.

'Where could I find Louis?' Chemo tried again.

'Raiford,' said two of the kids, simultaneously.

'Raiford,' Chemo repeated. 'That's a prison, isn't it?'

With this, all the teenagers doubled up, slapping fives, howling hysterically at this gangly freak with the fuzzballs on his head.

'Fuck, yeah, it's a prison,' one of them said finally.

Chemo scratched the top two Stranahans off his list. As he opened the door of the Bonneville, the black kid who was dribbling the basketball hollered, 'Hey, big man, you a movie star?'

'No,' Chemo said.

'I swear you are.'

'I swear I'm not.'

'Then how come I saw you in *Halloween III*?'

The kid bent over in a deep wheeze; he thought this was so damn funny. Chemo reached under the car seat and got a .22-caliber pistol, which was fitted with a cheap mail-order suppressor. Without saying a word, he took aim across the roof of the Bonneville and shot the basketball clean out of the kid's hands. The explosion sounded like the world's biggest fart, but the kids from the project didn't think it was funny. They ran like hell.

As Chemo drove away, he decided he had taught the youngsters a valuable lesson: Never make fun of a man's complexion.

It was half-past noon when Chemo found the third address, a two-story Mediterranean-style house in Coral Gables. An ill-tempered Rottweiler was chained to the trunk of an olive tree in the front yard, but Chemo ambled past the big dog without incident; the animal merely cocked its head and watched, perhaps not sure if this odd extenuated creature was the same species he'd been trained to attack.

Chloe Simpkins Stranahan was on the phone to her husband's secretary when the doorbell rang.

'Tell him, if he's not home by eight, I sell the Dali. Tell him that right now.' Chloe slammed down the phone and stalked to the door. She looked up at Chemo and said, 'How'd you get past the pooch?'

Chemo shrugged. He was wearing black Raybans, which he hoped would lessen the effect of his facial condition. If necessary, he was prepared to explain what had happened; it wouldn't be the first time.

Yet Chloe Simpkins Stranahan didn't mention it. She said, 'You selling something?'

'I'm looking for a man named Mick Stranahan.'

'He's a dangerous lunatic,' Chloe said. 'Come right in.'

Chemo removed the sunglasses and folded them into the top pocket of his shirt. He sat down in the living room, and put a hand on each of his bony kneecaps. At the wet bar Chloe fixed him a cold ginger ale. She acted like she didn't even notice what was wrong with his appearance.

'Who are you?' she asked.

'Collection agent,' Chemo said. Watching Chloe move around the house, he saw that she was a very beautiful woman: auburn hair, long legs, and a good figure. Listening to her, he could tell she was also hard as nails.

'Mick is my ex,' Chloe said. 'I have nothing good to say about him. Nothing.'

'He owe you money, too?'

She chuckled harshly. 'No, I took him for every goddamn dime. Cleaned his clock.' She drummed her ruby fingernails on the side of the ginger ale glass. 'I'm now married to a CPA,' she said. 'Has his own firm.'

'Nice to hear it,' Chemo said.

'Dull as a dog turd, but at least he's no lunatic.'

Chemo shifted in the chair. 'Lunatic, you keep saying that word. What do you mean? Is Mr. Stranahan violent? Did he hit you?'

'Mick? Never. Not me,' Chloe said. 'But he did attack a friend of mine. A male-type friend.'

Chemo figured he ought to learn as much as possible about the man he was supposed to kill. He said to Chloe, 'What exactly did Mick do to this male-type friend?'

'It's hard for me to talk about it.' Chloe got up and dumped a jigger of vodka into her ginger ale. 'He was always on the road, Mick was. Never home. No doubt he was screwing around.'

'You know for a fact?'

'I'm sure of it.'

'So you got a . . . boyfriend.'

'You're a smart one,' Chloe said mordantly. 'A goddamn rocket scientist, you are. Yes, I got a *boyfriend*. And he loved me, this guy. He treated me like a queen.'

Chemo said, 'So one night Mr. Stranahan gets home early from a trip and catches the two of you—'

'In action,' Chloe said. 'Don't get me wrong, I didn't plan it that way. God knows I didn't want him to walk in on us—you gotta know Mick, it's just not a safe situation.'

'Short fuse?'

'No fuse.'

'So then what?'

Chloe sighed. 'I can't believe I'm telling this to some stranger, a bill collector! Unbelievable.' She polished off her drink and got another. This time when she came back from the bar, she sat down on the divan next to Chemo; close enough that he could smell her perfume.

'I'm a talker,' she said with a soft smile. The smile certainly didn't go with the voice.

'And I'm a listener,' Chemo said.

'And I like you.'

'You do?' This broad is creepy, he thought, a real head case.

'I like you,' Chloe went on, 'and I'd like to help you with your problem.'

'Then just tell me,' Chemo said, 'where I can find your ex-husband.'

'How much are you willing to pay?'

'Ah, so that's it.'

'Everything's got a price,' Chloe said, 'especially good information.'

'Unfortunately, Mrs. Stranahan, I don't have any money. Money is the reason I'm looking for Mick.'

Chloe crossed her legs, and Chemo noticed a very fine run in one of her nylon stockings; it seemed to go on forever, all the way up her thigh. Who knew where it ended? Internally he cautioned himself against such distractions. Any moment now, she was going to say something about his Rice Krispie face— Chemo knew it.

'You're not a bill collector,' Chloe said sharply, 'so cut the shit.'

'All right,' Chemo said. Feverishly he set his limited imagination to work, trying to come up with another story.

'I don't care what you are.'

'You don't?'

'Nope. Long as you're not a friend of Mick's.'

Chemo said, 'I'm not a friend.'

'Then I'll help,' Chloe said, 'maybe.'

'What about the money?' Chemo said. 'The most I can do is a hundred dollars, maybe one fifty.'

'Fine.'

'Fine?' Christ, he couldn't believe this woman. A hundred bucks.

She said, 'But before I agree to help, you ought to know everything. It would be irresponsible for me not to warn you what you're up against.'

'I can handle myself,' Chemo said with a cold smile. Even that—his fractured, cadaverous leer—didn't seem to bother Chloe Simpkins Stranahan.

She said, 'So you really don't want to know?'

'Go ahead, then, shoot. What did Stranahan do to your precious boyfriend?'

'He put Krazy Glue on his balls.'

'What?'

'A whole tube,' Chloe said. 'He glued the man to the hood of his car. By the balls. Stark naked, glued to the hood of an Eldorado convertible.'

'Jesus H. Christ,' Chemo said.

'Ever seen the hood ornament on a Cadillac?'

Chemo nodded.

'Think about it,' Chloe said grimly.

'And glue burns like hell,' Chemo remarked.

'Indeed it does.'

'So Mick came home, caught you two in the sack—'

'Right here on the divan.'

'Wherever,' Chemo said. 'Anyway, he hauls Mr. Studhunk outside and glues him buck naked to the hood of his Caddy.'

'By the testicles.'

'Then what?'

'That's it,' Chloe said. 'Mick packed his suitcase and left. The paramedics came. What more is there?'

'Your male friend—is this the same guy you're married to?'

'No, it isn't,' Chloe said. 'My male-type friend never recovered from his encounter with Mick Stranahan. I mean *never recovered*. You understand what I'm saying?'

'I think so.'

'The doctors insisted there was nothing wrong, medically speaking. I mean, the glue peeled off with acetone, and in a few days the skin healed just like new. But, still, the man was never the same.'

Chemo said, 'It's a major trauma, Mrs. Stranahan. It probably takes some time—'

He flinched as Chloe threw her cocktail glass against the wall. 'Time?' she said. 'I gave him plenty of time, mister. And I tried every trick I knew, but he was a dead man after that night with Mick. It was like trying to screw linguini.'

Chemo could imagine the hellish bedroom scene. He felt himself shrivel, just thinking about it.

'I loved that man,' Chloe went on. 'At least, I was getting there. And Mick ruined everything. He couldn't just beat the shit out of him, like other jealous husbands. No, he had to torture the guy.'

In a way, Chemo admired Stranahan's style. Murder is the way Chemo himself would have handled the situation: A bullet in the base of the skull. For both of them.

Chloe Simpkins Stranahan was up and pacing now, arms folded across her chest, heels clicking on the Spanish tile. 'So you see,' she said, 'this is why I hate my ex-husband so much.'

There had to be more, but who cared. Chemo said, 'You want to get even?'

'Boy, are you a swifty. Yes, I want to get even.'

'Then why should I pay you anything? You should pay *me*.'

Chloe had to smile. 'Good point.' She bent over and picked a chunk of broken glass out of the deep-pile carpet. She looked up at Chemo and asked, 'Who are you, anyway?'

'Doesn't matter, Mrs. Stranahan. The question is, how bad do you want revenge on your ex-husband?'

'I guess that is the question,' Chloe said thoughtfully. 'How about another ginger ale?'

7

Of the four plastic surgeons who had worked with Dr. Rudy Graveline at the Durkos Center, only one had remained in Miami after the clinic closed. His name was George Ginger, and Stranahan found him on a tennis court at Turnberry Isle in the middle of a weekday afternoon. Mixed doubles, naturally.

Stranahan watched the pudgy little man wheeze back and forth behind the baseline, and marveled at the atrociousness of his hairpiece. It was one of those synthetic jobs, the kind you're supposed to be able to wear in the shower. In Dr. George Ginger's case, the thing on his head looked a lot like a fresh road kill.

Each point in the tennis game became its own little comedy, and Stranahan wondered if this stop was a waste of time, an unconscious stall on his part. By now he knew exactly where to locate Rudy Graveline; the problem was, he didn't know what to ask him that would produce the truth. It was a long way from Vicky Barletta to Tony the Eel, and Stranahan still hadn't found the thread, if there was one. One way or another, Dr. Graveline was central to the mystery, and Stranahan didn't want to spook him. For now, he wanted him safe and contented at Whispering Palms.

Stranahan strolled into the dead lane of the tennis court and said, 'Dr. Ginger?'

'Yo!' said the doctor, huffing.

Stranahan knew about guys who said yo.

'We need to talk.'

'Do we now?' said Dr. Ginger, missing an easy backhand. His doubles partner, a lanky, overtanned woman, shot Stranahan a dirty look.

'Just take a minute,' Stranahan said.

Dr. Ginger picked up two of the tennis balls. 'Sorry, but I'm on serve.'

'No, you're not,' Stranahan said. 'And besides, that was the set.' He'd been following the match from a gazebo two courts over.

As Dr. Ginger intently bounced one of the balls between his feet, the other players picked up their monogrammed club towels and calfskin racket covers and ambled off the court.

Solemnly George Ginger said, 'The tall fellow was my lawyer.'

'Every doctor should have a lawyer,' said Mick Stranahan. 'Especially surgeons.'

Ginger jammed the tennis balls into the pockets of his damp white shorts. 'What's this all about?'

'Rudy Graveline.'

'I've heard of him.'

This was going to be fun, Stranahan thought. He loved it when they played cool.

'You worked for him at the Durkos Center,' Stranahan said to George Ginger. 'Why don't you be a nice fellow and tell me about it?'

George Ginger motioned Stranahan to follow. He picked a quiet patio table with an umbrella, not far from the pro shop.

'Who are you with?' the doctor inquired in a low voice.

'The board,' Stranahan said. Any board would do; Dr. Ginger wouldn't press it.

After wiping his forehead for the umpteenth time, the doctor said, 'There were four of us—Kelly, Greer, Shulman, and me. Graveline was the managing partner.'

'Business was good?'

'It was getting there.'

'Then why did he close the place?'

'I'm still not certain,' George Ginger said.

'But you heard rumors.'

'Yes, we heard there was a problem with a patient. The sort of problem that might bring in the state.'

'One of Rudy's patients?'

George Ginger nodded. 'A young woman is what we heard.'

'Her name?'

'I don't know.' The doctor was quite a lousy liar.

'How bad a problem?' Stranahan went on.

'I don't know that either. We assumed it was a major fuckup, or else why would Graveline pull out so fast?'

'Didn't any of you guys bother to ask?'

'Hell, no. I've been to court before, buddy, and it's no damn fun. None of us wanted to get dragged down that road. Anyway, we show up for work one day and the place is empty. Later we get a certified check from Rudy with a note saying he's sorry for the inconvenience, but good luck with our careers. Before you know it, he's back in business at Bal Harbour—of all places—with a frigging assembly-line operation. A dozen boob jobs a day.'

Stranahan said, 'Why didn't you call him?'

'What for? Old time's sake?'

'That certified check, it must've been a good one.'

'It was,' Dr. Ginger conceded, 'very generous.'

Stranahan picked up the doctor's graphite tennis racket and plucked idly at the strings. George Ginger eyed him worriedly. 'Do you remember the day the police came?' Stranahan asked. 'The day a young female patient disappeared from a bus bench in front of the clinic?'

'I was off that day.'

'That's not what I asked.' Stranahan studied him through the grid of the racket strings.

'I remember hearing about it,' George Ginger said lamely.

'That happened right before Dr. Graveline split, didn't it?'

'I think so, yes.'

Stranahan said, 'You consider yourself a bright man, Dr. Ginger? Don't look so insulted, it's a serious question.' He put the tennis racket down on the patio table.

'I consider myself to be intelligent, yes.'

'Well, then, didn't you wonder about the timing? A girl gets snatched from in front of your office, and a few weeks later the boss closes up shop. Could that be the fuckup you guys heard about? What do you think?'

Sourly, George Ginger said, 'I can't imagine a connection.' He picked up his tennis racket and, with a touch of pique, zipped it into its carry case.

Stranahan stood up. 'Well, the important thing is, you still got your medical license. Now, where can I find the rest of the stooges?'

Dr. Ginger wrapped the towel around his neck, a real jock gesture. 'Kelly moved to Michigan. Shulman's up in Atlanta, working for some HMO. Dr. Greer is deceased, unfortunately.'

'Do tell.'

'Don't you guys have it in your files? I mean, when a doctor dies?'

'Not in every case,' Stranahan bluffed.

George Ginger said, 'It happened maybe six months after Durkos closed. A hunting accident up around Ocala.'

'Who else was there?'

'I really don't know,' the doctor said with an insipid shrug. 'I'm afraid I'm not clear about all the details.'

'Why,' said Mick Stranahan, 'am I not surprised?'

The Rudy Graveline system was brilliant in its simplicity: Sting, persuade, operate, then flatter.

On the wall of each waiting room at Whispering Palms hung a creed: VANITY IS BEAUTIFUL. Similar maxims were posted in the hallways and examining rooms. WHAT'S WRONG WITH PERFECTION? was one of Rudy's favorites. Another: TO IMPROVE ONE'S SELF, IMPROVE ONE'S FACE. This one was framed in the spa, where post-op patients relaxed in the crucial days following their plastic surgery, when they didn't want to go out in public. Rudy had shrewdly recognized that an after-surgery spa would not only be a tremendous money-maker, it would also provide important positive feedback during recovery. Everyone there had fresh scars and bruises, so no patient was in a position to criticize another's results.

As best he could, Reynaldo Flemm made mental notes of Whispering Palms during his tour. He was posing as a male exotic dancer who needed a blemish removed from his right buttock. For the purpose of disguise, Flemm had dyed his hair brown and greased it straight back; that was all he could bear to do to alter his appearance. Secretly, he loved it when people stared because they recognized him from television.

As it happened, the nurse who greeted him at Whispering

Palms apparently never watched *In Your Face*. She treated Flemm as any other prospective patient. After a quick tour of the facilities, she led him to a consultation room, turned off the lights and showed him a videotape about the wonders of cosmetic surgery. Afterwards she turned the lights back on and asked if he had any questions.

'How much will it cost?' Reynaldo Flemm said.

'That depends on the size of the mole.'

'Oh, it's a big mole,' Reynaldo said. 'Like an olive.' He held up his thumb and forefinger to show her the size of his fictional growth.

The nurse said, 'May I see it?'

'No!'

'Surely you're not shy,' she said. 'Not in your line of work.'

'I'll show it to the doctor,' Flemm said. 'No one else.'

'Very well, I'll arrange for an appointment.'

'With Dr. Graveline, please.'

The nurse smiled. 'Really, Mr. LeTigre.'

Flemm had come up with the name Johnny LeTigre all by himself. It seemed perfect for a male go-go dancer.

'Dr. Graveline doesn't do moles,' the nurse said in a chilly tone. 'One of our other excellent surgeons can take care of it quite easily.'

'It's Dr. Graveline or nobody,' Flemm said firmly. 'This is my dancing career, my life we're talking about.'

'I'm sorry, but Dr. Graveline is not available.'

'For ten grand I bet he is.'

The nurse tried not to seem surprised. 'I'll be right back,' she said lightly.

When he was alone, Reynaldo Flemm checked himself in the mirror to see how the disguise was holding up. All he needed was a date and time to see the doctor, then he'd come back with Willie and a camera for the showdown—not out on the street, but inside the clinic. And if Graveline ordered them out, Reynaldo and Willie would be sure to leave through the spa exit, tape rolling. It would be dynamite stuff; even Christina would have to admit it.

The nurse returned and said, 'Come with me, Mr. LeTigre.'

'Where to?'

'Dr. Graveline has agreed to see you.'

'Now?' Flynn squeaked.

'He only has a few minutes.'

A cold prickle of panic accompanied Reynaldo Flemm as he followed the nurse down a long pale-blue hallway. About to meet the target of his investigation and here he was, defenseless—no camera, no tape, no note-books. He could blow the whole story if he wasn't careful. The only thing in Flemm's favor was the fact that he also had no script. He wouldn't know what to ask even if the opportunity presented itself.

The nurse abandoned him in a spacious office with a grand view of north Biscayne Bay, foamy with whitecaps. Reynaldo Flemm barely had time to snoop the joint over before Dr. Rudy Graveline came in and introduced himself. Reynaldo took a good close look, in case he might later have to point him out to Willie from the TV van: Lean build, medium height, sandy brown hair. Had a golfer's tan but not much muscle. Overall, not a bad-looking guy.

Rudy Graveline didn't waste any time. 'Let's see your little problem, Mr. LeTigre.'

'Hold on a minute.'

'It's only a mole.'

'To you maybe,' Reynaldo Flemm said. 'Before we go any further, I'd like to ask you some questions.' He paused, then: 'Questions about your background.'

Dr. Graveline settled in behind a gleaming onyx desk and folded his hands. 'Fire away,' he said amiably.

'What medical school did you go to?'

'Harvard,' Rudy replied.

Reynaldo nodded approvingly.

He asked, 'How long have you been in practice?'

'Sixteen years,' Dr. Graveline said.

'Ah,' said Reynaldo Flemm. He couldn't think of much else to ask, which was fine with Rudy. Sometimes patients wanted to know how high the doctor had placed in his med school class (dead last), or whether he was certified by a national board of plastic and reconstructive surgeons (he was not). In truth, Rudy had barely squeaked through a residency in radiology and had never been trained in plastic surgery. Still, no law prevented him from declaring it to be his specialty; that was the beauty of the medical profession—once you got a degree, you could try whatever you damn well pleased, from brain surgery to gynecology. Hospitals might do some checking, but never the patients. And failing at one or more specialties (as Rudy had), you could always leave town and try something else.

Still stalling, Reynaldo Flemm said, 'What's involved in an operation like this?'

'First we numb the area with a mild anesthetic, then we use a small knife to remove the mole. If you need a couple sutures afterward, we do that, too.'

'What about a scar?'

'No scar, I guarantee it,' said Dr. Graveline.

'For ten grand, you're damn right.'

The doctor said, 'I didn't realize male strippers made that much money.'

'They don't. It's inheritance.'

If Flemm had been paying attention, he would have noticed a hungry flicker in Dr. Graveline's expression.

'Mr. LeTigre, you won't mind some friendly professional advice?'

'Of course not.'

'Your nose,' Rudy ventured. 'I mean, as long as you're going to all the trouble of surgery.'

'What the hell is wrong with my nose?'

'It's about two sizes too large for your face. And, to be honest, your tummy could probably come down an inch or three. I can do a liposuction after we excise the mole.'

Reynaldo Flemm said, 'Are you kidding? There's nothing wrong with me.'

'Please don't be embarrassed,' Rudy said. 'This is my specialty. I just thought someone in a job like yours would want to look their very best.'

Flemm was getting furious. 'I *do* look my very best!'

Dr. Graveline put his elbows on the desk and leaned forward. Gently he said, 'With all respect, Mr. LeTigre, we seldom choose to see ourselves the way others do. It's human nature.'

'I've heard enough,' Reynaldo Flemm snapped.

'If it's the money, look, I'll do the mole and the fat suction as a package. Toss in the rhinoplasty for nothing, okay?'

Flemm said, 'I don't need a goddamn rhinoplasty.'

'Please,' said Dr. Graveline, 'go home and think about it. Take a good critical look at yourself in the mirror.'

'Fuck you,' said Reynaldo Flemm, and stormed out of the office.

'It's no sin to have a big honker,' Rudy Graveline called after him. 'Nobody's *born* perfect!'

One hour later, as Rudy was fitting a Mentor Model 7000 Gel-Filled Mammary Prosthesis into the left breast of the future Miss Ecuador, he was summoned from the operating suite to take an urgent phone call from New York.

The semi-hysterical voice on the other end belonged to Maggie Gonzalez.

'Take some deep breaths,' Rudy advised.

'No, you listen. I got a message on my machine,' Maggie said. 'The phone machine at my house.'

'Who was it from?'

'Stranahan. That investigator.'

'Really.' Dr. Graveline worked hard at staying calm; he took pride in his composure. He asked, 'What was the message, Maggie?'

'Three words: *"It won't work."* '

Dr. Graveline repeated the message out loud. Maggie sounded like she was bouncing off the walls.

'Don't come back here for a while,' Rudy said. 'I'll wire you some more money.' He couldn't think clearly with Maggie hyperventilating into the phone, and he did need to think. *It won't work.* Damn, he didn't like the sound of that. How much did Stranahan know? Was it a bluff? Rudy Graveline wondered if he should call Chemo and tell him to speed things up.

'What are we going to do?' Maggie demanded.

'It's being done,' the doctor said.

'Good.' Maggie didn't ask specifically what was being done. Specifically, she didn't want to know.

After lunch, Mick Stranahan stopped by the VA hospital, but for the second day in a row the nurses told him that Timmy Gavigan was asleep. They said it had been another poor night, that the new medicine was still giving him fevers.

Stranahan was eager to hear what his friend remembered about Dr. Rudy Graveline. Like most good cops, Timmy never forgot an interview; and like most cops, Timmy was the only one who could read his own handwriting. The Barletta file was full of Gavigan-type scribbles.

After leaving the VA, Stranahan drove back to the marina at Key Biscayne. On the skiff out to Stiltsville, he mentally catalogued everything he knew so far.

Vicky Barletta had disappeared, and was probably dead.

Her doctor had closed up shop a few weeks later and bought out his four partners for fifty thousand dollars apiece.

One of those partners, Dr. Kenneth Greer, had never cashed his check—this according to microfiche records at the bank.

Approximately seven months after Rudy Graveline closed the Durkos Center, Dr. Kenneth Greer was shot to death while hunting deer in the Ocala National Forest. The sheriff's office had ruled it an accident.

The hunter who had somehow mistaken Kenneth Greer for a white-tail buck had given his name as T. B. Luckner of 1333 Carter Boulevard in Decatur, Georgia. If the sheriff in Ocala had troubled himself to check, he would have found that there was no such person and no such address.

The nurse who participated in Victoria Barletta's surgery had recently gone to New York to sell her story to a TV producer.

Shortly afterwards, a paid killer named Tony the Eel showed up to murder Mick Stranahan. Tony, with a brand-new face.

Then the TV producer arrived in Miami to take Stranahan's picture for a prime-time special.

All traced to a four-year-old kidnapping that Mick Stranahan had never solved.

As he steered the boat into the Biscayne Channel, angling out of the messy following chop, he gunned the outboard and made a beeline for his stilt house. The tide was up, making it safe to cross the flats.

On the way, he thought about Rudy Graveline.

Suppose the doctor had killed Vicky. Stranahan checked himself—make that Victoria, not Vicky. Better yet, just plain Barletta. No sense personalizing.

But suppose the doctor had killed her, and suppose Greer knew, or found out. Greer was the only one who didn't cash the buyout check—maybe he was holding out for more money, or maybe he was ready to blab to the authorities.

Either way, Dr. Graveline would have had plenty of motive to silence him.

And if, for some reason, Dr. Graveline had been led to believe that Mick Stranahan posed a similar threat, what would stop him from killing again?

Stranahan couldn't help but marvel at the possibility. Considering all the cons and ex-cons who'd love to see him dead—hoods, dopers, scammers, bikers and stickup artists—it was ironic that the most likely suspect was some rich quack he'd never even met.

The more Stranahan learned about the case, and the more he thought about what he'd learned, the lousier he felt.

His spirits improved somewhat when he spotted his model friend Tina stretched out on the sun deck of the stilt house. He was especially pleased to notice that she was alone.

8

Stranahan caught four small snappers and fried them up for supper.

'Richie left me,' Tina was explaining. 'I mean, he put me out on your house and left. Can you believe that?'

Stranahan pretended to be listening as he foraged in the refrigerator. 'You want lemon or garlic salt?'

'Both,' Tina said. 'We had a fight and he ordered me to get off the boat. Then he drove away.'

She wore a baggy Jimmy Buffett T-shirt over a cranberry bikini bottom. Her wheat colored hair was pulled back in a ponytail, and a charm glinted at her throat; a tiny gold porpoise, it looked like.

'Richie deals a little coke,' Tina went on. 'That's what we were fighting about. Well, part of it.'

Stranahan said, 'Keep an eye on the biscuits so they don't burn.'

'Sure. Anyway, know what else we were fighting about? This is so dumb you won't believe it.'

Stranahan was dicing a pepper on the kitchen countertop. He was barefoot, wearing cutoff jeans and a khaki short-sleeved shirt, open to the chest. His hair was still damp from the shower. Overall, he felt much better about his situation.

Tina said, 'I got this modeling job and Richie, he went crazy. All because I had to do some, you know, nudes. Just beach stuff, nobody out there but me and the photog. Richie says no way, you can't do it. And I said, you can't tell me what to do. Then—then!—he calls me a slut, and I say that's pretty rich coming from a two-bit doper. So then he slugs me in the stomach and tells me to get my butt out of the boat.' Tina paused for a sigh. 'Your house was closest.'

'You can stay for the night,' Stranahan said, sounding down-right fatherly.

'What if Richie comes back?'

'Then we teach him some manners.'

Tina said, 'He's still pissed about the last time, when you drag-ged him through the water.'

'The biscuits,' Stranahan reminded her.

'Oh, yeah, sorry.' Tina pulled the hot tray out of the oven.

For at least thirteen minutes she didn't say anything, because the snapper was excellent and she was hungry. Stranahan found a bottle of white wine and poured two glasses. It was then Tina smiled and said, 'Got any candles?'

Stranahan played along, even though darkness still was an hour away. He lighted two stubby hurricane candles and set them on the oilskin tablecloth.

'This is really nice,' Tina said.

'Yes, it is.'

'I haven't found a single bone,' she said, chewing intently.

'Good.'

'Are you married, Mick?'

'Divorced,' he replied. 'Five times.'

'Wow.'

'My fault, every one,' he added. To some degree, he believed it. Each time the same thing happened: He'd awakened one morning and felt nothing; not guilt or jealousy or anger, but an implacable numbness, which was worse. Like his blood had turned to novocaine overnight. He'd stared at the woman in his bed and become incredulous at the notion that this was a spouse, that he had married this person. He'd felt trapped and done a poor job of concealing it. By the fifth go-round, divorce had become an eerie out-of-body experience, except for the part with the lawyers.

'Were you fooling around a lot, or what?' Tina asked.

'It wasn't that,' Stranahan said.

'Then what? You're a nice-looking guy, I don't know why a girl would cut and run.'

Stranahan poured more wine for both of them.

'I wasn't much fun to be around.'

'Oh, I disagree,' Tina said with a perkiness that startled him.

Her eyes wandered up to the big mount on the living room wall. 'What happened to Mr. Swordfish?'

'That's a marlin,' Stranahan said. 'He fell off the wall and broke his beak.'

'The tape looks pretty tacky, Mick.'

'Yeah, I know.'

After dinner they went out on the deck to watch the sun go down behind Coconut Grove. Stranahan tied a size 12 hook on his fishing line and baited it with a lint-sized shred of frozen shrimp. In fifteen minutes he caught five lively pinfish, which he dropped in a plastic bait bucket. Entranced, Tina sat cross-legged on the deck and watched the little fish swim frenetic circles inside the container.

Stranahan stowed the rod in the stilt house, came out, and picked up the bucket. 'I'll be right back.'

'Where you off to?'

'Downstairs, by the boat.'

'Can I come?'

He shrugged. 'You might not like it.'

'Like what?' Tina asked and followed him tentatively down the wooden stairs toward the water.

Liza hovered formidably in the usual place. Stranahan pointed at the huge barracuda and said, 'See there?'

'Wow, is that a shark?'

'No.'

He reached into the bucket and grabbed one of the pinfish, carefully folding the dorsal so it wouldn't prick his fingers.

Tina said, 'Now I get it.'

'She's like a pet,' Stranahan said. He tossed the pinfish into the water, and the barracuda devoured it in a silent mercury flash, all fangs. When the turbulence subsided, they saw that the big fish had returned to its station; it hung there as if it had never moved.

Impassively Stranahan tossed another pinfish and the barracuda repeated the kill.

Tina stood so close that Stranahan could feel her warm breath on his bare arm. 'Do they eat people?' she asked.

He could have hugged her right then.

'No,' he said, 'they don't eat people.'

'Good!'

'They do strike at shiny objects,' he said, 'so don't wear a bracelet if you're diving.'

'Seriously?'

'It's been known to happen.'

This time he scooped up two pinfish and lobbed them into the water simultaneously; the barracuda got them both in one fierce swipe.

'I call her Liza,' Stranahan said. 'Liza with a z.'

Tina nodded as if she thought it was a perfectly cute name. She asked if she could try a toss.

'You bet.' Stranahan got the last pinfish from the bucket and placed it carefully in the palm of her hand. 'Just throw it anywhere,' he said.

Tina leaned forward and called out, 'Here Liza! Here you go!'

The little fish landed with a soft splash and spun a dizzy figure eight under the dock. The barracuda didn't move.

Stranahan smiled. In slow motion the addled pinfish corkscrewed its way to the bottom, taking refuge inside an old horse conch.

'What'd I do wrong?' Tina wondered.

'Not a thing,' Stranahan said. 'She wasn't hungry anymore, that's all.'

'Maybe it's just me.'

'Maybe it is,' Stranahan said.

He took her by the hand and led her upstairs. He turned on the lights in the house and vented the shutters on both sides to catch the cool night breeze. On the roof, the windmill creaked as it picked up speed.

Tina made a place for herself on a faded lumpy sofa. She said, 'I always wondered what it's like out here in the dark.'

'Not much to do, I'm afraid.'

'No TV?'

'No TV,' Stranahan said.

'You want to make love?'

'There's an idea.'

'You already saw me naked.'

'I haven't forgotten,' Stranahan said. 'The thing is—'

'Don't worry about Richie. Anyway, this is just for fun. We'll keep it casual, okay?'

'I don't do anything casually,' Stranahan said. 'This is my problem.' He was constantly falling in love; how else would you explain five marriages, all to cocktail waitresses?

Tina peeled off the tropical T-shirt and draped it across a bar-stool. Rockette-style, she kicked her way out of her bikini bottoms and left them in a rumple on the floor.

'How about these tan lines, huh?'

'What tan lines?' he asked.

'Exactly.' Tina pulled the rubber band out of her ponytail and shook her hair free. Then she got back on the sofa and said, 'Watch this.' She stretched out and struck a smokey-eyed modeling pose—a half-turn up on one elbow, legs scissored, one arm shading her nipples.

'That looks great,' Stranahan said, amused but also uneasy.

'It's tough work on a beach,' Tina remarked. 'Sand sticks to places you wouldn't believe. I did a professional job, though.'

'I'm sure.'

'Thanks to you, I got my confidence back. About my boobs, I mean.' She glanced down at herself appraisingly.

'Confidence is everything in the modeling business,' she said. 'Somebody tells you that your ass is sagging or your tits don't match up, it's like an emotional disaster. I was worried sick until you measured them with that carpenter's thing.'

'Glad I could help,' Stranahan said, trying to think of something, anything, more romantic.

She said, 'Anyone ever tell you that you've got Nick Nolte's nose?'

'That's all?' Stranahan said. Nick Nolte was a new one.

'Now the eyes,' Tina said, 'your eyes are more like Sting's. I met him one time at the Strand.'

'Thank you,' Stranahan said. He didn't know who the hell she was talking about. Maybe one of those pro wrestlers from cable television.

Holding her pose, Tina motioned him to join her on the old sofa. When he did, she took his hands, placed them on her staunch new breasts, and held them there. Stranahan assumed a compliment was in order.

'They're perfect,' he said, squeezing politely.

Urgently Tina arched her back and rolled over, Stranahan hanging on like a rock climber.

'While we're on the subject,' he said, 'could I get the name of your surgeon?'

Even before the electrolysis accident, Chemo had led a difficult life. His parents had belonged to a religious sect that believed in bigamy, vegetarianism, UFOs, and not paying federal income taxes; his mother, father, and three of their respective spouses were killed by the FBI during a bloody ten-day siege at a post office outside Grand Forks, North Dakota. Chemo, who was only six at the time, went to live with an aunt and uncle in the Amish country of western Pennsylvania. It was a rigorous and demanding period, especially since Chemo's aunt and uncle were not actually Amish themselves, but fair-weather Presbyterians fleeing a mail-fraud indictment out of Bergen County, New Jersey.

Using their hard-won embezzlements, the couple had purchased a modest farm and somehow managed to infiltrate the hermetic social structure of an Amish township. At first it was just another scam, a temporary cover until the heat was off. As the years passed, though, Chemo's aunt and uncle got authentically converted. They grew to love the simple pastoral ways and hearty fellowship of the farm folk; Chemo was devastated by their transformation. Growing up, he had come to resent the family's ruse, and consequently the Amish in general. The plain baggy clothes and strict table manners were bad enough, but it was the facial hair that drove him to fury. Amish men do not shave their chins, and Chemo's uncle insisted that, once attaining puberty, he adhere to custom. Since religious arguments held no sway with Chemo, it was the practical view that his uncle propounded: All fugitives need a disguise, and a good beard was hard to beat.

Chemo sullenly acceded, until the day of his twenty-first birthday when he got in his uncle's pickup truck, drove down to the local branch of the Chemical Bank, threatened a teller with a pitchfork (the Amish own no pistols), and strolled off with seven thousand dollars and change. The first thing he bought was a Bic disposable safety razor.

The *Philadelphia Inquirer* reported that it was the only bank robbery by an Amish in the entire history of the commonwealth. Chemo himself was never arrested for the crime, but his aunt and uncle were unmasked, extradited back to New Jersey, tried and convicted of mail fraud, then shipped off to a country-club prison in north Florida. Their wheat farm was seized by the U.S. government and sold at auction.

Once Chemo was free of the Amish, the foremost challenge of adulthood was avoiding manual labor, to which he had a chronic aversion. Crime seemed to be the most efficient way of making money without working up a sweat, so Chemo gave it a try. Unfortunately, nature had dealt him a cruel disadvantage: While six foot nine was the perfect height for an NBA forward, for a burglar it was disastrous. Chemo got stuck in the very first window he ever jimmied; he could break, but he could not enter.

Four months in a county jail passed too slowly. He thought often of his aunt and uncle, and upbraided himself for not taking advantage of their vast expertise. They could have taught him many secrets about white-collar crime, yet in his rebellious insolence he had never bothered to ask. Now it was too late—their most recent postcard from the Eglin prison camp had concluded with a religious limerick and the drawing of a happy face. Chemo knew they were lost forever.

After finishing his stretch for the aborted burglary, he moved to a small town outside of Scranton and went to work for the city parks and recreation department. Before long, he parlayed a phony but impressive résumé into the post of assistant city manager, a job that entitled him to a secretary and a municipal car.

While the salary was only twenty thousand dollars a year, the secondary income derived from bribes and kickbacks was substantial. Chemo prospered as a shakedown artist, and the town prospered, too. He was delighted to discover how often the mutual interests of private enterprise and government seemed to intersect.

The high point of Chemo's municipal career was his savvy trashing of local zoning laws to allow a Mafia-owned-and-operated dog food plant to be built in the suburbs. Three hundred new jobs were created, and there was talk of running Chemo for mayor.

He greatly liked the idea and immediately began gouging illegal political contributions out of city contractors. Soon a campaign poster was designed, but Chemo recoiled when he saw the finished product: the four-foot photographic blowup of his face magnified the two ingrown hair follicles on the tip of his otherwise normal nose; the blemishes looked, in Chemo's own distraught simile, 'like two ticks fucking.' He ordered the campaign posters shredded, scheduled a second photo session, and drove straight to Scranton for the ill-fated electrolysis treatment.

The grisly mishap and subsequent murder of the offending doctor put an end to Chemo's political career. He swore off public service forever.

They rented an Aquasport and docked it at Sunday's-on-the-Bay. They chose a table under the awning, near the water. Chemo ordered a ginger ale and Chloe Simpkins Stranahan got a vodka tonic, double.

'We'll wait till dusk,' Chemo said.

'Fine by me.' Chloe slurped her drink like a parched coyote. She was wearing a ridiculous white sailor's suit from Lord and Taylor's; she even had the cap. It was not ideal boatwear.

'I used to work in this joint,' Chloe said, as if to illustrate how far she'd come.

Chemo said, 'This is where you met Mick?'

'Unfortunately.'

The bar was packed for ladies' night. In addition to the standard assembly of slick Latin studs in lizard shoes, there were a dozen blond, husky mates off the charter boats. In contrast to the disco Dannies, the mates wore T-shirts and sandals and deep Gulf Stream tans, and they drank mostly beer. The competition for feminine attention was fierce, but Chemo planned to be long gone before any fights broke out. Besides, he didn't like sitting out in the open, where people could stare.

'Have you got your plan?' Chloe asked.

'The less you know, the better.'

'Oh, pardon me,' she said caustically. 'Pardon me, Mister James Fucking Bond.'

He blinked neutrally. A young pelican was preening itself on a nearby dock piling, and Chemo found this infinitely more fascinating than watching Chloe Simpkins Stranahan in a Shirley Temple sailor cap, sucking down vodkas. It offended him that someone so beautiful could be so repellent and obnoxious; it seemed damned unfair.

On the other hand, she had yet to make the first wisecrack about his face, so maybe she had one redeeming quality.

'This isn't going to get too heavy?' she said.

'Define heavy.'

Chloe stirred her drink pensively. 'Maybe you could just put a good scare in him.'

'Bet on it,' Chemo said.

'But you won't get too tough, right?'

'What is this, all of a sudden you're worried about him?'

'You can hate someone's guts and still worry about him.'

'Jesus H. Christ.'

Chloe said, 'Chill out, okay? I'm not backing down.'

Chemo toyed with one of the infrequent black wisps attached to his scalp. He said: 'Where does your husband think you are?'

'Shopping,' Chloe replied.

'Alone?'

'Sure.'

Chemo licked his lips and scanned the room. 'You see anybody you know?'

Chloe looked around and said, 'No. Why do you ask?'

'Just making sure. I don't want any surprises; neither do you.'

Chemo paid the tab, helped Chloe into the bow of the Aquasport and cast off the ropes. He checked his wristwatch: 5:15. Give it maybe an hour before nightfall. He handed Chloe a plastic map of Biscayne Bay with the pertinent channel markers circled in red ink. 'Keep that handy,' he shouted over the engine, 'case I get lost.'

She tapped the map with one of her stiletto fingernails. 'You can't miss the goddamn things, they're sticking three stories out of the water.'

Fifteen minutes later, they were drifting through a Stiltsville channel with the boat's engine off. Chloe Simpkins Stranahan was complaining about her hair getting salty, while Chemo untangled the anchor ropes. The anchor was a big rusty clunker with a bent tongue. He hauled it out of the Aquasport's forward hatch and laid it on the deck.

Then he took some binoculars from a canvas duffel and began scouting the stilt houses. 'Which one is it?' he asked.

'I told you, it's got a windmill.'

'I'm looking at three houses with windmills, so which is it? I'd like to get the anchor out before we float to frigging Nassau.'

Chloe huffed and took the binoculars. After a few moments she said, 'Well, they all look alike.'

'No shit.'

She admitted she had never been on her ex-husband's house before. 'But I've been by there in a boat.'

Chemo said, 'How do you know it was his?'

'Because I saw him. He was outside, fishing.'

'How long ago was this?'

'Three, maybe four months. What's the difference?'

Chemo said, 'Did Mick know it was you in the boat?'

'Sure he did, he dropped his damn pants.' Chloe handed Chemo the binoculars and pointed. 'That's the one, over there.'

'You sure?'

'Yes, Captain Ahab, I am.'

Chemo studied the stilt house through the field glasses. The windmill was turning and a skiff was tied up under the water tanks, but no one was outside.

'So now what?' Chloe asked.

'I'm thinking.'

'Know what I wish you'd do? I wish you'd do to him what he did to my male friend. Krazy Glue the bastard.'

'That would settle things, huh?'

Chloe's tone became grave. 'Mick Stranahan destroyed a man without killing him. Can you think of anything worse?'

'Well,' Chemo said, reaching for the duffel, 'I didn't bring any glue. All I brought was this.' He took out the .22 pistol and screwed on the silencer.

Chloe made a gulping noise and grabbed the bow rail for support. So much for poise, Chemo thought.

'Don't worry, Mrs. Stranahan, this is my just-in-case.' He laid the pistol on top of the boat's console. 'All I really need is a little friction.' Smiling, he held up a book of matches from Sunday's bar.

'You're going to burn the house down? That's great!' Chloe's eyes shone with relief. 'Burning the house, that'll freak him out.'

'Big-time,' Chemo agreed.

'Just what that dangerous lunatic deserves.'

'Right.'

Chloe looked at him mischievously. 'You promised to tell me who you really are.'

'No, I didn't.'

'At least tell me why you're doing this.'

'I'm being paid,' Chemo said.

'By who?'

'Nobody you know.'

'Another ex-wife, I'll bet.'

'What did I say?'

'Oh, all right.' Chloe stood up and peered over the gunwale at the slick green water. Chemo figured she was checking out her own reflection.

'Did you bring anything to drink?'

'No,' Chemo replied. 'No drinks.'

She folded her arms to show how peeved she was. 'You mean, I've got to stay out here till dark with nothing to drink.'

'Longer than that,' Chemo said. 'Midnight.'

'But Mick'll be asleep by then.'

'That's the idea, Mrs. Stranahan.'

'But how will he know to get out of the house?'

Chemo laughed gruffly. 'Now who's the rocket scientist?'

Chloe's expression darkened. She pursed her lips and said, 'Wait a minute, I don't want you to kill him.'

'Who asked you?'

A change was taking place in Chloe's attitude, the way she regarded Chemo. It was as if she was seeing the man for the first time, and she was staring, which Chemo did not appreciate. Her and her tweezered eyebrows.

'You're a killer,' she said, reproachfully.

Chemo blinked amphibiously and plucked at one of the skin tags on his cheek. His eyes were round and wet and distant.

'You're a killer,' Chloe repeated, 'and you tricked me.'

Chemo said, 'You hate him so much, what do you care if he's dead or not?'

Her eyes flashed. 'I care because I still get a check from that son of a bitch as long as he's alive. He's dead, I get zip.'

Chemo was dumbstruck. 'You get alimony? But you're remarried! To a frigging CPA!'

'Let's just say Mick Stranahan didn't have the world's sharpest lawyer.'

'You are one greedy twat,' Chemo said acidly.

'Hey, it's one-fifty a month,' Chloe said. 'Barely covers the lawn service.'

She did not notice the hostility growing in Chemo's expression. 'Killing Mick Stranahan is out of the question,' she declared. 'Burn up the house, fine, but I don't want him dead.'

'Tough titties,' Chemo said.

'Look, I don't know who you are—'

'Sit,' Chemo said. 'And keep your damn voice down.'

The wind was kicking up, and he was afraid the argument might carry across the flats to the house.

Chloe sat down but was not about to shut up. 'You listen to me—'

'I said, keep your damn voice down!'

'Screw you, Velcro face.'

Chemo's brow crinkled, his cheeks fluttered. He probably even flushed, though this was impossible to discern.

Velcro-face—there it was, finally. The insult. The witch just couldn't resist after all.

'Now what's the matter?' Chloe Simpkins Stranahan said. 'You look seasick.'

'I'm fine,' Chemo said. 'But you shouldn't call people names.'

Then he heaved the thirty-pound anchor into her lap, and watched her pitch over backwards in her silky sailor suit. The staccato trail of bubbles suggested that she was cursing him all the way to the bottom of the bay.

9

Tina woke up alone in bed. She wrapped herself in a sheet and padded groggily around the dark house, looking for Mick Stranahan. She found him outside, balanced on the deck rail with his hands on his hips. He was watching Old Man Chitworth's stilt house light up the sky; a crackling orange torch, visible for miles. The house seemed to sway on its wooden legs, an illusion caused by blasts of raw heat above the water.

Tina thought it was the most breathtaking thing she had ever seen, even better than Old Faithful. In the glow from the blaze she looked up at Stranahan's face and saw concern.

'Somebody living there?' she said.

'No.' Stranahan watched Old Man Chitworth's windmill fall, the flaming blades spinning faster in descent. It hit the water with a sizzle and hiss.

'What started the fire?' Tina asked.

'Arson,' Stranahan said matter-of-factly. 'I heard a boat.'

'Maybe it was an accident,' she suggested. 'Maybe somebody tossed a cigarette.'

'Gasoline,' Stranahan said. 'I smelled it.'

'Wow. Whoever owns that place has some serious enemies, I guess.'

'The man who owns that place just turned eighty-three,' Stranahan said. 'He's on tubes in a nursing home, all flaked out. Thinks he's Eddie Rickenbacker.'

A gust of wind prompted Tina to rearrange her sheet. She got a shiver and edged closer to Mick. She said, 'Some harmless old geezer. Then I don't get it.'

Stranahan said, 'Wrong house, that's all.' He hopped off the rail. 'Somebody fucked up.' So much for paradise, he thought; so much for peace and tranquility.

Across the bay, from Dinner Key, came the whine of toy-like sirens. Stranahan didn't need binoculars to see the flashing blue dots from the advancing police boats.

Tina clutched his hand. She couldn't take her eyes off the fire. 'Mick, have you got enemies like that?'

'Hell, I've got *friends* like that.'

By midmorning the Chitworth house had burned to the water-line, and the flames died. All that remained sticking out were charred tips of the wood pilings, some still smoldering.

Tina was reading on a deck chair and Stranahan was doing push-ups when the marine patrol boat drove up and stopped. It was Luis Córdova and another man whom Stranahan did not expect.

'Now, there's something you don't see every day,' Stranahan announced, plenty loud. 'Two Cubans in a boat, and no beer.'

Luis Córdova grinned. The other man climbed noisily up on the dock and said, 'And here's something else you don't see every day: An Irishman up before noon, and still sober.'

The man's name was Al García, a homicide detective for the Metro-Dade police. His J. C. Penney coat jacket was slung over one arm, and his shiny necktie was loosened halfway down his chest. García was not wild about boat rides, so he was in a gruff and unsettled mood. Also, there was the matter of the dead body.

'What dead body?' Mick Stranahan said.

Badger-like, García shuffled up the stairs to the house, with Stranahan and Luis Córdova following single file. García gave the place the once-over and waved courteously to Tina on her lounge chair. The detective half-turned to Stranahan and in a low voice said, 'What, you opened a halfway house for bimbos! Mick, you're a freaking saint, I swear.'

They went inside the stilt house and closed the door. 'Tell me about the dead body,' Stranahan said.

'Sit down. Hey, Luis, I could use some coffee.'

'A minute ago you were seasick,' Luis Córdova said.

'I'm feeling much better, okay?' García scowled theatrically as the young marine patrol officer went to the kitchen. 'Interdepartmental cooperation, that's the buzzword these days. Coffee's a damn good place to start.'

'Easy, man, Luis is a sharp kid.'

'He sure is. I wish he was ours.'

Stranahan said, 'Now about the body . . .'

García waved a meaty brown hand in the air, as if shooing an invisible horsefly. 'Mick, what are you doing way the fuck out here? Somehow I don't see you as Robinson Crusoe, sucking the milk out of raw coconuts.'

'It's real quiet out here.'

Luis Córdova brought three cups of hot coffee.

Al García smacked his lips as he drank. 'Quiet—is that what you said? Jeez, you got dead gangsters floating around, not to mention burning houses—'

'Is this about Tony the Eel?'

'No,' Luis said seriously.

García put down his coffee cup and looked straight at Stranahan. 'When's the last time you saw Chloe?'

Suddenly Mick Stranahan did not feel so well.

'A couple of months back,' he said. 'She was on a boat with some guy. I assumed it was her new husband. Why?'

'You mooned her.'

'Can you blame me?'

'We heard about it from the mister this morning.'

Stranahan braced to hear the whole story. Luis Córdova opened a spiral notebook but didn't write much. Stranahan listened somberly and occasionally looked out the window toward the channel where Al García said it had happened.

'A rusty anchor?' Stranahan said in disbelief.

'It got tangled in this silky thing she was wearing,' the detective explained. 'She went down like a sack of cement.' Sensitivity was not García's strong suit.

'The rope is what gave it away,' added Luis Córdova. 'One of the guys coming out to the fire saw the rope drifting up out of the current.'

'Hauled her right in,' García said, 'like a lobster pot.'

'Lord.'

García said, 'Fact is, we really shouldn't be telling you all this.'

'Why not?'

'Because you're the prime suspect.'

'That's very funny.' Stranahan looked at Luis Córdova. 'Is he kidding?'

The young marine patrolman shook his head.

García said, 'Mick, your track record is not so hot. I mean, you already got a few notches in your belt.'

'Not murder.'

'Chloe hated your guts,' Al García said, in the tone of a reminder.

'That's my motive? She hated my guts?'

'Then there's the dough.'

'You think I'd kill her over a crummy one-hundred fifty dollars a month?'

'The principle,' Al García said, unwrapping a cigar. 'I think you just might do it over the principle of the thing.'

Stranahan leaned back with a tired sigh. He felt bad about Chloe's death, but mostly he felt curious. What the hell was she doing out here at night?

'I always heard good things about you,' Al García said, 'mainly from Timmy Gavigan.'

'Yeah, he said the same for you.'

'And the way Eckert dumped you from the State Attorney's, that was low.'

Stranahan shrugged. 'They don't forget it when you shoot a judge. It's bound to make people nervous.'

García made a great ceremony of lighting the cigar. Afterwards, he blew two rings of smoke and said, 'For what it's worth, Luis here doesn't think you did it.'

'It's the anchor business,' Luis Córdova explained, 'very strange.' He was trying to sound all business, as if the friendship meant nothing.

Stranahan said, 'The murder's got to be connected to the fire.'

'The fire was an arson,' Luis said. 'Boat gas and a match. These houses are nothing but tinder.' To make his point, he tapped the rubber heel of his shoe on the pine floor.

Stranahan said, 'I think you both ought to know: Somebody wants to kill me.'

García's eyebrows shot up and he rolled the cigar from one side of his mouth to the other. 'Who is it, *chico*? Please, make my job easier.'

'I think it's a doctor. His name is Rudy Graveline. Write this down, Luis, please.'

'And why would this doctor want you dead?'

'I'm not sure, Al.'

'But you want me to roust him on a hunch.'

'No, I just want his name in a file somewhere. I want you to know who he is, just in case.'

García turned to Luis Córdova. 'Don't you love the fucking sound of that? *Just in case*. Luis, I think this is where we're supposed to give Mr. Stranahan a lecture about taking the law into his own hands.'

Luis said, 'Don't take the law into your own hands, Mick.'

'Thank you, Luis.'

Al García flicked a stubby thumb through his black mustache. 'Just for the record, you didn't invite the lovely Chloe Simpkins Stranahan out here for a romantic reconciliation over fresh fish and wine?'

'No,' Stranahan said. Fish and wine—that fucking García must have scoped out the dirty dinner dishes.

'And the two of you didn't go for a boat ride?'

'No, Al.'

'And you didn't get in a sloppy drunken fight?'

'No.'

'And you didn't hook her to the anchor and drop her overboard?'

'Nope.'

'Luis, you get all that?'

Luis Córdova nodded as he jotted in the notebook. Shorthand, too; Stranahan was impressed.

García got up and went knocking around the house, making

Stranahan very nervous. When the detective finally stopped prowling, he stood directly under the stuffed blue marlin. 'Mick, I don't have to tell you there's some guys in Homicide think you aced old Judge Goomer without provocation.'

'I know that, Al. There's some guys in Homicide used to be in business with Judge Goomer.'

'And I know *that*. Point is, they'll be looking at this Chloe thing real hard. Harder than normal.'

Stranahan said, 'There's no chance it was an accident?'

'No,' Luis Córdova interjected. 'No chance.'

'So,' said Al García, 'you see the position I'm in. Until we get another suspect, you're it. The good news is, we've got no physical evidence connecting you. The bad news is, we've got Chloe's manicurist.'

Stranahan groaned. 'Jesus, let's hear it.'

García ambled to a window, stuck his arm out and tapped cigar ash into the water.

'Chloe had her toenails done yesterday morning,' the detective said. 'Told the girl she was coming out here to clean your clock.'

'Lovely,' said Mick Stranahan.

There was a small rap on the door and Tina came in, fiddling with the strap on the top piece of her swimsuit. Al García beamed like he'd just won the lottery; a dreary day suddenly had been brightened.

Stranahan stood up. 'Tina, I want you to meet Sergeant García and Officer Córdova. They're here on police business. Al, Luis, I'd like you to meet my alibi.'

'How do you do,' said Luis Córdova, shaking Tina's hand in a commendably official way.

García gave Stranahan another sideways look. 'I love it,' said the detective. 'I absolutely love this job.'

Christina Marks heard about the death of Chloe Simpkins Stranahan on the six o'clock news. The only thing she could think was that Mick had done it to pay Chloe back for siccing the TV crew on him. It was painful to believe, but the only other possibility was too far-fetched—that Chloe's murder was a coincidence of timing and had nothing to do with Mick or Victoria Barletta. This Christina Marks could not accept; she had to plan for the worst.

If Mick was the killer, that would be a problem.

If Chloe had blabbed about getting five hundred in tipster money from the Reynaldo Flemm show, that would be a problem too. The police would want to know everything, then the papers would get hold of it and the Barletta story would blow up prematurely.

Then there was the substantial problem of Reynaldo himself; Christina could just hear him hyping the hell out of Chloe's murder in the intro: 'The story you are about to see is so explosive that a confidential informant who provided us with key information was brutally murdered only days later . . .' *Brutally murdered* was one of Reynaldo's favorite on-camera redundancies. Once Christina had drolly asked Reynaldo if he'd ever heard of anyone being *gently* murdered, but he missed the point.

Sometimes, when he got particularly excited about a story, Reynaldo Flemm would actually try to write out the script himself, with comic results. The murder of Stranahan's ex-wife was just the sort of bombshell to inspire Reynaldo's muse, so Christina decided on a preemptive attack. She was reaching across the bed for the telephone when it rang.

It was Maggie Gonzalez, calling collect from somewhere in Manhattan.

'Miss Marks, I got a little problem.'

Christina said: 'We've been looking all over for you. What happened to your trip to Miami?'

'I went, I came back,' Maggie said. 'I told you, there's a problem down there.'

'So, what've you been doing the last few weeks,' Christina said, 'besides spending our money?' Christina had just about had it with this ditz; she was beginning to think Mick was right, the girl was ripping them off.

Maggie said, 'Hey, I'm sorry I didn't call sooner. I was scared. Scared out of my mind.'

'We thought you might be dead.'

'No,' said Maggie, barely audible. A long pause suggested that she was fretting over the grim possibility.

'Don't you even want to know how the story is going?' Christina asked warily.

'That's the problem,' Maggie replied. 'That's what I want to talk to you about.'

'Oh?'

Then, almost as an afterthought, Maggie asked, 'Who've you interviewed so far?'

'Nobody,' Christina said. 'We've got a lot of legwork to do first.'

'I can't believe you haven't interviewed anybody!'

Maggie was trolling for something, Christina could tell. 'We're taking it slow,' Christina said. 'This is a sensitive piece.'

'No joke,' Maggie said. 'Real sensitive.'

Christina held the phone in the crook of her shoulder and dug a legal pad and felt-tip pen from her shoulder bag on the bed table.

Maggie went on: 'This whole thing could get me killed, and I think that's worth more than five thousand dollars.'

'But that was our agreement,' Christina said, scribbling along with the conversation.

'That was before I started getting threatening calls on my machine,' said Maggie Gonzalez.

'From who?'

'I don't know who,' Maggie lied. 'It sounded like Dr. Graveline.'

'What kind of threats? What did they say?'

'*Threat* threats,' Maggie said impatiently. 'Enough to scare me shitless, okay? You guys tricked me into believing this was safe.'

'We did nothing of the sort.'

'Yeah, well, five thousand dollars isn't going to cut it anymore. By the time this is finished, I'll probably have to pack up and move out of Miami. You got any idea what that'll cost?'

Christina Marks said, 'What's the bottom line here, Maggie?'

'The bottom line is, I talked to *20/20*.'

Perfect, Christina thought. The perfect ending to a perfect day.

'I met with an executive producer,' Maggie said.

'Lucky you,' said Christina Marks. 'How much did they offer?'

'Ten.'

'Ten thousand?'

'Right,' Maggie said. 'Plus a month in Mexico after the program airs . . . you know, to let things cool off.'

'You thought of this all by yourself, or did you get an agent?'

'A what?'

'An agent. Every eyewitness to a murder ought to have his own booking agent, don't you think?'

Maggie sounded confused. 'Ten seemed like a good number,' she said. 'Could be better, of course.'

Christina Marks was dying to find out how much Maggie Gonzalez had told the producer at *20/20*, but instead of asking she said: 'Ten sounds like a winner, Maggie. Besides, I don't think we're interested in the story anymore.'

During the long silence that followed, Christina tried to imagine the look on Maggie's face.

Finally: 'What do you mean, "not interested"?'

'It's just too old, too messy, too hard to prove,' Christina said. 'The fact that you waited four years to speak up really kills us in the credibility department . . .'

'Hold on—'

'By the way, are they still polygraphing all their sources over at *20/20*?'

But Maggie was too sharp. 'Getting back to the money,' she said, 'are you saying you won't even consider a counteroffer?'

'Exactly.'

'Have you talked this over with Mr. Flemm?'

'Of course,' Christina Marks bluffed, forging blindly ahead.

'That's very weird,' remarked Maggie Gonzalez, 'because I just talked to Mr. Flemm myself about ten minutes ago.'

Christina sagged back on the bed and closed her eyes.

'And?'

'And he offered me fifteen grand, plus six weeks in Hawaii.'

'I see,' Christina said thinly.

'Anyway, he said I should call you right away and smooth out the details.'

'Such as?'

'Reservations,' said Maggie Gonzalez. 'Maui would be my first choice.'

10

One of the wondrous things about Florida, Rudy Graveline thought as he chewed on a jumbo shrimp, was the climate of unabashed corruption: There was absolutely no trouble from which money could not extricate you.

Rudy had learned this lesson years earlier when the state medical board had first tried to take away his license. For the board it had been a long sticky process, reviewing the complaints of disfigured patients, comparing the 'before' and 'after' photographs, sifting through the minutiae of thirteen separate malpractice suits. Since the medical board was made up mostly of other doctors, Rudy Graveline had fully expected exoneration—physicians stick together like shit on a shoe.

But the grossness of Rudy's surgical mistakes was so astounding that even his peers could not ignore it; they recommended that he be suspended from the practice of medicine forever. Rudy hired a Tallahassee lawyer and pushed the case to a state administrative hearing. The hearing officer acting as judge was not a doctor himself, but some schlump civil servant knocking down twenty-eight thousand a year, tops. At the end of the third day of testimony—some of it so ghastly that Rudy's own attorney became nauseated—Rudy noticed the hearing officer getting into a decrepit old Ford Fairmont to go home to his wife and four kids. This gave Rudy an idea. On the fourth day, he made a phone call. On the fifth day, a brand new Volvo station wagon with cruise control was delivered to the home of the hearing officer. On the sixth day, Dr. Rudy Graveline was cleared of all charges against him.

The board immediately reinstated Rudy's license and sealed all the records from the public and the press—thus honoring the long-held philosophy of Florida's medical establishment that the last persons who need to know about a doctor's incompetence are the patients.

Safe from the sanctions and scrutiny of his own profession, Dr. Rudy Graveline viewed all outside threats as problems that could be handled politically, that is, with bribery. Which is why he was having a long lunch with Dade County Commissioner Roberto Pepsical, who was chatting about the next election.

'Shrimp good, no?' said Roberto, who pocketed one in each cheek.

'Excellent,' Rudy agreed. He pushed the cocktail platter aside and dabbed the corners of his mouth with a napkin. 'Bobby, I'd like to give each of you twenty-five.'

'Grand?' Roberto Pepsical flashed a mouthful of pink-flecked teeth. 'Twenty-five grand, are you serious?'

The man was a hog: a florid, jowly, pug-nosed, rheumy-eyed hog. A cosmetic surgeon's nightmare. Rudy Graveline couldn't bear to watch him eat. 'Not so loud,' he said to the commissioner. 'I know what the campaign law says, but there are ways to duck it.'

'Great!' said Roberto. He had an account in the Caymans; all the commissioners did, except for Lillian Atwater, who was trying out a phony blind trust in the Dominican Republic.

Rudy said, 'First I've got to ask a favor.'

'Shoot.'

The doctor leaned forward, trying to ignore Roberto's hot gumbo breath. 'The vote on Old Cypress Towers,' Rudy said, 'the rezoning thing.'

Roberto Pepsical lunged for a crab leg and cracked it open with his front teeth. 'Nooooo problem,' he said.

Old Cypress Towers was one of Dr. Rudy Graveline's many real estate projects and tax shelters: a thirty-three story luxury apartment building with a nightclub and health spa planned for the top floor. Only trouble was, the land currently was zoned for low-density public use—parks, schools, ball fields, shit like that. Rudy needed five votes on the county commission to turn it around.

'No sweat,' Roberto reiterated. 'I'll talk to the others.'

The 'others' were the four commissioners who always got pieced out in Roberto Pepsical's crooked deals. The way the system was set up, each of the nine commissioners had his own crooked deals and his own set of locked votes. That way the tally always came out 5–4, but with different players on each side. The idea was to confuse the hell out of the newspaper reporters, who were always trying to figure out who on the commission was honest and who wasn't.

'One more thing,' Dr. Rudy Graveline said.

'How about another beer?' asked Roberto Pepsical, eyeing his empty sweaty glass. 'You don't mind if I get one.'

'Go ahead,' Rudy said, biting back his disgust.

'Crab?' The commissioner brandished another buttery leg.

'No thanks.' Rudy waited for him to wedge it in his mouth, then said: 'Bobby, I also need you to keep your ears open.'

'For what?'

'Somebody who used to work for me is threatening to go to the cops, trying to bust my balls. They're making up stuff about some old surgical case.'

Roberto nodded and chewed in synchronization, like a mechanical dashboard ornament. Rudy found it very distracting.

He said, 'The whole thing's bullshit, honestly. A disgruntled employee.'

Roberto said, 'Boy I know how it is.'

'But for a doctor, Bobby, it could be a disaster. My reputation, my livelihood, surely you can understand. That's why I need to know if the cops ever go for it.'

Roberto Pepsical said, 'I'll talk to the chief myself.'

'Only if you hear something.'

Roberto winked. 'I'll poke around.'

'I'd sure appreciate it,' Dr. Graveline said. 'I can't afford a scandal, Bobby. Something like that, I'd probably have to leave town.'

The commissioner's brow furrowed as he contemplated his twenty-five large on the wing. 'Don't sweat it,' he said confidently to the doctor. 'Here, have a conch fritter.'

Chemo was in the waiting room when Rudy Graveline got back to Whispering Palms.

'I did it,' he announced.

Rudy quickly led him into the office.

'You got Stranahan?'

'Last night,' Chemo said matter-of-factly. 'So when can we get started on my face?'

Unbelievable, Rudy thought. Very scary, this guy.

'You mean the dermabrasion treatments.'

'Fucking A,' Chemo said. 'We had a deal.'

Rudy buzzed his secretary and asked her to bring him the morning *Herald*. After she went out again, Chemo said, 'It happened so late, probably didn't make the paper.'

'Hmmmm,' said Rudy Graveline, scanning the local news page. 'Maybe that's it—must have happened too late. Tell me about it, please.'

Chemo wet his dead-looking lips. 'I torched his house.' No expression at all. 'He was asleep.'

'You know this for a fact?'

'I watched it go up,' Chemo said. 'Nobody got out.' He crossed his long legs and stared dully at the doctor. The droopy lids made him look like he was about to doze off.

Rudy folded up the newspaper. 'I believe you,' he said to Chemo, 'but I'd like to be sure. By tomorrow it ought to be in the papers.'

Chemo rubbed the palm of one hand along his cheeks, making sandpaper sounds. Rudy Graveline wished he would knock it off.

'What about the TV?' Chemo asked. 'Does that count, if it makes the TV?'

'Of course.'

'Radio, too?'

'Certainly,' Rudy said. 'I told you before, no big deal. I don't need to see the actual corpse, okay, but we do need to be sure. It's very important, because this is a dangerous man.'

'*Was*,' Chemo said pointedly.

'Right. This was a dangerous man.' Rudy didn't mention Stranahan's ominous phone call on Maggie Gonzalez's answering machine. Better to limit the cast of characters, for Chemo's sake. Keep him focused.

'Maybe it's already on the radio,' Chemo said hopefully.

Rudy didn't want to put the guy in a mood. 'Tell you what,' he said in a generous tone. 'We'll go ahead and do the first treatment this afternoon.'

Chemo straightened up excitedly. 'No shit?'

'Why not?' the doctor said, standing. 'We'll try a little patch on your chin.'

'How about the nose?' Chemo said, touching himself there.

Rudy slipped on his glasses and came around the desk to where Chemo was sitting. Because of Chemo's height, even in the chair, the surgeon didn't have to lean over far to get a close-up look at the corrugated, cheesy mass that passed for Chemo's nose.

'Pretty rough terrain,' Rudy Graveline said, peering intently. 'Better to start slow and easy.'

'Fast and rough is fine with me.'

Rudy took off his glasses and struck an avuncular pose, a regular Marcus Welby. 'I want to be very careful,' he told Chemo. 'Yours is an extreme case.'

'You noticed.'

'The machine we use is a Stryker dermabrader—'

'I don't care if it's a fucking Black and Decker, let's just do it.'

'Scar tissue is tricky,' Rudy persisted. 'Some skin reacts better to sanding than others.' He couldn't help remembering what had happened to the last doctor who had screwed up Chemo's face. Getting murdered was even worse than getting sued for malpractice.

'One little step at a time,' Rudy cautioned. 'Trust me.'

'Fine, then start on the chin, whatever,' Chemo said with a wave of a pale hand. 'You're the doctor.'

Those magic words.

How Rudy Graveline loved to hear them.

Compared to other law firms, Kipper Garth's had the overhead problem dicked. He had one central office, no partners, no associates, no 'of counsels.' His major expenses were billboard advertising, cable, telephones (he had twenty lines), and, of course, secretaries (he called them legal aides, and employed fifteen). Kipper Garth's law practice was, in essence, a high-class boiler room.

The phones never stopped ringing. This was because Kipper Garth had shrewdly put up his billboards at the most dangerous traffic intersections in South Florida, so that the second thing every noncomatose accident victim saw (after the Jaws of Life) was Kipper Garth's phone number in nine-foot red letters: 555-TORT.

Winnowing the incoming cases took most of the time, so Kipper Garth delegated this task to his secretaries, who were undoubtedly more qualified anyway. Kipper Garth saved his own energy for selecting referrals; some P.I. lawyers specialized in spinal cord injuries, others in orthopedics, still others in death-and-dismemberment. Though Kipper Garth was not one to judge a colleague's skill in the courtroom (not having *been* in a courtroom in at least a decade), he knew a fifty-fifty fee split when he saw it, and made his referrals accordingly.

The phone bank at Kipper Garth's firm looked and sounded like the catalog-order department at Montgomery Ward. By contrast, the interior of Kipper Garth's private office was rich and staid, lit like an old library and just as quiet. This is where Mick Stranahan found his brother-in-law, practicing his putting.

'You don't knock anymore?' said Kipper Garth, eyeing a ten-footer into a Michelob stein.

'I came to make a little deal,' Stranahan said.

'This I gotta hear.' Kipper Garth wore gray European-cut slacks, a silk paisley necktie and a bone-colored shirt, the French cuffs rolled up to his elbows. His salt-and-pepper hair had been dyed silver to make him look more trustworthy on the billboards.

'Let's forget this disbarment thing,' Stranahan said.

Kipper Garth chuckled. 'It's a little late, Mick. You already testified, remember?'

'How about if I agree not to testify next time?'

Kipper Garth backed away from the next putt and looked up. 'Next time?'

'There's other cases kicking around the grievance committee, am I right?'

'But how do you—'

'Lawyers talk, Jocko.' Stranahan emptied the golf balls out of the beer stein and rolled them back across the carpet toward his brother-in-law. 'I've still got a few friends in town,' he said. 'I'm still plugged in.'

Kipper Garth leaned his putter in the corner behind his desk. 'I'm suing *you* remember? Defamation, it's called.'

'Don't make me laugh.'

The lawyer's eyes narrowed. 'Mick, I know why you're here. Chloe's been killed and you're afraid you'll take the fall. You need a lawyer, so here you are, looking for a goddamn freebie.'

'I said don't make me laugh.'

'Then what is it?'

'Who's getting your malpractice stuff these days?'

Kipper Garth started flicking through his Rolodex; it was the biggest Rolodex that Stranahan had ever seen, the size of a pot roast. Kipper Garth said, 'I've got a couple main guys, why?'

'These guys you've got, can they get state records?'

'What kind of records?'

Christ, the man was lame. 'Discipline records,' Stranahan explained, 'from the medical board.'

'Gee, I don't know.'

'There's a shocker.'

'What's going on, Mick?'

'This: You help me out, I'll lay off of you. Permanently.'

Kipper Garth snorted. 'I'm supposed to be grateful? Pardon me if I don't give a shit.'

Naturally, thought Stranahan, it would come to this. The pertinent papers were wadded in his back pocket. He got them out, smoothed them with the heel of one hand and laid them out carefully, like solitaire cards, on Kipper Garth's desk.

The lawyer muttered, 'What the hell?'

'Pay attention,' Stranahan said. 'This one here is the bill of sale for your spiffy new Maserati. That's a Xerox of the check—fifty-seven thousand, eight something, what a joke. Anyway, the account that check was written on is your clients' trust account, Jocko. We're talking deep shit. Forget disbarment, we're talking felony.'

Kipper Garth's upper lip developed an odd tic.

'I'm paying it back,' he said hoarsely.

'Doesn't matter,' Mick Stranahan said. 'Now, some of this other crap—that's a hotel bill from the Grand Bay in Coconut Grove. Same weekend you told Katie you were in Boston with the ABA. Anyway, it's none of my business but you don't look like a man that could drink three bottles of Dom all by your lonesome. See, it's right there on the bill.' Stranahan pointed, but Kipper Garth's eyes were focused someplace else, someplace far away. By now his lip was twitching like a porch lizard.

'You,' he said to Stranahan. 'You jerk.'

'Now what's this dinner for two, Jocko? My sister was at Grandma's with the kids that night, if memory serves. Dinner for two at Max's Place, what exactly was that? Probably just a client, no?'

Kipper Garth collected himself and said, 'All right, Mick.'

'You understand this situation.'

'Yes.'

'It was easier than you think,' Stranahan said. 'See, once you're plugged in, it's hard to get unplugged. I mean, once you know this stuff is out there, it's real easy to find.' A half-dozen phone calls was all it took.

Kipper Garth began folding the papers, creasing each one with a great deal of force.

Stranahan said, 'What scares you more, Jocko, the Florida Bar, the county jail, or an expensive divorce?'

Wearily, Kipper Garth said, 'Did you mean what you said before, about the disbarment and all that?'

'You're asking because you know I don't have to deal, isn't that right? Maybe that's true—maybe you'd do me this favor for nothing. But fair is fair, and you ought to get something in return. So, yeah, I'll lay off. Just like I promised.'

Kipper Garth said, 'Then I'll talk to my guys about getting the damn state files. Give me a name, please.'

'Graveline,' said Stranahan. 'Dr. Rudy Graveline.'

Kipper Garth winced. 'Jeez, I've heard that name. I think he's in my yacht club.'

Mick Stranahan clapped his hands. 'Yo ho ho,' he said.

Later, on the way to see her plastic surgeon, Tina asked Mick: 'Why didn't you make love to me last night?'

'I thought you enjoyed yourself.'

'It was sweet, but why'd you stop?'

Stranahan said: 'Because I've got this terrible habit of falling in love.'

Tina rolled her eyes. 'After one night?'

'True story,' Stranahan said. 'All five of the women I married, I proposed to them the first night we went to bed.'

'Before or after?' Tina asked.

'After,' he said. 'It's like a disease. The scary part is, they tend to say yes.'

'Not me.'

'I couldn't take that chance.'

'You're nuts,' Tina said. 'Does this mean we're never gonna do it?'

Stranahan sighed, feeling old and out of it. His ex-wife just gets murdered, some asshole doctor's trying to kill him, a TV crew is lurking around his house—all this, and Tina wants to know about getting laid, wants a time and date. Why didn't she believe him about the others?

He stopped at a self-service Shell station and filled three plastic Farm Stores jugs with regular unleaded. When he went up to pay, nobody said a word. He put the gallon jugs in the trunk of the Imperial and covered them with a bunch of boat rags.

Back in the car, Tina gave him a look. 'You didn't answer my question.'

'You've got a boyfriend,' Stranahan said, wishing he could've come up with something better, more original.

'Richie? Richie's history,' said Tina. *'No problema.'*

It always amazed Stranahan how they could make boyfriends disappear, snap, just like that.

'So,' Tina said, 'how about tonight?'

'How about I call you,' he said, 'when things cool off?'

'Yeah,' Tina muttered. 'Sure.'

Stranahan was glad when they got to the doctor's office. It was a two-story peach stucco building in Coral Gables, a refurbished old house. The plastic surgeon's name was Dicer. Craig E. Dicer; a nice young fellow, too nice to say anything nasty about Rudy Graveline at first. Stranahan badgered him and tried again. Dr.

Dicer took a good hard look at the gold State Attorney's investigator shield before he said: 'Is this off the record?'

'Sure,' said Stranahan, wondering: Where do these guys learn to talk like this?

'Graveline's a butcher,' Dr. Dicer said. 'A hacker. Everybody in town's mopped up after him, one time or another. Fortunately, he doesn't do much surgery himself anymore. He got wise, hired a bunch of young sharpies, all board certified. It's like a damn factory up there.'

'Whispering Palms?'

'You've seen it?' Dr. Dicer asked.

Stranahan said no, but it was his next stop. 'If everybody in Miami knows that Graveline's a butcher, how does he get any patients?'

Dr. Dicer laughed caustically. 'Hell, man, the patients don't know. You think some housewife wants her tits poofed goes downtown to the courthouse and looks up the lawsuits? No way. Rudy Graveline's got a big rep because he's socially connected. He did the mayor's niece's chin, this I know for a fact. And old Congressman Carberry? Graveline did his girlfriend's eyelids. Or somebody at Whispering Palms did; Rudy always takes the credit.'

Tina, who hadn't been saying much since the car, finally cut in. 'Talk to models and actresses,' she said. 'Whispering Palms is in. Like tofu.'

'Jesus,' said Stranahan.

Dr. Dicer said, 'Can I ask why you're interested?'

'Really, you don't want to know,' Stranahan said.

'I guess not.'

'*I* want to know,' Tina said.

Stranahan pretended not to hear her. He said to Dr. Dicer: 'One more question, then we'll let you get back to work. This is hypothetical.'

Dr. Dicer nodded, folded his hands, got very studious looking.

Stranahan said: 'Is it possible to kill somebody during a nose job?'

By way of an answer, Dr. Dicer took out a pink neoprene replica of a bisected human head, a bronze Crane mallet, and a small Cottle chisel. Then he demonstrated precisely how you could kill somebody during a nose job.

When Chemo got to the Gay Bidet, a punk band called the Chicken Chokers had just finished wringing their sweaty jock straps into a cocktail glass and guzzling it down on stage.

'You're late,' said Chemo's boss, a man named Freddie. 'We already had three fights.'

'Car trouble,' said Chemo. 'Radiator hose.' Not an apology, an explanation.

Freddie pointed at the small bandage and said, 'What happened to your chin?'

'A zit,' Chemo said.

'A zit, that's a good one.'

'What's that supposed to mean?'

'Nothing,' Freddie said. 'Don't mean nothing.' He had to watch the wisecracks around Chemo. The man made him nervous as a gerbil. Freaking seven-foot cadaver, other clubs would kill for a bouncer like that.

Freddie said, 'Here, you got a message.'

Chemo said thank you, went outside to a pay phone on Collins and called Dr. Rudy Graveline's beeper. At the tone, Chemo punched in the number of the pay phone, hung up, and waited. All the way out here, he could hear the next band cranking up. The Crotch Rockets, it sounded like. Their big hit was *Lube-Job Lover*. Chemo found it somewhat derivative.

The telephone rang. Chemo waited for the third time before picking up.

'We have got a problem,' said Rudy Graveline, raspy, border-line terrified.

Chemo said, 'Aren't you going to ask about my chin?'

'No!'

'Well, it stings like hell.'

Dr. Graveline said, 'I told you it would.'

Chemo said, 'How long've I gotta wear the Band-Aid?'

'Till it starts to heal, for Chrissakes. Look, I've got a major situation here and if you don't fix it, the only person's going to care about your complexion is the goddamn undertaker. One square inch of perfect chin, maybe you're thinking how gorgeous you look. Well, think open casket. How's that for gorgeous?'

Chemo absently touched his new bandage. 'Why're you so upset?'

'Mick Stranahan's alive.'

Chemo thought: The bitch in the sailor suit, she got the wrong house.

'By the way,' Rudy Graveline said angrily, 'I'd like to thank you for not telling me how you drowned the man's wife in the middle of Biscayne Bay. From what was on TV, I'm assuming it was you. Had your subtle touch.' When Chemo didn't respond for several moments, the doctor said: 'Well?'

Chemo asked, 'Is that a siren at your end?'

'Yes,' Rudy said archly, 'yes, that would be a siren. Now, aren't you going to ask how I know that Stranahan's still alive?'

'All right,' Chemo said, 'how do you know?'

'Because,' the doctor said, 'the bastard just blew up my Jag.'

11

Christina Marks knocked twice, and when no one answered she walked in. The man in the hospital bed had a plastic oxygen mask over his mouth. Lying there he looked as small as a child. The covers were pulled up to the folds of his neck. His face was mottled and drawn. When Christina approached the bed, the man's blue eyes opened slowly and he waved. When he lifted the oxygen mask away from his mouth, she saw that he was smiling.

'Detective Gavigan?'

'The one and only.'

'I'm Christina Marks.' She told him why she had come, what she wanted. When she mentioned Vicky Barletta, Timmy Gavigan made a zipper motion across his lips.

'What's the matter?' Christina asked.

'That's an open case, lady. I can't talk about it.' Timmy Gavigan's voice was hollow, like it was coming up a pipe from his dead lungs. 'We got regulations about talking to the media,' he said.

'Do you know Mick Stranahan?' Christina said.

'Sure I know Mick,' Timmy Gavigan said. 'Mick came to see me a while back.'

'About this case?'

'Mick's in my scrapbook,' Timmy Gavigan said, looking away.

Christina said, 'He's in some trouble.'

'He didn't get married again, the dumb bastard?'

Not that kind of trouble, Christina said. This time it was the Barletta case.

'Mick's a big boy,' said Timmy Gavigan. 'My guess is, he can handle it.' He was smiling again. 'Honey, you sure are pretty.'

'Thank you,' said Christina.

'Can you believe, six months ago I'd be trying to charm you right into the sack. Now I can't even get up to take a whizz. Here a gorgeous woman comes to my room and I can't raise my goddamn head, much less anything else.'

She said, 'I'm sorry.'

'I know what you're thinking—a dying man, he's likely to say anything. But I mean it, you're something special. I got high standards, always did. I mean, hell, I might be dead, but I ain't blind.'

Christina laughed softly. Timmy Gavigan reached for the oxygen mask, took a couple of deep breaths, put it down again. 'Give me your hand,' he said to Christina Marks. 'Please, it's all right. What I got, you can't catch.'

Timmy Gavigan's skin was cold and papery. Christina gave a little squeeze and tried to pull away, but he held on. She noticed his eyes had a sparkle.

'You've been to the file?'

She nodded.

'I took a statement from that doctor, Rudy Something.'

Christina said, 'Yes, I read it.'

'Help me out,' said Timmy Gavigan, squinting in concentration. 'What the hell did he say again?'

'He said it was a routine procedure, nothing out of the ordinary.'

'Yeah, I remember now,' Timmy Gavigan said. 'He was a precious thing, too, all business. Said he'd done five thousand nose jobs and this was no different from the others. And I said maybe not, but this time your patient vanished from the face of the earth. And he said she was fine last time he saw her. Walked out of the office all by herself. And I said yeah, walked straight into the fucking twilight zone. Pardon my French.'

Christina Marks said, 'You've got a good memory.'

'Too bad I can't breathe with it.' Timmy Gavigan took another hit of oxygen. 'Fact is, we had no reason to think the doctor was involved. Besides, the nurse backed him up. What the hell was his name again?'

'Graveline.'

Timmy Gavigan nodded. 'Struck me as a little snot. If only you could arrest people for that.' He coughed, or maybe it was a chuckle. 'Did I mention I was dying?'

Christina said yes, she knew.

'Did you say you were on TV?'

'No, I'm just a producer.'

'Well, you're pretty enough to be on TV.'

'Thank you.'

'I'm not being very much help, I know,' said Timmy Gavigan. 'They got me loaded up on morphine. But I'm trying to think if there was something I left out.'

'It's all right, you've been helpful.'

She could tell that each breath was torture.

He said, 'Your idea is that the doctor did it, is that right? See, that's a new angle—let me think here.'

Christina said, 'It's just a theory.'

Timmy Gavigan shifted under the covers and turned slightly to face her. 'He had a brother, was that in the file?'

No, Christina said. Nothing about a brother.

'Probably not,' Timmy Gavigan said. 'It didn't seem important at the time. I mean, the doc wasn't even a suspect.'

'I understand.'

'But he did have a brother, I talked to him maybe ten minutes. Wasn't worth typing it up.' Timmy Gavigan motioned for a cup of water and Christina held it to his lips.

'Jesus, I must be a sight,' he said. 'Anyway, the reason I mention it—let's say the doctor croaked Vicky. Don't know why, but let's say he did. What to do about the body? That's a big problem. Bodies are damn tough to get rid of, Jimmy Hoffa being the exception.'

'What does the doctor's brother do?'

Timmy Gavigan grinned, and color flashed to his cheeks. 'That's my point, honey. The brother was a tree trimmer.'

Christina tried to look pleased at this new information, but mostly she looked puzzled.

'You don't know much about tree trimming, do you?' Timmy

Gavigan said in a teasing tone. Then he gulped more oxygen.

She said, 'Why did you go see the doctor's brother?'

'I didn't. Didn't have to. I met him right outside the clinic—I forget the damn name.'

'The Durkos Medical Center.'

'Sounds right.' Timmy Gavigan paused, and his free hand moved to his throat. When the pain passed, he continued. 'Outside the clinic, I saw this guy hacking on the black olive trees. Asked him if he was there the day Vicky disappeared, if he saw anything unusual. Naturally he says no. After, I ask his name and he tells me George Graveline. So like the genius I am, I say: You related to the doctor? He says yeah, and that's about it.'

'George Graveline.' Christina Marks wrote the name down.

Timmy Gavigan lifted his head and eyed the notebook. 'Tree trimmer,' he said, 'make sure you put that down.'

'Tell me what it means, please.'

'No, you ask Mick.'

She said, 'What makes you so sure I'll see him?'

'Wild hunch.'

Then Timmy Gavigan said something that Christina Marks couldn't quite hear. She leaned over and asked him, in a whisper, to repeat it.

'I said, you sure are beautiful.' He winked once, then closed his eyes slowly.

'Thanks for holding my hand,' he said.

And then he let go.

Whenever there was a bombing in Dade County, somebody in the Central Office would call Sergeant Al García for help, mainly because García was Cuban and it was automatically assumed that the bombing was in some way related to exile politics. García had left orders that he was not to be bothered about bombings unless somebody actually died, since a dead body was the customary prerequisite of homicide investigation. He also sent detailed memoranda explaining that Cubans were not the only ones who tried to bomb each other in South Florida, and he listed all the mob and labor and otherwise non-Cuban bombings over the last ten years. Nobody at the Central Office paid much attention to García's pleadings, and they still summoned him over the most chickenshit of explosions.

This is what happened when Dr. Rudy Graveline's black Jaguar sedan blew up. García was about to tell the dispatcher to piss off, until he heard the name of the complainant. Then, fifteen minutes behind the fire trucks, he drove straight to Whispering Palms.

What had happened was: Rudy had gone to the airport to pick up a potentially important patient, a world-famous actress who had awakened one morning in her Bel Air mansion, glanced at herself naked in the mirror, and burst into tears. She got Dr. Graveline's name from a friend of a friend of Pernell Roberts's poolboy, and called to tell the surgeon that she was flying to Miami for an emergency consultation. Because of the actress's fame and wealth (most of it accumulated during a messy divorce from one of the Los Angeles Dodgers), Rudy agreed to meet the woman at the airport and give a personal tour of Whispering Palms. He was double-parked in front of the Pan Am terminal when he first noticed the beat-up old Chrysler pull in behind him, its rear end sticking into traffic. Rudy noticed the car again on his way back to the beach—the actress yammering away about the practical joke she once played on Richard Chamberlain while they were shooting some miniseries; Rudy with a worried eye on the rearview, because the Imperial was right there, on his bumper.

The other car disappeared somewhere on Alton Road, and Rudy didn't think about it again until he and the actress walked out of Whispering Palms; Rudy with a friendly hand on her elbow, she with a fistful of glossy surgery brochures. The Imperial was parked right across from Rudy's special reserved slot. The same big man was behind the wheel. The actress didn't know anything was wrong until the man got out of the Chrysler and whistled at a Yellow Cab, which was conveniently parked under a big ficus tree at the north end of the lot. When the taxi pulled up, the man from the Imperial opened the back door and told the actress to get in. He said the cabbie would take her straight to the hotel. She said she wasn't staying in any *hotel*, that she'd

rented a villa in Golden Beach where Eric Clapton once lived;
the big man said fine, the cabbie knew the way.

Finally the actress got in, the taxi drove off, and it was just the
stranger and Rudy Graveline alone in the parking lot. When
the man introduced himself, Rudy tried very hard not to act
terrified. Mick Stranahan said that he wasn't yet certain why Dr.
Graveline was trying to have him killed, but that it was a very
bad idea, overall. Dr. Graveline replied that he didn't know what
on earth the man was talking about. Then Mick Stranahan walked
across the parking lot, got in his Chrysler, turned on the ignition,
placed a coconut on the accelerator, got out of the car, reached
through the driver's window and slipped it into Drive. Then he
jumped out of the way and watched the Imperial plow directly
into the rear of Dr. Rudy Graveline's black Jaguar sedan. The
impact, plus the three jugs of gasoline that Mick Stranahan had
strategically positioned in the Jaguar's trunk, caused the automobile to explode in a most spectacular way.

When Rudy Graveline recounted this story to Detective
Sergeant Al García, he left out two details—the name of the man
who did it, and the reason.

'He never said why?' said Al García, all eyebrows.

'Not a word,' lied Dr. Graveline. 'He just destroyed my car and
walked away. The man was obviously deranged.'

García grunted and folded his arms. Smoke was still rising from
the Jag, which was covered with foam from the firetrucks. Rudy
acted forlorn about the car, but García knew the truth. The only
reason the asshole even bothered with the police was for the
insurance company.

The detective said, 'You don't know the guy who did this?'

'Never saw him before.'

'That's not what I asked.'

Rudy said, 'Sergeant, I don't know what you mean.'

García was tempted to come out and ask the surgeon if it
were true that he was trying to bump off Mick Stranahan, like
Stranahan had said. That was a fun question, the kind García
loved to ask, but the timing wasn't right. For now, he wanted
Rudy Graveline to think of him as a big, dumb cop, not a threat.

'A purely random attack,' García mused.

'It would appear so,' Rudy said.

'And you say the man was short and wiry?'

'Yes,' Rudy said.

'How short?'

'Maybe five one,' Rudy said. 'And he was black.'

'How black?'

'Very black,' the doctor said. 'Black as my tires.'

Al García dropped to a crouch and shone his flashlight on the front hub of the molten Jag. 'Michelins,' he noted. 'The man was as black as Michelins.'

'Yes, and he spoke no English.'

'Really. What language was it?'

'Creole,' Rudy Graveline said. 'I'm pretty sure.'

García rubbed his chin. 'So what we've got in the way of an arsonist,' he said, 'is a malnourished Haitian midget.'

Rudy frowned. 'No,' he said seriously, 'he was taller than that.'

García said the man apparently had picked the trunk lock in order to put the containers of gasoline inside the doctor's car. 'That shows some thinking,' the detective said.

'Could still be crazy,' Rudy said. 'Crazy people can surprise you.'

One tow truck driver put the hooks on what was left of Rudy's black Jaguar. Another contemplated the remains of the Chrysler Imperial, which García kept referring to as 'that ugly piece of elephant shit.' His hatred for Chryslers went back to his patrol days.

Lennie Goldberg, a detective from Intelligence, came up and said, 'So, what do you think, Al? Think it was Cubans?'

'No, Lennie, I think it was the Shining Path. Or maybe the freaking Red Brigade.' It took Lennie Goldberg a couple of beats to catch on. Irritably García said, 'Would you stop this shit about the Cubans? This was a routine car bomb, okay? No politics, no Castro, no CIA. No fucking Cubans, got it?'

'Jeez, Al, I was just asking.' Lennie thought García was getting very touchy on the subject.

'Use your head, Lennie.' García pointed at the wreck. 'This look like an act of international terrorism? Or does it look like some dirtball in a junker went nuts?'

Lennie said, 'Could be either, Al. With bombings, sometimes you got to look closely for the symbolism. Maybe there's a message in this. Aren't Jaguars manufactured in Britain? Maybe this is the IRA.'

García groaned. A message, for Christ's sake. And symbolism! This is what happens when you put a moron in the intelligence unit: he gets even dumber.

A uniformed cop handed Rudy Graveline a copy of the police report. The doctor folded it carefully with three creases, like a letter, and placed it in the inside pocket of his jacket.

Al García turned his back on Lennie Goldberg and said to Rudy, 'Don't worry, we'll find the guy.'

'You will?'

'No sweat,' said García, noticing how uncomfortable Rudy seemed. 'We'll run the V.I.N. number on the Chrysler and come up with our Haitian dwarf, or whatever.'

'Probably a stolen vehicle,' Rudy remarked.

'Probably not,' said Al García. *Vehicle?* Now the guy was doing Jack Webb. García said: 'No, sir, this definitely was a premeditated act, the act of a violent and unstable perpetrator. We'll do our best to solve it, Doctor, you've got my word.'

'Really, it's not that big a deal.'

'Oh, it is to us,' García said. 'It is indeed a big deal.'

'Well, I know you're awfully busy.'

'Oh, not too busy for something like this,' García said in the heartiest of tones. 'The firebombing of a prominent physician— are you kidding? Starting now, Dr. Graveline, your case is priority one.'

García was having a ball, acting so damn gung ho; the doctor looked wan and dyspeptic.

The detective said, 'You'll be hearing back from me real soon.'

'I will?' said Rudy Graveline.

Reynaldo Flemm had been in a dark funk since his clandestine visit to Whispering Palms. Dr. Graveline had lanced his ego; this, without knowing Reynaldo's true identity or the magnitude of his fame. Three days had passed, and Flemm had scarcely been able to peek out the door of his Key Biscayne hotel room. He had virtually stopped eating most solid food, resorting to a diet of protein cereal and lemon Gatorade. Every time Christina Marks knocked, Reynaldo would call out that he was in the bathroom, sick to his stomach, which was almost true. He couldn't tear himself away from the mirror. The surgeon's dire assessment of Reynaldo's nose—'two sizes too large for your face'—was savage by itself, but the casual criticism of his weight was paralyzing.

Flemm was examining himself naked in the mirror when Christina came to the door again.

'I'm sick,' he called out.

'Ray, this is stupid,' Christina scolded from the hallway. She didn't know about his trip to the clinic. 'We've got to talk about Maggie,' she said.

There was the sound of drawers being opened and closed, and maybe a closet. For a moment Christina thought he might be getting ready to emerge.

'Ray?'

'What about Maggie?' he said. Now it sounded like he was inches from the door. 'Didn't you straighten out that shit about 20/20?'

Christina said, 'That's what we have to talk about. Fifteen thousand is ludicrous. Let me in, Ray.'

'I'm not well.'

'Open the damn door or I'm calling New York.'

'No, Chris, I'm not at my best.'

'Ray, I've seen you at your best, and it's not all that great. Let me in, or I start kicking.' And she did. Reynaldo Flemm couldn't believe it, the damn door was jumping off its hinges.

'Hey, stop!' he cried, and opened it just a crack.

Christina saw that he wore a towel around his waist, and nothing else. A bright green pair of elastic cyclist shorts lay on the floor.

'Hawaii?' Christina said. 'You told that bimbette we'd send her to Hawaii.'

Reynaldo said, 'What choice did I have? You want to lose this story?'

'Yes,' Christina said, 'this story is serious trouble, Ray. I want to pack up and go home.'

'And give it to ABC? Are you nuts?' He opened the door a little more. 'We're getting so close.'

Christina tried to bait him. 'How about we fly up to Spartanburg tomorrow? Do the biker segment, like we planned?'

Reynaldo loved to do motorcycle gangs, since they almost always attacked him while the tape was rolling. The Spartanburg story had a sex-slavery angle as well, but Flemm still didn't bite.

'That'll wait,' he said.

Christina checked both ways to make sure no one was coming down the hall. 'You heard about Chloe Simpkins?'

Reynaldo Flemm shook his head. 'I haven't seen the news,' he admitted, 'in a couple of days.'

'Well, she's dead,' Christina said. 'Murdered.'

'Oh, God.'

'Out by the stilt houses.'

'No shit? What an opener.'

'Forget it, Ray, it's a mess.' She shouldered her way into his room. He sat down on the bed, his knees pressed together under the towel. A tape measure was coiled in his left hand. 'What's that for?' Christina asked, pointing.

'Nothing,' Flemm said. He wasn't about to tell her that he had been measuring his nose in the mirror. In fact, he had been taking the precise dimensions of all his facial features, to compare proportions.

He said, 'When is Chloe's funeral? Let's get Willie and shoot the stand-up there.'

'Forget it.' She explained how the cops would probably be looking for them anyway, to ask about the five hundred dollars. In its worst light, somebody might say that they contributed to Chloe's death, put her up to something dangerous.

'But we didn't,' Reynaldo Flemm whined. 'All we got from her was Stranahan's location, and barely that. A house in the bay, she said. A house with a windmill. Easiest five bills that woman ever made.'

Christina said, 'Like I said, it's a big mess. It's time to pull out. Tell Maggie to go fly her kite for Hugh Downs.'

'Let's wait a couple more days.' He couldn't stand the idea of giving up; he hadn't gotten beat up once on this whole assignment.

'Wait for what?' Christina said testily.

'So I can think. I can't think when I'm sick.'

She resisted the temptation to state the obvious. 'What exactly is the matter?' she asked.

'Nothing I care to talk about,' Flemm said.

'Ah, one of those male-type problems.'

'Fuck you.'

As she was leaving, Christina asked when he would be coming out of his hotel room to face the real world. 'When I'm good and ready,' Flemm replied defensively.

'Take your time, Ray. Tomorrow's interview is off.'

'You canceled it—why?'

'It canceled itself. The man died.'

Flemm gasped. 'Another murder!'

'No, Ray, it wasn't murder.' Christina waved good-bye. 'Sorry to disappoint you.'

'That's okay,' he said, sounding like a man on the mend, 'we can always fudge it.'

12

After Timmy Gavigan's funeral, García offered Mick Stranahan a ride back to the marina.

'I noticed you came by cab,' the detective said.

'Al, you got eyes like a hawk.'

'So where's your car?'

Stranahan said, 'I guess somebody stole it.'

It was a nice funeral, although Timmy Gavigan would have made fun of it. The chief stood up and said some good things, and afterwards some cops young enough to be Timmy's grandchildren shot off a twenty-one-gun salute and accidentally hit a power transformer, leaving half of Coconut Grove with no electricity. Stranahan had worn a pressed pair of jeans, a charcoal sports jacket, brown loafers and no socks. It was the best outfit he owned; he'd thrown out all his neckties when he moved to the stilt house. Stranahan caught himself sniffling a little toward the end of the service. He made a mental note to clip the obit from the newspaper and glue it in Timmy Gavigan's scrapbook, the way he promised. Then he would mail the scrapbook up to Boston, where Timmy's daughters lived.

Driving back out the Rickenbacker Causeway, García was saying, 'Didn't you have an old Chrysler? Funny thing, we got one of those shitheaps in a fire the other night. Somebody filed off the V.I.N. numbers, so we can't trace the damn thing—maybe it's yours, huh?'

'Maybe,' said Mick Stranahan, 'but you keep it. The block was cracked. I was ready to junk it anyway.'

García drummed his fingers on the steering wheel, which meant he was running out of patience.

'Hey, Mick?'

'What?'

'Did you blow up that asshole's Jag?'

Stranahan stared out at the bay and said, 'Who?'

'The doctor. The one who wants to kill you.'

'Oh.'

Something was not right with this guy, García thought. Maybe the funeral had put him in a mood, maybe it was something else.

'We're getting into an area,' the detective said, 'that makes me very nervous. You listening, *chico*?'

Stranahan pretended to be watching some topless girl on a sailboard.

García said, 'You want to play Charlie Bronson, okay, but let me tell you how serious this is getting. Forget the doctor for a second.'

'Yeah, how? He's trying to kill me.'

'Well, chill on that for a minute and think about this: Murdock and Salazar got assigned to Chloe's murder. Do I have to spell it out, or you want me to stop the car so you can go ahead and puke?'

'Jesus,' said Mick Stranahan.

Detectives John Murdock and Joe Salazar had been tight with the late Judge Raleigh Goomer, the one Stranahan had shot. Murdock and Salazar had been in on the bond fixings, part of the A-team. They were not Mick Stranahan's biggest fans.

'How the hell did they get the case?'

'Luck of the draw,' García said. 'Nothing I could do without making it worse.'

Stranahan slammed a fist on the dashboard. He was damn tired of all this bad news.

García said, 'So they come out here to do a canvass, right? Talk to people at the boat ramp, the restaurant, anyone who might have seen your ex on the night she croaked. They come back with statements from two waitresses and a gas attendant, and guess who they say was with Chloe? You, Blue Eyes.'

'That's a goddamn lie, Al.'

'You're right. I know it's a lie because I drive out here the next day on my lunch hour and talked to these same people myself.

On my lunch hour! Show them two mugs, including yours, and strike out. Oh for ten. So Frick and Frack are lying. I don't know what I can do about it yet—it's a tricky situation, them sticking together on their story.' García took a cigar from his breast pocket. Wrapper and all, he jammed it in the corner of his mouth. 'I'm telling you this so you know how goddamn serious it's getting, and maybe you'll quit this crazy car-bombing shit and give me a chance to do my job. How about it?'

Absently, Stranahan said, 'This is the worst year of my life, and it's only the seventeenth of January.'

García chewed the cellophane off the cigar. 'I don't know why I even bother to tell you anything,' he grumbled. 'You're acting like a damn zombie.'

The detective made the turn into the marina with a screech of the tires. Stranahan pointed toward the slip where his aluminum skiff was tied up, and García parked right across from it. He kept the engine running. Stranahan tried to open the door, but García had it locked with a button on the driver's side.

The detective punched the lighter knob in the dashboard and said, 'Don't you have anything else you want to ask? Think real hard, Mick.'

Stranahan reached across and earnestly shook García's hand. 'Thanks for everything, Al. I mean it.'

'Hey, are we having the same conversation? What the fuck is the matter with you?'

Stranahan said, 'It's been a depressing week.'

'Don't you even want to know what the waitresses and the pump jockey really said? About the guy with Chloe?'

'What guy?'

García clapped his hands. 'Good, I got your attention. Excellent!' He pulled the lighter from the dash and fired up the cigar.

'What guy?' Stranahan asked again.

Making the most of the moment, García took his notebook from his jacket and read aloud: 'White male, early thirties, approximately seven feet tall, two hundred fifty pounds, freckled, balding—'

'Holy shit.'

'—appeared to be wearing fright make-up, or possibly some type of Halloween mask. The waitresses couldn't agree on what, but they all said basically the same thing about the face. Said it looked like somebody dragged it across a cheese grater.'

Mick Stranahan couldn't recall putting anybody in jail who matched that remarkable description. He asked García if he had any leads.

'We're busy calling the circuses to see who's escaped lately,' the detective said sarcastically. 'I swear, I don't know why I tell you anything.'

He pushed the button to unlock the doors. 'We'll be in touch,' he said to Stranahan, waving him out of the police car. 'And stay away from the damn doctor, okay?'

'You bet,' said Mick Stranahan. All he could think of was: *Seven feet tall*. Poor Chloe.

Dr. Rudy Graveline now accepted the possibility that his world was imploding, and that he must prepare for the worst. Bitterly he thought of all the crises he had survived, all the professional setbacks, the lawsuits, the peer review hearings, the hospital expulsions, the hasty relocations from one jurisdiction to another. There was the time he augmented the breasts of a two-hundred-pound woman who had wanted a reduction instead; the time he nearly liposuctioned a man's gall bladder right out of his abdomen; the time he mistakenly severed a construction worker's left ear while removing a dime-sized cyst—Rudy Graveline had survived all these. He believed he'd found a safe haven in South Florida; having figured out the system, and how to beat it, he was sure he had it made. And suddenly a botched nose job had come back to spoil it all. It didn't seem fair.

Rudy sat at his desk and leafed dispiritedly through the most recent bank statements. The Whispering Palms surgical complex was raking in money, but the overhead was high and the mortgage was a killer. Rudy had not been able to siphon off nearly as much as he had hoped. Once his secret plan had been to retire in four years with six million put away; it now seemed likely that he would be forced to get out much sooner, and with much less. Having already been banned from practicing medicine in

California and New York—by far the most lucrative markets for
a plastic surgeon—Rudy Graveline's thoughts now turned to the
cosmopolitan cities of South America, a new frontier of vanity,
sun-baked and ripe with wrinkles; a place where a Harvard medical degree still counted for something. Riffling through his CDs,
he wondered if it was too late to weasel out of the Old Cypress
Towers project: get liquid and get gone.

He was studying a map of Brazil when Heather Chappell, the
famous actress, came into the office. She wore the pink terrycloth
robe and bath slippers that Whispering Palms provided to all its
VIP guests. Heather's lipstick was candy apple, her skin had a
caramel tan, and her frosted blond hair was thick and freshly
brushed. She was a perfectly beautiful thirty-year-old woman
who, for reasons unfathomable, despised her own body. A dream
patient, as far as Rudy Graveline was concerned.

She sat in a low-backed leather chair and said, 'I've had it with
the spa. Let's talk about my operation.'

Rudy said, 'I wanted you to unwind for a couple days, that's all.'

'It's been a couple days.'

'But aren't you more relaxed?'

'Not really,' Heather said. 'Your masseur, what's his name—'

'Niles?'

'Yeah, Niles. He tried to cornhole me yesterday. Aside from
that, I've been bored to tears.'

Rudy smiled with practiced politeness. 'But you've had a
chance to think about the different procedures.'

'I didn't need to think about anything, Dr. Graveline. I was
ready the first night off the plane. Have you been dodging me?'

'Of course not.'

'I heard your car got blown up.' She said it in a schoolgirl's
voice, like it was gossip she'd picked up in study hall.

Rudy tried to neutralize his inflection. 'There was an accident,'
he said. 'Very minor.'

'The night I came, wasn't it? That hunk in the parking lot, the
guy who put me in the taxi. What's going on with him?'

Rudy ignored the question. 'I can schedule the surgery for
tomorrow,' he said.

'Fine, but I want you to do it,' Heather said. 'You personally.'

'Of course,' Rudy said. He'd stay in the O.R. until they put her under, then he'd head for the back nine at Doral. Let one of the young hotshots do the knife work.

'What did you decide?' he asked her.

Heather stood up and stepped out of her slippers. Then she let the robe drop to the carpet. 'You tell me,' she said.

Rudy's mouth went dry at the sight of her.

'Well,' he said. 'Let's see.' The problem was, she didn't need any surgery. Her figure, like her face, was sensational. Her tan breasts were firm and large, not the least bit droopy. Her tummy was tight and flat as an iron. There wasn't an ounce of fat, a trace of a stretch mark, the slenderest serpentine shadow of a spider vein—not on her thighs, her legs, not anywhere. Nothing was out of proportion. Naked, Heather looked like an 'after,' not a 'before.'

Rudy was really going to have to scramble on this one. He put on his glasses and said, 'Come over here, Miss Chappell, let me take a closer look.'

She walked over and, to his stupefaction, climbed up on the onyx desk, her bare feet squeaking on the slick black surface. Standing, she vamped a movie pose—one hand on her hip, the other fluffing her hair. As Rudy's eyes traveled up those long legs, he nearly toppled over backwards in his chair.

'The nose, obviously,' Heather said.

'Yes,' said Rudy, thinking: She has a great straight nose. What the hell am I going to do?

'And the breasts,' Heather said, taking one in each hand and studying them. Like she was in the produce section, checking out the grapefruits.

Bravely Rudy asked, 'Would you like them larger or smaller?'

Heather glared at him. 'Bigger, of course! And brand-new nipples.'

Jesus, Rudy muttered under his breath. 'Miss Chappell,' he said, 'I wouldn't advise new nipples. There could be serious complications and, really, it isn't necessary.' Little pink rosebuds, that's what her nipples looked like. Why, Rudy wondered, would she ever want new ones?

In a pouty voice, Heather said all right, leave the nipples. Then she pivoted on the desktop and patted her right thigh. 'I want two inches off here.'

'That much?' Rudy was sweating. He didn't see it, plain and simple. Two inches of what?

'Stand up,' Heather told him. 'Look here.'

He did, he looked hard. His chin was about three inches from her pubic bone. 'Two inches,' Heather repeated, turning to show him the other thigh, 'from both sides.'

'As you wish,' the doctor said. What the hell, he'd be on the golf course anyway. Let the whizz kids figure it out.

Heather dropped to her knees on the desk, so the two of them were nearly face to face. 'And I want my eyelids done,' she said, pointing with a long cranberry fingernail, 'and my neck, too. You said no scars, remember?'

'Don't worry,' Rudy assured her.

'Good,' Heather said. 'Anything else?'

'Not that I can see.'

'How about my butt?' She spun around on the desk, showing it to Rudy; looking over one shoulder, waiting for his professional opinion.

'Well,' said Rudy, running his fingers along the soft round curves.

'Hey,' said Heather, 'easy there.' She squirmed around to face him. 'Are you getting worked up?'

Rudy Graveline said, 'Of course not.' But he was. He couldn't figure it out, either; all the thousands of female bodies he got to see and feel. This was no ordinary lust, this was something fresh and wondrous. Maybe it was the way she bossed him around.

'I saw you in *Fevers of the Heart*,' Rudy said, idiotically. He had rented the cassette for a pool party. 'You were quite good, especially the scene on the horse.'

'Sit down,' Heather told him, and he did. She was bare-assed on the desk, legs swinging mischievously on either side of him. He put a clammy hand on each knee. 'Maybe now's a good time to talk about money,' she said.

For Rudy Graveline, the ultimate test of sobriety. In his entire career he had never traded sex for his surgical services, never even discounted. Money was money, pussy was pussy—a credo he drilled into his sure-handed young assistants. Some things in life you just don't give away.

To Heather Chappell, he said, 'I'm afraid it's going to be expensive.'

'Is it?' She swung one leg up and propped her foot on his right shoulder.

'All these procedures at once, yes, I'm afraid so.'

'How much, Dr. Graveline?'

Up came the other leg, and Rudy was scissored.

'Come here a second,' Heather said.

Rudy Graveline was torn between the thing he loved most and the thing he needed most: Sex and money. The warm feel of Heather's bare heels on his shoulders was like the weight of the world. And heaven, too.

Her toes tickled his ears. 'I said, come here.'

'Where?' Rudy peeped, reaching out.

'God, are you blind?'

Chemo bought an Ingram submachine gun to go with his .22 pistol. He got it from a man who had come to the club one night with a bunch of Jamaicans. The man himself was not a Jamaican; he was from Colombia. Chemo found this out when he stopped him at the door and told him he couldn't come inside the Gay Bidet with a machine gun.

'But this is Miami,' the man had said with a Spanish accent.

'I've got my orders,' Chemo said.

The man agreed to let Chemo take the gun while he and his pals went inside, which turned out to be a smart thing. As the band was playing a song called *Suck Till You're Sore*, a local skinhead gang went into a slam-dance frenzy, and fights broke out all over the place. The Jamaicans took off, but the Colombian stayed behind to do battle. At one point he produced a pocket knife and tried to surgically remove the swastika tattoo off the proud but hairless chest of a teenaged skinhead. The band took a much-needed break while the Beach police rushed in for the arrests. Later, when Chemo spotted the Colombian in the back of the squad car, he tapped on the window and asked about the Ingram. The Colombian said keep it and Chemo said thanks, and slipped a twenty-dollar bill through the crack of the window.

The thing Chemo liked best about the Ingram was the shoulder strap. He put it on and showed it to his boss, Freddie, who said, 'Get the fuck outta here with that thing!'

The next day, the eighteenth of January, Chemo got up early and drove out to Key Biscayne. He knew it would be unwise to go to the same marina where he had taken Chloe, so he looked around for another boat place. He found one near the Marine Stadium, where they race the big Budweiser speedboats. At first a kid with badly bleached hair tried to rent him a twenty-foot Dusky for a hundred ten dollars a day, plus a hundred fifty security deposit. Chemo didn't have that kind of money.

'Got a credit card?' the kid asked.

'No,' said Chemo. 'What about that thing over there?'

'That's a jet ski,' the kid said.

It was designed like a waterbug with handlebars. You drove it like a motorcycle, only standing up. This one was yellow, with the word *Kawasaki* on the front.

'You don't want to try it,' the kid with yellow hair said.

'Why not?'

'Because,' the kid said, laughing, 'you're too tall, man. Hit a wake, it'll snap your spine.'

Chemo figured the guy was just trying to talk him into renting something bigger, something he didn't need.

'How much is the jet ski?' he said.

'Twenty an hour, but you got to sign a waiver.' The kid was thinking that, as tall as this guy is, he doesn't look healthy enough to ride a jet ski; he looks kind of tapped-out and sickly, like he's been hanging from the wall of some dungeon for a couple of months. The kid was thinking maybe he ought to ask if the guy knew how to swim, just in case.

Chemo handed him two twenties.

The kid said, 'I'll still need a deposit.'

Chemo said he didn't have any more money. The kid said he'd

take Chemo's wristwatch, but Chemo said no, he didn't want to give it up. It was a Heuer diving watch, silver and gold links, made in Switzerland. Chemo had swiped it off a young architect who was overdosing in the men's room at the club. While the jerk was lying there in the stall, trying to swallow his tongue, Chemo grabbed his wrist and replaced the Heuer with his own thirty-dollar Seiko with the fake alligator band.

'No jet ski without a deposit,' said the kid with yellow hair.

'How about a gun?' Chemo said.

'What kind?'

Chemo showed him the .22 and the kid said okay, since it was a Beretta he'd hang onto it. He stuck it in the front of his chinos and led Chemo to the jet ski. He showed Chemo how the choke and the throttle worked, and tossed him a bright red life vest.

'You can change in the shed,' the kid said.

'Change?'

'You got a swimsuit, right?' The kid hopped back on the dock and gave Chemo the keys. 'Man, you don't want to ride these things in heavy pants.'

'I guess not,' said Chemo, unbuckling his trousers.

A shrimper named Joey agreed to take Christina Marks anywhere she wanted. When she gave him a hundred-dollar bill, Joey looked at it and said, 'Where you going, Havana?'

'Stiltsville,' Christina said, climbing into the pungent shrimp boat. 'And I need a favor.'

'You bet,' said Joey, tossing off the ropes.

'After you drop me off, I need you to stay close. Just in case.'

Joey aimed the bow down the canal, toward the mouth of Norris Cut. 'In case what?' he asked.

'In case the man I'm going to see doesn't want me to stay.'

Joey grinned and said, 'I can't imagine that. Here, you want a beer?'

He motored down the ocean side of Key Biscayne in amiable silence. Christina stood next to him at the wheel, guardedly watching the swarm of hungry seagulls that wailed and dove behind the stern. When the shrimp boat passed the Cape Florida lighthouse at the tip of the island, Christina saw the stilt houses to the south.

'Which one?' Joey shouted over the engines. When Christina pointed, Joey smiled and gave her a crusty wink.

'What's that mean?'

'Him,' Joey said. 'Why didn't you say so?'

They were maybe two hundred yards off the radio towers and making the wide turn into the channel when Joey nudged Christina Marks and pointed with his chin. Up ahead, something swift and yellow was crossing one of the tidal flats, bouncing severely in the choppy water. It was an odd, gumdrop-shaped craft, and a tall pale figure appeared to be standing in the middle, holding on with both arms.

Joey eased back on the throttle to give way.

'I hate those fool things,' he said. 'Damn tourists don't know where the hell they're going.'

They watched it cross from the starboard side, no more than thirty yards ahead of them. Joey frowned and said, 'I'll be goddamned.' He snatched a rag from his tool box and wiped the salty film from the shrimp boat's windshield.

'Look,' he said to Christina. 'Now you've seen it all.'

The tall pale man driving the jet ski was nude except for his soggy Jockey shorts.

And black sunglasses.

And a gleaming wristwatch.

And an Ingram .45 submachine gun strapped on his bare shoulder.

Christina Marks was astonished. 'What do you suppose he's doing out here with *that*?'

'Whatever the hell he wants,' said Joey the shrimper.

13

Earlier that day, Tina and two of her girlfriends had appeared at the stilt house in a borrowed Bayliner Capri. They saw Mick Stranahan sleeping on the roof beneath the windmill, the Remington shotgun at his side.

Tina's friends were alarmed. They voted to stay in the boat while Tina went up on the dock and approached the house.

'Richie wants me back,' she called to Stranahan.

He sat up and rubbed his eyes. 'What?'

'I said, Richie wants me back. I wanted you to be the first to know.'

'Why?' Stranahan said, his voice thick.

'So you could change my mind.'

Stranahan noticed that a seagull had crapped all over the shotgun while he was asleep. 'Damn,' he said under his breath. He took a black bandanna from the pocket of his jeans and wiped the gunstock.

'Well?' came Tina's voice from below. 'You going to change my mind or not?'

'How?'

'Sleep with me.'

'I already did,' Stranahan said.

'You know what I mean.'

'Go back to Richie,' Stranahan advised. 'If he hits you again, file charges.'

'Why are you so afraid?'

Stranahan slid butt-first down the grainy slope of the roof, to a spot from which Tina was visible in her tiny tangerine thong swimsuit.

'We've been over this,' Stranahan said to her.

'But I don't want to marry you,' she said. 'I promise. Even if you ask me afterwards, I'll say no—no matter how great it was. Besides, I'm not a waitress. You said all the others were waitresses.'

He groaned and said, 'Tina, I'm sorry. It just won't work.'

Now she looked angry. One of the other girls in the Bayliner turned on the radio and Tina snapped at her, told her to shut off the damn music. 'How do you know it won't work?' she said to Stranahan.

'I'm too old.'

'Bullshit.'

'And you're too young.'

'Double bullshit.'

'Okay,' he said. 'Then name the Beatles.'

'What?' Tina forced a caustic laugh. 'Are you serious?'

'Dead serious,' Stranahan said, addressing her from the edge of the roof. 'If you can name all the Beatles, I'll make love to you right now.'

'I don't believe this,' Tina said. 'The fucking Beatles.'

Stranahan had done the math in his head: She was nineteen, which meant she had been born the same year that the band broke up.

'Well, there's Paul,' Tina said.

'Last name?'

'Come on!'

'Let's hear it.'

'McCartney, okay? I don't believe this.'

Stranahan said, 'Go on, you're doing fine.'

'Ringo,' Tina said. 'Ringo Starr. The drummer with the nose.'

'Good.'

'And then there's the guy who died. Lennon.'

'First name?'

'I know his son is Julian.'

'His son doesn't count.'

Tina said, 'Yeah, well, you're an asshole. It's *John*. John Lennon.'

Stranahan nodded appreciatively. 'Three down, one to go. You're doing great.'

Tina folded her arms and tried to think of the last Beatle. Her lips were pursed in a most appealing way, but Stranahan stayed on the roof. 'I'll give you a hint,' he said to Tina. 'Lead guitar.'

She looked up at him, triumph shining in her gray eyes. 'Harrison,' she declared. 'Keith Harrison!'

Muttering, Stranahan crabbed back up to his vantage beneath the legs of the windmill. Tina said some sharp things, all of which he deserved, and then got on the boat with her friends and headed back across the bay toward Dinner Key and, presumably, Richie.

Joey the shrimper spit over the transom and said, 'Well, there's your boy.'

Christina Marks frowned. Mick Stranahan lay naked in the shape of a T on the roof of the house. His tan legs were straight, and each arm was extended. He had a bandanna pulled down over his eyes to shield them from the white rays of the sun. Christina Marks thought he looked like the victim of a Turkish firing squad.

'He looks like Christ,' said Joey. 'Don't you think he looks like Christ? Christ without a beard, I mean.'

'Take me up to the house,' Christina said. 'Do you have a horn on this thing?'

'Hell, he knows we're here.'

'He's sleeping.'

'No, ma'am,' Joey said. 'You're wrong.' But he sounded the horn anyway. Mick Stranahan didn't stir.

Joey idled the shrimp boat closer. The tide was up plenty high, rushing sibilantly under the pilings of the house. Clutching a brown grocery bag, Christina stepped up on the dock and waved the shrimper away.

'Thanks very much.'

Joey said, 'You be sure to tell him what we saw. About that big freak on the water scooter.'

She nodded.

'Tell him first thing,' Joey said. He pulled back on the throttle and the old diesel moaned into reverse. The engine farted an odious cloud of blue smoke that enveloped Christina Marks. She coughed all the way up the stairs.

When she got to the main deck, Stranahan was sitting on the edge of the roof, legs dangling.

'What's in the bag?'

'Cold cuts, wine, cheese. I thought you might be hungry.'

'This how they do it in New York?'

The sack was heavy, but Christina didn't put it down. She held it like a baby, with both arms, but not too tightly. She didn't want him to think it was a chore. 'What are you talking about?' she asked.

'The wine and cheese,' Stranahan said. 'There's a sense of ceremony about it. Maybe it's necessary where you come from, but not here.'

'Fuck you,' said Christina Marks. 'I'm on expense account, hotshot.'

Stranahan smiled. 'I forgot.' He hopped off the roof and landed like a cat. She followed him into the house and watched him slip into blue jean cutoffs, no underwear. She put the bag on the kitchen counter and he went to work, fixing lunch. From the refrigerator he got some pickles and a half pound of big winter shrimp, still in the shell.

As he opened the wine, he said, 'Let's get right to it: You've heard something.'

'Yes,' Christina said. 'But first: You won't believe what we just saw. A man with a machine gun, on one of those water-jet things.'

'Where?'

She motioned with her chin. 'Not even a mile from here.'

'What did he look like?'

Christina described him. Stranahan popped the cork.

'I guess we better eat fast,' he said. He was glad he'd brought the shotgun down from the roof after Tina and her friends had left, when he went to find a fresh bandanna. Subconsciously he glanced at the Remington, propped barrel-up in the corner of the same wall with the stuffed marlin head.

Christina peeled a shrimp, dipped it tail-first into a plastic thimble of cocktail sauce. 'Are you going to tell me who he is, the man in the underwear?'

'I don't know,' Stranahan said. 'I honestly don't. Now tell me what else.'

This would be the most difficult part. She said, 'I went to see your friend Tim Gavigan at the hospital.'

'Oh.'

'I was there when he died.'

Stranahan cut himself three fat slices of cheddar. 'Extreme unction,' he said. 'Too bad you're not a priest.'

'He wanted me to tell you something. Something he remembered about the Vicky Barletta case.'

With a mouthful of cheese, Stranahan said, 'Tell me you didn't take that asshole up to the VA. Flemm—you didn't let him have a crack at Timmy in that condition, did you?'

'Of course not,' she said sharply. 'Now listen: Tim Gavigan remembered that the plastic surgeon has a brother. George Graveline. He saw him working outside the clinic.'

'Doing what?' Stranahan asked.

'This is what Tim wanted me to tell you: The guy is a tree trimmer. He said you'd know what that means. He was going on about Hoffa and dead bodies.'

Stranahan laughed. 'Yeah, he's right. It's perfect.'

Impatiently Christina said, 'You want to fill me in?'

Stranahan chomped on a pickle. 'You know what a wood chipper is? It's like a king-sized sideways Cuisinart, except they use it to shred wood. The companies tow them around like a U-Haul. Throw the biggest branches down this steel chute and they come out sawdust and barbecue chips.'

'Now I get it,' Christina said.

'Something can pulverize a mahogany tree, think of what it could do to a human body.'

'I'd rather not.'

'There was a famous murder case up in New Jersey, they had everything but the corpse. The corpse was ground up in a wood chipper so basically all they found was splinters of human bone—not enough for a good forensic I.D. Finally somebody found a molar, and the tooth had a gold filling. That's how they made the case.'

Christina was still thinking about bone splinters.

'At any rate,' Stranahan said, 'it's a helluva good lead. Hurry now, finish up.' He wedged the cork into the half-empty wine bottle and started wrapping the leftover cold cuts and cheese in wax paper. Christina was reaching for one last shrimp when he snatched the dish away and put it in the refrigerator.

'Hey!'

'I said hurry.'

She noticed how deliberately he was moving, and it struck her that something was happening. 'What is it, Mick?'

'You mean you don't hear it?'

Christina said no.

'Just listen,' he said, and before she knew it the stilt house was shuttered, and the door closed, and the two of them were alone in the corner of the bedroom, sitting on the wooden floor. At first the only sound Christina Marks heard was the two of them breathing, and then came some scratching noises that Stranahan said were seagulls up on the roof. Finally, when she leaned her head against the plywood wall, she detected a faraway hum. The longer she listened, the more distinct it became. The pitch of the motor was too weak to be an airplane and too high to be much of a boat.

'Jesus, it's him,' she said with a tremble.

Stranahan acknowledged the fact with a frown. 'You know,' he said, 'this used to be a pretty good neighborhood.'

Chemo wondered about the Ingram, about the effects of salt spray on the firing mechanism. He didn't know much about machine guns, but he suspected that it was best not to get them wet. The ride out to Stiltsville had been wetter than he'd planned.

He parked the jet ski beneath one of the other stilt houses to wait for the shrimp boat to leave Mick Stranahan's place. He saw a good-looking woman in a white cottony top and tan safari shorts hop off the shrimp boat and go upstairs, so Chemo began to work her into the scenario. He didn't know if she was a wife

or a girlfriend or what, but it didn't matter. She was there, and
she had to die. End of story.

Chemo pried open a toolshed and found a rag for the Ingram.
Carefully he wiped off the moisture and salt. The gun looked
fine, but there was only one way to be sure. He took an aluminum
mop handle from the shed and busted the padlock off the door
of the house. Once inside, he quickly found a target: an old
convertible sofa, its flowered fabric showing traces of mold and
mildew. Chemo shut the door to trap the noise. Then he knelt in
front of the sofa, put the Ingram to his shoulder and squeezed
off three rounds. Dainty puffs of white fuzz and dust rose with
the impact of each bullet. Chemo lowered the gun and carefully
examined the .45-caliber holes in the cushions.

Now he was ready. He slung the gun strap over his shoulder
and pulled his soggy Jockey shorts up snugly on his waist. He
was about to go when he thought of something. Quickly he
moved through the house, opening doors until he found a
bathroom.

At the sink Chemo took off his sunglasses and put his face to
the mirror. With a forefinger he tested the tiny pink patch of
flesh that Dr. Rudy Graveline had dermabraded. The patch no
longer stung; in fact, it seemed to be coming along nicely. Chemo
was extremely pleased, and ventured forth in bright spirits.

Someplace, maybe it was *Reader's Digest*, he had read where
salt walter actually expedited the healing process.

'Don't move,' Mick Stranahan whispered.

'I wasn't planning on it.'

'Unless I tell you.'

From the hum of the engine, Christina Marks guessed that the
jet ski was very close: no more than thirty yards.

Stranahan held the shotgun across his knees. She looked at his
hands and noticed they were steady. Hers were shaking like an
old drunk's.

'Do you have a plan?' she asked.

'Basically, my plan is to stay alive.'

'Are you going to shoot him?'

Stranahan looked at her as if she were five years old. 'Now what do you think? *Of course* I'm going to shoot him. I intend to blow the motherfucker's head off, unless you've got some objection.'

'Just asking,' Christina said.

Chemo was thinking: Damn Japanese.

Whoever designed these jet skis must have been a frigging dwarf.

His back was killing him; he had to hunch over like a washerwoman to reach the handlebars. Every time he hit a wave, the gun strap slipped off his bony shoulder. A couple times he thought for sure he'd lost the Ingram, or at least broken it. Damn Japanese.

As he approached Stranahan's stilt house, Chemo started thinking something else. He had already factored the girl into the scenario, figured he'd shoot her first and get it over with. But then he realized he had another problem: Surely she had seen him ski past the shrimp boat, probably noticed the machine gun, probably told Stranahan.

Who had probably put it together.

So Chemo anticipated a fight. Screw the element of surprise; the damn jet scooter was as loud as a Harley. Stranahan could hear him coming two miles away.

But where was he?

Chemo circled the stilt house slowly, eventually riding the curl of his own wake. The windows were down, the door shut. No sign of life, except for a pair of ratty looking gulls on the roof.

A thin smile of understanding came to his lips. Of course— the man was waiting inside. A little ambush action.

Chemo coasted the jet ski up to the dock and stepped off lightly. He took the Ingram off his shoulder and held it in front of him as he went up the stairs, thinking: Where's the logical place for Stranahan to be waiting? In a corner, of course.

He was pleased to find that the wooden deck went around Stranahan's entire house. Walking cautiously on storklike legs, Chemo approached the southwest corner first. Calmly he fired one shot, waist level, through the wall. He repeated the same procedure at each of the other corners, then sat on the rail of the deck and waited. When nothing happened after three minutes, he walked up to the front door and fired twice more.

Then he went in.

Christina Marks was not aware that Stranahan had been hit until she felt something warm on her bare arm. She opened her mouth to scream but Stranahan covered it with his hand and motioned for her to be quiet. She saw that his eyes were watering from the pain of the bullet wound. He removed his hand from her mouth and pointed at his left shoulder. Christina nodded but didn't look.

They heard three more gunshots, each in a different part of the house. Then came a silence that lasted a few agonizing minutes. Finally Stranahan rose to his feet with the shotgun cradled in his right arm. The left side of his body was numb and wet with blood; in the twilight of the shuttered house, he looked two-tone.

From the floor Christina watched him move. He pressed his back to the wall and edged toward the front of the house. The next shots made Christina shut her eyes. When she opened them, she saw two perfect holes through the front door; twin sunbeams, sharp as lasers, perforated the shadows. Beneath the light shafts, Mick Stranahan lay prone on his belly, elbows braced on the wooden floor. He was aiming at the front door when Chemo opened it.

Stranahan's shotgun was a Remington 1100, a semi-automatic twelve-gauge, an excellent bird gun that holds up to five shells. Later, when Stranahan measured the distance from the door to where he had lain, he would marvel at how any human being with two good eyes could miss a seven-foot target at a distance of only nineteen feet four inches. The fact that Stranahan was bleeding to death at the time was not, in his view, a mitigating excuse.

In truth, it was the shock of the intruder's appearance that had caused Stranahan to hesitate—the sight of this gaunt, pellucid, frizzle-haired freak with a moonscape face that could stop a freight train.

So Stranahan had stared for a nanosecond when he should have squeezed the trigger. For someone who looked so sickly, Chemo moved deceptively fast. As he dove out of the doorway, the first blast from the Remington sprinkled its rain of birdshot into the bay.

'Shit,' Stranahan said, struggling to his feet. On his way toward the door he slipped on his own blood and went down again, his right cheek slamming hard on the floor; this, just as Chemo craned around the corner and fired a messy burst from the Ingram. Rolling in a sticky mess, Stranahan shot back.

Chemo slammed the door from the outside, plunging the house into darkness once more.

Stranahan heard the man running on the outside deck, following the apron around the house. Stranahan took aim through the walls. He imagined that the man was a rising quail, and he led accordingly. The first blast tore a softball-sized hole in the wall of the living room. The second punched out the shutter in the kitchen. The third and final shot was followed by a grunt and a splash outside.

'Christina!' Stranahan shouted. 'Quick, help me up.'

But when she got there, biting back tears, crawling on bare knees, he had already passed out.

Chemo landed on his back in the water. He kicked his legs just to make sure he wasn't paralyzed; other than a few splinters in his scalp, he seemed to be fine. He figured that the birdshot must have missed him, that the concussion so close to his head was what threw him off balance.

Instinctively he held the Ingram high out of the water with his right hand, and paddled furiously with his left. He knew he had to make it under cover of the house before Stranahan came out; otherwise he'd be a sitting duck. Chemo saw that the machine gun was dripping, so he figured it must have gotten dunked in the fall. Would it still fire? And how many rounds were left? He had lost count.

These were his concerns as he made for the pilings beneath the stilt house. Progress was maddeningly slow; by paddling with only one hand, Chemo tended to move himself in a frothy circle.

In frustration he paddled more frenetically, a tactic that decreased the perimeter of his route but brought him no closer to safety. He expected at any second to see Stranahan burst onto the deck with the shotgun.

Beneath Chemo there appeared in the water a long gray-blue shadow, which hung there as if frozen in glass. It was Stranahan's silent companion, Liza, awakened from its afternoon siesta by the wild commotion.

A barracuda this age is a creature of sublime instinct and flawless precision, an eating machine more calculating and efficient than any shark in the ocean. Over time the great barracuda had come to associate human activity with feeding; its impulses had been tuned by Stranahan's evening pinfish ritual. As Chemo struggled in the shallows, the barracuda was on full alert, its cold eyes trained upward in anticipation. The blue-veined legs that kicked impotently at its head, the spastic thrashing—these posed no threat.

Something else had caught its attention: the familiar rhythmic glint of stunned prey on the water's surface. The barracuda struck with primitive abandon, streaking up from the deep, slashing, then boring back toward the pilings.

There, beneath the house, the great fish flared its crimson gills in a darkening sulk. What it had mistaken for an easy meal of silver pinfish turned out to be no such thing, and the barracuda spit ignominiously through its fangs.

It was a testimony to sturdy Swiss craftsmanship that the Heuer diving watch was still ticking when it came to rest on the bottom. Its stainless silver and gold links glistened against Chemo's pale severed hand, which reached up from the turtle grass like some lost piece of mannequin.

14

On Washington Avenue there was a small shop that sold artificial limbs. Dr. Rudy Graveline went there on his lunch hour and purchased four different models of prosthetic hands. He paid cash and made sure to get a receipt.

Later, back at Whispering Palms, he arranged the artificial hands in an attractive row on the top of his onyx desk.

'What about this one?' he asked Chemo.

'It's a beaut,' Chemo said trenchantly, 'except I've already got one on *that* arm.'

'Sorry.' Rudy Graveline picked up another. 'Then look here— state-of-the-art technology. Four weeks of therapy, you can deal blackjack with this baby.'

'Wrong color,' Chemo remarked.

Rudy glanced at the artificial hand and thought: Of course it's the wrong color, they're *all* the wrong damn color. 'It's a tough match,' the doctor said. 'I looked for the palest one they had.'

'I hate them all,' Chemo said. 'Why does it have to be a hand, anyway?'

'You didn't like the mechanical hooks,' Rudy Graveline reminded him. 'Talk about advanced, you could load a gun, even type with those things. But you said no.'

'Damn right I said no.'

Rudy put down the prosthesis and said: 'I wish you wouldn't take that tone with me. I'm doing the best I can.'

'Oh, yeah.'

'Look, didn't I advise you to see a specialist?'

'And didn't I advise you, you're crazy? The cops'll be hunting all over.'

'All right,' Rudy said in a calming voice. 'Let's not argue.'

It had been three weeks since Chemo had shown up behind Whispering Palms on a blood-streaked water scooter—a vision that Dr. Rudy Graveline would carry with him for the rest of his life. It had happened during an afternoon consult with Mrs. Carla Crumworthy, heiress to the Crumworthy panty-shield fortune. She had come to complain about the collagen injections that Rudy Graveline had administered to give her full, sensual lips, which is just what every rheumatoid seventy-one-year-old woman needs. Mrs. Crumworthy had lamented that the results were nothing like she had hoped, that she now resembled one of those Ubangi tribal women from the *National Geographic*, the ones with the ceramic platters in their mouths. And, in truth, Dr. Rudy Graveline was concerned about what had happened, because Mrs. Crumworthy's lips had indeed grown bulbous and unwieldy and hard as cobblestones. As he examined her (keeping his doubts to himself), Rudy wondered if maybe he had injected too much collagen, or not enough, or if maybe he'd zapped it into the wrong spots. Whatever the cause, the result was undeniable: Mrs. Carla Crumworthy looked like a duck wearing mauve lipstick. A malpractice jury could have a ball with this one.

Dr. Graveline had been whisking through his trusty Rolodex, searching for a kind-hearted colleague, when Mrs. Crumworthy suddenly rose to her feet and shrieked. Pointing out the picture window toward Biscayne Bay, the old woman had blubbered in terror, her huge misshapen lips slapping together in wet percussion. Rudy had no idea what she was trying to say.

He spun around and looked out the window.

The yellow jet ski lay on its side, adrift in the bay. Somehow Chemo had dragged himself, soaking wet and stark naked, over the ledge of the seawall behind the clinic. He didn't look well enough to be dead. His gray shoulders shivered violently in the sunshine, and his eyes flickered vaguely through puffy purple slits. Chemo swung the bloody stump to show Dr. Graveline what had happened to his left hand. He pointed gamely at the elastic wrist tourniquet that he had fashioned from his Jockey shorts, and Rudy would later concede that it had probably saved his life.

Mrs. Carla Crumworthy was quickly ushered to a private recovery suite and oversedated, while Rudy and two young assistant surgeons led Chemo to an operating room. The assistants argued that he belonged at a real trauma center in a real hospital, but Chemo adamantly refused. This left the doctors with no choice but to operate or let him bleed to death.

Gently discouraged from participating in the surgery, Rudy had been content to let the young fellows work unimpeded. He spent the time making idle conversation with the woozy Chemo, who had rejected a general anesthetic in favor of an old-fashioned intravenous jolt of Demerol.

Since that evening, Chemo's post-op recovery had progressed swiftly and in relative luxury, with the entire staff of Whispering Palms instructed to accommodate his every wish. Rudy Graveline himself was exceedingly attentive, as he needed Chemo's loyalty now more than ever. He had hoped that the killer's spirits would improve at the prospect of reconstructing his abbreviated left arm.

'A new hand,' Rudy said, 'would be a major step back to a normal life.'

'I never had a normal life,' Chemo pointed out. Sure, he would miss the hand, but he was more pissed off about losing the expensive wrist-watch.

'What are my other options?' Chemo asked.

'What do you mean?'

'I mean, besides these things.' He waved his stump contemptuously at the artificial hands.

'Well,' Rudy said, 'frankly, I'm out of ideas.' He gathered the prostheses from his desk and put them back in the box. 'I told you this isn't my field,' he said to Chemo.

'You keep trying to dump me off on some other surgeon, but it won't work. It's you or nobody.'

'I appreciate your confidence,' Rudy said. He leaned forward in his chair and put on his glasses. 'Can I ask, what's that on your face?'

Chemo said, 'It's Wite-Out.'

After a careful pause, Dr. Graveline said, 'Can I ask—'

'I might go out to the club later. I wanted to cover up these darn patches.'

Out of pity Rudy had agreed to dermabrade several more one-inch squares along Chemo's chin.

'You covered them with Wite-Out?'

Chemo said, 'Your secretary loaned me a bottle. The color's just right.'

Rudy cleared his throat. 'It's not so good for your skin. Please, let me prescribe a mild cosmetic ointment.'

'Forget it,' said Chemo. 'This'll do fine. Now what about a new thing for my arm?' With his right hand he gestured at the bandaged limb.

Rudy folded his hands in his lap, a relaxed gesture that damn near exuded professional confidence. 'As I said before, we've gone over most of the conventional options.'

Chemo said, 'I don't like therapy. I want something easy to use, something practical.'

'I see,' said Rudy Graveline.

'And durable, too.'

'Of course.'

'Also, I don't want people to stare.'

Rudy thought: Beautiful. A seven-foot, one-handed geek with Wite-Out painted on his face, and he's worried about people staring.

'So what do you think?' Chemo pressed.

'I think,' said Dr. Rudy Graveline, 'we've got to use our imaginations.'

Detective John Murdock bent his squat, porky frame over the rail of the hospital bed and said, 'Wake up, fuckwad.'

Which was pretty much his standard greeting.

Mick Stranahan did not open his eyes.

'Get out of here,' said Christina Marks.

Detective Joe Salazar lit a Camel and said, 'You don't look like a nurse. Since when do nurses wear blue jeans?'

'Good point,' said John Murdock. 'I think you're the one should get out of here.'

'Yeah,' said Joe Salazar. 'We got official business with this man.' Salazar was as short as his partner, only built like a stop sign. Fat, florid face stuck on a pipestem body.

'Now I know who you are,' Christina said. 'You must be Murdock and Salazar, the crooked cops.'

Stranahan nearly busted out laughing, but he pressed his eyes closed, trying to look asleep.

'I see what we got here,' said Murdock. 'What we got here is some kinda Lily Tomlin.'

'Sure,' said Joe Salazar, though he didn't know who his partner was talking about. He assumed it was somebody they'd arrested together. 'Sure,' he chimed in, 'a regular Lily Thomas.'

Christina Marks said, 'The man's asleep, so why don't you come back another time?'

'And why don't you go change your tampon or something?' snapped John Murdock. 'We've got business here.'

'We got questions,' Joe Salazar added. When he took the Camel cigarette out of his mouth, Christina noticed, the end was all soggy and mulched.

She said, 'I was there when it happened, if you want to ask me about it.'

Salazar had brought a Xerox of the marine patrol incident report. He took it out of his jacket, unfolded it, ran a sticky brown finger down the page until he came to the box marked Witnesses. 'So you're Initial C. Marks?'

'Yes,' Christina said.

'We've been looking all over Dade County for you. Two, three weeks we've been looking.'

'I changed hotels,' she said. She had moved from Key Biscayne over to the Grove, to be closer to Mercy Hospital.

John Murdock, the senior of the two detectives, took a chair from the corner, twirled it around, and sat down straddling it.

'Just like in the movies,' Christina said. 'You think better, sitting with your legs like that?'

Murdock glowered. 'What suppose we just throw your tight little ass in the women's annex for a night or two, would you enjoy that? Just you and all the hookers, maybe a lesbo or two.'

'Teach you some manners,' Joe Salazar said, 'and that's not all.'

Christina smiled coolly. 'And here I thought you boys wanted a friendly chat. Maybe I'll just call hospital security and tell them what's going on up here. After that, maybe I'll call the newspapers.'

Mick Stranahan was thinking: She'd better be careful. These guys aren't nearly as dumb as they look.

Murdock said, 'One time we booked a big lesbo looked just like Kris Kristofferson. I'm not kidding, we're talking major facial hair. And mean as a bobcat.'

'Resisting with violence, two counts,' Salazar recalled. 'On top of the murder.'

'Manslaughter,' John Murdock cut in. 'Actually, woman-slaughter, if there is such a thing. Jesus, what a mess. I can't even think about it, so close to lunch.'

'Involved a fire hose,' Salazar said.

'I said enough,' Murdock protested. 'Anyhow, I think she's still in the annex. The one who looks like Kristofferson. I think she runs the drama group.'

Salazar said, 'You like the theater, Miss Marks?'

'Sure,' Christina said, 'but mainly I like television. You guys ever been on TV? Maybe you've heard of the Reynaldo Flemm show.'

'Yeah,' Joe Salazar said, excitedly. 'One time I saw him get his ass pounded by a bunch of Teamsters. In slow motion, too.'

'*That* asshole,' Murdock muttered.

'We finally agree,' Christina said. 'Unfortunately, he happens to be my boss. We're in town taping a big story.'

The two detectives glanced at one another, trying to decide on a plan without saying it. Salazar stalled by lighting up another Camel.

Lying in bed listening, Mick Stranahan figured they'd back off now, just to be safe. Neither of these jokers wanted to see his own face on prime-time TV.

Murdock said, 'So tell us what happened.' Salazar stood in the empty corner, resting his fat head against the wall.

Christina said, 'You've got photographic memories, or maybe you'd prefer to take some notes?' Murdock motioned to his part-ner, who angrily stubbed out his cigarette and dug a worn spiral notebook from his jacket.

She began with what she had seen from the wheelhouse of Joey's shrimp boat—the tall man toting a machine gun on the jet scooter. She told the detectives about how Stranahan had battened down the stilt house, and how the man had started shooting into the corners. She told them how Stranahan had been wounded in the shoulder, and how he had fired back with a shotgun until he passed out. She told them she had heard a splash outside, then a terrible cry; ten, maybe fifteen minutes later she'd heard somebody rev up the jet ski, but she was too scared to go to a window. Only when the engine was a faint whine in the distance did she peer through the bullet holes in the front door to see if the gunman had gone. She told the detectives how she had half-carried Stranahan down the stairs to where his skiff was docked, and how she had hand-cranked the outboard by herself. She told them how he had groggily pointed across the bay and said there was a big hospital on the mainland, and by the time they got to Mercy there was so much blood in the bottom of the skiff that she was bailing with a coffee mug.

After Christina had finished, Detective John Murdock said, 'That's quite a story. I bet *Argosy* magazine would go for a story like that.'

Joe Salazar leafed through his notebook and said, 'I think I missed something, lady. I think I missed the part where you explained why you're at Stranahan's house in the first place. Maybe you could repeat it.'

Murdock said, 'Yeah, I missed that, too.'

'I'd be happy to tell you why I was there,' Christina said. 'Mr. Flemm wanted Mr. Stranahan to be interviewed for an upcoming broadcast, but Mr. Stranahan declined. I went to his house in the hopes of changing his mind.'

'I'll bet,' Salazar said.

'Joe, be nice,' said his partner. 'Tell me, Miss Marks, why'd you want to interview some dweeb P.I.? I mean, he's nobody. Hasn't been with the State Attorney for years.'

From his phony coma Stranahan wondered how far Christina Marks would go. Not too far, he hoped.

'The interview involved a story we were working on, and that's all I can say.'

Murdock said, 'Gee, I hope it didn't concern a murder.'

'I really can't—'

'Because murder is our main concern. Me and Joe.'

Christina Marks said, 'I've cooperated as much as I can.'

'And you've been an absolute peach about it,' said Murdock. 'Fact, I almost forgot why we came in the first place.'

'Yeah,' said Detective Joe Salazar, 'the questions we got, you can't really answer. Thanks just the same.'

Murdock slid the chair back to the corner. 'See, we need to talk to Rip Van Rambo here. So I think you'd better go.' He smiled for the first time. 'And I apologize for that wisecrack about the Kotex. Not very professional, I admit.'

'It was tampons,' Joe Salazar said.

'Whatever.'

Christina Marks said, 'I'm not leaving this room. This man is recovering from a serious gunshot wound and you shouldn't disturb him.'

'We spoke to his doctor—'

'You're lying.'

'Okay, we put in a call. The guy never called back.'

Salazar walked up to the hospital bed and said, 'He don't look so bad. Anyway, three weeks is plenty of time. Wake him up, Johnny.'

'Have it your way,' Christina said. She got a legal pad from her shoulder bag, uncapped a felt-tip pen, and sat down, poised to write.

'Now what the hell are you doing?' Salazar said.

'Forget about her,' Murdock said. He leaned close to Stranahan's face and sang, 'Mi-ick? Mick, buddy? Rise and shine.'

Stranahan growled sleepily, blowing a mouthful of stale, hot breath directly into Murdock's face.

'Holy Christ,' the detective said, turning away.

Salazar said, 'Johnny, I swear he's awake.' He cupped his hand at Stranahan's ear and shouted: '*Hey, fuckwad, you awake?*'

'Knock it off,' Christina said.

'I know how you can tell,' Salazar went on. 'Grab his dick. If he's asleep, he won't do nothing. If he's awake he'll jump ten feet out of this frigging bed.'

Murdock said, 'Aw, you're crazy.'

'You think he'd let one of us grab his schlong if he was wide awake? I'm telling you, Johnny, it's a sure way to find out.'

'Okay, you do it.'

'Nuh-uh, we flip a coin.'

'Screw you, Joe. I ain't touching the man's privates. The county doesn't pay me enough.'

Stranahan was lying there, thinking: Thattaboy, Johnny, stick to the book.

From the corner Christina said, 'Lay a finger on him, I'll see that Mr. Stranahan sues the living hell out of both of you. When he wakes up.'

'Not that old line,' Salazar said with a laugh.

She said, 'Beat the shit out of some jerk on the street, that's one thing. Grab a man's sexual organs while he's lying unconscious in a hospital bed—try to get the union worked up about *that*. You guys just kiss your pensions good-bye.'

Murdock shot Christina Marks a bitter look. 'When he wakes up, you be sure to tell him something. Tell him we know he drowned his ex-wife, so don't be surprised if we show up in Stiltsville with a waterproof warrant. Tell him he'd be smart to sell that old house, too, case a storm blows it down while he's off at Raiford.'

With secretarial indifference, Christina jotted every word on the legal pad. Murdock snorted and stalked out the door. Joe Salazar followed two steps behind, pocketing his own notebook, fumbling for a fresh Camel.

'Lady,' he said out the side of his mouth, 'you got to learn some respect for authority.'

That weekend, a notorious punk band called the Fudge Packers was playing the Gay Bidet. Freddie didn't like them at all. There were fights every night; the skinheads, the Latin Kings, the 34th Street Players. This is what Freddie couldn't understand: Why the spooks and spics even showed up for a band like this. Usually they had better taste. The Fudge Packers were simply dreadful—four frigging bass guitars, now what the hell kind of music was that? No wonder everybody was fighting: take their minds off the noise.

Since Chemo had disappeared, Freddie had hired a new head bouncer named Eugene, guy used to play in the World Football League. Eugene was all right, big as a garbage dumpster, but he couldn't seem to get people's attention the way Chemo did. Also, he was slow. Sometimes it took him five minutes to get down off the stage and pound heads in the crowd. By comparison Chemo had moved like a cat.

Freddie also was worried about Eugene's pro-labor leanings. One week at the Gay Bidet and already he was complaining about how loud the music was, could they please turn it down? You're kidding, Freddie had said, turn it down? But Eugene said damn right, his eardrums were fucking killing him. He said if his ears kept hurting he might go deaf and have to file a workman's comp, and Freddie said what's that? Then Eugene started going on about all his football injuries and, later, some shit that had happened to him working construction down in Homestead. He told Freddie about how the unions always took care of him, about how one time he was laid up for six weeks with a serious groin pull and never missed a paycheck. Not one.

Freddie could scarcely believe such a story. To him it sounded like something out of Communist Russia. He was delighted the night Chemo came back to work.

'Eugene, you're fired,' Freddie said. 'Go pull your groin some-place else.'

'What?' said Eugene, cocking his head and leaning closer.

'Don't pull that deaf shit with me,' Freddie warned. 'Now get lost.'

On his way out of Freddie's office, Eugene sized up his towering replacement. 'Man, what happened to you?'

'Gardening accident,' Chemo replied. Eugene grimaced sympathetically and said good-bye.

Freddie turned to Chemo. 'Thank God you're back. I'm afraid to ask.'

'Go ahead. Ask.'

'I don't think so,' Freddie said. 'Just tell me, you okay?'

Chemo nodded. 'Fine. The new band sounds like vomit.'

'Yeah, I know,' Freddie said. 'Geez, you should see the crowd. Be careful in there.'

'I'm ready for them,' Chemo said, hoisting his left arm to show Freddie the new device. He and Dr. Rudy Graveline had found it on sale at a True Value hardware store.

'Wow,' said Freddie, staring.

'I got it rigged special for a six-volt battery,' Chemo explained. He patted the bulge under his arm. 'Strap it on with an Ace bandage. Only weighs about nine pounds.'

'Neat,' said Freddie, thinking: Sweet Jesus, this can't be what I think it is.

A short length of anodyzed aluminum piping protruded from the padding over Chemo's amputation. Bolted to the end of the pipe was a red saucer-sized disc made of hard plastic. Coiled tightly on a stem beneath the disc was a short length of eighty-pound monofilament fishing line.

Freddie said, 'Okay, now I'm gonna ask.'

'It's a Weed Whacker,' Chemo said. 'See?'

15

George Graveline was sun-tanned and gnarled and sinewy, with breadloaf arms and wide black Elvis sideburns. The perfect tree trimmer.

George was not at all jealous of his younger brother, the plastic surgeon. Rudy deserved all the fine things in life, George reasoned, because Rudy had gone to college for what seemed like eternity. In George's view, no amount of worldly riches was worth sitting in a stuffy classroom for years at a stretch. Besides, he loved his job as a tree trimmer. He loved the smell of sawdust and fresh sap, and he loved gassing yellow jacket nests; he loved the whole damn outdoors. Even Florida winters could get miserably hot, but a person could adjust. George Graveline had a motto by which he faithfully lived: *Always park in the shade.*

He did not often see his wealthy brother, but that was all right. Dr. Rudy was a busy man, and for that matter so was George. In Miami a good tree trimmer always had his hands full: year-round growth, no real seasons, no time for rest. Mainly you had your black olives and your common ficus tree, but the big problem there wasn't the branches so much as the roots. A twenty-year-old ficus had a root system could swallow the New York subway. Digging out a big ficus was a bitch. Then you had your exotics: the Australian pines, the melaleucas, and those God-forsaken Brazilian pepper trees, which most people mistakenly called a holly. Things grew like fungus, but George loved them because the roots weren't so bad and a couple good men could rip one out of the ground, no sweat. His favorite, though, was when people wanted their Brazilian pepper trees trimmed. Invariably these were customers new to Florida, novice suburbanites who didn't have the heart or the brains to actually *kill* a living tree.

So they'd ask George Graveline to please just trim it back a little, and George would say sure, no problem, knowing that in three months it'd shoot out even bushier than before and strangle their precious hibiscus as sure as a coathanger. No denying there was damn good money in the pepper-tree racket.

On the morning of February tenth, George Graveline and his crew were chopping a row of Australian pines off Krome Avenue to make room for a new medium-security federal prison. George and his men were not exactly busting their humps, since it was a government contract and nobody ever came by to check. George was parked in the shade, as usual, eating a roast-beef hoagie and drinking a tall Budweiser. The driver's door of the truck was open and the radio was on a country-music station, though the only time you could hear the tunes was between the grinding roars of the wood chipper, which was hooked to the bumper of George Graveline's truck. The intermittent screech of the machine didn't disturb George at all; he had grown accustomed to hearing only fragments of Merle Haggard on the radio and to letting his imagination fill in the musical gaps.

Just as he finished the sandwich, George glanced in the rear-view and noticed a big blond man with one arm in a sling. The man wore blue jeans, boots, and a flannel shirt with the left sleeve cut away. He was standing next to the wood chipper, watching George's crew chief toss pine stumps into the steel maw.

George swung out of the truck and said, 'Hey, not so close.'

The man obligingly took a step backward. 'That's some machine.' He gestured at the wood chipper. 'Looks brand new.'

'Had her a couple years,' George Graveline said. 'You looking for work?'

'Naw,' the man said, 'not with this bum wing. Actually I was looking for the boss. George Graveline.'

George wiped the hoagie juice off his hands. 'That's me,' he said.

The crew chief heaved another pine limb into the chipper. The visitor waited for the buzzing to stop, then he said, 'George, my name is Mick Stranahan.'

'Howdy, Mick.' George stuck out his right hand. Stranahan shook it.

'George, we don't know each other, but I feel like I can talk to you. Man to man.'

'Sure.'

'It's about your little brother.'

'Rudolph?' Warily George folded his big arms.

'Yes, George,' Stranahan said. 'See, Rudy's been trying to kill me lately.'

'Huh?'

'Can you believe it? First he hires some mobster to do the hit, now he's got the world's tallest white man with the world's worst case of acne. I don't know what to tell you, but frankly it's got me a little pissed off.' Stranahan looked down at his sling. 'This is from a .45-caliber machine gun. Honestly, George, wouldn't you be upset, too?'

George Graveline rolled the tip of his tongue around the insides of his cheeks, like he was probing for a lost wad of Red Man. The crew chief automatically kept loading hunks of pine into the wood chipper, which spit them out the chute as splinters and sawdust. Stranahan motioned to George that they should go sit in the truck and talk privately, where it was more quiet.

Stranahan settled in on the passenger side and turned down the country music. George said, 'Look, mister, I don't know who you are but—'

'I told you who I am.'

'Your name is all you said.'

'I'm a private investigator, George, if that helps. A few years back I worked for the State Attorney. On murder cases, mostly.'

George didn't blink, just stared like a toad. Stranahan got a feeling that the man was about to punch him.

'Before you do anything incredibly stupid, George, listen for a second.'

George leaned out the door of the truck and hollered for the crew chief to take lunch. The whine of the wood chipper died, and suddenly the two men were drenched in silence.

'Thank you,' Stranahan said.

'So talk.'

'On March 12, 1986, your brother performed an operation

on a young woman named Victoria Barletta. Something terrible happened, George, and she died on the operating table.'

'No way.'

'Your brother Rudy panicked. He'd already been in a shitload of trouble over his state medical license—and killing a patient, well, that's totally unacceptable. Even in Florida. I think Rudy was just plain scared.'

George Graveline said, 'You're full of it.'

'The case came through my office as an abduction-possible-homicide. Everybody assumed the girl was snatched from a bus bench in front of your brother's clinic because that's what he told us. But now, George, new information has come to light.'

'What kind of information?'

'The most damaging kind,' Mick Stranahan said. 'And for some reason, your brother thinks that I am the one who's got it. But I'm not, George.'

'So I'll tell him to leave you alone.'

'That's very considerate, George, but I'm afraid it's not so simple. Things have gotten out of hand. I mean, look at my damn shoulder.'

'Mmmm,' said George Graveline.

Stranahan said, 'Getting back to the young woman. Her body was never found, not a trace. That's highly unusual.'

'It is?'

'Yes, it is.'

'So?'

'So, you wouldn't happen to know anything about what happened, would you?'

George said, 'You got some nerve.'

'Yes, I suppose I do. But how about answering the question?'

'How about this,' said George Graveline, reaching for Mick Stranahan's throat.

With his good arm Stranahan intercepted George's toad-eyed lunge. He seized one of the tree-trimmer's stubby thumbs and twisted it clean out of the socket. It made a faintly audible pop, like a bottle of flat champagne. George merely squeaked as the color flooded from his face. Stranahan let go of the limp purple thumb, and George pinched it between his knees, trying to squeeze away the pain.

'Boy, I'm really sorry,' Stranahan said.

George grabbed at himself and gasped, 'You get out of here!'

'Don't you want to hear the rest of my theory, the one I'm going to tell the cops? About how you tossed that poor girl's body into the wood chipper just to save your brother's butt?'

'Go on,' George Graveline cried, 'before I shoot you myself.'

Mick Stranahan got out of George's truck, shut the door and leaned in through the open window. 'I think you're overreacting,' he said to the tree trimmer. 'I really do.'

'Eat shit,' George replied, wheezing.

'Fine,' Stranahan said. 'I just hope you're not this rude to the police.'

Christina Marks was dreading her reunion with Reynaldo Flemm. They met at twelve-thirty in the lobby of the Sonesta.

She said, 'You've done something to your hair.'

'I let it grow,' Flemm said self-consciously. 'Where've you been, anyway? What's the big secret?'

Christina couldn't get over the way he looked. She circled him twice, staring.

'Ray, nobody's hair grows that fast.'

'It's been a couple weeks.'

'But it's all the way to your shoulders.'

'So what?'

'And it's so yellow.'

'Blond, goddammit.'

'And so . . . kinky.'

Stiffly, Reynaldo Flemm said, 'It was time for a new look.'

Christina Marks fingered his locks and said, 'It's a bloody wig.'

'Thank you, Agatha Christie.'

'Don't get sore,' she said. 'I kind of like it.'

'Really?'

Despairing of his physical appearance since his visit to Whispering Palms, Reynaldo Flemm had flown back to New York and consulted a famous colorologist, who had advised him that blond hair would make him look ten years younger. Then a make-up man at ABC had told Reynaldo that long hair would make his nose look thinner, while *kinked* long hair would take twenty pounds off his waist on camera.

Armed with this expert advice, Reynaldo had sought out Tina Turner's wig stylist, who was booked solid but happy to recommend a promising young protégé in the SoHo district. The young stylist's name was Leo, and he pretended to recognize Reynaldo Flemm from television, which was all the salesmanship he needed. Reynaldo told Leo the basics of what he wanted, and Leo led him to a seven-hundred-dollar wig that looked freshly hacked off the scalp of Robert Plant, the rock singer. Or possibly Dyan Cannon.

Reynaldo didn't care. It was precisely the look he was after.

'I do kind of like it,' Christina Marks said, 'only we've got to do something about the Puerto Rican mustache.'

Flemm said, 'The mustache stays. I've had it since my first local Emmy.' He put his hands on her shoulders. 'Now, suppose you tell me what the hell's been going on.'

Christina hadn't talked to Reynaldo since the day Mick Stranahan was shot, and then she had told him next to nothing. She had called from the emergency room at Mercy Hospital, and said something serious had happened. Reynaldo had asked if she were hurt, and Christina said no. Then Reynaldo had asked what was so damn serious, and she said it would have to wait for a few weeks, that the police were involved and the whole Barletta story would blow up if they didn't lay low. She had promised to get back to him in a few days, but all she did was leave a message in Reynaldo's box at the hotel. The message had begged him to be patient, and Reynaldo had thought what the hell and gone back to Manhattan to hunt for some new hair.

'So,' he said to Christina, 'let's hear it.'

'Over here,' she said, and led him to a booth in the hotel coffee shop. She waited until he'd stuffed a biscuit in his mouth before telling him about the shooting.

'Theesus!' Flemm exclaimed, spitting crumbs. He looked as if he were about to cry, and in fact he was. 'You got shot at? Really?'

Christina nodded uneasily.

'With a machine gun? Honest to God?' Plaintively he added, 'Was it an Uzi?'

'I'm not sure, Ray.'

Christina knew his heart was breaking; Reynaldo had been waiting his entire broadcast career for an experience like that. Once he had drunkenly confided to Christina that his secret dream was to be shot in the thigh—live on national television. Not a life-threatening wound, just enough to make him go down. 'I'm tired of getting beat up,' he had told Christina that night. 'I want to break some new ground.' In Reynaldo's secret dream, the TV camera would jiggle at the sound of gunshots, then pan dramatically to focus on his prone and blood-splattered form sprawled on the street. In the dream, Reynaldo would be clutching his microphone, bravely continuing to broadcast while paramedics worked feverishly to save his life. The last clip, as Reynaldo dreamed it, was a close-up of his famous face: the lantern jaw clenched in agony, a grimace showcasing his luxurious capped teeth. Then the trademark sign-off: *This is Reynaldo Flemm, reporting In Your Face!*—just as the ambulance doors swung shut.

'I can't believe this,' Reynaldo moaned over his breakfast. 'Producers aren't supposed to get shot, the talent is.'

Christina Marks sipped a three-dollar orange juice. 'In the first place, Ray, I wasn't the one who got shot—'

'Yeah but—'

'In the second place, you would've pissed your pants if you'd been there. This is no longer fun and games, Ray. Somebody is trying to murder Stranahan. Probably the same goon who killed his ex-wife.'

Flemm was still pouting. 'Why didn't you tell me you were going out to Stiltsville?'

'You were locked in your room, remember? Measuring your body parts.' Christina patted his arm. 'Have some more marmalade.'

Worriedly, Reynaldo asked, 'Does this mean you get to do the stand-up? I mean, since you eyewitnessed the shooting and not me.'

'Ray, I have absolutely no interest in doing a stand-up. I don't want to be on camera.'

'You mean it?' His voice dripped with relief. Pathetic, Christina thought; the man is pathetic.

Clearing his throat, Reynaldo Flemm said, 'I've got some bad news of my own, Chris.'

Christina dabbed her lips with the corner of the napkin. 'Does it involve your trip to New York?'

Flemm nodded yes.

'And, perhaps, Maggie Gonzalez?'

'I'm afraid so,' he said.

'She's missing again, isn't she, Ray?'

Flemm said, 'We had a dinner set up at the Palm.'

'And she never showed.'

'Right,' he said.

'Was this before or after you wired her the fifteen thousand?' Christina asked.

'Hey, I'm not stupid. I only sent half.'

'Shit.' Christina drummed her fingernails on the table.

Reynaldo Flemm sighed and turned away. Absently he ran a hand through his new golden tendrils. 'I'm sorry,' he said finally. 'You still want to dump this story?'

'No,' Christina said. 'No, I don't.'

Mick Stranahan looked through mug shots all morning, knowing he would never find the killer's face.

'Look anyway,' said Al García.

Stranahan flipped to another page. 'Is it just my imagination,' he said, 'or are these assholes getting uglier every year?'

'I've noticed that, too,' García said.

'Speaking of which, I got a friendly visit from Murdock and Salazar at the hospital.' Stranahan told García what had happened.

'I'll report it to I.A., if you want,' García said.

I.A. was Internal Affairs, where detectives Murdock and Salazar probably had files as thick as the Dade County Yellow Pages.

'Don't push it,' said Stranahan. 'I just wanted you to know what they're up to.'

'Pricks,' García grunted. 'I'll think of something.'

'I thought you had clout.'

'Clout? All I got is a ten-cent commendation and a gimp arm, same as you. Only mine came from a sawed-off.'

'I'm impressed,' said Mick Stranahan. He closed the mug book and pushed it across the table. 'He's not in here, Al. You got one for circus freaks?'

'That bad, huh?'

Stranahan said, 'Bad's not the word.' It wasn't.

'Want to try a composite? Let me call one of the artists.'

'No, that's all right,' Stranahan said. 'I wouldn't know where to start. Al, you wouldn't believe this guy.'

The detective gnawed the tip off a cigar. 'He's got to be the same geek who did Chloe. Thing is, I got witnesses saw them out at the marina having a drink, chatting like the best of friends. How do you figure that?'

'She always had great taste in men.' Stranahan stood up, gingerly testing the strap of his sling.

'Where you going?'

'I'm off to do a B-and-E.'

'Now don't say shit like that.'

'It's true, Al.'

'I'm not believing this. Tell me you're bullshitting, Mick.'

'If it makes you feel better.'

'And call me,' García said in a low voice, 'if you turn up something good.'

At half-past three, Mick Stranahan broke into Maggie Gonzalez's duplex for the second time. The first thing he did was play back the tape on the answering machine. There were messages from numerous relatives, all demanding to know why Maggie had missed her cousin Gloria's baby shower. The only message that Mick Stranahan found interesting was from the Essex House hotel in downtown New York. A nasal female clerk requested that Miss Gonzalez contact them immediately about a forty-three-dollar dry-cleaning bill, which Maggie had forgotten to pay before checking out. The Essex House clerk had efficiently left the time and date of the phone message: January twenty-eighth at ten o'clock in the morning.

The next thing Mick Stranahan did was to sift through a big stack of Maggie's mail until he found the most recent Visa card bill, which he opened and studied at her kitchen table. That Maggie was spending somebody else's money in Manhattan was obvious: She had used her personal credit card only twice. One entry was $35.50 at Ticketron, probably for a Broadway show; the other charge was from a clothing shop for $179.40, more than Maggie was probably carrying in cash at the time. The clothing store was in the Plaza Hotel; the transaction was dated February 1.

Mick Stranahan was getting ready to leave the duplex when Maggie's telephone rang twice, then clicked over to the machine. He listened as a man came on the line. Stranahan thought he recognized the voice, but he wasn't certain. He had only spoken with the man once.

The voice on the machine said: 'Maggie, it's me. I tried the Essex but they said you checked out . . . Look, we've really got to talk. In person. Call me at the office right away, collect. Wherever you are, okay? Thanks.'

As the man gave the number, Stranahan copied it in pencil on the Formica counter. After the caller hung up, Stranahan dialed 411 and asked for the listing of the Whispering Palms Spa and Surgery Center in Bal Harbour. A recording gave the main number as 555–7600. The phone number left by Maggie's male caller was 555–7602.

Rudy Graveline, Stranahan thought, calling on his office line.

The next number Stranahan dialed was 1–212–555–1212. Information for Manhattan. He got the number of the Plaza, dialed the main desk, and asked for Miss Maggie Gonzalez's room. A woman picked up on the fourth ring.

'Is this Miss Gonzalez?' Stranahan asked, trying to mimic a Brooklyn accent.

'Yes, it is.'

'This is the concierge downstairs.' Like there was an *upstairs* concierge. 'We were just wondering if you had any dry cleaning you needed done this evening.'

'What are you talking about, I'm still waiting for those three dresses I sent out Sunday,' Maggie said, not pleasantly.

'Oh, I'm very sorry,' Mick Stranahan said. 'I'll see to it immediately.'

Then he hung up, grabbed the white pages off the kitchen counter, and looked up the number for Delta Airlines.

16

On his way to Miami International, Mick Stranahan stopped at his brother-in-law's office. Kipper Garth was on the speaker phone, piecing out a slip-and-fall to one of the Brickell Avenue buzzards.

Mick Stranahan walked in and said, 'The files?'

Kipper Garth motioned to a wine-colored chair and put a finger to his waxy lips. 'So, Chuckie,' he said to the speaker phone, 'what're you thinking?'

'Thinking maybe two hundred if we settle,' said the voice on the other end.

'Two hundred!' Kipper exclaimed. 'Chuckie, you're nuts. The woman tripped over her own damn dachshund.'

'Kip, they'll settle,' the other lawyer said. 'It's the biggest grocery chain in Florida, they always settle. Besides, the dog croaked—that's fifty grand right there for mental anguish.'

'But dogs aren't even allowed in the store, Chuckie. If it was somebody else's dachshund she tripped on, then we'd really have something. But this was her own fault.'

Sardonic laughter crackled over the speaker box. 'Kip, buddy, you're not thinking like a litigator,' the voice said. 'I went to the supermarket myself and guess what: No signs!'

'What do you mean?'

'I mean no No Dogs Allowed-type signs. Not a one posted in Spanish. So how was our poor Consuelo to know?'

'Chuckie, you're beautiful,' said Kipper Garth. 'If that ain't negligence—'

'Two hundred thou,' Chuckie said, 'that's my guess. We'll split sixty-forty.'

'Nope,' Kipper Garth said, staring coldly at the speaker box. 'Half-and-half. Same as always.'

'Excuse me.' It was Mick Stranahan. Kipper Garth frowned and shook his head; not now, not when he was closing the deal.

The voice on the phone said: 'Kip, who's that? You got somebody there?'

'Relax, Chuckie, it's just me,' Stranahan said to the box. 'You know—Kipper's heroin connection? I just dropped by with a briefcase full of Mexican brown. Can I pencil you in for a kilo?'

Frantically Kipper Garth jabbed two fingers at the phone buttons. The line went dead and the speaker box hummed the dial tone. 'You're fucking crazy,' he said to Mick Stranahan.

'I've got a plane to catch, Jocko. Where are the Graveline files?'

'You're crazy,' Kipper Garth said again, trying to stay calm. He buzzed for a secretary, who lugged in three thick brown office folders.

'There's a conference room where you can read this shit in private.'

Mick Stranahan said, 'No, this is fine.' With Kipper Garth stewing, Stranahan skimmed quickly through the files on Rudy Graveline. It was worse than he thought—or better, depending on one's point of view.

'Seventeen complaints to the state board,' Stranahan marveled.

'Yeah, but no action,' Kipper Garth noted. 'Not even a reprimand.'

Stranahan looked up, lifting one of the files. 'Jocko, this is a gold mine.'

'Well, Mick, I'm glad I could help. Now, if you don't mind, it's getting late and I've got a few calls to make.'

Stranahan said, 'You don't understand, I wanted this stuff for you, not me.'

Peevishly Kipper Garth glanced at his wristwatch. 'You're right, Mick, I *don't* understand. What the hell do I want with Graveline's files?'

'Names, Jocko.' Stranahan opened the top folder and riffled the pages dramatically. 'You got seventeen names, seventeen leads on a silver platter. You got Mrs. Susan Jacoby and her boobs that don't match. You got Mr. Robert Mears with his left eye that won't close and his right that won't open. You got, let's see, Julia Kelly with a shnoz that looks like a Philips screwdriver—Jesus, you see the Polaroid of that thing? What else? Oh, you got Ken Martinez and his lopsided scrotum . . .'

Kipper Garth waved his arms. 'Mick, that's enough! What would I want with all this crap?'

'I figured you'll need it, Jocko.'

'For what?'

'For suing Doctor Rudy Graveline.'

'Very funny,' Kipper Garth said. 'I told you, the man's in my yacht club. Besides, he's been sued before.'

'Sue him again,' Mick Stranahan said. 'Sue the mother like he's never been sued before.'

'He'd settle out. Doctors always settle.'

'Don't let him. Don't settle for anything. Not for ten million dollars. Sign up one of these poor misfortunate souls and go to the frigging wall.'

Kipper Garth stood up and adjusted his necktie, suddenly on his way to some important meeting. 'I can't help you, Mick. Get yourself another lawyer.'

'You don't do this favor for me,' said Stranahan, 'and I'll go tell Katie about your trip to Steamboat next month with Inga or Olga or whatever the hell her name is, I got it written down here somewhere. And for future reference, Jocko, don't ever put your ski bunny's plane tickets on American Express. I know it's convenient and all, but it's very, very risky. I mean, with the computers they got these days, I can pull out your goddamned seat assignments—5A and 5B, I think it is.'

All Kipper Garth could say was: 'How'd you do that?'

'I told you before, I'm still plugged in.' A travel agent in Coral Gables who owed him one. It was so damn easy Stranahan couldn't bear to tell his brother-in-law.

'What's the point of all this?' Kipper Garth asked.

'Never mind, just do it. Sue the asshole.'

The lawyer lifted his pinstriped coat off the back of the chair and checked it for wrinkles. 'Mick, let me shop this around and get back to you.'

'No, Jocko. No referrals. You do this one all by yourself.'

The lawyer sagged as if struck by a brick.

'You heard me right,' Stranahan said.

'Mick, please.' It was a pitiable peep. 'Mick, I don't do this sort of thing.'

'Sure you do. I see the billboards all over town.'

Kipper Garth nibbled on a thumbnail to mask the spastic twitching of his upper lip. The thought of actually going to court had pitched him into a cold sweat. A fresh droplet made a shiny trail from the furrow of his forehead to the tip of his well-tanned nose.

'I don't know,' he said, 'it's been so long.'

'Aw, it's easy,' Stranahan said. 'One of your paralegals can draw up the complaint. That'll get the ball rolling.' With a thud he stacked the Graveline files on Kipper Garth's desk; the lawyer eyed the pile as if it were nitroglycerine.

'A gold mine,' Stranahan said encouragingly. 'I'll check back in a few days.'

'Mick?'

'Relax. All you've got to do is go down to the courthouse and sue.'

Wanly, Kipper Garth said, 'I don't have to win, do I?'

'Of course not,' Stranahan said, patting his arm. 'It'll never get that far.'

Dr. Rudy Graveline lived in a palatial three-story house on northern Biscayne Bay. The house had Doric pillars, two spiral staircases, and more imported marble than the entire downtown art museum. The house had absolutely no business being on Miami Beach, but in fairness it looked no more silly or out of place than any of the other garish mansions. The house was on the same palm-lined avenue where two of the Bee Gees lived, which meant that Rudy had been forced to pay about a hundred thousand more than the property was worth. For the first few years, the women whom Rudy dated were impressed to be in the Bee Gees' neighborhood, but lately the star value had worn off and Rudy had quit mentioning it.

It was Heather Chappell, the actress, who brought it up first.

'I think Barry lives around here,' she said as they were driving back to Rudy's house after dinner at the Forge.

'Barry who?' Rudy asked, his mind off somewhere.

'Barry Gibb. The singer. *Staying alive, staying alive, ooh, ooh, ooh.*'

As much as he loved Heather, Rudy wished she wouldn't try to sing.

'You know Barry personally?' he asked.

'Oh sure. All the guys.'

'That's Barry's place there,' Rudy Graveline said, pointing. 'And Robin lives right here.'

'Let's stop over,' Heather said, touching his knee. 'It'll be fun.'

Rudy said no, he didn't know the guys all that well. Besides, he never really liked their music, especially that disco shit. Immediately Heather sank into a deep pout, which she heroically maintained all the way back to Rudy's house, up the stairs, all the way to his bedroom. There she peeled off her dress and panties and lay face down on the king-sized bed. Every few minutes she would raise her cheek off the satin pillow and sigh disconsolately, until Rudy couldn't stand it anymore.

'Are you mad at me?' he asked. He was in his boxer shorts, standing in the closet where he had hung his suit. 'Heather, are you angry?'

'No.'

'Yes, you are. Did I say something wrong? If I did, I'm sorry.' He was blubbering like a jerk, all because he wanted to get laid in the worst way. The sight of Heather's perfect bare bottom— the one she wanted contoured—was driving him mad.

In a tiny voice she said, 'I love the Bee Gees.'

'I'm sorry,' Rudy said. He sat on the corner of the bed and stroked her peachlike rump. 'I liked their early stuff, I really did.'

Heather said, 'I loved the disco, Rudy. It just about killed me when disco died.'

'I'm sorry I said anything.'

'You ever made love to disco music?'

Rudy thought: What is happening to my life?

'Do you have any Village People tapes?' Heather asked, giving him a quick saucy look over the shoulder. 'There's a song on their first album, I swear, I could fuck all night to it.'

Rudy Graveline was nothing if not resourceful. He found the Village People tape in the discount bin of an all-night record store across from the University of Miami campus in Coral Gables. He sped home, popped the cassette into the modular sound system, cranked up the woofers, and jogged up the spiral staircase to the bedroom.

Heather said, 'Not here.' She took him by the hand and led him downstairs. 'The fireplace,' she whispered.

'It's seventy-eight degrees,' Rudy remarked, kicking off his underwear.

'It's not the fire,' Heather said, 'it's the marble.'

One of the selling points of the big house was an oversized fireplace constructed of polished Italian marble. Fireplaces were considered a cozy novelty in South Florida, but Rudy had never used his, since he was afraid the expensive black marble would blister in the heat.

Heather crawled in and got on her back. She had the most amazing smile on her face. 'Oh, Rudy, it's so cold.' She lifted her buttocks off the marble and slapped them down; the squeak made her giggle.

Rudy stood there, naked and limp, staring like an idiot. 'We could get hurt,' he said. He was thinking of what the marble would do to his elbows and kneecaps.

'Don't be such a geezer,' Heather said, hoisting her hips and wiggling them in his face. She rolled over and pointed to the twin smudges of condensation on the black stone. 'Look,' she said. 'Just like finger-prints.'

'Sort of,' Rudy Graveline mumbled.

She said, 'I must be hot, huh?'

'I guess so,' Rudy said. His skull was ready to split; the voices of the Village People reverberated in the fireplace like mortar fire.

'Oh, God,' Heather moaned.

'What is it?' Rudy asked.

'The song. That's my song.' She squeaked to her knees and

seized him ferociously around the waist. 'Come on down here,' she said. 'Let's dance.'

In order to prolong his tumescence, Dr. Rudy Graveline had trained himself to think of anything but sex while he was having sex. Most times he concentrated on his unit trusts and tax shelters, which were complicated enough to keep orgasm at bay for a good ten to fifteen minutes. Tonight, though, he concentrated on something different. Rudy Graveline was thinking of his daunting predicament—of Victoria Barletta and the up-coming television documentary about her death; of Mick Stranahan, still alive and menacing; of Maggie Gonzalez, spending his money somewhere in New York.

More often than not, Rudy found he could ruminate with startling clarity during the throes of sexual intercourse. He had arrived at many crucial life decisions in such moments—the clutter of the day and the pressure from his patients seemed to vanish in a crystal vacuum, a mystic physical void that permitted Rudy to concentrate on his problems in a new light and from a new angle.

And so it was that—even with Heather Chappell clawing his shoulders and screaming disco drivel into his ear, even with the flue vent clanging in the chimney above his head, and even with his knees grinding mercilessly on the cold Italian marble—Rudy was able to focus on the most important crisis of his life. Both pain and pleasure dissipated; it was as if he were alone, alert and sensitized, in a cool dark chamber. Rudy thought about everything that had happened so far, and then about what he must do now. It wasn't a bad plan. There was, however, one loose end.

Rudy snapped out of his cognitive trance when Heather cried, 'Enough already!'

'What?'

'I said you can stop now, okay? This isn't a damn rodeo.' She was all out of breath. Her chest was slick with sweat.

Rudy quit moving.

'What were you thinking of?' Heather asked.

'Nothing.'

'Did you come?'

'Sure,' Rudy lied.

'You were thinking of some other girl, weren't you?'

'No, I wasn't.' Another lie.

He had been thinking of Maggie Gonzalez, and how he should have killed her two months ago.

The next day at noon, George Graveline arrived at the Whispering Palms surgery clinic and demanded to see his brother, said it was an emergency. When Rudy heard the story, he agreed.

The two men were talking in hushed, worried tones when Chemo showed up an hour later.

'So what's the big rush?' he said.

'Sit down,' Rudy Graveline told him.

Chemo was dressed in a tan safari outfit, the kind Jim Fowler wore on the *Wild Kingdom* television show.

Rudy said, 'George, this is a friend of mine. He's working for me on this matter.'

Chemo raised his eyebrows. 'Happened to your thumb?' he said to George.

'Car door.' Rudy's brother did not wish to share that painful detail of his encounter with Mick Stranahan.

George Graveline had a few questions of his own for the tall stranger, but he held them. Valiantly he tried not to stare at Chemo's complexion, which George assessed as some tragic human strain of Dutch elm disease. What finally drew the tree trimmer's attention away from Chemo's face was the colorful Macy's shopping bag in which Chemo concealed his newly extended left arm.

'Had an accident,' Chemo explained. 'I'm only wearing this until I get a customized cover.' He pulled the shopping bag off the Weed Whacker. George Graveline recognized it immediately—the lightweight household model.

'Hey, that thing work?'

'You bet,' Chemo said. He probed under his arm until he found the toggle switch that jolted the Weed Whacker to life. It sounded like a blender without the top on.

George grinned and clapped his hands.

'That's enough,' Rudy said sharply.

'No, watch,' said Chemo. He ambled to the corner of the office where Rudy kept a beautiful potted rubber plant.

'Oh no,' the doctor said, but it was too late. Gleefully Chemo chopped the rubber plant into slaw.

'Yeah!' said George Graveline.

Rudy leaned over and whispered, 'Don't encourage him. He's a dangerous fellow.'

Basking in the attention, Chemo left the Weed Whacker unsheathed. He sat down next to the two men and said, 'Let's hear the big news.'

'Mick Stranahan visited George yesterday,' Rudy said. 'Apparently the bastard's not giving up.'

'What'd he say?'

'All kinds of crazy shit,' George said.

Rudy had warned his brother not to tell Chemo about Victoria Barletta or the wood chipper or Stranahan's specific accusation about what had happened to the body.

Rudy twirled his eyeglasses and said: 'I don't understand why Stranahan is so damn hard to kill.'

'Least we know he's out of the hospital,' Chemo said brightly. 'I'll get right on it.'

'Not just yet,' Rudy said. He turned to his brother. 'George, could I speak to him alone, please?'

George Graveline nodded amiably at Chemo on his way out the door. 'Listen, you ever need work,' he said, 'I could use you and that, uh . . .'

'Prothesis,' Chemo said. 'Thanks, but I don't think so.'

When they were alone, Rudy opened the top drawer of his desk and handed Chemo a large brown envelope. Inside the envelope were an eight-by-ten photograph, two thousand dollars in traveler's checks, and an airline ticket. The person in the picture was a handsome, sharp-featured woman with brown eyes and brown hair; her name was printed in block letters on the back of the photograph. The plane ticket was round-trip, Miami to La Guardia and back.

Chemo said, 'Is this what I think it is?'

'Another job,' Dr. Rudy Graveline said.

'It'll cost you.'

'I'm prepared for that.'

'Same as the Stranahan deal,' Chemo said.

'Twenty treatments? You don't *need* twenty more treatments. Your face'll be done in two months.'

'I'm not talking about dermabrasion,' Chemo said. 'I'm talking about my ears.'

Rudy thought: Dear God, will it never end? 'Your ears,' he said to Chemo, 'are the last things that need surgical attention.'

'The hell is that supposed to mean?'

'Nothing, nothing. All I'm saying is, once we finish the dermabrasions you'll look as good as new. I honestly don't believe you'll want to touch a thing, that's how good your face is going to look.'

Chemo said, 'My ears stick out too far and you know it. You want me to do this hit, you'll fix the damn things.'

'Fine,' Rudy Graveline sighed, 'fine.' There was nothing wrong with the man's ears, only what was between them.

Chemo tucked the envelope into his armpit and bagged up the Weed Whacker. 'Oh yeah, one more thing. I'm out of that stuff for my face.'

'What stuff?'

'You know,' Chemo said, 'the Wite-Out.'

Rudy Graveline found a small bottle in his desk and tossed it to Chemo, who slipped it into the breast pocket of his Jim Fowler safari jacket. 'Call you from New York,' he said.

'Yes,' said Rudy wearily. 'By all means.'

17

Christina Marks slipped out of the first-class cabin while Reynaldo Flemm was autographing a cocktail napkin for a flight attendant. The flight attendant had mistaken the newly bewigged Reynaldo for David Lee Roth, the rock singer. The Puerto Rican mustache looked odd with all that blond hair, but the flight attendant assumed it was meant as a humorous disguise.

Mick Stranahan was sitting in coach, a stack of outdoors magazines on the seat next to him. He saw Christina coming down the aisle and smiled. 'My shadow.'

'I'm not following you,' she said.

'Yes, you are. But that's all right.' He moved the magazines and motioned her to sit down.

'You look very nice.' It was the first time he had seen her in a dress. 'Some coincidence, that you and the anchorman got the same flight as I did.'

Christina said, 'He's not an anchorman. And no, it's not a coincidence that we're on the same plane. Ray thinks it is, but it's not.'

'Ray thinks it is, huh? So this was your idea, following me.'

'Relax,' Christina said. Ever since the shooting she had stayed close; at first she rationalized it as a journalist's instinct—the Barletta story kept coming back to Stranahan, didn't it? But then she had found herself sleeping some nights at the hospital, where nothing newsworthy was likely to happen; sitting in the corner and watching him in the hospital bed, long after it was obvious he would make a full recovery. Christina couldn't deny she was attracted to him, and worried about him. She also had a feeling he was moderately crazy.

Stranahan said, 'So you guys are going to trail me all around New York. A regular tag team, you and Ray.'

'Ray will be busy,' Christina said, 'on other projects.'

The jetliner dipped slightly, and a shaft of sunlight caught the side of her face, forcing her to look away. For the first time Stranahan noticed a sprinkling of light freckles on her nose and cheeks: cinnamon freckles, the kind that children have.

'Did I ever thank you for saving my life?' he asked.

'Yes, you did.'

'Well, thanks again.' He poured some honey-roasted peanuts into the palm of her hand. 'Why are you following me?'

'I'm not,' she said.

'If it's only to juice up your damn TV show, then I'm going to get angry.'

Christina said, 'It's not that.'

'You want to keep an eye on me.'

'You're an interesting man. You make things happen.'

Stranahan popped a peanut and said, 'That's a good one.'

Christina Marks softened her tone. 'I'll help you find her.'

'Find who?'

'Maggie Gonzalez.'

'Who said she was lost? Besides, you got her on tape, right? The whole sordid story.'

'Not yet,' Christina admitted.

Stranahan laughed caustically. 'Oh brother,' he said.

'Listen, I got a trail of bills she's been sending up to the office. Between the two of us, we could find her in a day. Besides, I think she'll talk to me. The whole sordid story, on tape—like you said.'

Stranahan didn't mention that he already knew where Maggie Gonzalez was staying, and that he was totally confident that he could persuade her to talk.

'You're the most helpful woman I ever met,' he said to Christina Marks. 'So unselfish, too. If I didn't know better, I'd think maybe you were hunting for Maggie because she beat you and the anchorman out of some serious dough.'

Christina said, 'I liked you better unconscious.'

Stranahan chuckled and took her hand. He didn't let go like she thought he would, he just held it. Once, when the plane hit some turbulence, Christina jumped nervously. Without looking up from his *Field & Stream*, Stranahan gave her hand a squeeze. It was more comforting than suggestive, but it made Christina flush.

She retreated to the role of professional interviewer. 'So,' she said, 'tell me about yourself.'

'You first,' Stranahan said; a brief smile, then back to the magazine.

Oddly, she found herself talking—talking so openly that she sounded like one of those video-dating tapes: Let's see, I'm thirty-four years old, divorced, born in Richmond, went to the University of Missouri journalism school, lettered on the swim team, graduated magna, got my first decent news job with the ABC affiliate in St. Louis, then three years at WBBM in Chicago until I met Ray at the Gacy trial and he offered me an assistant producer's job, and here I am. Now it's your turn, Mick.

'Pardon?'

'Your turn,' Christina Marks said. 'That's my life story, now let's hear yours.'

Stranahan closed the magazine and centered it on his lap. He said, 'My life story is this: I've killed five men, and I've been married five times.'

Christina slowly pulled her hand away.

'Which scares you more?' Mick Stranahan said.

When Dade County Commissioner Roberto Pepsical broke the news to The Others (that is, the other crooked commissioners), they all had the same reaction: Nope, sorry, too late.

Dr. Rudy Graveline had offered major bucks to rezone prime green space for the Old Cypress Towers project, and the commissioners had gone ahead and done it. They couldn't very well put it back on the agenda and reverse the vote—not without arousing the interest of those goddamned newspapers reporters. Besides, a deal was a deal. Furthermore, The Others wanted to know about the promised twenty-five thousand dollar bribe: specifically, where was it? Was Rudy holding out? One commissioner even suggested that a new vote to rescind the zoning and scrap the project could be obtained only by doubling the original payoff.

Roberto Pepsical was fairly sure that Dr. Rudy Graveline would not pay twice for essentially the same act of corruption. In addition, Roberto didn't feel like explaining to the doctor that if Old Cypress Towers were to expire on the drawing board, so would a plethora of other hidden gratuities that would have winged their way into the commissioners' secret accounts. From downtown bankers to the zoning lawyers to the code inspectors, payoffs traditionally trickled upward to the commissioners. The ripple effect of killing a project as large as Rudy's was calamitous, bribery-wise.

Roberto hated being the middleman when the stakes got this high. By nature he was slow, inattentive, and somewhat easily confused. He hadn't taken notes during Rudy's late-night phone call, and maybe he should have. This much he remembered clearly: The doctor had said that he'd changed his mind about Old Cypress Towers, that he'd decided to move his money out of the country instead. When Roberto protested, the doctor told him there'd been all kinds of trouble, serious trouble—specifically, that hinky old surgical case he'd mentioned that day at lunch. The proverbial doo-doo was getting ready to hit the proverbial fan, Rudy had said; somebody was out to ruin him. He told Roberto Pepsical to pass along his most profound apologies to The Others, but there was no other course for the doctor to take. Since his problem wasn't going away, Old Cypress Towers would.

The solution was so obvious that even Roberto grasped it immediately. The apartment project could be rescued, and so could the commissioners' bribes. Once Roberto learned that Dr. Rudy Graveline's problem had a name, he began checking with his connections at the Metro-Dade Police Department.

Which led him straight to detectives John Murdock and Joe Salazar.

Roberto considered the mission of such significance that he took the radical step of skipping his normal two-hour lunch to stop by the police station for a personal visit. He found both detectives at their desks. They were eating hot Cuban sandwiches and cleaning their revolvers. It was the first time Roberto had ever seen Gulden's mustard on a .357.

'You're sure,' said the commissioner, 'that this man is a murder suspect?'

'Yep,' said John Murdock.

'Number one suspect,' added Joe Salazar.

Roberto said, 'So you're going to arrest him?'

'Of course,' Salazar said.

'Eventually,' said Murdock.

'The sooner the better,' Roberto said.

John Murdock glanced at Joe Salazar. Then he looked at Roberto and said, 'Commissioner, if you've got any information about this man . . .'

'He's been giving a friend of mine a hard time, that's all. A good friend of mine.' Roberto knew better than to mention Rudy Graveline's name, and John Murdock knew better than to ask.

Joe Salazar said, 'It's a crime to threaten a person. Did Stranahan make a threat?'

'Nothing you could prove,' Roberto said. 'Look, I'd appreciate it if you guys would keep me posted.'

'Absolutely,' John Murdock promised. He wiped the food off his gun and shoved it back in the shoulder holster.

'This is very important,' Roberto Pepsical said. 'Extremely important.'

Murdock said, 'Don't worry, we'll nail the fuckwad.'

'Yeah,' said Joe Salazar. 'It's only a matter of time.'

'Not much time, I hope.'

'We'll do what we can, Commissioner.'

'There might even be a promotion in it.'

'Oh boy, a promotion,' said John Murdock. 'Joey, you hear that? A promotion!' The detective burped at the commissioner and said, 'How about some green instead?'

Roberto Pepsical winced as if a hornet had buzzed into his ear. 'Jesus, are you saying—'

'Money,' said Joe Salazar, chomping a pickle. 'He means money.'

'Let me get this straight: You guys want a bribe for solving a murder?'

'No,' Murdock said, 'just for making the arrest.'

'I can't believe this.'

'Sure you can,' Joe Salazar said. 'Your friend wants Stranahan out of the way, right? The county jail, that's fucking out of the way.'

Roberto buried his rubbery chin in his hands. 'Money,' he murmured.

'I don't know what you guys call it over at Government Center, but around here we call it a bonus.' John Murdock grinned at the county commissioner. 'What *do* you guys call it?'

To Roberto it seemed reckless to be discussing a payoff in the middle of the detective squad room. He felt like passing gas.

In a low voice he said to John Murdock, 'All right, we'll work something out.'

'Good.'

The commissioner stood up. He was about to reach out and shake their hands, but he changed his mind. 'Look, we never had this meeting,' he said to the two detectives.

'Of course not,' John Murdock agreed.

Joe Salazar said, 'Hey, you can trust us.'

About as far as I can spit, thought Roberto Pepsical.

Three days before Mick Stranahan, Christina Marks, and Reynaldo Flemm arrived in Manhattan, and four days before the man called Chemo showed up, Maggie Gonzalez walked into a video-rental shop on West 52nd Street and asked to make a tape. She gave the shop clerk seventy-five dollars cash, and he led her to 'the studio,' a narrow backroom paneled with cheap brown cork. The studio reeked of Lysol. On the floor was a stained gray mattress and a bright clump of used Kleenex, which, at Maggie's insistence, the clerk removed. A Sony video camera was mounted on an aluminum tripod at one end of the room; behind it, on another stem, was a small bank of lights. The clerk opened a metal folding chair and placed it eight feet in front of the lens.

Maggie sat down, opened her purse and unfolded some notes

she had printed on Plaza stationery. While she read them to herself, the clerk was making impatient chewing-gum noises in his cheeks, like he had better things to do. Finally Maggie told him to start the tape, and a tiny red light twinkled over the Sony's cold black eye.

Maggie was all set to begin when she noticed the clerk hovering motionless in the darkest corner, a cockroach trying to blend into the cork. She told the guy to get lost, waited until the door slammed, then took a breath and addressed the camera.

'My name is Maggie Orestes Gonzalez,' she said. 'On the twelfth of March, 1986, I was a witness to the killifig of a young woman named Victoria Barletta . . .'

The taping took fourteen minutes. Afterwards Maggie got two extra copies made at twenty dollars each. On the way back to the hotel she stopped at a branch of the Merchant bank and rented a safe-deposit box, where she left the two extra videotapes. She took the original up to her room at the Plaza, and placed it in the nightstand, under the room-service menu.

The very next day Maggie Gonzalez took a cab to the office of Dr. Leonard Leaper on the corner of 50th Street and Lexington. Dr. Leaper was a nationally renowned and internationally published plastic surgeon; Maggie had read up on him in the journals. 'You have a decent reputation,' she told Dr. Leaper. 'I hope it's not just hype.' Her experiences in Dr. Rudy Graveline's surgical suite had taught her to be exceedingly careful when choosing a physician.

Neutrally Dr. Leaper said, 'What can I do for you, young lady?'

'The works,' Maggie replied.

'The works?'

'I want a bleph, a lift, and I want the hump taken out of this nose. Also, I want you to trim the septum so it looks like this.' With a finger she respositioned the tip of her nose at a perky, Sandy Duncan-type angle. 'See?'

Dr. Leaper nodded.

'I'm a nurse,' Maggie said. 'I used to work for a plastic surgeon.'

'I figured something like that,' Dr. Leaper said. 'Why do you want these operations?'

'None of your business.'

Dr. Leaper said, 'Miss Gonzalez, if indeed you worked for a surgeon then you understand I've got to ask some personal questions. There are good reasons for elective cosmetic surgery and bad reasons, good candidates and poor candidates. Some patients believe it will solve all their problems, and of course it won't—'

'Cut the crap,' Maggie said, 'and take my word: Surgery will definitely solve my problem.'

'Which is?'

'None of your business.'

Dr. Leaper stood up. 'Then I'm afraid I can't help.'

'You guys are all alike,' Maggie complained.

'No, we're not,' Dr. Leaper said. 'That's why you're here. You wanted somebody good.'

His composure was maddening. Maggie said, 'All right—will you do the surgery if I tell you the reason?'

'If it's a good one,' the doctor replied.

She said, 'I need a new face.'

'Why?'

'Because I am about to . . . testify against someone.'

Dr. Leaper said, 'Can you tell me more?'

'It's a serious matter, and I expect he'll send someone to find me before it's over. I don't want to be found.'

Dr. Leaper said, 'But surgery can only do so much—'

'Look, I've seen hundreds of cases, and I know good results from bad results. I also know the limitations of the procedures. You just do the nose, the neck, the eyes, maybe a plastic implant in the chin . . . and let me and Lady Clairol do the rest. I guarantee the bastard won't recognize me.'

Dr. Leaper locked his hands. In a grave voice he said, 'Let me understand: You're a witness in a criminal matter?'

'Undoubtedly,' Maggie said. 'A homicide, to be exact.'

'Oh, dear.'

'And I must testify, Doctor.' The word *testify* was a stretch, but it wasn't far from the truth. 'It's the right thing for me to do,' Maggie asserted.

'Yes,' said Dr. Leaper, without conviction.

'So, you see why I need your help.'

The surgeon sighed. 'Why should I believe you?'

Maggie said, 'Why should I lie? If it weren't an emergency, don't you think I would have had this done a long time ago, when I could've got a deal on the fees?'

'I suppose so.'

'Please, Doctor. It's not vanity, it's survival. Do my face, you'll be saving a life.'

Dr. Leaper opened his schedule book. 'I've got a lipo tomorrow at two, but I'm going to bump him for you. Don't eat or drink anything after midnight—'

'I know the routine,' Maggie Gonzalez said ebulliently. 'Thank you very much.'

'It's all right.'

'One more thing.'

'Yes?' said Dr. Leaper, cocking one gray eyebrow.

'I was wondering if there's any chance of a professional discount? I mean, since I *am* a nurse.'

Mick Stranahan stood on the curb outside La Guardia Airport and watched Reynaldo Flemm climb into a long black limousine. The limo driver, holding the door, eyed Reynaldo's new hair and looked to Christina Marks for a clue. She said something quietly to the driver, then waved good-bye to Reynaldo in the back seat. Through the smoked gray window Stranahan thought he saw Flemm shoot him a bitter look as the limo pulled away.

'I don't like this place,' Stranahan muttered, his breath frosty.

'What places *do* you like?' Christina asked.

'Old Rhodes Key. That's one place you won't see frozen spit on the sidewalk. Fact, you won't even see a sidewalk.'

'You old curmudgeon.' Christina said it much too sarcastically for Stranahan. 'Come on, let's get a cab.'

Her apartment was off 72nd Street on the Upper East Side. Third floor, one bedroom with a small kitchen and a garden patio scarcely big enough for a Norway rat. The furniture was low and modern: glass, chrome, and sharp angles. One of those sofas you put together like a jigsaw puzzle. Potted plants occupied three of the four corners in the living room. On the main wall hung a vast and frenetic abstract painting.

Stranahan took a step back and studied it. 'Boy, I don't know,' he said.

From the bedroom came Christina's voice. 'You like it?'

'Not really,' Stranahan said.

When Christina walked out, he saw that she had changed to blue jeans and a navy pullover sweater. She stood next to him in front of the painting and said, 'It's supposed to be springtime. Spring in the city.'

'Looks like an Amoco station on fire.'

'Thank you,' Christina said. 'Such a sensitive man.'

Stranahan shrugged. 'Let's go. I gotta check in.'

'Why don't you stay here?' She gave it a beat. 'On the sectional.'

'The sectional? I don't think so.'

'It's safer than a hotel, Mick.'

'I'm not so sure.'

Christina said, 'Don't flatter yourself.'

'It's not me I was thinking of. Believe it or not.'

'Sorry. Please stay.'

'The Great Reynaldo will not be pleased.'

'All the more reason,' Christina said.

They ate a late lunch at a small Italian restaurant three blocks from Christina's apartment. She ordered a pasta salad and Perrier, while Stranahan had spaghetti and meatballs and two beers. Then they took a taxi to the Plaza Hotel.

'She's here?' Christina asked, once in the lobby and again in the elevator.

Stranahan knocked repeatedly on the door to Maggie Gonzalez's room, but no one answered. Maggie was in bed, coasting through a codeine dreamland with a brand new face that she had not yet seen. The sound of Mick Stranahan's knocking was but a muffled drumbeat in her delicious pharmaceutical fog, and Maggie paid it no attention. It would be hours before the drumming returned, and by then she would be conscious enough to stumble toward the door.

Her big mistake had been to call Dr. Rudy Graveline four days earlier when she had gotten the message on her machine in Miami. Curiosity had triumphed over common sense; Maggie had been dying for an update on the Stranahan situation. She needed to stay close to Rudy, but not too close. It was a dicey act. She wanted the doctor to believe that they were on the same side, his side. She also wanted to keep the expense money coming.

The phone call, though, had been peculiar. At first Dr. Graveline had seemed relieved to hear her voice. But the more questions Maggie had asked—about Stranahan, the TV people, the money situation—the more remote the doctor had become, his voice getting tighter and colder on the other end. Finally Rudy had said that something had come up in the office, could he call her right back? Certainly, Maggie had said and—stupidly, it turned out—had given Rudy the phone number at the hotel. Days later the doctor still had not called back, and Maggie wondered why in the hell he had tried to reach her in the first place.

The answer was simple.

On the thirteenth of February, the man known as Chemo got off a Pan Am flight from Miami to New York. He wore a dusty broad-brimmed hat pulled down tightly to shadow his igneous face, a calfskin golf-bag cover snapped over his left arm to conceal the prosthesis, a pea-green woolen overcoat to protect against the winter wind, and heavy rubber-soled shoes to combat the famous New York City slush. He also had in his possession a Rapala fishing knife, the phone number of a man in Queens who would sell him a gun, and a slip of prescription paper on which were written these words in Dr. Rudy Graveline's spastic scrawl: 'Plaza Hotel, Rm. 966.'

18

When they returned from the Plaza to the apartment, Mick Stranahan said to Christina Marks: 'Sure you want a killer sleeping on the sectional?'

'Do you snore?'

'I'm serious.'

'Me, too.' From a closet she got a flannel sheet, a blanket, and two pillows. 'I've got a space heater that works, sometimes,' she said.

'No, this is fine.' Stranahan pulled off his shoes, turned on Letterman and stretched out on the sofa, which he had rearranged to contain his legs. He heard the shower running in the bathroom. After a few minutes Christina came out in a cloud of steam and sat down at the kitchen table. Her cheeks were flushed from the hot water. She wore a short blue robe, and her hair was wet. Stranahan could tell she'd brushed it out.

'We'll try again first thing in the morning,' he said.

'What?'

'Maggie's room at the hotel.'

'Oh, right.' She looked distracted.

He sat up and said, 'Come sit here.'

'I don't think so,' Christina said.

Stranahan could tell she had the radar up. He said, 'I must've scared you on the plane.'

'No, you didn't.' She wanted to ask about everything, his life; he was trying to make it easier and not doing so well.

'You didn't scare me,' Christina said again. 'If you did, I wouldn't let you stay.' But he had, and she did. That worried her even more.

Stranahan picked up the remote control and turned off the

television. He heard sirens passing on the street outside and wished he were home, asleep on the bay.

When Christina spoke again, she didn't sound like a seasoned professional interviewer. She said, 'Five men?'

Stranahan was glad she'd started with the killings. The marriages would be harder to justify.

'Are we off the record?'

She hesitated, then said yes.

'The men I killed,' he began, 'would have killed me first. You'll just have to take my word.' Deep down, he wasn't sure about Thomas Henry Thomas, the fried-chicken robber. That one was a toss-up.

'What was it like?' Christina asked.

'Horrible.'

She waited for the details; often men like Stranahan wanted to tell about it. Or needed to.

But all he said was: 'Horrible, really. No fun at all.'

She said, 'You regret any of them?'

'Nope.'

She had one elbow propped on the table, knuckles pressed to her cheek. The only sound was the hissing of the radiator pipes, warming up. Stranahan peeled off his T-shirt and put it in a neat pile with his other clothes.

'I'll get a hotel room tomorrow.'

'No, you won't,' she said. 'I'm not frightened.'

'You haven't heard about my wives.'

She laughed softly. 'Five already at your age. You must be going for the record.'

Stranahan lay back, hands locked behind his head. 'I fall in love with waitresses. I can't help it.'

'You're kidding.'

'Don't be a snob. They were all smarter than I was. Even Chloe.'

Christina said, 'If you don't mind me saying so, she seemed like a very cold woman.'

He groaned at the memory.

'What about the others, what were they like?'

'I loved them all, for a time. Then one day I didn't.'

Christina said, 'Doesn't sound like love.'

'Boy, are you wrong.' He smiled to himself.

'Mick, you regret any of them?'

'Nope.'

The radiator popped. The warmth of it made Stranahan sleepy, and he yawned.

'What about lovers?' Christina asked—a question sure to jolt him awake. 'All waitresses, no exceptions?'

'Oh, I've made some exceptions.' He scratched his head and pretended there were so many he had to add them up. 'Let's see, there was a lady probate lawyer. And an architect . . . make that two architects. Separately, of course. And an engineer for Pratt Whitney up in West Palm. An honest-to-God rocket scientist.'

'Really?'

'Yeah, really. And they were all dumber than I was.' Stranahan pulled the blanket up to his neck and closed his eyes. 'Good night, Christina.'

'Good night, Mick.' She turned off the lights, returned to the kitchen table, and sat in the gray darkness for an hour, watching him sleep.

When Maggie Gonzalez heard the knocking again, she got out of bed and weaved toward the noise. With outstretched arms she staved off menacing walls, doorknobs, and lampshades, but barely. She navigated through a wet gauze, her vision fuzzed by painkillers. When she opened the door, she found herself staring at the breast of a pea-green woolen overcoat. She tilted her throbbing head, one notch at a time, until she found the man's face.

'Uh,' she said.

'Jesus H. Christ,' said Chemo, shoving her back in the room, kicking the door shut behind him, savagely cursing his own rotten luck. The woman was wrapped from forehead to throat in white surgical tape—a fucking mummy! He took the photograph from his overcoat and handed it to Maggie Gonzalez.

'Is that you?' he demanded.

'No.' The answer came from parchment lips, whispering through a slit in the bandages. 'No, it's not me.'

Chemo could tell that the woman was woozy. He told her to sit down before she fell down.

'It's you, isn't it? You're Maggie Gonzalez.'

She said, 'You're making a big mistake.'

'Shut up.' He took off his broad-brimmed hat and threw it on the bed. Through the peepholes in the bandage, Maggie was able to get a good look at the man's remarkable face.

She said, 'My God, what happened to you?'

'Shut the fuck up.'

Chemo unbuttoned his overcoat, heaved it over a chair, and paced. The trip was turning into a debacle. First the man in Queens had sold him a rusty Colt .38 with only two bullets. Later, on the subway, he had been forced to flee a group of elderly Amish in the fear that they might recognize him from his previous life. And now this—confusion. While Chemo was reasonably sure that the bandaged woman was Maggie Gonzalez, he didn't want to screw up and kill the wrong person. Dr. Graveline would never understand.

'Who are you?' Maggie said thickly. 'Who sent you?'

'You ask too many questions.'

'Please, I don't feel very well.'

Chemo took the Colt from the waistband of his pants and pointed it at the bandaged tip of her new nose. 'Your name's Maggie Gonzalez, isn't it?'

At the sight of the pistol, she leaned forward and vomited all over Chemo's rubber-soled winter shoes.

'Jesus H. Christ,' he moaned and bolted for the bathroom.

'I'm sorry,' Maggie called after him. 'You scared me, that's all.'

When Chemo came back, the shoes were off his feet and the gun was back in his pants. He was wiping his mouth with the corner of a towel.

'I'm really sorry,' Maggie said again.

Chemo shook his head disgustedly. He sat down on the corner of the bed. To Maggie his legs seemed as long as circus stilts.

'You're supposed to kill me?'

'Yep,' Chemo said. With the towel he wiped a fleck of puke off her nightgown.

Blearily she studied him and said, 'You've had some derm-abrasion.'

'So?'

'So how come just little patches—why not more?'

'My doctor said that would be risky.'

'Your doctor's full of it,' Maggie said.

'And I guess you're an expert or something.'

'I'm a nurse, but you probably know that.'

Chemo said, 'No, I didn't.' Dr. Graveline hadn't told him a thing.

Maggie went on, 'I used to work for a plastic surgeon down in Miami. A butcher with a capital B.'

Subconsciously Chemo's fingers felt for the tender spots on his chin. He was almost afraid to ask.

'This surgeon,' he said to Maggie, 'what was his name?'

'Graveline,' she said. 'Rudy Graveline. Personally, I wouldn't let him trim a hangnail.'

Lugubriously Chemo closed his bulbous red eyes. Through the codeine, Maggie thought he resembled a giant nuclear-radiated salamander, straight from a monster movie.

'How about this,' he said. 'I'll tell you what happened to my face if you tell me what happened to yours.'

It was Chemo's idea to have breakfast in Central Park. He figured there'd be so many other freaks that no one would notice them. As it turned out, Maggie's Tut-like facial shell drew more than a few stares. Chemo tugged his hat down tightly and said, 'You should've worn a scarf.'

They were sitting near Columbus Circle on a bench. Chemo had bought a box of raisin bagels with cream cheese. Maggie said her stomach felt much better but, because of the surgical tape, she was able to fit only small pieces of bagel into her mouth. It was a sloppy process, but two fat squirrels showed up to claim the crumbs.

Chemo was saying, 'Your nose, your chin, your eyelids—Christ, no wonder you hurt.' He took out her picture and looked at it appraisingly. 'Too bad,' he said.

'What's that supposed to mean?'

'I mean, you were a pretty lady.'

'Maybe I still am,' Maggie said. 'Maybe prettier.'

Chemo put the photograph back in his coat. 'Maybe,' he said.

'You're going to make me cry and then everything'll sting.'

He said, 'Knock it off.'

'Don't you think I feel bad enough?' Maggie said. 'I get a whole new face—and for what! A month from now and you'd never have recognized me. I could've sat in your lap on the subway and you wouldn't know who I was.'

Chemo thought he heard sniffling behind the bandages. 'Don't fucking cry,' he said. 'Don't be a baby.'

'I don't understand why Rudy sent you,' Maggie whined.

'To kill you, what else?'

'But why now? Nothing's happened yet.'

Chemo frowned and said, 'Keep it down.' The pink patches on his chin tingled in the cold air and made him think about Rudy Graveline. Butcher with a capital B, Maggie had said. Chemo wanted to know more.

A thin young Moonie in worn corduroys came up to the park bench and held out a bundle of red and white carnations. 'Be happy,' the kid said to Maggie. 'Five dollars.'

'Get lost,' Chemo said.

'Four dollars,' said the Moonie. 'Be happy.'

Chemo pulled the calfskin cover off his Weed Whacker and flicked the underarm toggle for the battery pack. The Moonie gaped as Chemo calmly chopped the bright carnations to confetti.

'Be gone, Hop-sing,' Chemo said, and the Moonie ran away. Chemo recloaked the Weed Whacker and turned to Maggie. 'Tell me why the doctor wants you dead.'

It took her several moments to recover from what she had seen. Finally she said, 'Well, it's a long story.'

'I got all day,' Chemo said. 'Unless you got tickets to *Phantom* or something.'

'Can we go for a walk?'

'No,' Chemo said sharply. 'Remember?' He had thrown his vomit-covered shoes and socks out the ninth-floor window of Maggie's room at the Plaza. Now he was sitting in bare feet in Central Park on a forty-degree February morning. He wiggled his long bluish toes and said to Maggie Gonzalez: 'So talk.'

She did. She told Chemo all about the death of Victoria Barletta. It was a slightly shorter recital than she'd put on the videotape, but it was no less shocking.

'You're making this up,' Chemo said.

'I'm not either.'

'He killed this girl with a nose job?'

Maggie nodded. 'I was there.'

'Jesus H. Christ.'

'It was an accident.'

'That's even worse,' Chemo said. He tore off his hat and threw it on the sidewalk, spooking the squirrels. 'This is the same maniac who's working on my face. I can't fucking stand it!'

By way of consolation, Maggie said: 'Dermabrasion is a much simpler procedure.'

'Yeah, tell me about simple procedures.' Chemo couldn't believe the lousy luck he had with doctors. He said, 'So what does all this have to do with him wanting you dead?'

Maggie told Chemo about Reynaldo Flemm's TV investigation (without mentioning that she had been the tipster), told how she had warned Rudy about Mick Stranahan, the investigator. She was careful to make it sound as if Stranahan was the whistle-blower.

'Now it's starting to make sense,' Chemo said. 'Graveline wants me to kill *him*, too.' He held up the arm-mounted Weed Whacker. 'He's the prick that cost me this hand.'

'Rudy can't afford any witnesses,' Maggie explained, 'or any publicity. Not only would they yank his medical license, he'd go to jail. Now do you understand?'

Do I ever, thought Chemo.

The white mask that was Maggie's face asked: 'Are you still going to kill me?'

'We'll see,' Chemo replied. 'I'm sorting things out.'

'How much is that cheap bastard paying you?'

Chemo plucked his rumpled hat off the sidewalk. 'I'd rather

not say,' he muttered, clearly embarrassed. No way would he let that butcher fuck with his ears. Not now.

Christina Marks and Mick Stranahan got to the Plaza Hotel shortly before ten. From the lobby Stranahan called Maggie's room and got no answer. Christina followed him into the elevator and, as they rode to the ninth floor, she watched him remove a small serrated blade from his wallet.

'Master key,' he said.

'Mick, no. I could get fired.'

'Then wait downstairs.'

But she didn't. She watched him pick the lock on Maggie's door, then slipped into the room behind him. She said nothing and scarcely moved while he checked the bathroom and the closets to see if they were alone.

'Mick, come here.'

On the bedstand were two prescription bottles, a plastic bedpan, and a pink-splotched surgical compress. Stranahan glanced at the pills: Tylenol No. 3 and Darvocet. The bottle of Darvocets had not yet been opened. A professional business card lay next to the telephone on Maggie's nightstand. Stranahan chuckled drily when he read what was on the card:

> LEONARD R. LEAPER, M.D.
> *Certified by the American Board of Plastic Surgery*
> *Office: 555–6600   Nights and Emergencies: 555–6677*

'How nice,' Christina remarked. 'She took our money and got a facelift.'

Stranahan said, 'Something's not right. She ought to be in bed.'

'Maybe she went for a brunch at the Four Seasons.'

He shook his head. 'These scrips are only two days old, so that's when she had the surgery. She's still got to be swollen up like a mango. Would you go out in public looking like that?'

'Depends on how much dope I ate.'

'No,' Stranahan said, scanning the room, 'Something's not right. She ought to be here.'

'What do you want to do?'

Stranahan said they should go downstairs and wait in the lobby; in her condition, Maggie shouldn't be hard to spot. 'But first,' he said, 'let's really go through this place.'

Christina went to the dresser. Under a pile of Maggie's bras and panties she found three new flowered bikinis, the price tags from the Plaza Shops still attached. Maggie was definitely getting ready for Maui.

'Oh, Miss Marks,' Stranahan sang out. 'Lookie here.'

It was a video cassette in a brown plastic sleeve. The sleeve was marked with a sticker from Midtown Studio Productions.

Stranahan tossed Christina the tape. She tossed it back.

'We can't take that, it's larceny.'

He said, 'It's not larceny to take something you already own.'

'What do you mean?'

'If this is what I think it is, you've paid for it already. The Barletta story, remember?'

'We don't know that. Could be anything—home movies, maybe.'

Stranahan smiled and stuffed the cassette into his coat. 'Only one way to find out.'

'No,' Christina said.

'Look, you got a VCR at your place. Let's go watch the tape. If I'm wrong, then I'll bring it back myself.'

'Oh, I see. Just sneak in, put it back where you got it, tidy up the place.'

'Yeah, if I'm wrong. If it turns out to be Jane Fonda or something. But I don't think so.'

Christina Marks knew better; it was madness, of course. She could lose her job, blow a perfectly good career if they were caught. But, then again, this hadn't turned out to be the typical Reynaldo Flemm exposé. She had damn near gotten machine-gunned over this one, so what the hell.

Grudgingly she said, 'Is it Beta or VHS?'

Stranahan gave her a hug.

Then they heard the key in the door.

The two couples said nothing for the first few seconds, just stared. Mick Stranahan and Christina Marks had the most to contem-

plate: a woman wrapped in tape, and a beanpole assassin with
one arm down to his knees.

Maggie Gonzalez was the first to speak: 'It's him.'

'Who?' Chemo asked. He had never seen Stranahan up close,
not even at the stilt house.

'Him,' Maggie repeated through the bandages. 'What're you
doing in my room?'

'Hello, Maggie,' Stranahan said, 'assuming it's you under there.
It's sure been a long time.'

'And you!' Maggie grunted, pointing at Christina Marks.

'Hi, again,' said Christina. 'I thought you'd be in Hawaii by now.'

Chemo said, 'I guess everybody's old pals except me.' He pulled
the .38 out of his overcoat. 'Nobody move.'

'Another one who watches too much TV,' Stranahan whispered
to Christina.

Chemo blinked angrily. 'I don't like you one bit.'

'I assumed as much from the fact you keep trying to kill me.'
Stranahan had seen some bizarros in his day, but this one took
the cake. He looked like Fred Munster with bulimia. One eye
on the gun, Stranahan asked, 'Do you have a name?'

'No,' Chemo said.

'Good. Makes for a cheaper tombstone.'

Chemo told Maggie to close the door, but Maggie didn't move.
The sight of the pistol had made her nauseated all over again,
and she was desperately trying to keep down her breakfast bagels.

'What's the matter now?' Chemo snapped.

'She doesn't look so hot,' Christina said.

'And who the fuck are you, Florence Nightingale?'

'What happened to your arm?' Christina asked him. A cool
customer she was; Stranahan admired her poise.

Chemo got the impression that he was losing control, which
made no sense, since he was the one with the pistol. 'Shut up,
all of you,' he said, 'while I kill Mr. Stranahan here. *Finally.*'

At these words, Maggie Gonzalez upchucked gloriously all over
Chemo's gun arm. Given his general translucence, it was impossible to tell if Chemo blanched. He did, however, wobble per-
ceptibly.

Mick Stranahan stepped forward and punched him ferociously,

in the Adam's apple. The man went down like a seven-foot Tinkertoy, but did not release his grip on the gun. Maggie backed up and screamed, a primal wail that poured from the hole in her bandage and filled the hallway. Stranahan decided there was no time to finish the job. He pushed Christina Marks through the doorway and told her to go for the elevator. Gagging and spitting blood, Chemo rolled out of his fetal curl and took a wild shot at Christina as she ran down the hall. The bullet twanged impotently off a fire extinguisher and was ultimately stopped by the opulent Plaza wallpaper.

Before Chemo could fire again, Stranahan stomped on his wrist, still slippery from Maggie's used bagels. Chemo would not let go of the gun. With a growl he swung his refurbished left arm, like a fungo bat across his body. It caught Stranahan in the soft crease behind the knee and brought him down. The two men wrestled for the pistol while Maggie howled and clawed chimp-like at her swaddled head.

It was a clumsy fight. Tangled in the killer's gangliness, Stranahan could not shield himself from a clubbing by Chemo's over-sized left arm. Whatever it was—and it wasn't a human fist—it hurt like hell. His skull chiming, Stranahan tried to break free.

Suddenly he felt the dull barrel of the .38 against his throat. He flinched when he heard the click, but nothing else followed. No flash, no explosion, no smell. The bullet, Chemo's second and only remaining round, was a dud. Chemo couldn't believe it—that asshole in Queens had screwed him royal.

Stranahan squirmed loose, stood up, and saw that they had attracted an audience. All along the corridor, doors were cracked open, some more than others. Under Maggie's keening he could hear excited voices. Somebody was calling the police.

Stranahan groped at his coat to make sure that the videotape was still in his pocket, kicked Chemo once in the groin (or where he estimated that the giant's groin might be), then jogged down the hallway.

Christina Marks was considerate enough to hold the elevator.

19

Dr. Rudy Graveline was a fellow who distrusted chance and prided himself on preparation, but he had not planned a love affair with a Hollywood star. Heather Chappell was a distraction—a fragrant, gorgeous, elusive, spoiled, sulky bitch of a distraction. He couldn't get enough of her. Rudy had come to crave the tunnel of clear thinking that enveloped him while making love to Heather; it was like a sharp cool drug. She screwed him absolutely numb, left him aching and drained and utterly in focus with his predicament.

For a while he kept cooking up lame excuses for postponing Heather's elaborate cosmetic surgery—knowing it would put her out of action for weeks. Sex with Heather had become a crucial component of Rudy Graveline's daily regimen; like a long-distance runner, he had fallen into a physical rhythm that he could not afford to break. TV people were after him, his medical career was in jeopardy, a homicide rap was on the horizon—and salvation depended on a crooked halfwit politician and a one-armed, seven-foot hit man. Rudy needed to stay razor-sharp until the crisis was over, and Heather had become vital to his clarity.

He treated her like a queen and it seemed to work. Heather's initial urgency to schedule the surgery had subsided during the day-long shopping sprees, the four-star meals, the midnight yacht cruises up and down the Intracoastal. In recent days, though, she again had begun to press Rudy not only about the date for the operations, but the cost. She was dropping broad hints to the effect that for all her bedroom labors she deserved a special discount, and Rudy found himself weakening on the subject. Finally, one night, she waited until he was inside her to bring up the money again, and Rudy breathlessly agreed to knock forty percent off the usual fee. Afterwards he was furious at himself, and blamed his moment of weakness on stress and mental fatigue.

Deep down, the doctor knew better. He was trapped. While he dreaded the prospect of Heather Chappell's surgery, he feared that she would leave him if he didn't agree to do it. He probably would have done it for free. He had become addicted to her body—a radiantly perfect body that she now wanted him to *improve*. The task would have posed a career challenge for the most skillful of plastic surgeons; for a hack like Rudy Graveline, it was flat-out impossible. Naturally he planned to let his assistants do it.

Until Heather dropped another surprise.

'My agent says I should tape the operation, love.'

Rudy said, 'You're kidding.'

'Just to be on the safe side.'

'What, you don't trust me?'

'Sure I do,' Heather said. 'It's my damn agent, is all. She says since my looks are everything, my whole career, I should be careful, legal-wise. I guess she wants to make sure nothing goes wrong—'

Rudy sprung out of bed, hands on his hips. 'Look, I told you these operations are not necessary at all.'

'And I told you, I'm sick of doing sitcoms and *Hollywood Squares*. I need to get back in the movies, hon, and that means I need a new look. That's why I came down here.'

Rudy Graveline had never tried to talk anyone out of surgery before, so he was forced to improvise. By and large it was not such a terrible speech. He said, 'God was very good to you, Heather. I have patients who'd give fifty grand to look half as beautiful as you look: teenagers who'd kill for that nose you want me to chisel, housewives who'd trade their firstborn child for tits like yours—'

'Rudolph,' Heather said, 'save it.'

He tried to pull up his underwear but the elastic snagged on heavily bandaged kneecaps, the product of the disco tryst in the fireplace.

'I am appalled,' Rudy was huffing, 'at the idea of videotaping in my surgical suite.' In truth he wasn't appalled so much as afraid: A video camera meant he couldn't hand off to the other surgeons and duck out to the golf course. He'd have to perform every procedure himself, just as Heather had demanded. You couldn't drug a damn camera; it wouldn't miss a stitch.

'This just isn't done,' Rudy protested.

'Oh, it is too.' Heather said. 'I see stuff like that on PBS all the time. Once I saw them put a baboon heart inside a human baby. They showed the whole thing.'

'It isn't done *here*,' Rudy said.

Heather sat up, making sure that the bedsheets slipped off the slope of her breasts. 'Fine, Rudolph,' she said. 'If that's the way you want it, I'll fly back to California tonight. There's only about a dozen first-rate surgeons in Beverly Hills that would give anything to do me.'

The ice in her voice surprised him, though it shouldn't have. 'All right,' he said, pulling on his robe, 'we'll video the surgery. Maybe Robin Leach can use a clip on his show.'

Heather let the wisecrack pass; she was focused on business. She asked Rudy Graveline for a date they could begin.

'A week,' he said. He had to clear his mind a few more times. In another week he also would have heard something definite from Chemo, or maybe Roberto Pepsical.

'And we're not doing all this at once,' he added. 'You've got the liposuction, the breast augmentation, the rhinoplasty, the eyelids, and the rhytidectomy—that's a lot of surgery, Heather.'

'Yes, Rudolph.' She had won and she knew it.

'I think we'll start with the nose and see how you do.'

'Or how *you* do,' Heather said.

Rudy had a queasy feeling that she wasn't kidding.

The executive producer of *In Your Face* was a man known to Reynaldo Flemm only as Mr. Dover. Mr. Dover was in charge of the budget. Upon Reynaldo's return to New York, he found a message taped to his office door. Mr. Dover wanted to see him right away.

Immediately Reynaldo called the apartment of Christina Marks, but hung up when Mick Stranahan answered the phone. Reynaldo was fiercely jealous; beyond that, he didn't think it was fair that he should have to face Mr. Dover alone. Christina was the producer, she knew where all the money went. Reynaldo was merely the talent, and the talent never knew anything.

When he arrived at Mr. Dover's office, the secretary did not recognize him. 'The music division is on the third floor,' she said, scarcely making eye contact.

Reynaldo riffled his new hair and said, 'It's me.'

'Oh, hi, Ray.'

'What do you think?'

The secretary said, 'It's a dynamite disguise.'

'It's not a disguise.'

'Oh.'

'I wanted a new look,' he explained.

'Why?' asked the secretary.

Reynaldo couldn't tell her the truth—that a rude plastic surgeon told him he had a fat waist and a big honker—so he said: 'Demographics.'

The secretary looked at him blankly.

'Market surveys,' he went on. 'We're going for some younger viewers.'

'Oh, I see,' the secretary said.

'Long hair is making quite a comeback.'

'I didn't know,' she said, trying to be polite. 'Is that real, Ray?'

'Well, no. Not yet.'

'I'll tell Mr. Dover you're here.'

Mr. Dover was a short man with an accountant's pinched demeanor, a fishbelly complexion, tiny black eyes, and the slick, sloping forehead of a killer whale. Mr. Dover wore expensive dark suits and yuppie suspenders that, Reynaldo suspected, needed adjustment.

'Ray, what can you tell me about this Florida project?' Mr. Dover never wasted time with small talk.

'It's heavy,' Reynaldo replied.

'Heavy.'

'Very heavy.' Reynaldo noticed his expense vouchers stacked

in a neat pile on the corner of Mr. Dover's desk. This worried him, so he said, 'My producer was almost murdered.'

'I see.'

'With a machine gun,' Reynaldo added.

Mr. Dover pursed his lips. 'Why?'

'Because we're getting close to cracking this story.'

'You're getting close to cracking my budget, Ray.'

'This is an important project.'

Mr. Dover said, 'A network wouldn't blink twice, Ray, but we're not one of the networks. My job is to watch the bottom line.'

Indignantly Reynaldo thought: *I eat twits like you for breakfast.* He was good at thinking tough thoughts.

'Investigations cost money,' he said tersely.

With shiny pink fingernails Mr. Dover leafed through the receipts on his desk until he found the one he wanted. 'Jambala's House of Hair,' he said. 'Seven hundred and seventeen dollars.'

Reynaldo blushed and ground his caps. Christina should be here for this; she'd know how to handle this jerk.

Mr. Dover continued: 'I don't intend to interfere, nor do I intend to let these extravagances go on forever. As I understand it, the program is due to air next month.'

'All the spots have been sold,' Reynaldo said. 'They've been sold for six months.' He couldn't resist.

'Yes, well I suggest you try not to spend all that advertising revenue before the broadcast date—just in case it doesn't work out.'

'And when hasn't it worked out?'

Reynaldo regretted the words almost instantly, for Mr. Dover was only too happy to refresh his memory. There was the time Flemm claimed to have discovered the wreckage of Amelia Earhart's airplane (it turned out to be a crop duster in New Zealand); the time he claimed to have an exclusive interview with the second gunman from Dealey Plaza (who, it later turned out, was barely seven years old on the day of the Kennedy assassination); the time he uncovered a Congressional call-girl ring (only to be caught boffing two of the ladies in a mop closet at the Rayburn Building). These fiascos each resulted in a canceled broadcast, snide blurbs in the press, and great sums of lost revenue, which Mr. Dover could recall to the penny.

'Ancient history,' Reynaldo Flemm said defensively.

Unspoken was the fact that no such embarrassments had happened since Christina Marks had been hired. Every show had been finished on time, on budget. Reynaldo did not appreciate the connection, but Mr. Dover did.

'You understand my concern,' he said. 'How much longer do you anticipate being down in Miami?'

'Two weeks. We'll be editing.' Sounded good, anyway.

'So, shall we say, one more trip?'

'That ought to do it,' Reynaldo agreed.

'Excellent.' Mr. Dover straightened the stack of Reynaldo's expense receipts, lining up all the little corners in perfect angles. 'By the way, Miss Marks wasn't harmed, was she?'

'No, just scared shitless. She's not used to getting shot at.' As if he was.

'Did they catch this person?'

'Nope,' Reynaldo said, hard-bitten, like he wasn't too surprised.

'My,' said Mr. Dover. He hoped that Christina Marks was paid up on her medical plan and death benefits.

'I told you it was heavy,' Reynaldo said, rising. 'But it'll be worth it, I promise.'

'Good,' said Mr. Dover. 'I can't wait.'

Reynaldo was three steps toward the door when Mr. Dover said, 'Ray?'

'Yeah.'

'Forgive me, but I was just noticing.'

'That's all right.' He'd been wondering how long it would take the twerp to mention something about the hair.

But from behind the desk Mr. Dover smiled wickedly and patted his midsection. 'You've put on a pound or three, haven't you, Ray?'

In the elevator Reynaldo angrily tore off his seven-hundred-dollar wig and hurled it into a corner, where it lay like a dead pekinese. He took the limo back to his apartment, stripped off his clothes, and stood naked for a long time in front of the bedroom mirror.

Reynaldo decided that Dr. Graveline was right: His nose was too large. And his belly had thickened.

He pivoted to the left, then to the right, then back to the left. He sucked in his breath. He flexed. He locked his knuckles behind his head and tightened his stomach muscles, but his belly did not disappear.

In the mirror Reynaldo saw a body that was neither flabby nor lean: an average body for an average forty-year-old man. He saw a face that was neither dashing nor weak: small darting eyes balanced by a strong, heavy jaw, with a nose to match. He concluded that his instincts about preserving the mustache were sound: When Reynaldo covered his hairy upper lip with a bare finger, his nose assumed even greater prominence.

Of course, something radical had to be done. Confidence was the essence of Reynaldo's camera presence, the core of his masculine appeal. If he were unhappy with himself or insecure about his appearance, it would show up on his face like a bad rash. The whole country would see it.

Standing alone at the mirror, Reynaldo hatched a plan that would solve his personal dilemma and wrap up the Barletta story simultaneously. It was a bold plan because it would not include Christina Marks. Reynaldo Flemm would serve as his own producer and would tell Christina nothing, just as she had told him nothing for two entire weeks after the shooting in Stiltsville.

The shooting. Still it galled him, the sour irony that *she* would be the one to get the glory—after all his years on the streets. To have his producer nearly assassinated while he dozed on the massage table at the Sonesta was the lowest moment in Reynaldo's professional career. He had to atone.

In the past he had always counted on Christina to worry about the actual nuts-and-bolts journalism of the program. It was Christina who did the reporting, blocked out the interviews, arranged for the climactic confrontations—she even wrote the scripts. Reynaldo Flemm was hopelessly bored by detail, research, and the rigors of fact checking. He was an action guy, and he saved his energy for when the tape was rolling. Whereas Christina had filled three legal pads with notes, ideas, and questions about

Victoria Barletta's death, Reynaldo cared about one thing only: Who could they get on tape? Rudy Graveline was the big enchilada, and certainly Victoria's still-grieving mother was a solid bet. Mick Stranahan had been another obvious choice—the embarrassed investigator, admitting four years later that he had overlooked the prime suspect, the doctor himself.

But the Stranahan move had backfired, and nearly made a news-industry martyr of Christina Marks. Fine, thought Reynaldo, go ahead and have your fling. Meanwhile Willie and I will be kicking some serious quack ass.

Every time Dr. Rudy Graveline got a phone call from New York or New Jersey he assumed it was the mob. The mob had generously put him through Harvard Medical School, and in return Rudy occasionally extended his professional courtesies to mob guys, their friends or family. It was Rudy himself who had redone the face of Tony (The Eel) Traviola, the hit man who later washed up dead on Cape Florida beach with a marlin hole through his sternum. Fortunately for Rudy, most mob fugitives were squeamish about surgery, so he wound up doing mainly their wives, daughters, and mistresses. Noses, mostly, with the occasional face-lift.

That's the kind of call Rudy expected when his secretary told him that New York was on the line.

'Yes?'

'Hello, Doctor Graveline.'

The voice did not belong to Curly Eyebrows or any of his cousins.

'Who is this?'

'Johnny LeTigre, remember me?'

'Of course.' The hinky male stripper. Rudy said, 'What are you doing in New York?'

'I had a gig in the Village, but I'm on my way back to Miami.' This was Reynaldo Flemm's idea of being fast on his feet. He said, 'Look, I've been thinking about what you said that day at the clinic.'

Rudy Graveline could not remember exactly what he had said. 'Yes?'

'About my nose and abdomen.'

Then it came back to Rudy. 'Your nose and abdomen, yes, I remember.'

'You were right,' Reynaldo went on. 'We don't always see ourselves the way other people do.'

Rudy was thinking: Get to the damn point.

'I'd like for you to do my nose,' Reynaldo declared.

'All right.'

'And my middle—what's that operation called?'

'Suction-assisted lipectomy,' Rudy said.

'Yeah, that's it. How much'd that set me back?'

Rudy recalled that this was a man who offered ten grand to have a mole removed from his buttocks.

'Fifteen thousand,' Rudy said.

'Geez!' said the voice from New York.

'But that's if I perform the procedures myself,' Rudy explained. 'Keep in mind, I've got several very competent associates who could handle your case for, oh, half as much.'

The way that Rudy backed off on the word *competent* was no accident, but Reynaldo Flemm didn't need a sell job. Quickly he said, 'No, I definitely want you. Fifteen it is. But I need the work done this week.'

'Out of the question.' Rudy would be immersed in preparation for the Heather Chappell marathon.

'Next week at the latest,' Reynaldo pressed.

'Let me see what I can do. By the way, Mr. LeTigre, what is the status of your mole?'

Reynaldo had almost forgotten about the ruse that originally had gained his entry to Whispering Palms. Again he had to wing it. 'You won't believe this,' he said to Dr. Rudy Graveline, 'but the damn thing fell off.'

'Are you certain?'

'Swear to God, one morning I'm standing in the shower and I turn around and it's gone. Gone! I found it lying there in the bed. Just fell off, like an acorn or something.'

'Hmmm,' Rudy said. The guy was a flake, but who cared.

'I threw it away, is that okay?'

'The mole?'

'Yeah, I thought about saving it in the freezer, maybe having some tests run. But then I figured what the hell and I tossed it in the trash.'

'It was probably quite harmless,' Rudy Graveline said, dying to hang up.

'So I'll call you when I get back to Miami.'

'Fine,' said the doctor. 'Have a safe trip, Mr. LeTigre.'

Reynaldo Flemm was beaming when he put down the phone. This would be something. Maybe even better than getting shot on the air.

20

Maggie Gonzalez said: 'Tell me about your hand.'

'Shut up,' Chemo grumbled. He was driving around Queens, trying to find the sonofabitch who had sold him the bad bullets.

'Please,' Maggie said. 'I am a nurse.'

'Too bad you're not a magician, because that's what it's gonna take to make my hand come back. A fish got it.'

At a stop light he rolled down the window and called to a group of black teenagers. He asked where he could locate a man named Donnie Blue, and the teenagers told Chemo to go blow himself. 'Shit,' he said, stomping on the accelerator.

Maggie asked, 'Was it a shark that did it?'

'Do I look like Jacques Cousteau? I don't know what the hell it was—some big fish. The subject is closed.'

By now Maggie was reasonably confident that he wasn't going to kill her. He would have done it already, most conveniently during the scuffle back at the Plaza. Instead he had grabbed her waist and hustled her down the fire exit, taking four steps at a time. Considering the mayhem on the ninth floor, it was a miracle they got out of the place without being stopped. The lobby was full of uniformed cops waiting for elevators, but nobody looked twice at the Fun Couple of the Year.

As Chemo drove, Maggie said, 'What about your face?'

'Look who's talking.'

'Really, what happened?'

Chemo said, 'You always this shy with strangers? Jesus H. Christ.'

'I'm sorry,' she said. 'Professional curiosity, I guess. Besides, you promised to tell me.'

'Do the words *none of your fucking business* mean anything?'

From behind the bandages a chilly voice said, 'You don't have to be crude. Swearing doesn't impress me.'

Chemo found the street corner where he had purchased the rusty Colt .38 and the dead bullets, but there was no sign of Donnie Blue. Every inquiry was met by open derision, and Chemo's hopes for a refund began to fade.

As he circled the neighborhood Maggie said, 'You're so quiet.'

'I'm thinking.'

'Me, too.'

'I'm thinking I was seriously gypped by your doctor pal.' Chemo didn't want to admit that he had agreed to murder two people in exchange for a discount on minor plastic surgery.

'If I had known about this dead girl—'

'Vicky Barletta.'

'Right,' Chemo said. 'If I had known that, I would have jacked my price. Jacked it way the hell up.'

'And who could blame you,' Maggie said.

'Graveline never told me he killed a girl.'

They were heading out the highway toward La Guardia. Maggie assumed there were travel plans.

She said, 'Rudy's a very wealthy man.'

'Sure, he's a doctor.'

'I can ruin him. That's why he wanted me dead.'

'Sure, you're a witness,' Chemo said.

Something dismissive in his tone alarmed her once again. She said, 'Killing me won't solve anything now.'

Chemo's forehead crinkled where an eyebrow should have been. 'It won't?'

Maggie shook her head from side to side in dramatic emphasis. 'I made my own tape. A videotape, at a place in Manhattan. Everything's on it, everything I saw that day.'

Chemo wasn't as rattled as she thought he might be; in fact, his mouth curled into a dry smile. His lips looked like two pink snails crawling up a sidewalk.

'A video,' he mused.

Maggie teased it along. 'You have any idea what that bastard would pay for it?'

'Yes,' Chemo said. 'Yes, I think I do.'

At the airport, Maggie told Chemo she had to make a phone call. To eavesdrop he squeezed inside the same booth, his chin digging into the top of her head. She dialed the number of Dr. Leonard Leaper and informed the service that she had to leave town for a while, but that the doctor should not be concerned.

'I already told him I was a witness in a murder,' Maggie explained to Chemo. 'If what happened at the hotel turns up in the newspapers, he'll think I was kidnapped.'

'But you were,' Chemo pointed out.

'Oh, not really.'

'Yes, *really*.' Chemo didn't care for her casual attitude; just who did she take him for?

Maggie said, 'Know what I think? I think we could be partners.'

They got on line at the Pan Am counter, surrounded by a typical Miami-bound contingent—old geezers with tubas for sinuses; shiny young hustlers in thin gold chains; huge hollow-eyed families that looked like they'd staggered out of a Sally Struthers telethon. Chemo and Maggie fit right in.

He told her, 'I only got one plane ticket.'

She smiled and stroked her handbag, which had not left her arm since their breakfast in Central Park. 'I've got a Visa card,' she said brightly. 'Where we headed?'

'Me, I'm going back to Florida.'

'Not like that, you're not. They've got rules against bare feet, I'm sure.'

'Hell,' Chemo said, and loped off to locate some cheap shoes. He came back wearing fuzzy brown bathroom slippers, size 14, purchased at one of the airport gift shops. Maggie was saving him a spot at the ticket counter. She had already arranged for him to get an aisle seat (because of his long legs), and she would be next to him.

Later, waiting in the boarding area, Maggie asked Chemo if his name was Rogelio Luz Sanchez.

'Oh, sure.'

'That's what it says on your ticket.'

'Well, there you are,' Chemo said. He couldn't even *pronounce*

Rogelio Luz Sanchez—some alias cooked up by Rudy Graveline, the dumb shit. Chemo looked about as Hispanic as Larry Bird.

After they took their seats on the airplane, Maggie leaned close and asked, 'So, can I call you Rogelio? I mean, I've got to call you *something*.'

Chemo's hooded lids blinked twice very slowly. 'The more you talk, the more I want to spackle the holes in that fucking mask.'

Maggie emitted a reedy, birdlike noise.

'I think we can do business,' Chemo said, 'but only on two conditions. One, don't ask any more personal questions, is that clear? Two, don't ever puke on me again.'

'I said I was sorry.'

The plane had started to taxi and Chemo raised his voice to be heard over the engines. 'Once I get some decent bullets I'll be using that gun, and God help you if you toss your cookies when I do.'

Maggie said, 'I'll do better next time.'

One of the flight attendants came by and asked Maggie if she needed a special meal because of her medical condition, and Maggie remarked that she wasn't feeling particularly well. She said the coach section was so crowded and stuffy that she was having trouble breathing. The next thing Chemo knew, they were sitting up in first class and sipping red wine. Having noticed his disability, the friendly flight attendant was carefully cutting Chemo's surf-and-turf into bite-sized pieces. Chemo glanced at Maggie and felt guilty about coming down so hard.

'That was a slick move,' he said, the closest he would come to a compliment. 'I never rode up here before.'

Maggie exhibited no surprise at this bit of news. Her eyes looked sad and moist behind the white husk.

Chemo said, 'You still want to be partners?'

She nodded. Carefully she aimed a forkful of lobster for the damp hole beneath her nostrils in the surgical bandage.

'Graveline's gonna scream when he learns about your video-tape,' Chemo said with a chuckle. 'Where is it, anyway?'

When Maggie finished chewing, she said, 'I've got three copies.'

'Good thinking.'

'Two of them are locked up at the bank. The third one, the original tape, that's for Rudy. That's how we get his attention.'

Chemo smiled a yellow smile. 'I like it.'

'You won't like this part,' Maggie said. 'Stranahan swiped the tape from the hotel room. We can't show it to Rudy until we get it back.'

'Hell,' Chemo said. This was terrible—Mick Stranahan and that TV bitch loose with the blackmail goodies. Just terrible. He said, 'I've got to get to them before they get to Graveline, otherwise we're blown out of the water. He'll be on the first flight to Panama and we'll be holding our weenies.'

From Maggie came a muffled, disapproving noise.

'It's just an expression,' Chemo said. 'Lighten up, for Chrissakes.'

After the flight attendants removed the meal trays, Chemo lowered the seat back and stretched his endless legs. Almost to himself, he said, 'I don't like this Stranahan guy one bit. When we get to Miami, we hit the ground running.'

'Yes,' Maggie agreed, easing into the partnership, 'we've got to get the tape.'

'That, too,' said Chemo, tugging his hat down over his eyes.

The news of gunshots and a possible kidnapping at the Plaza Hotel rated five paragraphs in the *Daily News*, a page of photos in the *Post* and nothing in the *Times*. That morning New York detectives queried a teletype to the Metro-Dade Police Department stating that the victim of the abduction was believed to be a Miami woman named Margaret Orestes Gonzalez, a guest at the hotel. The police teletype described her assailant as a white male, age unknown, with possible burn scars on his face and a height of either six foot four or eight foot two, depending on which witness you believed. The teletype further noted that a Rapala fishing knife found on the carpet outside the victim's room was traced to a shipment that recently had been sold to a retail establishment known as Bubba's Bait and Cold Beer, on Dixie Highway in South Miami. Most significantly, a partial thumb-print lifted from the blade of the knife was identified as belonging to one

Blondell Wayne Tatum, age thirty-eight, six foot nine, one hundred eighty-one pounds. Mr. Tatum, it seemed, was wanted in the state of Pennsylvania for the robbery-at-pitchfork of a Chemical Bank, and for the first-degree murder of Dr. Kyle Kloppner, an elderly dermatologist. Tatum was to be considered armed and dangerous. Under AKAs, the police bulletin listed one: Chemo.

'Chemo?' Sergeant Al García read the teletype again, then pulled it off the bulletin board and took it to the Xerox machine. By the time he got back, a new teletype had been posted in its place.

This one was even more interesting, and García's cigar bobbed excitedly as he read it.

The new teletype advised Metro-Dade police to disregard the kidnap query. Miss Margaret Gonzalez had phoned the New York authorities to assure them that she was in no danger, and to explain that the disturbance at the Plaza Hotel was merely a dispute between herself and a male companion she had met in a bar.

Maggie had hung up before detectives could ask if the male companion was Mr. Blondell Wayne Tatum.

Commissioner Roberto Pepsical arranged to meet the two crooked detectives at a strip joint off LeJeune Road, not far from the airport. Roberto got there early and drank three strong vodka tonics to give him the courage to say what he'd been told to say. He figured he was so far over his head that being drunk couldn't make it any worse.

Dutifully the commissioner had carried Detective Murdock's proposal to Dr. Rudy Graveline, and now he had returned with the doctor's reply. It occurred to Roberto, even as a naked woman with gold teeth delivered a fourth vodka, that the role of an elected public servant was no longer a distinguished one. He found himself surrounded by ruthless and untrustworthy people—nobody played a straight game anymore. In Miami, corruption had become a sport of the masses. Roberto had been doing it for years, of course, but jerks like Salazar and Murdock and even Graveline—they were nothing but dilettantes. Moochers. They didn't know when to back off. The word *enough* was not in their vocabulary. Roberto hated the idea that his future depended on such men.

The crooked cops showed up just as the nude Amazonian mud-wrestling match began on stage. 'Very nice place,' Detective John Murdock said to the commissioner. 'Is that your daughter up there?'

Joe Salazar said, 'The one on the right, she even looks like you. Except I think you got bigger knockers.'

Roberto Pepsical flushed. He was sensitive about his weight. 'You're really funny,' he said to the detectives. 'Both of you should've been comedians instead of cops. You should've been Lawrence and Hardy.'

Murdock smirked. 'Lawrence and Hardy, huh? I think the commissioner has been drinking.'

Salazar said, 'Maybe we hurt his feelings.'

The vodka was supposed to make Roberto Pepsical cool and brave; instead it was making him hot and dizzy. He started to tell the detectives what Rudy Graveline had said, but he couldn't hear himself speak over the exhortations of the wrestling fans. Finally Murdock seized him by the arm and led him to the restroom. Joe Salazar followed them in and locked the door.

'What's all this for?' Roberto said, belching in woozy fear. He thought the detectives were going to beat him up.

Murdock took him by the shoulders and pinned him to the condom machine. He said, 'Joe and I don't like this joint. It's noisy, it's dirty, it's a shitty fucking joint to hold a serious conversation. We are offended, Commissioner, by what we see taking place on the stage out there—naked young females with wet mud all over their twats. You shouldn't have invited us here.'

Joe Salazar said, 'That's right. Just so you know, I'm a devoted Catholic.'

'I'm sorry,' said Roberto Pepsical. 'It was the darkest place I could think of on short notice. Next time we'll meet at St. Mary's.'

Someone knocked on the restroom door and Murdock told him to go away if he valued his testicles. Then he said to Roberto: 'What is it you wanted to tell us?'

'It's a message from my friend. The one with the problem I told you about—'

'The problem named Stranahan?'

'Yes. He says five thousand each.'

'Fine,' said John Murdock.

'Really?'

'Long as it's cash.'

Salazar added, 'Not in sequence. And not bank-wrapped.'

'Certainly,' Roberto Pepsical said. Now came the part that made his throat go dry.

'There's one part of the plan that my friend wants to change,' he said. 'He says it's no good just arresting this man and putting him in jail. He says this fellow has a big mouth and a vivid imagination.' Those were Rudy's exact words; Roberto was proud of himself for remembering.

Joe Salazar idly tested the knobs on the condom machine and said, 'So you got a better idea, right?'

'Well . . .' Roberto said.

Murdock loosened his grip on the commissioner and straightened his jacket. 'You're not the idea man, are you? I mean, it was your idea to meet at this pussy parlor.' He walked over to the urinal and unzipped his trousers. 'Joe and I will think of something. We're idea-type guys.'

Salazar said, 'For instance, supposing we get a warrant to arrest the suspect for the murder of his former wife. Supposing we proceed to his residence and duly identify ourselves as sworn police officers. And supposing the suspect attempts to flee.'

'Or resists with violence,' Murdock hypothesized.

'Yeah, the manual is clear,' Salazar said.

Murdock shook himself off and zipped up. 'In a circumstance such as that, we could use deadly force.'

'I imagine you could,' said Roberto Pepsical, sober as a choirboy.

The three of them stood there in the restroom, sweating under the hot bare bulb. Salazar examined a package of flamingo-pink rubbers that he had shaken loose from the vending machine.

Finally Murdock said, 'Tell your friend it sounds fine, except for the price. Make it ten apiece, not five.'

'Ten,' Roberto repeated, though he was not at all surprised. To close the deal, he sighed audibly.

'Come on,' said Joe Salazar, unlocking the door. 'We're missing the fingerpaint contest.'

Over the whine of the outboard Luis Córdova shouted: 'There's no point in stopping.'

Mick Stranahan nodded. Under ceramic skies, Biscayne Bay unfolded in a dozen shifting hues of blue. It was a fine, cloudless morning: seventy degrees, and a northern breeze at their backs. Luis Córdova slowed the patrol boat a few hundred yards from the stilt house. He leaned down and said: 'They tore the place up pretty bad, Mick.'

'You sure it was cops?'

'Yeah, two of them. Not uniformed guys, though. And they had one of the sheriff boats.'

Stranahan knew who it was: Murdock and Salazar.

'Those goons from the hospital,' said Christina Marks. She stood next to Luis Córdova at the steering console, behind the Plexiglas windshield. She wore a red windbreaker, baggy knit pants, and high-top tennis shoes.

From a distance Stranahan could see that the door to his house had been left open, which meant it had probably been looted and vandalized. What the kids didn't wreck, the seagulls would. Stranahan stared for a few moments, then said: 'Let's go, Luis.'

The trip to Old Rhodes Key took thirty-five minutes in a light, nudging sea. Christina got excited when they passed a school of porpoises off Elliott Key, but Stranahan showed no interest. He was thinking about the video-tape they had watched at Christina's apartment—Maggie Gonzalez, describing the death of Vicky Barletta. Twice they had watched it. It made him mad but he wasn't sure why. He had heard of worse things, seen worse things. Yet there was something about a doctor doing it, getting away with it, that made Stranahan furious.

When they reached the island, Luis Córdova dropped them at a sagging dock that belonged to an old Bahamian conch fisherman named Cartwright. Cartwright had been told they were coming.

'I got the place ready,' he told Mick Stranahan. 'By the way, it's good to see you, my friend.'

Stranahan gave him a hug. Cartwright was eighty years old. His hair was like cotton fuzz and his skin was the color of hot tar. He had Old Rhodes Key largely to himself and seldom entertained, but he had happily made an exception for his old friend. Years ago Stranahan had done Cartwright a considerable favor.

'White man tried to burn me out,' he told Christina Marks. 'Mick took care of things.'

Stranahan hoisted the duffel bags over his shoulders and trudged toward the house. He said, 'Some asshole developer wanted Cartwright's land but Cartwright didn't want to sell. Things got sticky.'

The conch fisherman cut in: 'I tell the story better. The man offered me one hunnert towsind dollars to move off the island and when I says no thanks, brother, he had some peoples pour gasoline all on my house. Luckily it rain like hell. Mick got this man arrested and dey put him in the big jail up Miami. That's the God's truth.'

'Good for Mick,' Christina said. Naturally she had assumed that Stranahan had killed the man.

'Asshole got six years and did fifteen months. He's out already.' Stranahan laughed acidly.

'That I didn't know,' Cartwright said thoughtfully.

'Don't worry, he won't ever come back to this place.'

'You don't tink so?'

'No, Cartwright, I promise he won't. I had a long talk with the man. I believe he moved to California.'

'Very fine,' Cartwright said with obvious relief.

House was a charitable description for where the old fisherman lived: bare cinderblock walls on a concrete foundation; no doors in the doorways, no glass in the windows; a roof woven from dried palm fronds.

'Dry as a bone,' Cartwright said to Christina. 'I know it don't look like much, but you be dry inside here.'

Gamely she said, 'I'll be fine.'

Stranahan winked at Cartwright. 'City girl,' he said.

Christina jabbed Stranahan in the ribs. 'And you're Daniel Boone, I suppose. Well, fuck you both. I can handle myself.'

Cartwright's eyes grew wide.

'Sorry,' Christina said.

'Don't be,' Cartwright said with a booming laugh. 'I love it. I love the sound of a womanly voice out here.'

For lunch he fixed fresh lobster in a conch salad. Afterwards he gathered some clothes in a plastic garbage bag, told Mick goodbye and headed slowly down to the dock.

Christina said, 'Where's he going?'

'To the mainland,' Stranahan replied. 'He's got a grandson in Florida City he hasn't seen in a while.'

From where they sat, they could see Cartwright's wooden skiff motoring westward across the bay; the old man had one hand on the stem of the throttle, the other shielding his eyes from the low winter sun.

Christina turned to Stranahan. 'You arranged it this way.'

'He's a nice guy. He doesn't deserve any trouble.'

'You really think they'll find us all the way out here?'

'Yep,' Stranahan said. He was counting on it.

21

The clerical staff of Kipper Garth's law office was abuzz: Clients—real live clients—were coming in for a meeting. Most of the secretaries had never seen any of Kipper Garth's clients because he generally did not allow them to visit. Normally all contact took place over the telephone, since Kipper Garth's practice was built exclusively on referrals to other lawyers. The rumor this day (and an incredible one, at that) was that Kipper Garth was going to handle a malpractice case all by himself; one of the senior paralegals had been vaguely instructed to prepare a complaint for civil court. The women who worked Kipper Garth's phone bank figured that it must be a spectacularly egregious case if their boss would tackle it solo, for his fear of going to court was well known. Kipper Garth's staff couldn't wait to get a look at the new clients.

They arrived at eleven sharp, a man and a woman. The clerks, secretaries, and paralegals were startled: It was an unremarkable couple in their mid-thirties. The man was medium-build and ordinary looking, the woman had long ash-blond hair and a nice figure. Neither displayed any obvious scars, mutilations, or crippling deformities. Kipper Garth's staff was baffled—the hushed wagering shifted back and forth between psychiatric aberration and sexual dysfunction.

Both guesses were wrong. The problem of John and Marie Nordstrom was far more peculiar.

Kipper Garth greeted them crisply at the door and led them to two high-backed easy chairs positioned in front of his desk. The lawyer was extremely nervous and hoped it didn't show. He hoped he would ask the right questions.

'Mr. Nordstrom,' he began, 'I'd like to review some of the material in the state files.'

Nordstrom looked around the elegant office and said: 'Are we the only ones?'

'What do you mean?'

'Are we the only ones to sue? Over the phone you said a whole bunch of his patients were suing.'

Kipper Garth tugged restlessly at the sleeves of his coat. 'Well, we've been talking to several others with strong cases. I'm sure they'll come around. Meanwhile you and your wife expressed an interest—'

'But not alone,' John Nordstrom said. 'We don't want to be the only ones.' His wife reached across and touched his arm.

'Let's listen to him,' she said. 'It can't hurt.'

Kipper Garth waited for the moment of tension to pass. It didn't. He motioned toward the walnut credenza behind his desk. 'See all those files, Mr. Nordstrom? Patients of Dr. Rudy Graveline. Most of them have suffered more than you and your wife. Much more.'

Nordstrom said, 'So what's your point?'

'The point is, Mr. Nordstrom, a monster is loose. Graveline is still in business. On a good day his clinic takes in a hundred grand in surgical fees. One hundred grand! And every patient walks in there thinking that Dr. Graveline is one brilliant surgeon, and some of them find out the hard way that he's not. He's a putz.'

Mrs. Nordstrom said: 'You don't have to tell us.'

Kipper Garth leaned forward and, ministerially, folded his hands. 'For me, this case isn't about money.' He sounded so damn earnest that he almost believed himself. 'It isn't about money, it's about morality. And conscience. And concern for one's fellow man. I don't know about you folks, but my stomach churns when I think how a beast like Rudolph Graveline is allowed to continue to destroy the lives of innocent, trusting people.' Kipper Garth swiveled his chair slowly and gestured again at the stacks of files. 'Look at all these victims—men and women just like yourselves. And to think that the state of Florida has done nothing to stop this beast. It makes me nauseous.'

'Me, too,' said Mrs. Nordstrom.

'My mission,' continued Kipper Garth, 'is to find someone with the courage to go after this man. Shut him down. Bring to light his incompetence so that no one else will have to suffer. The place to do that is the courtroom.'

John Nordstrom sniffed. 'Don't tell me the sonofabitch's never been sued before.'

Kipper Garth smiled. 'Oh yes. Yes, indeed, Dr. Graveline has been sued before. But he's always escaped the glare of publicity and the scrutiny of his peers. How? By settling the cases out of court. He buys his way out, never goes to trial. This time he won't get off so lightly, Mr. Nordstrom. This time, with your permission, I want to take him to the wall. I want to go all the way. I'm talking about a trial.'

It was a damn mellifluous speech for a man accustomed to bellowing at a speaker box. If not moved, the Nordstroms were at least impressed. A self-satisfied Kipper Garth wondered if he could ever be so smooth in front of a jury.

Marie Nordstrom said: 'In person you look much younger than on your billboards.'

The lawyer acknowledged the remark with a slight bow.

Mrs. Nordstrom nudged her husband. 'Go ahead, tell him what happened.'

'It's all in the file,' John Nordstrom said.

'I'd like to hear it again,' Kipper Garth said, 'in your own words.' He pressed a button on the telephone console, and a stenographer with a portable machine entered the office. She was followed by a somber-looking paralegal wielding a long yellow pad. Mutely they took positions on either side of Kipper Garth. Nordstrom scanned the trio warily.

His wife said: 'It's a little embarrassing for us, that's all.'

'I understand,' Kipper Garth said. 'We'll take our time.'

Nordstrom shot a narrow look at his wife. 'You start,' he said.

Calmly she straightened in the chair and cleared her throat. 'Two years ago, I went to Dr. Graveline for a routine breast augmentation. He came highly recommended.'

'Your manicurist,' John Nordstrom interjected, 'a real expert.'

Kipper Garth raised a tanned hand. 'Please.'

Marie Nordstrom continued: 'I insisted that Dr. Graveline himself do the surgery. Looking back on it, I would've been better off with one of the other fellows at the clinic—anyway, the surgery was performed on a Thursday. Within a week it was obvious that something was very wrong.'

Kipper Garth said, 'How did you know?'

'Well, the new breasts were quite . . . hard.'

'Try concrete,' John Nordstrom said.

His wife went on. 'They were extremely round and tight. Too tight. I mean, they didn't even bounce.'

A true professional, Kipper Garth never let his eyes wander below Mrs. Nordstrom's neckline.

She said: 'When I saw Dr. Graveline again, he assured me that this was normal for cases like mine. He had a name for it and everything.'

'Capsular contracture,' said the paralegal, without looking up from her notes.

'That's it,' Mrs. Nordstrom said. 'Dr. Graveline told me everything would be fine in a month or two. He said they'd be soft as little pillows.'

'And?'

'And we waited, just like he told us. In the meantime, of course, John kept wanting to try them out.'

'Hey,' Nordstrom said, 'I paid for the damn things.'

'I understand,' said Kipper Garth. 'So you made love to your wife?'

Nordstrom's cheeks reddened. 'You know the rest.'

With his chin Kipper Garth pointed toward the stenographer and the paralegal, both absorbed in transcribing the incident. Nordstrom sighed and said, 'Yeah, I made love to my wife. Or tried to.'

'That's when the accident happened between John and my breasts,' continued Mrs. Nordstrom. 'I'm not sure if it was the left one or the right one that got him.'

Nordstrom muttered, 'I'm not sure, either. It was a big hard boob, that's all I know.'

Kipper Garth said, 'And it actually put your eye out?'

John Nordstrom nodded darkly.

His wife said: 'Technically they called it a detached retina. We didn't know it was so serious right away. John's eye got all swollen up and then there was some bleeding. When his vision didn't come back after a few days, we went to a specialist . . . but it was already too late.'

Gently Kipper Garth said, 'I noticed that you told the ophthalmic surgeon a slightly different story. You told him you were poked by a Christmas tree branch.'

Nordstrom glared, with his good eye, at the lawyer. 'What the hell would *you* have told him—that you were blinded by a tit?'

'It must have been difficult,' Kipper Garth said, his voice rich with sympathy. 'And this was your right eye, according to the file.'

'Yeah,' said Nordstrom, pointing.

'They gave him a glass one,' his wife added. 'You can hardly tell.'

'*I* can sure as hell tell,' Nordstrom said.

Kipper Garth asked: 'Did it affect your work?'

'Are you kidding? I lost my job.'

'Really?' The lawyer suppressed a grin of delight, but mentally tacked a couple more zeros to the pain-and-suffering demand.

Mrs. Nordstrom said: 'John was an air-traffic controller. You can well imagine the problems.'

''Yeah, and the jokes,' Nordstrom said bitterly.

Kipper Garth leaned back and locked his hands across his vest. 'Folks, how does ten million sound?'

Nordstrom snorted. 'Come off it.'

'We get the right jury, we can probably do twelve.'

'Twelve million dollars—no shit?'

'No shit,' said Kipper Garth. 'Mrs. Nordstrom, I need to ask you something. Did this, uh, condition with your breasts ever improve?'

She glanced down at her chest. 'Not much.'

'Not much is right,' said her husband. Take my word, they're like goddamn bocci balls.'

The guy would be poison as a witness, Kipper Garth decided;

the jury would hate his guts. No wonder other lawyers had balked at taking the case. Kipper Garth thanked the Nordstroms for their time and showed them to the door. He promised to get back to them in a few days with some important papers to review.

After the couple had gone, Kipper Garth ordered the stenographer to transcribe the interview and make a half-dozen copies. Then he told the paralegal to type up a malpractice complaint against Dr. Rudy Graveline and the Whispering Palms Spa and Surgery Center.

'Can you handle that?' Kipper Garth asked.

'I think so,' the paralegal said, coolly.

'And afterwards go down to the courthouse and do . . . whatever it is needs to be done.'

'We'll go together,' the paralegal said. 'You might as well learn your way around.'

Kipper Garth agreed pensively. If only his ski bunny knew what their dalliance had cost him. That his blackmailer was his own frigging brother-in-law compounded the humiliation. 'One more question,' Kipper Garth said to his paralegal. 'After we file the lawsuit, then what?'

'We wait,' she replied.

The lawyer giggled with relief. 'That's all?'

'Sure, we wait and see what happens,' the paralegal said. 'It's just like dropping a bomb.'

'I see,' said Kipper Garth. Just what he needed in his life. A bomb.

Freddie was napping in his office at the Gay Bidet when one of the ticket girls stuck her head in the doorway and said there was a man wanted to see him. Right away Freddie didn't like the looks of the guy, and would have taken him for a cop except that cops don't dress so good. The other thing Freddie didn't like about the guy was the way he kept looking around the place with his nose twitching up in the air like a swamp rabbit, like there was something about the place that really stunk. Freddie didn't appreciate that.

'This isn't what I expected,' the man said.

'The fuck you expect, Regine's?' Boldly Freddie took the offensive.

'This isn't a gay bar?' the man asked. 'I assumed from the name . . .'

Freddie said, 'I didn't name the place, pal. All I know is, it rhymes. That doesn't automatically make it no fruit bar. Now state your business or beat it.'

'I need to see one of your bouncers.'

'What for?'

The man said, 'I'm his doctor.'

'He sick?'

'I don't know until I see him,' said Rudy Graveline.

Freddie was skeptical. Maybe the guy was a doctor, maybe not; these days everybody was wearing white silk suits.

'Which of my security personnel you want to see?' asked Freddie.

'He's quite a big man.'

'They're all big, mister. I don't hire no munchkins.'

'This one is extremely tall and thin. His face is heavily scarred, and he's missing his left hand.'

'Don't know him,' Freddie said, playing it safe. In case the guy was a clever bail bondsman or an undercover cop with a wardrobe budget.

Rudy said: 'But he told me he works here.'

Freddie shook his head and made sucking sounds through his front teeth. 'I have a large staff, mister, and turnover to match. Not everybody can take the noise.' He jerked a brown thumb toward the fiberboard wall, which was vibrating from the music on the other side.

'Sounds like an excellent band,' Rudy said lamely.

'Cathy and the Catheters,' Freddie reported with a shrug. 'Queen of slut rock, all the way from London.' He pushed himself to his feet and stretched. 'Sorry I can't help you, mister—'

At that instant the ticket girl flung open the door and told Freddie that a terrible fight had broken out and he better come quick. Rudy Graveline was huffing at Freddie's heels by the time a path had been cleared to the front of the stage. There a gang of anorectic Nazi skinheads had taken on a gang of flabby redneck bikers in a dispute over tattoos—specifically, whose was the baddest. The battle had been joined by a cadre of heavy-set bouncers, each sporting a pink Gay Bidet T-shirt with the word *SECURITY* stenciled on the back. The vicious fighting seemed only to inspire more volume from the band and more random slam-dancing from the other punkers.

Towering above the melee was Chemo himself, his T-shirt ragged and bloody, and a look of baleful concentration on his face. Even through the blinding strobes, Rudy Graveline could see the Weed Whacker attached to Chemo's stub was unsheathed and fully operative; the monofilament cutter was spinning so rapidly that it appeared transparent and harmless, like a hologram. In horror Rudy watched Chemo lower the buzzing device into the tangle of humanity—the ensuing screams rose plangently over the music. As if by prearrangement, the other bouncers backed off and let Chemo work, while Freddie supervised from atop an overturned amplifier.

The fighting subsided quickly. Splints and bandages were handed out to fallen bikers and skinheads alike, while the band took a break. An expression of fatherly admiration in his shoe-button eyes, Freddie patted Chemo on the shoulder, then disappeared backstage. Rudy Graveline worked his way through the sweaty crowd, stepping over the wounded and semiconscious until he reached Chemo's side.

'Well, that was amazing,' Rudy said.

Chemo glanced down at him and scowled. 'Fucking battery died. I hope that's it for the night.'

The surgeon said, 'We really need to talk.'

'Yes,' Chemo agreed. 'We sure do.'

As soon as Chemo and Rudy went backstage, they ran into Freddie, Cathy, and two of the Catheters sharing some hash in a glass pipe. Through a puff of blue smoke Freddie said to Chemo: 'This jerkoff claimed he's your doctor.'

'Was,' Chemo said. 'Can we use the dressing room?'

'Anything you want,' Freddie said.

'Watch out for my python,' Cathy cautioned.

The dressing room was not what Rudy had expected. There was a folding card table, an old-fashioned coat rack, a blue velour sofa, a jagged triangle of broken mirror on the wall and, in one corner, an Igloo cooler full of Heinekens. On the naked floor was a low flat cage made from plywood and chicken wire in which resided a nine-foot Burmese python, the signature of Cathy's big encore.

Rudy Graveline took a chair at the card table while Chemo stretched out on the whorehouse sofa.

Rudy said: 'I was worried when you didn't call from New York. What happened?'

Chemo ran a whitish tongue across his lips. 'Aren't you even going to ask about my face, how it's healing?'

The doctor seemed impatient. 'It looks fine from here. It looks like the dermabrasion is taking nicely.'

'As if you'd know.'

Rudy's mouth twitched. 'Now what is that supposed to mean?'

'It means you're a fucking menace to society. I'm getting myself another doctor—Maggie's picking one out for me.'

Rudy Graveline felt the back of his neck go damp. It wasn't as if he had not expected problems with Chemo—that was the reason for choosing Roberto Pepsical and his crooked cops as a contingency. But it was merely failure, not betrayal, that Rudy had anticipated from his homicidal stork.

'Maggie?' the doctor said. 'Maggie Gonzalez?'

'Yeah, that's the one. We had a long talk, she told me some things.'

'Talking to her wasn't the plan,' Rudy said.

'Yeah, well, the plan has been changed.' Chemo reached into the Igloo cooler and got a beer. He twisted off the cap, tilted the bottle to his lips, and glowered at the doctor the whole time he gulped it down. Then he belched once and said: 'You tried to gyp me.'

Rudy said, 'That's simply not true.'

'You didn't tell me the stakes. You didn't tell me about the Barletta girl.'

The color washed from Rudy's face. Stonily he stared into his own lap. Suddenly his silk Armani seemed as hot and heavy as an army blanket.

Chemo rolled the empty Heineken bottle across the bare terrazzo floor until it clanked to rest against the snake cage. The sleek green python flicked its tongue once, then went back to sleep.

Chemo said, 'And all this time, I thought you knew what the fuck you were doing. I trusted you with my own face.' He laughed harshly and burped again. 'Jesus H. Christ, I bet your own family won't let you carve the bird on Thanksgiving, am I right?'

In a thin abraded voice, Rudy Graveline said: 'So Maggie is still alive.'

'Yeah, and she's going to stay that way as long as I say so.' Chemo swung his spidery legs off the sofa and sat up, straight as a lodgepole. 'Because if anything should happen to her, you are going to be instantly famous. I'm talking TV, Dr. Frankenstein.'

By now Rudy was having difficulty catching his breath.

Chemo went on. 'Your nurse is a smart girl. She made three videotapes for insurance. Two of them are locked up safe and sound in New York. The other . . . well, you'd better pray that I find it before it finds you.'

'Go do it.' Rudy's voice was toneless and weak.

'Naturally this will be very expensive.'

'Whatever you need,' the doctor croaked. This was a scenario he had never foreseen, something beyond his worst screaming nightmares.

'I didn't realize plastic surgeons made so much dough,' Chemo remarked. 'Maggie was telling me.'

'The overhead,' Rudy said, fumbling, 'is sky-high.'

'Well, yours just got higher by seven feet.' Chemo produced a small aerosol can of WD–40 and began lubricating the rotor mechanism of the Weed Whacker. Without glancing up from his chore, he said, 'By the way, Frankenstein, you're getting off easy. Last time a doctor screwed me over, I broke his frigging neck.'

In his mental catacomb Rudy clearly heard the snap of the old dermatologist's spine, watched as the electrolysis needle fell from the old man's lifeless hand and clattered on the office floor.

As soon as he regained his composure, Rudy asked, 'Who's got the missing tape?'

'Oh, take a wild guess.' There was amusement in Chemo's dry tone.

'Shit,' said Rudy Graveline.

'My sentiments exactly.'

22

Reynaldo Flemm hadn't even finished explaining the plan before Willie, the cameraman, interrupted. 'What about Christina?' he asked. 'What does she say?'

'Christina is tied up on another project.'

Willie eyed him skeptically. 'What project?'

'That's not important.'

Willie didn't give up; he was accustomed to Reynaldo treating him like hired help. 'She in New York?'

Reynaldo said, 'She could be in New Delhi for all I care. Point is, I'm producing the Barletta segment. Get used to it, buddy.'

Willie settled back to sip his planter's punch and enjoy the rosy tropical dusk. They had a deck table facing the ocean at an outdoor bar, not far from the Sonesta on Key Biscayne. Reynaldo Flemm was nursing a Perrier, so Willie was confident of having the upper hand. Reynaldo was the only person he knew who blabbed more when he was sober than when he was drunk. Right now Reynaldo was blabbing about his secret plan to force Dr. Rudy Graveline to confess in front of the television camera. It was the most ludicrous scheme that Willie had ever heard, the sort of thing he'd love to watch, not shoot.

After a decent interval, Willie put his rum drink on the table and said: 'Who's blocking out the interview?'

'Me.'

'The questions, too?'

Reynaldo Flemm reddened.

Willie said, 'Shouldn't we run this puppy by the lawyers? I think we got serious trespass problems.'

'Ha,' Reynaldo scoffed.

Sure, Willie thought sourly, go ahead and laugh. I'm the one who always gets tossed in the squad car. I'm the one gets blamed when the cops bang up the camera.

Reynaldo Flemm said, 'Let me worry about the legalities, Willie. The question is: Can you do it?'

'Sure, I can do it.'

'You won't need extra lights?'

Willie shook his head. 'Plenty of light,' he said. 'Getting the sound is where I see the problem.'

'I was wondering about that, too. I can't very well wear the wireless.'

Willie chuckled in agreement. 'No, not hardly.'

Reynaldo said, 'You'll think of something, you always do. Actually, I prefer the hand-held.'

'I know,' Willie said. Reynaldo disliked the tiny cordless clip-on microphones; he favored the old baton-style mikes that you held in your hand—the kind you could thrust in some crooked politician's face and make him pee his pants. Christina Marks called it Reynaldo's 'phallic attachment.' She postulated that, in Reynaldo's mind, the microphone had become a substitute for his penis.

As Willie recalled, Reynaldo didn't think much of Christina's theory.

He said to Willie: 'This'll be hairy, but we've done it before. We're a good team.'

'Yeah,' said Willie, half-heartedly draining his glass. Some team. The basic plan never changed: Get Reynaldo beat up. *Now remember*, he used to tell Willie, *we got to live up to the name of the show. Stick it right in his motherloving face, really piss him off.* Willie had it down to an art: He'd poke the TV camera directly at the subject's nose, the guy would push the camera away and tear off in a fury after Reynaldo Flemm. *Now remember*, Reynaldo would coach, *when he shoves you, jiggle the camera like you were really shaken up. Make the picture super jerky looking, the way they do on 'Sixty Minutes.'* If by chance the interview subject lunged after Willie instead of Reynaldo, Willie had standing orders to halt taping, shield the camera and defend himself—in that order. Invariably the person doing the pummeling got tired of banging his fists on a bulky, galvanized Sony and redirected his antagonism toward the arrogant puss of Reynaldo Flemm. *It's me they're tuning in to see*, Reynaldo would say, *I'm the talent here.* But if the beating became too severe or if Reynaldo got outnumbered, Willie's job then was to stow the camera (carefully) and start swinging away. Many times he had felt like a rodeo clown, diverting Reynaldo's enraged attackers until Reynaldo could escape, usually by locking himself in the camera van. The van was where, at Reynaldo's insistence, Christina Marks waited during ambush interviews. Reynaldo maintained that this was for her own safety, but in reality he worried that if something happened to her, it might end up on tape and steal his thunder.

Reflecting upon all this, Willie ordered another planter's punch. This time he asked the waitress for more dark rum on the top. He said to Reynaldo, 'What makes you think this doctor guy'll break?'

'I've met him. He's weak.'

'That's what you said about Larkey McBuffum.'

Larkey McBuffum was a crooked Chicago pharmacist who had been selling steroid pills to junior high school football players. When Reynaldo and Willie had burst into Larkey's drug store to confront him, the old man had maced Willie square in the eyes with an aerosol can of spermicidal birth-control foam.

'I'm telling you, the surgeon's a wimp,' Reynaldo was saying. 'Put a mike in his face and he'll crack like a fucking Triscuit.'

'I'll stay close on him,' Willie said.

'Not too close,' Reynaldo Flemm cautioned. 'You gotta be ready to pull back and get us both in the shot, right before it happens.'

Willie stirred the dark rum with his little finger. 'You mean, when he slugs you?'

'Of course,' Reynaldo said curtly. 'Christ, you ought to know the drill by now. *Of course* when he slugs me.'

'Will that be,' Willie asked playfully, 'before or after the big confession?'

Reynaldo gnawed on this one a few seconds before giving up. 'Just get it, that's all,' he said stiffly. 'Whenever it happens, get every bloody second on tape. Understand?'

Willie nodded. Sometimes he wished he were still free-lancing for the networks. A coup in Haiti was a picnic compared to this.

The Pennsylvania State Police were happy to wire a photograph of Blondell Wayne Tatum to Sergeant Al García at the Metro-Dade Police Department. García was disappointed, for the photograph was practically useless. It had been taken more than twenty years earlier by a feature photographer for a small rural newspaper. At the time, the paper was running a five-part series on how the Amish sect was coping with the social pressures of the twentieth century. Blondell Wayne Tatum was one of several teenaged Amish youths who were photographed while playing catch with a small pumpkin. Of the group, Blondell Wayne Tatum was the only one wearing a brand-new Rawlings outfielder's mitt.

For purposes of criminal identification, the facsimile of the newspaper picture was insufficient. García knew that the man named Chemo no longer wore a scraggly pubescent beard, and that he since had suffered devastating facial trauma as a result of a freak dermatology accident. Armed with these revisions, García enlisted the help of a police sketch artist named Paula Downs. He tacked the newspaper picture on Paula's easel and said: 'Third one from the left.'

Paula slipped on her eyeglasses, but that wasn't enough. She took a photographer's loupe and peered closely at the picture. 'Stringbean,' she said. 'Sixteen, maybe seventeen years old.'

García said: 'Make him thirty-eight now. Six foot nine, one hundred eighty pounds.'

'No sweat,' Paula said.

'And lose the beard.'

'Let's hope so. Yuk.'

With an unwrapped cigar, García tapped on the photograph. 'Here's the hard part, babe. A few years ago this turkey had a bad accident, got his face all fried up.'

'Burns?'

'Yup.'

'What kind—gas or chemical?'

'Electrolysis.'

Paula peered at the detective over the rim of her spectacles and said, 'That's very humorous, Al.'

'I swear. Got it straight from the Pennsylvania cops.'

'Hmmmm.' Paula chewed on the eraser of her pencil as she contemplated the photograph.

Al García described Chemo's face to Paula the way that Mick Stranahan had described it to him. As García spoke, the artist began to draw a freehand composite. She held the pencil at a mild angle and swept it in light clean ovals across the onionskin paper. First came the high forehead, the sharp chin, then the cheekbones and the puffy blowfish eyes and the thin cruel lips. Before long, the gangly young Amish kid with the baseball mitt became a serious-looking felon.

Paula got up and said, 'Be right back.' Moments later she returned with a salt shaker from the cafeteria. She lifted the onionskin and copiously sprinkled salt on the drawing pad. With the heel of her left hand she spread the grains evenly. After replacing the onionskin that bore Chemo's likeness, Paula selected a stubby fat pencil with a soft gray lead. She held it flat to the paper, as if it were a hunk of charcoal, and began a gentle tracing motion across the drawing. Instantly the underlying salt crystals came into relief. García smiled: The effect was perfect. It gave Chemo's portrait a harsh granular complexion, just as Mick Stranahan had described.

'You're a genius,' García told Paula Downs.

She handed him the finished composite. 'You get some winners, Al.'

He went to the Xerox room and made a half-dozen copies of the sketch. He stuck one in John Murdock's mailbox. On the back of Murdock's copy García had printed the name Blondell Wayne Tatum, the AKA, and the date of birth. Then García had written: 'This is your guy for the Simpkins case!!!!'

Murdock, he knew, would not appreciate the help.

García spent the rest of the afternoon on Key Biscayne, showing Chemo's composite to dock boys, bartenders, and cocktail waitresses at Sunday's-on-the-Bay. By four o'clock the detective had three positive I.D.s saying that the man in the drawing was

the same one who had been drinking with Chloe Simpkins Stranahan on the evening she died.

Now Al García was a happy man. When he got back to police
headquarters, he called a florist and ordered a dozen long-stem-
med roses for Paula Downs. While he was on the phone, he
noticed a small UPS parcel on his desk. García tore it open with
his free hand.

Inside was a videotape in a plastic sleeve. On the sleeve was a
scrap of paper, attached with Scotch tape. A note.

'I told you so. Regards, Mick.'

García took the videotape to the police audio room, where a
couple of the vice guys were screening the very latest in bestiality
vérité. García told them to beat it and plugged Stranahan's tape
into a VHS recorder. He watched it twice. The second time, he
stubbed out his cigar and took notes.

Then he went searching for Murdock and Salazar.

In the detective room, nobody seemed to know where they
were. García didn't like the looks of things.

The copy of Paula's sketch of Blondell Wayne Tatum lay crumpled next to an empty Doritos bag on John Murdock's desk.
'Asshole,' García hissed. He didn't care who heard him. He pawed
through the rest of Murdock's debris until he found a pink
message slip. The message was from the secretary of Circuit Judge
Cassie B. Ireland.

García groaned. Cassie Ireland had been a devoted golfing partner of the late and terminally crooked Judge Raleigh Goomer.
Cassie himself was known to have serious problems with drinking
and long weekends in Las Vegas. The problems were in the area
of chronic inability to afford either vice.

The message to Detective John Murdock from Judge Cassie
Ireland's secretary said: 'Warrant's ready.'

Al García used Murdock's desk phone to call the judge's chambers. He told the secretary who he was. Not surprisingly, the
judge was gone for the day. Gone straight to the tiki bar at
the Airport Hilton, García thought.

To the judge's secretary he said, 'There's been a little mixup
down here. Did Detective Murdock ask Judge Ireland to sign
a warrant?'

'Sure did,' chirped the secretary. 'I've still got the paperwork right here. John and his partner came by and picked it up yesterday morning.'

Al García figured he might as well ask, just to make sure. 'Can you tell me the name on the warrant?'

'Mick Stranahan,' the secretary replied. 'First-degree murder.'

Christina Marks found the darkness exciting. As she floated naked on her back, the warm water touched her everyplace. Sometimes she stood up and curled her toes in the cool, rough sand, to see how deep it was. A few yards away, Mick Stranahan broke the surface with a swoosh, a glistening blond sea creature. He sounded like a porpoise when he blew the air from his lungs.

'This is nice,' Christina called to him.

'No hot showers on the key,' he said. 'No shower, period. Cartwright is a no-frills guy.'

'I said it's nice. I mean it.'

Stranahan swam closer and rose to his feet. The water came up to his navel. In the light from a quarter moon Christina could make out the fresh bullet scar on his shoulder; it looked like a smear of pink grease. She found herself staring—he was different out here on the water. Not the same man whom she had seen in the hospital or at her apartment. On the island he seemed larger and more feral, yet also more serene.

'It's so peaceful,' Christina said. They were swimming on a marly bonefish flat, forty yards from Cartwright's dock.

'I'm glad you can relax,' Stranahan said. 'Most women would be jittery, having been shot at twice by a total stranger.'

Christina laughed easily, closed her eyes and let the wavelets tickle her neck. Mick was right; she ought to be a nervous wreck by now. But she wasn't.

'Maybe I'm losing my mind,' she said to the stars. She heard a soft splash as he went under again. Seconds later something cool brushed against her ankle, and she smiled. 'All right, mister, no funny business.'

From a surprising distance came his voice: 'Sorry to disappoint you, but that wasn't me.'

'Oh no.' Christina rolled over and kicked hard for the deep

channel, but she didn't get far. Like a torpedo he came up beneath her and slid one arm under her hips, the other around her chest. As he lifted her briskly out of the water, she let out a small cry.

'Easy,' Stranahan said, laughing. 'It was only a baby bonnet shark—I saw it.'

He was standing waist-deep on the flat, holding her like an armful of firewood. 'Relax,' he said. 'They don't eat bigshot TV producers.'

Christina turned in his arms and held him around the neck. 'Is it gone?' she asked.

'It's gone. Want me to put you down?'

'Not really, no.'

In the moonlight he could see enough of her eyes to know what she was thinking. He kissed her on the mouth.

She thought: This is crazy. I love it.

Stranahan kissed her again, longer than the first time.

'A little salty,' she said, 'but otherwise very nice.'

Christina let her hands wander. 'Say there, what happened to your jeans?'

'I guess they came off in the undertow.'

'What undertow?' She started kissing him up and down the neck; giggling, nipping, using the tip of her tongue. She could feel the goose flesh rise on his shoulders.

'There really *was* a shark,' he said.

'I believe you. Now take me back to the island. Immediately.'

Stranahan said, 'Not right this minute.'

'You mean we're going to do it out here?'

'Why not?'

'Standing up?'

'Why not?'

'Because of the sharks. You said so yourself.'

Stranahan said, 'You'll be safe, just put your legs around me.'

'Nice try.'

He kissed her again. This was a good one. Christina wrapped her legs around his naked hips.

Stranahan stopped kissing long enough to catch his breath and say, 'I almost forgot. Can you name the Beatles?'

'Not right this minute.'

'Yes, now. Please.'

'You're a damn lunatic.'

'I know,' he said.

Christina pressed so close and so hard that water sluiced up between her breasts and splashed him on the chin. 'That's what you get,' she said. Then, nose to nose: 'John, Paul, George, and Ringo.'

'You're terrific.'

'And don't forget Pete Best.'

'I think I love you,' Stranahan said.

Later he caught a small grouper from the dock, and fried it for dinner over an open fire. They ate on the ocean side of the island, under a stand of young palms. Stranahan used a pair of old lobster traps for tables. The temperature had dropped into the low seventies with a sturdy breeze. Christina wore a tartan flannel shirt, baggy gray workout trousers, and running shoes. Stranahan wore jeans, sneakers, and a University of Miami sweatshirt. Tucked in the waist of his jeans was a Smith .38 he had borrowed from Luis Córdova. Stranahan was reasonably certain that he would not have to fire it.

Christina was on her second cup of coffee when she said, 'I've been a pretty good sport about all this, don't you agree?'

'Sure.' He had his eyes on the faraway lights of a tramp freighter plowing south in the Gulf Stream.

Christina said, 'I know I've asked before, but I'm going to try again: What the hell are we doing out here?'

'I thought you liked this place.'

'I love it, Mick, but I still don't understand.'

'We can't go back to the stilt house. Not yet, anyway.'

'But why come here?' She was nearly out of patience with the mystery.

'Because I needed a place where something could happen, and no one would see it. Or hear it.'

'Mick—'

'There's no other way.' He stood up and poured out the cold

dregs of his coffee, which splattered against the bare serrated coral. He noticed that the tide was slipping out. 'There's no other way to deal with people like this,' he said.

Christina turned to him. 'You don't understand. I can't do this, I can't be a part of this.'

'You wanted to come along.'

'To observe. To report. To get the story.'

Stranahan's laugh carried all the way to Hawk Channel. 'Story?'

She knew how silly it sounded, and was. Willie had the television cameras, and Reynaldo Flemm had Willie. Reynaldo . . . another macho head case. He had sounded so odd when she had phoned from the mainland; his voice terse and icy, his laugh thin and ironic. He was cooking up something, although he denied it to Christina. Even when she told him about the wild incident at the Plaza, about how she had almost been shot *again*, Reynaldo's reaction was strangely muted and unreadable. When she had called again two hours later from a pay booth at the marina, the secretary in New York told Christina that Reynaldo had already left for the airport. The secretary went on to report, in a snitchy tone, that Reynaldo had withdrawn fifteen thousand dollars from the emergency weekend travel account—the account normally reserved for commercial airline disasters, killer earthquakes, political assassinations, and other breaking news events. Christina Marks could not imagine what Reynaldo intended to do with fifteen grand, but she assumed it would be a memorable folly.

And there she was in Florida: no camera, no crew, no star. So she had boarded the marine patrol boat with Mick Stranahan and Luis Córdova.

Standing in the moonglow, watching the tide lick the coral under her feet, Christina said again: 'I can't be a part of this.'

Stranahan put an arm around her. It reminded Christina of the hugs her father sometimes gave her when she was a child and something sad had made her cry. A gesture that said he was sorry, but nothing could be done; sometimes the world was not such a good place.

'Mick, let's just go to the police.'

'These *are* the police. Remember?'

She looked at his face, searching the shadows for his expression. 'So that's who you're waiting for.'

'Sure. Who'd you think?'

Christina pretended to slap herself on the forehead. 'Oh, silly me—I thought it might be that huge skinny freak who keeps trying to shoot us.'

Stranahan shook his head. 'Him, we don't wait for.'

'Mick, this still isn't right.'

But the hug was finished, and so was the discussion. 'There's a lantern back at the house,' he told her. 'I want you to take a walk around the island. A long walk, okay?'

23

Joe Salazar said, 'You got to steer yesterday.'

'For Christ's sake,' mumbled Murdock.

'Come on, Johnny, it's my turn.'

They were gassing up the boat at Crandon Marina on Key Biscayne. It was the sheriff's department's boat, a nineteen-foot Aquasport with a forest-green police stripe down the front. It was the same boat that the two detectives had borrowed the day before. The sergeant in charge of the marine division had not wanted to loan the boat to Murdock or Salazar because it was obvious that neither knew how to navigate. The sergeant wondered if they even knew how to swim. Both men were wearing new khaki deck shorts that revealed pale legs, chubby legs that had seldom been touched by salt or sunlight: landlubber's legs. The sergeant had surrendered the Aquasport only when John Murdock flashed the murder warrant and said the suspect had been spotted on a house way out in Stiltsville. The sergeant had asked why they weren't taking any backups along, since there was room on the boat, but Murdock hadn't seemed to hear the question.

When the two detectives had returned to the dock a few hours later, the sergeant had been pleasantly surprised to find no major structural damage to the Aquasport or its drive shaft. But when Murdock and Salazar in their stupid khakis showed up again the following afternoon, the sergeant wondered how long their luck would hold out on the water.

'Go ahead and drive,' Murdock grumped at the gas dock. 'I don't give a shit.'

Joe Salazar took a stance behind the steering console. He tried not to gloat. Then it occurred to him: 'Where do we look now?'

The day before, Stranahan's stilt house had been empty. They had torn the rooms apart for clues to his whereabouts, found none, and departed in frustration. The whole way back, Murdock had complained about how the shoulder holster was chafing through his mesh tank top. Twice they had run the boat aground on bonefish flats, and both times Murdock had forced Salazar to hop out in the mud and push. For this, if for nothing else, Salazar figured that he deserved to be the captain today.

Murdock said: 'I tell you where we look. We look in every goddamned stilt house on the bay.'

'Yeah, like a regular canvass.'

'Door to door, except by boat. You know the fuckwad's out there somewhere.'

Joe Salazar felt better now that they had a plan. He paid the dock attendant for the gasoline, cranked up the big Evinrude on the back of the Aquasport, and aimed the bow towards Bear Cut. Or tried. The boat didn't want to move.

The dock attendant snickered. 'Helps to untie it,' he said, pointing with one of his bright white sneakers.

Sheepishly Joe Salazar unhitched the lines off the bow and stern and shoved off. John Murdock said, 'What a wiseass that guy was. Didn't he see we had guns?'

'Sure he did,' Salazar replied, steering tentatively towards the channel.

'This town is gone to shit,' Murdock said, spitting over the gunwale, 'when a guy with a gun has to put up with that kind of bull.'

'Everybody's a wiseass,' Joe Salazar agreed. Nervously he was watching a gray outboard coming in the other direction along the opposite side of the channel. The boat had a blue police light mounted in the center. A young Latin man in a gray uniform stood behind the windshield. He waved to them: the world-weary wave of one cop to another.

'What do I do?' Salazar asked.

'Try waving back,' said Murdock.

Salazar did. The man in the gray boat changed his course and idled towards them.

'Grouper trooper,' John Murdock whispered. Salazar nodded as if he knew what his partner was talking about. He didn't. He also didn't know how to stop the Aquasport. Every time he pulled down on the throttle, the engine jolted into reverse. When he pushed the lever the other way, the boat would shudder and shoot forward. Backward, forward, backward again. The big Evinrude sounded like it was about to blow up. Joe Salazar could tell that Murdock was seething.

'Try neutral,' the young marine patrolman called. 'Move the throttle sideways till it clicks.'

Salazar did as he was told, and it worked.

'Thanks!' he called back.

Under his breath, Murdock said: 'Yeah, thanks for making us look like a couple of jerkoffs.'

The marine patrol boat coasted up on the port side of the Aquasport. The young officer introduced himself as Luis Córdova. He asked where the two detectives were headed, and if he could help. Joe Salazar told him they were going to Stiltsville to serve a murder warrant.

'Only one guy lives out there that I know of,' Luis Córdova said.

Murdock said: 'That's the guy we want.'

'Mick Stranahan?'

'You know him?'

'I know where he lives,' said Luis Córdova, 'but he's not there now. I saw him only yesterday.'

'Where?' blurted Joe Salazar. 'Was he alone?'

'Yeah, he was alone. Sitting on the conch dock down at Old Rhodes Key.'

Murdock said, 'Where the hell's that?'

'South of Elliott.'

'Where the hell's Elliott?'

The marine patrolman said, 'Why don't you guys just wait a few hours and follow me down? The tide won't be right until dusk. Besides, you might need some extra muscle with this guy.'

'No. Thanks anyway.' John Murdock's tone left no chance for discussion. 'But we could use a map, if you got one.'

Luis Córdova disappeared briefly behind the steering console. When he stood up again, he was smiling. 'Just happened to have an extra,' he said.

A half-hour out of the marina, Joe Salazar said to his partner: 'Maybe we should've asked what he meant about the tides.'

The Aquasport was stuck hard on another mud flat, this one a mile south of Soldier Key. John Murdock cracked open his third can of beer and said: 'You're the one wanted to drive.'

Salazar leaned over the side of the boat and studied the situation. He decided there was no point in getting out to push. 'It's only six inches deep,' he said, a childlike marvel in his voice. 'On the map it sure looked like plenty of water, didn't it?'

Murdock said, 'If you're a starfish, it's plenty of water. If you're a boat, it's a goddamn beach. Another thing: I told you to get three bags of ice. Look how fast this shit is melting.' He kicked angrily at the cooler.

Joe Salazar continued to stare at the shallow gin-clear water. 'I think the tide's coming in,' he said hopefully.

'Swell,' said Murdock. 'That means it's only what?—another four, five hours in the mud. Fanfuckingtastic. By then it'll be good and dark, too.'

Salazar pointed out that the police boat was equipped with excellent lights. 'Once we get off the flat, it's a clean shot down to the island. Deep water the whole trip.'

He had never seen his partner so jumpy and short-tempered. Normally John Murdock was the picture of a cool tough cop, but Salazar had watched a change come over him beginning the night they took the down payment from Commissioner Roberto Pepiscal. Five thousand cash, each. Five more when it was done. To persuade the detectives that he was not the booze-swilling lech that he had appeared to be at the nudie joint, the commissioner had arranged the payoff meeting to take place in one of the empty confessionals at St. Mary's Catholic Church in Little Havana. The confessional was dimly lit and no bigger than a broom closet; the three conspirators had to stand sidewise to fit. It had been a dozen years since Joe Salazar had stepped inside a confessional and not much had changed. The place reeked of damp linen and guilt, just as he remembered. He and Murdock stuffed the cash in their jackets and bolted out the door together, nearly trampling a quartet of slow-footed nuns. Commissioner Roberto Pepsical stayed alone in the confessional and recited three Hail Marys. He figured it couldn't hurt.

Back in the car, John Murdock had not displayed the crude and cocky ebullience that usually followed the taking of a hefty bribe; rather, his mood had been taciturn and apprehensive. It had stayed that way for two days.

Now, with the boat stuck fast on the bonefish flat, Murdock sulked alone in the stern, glaring at the slow crawl of the incoming tide. Joe Salazar lit a Camel and settled in for a long, tense afternoon. He didn't feel so well himself, but at least he knew why. This was the biggest job they'd ever done, and the dirtiest. By a mile.

In fact, the tides would not have mattered if either of the two detectives had known how to read a marine chart. Even at dead low, there was plenty of water from Cape Florida all the way to Old Rhodes Key. All you had to do was follow the channels, which were plainly marked on Luis Córdova's map.

Mick Stranahan knew that Murdock and Salazar would run the boat aground. He also knew that it would be nighttime before they could float free, and that they would make the rest of the trip at a snail's pace, fearful of repeating the mishap.

He and Luis Córdova had talked this part out. Together they had calculated that the two detectives would reach the island between nine and midnight, provided they didn't hit the shoal off Boca Chita and shear the prop off the Evinrude. Luis had offered to tail the Aquasport at a discreet distance, but Stranahan told him no. He didn't want the marine patrolman anywhere near Old Rhodes Key when it happened. If Luis was there, he'd want to do it by the book. Wait for the assholes to make their move, then try to arrest them. Stranahan knew it would never work that way—they'd try to kill Luis, too. And even if Luis was as sharp as Stranahan thought, it would be a mess for him afterwards. An automatic suspension, a grand jury, his name all over the newspapers. No way, Stranahan told him, no hero stuff. Just give them the map and get lost.

Besides, Stranahan already had his hands full with Christina Marks on the island.

'I don't want to go for a walk,' she said. 'Grandmothers and widows go for walks. I'm staying here with you.'

'So you can take notes, or what?' He handed her a Coleman lantern. The jumpy white light made their shadows clash on the cinderblock walls. Stranahan said, 'You're not a reporter anymore, you're a goddamn witness.'

She said, 'Is this your idea of pillow talk? Half an hour ago we were making love, and now I'm a "goddamn witness." You ever thought of writing poetry, Mick?'

He was down on one knee, pulling items from one of the duffel bags. Without looking up, he said, 'You said you couldn't be a part of this, I'm trying to accommodate you. As for the afterglow, you want to waltz in the moonlight, we'll do that later. Right now there's a pair of bad cops on their way out here to shoot me.'

'You don't know that.'

'Yeah, you're right,' Stranahan said. 'They're probably just collecting Toys for Tots. Now go.'

He stood up. In the lantern light, Christina saw that his arms were full: binoculars, a poplin windbreaker, a pair of corduroys, an Orioles cap, a fishing knife, and a round spool of some kind.

She said, 'It's not for the damn TV show that I want to stay. I'm scared for you. I don't know why—since you're being such a prick—but I'm worried about you, I admit it.'

When Stranahan spoke again, the acid was gone from his voice. 'Look, if you stay . . . if you were to see something, they'd make you testify. Forget reporter's privilege and First Amendment—doesn't count for a damn thing in a situation like this. If you witness a crime, Chris, they put you under oath. You don't want that.'

'Neither do you.'

He smiled drily. She had him on that one. It was true: He didn't want any witnesses. 'You've had enough excitement,' he told her. 'Twice I've nearly gotten you killed. If I were you, I'd take that as a hint.'

Christina said, 'What if you're wrong about them, Mick? What if they only want to ask more questions? Even if they're coming to arrest you, you can't just—'

'Go,' he said. Later he would explain that these cops were buddies of the late Judge Raleigh Goomer, and that what they wanted from Mick Stranahan was payback. Asking questions was not at all what they had in mind. 'Take the path I showed you. Follow the shoreline about halfway down the island and you'll come to a clearing. You'll see some plastic milk crates, an empty oil drum, an old campfire hole. Wait there for me.'

Christina gave him a frozen look, but he didn't feel it. His mind was in overdrive, long gone.

'There's some fruit and candy bars in the Tupperware,' he said. 'But don't feed the raccoons, they bite like hell.'

She was twenty yards down the path when she heard him call, 'Hey, Chris, you forgot the bug spray.'

She shook her head and kept walking.

Fifteen minutes later, when Stranahan was sure she was gone, he carried his things down to Cartwright's dock. There he lit another lantern and hung it on a nail in one of the pilings. Then he pulled off his sneakers, kicked out of his jeans, and slid naked into the cool flowing tides.

For Joe Salazar, it was a moment of quiet triumph at the helm. 'By God, we did it.'

John Murdock made a snide chuckle. 'Yeah, we found it,' he said. 'The Atlantic fucking Ocean. A regular needle in a haystack, Joe. And all it took was three hours of dry humping these islands.'

Salazar didn't let the sarcasm dampen his newfound confidence. The passage through Sand Cut had been hairy; even at a slow speed, navigating the swift serpentine channel at night was an accomplishment worth savoring. Murdock knew it, too; not once had he tried to take the wheel.

'So this is the famous Elliott Key.' Murdock scratched his sunburned cheeks. The Aquasport idled half a mile offshore, rocking in a brisk chop. The beer was long gone, the ice melted. In the cool breeze Murdock had slipped into a tan leather jacket, the one he always wore to work; it looked ridiculous over his khaki shorts. Dismally he slapped at his pink shins, where a horsefly was eating supper.

Joe Salazar held the chart on his lap, a flashlight in his right hand. With the other hand he pointed: 'Like I said, Johnny, from here it's a straight nine-mile run to Rhodes. Twelve feet of water the whole way.'

Murdock said, 'So let's go, Señor Columbus. Maybe we can make it before Christmas.' He readjusted his shoulder holster for the umpteenth time.

Salazar hesitated. 'Once we get there, what exactly is the plan?'

'Get that goddamn flashlight out of my face.' Murdock's eyelids were swollen and purple. Too much sun, too much beer. It worried Salazar; he wanted his partner to be sharp.

'The plan is simple,' Murdock said. 'We arrive with bells on—sirens, lights, the works. We yell for Stranahan to come out with his hands up. Go ahead with the whole bit—serve the warrant, do the Miranda, all that shit. Then we shoot him like he was trying to get away.'

'Do we cuff him first?'

'Now, how would that look? No, we don't cuff him first. Jesus Christ.' Murdock spit into the water. He'd been spitting all after-noon. Salazar hoped this wasn't a new habit.

Murdock said, 'See, Joe, we shoot him in the back. That way it looks like he's running away. Then we get on this boat radio, if one of us can figure out how to use the goddamn thing, and call for air rescue.'

'Which'll take forever to get here.'

'Exactly. But then we're covered, procedure-wise.'

It sounded like a solid plan, with only one serious variable. Joe Salazar decided to put the variable out of his mind. He stowed the flashlight, reclaimed his post at the wheel of the police boat and steered a true course for Old Rhodes Key.

A straight line through open seas. No sweat.

The channel that leads from the ocean to the cut of Old Rhodes Key is called Caesar Creek. It is deep and fairly broad, and well charted with lighted markers. For this Joe Salazar was profoundly thankful. Having mastered the balky throttle, he guided the Aquasport in at half-speed, with John Murdock standing (or trying to) in the bow. Murdock cupped his hands around his eyes to block the peripheral light; he was peering at the island, searching for signs of Mick Stranahan. Two hundred yards from the mouth of the cut, Salazar killed the engine and joined his chubby partner on the front of the boat.

'There he is!' Murdock's breathing was raspy, excited.

Salazar squinted into the night. 'Yeah, Johnny, sitting under that light on the dock.'

They could see the lantern and, in its white penumbra, the figure of a man with his legs hanging over the planks. The figure wore a baseball cap, a tan jacket, and long pants. From the angle of the cap, the man's head appeared to be down, chin resting on his chest.

'Dumb fuckwad's asleep.' Murdock's laugh was high and brittle. He already had his pistol out.

'Then I guess we better do it,' Salazar said.

'By all means.' Murdock dropped to a crouch.

They had tested the blue lights and siren on the way down, so Salazar knew where the switches were. He flipped them simultaneously, then turned the ignition key. As the Evinrude growled to life, Salazar put all his weight to the throttle.

Gun in hand, John Murdock clung awkwardly to the bow rail as the Aquasport planed off and raced toward the narrow inlet. The wind spiked Murdock's hair and flattened his cheeks. His teeth were bared in a wolfish expression that might have passed for a grin.

As the boat got closer, Joe Salazar expected Mick Stranahan to wake up at any moment and look in their direction—but the man didn't move.

A half-mile away, sitting on a milk crate under some trees, Christina Marks heard the police siren. With a shiver she closed her eyes and waited for the sound of gunfire.

They could have come one of several ways. The most likely was the oceanside route, following Caesar Creek into the slender fork between tiny Hurricane Key and Old Rhodes. This was the easiest way to Cartwright's dock.

But a westward approach, out of Biscayne Bay, would leave more options and offer more cover. They could come around Adams Key, or circle the Rubicons and sneak through the grassy flats behind Totten. But that would be a tricky and perilous passage, almost unthinkable for someone who had never made the trip.

Not at night, Stranahan decided, not these guys.

He had gambled that they would come by the ocean.

In the water he had carried only the knife and the spool. Four times he made the swim between Old Rhodes and Hurricane Key; not a long swim, but enervating against a strong outbound current. After pulling himself up on Cartwright's dock for the last time, Stranahan had rubbed the cold ache from his legs and arms. It had taken a long time to catch his breath.

Then he pulled on some dry clothes, got the .38 that Luis Córdova had loaned him, and sat down to wait.

The spool in Stranahan's duffel had contained five hundred yards of thin plastic monofilament. The line was calibrated to a tensile strength of one hundred twenty pounds, for it was designed to withstand the deep-water surges of giant marlin and bluefin tuna. It was the strongest fishing line manufactured in the world, tournament quality. For further advantage it was lightly tinted a charcoal gray, which made it practically invisible underwater.

Even out of the water, the line was sometimes impossible to see.

At night, for instance. Stretched across a mangrove creek.

Undoubtedly John Murdock never saw it.

He was squatting toad-like on the front of the boat, training his .357 at the figure on the dock as they made their approach. Under Joe Salazar's hand, the Aquasport was moving at exactly forty-two miles per hour.

Mick Stranahan had strung three taut vectors between the islands. The lines were fastened to the trunks of trees and crossed the water at varying heights. The lowest of the lines was snapped immediately by the bow of the speeding police boat. The other two garrotted John Murdock in the belly and the neck, respectively.

Joe Salazar, in the bewildering final millisecond of his life, watched his partner thrown backwards, bug-eyed and gurgling, smashed to the deck by unseen hands. Then the same spectral claw seized Salazar by the throat, chopped him off his feet, bounced his overripe skull off the howling Evintrude and twanged him directly into the creek.

The noise made by the fishing line when it snapped on Joe Salazar's neck was very much like that of a gunshot.

Christina Marks ran all the way back to Cartwright's dock. Along the way she dropped the Coleman lantern, hissing, on some rocks. But she kept running. When she got there, Caesar Creek was black and calm. She saw no boat, no sign of intruders.

On the dock, the familiar figure of a man in a baseball cap slouched beneath another lantern, this one glowing brightly.

'Mick, what happened?'

Then Christina realized that it wasn't a man at all, but a scarecrow wearing Stranahan's poplin jacket and long corduroys. The body of the scarecrow was stuffed with palm leaves and dried seaweed. The head was a green coconut. The baseball cap fit like a charm.

24

The Aquasport wedged itself deep in the mangroves on Totten Key. The engine was dead, but the prop was still twirling when Mick Stranahan got there. Barefoot, he monkeyed through the slick branches until he could see over the side of the battered boat. In his right hand he held Luis Córdova's .38.

He didn't need it. Detective John Murdock wasn't dead, but he would be soon. He lay motionless on the deck, his knees drawn up in pain. Blackish blood oozed from his nose. Only one eye was open, rhythmically illuminated by the strobing blue police light. Cracked but still flashing, the light dangled from a nest of loose wires on the console. It looked like a fancy electric Christmas ornament.

Stranahan felt his stomach shrink to a knot. He put the pistol in his jeans and swung his legs over the gunwale. 'John?'

Murdock's eye blinked, and he grunted weakly.

Stranahan said, 'Try to take it easy.' Like the guy had a choice. 'One quick question, I've got to ask. You fellows were going to kill me, weren't you?'

'Damn right,' rasped the dying detective.

'Yeah, that's what I thought. I can't believe you're still sore about Judge Goomer.'

Murdock managed a bloody grin and said, 'You dumb fuckwad.'

Stranahan leaned forward and brushed a horsefly off Murdock's forehead. 'But if it wasn't revenge for the judge, then why pull something like this?' Silence gave him the answer. 'Don't tell me somebody paid you.'

Murdock nodded, or tried. His neck wasn't working so well; it looked about twice as long as it was supposed to be.

Stranahan said, 'You took money for this? From who?'

'Eat me,' Murdock replied.

'It was probably the doctor,' Stranahan speculated. 'Or a go-between. That would make more sense.'

Murdock's reply came out as a dank rattle. Mick Stranahan sighed. Queasiness at the sight of Murdock had given way to emotional exhaustion.

'John, it's some kind of city, isn't it? All I wanted out here was some peace and solitude. I was through with all this crap.'

Murdock gave a hateful moan, but Stranahan needed to talk. 'Here I'm minding my own business, feeding the fish, not bothering a soul, when some guy shows up to murder me. At my very own house, John, in the middle of the bay! All because some goddamn doctor thinks I'm going to break open a case that's so old it's mildewed.'

The dying Murdock seemed hypnotized by the flashing blue light. It was ticking much faster than his own heart. One of the detective's hands began to crawl like an addled blue crab, tracking circles on the blood-slickened deck.

Stranahan said, 'I know it hurts, John, but there's nothing I can do.'

In a slack voice Murdock said, 'Fuck you, shithead.' Then his eye closed for the last time.

Mick Stranahan and Christina Marks were waiting when Luis Córdova pulled up to the dock at nine sharp the next morning.

'Where to?' he asked Stranahan.

'I'd like to go back to my house, Luis.'

'Not me,' said Christina Marks. 'Take me to Key Biscayne. The marina is fine.'

Stranahan said, 'I guess that means you still don't want to marry me.'

'Not in a million years,' Christina said. 'Not in your wildest dreams.'

Stranahan turned to Luis Córdova. 'She didn't get much sleep. The accommodations were a bit too . . . rustic.'

'I understand,' said the marine patrolman. 'But, otherwise, a quiet night?'

'Fairly quiet,' Stranahan said.

The morning was sunny and cool. The bay had a light wash-board ripple that made the patrol boat seem to fly. As they passed the Ragged Keys, Stranahan nudged Luis Córdova and pointed to the white-blue sky. 'Choppers!' he shouted over the engine noise. Christina Marks saw them, too: three Coast Guard rescue helicopters, chugging south at a thousand feet.

Without glancing from the wheel, Luis Córdova said, 'There's a boat overdue from Crandon. Two cops.'

'No shit?'

'They found a body this morning floating off Broad Creek. Homicide man named Salazar.'

'What happened?'

'Drowned,' yelled Luis Córdova. 'Who knows how.'

Christina Marks listened to the two men going back and forth. She wasn't sure how much Luis Córdova knew, but it was more than Stranahan would ever tell her. She felt angry and insulted and left out.

When they arrived at the stilt house, Stranahan took out the Smith .38 and returned it to Luis. The marine patrolman was relieved to see that it had not been fired.

Stranahan hoisted two of the duffel bags and hopped off the patrol boat.

From the dock he said, 'Take care, Chris.' He wanted to say more, but it was the wrong time. She was still fuming about last night, furious because he wouldn't tell her what had happened. She had kicked the coconut head off the scarecrow, that's how mad she had gotten. It was at that moment he'd asked her to marry him. Her reply had been succinct, to say the least.

Now she turned away coldly and said to Luis Córdova: 'Can we get going, please.'

Stranahan waved them off and trudged up the steps to inspect the looted house. The first thing he saw on the floor was the big marlin head; the tape on the fractured bill had been torn off in the fall. Stranahan stepped over the stuffed fish and went to the bedroom to check for the shotgun. It was still wedged up in the box spring where he had hidden it.

The whole place was a mess all right, depressing but not irreparable. Stranahan was glad, in a way, to have such a large chore ahead of him. Take his mind off Murdock and Salazar and Old Rhodes Key. And Christina Marks, too.

She was the first woman he had loved who had ever said no to marriage. It was quite a feeling.

Luis Córdova came back to the stilt house as Mick Stranahan was finishing lunch. There was a burly new passenger on the boat: Sergeant Al García.

Stranahan greeted them at the door and said, 'Two Cubans with guns is never good news.'

Luis Córdova said, 'Al is working the dead cops.'

'Cops plural?' Stranahan's eyebrows arched.

García sat down heavily on one of the barstools. 'Yeah, we found Johnny Murdock inside the boat. The boat was up in a frigging tree.'

'Where?' Stranahan asked impassively.

'Not far from where you and your lady friend went camping last night.' García patted his pockets and cursed. He was out of cigars. He took out a pack of Camels and lit one half-heartedly. He glanced up at the beakless marlin hanging from a new nail on the wall.

Luis Córdova said, 'I told Al about how I gave you a lift down to the island after your house got trashed.'

Stranahan wasn't upset. If asked, Luis would tell the truth about what he saw, what he knew for a fact. Most likely he had already told García about loaning the two detectives a map of the bay. Nothing strange about that.

'You hear anything funny last night?' Al García asked. 'By the way, where's the girl?'

'I don't know,' Stranahan said.

'What about last night?'

'A boat went by about eleven. Maybe a little later. Sounded like an outboard. What the hell happened, Al—somebody do these guys?'

García was puffing hard on the cigarette, and blowing circles of smoke, like he did with his stogies. 'Way it looks,' he said, 'they were going wide open. Missed the channel completely.'

'You said the boat was in a tree.'

'That's how fast the bozos were going. Way it looks, Salazar got thrown, hit his head. He drowned right away but the tide took him south.'

'Broad Creek,' Luis Córdova said. 'A mullet man found the body.'

García went on: 'Murdock stayed in the boat, but it didn't save him. We're talking major head trauma. The medical examiner thinks a mangrove branch or something snapped his neck. Same with Salazar. Figures it happened when they hit the trees.'

'Wide open?'

Luis Córdova said, 'The throttle was all the way down. You got to be nuts to run that creek wide open at night.'

'Or amazingly stupid,' Stranahan said. 'Let me guess who they were looking for.'

García nodded. 'You're on some roll, Mick. A regular archangel of death, you are. First your ex, now Murdock and Salazar. I'm noticing that bad things happen to people who fuck with you. Seems to be a pattern going way back.'

Stranahan said, 'I can't help it these jerks don't know how to drive a boat.'

Luis Córdova said, 'It was an accident, that's all.'

'I just find it interesting,' said Al García. 'Maybe the word is ironic, I don't know. Anyway, you're right, Mick. The two boys were coming to pay you a visit. They kept it real quiet around the shop, too. I can only guess why.' He reached in his jacket and took out a soggy white piece of paper. The paper was folded three times, pamphlet sized.

García showed it to Stranahan. 'We found this in Salazar's back pocket.'

Stranahan knew what it was. He'd seen a thousand just like it. The word *warrant* was still legible in the standard judicial calligraphy. As he handed it back to García, Stranahan wondered whether he was about to be arrested.

'What is this?' he asked.

'Garbage,' García replied. He crumpled the sodden document in his right hand and lobbed it out a window into the water.

Stranahan smiled. 'You liked the videotape.'

'Obviously,' said the detective.

At the Holiday Inn where they got a room, Maggie Gonzalez was going through the yellow pages column by column, telling Chemo which plastic surgeons were good enough to finish the dermabrasion treatments on his face; some of the names were new to her, but others she remembered from her nursing days. Chemo was stooped in front of the bathroom mirror, picking laconically at the patches left on his chin by Dr. Rudy Graveline.

Out of the side of his mouth, Chemo said, 'Fucker's not returning my calls.'

'It's early,' Maggie said. 'Rudy sleeps late on his day off.'

'I want to see some cash. Today.'

'Don't worry.'

'The sooner I get the money, the sooner I can take care of this.' Meaning his skin. In the mirror, Chemo could see Maggie's expression—at least, as much of it as the bandages revealed—and something that resembled genuine sympathy in her eyes. Not pity, sympathy.

She was the first woman who had ever looked at him that way. Certainly she seemed sincere about helping him find a new plastic surgeon. Chemo thought: She's either a truly devoted nurse or a sneaky little actress.

Maggie ripped a page of physicians from the phone book and said off-handedly, 'How much are we hitting him for?'

'A million dollars,' Chemo said. His sluglike lips quivered into a smile. 'You said he's loaded.'

'Yeah, he's also cheap.'

'A minute ago you said don't worry.'

'Oh, he'll pay. Rudy's cheap, but he's also a coward. All I'm saying is, he'll try to play coy at first. That's his style.'

'Coy?' Chemo thought: What in the fuck is she talking about? 'I wouldn't know about coy,' he said. 'I got a Weed Whacker strapped to my arm.'

Maggie said, 'Hey, I'm on your side. I'm just telling you, he can be stubborn when he wants.'

'You know what I think? I think you're in this for more than the money. I think you want to see a show.'

Maggie's brown eyes narrowed above the gauze. 'Don't be ridiculous.'

'Yeah,' Chemo said, 'I think you'd enjoy it if the boys got nasty with each other. I think you've got your heart set on blood.'

He was beaming as if he had just discovered the secret of the universe.

Dr. Rudy Graveline stared at the vaulted ceiling and contemplated his pitiable existence. Chemo had turned blackmailer. Maggie Gonzalez, the bitch, was still alive. So was Mick Stranahan. And somewhere out there a television crew was lurking, waiting to grill him about Victoria Barletta.

Aside from that, life was peachy.

When the phone rang, Rudy pulled the bedsheet up to his chin. He had a feeling it was more bad news.

'Answer it.' Heather Chappell's muffled command came from beneath a pillow. 'Answer the damn thing.'

Rudy reached out from the covers and seized the receiver fiercely, as if it were the neck of a cobra. The grim grassy voice on the other end of the line belonged to Commissioner Roberto Pepsical.

'You see the news on TV?'

'No,' Rudy said. 'But I got the paper here somewhere.'

'There's a story about two policemen who died.'

'Yeah, so?'

'In a boat accident,' Roberto said.

'Cut to the punch line, Bobby.'

'Those were the guys.'

'What guys?' asked Rudy. Next to him, Heather mumbled irritably and wrapped the pillow tightly around her ears.

'The guys I told you about. *My* guys.'

'Shit,' said Rudy.

Heather looked up raggedly and said: 'Do you mind? I'm trying to sleep.'

Rudy told Roberto that he would call him right back from another phone. He put on a robe and hurried down the hall to his den, where he shut the door. Numbly he dialed Roberto's private number, the one reserved for bagmen and lobbyists.

'Let me make sure I understand,' Rudy said. 'You were using police officers as hit men?'

'They promised it would be a cinch.'

'And now they're dead.' Rudy was well beyond the normal threshold of surprise. He had become conditioned to expect the worst. He said, 'What about the money—can I get it back?'

Roberto Pepsical couldn't believe the nerve of this cheapskate. 'No, you can't get it back. I paid them. They're dead. You want the money back, go ask their widows.'

The commissioner's tone had become impatient and firm. It made Rudy nervous; the fat pig should have been apologizing all over himself.

Rudy said, 'All right, then, can you get somebody else to do it?'

'Do what?'

'Do Stranahan. The offer's still open.'

Roberto laughed scornfully on the other end; Rudy was baffled by this change of attitude.

'Listen to me,' the commissioner said. 'The deal's off, forever. Two dead cops is major trouble, Doctor, and you just better hope nobody finds out what they were up to.'

Rudy Graveline wanted to drop the subject and crawl back to bed. 'Fine, Bobby,' he said. 'From now on, we never even met. Good-bye.'

'Not so fast.'

Oh brother, Rudy thought, here we go.

Roberto said, 'I talked to The Others. They still want the original twenty-five.'

'That's absurd. Cypress Towers is history, Bobby. I'm through with it. Tell your pals they get zippo.'

'But you got your zoning.'

'I don't need the damn zoning,' Rudy protested. 'They can have it back, understand? Peddle it to some other dupe.'

Roberto's voice carried no trace of understanding, no patience for a compromise. 'Twenty-five was the price of each vote. You agreed. Now The Others want their money.'

'Don't you ever get sick of being an errand boy?'

'It's my money, too,' Roberto said soberly. 'But yeah, I do get sick of being an errand boy. I get sick a dealing with cheap scuzzbuckets like you. When it comes to paying up, doctors are the fucking worst.'

'Hey,' Rudy said, 'it doesn't grow on trees.'

'A deal is a deal.'

In a way, Roberto was glad that Dr. Graveline was being such a prick. It felt good to be the one to drop the hammer for a change. He said, 'You got two business days to cover me and The Others.'

'What?' Rudy bleated.

'Two days, I'm calling my banker in the Caymans and having him read me the balance in my account. If it's not heavier by twenty-five, you're toast.'

Rudy thought: This can't be the same man, not the way he's talking to me.

Roberto Pepsical went on, detached, businesslike: 'Me and The Others got this idea that we—meaning the county—should start certifying all private surgical clinics. Have our own testing, license hearings, bi-monthly inspections, that sort of thing. It's our feeling that the general public needs to be protected.'

'Protected?' Rudy said feebly.

'From quacks and such. Don't you agree?'

Rudy thought: The whole world has turned upside down.

'Most clinics won't have anything to worry about,' Roberto said brightly, 'once they're brought up to county standards.'

'Bobby, you're a bastard.'

After Rudy Graveline slammed down the phone, his hand was shaking. It wouldn't stop.

At the breakfast table, Heather stared at Rudy's trembling fingers and said, 'I sure don't like the looks of that.'

'Muscle spasms,' he said. 'It'll go away.'

'My surgery is tomorrow,' Heather said.

'I'm aware of that, darling.'

They had spent the better part of the morning discussing breast implants. Heather had collected testimonials from all her Hollywood actress friends who ever had boob jobs. Some of them favored the Porex line of soft silicone implants, others liked the McGhan Biocell 100, and still others swore by the Replicon. Heather herself was leaning toward the Silastic II Teardrop model, because they came with a five-year written warranty.

'Maybe I better check with my agent,' she said.

'Why?' Rudy asked peevishly.

'This is my body we're talking about. My career.'

'All right,' Rudy said. 'Call your agent. What do I know? I'm just the surgeon.' He took the newspaper to the bathroom and sat down on the john. Ten minutes later, Heather knocked lightly on the door.

'It's too early on the coast,' she said. 'Melody's not in the office.'

'Thanks for the bulletin.'

'But a man called for you.'

Rudy folded the newspaper across his lap and braced his chin in his hands. 'Who was it, Heather?'

'He didn't give his name. Just said he was a patient.'

'That certainly narrows it down.'

'He said he came up with a number. I think he was talking about money.'

Crazy Chemo. It had to be. 'What did you tell him?' Rudy asked through the door.

'I told him you were unavailable at the moment. He didn't sound like he believed me.'

'Gee, I can't imagine,' said Rudy.

'He said he'll come by the clinic later.'

'Splendid.' He could hear her breathing at the door. 'Heather, is there something else?'

'Yes, there was a man out front. A process server from the courthouse.'

Rudy felt himself pucker at both ends.

Heather said, 'He rang the bell about a dozen times, but I wouldn't open the door. Finally he went away.'

'Good girl,' Rudy said. He sprang off the toilet, elated. He flung open the bathroom door, carried Heather into the shower, and turned on the water, steamy hot. Then he got down on his bare knees and began kissing her silky, perfect thighs.

'This is our last day,' she said in a whisper, 'before the operation.'

Rudy stopped kissing and looked up, the shower stream hitting him squarely in the nostrils. Through the droplets he could see the woman of his dreams squeezing her perfect breasts in her perfect hands. With a playful laugh, she said, 'Say so long to these little guys.'

God, Rudy thought, what am I doing? The irony was wicked. All the rich geezers and chunky bimbos he had conned into plastic surgery, patients with no chance of transforming their looks or improving their lives—now he finds one with a body and face that are absolutely flawless, perfect, classic, and she's begging for the knife.

A crime against nature, Rudy thought; and he, the instrument of that crime.

He stood up and made reckless love to Heather right there in the shower. She braced one foot on the bath faucet, the other on the soap dish, but Rudy was too lost in his own locomotions to appreciate the artistry of her balance.

The faster he went, the easier it was to concentrate. His mind emptied of Chemo and Roberto and Stranahan and Maggie. Before long Rudy Graveline was able to focus without distraction on his immediate crisis: the blond angel under the shower, and what she had planned for the next day.

Before long, an idea came to Rudy. It came to him with such brilliant ferocity that he mistook it for an orgasm.

Heather Chappell didn't particularly care what it was, as long as it was over. The hot water had run out, and she was freezing the orbs of her perfect bottom against the clammy bathroom tiles.

25

Mick Stranahan asked Al García to wait in the car while he went to see Kipper Garth. The law office was a chorus of beeping telephones as Stranahan made his way through the labyrinth of modular desks. The secretaries didn't bother to try to stop him. They could tell he wasn't a client.

Inside his personal sanctum, Kipper Garth sat in a familiar pose, waiting for an important call. He was tapping a Number 2 pencil and scowling at the speaker box. 'I did exactly what you wanted,' he said to Stranahan. 'See for yourself.'

The Nordstroms' malpractice complaint was clipped in a thin brown file on the corner of Kipper Garth's desk. He had been waiting all day for the moment to show his brother-in-law how well he had done. He handed Stranahan the file and said, 'Go ahead, it's all there.'

Stranahan remained standing while he read the lawsuit. 'This is very impressive,' he said, halfway down the second page. 'Maybe Katie's right, maybe you do have some genuine talent.'

Kipper Garth accepted the compliment with a cocky no-sweat shrug. Stranahan resisted the impulse to inquire which bright young paralegal had composed the document, since the author could not possibly be his brother-in-law.

'This really happened?' Stranahan asked. 'The man lost an eye to a . . .'

'Hooter,' Kipper Garth said. 'His wife's hooter, fortunately. Means we can automatically double the pain-and-suffering.'

Stranahan was trying to imagine a jury's reaction to such a mishap. The case would never get that far, but it was still fun to think about.

'Has Dr. Graveline been served?'

'Not yet,' Kipper Garth reported. 'He's ducked us so far, but that's fine. We've got a guy staking out the medical clinic, he'll grab him on the way in or out. The lawsuit's bad enough, but your man will go ape when he finds out we've got a depo scheduled already.'

'Excellent,' Stranahan said.

'He'll get it postponed, of course.'

'It doesn't matter. The whole idea is to keep the heat on. That's why I brought this.' Stranahan handed Kipper Garth a page of nine names, neatly typed.

'The witness list,' Stranahan explained. 'I want you to file it with the court as soon as possible.'

Skimming it, Kipper Garth said, 'This is highly unusual.'

'How would you know?'

'It *is*, dammit. Nobody gives up their witnesses so early in the case.'

'You do,' said Mick Stranahan. 'As of now.'

'I don't get it.'

'Heat, Jocko, remember? Send one of the clerks down to the courthouse and put this list in the Nordstrom file. You might even courier a copy over to Graveline's place, just for laughs.'

Kipper Garth noticed that all but one of the names on the witness list belonged to other doctors—specifically, plastic and reconstructive surgeons: experts who would presumably testify to Rudy Graveline's shocking incompetence in the post-op treatment of Mrs. Nordstrom's encapsulated breast implants.

'Not bad,' said Kipper Garth, 'but who's this one?' With a glossy fingernail he tapped the last name on the list.

'That's a former nurse,' Stranahan said.

'Disgruntled?'

'You might say that.'

'And about what,' said Kipper Garth, 'is she prepared to testify?'

'The defendant's competence,' Stranahan replied, 'or lack thereof.'

Kipper Garth stroked a chromium sideburn. 'Witness-wise, I think we're better off sticking with these hotshot surgeons.'

'Graveline won't give a shit about them. The nurse's name is what will get his attention. Trust me.'

With feigned authority, the lawyer remarked that testimony

from an embittered ex-employee wouldn't carry much weight in court.

'We're not going to court,' Stranahan reminded him. 'Not for malpractice, anyway. Maybe for a murder.'

'You're losing me again,' Kipper Garth admitted.

'Stay lost,' said Stranahan.

George Graveline's tree-trimming truck was parked off Crandon Boulevard in a lush tropical hammock. Buttonwoods, gumbo limbo, and mahogany trees—plenty of shade for George Graveline's truck. The county had hired him to rip out the old trees to make space for some tennis courts. Before long a restaurant would spring up next to the tennis courts and, after that, a major resort hotel. The people who would run the restaurant and the hotel would receive the use of the public property for practically nothing, thanks to their pals on the county commission. In return, the commissioners would receive a certain secret percentage of the refreshment concessions. And the voters would have brand-new tennis courts, whether they wanted them or not.

George Graveline's role in this civil endeavor was small, but he went at it with uncharacteristic zest. In the first two hours he and his men cleared two full acres of virgin woods. Afterwards George Graveline sat down in the truck cab to rest, while his workers tossed the uprooted trees one at a time into the automatic wood chipper.

All at once the noise died away. George Graveline opened his eyes. He could hear his foreman talking to an unfamiliar voice behind the truck. George stuck his head out the window and saw a stocky Cuban guy in a brown suit. The Cuban guy had a thick mustache and a fat unlit cigar in one corner of his mouth.

'What can I do for you?' George Graveline asked.

The Cuban guy reached in his coat and pulled out a gold police badge. As he walked up to the truck, he could see George Graveline's Adam's apple sliding up and down.

Al García introduced himself and said he wanted to ask a few questions.

George Graveline said, 'You got a warrant?'

The detective smiled. 'I don't need a warrant, *chico*.'

'You don't?'

García shook his head. 'Nope. Here, take a look at this.' He showed George Graveline the police composite of Blondell Wayne Tatum, the man known as Chemo. 'Ever see this bird before?'

'No, sir,' said the tree trimmer, but his expression gave it away. He looked away too quickly from the drawing; anyone else would have stared.

García said, 'This is a friend of your brother's.'

'I don't think so.'

'No?' García shifted the cigar to the other side of his mouth. 'Well, that's good to know. Because this man's a killer, and I can't think of one good reason why he'd be hanging out with a famous plastic surgeon.'

George Graveline said, 'Me neither.' He turned on the radio and twirled the tuner knob back and forth, pretending to look for his favorite country station. García could sense the guy was about to wet his pants.

The detective said, 'I'm not the first homicide man you ever met, am I?'

'Sure. What do you mean?'

'Hell, it was four years ago,' García said. 'You probably don't even remember. It was outside your brother's office, the place he had before he moved over to the beach.'

With a fat brown finger George Graveline scratched his neck. He scrunched his eyebrows, as if trying to recall.

García said: 'Detective's name was Timmy Gavigan. Skinny Irish guy, red hair, about so big. He stopped to chat with you for a couple minutes.'

'No, I surely don't remember,' George said, guardedly.

'I'll tell you exactly when it was—it was right after that college girl disappeared,' García said. 'Victoria Barletta was her name. Surely you remember. There must've been cops all over the place.'

'Oh yeah.' Slowly it was coming back to George; that's what he wanted the cop to think.

'She was one of your brother's patients, the Barletta girl.'

'Right,' said George Graveline, nodding. 'I remember how upset Rudolph was.'

'But you don't remember talking to Detective Gavigan?'

'I talked to lots of people.'

García said, 'The reason I mention it, Timmy remembered you.'

'Yeah, so?'

'You know, he never solved that damn case. The Barletta girl, after all these years. And now he's dead, Timmy is.' García stepped to the rear of the truck. Casually he put one foot on the bumper, near the hitch of the wood chipper. George Graveline opened the door of the truck and leaned out to keep an eye on the Cuban detective.

The two men were alone. George's workers had wandered off to find a cool place to eat lunch and smoke some weed; it was hard to unwind with a cop hanging around.

Curiously Al García bent over the wood chipper and peered at a decal on the engine mount. The decal was in the cartoon likeness of a friendly raccoon. 'Brush Bandit—is that the name of this mother?'

'That's right,' said George Graveline.

'How does it work exactly?'

George motioned sullenly. 'You throw the wood into that hole and it comes out here, in the back of the truck. All grinded up.'

García whistled over his cigar. 'Must be some nasty blade.'

'It's a big one, yessir.'

García took his foot off the truck bumper. He held up the drawing of Chemo one more time. 'You see this guy, I want you to call us right away.'

'Surely,' said George Graveline. The detective gave him a business card. The tree trimmer glanced at it, decided it was authentic, slipped it into the back pocket of his jeans.

'And warn your brother,' García said. 'Just in case the guy shows up.'

'You betcha,' said George Graveline.

Back in the unmarked county car, parked a half-mile down the boulevard at the Key Biscayne fire station, Mick Stranahan said: 'So how'd it go?'

'Just like we figured,' García replied. *'Nada.'*

'What do you think of Timmy's theory? About how they got rid of the body?'

'If the doctor really killed her then, yeah, it's possible. That's quite a machine brother George has got himself.'

Stranahan said, 'Too bad brother George won't flip.'

García rolled up the windows and turned on the air-conditioning to cool off. He knew what Stranahan was thinking and he was right: Brother George could blow the whole thing wide open. If Maggie were dead or gone, the videotape alone would not be enough for an indictment. They would definitely need George Graveline to talk about Vicky Barletta.

'I'm going for some fresh air,' Stranahan said. 'Why don't you meet me back here in about an hour?'

García said, 'Where the hell you off to?'

Stranahan got out of the car. 'For a walk, do you mind? Go get some coffee or flan or something.'

'Mick, don't do anything stupid. It's too nice a day for being stupid.'

'Hey, it's a lovely day.' Stranahan slammed the car door and crossed the boulevard at a trot.

'Shit,' García muttered. *'Mierda!'*

He drove down to the Oasis restaurant and ordered a cup of overpowering Cuban coffee. Then he ordered another.

George Graveline was still alone when Mick Stranahan got there. He was leaning against the truck fender, staring at his logger boots. He looked up at Stranahan, straightened, and said, 'You put that damn cop on my ass.'

'Good morning, George,' said Stranahan. 'It's certainly nice to see you again.'

'Fuck you, hear?'

'Are we having a bad day? What is it—cramps?'

George Graveline was one of those big, slow guys who squint when they get angry. He was squinting now. Methodically he clenched and unclenched his fists, as if he were practicing isometrics.

Stranahan said, 'George, I've still got that problem I told you about last time. Your brother's still got some goon trying to murder me. I'm really at the end of my rope.'

'You got that right.'

'My guess,' continued Stranahan, 'is that you and Rudy had a brotherly talk after last time. My guess is that you know exactly where I can locate this goony hit man.'

'Screw you,' said George Graveline. He kicked the switch on the wood chipper and the motor growled to life.

Stranahan said, 'Aw, what'd you do that for? How'm I supposed to hear you over all that damn racket?'

George Graveline lunged with both arms raised stiff in fury, a Frankenstein monster with Elvis jowls. He was clawing for Stranahan's neck. Stranahan ducked the grab and punched George Graveline hard under the heart. When the tree trimmer didn't fall, Stranahan punched him twice in the testicles. This time George went down.

Stranahan placed his right foot on the husky man's neck and applied the pressure slowly, shifting his weight from heel to toe. By reflex George's hands were riveted to his swollen scrotum. He was helpless to fight back. He made a noise like a tractor tire going flat.

'I can't believe you did that,' Stranahan muttered. 'Isn't it possible to have a civilized conversation in this town without somebody trying to kill you?'

It was a rhetorical question but George Graveline couldn't hear it over the wood chipper, anyway. Stranahan leaned over and shouted: 'Where's the goon?'

George did not answer promptly, so Stranahan added more weight on the Adam's apple. George was not squinting anymore; both eyes were quite large.

'Where is he?' Stranahan repeated.

When George's lips started moving, Stranahan let up. The voice that came out of the tree trimmer's mouth had a fuzzy electronic quality. Stranahan knelt to hear it.

'Works on the beach,' said George Graveline.

'Can we be more specific?'

'At a club.'

'What club, George? There's lots of nightclubs on Miami Beach.'

George blinked and said, 'Gay Bidet.' Now it was done, he thought. His brother Rudy was a goner.

'Thank you, George,' said Stranahan. He removed his shoe from the tree trimmer's throat. 'This is a good start. I'm very encouraged. Now let's talk about Vicky Barletta.'

George Graveline lay there with his head in the moist dirt, his groin throbbing. He lay there worrying about his brother the doctor, about what horrible things would happen to him all because of George's big mouth. Rudy had confided in him, trusted him, and now George had let his brother down. Lying there dejectedly, he decided that no matter how much pain was inflicted upon him, he wasn't going to tell Mick Stranahan what had happened to that college girl. Rudy had made a mistake, everybody makes mistakes. Why, one time George himself got a work order mixed up and cut down a whole row of fifty-foot royal palms, when it was mangy old Brazilians he was supposed to chop. Still, they didn't put him in jail or anything, just made him pay a fine. Hundred bucks a tree, something like that. Why should a doctor be treated any different? As he reflected upon Rudy's turbulent medical career, George Graveline removed one of his hands from his swollen scrotum. The free hand happened to settle on a hunk of fresh-cut mahogany concealed by his left leg. The wood was heavy, the bark coarse and dry. George closed his fingers around it. It felt pretty good.

Still kneeling, Mick Stranahan nudged George Graveline's shoulder and said, 'Penny for your thoughts.'

And George hit him square on the back of the skull.

Stranahan didn't see the blow, and at first he thought he'd been shot. He heard a man shouting and what sounded like an ambulance. The rescue scene played vividly in his imagination. He waited to feel the paramedics' hands ripping open his shirt. He waited for the cold clap of the stethoscope on his chest, for the sting of the I.V. needle in his arm. He waited for the childlike sensation of being lifted onto the stretcher.

None of this came, yet the sound of the ambulance siren would not go away. In his crashing sleep, Stranahan grew angry. Where were the goddamn EMTs? A man's been shot here!

Then, blessedly, he felt someone lifting him. Lifting him under the arms, someone strong. It hurt, oh, God, how it hurt, but that was all right—at least they had come. But then he was falling again, falling or dying, he couldn't be sure. And in his crashing sleep he heard the moan of the siren rise to such a pitch that he wanted to cover his ears and scream for it to stop, please God.

And it did stop.

Somebody shut off the wood chipper.

Stranahan awoke to the odd hollow silence that follows a sharp echo. His eardrums fluttered. The air smelled pungently of cordite. He found himself on his knees, weaving, a drunk waiting for communion. His shirt was damp, his pulse rabbity. He checked himself and saw he was mistaken, he hadn't been shot. There was no ambulance, either, just the tree truck.

Al García sat on the bumper. His gun was in his right hand, which hung heavily at his side. He was as pale as a flounder.

There was no sign of George Graveline anywhere.

'You all right?' Stranahan asked.

'No,' said the detective.

'Where's the tree man?'

With the gun García pointed toward the bin of the tree truck, where the wood chipper had spit what bone and jelly was left of George Graveline.

After he had tried to feed Mick Stranahan into the maw.

And Al García had shot him twice in the back.

And the impact of the bullets had slammed him face-forward down the throat of the tree-eating machine.

26

Chemo got the Bonneville out of the garage and drove out to Whispering Palms, but the receptionist said that Dr. Graveline wasn't there. Noticing the dramatic topography of Chemo's face, the receptionist told him she could try the doctor at home for an emergency. Chemo said thanks, anyway.

After leaving the clinic, he walked around to the side of the building where the employees parked. Dr. Graveline's spiffy new Jaguar XJ–6 was parked in its space. This was the Jaguar that the doctor had purchased immediately after Mick Stranahan had blown up his other one. The sedan was a rich shade of red; candy apple, Chemo guessed, though the Jaguar people probably had a fancier name for it. The windows of the car were tinted gray so that you couldn't see inside. Chemo assumed that Dr. Graveline had a burglar alarm wired on the thing, so he was careful not to touch the doors or the hood.

He ambled to the rear of the clinic, by the water, and peeked through the bay window into Rudy's private office. There was the doctor, yakking on the phone. Chemo was annoyed; it was rude of Graveline to be ducking him this way. Rude, hell. It was just plain stupid.

When Chemo turned the corner of the building, he saw a short man in an ill-fitting gray suit standing next to Rudy's car. The man wore dull brown shoes and black-rimmed eyeglasses. He looked to be in his mid-fifties. Chemo walked up to him and said, 'Are you looking for Graveline?'

The man in the black-rimmed glasses appraised Chemo skittishly and said, 'Are you him?'

'Fuck no. But this is his car.'

'They told me he wasn't here.'

'They lied,' Chemo said. 'Hard to believe, isn't it?'

The man opened a brown billfold to reveal a cheap-looking badge. 'I work for the county,' he said. 'I'm trying to serve some papers on the doctor. I been trying two, three days.'

Chemo said, 'See that side door? You wait there, he'll be out soon. It's almost five o'clock.'

'Thanks,' said the process server. He went over and stood, idiotically, by the side entrance to the clinic. He clutched the court papers rolled up in one hand, as if he were going to sap the doctor when he came out.

Chemo slipped the calfskin sheath off the Weed Whacker and turned his attention to Rudy's new Jaguar. He chose as his starting place the left front fender.

Initially it was slow going—those British sure knew how to paint an automobile. At first the Weed Whacker inflicted only pale stripes on the deep red enamel. Chemo tried lowering the device closer to the fender and bracing it in position with his good arm. It took fifteen minutes for the powerful lawn cutter to work its way down to the base steel of the sedan. Chemo moved its buzzing head back and forth in a sweeping motion to enlarge the scar.

From his waiting post outside the clinic door, the process server watched the odd ceremony with rapt fascination. Finally he could stand it no longer, and shouted at Chemo.

Chemo turned away from the Jaguar and looked at the man in the black-rimmed glasses. He flicked the toggle switch to turn off the Weed Whacker, then cupped his right hand to his ear.

The man said, 'What are you doing with that thing?'

'Therapy,' Chemo answered. 'Doctor's orders.'

Like many surgeons, Dr. Rudy Graveline was a compulsive man, supremely organized but hopelessly anal retentive. The day after the disturbing phone call from Commissioner Roberto Pepsical, Rudy meticulously wrote out a list of all his career-threatening problems. By virtue of the scope of his extortion, Roberto Pepsical was promoted to the number three spot, behind Mick Stranahan and Chemo. Rudy studied the list closely. In the larger context of a possible murder indictment, Roberto Pepsical was chickenshit. Expensive chickenshit, but chickenshit just the same.

Rudy Graveline dialed the number in New Jersey and waited for Curly Eyebrows to come on the line.

'Jeez, I told you not to call me here. Let me get to a better phone.' The man hung up, and Rudy waited. Ten minutes later the man called back.

'Lemme guess, your problem's got worse.'

'Yes,' said Rudy.

'That local talent you hired, he wasn't by himself after all.'

'He was,' Rudy said, 'but not now.'

'That's pretty funny.' Curly Eyebrows laughed flatulently. Somewhere in the background a car blasted its horn. The man said, 'You rich guys are something else. Always trying to do it on the cheap.'

'Well, I need another favor,' Rudy said.

'Such as what?'

'Remember the hunting accident a few years ago?'

Curly Eyebrows said, 'Sure. That doctor. The one was giving you a hard time.'

The man in New Jersey didn't remember the name of the dead doctor, but Rudy Graveline certainly did. It was Kenneth Greer, one of his former partners at the Durkos Center. The one who figured out what had happened to Victoria Barletta. The one who was trying to blackmail him.

'That was a cinch,' said Curly Eyebrows. 'I wish they all could be hunters. Every deer season we could clean up the Gambinos that way. Hunting accidents.'

The man in New Jersey had an itch—on the line Rudy Graveline heard the disgusting sound of fat fingers scratching hairy flesh. He tried not to think about it.

'Somebody new is giving me a hard time,' the doctor said. 'I don't know if you can help, but I thought I'd give it a shot.'

'I'm listening.'

'It's the Dade County Commission,' Rudy said. 'I need somebody to kill them. Can you arrange it?'

'Wait a minute—'

'All of them,' Rudy said, evenly.

'Excuse me, Doc, but you're fucking crazy. Don't call me no more.'

'Please,' Rudy said. 'Five of them are shaking me down for twenty-five grand each. The trouble is, I don't know which five. So my idea is to kill all nine.'

Curly Eyebrows grunted. 'You got me confused.'

Patiently Rudy explained how the bribe system worked, how each commissioner arranged for four crooked colleagues to go along on each controversial vote. Rudy told the man in New Jersey about the Old Cypress Towers project, about how the commissioners were trying to pinch him for the zoning decision he no longer needed.

'Hey, a deal is a deal,' Curly Eyebrows said unsympathetically. 'Seems to me you got yourself in a tight situation.' Now it sounded like he was picking his teeth with a comb.

Rudy said, 'You won't help?'

'Won't. Can't. Wouldn't.' The man coughed violently, then spit. 'Much as the idea appeals to me personally—killing off an entire county commission—it'd be bad for business.'

'It was just an idea,' Rudy said. 'I'm sorry I bothered you.'

'Want some free advice?'

'Why not.'

Curly Eyebrows said, 'Who's the point man in this deal? You gotta know his name, at least.'

'I do.'

'Good. I suggest something happens to the bastard. Something awful bad. This could be a lesson to the other eight pricks, you understand?'

Rudy Graveline said yes, he understood.

'Trust me,' said the man in New Jersey. 'I been in this end of it for a long time. Sort of thing makes an impression, especially dealing with your mayors and aldermen and those types. These are not exactly tough guys.'

'I suppose not.' Rudy cleared his throat. 'Listen, that's a very good idea. Just do one of them.'

'That's my advice,' said the man in New Jersey.

'Could you arrange it?'

'Shit. I ain't risking my boys on some lowlife county pol. No way. Talent's too hard to come by these days—you found that out yourself.'

Rudy recalled the newspaper story about Tony the Eel, washed up dead on the Cape Florida beach. 'I still feel bad about that fellow last month,' the doctor said.

'Hey, it happens.'

'But still,' said Rudy morosely.

'You ought to get out of Florida,' advised Curly Eyebrows. 'I been telling all my friends, it's not like the old days. Fuck the pretty beaches, Doc, them Cubans are crazy. They're not like you and me. And then there's the Jews and the Haitians, Christ!'

'Times change,' said Rudy.

'I was reading up on it, some article about stress. Florida is like the worst fucking place in America for stressing out, besides Vegas. I'm not making this up.'

Dispiritedly, Rudy Graveline said, 'It seems like everybody wants a piece of my hide.'

'Ain't it the fucking truth.'

'I swear, I'm not a violent person by nature.'

'Costa Rica,' said the man in New Jersey. 'Think about it.'

Commissioner Roberto Pepsical got to the church fifteen minutes early and scouted the aisles: a bag lady snoozing on the third pew, but that was it. To kill time Roberto lit a whole row of devotional candles. Afterwards he fished through his pocket change and dropped a Canadian dime in the coin box.

When the doctor arrived, Roberto waddled briskly to the back of the church. Rudy Graveline was wearing a tan sports jacket and dark, loose-fitting pants and a brown striped necktie. He looked about as calm as a rat in a snake hole. In his right hand was a black Samsonite suitcase. Wordlessly Roberto brushed past him and entered one of the dark confessionals. Rudy waited about three minutes, checked over both shoulders, opened the door, and went in.

'God,' he exclaimed.

'He's here somewhere.' The commissioner chuckled at his own joke. Rudy had never been inside a confession booth before. It was smaller and gloomier than he had imagined; the only light was a tiny amber bulb plugged into a wall socket.

Roberto had planted his fat ass on the kneeling cushion with his back to the screen. Rudy checked to make sure there wasn't a priest on the other side, listening. Priests could be awful quiet when they wanted.

'Remember,' the commissioner said, raising a finger. 'Whisper.'

Right, Rudy thought, like I was going to belt out a Gershwin tune. 'Of all the screwy places to do this,' he said.

'It's quiet,' Roberto Pepsical said. 'And very safe.'

'And very small,' Rudy added. 'You had anchovies for dinner, didn't you?'

'There are no secrets here,' said Roberto.

With difficulty, Rudy wedged himself and the Samsonite next to the commissioner on the kneeling bench. Roberto's body heat bathed both of them in a warm acrid fog, and Rudy wondered how long the oxygen would hold out. He had never heard of anyone suffocating in confession; on the other hand, that was exactly the sort of incident the Catholics would cover up.

'You ready?' Roberto asked with a wink. 'What's that in your pocket?'

'Unfortunately, that's a subpoena. Some creep got me on the way out of the clinic tonight.' Rudy had been in such a hurry that he hadn't even looked at the court papers; he was somewhat accustomed to getting sued.

Roberto said, 'No wonder you're in such a lousy mood.'

'It's not that so much as what happened to my new car. It got vandalized—actually, scoured is the word for it.'

'The Jag? That's terrible.'

'Oh, it's been a splendid day,' Rudy said. 'Absolutely splendid.'

'Getting back to the money . . .'

'I've got it right here.' The doctor opened the suitcase across both their laps, and the confessional was filled with the sharp scent of new money. Rudy Graveline was overwhelmed—it really did *smell*. Roberto picked up a brick of hundred-dollar bills. 'I thought I said twenties.'

'Yeah, and I would've needed a bloody U-Haul.'

Roberto Pepsical snapped off the bank wrapper and counted out ten thousand dollars on the floor between his feet. Then he added up the other bundles in the suitcase to make sure the total came to one twenty-five.

Grinning, he held up one of the loose hundreds. 'I don't see many of these. Whose picture is that—Eisenhower's?'

'No,' said Rudy, stonily.

'What'd the bank say? About you taking all these big bills.'

'Nothing,' Rudy said. 'This is Miami, Bobby.'

'Yeah, I guess.' Ebulliently the commissioner restacked the cash bundles and packed them in the Samsonite. He scooped up the loose ten thousand dollars and shoved the thick wad into the pockets of his suit. 'This was a smart thing you did.'

Rudy said, 'I'm not so sure.'

'You know that plan I told you about . . . about licensing the medical clinics and all that? Me and The Others, we decided to drop the whole thing. We figure that doctors like you got enough rules and regulations as it is.'

'Glad to hear it,' said Rudy Graveline. He wished he had brought some Certs. Roberto could use a whole roll.

'How about a drink?' the commissioner asked. 'We could stop at the Versailles, get a couple pitchers a sangría.'

'Yum.'

'Hey, it's my treat.'

'Thanks,' said the doctor, 'but first you know what I'd like to do? I'd like to say a prayer. I'd like to thank the Lord that this problem with Cypress Towers is finally over.'

Roberto shrugged. 'Go ahead.'

'Is it all right, Bobby? I mean, since I'm not Catholic.'

'No problem.' The commissioner grunted to his feet, turned around in the booth and got to his knees. The cushion squeaked under his weight. 'Do like this,' he said.

Rudy Graveline, who was slimmer, had an easier time with the turnaround maneuver. With the suitcase propped between them, the two men knelt side by side, facing the grated screen through which confessions were heard.

'So pray,' Roberto Pepsical said. 'I'll wait till you're done. Fact,

I might even do a couple Hail Marys myself, long as I'm here.'

Rudy shut his eyes, bowed his head, and pretended to say a prayer.

Roberto nudged him. 'I don't mean to tell you what to do,' he said, 'but in here it's not proper to pray with your hands in your pockets.'

'Of course,' said Rudy, 'I'm sorry.'

He took his right hand from his pants and placed it on Roberto's doughy shoulder. It was too dark for the commissioner to see the hypodermic syringe.

'Hail Mary,' Roberto said, 'full of grace, the Lord is with thee. Blessed ar—ow!'

The commissioner pawed helplessly at the needle sticking from his jacket at the crook of the elbow. Considering Rudy's general clumsiness with injections, it was a minor miracle that he hit the commissioner's antecubital vein on the first try. Roberto Pepsical hugged the doctor desperately, a panting bear, but already the deadly potassium was streaming toward the valves of his fat clotty heart.

Within a minute the seizure killed him, mimicking the symptoms of a routine infarction so perfectly that the commissioner's relatives would never challenge the autopsy.

Rudy removed the spent syringe, retrieved the loose cash from Roberto's pocket, picked up the black suitcase, and slipped out of the stuffy confessional. The air in the church seemed positively alpine, and he paused to breathe it deeply.

In the back row, an elderly Cuban couple turned at the sound of his footsteps on the terrazzo. Rudy nodded solemnly. He hoped they didn't notice how badly his legs were shaking. He faced the altar and tried to smile like a man whose soul had been cleansed of all sin.

The old Cuban woman raised a bent finger to her forehead and made the sign of the cross. Rudy worried about Catholic protocol and wondered if he was expected to reply. He didn't know how to make the sign of the cross, but he put down the suitcase and gave it a gallant try. With a forefinger he touched his brow, his breast, his right shoulder, his left shoulder, his navel, then his brow again.

'Live long and prosper,' he said to the old woman and walked out the doors of the church.

When he got home, Rudy Graveline went upstairs to see Heather Chappell. He sat next to the bed and took her hand. She blinked moistly over the edge of the bandages.

Rudy kissed her knuckles and said, 'How are you feeling?'

'I don't know about you,' Heather said, 'but I'm feeling a hundred years old.'

'That's to be expected. You had quite a day.'

'You sure it went okay?'

'Beautifully,' Rudy said.

'The nose, too?'

'A masterpiece.'

'But I don't remember a thing.'

The reason Heather couldn't remember the surgery was because there had been no surgery. Rudy had drugged her copiously the night before and kept her drugged the whole day. Heather had lain unconscious for seven hours, whacked out on world-class pharmaceutical narcotics. By the time she awoke, she felt like she'd been sleeping for a month. Her hips, her breasts, her neck, and her nose were all snugly and expertly bandaged, but no scalpel had touched her fine California flesh. Rudy hoped to persuade Heather that the surgery was a glowing success; the absence of scars, a testament to his wizardry. Obviously he had weeks of bogus post-operative counseling ahead of him.

'Can I see the video?' she asked from the bed.

'Later,' Rudy promised. 'When you're up to snuff.'

He had ordered (by FedEx) a series of surgical training cassettes from a medical school in California. Now it was simply a matter of editing the tapes into a plausible sequence. Gowned, masked, and anesthetized on the operating table, all patients looked pretty much alike to a camera. Meanwhile, all you ever saw of the surgeon was his gloved hands; Heather would never know that the doctor on the videotape was not her lover.

She said, 'It's incredible, Rudolph, but I don't feel any pain.'

'It's the medication,' he said. 'The first few days, we keep you pretty high.'

Heather giggled. 'Eight miles high?'

'Nine,' said Rudy Graveline, 'at least.'

He tucked her hand beneath the sheets and picked up something from the bedstand. 'Look what I've got.'

She squinted through the fuzz of the drugs. 'Red and blue and white,' she said dreamily.

'Plane tickets,' Rudy said. 'I'm taking you on a trip.'

'Really?'

'To Costa Rica. The climate is ideal for your recovery.'

'For how long?'

Rudy said, 'A month or two, maybe longer. As long as it takes, darling.'

'But I'm supposed to do a *Password* with Jack Klugman.'

'Out of the question,' said Rudy. 'You're in no condition for that type of stress. Now get some sleep.'

'What's that noise?' she asked, lifting her head.

'The doorbell, sweetheart. Lie still now.'

'Costa Rica,' Heather murmured. 'Where's that, anyhow?'

Rudy kissed her on the forehead and told her he loved her.

'Yeah,' she said. 'I know.'

Whoever was at the door was punching the button like it was a jukebox. Rudy hurried down the stairs and checked through the glass peephole.

Chemo signaled mirthlessly back at him.

'Shit.' Rudy sighed, thought of his Jaguar, and opened the door.

'Why did you destroy my car?'

'Teach you some manners,' Chemo said. Another bandaged woman stood at his side.

'Maggie?' Rudy Graveline said. 'Is that you?'

Chemo led her by the hand into the big house. He found the living room and made himself comfortable in an antique rocking chair. Maggie Gonzalez sat on a white leather sofa. Her eyes, which were Rudy's only clue to her mood, seemed cold and hostile.

Chemo said, 'Getting jerked around is not my favorite thing. I ought to just kill you.'

'What good would that do?' Rudy said. He stepped closer to Maggie and asked, 'Who did your face?'

'Leaper,' she said.

'Leonard Leaper? Up in New York? I heard he's good—mind if I look?'

'Yes,' she said, recoiling. 'Rogelio, make him get away!'

'Rogelio?' Rudy looked quizzically at Chemo.

'It's your fucking fault,' he said. 'That's the name you put on the tickets. Now leave her alone.' Chemo stopped rocking. He eyed Rudy Graveline as if he were a palmetto bug.

The surgeon sat near Maggie on the white leather sofa and said to Chemo, 'So how're the dermabrasions healing?'

Self-consciously the killer's hand went to his chin. 'All of a sudden you're concerned about my face. Now that you're afraid.'

'Well, you look good,' Rudy persisted. 'Really, it's a thousand percent improvement.'

'Jesus H. Christ.'

Irritably Maggie said, 'Let's get to the point, okay? I want to get out of here.'

'The money,' Chemo said to the doctor. 'We decided on one million, even.'

'For what!' Rudy was trying to stay cool, but his tone was trenchant.

Chemo started rocking again. 'For everything,' he said. 'For Maggie's videotape. For Stranahan. For stopping that TV show about the dead girl. That's worth a million dollars. In fact, the more I think about it, I'd say it's worth two.'

Rudy folded his arms and said, 'You do everything you just said, and I'll gladly give you a million dollars. As of now, you get nothing but expenses because you haven't done a damn thing but stir up trouble.'

'That's not true,' Maggie snapped.

'We've been busy,' Chemo added. 'We got a big surprise.'

Rudy said, 'I've got a big surprise, too. A malpractice suit. And guess whose name is on the witness list?'

He jerked an accusing thumb at Maggie, who said, 'That's news to me.'

Rudy went on, 'Some fellow named Nordstrom. Lost his eye in some freak accident and now it's all my fault.'

Maggie said, 'I never heard of a Nordstrom.'

'Well, your name is right there in the file. Witness for the plaintiff. Why should I pay you people a dime?'

'All the more reason,' Chemo said. 'I believe its called hush money.'

'No,' said the doctor, 'that's not the way it goes.'

Chemo stood up from the rocker. He took two large steps across the living room and punched Rudy Graveline solidly in the gut. The doctor collapsed in a gagging heap on the Persian carpet. Chemo turned him over with one foot. Then he cranked up the Weed Whacker.

'Oh God,' cried Rudy, raising his hand to shield his eyes. Quickly Maggie moved out of the way, her facial bandages crinkled in trepidation.

'I got a new battery,' Chemo said. 'A Die-Hard. Watch this.'

He started weed-whacking Rudy's fine clothes. First he shredded the shirt and tie, then he tried trimming the curly brown hair on Rudy's chest. The doctor yelped pitiably as nasty pink striations appeared beneath his nipples.

Chemo was working the machine towards Rudy's pubic zone when he spied something inside the tattered lining of the surgeon's tan coat. He turned off the Weed Whacker and leaned down for a closer look.

With his good hand Chemo reached into the silky entrails of Rudy's jacket and retrieved the severed corner of a one-hundred-dollar bill. Excitedly he probed around until he found more: handfuls, blessedly unshredded.

Chemo spread the money on the coffee table, beneath which Rudy thrashed and moaned impotently. The stricken surgeon observed the accounting firsthand, gazing up through the frosted glass. As the cash grew to cover the table, Rudy's face hardened into a mask of abject disbelief. On his way back from the church he had meant to stop at the clinic and return the money to the drop safe. Now it was too late.

'Count it,' Chemo said to Maggie.

Excitedly she riffled through the bills. 'Nine thousand two hundred,' she reported. 'The rest is all chopped up.'

Chemo dragged Dr. Graveline from under the coffee table. 'Why you carrying this much cash?' he said. 'Don't tell me the Jag dealer won't take credit cards.' His moist salamander eyes settled on the black Samsonite, which Rudy had stupidly left in the middle of the hallway.

Rudy sniffled miserably as he watched Chemo kick open the suitcase and crouch down to count the rest of the money. 'Well, well,' said the killer.

'What are you going to do with it?' the doctor asked.

'Gee, I think we'll give it to the United Way. Or maybe Jerry's kids.' Chemo walked over to Rudy and poked his bare belly with the warm head of the Weed Whacker. 'What the hell you think we're going to do with it? We're gonna spend it, and then we're gonna come back for more.'

After they had gone, Dr. Rudy Graveline sprawled on the rumpled Persian carpet for a long time, thinking: This is what a Harvard education has gotten me—extorted, beaten, stripped, scandalized, and chopped up like an artichoke. The doctor's fingers gingerly explored the tumescent stripes that crisscrossed his chest and abdomen. If it didn't sting so much, the sight would be almost comical.

It occurred to Rudy Graveline that Chemo and Maggie had forgotten to tell him their big secret, whatever it was they had done, whatever spectacular felony they had committed to earn this first garnishment.

And it occurred to Rudy that he wasn't all that curious. In fact, he was somewhat relieved not to know.

27

The man from the medical examiner's office took one look in the back of the tree truck and said: 'Mmmm, lasagna.'

'That's very funny,' said Al García. 'You oughta go on the Carson show. Do a whole routine on stiffs.'

The man from the medical examiner's office said, 'Al, you gotta admit—'

'I told you what happened.'

'—but you gotta admit, there's a humorous aspect.'

Coroners made Al García jumpy; they always got so cheery when somebody came up with a fresh way to die.

The detective said, 'If you think it's funny, fine. You're the one's gotta do the autopsy.'

'First I'll need a casserole dish.'

'Hilarious,' said García. 'Absolutely hilarious.'

The man from the medical examiner's office told him to lighten up, said everybody needs a break in the monotony, no matter what line of work. 'I get tired of gunshot wounds,' the coroner said. 'It's like a damn assembly line down there. GSW head, GSW thorax, GSW neck—it gets old, Al.'

García said, 'Listen, go ahead, make your jokes. But I need you to keep this one outta the papers.'

'Good luck.'

The detective knew it wouldn't be easy to keep the lid on George Graveline's death. Seven squad cars, an ambulance, and a body wagon—even in Miami, that'll draw a crowd. The gawkers were being held behind yellow police ribbons strung along Crandon Boulevard. Soon the minicams would arrive, and the minicams could zoom in for close-ups.

'I need a day or two,' García said. 'No press, and no next of kin.'

The man from the medical examiner shrugged. 'It'll take at least that long to make the I.D., considering what's left. I figure we'll have to go dental.'

'Whatever.'

'I'll need to impound the truck,' the coroner said. 'And this fancy toothpick machine.'

García said he would have them both towed downtown.

The coroner stuck his head into the maw of the wood chipper and examined the blood-smeared blades. 'There ought to be bullet fragments,' he said, 'somewhere in this mess.'

García said, 'Hey, Sherlock, I told you what happened. I shot the asshole, okay? My gun, my bullets.'

'Al, don't take all the fun out of it.' The man from the medical examiner reached into the blades of the wood chipper and carefully plucked out an item that the untrained eye would have misidentified as a common black woolly-bear caterpillar.

The coroner held it up for Al García to see.

The detective frowned. 'What, do I get a prize or something? It's a sideburn, for Chrissakes.'

'Very good,' said the coroner.

García flicked the soggy nub of his cigar into the bushes and went looking for George Graveline's crew of tree trimmers. There were three of them sitting somberly in the back seat of a county patrol car. Al García got in front, on the passenger side. He turned around and spoke to them through the cage. The men's clothes smelled like pot. García asked if any of them had seen what had happened, and to a one they answered no, they'd been on their lunch break. The officers from Internal Review had asked the same thing.

'If you didn't see anything,' García said, 'then you don't have much to tell the reporters, right?'

In unison the tree trimmers shook their heads.

'Including the name of the alleged victim, right?'

The tree trimmers agreed.

'This is damned serious,' said García. 'I don't believe you boys would purposely obstruct a homicide investigation, would you?'

The tree trimmers promised not to say a word to the media. Al

García asked a uniformed cop to give the men a lift home, so they wouldn't have to walk past the minicams on their way to the bus stop.

By this time, the ambulance was backing out, empty. García knocked on the driver's window. 'Where's the guy you were working on?'

'Blunt head wound?'

'Right. Big blond guy.'

'Took off,' said the ambulance driver. 'Gobbled three Darvocets and said so long. Wouldn't even let us wrap him.'

García cursed and bearishly swatted at a fresh-cut button-wood branch.

The ambulance driver said, 'You see him, be sure and tell him he oughta go get a skull X-ray.'

'You know what you'd find?' García said. 'Shit for brains, that's what.'

Reynaldo Flemm picked up an attractive young woman at a nightclub called Biscayne Baby in Coconut Grove. He took her to his room at the Grand Bay Hotel and asked her to wait while he ran the water in the Roman tub. Still insecure about his impugned physique, Reynaldo didn't want the young woman to see him naked in the bright light. He lowered himself into the bath, covered the vital areas with suds, double-checked himself in the mirrors, then called for the young woman to join him. She came in the bathroom, stripped, and climbed casually into the deep tub. When Reynaldo tickled her armpits with his toes, the young woman politely pushed his legs away.

'So, what do you do?' he asked.

'I told you, I'm a legal secretary.'

'Oh, yeah.' When Reynaldo got semi-blitzed on screwdrivers, his short-term memory tended to vapor-lock. 'You probably recognize me,' he said to the young woman.

'I told you already—no.'

Reynaldo said, 'Normally my hair's black. I colored it this way for a reason.'

He had revived the Johnny Le Tigre go-go dancer disguise for his confrontation with Dr. Rudy Graveline. He had dyed his hair brown and slicked it straight back with a wet comb. He looked like a Mediterranean sponge diver.

'Imagine me with black hair,' he said to the legal secretary, who flicked a soap bubble off her nose and said no, she still wouldn't recognize him.

He said, 'You get TV, right? I'm Reynaldo Flemm.'

'Yeah?'

'From *In Your Face*.'

'Oh, sure.'

'Ever seen it?'

'No,' said the secretary, 'but I don't watch all that much television.' She was trying to be nice. 'I think I've seen your commercials,' she said.

Flemm shrunk lower in the tub.

'Is it, like, a game show?' the woman asked.

'No, it's a news show. I'm an investigative reporter.'

'Like that guy on *Sixty Minutes*?'

Reynaldo bowed his head. Feeling guilty, the secretary slid across the tub and climbed on his lap. She said, 'Hey, I believe you.'

'Thanks a bunch.'

She felt a little sorry for him; he seemed so small and wounded among the bubbles. She said, 'You certainly look like you could be on television.'

'I *am* on fucking television. I've got my own show.'

The woman said, 'Okay, whatever.'

'I could loan you a tape—you got a VCR?'

The secretary told him to hush. She put her lips to his ear and said, 'Why don't we try it right here?'

Reynaldo half-heartedly slipped one arm around her waist and began kissing her breasts. They were perfectly lovely breasts, but Reynaldo's heart wasn't in it. After a few moments the woman said, 'You're not really in the mood, huh?'

'I *was*.'

'I'm sorry. Here, let me do your back.'

Reynaldo's buttocks squeaked as he turned around in the tub

so the secretary could scrub him. He watched her in the mirror; her hands felt wondrously soothing. Eventually he closed his eyes.

'There you go,' she said, kneading his shoulder blades. 'My great big TV star.'

Reynaldo found he was getting excited again. He touched himself underwater, just to make sure. He was smiling until he opened his eyes and saw something new in the mirror.

A man standing in the doorway. The man with the tarpon gaff.

'Sorry to interrupt,' said Mick Stranahan.

The woman squealed and dove for a towel. Reynaldo Flemm groped for floating suds to cover his withering erection.

'I was looking for Christina,' Stranahan said. He walked up to the Roman tub with the gaff held under one arm, like a riding crop. 'She's not in her hotel room.'

'How'd you find me?' Reynaldo's voice was reedy and taut, definitely not an anchorman's voice.

'Miami is not one of the world's all-time great hotel towns,' Stranahan said. 'Hotshot celebrities like you always end up in the Grove. But tell me: Why's Christina still registered out at Key Biscayne?'

Nervously the secretary said, 'Who's Christina?'

Stranahan said: 'Ray, I asked you a question.' He poked the fish gaff under the suds and scraped the point across the bottom of the tub. The steel screeched ominously against the ceramic. Reynaldo Flemm drew up his knees and sloshed protectively into a corner.

'Chris doesn't know I'm here,' he said. 'I ditched her.'

Stranahan told the legal secretary to get dressed and go home. He waited until she was gone from the bathroom before he spoke again.

'I checked Christina's room at the Sonesta. She hasn't been there for two days.'

Reynaldo said, 'What're you going to do to me?' He couldn't take his eyes off the tarpon gaff. Wrapping his arms around his knees, he said, 'Don't hurt me.'

'For Christ's sake.'

'I mean it!'

'Are you crying?' Stranahan couldn't believe it—another dumb twit overreacting. 'Just tell me about Christina. Her notebooks were still in the room, and so was her purse. Any ideas?'

'Uuunnngggh.' The pink of Flemm's tongue showed between his front teeth. It was a cowering, poodle-like expression, amplified by trembling lips and liquid eyes.

'Settle down,' said Stranahan. His head felt like it was full of wet cement. The Darvocets had barely put a ripple in the pain. What a shitty day.

He said, 'You haven't seen her?'

Violently Reynaldo shook his head no.

They heard a door slam—the secretary, making tracks. Stranahan used the gaff to pull the plug in the Roman tub. Wordlessly he watched the soapy water drain, leaving Reynaldo bare and shriveled and flecked with suds.

'What's with the hairdo?' Stranahan asked.

Reynaldo composed himself and said, 'For a show.'

Stranahan tossed him a towel. He said, 'I know what you're doing. You're acing Christina out of the Barletta story. I saw your notes on the table.'

Flemm reddened. It had taken him three hours to come up with ten questions for Dr. Rudy Graveline. Carefully he had printed the questions on a fresh legal pad, the way Christina Marks always did. He had spent the better part of the afternoon trying to memorize them before calling it quits and heading over to Biscayne Baby for some action.

'I don't care about your show,' Stranahan said, 'but I care about Christina.'

'Me, too.'

'It looked like somebody pushed his way into her hotel room. There was a handprint on the door.'

Reynaldo said, 'Well, it wasn't mine.'

'Stand up,' Stranahan told him.

Flemm wrapped himself into the towel as he stood up in the tub. Stranahan measured him with his eyes. 'I believe you,' he said. He went back to the living room to wait for Reynaldo to dry off and get dressed.

When Flemm came out, wearing an absurd muscle shirt and

tight jeans, Stranahan said, 'When are you going to see the doctor?'

'Soon,' Reynaldo replied. Then, blustery: 'None of your business.' He felt so much tougher with a shirt on.

Stranahan said, 'If you wait, you'll have a better story.'

Reynaldo rolled his eyes—how many times had he heard that one! 'No way,' he said. The snide pomposity had returned to his voice.

'Ray, I'm only going to warn you once. If something's happened to Christina because of you, or if you do something that brings her any harm, you're done. And I'm not talking about your precious TV career.'

Flemm said, 'You sound pretty tough, long as you've got that hook.'

Stranahan tossed the tarpon gaff at Reynaldo and said, 'There— see if it works for you, too.'

Reynaldo quickly dropped it on the carpet. As a rule he didn't fight with crazy people unless cameras were rolling. Otherwise, what was the point?

'I hope you find her,' Reynaldo said.

Stranahan stood to leave. 'You better pray that I do.'

At the Gay Bidet, Freddie didn't even bother to get up from the desk to introduce himself. 'I'm gonna tell you the same as I told that Cuban cop, which is nothing. I got a policy not to talk about employees, past or present.'

Stranahan said, 'But you know the man I'm asking about.'

'Maybe, maybe not.'

'Is he here?'

'Ditto,' said Freddie. 'Now get the fuck gone.'

'Actually, I'm going to look around.'

'Oh, you are?' Freddie said. 'Like hell.' He punched a black buzzer under the desk. The door opened and Stranahan momentarily was drowned by the vocal stylings of the Fabulous Foreskins, performing their opening set. The man who entered Freddie's office was a short muscular Oriental. He wore a pink Gay Bidet security T-shirt, stretched to the limit.

Freddie said, 'Wong, please get this dog turd out of my sight.'

Stranahan waved the tarpon gaff and its sinister glint caused Wong to hesitate. Disdainfully Freddie glowered at the bouncer and said, 'What happened to all that kung-fu shit?'

Wong's chest began to swell.

Stranahan said, 'I've had a lousy day, and I'm really in no mood. You like having a liquor license?'

Freddie said, 'What're you talkin' about, do I like it?'

'Because you oughta enjoy it tonight, while you can. If you don't answer my questions, here's what happens to you and this toilet bowl of a nightclub: First thing tomorrow, six nasty bastards from Alcohol and Beverage come by and shut your ass down. Why? Because you lied when you got your liquor license, Freddie. You got a felony record in Illinois and Georgia, and you lied about that. Also, you've been serving to minors, big time. Also, your bartender just tried to sell me two grams of Peruvian. You want, I can keep going.'

Freddie said, 'Don't bother.' He instructed Wong to get lost. When they were alone again, he said to Stranahan, 'That rap in Atlanta was no good.'

'So you're not a pimp. Excellent. The beverage guys will be very impressed, Freddie. Be sure to tell them you're not a pimp, no matter what the FBI computer says.'

'What the fuck is it you want?'

'Just tell me where I can find my tall, cool friend. The one with the face.'

Freddie said, 'Truth is, I don't know. He took off a couple days ago. Picked up his paycheck and quit. Tried to give me back the T-shirt, the dumb fuck—like somebody else would wear the damn thing. I told him to keep it for a souvenir.'

'Did he say where he was going?' Stranahan asked.

'Nope. He had two broads with him, you figure it out.' Freddie flashed a mouthful of nubby yellow teeth. 'Creature from the Black Lagoon, and still he gets more poon than me.'

'What did the women look like?' Stranahan asked.

'One, I couldn't tell. Her face was all busted up, cuts and bruises and Band-Aids. He must've beat the hell out of her for something.

The other was a brunette, good-looking, on the thin side. Not humongous titties but nice pointy ones.'

Stranahan couldn't decide whether it was Freddie or the music that was aggravating his headache. 'The thin one—was she wearing blue jeans?'

Freddie said he didn't remember.

'Did they say anything?'

'Nope, not a word.'

'Did he have a gun?'

Freddie laughed again. 'Man, he doesn't need a gun. He has that whirly thing on his arm.' Freddie told Stranahan what the thing was and how the man known as Chemo would use it.

'You're kidding.'

'Like hell,' said Freddie. 'Guy was the best goddamn bouncer I ever had.'

Stranahan handed the club owner a fifty-dollar bill and the phone number of the bait shop at the marina. 'This is in case he comes back. You call me before you call the cops.'

Freddie pocketed the money. Reflectively he said: 'Freak like that with two broads, man, it just proves there's no God.'

'We'll see,' said Stranahan.

28

Chemo's first instinct was to haul ass with the doctor's cash, which was more than he would see in a couple of Amish lifetimes. Forget about the Stranahan hit, just blow town. Maggie Gonzalez told him, don't be such a small-timer, remember what we've got here: A surgeon on the hook. A money machine, for God's sake. Maggie assured him that a million, even two million, was do-able. There wasn't anything that Rudy Graveline wouldn't give to save his medical license.

Goosing the Bonneville along Biscayne Boulevard, Chemo said, 'What I've got now, I could get my face patched and still have enough for a year in Barbados. Maybe even get some real hair—those plug deals they stick in your scalp. I read where that's what they did to Elton John.'

'Sure,' Maggie said. 'I know some doctors who do hair.'

She was trying to play Chemo the way she had played all her men, but it wasn't easy. Beyond his desire for a clear complexion, she had yet to discover what motivated him. While Chemo appreciated money, he hardly displayed the proper lust for it. As for sex, he expressed no interest whatsoever. Maggie chose to believe that he was deterred by her bruises and bandages; once the facelift had healed, her powers of seduction would return. Then the only obstacle would be a logistical one: What would you do with the Weed Whacker under the sheets?

As Chemo pulled up to the Holiday Inn at 125th Street, Maggie said, 'If it would make you feel better, we could move to a nicer hotel.'

'What would make me feel better,' Chemo said, 'is for you to give me the keys to the suitcase.' He turned off the ignition and held out his right hand.

Maggie said, 'You think I'm dumb enough to try and rip you off?'

'Yes,' said Chemo, reaching for her purse. 'Plenty dumb enough.'

Christina Marks heard the door open and prayed it was the maid. It wasn't.

The lights came on and Chemo loomed incuriously over the bed. He checked the knots at Christina's wrists and ankles, while Maggie stalked into the bathroom and slammed the door.

After Chemo removed the towel from her mouth, Christina said, 'What's the matter with her?'

'She thinks I don't trust her. She's right.'

'For what it's worth,' Christina said, 'she already conned my boss out of a bundle.'

'I'll keep that in mind.' Chemo sat on the corner of the bed, counting the cash that he had taken from Dr. Rudy Graveline's pockets. Counting wasn't easy with only one hand. Christina watched inquisitively. After he was finished, Chemo put five thousand in the suitcase with the rest of the haul; forty-two hundred went down the heels of his boots. He slid the suitcase under the bed.

'How original,' Christina said.

'Shut up.'

'Could you untie me, please? I have to pee.'

'Jesus H. Christ.'

'You want me to wet the bed?' she said. 'Ruin all your cash?'

Chemo got Maggie out of the bathroom and made her help undo the knots. They had bound Christina to the bed frame with nylon clothesline. Once freed, she rubbed her wrists and sat up stiffly.

'Go do your business,' Chemo said. Then, to Maggie: 'Stay with her.'

Christina said, 'I can't pee with somebody watching.'

'What?'

'She's right,' Maggie said. 'I'm the same way. I'll just wait outside the door.'

'No, do what I told you,' Chemo said.

'There's no window in there,' Christina said. 'What'm I going to do, escape down the toilet?'

When she came out of the bathroom, Chemo was standing by the door. He led her back to the bed, made her lie down, then tied her again—another tedious chore, one-handed.

'No gag this time,' Christina requested. 'I promise not to scream.'

'But you'll talk,' said Chemo. 'That's even worse.'

Since the morning he had kidnapped her from the hotel on Key Biscayne, Chemo had said practically nothing to Christina Marks. Nor had he menaced or abused her in any sense—it was as if he knew that the mere sight of him, close up, was daunting enough. Christina had spied the butt of a revolver in Chemo's baggy pants pocket, but he had never pulled it; this was a big improvement over the two previous encounters, when he had nearly shot her.

She said, 'I just want to know why you're doing this, what exactly you want.'

He acted as if he never heard her. Maggie handed Christina a small cup of Pepsi.

'Don't let her drink too much,' Chemo cautioned. 'She'll be going to the head all night.'

He turned on the television set and grimaced: pro basketball—the Lakers and the Pistons. Chemo hated basketball. At six foot nine, he had spent his entire adulthood explaining to rude strangers that no, he didn't play pro basketball. Once a myopic Celtics fan had mistaken him for Kevin McHale and demanded an autograph; Chemo had savagely bitten the man on the shoulder, like a horse.

He began switching channels until he found an old *Miami Vice*. He turned up the volume and scooted his chair closer to the tube. He envied Don Johnson's three-day stubble; it looked rugged and manly. Chemo himself had not shaved, for obvious reasons, since the electrolysis accident.

He turned to Maggie and asked, 'Can they do hair plugs on your chin, too?'

'Oh, I'm sure,' she said, though in fact she had never heard of such a procedure.

Pinned to the bed like a butterfly, Christina said, 'Before long, somebody's going to be looking for me.'

Chemo snorted. 'That's the general idea.' Didn't these women ever shut up? Didn't they appreciate his potential for violence?

Maggie sat next to Christina and said, 'We need to get a message to your boyfriend.'

'Who—Stranahan? He's not my boyfriend.'

'Still, I doubt if he wants to see you get hurt.'

Christina appraised herself—strapped to a bed, squirming in her underwear—and imagined what Reynaldo Flemm would say if he came crashing through the door. For once she'd be happy to see the stupid sonofabitch, but she knew there was no possibility of such a rescue. If Mick couldn't find her, Ray didn't have a prayer.

'If it's that videotape you're after, I don't know where it is—'

'But surely your boyfriend does,' said Maggie.

Chemo pointed at the television. 'Hey, lookie there!' On the screen, Detective Sonny Crockett was chasing a drug smuggler through Stiltsville in a speedboat. This was the first time Christina had seen Chemo smile. It was a harrowing experience.

Maggie said, 'So how do you get in touch with him?'

'Mick? I don't know. There's no phone out there. Anytime I wanted to see him, I rented a boat.'

A commercial came on the television, and Chemo turned to the women. 'Jesus, I don't want to go back to that house— enough of that shit. I want him to come see me. And he will, soon as he knows I've got you.'

In her most lovelorn voice, Christina said to Maggie, 'I really don't think Mick cares one way or the other.'

'You better hope he does,' said Chemo. He pressed the towel firmly into Christina's mouth and turned back to watch the rest of the show.

On the morning of February eighteenth, the last day of Kipper Garth's law career, he filed a motion with the Circuit Court of

Dade County in the cause of Nordstrom v. Graveline, Whispering Palms, *et al.*

The motion requested an emergency court order freezing all the assets of Dr. Rudy Graveline, including bank accounts, certificates of deposit, stock portfolios, municipal bonds, Keogh funds, Individual Retirement Accounts, and real estate holdings. Submitted to the judge with Kipper Garth's motion was an affidavit from the Beachcomber Travel Agency stating that, on the previous day, one Rudolph Graveline had purchased two first-class airplane tickets to San José, Costa Rica. In the plea (composed entirely by Mick Stranahan and one of the paralegals), Kipper Garth asserted that it was Dr. Graveline's intention to flee the United States permanently.

Normally, a request involving a defendant's assets would have resulted in a full-blown hearing and, most likely, a denial of the motion. But Kipper Garth's position (and thus the Nordstroms') was buttressed by a discreet phone call from Mick Stranahan to the judge, whom Stranahan had known since his days as a young prosecutor in the DUI division. After a brief reminiscence, Stranahan told the judge the true reason for his call: that Dr. Rudy Graveline was a prime suspect in an unsolved four-year-old abduction case that might or might not be a homicide. Stranahan assured his friend that, rather than face the court, the surgeon would take his dough and make a run for it.

The judge granted the emergency order shortly after nine o'clock in the morning. Kipper Garth was astonished at his own success; he never dreamed litigation could be so damn easy. He fantasized a day when he could get out of the referral racket altogether, when he would be known and revered throughout Miami as a master trial attorney. Kipper Garth liked the billboards, though. However high he might soar among the eagles of Brickell Avenue, the billboards definitely had to stay. . . .

At ten forty-five, Rudy Graveline arrived at his bank in Bal Harbour and asked to make a wire transfer of $250,000 from his personal account to a new account in Panama. He also requested $60,000 in U.S. currency and traveler's cheques. The young bank officer who was assisting Rudy Graveline left his office for several minutes. When he returned, one of the bank's vice-presidents stood solemnly at his side.

Rudy took the news badly.

First he wept, which was merely embarrassing. Then be became enraged and hysterical and, finally, incoherent. He staggered, keening, into the bank lobby, at which point two enormous security guards were summoned to escort the surgeon from the premises.

By the time they deposited Rudy in the parking lot, he had settled himself and stopped crying.

Until one of the bank guards had pointed at the fender of the car and said, 'The hell happened to your Jag, brother?'

Perhaps it was the euphoria of a legal triumph, or perhaps it was simple prurient curiosity that impelled Kipper Garth to drop by the Nordstrom household during his lunch hour. The address was in Morningside, a pleasant old neighborhood of bleached stucco houses located a few blocks off the seediest stretch of Biscayne Boulevard.

Marie Nordstrom was surprised to see Kipper Garth, but she welcomed him warmly at the door, led him to the Florida room, and offered him a cup of coffee. She wore electric-blue Lycra body tights, and her ash-blond hair was pulled back in a girlish ponytail. Kipper couldn't take his eyes off the subject of litigation, her breasts. The exercise outfit left nothing to the imagination; these were the merriest-looking breasts that Kipper Garth had ever seen. It was difficult to think of them as weapons.

'John's not here,' Mrs. Nordstrom said. 'He got a job interview over at the jai-alai fronton. You take cream?'

Kipper Garth took cream. Mrs. Nordstrom placed the coffee pot on a glass tray. Kipper Garth made space for her on the sofa, but she moved to a love seat, facing him from across the coffee table.

Kipper Garth said, 'I just wanted to bring you up to date on the malpractice case.' Matter-of-factly he told Mrs. Nordstrom about the emergency court order to freeze Dr. Graveline's assets.

'What exactly does that mean?'

'It means his money won't be going anywhere, even if he does.'

Mrs. Nordstrom was not receiving the news as exuberantly as Kipper Garth had hoped; apparently she could not appreciate the difficulty of what he had done.

'John and I were talking just last night,' she said. 'The idea of going to trial . . . I don't know, Mr. Garth. This has been so embarrassing for both of us.'

'We're in it now, Mrs. Nordstrom. There's no turning back.' Kipper Garth tried to suppress the exasperation in his voice: Here Rudy Graveline was on the ropes and suddenly the plaintiffs want to back out.

'Maybe the doctor would be willing to settle the case,' ventured Mrs. Nordstrom.

Kipper Garth put down the coffee cup with a clack and folded his arms. 'Oh, I'm sure he would. I'm sure he'd be delighted to settle. That's exactly why we won't hear of it. Not yet.'

'But John says—'

'Trust me,' the lawyer said. He paused and lowered his eyes. 'Forgive me for saying so, Mrs. Nordstrom, but settling this case would be very selfish on your part.'

She looked startled at the word.

Kipper Garth went on: 'Think of all the patients this man has harmed. This *alleged* surgeon. If we don't stop him, nobody will. If you settle the case, Mrs. Nordstrom, the butchery will continue. You and your husband will be wealthy, yes, but Rudy Graveline's butchery will continue. At his instruction, the court file will be sealed and his reputation preserved. Again. Is that really what you want?'

Kipper Garth had listened intently to his own words, and was impressed by what he had heard; he was getting damn good at oratory.

A few awkward moments passed and Mrs. Nordstrom said, 'They've got an opening for a coach over at the jai-alai. John used to play in college, he was terrific. He even went to Spain one summer and trained with the Basques.'

Kipper Garth had never heard of a Scandinavian jai-alai coach, but his knowledge of the sport was limited. Oozing sincerity, he told Mrs. Nordstrom that he hoped her husband got the job.

She said, 'Thing is, he can't tell anybody about his eye. They'd never hire him.'

'Why not?'

'Too dangerous,' Mrs. Nordstrom said. 'The ball they use is like a rock. A *pelota* it's called. John says it goes like a hundred sixty miles an hour off those walls.'

Kipper Garth finished his coffee. 'I've never been to a jai-alai game.' He hoped she would take the hint and change the conversation.

'If you're playing, it helps to have two good eyes,' Mrs. Nordstrom explained. 'For depth perception.'

'I think I understand.'

'John says they won't let him coach if they find out about the accident.'

Now Kipper Garth got the picture. 'That's why you want to settle the lawsuit, isn't it?'

Mrs. Nordstrom said yes, they were worried about publicity. 'John says the papers and TV will go crazy with a story like this.'

Kipper thought: John is absolutely right.

'But you're a victim, Mrs. Nordstrom. You have the right to be compensated for this terrible event in your life. It says so in the Constitution.'

'John says they let cameras in the courtrooms. Is that true?'

'Yes, but let's not get carried away—'

'If it were your wife, would you want the whole world to see her tits on the six o'clock news?' Her tone was prideful and indignant.

'I'll speak to the judge, Mrs. Nordstrom. Please don't be upset. I know you've been through hell already.' But Kipper Garth was excited by the idea of TV cameras in the courtroom—it would be better than billboards!

Marie Nordstrom was trying not to cry and doing stolidly. She said, 'I blame that damn Reagan. He hadn't busted up the union, John'd still have his job in the flight tower.'

Kipper Garth said, 'Leave it to me and the two of you will be set for life. John won't need a job.'

Mrs. Nordstrom wistfully gazed at the two sturdy, silicon-

enhanced, Lycra-covered cones on her chest. 'They say contrac-
tures are easy to fix, but I don't know.'

Kipper Garth circled the coffee table and joined her on the love
seat. He put an unpracticed arm around her shoulders. 'For what
it's worth,' he said, 'they *look* spectacular.'

'Thank you,' she whispered, 'but you just don't know—how
could you?'

Kipper Garth removed the silk handkerchief from his breast
pocket and gave it to Mrs. Nordstrom, who sounded like the SS
Norway when she blew her nose.

'Know what I think?' said Kipper Garth. 'I think you should
let me feel them.'

Mrs. Nordstrom straightened and gave a stern sniffle.

The lawyer said: 'The only way I can begin to understand, the
only way I can convey the magnitude of this tragedy to a jury, is
if I can experience it myself.'

'Wait a minute—you want to feel my boobs?'

'I'm your lawyer, Mrs. Nordstrom.'

She eyed him doubtfully.

'If it were a burn case, I'd have to see the scar. Dismemberment,
paraplegia, same goes.'

'Looking is one thing, Mr. Garth. Touching is something else.'

'With all respect, Mrs. Nordstrom, your husband is going to
make a lousy witness in this case. He's going to come across as a
selfish prick. Remember what he said that day in my office? Bocci
balls, Mrs. Nordstrom. He said your breasts were hard as bocci
balls. This is not the testimony of a sensitive, caring spouse.'

She said, 'You'd be bitter, too, if it was your eye that got
poked out.'

'Granted. But let me try to come up with a more gentle description of your condition. Please, Mrs. Nordstrom.'

'All right, but I won't take my clothes off.'

'Of course not!'

She slid a little closer on the love seat. 'Give me your hands,'
she said. 'There you go.'

'Wow,' said Kipper Garth.

'What'd I tell you?'

'I had no idea.'

'You can let go now,' Mrs. Nordstrom said.

'Just a second.'

But one second turned into ten seconds, and ten seconds turned into thirty, which was plenty of time for John Nordstrom to enter the house and size up the scene. Without a word he loaded up the wicker *cesta* and hurled a goatskin jai-alai ball at the slimy lawyer who was feeling up his wife. The first shot sailed wide to the left and shattered a jalousie window. The second shot dimpled the arm of the love seat with a flat *thunk*. It was then that Kipper Garth released his grip on Marie Nordstrom's astoundingly stalwart breasts and made a vain break for the back door. Whether the lawyer fully comprehended his ethical crisis or fled on sheer animal instinct would never be known. John Nordstrom's third and final jai-alai shot struck the occipital seam of Kipper Garth's skull. He was unconscious by the time his silvery head smacked the floor.

'Ha!' Nordstrom exclaimed.

'I take it you got the job,' said his wife.

Willie the cameraman said they had two ways to go: they could crash the place or sneak one in.

Reynaldo Flemm said: 'Crash it.'

'Think of the timing,' Willie said. 'The timing's got to be flawless. We've never tried anything like this.' Willie was leaning toward trying a hidden camera.

Reynaldo said: 'Crash it. There's no security, it's a goddamn medical clinic. Who's gonna stop you, the nurse?'

Willie said he didn't like the plan; too many holes. 'What if the guy makes a run for it? What if he calls the police?'

Reynaldo said: 'Where's he gonna go, Willie? That's the beauty of this thing. The sonofabitch can't run away, and he knows it. Not with the tape rolling. They got laws.'

'Jesus,' Willie said, 'I don't like it. We've got to have a signal, you and me.'

'Don't worry,' Reynaldo said, 'we'll have a signal.'

'But what about the interview?' Willie asked. It was another way of bringing up Christina Marks.

'I wrote my own questions,' Reynaldo said sharply. 'Ball busters, too. You just wait.'

'Okay,' Willie said. 'I'll be ready.'

'Seven sharp,' Reynaldo said. 'I can't believe you're so nervous—this isn't the Crips and Bloods, man, it's a candyass doctor. He'll go to pieces, I guarantee it. True confessions, you just wait.'

'Seven sharp,' Willie said. 'See you then.'

After the cameraman had gone, Reynaldo Flemm called the Whispering Palms Spa and Surgery Center to confirm the appointment for Johnny LeTigre. To his surprise, the secretary put him through directly to Dr. Graveline.

'We still on for tomorrow morning?'

'Certainly,' the surgeon said. He sounded distracted, subdued. 'Remember: Nothing to eat or drink after midnight.'

'Right.'

'I thought we'd start with the rhinoplasty and go on to the liposuction.'

'Fine by me,' said Reynaldo Flemm. That's exactly how he had planned it, the nose job first.

'Mr. LeTigre, I had a question regarding the fee . . .'

'Fifteen thousand is what we agreed on.'

'Correct,' said Rudy Graveline, 'but I just wanted to make sure—you said something about cash?'

'Yeah, that's right. I got cash.'

'And you'll have it with you tomorrow?'

'You bet.' Reynaldo couldn't believe this jerk. Probably grosses two million a year, and here he is drooling over a lousy fifteen grand. It was true what they said about doctors being such cheap bastards.

'Anything else I need to remember?'

'Just take plenty of fluids,' Rudy said mechanically, 'but nothing after midnight.'

'I'll be a good boy,' Reynaldo Flemm promised. 'See you tomorrow.'

29

The wind kicked up overnight, whistled through the planks of the house, slapped the shutters against the walls. Mick Stranahan climbed naked to the roof and lay down with the shotgun at his right side. The bay was noisy and black, hissing through the pilings beneath the house. Above, the clouds rolled past in churning gray clots, celestial dust devils tumbling across a low sky. As always, Stranahan lay facing away from the city, where the halogen crime lights stained an otherwise lovely horizon. On nights such as this, Stranahan regarded the city as a malignancy and its sickly orange aura as a vast misty bubble of pustular gas. The downtown skyline, which had seemed to sprout overnight in a burst of civic priapism, struck Stranahan as a crass but impressive prop, an elaborate movie set. Half the new Miami skyscrapers had been built with coke money and existed largely as an inside joke, a mirage to please the banks and the Internal Revenue Service and the chamber of commerce. Everyone liked to say that the skyline was a monument to local prosperity, but Stranahan recognized it as a tribute to the anonymous genius of Latin American money launderers. In any case, it was nothing he wished to contemplate from the top of his stilt house. Nor was the view south of downtown any kinder, a throbbing congealment from Coconut Grove to the Gables to South Miami and beyond. Looking westward on a clearer evening, Stranahan would have fixed on the newest coastal landmark: A sheer ten-story cliff of refuse known as Mount Trashmore. Having run out of rural locations in which to conceal its waste, Dade County had erected a towering fetid landfill along the shore of Biscayne Bay. Stranahan could not decide which sight was more offensive, the city skyline or the mountain of garbage. The turkey buzzards, equally ambivalent, commuted regularly from one site to the other.

Stranahan was always grateful for a clean ocean breeze. He sprawled on the eastern slope of the roof, facing the Atlantic. A DC-10 took off from Miami International and passed over Stilts-ville, rattling the windmill on Stranahan's house. He wondered what it would be like to wake up and find the city vaporized, the skies clear and silent, the shoreline lush and virginal! He would have loved to live here at the turn of the century, when nature owned the upper hand.

The cool wind tickled the hair on his chest and legs. Stranahan tasted salt on his lips and closed his eyes. One of his ex-wives, he couldn't remember which, had told him he ought to move to Alaska and become a hermit. You're such an old grump, she had said, not even the grizzly bears'd put up with you. Now Stranahan recalled which wife had said this: Donna, his second. She had eventually grown tired of all his negativity. Every big city has crime, she had said. Every big city has corruption. Look at New York, she had said. Look at Chicago. Those are great goddamn cities, Mick, you gotta admit. Like so many cocktail waitresses, Donna steadfastly refused to give up on humanity. She believed that the good people of the world outnumbered the bad, and she got the tips to prove it. After the divorce, she had enrolled in night school and earned her Florida real estate license; Stranahan had heard she'd moved to Jacksonville and was going great guns in the waterfront condo market. Bleakly it occurred to him that all his former wives (even Chloe, who had nailed a CPA for a husband) had gone on to greater achievements after the divorce. It was as if being married to Stranahan had made each of them realize how much of the real world they were missing.

He thought of Christina Marks. How did he get mixed up with such a serious woman? Unlike the others he had loved and married, Christina avidly pursued that which was evil and squalid and polluted. Her job was to expose it. There was not a wisp of true innocence about her, not a trace of cheery waitress-type optimism ... yet something powerful attracted him. Maybe because she slogged through the same moral swamps. Crooked cops, crooked lawyers, crooked doctors, crooked ex-wives, even crooked tree trimmers—these were the spawn of the city bog.

Stranahan's fingers found the stock of the shotgun, and he moved it closer. Soon he fell asleep, and he dreamed that Victoria Barletta was alive. He dreamed that he met her one night in the Rathskellar on the University of Miami campus. She was working behind the bar, wearing a pink butterfly bandage across the bridge of her nose. Stranahan ordered a beer and a cheeseburger medium, and asked her if she wanted to get married. She said sure.

The boat woke him up. It was a familiar yellow skiff with a big outboard. Stranahan saw it a mile away, trimmed up, running the flats. He smiled—the bonefish guide, his friend. With all the low dirty clouds it was difficult to estimate the time, but Stranahan figured the sun had been up no more than two hours. He dropped from the roof, stowed the Remington inside the house, and pulled on a pair of jeans so as not to startle the guide's customers, who were quite a pair. The man was sixty-five, maybe older, obese and gray, with skin like rice parchment; the woman was twenty-five tops, tall, dark blond, wearing bright coral lip gloss and a gold choker necklace.

The guide climbed up to the stilt house and said, 'Mick, take a good look. Fucking lipstick on a day like this.'

From the skiff, tied up below, Stranahan could hear the couple arguing about the weather. The woman wanted to go back, since there wasn't any sun for a decent tan. The old man said no, he'd paid his money and by God they would fish.

Stranahan said to his friend, 'You've got the patience of Job.'

The guide shook his head. 'A killer mortgage is what I've got. Here, this is for you.'

It was an envelope with Stranahan's name printed in block letters on the outside. 'Woman with two black eyes told me to give it to you,' the guide said. 'Cuban girl, not bad looking, either. She offered me a hundred bucks.'

'Hope you took it.'

'I held out for two,' the guide said.

Stranahan folded the envelope in half and tucked it in the back pocket of his jeans.

The guide said, 'You in some trouble?'

'Just business.'

'Mick, you don't have a business.'

Stranahan grinned darkly. 'True enough.' He knew what his friend was thinking: Single guy, cozy house on the water, a good boat for fishing, a monthly disability check from the state—how could anybody fuck up a sweet deal like that?

'I heard some asshole shot hell out of the place.'

'Yeah.' Stranahan pointed to a sheet of fresh plywood on the door. The plywood covered two of Chemo's bullet holes. 'I've got to get some red paint,' Stranahan said.

The guide said, 'Forget the house, what about your shoulder?'

'It's fine,' Stranahan said.

'Don't worry, it was Luis who told me.'

'No problem. You want some coffee?'

'Naw.' The bonefish guide jerked a thumb in the direction of his skiff. 'This old fart, he's on the board of some steel company up north. That's his secretary.'

'God bless him.'

The guide said, 'Last time they went fishing, I swear, she strips off the bottom of her bathing suit. Not the top, Mick, the bottom part. All day long, flashing her bush in my face. Said she was trying to bleach out her hair. Here I'm poling like a maniac after these goddamn fish, and she's turning somersaults in front of the boat, trying to keep her bush in the sun.'

Stranahan said, 'I don't know how you put up with it.'

'So today there's no sunshine and of course she's throwin' a fit. Meanwhile the old fart says all he wants is a world-record bonefish on fly. That's all. Mick, I'm too old for this shit.' The guide pulled on his cap so tightly that it crimped the tops of his ears. Lugubriously he descended the stairs to the dock.

'Good luck,' Stranahan said. Under the circumstances, it sounded ridiculous.

The guide untied the yellow skiff and hopped in. Before starting the engine, he looked up at Stranahan and said, 'I'll be out here tomorrow, even if the weather's bad. The next day, too.'

Stranahan nodded; it was good to know. 'Thanks, Captain,' he said.

After the skiff was gone, Stranahan returned to the top of the house and took the envelope out of his pocket. He opened it calmly because he knew what it was and who it was from. He'd been waiting for it.

The message said: 'We've got your girlfriend. No cops!'

And it gave a telephone number.

Mick Stranahan memorized the number, crumpled the paper, and tossed it off the roof into the milky waves. 'Somebody's been watching too much television,' he said.

That afternoon, Mick Stranahan received another disturbing message. It was delivered by Luis Córdova, the young marine patrol officer. He gave Stranahan a lift by boat from Stiltsville to the Crandon Marina, where Stranahan got a cab to his sister Kate's house in Gables-by-the-Sea.

Sergeant Al García was fidgeting on the front terrace. Over his J. C. Penney suit he was wearing what appeared to be an authentic London Fog trenchcoat. Stranahan knew that García was upset because he was smoking those damn Camels again. Even before Stranahan could finish paying the cabbie, García was charging down the driveway, blue smoke streaming from his nostrils like one of those cartoon bulls.

'So,' the detective said, 'Luis fill you in?'

Stranahan said yes, he knew that Kipper Garth had been gravely injured in a domestic dispute.

García blocked his path up the drive. 'By a client, Mick. Imagine that.'

'I didn't know the client, Al.'

'Name of Nordstrom, John Nordstrom.' García was working the sodden nub of the Camel the same way he worked the cigars, from one side of his mouth to the other. Stranahan found it extremely distracting.

'According to the wife,' García said, 'the assailant returned home unexpectedly and found your brother-in-law, the almost deceased—'

'Thank you, Al.'

'—found the almost deceased fondling his wife. Whereupon, the assailant attempted to strike the almost deceased at least three times with *pelotas*. That's a jai-alai ball, Mick. The third shot struck your brother-in-law at the base of the skull, rendering him unconscious.'

'The dumb shit. How's Kate?'

'Puzzled,' García said. 'But then, aren't we all?'

'I want to see her.' Stranahan sidestepped the detective and made for the front door. His sister was standing by the bay window of the Florida room and staring out at Kipper Garth's sailboat, the *Pain-and-Suffering*, which was rocking placidly at the dock behind the house, Stranahan gave Kate a hug and kissed her on the forehead.

She sniffled and said, 'Did they tell you?'

'Yes, Kate.'

'That he was groping a client—did they tell you?'

Stranahan said, 'That's the woman's story.'

Kate gave a bitter chuckle. 'And you don't believe it? Come on, Mick, *I* believe it. Kipper was a pig, let's face it. You were right, I was wrong.'

Stranahan didn't know what to say. 'He had some good qualities.' Jesus, how stupid. '*Has* some good qualities, I mean.'

'The doctors say it's fifty-fifty, but I'm ready for the worst. Kipper's not a fighter.'

'He might surprise you,' Stranahan said without conviction.

'Mick, just so you know—I was aware of what he was up to. Some of the excuses, God, you should have heard them. Late nights, weekends, trips to God knows where. I pretended to believe him because . . . because I liked this life, Mick. The house . . . this great yard. I mean, it sounds selfish, but it felt *good* here. Safe. This is a wonderful neighborhood.'

'Katie, I'm sorry.'

'Neighborhoods like this are hard to find, Mick. You know, we've only been burglarized twice in four years. That's not bad for Miami.'

'Not at all,' Stranahan said.

'See, I had to weigh these things every time I thought about leaving.' Kate put a hand on his arm and said, 'You knew about all his fooling around.'

'Not everything.'

'Thanks for not mentioning it.' She was sincere.

Stranahan felt like a complete shit, which he was. 'This is my fault,' he said. 'I told Kipper to take this case. I *made* him take it.'

'How?' she asked. 'And why?'

'Whatever you're thinking, it's even worse. I can't tell you the details, Kate, because there's going to be trouble and I want you clear of it. But you ought to know that I'm the one who got Kipper involved.'

'But you're not the one who played grab-the-tittie with your client. *He* did.' She turned back to the big window and folded her arms. 'It's so . . . tacky.'

'Yes,' Stranahan agreed. 'Tacky's the word.'

When he came out of the house, García was waiting.

'Wasn't that courteous of me, not barging in and making a big Cuban scene in front of your sister?'

'Al, you're a fucking prince among men.'

'Know why I'm wearing this trenchcoat? It's brand-new, by the way. I hadda go to another funeral: Bobby Pepsical, the county commissioner. Dropped dead in confession.'

'Good place for it. He was a stone crook.'

'Course he was, Mick. But I got a feeling he didn't get his penance.'

'Why not?'

'Because there wasn't a priest in there. Bobby's confessing to an empty closet—that's pretty weird, huh? Anyway, they make a bunch of us go to the fucking funeral, because of who he was. That's why I've got the new coat. It was raining.'

Stranahan said, 'How was it? Did they screw him into the ground? That's about how crooked he was.'

'I know but, Christ, have some respect for the dead.' García rubbed his temples like he was massaging a cramp. 'See, this is what's got me so agitated, Mick. Ever since I got into this thing with you and the doctor, so many people are dying. Dying weird, too. There's your ex, and Murdock and Salazar—another funeral! Then the business with that goddamn homicidal tree man. So after all that, here I am standing in the rain, watching them plant some scuzzbucket politician who croaks on his knees in an empty confessional, and my frigging beeper goes off. Lieutenant says some big-shot lawyer got beaned by a jai-alai ball and could be a homicide any second. A jai-alai ball! On top of which the big-shot lawyer turns out to be *your* brother-in-law. It's like a nightmare of weirdness!'

'It's been a bad month,' Stranahan conceded.

'Yeah, it sure has. So what about these Nordstroms?'

'I didn't know them, I told you.'

García lit up another cigarette and Stranahan made a face. 'Know why I'm smoking these things? Because I'm agitated. I get agitated whenever I get jerked around, and I hate to waste a good cigar on agitation.'

Stranahan said, 'Can you please not blow it in my face? That's all I ask.'

The detective took the cigarette out of his mouth and held it behind his back. 'There, you happy? Now help me out, Mick. The assailant's wife, she says Kipper Garth phones her out of the blue and asks if she wants to sue—guess who—Rudy Graveline! Since he's the quack who gave her the encapsulated whatcha-macallits.'

'If that's what she says, fine.'

'But lawyers aren't supposed to solicit.'

'Al, this is Miami.'

García took a quick drag and hid the Camel again. 'My theory is you somehow got your sleazy, almost-deceased brother-in-law to sue Graveline, just to bust his balls. Shake things up. Maybe flush the giant Mr. Blondell Tatum out of his fugitive gutter. I don't expect you to open up your heart, Mick, but just tell me this: Did it work? Because if it did, you're a fucking genius and I apologize for all the shitty things I've been saying about you in my sleep.'

'Did what work?'

García grinned venomously. 'I thought we were buddies.'

'Al, I'm not going to shut you out,' Stranahan said. 'For God's sake, you saved my life.'

'Aw, shucks, you remembered.'

Stranahan said: 'Which one do you want, Al? The freaky hit man or the doctor?'

'Both.'

'No, I'm sorry.'

'Hey, I could arrest your ass right now. Obstruction, tampering, I'd think of something.'

'And I'd be out in an hour.'

García's jaw tightened for a moment and he turned away, stewing. When he turned back, he seemed more amused than angry.

'The problem is, Mick, you're too smart. You know the system too damn well. You know there's only so much I can get away with.'

'Believe me, we're on the same side.'

'I know, *chico*, that's what scares me.'

'So, which of these bastards do you want for yourself—the surgeon or the geek?'

'Don't rush me, Mick.'

30

Early on the morning of February nineteenth, Reynaldo Flemm, the famous Shock Television journalist, arrived at the Whispering Palms Spa and Surgery Center for the most sensational interview of his sensational career. A sleepy receptionist collected the $15,000 cash and counted it twice; if she was surprised by the size of the surgeon's fee, she didn't show it. The receptionist handed Reynaldo Flemm two photocopied consent forms, one for a rhinoplasty and one for a suction-assisted lipectomy. Reynaldo skimmed the paperwork and extravagantly signed as 'Johnny LeTigre.'

Then he sat down to wait for his moment. On a buff-colored wall hung a laminated carving of one of Rudy Graveline's pet sayings: TO IMPROVE ONE'S SELF, IMPROVE ONE'S FACE. That wasn't Reynaldo's favorite Rudyism. His favorite was framed in quilted Norman Rockwell-style letters above the water fountain: VANITY IS BEAUTIFUL. That's the one Reynaldo had told Willie about. Be sure to get a quick shot on your way in, he had told him. What for? Willie had asked. For the irony, Reynaldo Flemm had exclaimed. For the irony! Reynaldo was proud of himself for thinking up that camera shot; usually Christina Marks was in charge of finding irony.

Soon an indifferent young nurse summoned Reynaldo to a chilly examining room and instructed him to empty his bladder, a tedious endeavor that took fifteen minutes and produced scarcely an ounce. Reynaldo Flemm was a very nervous man. In his professional life he had been beaten by Teamsters, goosed by white supremacists, clubbed by Mafia torpedoes, pistol-whipped by Bandito bikers, and kicked in the groin by the Pro-Life Posse. But he had never undergone surgery. Not even a wart removal.

Flemm stiffly removed his clothes and pulled off his hightop

Air Jordans. He changed into a baby-blue paper gown that hung to his knees. The nurse gave him a silly paper cap to cover his silly dyed hair, and paper shoe covers for his bare feet.

A nurse anesthetist came out of nowhere, brusquely flipped up the tail of Reynaldo's gown and stuck a needle in his hip. The hypodermic contained a drug called Robinul, which dries up the mouth by inhibiting oral secretions. Next the nurse seized Reynaldo's left arm, swabbed it, and stuck it cleanly with an I.V. needle that dripped into his veins a lactated solution of five percent dextrose and, later, assorted powerful sedatives.

The anesthetist then led Reynaldo Flemm and his I.V. apparatus into Suite F, one of four ultramodern surgical theaters at Whispering Palms. She asked him to lie on his back and, as he stretched out on the icy steel, Reynaldo frantically tried to remember the ten searing questions he had prepared for the ambush of Dr. Rudy Graveline.

One, did you kill Victoria Barletta on March 12, 1986?

Two, why would one of your former nurses say that you did?

Three, isn't it true that you've repeatedly gotten into trouble for careless and incompetent surgery?

Four, how do you explain . . .

Explain?

Explain this strap on my fucking legs!

'Please quiet down, Mr. LeTigre.'

And my arms! What've you done to my arms? I can't move my goddamn arms!

'Try to relax. Think pleasant thoughts.'

Wait, wait, wait, wait, wait!

'You ought to be feeling a little drowsy.'

This is wrong. This is not right. I read up on this. I got a fucking pamphlet. You're supposed to tape my eyes, not my arms. What are you smiling at, you dumb twat? Lemme talk to the doctor! Where's the doctor? Jesus Christ, that's cold. What are you *doing* down there!

'Good morning, Mr. LeTigre.'

Doctor, thank God you're here! Listen good now: These Nazi nurse bitches are making a terrible mistake. I don't wanna general, I wanna local. Just pull the I.V., okay? I'll be fine, just pull the tubes before I pass out.

'John, we're having a little trouble understanding you.'

No shit, Sherlock, my tongue's so dry you could light a match on it. Please yank the needles, I can't think with these damn needles. And make 'em quit fooling around with me down there. Christ, it's cold! What're they doing!

'I assumed they told you—there's been a change of plans. I've decided to do the lipectomy first, then the rhinoplasty. It'll be easier that way.'

No no no, you gotta do the nose first. Do the fucking nose.

'You should try to relax, John. Here, hold still, we're going to give you another injection.'

No no no no no no no.

'That didn't hurt a bit, did it?'

I wanna ask I gotta ask right now . . .

'Go ahead, push the Sublimaze.'

Did you kill . . . ?

'What did he say?'

Is it true you killed . . . ?

'This guy looks sort of familiar.'

Did you . . . kill Victoria . . . Principal?

'Victoria Principal! Boy, is he whacked out.'

Well did you?

'Where's the mask? Start the Forane. Give him the mask.'

Willie hadn't slept much, fretting about Reynaldo's big plan. He had tried to call Christina Marks in New York, but the office said she was in Miami. But where? Reynaldo's plan was the craziest thing Willie had ever heard, starting with the signal. Willie needed a signal to know when to come crashing into the operating room with the camera. The best that Reynaldo could come up with was a scream. Willie would be in the waiting room, Reynaldo would scream.

'What exactly will you scream?' Willie had asked.

'I'll scream: WILLIE!'

Willie thought Reynaldo was joking. He wasn't.

'What about the other patients in the waiting room? I mean, here I am with a TV camera and a sound pack—what do I tell these people?'

'Tell 'em you're from PBS,' Reynaldo had said. 'Nobody hassles PBS.'

The shot that Reynaldo Flemm most fervently wanted was this: Himself prone, prepped, cloaked in blue, preferably in the early stages of rhinoplasty and preferably bloody. That was the good thing about a nose job, you could ask for a local. Most plastic surgeons want their rhinoplasty patients to be all the way zonked, but you could get it done with a local and a mild I.V. if you could stand a little pain. Reynaldo Flemm had no doubt he could stand it.

Willie would burst like a fullback into the operating room, tape rolling, toss the baton mike to Reynaldo on the table, Reynaldo would poke it in Rudy Graveline's face and pop the questions. Bam bam bam. The nurses and scrub techs would drop whatever they were doing and run, leaving the hapless surgeon to dissolve, alone, before the camera's eye.

Wait'll he realizes who I am, Reynaldo had chortled. Be sure you go extra tight on his face.

Willie had said he needed a soundman, but Reynaldo said no, out of the question; this was to be a streamlined attack.

Willie had said all right, then we need a better signal. Just screaming isn't good enough, he had said. What if somebody else starts screaming first, some other patient?

'Who else would scream your name?' Reynaldo had asked in a caustic tone. 'Listen to what I'm saying.'

The plan was bold and outrageous, Willie had to admit. No doubt it would cause a national sensation, stir up all the TV critics, not to mention Johnny Carson's gag writers. There would be a large amount of cynical speculation among Ray's colleagues that what he really wanted out of this caper was a free nose job— a theory that occurred even to Willie as he listened to Reynaldo map out the big ambush. The possibility of coast-to-coast media ridicule was no deterrent; the man seemed to relish being maligned as a hack and a clown and a shameless egomaniac. He

said they were jealous, that's what they were. What other broadcast journalist in America had the guts to go under the knife just
to get an interview? Mike Wallace? Not in a million years, the
arrogant old prune. Bill Moyers? That liberal pussy would faint
if he got a hangnail!

Yeah, Willie had said, it's quite a plan.

Brilliant, Reynaldo had crowed. Try brilliant.

However inspired, the plan's success depended on several crucial factors, not the least of which was the premise that Reynaldo
Flemm would be conscious for the interview.

Although the surgical procedure known as liposuction, or fat
sucking, was developed in France, it has achieved its greatest
mass-market popularity in the United States. It is now the most
common cosmetic procedure performed by plastic surgeons in
this country, with more than 100,000 operations every year.
The mortality rate for suction-assisted lipectomy is relatively low,
about one death for every 10,000 patients. The odds of complications—which include blood clots, fat embolisms, chronic numbness, and severe bruising—increase considerably if the surgeon
performing the liposuction has had little or no training in the
procedure. Rudy Graveline fell decisively into this category—a
doctor who had taken up liposuction for the simple reason that
it was exceedingly lucrative. No state law or licensing board or
medical review committee required Rudy to study liposuction
first, or become proficient, or even be tested on his surgical
competence before trying it. The same libertarian standards
applied to rhinoplasties or hemorrhoidectomies or even brain
surgery: Rudy Graveline was a licensed physician, and legally
that meant he could try any damn thing he wanted.

He did not give two hoots about certification by the American
Board of Plastic Surgery, or the American Academy of Facial
Plastic and Reconstructive Surgery, or the American Society of
Plastic and Reconstructive Surgeons. What were a couple more
snotty plaques on the wall? His patients could care less. They
were rich and vain and impatient. In some exclusive South
Florida circles, Rudy's name carried the glossy imprimatur of a

Gucci or de La Renta. The lacquered old crones at La Gorce or the Biltmore would point at each other's shiny chins and taut necks and sculpted eyelids and ask, not in a whisper but a haughty bray, 'Is that a Graveline?'

Rudy was a designer surgeon. To have *him* suck your fat was an honor, a social plum, a mark (literally) of status. Only a boor, white trash or worse, would ever question the man's techniques or complain about the results.

Ironically, most of the surgeons who worked for Rudy Graveline at Whispering Palms were completely qualified to do suction lipectomies; they had actually trained for it—studied, observed, practiced. While Rudy admired their dedication, he thought they were overdoing things—after all, how difficult could such an operation really be? The fat itself was abundantly easy to find. Suck it out, close 'em up, next case! Big deal.

To be on the safe side, Rudy read two journal articles about liposuction and ordered an instructional video cassette for $26.95 from a medical-supply firm in Chicago. The journal articles turned out to be dense and fairly boring, but the video was an inspiration. Rudy came away convinced that any fool doctor with half a brain could vacuum fat with no problem.

The typical lipectomy patient was not a grotesque hypertensive blimp but—like Johnny LeTigre—a healthy person of relatively normal stature and weight. The object of their complaint was medically mundane—bumper-car hips, droopy buttocks, gelatinous thighs, or old-fashioned 'love handles' at the waist. Properly performed, liposuction would remove localized pockets of excess fat to improve and smooth the body's natural contour. Improperly performed, the surgery would leave a patient lumpy and lopsided and looking for a lawyer.

On the morning of Reynaldo Flemm's undercover mission, nothing as sinister as a premonition caused Rudy Graveline to change his mind about doing the nose job first. What changed the doctor's mind, as usual, was money. Because a lipectomy usually required general anesthesia, it was more labor-intensive (and costly) than a simple rhinoplasty. Rudy figured the sooner he could get done with the heavy stuff, the sooner he could get the anesthetist and her gas machine off the clock. He could do the rhino later with intravenous sedation, which was much cheaper.

That Rudy Graveline could still worry about overhead at this point, with his career crumbling, was a tribute both to his power of concentration and his ingrained devotion to profit.

He grabbed a gloveful of Reynaldo Flemm's belly roll and gave a little squeeze. Paydirt. Fat city.

Rudy selected a Number 15 blade and made a one-quarter inch incision in Reynaldo's navel. Through this convenient aperture Rudy inserted the cannula, a long tubular instrument that resembled in structure the nose of an anteater. Rudy rammed the blunt snout of the cannula into the soft meat of Reynaldo's abdomen, then scraped the instrument back and forth to break up the tissue. With his right foot the surgeon tapped a floor pedal that activated a suction machine, which vacuumed the fat particles through small holes in the tip of the cannula, down a long clear plastic tube to a glass bottle.

Within moments, the first yellow glops appeared.

Johnny LeTigre's spare tire!

Soon he would be a new man.

In the waiting room, Willie got to talking with some of the other patients. There was a charter-boat captain with a skin cancer the size of a toad on his forehead. There was a dancer from the Miami ballet who was getting her buttocks suctioned for the second time in as many years. There was a silver-haired Nicaraguan man whom Willie had often seen on television—one of the *contra* leaders—who was getting his eyelids done for eighteen hundred dollars. He said the CIA was picking up the tab.

The one Willie liked best was a red-haired stripper from the Solid Gold club up in Lauderdale. She was getting new boobs, of course, but she was also having a tattoo removed from her left thigh. When the stripper heard that Willie was from PBS, she asked if she could be in his documentary and hiked up her corduroy miniskirt to show off the tattoo. The tattoo depicted a green reticulated snake eating itself. Willie said, in a complimentary way, that he had never seen anything like it. He made sure to get the stripper's phone number so that he could call her about the imaginary program.

The hour passed without a peep from Reynaldo Flemm, and Willie began to get jittery. Reynaldo had said give it to nine o'clock before you freak, and now it was nine o'clock. The halls of Whispering Palms were quiet enough that Willie was certain he would have heard a scream. He asked the ballet dancer, who had been here before, how far it was from the waiting area to the operating room.

'Which operating room?' she replied. 'They've got four.'

'Shit,' said Willie. 'Four?'

This was shocking news. Reynaldo Flemm had made it sound like there was only one operating room, and that he would be easy to find. More worried than ever, Willie decided to make his move. He hoisted the Betacam to his shoulder, checked the mike and the cables and the belt pack and the battery levels, turned on the Frezzi light (which caused the other patients to mutter and shield their eyes), and went prowling through the corridors in search of Reynaldo Flemm.

When the telephone on the wall started tweeting, Dr. Rudy Graveline glanced up from Johnny LeTigre's gut and said: 'Whoever it is, I'm not here.'

The circulating nurse picked up the phone, listened for several moments, then turned to the doctor. 'It's Ginny at the front desk. There's a man with a minicam running all over the place.'

Rudy's surgical mask puckered. 'Tell her to call the police. . . . No! Wait—' Oh Jesus. Stay calm. Stay extremely calm.

'He just crashed in on Dr. Kloppner in Suite D.'

Rudy grunted unhappily. 'What does he want? Did he say what he wants?'

'He's looking for you. Should I tell Ginny to call the cops or what?'

The nurse-anesthetist interrupted: 'Let's not do anything until we finish up here. Let's close up this patient and get him off the table.'

'She's right,' Rudy said. 'She's absolutely right. We're almost done here.'

'Take your time,' the anesthetist said with an edge of concern. Under optimum conditions, Rudy Graveline scared the daylights out of her. Under stress, there was no telling how dangerous he could be.

He said, 'What're we looking at here?'

'One more pocket, maybe two hundred cc's.'

'Let's do it, okay?'

The wall phone started tweeting again.

'Screw it,' said Rudy. 'Let it go.'

He gripped the cannula like a carving knife, scraping frenetically at the last stubborn colony of fat inside Reynaldo's midriff. The suction machine hummed contentedly as it filled the glass jar with gobs of unwanted pudge.

'One more minute and we're done,' Rudy said.

Then the doors opened and an awesome white light bathed the operating room. The beam was brighter and hotter than the surgical lights, and it shone from the top of a camera, which sat like a second head on the shoulder of a man. A man who had no business in Rudy Graveline's operating room.

The man with the camera cried out: 'Ray!'

Rudy said, 'Get out of here this minute.'

'Are you Dr. Graveline?'

Rudy's hand continued to work on Reynaldo Flemm's belly. 'Yes, I'm Dr. Graveline. But there's nobody named Ray here. Now get out before I phone the police.'

But the man with the camera on his shoulder shuffled closer, scorching the operating team with his fierce, hot light. The anesthetist, the scrub nurse, the circulating nurse, even Rudy flinched from the glare. The camera-headed man approached the table and zoomed in on the sleeping patient's face, which was partially concealed by a plastic oxygen mask. The voice behind the camera said, 'Yeah, that's him!'

'Who?' Rudy said, rattled. 'That's Ray?'

'Reynaldo Flemm!'

The scrub nurse said: 'I told you he looked familiar.'

Again Rudy asked: 'Who? Reynaldo who?'

'That guy from the TV.'

'This has gone far enough,' Rudy declared, fighting panic.

'You better . . . just get the hell out of my operating room.'

Willie pushed forward. 'Ray, wake up! It's me!'

'He can't wake up, you asshole. He's gassed to the gills. Now turn off that spotlight and get lost.'

The scope of the journalistic emergency struck Willie at once. Reynaldo was unconscious. Christina was gone. The tape was rolling. The batteries were running out.

Willie thought: It's up to me now.

The baton microphone, Ray's favorite, the one Willie was supposed to toss to him at the moment of ambush, was tucked in Willie's left armpit. Grunting, contorting, shifting the weight of the Betacam on his shoulder, Willie was able to retrieve the mike with his right hand. In an uncanny imitation of Reynaldo Flemm, Willie thrust it toward the face of the surgeon.

Above the surgical mask, Rudy Graveline's eyes grew wide and fearful. He stared at the microphone as if it were the barrel of a Mauser. From behind the metallic hulk of the minicam, the voice asked: 'Did you kill Victoria Barletta?'

A bullet could not have struck Rudy Graveline as savagely as those words.

His spine became rigid.

The pupils of his eyes shrunk to pinpricks.

His muscles cramped, one by one, starting in the toes. His right hand, the one that held the cannula, the one buried deep in the livid folds of Reynaldo Flemm's freshly vacuumed tummy—his right hand twisted into a spastic nerveless talon.

With panic welling in her voice, the anesthetist said: 'All right, that's it!'

'Almost done,' the surgeon said hoarsely.

'No, that's enough!'

But Dr. Rudy Graveline was determined to finish the operation. To quit would be an admission of . . . *something*. Composure— that's what they taught you at Harvard. Above all, a physician must be composed. In times of crisis, patients and staff relied on a surgeon to be cool, calm, and composed. Even if the man lying on the operating table turned out to be . . . Reynaldo Flemm, the notorious undercover TV reporter! That would explain the woozy babbling while he was going under—the jerkoff wasn't talking about Victoria Principal, the actress. He was talking about Victoria Barletta, she of the fateful nose job.

The pain of the muscle cramps was so fierce that it brought viscous tears to Rudy Graveline's eyes. He forced himself to continue. He lowered his right shoulder into the rhythm of the liposuction, back and forth in a lumberjack motion, harder and harder.

Again, the faceless voice from behind the TV camera: 'Did you kill that girl?'

The black eye of the beast peered closer, revolving clockwise in its socket—Willie, remembering Ray's instructions to zoom tight on Rudy's face. The surgeon stomped on the suction pedal as if he were squashing a centipede. The motor thrummed. The tube twitched. The glass jar filled.

Time to stop.

Time to stop!

But Dr. Rudy Graveline did not stop.

He kept on poking and sucking . . . the long hungry snout of the mechanical anteater slurping through the pit of Reynaldo's abdomen . . . down, down, down through the fascia and the muscle . . . snorkeling past the intestines, nipping at the transverse colon . . . down, down, down the magic anteater burrowed.

Until it glomped the aorta.

And the plastic tube coming out of Reynaldo's navel suddenly turned bright red.

The jar at the other end turned red.

Even the doctor's arm turned red.

Willie watched it all through the camera's eye. The whole place, turning red.

31

The first thing Chemo bought with Rudy's money was a portable phone for the Bonneville. No sooner was it out of the box than Maggie Gonzalez remarked, 'This stupid toy is worth more than the car.'

Chemo said, 'I need a private line. You'll see.'

They were driving back to the Holiday Inn after spending the morning at the office of Dr. George Ginger, the plastic surgeon. Maggie knew Dr. Ginger from his early days as one of Rudy's more competent underlings at the Durkos Center. She trusted George's skill and his discretion. He could be maddeningly slow, and he had terrible breath, but technically he was about as good as cosmetic surgeons come.

Chemo had prefaced the visit to Dr. Ginger with this warning to Maggie: 'If he messes up my face, I'll kill him on the spot. And then I'll kill you.'

The second thing that Chemo had bought with Rudy's money was a box of bullets for the rusty colt .38. Brand-new rounds, Federals. The good stuff.

Maggie had said, 'You're going into this with the wrong attitude.'

Chemo frowned. 'I've had rotten luck with doctors.'

'I know, I know.'

'I don't even like this guy's name, George Ginger. Sounds like a fag name to me.' Then he had checked the chambers on the Colt and slipped it into his pants.

'You're hopeless,' Maggie had said. 'I don't know why I even bother.'

'Because otherwise I'll shoot you.'

Fortunately the dermabrasion went smoothly. Dr. George

Ginger had never seen a burn case quite like Chemo's, but he wisely refrained from inquiry. Once, when Chemo wasn't looking, the surgeon snuck a peek at the cumbersome prosthesis attached to the patient's left arm. An avid gardener, Dr. Ginger recognized the Weed Whacker instantly, but resisted the impulse to pry.

The sanding procedure took about two hours, and Chemo endured stoically, without so much as a whimper. When it was over, he no longer looked as if someone had glued Rice Krispies all over his face. Rather, he looked as if he had been dragged for five miles behind a speeding dump truck.

His forehead, his cheeks, his nose, his chin all glowed with a raw, pink, oozing sheen. The spackled damage of the errant electrolysis needle had been scraped away forever, but now it was up to Chemo to grow a new skin. While he might never enjoy the radiant peachy complexion of, say, a Christie Brinkley, at least he would be able to stroll through an airport or a supermarket or a public park without causing small children to cringe behind their mothers' skirts. Chemo conceded that this alone would be a vast improvement, socially.

Before leaving the office, Maggie Gonzales had asked Dr. George Ginger to remove her sutures and inspect the progress of her New York facelift. He reported—with toxic breath—that everything was healing nicely, and gave Maggie a make-up mirror to look for herself. She was pleased by what she saw: The angry purple bruises were fading shadows under the eyes, and the incision scars had shrunk to tender rosy lines. She was especially delighted with her perky new nose.

Dr. Ginger studied the still-swollen promontory from several angles and nodded knowingly. 'The Sandy Duncan.'

Maggie smiled. 'Exactly!'

Popping a codeine Tylenol, Chemo said, 'Who the fuck is Sandy Duncan?'

In the Bonneville, on the way back to the motel, Chemo remarked, 'Three grand seems like a lot for what he did.'

'All he did was make you look human again,' Maggie said. 'Three grand was a bargain, if you ask me. Besides, he even gave a professional discount—fifteen percent off because I'm a nurse.'

As he steered, Chemo kept leaning toward the middle of the seat to check himself in the rearview. It was difficult to judge the result of the dermabrasion, since his face was slathered in a glue-colored ointment. 'I don't know,' he said. 'It's still pretty broken out.'

Maggie thought: Broken out? It's seeping, for God's sake. 'You heard what the doctor said. Give it a couple weeks to heal.' With that she leaned over and commandeered the rearview to examine her own refurbished features.

A beep-beep noise came chirping out of the dashboard; the car phone. With a simian arm Chemo reached into the glove compartment and snatched it on the second ring.

With well-acted nonchalance, he wedged the receiver between his ear and his left shoulder. Maggie thought it looked ridiculous to be riding in a junker like this and talking on a fancy car phone. Embarrassed, she scooted lower in the seat.

'Hullo,' Chemo said into the phone.

'Hello, Funny Face.' It was Mick Stranahan. 'I got your message.'

'Yeah?'

'Yeah.'

'And?'

'And you said to call, so I am.'

Chemo was puzzled at Stranahan's insulting tone of voice. The man ought to be scared. Desperate. Begging. At least polite.

Chemo said, 'I got your lady friend.'

'Yeah, yeah, I read the note.'

'So, you're waiting to hear my demands.'

'No,' said Stranahan, 'I'm waiting to hear you sing the fucking aria from *Madame Butterfly* . . . *Of course* I want to hear your demands.'

'Christ, you're in a shitty mood.'

'I can barely hear you,' Stranahan complained. 'Don't tell me you got one of those yuppie Mattel car phones.'

'It's a Panasonic,' Chemo said, sharply.

Maggie looked over at him with an impatient expression, as if to say: Get on with it.

As he braked for a stop light, the phone slipped from Chemo's ear. He took his good hand off the wheel to grab for it.

'Hell!' The receiver was gooey with the antibiotic ointment from his cheeks.

Stranahan's voice cracked through the static. 'Now what's the matter?'

'Nothing. Not a damn thing.' Chemo carefully propped the receiver on his shoulder. 'Look, here's the deal. You want to see your lady friend alive, meet me at the marina at midnight tonight.'

'Fuck you.'

'Huh?'

'That means no, Funny Face. No marina. I know what you want and you can have it. Me for her, right?'

'Right.' Chemo figured there was no sense trying to bullshit this guy.

'It's a deal,' Stranahan said, 'but I'm not going anywhere. You come to me.'

'Where are you now?'

'I'm at a pay phone on Bayshore Drive, but I won't be here long.'

Impatiently Chemo said, 'So where's the meet?'

'My place.'

'That house? No fucking way.'

' 'Fraid so.'

The car phone started sliding again. Chemo groped frantically for it, and the Bonneville began to weave off the road. Maggie reached over and steadied the wheel.

Chemo got a grip on the receiver and snarled into it: 'You hear what I said? No way am I going back to that damn stilt house.'

'Yes, you are. You'll be getting another call with more information.'

'Tell me now!'

'I can't,' Stranahan said.

'I'll kill the Marks girl, I swear.'

'You're not quite that stupid, are you?'

The hot flush of anger made Chemo's face sting even worse.

He said, 'We'll talk about this later. What time you gonna call?'

'Oh, not me,' Mick Stranahan said. 'I won't be the one calling back.'

'Then who?' Chemo demanded.

But the line had gone dead.

Willie played the videotape for his friend at WTVJ, the NBC affiliate in Miami. Willie's friend was sufficiently impressed by the blood on his shirt to let him use one of the editing rooms. 'You gotta see this,' Willie said.

He punched the tape into the machine and sat back to chew on his knuckles. He felt like an orphan. No Christina, no Reynaldo. He knew he should call New York, but he didn't know what to say or who to tell.

Willie's friend, who was a local news producer, pointed to the monitor. 'Where's that?' he asked.

'Surgery clinic over in Bal Harbour. That's the waiting room.'

The friend said, 'You were portable?'

'Right. Solo the whole way.'

'So where's Flemm? That doesn't look like him.'

'No, that's somebody else.' The monitor showed an operating room where a tall bald doctor was hunched over a chubby female patient. The bald doctor was gesticulating angrily at the camera and barking for a nurse to call the authorities. 'I don't know who that was,' Willie said. 'Wrong room.'

'Now you're back in the hallway, walking. People are yelling, covering their faces.'

'Yeah, but here it comes,' Willie said, leaning forward. 'Bingo. That's Ray on the table.'

'Jeez, what're they doing?'

'I don't know.'

'It looks like a goddamn Caesarean.'

Willie said, 'Yeah, but it was supposed to be a nose job.'

'Go on!'

The audio portion of the tape grew louder.

'Yeah, that's him!'

'Who? That's Ray?'

'Reynaldo Flemm.'
'I told you he looked familiar.'
'Who? Reynaldo who?'
'That guy from the TV.'
'This has gone far enough. . . .'

When the frame filled with Reynaldo Flemm's gaping muzzled face, Willie's friend hit the Pause button and said, 'Fucker never looked better.'

'You know him?'

'I knew him back from Philadelphia. Back when he was still Ray Fleming.'

'You're kidding,' Willie said.

'No, man, that's his real name. Raymond Fleming. Then he got on this bi-ethnic kick . . . 'Reynaldo Flemm'—half Latin, half Eastern bloc. Told everybody in the business that his mother was a Cuban refugee and his father was with the Yugoslavian resistance. Shit, I laugh about it but that's when his career really took off.'

Willie said, 'Romania. What he told me, his old man was with the Romanian underground.'

'His old man sold Whirlpools in Larchmont, I know for a fact. Let's see the rest.'

Willie pressed the Fast Forward and squeaked the tape past the part when he confronted Dr. Rudy Graveline about Victoria Barletta; he didn't want his producer friend to hear the dead woman's name, on the off-chance that the story could be salvaged. Willie slowed the tape to normal speed just as he zoomed in on the doctor's quavering eyes.

'Boris Karloff,' said Willie's friend.

'Watch.'

The camera angle widened to show Rudy Graveline feverishly toiling over Reynaldo's belly. Then came a mist of blood, and one of the nurses began shouting for the surgeon to stop.

'Geez,' said Willie's friend, looking slightly queasy. 'What's happening?'

The doctor abruptly wheeled from the operating table to confront the camera directly. In his bloody right hand was a wicked-looking instrument connected to a long plastic tube. The device was making an audible slurp-slurp noise.

'*Your turn, fat boy!*'

Willie's friend gestured at the monitor and said: 'He called you fat boy?'

'Watch!'

On the screen, the surgeon lunged forward with the pointy slurp-slurping device. There was a cry, a dull clunk. Then the picture got jerky and went gray.

Willie pressed the Stop button. 'I hauled ass,' he explained to his friend. 'He came at me with that sucking . . . *thing*, so I took off.'

'Don't blame you, man. But what about Ray?'

Willie took the videotape out of the editing console. 'That's what's got me scared. I get in the van and take off, right? Stop at the nearest phone booth and call this clinic. Whispering Palms is the name.'

'Yeah, I've heard of it.'

'So I call. Don't say who I am. I ask about Reynaldo Flemm. I say he's my brother. I'm s'posed to pick him up after the operation. Ask can I come by and get him. Nurse gets on the line and wants to know what's going on. She wants to know how come Ray was using a phony name when he checks in at the place. Johnny Tiger, some shit like that. I tell her I haven't got the faintest—maybe he was embarrassed, didn't want his nose job to turn up in the gossip columns. Then she says, well, he's not here. She says the doctor, this Rudy Graveline, the nurse says he drove Ray to Mount Sinai. She says she's not allowed to say anything more on the phone. So I haul ass over to Emergency at Sinai and guess what? No Ray anywhere. Fact there's nothing but strokes and heart attacks. No Reynaldo Flemm!'

Willie's friend said, 'This is too fucking weird. Even for Miami.'

'Best part is, now I gotta call New York and break the news.'

'Oh, man.'

Willie said, 'Maybe I'll ship the tape first.'

'Might as well,' agreed the producer. 'What about Ray? Think he's all right?'

'No,' said Willie. 'You want the truth, I'd be fucking amazed if he was all right.'

The nurses had wanted to call 911, but Rudy Graveline had said no, there wasn't time. I'll take him myself, Rudy had said. He had run to the parking lot (stopping only at the front desk to pick up Reynaldo's $15,000), got the Jag and pulled up at the staff entrance.

Back in the operating suite, the anesthetist had said: 'Everything's going flat.'

'Then hurry, goddammit!'

They had gotten Reynaldo on a gurney and wheeled him to Rudy's car and bundled him in the passenger seat. The scrub nurse even tried to hook up the safety belt.

'Oh, forget it,' Rudy had said.

'But it's a law.'

'Go back to work!' Rudy had commanded. The Jaguar had peeled rubber on its way out.

Naturally he had no intention of driving to Mount Sinai Hospital. What was the point? Rudy glanced at the man in the passenger seat and still did not recognize him from television. True, Reynaldo Flemm was not at his telegenic best. His eyes were half-closed, his mouth was half-open, and his skin was the color of bad veal.

He was also exsanguinating all over Rudy's fine leather seats and burled walnut door panels. 'Great,' Rudy muttered. 'What else.' As the surgeon sped south on Alton Road, he took out the portable telephone and called his brother's tree company.

'George Graveline, please. It's an emergency.'

'Uh, he's not here.'

'This is his brother. Where's he working today?'

The line clicked. Rudy thought he had been cut off. Then a lady from an answering service came on and asked him to leave his number. Rudy hollered, but she wouldn't budge. Finally he surrendered the number and hung up.

He thought: I must find George and his wood-chipping machine. This is very dicey, driving around Miami Beach in a

$47,000 sedan with a dead TV star in the front seat. *Bleeding* on the front seat.

The car phone beeped and Rudy grabbed at it in frantic optimism. 'George!'

'No, Dr. Graveline.'

'Who's this?'

'Sergeant García, Metro Homicide. You probably don't remember, but we met that night the mysterious midget Haitian blew up your car.'

Rudy's heart was pounding. Should he hang up? Did the cops know about Flemm already? But how—the nurses? Maybe that moron with the minicam!

Al García said: 'I got some bad news about your brother George.'

Rudy's mind was racing. The detective's words didn't register. 'What—could you give me that again?'

'I said I got bad news about George. He's dead.'

Rudy's foot came off the accelerator. He was coasting now, trying to think. Which way? Where?

García went on: 'He tried to kill a man and I had to shoot him. Internal Review has the full report, so I suggest you talk to them.'

Nothing.

'Doctor? You there?'

'Yuh.'

No questions, nothing.

'The way it went down, I had no choice.'

Rudy said dully, 'I understand.' He was thinking: It's awful about George, yes, but what am I going to do with this dead person in my Jaguar?

García could sense that something strange was going on at the end of the line. He said, 'Look, I know it's a bad time, but we've got to talk about a homicide. A homicide that may involve you and your brother. I'd like to come over to the clinic as soon as possible.'

'Make it tomorrow,' Rudy said.

'It's about Victoria Barletta.'

'I'm eager to help in any way I can. Come see me tomorrow.'

The surgeon sounded like a zombie. A heavily sedated zombie. If there was a realm beyond sheer panic, Rudy Graveline had entered it.

'Doctor, it really can't wait—'

'For heaven's sake, Sergeant, give me some time. I just found out my brother's dead, I need to make the arrangements.'

'To be blunt,' García said, 'as far as George goes, there's not a whole lot left to arrange.'

'Call me tomorrow,' Rudy Graveline said curtly. Then he threw the car phone out the window.

When the phone rang again in the Bonneville, Chemo gloated at Maggie Gonzalez. 'I told you this would come in handy.'

'Quit picking at your face.'

'It itches like hell.'

'Leave it be!' Maggie scolded. 'You want it to get infected? Do you?'

On the other end of the phone was Rudy Graveline. He sounded worse than suicidal.

Chemo said, 'Hey, Doc, you in your car? I'm in mine.'

He felt like the king of the universe.

'No, I'm home,' Rudy said. 'We have a major problem.'

'What's this *we* stuff? I don't have a problem. I got a hundred-twenty-odd grand, a brand-new face, a brand-new car phone. Life's looking better every day.'

Rudy said, 'I'm delighted for you, I really am.'

'You don't sound too damn delighted.'

'He got Heather.' The doctor choked out the words.

'Who's Heather?' Chemo said.

'My . . . I can't believe . . . when I got home, she was gone. He took her away.'

Maggie asked who was on the line and Chemo whispered the doctor's name. 'All right,' he said to Rudy, 'you better tell me what's up.'

Suddenly Rudy Graveline remembered what Curly Eyebrows had warned him about cellular phones, about how private conversations sometimes could be picked up on outside frequencies.

In his quickening state of emotional deterioration, Rudy clearly envisioned—as if it were real—some nosy Coral Gables housewife overhearing his felonious litany on her Amana toaster oven.

'Come to my house,' he instructed Chemo.

'I can't, I'm waiting on a call.'

'This is it.'

'What? You mean this is the phone call he—'

'Yes,' Rudy said. 'Get out here as fast as you can. We're going on a boat ride.'

'Jesus H. Christ.'

32

Maggie and Chemo left Christina Marks tied up in the trunk of the Bonneville, which was parked in Rudy Graveline's flagstone driveway. Miserable as she was, Christina didn't worry about suffocating inside the car; there were so many rust holes, she could actually feel a breeze.

For an hour Maggie and Chemo sat on the white leather sofa in Rudy's living room and listened to the doleful story of how he had come home to find his lover, his baby doll, his sweetie pie, his Venus, his sugar bunny, his punkin, his blond California sunbeam missing from the bedroom.

They took turns studying the kidnap note, which said:

'Ahoy! You're Invited to a Party!'

On the front of the note was a cartoon pelican in a sailor's cap. On the inside was a hand-drawn chart of Stiltsville. Chemo and Rudy grimly agreed that something had to be done permanently about Mick Stranahan.

Chemo asked about the fresh dark drops on the foyer, and Rudy said that it wasn't Heather's blood but someone else's. In chokes and sighs he told them about the mishap at the clinic with Reynaldo Flemm. Maggie Gonzalez listened to the gruesome account with amazement; she had never dreamed her modest extortion scheme would come to this.

'So, where is he?' she asked.

'In there,' Rudy replied. 'The Sub-Zero.'

Chemo said, 'The what? What're you talking about?'

Rudy led them to the kitchen and pointed at the cabinet-sized refrigerator. 'The Sub-Zero,' he said.

Maggie noticed that the aluminum freezer trays had been stacked on the counter, along with a half-dozen Lean Cuisines and three pints of chocolate Häagen-Dazs.

Chemo said, 'That's a big fridge, all right.' He opened the door and there was Reynaldo Flemm, upright and frosty as a Jell-O pop.

'It was the only way he could fit,' explained Rudy. 'See, I had to tear out the damn ice maker.'

Chemo said, 'He sure looks different on TV.' Chemo propped open the refrigerator door with one knee; the cold air made his face feel better.

Maggie said nothing. This wasn't part of the plan. She was trying to think of a way to sneak out of Rudy's house and run. Go back to the motel room, grab the black Samsonite, and disappear for about five years.

Chemo closed the freezer door. He pointed to more brownish spots on the bone-colored tile and said, 'If you got a mop, she can clean that up.'

'Wait a second,' Maggie said. 'Do I look like a maid?'

'You're gonna look like a cabbage if you don't do what I say.' Balefully Chemo brandished the Weed Whacker.

Maggie recalled the savage thrashing of Rudy Graveline and said, 'All right, put that stupid thing away.'

While Maggie mopped, Rudy moped. He seemed shattered, listless, inconsolable. He needed to think; he needed the soothing rhythm of athletic copulation, the sweet crystal tunnel of clarity that only Heather's loins could give him.

The day had begun with such promise!

Up before dawn to pack their bags. And the airline tickets—he had placed them in Heather's purse while she slept. He would drive to the clinic, perform the operation on the male go-go dancer, collect the fifteen grand, and come home for Heather. Then it was off to the airport! Fifteen thousand was plenty for starters—a month or two in Costa Rica in a nice apartment. Time enough for Rudy's Panamanian lawyer to liquidate the offshore trusts. After that, Rudy and Heather could breathe again. Get themselves some land up in the mountains. Split-level ranch house on the side of a hill. A stable, too; she loved to ride. Rudy envisioned himself opening a new surgery clinic; he had even packed his laminated Harvard diploma, pillowing it tenderly in the suitcase among his silk socks and designer underwear. San José was crawling with wealthy expatriates and aspiring international jet-setters. An American plastic surgeon would be welcomed vivaciously.

Now, disaster. Heather—fair, nubile, perfectly apportioned Heather—had been snatched from her sickbed.

'We need a boat,' Rudy Graveline croaked. 'For tonight.'

Chemo said, 'Yeah, a big one. If I'm going back to that damn house I want to stay dry. See if you can find us a Scarab thirty-eight.'

'Are you nuts?'

'Just like they had on *Miami Vice*.'

'You *are* nuts. Who's going to drive it?' Rudy stared pointedly at the unwieldy garden tool attached to Chemo's left arm. 'You?'

'Yeah, me. Just get on the phone, see what you can do. We've gotta move before the cops show up.'

Rudy looked stricken by the mention of police.

'Well, Jesus,' Chemo said, 'you got a dead man in your fridge. This is a problem.'

Maggie was rinsing the mop in the kitchen sink. She said, 'I've got an idea about that. You might not like it, but it's worth a try.'

Rudy shrugged wearily. 'Let's hear it.'

'I used to work for a surgeon who knew this guy . . . this guy who would buy certain things.'

'Surely you're not suggesting—'

'It's up to you,' Maggie said. 'I mean, Dr. Graveline, you've got yourself a situation here.'

'Yeah,' said Chemo. 'Your ice cream is melting.'

The man's name was Kimbler, and his office was in Miami's hospital district; a storefront operation on 12th Street, a purse-snatcher's jog from Jackson Hospital or the Medical Examiner's Office. The magnetic sign on the door of the office said: 'International Bio-Medical Exports, Inc.' The storefront window was tinted dark blue and was obscured by galvanized burglar mesh.

Kimbler was waiting for them when they arrived—Rudy, Chemo, Maggie, and Christina. Chemo had the Colt .38 in his pants pocket, pointed at Christina the whole time. He had wanted to leave her in the trunk of the Pontiac, but there was not enough room.

Kimbler was a rangy thin-haired man with tortoise-shell glasses and a buzzard's-beak nose. The office was lighted like a stockroom, with cheap egg-carton overheads. Rows of gray steel shelves covered both walls. The shelves were lined with old-fashioned Mason jars, and preserved in the Mason jars were assorted human body parts: ears, eyeballs, feet, hands, fingers, toes, small organs, large organs.

Chemo looked around and, under his breath, said, 'What the fuck.'

Kimbler gazed with equal wonderment at Chemo, who was truly a sight—his freshly sanded face glistening with Neosporin ointment, his extenuated left arm cloaked with its calfskin golf-bag cover, his radish-patch scalp, his handsome Jim Fowler safari jacket. Kimbler examined Chemo as if he were a prized future specimen.

'This is some hobby you got,' Chemo said, picking up a jar of gall bladders. 'This is better than baseball cards.'

Kimbler said, 'I've got the proper permits, I assure you.'

Maggie explained that Kimbler sold human tissue to foreign medical schools. She said it was perfectly legal.

'The items come from legitimate sources,' Kimbler added. 'Hospitals. Pathology labs.'

Items. Christina was nauseated at the concept. Or maybe it was just the sweet dead smell of the place.

Kimbler said, 'It may sound ghoulish, but I provide a much-needed service. These items, discarded organs and such, they would otherwise go to waste. Be thrown away. Flushed. Incinerated. Overseas medical schools are in great need of clinical teaching aids—the students are extremely grateful. You should see some of the letters.'

'No thanks,' Chemo said. 'What's a schlong go for these days?'

'Pardon me?'

Maggie cut in: 'Mr. Kimbler, we appreciate you seeing us on short notice. We have an unusual problem.'

Kimbler peered theatrically over the tops of his glasses. A slight smile came to his lips. 'I assumed as much.'

Maggie went on, 'What we have is an entire . . . *item.*'

'I see.'

'It's a pauper-type situation. Very sad—no family, no funds for a decent burial. We're not even sure who he is.'

Christina could scarcely contain herself. She had gotten a quick glimpse of a body as they angled it into the trunk of the Bonneville. A young man; that much she could tell.

Kimbler said to Maggie: 'What can you tell me of the circumstances? The manner of death, for instance.'

She said, 'An indigent case, like I told you. Emergency surgery for appendicitis.' She pointed at Rudy. 'Ask him, he's the doctor.'

Rudy Graveline was stupefied. He scrambled to catch up with Maggie's yarn. 'I was doing . . . he had a chronic heart condition. Bad arrhythmia. He should've said something before the operation, but he didn't.'

Kimbler pursed his lips. 'You're a surgeon?'

'Yes.' Rudy wasn't dressed like a surgeon. He was wearing Topsiders, tan cotton pants, and a Bean crewneck pullover. He was dressed for a boat ride. 'Here, wait.' He took out his wallet and showed Kimbler an I.D. card from the Dade County Medical Society. Kimbler seemed satisfied.

'I realize this is out of the ordinary,' Maggie said.

'Yes, well, let's have a look.'

Chemo pinched Christina by the elbow and said, 'We'll wait here.' He handed Maggie the keys to the Bonneville. She and Rudy led the man named Kimbler to the car, which was parked in a city lot two blocks away.

When Maggie opened the trunk, Rudy turned away. Kimbler adjusted his glasses and craned over the corpse as if he were studying the brush strokes on a fine painting. 'Hmmmmm,' he said. 'Hmmmmmm.'

Rudy edged closer to block the view of the trunk, in case any pedestrians got curious. His concern was groundless, for no one gave the trio a second look; half the people in Miami did their business out of car trunks.

Kimbler seemed impressed by what he saw. 'I don't get many whole cadavers,' he remarked. 'Certainly not of this quality.'

'We tried to locate a next of kin,' Rudy said, 'but for some reason the patient has given us a phony name.'

Kimbler chuckled. 'Probably had a very good reason. Probably a criminal of some type.'

'Every place we called was a dead end,' Rudy said, lamely embellishing the lie.

Maggie stepped in to help. 'We were going to turn him over to the county, but it seemed like such a waste.'

'Oh, yes,' said Kimbler. 'The shortage of good cadavers . . . by good, I mean white and well-nourished. Most of the schools I deal with—for instance, one place in the Dominican, they had only two cadavers for a class of sixty medical students. Tell me how those kids are ever going to learn gross anatomy.'

Rudy started to say something but thought better of it. The whole deal was illegal as hell, no doubt about it. But what choice did he have? For the first time in his anal-retentive, hyper-compulsive professional life he had lost control of events. He had surrendered himself to the squalid street instincts of Chemo and Maggie Gonzalez.

Kimbler was saying, 'Two measly cadavers, both dysenteries. Weighed about ninety pounds each. For sixty students! And this is not so unusual in some of these poor countries. There's a med school on Guadeloupe, the best they could do was monkey skeletons. To help out I shipped down two hearts and maybe a half-dozen lungs, but it's not the same as having whole human bodies.'

Shrewd haggler that she was, Maggie had heard enough. Slowly she closed, but did not lock, the rusty trunk of the Bonneville; Reynaldo Flemm had begun to thaw.

'So,' she said, 'you're obviously interested.'

'Yes,' said Kimbler. 'How does eight hundred sound?'

'Make it nine,' said Maggie.

Kimbler frowned irritably. 'Eight-fifty is pushing it.'

'Eight seventy-five. Cash.'

Kimbler still wore a frown, but he was nodding. 'All right. Eight seventy-five it is.'

Rudy Graveline was confused. 'You're paying *us*?'

'Of course,' Kimbler replied. He studied Rudy doubtfully. 'Just so there's no question later, you *are* a medical doctor? I mean, your state license is current. Not that you need to sign anything, but it's good to know.'

'Yes,' Rudy sighed. 'Yes, I'm a doctor. My license is up to date.' As if it mattered. If all went as planned, he'd be gone from the country by this time tomorrow. He and Heather, together on a mountaintop in Costa Rica.

The man named Kimbler tapped cheerfully on the trunk of the Bonneville. 'All right, then. Why don't you pull around back of the office. Let's get this item on ice straightaway.'

Mick Stranahan brought Heather Chappell a mug of hot chocolate. She pulled the blanket snugly around her shoulders and said, 'Thanks. I'm so damn cold.'

He asked how she was feeling.

'Beat up,' she replied. 'Especially after that boat ride.'

'Sorry,' Stranahan said. 'I know it's rough as hell—there's a front moving through so we got a big westerly tonight.'

Heather sipped tentatively at the chocolate. The kidnapper, whoever he was, watched her impassively from a wicker barstool. He wore blue jeans, deck shoes, a pale yellow cotton shirt and a poplin windbreaker. To Heather the man looked strong, but not particularly mean.

In the middle of the living room was a card table, covered by an oilskin cloth. On the table was a red Sears Craftsman toolbox. The kidnapper had been carrying it when he broke into Dr. Graveline's house.

Heather nodded toward the toolbox and said, 'What's in there?'

'Just some stuff I borrowed from Rudy.'

The furniture looked like it came from the Salvation Army, but still there was a spartan coziness about the place, especially with the soft sounds of moving water. Heather said, 'I like your house.'

'The neighborhood's not what it used to be.'

'What kind of fish is that on the wall?'

'It's a blue marlin. The bill broke off, I've got to get it fixed.'

Heather said, 'Did you catch it yourself?'

'No,' Stranahan smiled. 'I'm no Hemingway.'

'I read for *Islands in the Stream*. With George C. Scott—did you see it?'

Stranahan said no, he hadn't.

'I didn't get the part, anyway,' said Heather. 'I forget now who played the wife. George C. Scott was Hemingway, and there was lots of fishing.'

The beakless marlin stared down from the wall. Stranahan said, 'It used to be paradise out here.'

Heather nodded; she could picture it. 'What're you going to do with me?'

'Not much,' said Stranahan.

'I remember you,' she said. 'From the surgery clinic. That night in the parking lot, you put me in the cab. The night Rudolph's car caught fire.'

'My name is Mick.'

Being a famous actress, Heather didn't customarily introduce herself. This time she felt like she had to.

Stranahan said, 'The reason I asked how you're feeling is this.' He held up three pill bottles and gave them a rattle. 'These were on the nightstand by your bed. Young Dr. Rudy was keeping you loaded.'

'Painkillers, probably. See, I just had surgery.'

'Not painkillers,' Stranahan said. 'Seconal 100s. Industrial-strength, enough to put down an elephant.'

'What . . . why would he do that?'

Stranahan got off the barstool and walked over to Heather Chappell. In his right hand was a small pair of scissors. He knelt down in front of her and told her not to move.

'Oh, God,' she said.

'Be still.'

Carefully he clipped the bandages off her face. Heather expected the salty cool air to sting the incisions, but she felt nothing but an itchy sensation.

Stranahan said, 'I want to show you something.' He went to the bathroom and came back with a hand mirror. Heather studied herself for several moments.

In a puzzled voice she said, 'There's no marks.'

'Nope. No scars, no bruises, no swelling.'

'Rudolph said . . . See, he mentioned something about micro-surgery. Lasers, I think he said. He said the scars would be so small—'

'Bullshit.' Stranahan handed her the scissors. She gripped them in her right hand like a pistol.

'I'm going in the other room for a little while,' he said. 'Call me when you're done and I'll explain as much as I can.'

Ten minutes later Heather was pounding on the bedroom door. She had cut off the remaining bandages and phony surgical dressings. She was standing there naked, striped with gummy adhesive, and crying softly. Stranahan bundled her in the blanket and sat her on the bed.

'He was s'posed to do my boobs,' she said. 'And my hips. My nose, eyelids . . . everything.'

'Well, he lied,' said Stranahan.

'Please, I wanna go back to L.A.'

'Maybe tomorrow.'

'What's going on?' Heather cried. 'Can I use your phone, I've got to call my manager. Please?'

'Sorry,' said Stranahan. 'No telephone. No ship-to-shore. No fax. The weather's turned to shit, so we're stuck for the night.'

'But I'm s'posed to do a *Password* with Jack Klugman. God, what day is it?'

Stranahan said: 'Can I ask you something? You're a beautiful girl—you get points for that, okay—but how could you be so fucking dumb?'

Heather stopped crying instantly, gulped down her sobs. No man had ever talked to her this way. Well, wait; Patrick Duffy had, once. She was playing a debutante on *Dallas* and she forgot one lousy line. One out of seventeen! But later at least Patrick Duffy had said he was sorry for blowing his stack.

Mick Stranahan said, 'To trust yourself to a hack like Graveline, Jesus, it's pathetic. And for what? Half an inch off your hips. A polyurethane dimple in your chin. Plastic bags inside your breasts. Think about it: A hundred years from now, your coffin cracks open and there's nothing inside but two little bags of silicone. No flesh, no bones, everything's turned to ashes except for your boobs. They're bionic. Eternal!'

In a small voice Heather said, 'But everybody does it.'

Stranahan tore off the blanket, and for the first time Heather was truly afraid. He told her to stand up.

'Look at yourself.'

Diffidently she lowered her eyes.

'There's not a thing wrong with you,' Stranahan said. 'Tell me what's wrong with you.'

The wind shook the shutters, and shafts of cold air sliced the room. Heather shivered, sat down, and put her hands over her nipples. Stranahan folded his arms as if he were awaiting something: An explanation.

'You're a man, I don't expect you to understand.' She wondered if he would try to touch her in some way.

'Vanity I understand,' Stranahan said. 'Men are experts on the subject.' He picked the blanket off the floor. Indifferently he draped it across her lap. 'I think there's some warm clothes in one of the drawers.'

He found a gray sweatsuit with a hood and a pair of men's woolen socks. Hurriedly Heather got dressed. 'Just tell me,' she said, still trembling, 'why did Rudolph lie about this? I can't get over it—why didn't he do the operation?'

'I guess he was scared. In case you didn't notice, he's crazy about you. He probably couldn't bear the thought of something going wrong in surgery. It's been known to happen.'

'But I paid him,' Heather said. 'I wrote the bastard a personal check.'

'Stop it, you're breaking my heart.'

Heather glared at him.

'Look,' said Stranahan, 'I've seen his Visa bill. Swanky restaurants, designer clothes, a diamond here and there—you made out pretty well. Did he mention he was going to fly you away on a tropical vacation?'

'I remember him saying something about Costa Rica, of all places.'

'Yeah, well, don't worry. The trip's off. Rudy's had a minor setback.'

Heather said, 'So tell me what's going on.'

'Just consider yourself damn lucky.'

'Why? What are you talking about?'

'Rudy killed a young woman just like you. No, I take that back—she wasn't just like you, she was innocent. And he killed her with a nose job.'

Heather Chappell cringed. Unconsciously her hand went to her face.

'That's what this is all about,' Stranahan said. 'You don't believe me, ask him yourself. He's on his way.'

'Here?'

'That's right. To save you and to kill me.'

'Rudolph? No way.'

'You don't know him like I do, Heather.'

Stranahan went from room to room, turning off the lights. Heather followed, saying nothing. She didn't want to be left alone, even by him. Carrying a Coleman lantern, Stranahan led her out of the stilt house and helped her climb to the roof. The windmill whistled and thrummed over their heads.

Heather said, 'God, this wind is really getting nasty.'

'Sure is.'

'What kind of gun is that?'

'A shotgun, Heather.'

'I can't believe Rudolph is coming all the way out here on a night like this.'

'Yep.'

'What's the shotgun for?'

'For looks,' said Stranahan. 'Mostly.'

33

Al García was feeling slightly guilty about lying to Mick Stranahan until Luis Córdova's patrol boat conked out. Now Luis was hanging over the transom, poking around the lower unit; García stood next to him, aiming a big waterproof spotlight and cursing into the salt spray.

García thought: I hate boats. Car breaks down, you just walk away from it. With a damn boat, you're stuck.

They were adrift about half a mile west of the Seaquarium. It was pitch black and ferociously choppy. A chilly northwesterly wind cut through García's plastic windbreaker and made him wish he had waited until dawn, as he had promised Stranahan.

It did not take Luis Córdova long to discover the problem with the engine. 'It's the prop,' he said.

'What about it?'

'It's gone,' said Luis Córdova.

'We hit something?'

'No, it just fell off. Somebody monkeyed with the pin.'

García considered this for a moment. 'Does he know where you keep the boat?'

'Sure,' said Luis Córdova.

'Shit.'

'I better get on the radio and see if we can get help.'

Al García stowed the spotlight, sat down at the console and lit a cigarette. He said, 'That bastard. He didn't trust us.'

Luis Córdova said, 'We need a new prop or a different boat. Either way, it's going to take a couple hours.'

'Do what you can.' To the south García heard the sound of another boat on the bay; Luis Córdova heard it, too—the hull slapping heavily on the waves. The hum of the engine receded as the craft moved farther away. They knew exactly where it was going.

'Goddamn,' said García.

'You really think he did this?'

'I got no doubt. The bastard didn't trust us.'

'I can't imagine why,' said Luis Córdova, reaching for the radio.

Driving across the causeway to the marina, Chemo kept thinking about the stilt house and the monster fish that had eaten off his hand. As hard as he tried, he could not conceal his trepidation about going back.

When he saw the boat that Rudy Graveline had rented, Chemo nearly called off the expedition. 'What a piece a shit,' he said.

It was a twenty-one-foot outboard, tubby and slow, with an old sixty-horse Merc. A cheap hotel rental, designed for abuse by tourists.

Chemo said, 'I'm not believing this.'

'At this hour I was lucky to find anything,' said Rudy.

Maggie Gonzalez said, 'Let's just get it over with.' She got in the boat first, followed by Rudy, then Christina Marks.

Chemo stood on the pier, peering across the bay toward the amber glow of the city. 'It's blowing like a fucking typhoon,' he said. He really did not want to go.

'Come on,' Rudy said. He was frantic about Heather; more precisely, he was frantic about what he would have to do to get her back. He had a feeling that Chemo didn't give a damn one way or another, as long as Mick Stranahan got killed.

As Chemo was unhitching the bow rope, Christina Marks said, 'This is really a bad idea.'

'Shut up,' said Chemo.

'I mean it. You three ought to get away while you can.'

'I said shut up.'

Maggie said, 'She might be right. This guy, he's not exactly a stable person.'

Chemo clumped awkwardly into the boat and started the engine. 'What, you want to spend the rest of your life in jail? You think he's gonna forget about everything and let us ride off into the sunset?'

Rudy Graveline shivered. 'All I want is Heather.'

Christina said, 'Don't worry, Mick won't hurt her.'

'Who gives a shit,' said Chemo, gunning the throttle with his good hand.

By the time they made it to Stiltsville, Chemo felt like his face was aflame. The rental boat rode like a washtub, each wave slopping over the gunwale and splashing spray against the raw flesh of his cheeks. The salt stung like cold acid. Chemo soon ran out of profanities. Rudy Graveline was no help, nor were the women; they were all soaking wet, queasy, and glum.

As he made a wide weekend-sailor's turn into the Biscayne Channel, Chemo slowed down and pointed with the Weed Whacker. 'What the fuck?' he said. 'Look at that.'

Across the bonefish flats, Stranahan's stilt house was lit up like a used-car lot. Lanterns hung off every piling, and swung eerily in the wind. The brown shutters were propped open and there was music, too, fading in and out with each gust.

Christina Marks laughed to herself. 'The Beatles,' she said. He was playing 'Happiness Is a Warm Gun.'

Chemo snorted. 'What, he's trying to be cute?'

'No,' Christina said. 'Not him.'

Maggie Gonzalez swept a whip of wet hair out of her face. 'He's nuts, obviously.'

'And we're not?' Rudy said. He got the binoculars and tried to spot Heather Chappell on the stilt house. He could see no sign of life, human or otherwise. He counted a dozen camp lanterns aglow.

The sight of the place brought back dreadful memories for Chemo. Too clearly he could see the broken rail where he had fallen to the water that day of the ill-fated jet ski assault. He wondered about the fierce fish, whatever it was, dwelling beneath the stilt house. Inwardly he speculated about its nocturnal feeding habits.

Maggie said, 'How are we going to handle this?'

Rudy looked at her sternly. 'We don't do anything until Heather's safe in this boat.'

Chemo grabbed Christina's arm and pulled her to the console. 'Stand here, next to me,' he said. 'Real close, in case your jerkoff boyfriend gets any ideas.' He pressed the barrel of the Colt .38 to her right breast. With the stem of the Weed Whacker he steadied the wheel.

As the boat bucked and struggled across the shallow bank toward Mick Stranahan's house, Christina Marks accepted the probability that she would not live through the next few moments. 'For the record,' she said, 'he's *not* my boyfriend.'

Maggie nudged her with an elbow and whispered, 'You could've done worse.'

Chemo stopped the boat ten yards from the dock.

The stereo had died. The only sound was the thrum of the windmill and the chalkboard squeak of the Colemans, swinging in the gusts. The house scorched the sky with its watery brightness; a white torch in the blackest middle of nowhere. Christina wondered: Where did he get so many bloody lanterns?

Chemo looked down at Rudy Graveline. 'Well? You're the one who got the invitation.'

Rudy nodded grimly. On rubbery legs he made his way to the bow of the boat; the rough, wet ride had drubbed all the nattiness out of his L. L. Bean wardrobe. The doctor cupped both hands to his mouth and called out Stranahan's name.

Nothing.

He glanced back at Chemo, who shrugged. The .38 was still aimed at Christina Marks.

Next Rudy called Heather's name and was surprised to get a reply.

'Up here!' Her voice came from the roof, where it was darker.

'Come on down,' Rudy said excitedly.

'No, I don't think so.'

'Are you all right?'

'I'm fine,' said Heather. 'No thanks to you.'

Chemo made a sour face at Rudy. 'Now what?'

'Don't look at me,' the doctor said.

Chemo called out to Heather: 'We're here to save you. What's your fucking problem?'

Suddenly Heather appeared on the roof. For balance she held onto the base of the windmill. She was wearing a gray sweatsuit with a hood. 'My problem? Ask him.' She pulled the hood off her head, and Rudy Graveline saw that the bandages were gone.

'Damn,' he said.

'Let's hear it,' Chemo muttered.

'I was supposed to do some surgery, but I didn't. She thought— see, I told her I did it.'

Maggie Gonzalez said, 'You're right. Everybody out here is crazy.'

'I paid you, you bastard!' Heather shouted.

'Please, I can explain,' Rudy pleaded.

Chemo was disgusted. 'This is some beautiful moment. She doesn't want to be rescued, she hates your damn guts.'

Heather disappeared from the roof. A few moments later she emerged, still alone, on the deck of the stilt house. Rudy Graveline tossed her the bow rope and she wrapped it around one of the dock cleats. The surgeon stepped out of the boat and tried to give her a hug, but Heather backed up and said, 'Don't you touch me.'

'Where's Stranahan?' Chemo demanded.

'He's around here somewhere,' Heather said.

'Can he hear us?'

'I'm sure.'

Chemo's eyes swept back and forth across the house, the deck, the roof. Every time he glanced at the water he thought of the terrible fish and how swiftly it had happened before. His knuckles were blue on the grip of the pistol.

A voice said: 'Look here.'

Chemo spun around. The voice had come from beneath the stilt house, somewhere in the pilings, where the tide hissed.

Mick Stranahan said: 'Drop the gun.'

'Or what?' Chemo snarled.

'Or I'll blow your new face off.'

Chemo saw an orange flash, and instantly the lantern nearest his head exploded. Maggie shrieked and Christina squirmed from

Chemo's one-armed clasp. On the deck of the house, Rudy Grave-line dropped to his belly and covered his head.

Chemo stood alone with his lousy pistol. His ears were roaring. Shards of hot glass stuck to his scalp. He thought: That damn shotgun again.

When the echo from the gunfire faded, Stranahan's voice said: 'That's buckshot, Mr. Tatum. In case you were wondering.'

Chemo's face was killing him. He contemplated the damage that a point-blank shotgun blast would do to his complexion, then tossed the Colt .38 into the bay. Perhaps a deal could be struck; even after splurging on the car phone, there was still plenty of money to go around.

Stranahan ordered Chemo to get out of the boat. 'Carefully.'

'No shit.'

'Remember what happened last time with the 'cuda.'

'So that's what it was.' Chemo remembered seeing pictures of barracudas in sports magazines. What he remembered most were the incredible teeth. 'Jesus H. Christ,' he said.

Stranahan didn't mention that the big barracuda was long gone—off to deeper water to wait out the cold. Probably laid up in Fowey Rocks.

Chemo moved with crab-like deliberation, one gangly limb at a time. Between the rocking of the boat and the lopsided weight of his prosthesis, he found it difficult to balance on the slippery gunwale. Maggie Gonzalez came up from behind and helped boost him to the dock. Chemo looked surprised.

'Thanks,' he said.

From under the house, Stranahan's voice: 'All right, Heather, get in the boat.'

'Wait a second,' said Rudy.

'Don't worry, she'll be all right.'

'Heather, don't!' Rudy was thinking about that night in the fireplace, and that morning in the shower. And about Costa Rica.

'Hands off,' said Heather, stepping into the boat.

By now Christina Marks had figured out the plan. She said, 'Mick, I want to stay.'

'Ah, you changed your mind.'

'What—'

'You want to get married after all?'

The words hung in the night like the mischievous cry of a gull. Then, from under the stilt house, laughter. 'Everything's just a story to you,' Stranahan said. 'Even me.'

Christina said, 'That's not true.' No one seemed particularly moved by her sincerity.

'Don't worry about it,' Stranahan said. 'I'll still love you, no matter what.'

Rudy cautiously got to his feet and stood next to Chemo. In the flickering lantern glow, Chemo looked more waxen than ever. He seemed hypnotized, his puffy blowfish eyes fixed on the surging murky waves.

Heather said, 'Should I untie the boat now?'

'Not just yet,' Stranahan called back. 'Check Maggie's jacket, would you?'

Maggie Gonzalez was wearing a man's navy pea jacket. When Heather reached for the pockets, Maggie pushed her arm away.

There was a metallic clunking noise under the house: Stranahan, emerging from his sniper hole. Quickly he clambered out of the aluminum skiff, over the top of the water tank, pulling himself one-handed to the deck of the house. His visitors got a good long look at the Remington.

'Maggie, be a good girl,' Stranahan said. 'Let's see what you've got.'

Christina took one side of the coat and Heather took the other. 'Keys,' Christina announced, holding them up for Stranahan to see. One was a tiny silver luggage key, the other was from a room at the Holiday Inn.

Chemo blinked sullenly and patted at his pants. 'Jesus H. Christ,' he said. 'The bitch picked my pockets.'

He couldn't believe it: Maggie had lifted the keys while helping him out of the boat! She planned to sneak back to the motel and steal all the money.

'I know how you feel,' Stranahan said to Chemo. He reached into the boat and plucked the keys from Christina's hand. He put them in the front pocket of his jeans.

'What now?' Rudy whined, to anyone who might have a clue.

Chemo's right hand crept to his left armpit and found the toggle switch for the battery pack. The Weed Whacker buzzed, stalled once, then came to life.

Stranahan said, 'I'm impressed, I admit it.' He aimed the Remington at Chemo's head and told him not to move.

Chemo paid no attention. He took two giraffe-like steps across the dock and, with a vengeful groan, dove into the stern of the boat after Maggie. They all went down in a noisy tangle—Chemo, Maggie, Heather and Christina—the boat listing precariously against the pilings.

Mick Stranahan and Rudy Graveline watched the melee from the lower deck of the stilt house. One woman's scream, piercing and feline, rose above the uproar.

'Do something!' the doctor cried.

'All right,' said Stranahan.

Later, Stranahan gathered all the lanterns and brought them inside. Rudy Graveline lay in his undershorts on the bed; he was handcuffed spreadeagle to the bedposts. Chemo was unconscious on the bare floor, folded into a corner. With the shutters latched, the lanterns made the bedroom as bright as a television studio.

Rudy said, 'Are they gone?'

'They'll be fine. The tide's running out.'

'I'm not sure if Heather can swim.'

'The boat won't sink. They'll all be fine.'

Rudy noticed fresh blood on Stranahan's forehead, where he had been grazed by the Weed Whacker. 'You want me to look at that?'

'No,' Stranahan said acidly. 'No, I don't.' He left the bedroom and returned with the red Sears Craftsman toolbox. 'Look what I've got,' he said to Rudy.

Rudy craned to see. Stranahan opened the toolbox and began to unpack. 'Recognize any of this stuff?'

'Yes, of course . . . what're you doing?'

'Before we get started, there's something I ought to tell you. The cops have Maggie's videotape, so they know about what you did to Vicky Barletta. Whether they can convict you is another matter. I mean, Maggie is not exactly a prize witness. In fact, she'd probably change her story again for about twenty-five cents.'

Rudy Graveline swallowed his panic. He was trying to figure out what Stranahan wanted and how to give it to him. Rudy could only asume that, deep down, Stranahan must be no different than the others: Maggie, Bobby Pepsical, or even Chemo. Surely Stranahan had a scam, an angle. Surely it involved money.

Stranahan went out again and returned with the folding card table. He placed it in the center of the room, covered with the oilskin cloth.

'What is it?' the doctor said. 'What do you want?'

'I want you to show me what happened.'

'I don't understand.'

'To Vicky Barletta. Show me what went wrong.' He began placing items from the toolbox on the card table.

'You're insane,' said Rudy Graveline. It seemed the obvious conclusion.

'Well, if you don't help,' Stranahan said, 'I'll just have to wing it.' He tore open a package of sterile gloves and put them on. Cheerily he flexed the latex fingers in front of Rudy's face.

The surgeon stared back, aghast.

Stranahan said, 'Don't worry, I did some reading up on this. Look here, I got the Marcaine, plenty of cotton, skin hooks, a whole set of new blades.'

From the toolbox he selected a pair of doll-sized surgical scissors and began trimming the hairs in Rudy Graveline's nose.

'Aw, no!' Rudy said, thrashing against the bedposts.

'Hold still.'

Next Stranahan scrubbed the surgeon's face thoroughly with Hibiclens soap.

Rudy's eyes began to water. 'What about some anesthesia?' he bleated.

'Oh yeah,' said Stranahan. 'I almost forgot.'

Chemo awoke and rolled over with a thonk, the Weed Whacker bouncing on the floor planks. He sat up slowly, groping under his shirt. The battery sling was gone; the Weed Whacker was dead.

'Ah!' said Mick Stranahan. 'The lovely Nurse Tatum.'

A knot burned on the back of Chemo's head, where Stranahan had clubbed him with the butt of the Remington. Teetering to his feet, the first thing Chemo focused upon was Dr. Rudy Graveline—cuffed half-naked to the bed. His eyes were taped shut and a frayed old beach towel had been tucked around his neck. A menacing tong-like contraption lay poised near the surgeon's face: a speculum, designed for spreading the nostrils. It looked like something Moe would have used on Curly.

Stranahan stood at a small table cluttered with tubes and gauze and rows of sharp stainless-steel instruments. In one corner of the table was a heavy gray textbook, opened to the middle.

'What the fuck?' said Chemo. His voice was foggy and asthmatic.

Stranahan handed him a sterile glove. 'I need your help,' he said.

'No, not him,' objected Rudy, from the bed.

'This is where we are,' Stranahan said to Chemo. 'We've got his nose numb and packed. Got the eyes taped to keep out the blood. Got plenty of sponges—I'm sorry, you look confused.'

'Yeah, you could say that.' Scraggles of hair rose on the nape of Chemo's scalp. His stomach heaved against his ribs. He wanted out—but where was the goddamn shotgun?

'Put the glove on,' Stranahan told him.

'What for?'

'The doctor doesn't want to talk about what happened to Victoria Barletta—she died during an operation exactly like this. I know it's been four years, and Dr. Graveline's had hundreds of patients since then. But my idea was that we might be able to refresh his memory by re-enacting the Barletta case. Right here.'

Rudy fidgeted against the handcuffs.

Chemo said, 'For Christ's sake, just tell him what he wants to hear.'

'There's nothing to tell,' said Rudy. By now he was fairly certain that Stranahan was bluffing. Already Stranahan had skipped several fundamental steps in the rhinoplasty. He had not attempted to file the bony dorsum, for example. Nor had he tried to make any incisions inside of Rudy's nostrils. This led Rudy to believe that Stranahan wasn't serious about doing a homemade nose job, that he was merely trying to frighten the doctor into a cheap confession.

To Chemo, of course, the makeshift surgical suite was a gulag of horrors. One glimpse of Rudy, blindfolded and splayed like a pullet on a bed, convinced Chemo that Mick Stranahan was monstrously deranged.

Stranahan was running a forefinger down a page of the surgical text. 'Apparently this is the most critical part of the operation— fracturing the nasal bones on both sides of the septum. This is very, very delicate.' He handed Chemo a small steel mallet and said, 'Don't worry, I've been reading up on this.'

Chemo tested the weight of the mallet in his hand. 'This isn't funny,' he said.

'Is it supposed to be? We're talking about a young woman's death.'

'Probably it was an accident,' Chemo said. He gestured derisively at Rudy Graveline. 'The guy's a putz, he probably just fucked up.'

'But you weren't there. You don't know.'

Chemo turned to Rudy. 'Tell him, you asshole.'

Rudy shook his head. 'I'm an excellent surgeon,' he insisted.

Stranahan foraged through the toolbox until he found the proper instrument.

'What's that, a chisel?' Chemo asked.

'Very good,' Stranahan said. 'Actually, it's called an osteotome. A Storz number four. But basically, yeah, it's just a chisel. Look here.'

He leaned over the bed and pinched the bridge of Rudy Graveline's nose. With the other hand he gingerly slipped the osteotome into the surgeon's right nostril, aligning the instrument lengthwise along the septum. 'Now, Mr. Tatum, I'll hold this steady while you give it a slight tap—'

'Nuggghhh,' Rudy protested. The dull pressure of the chisel reawakened the fear that Stranahan was really going to do it.

'Did you say something?' Stranahan asked.

'You were right,' the surgeon said. His voice came out in a wheeze. 'About the Barletta girl.'

'You killed her?'

'I didn't mean to, I swear to God.' Between the pinch of Stranahan's fingers and the poke of the osteotome, Rudy Graveline talked like he had a terrible cold.

He said, 'What happened was, I let go of her nose. It was . . . terrible luck. I let go just when the nurse hit the chisel, so—'

'So it went all the way up.'

'Yes. The radio was on, I lost my concentration. The Lakers and the Sonics. I didn't do it on purpose.'

Stranahan said, 'And afterwards you got your brother to destroy the body.'

'Uh-huh.' Rudy couldn't nod very well with the Number 4 osteotome up his nostril.

'And what about my assistant?' Stranahan glanced over at Chemo. 'You hired him to kill me, right?'

Rudy's Adam's apple hopped up and down like a scalded toad. Sightless, he imagined the scene by what he could hear: The plink of the instruments, the two men breathing, the wind and the waves shaking the house, or so it seemed.

Stranahan said, 'Look, I know it's true. I'd just like to hear the terms of the deal.'

Rudy felt the chisel nudge the bony plate between the eye sockets, deep in his face. He was, understandably, reluctant to give Mick Stranahan the full truth—that the price on his head was to be paid in discount dermatological treatments.

Rudy said, 'It was sort of a trade.'

'This I gotta hear.'

'Tell him,' Rudy said blindly to Chemo. 'Tell him the arrangement with the dermabrasion, tell—'

Chemo reacted partly out of fear of incrimination and partly out of embarrassment. He let out a feral grunt and swung the mallet with all his strength. It was a clean blow to the butt of the osteotome, precisely the right spot.

Only much too hard. So hard that it knocked the chisel out of Stranahan's hand.

So hard that the instrument disappeared entirely, as if inhaled by Rudy Graveline's nose.

So hard that the point of the chisel punched through the brittle plate of the ethmoid bone and penetrated Rudy Graveline's brain.

The hapless surgeon shuddered, kicked his left leg, and went limp. 'Damn,' said Stranahan, jerking his hand away from the blood.

This he hadn't planned. Stranahan had anticipated having to kill Chemo, at some point, because of the man's stubborn disposition to violence. He had figured that Chemo would grab for the shotgun or maybe a kitchen knife, something dumb and obvious; then it would be over. But the doctor, alive and indictable, Stranahan had promised to Al García.

He looked up from the body and glared at Chemo. 'You happy now?'

Chemo was already moving for the door, wielding the mallet and neutered Weed Whacker as twin bludgeons, warning Stranahan not to follow. Stranahan could hear the seven-foot killer clomping through the darkened house, then out on the wooden deck, then down the stairs toward the water.

When Stranahan heard the man coming back, he retrieved the Remington from under the bed and waited.

Chemo was panting as he ducked through the doorway. 'The fuck did you do to your boat?'

'I shot a hole in it,' Stranahan said.

'Then how do we got off this goddamn place?'

'Swim.'

Chemo's lips curled. He glowered at the bulky lawn appliance strapped to the stump of his arm. He could unfasten it, certainly, but how far would he get? Paddling with one arm at night, in these treacherous waters! And what about his face—it would be excruciating, the stringent salt water scouring his fresh abrasions. Yet there was no other way out. It would be lunacy to stay.

Stranahan lowered the gun and said, 'Here, I think this belongs to you.'

He took something out of his jacket and held it up, so the gold and silver links caught the flush of the lantern lights. Chemo's knees went to rubber when he saw what it was.

The Swiss diving watch. The one he lost to the barracuda.

'Still ticking,' said Mick Stranahan.

34

At dawn the cold front arrived under a foggy purple brow, and the wind swung dramatically to the north. The waves off the Atlantic turned swollen and foamy, nudging the boat even farther from the shore of Cape Florida. The tide was still creeping out.

The women were weary of shouting and waving for help, but they tried once more when a red needlenose speedboat rounded the point of the island. The driver of the speedboat noticed the commotion and cautiously slowed to approach the other craft. A young woman in a lemon cotton pullover sat beside him.

She stood up and called out: 'What's the matter?'

Christina Marks waved back. 'Engine trouble! We need a tow to the marina.'

The driver, a young muscular Latin, edged the speedboat closer. He offered to come aboard and take a look at the motor.

'Don't bother,' said Christina. 'The gas line is cut.'

'How'd that happen?' The young man couldn't imagine.

It was a strange scene so early on a cold morning. Three women alone on rough water. The one, a slender brunette, looked pissed off about something. The blonde in a sweatsuit was unsteady, maybe seasick. Then there was a Cuban woman, attractive except for an angry-looking bald patch on the crown of her head.

'You all right?' the young man asked.

The Cuban woman nodded brusquely. 'How about giving us a lift?'

The young man in the speedboat turned to his companion and quietly said, 'Tina, I don't know. Something's fucked up here.'

'We've got to help,' the young woman said. 'I mean, we can't just leave them.'

'There'll be other boats.'

Christina Marks said, 'At least can we borrow your radio? Something happened out there.' She motioned toward the distant stilt houses.

'What was it?' said Tina, alarmed.

Maggie Gonzalez, who had prison to consider, said firmly: 'Nothing happened. She's drunk out of her mind.'

And Heather Chappell, who had her career to consider, said: 'We were s'posed to meet some guys for a party. The boat broke down, that's all.'

Christina's eyes went from Heather to Maggie. She felt like crying, and then she felt like laughing. She was as helpless and amused as she could be. So much for sisterhood.

'I know how that goes,' Tina was saying, 'with parties.'

Heather said, 'Please, I don't feel so hot. We've been drifting for hours.' Her face looked familiar, but Tina wasn't sure.

The Cuban woman with the bald patch said, 'Do you have an extra soda?'

'Sure,' said Tina. 'Richie, throw them a rope.'

Sergeant Al García bent over the rail and got rid of his breakfast muffins.

'I thought you were a big fisherman,' needled Luis Córdova. 'Who was it told me you won some fishing tournament?'

'That was different.' García wiped his mustache with the sleeve of the windbreaker. 'That was on a goddamn lake.'

The journey out to Stiltsville had been murderously rough. That was García's excuse for getting sick—the boat ride, not what they had found inside the house.

Luis Córdova chucked him on the arm. 'Anyway, you feel better now.'

The detective nodded. He was still smoldering about the patrol boat, about how it had taken three hours to get a new pin for the prop. Three crucial hours, it turned out.

'Where's Wilt?' García asked.

'Inside. Pouting.'

The man known as Chemo was standing up, his right arm suspended over his head. Luis Córdova had handcuffed him to

the overhead water pipes in the kitchen. As a security precaution, the Weed Whacker had been unstrapped from the stump
of Chemo's left arm. Trailing black and red cables, the yard clipper
lay on the kitchen bar.

Luis Córdova pointed at the monofilament coil on the rotor.
'See that—human hair,' he said to Al García. 'Long hair, too; a
brunette. Probably a woman's.'

García turned to the killer. 'Hey, Wilt, you a barber?'

'Fuck you.' Chemo blinked neutrally.

'He says that a lot,' said Luis Córdova. 'It's one of his favorite
things. All during the Miranda, he kept saying it.'

Al García walked over to Chemo and said, 'You're aware that
there's a dead doctor in the bedroom?'

'Fuck you.'

'See,' said Luis Córdova. 'That's all he knows.'

'Well, at least he knows *something*.' García groped in his
pocket and came out with a wrinkled handkerchief. He put the
handkerchief to his face and returned to the scene in the bedroom. He came out a few minutes later and said, 'That's very
unpleasant.'

'Sure is,' agreed Luis Córdova.

'Mr. Tatum, since you're not talking, you might as well listen.'
García arranged himself on one of the wicker barstools and stuck
a cigar in his mouth. He didn't light it.

He said, 'Here's what's happened. You and the doctor have a
serious business disagreement. You lure the dumb bastard out
here and try to torture some dough out of him. But somehow
you screw it up—you kill him.'

Chemo reddened. 'Horse shit,' he said.

Luis Córdova looked pleased. 'Progress,' he said to García.
'We're making progress.'

Chemo clenched his fist, causing the handcuff to rattle against
the rusty pipe. He said, 'You know damn well who it was.'

'Who?' García raised the palms of his hands. 'Where is this
mystery man?'

'Fuck you,' Chemo said.

'What I can't figure out,' said the detective, 'is why you didn't take off. After all this mess, why'd you stay on the house? Hell, *chico*, all you had to do was jump.'

Chemo lowered his head. His cheeks felt hot and prickly; a sign of healing, he hoped.

'Maybe he can't swim,' suggested Luis Córdova.

'Maybe he's scared,' García said.

Chemo said nothing. He closed his eyes and concentrated on the soothing sounds of freedom: the wind and the waves and the gulls, and the ticking of his waterproof wristwatch.

Al García waited until he was outside to light up the cigar. He turned a shoulder to the wind and cupped the match in his hand.

'I called for the chopper,' said Luis Córdova. 'And a guy from the M.E.'

'Gives us what, maybe half an hour?'

'Maybe,' said the young marine patrolman. 'We got time to check the other houses. Wilt's not going anywhere.'

García tried to blow a smoke ring, but the wind sucked it away. The cusp of the front had pushed through, and the sky over Biscayne Bay was clearing. The first sunlight broke out of the haze in slanted golden shafts that fastened to the water like quartz, lighting up the flats.

'I see why you love it out here,' García said.

Luis Córdova smiled. 'Some days it's like a painting.'

'Where do you think he went?'

'Mick? He might be dead. Guy that size could probably take him. Dump the body off the house.'

García gnawed skeptically at the end of the cigar. 'It's possible. Or he could've got away. Don't forget, he had that pump gun.'

'His skiff's sunk,' Luis Córdova noted. 'Somebody blasted a hole in the bottom.'

'Weird,' said Al García. 'But I had to guess, I'd say he probably wasn't around when all this happened. I'd say he got off the house.'

'Maybe.'

'Whatever happened out here, it was between Tatum and the

doctor. Maybe it was money, maybe it was something to do with surgery. Christ, you notice that guy's arm?'

'His face, too,' said Luis Córdova. 'What you're saying makes sense. Just looking at him, he's not the type to file a lawsuit.'

'But doing it with a hammer, that's cold,' García puffed his cheeks as if to whistle. 'On the other hand, your victim ain't exactly Marcus Welby . . . whatever. It all fits.'

That was the main thing.

A small boat, a sleek yellow outboard, came speeding across the bonefish flats. It was headed south on a line toward Soldier Key. García watched the boat intently, walked around the house to keep it in view.

'Don't worry, I know him,' said Luis Córdova. 'He's a fishing guide.'

'Wonder why he's out here alone.'

'Maybe his clients didn't show. That happens when it blows hard—these rubes'll chicken out at the dock. Meanwhile it turns into a nice day.'

Just south of Stiltsville, the yellow skiff angled off the flats and stopped in a deep blue channel. The guide took out a rod and casted a bait over the side. Then he sat down to wait.

'See?' said Luis Córdova. 'He's just snapper fishing.'

García was squinting against the sun. 'Luis, you see something else out there?'

'Whereabouts?'

The detective pointed. 'I'd say a quarter mile. Something in the water, between us and that island.'

Luis Córdova raised one hand to block the glare. With the other hand he adjusted his sunglasses. 'Yeah, now I see it,' he said. 'Swimming on top. Looks like a big turtle.'

'Yeah?'

'Grandpa loggerhead. Or maybe it's a porpoise. You want me to get the binoculars?'

'No, that's okay.' García turned around and leaned his back against the wooden rail. He was grinning broadly, the stogie bobbing under his mustache. 'I've never seen a porpoise before, except for the Seaquarium.'

'Well, there's still a few wild ones out here,' Luis Córdova said. 'If that's what it was.'

'That's what it was,' said Al García. 'I'm sure of it.'

He tapped the ashes off the cigar and watched them swirl and scatter in the sea breeze. 'Come on,' he said, 'let's go see if Wilt's learned any new words.'

EPILOGUE

BLONDELL WAYNE TATUM, also known as Chemo, pleaded guilty in Dade Circuit Court to the murders of Dr. Rudy Graveline and Chloe Simpkins Stranahan. He later was extradited to Pennsylvania, where he confessed to the unsolved slaying of Dr. Gunther MacLeish, a semiretired dermatologist and pioneer in the use of electrolysis to remove unwanted facial hair. Because of his physical handicap, and because of favorable testimony from sympathetic Amish elders, Tatum received a relatively lenient sentence of three seventeen-year terms, to be served concurrently. He is now a trusty in charge of the winter vegetable garden at the Union Correctional Institution at Raiford, Florida.

MAGGIE ORESTES GONZALEZ pleaded no contest to one count of obstruction for lying to investigators after Victoria Barletta's death. She received a six-month suspended sentence, but was ordered to serve one hundred hours of community service as a volunteer nurse at the Dade County Stockade, where she was taken hostage and killed during a food-related riot.

HEATHER CHAPPELL continued to appear in numerous television shows, including *Matlock*, *L.A. Law* and *Murder, She Wrote*. Barely five months after Dr. Rudy Graveline's death, Heather quietly entered an exclusive West Hollywood surgical clinic and underwent a breast augmentation, a blepharoplasty, a rhinoplasty, a complete rhytidectomy, a chin implant, and suction lipectomies of the thighs, abdomen and buttocks. Soon afterward, Heather's movie career was revived when she was offered—and accepted—the role of Triana, a Klingon prostitute, in *Star Trek VII: The Betrayal of Spock*.

KIPPER GARTH never fully recovered from his *pelota* injuries and retired from the law. His lucrative personal-injury practice was purchased by a prominent Miami Beach firm, which sought—and received—permission to retain the use of Kipper Garth's name and likeness in all future advertising and promotion.

The Dade County Grand Jury refused to indict JOHN NORDSTROM for assaulting his lawyer. Nordstrom and his wife pursued their malpractice claim against the Whispering Palms Spa and Surgery Center and eventually settled out of court for $315,000, forty percent of which went straight to their new attorney.

MARIE NORDSTROM'S contractured breast implants were repaired in a simple out-patient procedure performed by Dr. George Ginger. The operation took only ninety minutes and was a complete success.

The seat held on the County Commission by ROBERTO PEPSICAL was filled by his younger brother, Charlie. The zoning rights to the Old Cypress Towers project were eventually picked up by a group of wealthy South American investors. Ignoring protests from environmentalists and local homeowners, the developers paved over the ballpark and playground to construct a thirty-three-story luxury condominium tower, with a chic rooftop nightclub called Freddie's. Nine weeks after it opened, the entire building was seized by the Drug Enforcement Administration in a money-laundering probe that was code-named 'Operation Piranha.'

The popular television show *In Your Face* was canceled after the disappearance and presumed death of its star, REYNALDO FLEMM. The program's executive producers soon announced that a $25,000 scholarship in Reynaldo's name would be awarded to the Columbia University School of Journalism, from which, ironically, he had been twice expelled.

Exporter J. W. KIMBLER received a personal letter from the vice-chancellor of the Leeward Islands Medical University in Guadeloupe. The note said: 'Thank you for your most recent shipment, which has become the highlight of our spring semester. On behalf of the faculty and of the future surgeons who study here, accept my deepest gratitude for a superior product.'

For his dramatic videotaped footage of Reynaldo Flemm's cosmetic surgery, cameraman WILLIE VELASQUEZ was offered— and accepted—his own news-documentary program on the Fox Television Network. *Eye-Witness Undercover!* premiered in the 8 P.M. time slot on Thursdays, and in four major markets decisively beat out *The Cosby Show* in both the Nielsens and Arbitrons.

CHRISTINA MARKS declined an offer to become a producer for Willie's new program. Instead, she left television and took a job as an assistant city editor at the *Miami Herald*, and with it a pay cut of approximately $135,000. Soon after moving to Miami, she purchased a second-hand Boston Whaler and a nautical chart of South Biscayne Bay.

The parents of Victoria Barletta were puzzled to receive, via UPS, a black Samsonite suitcase containing approximately $118,400 in cash. A letter accompanying the money described it as a gift from the estate of Dr. Rudy Graveline. The letter was signed by a retired investigator named MICK STRANAHAN and bore no return address.

CARL HIAASEN

Carl Hiaasen is a native of Florida with an outstanding reputation as an investigative journalist exposing local scandals. He is the author of *Tourist Season, Double Whammy, Skin Tight, Native Tongue, Strip Tease* and *Stormy Weather*, and has co-written *Powder Burn* and *Trap Line* with Bill Montalbano.